Robert Barr (16 September 1849 – 21 October 1912) was a Scottish-Canadian short story writer and novelist. Robert Barr was born in Barony, Lanark, Scotland to Robert Barr and Jane Watson. In 1854, he emigrated with his parents to Upper Canada at the age of four years old. His family settled on a farm near the village of Muirkirk. Barr assisted his father with his job as a carpenter, and developed a sound work ethic. Robert Barr then worked as a steel smelter for a number of years before he was educated at Toronto Normal School in 1873 to train as a teacher. After graduating Toronto Normal School, Barr became a teacher, and eventually headmaster/principal of the Central School of Windsor, Ontario in 1874. While Barr worked as head master of the Central School of Windsor, Ontario, he began to contribute short stories—often based on personal experiences, and recorded his work. On August 1876, when he was 27, Robert Barr married Ontario-born Eva Bennett, who was 21. (Source: Wikipedia)

Literary works:
"The Face And The Mask" (1894)
In the Midst of Alarms (1894, 1900, 1912)
From Whose Bourne (1896)
One Day's Courtship (1896)
Revenge!
The Strong Arm
A Woman Intervenes (1896)
Tekla: A Romance of Love and War (1898)
Jennie Baxter, Journalist (1899)
The Unchanging East (1900)
The Victors (1901)
A Prince of Good Fellows (1902)
Over The Border: A Romance (1903)
The O'Ruddy, A Romance, with Stephen Crane

THORNE CLASSICS

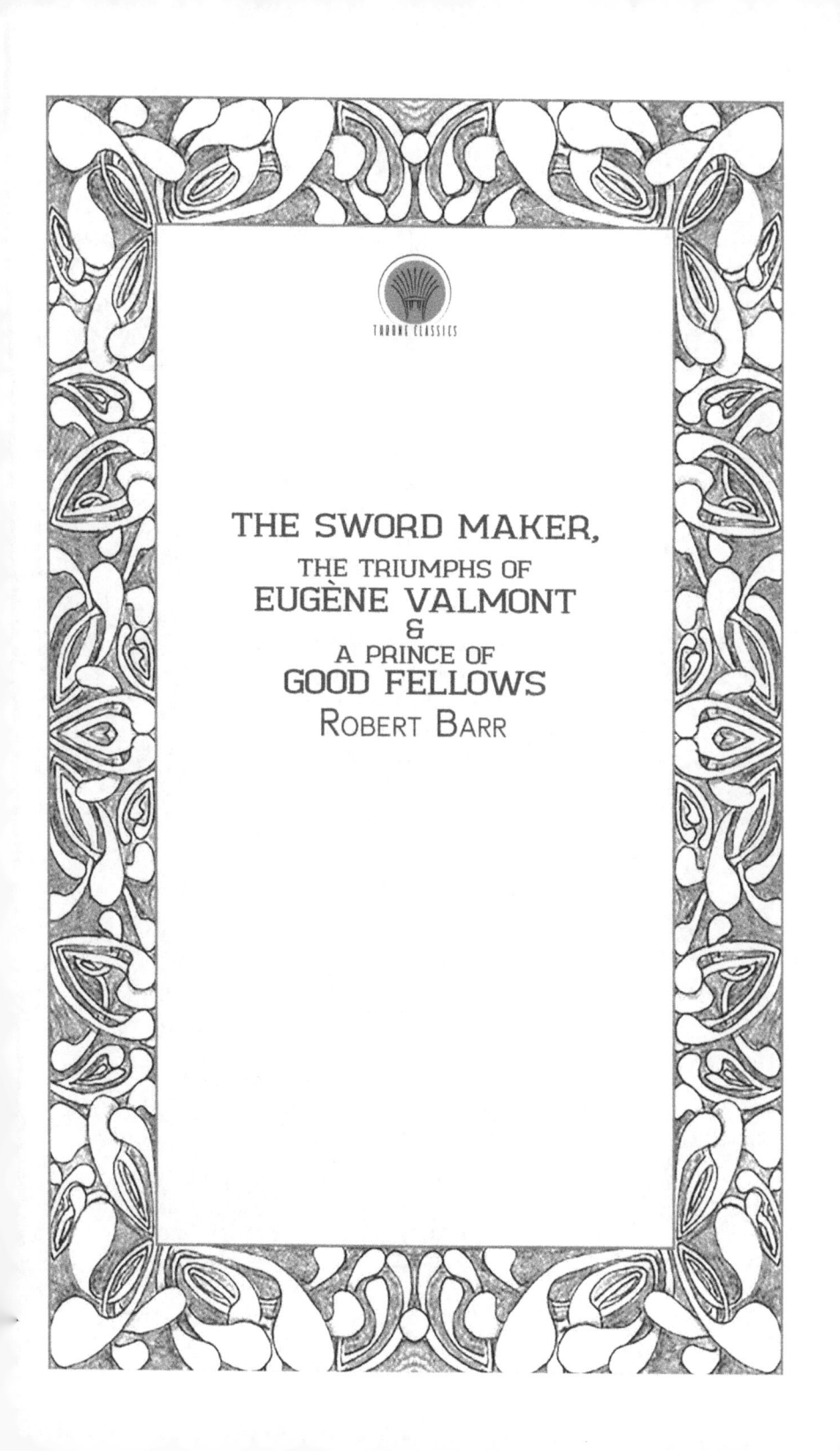

THE SWORD MAKER,
THE TRIUMPHS OF
EUGÈNE VALMONT
&
A PRINCE OF
GOOD FELLOWS
Robert Barr

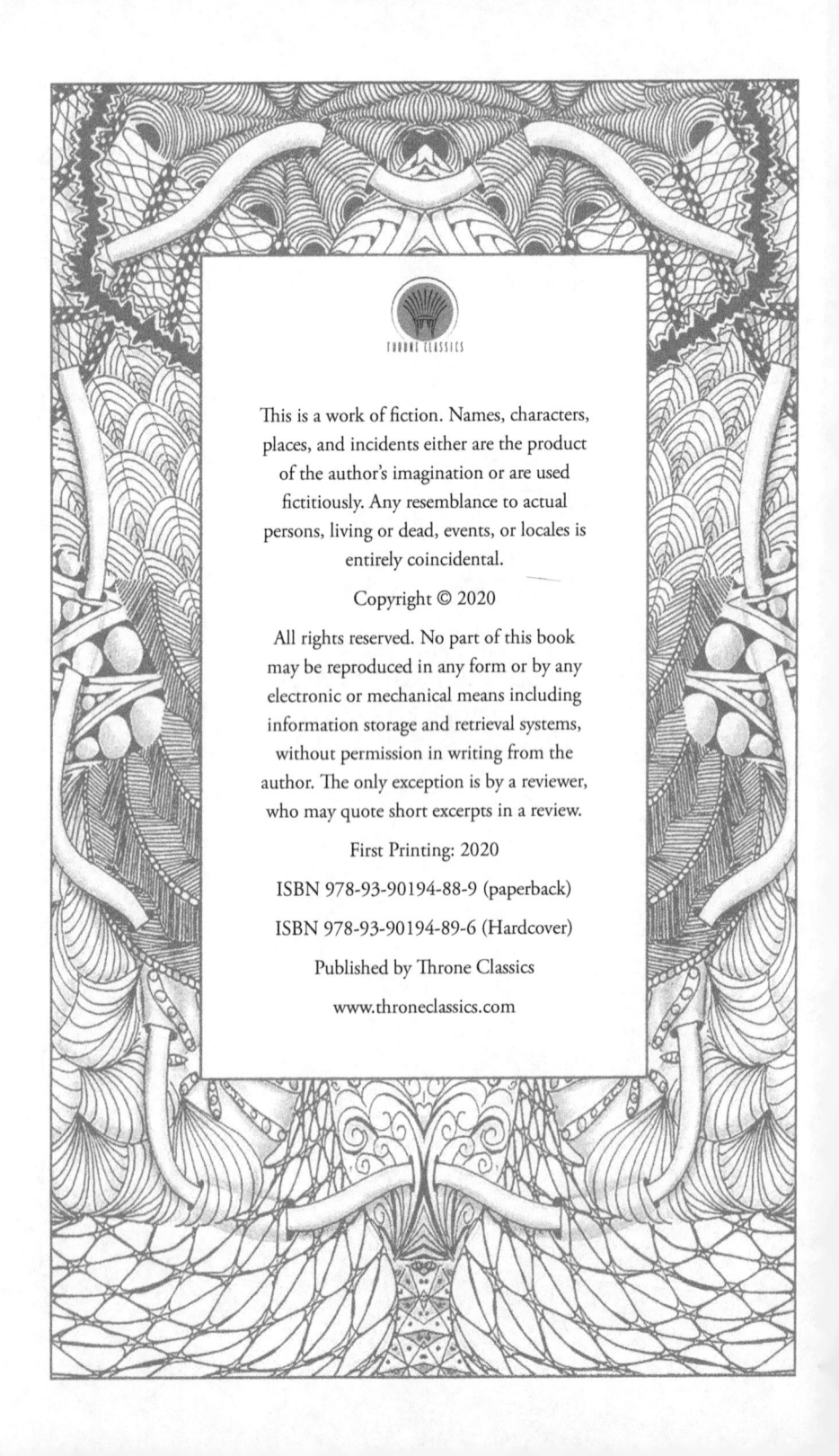

This is a work of fiction. Names, characters, places, and incidents either are the product of the author's imagination or are used fictitiously. Any resemblance to actual persons, living or dead, events, or locales is entirely coincidental.

Copyright © 2020

All rights reserved. No part of this book may be reproduced in any form or by any electronic or mechanical means including information storage and retrieval systems, without permission in writing from the author. The only exception is by a reviewer, who may quote short excerpts in a review.

First Printing: 2020

ISBN 978-93-90194-88-9 (paperback)

ISBN 978-93-90194-89-6 (Hardcover)

Published by Throne Classics

www.throneclassics.com

Contents

THE SWORD MAKER	11
I. AN OFFER TO OPEN THE RIVER	13
II. THE BARGAIN IS STRUCK	31
III. DISSENSION IN THE IRONWORKERS' GUILD	53
IV. THE DISTURBING JOURNEY OF FATHER AMBROSE	73
V. THE COUNTESS VON SAYN AND THE ARCHBISHOP OF COLOGNE	93
VI. TO BE KEPT SECRET FROM THE COUNTESS	100
VII. MUTINY IN THE WILDERNESS	111
VIII. THE MISSING LEADER AND THE MISSING GOLD	131
IX. A SOLEMN PROPOSAL OF MARRIAGE	149
X. A CALAMITOUS CONFERENCE	164
XI. GOLD GALORE THAT TAKES TO ITSELF WINGS	187
XII. THE LAUGHING RED MARGRAVE OF FURSTENBERG	205
XIII. "A SENTENCE; COME, PREPARE!"	225
XIV. THE PRISONER OF EHRENFELS	235
XV. JOURNEYS END IN LOVERS' MEETING	253
XVI. MY LADY SCATTERS THE FREEBOOTERS AND CAPTURES THEIR CHIEF	260
XVII. "FOR THE EMPRESS, AND NOT FOR THE EMPIRE"	281
XVIII. THE SWORD MAKER AT BAY	292
XIX. THE BETROTHAL IN THE GARDEN	307
XX. THE MYSTERY OF THE FOREST	316
XXI. A SECRET MARRIAGE	325
XXII. LONG LIVE THEIR MAJESTIES	337

THE TRIUMPHS OF EUGÈNE VALMONT — 351

1. The Mystery of the Five Hundred Diamonds — 353

2. The Siamese Twin of a Bomb-Thrower — 381

3. The Clue of the Silver Spoons — 421

4. Lord Chizelrigg's Missing Fortune — 441

5. The Absent-Minded Coterie — 465

6. The Ghost with the Club-Foot — 508

7. The Liberation of Wyoming Ed — 538

8. Lady Alicia's Emeralds — 560

APPENDIX: TWO SHERLOCK HOLMES PARODIES — 583

1. The Adventures of Sherlaw Kombs — 583

2. The Adventure of the Second Swag — 594

A PRINCE OF GOOD FELLOWS	**607**
The King Intervenes	611
The King Dines	626
The King's Tryst	635
The King Investigates	651
The King's Gold	671
The King A-Begging	690
The King's Visit	710
The King Explores	724
The King Drinks	740
The King Sails	754
The King Weds	770
About Author	**795**
NOTABLE WORKS	**798**

THE SWORD MAKER,
THE TRIUMPHS OF
EUGÈNE VALMONT
&
A PRINCE OF
GOOD FELLOWS

THE SWORD MAKER

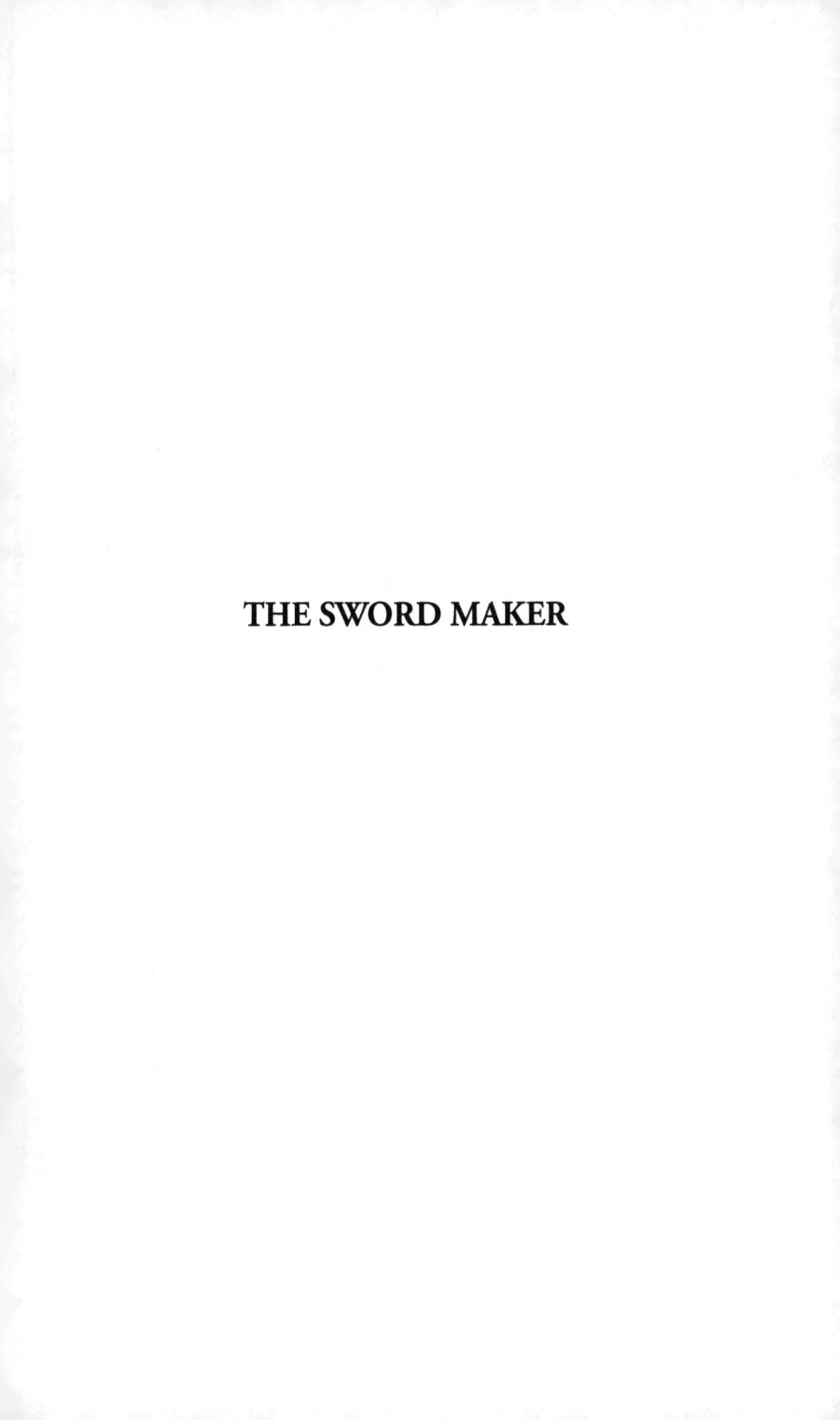

I. AN OFFER TO OPEN THE RIVER

Considering the state of the imperial city of Frankfort, one would not expect to find such a gathering as was assembled in the Kaiser cellar of the Rheingold drinking tavern. Outside in the streets all was turbulence and disorder; a frenzy on the part of the populace taxing to the utmost the efforts of the city authorities to keep it within bounds, and prevent the development of a riot that might result in the partial destruction at least of this once prosperous city. And indeed, the inhabitants of Frankfort could plead some excuse for their boisterousness. Temporarily, at any rate, all business was at a standstill. The skillful mechanics of the town had long been out of work, and now to the ranks of the unemployed were added, from time to time, clerks and such-like clerical people, expert accountants, persuasive salesmen, and small shopkeepers, for no one now possessed the money to buy more than the bare necessities of life. Yet the warehouses of Frankfort were full to overflowing, with every kind of store that might have supplied the needs of the people, and to the unlearned man it seemed unjust that he and his family should starve while granaries were packed with the agricultural produce of the South, and huge warehouses were glutted with enough cloth from Frankfort and the surrounding districts to clothe ten times the number of tatterdemalions who clamored through the streets.

The wrath of the people was concentrated against one man, and he the highest in the land; to blame, of course, in a secondary degree, but not the one primarily at fault for this deplorable state of things. The Emperor, always indolent from the time he came to the throne, had grown old and crabbed and fat, caring for nothing but his flagon of wine that stood continually at his elbow. Laxity of rule in the beginning allowed his nobles to get the upper hand, and now it would require a civil war to bring them into subjection again. They, sitting snug in their strongholds, with plenty of wine in their cellars and corn in their bins, cared nothing for the troubles of the city. Indeed, those who inhabited either bank of the Rhine, watching from their elevated castles the main avenue of traffic between Frankfort and Cologne, her chief market, had throughout that long reign severely taxed the merchants conveying goods downstream. During the last five years, their exactions became so piratical that finally they killed the goose that laid the golden eggs, so now the Rhine was without a boat, and Frankfort without a buyer.

For too long Frankfort had looked to the Emperor, whose business it was to keep order in his domain, and when at last the merchants, combining to help themselves, made an effort towards freedom, it was too late. The result of their combination was a flotilla of nearly a hundred boats, which, gathering at Frankfort and Mayence, proceeded together down the river, convoyed by a fleet containing armed men, and thus they thought to win through to Cologne, and so dispose of their goods. But the robber Barons combined also, hung chains across the river at the Lorely rocks, its narrowest part, and realizing that this fleet could defeat any single one of them, they for once acted in concert, falling upon the boats when their running against the chains threw them into confusion.

The nobles and their brigands were seasoned fighters all, while the armed men secured by the merchants were mere hirelings, who fled in panic; and those not cut to pieces by their savage adversaries became themselves marauders on a small scale, scattered throughout the land, for there was little use of tramping back to the capital, where already a large portion of the population suffered the direst straits.

Not a single bale of goods reached Cologne, for the robbers divided everything amongst themselves, with some pretty quarrels, and then they sank the boats in the deepest part of the river as a warning, lest the merchants of Frankfort and Mayence should imagine the Rhine belonged to them. Meantime, all petitions to the Emperor being in vain, the merchants gave up the fight. They were a commercial, not a warlike people. They discharged their servants and underlings, and starvation slowly settled down upon the distressed city.

After the maritime disaster on the Rhine, some of the merchants made a futile attempt to amend matters, for which their leaders paid dearly. They appealed to the seven Electors, finding their petitions to the Emperor were in vain, asking these seven noblemen, including the three warlike Archbishops of Cologne, Treves, and Mayence, to depose the Emperor, which they had power to do, and elect his son in his stead. But they overlooked the fact that a majority of the Electors themselves, and probably the Archbishops also, benefited directly or indirectly by the piracies on the Rhine. The answer to this request was the prompt hanging of three leading merchants, the imprisonment of a score of others, and a warning to the rest that the shoemaker should stick to his last, leaving high politics to those born to rule. This misguided effort caused the three Archbishops to arrest Prince Roland, the Emperor's only son, and incarcerate him in Ehrenfels, a strong castle on the Rhine belonging to the Archbishop of Mayence, who was thus made custodian of the young man, and responsible to his brother prelates of Cologne and Treves for the safe-keeping of the Prince. The Archbishops, as has been said, were too well satisfied with the weak administration then established at Frankfort to wish a change, so the lad was removed from the capital, that the citizens of Frankfort might be under no temptation to place him at their head, and endeavor to overturn the existing order of things.

This being the state of affairs in Frankfort, with every one gloomy, and a majority starving, it was little wonder that the main cellar of the Rheingold tavern should be empty, although when times were good it was difficult to find a seat there after the sun went down. But in the smaller Kaiser cellar, along each side of the single long table, sat young men numbering a score, who ate black bread and drank Rhine wine, to the roaring of song and the telling of story. They formed a close coterie, admitting no stranger to their circle if one dissenting voice was raised against his acceptance, yet in spite of this exclusiveness there was not a drop of noble blood in the company. They belonged, however, to the aristocracy of craftsmen; metal-workers for the most part, ingenious artificers in iron, beaters of copper, fashioners of gold and silver. Glorious blacksmiths, they called themselves; but now, like every one else, with nothing to do. In spite of their city up-bringing all were stalwart, well-set-up young men; and, indeed, the swinging of hammers is good exercise for the muscles of the arm, and in those turbulent days a youth who could not take care of himself with his stick or his fists was like to fare ill if he ventured forth after nightfall.

This, indeed, had been the chief reason for the forming of their guild, and if one of their number was set upon, the secret call of the organization shouted aloud brought instant help were any of the members within hearing. Belonging neither to the military nor the aristocracy, they were not allowed to wear swords, and to obtain this privilege was one of the objects of their organization. Indeed, each member of the guild secretly possessed a weapon of the best, although he risked his neck if ever he carried it abroad with him. Among their number were three of the most expert sword makers in all Germany.

These three sword makers had been instrumental in introducing to their order the man who was now its leader. This youth came to one of them with ideas concerning the proper construction of a sword, and the balancing of it, so that it hung easily in the hand as though part of the fore-arm. Usually, the expert has small patience with the theories of an amateur; but this young fellow, whose ambition it was to invent a sword, possessed such intimate knowledge of the weapon as it was used, not only in Germany, but also in France and Italy, that the sword maker introduced him to fellow-craftsmen at other shops, and they taught him how to construct a sword. These instructors, learning that although, as Roland laughingly said, he was not allowed to wear a sword, he could wield it with a precision little short of marvelous, the guild gave permission for this stranger to be a guest at one of their weekly meetings at the Kaiser cellar, where he exhibited his wonderful skill.

Not one of them, nor, indeed, all of them together, stood any chance when confronting him. They clamored to be taught, offering good money for the lessons, believing that if they acquired but a tithe of his excellence with the blade they might venture to wear it at night, and let their skill save them from capture. But the young fellow refused their money, and somewhat haughtily declined the rôle of fencing-master, whereupon they unanimously elected him a member of the coterie, waiving for this one occasion the rule which forbade the choice of any but a metal-worker. When the stranger accepted the election, he was informed that it was the duty of each member to come to the aid of his brethren when required, and they therefore requested him to teach them swordsmanship. Roland, laughing, seeing how he had been trapped, as it were, with his own consent, acceded to the universal wish, and before a year had passed his twenty comrades were probably the leading swordsmen in the city of Frankfort.

Shortly after the disaster to the merchants' fleet at the Lorely, Roland disappeared without a word of farewell to those who had come to think so much of him. He had been extremely reticent regarding his profession, if he had one, and no one knew where he lodged. It was feared that the authorities had arrested him with the sword in his possession, for he grew more reckless than any of the others in carrying the weapon. One night, however, he reappeared, and took his seat at the head of the table as if nothing had happened. Evidently he had traveled far and on foot, for his clothes were dusty and the worse for wear. He refused to give any account of himself, but admitted that he was hungry, thirsty, and in need of money.

His hunger and thirst were speedily satisfied, but the money scarcity was not so easily remedied. All the score were out of employment, with the exception of the three sword makers, whose trade the uncertainty of the times augmented rather than diminished. To cheer up Roland, who was a young fellow of unquenchable geniality, they elected him to the empty honor of being their leader, Kurzbold's term of office having ended.

The guild met every night now, instead of once a week, and it may be shrewdly suspected that the collation of black bread and sausage formed the sole meal of the day for many of them. Nevertheless, their hilarity was undiminished, and the rafters rang with song and laugh, and echoed also maledictions upon a supine Government, and on the rapacious Rhine lords. But the bestowal of even black bread and the least expensive of wine could not continue indefinitely. They owed a bill to the landlord upon which that worthy, patient as he had proved himself, always hoping for better times, wished for at least something on account. All his other customers had deserted him, and if they drank at all, chose some place where the wine was thin and cheap. The landlord held out bravely for three months after Roland was elected president, then, bemoaning his fate, informed the guild that he would be compelled to close the Rheingold tavern.

"Give me a week!" cried Roland, rising in his place at the head of the table, "and I will make an effort to get enough gold to settle the bill at least, with perhaps something over for each of our pockets."

This promise brought forth applause and a rattle of flagons on the table, so palpably empty that the ever-hopeful landlord proceeded forthwith to fill them.

"There is one proviso," said Roland, as they drank his health in the wine his offer produced. "To get this money I must do something in return. I have a plan in mind which it would be premature to disclose. If it succeeds, none of us will ever need to bend back over a workman's bench again, or hammer metal except for our own pleasure. But acting alone I am powerless, so I must receive your promise that you will stand by any pledge I make on your behalf, and follow me into whatever danger I choose to lead you."

There was a great uproar at this, and a boisterous consent.

"This day week, then," said Roland, as he strapped sword to side, threw cloak over shoulders, so that it completely concealed the forbidden weapon, waved a hand to his cheering comrades, and went out into the night.

Once ascended the cellar steps, the young man stood in the narrow street as though hesitating what to do. Faintly there came to him the sound of singing from the cellar he had quitted, and he smiled slightly as he listened to the rousing chorus he knew so well. From the direction of the Palace a more sinister echo floated on the night air; the unmistakable howl of anger, pain, and terror; the noise that a pursued and stricken mob makes when driven by soldiers. The populace had evidently been engaged in its futile and dangerous task of demonstrating, and proclaiming its hunger, and the authorities were scattering it; keeping it ever on the move.

It was still early; not yet ten o'clock, and a full moon shone over the city, unlighted otherwise. Drawing his cloak closer about him, Roland walked rapidly in an opposite direction to that from which the tumult of the rabble came, until he arrived at the wide Fahrgasse, a street running north and south, its southern end terminating at the old bridge. Along this thoroughfare lived the wealthiest merchants of Frankfort.

Roland turned, and proceeded slowly towards the river, critically examining the tall, picturesque buildings on either hand, cogitating the question which of them would best answer his purpose. They all seemed uninviting enough, for their windows were dark, most of them tightly shuttered; and, indeed, the thoroughfare looked like a street of the dead, the deserted appearance enhanced, rather than relieved, by the white moonlight lying on its cobble-stones.

Nearing the bridge, he discovered one stout door ajar, and behind it shone the yellow glow of a lamp. He paused, and examined critically the façade of the house, which, with its quiet, dignified architectural beauty, seemed the abode of wealth. Although the shutters were closed, his intent inspection showed him thin shafts of light from the chinks, and he surmised that an assemblage of some sort was in progress, probably a secret convention, the members of which entered unannounced, and left the door ajar ready for the next comer.

For a moment he thought of venturing in, but remembering his mission required the convincing of one man rather than the persuasion of a group, he forbore, but noted in his mind the position and designation of the house, resolving to select this building as the theater of his first effort, and return to it next morning. It would serve his purpose as well as another.

Roland's attention was then suddenly directed to his own position, standing in the bright moonlight, for there swung round from the river road, into the Fahrgasse, a small and silent company, who marched as one man. The moon was shining almost directly up the street, but the houses to the west stood in its radiance, while those in the east were still in shadow. Roland pressed himself back against the darkened wall to his left, near the partially opened door; between it and the river. The silent procession advanced to the door ajar, and there paused, forming their ranks into two lines, thus making a passage for a tall, fine-looking, bearded man, who walked to the threshold, then turned and raised his bonnet in salute.

"My friends," he said, "this is kind of you, and although I have been silent, I ask you to believe that deeply I appreciate your welcome escort. And now, enter with me, and we will drink a stoup of wine together, to the somber toast, 'God save our stricken city!'"

"No, no, Herr Goebel. To-night is sacred. We have seen you safely to your waiting family, and at that reunion there should be no intruders. But to-morrow night, if you will have us, we will drink to the city, and to your own good health, Herr Goebel."

This sentiment was applauded by all, and the merchant, seeing that they would not accept his present invitation, bowed in acquiescence, and bade them good-by. When the door closed the delegation separated into units, and each went his own way. Roland, stepping out of the shadow, accosted the rearmost man.

"Pardon me, mein Herr," he said, "but may I ask what ceremony is this in which you have been taking part?"

The person accosted looked with some alarm at his questioner, but the moonlight revealed a face singularly gentle and winning; a face that in spite of its youth inspired instinctive confidence. The tone, too, was very persuasive, and seemed devoid even of the offense of curiosity.

"'Tis no ceremony," said the delegate, "but merely the return home of our friend, Herr Goebel."

"Has he, then, been on a journey?"

"Sir, you are very young, and probably unacquainted with Frankfort."

"I have lived here all my life," said Roland. "I am a native of Frankfort."

"In that case," replied the other, "you show yourself amazingly ignorant of its concerns; otherwise you would know that Herr Goebel is one of the leading merchants of the city, a man honorable, enlightened, and energetic—an example to us all, and one esteemed alike by noble or peasant. We honor ourselves in honoring him."

"Herr Goebel should be proud of such commendation, mein Herr, coming I judge, from one to whom the words you use might also be applied."

The merchant bowed gravely at this compliment, but made no remark upon it.

"Pardon my further curiosity," continued the young man, "but from whence does Herr Goebel return?"

"He comes from prison," said the other. "He made the mistake of thinking that our young Prince would prove a better ruler than his father, our Emperor, and but that the Archbishops feared a riot if they went to extremes, Herr Goebel ran great danger of losing his life rather than his liberty."

"What you say, mein Herr, interests me very much, and I thank you for your courtesy. My excuse for questioning you is this. I am moved by a desire to enter the employ of such a man as Herr Goebel, and I purpose calling upon him to-morrow, if you think he would be good enough to receive me."

"He will doubtless receive you," replied the other, "but I am quite certain your mission will fail. At the present moment none of us are engaging clerks, however competent. Ignorant though you are of civic affairs, you must be aware that all business is at a standstill in Frankfort. Although Herr Goebel has said nothing about it, I learn from an unquestionable source that he himself is keeping from starvation all his former employees, so I am sure he would not take on, for a stranger, any further obligation."

"Sir, I am well acquainted with the position of affairs, and it is to suggest a remedy that I desire speech with Herr Goebel. I do not possess the privilege of acquaintance with any merchant in this city, so one object of my accosting you was to learn, if possible, how I might secure some note of introduction to the merchant that would ensure his receiving me, and obtain for me a hearing when once I had been admitted to his house."

If Roland expected the stranger to volunteer such a note, he quite underestimated the caution of a Frankfort merchant.

"As I said before, you will meet with no difficulty so far as entrance to the house is concerned. May I take it that you yourself understand the art of writing?"

"Oh yes," replied Roland.

"Then indite your own letter of introduction. Say that you have evolved a plan for the redemption of Frankfort, and Herr Goebel will receive you without demur. He will listen patiently, and give a definite decision regarding the feasibility of your project. And now, good sir, my way lies to the left. I wish you success, and bid you good-night."

The stranger left Roland standing at the intersection of two streets, one of which led to the Saalhof. They had been approaching the Romerberg, or market-place, the center of Frankfort, when the merchant so suddenly ended the conversation and turned aside. Roland remembered that no Jew was allowed to set foot in the Romerberg, and now surmised the nationality of his late companion. The youth proceeded alone through the Romerberg, and down directly to the river, reaching the spot where the huge Saalhof faced its flood. Roland saw that triple guards surrounded the Emperor's Palace. The mob had been cleared away, but no one was allowed to linger in its precincts, and the youth was gruffly ordered to take himself elsewhere, which he promptly did, walking up the Saalgasse, and past the Cathedral, until he came once more into the Fahrgasse, down which he proceeded, pausing for another glance at Goebel's house, until he came to the bridge, where he stood with arms resting on the parapet, thoughtfully shaping in his mind what he would say to Herr Goebel in the morning.

Along the opposite side of the river lay a compact mass of barges; ugly, somber, black in the moonlight, silent witnesses to the ruin of Frankfort. The young man gazed at this melancholy accumulation of useless floating stock, and breathed the deeper when he reflected that whoever could set these boats in motion again would prove himself, temporarily at least, the savior of the city.

When the bells began to toll eleven, Roland roused himself, walked across the bridge to Sachsenhausen, and so to his squalid lodging, consoling himself with the remembrance that the great King Charlemagne had made this his own place of residence. Here, before retiring to bed, he wrote the letter which he was to send in next day to Herr Goebel, composing it with some care, so that it aroused curiosity without satisfying it.

It was half-past ten next morning when Roland presented himself at the door of the leading merchant in the Fahrgasse, and sent in to that worthy his judiciously worded epistle. He was kept waiting in the hall longer than he expected, but at last the venerable porter appeared, and said Herr Goebel would be pleased to receive him. He was conducted up the stair to the first floor, and into a front room which seemed to be partly library and partly business office. Here seated at a stout table, he recognized the grave burgher whose home-coming he had witnessed the night before.

The keen eyes of the merchant seemed to penetrate to his inmost thought, and it struck Roland that there came into them an expression of disappointment, for he probably did not expect so youthful a visitor.

"Will you be seated, mein Herr," said his host; and Roland, with an inclination of the head, accepted the invitation. "My time is very completely occupied to-day," continued the elder man, "for although there is little business afoot in Frankfort, my own affairs have been rather neglected of late, and I am endeavoring to overtake the arrears."

"I know that," said Roland. "I stood by your doorcheek last night when you returned home."

"Did you so? May I ask why?"

"There was no particular reason. It happened that I walked down the Fahrgasse, endeavoring to make up my mind upon whom I should call to-day."

"And why have I received the preference?"

"Perhaps, sir, it would be more accurate to say your house received the preference, if it is such. I was struck by its appearance of solidity and wealth, and, differing from all others in the door being ajar, I lingered before it last night with some inclination to enter. Then the procession which accompanied you came along. I heard your address to your friends, and wondered what the formality was about. After the door was closed I accosted one of those who escorted you, and learned your name, business, and reputation."

"You must be a stranger in Frankfort when you needed to make such inquiry."

"Those are almost the same words that my acquaintance of last night used, and he seemed astonished when I replied that I was born in Frankfort, and had lived here all my life."

"Ah, I suppose no man is so well known as he thinks he is, but I venture to assert that you are not engaged in business here."

"Sir, you are in the right. I fear I have hitherto led a somewhat useless existence."

"On money earned by some one else, perhaps."

"Again you hit the nail on the head, Herr Goebel. I lodge on the other side of the river, and coming to and fro each day, the sight of all those useless barges depresses me, and I have formulated a plan for putting them in motion again."

"I fear, sir, that wiser heads than yours have been meditating upon that project without avail."

"I should have been more gratified, Herr Goebel, if you had said 'older heads.'"

The suspicion of a smile hovered for a brief instant round the shrewd, firm lips of the merchant.

"Young sir, your gentle reproof is deserved. I know nothing of your wisdom, and so should have referred to the age, and not to the equipment of your head. It occurs to me, as I study you more closely, that I have met you before. Your face seems familiar."

"'Tis but a chance resemblance, I suspect. Until very recently I have been absorbed in my studies, and rarely left my father's house."

"I am doubtless mistaken. But to return to our theme. As you are ignorant of my name and standing in this city, you are probably unaware of the efforts already made to remove the deadlock on the Rhine."

"In that, Herr Goebel, you are at fault. I know an expedition of folly was promoted at enormous expense, and that the empty barges, numbering something like fivescore, now rest in the deepest part of the Rhine."

"Why do you call it an expedition of folly?"

"Surely the result shows it to be such."

"A plan may meet with disaster, even where every precaution has been taken. We did the best we could, and if the men we had paid for the protection of the flotilla had not, with base cowardice, deserted their posts, these barges would have reached Cologne."

"Never! The defenders you chose were riff-raff, picked up in the gutters of Frankfort, and you actually supposed such cattle, undisciplined and untrained, would stand up against the fearless fighters of the Barons, swashbucklers, hardened to the use of sword and pike. What else was to be expected? The goods were not theirs, but yours. They had received their pay, and so speedily took themselves out of danger."

"You forget, sir, or you do not know, that several hundred of them were cut to pieces."

"I know that, also, but the knowledge does not in the least nullify my contention. I am merely endeavoring to show you that the heads you spoke of a moment ago were only older, but not necessarily wiser than mine. It would be impossible for me to devise an expedition so preposterous."

"What should we have done?"

"For one thing, you should have gone yourselves, and defended your own bales."

The merchant showed visible signs of a slowly rising anger, and had the young man's head contained the wisdom he appeared to claim for it, he would have known that his remarks were entirely lacking in tact, and that he was making no progress, but rather the reverse. "You speak like a heedless, untutored youth. How could we defend our bales, when no merchant is allowed to wear a sword?"

Roland rose and put his hands to the throat of his cloak.

"I am not allowed to wear a sword;" and saying this, he dramatically flung wide his cloak, displaying the prohibited weapon hanging from his belt. The merchant sat back in his chair, visibly impressed.

"You seem to repose great confidence in me," he said. "What if I were to inform the authorities?"

The youth smiled.

"You forget, Herr Goebel, that I learned much about you from your friend last night. I feel quite safe in your house."

He flung his cloak once more over the weapon, and sat down again.

"What is your occupation, sir?" asked the merchant.

"I am a teacher of swordsmanship. I practice the art of a fencing-master."

"Your clients are aristocrats, then?"

"Not so. The class with which I am now engaged contains twenty skilled artisans of about my own age."

"If they do not belong to the aristocracy, your instruction must be surreptitious, because it is against the law."

"It is both surreptitious and against the law, but in spite of these disadvantages, my twenty pupils are the best swordsmen in Frankfort, and I would willingly pit them against any twenty nobles with whom I am acquainted."

"So!" cried the merchant. "You are acquainted with twenty nobles, are you?"

"Well, you see," explained the young man, flushing slightly, "these metal-workers whom I drill, being out of employment, cannot afford to pay for their lessons, and naturally, as you indicated, a fencing-master must look to the nobles for his bread. I used the word acquaintance hastily. I am acquainted with the nobles in the same way that a clerk in the woolen trade might say he was acquainted with a score of merchants, to none of whom he had ever spoken."

"I see. Am I to take it that your project for opening the Rhine depends for its success on those twenty metal-workers, who quite lawlessly know how to handle their swords?"

"Yes."

"Tell me what your plan is."

"I do not care to disclose my plan, even to you."

"I thought you came here hoping I should further your project, and perhaps finance it. Am I wrong in such a surmise?"

"Sir, you are not. The very first proviso is that you pay to me across this table a thousand thalers in gold."

The smile came again to the lips of the merchant.

"Anything else?" he asked.

"Yes. You will select one of your largest barges, and fill it with whatever class of goods you deal in."

"Don't you know what class of goods I deal in?"

"No! I do not."

Goebel's smile broadened. That a youth so ignorant of everything pertaining to the commerce of Frankfort, should come in thus boldly and demand a thousand thalers in gold from a man whose occupation he did not know, seemed to the merchant one of the greatest pieces of impudence he had encountered in his long experience of men.

"After all, my merchandise," he said, "matters little one way or another when I am engaged with such a customer as you. What next?"

"You will next place a price upon the shipload; a price such as you would accept if the boat reached Cologne intact. I agree to pay you that money, together with the thousand thalers, when I return to Frankfort."

"And when will that be, young sir?"

"You are better able to estimate the length of time than I. I do not know, for instance, how long it takes a barge to voyage from Frankfort to Cologne."

"Given fair weather, which we may expect in July, and premising that there are no interruptions, let us say a week."

"Would a man journeying on horseback from Cologne to Frankfort reach here sooner than the boat?"

"The barge having to make headway against a strong current, I should say the horseman would accomplish the trip in a third of the time."

"Very well. To allow for all contingencies, I promise to pay the money one month from the day we leave the wharf at Frankfort."

"That would be eminently satisfactory."

"I forgot to mention that I expect you, knowing more about navigation than I, to supply a trustworthy captain and an efficient crew for the manning of the barge. I should like men who understand the currents of the river, and who, if questioned by the Barons, would not be likely to tell more than they were asked."

"I can easily provide such a set of sailors."

"Very well, Herr Goebel. Those are my requirements. Will you agree to supply them?"

"With great pleasure, my young and enthusiastic friend, provided that you comply with one of the most common of our commercial rules."

"And what is that, mein Herr?"

"Before you depart you will leave with me ample security that if I never see you again, the value of the goods, plus the thousand thalers, will be repaid to me when the month is past."

"Ah," said the young man, "you impose an impossible condition."

"Give me a bond, then, signed by three responsible merchants."

"Sir, as I am acquainted with no merchant in this city except yourself, how could I hope to obtain the signature of even one responsible man?"

"How, then, do you expect to obtain my consent to a project which I know cannot succeed, while I bear all the risk?"

"Pardon me, Herr Goebel. I and my comrades risk our lives. You risk merely your money and your goods."

"You intend, then, to fight your way down the Rhine?"

"Surely. How else?"

"Supported by only twenty followers?"

"Yes."

"And you hope to succeed where a thousand of our men failed?"

"Yes; they were hirelings, as I told you. With my twenty I could put them all to flight. Aside from this, I should like to point out to you that the merchants of Frankfort formed their combination at public meetings, called together by the burgomaster. There was no secrecy about their deliberations. Every robber Baron along the Rhine knew what you were going to attempt, and was prepared for your coming. I intend that your barge shall leave Frankfort at midnight. My company will proceed across country, and join her at some agreed spot, probably below Bingen."

"I see. Well, my young friend, you have placed before me a very interesting proposal, but I am a business man, and not an adventurer. Unless you can furnish me with security, I decline to advance a single thaler, not to mention a thousand."

The young man rose to his feet, and the merchant, with a sigh, seemed glad that the conference was ended.

"Herr Goebel, you deeply disappoint me."

"I am sorry for that, and regret the forfeiting of your good opinion, but despite that disadvantage I must persist in my obstinacy."

"I do not wonder that this fair city lies desolate if her prosperity depends upon her merchants, and if you are chief among them; yet I cannot forget that you risked life and liberty on my behalf, though now you will not venture a miserable thousand thalers on my word of honor."

"On your behalf? What do you mean?"

"I mean, Herr Goebel, that I am Prince Roland, only son of the Emperor, and that you placed your neck in jeopardy to elevate me to the throne."

II. THE BARGAIN IS STRUCK

Every epoch seems to have possessed a two-word phrase that contained, as it were, the condensed wisdom of the age, and was universally believed by the people. For instance, the aphorism "Know thyself" rose to popularity when cultured minds turned towards science. In the period to which this recital belongs the adage "Blood tells" enjoyed universal acceptance. It was, in fact, that erroneous statement "The King can do no wrong" done up into tabloid form. From it, too, sprang that double-worded maxim of the days of chivalry, "Noblesse oblige."

In our own time, the two-worded phrase is "Money talks," and if diligent inquirers probe deeply into the matter, they will find that the aspirations of the people always correspond with reasonable accuracy to the meaning of the phrase then in use. Nothing could be more excellent, for instance, than the proverb "Money talks" as representing two commercial countries like America and England. In that short sentence is packed the essence of many other wise and drastic sayings, as, for instance, "The devil take the hindmost;" for, of course, if money talks, then the man without it must remain silent, and his place is at the tail of the procession, where the devil prowls about like a Cossack at the rear of Napoleon's army.

Confronting each other in that ancient house on the Fahrgasse, we witness, then, the personification of the two phrases, ancient and modern: blood represented by the standing lad, and money by the seated merchant.

"I am Prince Roland, only son of the Emperor," the young man had said, and he saw at once by the expression on the face of his host that, could he be convinced of the truth of the assertion, the thousand thalers that the Prince had demanded would be his on the instant.

For a full minute Roland thought he had succeeded, but as the surprise died out of the merchant's countenance, there replaced it that mask of caution which had had so much to do with the building of his fortune. During their conference Herr Goebel cudgeled his brain, trying to remember where he had seen this young man before, but memory had roamed among clerks, salesmen, and industrious people of that sort where, somehow, this young fellow did not fit in. When Roland suddenly sprung on him the incredible statement that he was a member of the Imperial family, the merchant's recollection then turned towards pageants he had seen, in one of which this young stranger might very well have borne a part. Blood was beginning to tell.

But now experience came to the merchant's aid. Only in romances did princes of the blood royal wander about like troubadours. Even a member of the lesser nobility did not call unheralded at the house of a merchant. The aristocracy always wanted money, it is true, "but what they thought they might require, they went and took," as witness the piratical Barons of the Rhine, whose exactions brought misery on the great city of Frankfort.

Then all at once came the clinching remembrance that when the Electors were appealed to on behalf of the young Prince, the three Archbishops had promptly seized his Royal Highness, and, in spite of the pleadings of the Empress (the Emperor was drunk and indifferent) placed him in the custody of the Archbishop nearest to Frankfort, the warrior prelate of Mayence, who imprisoned him in the strong fortress of Ehrenfels, from which, well guarded and isolated as it was upon a crag over-hanging the Rhine, no man could escape.

"Will you kindly be seated again, sir," requested the merchant, and if he had spoken a short time before, he would have put the phrase "your Royal Highness" in the place of the word "sir."

Roland, after a moment's hesitation, sat down. He saw that his coup had failed, because he was unable to back it up by proofs. His dramatic action had been like a brilliant cavalry charge, for a moment successful, but coming to naught because there was no solid infantry to turn the temporary confusion of the enemy into complete rout. Realizing that the battle must be fought over again, the Prince sat back with a sigh of disappointment, a shade of discontent on his handsome face.

"I find myself in rather a quandary," proceeded the merchant. "If indeed you are the Emperor's son, it is not for such as I to cross-examine you."

"Ask me any questions you like, sir. I shall answer them promptly enough."

"If I beg you to supply proof of the statement you make, you would be likely to reply that as you dared not enter your father's Palace, you are unable to furnish me with corroboration."

"Sir, you put the case in better language than I could employ. In more halting terms that is what I should have said."

"When were you last in the Palace?"

"About the same time, sir, that you took up your residence in prison."

"Ah, yes; that naturally would be your answer. Now, my young friend, you have shown me that you know nothing of mercantile practice; therefore it may perhaps interest you if I explain some of our methods."

"Herr Goebel, you may save your breath. Such a recital must not only fail to interest me, but will bore me extremely. I care nothing for your mercantile procedure, and, to be quite plain with you, I despise your trade, and find some difficulty in repressing my contempt for those who practice it."

"If an emissary of mine," returned Goebel, unperturbed, "approached a client or customer for the purpose of obtaining a favor, and used as little tact as you do, I should dismiss him."

"I'm not asking any favors from you."

"You wish me to hand over to you a thousand thalers, otherwise why came you here?"

"I desire to bestow upon you the greatest of boons, namely to open up the Rhine, and bring back prosperity to Frankfort, which you brainless, cowardly merchants have allowed to slip through your fingers, blaming now the Barons, now the Emperor, now the Electors; censuring everybody, in fact, except the real culprits ... yourselves. You speak of the money as a favor, but it is merely an advance for a few weeks, and will be returned to you; yet because I desire to confer this inestimable gift upon you and your city, you expect me to cringe to you, and flatter you, as if I were a member of your own sycophantic league. I refuse to do anything of the kind, and yet, by God, I'll have the money!"

The merchant, for the first time during their conference, laughed heartily. The young man's face was aflame with anger, yet the truculent words he used did more to convince Herr Goebel that he belonged to the aristocracy than if he had spoken with the most exemplary humility. Goebel felt convinced he was not the Prince, but some young noble, who, intimate with the Royal Family, and knowing the Emperor's son to be out of the way, thought it safe to assume his name, the better to carry forward his purpose, whatever that purpose might actually be. That it was to open the Rhine he did not for a moment credit, and that he would ever see his cash again, if once he parted with it, he could not believe.

"At the risk of tiring you, I shall nevertheless proceed with what I was about to say. We merchants, for our own protection, contribute to a fund which might be entitled one for secret service. This fund enables us to procure private information that may be of value in our business. Among other things we need to know are accurate details pertaining to the intentions and doings of our rulers, for whatever our own short-comings may be, the actions of those above us affect business one way or the other. May I read you a short report that came in while I was serving my term of imprisonment?"

"Oh, read what you like," said Roland indifferently, throwing back his head, and partially closing his eyes, with an air of ennui.

The merchant drew towards him a file of papers, and going through them carefully, selected a document, and drew it forth, then, clearing his throat, he read aloud—

"'At an hour after midnight, on St. Stanislas' Day, three nobles, one representing the Archbishop of Mayence, the second the Archbishop of Treves, and the third the Archbishop of Cologne, armed with authority from these three Electors and Princes of the Church, entered the Saalhof from the side facing the river, and arrested in his bed the young Prince Roland. They assured the Empress, who protested, that the Prince would be well cared for, and that, as an insurrection was feared in Frankfort, it was considered safer that the person whom they intended to elevate to the throne on the event of the Emperor's death, should be out of harm's way, being placed under the direct care of the Archbishop of Mayence. They informed the Empress that the Archbishops would not remove the Prince from the Palace in opposition to the wishes of either the Emperor or herself, but if this permission was not given, a meeting of the Electors would at once be called, and some one else selected to succeed the present ruler.

"'This consideration exerted a great influence upon the Empress, who counseled her son to acquiesce. The young man was led to a boat then in waiting by the river steps of the Palace, and so conveyed down the Main to the Rhine, which was reached just after daybreak. Without landing, and keeping as much as possible to the middle of the river, the party proceeded down the Rhine, past Bingen, to the foot of the crag on which stands the castle of Ehrenfels. The Prince was taken up to the Castle, where he now remains.

"'The Archbishops from their revenues allot to him seven hundred thalers a month, in addition to his maintenance. It is impossible for him to escape from this stronghold unaided, and as the Emperor takes no interest in the matter, and the Empress has given her consent, he is like to be an inmate of Ehrenfels during the pleasure of the Archbishops, who doubtless will not elect him to the throne in succession unless he proves compliant to their wishes. The Prince being a young man of no particular force of character'" (the merchant paused in his reading, and looked across at his vis-à-vis with a smile, but the latter appeared to be asleep), "'he will probably succumb to the Archbishops, therefore merchants are advised to base no hopes upon an improvement in affairs, even though the son should succeed the father. Despite the precautions taken, the arrest and imprisonment of the Prince, and even the place of his detention, became rather generally known in Frankfort, but the news is in the form of rumor only, and excites little interest throughout the city.'

"There, Sir Roland, what do you say to that?"

"Oh, nothing much," replied Roland. "The account might have stated that in the boat were five rowers, who worked lustily until we reached the Rhine, when, the wind being favorable, a sail was hoisted, and with the current assisting the wind, we made excellent time to Ehrenfels. I observe, further, that your secret service keeps you very well informed, and therefore withdraw a tithe of the harsh things I said regarding the stupidity of the merchants."

"Many thanks for the concession," said Goebel, replacing the document with its fellows. "Now, as a plain and practical man, what strikes me is this: you need only return to Ehrenfels for two months, and as there is little use for money in that fortress, your maintenance being guaranteed, and seven hundred thalers allowed, you can come away with four hundred thalers more than the sum you demand from me, and thus put your project into force without being under obligations to any despised merchant."

"True, Herr Goebel, but can you predict what will happen in Frankfort before two months are past? You learn from that document that the shrewd Archbishops anticipate an insurrection, and doubtless they command the force at hand ready to crush it, but during this conflict, which you seem to regard so lightly, does it ever occur to you that the merchants' palaces along the Fahrgasse may be sacked and burnt?"

"That, of course, is possible," commented the merchant.

"Nay, it is absolutely certain. Civil war means ruin, to innocent and guilty alike."

"You are in the right. Now, will you tell me how you escaped from Ehrenfels?"

"Yes; if you agree to my terms without further haggling."

"I shall agree to your terms if I believe your story."

"It seems impossible, sir, to pin you down to any definite bargain. Is this the way you conduct your business?"

"Yes; unless I am well assured of the good faith of my customer. I offered you ordinary business terms when I asked for security, or for the signature of three responsible merchants to your bond. It is because I am a merchant, and not a speculator, that I haggle, as you term it."

"Very well, then, I will tell you how I got away, but I begin my recital rather hopelessly, for you always leave yourself a loophole of escape. If you believe my story, you say! Yes: could I weave a romance about tearing my sheets into ropes; of lowering myself in the dark from the battlements to the ground; of an alarm given; of torches flashing; of diving into the Rhine, and swimming under the water until I nearly strangled; of floating down over the rapids, with arrows whizzing round me in the night; of climbing dripping to the farther shore, far from sight of Ehrenfels, then, doubtless, you would believe. But my escape was prosaically commonplace, depending on the cupidity of one man. The material for it was placed in my hands by the Archbishops themselves. Your account states that the Castle is well guarded. So it is, but when the Archbishop needs an augmentation of his force, he withdraws his men from Ehrenfels to Mayence, as my prison is the nearest of his possessions to his capital city, and thus at times it happens that the Castle is bereft of all save the custodian and his family. His eldest son happens to be of my own age, and not unlike me in appearance. None of the guards saw me, except the custodian, and you must remember he was a very complacent jailer, for the reason that he knew well every rising sun might bring with it tidings that I was his Emperor, so he cultivated my acquaintance, to learn in his own thrifty, peasant way what manner of ruler I might become, and I, having no one else to talk to, made much of his company.

"Frequently he impressed upon me that his task of jailer was most irksome to him, but poverty compelling, what could he do? He swore he would accomplish whatever was in his power to mitigate my captivity, and this indeed did; so at last when the Castle was empty I made him a proposal. Now remember, Sir Merchant, that what I tell you is in confidence, and should you break faith with me, I will have you hanged if I become Emperor, or slit your throat with my own sword if I don't."

"Go on. I shall tell no one."

"I said to my jailer: 'There are not half a dozen people in this world who know me by sight, and among that half-dozen no Elector is included. Outside the Palace at Frankfort I am acquainted with a sword maker or two, and about a score of good fellows who are friends of theirs, but to them I am merely a fencing-master. Now, seven hundred thalers a month pass through your honest hands to mine, and will continue to do so. Your son seems to be even more silent than yourself, and he is a young fellow whom I suspect knows the difference between a thaler and a button on his own coat. If you do what I wish, there will be some slight risk, but think of the reward immediate and in future! At once you come into an income of seven hundred thalers a month. If I am elected Emperor, I shall ennoble you, and present you with the best post in the land. If you don't do what I wish, I shall cause your head cut off as the first act of my first day of power.'"

"You did not threaten to slit his throat with your own sword, failing your elevation?" asked the merchant, with a smile.

"No. He was quite safe from my vengeance unless I came to the throne."

"In that case I should say the custodian need not fear the future. But please go on with your account."

"I proposed that his son and I should exchange costumes; in short, the young man was to take my place, occupying the suite of rooms assigned to me in the Castle. I told his father there was not the slightest fear of discovery, for if the Archbishop of Mayence sent some one to see that the Prince was safe, or even came himself, all the young man need do was to follow my example and keep silent, for I had said nothing from the time I was roused in my room in the Saalhof until I was lodged in Ehrenfels. I promised, if set at liberty, to keep within touch of Frankfort, where, at the first rumor of any crisis, I could return instantly to Ehrenfels.

"The custodian is a slow-minded man, although not so laggard in coming to an agreement as yourself. He took a week to turn the matter over in his mind, and then made the plunge. He is now jailer to his own son, and that young peasant lives in a style he never dreamed of before. The Archbishops are satisfied, because they believe I cannot escape from the stronghold— like yourself, holding but a poor opinion of my abilities; and their devout

Lordships know that outside the fortress no person, not even my mother, wishes me forth. I took in my wallet five hundred thalers, and fared like the peasant I seemed to be, down the Rhine, now on one side, now on the other, until I came to the ancient town of Castra Bonnensia of the Romans, which name the inhabitants now shorten to Bonn. There I found the Archbishop in residence, and not at Cologne, as I had supposed. The town being thronged with soldiers and inquisitive people of Cologne's court, I returned up the Rhine again, remembering I had gone rather far afield, and although you may not believe it, I called upon my old friend the custodian of Ehrenfels, and enjoyed an excellent meal with him, consuming some of the seductive wine that is grown on the same side of the river about a league above Ehrenfels."

"I dare say," said the merchant, "that I can give the reason for this apparently reckless visit of yours to Ehrenfels. You were in want of money, the five hundred thalers being spent."

"Sir, you are exactly in the right, and I got it, too, without nearly so much talk as I have been compelled to waste on the present occasion."

"What was your object in going down the river instead of turning to Frankfort?"

"I had become interested in my prison, and had studied methods by which it could be successfully attacked. I knew that my father allowed the Barons of the Rhine to override him, and I wondered if his wisdom was greater than I thought. Probably, said I to myself, he knew their castles to be impregnable, but, with the curiosity of youth, I desired to form an opinion of my own. I therefore lodged as a wayfarer at every castle to I could gain admittance, making friends with some underling, and getting a bed on occasion in the stables, although often I lodged within the castle itself. Thus I came to the belief, which I bring to you, that assisted by twenty fearless men I can capture any castle on the Rhine with the exception of three. And now, Herr Goebel, I have said all I intend to say. Do you discredit my story?"

The merchant gazed across at him quizzically for some time without making any reply, then he said:

"Do you think I believe you?"

"Frankly, I do not."

"If I am unable to give you the gold, I can at least furnish some good advice. Set up as a poet, good Master Roland, and weave for our delectation stories of the Rhine. I think your imagination, if cultivated, would give you a very high place among the romancers of our time."

With a patience that Herr Goebel had not expected, Roland replied:

"It grieves me to return empty-handed to my twenty friends, who last night bade me a very confident adieu."

"Yes, they will be disappointed, and I shrewdly suspect that my thousand thalers would not go towards the prosecuting of the expedition you have outlined, but rather in feasting and in wine."

"Again, sir, you are right. It is unfortunate that I am so often compelled to corroborate your statements, when all the acumen with which you credit my mind is turned towards the task of proving you a purse-proud fool, puffed up in your own conceit, and as short-sighted as an owl in the summer sunlight. However, let us stick to our text. If what I said had been true, although of course you know it isn't, you have nevertheless enough common sense to be aware that I would certainly show a pardonable reluctance about visiting my father's Palace. It is thronged with spies of the Archbishop, and although, as I have said, I am not very well known, there is a chance that one or another might recognize me, and then, almost instantly, a man on a swift horse would be on his way to Mayence. If I knew that I had been discovered, I should make at once for Ehrenfels, arriving there before an investigation was held. But my twenty comrades would wait for me in vain. Nevertheless, I shall venture into the Saalhof this very afternoon, and bring to you a letter written by my mother certifying that I am her son. Would that convince you?"

"Yes; were I sure the signature was genuine."

"Ah, there you go again! Always a loophole!"

The young man spoke in accents of such genuine despair that his host was touched despite his incredulity.

"Look you here," he said, bending across the table. "There is, of course, one chance in ten thousand that you are what you say. I have never seen the signature of the Empress, and such a missive could easily be forged by a scholar, which I take you to be. If, then, you wish to convince me, I'll put before you a test which will be greatly to your advantage, and which I will accept without the loophole."

"In Heaven's name, let's hear what it is."

"There is something that you cannot forge: the Great Seal of the Realm, attached to all documents signed by the Emperor."

"I have had no dealings with my father for years," cried the young man. "I have not even seen him these many months past. I can obtain the signature of my mother to anything I like to write, but not that of my father."

"Patience, patience," said the merchant, holding up his hand. "'Tis well known that the Empress can bend the Emperor to her will when she chooses to exert it. You see, in spite of all, I am quite taking it for granted that you are the Prince, otherwise 'twere useless to waste time in this talk. You display all the confidence of youth in speaking of the exploits you propose, and, indeed, it is cheering for a middle-aged person like myself to meet one so confident of anything in these pessimistic days. But have you considered what will happen if something goes wrong during one of your raids?"

"Nothing can go wrong. I feel no fear on that score."

"I thought as much. Very well, I will tell you what could go wrong. Some Baron may entrap you and your score, and forthwith hang you all from his battlements. Now, it is but common sense to prevent such a termination, if it be possible. Therefore seek out the Empress. Tell her that you and your twenty companions are about to embark on an enterprise greatly beneficial to the land. Say that you go incognito, and that, even should you fail, 'twill bring no discredit to your Royal House. But point out the danger of which I forewarn you. Ask her to get the signature of the Emperor attached to a safe-conduct, together with the device of the Great Seal; then if the Baron who captures you cannot read, he will still know the potency of the picture, and as there is no loophole to my acceptance of this proof, I will, for your convenience, and for my own protection, write the safe-conduct on as sound a bit of parchment as ever was signed in a palace."

Saying this, Herr Goebel rose, and went to his desk in a corner of the room, where he indited the memorial he had outlined, and, after sprinkling it with sand, presented it to Roland, who read:

"These presents warn him to whom they are presented that Roland the bearer is my son, and that what he has done has been done with my sanction, therefore he and his twenty comrades are to be held scathless, pending an appeal to me in my capital city of Frankfort.

"Whomsoever disobeys this instrument forfeits his own life, and that of his family and followers, while his possessions will be confiscated by the State."

Roland frowned.

"Doesn't it please you?" asked Goebel, his suspicions returning.

"Well, it seems to me rather a plebeian action, to attack a man's castle, and then, if captured, crawl behind a drastic threat like this."

The merchant shrugged his shoulders.

"That's a sentimental objection, but of course you need not use the document unless you wish, though I think if you see twenty-one looped ropes dangling in the air your hesitation will vanish. Oh, not on your own account," cried Goebel, as a sign of dissent from his visitor, "but because of those twenty fine young fellows who doubtless wait to drink wine with you."

"That is true," said Roland, with a sigh, folding up the stiff parchment, opening his cloak, and thrusting it under his belt, standing up as he did this.

"Bring me that parchment, bearing the Emperor's signature and the Great Seal, and you will find the golden coins awaiting you."

"Very well. At what time this evening would it please you to admit me?"

"Friends of mine are coming to-night, but they are not likely to stop long; merely a few handshakes, and a few cups of wine. I shall be ready for you when the Cathedral clock strikes ten."

With this the long conference ended, and the aged servitor in the hall showed Roland into the Fahrgasse.

As the young man proceeded down the Weckmarkt into the Saalgasse, he muttered to himself:

"The penurious old scoundrel! God keep me in future from dealing with such! To the very last he suspects me of being a forger, and has written this with his own hand, doubtless filling it with secret marks. Still, perhaps it is as well to possess such a safeguard. This is my loophole out of the coming enterprise, I fear we are all cowards, noble and merchant alike."

He walked slowly past the city front of the Palace, cogitating some means of entering without revealing his identity, but soon found that even this casual scrutiny made him an object of suspicion. He could not risk being accosted, for, if taken to the guard-room and questioned—searched, perhaps, and the sword found on him—a complication would arise adding materially to the difficulties already in his way. Quickening his pace, he passed through the Fahrthor, and so to the river-bank, where he saw that the side of the Saalhof fronting the Main was guarded merely by one or two sentries, for the mob could not gather on the surface of the waters, as it gathered on the cobble-stones of the Saalgasse and the Fahrthor.

Retracing his steps, the Prince walked rapidly until he came to the bridge, advancing to the iron Cross which commemorates the fowl sacrifice to the devil, as the first living creature venturing upon that ancient structure. Here he leaned against the parapet, gazed at the river façade of the Palace, and studied his problem. There were three sets of steps from the terrace to the water, a broad flight in the center for use upon state occasions, and a narrow flight at either end; the western staircase being that in ordinary use, and the eastern steps trodden by the servants carrying buckets of water from the river to the kitchen.

"The nearer steps," he said to himself, "offer the most feasible opportunity. I'll try them."

He counted his money, for here was probably a case for bribery. He found twenty-four gold pieces, and some loose silver. Returning the coins to his pouch, he walked to the land, and proceeded up the river until he reached a wharf where small skiffs were to let. One of these he engaged, and refusing the services of a waterman, stepped in, and drifted down the stream. He detached sword and scabbard from his belt, removed the cloak and wrapped the weapon in it, placing the folded garment out of sight under the covering at the prow. With his paddle he kept the boat close to the right bank, discovering an excellent place of concealment under the arch supporting the steps, through which the water flowed. He waited by the steps for a few moments until a scullion in long gabardine came down and dipped his bucket in the swift current.

"Here, my fine fellow," accosted Roland, "do you wish to earn a pair of gold pieces?" and he showed the yellow coins in the palm of his hand.

The menial's eyes glistened, and he cast a rapid glance over his shoulder.

"Yes," he replied breathlessly.

"Then leave your bucket where it is, and step into this wherry."

The underling, again with a cautious look around, did as he was ordered.

"Now throw off that outer garment, and give it to me."

Roland put it on over his own clothes, and flung his bonnet beside the cloak and sword, for the servant was bareheaded.

"Get under that archway, and keep out of sight until you hear me whistle."

Taking the bucket, Roland mounted the steps, and strode out of the brilliant sunlight into the comparative gloom of the corridor that led to the kitchen. He had been two hours with the merchant, and it was now the time of midday eating. Every one was hurrying to and fro, with no time to heed anything that did not pertain to the business in hand, so placing the bucket in a darkened embrasure, the intruder flung off the gabardine beside it, and searching, found a back stair which he ascended.

Once in the upper regions, he knew his way about, and proceeded directly to his mother's room, being sure at this hour to find her within. On his unannounced entrance the Empress gave utterance to an exclamation that indicated dismay rather than pleasure, but she hurried forward to meet and embrace him.

"Oh, Roland!" she cried, "what do you here? How came you to the Palace?"

"By way of the river. My boat is under the arch of the servants' stairway, and I have not a moment to lose."

"How did you escape from Ehrenfels, and why have you come here? Surely you know the Palace will be the first place searched for you?"

"There will be no search, mother. Take my word for it that no one is aware of my absence from Ehrenfels but the custodian, and for the best of reasons he dare not say a word. Do not be alarmed, I beg of you. I am free by his permission, and shall return to the Castle before he needs me. Indeed, mother, so far from jeopardizing my own safety, I am here to preserve it."

He drew from under his belt Herr Goebel's parchment, and handed it to her.

"In case it should occur to the good Archbishop, or any other noble, to hang me, I thought it best to get such a declaration signed by the Emperor, and decorated with the Great Seal of the Empire. Then, if any attempt is made on my life, as well as on my liberty, I may produce this Imperial decree, and bring my case to Frankfort."

"Surely, surely," exclaimed the agitated lady, her hands trembling as she held the document and tried to read it; "I can obtain your father's signature, but the Great Seal must be attached by the Chamberlain."

"Very good, mother. The Chamberlain will do as his Majesty orders. The seal is even more important than the signature, if it comes to that, and I am sure the Chamberlain will make no objection when the instrument is for the protection of your son's life. It is not necessary to say that I am here, or have anything to do with the matter. But lose not a moment, and give orders that no one shall enter this room."

The empress hastened away with the parchment, while the young man walked impatiently up and down the room. It seemed hours before she returned, but at last she came back with the document duly executed. Roland thrust it under his belt again, and reassuring his mother, who was now weeping on his shoulder, he tried to tear himself away. The Empress detained him until, with fumbling hands, she unlocked a drawer in a cabinet, and took from it a bag that gave forth a chink of metal as she pressed it on her son.

"I must not take it," he said. "I am quite well provided. The generous Archbishops allow me seven hundred thalers a month, which is paid with exemplary regularity."

"There are only five hundred thalers here," replied the Empress. "I wish there were more, but you must accept it, for I should feel easier in my mind to know that you possess even that much. Do they misuse you at Ehrenfels, my son?"

"Oh, no, no, no! I live like a burgomaster. You need feel no fear on my account, mother. Ehrenfels is a delightful spot, with old Bingen just across the water. I like it much better than I did Frankfort, with its howling mobs, and shall be very glad to get quit again of the city."

Then, with a hurried farewell, he left the weeping woman, and descending the back stair, secured the abandoned gabardine, put it on, and so came to the water's edge, entering into possession of his boat again. Returning the craft to its owner, he resumed sword and cloak once more, and found his way to a tavern, where he ordered a satisfactory meal.

In the evening he arrived at the Rheingold, and meeting the landlord in the large, empty, public cellar, asked that worthy if his friends had assembled yet, and was told they were all within the Kaiser cellar.

"Good!" he cried. "I said I would be gone a week, but here I am within a day. If that's not justifying a man's word, I should like to know what is. And now, landlord, set forth the best meal you can provide, with a double quantity of wine."

"For yourself, sir?"

"For all, landlord. What else? The lads have had no supper, I'll warrant."

"A little black bread has gone the rounds."

"All the more reason that we should have a huge pasty, steaming hot, or two or three of them if necessary. And your best wine, landlord. That from the Rheingau."

But the landlord demurred.

"A meal for yourself, sir, as leader, I could venture upon, but feeding a score of hungry men is a different matter. Remember, sir, I have not seen the color of their silver for many a long day, and, since these evil times have set in, I am a poor man."

"Sordid silver? Out upon silver! unless it is some silvery fish from the river, fresh and firm; and that's a good idea. We will begin with fish while you prepare the meat. 'Tis gold I deal with to-night, and most of it is for your pouch. Run your hand in here and enjoy the thrill," and Roland held open the mouth of the bag which contained his treasure.

"Ah!" cried the inn-keeper, his face aglow. "No such meal is spread to-night in Frankfort as will be set before you."

There was a great shout as Roland entered the Kaiser cellar, and a hurrah of welcome.

"Ha, renegade!" cried one. "Have you shirked your task so soon?"

"Coward, coward, poltroon!" was the cry. "I see by his face he has failed. Never mind them, Roland. Your chair at the head of the table always awaits you. There is a piece of black bread left, and though the wine is thin, it quenches thirst."

Roland flung off his cloak, hung it and the sword on a peg, and took his seat at the head of the table. Pushing away the flagons that stood near him, he drew the leathern bag from his belt, and poured the shining yellow coins on the table, at the sight of which there arose such a yell that the stout beams above them seemed to quake.

"Apologize!" demanded Roland, when the clamor quieted down. "The man who refuses to apologize, and that abjectly, must take down his sword from the peg and settle with me!"

A shout of apology was the response.

"We grovel at your feet, High Mightiness!" cried the man who had called him poltroon.

"I have taken the liberty of ordering a fish and meat supper, with a double quantity of Rudesheimer wine. Again I offer to fight any man who resents this encroachment on my part."

"I could spit you with a hand tied behind my back," cried one, "but I am of a forgiving nature, and will wait instead for the spitted fowl."

"Most of this money," continued Roland quietly, "goes, I suspect, to the landlord, as a slight recognition of past kindness, but I am promised a further supply this evening, which will be divided equally among ourselves. I ask you, therefore, to be sparing of the wine." Here he was compelled to pause for some moments, and listen to groans, hoots, howls, and the rapping of empty flagons on the stout table.

The commotion was interrupted by the entrance of the landlord, who brought with him the promised Rhine wine; for, hearing the noise, he supposed it represented impatience of the company at the delay, a mistake which no one thought it worth while to rectify. He promised that the fish would follow in a very few minutes, and went out to see that his word was kept.

"Why should we be sparing of the wine?" asked a capable drinker, who had drained his flagon before asking the question. "With all that money on the table it seems to me a scandalous proviso."

"'Tis not a command at all," replied Roland, "but merely a suggestion.

I spoke in the interests of fair-play. An appointment was made by me for ten o'clock this evening, and I wish to keep it and remain uninfluenced by wine."

"What's her name, Roland?" inquired the wine-bibber.

"I was about to divulge that secret when you interrupted me. The name is Herr Goebel."

"What! the cloth merchant on the Fahrgasse?"

"Is it cloth he deals in? I didn't know the particulars of his occupation beyond the facts that he is a merchant, and lives in the Fahrgasse. This morning I enjoyed the privilege of presenting to Herr Goebel a mutually beneficial plan which would give us all something to do."

"Oh, is Goebel to be our employer? I'm a sword forger, and work for no puny cloth merchant," said Kurzbold.

"This appointment," continued Roland, unheeding, "is set for ten o'clock, and I expect to return here before half-past, therefore—"

"Therefore we're not to drink all the wine."

"Exactly."

Their leader sat down as the landlord, followed by an assistant, entered, carrying the paraphernalia for the substantial repast, and proceeded to set the table.

When the hilarious meal was finished, the company sat for another half-hour over its wine, then Roland rose, buckled on his sword, and flung his cloak over his shoulders.

"Roland, I hope you have not sold your soul for this gold?"

"No; but I have pledged your bodies, and my own as well. Greusel, will you act as secretary and treasurer? Scrutinize the landlord's bill with a generous eye, and pay him the amount we owe. If anything is left, we will divide it equally," and with that he waved his hand to them, departing amidst a round of cheers, for the active youths were tired of idleness.

Punctuality is the politeness of kings, and as the bells of Frankfort were ringing ten o'clock, Roland knocked at the door of the merchant's house in the Fahrgasse. It was promptly opened by the ancient porter, who, after securing it again, conducted the young man up the solid stairway to the office-room on the first floor.

Ushered in, the Prince found the merchant seated in his usual chair, as if he had never moved from the spot where Roland had left him at noon that day. Half a dozen candles shed their soft radiance over the table, and on one corner of it, close by Herr Goebel's right elbow, the visitor saw a well-filled doeskin bag which he fancied might contain the thousand thalers.

"Good even to you, Herr Goebel," said the young man, doffing his bonnet. "I hope I have not trodden too closely on the heels of my appointment, thus withdrawing you prematurely from the festivities, which I trust you enjoyed all the more that you breathed the air of liberty again."

"The occasion, sir, was solemn rather than festive, for although I was glad to see my old friends again, and I believe they were glad to see me, the condition of the city is such, and growing rapidly worse, that merchants cannot rejoice when they are gathered together."

"Ah, well, Herr Goebel, we will soon mend all that. How long will it require to load your boat and choose your crew?"

"Everything can be ready by the evening of the day after to-morrow."

"You will select one of your largest barges. Remember, it must house twenty-one men besides the crew and the goods."

"Yes; I shall see that complete arrangements are made for your comfort."

"Thank you. But do not provide too much luxury. It might arouse suspicion from the Barons who search the boat."

"But the Barons will see you and your men in the boat."

"I think not. At least, we don't intend to be seen. I will call upon you again to-morrow at ten o'clock. Will you kindly order your captain to be here to meet me? I wish you to give him instructions in my presence that he is to do whatever I ask of him. We will join the boat on the Rhine between Ehrenfels and Assmannshausen. Instruct him to wait for us midway between the two places, on the right bank. And now the money, if you please."

"The money is here," said the merchant, sitting up a little more stiffly in his chair as he patted the well-stuffed bag. "The money is here if you have brought the instrument that authorizes you to take it."

"I have brought it with me, mein herr."

"Then show it to me," demanded the merchant, adjusting his horn glasses with the air of one who will not allow himself to be hoodwinked.

"With the greatest pleasure," returned the young man, standing before him. He unfastened his cloak, and allowed it to fall at his feet, then whisked out his sword, and presented the point of it to the merchant's throat.

Goebel, who had been fumbling with his glasses, suddenly became aware of his danger, and shrank back so far as his chair allowed, but the point of the sword followed him.

"What do you mean by that?" he gasped.

"I mean to show you that in this game iron is superior to gold. Your card is on the table, represented by that bag. Mine is still in my hand, and unplayed, but it takes the trick, I think. I hope you see the uselessness of resistance. You cannot even cry out, for at the first attempt a thrust of this blade cuts the very roots of utterance. It will be quite easy for me to escape, because I shall go quietly out with the bag under my cloak, telling the porter that you do not wish to be disturbed."

"It is the Prince of Thieves you are, then," said Herr Goebel.

"So it would appear. With your right hand pass that bag of gold across the table, and beg of me to accept it."

The merchant promptly did what he was told to do.

The young man put his sword back in its place, laughing joyously, but there was no answering smile on the face of Herr Goebel. As he had said, the condition of things in Frankfort, especially in that room, failed to make for merriment. Roland, without being invited, drew up a chair, and sat down at the opposite side of the table.

"Please do not attempt to dash for the door," he warned, "because I can quite easily intercept you, as I am nearer to it than you are, and more active. Call philosophy to your aid, and take whatever happens calmly. I assure you, 'tis the best way, and the only way."

He untied the cord, and poured the bulk of the gold out upon the table. The merchant watched him with amazement. For all the robber knew, the door might be opened at any moment, but he went on with numbering the coins as nonchalantly as if seated in the treasury of the Corn Exchange. When he had counted half the sum the bag contained, he poured the loose money by handfuls into the wallet that had held his mother's contribution, and pushed towards the merchant the bag, in which remained five hundred thalers.

"You are to know," he said with a smile, abandoning his bent-forward posture, "that when I visited my mother this afternoon, she quite unexpectedly gave me five hundred thalers, so I shall accept from you only half the sum I demanded this morning."

"Your mother!" cried the merchant. "Who is your mother?"

"The Empress, as I told you. Oh, at last I understand your uneasiness. You wished to see that document! Why didn't you ask for it? I asked for the money plainly enough. Well, here it is. Examine Seal and sign-manual."

The merchant minutely scrutinized the Great Seal and the signature above it.

"I don't know what to think," stammered Herr Goebel at last, gazing across the table with bewildered face.

"Think of your good fortune. A moment ago you imagined a thousand thalers were lost. Now it is but five hundred thalers invested, and you are a partner with the Royal House of the Empire."

III. DISSENSION IN THE IRONWORKERS' GUILD

Up to the time of his midnight awakening, Prince Roland had led a care-free, uneventful life. Although he received the general education supposed to be suitable for a youth of his station, he interested himself keenly in only two studies, but as one of these challenged the other, as it were, the result was entirely to the good. He was a very quiet boy, much under the influence of his mother, seeing little or nothing of his easy-going, inebriated father. It was his mother who turned her son's attention towards the literature of his country, and he became an omnivorous reader of the old monkish manuscripts with which the Palace was well supplied. Especially had his mind been attracted by the stories and legends of the Rhine. The mixture of history, fiction, and superstition which he found in these vellum pages, so daintily limned, and so artistically embellished with initial letters in gold and crimson and blue, fascinated him, and filled him with that desire to see those grim strongholds on the mountain-sides by the river, which later on resulted in his journey from Ehrenfels to Bonn, when his ingenuity, and the cupidity of his custodian, freed him from the very slight thraldom in which he was held by the Archbishop of Mayence.

If his attention had been entirely absorbed by the reading of these tomes, he might have become a mere dreamy bookworm, his intellect saturated with the sentimental and romantic mysticism permeating Germany even unto this day, and, as he cared nothing for the sports of boyhood, body might have suffered as brain developed.

But, luckily, he had been placed under the instruction of Rinaldo, the greatest master of the sword that the world had up to that period produced. Rinaldo was an Italian from Milan, whom gold tempted across the Alps for the purpose of instructing the Emperor's son in Frankfort. He was a man of grace and politeness, and young Roland took to him from the first, exhibiting such aptitude in the art of fencing that the Italian was not only proud of one who did such credit to his tuition, but came to love the youth as if he were his own son.

For the sword-making of Germany the Italian expressed the utmost contempt. The coarse weapons produced by the ironworkers of Frankfort needed strength rather than skill in their manipulation. Between the Italian method and the German was all the contrast that exists between the catching of salmon with a delicate line and a gossamer fly, or clubbing the fish to death as did the boatmen at that fishery called the Waag down the Rhine by St. Goar.

Roland listened intently and without defense to the diatribe against his country's weapons and the clumsy method of using them, but although he said nothing, he formed opinions of his own, believing there was some merit in strength which the Italian ignored; so, studying the subject, he himself invented a sword which, while lacking the stoutness of the German weapon, retained some of its stability, and was almost as easily handled as the Italian rapier, without the disadvantage of its extreme frailty.

Thus it came about that young Roland stole away from the Palace and made the acquaintance of the sword makers. The practice of fencing exercises every muscle in the body, and Roland's constant bouts with Rinaldo did more than make him a master of the weapon, with equal facility in his right arm or his left; it produced an athlete of the first quality; agile and strong, developing his physical powers universally, and not in any one direction.

Meanwhile Roland remained deplorably ignorant regarding affairs of State, this being a subject of which his mother knew nothing. The Emperor, who should have been his son's natural teacher, gave his whole attention to the wine-flagon, letting affairs drift towards disaster, allowing the power that deserted his trembling fingers to be grasped by stronger but unauthorized hands. Roland's surreptitious excursions into the city to confer with the sword makers taught him little of politics, for his conversations with these mechanics were devoted entirely to metal-working. He was hustled now and again by the turbulent mob, in going to and fro, but he did not know why it clamored, and, indeed, took little interest in the matter, conscious only that he came more and more to hate the city and loathe its inhabitants. When he could have his own way, he said to himself, he would retire to some country castle which his father owned, and there devote himself to such employment as fell in with his wishes.

But he was to receive a sharp lesson that no man, however highly placed, is independent of his fellows. He was unaware of the commotion that arose round his own name, and of the grim hanging of the leaders who chose him as their supreme head. When, bewildered and sleepy, he was aroused at midnight, and saw three armed men standing by his bedside, he received a shock that did more to awaken him than the grip of alien hands on his shoulders. During that night ride in the boat he said nothing but thought much. He had heard his mother plead for him without for a moment delaying his departure. She, evidently, was powerless. There was then in the land a force superior to that of the Throne. Something that had been said quieted his mother's fears, for at last she allowed him to go without further protest, but weeping a little, and embracing him much. There was no roughness or rudeness on the part of those who conveyed him down the river Main, and finally along the Rhine to Ehrenfels, but rather the utmost courtesy and deference, yet Roland remained silent throughout the long journey, agitated by this new, invisible, irresistible sovereignty animated with the will and power to do what it liked with him.

At the Castle of Ehrenfels he found awaiting him no rigorous imprisonment. He was treated as a welcome guest of an invisible host. It was his conversations with the garrulous custodian, who was a shrewd observer of the passing show, that gradually awakened the young Prince to some familiarity with the affairs of the country. He learned now in what a deplorable state the capital stood, through the ever-increasing exactions of the robber Barons along the Rhine. He asked his instructor why the merchants did not send their goods by some other route, which was a very natural query, but was told there existed no other route. A great forest extended for the most part between Frankfort and Cologne, and through the wilderness were no roads, for even those constructed by the Romans had been allowed to fall into decay; overgrown with trees, Nature thus destroying the neglected handiwork of man; the forest reclaiming its own.

"Indeed," continued the custodian, "for the last ten years things have been going to the devil, for the lack of a strong hand in the capital. A strong hand is needed by nobles and outlaws alike. We want a new Frederick

Barbarossa; the hangman's rope and the torch judiciously applied might be the saving of the country."

Ehrenfels, belonging to the Archbishop, was not a nest of piracy, and so its guardian could talk in this manner if he chose, but had he uttered these sentiments farther down the Rhine, he would himself have experienced the utility of the hangman's rope. Roland, knowing by this time who had taken him into custody, said:

"Why do not the three Archbishops put a stop to it? They possess the power."

The old jailer shrugged his shoulders.

"My chief, the great prelate of Mayence, would do it speedily enough if he stood alone, but the Archbishops of Treves have ever been robbers themselves, and Cologne is little better, therefore they neutralize one another. No two of them will allow the other to act, fearing he may gain in power, and thus upset the balance of responsibility, which I assure your Highness is very nicely adjusted. Each of the three claim allegiance from this Baron or the other, and although the Archbishops themselves may not lay toll directly on the Rhine, their ardent partisans do, which produces a deadlock."

Thus Roland received an education not to be had in palaces, and, saying little beyond asking an occasional question, he thought much, and came to certain conclusions. He arrived at an ambition to open the lordly Rhine and spent his time gathering knowledge and forming plans.

Twelve hours after receiving the five hundred thalers from the merchant, he again presented himself at the now familiar door in the Fahrgasse. In the room on the first floor he found with Herr Goebel a thick-set, heavily-bearded, weather-beaten man, who stood bonnet in hand while the merchant gave him final instructions.

"Good-morning, Sir Roland," cried Herr Goebel cheerfully. He exhibited no resentment for his treatment of the night before, and apparently daylight brought with it renewed confidence that the young man might succeed in his mission. There was now no hesitation in the merchant's manner; alert and decided, all mistrust seemed to have vanished. "This is Captain Blumenfels, whom I put in charge of the barge, and who has gathered together a crew on which he can depend although, of course, you must not expect them to fight."

"No," said Roland, "I shall attend to that portion of the enterprise."

"Now, Captain Blumenfels," continued Herr Goebel, "this young man is commander. You are to obey him in every particular, just as you would obey me."

The captain bowed without speaking.

"I shall not detain you any longer, captain, as you will be anxious to see the bales disposed of to your liking on the barge."

The captain thereupon took himself off, and Roland came to the conclusion that he liked this rough-and-ready mariner with so little to say for himself; a silent man of action, evidently.

Herr Goebel turned his attention to Roland.

"I have ordered bales of cloth to the value of a trifle more than four thousand thalers to be placed in the barge," he said. "The bales are numbered, and I have given the captain an inventory showing the price of each. I suppose you despise our vulgar traffic, and, indeed, I had no thought of asking so highly placed a person as yourself to sell my goods, therefore Blumenfels will superintend the marketing when you reach Cologne—that is, if you ever get so far."

"Your pardon, Herr Goebel, but I have my own plans regarding the disposal of your goods. I intend to be quit of them long before I see Cologne. Indeed, should I prosper, I hope your boat will set its nose southward for the return journey some distance this side of Coblentz."

The merchant gazed up at him in astonishment.

"Your design is impossible. There is no sale for cloth nearer than Coblentz. Your remarks prove you unacquainted with the river."

"I have walked every foot of both sides of the river between Ehrenfels and Bonn. There are many wealthy castles on this side of Coblentz."

"True, my good sir, true; but how became they wealthy? Simply by robbing the merchants. Are you not aware that each of these castles is inhabited by a titled brigand? You surely do not expect to sell my cloth to the Barons?"

"Why not? Remember how long it is since a cloth-barge went down the Rhine. Think for a moment of the arduous life which these Barons lead, hunting the boar, the bear, and the deer, tearing recklessly through thicket and over forest-covered ground. Why, our noble friends must be in rags by this time, or clad in the skins of the beasts they kill! They will be delighted to see and handle a piece of well-woven cloth once more."

For a full minute the merchant gaped aghast at this senseless talk so seriously put forward; then a smile came to his lips.

"Prince Roland, I begin to understand you. Your words are on a par with the practical joke you played upon me so successfully last night. Of course, you know as well as I that the Barons will buy nothing. They will take such goods as they want if you but give them opportunity. What you say is merely your way of intimating it is none of my affair how the goods are disposed of, so long as you hand over to me four thousand thalers."

"Four thousand five hundred, if you please."

"I shall be quite content with the four thousand, regarding the extra five hundred as paid for services rendered. Now, can I do anything further to aid you?"

"Yes. I wish you to send a man on horseback to Lorch, there to await the barge. Choose a man as silent as your captain; one whom you trust implicitly, for I hope to send back with him four thousand five hundred thalers, and also some additional gold, which I beg of you to keep safely for me until I return."

"Prince Roland, there can be no gold for me at Lorch."

"Dispatch a trustworthy man in case I receive the money. You will be anxious to know how we prosper, and I can at least forward a budget of news."

"But should there be gold, he cannot return safely with it to Frankfort."

"Oh, yes, if he keeps to the eastern bank of the Rhine. There is no castle between Lorch and Frankfort except Ehrenfels, and that, being the property of the Archbishop, may be passed safely."

"Very well. The man shall await you at Lorch. Inquire for Herr Kruger at Mergler's Inn."

That night, in the Kaiser cellar, another excellent supper was spread before the members of the metal-workers' league. It was quite as hilarious as the banquet of the night before; perhaps more so, because now, for the first time in months, the athletic young men were well fed, with money in their pouches. Each was clad in a new suit of clothes. Nothing like uniformity in costume had been attempted, there being but one day in which to replenish the wardrobes, which involved the acquiring of garments already made. However no trouble was experienced about this, for each branch of the metal-workers had its own recognized outfit, which was kept on hand in all sizes by various dealers catering to the wants of artisans, from apprentices to masters of their trade. The costumes were admirably adapted to the use for which they were intended. There was nothing superfluous in their make-up, and, being loosely cut, they allowed ample play to stalwart limbs. For dealing with metal the wearers required a cloth tightly woven, of a texture as nearly as possible resembling leather, and better accouterment for a rough-and-tumble, freebooter's excursion could not have been found, short of coats of mail, or, failing that, of leather itself.

Roland appeared in the trousers and doublet of a sword maker, and his comrades cheered loudly when he threw off his cloak and displayed for the first time that he was actually one of themselves. Hitherto something in the fashioning of his wearing apparel had in a manner differentiated him from the rest of the company, but now nothing in his dress indicated that he was leader of the coterie, and this pleased the independent metal-workers.

The previous night, after the landlord's bill was generously liquidated, each man had received upwards of thirty thalers. Roland then related to them his adventure with the merchant, and the result of his sword-play in the vicinity of Herr Goebel's throat. Two accomplishments he possessed endeared Roland to his comrades: first, the ability to sing a good song; and second, his talent for telling an interesting story, whether it was a personal adventure, a legend of the Rhine, or some tale of the gnomes which, as every one knows, haunt the gloomy forests in the mountain regions. His account of the evening spent with Herr Goebel aroused much laughter and applause, which greatly augmented when the material advantages of the interview were distributed among the guild.

This evening he purposed making a still more important disclosure; thus when the meal was finished, and the landlord, after replenishing the flagons, had retired, the new sword maker rose in his place at the head of the table.

"I crave your strict attention for a few minutes. Although I refused to confide my plans to Herr Goebel, I consider it my duty to inform you minutely of what is before us, and if I speak with some solemnity, it is because I realize we may never again meet around this table. We depart from Frankfort to-morrow upon a hazardous expedition, and some of us may not return."

"Oh, I say, Roland," protested Conrad Kurzbold, "don't mar a jovial evening with a note of tragedy. It's bad art, you know."

Kurzbold was one of the three actual sword makers, and had been president of the guild until he gave place to Roland. He was the oldest of the company; an ambitious man, a glib talker, with great influence among his fellows, and a natural leader of them. What he said generally represented the opinion of the gathering.

"For once, Kurzbold, I must ask you to excuse me," persisted Roland. "It is necessary that on this, the last, opportunity I should place before you exactly what I intend to do. I am very anxious not to minimize the danger. I wish no man to follow me blindfold, thus I speak early in the evening, that you may not be influenced by the enthusiasm of wine in coming to a decision. I desire each man here to estimate the risk, and choose, before we separate to-night, whether or not he will accompany the expedition.

"Here is the compact made with Herr Goebel: I promised that, with the help of my comrades, I would endeavor to open the Rhine to mercantile traffic. On the strength of such promise he gave me the money."

At this announcement rose a wild round of applause, and with the thunder of flagons on the table, and the shouting of each member, no single voice could make itself heard above the tumult. These lads had no conception of the perils they were to face, and Roland alone remained imperturbable, becoming more and more serious as the uproar went on. When at last quiet was restored, he continued, with a gravity in striking contrast to the hilarity of his audience:

"Herr Goebel is filling his largest barge with bales of cloth, and he has engaged an efficient crew, and a capable captain who will assume charge of the navigation. The barge will proceed to-morrow night down the Main, leaving Frankfort as unostentatiously as possible, while we march across the country to Assmannshausen, and there join this craft. It is essential that no hint of our intention shall spread abroad in gossipy Frankfort, therefore, depending on Captain Blumenfels to get his boat clear of the city without observation, and before the moon rises, I ask you to leave to-morrow separately by different gates, meeting me at Hochst, something more than two leagues down the river. I dare say you all know the Elector's palace, whose beautiful tower is a landmark for the country round."

"I protest against such a rendezvous," objected Kurzbold. "Make it the tavern of the Nassauer Hof, Roland. We shall all be thirsty after a walk of two leagues."

"Not at that time in the morning, I hope," said Roland, "for I shall await you in the shadow of the tower at nine o'clock. Let every man drink his fill to-night, for I intend to lead a sober company from Hochst to-morrow."

"Oh, you're optimistic, Roland," cried John Gensbein. "Give us till twelve o'clock to cool our heads."

"Drink all you wish this evening," repeated Roland, "but to-morrow we begin our work, with a long day's march ahead of us, so nine is none too early for a start from Hochst."

"Sufficient to the day is the wine thereof," said Conrad Kurzbold, rising to his feet. "Wine, blessed liquor as it is, possesses nevertheless one defect, which blot on its escutcheon is that it cannot carry over till next day, except in so far as a headache is concerned, and a certain dryness of the mouth. It is futile to bid us lay in a supply to-night that will be of any use to-morrow morning. For my part, I give you warning, Roland, that I shall make directly for the Nassauer Hof, or for the Schone Aussicht, where they keep most excellent vintages."

To this declaration Roland made no reply, but continued his explanatory remarks.

"We shall join the barge, as I have said, above Assmannshausen, probably at night, and then cross directly over the river. The first castle with which I intend to deal is that celebrated robber's roost, Rheinstein, standing two hundred and sixty feet above the water. Disembarking about a league up the river from Rheinstein, before daybreak we will all lie concealed in the forest within sight of the Castle gates. When the sun is well risen, Captain Blumenfels will navigate his boat down the river, and as it approaches Rheinstein we shall probably enjoy the privilege of seeing the gates open wide, as the company from the Castle descend precipitously to the water. While they rifle the barge we shall rifle the Castle, overpowering whoever we may find there, and taking in return for the cloth they steal such gold or silver as the treasury affords. We will then imprison all within the Castle, so that a premature alarm may not be given. If we are hurried, we may lock them in cellars, or place them in dungeons, then leave the Castle with our booty, but I do not purpose descending to the river until we have traversed a league or more of the mountain forest, where we may remain concealed until the barge appears, and so take ship again.

"The next castle is Falkenberg, the third Sonneck, both on the same side of the river as Rheinstein, and within a short distance from the stronghold, but the plan with each being the same as that already outlined, it is not necessary for me to repeat it."

"An excellent arrangement!" cried several; but John Gensbein spoke up in criticism.

"Is there to be no fighting?" he asked. "I expected you to say that after we had secured the gold we would fall on the robbers to the rear, and smite them hip and thigh."

"There is likely to be all the fighting you can wish for," replied Roland, "for at some point our scheme may go awry. It is not my intention to attack, but I expect you to fight like heroes in our own defense."

"I agree with Herr Roland," put in Conrad Kurzbold, rising to his feet. "If we purpose to win our way down to Cologne, it is unnecessary to search for trouble, because we shall find enough of it awaiting us at one point or another. But Roland stopped his account at what seems to me the most interesting juncture. What is the destination of the gold we loot from the castles?"

"The first call upon our accumulation will be the payment of four thousand five hundred thalers to Herr Goebel."

"Oh, damn the merchant!" cried Conrad. "We are risking our lives, and I don't see why he should reach out his claws. He will profit enough through our exertions if we open the Rhine."

"True; but that was the bargain I made with him. We risk our lives, as you say, but he risks his goods, besides providing barge, captain, and crew. He also furnished us with the five hundred thalers now in our pockets. We must deal honestly with the man who has supported us in the beginning."

"Oh, very well," growled Kurzbold, "have it your own way; but in my opinion the merchants should combine and raise a fund with which to reward us for our exertions if we succeed. Still, I shall not press my contention in the face of an overwhelming sentiment against me. However, I should like to speak to our leader on one matter which it seemed ungracious to mention last night. The merchant offered him a thousand thalers in gold, and he, with a generosity which I must point out to him was exercised at our expense, returned half that money to Herr Goebel. I confess that all I received has been spent; my hand is lonesome when it enters my pouch. I should be glad of that portion which might have been mine (and when I speak for myself, I speak for all) were it not for the misplaced prodigality of our leader who, possessing the money, was so thoughtless of our fellowship that he actually handed over five hundred thalers to a man who had not the slightest claim upon it."

"Herr Kurzbold," said Roland, with some severity, "many penniless nights passed over our heads in this room. If you know so much better than I how to procure money, why did you not do so? I should not venture to criticise a man who, without any effort on my part, placed thirty thalers at my disposal."

There was a great clamor at this, every one except Kurzbold, who stood stubbornly in his place, and Gensbein, who sat next to him, becoming vociferous in defense of their leader.

"It is uncomrade-like," cried Ebearhard above the din, "to spend the money and then growl."

"I speak in the interests of us all," shouted Kurzbold. "In the interests of our leader, no less than ourselves," but the others howled him down.

Roland, holding up his right hand, seemed to request silence and obtained it.

"I am rather glad," he said, "that this discussion has arisen, because there is still time to amend our programme. Herr Goebel's barge will not be loaded until to-morrow night, so the order may even yet be countermanded. The five hundred thalers which belonged to me I say nothing about, but the five hundred advanced by Herr Goebel must be returned to him unless we are in perfect unanimity."

At this suggestion Kurzbold sat down with some suddenness.

"I told you, when I left this room, promising to find the money within a week, that one condition was the backing of my fellows. You empowered me to pledge the efforts of our club as though it contained but one man. If that promise is not to be kept in spirit as well as in letter, I shall retire from the position I now hold, and you may elect in my stead Conrad Kurzbold, John Gensbein, or any one else that pleases you. But first I must be in a position to give back intact Herr Goebel's money; then, as I have divulged to you my plans, Conrad Kurzbold may approach him, and make better terms than I was able to arrange."

There were cries of "Nonsense! Nonsense!" "Don't take a little opposition in that spirit, Roland." "We are all free-speaking comrades, you know." "You are our leader, and must remain so."

Kurzbold rose to his feet for the third time.

"Literally and figuratively, my friend Roland has me on the hip, for my hip-pocket contains no money, and it is impossible for me to refund. I imagine, if the truth were told, we are all more or less in the same condition, for we have had equipment to buy, and what-not."

"Also Hochheimer," said one, at which there was a laugh, as Kurzbold was noted for his love of good wine. Up to this point Roland had carried the assemblage with him, but now he made an injudicious remark that instantly changed the spirit of the room.

"I am astonished," he said, "that any objection should be made to the fair treatment of Herr Goebel, for you are all of the merchant class, and should therefore hold by one of your own order."

He could proceed no farther. Standing there, pale and determined, he was simply stormed down. His ignorance of affairs, of which on several occasions the merchant himself had complained, led him quite unconsciously to touch the pride of his hearers. It was John Gensbein who angrily gave expression to the sentiment of the meeting.

"To what class do you belong, I should like to know? Do you claim affinity with the merchant class? If you do, you are no leader of ours. I inform you, sir, that we are skilled artisans, with the craft to turn out creditable work, while the merchants are merely the vendors of our products. Which, therefore, takes the higher place in a community, and which deserves it better: he who with artistic instinct unites the efforts of brain and hand to produce wares that are at once beautiful and useful, or he who merely chaffers over his counter to get as much lucre as he can for the creations that come from our benches?"

To Roland's aristocratic mind, every man who lacked noble blood in his veins stood on the same level, and it astonished him that any mere plebeian should claim precedence over another. He himself felt immeasurably superior to those present, sensible of a fathomless gulf between him and them, which he, in his condescension, might cross as suited his whim, but over which none might follow him back again; and this, he was well aware, they would be the first to admit did they but know his actual rank.

For a moment he was tempted to acknowledge his identity, and crush them by throwing the crown at their heads, but some hitherto undiscovered stubbornness in his nature asserted itself, arousing a determination to stand or fall by whatever strength of character he might possess.

"I withdraw that remark," he said, as soon as he could obtain a hearing. "I not only withdraw it, but I apologize to you for my folly in making it. It was merely thoughtlessness on my part, and, resting on your generosity, I should like you to consider the words unsaid."

Once more eighteen of the twenty swung round to his side. Roland now turned his attention to Conrad Kurzbold, ignoring John Gensbein, who had sat down flushed after his declamation, bewildered by the mutability of the many as Coriolanus had been before him.

"Herr Kurzbold," began Roland sternly, "have you any further criticism to offer?"

"No; but I stand by what I have already said."

"Well, I thank you for your honest expression of that determination, and I announce that you cannot accompany this expedition."

Again Roland instantaneously lost the confidence of his auditors, and they were not slow in making him of the fact.

"This is simply tyranny," said Ebearhard. "If a man may not open his mouth without running danger of expulsion, then all comradeship is at an end, and I take it that good comradeship is the pivot on which this organization turns. I do not remember that we ever placed it in the power of our president merely by his own word to cast out one of us from the fellowship. I may add, Roland, that you seem to harbor strange ideas concerning rank and power. I have been a member of this guild much longer than you, and perhaps understand better its purpose. Our leader is not elected to govern a band of serfs. Indeed, and I say it subject to correction from my friends, the very opposite is the case. Our leader is our servant, and must conduct himself as we order. It is not for him to lay down the law to us, but whatever laws exist for our governance, and I thank Heaven there are few of them, must be settled in conclave by a majority of the league."

"Right! Right!" was the unanimous cry, and when Ebearhard sat down all were seated except Roland, who stood at the end of the table with pale face and compressed lips.

"We are," he said, "about to set out against the Barons of the Rhine, entrenched in their strong castles. Hitherto these men have been completely successful, defying alike the Government and the people. It was my hope that we might reverse this condition of things. Now, Brother Ebearhard, name me a single Baron along the whole length of the Rhine who would permit one of his men-at-arms to bandy words with him on any subject whatever."

"I should hope," replied Ebearhard, "that we do not model our conduct after that of a robber."

"The robbers, I beg to point out to you, Ebearhard, are successful. It is success we are after, also a portion of that gold of which Herr Kurzbold has pathetically proclaimed his need."

"Do you consider us your men-at-arms, then, in the same sense that a Rhine Baron would employ the term?"

"Certainly."

"You claim the liberty of expelling any one you choose?"

"Yes; I claim the liberty to hang any of you if I find it necessary."

"Oh, the devil!" cried Ebearhard, sitting down as if this went beyond him. He gazed up and down the table as much as to say, "I leave this in your hands, gentlemen."

The meeting gave immediate expression of its agreement with Ebearhard.

"Gentlemen," said Roland, "I insist that Conrad Kurzbold apologizes to me for the expressions he has used, and promises not again to offend in like manner."

"I'll do nothing of the sort," asserted Kurzbold, with equal firmness.

"In that case," exclaimed Roland, "I shall retire, and I ask you to put me in a position to repay Herr Goebel the money I extracted from him. I resign the very thankless office of so-called leadership."

At this several wallets came out upon the table, but their contents clinked rather weakly. The majority of the guild sat silent and sobered by the crisis that had so unexpectedly come upon them. Joseph Greusel, seeing that no one else made a move, uprose, and spoke slowly. He was a man who never had much to say for himself; a listener rather than a talker, in whom Roland reposed great confidence, believing him to be one who would not flinch if trial came, and he had determined to make Greusel his lieutenant if the expedition was not wrecked before it set out.

"My friends," said Greusel gloomily, "we have arrived at a deadlock, and I should not venture to speak but that I see no one else ready to make a suggestion. I cannot claim to be non-partisan in the matter. This crisis has been unnecessarily brought about by what I state firmly is a most ungenerous attack on the part of Conrad Kurzbold."

There were murmurs of dissent, but Greusel proceeded stolidly, taking no notice.

"It is not disputed that Kurzbold accepted the money from Roland last night, spent it to-day, and now comes penniless amongst us, quite unable to refund the amount when his unjust remarks produce their natural effect. He is like a man who makes a wager knowing he hasn't the money to pay should he lose. If Roland retires from this guild, I retire also, ashamed to keep company with men who uphold a trick worthy of a ruined gambler."

"My dear Joseph," cried Ebearhard, springing up with a laugh, "you were misnamed in your infancy. You should have been called Herod, practically justifying a slaughter of us innocents."

"I stand by Benjamin," growled Gruesel, "the youngest and most capable of our circle; the one who produced the money while all the rest of us talked."

"You never talked till now, Joseph," said Ebearhard, still trying to ease the situation with a laugh, "and what you say is not only deplorably severe, but uttered, as I will show you, upon entirely mistaken grounds. We did not, and do not, support Conrad Kurzbold in what he said at first. Now you rate us as if we were no better than thieves. Dishonest gamblers, you call us, and Lord knows what else, and then you threaten withdrawal. I submit that your diatribe is quite undeserved. We all condemn Kurzbold for censuring Roland's generosity to the merchant, unanimously upholding Roland in that action, and have said so plainly enough. What we object to is this: Roland arrogates to himself power which he does not possess, of peremptorily expelling any member whose remarks displease him. Surely you cannot support him in that any more than we."

"Let us take one thing at a time," resumed Greusel, "not forgetting from whom came the original provocation. I must know where we stand. I therefore move a vote of censure on Conrad Kurzbold for his unmerited attack upon our president anent his dealings with Herr Goebel."

"I second that with great pleasure," said Ebearhard.

"Now, as we cannot ask our leader to put that motion, I shall take the liberty of submitting it myself," continued Greusel. "All in favor of the vote of censure which you have heard, make it manifest by standing up."

Every one arose except Roland, Gensbein, and Kurzbold.

"There, we have removed that obstacle to a clear understanding of the case, and before I formally deliver this vote of censure to Herr Kurzbold, I request him to reconsider his position, and of his own motion to make such delivery unnecessary.

"If it is the case that Roland assumes authority to expel whom he pleases from this guild, I shall not support him."

"It is the case! It is the case!" shouted several.

"Pardon me, comrades; I have the floor," continued Greusel. "I am not attempting oratory, but trying to disentangle a skein in which we have involved ourselves. I wish to receive neither applause nor hissing until I have finished the business. You say it is the case. I say it is not. Roland gave Herr Kurzbold the alternative either of apologizing or of paying over the money, so that it might be returned to the merchant. As I understand the matter, our president does not insist on Kurzbold leaving the guild, but merely announces his own withdrawal from it. You have allowed Kurzbold to put you in the position of being compelled to choose between himself and Roland. If you are logical men you cannot pass a vote of censure on Kurzbold, and then choose him instead of Roland. I therefore move a vote of confidence in our chief, the man who has produced the money, a thousand thalers in all, half of which was his own, and has divided it equally amongst us, when the landlord's bill was paid, withholding not a single thaler, nor arrogating—I think that was your word, friend Ebearhard—to himself a stiver more of the money than each of the others received. While Kurzbold has prated of comradeship, Roland has given us an excellent example of it, and I think he deserves our warmest thanks and our cordial support. I therefore submit to you the following motion: This meeting tenders to the president its warmest thanks for his recent efforts on behalf of the guild, and begs to assure him of its most strenuous assistance in carrying out the project he has put before it to-night."

"Joseph," said Ebearhard, rising, with his usual laugh, "you are a very clever man, although you usually persist in hiding your light under a bushel. I desire to associate myself with the expressions you have used, and therefore second your motion."

"I now put the resolution which you have all heard," said Greusel, "and I ask those in favor of it to stand."

Every one stood up promptly enough except the two recalcitrants, and of those two John Gensbein showed signs of hesitation and uneasiness. He half rose, sat down again; then, apparently at the urging of the man next him, stood up, a picture of irresolution. Kurzbold, finding himself now alone, laughed, and got upon his feet, thus making the vote unanimous. As the company seated itself, Greusel turned to the president.

"Sir, it is said that all's well that ends well. It gives me pleasure to tender you the unanimous vote of thanks and confidence of the iron-workers' guild, and before calling upon you to make any reply, if such should be your intention, I will ask Conrad Kurzbold to say a few words, which I am sure we shall all be delighted to hear."

Kurzbold rose bravely enough, in spite of the fact that Joseph Greusel's diplomacy had made a complete separation between him and all the others.

"I should like to say," he began, with an air of casual indifference, "that my first mention of the money was wholly in jest. Our friend Roland took my remarks seriously, which, of course, I should not have resented, and there is little use in recapitulating what followed. As, however, my utterances gave offense which was not intended by me, I have no hesitation in apologizing for them, and withdrawing the ill-advised sentences. No one here feels a greater appreciation of what our president has done than I, and I hope he will accept my apology in the same spirit in which it is tendered."

"Now, Master of the Guild," said Greusel, and Roland took the floor once more.

"I have nothing to say but 'Thank you.' The antagonists whom we hope to meet are men brave, determined, and ruthless. If any one in this company holds rancor against me, I ask him to turn it towards the Barons, and punish me after the expedition is accomplished. Let us tolerate no disagreements in face of the foe."

The young man took his cloak and sword from the peg on which they hung, passed down along the table, and thrust across his hand to Kurzbold, who shook it warmly. Arriving at the door, Roland turned round.

"I wish to see Captain Blumenfels, and give him final instructions regarding our rendezvous on the Rhine, so good-night. I hope to meet you all under the shadow of the Elector's tower in Hochst to-morrow morning at nine," and with that the president departed, being too inexperienced to know that soft words do not always turn away wrath, and that mutiny is seldom quelled with a handshake.

IV. THE DISTURBING JOURNEY OF FATHER AMBROSE

The setting summer sun shone full on the western side of Sayn Castle, sending the shadow of that tenth-century edifice far along the greensward of the upper valley. Upon a balcony, perched like a swallow's nest against the eastern end of Sayn Castle, a lovely girl of eighteen leaned, meditating, with arms resting on the balustrade, the harshness of whose stone surface was nullified by the soft texture of a gaudily-covered robe flung over it. This ample cloth, brought from the East by a Crusading ancestor of the girl, made a gay patch of scarlet and gold against the somber side of the Castle.

The youthful Countess Hildegunde von Sayn watched the slow oncoming of a monk, evidently tired, who toiled along the hillside deep in the shadow of the Castle, as if its cool shade was grateful to him. Belonging, as he did, to the very practical Order of the Benedictines, whose belief was in work sanctioned by prayer, the Reverend Father did not deny himself this temporary refuge from the hot rays of the sun, which had poured down upon him all day.

Looking up as he approached the stronghold, and seeing the girl, little dreaming of the frivolous mission she would propose, he waved his hand to her, and she responded gracefully with a similar gesture.

Indeed, however strongly the monk might disapprove, there was much to be said in favor of the resolution to which the young lady had come. She was well educated, probably the richest heiress in Germany, and carefully as the pious Sisters of Nonnenwerth Convent may have concealed the fact from her, she was extremely beautiful, and knew it, and although the valley of the Saynbach was a very haven of peace and prosperity, the girl became just a trifle lonely, and yearned to know something of life and the Court in Frankfort, to which her high rank certainly entitled her.

It is true that very disquieting rumors had reached her concerning the condition of things in the capital city; nevertheless she determined to learn from an authoritative source whether or not it was safe to take up a temporary residence in Frankfort, and for this purpose the reluctant Father Ambrose would journey southward.

Father Ambrose was more than sixty years old, and if he had belonged to the world, instead of to religion, would have been entitled to the name Henry von Sayn. His presence in the Benedictine Order was proof of the fact that money will not accomplish everything. His famous, or perhaps we should say infamous, ancestor, Count Henry III. of Sayn, who died in 1246, was a robber and a murderer, justly esteemed the terror of the Rhine. Concealed as it was in the Sayn valley, half a league from the great river, the situation of his stronghold favored his depredations. He filled his warehousing rooms with merchandise from barges going down the river, and with gold seized from unhappy merchants on their way up. He thought no more of cutting a throat than of cutting a purse, and it was only when he became amazingly wealthy that the increase of years brought trouble to a conscience which all men thought had ceased to exist. Thereupon, for the welfare of his soul, he built the Abbey of Sayn, and provided for the monks therein. Yet, when he came to die, he entertained fearsome, but admittedly well-founded doubts regarding his future state, so he proceeded to sanctify a treasure no longer of any use to him, by bequeathing it to the Church, driving, however, a bargain by which he received assurance that his body should rest quietly in the tomb he had prepared for himself within the Abbey walls.

He was buried with impressive ceremony, and the monks he had endowed did everything to carry out their share of the pact. The tomb was staunchly built with stones so heavy that no ordinary ghost could have emerged therefrom, but to be doubly sure a gigantic log was placed on top of it, strongly clamped down with concealed bands of iron, and, so that this log might not reveal its purpose, the monks cunningly carved it into some semblance of Henry himself, until it seemed a recumbent statue of the late villainous Count.

But despite such thoughtfulness their plan failed, for when next they visited the tomb the statue lay prone, face downwards, as if some irresistible, unseen power had flung it to the stone flags of the floor. Replacing the statue, and watching by the tomb, was found to be of little use. The watchers invariably fell asleep, and the great wooden figure, which during their last waking moments lay gazing towards the roof, was now on its face on the monastery floor, peering down in the opposite direction, and this somehow was regarded by the brethren as a fact of ominous significance.

The new Count von Sayn, heir to the title and estate of the late Henry III. was a gloomy, pious man, very different indeed from his turbulent predecessor. Naturally he was much perturbed by the conduct of the wooden statue. At first he affected disbelief in the phenomena despite the assurances of the monks, and later on the simple brethren deeply regretted they had made any mention of the manifestations. The new Count himself took up the task of watching, and paced all night before the tomb of the third Henry. He was not a man to fall asleep while engaged on such a somber mission, and the outcome of his vigil was so amazing that in the morning he gathered the brethren together in the great hall of the Abbey, that he might relate to them his experience.

The wooden statue had turned over, and fallen to the floor, as was its habit, but on this occasion it groaned as it fell. This mournful sound struck terror into the heart of the lonely watcher, who now, he confessed, regretted he had not accepted the offer of the monks to share his midnight surveillance. The courage of the House of Sayn is, however, a well-known quality, and, notwithstanding his piety, the new holder of the title was possessed of it, for although admitting a momentary impulse towards flight, and the calling for assistance which the monks would readily have given, he stood his ground, and in trembling voice asked what he could do to forward the contentment of his deceased relative.

The statue replied, still face downward on the stone floor, that never could the late wicked Count rest in peace unless the heir to his titles and lands should take upon himself the sins Henry had committed during his life, while a younger member of the family should become a monk of the Benedictine Order, and daily intercede for the welfare of his soul.

"With extreme reluctance," continued the devout nobleman, "I gave my assent to this unwelcome proposal, providing only that it should receive the sanction of the Abbot and brethren of the Monastery of Sayn, hoping by a life of continuous rectitude to annul, in some measure at least, the evil works of Henry III.; and that holy sanction I now request, trusting if given it may remove any doubts regarding the righteousness of my promise."

Here the Count bowed low to the enthroned Abbot and, with less reverence, to the assembled brethren. The Abbot rose to his feet, and in a few well-chosen words complimented the nobleman on the sacrifice he made, predicting that it would redound greatly to his spiritual welfare. Speaking for himself, he had no hesitation in giving the required sanction, but as the Count made it a proviso that the brethren should concur, he now requested their acquiescence.

This was accorded in silent unanimity, whereupon Count von Sayn, deeply sighing as one accepting a burden almost too heavy to bear, spoke with a tremor of grief in his voice.

"It is not for me," he said, "to question your wisdom, nor shrink from my allotted task. After all, I am but human, and up to this decisive moment had hoped, alas! in vain, that some one more worthy than I might be chosen in my place. The most grievous part of the undertaking, so far as I am concerned, was outlined in the last words spoken by the wooden statue. The evil deeds my ancestor has committed will in time be obliterated by the prayers of the younger member of my family who becomes a monk, but the accumulated gold carries with it a continual curse, which can be wiped off each coin only by that coin benefiting the merchants who have been robbed. The contamination of this metal, therefore, I must bear, for it adds to the agony of my ancestor that, little realizing what he was doing, he bequeathed this poisonous dross to the Abbey he founded. I am required to lend it in Frankfort, upon undoubted security and suitable usury, that it may stimulate and fertilize the commerce of the land, much as the contents of a compost heap, disagreeable in the senses, and defiling to him who handles it, when spread upon the fields results in the production of flower, fruit, and food, giving fragrance, delight, and sustenance to the human frame."

The count, bowing for the third time to the conclave, passed from its presence with mournful step and sorrowful countenance; whereupon the brethren, seeing themselves thus denuded of wealth they had hoped to enjoy, gave utterance to a groan doubtless much greater in volume than that emitted by the carven statue, which wooden figure may be seen to-day in the museum of the modern Castle of Sayn by any one who cares to spend the fifty pfennigs charged for admission.

All that has been related happened generations before the time when the Countess Hildegunde reigned as head of the House of Sayn, but Father Ambrose formed a link with the past in that he was the present scion of Sayn who, as a Benedictine, daily offered prayer for the repose of the wicked Henry III. The gold which Henry's immediate successor so craftily deflected from the monks seemed to be blessed rather than cursed, for under the care of that subtle manager it multiplied greatly in Frankfort, and scandal-mongers asserted that besides receiving the usury exacted, the pietistic Count tapped the treasure-casks of upward-sailing Rhine merchants quite as successfully, if more quietly, than the profane Henry had done. Thus the House of Sayn was one of the richest in Germany.

The aged monk and the youthful Countess were distant relatives, but he regarded her as a daughter, and her affection was given to him as to a father, in other than the spiritual sense.

In his youth Ambrose the Benedictine, because of his eloquence in discourse, and also on account of his aristocratic rank, officiated at the court in Frankfort. Later, he became spiritual and temporal adviser to that great prelate, the Archbishop of Cologne, and the Archbishop, being guardian of the Countess von Sayn, sent Father Ambrose to the castle of his ancestor to look after the affairs of Sayn, both religious and material. Under his gentle rule the great wealth of his House increased, although he, the cause of prosperity, had no share in the riches he produced, for, as has been written of the Benedictines:

"It was as teachers of ... scientific agriculture, as drainers of fens and morasses, as clearers of forests, as makers of roads, as tillers of the reclaimed soil, as architects of durable and even stately buildings, as exhibiting a visible type of orderly government, as establishing the superiority of peace over war as the normal condition of life, as students in the library which the rule set up in every monastery, as the masters in schools open not merely to their own postulants but to the children of secular families also, that they won their high place in history as benefactors of mankind."

"Oh, Father Ambrose," cried the girl, when at last he entered her presence, "I watched your approach from afar off. You walked with halting step, and shoulders increasingly bowed. You are wearing yourself out in my service, and that I cannot permit. You return this evening a tired man."

"Not physically tired," replied the monk, with a smile. "My head is bowed with meditation and prayer, rather than with fatigue. Indeed, it is others who do the harassing manual labor, while I simply direct and instruct. Sometimes I think I am an encumberer in the vineyard, lazily using brain instead of hand."

"Nonsense!" cried the girl, "the vineyard would be but a barren plantation without you; and speaking of it reminds me that I have poured out, with my own hand, a tankard of the choicest, oldest wine in our cellars, which I allow no one but yourself to taste. Sit down, I beg of you, and drink."

The wise old man smiled, wondering what innocent trap was being set for him. He raised the tankard to his lips, but merely indulged in one sip of the delectable beverage. Then he seated himself, and looked at the girl, still smiling. She went on speaking rapidly, a delicate flush warming her fair cheeks.

"Father, you are the most patient and indefatigable of agriculturists, sparing neither yourself nor others, but there is danger that you grow bucolic through overlong absence from the great affairs of this world."

"What can be greater, my child, than increasing the productiveness of the land; than training men to supply all their needs from the fruitful earth?"

"True, true," admitted the girl, her eyes sparkling with eagerness, "but to persist overlong even in well-doing becomes ultimately tedious. If the laborer is worthy of his hire, so, too, is the master. You should take a change, and as I know your fondness for travel, I have planned a journey for you."

The old man permitted himself another sip of the wine.

"Where?" he asked.

"Oh, an easy journey; no farther than the royal city of Frankfort, there to wander among the scenes of your youth, and become interested for a time in the activities of your fellow-men. You have so long consorted with those inferior to you in intellect and learning that a meeting with your equals—though I doubt if there are any such even in Frankfort—must prove as refreshing to your mind as that old wine would to your body, did you but obey me and drink it."

Father Ambrose slowly shook his head.

"From what I hear of Frankfort," he said, "it is anything but an inspiring town. In my day it was indeed a place of cheer, learning, and prosperity, but now it is a city of desolation."

"The rumors we hear, Father, may be exaggerated; and even if the city itself be doleful, which I doubt, there is sure to be light and gayety in the precincts of the Court and in the homes of the nobility."

"What have I to do with Court or palaces? My duty lies here."

"It may be," cried the girl archly, "that some part of your duty lies there. If Frankfort is indeed in bad case, your sage advice might be of the greatest benefit. Prosperity seems to follow your footsteps, and, besides, you were once a chaplain in the Court, and surely you have not lost all interest in your former charge?"

Again that quiet, engaging smile lit up the monk's emaciated features, and then he asked a question with that honest directness which sometimes embarrassed those he addressed:

"Daughter Hildegunde, what is it you want?"

"Well," said the girl, sitting very upright in her chair, "I confess to loneliness. The sameness of life in this castle oppresses me, and in its continuous dullness I grow old before my time. I wish to enjoy a month or two in Frankfort, and, as doubtless you have guessed, I send you forth as my ambassador to spy out the land."

"In such case, daughter, you should present your petition to that Prince of the Church, the Archbishop of Cologne, who is your guardian."

"No, no, no, no!" cried the girl emphatically; "you are putting the grapes into the barrel instead of into the vat. Before I trouble the worthy Archbishop with my request, I must learn whether it is practicable or not. If the city is indeed in a state of turbulence, of course I shall not think of going thither. It is this I wish to discover, but if you are afraid." She shrugged her shoulders and spread out her hands.

And now the old monk came as near to laughing as he ever did.

"Clever, Hildegunde, but unnecessary. You cannot spur me to action by slighting the well-known valor of our race. I will go where and when you command me, and report to you faithfully what I see and hear. Should the time seem favorable for you to visit Frankfort, and if your guardian consents, I shall raise not even one objection."

"Oh, dear Father, I do not lay this as a command upon you."

"No; a request is quite sufficient. To-morrow morning I shall set out."

"Along the Rhine?" queried the girl, so eagerly that the old man's eyes twinkled at the celerity with which she accepted his proposition.

"I think it safer," he said, "to journey inland over the hills. The robbers on the Rhine have been so long bereft of the natural prey that one or other of them may forget I am Father Ambrose, a poor monk, remembering me only as Henry of the rich House of Sayn, and therefore hold me for ransom. I would not willingly be a cause of strife, so I shall go by way of Limburg on the Lahn, and there visit my old friend the Bishop, and enjoy once more a sight of the ancient Cathedral on the cliff by the river."

When the young Countess awoke next morning, and reviewed in her mind the chief event of the preceding day, remembering the reluctance of

Father Ambrose to undertake the quest she had outlined without the consent of his overlord the Archbishop, a feeling of compunction swept over her. She berated her own selfishness, resolving to send her petition to her guardian, the Archbishop, and abide by his decision.

When breakfast was finished, she asked her lady-in-waiting to request the presence of Father Ambrose, but instead of the monk came disturbing news.

"The seneschal says that Father Ambrose left the Castle at daybreak this morning, taking with him frugal rations for a three days' journey."

"In which direction did he go?" asked the lady of Sayn.

"He went on horseback up the valley, after making inquiries about the route to Limburg on the Lahn."

"Ah!" said the Countess. "He spoke yesterday of taking such a journey, but I did not think he would leave so early."

This was the beginning of great anxiety for the young lady of the Castle. She knew at once that pursuit was useless, for daybreak comes early in summer, and already the good Father had been five hours on his way—a way that he was certain to lose many times before he reached the capital city. An ordinary messenger might have been overtaken, but the meditative Father would go whither his horse carried him, and when he awoke from his thoughts and his prayers, would make inquiries, and so proceed. A day or two later came a message that he had achieved the hospitality of Limburg's bishop, but after that arrived no further word.

Nearly two weeks had elapsed when, from the opposite direction, Hildegunde received a communication which added to her already painful apprehension. It was a letter from her guardian in Cologne, giving warning that within a week he would call at her Castle of Sayn.

"Matters of great import to you and me," concluded the Archbishop, "are toward. You will be called upon to meet formally my two colleagues of Mayence and Treves, at the latter's strong Castle of Stolzenfels, above Coblentz.

81

From the moment we enter that palace-fortress, I shall, temporarily, at least, cease to be your guardian, and become merely one of your three overlords. But however frowningly I may sit in the throne of an Elector, believe me I shall always be your friend. Tell Father Ambrose I wish to consult with him the moment I arrive at your castle, and that he must not absent himself therefrom on any pretext until he has seen me."

Here was trouble indeed, with Father Ambrose as completely disappeared as if the dragons of the Taunus had swallowed him. Never before on his journeys had he failed to communicate with her, even when his travels were taken on account of the Archbishop, and not, as in this case, on her own. She experienced the darkest forebodings from this incredible silence. Imagine, then, her relief, when exactly two weeks from the day he had left Schloss Sayn, she saw him coming down the valley. As when she last beheld him, he traveled on foot, leading his horse, that had gone lame.

Throwing etiquette to the wind, she flew down the stairway, and ran to meet her thrice-welcome friend.

She realized with grief that he was haggard, and the smile he called up to greet her was wan and pitiful.

"Oh, Father, Father!" she cried, "what has happened to you? I have been nearly distraught with doubt and fear, hearing nothing of you since your message from Limburg."

"I was made a prisoner," said the old man quietly, "and allowed to communicate with no one outside my cell. 'Tis a long and sad story, and, worse than all one that bodes ill for the Empire. I should have arrived earlier in the day, but my poor, patient beast has fallen lame."

"Yes!" said the girl indignantly, "and you spare him instead of yourself!"

The monk laid his left hand affectionately on her shoulder.

"You would have done the same, my dear," he said, and she looked up at him with a sweet smile. They were kin, and if she censured any quality in him, the comment carried something of self-reproach.

A servitor took away the lame horse; another waited on Father Ambrose in his small room, which was simple as that of a monastery cell, and as meagerly furnished. After a slight refection, Father Ambrose received peremptory command to rest for three full hours, the lady of the Castle saying it was impossible for her to receive him until that time had elapsed. The order was welcome to the tired monk, although he knew how impatient Hildegunde must be to unpack his budget of news, and he fell asleep even as he gave instructions that he should be awakened at nine.

Descending at that time, the supper hour of the Castle, he found a dainty meal awaiting him, flanked by a flagon of that rare wine which he sipped so sparingly.

"I lodged with my brethren in their small and quiet monastery on the opposite side of the Main from Frankfort, in that suburb of the workingmen which is called Sachsenhausen. Even if my eyes had not seen the desolation of the city, with the summer grass growing in many of its streets, the description given of its condition by my brethren would have been saddening enough to hear. All authority seems at an end. The nobles have fled to their country estates, for defense in the city is impossible should once a universal riot break out, and thinking men look for an insurrection when continued hunger has worn down the patience of the people. Up to the present sporadic outbreaks have been cruelly suppressed, starving men falling mutilated before the sword-cuts of the soldiers; but now disaffection has penetrated the ranks of the Army itself, through short rations and deferred pay, and when the people learn that the military are more like to join them than oppose, destruction will fall upon Frankfort. The Emperor sits alone in drunken stupor, and it is said cannot last much longer, he who has lasted too long already; while the Empress is as much a recluse as a nun in a convent."

"But the young Prince?" interrupted the Countess. "What of him? Is there no hope if he comes to the throne?"

"Ah!" cried the monk, with a long-drawn sigh, dolefully shaking his head.

"But, Father Ambrose, you knew him as a lad, almost as a young man. I have heard you speak highly of his promise."

"He denied me; denied his own identity; threatened my life with his sword, and finally flung me into the most loathsome dungeon in all Frankfort!"

The girl uttered an ejaculation of dismay. If so harsh an estimate of the heir-presumptive came from so mild and gentle a critic as Father Ambrose, then surely was this young man lower in the grade of humanity than even his bestial father.

"And yet," said the girl to herself, "what else was to be expected? Go on," she murmured; "tell me from the beginning."

"One evening, crossing the old bridge from Frankfort to Sachsenhausen, I saw approach me a swaggering figure that seemed familiar, and as he drew nearer I recognized Prince Roland, son of the Emperor, despite the fact that he held his cloak over the lower part of his face, as if, in the gathering dusk, to avoid recognition.

"'Your Highness!' I cried in surprise. On the instant his sword was out, and as the cloak fell from his face, displaying lips which took on a sinister firmness, I saw that I was not mistaken in so accosting him. He threw a quick glance from side to side, but the bridge, like the silent streets, was deserted. We stood alone, beside the iron Cross, and there under the Figure of Christ he denied me, with the sharp point of his sword against my breast.

"'Why do you dare address me by such a title?'

"'You are Prince Roland, son of the Emperor.'

"The sword-point pressed more sharply.

"'You lie!' he cried, 'and if you reiterate that falsehood, you will pay the penalty instantly with your life, despite your monkish cowl. I am nobody. I have no father.'

"'May I ask, then, sir, who you are?'

"'You may ask, but there is no reason for me to answer. Nevertheless, to satisfy your impertinent curiosity, I inform you that I am an ironworker, a maker of swords, and if you desire a taste of my handiwork, you have but to persist in your questioning. I lodge in the laboring quarter of Sachsenhausen, and am now on my way into Frankfort, which surely I have the right to enter free from any inquiry unauthorized by the law.'

"'In that case I beg your pardon,' said I. 'The likeness is very striking. I had once the honor to be chaplain at Court, where frequently I saw the young Prince in company with that noble lady, noble in every sense of the word, his mother, the Empress.'

"I watched the young man narrowly as I said this, and despite his self-control, he winced perceptibly, and I thought I saw a gleam of recognition in his eyes. He thrust the sword back into its scabbard, and said with a light laugh:

"''Tis I that should beg your pardon for my haste and roughness. I assure you I honor the cloth you wear, and would not willingly offer it violence. We are all liable to make mistakes at times. I freely forgive yours and trust you will extend a like leniency to mine.'

"With that he doffed his hat, and left me standing there."

"Surely," said the Countess, deeply interested in the recital, "so far as speech was concerned he made amends?"

"Yes, my daughter; such speech never came from the lips of an ironworker."

"You are convinced he was the Prince?"

"Never for one instant did I doubt it."

"Be that as it may, Father Ambrose, why should not the young man walk the streets of his own capital city, and even explore the laborers' quarter of Sachsenhausen, if he finds it interesting to do so? Is it not his right to wear a sword, and go where he lists; and is it such a very heinous thing that, being accosted by a stranger, he should refuse to make the admission demanded? You took him, as one might say, unaware."

The monk bowed his head, but did not waste time in offering any defense of his action.

"I followed him," he went on, "through the narrow and tortuous streets of Frankfort, an easy adventure, because darkness had set in, but even in daylight my course would have been safe enough, for never once did he look over his shoulder, or betray any of that suspicion characteristic of our laboring classes."

"I think that tells in his favor," persisted the girl.

"He came to the steps of the Rheingold, a disreputable drinking cellar, and disappeared from my sight down its steps. A great shout greeted him, and the rattle of tankards on a table, as he joined what was evidently his coterie. Standing outside, I heard song and ribaldry within. The heir-presumptive to the throne of the Empire was too obviously a drunken brawler; a friend and comrade of the lowest scum in Frankfort.

"After a short time he emerged alone, and once more I followed him. He went with the directness of a purposeful man to the Fahrgasse, the street of the rich merchants, knocked at a door, and was admitted. Along the first-floor front were three lighted windows, and I saw his form pass the first two of these, but from my station in the street could not witness what was going on within. Looking about me, I found to my right a narrow alley, occupied by an outside stairway. This I mounted, and from its topmost step I beheld the interior of the large room on the opposite side of the way.

"It appeared to me that Prince Roland had been expected, for the elderly man seated at the table, his calm face toward me, showed no surprise at the Prince's entrance. His Highness sat with his back towards me, and for a time it seemed that nothing was going forward but an amiable conversation. Suddenly the Prince rose, threw off his cloak, whisked out his sword, and presented its point at the throat of the merchant.

"It was clear, from the expression of dismay on the merchant's face, that this move on the part of his guest was entirely unexpected, but its object was speedily manifested. The old man, with trembling hand, pushed across the table to his assailant a well-filled bag, which the Prince at once untied.

Pouring out a heap of yellow gold, he began with great deliberation to count the money, which, when you consider his precarious situation, showed the young man to be old in crime. Some portion of the gold he returned to the merchant; the rest he dropped into an empty bag, which he tied to his belt.

"I did not wait to see anything more, but came down to the foot of the stairs, that I might learn if Roland took his money to his dissolute comrades. He came out, and once more I followed him, and once more he led me to the Rheingold cellar. On this occasion, however, I took step by step with him until we entered the large wineroom at the foot of the stairs, he less than an arm's length in front of me, still under the illusion that he was alone. Prince though he was, I determined to expostulate with him, and if possible persuade a restitution of the gold.

"'Your Highness!' I began, touching him lightly on the shoulder.

"Instantly he turned upon me with a savage oath, grasped me by the throat, and forced me backward against the cellar wall.

"'You spying sneak!' he cried. 'In spite of my warning you have been hounding my footsteps!'

"The moment I attempted to reply, he throttled me so as to choke every effort at utterance. There now approached us, with alarm in his wine-colored face, a gross, corpulent man, whom the Prince addressed as proprietor of the place, which doubtless he was.

"'Landlord,' said Roland very quietly, 'this unfortunate monk is weak in the head, and although he means no harm with his meddling, he may well cause disaster to my comrades and myself. Earlier in the evening he accosted on the bridge, but I spared him, hoping never to see his monkish costume again. You may judge the state of his mind when I tell you he accuses me of being the Emperor's son, and Heaven only knows what he would estimate to be the quality of my comrades were he to see them.'

"Two or three times I attempted to speak, but the closing of his fingers upon my throat prevented me, and even when they were slightly relaxed I was scarcely able to breathe."

The Countess listened with the closest attention, fixing upon the narrator her splendid eyes, and in them, despite their feminine beauty and softness, seemed to smoulder a deep fire of resentment at the treatment accorded her kinsman, a luminant of danger transmitted to her down the ages from ancestors equally ready to fight for the Sepulcher in Palestine or for the gold on the borders of the Rhine. In the pause, during which the monk wiped from his wrinkled brow the moisture brought there by remembrance of the indignity he had undergone, kindliness in the eyes of the Countess overcame their menace, and she said gently:

"I am quite confident, Father, that such a ruffian could not be Prince Roland. He was indeed the rude mechanic he proclaimed himself. No man of noble blood would have acted thus."

"Listen, my child, listen," resumed Father Ambrose. "Turning to the landlord, the Prince asked:

"'Is there a safe and vacant room in your establishment where I could bestow this meddlesome priest for a few days?'

"'There is a wine vault underneath this drinking cellar,' responded the landlord.

"'Does anyone enter that vault except yourself?'

"'No one,'

"'Will you undertake charge of the priest, seeing that he communicates with none outside?'

"'Of a surety, Captain,'

"'Good. I will pay you well, and that in advance.'"

"This ruffian was never the Prince," interrupted the Countess firmly.

"I beg you to listen, Hildegunde, and my next sentence will convince you. The Prince continued:

"'Not only prevent his communication with others, but do not listen to him yourself. He will endeavor to persuade you that his name is Father Ambrose, and that he is a monk in good standing with the Benedictine Order. If he finds you care little for that, he may indeed pretend he is of noble origin himself; that he is Henry von Sayn, and thus endeavor to work on whatever sympathy you may feel for the aristocrats. But I assure you he is no more a Sayn than I am Prince Roland.'

"'Indeed, Captain,' replied the host, 'I have as little liking for an aristocrat as for a monk, so you may depend that I will keep him safe enough until you order his release.'

"Now, my dear Hildegunde, you see there was no mistake on my part. This young man asserted he knew nothing of me, and indeed, I believed he had forgotten the time of my chaplaincy at the Court, often as he listened to my discourses, yet all the time he knew me, and now, with an effrontery that seems incredible, he showed no hesitation in proving me right when I accosted him as son of the Emperor. I must in justice, however, admit that he instructed the landlord when he paid him, to treat me with gentleness, and to see that I had plenty to eat and drink. When three days had expired, I was to be allowed my liberty.

"'He can do no harm then,' concluded the Prince, in his talk with the landlord, 'for by that time I shall have succeeded or failed.'

"I was led down a narrow, broken stairway by the proprietor, and thrust into a dark and damp cellar, partially filled with casks of wine, and there I remained until set at liberty a few days ago.

"I returned at once to the Benedictine Monastery where I had lodged, expecting to find my brethren filled with anxiety concerning me, but such was not the case. Any one man is little missed in this world, and my comrades supposed that I was invited to the Court, and had forgotten them as I saw they had forgotten me, so I said nothing of my adventure, but mounted my waiting horse and journeyed back to the Castle of Sayn."

For a long time there was silence between the two, then the younger spoke.

"Do you intend to take any action regarding your unauthorized imprisonment?"

"Oh, no," replied the forgiving monk.

"Is it certain that this dissolute young man will be chosen Emperor?"

"There is a likelihood, but not a certainty."

"Would not the election of such a person to the highest position in the State prove even a greater misfortune to the land than the continuance of the present regime, for this young man adds to his father's vice of drunkenness the evil qualities, of dishonesty, cruelty, ribaldry, and a lack of respect for the privileges both of Church and nobility?"

"Such indeed is my opinion, daughter."

"Then is it not your duty at once to acquaint the three Archbishops with what you have already told me, so that the disaster of his election may be avoided?"

"It is a matter to which I gave deep thought during my journey thither, and I also invoked the aid of Heaven in guiding me to a just conclusion."

"And that conclusion, Father?"

"Is to say nothing whatever about my experiences in Frankfort."

"Why?"

"Because it is not given to a humble man like myself, occupying a position of no authority, to fathom what may be in the minds of those great Princes of the Church, the Archbishops. In effect they rule the country, and it is possible that they prefer to place on the throne a drunken nonentity who will offer no impediment to their ambitions, rather than to elect a moral young man who might in time prove too strong for them."

"I am sure no such motive would actuate the Archbishop of Cologne."

"His Lordship of Cologne, my child, dare not break with their Lordships of Treves and Mayence, so you may be sure that if these two wish to elect

Prince Roland Emperor, nothing I could say to the Archbishop of Cologne would prevent that choice."

"Oh, I had forgotten, in the excitement of listening to your adventures, but talking of the Archbishop reminds me his Highness of Cologne will visit us to-morrow, and he especially wishes to see you. You may imagine my anxiety when I received his message a few days ago, knowing nothing of your whereabouts."

"Wishes to see me?" ejaculated Father Ambrose, wrinkling a perplexed brow. "I wonder what for. Can he have any knowledge of my visit to Frankfort?"

"How could he?"

"The Archbishops possess sources of enlightenment that we wot not of. If he charges me with being absent from my post, I must admit the fact."

"Of course. Let me confess to him as soon as he arrives; your journey was entirely due to my persistence. I alone am to blame."

The old man slowly shook his head.

"I am at least equally culpable," he said. "I shall answer truthfully any question asked me, but I hope I am not in the wrong if I volunteer no information."

The girl rose.

"You could do no wrong, Father, even if you tried; and now good-night. Sleep soundly and fear nothing. On the rare occasions when the good Archbishop was angry with me, I have always managed to placate him, and I shall not fail in this instance."

Father Ambrose bade her good-night, and left the room with the languid air of one thoroughly tired. As the young Countess stood there watching his retreat and disappearance, her dainty little fist clenched, and her eyebrows came together, bringing to her handsome face the determined expression which marked the countenances of some of her Crusader ancestors whose portraits decorated the walls.

"If ever I get that ruffian Prince Roland into my power," she said to herself, "I will make him regret his treatment of so tolerant and forbearing a man as Father Ambrose."

V. THE COUNTESS VON SAYN AND THE ARCHBISHOP OF COLOGNE

It was high noon when that great Prince of the Church, the Archbishop of Cologne, arrived at Castle Sayn, with a very inconsiderable following, which seemed to indicate that he traveled on no affair of State, for on such occasions he led a small army. The lovely young Countess awaited him at the top of the Castle steps, and he greeted her with the courtesy of a polished man of the world, rather than with the more austere consideration of a great Churchman. Indeed, it seemed to the quick apprehension of the girl that as he raised her fair hand to his lips his obeisance was lower, more deferential, than their differing stations in life justified.

He shook hands with Father Ambrose in the manner of old friend accosting old friend, and nothing in his salutation indicated displeasure of any sort in the background.

Perhaps, then, that sense of uneasiness felt by both the aged Father Ambrose and the youthful Countess Hildegunde in the Archbishop's presence came from their consciousness of conspiracy, resulting in the ill-fated journey to Frankfort. Nevertheless, all that afternoon the two were oppressed by the shadow of some impending danger, and the good spirits of the Archbishop seemed to them assumed for the occasion, and indeed in this they were not far wrong. His Lordship of Cologne was keenly apprehensive regarding an important conference set down for the next day, and the exuberance of an essentially serious man in such a crisis is prone to be overdone.

Father Ambrose, who, in the midst of luxury and plenty, lived with the abstemiousness of an anchorite, and always partook of his scant refreshment alone in his cell, was invited by the Archbishop to a seat at the table in the dining-hall.

"So long as you cast no look of reproach upon me for my enjoyment of Sayn's most excellent cuisine, and my appreciation of its unequaled cellar, I shall not comment on your dinner of parched peas and your unexhilarating tankard of water. Besides, I wish to consult with Ambrose the librarian of Sayn, touching the archives of this house, rather than with Ambrose the superintendent of farms, or Father Ambrose the monk."

During the midday meal the Archbishop led, and at times monopolized, the conversation.

"While you were under the tutelage of the good Sisters at Nonnenwerth Convent, Hildegunde, the Abbess frequently spoke of your proficiency in historical studies. Did you ever turn your attention to the annals of your own House?"

"No, Guardian. From what I heard casually of my ancestors a record of their doings would be scarcely the sort of reading recommended to a young girl."

"Ah, very true, very true," agreed the Archbishop. "Some of the Counts of Sayn led turbulent lives, and except with a battle-ax it was difficult to persuade them not to meddle with the goods and chattels of their neighbors. A strenuous line they proved in those olden days; but many noble women have adorned the Castle of Sayn whose lives shine out like an inspiration against the dark background of medieval tumult. Did you ever hear of your forebear, the gracious Countess Matilda von Sayn, who lived some hundreds of years ago? Indeed, the letters I have been reading, written in her quaint handwriting, are dated about the middle of the thirteenth century. I cannot learn whether she was older or younger than the Archbishop of Cologne of that period, and thus I wish to enlist the interest of Father Ambrose in searching the archives of Sayn for anything pertaining to her. The Countess sent many epistles to the Archbishop which he carefully preserved, while documents of much more importance to the Archbishopric were allowed to go astray.

"Her letters breathe a deep devotion to the Church, and a warm kindliness to its chief ornament of that day, the then Archbishop of Cologne. She was evidently his most cherished adviser, and in points of difficulty her counsel exhibits all the clarity of a man's brain, to which is added a tenderness and a sense of justice entirely womanly. I could not help fancying that this great prelate's success in his Archbishopric was largely due to the disinterested advice of this noble woman. It is clearly to be seen that the Countess was the benignant power behind the throne, and she watched his continued advancement with a love resembling that lavished on a favorite son. Her writings now and then betray an affection of a quality so motherly that I came to believe she was much older than the great Churchman, but then there is the fact that she long outlived him, so it is possible she may have been the younger."

"Why, my Lord, are you about to weave us a romance?"

The Archbishop smiled, and for a moment placed his hand upon hers, which rested on the table beside him.

"A romance, perhaps, between myself and the Countess of long ago, for as I read these letters I used much of their contents for my own guidance, and found her precepts as wise to-day as they were in 1250, and to me ... to me," the Archbishop sighed, "she seems to live again. Yes, I confess my ardent regard for her, and if you call that romance, it is surely of a very innocent nature."

"But the other Archbishop? Your predecessor, the friend of Matilda; what of him?"

"There, Hildegunde, I have much less evidence to go upon, for his letters, if they exist, are concealed somewhere in the archives of Sayn Castle."

"To-morrow," cried the girl, "I shall robe myself in the oldest garments I possess, and will rummage those dusty archives until I find the letters of him who was Archbishop in 1250."

"I have bestowed that task upon one less impulsive. Father Ambrose is the searcher, and he and I will put our wise old heads together in consultation over them before entrusting them to the perusal of that impetuous young noblewoman, the present Countess von Sayn."

The impetuous person referred to brought down her hand with a peremptory impact upon the table, and exclaimed emphatically:

"My Lord Archbishop, I shall read those letters to-morrow."

Once more the Archbishop placed his hand on hers, this time, however, clasping it firmly in his own. There was no smile on his face as he said gravely:

"My lady, to-morrow you will face three living Archbishops, more difficult, perhaps, to deal with than one who is dust."

"Three!" she cried, startled, a gleam of apprehension troubling her fine eyes. "My Lords of Mayence, Treves, and yourself? Are they coming here?"

"The conclave of the Archbishops will be held at Castle Stolzenfels, the Rhine residence of my brother of Treves."

"Why is this Court convened?"

"That will be explained to you, Hildegunde, by his Highness of Mayence. I did not intend to speak to you about this until later, so I will merely say that there is nothing to fear. I, being your guardian, am sent to escort you to Stolzenfels, and as we ride there together I wish to place before you some suggestions which you may find useful when the meeting takes place."

"I shall faithfully follow any advice you give me, my Lord."

"I am sure of it, Hildegunde, and you will remember that I speak as guardian, not as Councilor of State. My observations will be requests and not commands. You see, we have reversed the positions of my predecessor and the Countess Matilda. It was always she who tendered advice, which he invariably accepted. Now I must take the rôle of advice-giver; thus you and I transpose the parts of the former Archbishop of Cologne, and the former Countess of Sayn, who, I am sorry to note, have been completely banished from your thoughts by my premature announcement regarding the three living Archbishops."

"Oh, not at all, not at all! I am still thinking of those two. Have you told me all you know about them?"

"Far from it. Although I was handicapped in my reconstitution of their friendship by lack of the Archbishop's letters, he had nevertheless made a note here and there upon the communications he received from the Countess. Throughout the letters certain paragraphs are marked with a cross, as if for reperusal, these paragraphs being invariably most delicately and charmingly written. But now I come to the last very important document, the only one of which a copy has been kept, written in the Archbishop's own hand.

"In the year 1250, the Countess von Sayn had ceded to him the Rhine town of Linz. Linz seems to have been a rebellious and troublesome fief, which the Sayns held by force of arms. When it came into the possession of the Archbishop, the foolish inhabitants, remembering that Cologne was a long distance down the river compared with the up-river journey to Sayn, broke out into open revolt. The Archbishop sent up his army, and most effectually crushed this outbreak, severely punishing the rebels. He returned from this subdued town to his own city of Cologne, and whether from the exposure of the brief campaign, or some other cause, he was taken ill and shortly after died.

"The new Archbishop was installed, and nearly two years passed, so far as I can learn, before the Countess Matilda made claim that the town of Linz should come again within her jurisdiction, saying that this restitution had been promised by the late Archbishop. His successor, however, disputed this claim. He possessed, he said, the deed of gift making over the town of Linz to his predecessor, and this document was definite enough. If then, it was the intention of the late Archbishop to return Linz to the House of Sayn, the Countess doubtless held some document to that effect, and in this case he would like to know its purport.

"The Countess replied that an understanding had existed between the late Archbishop and herself regarding the subjugation of the town of Linz and its return to her after the rebellion was quelled. But for the untimely death of the late Archbishop she did not doubt that his part of the contract would have been kept long since. Nevertheless, she did possess a document, in the late Archbishop's own hand, setting out the terms of their agreement, and of this manuscript she sent a copy.

"The crafty Archbishop, without casting doubt on the authenticity of the copy, said that of course it would be illegal for him to act upon it. He must have the original document. Matilda replied, very shrewdly, that on her part she could not allow the original document to quit her custody, as upon it rested her rights to the town of Linz. She would, however, exhibit this document to any ecclesiastical committee her correspondent might appoint, and the members of the committee so chosen should be men well acquainted with the late Archbishop's writing and signature. In reply the Archbishop regretted that he could not accept her suggestion. The people of Cologne, believing that their overlord had rightfully acquired Linz, cheerfully consented to make good their title by battle, thus having, as it were, bought the town with their blood, and indeed, a deplorable sacrifice of life, it would become a dangerous venture to give up the town unless indisputable documentary evidence might be exhibited to them showing that such a bargain was made by the deceased prelate.

"But before proceeding farther in this matter, he asked the Countess if she were prepared to swear that the copy forwarded to him was a full and faithful rendition of the original. Did it contain every word the late Archbishop had written in that letter?

"To this the Countess made no reply, and allowed to lapse any title she might have to the town of Linz."

"I think," cried the girl indignantly, "that my ancestress was in the right, refusing further communication with this ignoble Churchman who dared to impugn her good faith."

The Archbishop smiled at her vehemence.

"I shall make no attempt to defend my astute predecessor. A moneylender's soul tenanted his austere body, but what would you say if his implication of the Countess Matilda's good faith was justified?"

"You mean that the copy which she sent of the Archbishop's letter was fraudulent? I cannot believe it."

"Not fraudulent. So far as it went her copy was word perfect. She neglected to add, however, a final sentence, and rather than make it public forfeited her rightful claim to great possessions. Of the Archbishop's communications to her there remains in our archives a copy of this last epistle written in his own hand. I cannot imagine why he added the final clauses to what was in essence an important business communication. The premonition he admits may have set his thoughts upon things not of this world, but undoubtedly he believed that he would live long enough to conquer the rebels of Linz, and restore to the Countess her property. This is what he wrote, and she refused to publish:

"'Matilda, I feel that my days are numbered, and that their number is scant. To all the world my life seems to have been successful beyond the wishes of mortal man, but to me it is a dismal failure, in that I die bachelor Archbishop of Cologne, and you are the spinster Countess von Sayn.'"

VI. TO BE KEPT SECRET FROM THE COUNTESS

There are few favored spots occupied by blue water and greensward over which a greater splendor is cast by the rising sun on a midsummer morning than that portion of the Rhine near Coblentz, and as our little procession emerged from the valley of the Saynbach every member of it was struck with the beauty of the flat country across the Rhine, ripening toward a yellow harvest, flooded by the golden glory of the rising sun.

Their route led to the left by the foot of the eastern hills, and not yet along the margin of the great river. Gradually, however, as they journeyed in a southerly direction, the highlands deflected them westward until at last there was but scant room for the road between rock and water. Always they were in the shade, a comforting feature of a midsummer journey, an advantage, however, soon to be lost when they crossed the Rhine by the ferry to Coblentz. The distance from Sayn Castle to Schloss Stolzenfels was a little less than four leagues, so their early start permitted a leisurely journey.

The Archbishop and the Countess rode side by side. Following them at some distance came Father Ambrose, deep in his meditations, and paying little attention to the horse he rode, which indeed, faithful animal, knew more about the way than did his rider. Still farther to the rear rode half a dozen mounted lancemen, two and two, the scant escort of one who commanded many thousands of armed men.

"How lovely and how peaceful is the scene," said the Countess. "How beautiful are the fields of waving grain; their color of dawn softened by the deep green of interspersed vineyards, and the water without a ripple, like a slumbering lake rather than a strong river. It seems as though anger, contention, and struggle could not exist in a realm so heavenly."

"'Seems' is the word to use," commented the Archbishop gravely, "but the unbroken placidity of the river you so much admire is a peace of defeat. I had much rather see its flood disturbed by moving barges and the turmoil of commerce. It is a peace that means starvation and death to our capital city, and, indeed, in a lesser degree, to my own town of Cologne, and to Coblentz, whose gates we are approaching."

"But surely," persisted the girl, "the outlook is improving, when you and I travel unmolested with a mere handful of men to guard us. Time was when a great and wealthy Archbishop might not stir abroad with less than a thousand men in his train."

The Archbishop smiled.

"I suppose matters mend," he said, "as we progress in civilized usage. The number of my escort, however, is not limited by my own modesty, but stipulated by the Court of Archbishops. Mayence travels down the Rhine and Treves down the Moselle, each with a similar following at his heels."

"You are pessimistic this lovely morning, my Lord, and will not even admit that the world is beautiful."

"It all depends on the point of view, Hildegunde. I regard it from a position toward the end of life, and you from the charming station of youth: the far-apart outlook of an old man and a young girl."

"Nonsense, Guardian, you are anything but old. Nevertheless I am much disappointed with your attitude this morning. I fully expected to be complimented by you."

"Doesn't my whole attitude breathe of compliment?"

"Ah, but I expected a particular compliment to-day!"

"What have I overlooked?"

"You overlooked the fact that yesterday you aroused my most intense curiosity regarding the journey we are now taking together, and the conference which is to follow. Despite deep anxiety to learn what is before me I have not asked you a single question, nor even hinted at the subject until this moment. Now, I think I should be rewarded for my reticence."

"Ah, Countess, you are an exception among women, and I merely withheld the well-earned praise until such time as I could broach the subject occupying my mind ever since we left the Castle. With the awkwardness of a man I did not know how to begin until you so kindly indicated the way."

"Perhaps, after all, I make a false claim, because I have guessed your secret, and therefore my deep solicitude is assumed."

"Guessed it?" queried the Archbishop, a shade of anxiety crossing his face.

"Yes. Your story of the former Archbishop and the Countess Matilda gave me a clue. You have discovered a document proving my right to the town of Linz on the Rhine."

The Archbishop bowed his head, but said nothing.

"Your sense of justice urges you to make amends, but such a long time has elapsed that my claim is doubtless outlawed, and you do not quite know how restoration may be effected. You have, I take it, consulted with one or other of your colleagues, Mayence or Treves, or perhaps with both. They have made objection to your proposed generosity, and put forward the argument that you are but temporary trustee of the Cologne Archbishopric; that you must guard the rights of your successor; and this truism could not help but appeal to that quality of equity which distinguishes you, so a conference of the prelates has been called, and a majority of that Court will decide whether or not the town of Linz shall be tendered to me. Perhaps a suggestion will be made that I allow things to remain as they are, in which case I shall at once refuse to accept the town of Linz. Now, Guardian, how near have I come to solving the mystery?"

They rode along in silence together, the Archbishop pondering on the problem of her further enlightenment. At last he said:

"Cologne is ruled by its Archbishop, wisely or the reverse as the case may be. The Archbishop, much as he reveres the opinion of his distinguished colleagues, would never put them to the inconvenience of giving a decision on any matter not concerning them. Linz's fate was settled when the handwriting of my predecessor, prelate of 1250 A.D., convinced me that this Rhine town belonged to the House of Sayn. Restitution has already been accomplished in due legal form, and when next the Countess Hildegunde rides through Linz, she rides through her own town."

"I shall never, never accept it, Guardian."

"It is yours now, Countess. If you do not wish to hold the town, use it as a gift to the fortunate man you marry. And now, Hildegunde, this long-postponed advice I wish to press upon your attention, must be given, for we are nearing the ferry to Coblentz, and between that town and Stolzenfels we may have company. Of the three Archbishops you will meet to-day, there is only one of whom you need take account."

"Oh, I know that," cried the girl, "his Lordship of Cologne!"

The Archbishop smiled, but went on seriously:

"Where two or three men are gathered together, one is sure to be leader. In our case the chief of the trio supposed to be equal is his Highness of Mayence. Treves and I pretend not to be under his thumb, but we are: that is to say, Treves holds I am under his thumb, and I hold Treves is under his thumb, and so when one or the other of us join the Archbishop of Mayence, there is a majority of the Court, and the third member is helpless."

"But why don't you and Treves join together?"

"Because each thinks the other a coward, and doubtless both are right. The point of the matter is that Mayence is the iron man of the combination; therefore I beg you beware of him, and I also entreat you to agree with the proposal he will make. It will be of tremendous advantage to you."

"In that case, my Lord, how could I refuse?"

"I hope, my child, you will not, but if you should make objection, do so with all the tact at your disposal. In fact, refrain wholly from objection if you can, and plead for time to consider, so that you and I may consult together, thus affording me opportunity of bringing arguments to bear that may influence your decision."

"My dear Guardian, you alarm me by the awesome way in which you speak. What fateful choice hangs over my head?"

"I have no wish to frighten you, my daughter, and, indeed, I anticipate little chance of disagreement at the conference. I merely desire that you shall understand something of Mayence. He is a man whom opposition may drive to extremity, and being accustomed to crush those who disagree with him, rather than conquer by more diplomatic methods, I am anxious you should not be led into any semblance of dissent from his wishes. By agreement between Mayence, Treves, and myself, I am not allowed to enlighten you regarding the question at issue. I perhaps strain that agreement a little when I endeavor to put you on your guard. If, at any point in the discussion, you wish a few moments to reflect, glance across the table at me, and I shall immediately intervene with some interruption which must be debated by the three members of the Court. Of course, I shall do everything in my power to protect you should our grim friend Mayence lose his temper, as may happen if you thwart him."

"Why am I likely to thwart him?"

"Why indeed? I see no reason. I am merely an old person perhaps overcautious. Hence this warding off of a crisis which I hope will never arise."

"Guardian, I have one question to ask, and that will settle the matter here on the border of the Rhine, before we reach Stolzenfels. Do you thoroughly approve, with your heart, mind, and conscience, of the proposition to be made to me?"

"I do," replied the Archbishop, in a tone of conviction that none could gainsay. "Heart and soul, agree."

"Then, Guardian, your crisis that never came vanishes. I shall tell his Lordship of Mayence, in my sweetest voice and most ingratiating manner, that I will do whatever he requests."

Here the conversation ceased, for the solitude now gave way to a scene of activity, as they came to the landing alongside which lay the floating bridge, a huge barge, capable of carrying their whole company at one voyage. Several hundred persons, on horseback or on foot, gathered along the river-bank, raised a cheer as the Archbishop appeared. The Countess thought they waited to greet him, but they were merely travelers or market people who found their journey interrupted at this point. An emissary of the Archbishop had commanded the ferry-boat to remain at its eastern landing until his Lordship came aboard. When the distinguished party embarked, the crew instantly cast off their moorings, and the tethered barge, impelled by the swift current, gently swung across to the opposite shore.

A great concourse of people greeted their arrival at Coblentz, and if vociferous shouts and hurrahs are signs of popularity, the Archbishop had reason to congratulate himself upon his reception. The prelate bowed and smiled, but did not pause at Coblentz, and, to the evident disappointment of the multitude, continued his way up the Rhine. When the little cavalcade drew away from the mob, the Countess spoke:

"I had no thought," she said, "that Coblentz contained so many inhabitants."

"Neither does it," replied the Archbishop.

"Then is this simply an influx of people from the country, and is the conclave of the Archbishops of such importance that it draws so many sightseers?"

"The Court held by the Archbishops on this occasion is very important. I suspect, however, that those are no sightseers, for the general public is quite unaware that we meet to-day. They who cheered so lustily just now are, I think, men of Treves."

"Do you mean soldiers?"

"Aye. Soldiers in the dress of ordinary townsmen, but I dare say they all know where to find their weapons should a war-cry arise."

"Do you imply that the Archbishop of Treves has broken his compact? I understood that your escort was limited to the few men following you."

His Lordship laughed.

"The Archbishop of Treves," he said, "is not a great strategist, yet I surmise he is ready in case of trouble to seize the city of Coblentz."

"What trouble could arise?"

"The present moment is somewhat critical, for the Emperor lies dying in Frankfort. We three Electors hope to avoid all commotion by having our plans prepared and acting upon them promptly. But the hours between the death of an Emperor and the appointment of his successor are fateful with uncertainty. I suppose the good Sisters at Nonnenwerth taught you about the Election of an Emperor?"

"Indeed, Guardian, I am sorry to confess that if they did I have forgotten all about it."

"There are seven Electors; four high nobles of the Empire and three Archbishops, Lords Temporal and Lords Spiritual. The present Count Palatine of the Rhine is, like my friend Treves, completely under the dominion of the Archbishop of Mayence, so the three Lords Spiritual, with the aid of the Count Palatine, form a majority of the Electoral Court."

"I understand. And now I surmise that you assemble at Stolzenfels to choose our future Emperor."

"No; he has already been chosen, but his name will not be announced to any person save one before the Emperor dies."

"Doubtless that one is the Count Palatine."

"No, Countess, he remains ignorant; and I give you warning, Madam, I am not to be cross-questioned by indirection. You should be merciful: I am but clay in your hands, yet there is certain information I am forbidden to impart, so I will merely say that if the Archbishop happens to be in good-humor this afternoon, he is very likely to tell you who will be the future Emperor."

The girl gave an exclamation of surprise.

"To tell me? Why should he do so?"

"I said I was not to be cross-examined any further. I tremble now with apprehension lest I have let slip something I should not, therefore we will change the subject to one of paramount importance; namely, our midday meal. I intended to stop at Coblentz for that repast, but the Archbishop of Treves, whose guests we are, was good enough to accept a menu I suggested, therefore we will sit at table with him."

"You suggested a menu?"

"Yes; I hope you will approve of it. There is some excellent Rhine salmon, with a sauce most popular in Treves, a sauce that has been celebrated for centuries. Next some tender venison from the forest behind Stolzenfels, which is noted for its deer. There are, beside, cakes and various breads, also vegetables, and all are to be washed down by delicate Oberweseler wine. How does my speis-card please you, Countess?"

"I am committing it to memory, Guardian, so that I shall know what to prepare for you when next you visit my Castle of Sayn."

"Oh, this repast is not in my honor, but in yours. I feared you might object to the simplicity of it. It is upon record that this meal was much enjoyed by a young lady some centuries ago, at this very Castle of Stolzenfels, shortly after it was completed. Indeed, I think it likely she was the noble castle's first guest. Stolzenfels was built by Arnold von Isenberg, the greatest Archbishop that ever ruled over Treves, if I may except Archbishop Baldwin, the fighter. Isenberg determined to have a stronghold on the Rhine midway between Mayence and Cologne, and he made it a palace as well as a fortress, taking his time about it—in all seventeen years. He began its erection in 1242, and so was building at the time your ancestress Matilda ceded Linz to the Archbishop of Cologne, therefore I imagine Cologne probably wished to have a stronghold within striking distance of Treves' new castle.

"One of the first to visit Stolzenfels was a charming young English girl named Isabella, who was no other than the youngest daughter of John, King of England. Doubtless she came here with an imposing suite of attendants, and I surmise that the great prelate's castle saw impressive pageants and festivities, for the chronicler, after setting down the menu whose excellence I hope to test to-day, adds:

107

"'They ate well, and drank better, and the Royal maiden danced a great deal.'

"Her brother then occupied the English throne. He was Henry III., and of course much attention was paid over here to his dancing sister."

"Why, Guardian, what you say gives a new interest to old Stolzenfels. I have never been within the Castle, but now I shall view it with delight, wondering through which of the rooms the English Princess danced. Why did Isabella come from England all the way to the Rhine?"

"She came to meet the three Archbishops."

"Really? For what purpose?"

"That they might in ecclesiastical form, and upon the highest ecclesiastical authority, announce her betrothal."

"Announce in Stolzenfels the betrothal of an English Princess, the daughter of one king and sister of another! Did she, then, marry a German?"

"Yes; she married the Emperor, Frederick II.; Frederick of Hohenstaufen."

Slowly the girl turned her head, and looked steadfastly at the Archbishop, who was gazing earnestly up the road as if to catch a glimpse of the Castle which had been the scene of the events he related. Her face became pale, and a questioning wonder rose in her eyes. What did the Archbishop really mean by this latest historical recital? True, he was a man who had given much study to ancient lore; rather fond of exhibiting his proficiency therein when he secured patient listeners. Could there be any secret meaning in his story of the English Princess who danced? Was there any hidden analogy between the journey of the English Isabella, and the short trip taken that day by Hildegunde of Sayn? She was about to speak when the Archbishop made a slight signal with his right hand, and a horseman who had followed them all the way from Coblentz now spurred up alongside of his Lordship, who said sharply to the newcomer:

"How many of Treves' men are in Coblentz?"

"Eight hundred and fifty, my Lord."

"Enough to capture the town?"

"Coblentz is already in their possession, my Lord."

"They seem to be unarmed."

"Their weapons are stored under guard in the Church of St. Castor, and can be in the hands of the soldiers within a few minutes after a signal is rung by the St. Castor's bells."

"Are there any troops in Coblentz from Mayence?"

"No, my Lord."

"How many of my men have been placed behind the Castle of Stolzenfels?"

"Three thousand are concealed in the forest near the hilltop."

"How many men has my Lord of Mayence within call?"

"Apparently only the scant half-dozen that reached Stolzenfels with him yesterday."

"Are you sure of that?"

"Scouts have been sent all through the forest to the south, and have brought us no word of an advancing company. Other scouts have gone up the river as far as Bingen, but everything is quiet, and it would have been impossible for his Lordship to march a considerable number of men from any quarter towards Stolzenfels without one or other of our hundred spies learning of the movement."

"Then doubtless Mayence depends on his henchman Treves."

"It would seem so, my Lord."

"Thank you; that will do."

The rider saluted, turned his horse towards the north, and galloped away, and a few moments later the little procession came within sight of Stolzenfels, standing grandly on its conical hill beside the Rhine, against a background of green formed by the mountainous forests to the rear.

This conversation, which she could not help but hear, had driven entirely from the mind of Hildegunde the pretty story of the English Princess.

"Why, Guardian!" she said, "we seem to be in the midst of impending civil war."

The Archbishop smiled.

"We are in the midst of an assured peace," he replied.

"What! with Coblentz practically seized, and three thousand of your men lurking in the woods above us?"

"Yes. I told you that Treves was no strategist. I suppose he and Mayence imagine that by seizing the town of Coblentz they cut off my retreat to Cologne. They know it would be useless in a crisis for me to journey up the river, as I should then be getting farther and farther from my base of supplies both in men and provisions, therefore the Archbishop of Mayence has neglected to garrison that quarter."

"But, Guardian, you are surely entrapped, with Coblentz thus held?"

"Not so, my child, while I command three thousand men to their eight hundred."

"But that means a battle!"

"A battle that will never take place, Hildegunde, because I shall seize something much more valuable than any town, namely, the persons of the two Archbishops. With their Lordships of Treves and Mayence in my custody, cut off from communication with their own troops, I have slight fear of a leaderless army. The very magnitude of the force at my command is an assurance of peace."

They now arrived at the branching hill-road leading up to the gates of Stolzenfels just above them, and conversation ceased, but the Countess was fated to remember before the afternoon grew old the final words Cologne spoke so confidently.

VII. MUTINY IN THE WILDERNESS

It was a lovely morning in July when Prince Roland walked into the shadow of the handsome tower which to-day is all that survives of the Elector's palace at Hochst, on the river Main. He found Greusel there awaiting him, but none of the others. When the two had greeted one another, the Prince said:

"Joseph, I determined several days ago to appoint you my lieutenant on this expedition."

"If you take my advice, Roland, you will do nothing of the kind."

"Why?"

"Because it may be looked upon as favoritism, and so promote jealously in the ranks, which is a thing to avoid."

"Whom would you suggest for the place?"

"Conrad Kurzbold."

"What! and run the risk of divided authority? I am determined to be commander, you know."

"Kurzbold, even if made lieutenant, would be as much under your orders as the rest of us. He is an energetic man, and you may thus direct his energy along the right path. From being a critic, he will become one of the criticised, giving him something to think about. Then your appointment of him would show that you bear no ill-feeling for what he said last night."

"You appear to think, Greusel, that it is the duty of a commander to curry favor with his following."

"No; but I regard tact as a useful quality. You see, you are not in the position of a general with an army. The members of the guild can depose you whenever they like and elect a successor, or they may desert you in a body, and you have no redress. Your methods should not be drastic, but rather those of a man who seeks election to some high office."

"I fear I am not constituted for such a rôle, Greusel."

"If you are to succeed in the task you have undertaken, Roland, you must adapt yourself to your situation as it actually is, and not as you would wish to have it. I stood by you yesterday evening, and succeeded in influencing the others to do the same, yet there is no denying that you spoke to those men in a most overbearing manner. Why, you could not have been more downright had you been an officer of the Emperor himself. What passed through my mind as I listened was, 'Where did this youth get his swagger?' You ordered Kurzbold out of the ranks, you know."

"Then why favor my action?"

"Because I was reluctant to see a promising marauding adventure wrecked at the very outset for lack of a few soothing words."

Roland laughed heartily. The morning was inspiring, and he was in good fettle.

"Your words to Kurzbold were anything but soothing."

"Oh, I was compelled to crush him. He was the cause of the disturbance, and therefore I had no mercy so far as the affair impinged upon him. But the others, with the exception of Gensbein perhaps, are good, honest, sweet-tempered fellows, whom I did not wish to see misled. I think you must put out of your mind all thought of punishment, no matter what the offense against your authority may be."

"Then how would you deal with insubordination when it arises?"

"I should trust to the good sense of the remaining members of your company to make it uncomfortable for the offender."

"But suppose they don't?"

Greusel shrugged his shoulders.

"In that case you are helpless, I fear. At any rate, talking of hanging, or the infliction of any other punishment, is quite futile so long as you do not possess the power to carry out your sentence. To return to my simile of the general: a general can order any private in his army to be hanged, and the man is taken out and hanged accordingly, but if one of the guild is to be executed, he must be condemned by an overwhelming vote of his fellows, because even if a bare majority sentenced one belonging to the minority it would mean civil war among us. Suppose, for example, it was proposed to hang you, and eleven voted for the execution and nine against it. Do you think we nine would submit to the verdict of the eleven? Not so. I am myself the most peaceful of men, but the moment it came to that point, I should run my sword through the proposer of the execution before he had time to draw his weapon. In other words, I'd murder him to lessen the odds, and then we'd fight it out like men."

"Why didn't you say all this last night, Greusel?"

"Last night my whole attention was concentrated on inducing Kurzbold to forget that you had threatened the company with a hangman's rope. Had he remembered that, I could never have carried the vote of confidence. But you surely saw that the other men were most anxious to support you if your case was placed fairly before them, a matter which, for some reason, you thought it beneath your dignity to attempt."

"My dear Joseph, your wholesale censure this morning does much to nullify the vote I received last night."

"My dear Roland, I am not censuring you at all; I am merely endeavoring to place facts before you so that you will recognize them."

"Quite so, but what I complain of is that these facts were not exhibited in time for me to shoulder or shirk the responsibility. I do not believe that military operations can be successfully carried on by a little family party, the head of which must coddle the others in the group, and beg pardon before he says 'Devil take you!' I would not have accepted the leadership last night had I known the conditions."

"Well, it is not yet too late to recede. The barge does not leave Frankfort until this evening, and it is but two leagues back to that city. Within half an hour at the farthest, every man of us will be assembled here. Now is the time to have it out with them, because to-morrow morning the opportunity to withdraw will be gone."

"It is too late even now, Greusel. If last night the guild could not make up the money we owe to Goebel, what hope is there that a single coin remains in their pockets this morning? Do I understand, then, that you refuse to act as my lieutenant?"

"No; but I warn you it will be a step in the wrong direction. You are quite sure of me; and as merely a man-at-arms, as you called us last night, I shall be in a better position to speak in your favor than if I were indebted to you for promotion from the ranks."

"I see. Therefore you counsel me to nominate Kurzbold?"

"I do."

"Why not Gensbein, who was nearly as mutinous as Kurzbold?"

"Well, Gensbein, if you prefer him."

"He showed a well-balanced mind last night, being part of the time on one side and part on the other."

"My dear commander, we were all against you last night, when you spoke of hanging, and even when you only went as far as expulsion."

"Yes, I suppose you were, and the circumstances being such as you state, doubtless you were justified. I am to command, then, a regiment that may obey or not, according to the whim of the moment; a cheering prospect, and one I had not anticipated. When I received the promise of twenty men that they would carry out faithfully whatever I undertook on their behalf, I expected them to stand by it."

"I think you are unjust, Roland. No one has refused, and probably no one will. If any one disobeys a command, then you can act as seems best to you, but I wish you fully to realize the weakness of your status should it come to drastic punishment."

"Quite so, quite so," said Roland curtly. He clasped his hands behind his back, and without further words paced up and down along the bank of the river, head bowed in thought.

Ebearhard was the next arrival, and he greeted Greusel cordially, then one after another various members of the company came upon the scene. To the new-comers Roland made no salutation, but continued his meditating walk.

At last the bell in the tower pealed forth nine slow, sonorous strokes, and Roland raised his head, ceasing his perambulations. Greusel looked anxiously at him as he came forward to the group, but his countenance gave no indication whether or not he had determined to abandon the expedition.

"Are we all here?" asked Roland.

"No," was the reply; "Kurzbold, Eiselbert, Rasselstein, and Gensbein have not arrived yet."

"Then we will wait for them a few moments longer," said the commander, with no trace of resentment at their unpunctuality, and from this Greusel assumed that he not only intended to go on, but had taken to heart the warning given him. Ebearhard and a comrade walked up the road rapidly toward Frankfort, hoping for some sign of the laggards, and Roland resumed his stroll beside the river. At last Ebearhard and his companion returned, and the former approached Roland.

"I see nothing of those four," he said. "What do you propose to do?"

Roland smiled.

"I think sixteen good men, all of a mind, will accomplish quite as much as twenty who are divided in purpose. I propose, therefore, to go on, unless you consider the missing four necessary, in which case we can do nothing but wait."

"I am in favor of going forward," said Ebearhard; then turning to the rest, who had gathered themselves around their captain, he appealed to them. All approved of immediate action.

"Do you intend to follow the river road, Captain?" asked Ebearhard.

"Yes, for two or three leagues, but after that we strike across the country."

"Very well. We can proceed leisurely along the road, and our friends may overtake us if they have any desire to do so."

"Right!" said Roland. "Then let us set out."

The seventeen walked without any company formation through the village, then, approaching a wayside tavern, they were hailed by a loud shout from the drinkers in front of it. Kurzbold was the spokesman for the party of four, which he, with his comrades, made up.

"Come here and drink success to glory," he shouted. "Where have you lads been all the morning?"

"The rendezvous," said Roland sternly, "was at the Elector's tower."

"My rendezvous wasn't. I have been here for more than an hour," said Kurzbold. "I told you last night that when I arrived at Hochst I should be thirsty, and would try to mitigate the disadvantage at a tavern."

"Yes," said Ebearhard, with a laugh, "we can all see you have succeeded in removing the disadvantage."

"Oh, you mean I'm drunk, do you? I'll fight any man who says I'm drunk. It was a tremendous thirst caused by the dryness of my throat from last night, and the dust on the Frankfort road this morning. It takes a great deal of wine to overcome two thirsts. Come along, lads, and drink to the success of the journey. No hard feeling. Landlord, set out the wine here for seventeen people, and don't forget us four in addition."

The whole company strolled in under the trees that fronted the tavern, except Roland, who stood aloof.

"Here's a salute to you, Captain," cried Kurzbold. "I drink wine with you."

"Not till we return from a successful expedition," said Roland.

"Oh, nonsense!" hiccoughed Kurzbold. "Don't think that your office places you so high above us that it is infra dig. to drink with your comrades."

To this diatribe Roland made no reply, and the sixteen, seeing the attitude of their leader, hesitated to raise flagon to lip. The diplomatic Ebearhard seized a measure of wine and approached Roland.

"Drink with us, Commander," he said aloud; and then in a whisper, "Greusel and I think you should."

"Thank you, comrade," said Roland, taking the flagon from him. "And now, brethren, I give you a toast."

"Good, good, good!" cried Kurzbold, with drunken hilarity. "Here's to the success of the expedition. That's the toast, I make no doubt, eh, Captain?"

"The sentiment is included in the toast I shall offer you. Drink to the health of Joseph Greusel, whom I have this morning appointed my lieutenant. If we all conduct ourselves as honorably and capably as he, our project is bound to prosper."

Greusel, who was seated at a table, allowed his head to sink into his hands. Here was his advice scouted, and a direct challenge flung in the face of the company. He believed now that, after all, Roland had resolved to return to Frankfort, money or no money. If he intended to proceed to the Rhine, then even worse might happen, for it was plain he was bent on rule or ruin. Instantly the challenge was accepted. Kurzbold stood up, swaying uncertainly, compelled to maintain his upright position by grasping the top of the table at which he had been seated.

"Stop there, stop there!" he cried. "No man drinks to that toast just yet. Patience, patience! all things in their order. If we claim the power to elect our captain, by the cock-crowned Cross of the old bridge we have a right to name the lieutenant! This is a question for the companionship to decide, and a usurpation on the part of Roland."

"Sit down, you fool!" shouted Ebearhard savagely. "You're drunk. The Captain couldn't have made a better selection. What say you, comrades?"

A universal shout of "Aye!" greeted the question, and even Kurzbold's three comrades joined in it.

"And now, gentlemen, no more talk. Here's to the health of the new lieutenant, Joseph Greusel."

The toast was drunk enthusiastically, all standing, with the exception of Kurzbold, who came down in his seat with a thud.

"All right!" he cried, waving his hand. "All right; all right! That's what I said. Greusel's good man, and now he's elected by the companionship, he's all right. I drink to him. Drink to anybody, I will!"

In groping round for the flagon, he upset it, and then roared loudly for the landlord to supply him again.

"Now, comrades," said Roland sharply, "fall in! We've a long march ahead of us. Come, Greusel, we must lead the van, for I wish to instruct you in your duties."

It was rather a straggling procession that set out from Hochst.

"Perhaps," began Roland, as he strode along beside Greusel, "I should make some excuse for not following the advice you so strenuously urged upon me this morning regarding the appointment of a lieutenant. The truth is I wished to teach you a lesson, and could not resist the temptation of proving that a crisis firmly and promptly met disappears, whereas if you compromise with it there is a danger of being overwhelmed."

"I admit. Commander, that you were successful just now, and the reason is that most of our brigade are sane and sober this morning. But wait until to-night, when the wine passes round several times, and if you try conclusions with them then you are likely to fail."

"But the wine won't pass round to-night."

"How can you prevent it?"

"Wait, and you will see," said Roland, with a laugh.

By this time they arrived at a fork in the road, one section going southwest and the other straight west. The left branch was infinitely the better thoroughfare, for the most part following the Main until it reached the Rhine. Roland, however, chose the right-hand road.

"I thought you were going along by the river," said his lieutenant.

"I have changed my mind," replied Roland, without further explanation.

At first Kurzbold determined to set the pace. He would show the company he was not drunk, and tax them to follow him, but, his stout legs proving unable to carry out this excellent resolution, he gradually fell to the rear. As the sun rose higher, and grew hotter, the pace began to tell on him, and he accepted without protest the support of two comrades who had been drinking with him at Hochst. He retrograded into a condition of pessimistic dejection as the enthusiasm of the wine evaporated. A little later he wished to lie down by the roadside and allow a cruel and unappreciative world to pass on its own way, but his comrades encouraged him to further efforts, and in some manner they succeeded in dragging him along at the tail of the procession.

As they approached the village of Zeilsheim, Roland requested his lieutenant to inform the marchers that there would be no halt until mittagessen.

Zeilsheim is rather more than a league from Hochst, and Kurzbold allowed himself to wake up sufficiently to maintain that the distance earned another drink, but his supporters dragged him on with difficulty past those houses which displayed a bush over the door. At the larger town of Hofheim, five leagues from Frankfort, the same command was passed down the ranks, and at this there was some grumbling, for the day had become very hot, and the way was exceedingly trying, up hill and down dale.

Well set up as these city lads were, walking had never been their accustomed exercise. The interesting Taunus mountains, which to-day constitute an exercise ground full of delights to the pedestrian, forming, as they do, practically a suburb of Frankfort, were at that time an unexplored wilderness, whose forests were infested by roving brigands, where no man ventured except at the risk of an untimely grave. The mediæval townsman rarely trusted himself very far outside the city gates, and our enterprising marauders, whom to outward view seemed stalwart enough to stand great fatigue, proved so soft under the hot sun along the shadeless road that by the time they reached Breckenheim, barely six leagues from Frankfort, there was a mopping of brows and a general feeling that the limit of endurance had been reached.

At Breckenheim Roland called a halt for midday refreshment, and he was compelled to wait nearly half an hour until the last straggler of his woebegone crew limped from the road on to the greensward in front of the Weinstaube which had been selected for a feeding-place. Black bread and a coarse kind of country cheese were the only provisions obtainable, but of these eatables there was an ample supply, and, better than all to the jaded wayfarers, wine in abundance, of good quality, too, for Breckenheim stands little more than a league to the north of the celebrated Hochheim.

The wanderers came in by ones and twos, and sank down upon the benches before the tavern, or sprawled at full length on the short grass, where Kurzbold and his three friends dropped promptly off into sleep. A more dejected and amenable gang even Roland could not have wished to command. Every ounce of fight, or even discussion, was gone from them. They cared not where they were, or what any one said to them. Their sole desire was to be let alone, and they took not the slightest interest even in the preparing of their frugal meal. A mug of wine served to each mitigated the general depression, although Kurzbold showed how far gone he was by swearing dismally when roused even to drink the wine. He said he was resolved to lead a temperate life in future, but nevertheless managed to dispose of his allowance in one long, parched draught.

Greusel approached his chief.

"There will be some difficulty," he said, "when this meal has to be paid for. I find that the men are all practically penniless."

"Tell them they need anticipate no trouble about that," replied Roland. "I have settled the bill, and will see that they do not starve or die of thirst before we reach the Rhine."

"It is proposed," continued Greusel, "that each man should give all the money he possesses into a general fund to be dealt with by a committee the men will appoint. What do you say to this?"

"There is nothing to say. I notice that the proposal was not made until the proposers' pouches were empty."

"They know that some of us have money," Greusel went on, "myself, for instance, and they wish us to share as good comrades should—at least, that is their phrase."

"An admirable phrase, yet I don't agree with it. How much money have you, Greusel?"

"The thirty thalers are practically intact, and Ebearhard has about the same."

"Well, fifty thalers lie safe in my pouch, but not a coin goes into the treasury of any committee the men may appoint. If they choose a committee, let them finance it themselves."

"There will be some dissatisfaction at that decision, Commander."

"I dare say. Still, as you know, I am always ready to do anything conducive to good feeling, so you may inform them that you and Ebearhard and myself, that is, three of us, will contribute to the committee's funds an amount equal to that subscribed by the other eighteen. Such lavishness on our part ought to satisfy them."

"It won't, Commander, because there's not a single kreuzer among the eighteen."

"So be it. That's as far as I am willing to go. Appeal to their reasoning powers, Greusel. If each of the eighteen contributes one thaler, we three will contribute six thalers apiece. Ask them whether they do not think we are generous when we do six times more than any one of them towards providing capital for a committee."

"'Tis not willingness they lack, Commander, but ability."

"They are not logical, Joseph. They prate of comradeship, and when it comes to an exercise of power they demand equality. How, then, can they, with any sense of fairness, prove ungrateful to us when we offer to bear six times the burden they are asked to shoulder?"

The lieutenant said no more, but departed to announce the decision to the men, and either the commander's reasoning overcame all opposition, or else the company was too tired to engage in a controversy.

When the black bread and cheese were served, with a further supply of wine, all sat up and ate heartily. The banquet ended, Greusel made an announcement to the men. There would now be an hour's rest, he said, before taking to the road again. The meal and the wine had been paid for by the commander, so no one need worry on that account, but if any man wished more wine he must pay the shot himself. However, before the afternoon's march was begun flagons of wine would be served at the commander's expense. This information was received in silence, and the men stretched themselves out on the grass to make the most of their hour of rest. Roland strolled off alone to view the village. The lieutenant and Ebearhard sat together at a table, conversing in low tones.

"Well," said Ebearhard, "what do you think of it all?"

"I don't know what to think," replied Greusel. "If the Barons of the Rhine could see us, and knew that we intended to attack them, I imagine there would be a great roar of laughter."

Ebearhard emulated the Barons, and laughed. He was a cheerful person.

"I don't doubt it," he said; "and talking of prospects, what's your opinion of the Commander?"

"I am quite adrift on that score also. This morning I endeavored to give him some good advice. I asked him not to appoint me lieutenant, but to choose Kurzbold or Gensbein from among the malcontents, for I thought if responsibility were placed on their shoulders we should be favored with less criticism."

"A very good idea it seems to me," remarked Ebearhard.

"Well, you saw how promptly he ignored it, yet after all there may be more wisdom in that head of his than I suspected. Look you how he has made a buffer of me. He gives no commands to the men himself, but merely orders me to pass along the word for this or that. He appears determined to have his own way, and yet not to bring about a personal conflict between himself and his following."

"Do you suppose that to be cowardice on his part?"

"No; he is not a coward. He doubtless intends that I shall stand the brunt of any ill-temper on the part of the men. Should disobedience arise, it will be my orders that are disobeyed, not his. If the matter is of no importance one way or the other, I take it he will say nothing, but I surmise that when it comes to the vital point, he will brush me aside as though I were a feather, and himself confront the men regardless of consequences. This morning I thought they would win in such a case, but, by the iron Cross, I am not so confident now. Remember how he sprung my appointment on the crowd, counting, I am sure, on your help. He said to me, when we were alone by the tower, that you were the most fair-minded man among the lot, and he evidently played on that, giving them not a moment to think, and you backed him up. He carried his point, and since then has not said a word to them, all orders going through me, but I know he intended, as he told you, to take the river road, instead of which he has led us over this hilly district until every man is ready to drop. He is himself very sparing of wine, and is in fit condition. I understand he has tramped both banks of the Rhine, from Ehrenfels to Bonn, so this walk is nothing to him. At the end of it he was off for a stroll, and here are these men lying above the sod like the dead underneath it."

"I cannot make him out," mused Ebearhard. "What has been his training? He appears to be well educated, and yet in some common matters is ignorant as a child, as, for instance, not knowing the difference in status between a skilled artisan and a chaffering merchant! What can have been his up-bringing? He is obviously not of the merchant class, yet he persuades the chief of our merchants, and the most conservative, to engage in this wild goose chase, and actually venture money and goods in supporting him. This expedition will cost Herr Goebel at least five thousand thalers, all because of the blandishments of a youth who walked in from the street, unintroduced. Then he is not an artisan of any sort, for when he joined us his hands were quite useless, except upon the sword-hilt."

"He said he was a fencing-master," explained Greusel.

"I know he did, and yet when he was offered a fee to instruct us he wouldn't look at it. The first duty of a fencing-master, like the rest of us, is to make money. Roland quite evidently scorns it, and at the last instructs us for nothing. Fencing-masters don't promote freebooting expeditions, and, besides, a fencing-master is always urbane and polite, cringing to every one. I have watched Roland closely at times, trying to study him, and in doing so have caught momentary glimpses of such contempt for us, that, by the good Lord above us, it made me shrivel up. You know, Greusel, that youth has more of the qualities usually attributed to a noble than those which go to the make-up of any tradesman."

"He is a puzzle to me," admitted Greusel, "and if this excursion does not break up at the outset, I am not sure that it will be a success."

Noticing a look of alarm in Ebearhard's eyes, Greusel cast a glance over his shoulder, and saw Roland standing behind him. The young man said quietly:

"It hasn't broken up at the outset, for we are already more than five leagues from Frankfort. Our foray must be a success while I have two such wise advisers as I find sitting here."

Neither of the men replied. Both were wondering how much their leader had overheard. He took his place on the bench beside Ebearhard, and said to him:

"I wish you to act as my second lieutenant. If anything happens to me,

Greusel takes my place and you take his. This, by the way, is an appointment, rather than an election. It is not to be put before the guild. You simply act as second lieutenant, and that is all there is about it."

"Very good, Commander," said Ebearhard.

"Greusel, how much money have you?"

"Thirty thalers."

"Economical man! Will you lend me the sum until we reach Assmannshausen?"

"Certainly." Greusel pulled forth his wallet, poured out the gold, and Roland took charge of it.

"And you, Ebearhard? How are you off for funds?"

"I possess twenty-five thalers."

"May I borrow from you as well?"

"Oh, yes."

"I was thinking," continued the young man, as he put away the gold, "that this committee idea of the men has merits of its own; therefore I have formed myself into a committee, appointed, not elected, and will make the disbursements. How much money does our company possess?"

"Not a stiver, so far as I can learn."

"Ah, in that case there is little use in my attempting a collection. Now, as I was saying, Greusel, if anything happens to me, you carry on the enterprise along the lines I have laid down. The first thing, of course, is to reach Assmannshausen."

"Nothing can happen to you before we arrive there," hazarded Greusel.

"I'm not so sure. The sun is very powerful to-day, and should it beat me down, let me lie where I fall, and allow nothing to interrupt the march. Once at Assmannshausen, you two must keep a sharp lookout up the river. When you see the barge, gather your men and lead them up to it. It is to await us about half a league above Assmannshausen."

The three conversed until the hour was consumed, then Roland, throwing his cloak over his arm, rose, and said to his lieutenant:

"Just rouse the men, if you please; and you, Ebearhard, tell the landlord to give each a flagon of wine. We take the road to Wiesbaden. I shall walk slowly on ahead, so that you and the company may overtake me."

With this the young leader sauntered indifferently away, leaving to his subordinates the ungracious task of setting tired men to their work again. Greusel looked glum, but Ebearhard laughed.

Some distance to the east of Wiesbaden the leader deflected his company from the road, and thus they passed Wiesbaden to the left, arriving at the village of Sonnenberg. The straggling company made a halt for a short time, while provisions were purchased, every man carrying his own share, which was scantly sufficient for supper and breakfast, and a quantity of wine was acquired to gratify each throat with about a liter and a half; plenty for a reasonable thirst, but not enough for a carouse.

The company grumbled at being compelled to quit Sonnenberg. They had hoped to spend the night at Wiesbaden, and vociferously proclaimed themselves satisfied with the amount of country already traversed. Their leader said nothing, but left Greusel and Ebearhard to deal with them. He paid for the provisions and the wine, and then, with his cloak loosely over his arm, struck out for the west, as if the declining sun were his goal. The rest followed him slowly, in deep depression of spirits. They were in a wild country, unknown to any of them. The hills had become higher and steeper, and there was not even a beaten path to follow; but Roland, who apparently knew his way, trudged steadily on in advance even of his lieutenants. A bank of dark clouds had risen in the east, the heat of the day being followed by a thunderstorm that growled menacingly above the Taunus mountains, evidently accompanying a torrent of rain, although none fell in the line of march.

The sun had set when the leader brought his company down into the valley of the Walluf, about two and a half leagues from Sonnenberg. Here the men found themselves in a wilderness through which ran a brawling stream. Roland announced to them that this would be their camping place for the night. At once there was an uproar of dissent. How were they to camp out without tents? A heavy rain was impending. Listen to the thunder, and taking warning from the swollen torrent.

"Wrap your cloaks around you," said Roland, "and sleep under the trees. I have often done it myself, and will repeat the experience to-night. If you are not yet tired enough to ensure sound slumber, I shall be delighted to lead you on for another few leagues."

The men held a low-voiced, sullen consultation, gathered in a circle. They speedily decided upon returning to Sonnenberg, which it was the unanimous opinion of the company they should never have left. Townsmen all, who had not in their lives spent a night without a roof over their heads, such accommodation as their leader proposed they should endure seemed like being cast away on a desert island. The mystery of the forest affrighted them. For all they could tell the woods were full of wild animals, and they knew that somewhere near lurked outlaws no less savage. The eighteen, ignoring Greusel and Ebearhard, who stood on one side, watching their deliberations with anxious faces, moved in a body upon their leader, who sat on the bank of the torrent, his feet dangling down towards the foaming water.

"We have resolved to return to Sonnenberg," said the leader of the conclave.

"An excellent resolution," agreed Roland cheerfully. "It is a pleasant village, and I have passed through it several times. By the way, Wiesbaden, which is much larger, possesses the advantage to tired men of being half a league nearer."

The spokesman seemed taken aback by Roland's nonchalant attitude.

"We do not know the road to Wiesbaden, and, indeed, are in some doubt whether or no we can find our way to Sonnenberg with darkness coming on."

"Then if I were you, I shouldn't attempt it. Why not eat your supper, and drink your wine in this sheltering grove?"

"By that time it will be as dark as Erebus," protested the spokesman.

"Then remain here, as I suggested, for the night."

"No; we are determined to reach Sonnenberg. A storm impends."

"In that case, gentlemen, don't let me detain you. The gloom thickens as you spend your time in talk."

"Oh, that's all very well, but when we reach Sonnenberg we shall need money."

"So you will."

"And we intend to secure it."

"Quite right."

"We demand from you three thalers for each man."

"Oh, you want the money from me?"

"Yes, we do."

"That would absorb all the funds I possess."

"No matter. We mean to have it."

"You propose to take it from me by force?"

"Yes."

"Ah, well, such being the case, perhaps it would be better for me to yield willingly?"

"I think so."

"I quite agree with you. There are eighteen of you, all armed with swords, while I control but one blade."

Saying this he unfastened his cloak, which he had put on in the gathering chill of the evening, and untying from his belt a well-filled wallet, held it up to their gaze.

"As this bag undisputedly belongs to me, I have a right to dispose of it as I choose. I therefore give it to the brook, whose outcry is as insistent as yours, and much more musical."

"Stop, Roland, stop!" shouted Ebearhard, but the warning came too late. The young man flung the bag into the torrent, where it disappeared in a smother of foam. He rose to his feet and drew his sword.

"If you wish a fight now, it will be for the love of it, no filthy lucre being at stake."

"By Plutus, you are an accursed fool!" cried the spokesman, making no further show of aggression now that nothing but steel was to be gained by a contest.

"A fool; yes!" said Roland. "And therefore the better qualified to lead all such. Now go to Sonnenberg, or go to Hades!"

The men did neither. They sat down under the trees, ate their supper, and drank their wine.

"Will you dine with me?" said Roland, approaching his two gloomy lieutenants, who stood silent at some distance from the circle formed by the others.

"Yes," said Greusel sullenly, "but I would have dined with greater pleasure had you not proven the spokesman's words true."

"You mean about my being a fool? Oh, you yourself practically called me that this morning. Come, let us sit down farther along the stream, where they cannot overhear what we say."

This being done, Roland continued cheerfully:

"I may explain to you that a week ago I had only a wallet of my own, but before leaving on this journey I called upon my mother, and she presented me with another bag. I foresaw during mittagessen that a demand would be made upon us for money, therefore I borrowed all that you two possessed. Walking on ahead, I prepared for what I knew must come, filling the empty wallet with very small stones picked up along the road. That wallet went into the stream. It is surprising how prone human nature is to jump at conclusions. Why should any of you think that I am simpleton enough to throw away good money? Dear, dear, what a world this is, to be sure!"

Half an hour later all were lying down enveloped in their cloaks, sleeping soundly because of their fatigue, despite being out of doors. Next morning there was consternation in the camp, real or pretended. Roland was nowhere to be found, nor did further search reveal his whereabouts.

VIII. THE MISSING LEADER AND THE MISSING GOLD

Probably because of the new responsibility resting upon him, Joseph Greusel was the first to awaken next morning. He let his long cloak fall from his shoulders as he sat up, and gazed about him with astonishment. It seemed as if some powerful wizard of the hills had spirited him away during the night. He had gone to sleep in a place of terror. The thunder rolled threateningly among the peaks of Taunus, and the reflection of the lightning flash, almost incessant in its recurrence, had lit up the grove with an unholy yellow glare. The never-ceasing roar of the foaming torrent, which in the darkness gleamed with ghostly pallor, had somehow got on his nerves. Under the momentary illumination of the lightning, the waves appeared to leap up at him like a pack of hungry wolves, flecked with froth, and the noise strove to emulate the distant thunder. The grove itself was ominous in its gloom, and sinister shapes seemed to be moving about among the trees.

How different was the aspect now! The sun was still beneath the eastern horizon. The cloudless sky gave promise of another warm day, and the air, of crystalline clearness, was inspiring to breathe. To Greusel's mind, tinged with religious feeling, the situation in which he found himself seemed like a section of the Garden of Eden. The stream, which the night before had been to his superstitious mind a thing of terror, was this morning a placid, smiling, rippling brook that a man might without effort leap across.

He rubbed his eyes in amazement, thinking the mists of sleep must be responsible for this magic transformation, until he remembered the distant thunderstorm of the night before among the eastern mountains, and surmised that a heavy rainfall had deluged these speedily drained peaks and valleys.

"What a blessed thing," he said to himself fervently, "is the ever-recurring morning. How it clears away the errors and the passions of darkness! It is as if God desired to give man repeated opportunities of reform, and of encouragement. How sane everything seems now, as compared with the turbulence of the sulphurous night."

As he rose he became aware of an unaccustomed weight by his side, and putting down his hand was astonished to encounter a bag evidently filled with coin. It had been tied by its deerskin thong to his belt, just as was his own empty wallet. He sat down again, drew it round to the front of him, and unfastened it. Pouring out the gold, he found that the wallet contained a hundred and fifteen thalers, mostly in gold, with the addition of a few silver coins. At once it occurred to him that these were Roland's sixty thalers, his own thirty, and Ebearhard's twenty-five. For some reason, probably fearing the men would suspect the ruse practiced on them the night before, Roland had made him treasurer of the company. But why should he have done it surreptitiously?

Readjusting the leathern sack, he again rose to his feet, but now cast his cloak about him, thus concealing the purse. Ebearhard lay sound asleep near him. Farther away the eighteen remaining members of the company were huddled closely together, as if they had gone to rest in a room too small for them, although the whole country was theirs from which to choose sleeping quarters.

Remembering how the brook had decreased in size, and was now running clear and pellucid, he feared that the bag of stones Roland had so dramatically flung into it might be plainly visible. He determined to rouse his commander, and seek the bag for some distance downstream; for he knew that when the men awakened, all night-fear would have departed from them, and seeing the shrinkage of the brook they might themselves institute a search.

On looking round for Roland he saw no sign of him, but this caused little disquietude, for he supposed that the leader had risen still earlier than himself, wishing to stroll through the forest, or up and down the rivulet.

Greusel, with the purpose of finding the bag, and in the hope, also, of encountering his chief, walked down the valley by the margin of the waterway. Peering constantly into the limpid waters, he discovered no trace of what he sought. Down and down the valley, which was wooded all the way, he walked, and sometimes he was compelled to forsake his liquid guide, and clamber through thickets to reach its border again.

At last he arrived at a little waterfall, and here occurred a break in the woods, causing him to stand entranced by the view which presented itself. Down the declivity the forest lasted for some distance, then it gave place to ever-descending vineyards, with here and there a house showing among the vines. At the foot of this hill ran a broad blue ribbon, which he knew to be the Rhine, although he had never seen it before. Over it floated a silvery gauze of rapidly disappearing mist. The western shore appeared to be flat, and farther along the horizon was formed by hills, not so lofty as that on which he stood, but beautiful against the blue sky, made to seem nearer than they were by the first rays of the rising sun, which tipped the summits with crimson.

Greusel drew a long breath of deep satisfaction. He had never before realized that the world was so enchanting and so peaceful. It seemed impossible that men privileged to live in such a land could find no better occupation than cutting one another's throats.

The gentle plash of the waterfall at his right hand accentuated the stillness. From his height he glanced down into the broad, pellucid pool, into whose depths the water fell, and there, perfectly visible, lay the bag of bogus treasure. Cautiously he worked his way down to the gravelly border of the little lake, flung off his clothes, and plunged head-first into this Diana's pool. It was a delicious experience, and he swam round and round the circular basin, clambered up on the gravel and allowed the stream to fall over his glistening shoulders, reveling in Nature's shower-bath. Satisfied at length, he indulged in another rainbow plunge, grasped the bag, and rose again to the surface. Coming ashore, he unloosened the swollen thongs, poured out the stones along the strand, then, after a moment's thought, he wrung the water out of the bag itself, and tied it to his belt, for there was no predicting where the men would wander when once they awoke, and if he threw it away among the bushes, it might be found, breeding first wonder how it came there, and then suspicion of the trick.

Greusel walked back to camp by the other bank of the stream. Although the early rays of the sun percolated through the upper branches of the trees above them, the eighteen prone men slept as if they were but seven. He sprang over the brook, touched the recumbent Ebearhard with his foot, and so awoke him. This excellent man yawned, and stretched out his arms above his head.

"You're an early bird, Greusel," he said. "Have you got the worm?"

"Yes, I have," replied the latter. "I found it in the basin of a waterfall nearly a league from here," and with that he drew aside his cloak, showing the still wet but empty bag.

For a few moments Ebearhard did not understand. He rose and shook himself, glancing about him.

"Great Jove!" he cried, "this surely isn't the stream by which we lay down last night? Do you mean to tell me that thread of water struck terror into my heart only a few hours ago? I never slept out of doors before in all my life, and could not have imagined it would produce such an effect. I see what you mean now. You have found the bag which Roland threw into the foaming torrent."

"Yes; I was as much astonished at the transformation as you when I awoke, and then it occurred to me that when our friends saw the reduction of the rivulet, they would forthwith begin a treasure-hunt, so I determined to obliterate the evidence."

"Was the bag really full of stones?"

"Oh, yes."

"Well, that is a lesson to me. I believe after all that Roland is helplessly truthful, but last night I thought he befooled us. I was certain it was the bag of coin he had thrown away, and becoming ashamed of himself, had lied to us."

"How could you imagine that? He showed us both the bag of money."

"He produced a bag full of something, but I, being the doubting Thomas of the group, was not convinced it contained money."

"Ah, that reminds me, Ebearhard; here is the bag we saw last night. I discovered it attached to my belt this morning."

"He attached it to the wrong belt, then, for you believed him. He should have tied it to mine. What reason does he give for presenting it to you?"

"Ah, now you touch a point of anxiety in my own mind. I have seen nothing of Roland this morning. I surmised that he had arisen before me, and expected to meet him somewhere down the stream, but have not done so."

"He may have gone farther afield. As you found the bag, he of course, missed it, and probably continued his search."

"I doubt that, because I came upon a point of view reaching to the Rhine and the hills beyond. I could trace the stream for a considerable distance, and watched it for a long time, but there appeared to be nothing alive in the forest."

"You don't suppose he has gone back to Frankfort, do you?"

"I am at loss what to think."

"If he has abandoned this gang of malcontents, I should be the last to blame him. The way these pigs acted yesterday was disgraceful, ending up their day with rank mutiny and threats of violence. By the iron Cross, Greusel, he has forsaken this misbegotten lot, and it serves them perfectly right, prating about comradeship and carrying themselves like cut-throats. This is Roland's method of returning our money, for I suppose that bag contains your thirty thalers and my twenty-five."

"Yes, and his own sixty as well. Poor disappointed devil, generous to the last. It was he who obtained all the money at the beginning, then these drunken swine spend it on wine, and prove so generous and brave that eighteen of them muster courage enough to face one man, and he the man who had bestowed the gold upon them."

"Greusel, the whole situation fills me with disgust. I propose we leave the lot sleeping there, go to Wiesbaden for breakfast, and then trudge back to Frankfort. It would serve the brutes right."

"No," said Greusel quietly; "I shall carry out Roland's instructions."

"I thought you hadn't seen him this morning?"

"Not a trace of him. You heard his orders at Breckenheim."

"I don't remember. What were they?"

"That if anything happened to him, I was to drive the herd to Assmannshausen. I quite agree with you, Ebearhard, that he is justified in deserting this menagerie, but, on the other hand, you and I have stood faithfully by him, and it doesn't seem to me right that he should leave us without a word. I don't believe he has done so, and I expect any moment to see him return."

"You're wrong, Greusel. He's gone. That purse is sufficient explanation, and as you recall to my mind his instructions, I believe something of this must have suggested itself to him even that early in the day. He has divested himself of every particle of money in his possession, turning it over to you, but instead of returning to Frankfort he has made his way over the hills to Assmannshausen, and will await us there."

"What would be the object of that?"

"One reason may be that he will learn whether or not you have enough control over these people to bring them to the Rhine. He will satisfy himself that your discipline is such as to improve their manners. It may be in his mind to resign, and make you leader, if you prove yourself able to control them."

"Suppose I fail in that?"

"Well, then—this is all fancy, remember—I imagine he may look round Assmannshausen to find another company who will at least obey him."

"What you say sounds very reasonable. Still, I do not see why he should have left two friends like us without a word."

"A word, my dear Greusel, would have led to another, and another, and another. One of the first questions asked him would be 'But what are Ebearhard and I to do?' That's exactly what he doesn't wish to answer. He desires to know what you will do of your own accord. He is likely rather hopeless about this mob, but is giving you an opportunity, and then another chance. Why, his design is clear as that rivulet there, and as easily seen through.

You will either bring those men across the hills, or you won't. If you and I are compelled to clamber over to Assmannshausen alone, Roland will probably be more pleased to see us than if we brought this rogues' contingent straggling at our heels. He will appoint you chief officer of his new company, and me the second. If you doubt my conclusions, I'll wager twenty-five thalers against your thirty that I am in the right."

"I never gamble, Ebearhard, especially when certain to lose. You are a shrewder man than I, by a long bowshot."

In a work of fiction it would of course be concealed till the proper time came that all of these men were completely wrong in their prognostications regarding the fate of Roland, but this being history it may be stated that the young man had not the least desire to test Greusel's ability, nor would his lieutenants find him awaiting them when they reached Assmannshausen.

"Hello! Rouse up there! What have we for breakfast? Has all the wine been drunk? I hope not. My mouth's like a brick furnace!"

It was the brave Kurzbold who spoke, as he playfully kicked, not too gently, those of his comrades who lay nearest him. He was answered by groans and imprecations, as one by one the sleeping beauties aroused themselves, and wondered where the deuce they were.

"Who has stolen the river?" cried Gensbein.

"Oh, stealing the river doesn't matter," said a third. "It's only running water. Who drank all the wine? That's a more serious question."

"Well, whoever's taken away the river, I can swear without searching my pouch has made no theft from me, for I spent my last stiver yesterday."

"Don't boast," growled Kurzbold. "You're not alone in your poverty. We're all in the same case. Curse that fool of a Roland for throwing away good money just when it's most needed."

"Good money is always most needed," exclaimed the philosophic Gensbein.

He rose and shook himself, then looked down at the beautiful but unimportant rivulet.

"I say, lads, were we as drunk as all that last night? Was there an impassable torrent here or not?"

"How could we be drunk, you fool, on little more than a liter of wine each," cried Kurzbold.

"Please be more civil in your talk," returned his friend. "You were drunk all day. The liter and a half was a mere nightcap. If you are certain there was a torrent, then I must have been in the same condition as yourself."

The spokesman of the previous night, who had been chided for not springing on Roland before he succeeded in doing away with the treasure, here uttered a shout.

"This water," he said, "is clear as air. You can see every pebble at the bottom. Get to work, you sleepyheads, and search down the stream. We'll recover that bag yet, and then it's back to Sonnenberg for breakfast. Whoever finds it, finds it for the guild; a fair and equal division amongst us. That is, amongst the eighteen of us. I propose that Roland, Greusel, and Ebearhard do not share. They were all in the plot to rob us."

"Agreed!" cried the others, and the treasure-hunt impetuously began.

Greusel and Ebearhard watched them disappear through the forest down the stream.

"Greusel," said Ebearhard, "what a deplorable passion is the frantic quest for money in these days, especially money that we have not earned. Our excited treasure-hunters do not realize that at such a moment in the early morning the only subject worth consideration is breakfast. Being unsparing and prodigal last night, it would take a small miracle of the fishes to suffice them to-day. There is barely enough for two hungry men, and as we are rid of these chaps for half an hour at least, I propose we sit down to our first meal."

Greusel made no comment upon this remark, but the advice commended itself to him, for he followed it.

Some time after they had finished breakfast, the unsuccessful company returned by twos and threes. Apparently they had not wandered so far as the waterfall, for no one said anything of the amazing view of the Rhine. Indeed, it was plain that they considered themselves involved in a boundless wilderness, and were too perplexed to suggest a way out. After a storm of malediction over the breakfastless state of things, and a good deal of quarreling among themselves anent who had been most greedy the night before, they now turned their attention to the silent men who were watching them.

"Where's Roland?" they demanded.

"I don't know," replied Greusel.

"Didn't he tell you where he was going?"

"We have not seen him this morning," explained Ebearhard gently. "He seems to have disappeared in the night. Perhaps he fell into the stream. Perhaps, on the other hand, he has deliberately deserted us. He gave us no hint of his intentions last night, and we are as ignorant as yourselves regarding his whereabouts."

"This is outrageous!" cried Kurzbold. "It is the duty of a leader to provide for his following."

"Yes; if the following follows."

"We have followed," said Kurzbold indignantly, "and have been led into this desert, not in the least knowing where in Heaven's name we are. And now to be left like this, breakfastless, thirsty—" Here Kurzbold's language failed him, and he drew the back of his hand across parched lips.

"When you remember, gentlemen," continued Ebearhard, in accents of honey, "that your last dealings with your leader took place with eighteen swords drawn; when you recollect that you expressed your determination to rob him, and when you call to mind that you brave eighteen threatened him with personal violence if he resisted this brigandage on your part, I cannot understand why you should be surprised at his withdrawal from your fellowship."

"Oh, you always were a glib talker, but the question now is what are we to do?"

"Yes, and that is a question for you to decide," said Ebearhard. "When you mutinied last night, you practically deposed Roland from the leadership. To my mind, he had no further obligations towards you, so, having roughly taken the power into your own hands, it is for you to deal with it as you think best. I should never so far forget myself as to venture even a suggestion."

"As I hinted to you," said Kurzbold, "you are talking too much. You are merely one of ourselves, although you have kept yourself separate from us. Greusel has been appointed lieutenant by our unanimous vote, and if his chief proves a poltroon, he is the man to act. Therefore, Joseph Greusel, I ask on behalf of the company what you intend to do?"

"Before I can answer that question," replied Greusel, "I must know whether or not you will act as you did yesterday?"

"What do you mean by that?" Several, speaking together, put the question.

"I wish to know whether you will follow cheerfully and without demur where I lead? I refuse to act as guide if I run the risk of finding eighteen sword-points at my throat when I have done my best."

"Oh, you talk like a fool," commented Kurzbold. "We followed Roland faithfully enough until he brought us into this impasse. You make entirely too much of last night's episode. None of us intended to hurt him, as you are very well aware, and besides, we don't want a leader who is frightened, and runs away at the first sign of danger."

"Make up your minds what you propose to do," said Greusel stubbornly, "and give me your decision; then you will receive mine."

Greusel saw that although Kurzbold talked like the bully he was, the others were rather subdued, and no voice but his was raised in defense of their previous conduct.

"There is one thing you must tell us before we can come to a decision," went on Kurzbold. "How much money have you and Ebearhard?"

"At midday yesterday I had thirty thalers, and Ebearhard had twenty-five. While you were all sleeping on the grass, after our meal at Breckenheim, Roland asked us for the money."

"You surely were not such idiots as to give it to him?"

"He was our commander, and we both considered it right to do what he asked of us."

"He said," put in Ebearhard, "that your suggestion about a finance committee was a good one, and that he had determined to be that committee. He asked us if any of you had money, but I told him I thought it was all spent, which probably accounts for his restricting the application to us two."

"Then we are here in an unknown wilderness, twenty men, hungry, and without a florin amongst us," wailed Kurzbold, and the comments of those behind him were painful to hear.

"I am glad that at last you thoroughly appreciate our situation, and I hope that in addition you realize it has been brought about not through any fault of Roland's, who gave in to your whims and childishness until you came to the point of murder and robbery. Therefore blame yourselves and not him. You now know as much of our position as I do, so make up your minds about the next step, and inform me what conclusion you come to."

"You're a mighty courageous leader," cried Kurzbold scornfully, and with this the hungry ones retired some distance into the grove, from whence echoes of an angry debate came to the two men who sat by the margin of the stream. After a time they strode forward again. Once more Kurzbold was the spokesman.

"We have determined to return to Frankfort."

"Very good."

"I suppose you remember enough of the way to lead us at least as far as Wiesbaden. Beyond that point we can look to ourselves."

"I should be delighted," said Greusel, "to be your guide, but unfortunately

I am traveling in the other direction with Ebearhard."

"Why, in the name of starvation?" roared Kurzbold. "You know no more of the country ahead of us than we do. By going back we can get something to eat, and a drink, at one of the farmhouses we passed this side of Sonnenberg."

"How?" inquired Greusel.

"Why, if they ask for payment we will give them iron instead of silver. No man need starve with a sword by his side."

"Granted that this is feasible, and that the farmers yield instead of raising the country-side against you, when you reach Frankfort what are you going to do? Eat and drink with the landlord of the Rheingold until he becomes bankrupt? You must remember that it was Roland who liquidated our last debt there, without asking or receiving a word of thanks, and he did that not a moment too soon, for the landlord was at the end of his resources and would have closed his tavern within another week."

Kurzbold stormed at this harping on the subject of Roland and his generosity, but those with him were hungry, and they now remembered, too late, that what Greusel said was strictly true. If Roland had put in an appearance then, he would have found a most docile company to lead. They were actually murmuring against Kurzbold, and blaming him and his clan for the disaster that had overtaken them.

"Why will you not come back with us?" pleaded the penitents, with surprising mildness.

"Because the future in Frankfort strikes me as hopeless. Not one amongst us has the brains of Roland, whom we have thrown out. Besides, it is nine and a half long leagues to Frankfort, and only three and a half leagues to Assmannshausen. I expect to find Roland there, and although I know nothing of his intentions, I imagine he has gone to enlist a company of a score or thereabouts that will obey his commands. There is some hope by going forward to Assmannshausen; there is absolutely none in retreating to Frankfort. Then, as I said, Assmannshausen is little more than three leagues away; a fact worth consideration by hungry men. On the Rhine we are in the rich wine country, where there is plenty to eat and drink, probably for the asking, whereas if we turn our faces towards the east we are marching upon starvation."

The buzz of comment aroused by this speech proved to the two men that Kurzbold stood once more alone. Greusel, without seeming to care which way the cat jumped, had induced that unreasoning animal to leap as he liked. His air of supreme indifference aroused Ebearhard's admiration, especially when he remembered that under his cloak there rested a hundred and fifteen thalers in gold and silver.

"But you know nothing of the way," protested Kurzbold. "None of us are acquainted with the country to the west."

"We don't need to be acquainted with it," said Greusel. "We steer westward by glancing at the sun now and then, and cannot go astray, because we must come to the Rhine; then it's either up or down the river, as the case may be, to reach Assmannshausen."

"To the Rhine! To the Rhine!" was now the universal cry.

"Before we begin our journey," said Greusel, as if he accepted the leadership with reluctance, "I must have your promise that you will obey me without question. I am not so patient a man as Roland, but on my part I guarantee you an excellent meal and good wine as soon as we reach Assmannshausen."

"How can you promise that," growled Kurzbold, "when you have given away your money?"

"Because, as I told you, I expect to meet Roland there."

"But he threw away his bag."

"Yes; I told him it was a foolish thing to do, and perhaps that is why he left without saying a word, even to me. He is an ingenious man. Assmannshausen is familiar to him, and I dare say he would not have discarded his money without knowing where to get more."

"To the Rhine! To the Rhine! To the Rhine!" cried the impatient host, gathering up their cloaks, and tightening their belts, as the savage does when he is hungry.

"To the Rhine, then," said Greusel, springing across the little stream in company with Ebearhard.

"You did that very well, Greusel," complimented the latter.

"I would rather have gone alone with you," replied the new leader, "for I have condemned myself to wear this heavy cloak, which is all very well to sleep in, but burdensome under a hot sun."

"The sun won't be so oppressive," predicted his friend, "while we keep to the forest."

"That is very true, but remember we are somewhere in the Rheingau, and that we must come out into the vineyards by and by."

"Don't grumble, Greusel, but hold up your head as a great diplomatist. Roland himself could not have managed these chaps so well, you flaunting hypocrite, the only capitalist amongst us, yet talking as if you were a monk sworn to eternal poverty."

Greusel changed the subject.

"Do you notice," he said, "that we are following some sort of path, which we must have trodden last evening, without seeing it in the dusk."

"I imagine," said Ebearhard, "that Roland knew very well where he was going. He strode along ahead of us as if sure of his ground. I don't doubt but this will lead us to Assmannshausen."

Which, it may be remarked, it did not. The path was little more than a trail, which a sharp-eyed man might follow, and it led up-hill and down dale direct to the Archbishop's Castle of Ehrenfels.

The forest lasted for a distance that the men in front estimated to be about two leagues, then they emerged into open country, and saw the welcome vines growing. Climbing out of the valley, they observed to the right, near the top of a hill, a small hamlet, which had the effect of instantaneously raising the spirits of the woebegone company.

"Hooray for breakfast!" they shouted, and had it not been for their own fatigue, and the steepness of the hill, they would have broken into a run.

"Halt!" cried Greusel sternly, standing before and above them. At once they obeyed the word of command, which caused Ebearhard to smile.

"You will climb to the top of this hill," said Greusel, "and there rest under command of my lieutenant, Ebearhard. As we now emerge into civilization, I warn you that if we are to obtain breakfast it must be by persuasion, and not by force. Therefore, while you wait on the hilltop, I shall go alone into the houses on the right, and see what can be done towards providing a meal for eighteen men. Ebearhard and I will fast until we reach Assmannshausen. On the other hand, you should be prepared for disappointment; loaves of bread are not to be picked up on the point of a sword. If I return and order you to march on unfed, you must do so as cheerfully as you can."

This ultimatum called forth not a word of opposition, and Ebearhard led the van while Greusel deflected up the hill to his right, the sooner to reach the village.

He learned that the name of the place was Anton-Kap; that the route he had been following would take him to Ehrenfels, and that he must adopt a reasonably rough mountain-road to the right in order to reach Assmannshausen.

By somewhat straining the resources of the place, which proved to possess no inn, he collected bread enough for the eighteen, and there was no dearth of wine, although it proved a coarse drink that reflected little credit on the reputation of the Rheingau. He paid for this meal in advance, saying that they were all in a hurry to reach Assmannshausen, and wished to leave as soon as the frugal breakfast was consumed.

Mounting a small elevation to the west of the village, he signaled to the patient men to come on, which they lost no time in doing. The bread was eaten and the wine drunk without a word being said by any one. And now they took their way down the hill again, crossed the little Geisenheim stream, and up once more, traversing a high table-land giving them a view of the Rhine, finally descending through another valley, which led them into Assmannshausen, celebrated for its red wine, a color they had not yet met with.

Assmannshausen proved to be a city as compared with the hamlets they had passed, yet was small enough to make a thorough search of the place a matter that consumed neither much effort nor time. Greusel led his men to a Weinstaube a short distance out of the village, and, to their delight, succeeded in establishing a credit for them to the extent of one liter of wine each, with a substantial meal of meat, eggs, and what-not. Greusel and Ebearhard left them there in the height of great enjoyment, all the more delightful after the hunger and fatigue they had encountered, for the three and a half leagues had proved almost without a single stretch of level land. The two officers inquired for Roland, without success, at the various houses of entertainment which Assmannshausen boasted, then canvassed every home in the village, but no one had seen anything of the man they described.

Coming out to the river front, deeply discouraged, the two gazed across the empty water, from which all enlivening traffic had departed. It was now evident to both that Roland had not entered Assmannshausen, for in so small and gossipy a hamlet no stranger could even have passed through without being observed.

"Well, Joseph," asked Ebearhard, "what do you intend to do?"

"There is nothing to do but to wait until our money is gone. It is absolutely certain that Roland is not here. Can it be possible that after all he returned?"

"How could he have done so? We know him to have been without money; therefore why to Frankfort, even if such a trip were possible for a penniless man?"

"I am sorry now," said Greusel despondently, "that I did not follow a suggestion that occurred to me, which was to take the men direct down the valley where we encamped, to the banks of the Rhine, and there make inquiries."

"You think he went that way?"

"I did, until you persuaded me out of it."

"Again I ask what could be his object?"

"It seems to me that this mutiny made a greater impression on his mind than I had supposed. After all, he is not one of us, and never has been. You yourself pointed that out when we were talking of him at Breckenheim. If you caught glances of contempt for us while we were all one jolly family in the Kaiser cellar, what must be his loathing for the guild after such a day as yesterday?"

"That's true. You must travel with a man before you learn his real character."

"Meaning Roland?"

"Meaning this crew, guzzling up at the tavern. Meaning you, meaning me; yes, and meaning Roland also. I never knew until yesterday and to-day what a capable fellow you were, and when I remember that I nominated Kurzbold for our leader before Roland appeared on the scene, I am amazed at my lack of judgment of men. As for Roland himself, my opinion of him has fallen. Nothing could have persuaded me that he would desert us all without a word of explanation, no matter what happened. My predictions regarding his conduct are evidently wrong. What do you think has actually occurred?"

"It's my opinion that the more he thought over the mutiny, the angrier he became; a cold, stubborn anger, not vocal at all, as Kurzbold's would be. I think that after fastening the money to my belt he went down the valley to the Rhine. He knows the country, you must remember. He would then either wait there until the barge appeared, or more likely would proceed up along the margin of the river, and hail the boat when it came in sight. The captain would recognize him, and turn in, and we know the captain is under his command. At this moment they are doubtless poling slowly up the Rhine to the Main again, and will thus reach Frankfort. Herr Goebel has confidence in

Roland, otherwise he would never have risked so much on his bare word. He will confess to his financier that he has been mistaken in us, and doubtless tell him all that happened, and the merchant will appreciate that, even though he has lost his five hundred thalers, Roland would not permit him to lose his goods as well."

"Do you suppose Roland will enlist another company?"

"It is very likely, for Herr Goebel trusts him, and, goodness knows, there are enough unemployed men in Frankfort for Roland to select a better score than we have proved to be."

It was quite certain that Roland was not in Assmannshausen, yet Greusel was a prophet as false as Ebearhard.

IX. A SOLEMN PROPOSAL OF MARRIAGE

When Roland wrapped his cloak about him, and lay down on the sward at some distance from the spot where his officers already slept, he found that he could not follow their example. Although, he had remained outwardly calm when the attack was made upon him, his mind was greatly perturbed over the outlook. He reviewed his own conduct, wondering whether it would be possible for him so to amend it that he could acquire the respect and maintain the obedience of his men. If he could not accomplish this, then was his plan foredoomed to failure. His cogitations drove away sleep, and he called to mind the last occasion on which he made this same spot his bedroom. Then he had slumbered dreamlessly the night through. He was on the direct trail between Ehrenfels Castle and the town of Wiesbaden, the route over which supplies had been carried to the Castle time and again when the periodical barges from Mayence failed to arrive. It had been pointed out to him by the custodian of the Castle when the young man first became irked by the confined limits of the Schloss, and frequently since that time he had made his way through the forest to Wiesbaden and back.

Never before had he seen the little Walluf so boisterous, pretending that it was important, and he quite rightly surmised that the cause was a sudden downpour in the mountains farther east. The distant mutterings of thunder having long since ceased, he recognized that the volume of the stream was constantly lessening. As the brook gradually subsided to its customary level, the forest became more and more silent. The greater his endeavor to sleep, the less dormant Roland felt, and all his senses seemed unduly quickened by this ineffectual beckoning to somnolence. He judged by the position of the stars, as he lay on his back, that it was past midnight, when suddenly he became aware of a noise to the west of him, on the other side of the brook. Sitting up, and listening intently, he suspected, from the rustle of the underbrush, that some one was following the trail, and would presently come upon his sleeping men.

He rose stealthily, unsheathed his sword, leaped across the rivulet, and proceeded with caution up the acclivity, keeping on the trail as best he could in the darkness. He was determined to learn the business of the wayfarer, without disturbing his men, so crept rapidly up the hill. Presently he saw the glimmer of a light, and conjectured that some one was coming impetuously down, guided by a lanthorn swinging in his hand. Roland stood on guard with sword extended straight in front of him, and the oncomer's breast was almost at the point of it when he hauled himself up with a sudden cry of dismay, as the lanthorn revealed an armed man holding the path.

"I have no money," were the first words of the stranger.

"Little matter for that," replied Roland. "'Tis information I wish, not gear. Why are you speeding through the forest at night, for no sane man traverses this path in the darkness?"

"I could not wait for daylight," said the stranger, breathing heavily. "I carry a message of the greatest importance. Do not delay me, I beg of you. I travel on affairs of State; Imperial matters, and it is necessary I should reach Frankfort in time, or heads may fall."

"So serious as that?" asked Roland, lowering the point of his sword, for he saw the messenger was unarmed. "Whom do you seek?"

"That I dare not tell you. The message concerns those of the highest, and I am pledged to secrecy. Be assured, sir, that I speak the truth."

"Your voice sounds honest. Hold up the lanthorn at arm's length, that I may learn if your face corresponds with it. Ha, that is most satisfactory! And now, my hurrying youth, will you reveal your mission, or shall I be compelled to run my sword through your body?"

"You would not learn it even then," gasped the young man, shrinking still farther up the hill.

Roland laughed.

"That is true enough," he said, "therefore shall I not impale you, but will instead relate to you the secret you carry. You are making not for Frankfort—"

"I assure you, sir, by the sacred Word, that I am, and grieve my oath does not allow me to do your bidding, even though you would kill me, which is easily done, since I am unarmed."

"You pass through Frankfort, I doubt not, but your goal is a certain small room in the neighboring suburb of Sachsenhausen, and he whom you seek is a youth of about your own age, named Roland. You travel on the behest of your father, who was much agonized in mind when you left him, and he, I take it, is custodian of Ehrenfels Castle."

"In God's name!" cried the youth, aghast, "how did you guess all that?"

Again Roland laughed quietly.

"Why, Heinrich," he said, "your agitation causes you to forget old friends. Hold up your lanthorn again, and learn whether or not you recognize me, as I recognized you."

"Heaven be praised! Prince Roland!"

"Yes; your journey is at an end, my good Heinrich, thank the fortune that kept me awake this night. Do you know why you are sent on this long and breathless journey?"

"Yes, Highness. There has come to the Castle from the Archbishop of Mayence a lengthy document for you to sign, and you are informed that the day after to-morrow their Lordships of Mayence, Treves, and Cologne, meet together at the Castle to hold some conversation with you."

"By my sword, then, Heinrich, had you found me in Sachsenhausen we had never attained Ehrenfels in time."

"I think I could have accomplished it," replied the young man. "I should have reached Wiesbaden before daybreak, and there bought the fastest horse that could be found. My father told me to time myself, and if by securing another horse at Frankfort for you I could not make the return journey speedily enough, I was to engage a boat with twenty rowers, if necessary, and convey you to Ehrenfels before the Archbishops arrived."

"Then, Heinrich, you must have deluded me when you said you had no money."

"No, Highness, I have none, but I carry an order for plenty upon a merchant in Wiesbaden, who would also supply me with a horse."

"Heinrich, there are many stars burning above us to-night, and I have been watching them, but your star must be blazing the brightest of all. Sit you down and rest until I return. Make no noise, for there are twenty others asleep by the stream. My cloak is at the bottom of the hill, and I must fetch it. I shall be with you shortly, so keep your candle alight, that I may not miss you."

With that Roland returned rapidly down the slope, untying his bag of money as he descended. Cautiously he fastened it to the belt of Greusel, then, snatching his cloak from the ground, he sprang once more across the stream, and climbed to the waiting Heinrich.

It was broad daylight before they saw the towers of Ehrenfels, and they found little difficulty in rousing Heinrich's father, for he had slept as badly that night as Roland himself.

The caretaker flung his arms around the young prisoner.

"Oh, thank God, thank God!" was all he could cry, and "Thank God!" again he repeated. "Never before have I felt my head so insecure upon my shoulders. Had you not been here when they came, Highness, their Lordships would have listened to no explanation."

"Really you were in little danger with such a clever son. The Archbishops would never have suspected that he was not I, for none of the three has ever seen me. I am quite sure Heinrich would have effected my signature excellently, and answered to their satisfaction all questions they might ask. So long as he complied with their wishes, there would be no inquiries set afoot, for none would suspect the change. Indeed, custodian, you have missed the opportunity of your life in not suppressing me, thus allowing your son to be elected Emperor."

"Your Highness forgets that my poor boy cannot write his own name, much less yours. Besides, it would be a matter of high treason to forge your signature, so again I thank God you are here. Indeed, your Highness, I am in great trouble about my son."

"Oh, the danger is not so serious as you think."

"'Tis not the danger, Highness. That it is his duty to face, but he takes advantage of his position as prisoner. He knows I dare refuse him nothing, and he calls for wine, wine, wine, spending his days in revelry and his nights in stupor."

"You astonish me. Why not cudgel the nonsense out of him? Your arm is strong enough."

"I dare not lay stick on him, and I beg you to breathe nothing of what I have told you, for he holds us both in his grasp, and he knows it. If I called for help to put him in a real dungeon, he would blurt out the whole secret."

"In that case you must even make terms with him. 'Twill be for but a very short time, and after that we will reform him. He was frightened enough of my sword in the forest, and I shall make him dance to its point once this crisis is over."

"I shall do the best I can, Highness. But you must have been on your way to Ehrenfels. Had you heard aught of what is afoot?"

"Nothing. 'Twas mere chance that Heinrich and I met in the forest, and he was within a jot of impinging himself upon my sword in his hurry. I stood in the darkness, while he himself held a light for the better convenience of any chance marauder who wished to undo him."

"Unarmed, and without money," said the custodian, "I thought he was safer than otherwise. But you are surely hungry, Highness. Advance then within, and I will see to your needs."

So presently the errant Prince consumed an excellent, if early breakfast, and, without troubling to undress, flung himself upon a couch, sleeping dreamlessly through the time that Greusel and Ebearhard were conjuring up motives for him, of which he was entirely innocent.

When Roland woke in the afternoon, he had quite forgotten that a score of men who, nominally, at least, acknowledged him master, were wondering what had become of him. He called the custodian, and asked for a sight of the parchments that his Lordship of Mayence had sent across the river for his perusal. He found the documents to be a very carefully written series of demands disguised under the form of requests.

The pledges which were asked of the young Prince were beautifully engrossed on three parchments, each one a duplicate of the other two. If Roland accepted them, they were to be signed next day, in presence of the three Archbishops. Two certainties were impressed upon him when he had read the scroll: first, the Archbishops were determined to rule; and second, if he did not promise to obey they would elect some other than himself Emperor on the death or deposition of his father. The young man resolved to be acquiescent and allow the future to settle the question whether he or the Archbishops should be the head of the Empire. A strange exultation filled him at the prospect, and all thought of other things vanished from his mind.

Leaving the parchments on the table in the knights' hall, where he had examined them, he mounted to the battlements to enjoy the fresh breeze that, no matter how warm the day, blows round the towers of Ehrenfels. Here a stone promenade, hung high above the Rhine, gave a wonderful view up and down the river and along the opposite shore. From this elevated, paved plateau he could see down the river the strongholds of Rheinstein and Falkenberg, and up the river almost as far as Mayence. He judged by the altitude of the sun that it was about four o'clock in the afternoon. The sight of Rheinstein should have suggested to him his deserted company, for that was the first castle he intended to attack, but the prospect opened up to him by the communication of the Archbishops had driven everything else from his mind.

Presently the cautious custodian joined him in his eyrie, and Roland knew instinctively why he had come. The old man was wondering whether or not he would make difficulties about signing the parchments. He feared the heedless impetuosity and conceit of youth; the natural dislike on the part of a proud young prince to be restricted and bound down by his elders, and the jailer could not conceal his gratification when the prisoner informed him that of course he would comply with the desires of the three prelates.

"You see," he continued, with a smile, "I must attach my signature to those instruments in order to make good my promises to you."

He was interrupted by a cry of astonishment from his aged comrade.

"Will wonders never cease!" cried the old man. "Those merchants in Frankfort must be irredeemable fools. Look you there, Highness! Do you see that barge coming down the river, heavily laden, as I am a sinner, for she lies low in the water. It is one of the largest of the Frankfort boats, and those hopeful simpletons doubtless imagine they can make their way through to Cologne with enough goods left to pay for the journey. 'Tis madness! Why, the knights of Rheinstein and Falkenberg alone will loot them before they are out of our sight. If they think to avoid those rovers by hugging our shore, their mistake will be apparent before they have gone far."

Roland gazed at the approaching craft, and instantly remembered that he was responsible for its appearance on the Rhine. He recognized Herr Goebel's great barge, with its thick mast in the prow, on which no sail was hoisted because the wind blew upstream. On recollecting his deserted men, he wondered whether or not Greusel had brought them across the hills to Assmannshausen. Had they yet discovered that Joseph carried the bag of gold? He laughed aloud as he thought of the scrimmage that would ensue when this knowledge came to them. But little as he cared for the eighteen, he experienced a pang of regret as he estimated the predicament in which both Greusel and Ebearhard had stood on learning he had left them without a word. Still, even now he could not see how any explanation on his part was possible without revealing his identity, and that he was determined not to do.

Turning round, he said abruptly to the custodian:

"Were the seven hundred thalers paid to you each month?"

"Of a surety," was the reply.

"That will be two thousand one hundred thalers altogether. Did you spend the money?"

"I have not touched a single coin. That amount is yours, and yours alone, Prince Roland. If I have been of service I am quite content to wait for my reward, or should I not be here, I know you will remember my family."

"May the Lord forget me if I don't. Still, the twenty-one hundred thalers are all yours, remember, but I beg of you to lend me a thousand, for I possess not a single gold piece in my bag. Indeed, if it comes to that, I do not possess even a bag. I had two yesterday, but one I gave away and the other I threw away."

The old man hurried down, and presently returned with the bag of money that Roland had asked of him. Before this happened, however, Roland, watching the barge, saw it round to, and tie up at the shore some distance above Assmannshausen. He took the gold, and passed down the stone stair to the courtyard.

"I shall return," he said, "before the sun sets," and without more ado, this extraordinary captive left his prison, and descended the hill in the direction of the barge.

After greeting Captain Blumenfels, he learned that the boat had been delayed by running on a sandbank in the Main during the night, but they had got it off at daybreak, and here they were. As, standing on the shore, Roland talked with the captain on the barge, he saw approaching from Assmannshausen two men whom he recognized. Telling the captain he might not be ready for several days, he walked along the shore to meet his astonished friends, who, as was usual with them, jumped at an erroneous conclusion, and supposed that he arrived on the barge which they had seen rounding to for the purpose of taking up her berth by the river-bank.

Greusel and Ebearhard stood still until he came up to them.

"Good afternoon, gentlemen. Are you here alone, or have you brought the mob with you?"

"Your capable lieutenant, sir," said Ebearhard, before his slower companion could begin to frame a sentence, "allowed the men to think they were having their own way, but in reality diverted them into his, so they are now enjoying a credit of one liter each at the tavern of the Golden Anker."

"That," said Roland, "is but as a drop of water in a parched desert. Have they discovered you hold the money, Greusel?"

"No, not yet; but I fear they will begin to suspect by and by. I suppose you went down the valley of the brook to the Rhine, and overhauled the barge there?"

"I suppose so," said Roland. "What else did you think I could do?"

"I was sure you had done that, but I feared you would turn the barge back to Frankfort."

"I never thought of such a thing. Indeed, the captain told me he met difficulty enough navigating the shallow Main, and I think he prefers the deeper Rhine. Of course, you know why I left you."

The men looked at each other without reply, and Roland laughed.

"I see you have been harboring dark suspicions, but the case is very simple. The pious monks tell us that the Scriptures say if a man asks us to go one league with him, we should go two. My good friends of the guild last night made a most reasonable request, namely, that I should bestow upon them three thalers each, and surely, to quote the monks again, the laborer is worthy of his hire."

"Oh, that is the way you look upon it, then," said Greusel.

"From a scriptural point of view, yes; and I am going to better the teachings of my young days by giving each of the men ten times the amount he desired. Thirty thalers each are waiting in this bag for them."

"By my sword!" cried Ebearhard, "if that isn't setting a premium on mutiny it comes perilously close."

"Not so, Ebearhard; not so. You and Greusel did not mutiny, therefore to each of you I give a hundred and thirty thalers, which is the thirty thalers the mutineers receive, and a hundred thalers extra, as a reward of virtue because you did not join them. After all, there is much to be said for the men's point of view. I had led them ruthlessly under a burning July sun, along a rough and shadeless road, then dragged them away from the ample wine-vaults of

Sonnenberg; next guided them on through brambles, over streams, into bogs and out again; and lastly, when they were dog-tired, hungry and ill-tempered, I carelessly pointed to a section of the landscape, and said, 'There, my dear chaps, is your bedroom'; lads who had never before slept without blankets and a roof. No wonder they mutinied; but even then, by the love of God for His creatures, they did not actually attack me when I stood up with drawn sword in my hand."

"Of course you have that at least to be thankful for," said Ebearhard. "Eighteen to one was foul odds."

"I be thankful! Surely you are dreaming, Ebearhard. Why should I be thankful, except that I escaped the remorse for at least killing a dozen of them!"

Ebearhard laughed heartily.

"Oh, if so sure of yourself as all that, you need no sympathy from me."

"You thought I would be outmatched? By the Three Kings! do you imagine me such a fool as to teach you artisans the higher qualities of the sword? There would have been a woeful surprise for the eighteen had they ventured another step farther. However, that's all past and done with, and we'll say no more about it. Let us sit down here on the sward, and indulge in the more agreeable recreation of counting money."

He spread his cloak on the grass, and poured out the gold upon it.

"I am keeping two hundred thalers for myself, as leader of the expedition, and covetous. Here are your hundred and thirty thalers, Greusel, and yours, Ebearhard. You will find remaining five hundred and forty, which, if divided with reasonable accuracy, should afford thirty thalers to each of our precious eighteen."

"Aren't you coming with us to Assmannshausen, that you may give this money to the men yourself?" asked Greusel.

"No; that pleasure falls to my lieutenants, first and second. One may divide the money while the other delivers the moral lecture against mutiny, illustrated by the amount that good behavior gains. Say nothing to the men about the barge being here, merely telling them to prepare for action. Now that you are in funds, engage a large room, exclusively for yourselves, at the Golden Anker. Thus you will be the better able to keep the men from talking with strangers, and so prevent any news of our intentions drifting across the river to Rheinstein or Falkenberg. You might put it to them, should they object to the special room, that you are reconstituting, as it were, the Kaiser cellar of Frankfort in the village of Assmannshausen. Go forward, therefore, with your usual meetings of the guild, as it was before I lowered its tone by becoming a member. Knowing the lads as I do, I suggest that you make your bargain with them before you deliver the money. No promise; no thirty thalers. And now, good-by. I shall be exceedingly busy for some days arranging for a further supply of money, so do not seek me out no matter what happens."

With this Roland shook hands, and returned to Ehrenfels Castle.

The three sumptuous barges of the Archbishops hove in sight at midday, two coming up the river and one floating down. They maneuvered to the landing so that all reached it at the same time, and thus the three Archbishops were enabled to set foot simultaneously on the firm ground, as was right and proper, no one of them obtaining precedence over the other two. On entering the Castle of Ehrenfels in state, they proceeded to the large hall of the knights, and seated themselves in three equal chairs that were set along the solid table. Here a repast was spread before them, accompanied by the finest wine the Rheingau produced, and although the grand prelates ate lustily, they were most sparing in their drink, for when they acted in concert none dared risk putting himself at a disadvantage with the others. They would make up for their abstinence when each rested in the security of his own castle.

The board being cleared, Roland was summoned, and bowing deeply to each of the three he took his place, modestly standing on the opposite side of the table. The Archbishop of Mayence, as the oldest of the trio, occupied the middle chair; Treves, the next in age, at his right hand, and Cologne at his left. A keen observer might have noticed that the deferential, yet dignified, bearing of the young Prince made a favorable impression upon these rulers who, when they acted together, formed a power that only nominally was second in the realm.

It was Mayence who broke the silence.

"Prince Roland, some months ago turbulence in the State rendered it advisable that you, as a probable nominee to the throne, should be withdrawn from the capital to the greater safety which this house affords. I hope it has never been suggested to you that this unavoidable detention merited the harsh name of imprisonment?"

"Never, your Lordships," said Roland, with perfect truth.

The three slightly inclined their heads, and Mayence continued:

"I trust that in the carrying out of our behests you have been put to no inconvenience during your residence in my Castle of Ehrenfels, but if you find cause for complaint I shall see to it that the transgressor is sharply punished."

"My Lord, had such been the case I should at once have communicated with your Lordship at Mayence. The fact that you have received no such protest from me answers your question, but I should like to add emphasis to this reply by saying I have met with the greatest courtesy and kindness within these walls."

"I speak for my brothers and myself when I assert we are all gratified to hear the expression that has fallen from your lips. There was sent for your perusal a document in triplicate. Have you found time to read it?"

"Yes, my Lord, and I beg to state at once that I will sign it with the greater pleasure since in any case, if called to the high position you propose, I should have consulted your Lordships on every matter that I deemed important enough to be worthy of your attention, and in no instance could I think of setting up my own opinion against the united wisdom of your Lordships."

For a few minutes there ensued a whispered conversation among the three, then Mayence spoke again:

"Once more I voice the sentiments of my colleagues, Prince Roland, when I assure you that the words you have just spoken give us the utmost satisfaction. In the whole world to-day there is no prouder honor than that which it is in the Electors' power to bestow upon you, and it is a blessed augury for the welfare of our country when the energy and aspiration of youth in this high place associates itself with the experience of age."

Here he made a signal, and the aged custodian, who had been standing with his back against the door, well out of earshot, for the conversation was carried on in the most subdued and gentle tones, hurried forward, and Mayence requested him to produce the documents entrusted to his care. These were spread out before the young man, who signed each of them amidst a deep silence, broken only by the scratching of the quill.

Up to this point Roland had been merely a Prince of the Empire; now, to all practical purposes, he was heir-apparent to the throne. This distinction was delicately indicated by Mayence, who asked the attendant to bring forward a chair, and then requested the young man to seat himself. Roland had supposed the ceremonies at an end, but it was soon evident that something further remained, for the three venerable heads were again in juxtaposition, and apparently there was some whispered difference as to the manner of procedure. Then Cologne, as the youngest of the three, was prevailed upon to act as spokesman, and with a smile he regarded the young man before he began.

"I reside farther than my two colleagues from your fair, if turbulent, city of Frankfort, and perhaps that is one reason why I know little of the town and its ways from personal observation. You are a young man who, I may say, has greatly commended himself to us all, and so in whatever questions I may put, you will not, I hope, imagine that there is anything underneath them which does not appear on the surface."

Roland drew a long breath, and some of the color left his face.

"What in the name of Heaven is coming now," he said to himself, "that calls for so ominous a prelude? It must be something more than usually serious. May the good Lord give me courage to face it!"

But outwardly he merely inclined his head.

"We have all been young ourselves, and I trust none of us forget the temptations, and perhaps the dangers, that surround youth, especially when highly placed. I am told that Frankfort is a gay city, and doubtless you have mixed, to some extent at least, in its society." Here the Archbishop paused, and, as he evidently expected a reply, Roland spoke:

"I regret to say, my Lord, that my opportunities for social intercourse have hitherto been somewhat limited. Greatly absorbed in study, there has been little time for me to acquire companions, much less friends."

"What your Highness says, so far from being a drawback, as you seem to imagine, is all to the good. It leaves the future clear of complications that might otherwise cause you embarrassment." Here the Archbishop smiled again, and Roland found himself liking the august prelate. "It was not, however, of men that I desired to speak, but of women."

"Oh, is that all?" cried the impetuous youth. "I feared, my Lord, that you were about to treat of some serious subject. So far as women are concerned, I am unacquainted with any, excepting only my mother."

At this the three prelates smiled in differing degrees; even the stern lips of Mayence relaxing at the young man's confident assumption that consideration of women was not a matter of importance.

"Your Highness clears the ground admirably for me," continued Cologne, "and takes a great weight from my mind, because I am entrusted by my brethren with a proposal which I have found some difficulty in setting forth. It is this. The choice of an Empress is one of the most momentous questions that an Emperor is called upon to decide. In all except the highest rank personal preference has much to do with the selection of a wife, but in the case of a king do you agree with me that State considerations must be kept in view?"

"Undoubtedly, my Lord."

"This is a matter to which we three Electors have given the weightiest consideration, finally agreeing on one whom we believe to possess the necessary qualifications; a lady highly born, deeply religious, enormously wealthy, and exceedingly beautiful. She is related to the most noble in the land. I refer to Hildegunde Lauretta Priscilla Agnes, Countess of Sayn. If there is any reason why your preference should not coincide with ours, I beg you quite frankly to state it."

"There is no reason at all, your Lordships," cried Roland, with a deep sigh of relief on learning that his fears were so unfounded. "I shall be most happy and honored to wed the lady at any time your Lordships and she may select."

"Then," said the Archbishop of Mayence, rising to his feet and speaking with great solemnity, "you are chosen as the future Emperor of our land."

X. A CALAMITOUS CONFERENCE

The prelate and his ward were met at the doors of Stolzenfels by the Archbishop of Treves in person, and the welcome they received left nothing to be desired in point of cordiality. There were many servants, male and female, about the Castle, but no show of armed men.

The Countess was conducted to a room whose outlook fascinated her. It occupied one entire floor of a square tower, with windows facing the four points of the compass, and from this height she could view the Rhine up to the stern old Castle of Marksburg, and down past Coblentz to her own realm of Sayn, where it bordered the river, although the stronghold from which she ruled this domain was hidden by the hills ending in Ehrenbreitstein.

When she descended on being called to mittagessen, she was introduced to a sister of the Archbishop of Treves, a grave, elderly woman, and to the Archbishop's niece, a lady about ten years older than Hildegunde. Neither of these grand dames had much to say, and the conversation at the meal rested chiefly with the two Archbishops. Indeed, had the Countess but known it, her presence there was a great disappointment to the two noblewomen, for the close relationship of the younger to the Archbishop of Treves rendered it impossible that she should be offered the honor about to be bestowed upon the younger and more beautiful Countess von Sayn.

The Archbishop of Mayence, although a resident of the Castle, partook of refreshment in the smallest room of the suite reserved for him, where he was waited upon by his own servants and catered for by his own cook.

When the great Rhine salmon, smoking hot, was placed upon the table, Cologne was generous in his praise of it, and related again, for the information of his host and household, the story of the English Princess who had partaken of a similar fish, doubtless in this same room. Despite the historical bill of fare, and the mildly exhilarating qualities of the excellent Oberweseler wine, whose delicate reddish color the sentimental Archbishop compared to the blush on a bride's cheeks, the social aspect of the midday refection was overshadowed by an almost indefinable sense of impending danger. In the pseudogenial conversation of the two Archbishops there was something forced: the attitude of the elderly hostess was one of unrelieved gloom. After a few conventional greetings to her young guest, she spoke no more during the meal. Her daughter, who sat beside the Countess on the opposite side of the table from his Lordship of Cologne, merely answered "Yes" or "No" to the comments of the lady of Sayn praising the romantic situation of the Castle, its unique qualities of architecture, and the splendid outlook from its battlements, eulogies which began enthusiastically enough, but finally faded away into silence, chilled by a reception so unfriendly.

Thus cast back upon her own thoughts, the girl grew more and more uneasy as the peculiar features of the occasion became clearer in her own mind. Here was her revered, beloved friend forcing hilarity which she knew he could not feel, breaking bread and drinking wine with a colleague while three thousand of his armed men peered down on the roof that sheltered him, ready at a signal to pounce upon Stolzenfels like birds of prey, capturing, and if necessary, slaying. She remembered the hearty cheers that welcomed them on their arrival at Coblentz, yet every man who thus boisterously greeted them, waving his bonnet in the air, was doubtless an enemy. The very secrecy, the unknown nature of the danger, depressed her more and more as she thought of it; the fierce soldiers hidden in the forest, ready to leap up, burn and kill at an unknown sign from a Prince of religion; the deadly weapons concealed in a Church of Christ: all this grim reality of a Faith she held dear had never been hinted at by the gentle nuns among whom she lived so happily for the greater part of her life.

At last her somber hostess rose, and Hildegunde, with a sigh of relief, followed her example. The Archbishop of Cologne gallantly held back the curtain at the doorway, and bowed low when the three ladies passed through. The silent hostess conducted her guest to a parlor on the same floor as the dining-room; a parlor from which opened another door connecting it with a small knights' hall; the kleine Rittersaal in which the Court of the Archbishops was to be held.

The Archbishop's sister did not enter the parlor, but here took formal farewell of Countess von Sayn, who turned to the sole occupant of the room, her kinsman and counselor, Father Ambrose.

"Were you not asked to dine with us?" she inquired.

"Yes; but I thought it better to refuse. First, in case the three Archbishops might have something confidential to say to you; and second, because at best I am poor company at a banquet."

"Indeed, you need not have been so thoughtful: first, as you say, there were not three Archbishops present, but only two, and neither said anything to me that all the world might not hear; second, the rest of the company, the sister and the niece of Treves, were so doleful that you would have proved a hilarious companion compared with them. Did my guardian make any statement to you yesterday afternoon that revealed the object of this coming Court?"

"None whatever. Our conversation related entirely to your estate and my management of it. We spoke of crops, of cultivation, and of vineyards."

"You have no knowledge, then, of the reason why we are summoned hither?"

"On that subject, Hildegunde, I am as ignorant as you."

"I don't think I am wholly in the dark," murmured the Countess, "although I know nothing definite."

"You surmise, in spite of your guardian's disclaimer, that the discussion will pertain to your recovery of the town of Linz?"

"Perhaps; but not likely. Did you say anything of your journey to Frankfort?"

"Not a word. I understood from you that no mention should be made of my visit unless his Lordship asked questions proving he was aware of it, in which case I was to tell the truth."

"You were quite right, Father. Did my guardian ask you to accompany us to Stolzenfels?"

"Assuredly, or I should not have ventured."

"What reason did he give, and what instructions did he lay upon you?"

"He thought you should have by your side some one akin to you. His instructions were that in no circumstances was I to offer any remark upon the proceedings. Indeed, I am not allowed to speak unless in answer to a question directly put to me, and then in the fewest possible words."

Hildegunde ceased her cross-examination, and seated herself by a window which gave a view of the steep mountain-side behind the Castle, where, sheltered by the thick, dark forest, she knew that her guardian's men lay in ambush. She shuddered slightly, wondering what was the meaning of these preparations, and in the deep silence became aware of the accelerated beating of her heart. She felt but little reassured by the presence of her kinsman, whose lips moved without a murmur, and whose grave eyes seemed fixed on futurity, meditating the mystery of the next world, and completely oblivious to the realities of the earth he inhabited.

She turned her troubled gaze once more to the green forest, and after a long lapse of time the dual reveries were broken by the entrance of an official gorgeously appareled. This functionary bowed low, and said with great solemnity:

"Madam, the Court of my Lords the Archbishops awaits your presence."

The kleine Rittersaal occupied a fine position on the river-side front of Stolzenfels, its windows giving a view of the Rhine, with the strong Castle of Lahneck over-hanging the mouth of the Lahn, and the more ornamental Schloss Martinsburg at the upper end of Oberlahnstein. The latter edifice, built by a former Elector of Mayence, was rarely occupied by the present Archbishop, but, as he sat in the central chair of the Court, he had the advantage of being able to look across the river at his own house should it please him to do so.

The three Archbishops were standing behind the long table when the

Countess entered, thus acknowledging that she who came into their presence, young and beautiful, was a very great lady by right of descent and rank. She acknowledged their courtesy by a graceful inclination of the head, and the three Princes of the Church responded each with a bow, that of Mayence scarcely perceptible, that of Treves deferential and courtly, that of Cologne with a friendly smile of encouragement.

In the center of the hall opposite the long table had been placed an immense chair, taken from the grand Rittersaal, ornamented with gilded carving, and covered in richly-colored Genoa velvet. It looked like a throne, which indeed it was, used only on occasions when Royalty visited the Castle. To this sumptuous seat the scarcely less gorgeous functionary conducted the girl, and when she had taken her place, the three Archbishops seated themselves. The glorified menial then bent himself until his forehead nearly touched the floor, and silently departed. Father Ambrose, his coarse, ill-cut clothes of somber color in striking contrast to the richness of costume worn by the others, stood humbly beside the chair that supported his kinswoman.

The Countess gave a quick glance at the Archbishop of Mayence, then lowered her eyes. Cologne she had known all her life; Treves she had met that day, and rather liked, although feeling she could not esteem him as she did her guardian, but a thrill of fear followed her swift look at the man in the center.

"A face of great strength," she said to herself, "but his thin, straight lips, tightly compressed, seemed cruel, as well as determined." With a flash of comprehension she understood now her guardian's warning not to thwart him. It was easy to credit the acknowledged fact that this man dominated the other two. Nevertheless, when he spoke his voice was surprisingly mild.

"Madam," he said, "we are met here in an hour of grave anxiety. The Emperor, who has been ill for some time, is now upon his death-bed, and the physicians who attend him inform me that at any moment we may be called upon to elect his successor. That successor has already been chosen; chosen, I may add, in an informal manner, but his selection is not likely to be canceled, unless by some act of his own which would cause us to reconsider our decision.

Our adoption was made very recently in my castle of Ehrenfels, and we are come together again in the Castle of my brother Treves, not in our sacred office as Archbishops, but in our secular capacity as Electors of the Empire, to determine a matter which we consider of almost equal importance. It is our privilege to bestow upon you the highest honor that may be conferred on any woman in the realm; the position of Empress.

"When you have signified your acceptance of this great elevation, I must put to you several questions concerning your future duties to the State, and these are embodied in a document which you will be asked to sign."

The Countess did not raise her eyes. While the Archbishop was speaking the color flamed up in her cheeks, but faded away again, and her guardian, who watched her very intently across the table, saw her face become so pale that he feared she was about to faint. However, she rallied, and at last looked up, not at her dark-browed questioner, but at the Archbishop of Cologne.

"May I not know," she said, in a voice scarcely audible, "who is my future husband?"

"Surely, surely," replied her guardian soothingly, "but the Elector of Mayence is our spokesman here, and you must address your question to his Lordship."

She now turned her frightened eyes upon Mayence, whose brow had become slightly ruffled at this interruption, and whose lips were more firmly closed. He sat there imperturbable, refusing the beseechment of her eyes, and thus forced her to repeat her question, though to him it took another form.

"My Lord, who is to be the next Emperor?"

"Countess von Sayn, I fear that in modifying my opening address to accord with the comprehension of a girl but recently emerged from convent life, I have led you into an error. The Court of Electors is not convened for the purpose of securing your consent, but with the duty of imposing upon you a command. It is not for you to ask questions, but to answer them."

"You mean that I am to marry this unknown man, whether I will or no?"

"That is my meaning."

The girl sat back in her chair, and the moisture that had gathered in her eyes disappeared as if licked up by the little flame that burned in their depths.

"Very well," she said. "Ask your questions, and I will answer them."

"Before I put any question, I must have your consent to my first proposition."

"That is quite unnecessary, my Lord. When you hear my answer to your questions, you will very speedily withdraw your first proposition."

The Elector of Treves, who had been shifting uneasily in his chair, now leaned forward, and spoke in an ingratiating manner.

"Countess, you are a neighbor of mine, although you live on the opposite side of the river, and I am honored in receiving you as my guest. As guest and neighbor, I appeal to you on our behalf: be assured that we wish nothing but your very greatest good and happiness." The spark in her eyes died down, and they beamed kindly on the courtier Elector. "You see before you three old bachelors, quite unversed in the ways of women. If anything that has been said offends you, pray overlook our default, for I assure you, on behalf of my colleagues and myself, that any one of us would bitterly regret uttering a single word to cause you disquietude."

"My disquietude, my Lord, is caused by the refusal to utter the single name I have asked for. Am I a peasant girl to be handed over to the hind that makes the highest offer?"

"Not so. No such thought entered our minds. The name is, of course, a secret at the present moment, and I quite appreciate the reluctance of my Lord of Mayence to mention it, but I think in this instance an exception may safely be made, and I now appeal to his Lordship to enlighten the Countess."

Mayence answered indifferently:

"I do not agree with you, but we are here three Electors of equal power, and two can always outvote one."

The Elector of Cologne smiled slightly; he had seen this comedy enacted before, and never objected to it. The carrying of some unimportant point in opposition to their chief always gave Treves a certain sense of independence.

"My Lord of Cologne," said the latter, bending forward and addressing the man at the other end of the table "do you not agree with me?"

"Certainly," replied Cologne, with some curtness.

"In that case," continued Treves, "I take it upon myself to announce to you, Madam, that the young man chosen for our future ruler is Prince Roland, only son of the dying Emperor."

The hands of the Countess nervously clutched the soft velvet on the arms of her chair.

"I thank you," she said, addressing Treves, and speaking as calmly as though she were Mayence himself. "May I ask you if this marriage was proposed to the young man?"

Treves looked up nervously at the stern face of Mayence, who nodded to him, as much as to say:

"You are doing well; go on."

"Yes," replied Treves.

"Was my name concealed from him?"

"No."

"Had he ever heard of me before?"

"Surely," replied the diplomatic Treves, "for the fame of the Countess von Sayn has traveled farther than her modesty will admit."

"Did he agree?"

"Instantly; joyfully, it seemed to me."

"In any case, he has never seen me," continued the Countess. "Did he make any inquiry, whether I was tall or short, old or young, rich or poor, beautiful or ugly?"

"He seemed very well satisfied with our choice."

Treves had his elbows on the table, leaning forward with open palms supporting his chin. He had spoken throughout in the most ingratiating manner, his tones soft and honeyed. He was so evidently pleased with his own diplomacy that even the eye of the stern Mayence twinkled maliciously when the girl turned impulsively toward the other end of the table, and cried:

"Guardian, tell me the truth! I know this young man accepted me as if I were a sack of grain, his whole mind intent on one thing only: to secure for himself the position of Emperor. Is it not so?"

"It is not so, Countess," said Cologne solemnly.

"Prince Roland, it is true, made no stipulation regarding you."

"I was sure of it. Any Gretchen in Germany would have done just as well. I was merely part of the bargain he was compelled to make with you, and now I announce to the Court that no power on earth will induce me to marry Prince Roland. I claim the right of my womanhood to wed only the man whom I love, and who loves me!"

Mayence gave utterance to an exclamation that might be coarsely described as a snort of contempt. The Elector of Treves was leaning back in his chair discomfited by her abrupt desertion of him. The Elector of Cologne now leaned forward, dismayed at the turn affairs had taken, deep anxiety visible on his brow.

"Countess von Sayn," he began, and thus his ward realized how deeply she had offended, "in all my life I never met any young man who impressed me so favorably as Prince Roland of Germany. If I possessed a daughter whom I dearly loved, I could wish her no better fortune than to marry so honest a youth as he. The very point you make against him should have told most strongly in his favor with a young girl. My reading of his character is that so far as concerns the love you spoke of, he knows as little of it as yourself, and thus he agreed to our proposal with a seeming indifference which you entirely misjudge. If you, then, have any belief in my goodwill towards you, in my deep anxiety for your welfare and happiness, I implore you to agree to the suggestion my Lord of Mayence has made. You speak of love knowing nothing concerning it. I call to your remembrance the fact that one noble lady of your race may have foregone the happiness that love perhaps brings, in her desire for the advancement of one whom she loved so truly that she chose for her guide the more subdued but steadier star of duty. The case is presented to you, my dear, in different form, and I feel assured that duty and love will shine together."

As the venerable Archbishop spoke with such deep earnestness, in a voice she loved so well, the girl buried her face in her hands, and he could see the tears trickle between her fingers. A silence followed her guardian's appeal, disturbed only by the agitated breathing of Hildegunde.

The cold voice of the Elector of Mayence broke the stillness, like a breath from a glazier:

"Do you consent, Madam?"

"Yes," gasped the girl, her shoulders quivering with emotion, but she did not look up.

"I fear that the object of this convocation was like to be forgotten in the gush of sentiment issuing from both sides of me. This is a business meeting, and not a love-feast. Will you do me the courtesy, Madam, of raising your head and answering my question?"

The girl dashed the tears from her eyes, and sat up straight, grasping with nervous hands the arms of the throne, as if to steady herself against the coming ordeal.

"I scarcely heard what you said. Do you consent to marry Prince Roland of Germany?"

"I have consented," she replied firmly.

"Will you use your influence with him that he may carry out the behests of the three Archbishops?"

"Yes, if the behests are for the good of the country."

"I cannot accept any qualifications, therefore I repeat my question. Will you use your influence with him that he may carry out the behests of the three Archbishops?"

"I can have no influence with such a man."

"Answer my question, Madam."

"Say yes, Hildegunde," pleaded Cologne.

She turned to him swimming eyes.

"Oh, Guardian, Guardian!" she cried, "I have done everything I can, and all for you; all for you. I cannot stand any more. This is torture to me. Let me go home, and another day when I am calmer I will answer your questions!"

The perturbed Archbishop sat back again with a deep sigh. The ignorance of women with which his colleague of Treves had credited all three was being amazingly dispelled. He could not understand why this girl should show such emotion at the thought of marrying the heir to the throne, when assured the young man was all that any reasonable woman could desire.

"Madam, I pray you give your attention to me," said the unimpassioned voice of Mayence. "I have listened to your conversation with my colleagues, and the patience I exhibited will, I hope, be credited to me. This matter of business"—he emphasized the word—"must be settled to-day, and to clear away all misapprehension, I desire to say that your guardian has really no influence on this matter. It was settled before you came into the room. You are merely allowed a choice of two outcomes: first, marriage with Prince Roland; second, imprisonment in Pfalz Castle, situated in the middle of the Rhine."

"What is that?" demanded the Countess.

"I am tired of repeating my statements."

"You would imprison me—me, a Countess of Sayn?"

Again the tears evaporated, and in their place came the smoldering fire bequeathed to her by the Crusaders, and, if the truth must be known, by Rhine robbers as well.

"Yes, Madam. A predecessor of mine once hanged one of your ancestors."

"It is not true," cried the girl, in blazing wrath. "'Twas the Emperor Rudolph who hanged him; the same Emperor that chastised an Archbishop of Mayence, and brought him, cringing, to his knees, begging for pardon, which the Emperor contemptuously flung to him. You dare not imprison me!"

"Refuse to marry Prince Roland, and learn," said the Archbishop very quietly.

The girl sprang to her feet, a-quiver with anger.

"I do refuse! Prince Roland has hoodwinked the three of you! He is a libertine and a brawler, consorting with the lowest in the cellars of Frankfort; a liar and a thief, and not a brave thief at that, but a cutthroat who holds his sword to the breast of an unarmed merchant while he filches from him his gold. Added to that, a drunkard as his father is; and, above all, a hypocrite, as his father is not, yet clever enough, with all his vices, to cozen three men whose vile rule has ruined Frankfort, and left the broad Rhine empty of its life-giving commerce;" she waved her hand toward the vacant river.

The Archbishop of Cologne was the first to rise, horror-stricken.

"The girl is mad!" he murmured.

Treves rose also, but Mayence sat still, a sour smile on his lips, yet a twinkle of admiration in his eyes.

"No, my poor Guardian, I am not mad," she cried, regarding him with a smile, her wrath subsiding as quickly as it had risen. "What I say is true, and it may be that our meeting, turbulent as it has been, will prevent you from making a great mistake. He whom you would put on the throne is not the man you think."

"My dear ward!" cried Cologne, "how can you make such accusations against him? What should a girl living in seclusion as you live, know of what is passing in Frankfort."

"It seems strange, Guardian, but it is true, nevertheless. Sit down again, I beg of you, and you, my Lord of Treves. Even my Lord of Mayence will, I think, comprehend my abhorrence when such a proposal was made to me, and I hope, my Lord, you will forgive my outburst of anger just now."

She heard the trembling Treves mutter:

"Mayence never forgives."

"Now, Father Ambrose, come forward."

"Why?" asked Ambrose, waking from his reverie.

"Tell them your experiences in Frankfort."

"I am not allowed to speak," objected the monk.

"Speak, speak!" cried Cologne. "What, sir, have you had to do with this girl's misleading?"

"I thought," he said wistfully to his kinswoman, "that I was not to mention my visit to Frankfort unless my Lord the Archbishop brought up the subject."

"Have you not been listening to these proceedings?" cried the girl impatiently. "The subject is brought up before three Archbishops, instead of before one. Tell their Lordships what you know of Prince Roland."

Father Ambrose, with a deep sigh, began his recital, to which Treves and Cologne listened with ever-increasing amazement, while the sullen Mayence sat back in his chair, face imperturbable, but the thin lips closing firmer and firmer as the narrative went on.

When the monologue ended, his Reverence of Cologne was the first to speak:

"In the name of Heaven, why did you not tell me all this yesterday?"

Father Ambrose looked helplessly at his kinswoman, but made no reply.

"I forbade him, my Lord," said the girl proudly, and for the first time addressing him by a formal title, as if from now on he was to be reckoned with her enemies. "I alone am responsible for the journey to Frankfort and its consequences, whatever they may be. You invoked the name of Heaven just now, my Lord, and I would have you know that I am convinced Heaven itself intervened on my behalf to expose the real character of Prince Roland, who has successfully deluded three men like yourselves, supposed to be astute!"

The Archbishop turned upon her sorrowful eyes, troubled yet kindly.

"My dear Countess," he said, "I have not ventured to censure you; nevertheless I am, or have been, your guardian, and should, I think, have been consulted before you committed yourself to an action that threatens disaster to our plans."

The girl replied, still with the hauteur so lately assumed:

"I do not dispute my wardship, and have more than once thanked you for your care of me, but at this crisis of my life—a crisis transforming me instantly from a girl to a woman—you fail me, seeing me here at bay. I wished to spend a month or two at the capital city, but before troubling you with such a request I determined to learn whether or not the state of Frankfort was as disturbed as rumor alleged. Finding matters there to be hopeless, the project of a visit was at once abandoned, and knowing nothing of the honor about to be conferred on Prince Roland, I thought it best to keep what had been discovered regarding his character a secret between the Reverend Father and myself. I dare say an attempt will be made to cast doubt on the Reverend Father's story, and perhaps my three judges may convince themselves of its falseness, but they cannot convince me, and I tell you finally and formally that no power on earth will induce me to marry a marauder and a thief!"

This announcement effectually silenced the one friend she possessed among the three. Mayence slowly turned his head, and looked upon the colleague at his right, as much as to say, "Do you wish to add your quota to this inconsequential talk?"

Treves, at this silent appeal, leaned forward, and spoke to the perturbed monk, who knew that, in some way he did not quite understand, affairs were drifting towards a catastrophe.

"Father Ambrose," began the Elector of Treves, "would you kindly tell us the exact date when this encounter on the bridge took place?"

"Saint Cyrille's Day," replied Father Ambrose.

"And during the night of that day you were incarcerated in the cellar among the wine-casks?"

"Yes, my Lord."

"Would it surprise you to know, Father Ambrose, that during Saint Cyrille's Day, and for many days previous to that date, Prince Roland was a close prisoner in his Lordship of Mayence's strong Castle of Ehrenfels, and that it was quite impossible for you to have met him in Frankfort, or anywhere else?"

"Nevertheless, I did meet him," persisted Father Ambrose, with the quiet obstinacy of a mild man.

Treves smiled.

"Where did you lodge in Frankfort, Father?"

"At the Benedictine Monastery in Sachsenhausen."

"Do the good brethren supply their guests with a potent wine? Frankfort is, and always has been, the chief market of that exhilarating but illusion-creating beverage."

The cheeks of the Countess flushed crimson at this insinuation on her kinsman's sobriety. The old monk's hand rested on the arm of her throne, and she placed her own hand upon his as if to encourage him to resent the implied slander. After all, they were two Sayns hard pressed by these ruthless potentates. But Ambrose answered mildly:

"It may be that the monastery contains wine, my Lord, and doubtless the wine is good, but during my visit I did not taste it."

Cross-examination at an end, the Lord of Mayence spoke scarcely above a whisper, a trace of weariness in his manner.

"My Lords," he said, "we have wandered from the subject. The romance by Father Ambrose is but indifferently interesting, and nothing at all to the point. Even a child may understand what has happened, for it is merely a case of mistaken identity, and my sympathy goes out entirely towards the unknown; a man who knew his own mind, and being naturally indignant at an interference both persistent and uncalled for, quite rightly immured the meddler among the casks, probably shrewd enough to see that this practicer of temperance would not interfere with their integrity.

"Madam, stand up!"

The Countess seemed inclined to disobey this curt order, but a beseeching look from her now thoroughly frightened guardian changed her intention, and she rose to her feet.

"Madam, the greatest honor which it is in the power of this Empire to bestow upon a woman has been proffered to you, and rejected with unnecessary heat. I beg therefore, to inform you, that in the judgment of this Court you are considered unworthy of the exalted position which, before knowing your true character, it was intended you should fill. The various calumnies you have poured upon the innocent head of Prince Roland amount in effect to high treason."

"Pardon, my Lord!" cried the Archbishop of Cologne, "your contention will hold neither in law nor in fact. High treason is an offense that can be committed only against the realm as a whole, or against its ruler in person. Prince Roland is not yet Emperor of Germany, and however much we may regret the language used in his disparagement, it has arisen through a misunderstanding quite patent to us all. A good but dreamy man made a mistake, which, however deplorable, has been put forward with a sincerity that none of us can question; indeed, it was the intention of Father Ambrose to keep his supposed knowledge a secret, and you both saw with what evident reluctance he spoke when commanded to do so by my colleague of Treves. Whatever justice there may be in disciplining Father Ambrose, there is none at all for exaggerated censure upon my lady, the Countess of Sayn, and before pronouncing a further censure I beg your Lordship to take into consideration the circumstances of the case, by which a young girl, without any previous warning or preparation, is called upon suddenly to make the most momentous decision of her life. I say it is to her ladyship's credit that she refused the highest station in the land in the interests of what she supposes to be, however erroneously, the cause of honesty, sobriety, and, I may add, of Christianity; qualities for which we three men should stand."

"My Lord," objected Treves, "we meet here as temporal Princes, and not as Archbishops of the Church."

"I know that, my brother of Treves, and my appeal is to the temporal law. Prince Roland, despite his high lineage, is merely a citizen of the Empire, and a subject of his Majesty, the Emperor. It is therefore impossible that the crime of treason can be committed against him."

During this protest and discussion the Elector of Mayence had leaned back again in his usual attitude of tired indifference; his keen eyes almost closed. When he spoke he made no reference to what either of his two confrères had said.

"Madam," he began, without raising his voice, "it is the sentence of this Court that you shall be imprisoned during its pleasure in the Castle of Pfalzgrafenstein, which stands on a rock in the middle of the Rhine. Under the guardianship of the Pfalzgraf von Stahleck, who will be responsible for your safe keeping, I hope you will listen to the devout counsel of his excellent wife to such effect that when next you are privileged to meet a Court so highly constituted as this you may be better instructed regarding the language with which it should be addressed. You are permitted to take with you two waiting-women, chosen by yourself from your own household, but all communication with the outside world is forbidden. You said something to the effect that this Court dared not pronounce such sentence against you, but if you possessed that wisdom you so conspicuously lack, you might have surmised that a power which ventured to imprison the future Emperor of this land would not hesitate to place in durance a mere Countess von Sayn."

The Countess bowed her head slightly, and without protest sat down again. The Elector of Cologne arose.

"My Lord, I raised a point of law which has been ignored."

"This is the proper time to raise it," replied Mayence, "and you shall be instantly satisfied. This Court is competent to give its decision upon any point of law. If my Lord of Treves agrees with me, your objection is disallowed."

"I agree," said the Elector of Treves.

"My Lord of Cologne," said Mayence, turning towards the person addressed, "the decision of the Court is against you."

Hildegunde was already learning a lesson. Although dazed by the verdict, she could not but admire the quiet, conversational tone adopted by the three men before her, as compared with her own late vehemence.

"The decision of the Court is not unexpected," said Cologne, "and I regret that I am compelled to appeal."

"To whom will you appeal?" inquired Mayence mildly, "The Emperor, as you know, is quite unfit for the transaction of public business, and even if such were not the case, would hesitate to overturn a decision given by a majority of this Court."

"I appeal," replied Cologne, "to a power that even Emperors must obey; the power of physical force."

"You mean," said Mayence sadly, "to the three thousand men concealed in the forest behind this house in which you are an honored guest?"

The Elector of Cologne was so taken aback by this almost whispered remark that he was momentarily struck speechless. A sudden pallor swept the usual ruddiness from his face. The Lord of Mayence gently inclined his head as if awaiting an answer, and when it did not come, went on impassively:

"I may inform you, my Lord, that my army occupies the capital city of Frankfort, able and ready to quell any disturbance that may be caused by the announcement of the Emperor's death, but there are still plenty of seasoned troops ready to uphold the decisions of this Court. When your spies scoured the country in the forests, and along the river almost to the gates of my city of Mayence, they appeared to labor under the illusion that I could move my soldiers only overland. Naturally, they met no sign of such an incursion, because I had requisitioned a hundred barges which I found empty in the river Main by Frankfort. These were floated down the Main to Mayence, and there received their quota of a hundred men each. The night being dark they came down the Rhine, it seems, quite unobserved, and are now concealed in the mouth of the river Lahn directly opposite this Castle.

"When my flag is hoisted on the staff of the main tower this flotilla will be at the landing below us within half an hour. You doubtless have made similar arrangements for bringing your three thousand down upon Stolzenfels, but the gates of this Castle are now closed. Indeed, Stolzenfels was put in condition to withstand a siege very shortly after you and your ward entered it, and it is garrisoned by two hundred fighting men, kindly provided at my suggestion by my brother of Treves. I doubt if its capture is possible, even though you gave the signal, which we will not allow. Of course, your plan of capturing Treves and myself was a good one could it be carried out, for a man in jeopardy will always compromise, and as I estimate you are in that position I should be glad to know what arrangement you propose."

The Archbishop of Cologne did not reply, but stood with bent head and frowning brow. It was the Countess von Sayn who, rising, spoke:

"My Lord Archbishop of Mayence," she said, "I could never forgive myself if through action of mine a fatal struggle took place between my countrymen. I have no desire to enact the part of Helen of Troy. I am therefore ready and willing to be imprisoned, or to marry Prince Roland of Frankfort, whichever alternative you command, so long as no disadvantage comes to my friend, his Lordship of Cologne."

"Madam," said Mayence suavely, "there are not now two alternatives, as you suppose."

"In such case, your Highness, I betake myself instantly to Pfalz Castle, and I ask that my guardian be allowed to escort me on the journey."

"Madam, your determination is approved, and your request granted, but, as the business for which the three Electors were convened is not yet accomplished, I request you to withdraw until such time as an agreement has been arrived at. Father Ambrose is permitted to accompany you."

The gallant Elector of Treves sprang at once to his feet, pleading for the privilege of conducting the Countess to the apartments of his sister and her daughter. As the door to the ante-room opened the Elector of Cologne, whose eyes followed his departing ward, did not fail to observe that the lobby was thronged with armed men, and he realized now, if he had not done so from Mayence's observation, how completely he was trapped. Even had a hundred thousand of his soldiers stood in readiness on the hills, it was impossible for him to give the signal bringing them to his rescue.

A few minutes later the Elector of Treves returned, and took his place at Mayence's right hand. The latter spoke as though the conference had been unanimous and amiable.

"Now that we three are alone together, I think we shall discuss our problems under a feeling of less apprehension if the small army in the forest is bade God-speed on its way to Cologne. Such being the case," he went on, turning to Cologne, "would you kindly write an order to that effect to your commander. Inform him that we three Electors wish to review your troops from the northern balcony, and bid them file past from the hills to the river road. They are to cross the Moselle by the old bridge, and so return to your city. You will perhaps pledge faith that no signal will be made to your officers as they pass us. I make this appeal with the greater confidence since you are well aware three thousand men would but destroy themselves in any attempt to capture this Castle, with an army of ten thousand on their flank to annihilate them. Do you agree?"

"I agree," replied Cologne.

He wrote out the order required, and handed it to Mayence, who scrutinized the document with some care before passing it on to Treves. Mayence addressed Cologne in his blandest tones:

"Would you kindly instruct our colleague how to get that message safely into the hands of your commander."

"If he will have it sent to the head of my small escort, ordering him to take it directly up the hill behind this Castle until he comes to my sentinels, whom he knows personally, they will allow him to pass through, and deliver my written command to the officer in charge."

This being done, and Treves once more returned, Mayence said:

"I am sure we all realize that the Countess von Sayn, however admirable in other respects, possesses an independent mind and a determined will rendering her quite unsuited for the station we intended her to occupy. I think her guardian must be convinced now, even though he had little suspicion of it before, that this lady would not easily be influenced by any considerations we might place before her. The regrettable incidents of this conference have probably instilled into her mind a certain prejudice against us."

Here, for the first time, the Elector of Cologne laughed.

"It is highly probable, my Lord," he said, "and, indeed, your moderate way of putting the case is unanswerable. Her ladyship as an Empress under our influence is out of the question. I therefore make a proposal with some confidence, quite certain it will please you both. I venture to nominate for the position of Empress that very demure and silent lady who is niece of my brother the Elector of Treves."

Treves strangled a gasp in its birth, but could not suppress the light of ambition that suddenly leaped into his eyes. The elevation of his widowed sister's child to the Imperial throne was an advantage so tremendous, and came about so unexpectedly, that for the moment his slow brain was numbed by the glorious prospect. It seemed incredible that Cologne had actually put forward such a proposition.

The eyes of Mayence veiled themselves almost to shutting point, but in no other manner did emotion show. Like a flash his alert mind saw the full purport of the bombshell Cologne had so carelessly tossed between himself and his henchman. Cologne, having lost everything, had now proved clever enough to set by the ears those who overruled him by their united vote. If this girl were made Empress she would be entirely under the influence of her uncle, of whose household she had been a pliant member ever since childhood. Yet what was Mayence to do? Should he object to the nomination, he would at once obliterate the unswerving loyalty of Treves, and if this happened, Treves and Cologne, joining, would outvote him, and his objection would prove futile. He would enrage Treves without carrying his own point, and he knew that he held his position only because of the dog-like fidelity of the weaker man. Slow anger rose in his heart as he pictured the conditions of the future. Whatever influence he sought to exert upon the Emperor by the indirect assistance of the Empress, must be got at through the complacency of Treves, who would gradually come to appreciate his own increased importance.

All this passed through the mind of Mayence, and his decision had been arrived at before Treves recovered his composure.

"It gives me great pleasure," said the Elector of Mayence, firmly suppressing the malignancy of his glance towards the man seated on his left,— "it gives me very great pleasure indeed to second so admirable a nomination, the more so that I am thus permitted to offer my congratulations to an esteemed colleague and a valued friend. My Lord of Treves, I trust that you will make this nomination unanimous, for, to my delight, his Lordship of Cologne anticipated, by a few moments the proposal I was about to submit to you."

"My Lord," stammered Treves, finding his voice with difficulty, "I—I—of course will agree to whatever the Court decides. I—I thank you, my Lord, and you too, my brother of Cologne."

"Then," cried Mayence, almost joyfully, "the task for which we are convened is accomplished, and I declare this Court adjourned."

He rose from his chair. The overjoyed Prince at his right took no thought of the fact that their chairman had not called upon the lady that she might receive the decision of the conclave and answer the questions to be put to her, but Cologne perceived the omission, and knew that from that moment Mayence would set his subtility at work to nullify the nomination. Even though his bombshell had not exploded, and the two other Electors were apparently greater friends than ever, Cologne had achieved his immediate object, and was satisfied.

Through the open windows came the sound of the steady tramping of disciplined men, and the metallic clash of armor and arms in transit.

"Ah, now," cried Mayence, "we will enjoy the advantage of reviewing the brave troops of Cologne. Lead the way, my Lord of Treves. You know the Castle better than we do."

The proud Treves, treading on air, guided his guests to the northern balcony.

XI. GOLD GALORE THAT TAKES TO ITSELF WINGS

In the thick darkness Roland paced up and down the east bank of the Rhine at a spot nearly midway between Assmannshausen and Ehrenfels. The night was intensely silent, its stillness merely accentuated by the gentle ripple of the water current against the barge's blunt nose, which pointed upstream. Standing motionless as a statue, the massive figure of Captain Blumenfels appeared in deeper blackness against the inky hills on the other side of the Rhine. Long sweeps lay parallel to the bulwarks of the barge, and stalwart men were at their posts, waiting the word of command to handle these exaggerated oars, in defiance of wind and tide. On this occasion, however, the tide only would be against them, for the strong southern breeze was wholly favorable. Their voyage that night would be short, but strenuous; merely crossing the river, and tying up against the opposite bank; but the Rhine swirled powerfully round the rock of Ehrenfels above them, and the men at the sweeps must pull vigorously if they were not to be carried down into premature danger.

Roland, who when they left Frankfort was in point of time the youngest member of the guild, now seemed, if one could distinguish him through the gloom of the night, to have become years older, and there was an added dignity in his bearing, for, although now but a potential freebooter, he had received assurance that he would be eventually elected Emperor.

He had sent word that morning to Greusel at the Golden Anker, bidding him get together his men, and lead them up to the barge not later than an hour before the moon rose, for Roland was anxious to reach the other side of the Rhine unseen from either shore. He cautioned Greusel to make his march a silent one, and this order Joseph at first found some difficulty in carrying out, but in any case he need have entertained no fear. The strong red wine of Assmannshausen is a potent liquid, and the inhabitants of the town were accustomed to song and laughter on the one street of the place at all hours of the night.

When they arrived, the men were quiet enough, and speedily stowed themselves away in their quarters at the stern of the barge, whereupon Roland, the last to spring aboard, waved his hand at the captain to cast off. The nose of the boat was shoved away from land, and then the powerful sweeps dipped into the water. Slowly but surely she made her way across the river; silent and invisible from either bank. The current, however, swept them down opposite the twinkling lights of Assmannshausen, after which, in the more tranquil waters of the western shore, they rowed steadily upstream for about half a league, and then, with ropes tied round trees growing at the water's edge, laid up for the remainder of the night.

Roland now counseled his company to enjoy what sleep was possible, as they would be roused at the first glint of daybreak; so, with great good-nature, each man wrapped himself up in his cloak and lay down on the cabin floor.

When the eastern sky became gray, the slumberers were awakened, and a ration of bread and wine served to each. The captain already had received his instructions, and the men discarding their cloaks, followed their leader into the still gloomy forest. Here, with as little noise as might be, they climbed the steep wooded hill, and arriving at something almost like a path, a hundred yards up from the river, they turned to the right, and so marched, no man speaking above a whisper.

The forest became lighter and lighter, and at last Roland, holding up his hand to sign caution, turned to the left from the path, and farther up into the unbroken forest. They had traversed perhaps a league when another silent order brought them to a standstill, and peering through the trees to the east, the men caught glimpses of the grand, gray battlements of that famous stronghold, Rheinstein, seeing at the corner nearest them a square tower, next a machicolated curtain of wall, and a larger square tower almost as high as the first hanging over the precipice that descended to the Rhine. Inside this impregnable enclosure rose the great bulk of the Castle itself, and near at hand the massive square keep, with an octagonal turret on the southeast corner, the top of which was the highest point of the stronghold, although a round tower rising directly over the Rhine was not much lower.

Roland, advancing through the trees, but motioning his men to remain where they were, peered across to the battlements and down at the entrance gate.

Baron von Hohenfels sat so secure in his elevated robber's nest, which he deemed invincible—and, indeed, the cliff on which it stood, nearly a hundred yards high, made it so if approached from the Rhine—that he kept only one man on watch, and this sentinel was stationed on the elevated platform of the round tower. Roland saw him yawn wearily as he leaned against his tall lance, and was glad to learn that even one man kept guard, for at first he feared that all within the Castle were asleep, the round tower, until Roland had shifted his position to the north, being blotted out by the nearer square donjon keep. Now satisfied, he signaled his men to sit down, which they did. He himself took up a position behind a tree, where, unseen, he could watch the man with the lance.

So indolent was the sentry that Roland began to fear the barge would pass by unnoticed. Not for months had any sailing craft appeared on the river, and doubtless the warden regarded his office as both useless and wearisome. Brighter and brighter became the eastern sky, and at last a tinge of red appeared above the hills across the silent Rhine. Suddenly the guardian straightened up, then, shading his eyes with his right hand, he leaned over the battlements, peering to the south. A moment later the stillness was rent by a lusty shout, and the man disappeared as if he had fallen through a trap-door. Presently the notes of a bugle echoed within the walls, followed by clashes of armor and the buzzing sound of men, as though a wasp's nest had been disturbed. Half a dozen came into sight on top of the various towers and battlements, glanced at the river, and vanished as hastily as the sentinel had done.

At last the gates came ponderously open, and the first three men to emerge were on horseback, one of them hastily getting into an outer garment, but the well-trained horses, who knew their business quite as thoroughly as their riders, for they were accustomed to plunge into the river if any barge disobeyed the order commanding it to halt, turned from the gate, and dashed down the steep road that descended through the forest. The men-at-arms poured forth with sword or pike, and in turn went out of sight. They appeared to be leaderless, dashing forward in no particular formation, yet, like the horses, they knew their business. All this turmoil was not without its effect on Roland's following, who edged forward on hands and knees to discover what was going on, everyone breathless with excitement; but they saw their leader cool and motionless, counting on his fingers the number of men who passed out, for he knew exactly how many fighters the Castle contained.

"Not yet, not yet!" he whispered.

Finally three lordly individuals strode out; officers their more resplendent clothing indicated them to be, and the trio followed the others.

"Ha!" cried Roland, "old Baron Hugo drank too deeply last night to be so early astir."

He was speaking aloud now.

"Take warning from that, my lads, and never allow wine to interfere with business. Follow me, but cautiously, one after the other in single file, and look to your footing. 'Tis perilous steep between here and the gate;" and, indeed, so they found it, but all reached the level forecourt in safety, and so through the open portal.

"Close and bar those gates," was the next command, instantly obeyed.

Down the stone steps of the Castle, puffing and grunting, came a gigantic, obese individual, his face bloated with excess, his eyes bleary with the lees of too much wine. He was struggling into his doublet, assisted by a terrified old valet, and was swearing most deplorably. Seeing the crowd at the gate, and half-blindly mistaking them for his own men, he roared:

"What do you there, you hounds? To the river, every man of you, and curse your leprous, indolent souls! Why in the fiend's name—" But here he came to an abrupt stop on the lowest step, the sting of a sword's point at his throat, and now, out of breath, his purple face became mottled.

"Good morning to you, Baron Hugo von Hohenfels. These men whom you address so coarsely obey no orders but mine."

"And who, imp of Satan, are you?" sputtered the old man.

"By profession a hangman. From our fastnesses in the hills, seeing a barge float down the river, we thought it likely you would leave the Castle undefended, and so came in to execute the Prince of Robbers."

The Baron was quaking like a huge jelly. It was evident that, although noted for his cruelty, he was at heart a coward.

"You—you—you—" he stammered, "are outlaws! You are outlaws from the Hunsruck."

"How clever of you, Baron, to recognize us at once. Now you know what to expect. Greusel, unwind the rope I gave you last night. I will show you its purpose."

Greusel did as he was requested without comment, but Ebearhard approached closely to his chief, and whispered:

"Why resort to violence? We have no quarrel with this elephant. 'Tis his gold we want, and to hang him is a waste of time."

"Hush, Ebearhard," commanded Roland sternly. "The greater includes the less. I know this man, and am taking the quickest way to his treasure-house."

Ebearhard fell back, but by this time the useful Greusel had made a loop of the rope, and threw it like a cravat around the Baron's neck.

"No, no, no!" cried the frightened nobleman. "'Tis not my life you seek. That is of no use to such as you; and, besides, I have never harmed the outlaws."

"That is a lie," said Roland. "You sent an expedition against us just a year ago."

"'Twas not I," protested Hohenfels, "but the pirate of Falkenberg. Still, no matter. I'll buy my life from you. I am a wealthy man."

"How much?" asked Roland, hesitating.

"More than all of you can carry away."

191

"In gold?"

"Of a surety in gold."

"Where are the keys of your treasury?"

"In my chamber. I will bring them to you," and the Baron turned to mount the steps again.

"Not so," cried Roland. "Stand where you are, and send your man for them. If they are not here before I count twoscore, you hang, and nothing will save you."

The Baron told the trembling valet where to find the keys.

"Greusel, you and Ebearhard accompany him, and at the first sign of treachery, or any attempt to give an alarm, run him through with your swords. Does your man know where the treasury is?" he continued to the Baron.

"Oh, yes, yes!"

"How is your gold bestowed?"

"In leathern bags."

"Good. Greusel, take sixteen of the men, and bring down into the courtyard all the gold you can carry. Then we will estimate whether or not it is sufficient to buy the Baron's life, for I hold him in high esteem. He is a valuable man. See to it that there is no delay, Greusel, and never lose sight of this valet. Bring him back, laden with gold."

They all disappeared within the Castle, led by the old servitor.

"Sit you down, Baron," said Roland genially. "You seem agitated, for which there is no cause should there prove to be gold enough to outweigh you."

The ponderous noble seated himself with a weary sigh.

"And pray to the good Lord above us," went on Roland, "that your men may not return before this transaction is completed, for if they do, my first duty will be to strangle you. Even gold will not save you in that case. But still, you have another chance for your life, should such an untoward event take place. Shout to them through the closed gates that they must return to the edge of the river until you join them; then, if they obey, you are spared. Remember, I beg of you, the uselessness of an outcry, for we are in possession of Rheinstein, and you know that the Castle is unassailable from without."

The Baron groaned.

"Do not be hasty with your cord," he said dejectedly. "I will follow your command."

The robbers, however, did not return, but the treasure-searchers did, piling the bags in the courtyard, and again Hohenfels groaned dismally at the sight. Roland indicated certain sacks with the point of his sword, ordering them to be opened. Each was full of gold.

"Now, my lads," he cried, "oblige the Baron by burdening yourselves with this weight of metal, then we shall make for the Hunsruck. Open the gates. Lead the men to the point where we halted, Greusel, and there await me."

The rich company departed, and Roland beguiled the time and the weariness of the Baron by a light and interesting conversation to which there was neither reply nor interruption. At last, having allowed time for his band to reach their former halting-place, he took the rope from the Baron's neck, tied the old robber's hands behind him, then bound his feet, cutting the rope in lengths with his sword. He served the trembling valet in the same way, shutting him up within the Castle, and locking the door with the largest key in the bunch, which bunch he threw down beside his lordship.

"Baron von Hohenfels," he said, "I have kept my word with you, and now bid farewell. I leave you out-of-doors, because you seem rather scant of breath, for which complaint fresh air is beneficial. Adieu, my lord Baron."

The Baron said nothing as Roland, with a sweep of his bonnet, took leave of him, climbed the steep path and joined his waiting men. He led them along the hillside, through the forest for some distance, then descended to the water's edge. The river was blank, so they all sat down under the trees out of sight, leaving one man on watch. Here Roland spent a very anxious half-hour, mitigated by the knowledge that the men of Rheinstein were little versed in woodcraft, and so might not be able to trace the fugitives. It was likely they would make a dash in quite the opposite direction, towards the Hunsruck, because Hohenfels believed they were outlaws from that district, and did not in any way associate them with the plundered barge.

But if the robbers of Rheinstein took a fancy to sink the barge, an act only too frequently committed, then were Roland and his company in a quandary, without food, or means of crossing the river. However, he was sure that Captain Blumenfels would follow his instructions, which were to offer no resistance, but rather to assist the looters in their exactions.

"Within a league," said Roland to his men, "stand three pirate castles: Rheinstein, which we have just left; Falkenberg, but a short distance below, and then Sonneck. If nothing happens to the barge, I expect to finish with all three before nightfall; for, the strongholds being so close together, we must work rapidly, and not allow news of our doings to leap in advance of us."

"But suppose," said Kurzbold, "that Hohenfels' men hold the barge at the landing for their own use?"

"We will wait here for another half-hour," replied Roland, "and then, if we see nothing of the boat, proceed along the water's edge until we learn what has become of her. I do not think the thieves will interfere with the barge, as they have not been angered either by disobedience of their orders to land, or resistance after the barge is by the shore. Besides, I count on the fact that the officers, at least, will be anxious to let the barge proceed, hoping other laden boats may follow, and, indeed, I think for this reason they will be much more moderate in their looting than we have been."

Before he had finished speaking, the man on watch by the water announced the barge in sight, floating down with the current. At this they all emerged from the forest. Captain Blumenfels, carefully scanning the shore, saw them at once, and turned the boat's head towards the spot where they stood.

The bags of gold were bolted away in the stout lockers extending on each side of the cabin. While this was being done, Roland gave minute instructions to the captain regarding the next item in the programme, and once more entered the forest with his men.

The task before them was more difficult than the spoiling of Rheinstein, because the huge bulk of Falkenberg stood on a summit of treeless rock; the Castle itself, a gigantic, oblong gray mass, with a slender square campanile some distance from it, rising high above its battlements on the slope that went down towards the Rhine, forming thus an excellent watch-tower. But although the conical hill of rock was bare of the large trees that surrounded Rheinstein, there were plenty of bowlders and shrubbery behind which cover could be sought. On this occasion the marauding guild could not secure a position on a level with the battlements of the Castle, as had been the case behind Rheinstein, and, furthermore, they were compelled to make their dash for the gate up-hill.

But these disadvantages were counterbalanced by the fact that Falkenberg was situated much higher than Rheinstein, and was farther away from the river, so that when the garrison descended to the water's edge it could not return as speedily as was the case with Hohenfels' men. Rheinstein stood directly over the water, and only two hundred and sixty feet above it, while, comparatively speaking, Falkenberg was back in the country. Still all these castles had been so long unmolested, and considered themselves so secure, that adequate watching had fallen into abeyance, and at Falkenberg guard was kept by one lone man on the tall campanile. The attacking party saw no one on the battlements of the Castle, so worked their way round the hill until the man on the tower was hidden from them by the bulk of the Castle itself, and thus they crawled like lizards from bush to bush, from stone to stone, and from rock-ledge to rock-ledge, taking their time, and not deserting one position of obscurity until another was decided upon. The fact that the watchman was upon the Rhine side of the Castle greatly favored a stealthy approach from any landward point.

At last the alarm was given; the gate opened, and, as it proved, every man in the Castle went headlong down the hill. The amateur cracksmen therefore had everything their own way, and while this at first seemed an advantage, they speedily found it the reverse, for although they wandered from room to room, the treasure could not be discovered. The interior of Falkenberg was unknown to Roland, this being one of the strongholds where he had been compelled to sleep in an outhouse. At last they found the door to the treasure-chamber, for Roland suggested it was probably in a similar position to that at Rheinstein, and those who had accompanied Hohenfels' valet made search according to this hint, and were rewarded by coming upon a door so stoutly locked that all their efforts to force it open were fruitless.

Deeply disappointed, with a number of the men grumbling savagely, they were compelled to withdraw empty handed, warned by approaching shouts that the garrison was returning, so the men crawled away as they had come, and made for the river, where on this occasion the boat already awaited them.

The lord of Falkenberg proved as moderate in his exactions as the men of Rheinstein. Many bales had been cut open, and the thieves, with the knowledge of cloth-weavers, selected in every case only the best goods, but of these had taken merely enough for one costume each.

Although the company had made so early a beginning, it was past noon by the time they reached the barge on the second occasion. A substantial meal was served, for every man was ravenously hungry, besides being disgusted to learn that there were ups and downs even in the trade of thievery.

Early in the afternoon they made for the delicate Castle of Sonneck, whose slender turrets stood out beautifully against the blue sky. Here excellent cover was found within sight of the doorway, for Sonneck stood alone on its rock without the protection of a wall.

In this case the experience of Rheinstein was repeated, with the exception that it was not the master of the Castle they encountered, but a frightened warder, who, with a sharp sword to influence him, produced keys and opened the treasury. Not nearly so large a haul of gold was made as in the first instance, yet enough was obtained to constitute a most lucrative day's work, and with this they sought the barge in high spirits.

They waited in the shadow of the hills until dusk, then quietly made their way across the river behind the shelter of the two islands, and so came to rest alongside the bank, just above the busy town of Lorch, scarcely two leagues down the river from the berth they had occupied the night before. After the barge was tied up, Roland walked on deck with the captain, listening to his account of events from the level of the river surface. It proved that, all in all, Roland could suggest no amendment of the day's proceedings. So far as Blumenfels was concerned, everything had gone without a hitch.

As they promenaded thus, one of the men came forward, and said, rather cavalierly:

"Commander, your comrades wish to see you in the cabin."

Roland made no reply, but continued his conversation with the captain until he learned from that somewhat reticent individual all he wished to know. Then he walked leisurely aft, and descended into the cabin, where he found the eighteen seated on the lockers, as if the conclave were a deliberate body like the Electors, who had come to some momentous decision.

"We have unanimously passed a resolution," said Kurzbold, "that the money shall be divided equally amongst us each evening. You do not object, I suppose?"

"No; I don't object to your passing a resolution."

"Very good. We do not wish to waste time just now in the division, because we are going to Lorch, intending to celebrate our success with a banquet. Would Greusel, Ebearhard, and yourself care to join us?"

"I cannot speak for the other two," returned Roland quietly; "but personally I shall be unable to attend, as there are some plans for the future which need thinking over."

"In that case we shall not expect you," went on Kurzbold, who seemed in no way grieved at the loss of his commander's company.

"Perhaps," suggested John Gensbein, "our chief will drop in upon us later in the evening. We learned at Assmannshausen that the Krone is a very excellent tavern, so we shall sup there."

"How did you know we were to stop at Lorch?" asked Roland, wondering if in any way they had heard he was to meet Goebel's emissary in this village.

"We were not sure," replied Gensbein, "but we made inquiries concerning all the villages and castles down the Rhine, and have taken notes."

"Ah, in that case you are well qualified as a guide. I may find occasion to use the knowledge thus acquired."

"We are all equally involved in this expedition," said Kurzbold impatiently, "and you must not imagine yourself the only person to be considered. But we lose time. What we wish at the present moment is that you will unlock one of these chests, and divide amongst us a bag of gold. The rest is to be partitioned when we return this evening; and after that, Herr Roland, we shall not need to trouble you by asking for more money."

"Are the thirty thalers I gave you the other day all spent, Herr Kurzbold?"

"No matter for that," replied this insubordinate ex-president. "The money in the lockers is ours, and we demand a portion of it now, with the remainder after the banquet."

Without another word, Roland took the bunch of keys from his belt, opened one of the lockers, lifted out a bag of gold, untied the thongs, and poured out the coins on the lid of the chest, which he locked again.

"There is the money," he said to Kurzbold. "I shall send Greusel and Ebearhard to share in its distribution, and thus you can invite them to your banquet. My own portion you may leave on the lid of the locker."

With that he departed up on deck again, and said to his officers:

"Kurzbold, on behalf of the men, has demanded a bag of gold. You will go to the cabin and receive your share. They will also invite you to a banquet at the Krone. Accept that invitation, and if possible engage a private room, as you did at Assmannshausen, to prevent the men talking with any of the inhabitants. Keep them roystering there until all the village has gone to bed;

then convoy them back to the barge as quietly as you can. A resolution has been passed that the money is to be divided amongst our warriors on their return, but I imagine that they will be in no condition to act as accountants when I have the pleasure of beholding them again, so if anything is said about the apportionment, suggest a postponement of the ceremony until morning. I need not add that I expect you both to drink sparingly, for this is advice I intend to follow myself."

Roland paced the deck deep in thought until his difficult contingent departed towards the twinkling lights of the village, then he went to the cabin, poured his share of the gold into his pouch, and followed the company at a distance into Lorch. He avoided the Krone, and after inquiring his way, stopped at the much smaller hostelry, Mergler's Inn. Here he gave his name, and asking if any one waited for him, was conducted upstairs to a room where he found Herr Kruger just about to sit down to his supper. A stout lad nearing twenty years of age stood in the middle of the room, and from his appearance Roland did not need the elder man's word for it that this was his son.

"I took the precaution of bringing him with me," said Kruger, "as I thought two horsemen were better than one in the business I had undertaken."

"You were quite right," returned Roland, "and I congratulate you upon so stalwart a traveling companion. With your permission I shall order a meal, and sup with you, thus we may save time by talking while we eat, because you will need to depart as speedily as possible."

"You mean in the darkness? To-night?"

"Yes; as soon as you can get away. There are urgent reasons why you should be on the road without delay. How came you here?"

"On horseback; first down the Main, then along the Rhine."

"Very well. In the darkness you will return by the way you came, but only as far as the Castle of Ehrenfels, three leagues from here. There you are to rouse up the custodian, and in safety spend the remainder of the night. To-morrow morning he will furnish you a guide to conduct you through the forest to Wiesbaden, and from thence you know your way to Frankfort, which you should reach not later than evening."

At this point the landlord, who had been summoned, came in.

"I will dine with my friends here," said Roland. "I suppose I need not ask if you possess some of the good red wine of Lorch, which they tell me equals that of Assmannshausen?"

"Of the very best, mein Herr, the product of my own vineyard, and I can therefore guarantee it sound. As for equaling that of Assmannshausen, we have always considered it superior, and, indeed, many other good judges agree with us."

"Then bring me a stoup of it, and you will be enabled to add my opinion to that of the others."

When the landlord produced the wine, Roland raised it to his lips, and absorbed a hearty draught.

"This is indeed most excellent, landlord, and does credit alike to your vines and your inn. I wish to send two large casks of so fine a wine to a merchant of my acquaintance in Frankfort, and my friend, Herr Kruger, has promised to convey it thither. If you can spare me two casks of such excellent vintage, they will make an evenly balanced burden for the horse."

"Surely, mein Herr."

"Choose two of those long casks, landlord, with bung-holes of the largest at the sides. Do you possess such a thing as a pack-saddle?"

"Oh, yes."

"And you, my young friend," he said, turning to Kruger's son, "rode here on a saddle?"

"No," interjected his father; "I ride a saddle, but my son was forced to content himself with a length of Herr Goebel's coarse cloth, folded four times, and strapped to the horse's back."

"Then the cloth may still be used as a cushion for the pack-saddle, and you, my lad, will be compelled to walk, to which I dare venture you are well accustomed."

The lad grinned, but made no objection.

"Now, landlord, while we eat, fill your casks with wine, then place the pack-saddle on the back of this young man's horse, and the casks thereon, for I dare say you have men expert in such a matter."

"There are no better the length of the Rhine," said the landlord proudly.

"Lay the casks so that the bung-holes are upward, and do not drive the bungs more tightly in place than is necessary, for they are to be extracted before Frankfort is reached, that another friend of mine may profit by the wine. When this is done, bring me word, and let me know how much I owe you."

The landlord gone, the three men fell to their meal.

"There is more gold," said Roland, "than I expected, and it is impossible even for two of you to carry it in bags attached to your belts. Besides, if you are molested, such bestowal of it would prove most unsafe. A burden of wine, however, is too common either to attract notice or arouse cupidity. I propose, then, when we leave here, to bring you to the barge belonging to Herr Goebel, and taking out the bungs, we will pour the gold into the barrels, letting the wine that is displaced overflow to the ground. Then we will stoutly drive in the bungs, and should the guards question you at the gates of Frankfort, you may let them taste the wine if they insist, and I dare say it will contain no flavor of the metal."

"A most excellent suggestion," said Herr Kruger with enthusiasm. "An admirable plan; for I confess I looked forward with some anxiety to this journey, laden down with bags of gold under my cloak."

"Yes. You are simply an honest drinker, tired of the white wine of Frankfort, and providing yourself with the stronger fluid that Lorch produces. I am sure you will deliver the money safely to Herr Goebel, somewhat in drink, it is true, but, like the rest of us, none the worse for that when the fumes are gone."

The repast finished, and all accounts liquidated, the trio left the inn, and, leading the two horses, reached the barge without observation. Here the bungs were removed from the casks, and the three men, assisted by the captain, quietly and speedily opened bag after bag, pouring the coins down into the wine; surely a unique adulteration, astonishing even to so heady a fluid as the vintage of Lorch. From the whole amount Roland deducted two thousand thalers, which he divided equally between two empty bags.

"This thousand thalers," said he to Kruger, "is to be shared by your son and yourself, in addition to whatever you may receive from Herr Goebel. The other you will hand to the custodian of Ehrenfels Castle, saying it came from his friend Roland, and is recompense for the money he lent the other day. That will be an effective letter of introduction to him. Say that I ask him to send his son with you as guide through the forest to Wiesbaden; and so goodnight and good luck to you."

It was long after midnight when the guild came roystering up the bank of the Rhine to the barge. The moon had risen, and gave them sufficient light to steer a reasonably straight course without danger of falling into the water. Ebearhard was with them, but Greusel walked rapidly ahead, so that he might say a few words to his chief before the others arrived.

"I succeeded in preventing their talking with any stranger, but they have taken aboard enough wine to make them very difficult and rather quarrelsome if thwarted. When I proposed that they should leave the counting until to-morrow morning they first became suspicious, and then resented the imputation that they were not in fit condition for such a task. I recommend, therefore, that you allow them to divide the money to-night. It will allay their fear that some trick is to be played upon them, and if you hint at intoxication, they are likely to get out of hand. As it does not matter when the money is distributed, I counsel you to humor them to-night, and postpone reasoning until to-morrow."

"I'll think about it," said Roland.

"They have bought several casks of wine, and are taking turns in carrying them. Will you allow this wine to come aboard, even if you determine to throw it into the water to-morrow?"

"Oh, yes," said Roland, with a shrug of the shoulders. "Coax them into the cabin as quietly as possible, and keep them there if you can, for should they get on deck, we shall lose some of them in the river."

Greusel turned back to meet the bellowing mob, while Roland roused the captain and his men.

"Get ready," he said to Blumenfels, "and the moment I raise my hand, shove off. Make for this side of the larger island, and come to rest there for the remainder of the night. Command your rowers to put their whole force into the sweeps."

This was done accordingly, and well done, as was the captain's custom. The late moon threw a ghostly light over the scene, and the barren island proved deserted and forbidding, as the crew tied up the barge alongside. Most of the lights in Lorch had gone out, and the town lay in the silence of pallid moonbeams like a city of the dead. Roland stood on deck with Greusel and Ebearhard by his side, the latter relating the difficulties of the evening. There had been singing in the cabin during the passage across, then came a lull in the roar from below, followed by a shout that betokened danger. An instant later the crowd came boiling up the short stair to the deck, Kurzbold in command, all swords drawn, and glistening in the moonlight.

"You scoundrel!" he cried to Roland, "those lockers are full of empty bags."

"I know that," replied Roland, quietly. "The money is in safe keeping, and will be honestly divided at the conclusion of this expedition."

"You thief! You robber!" shouted Kurzbold, flourishing his weapon.

"Quite accurate," replied Roland, unperturbed. "I was once called a Prince of Thieves when I did not deserve the title. Now I have earned it."

"You have earned the penalty of thieving, and we propose to throw you into the Rhine."

"Not, I trust, before you learn where the money is deposited."

Drunk as they were, this consideration staggered them, but Kurzbold was mad with rage and wine.

"Come on, you poltroons!" he shouted. "There are only three of them."

"Draw your swords, gentlemen," whispered Roland, flashing his own blade in the moonlight.

Greusel and Ebearhard obeyed his command.

XII. THE LAUGHING RED MARGRAVE OF FURSTENBERG

Ebearhard laughed, and took two steps forward. Whenever affairs became serious, one could always depend on a laugh from Ebearhard.

"Excuse me, Commander," he said, "but you placed Greusel and me in charge of this pious and sober party; therefore I, being the least of your officers, must stand the first brunt of our failure to keep these lambs peaceable for the night. Greusel, stand behind me, and in front of the Commander. I, being reasonably sober, believe I can cut down six of the innocents before they finish with me. You will attend to the next six, leaving exactly half a dozen for Roland to eliminate in his own fashion. Now, Herr Conrad Kurzbold, come on."

"We have no quarrel with you," said Kurzbold. "Stand aside."

"But I force a quarrel upon you, undisciplined pig. Defend yourself, for, by the Three Kings, I am going to tap your walking wine-barrel!"

Kurzbold, however, retreating with more haste than caution, one or two behind him were sent sprawling, and the half-dozen which were Roland's portion tumbled over one another down the steep ladder into the cabin.

Ebearhard laughed again when the last man disappeared.

"I think," he said to Roland, "that you will meet no further trouble from our friends. They evidently broke open the lockers, alarmed because Greusel and I asked for a postponement of the counting, probably intending to make the division without our assistance."

"Have you hidden the money?" asked Greusel.

"Not exactly," replied Roland; "but, in case anything should happen to me, I will tell you what I have done with it."

When he finished his recital, he added:

"I will give each of you a letter to Herr Goebel, identifying you. He is entitled to four thousand five hundred thalers of the money. The balance you will divide among those of us who survive."

Roland slept on deck, wrapped in his cloak. His two lieutenants took turn in keeping watch, but nothing except snores came up from the cabin. The mutineers were not examples of early rising next morning. The sun gave promise of another warm day, and Roland walked up and down the deck, anxiety printed on his brow. He had made up his mind to knock at the door of the Laughing Baron, a giant in stature, reported to be the most ingenious, most cruel, and bravest of all the robber noblemen of the Rhine, whose Castle was notoriously the hardest nut to crack along the banks of that famous river. For several reasons it would not be wise to linger much longer in the neighborhood of Lorch. The three castles they had entered the day before were still visible on the western bank. News of the raid would undoubtedly travel to Furstenberg, also within sight down the river, and thus the hilarious Margrave would be put on his guard, overjoyed at the opportunity of trapping the moral marauders. Furstenberg was also a fief of Cologne, and any molestation of it would involve the meddler, if identified, in complications with the Church and the Archbishop.

It was necessary, therefore, to move with caution, and to retreat, if possible, unobserved. These difficulties alone were enough to give pause to the most intrepid, but Roland was further handicapped by his own following. How could he hope to accomplish any subtle movement requiring silence, prompt obedience, and great alertness, supported by men whose brains were muddled with drink, and whose conduct was saturated with conspiracy against him? They had wine enough on board to continue their orgy, and he was quite unable to prevent their carouse. With a deep sigh he realized that he would be compelled to forego Furstenberg, and thus leave behind him a virgin citadel, which he knew was bad tactics from a military point of view.

During his meditations his men were coming up from the fuming cabin into the fresh air and the sunlight. They appeared by twos and threes, yawning and rubbing their eyes, but no one ventured to interrupt the leader as, with bent head, he paced back and forth on the deck. The men, indeed, seemed exceedingly subdued. They passed with almost overdone nonchalance from the boat to the island, and sauntered towards its lower end, from which, in the clear morning air, the grim fortress of Furstenberg could be plainly discerned diagonally across the river. It was Ebearhard who broke in upon Roland's reverie.

"Our friends appear very quiet this morning, but I observe they have all happened to coincide upon the northern part of the island as a rendezvous for their before-breakfast walk. I surmise they are holding a formal meeting of the guild, but neither Greusel nor I have been invited, so I suppose that after last night's display we two are no longer considered their brethren. This meekness on their part seems to me more dangerous than last night's flurry. I think they will demand from you a knowledge of what has been done with the gold. Have you decided upon your answer?"

"Yes; it is their right to know, so I shall tell them the truth. By this time Kruger is on his way somewhere between Ehrenfels and Wiesbaden. He will reach Frankfort to-night, and cannot be overtaken."

"Is there not danger that they will desert in a body, return to Frankfort, and demand from Herr Goebel their share of the spoil?"

"No matter for that," returned Roland. "Goebel will not part with a florin except under security of such letters as I purpose giving you and Greusel, and even then only when you have proven to him that I am dead."

"That is all very well," demurred Ebearhard, "but don't you see what a dangerous power you put into the hands of the rebels? Goebel is merely a merchant, and, though rich, politically powerless. He has already come into conflict with the authorities, and spent a term in prison. Do not forget that the Archbishops have refused to take action against these robber Barons. Our men, if there happen to be one of brains among them, can easily terrify Goebel into parting with the treasure by threatening to confess their own and his complicity in the raids. Consider what an excellent case they can put forward, stating quite truly that they joined this expedition in ignorance of its purport, but on the very first day, learning what was afoot, they deserted their criminal leader, and are now endeavoring to make restitution. Goebel is helpless. If he says that they first demanded the gold from him, they as strenuously deny it, and their denial must be believed, because they come of their own free-will to the authorities. The merchant, already tainted with treason, having suffered imprisonment, and narrowly escaped hanging, proves on investigation to be up to the neck in this affair. There is no difficulty in learning that his barge went down the river, manned by a crew of his own choosing. Of course, it need never come to this, because Goebel, being a shrewd man, could at once see in what jeopardy he stood, and convinced from the men's own story that they were part, at least, of your contingent, would deliver up the treasure to them. Don't you see he must do so to save his own neck?"

Roland pondered deeply on what had been said to him, but for the moment made no reply. Greusel, who joined them during the conversation, remaining silent until Ebearhard had finished, now spoke:

"I quite agree with all that has been said."

"What, then, would you advise me to do?" asked Roland.

"I have been talking with one or two of the men," said Greusel. "(They won't speak to Ebearhard because he drew his sword on them.) I find they believe you took advantage of their absence to bury the gold in what you suppose to be a safe place. They are sure you are acquainted with no one in Lorch to whom you could safely entrust it, and of course do not suspect an emissary from Frankfort. I should advise you to say that arrangements have been made for every man to get his share so long as nothing untoward happens to you. This will preserve your life should they go so far as to threaten it, and compel them to stay on with us. After all, we are merely artisans, and not fighting men. I am convinced that if ever we are really attacked, we shall make a very poor showing, even though we carry swords. Remember how the men tumbled over one another in their haste to get out of reach when Ebearhard flourished his blade."

"I think Greusel's suggestion is an excellent one," put in Ebearhard.

"Very well," said Roland, "I shall adopt it, although I had made up my mind fully to enlighten them."

"There is one more matter that I should like to speak to you about," continued Ebearhard. "Both at Assmannshausen, and at Lorch last night, we heard a good deal anent Furstenberg. It is the most dangerous castle on the Rhine to meddle with. The Laughing Baron, as they call him, although he is a Margrave, is the only man who dared to stop a king on his way down the Rhine, and hold him for ransom."

"Yes," said Roland; "Adolf of Nassau, on his way to be crowned at Aix-la-Chapelle."

"Quite so. Well, this huge ruffian—I never can remember his name; can you, Greusel?"

"No, it beats me."

"Margrave Hermann von Katznellenbogenstahleck," said Roland, so solemnly that Ebearhard laughed and even Greusel smiled.

"That's the individual," agreed Ebearhard, "and you must admit the name itself is a formidable thing to attack, even without the giant it belongs to."

"Banish all apprehension," said Roland. "I have already decided to remain here through the day, and drop quietly down the river to-night in the darkness past Furstenberg."

"I think that is a wise decision," said Ebearhard.

"'Tis against all military rules," demurred Roland, "but nevertheless with such an army as I lead it seems the only way. Do the men know that Furstenberg is our point of greatest danger?"

"Yes; but they do not know so much as I. Last night I left them in Greusel's charge, being alarmed about what I heard of Furstenberg, and engaged a boatman to take me over there before the moon rose. I discovered that the Laughing Baron has caused a chain to be buoyed up just below the surface of the water, running diagonally up the river more than half-way across it, so that any boat coming down is caught and drawn into the landing, for the main flood of the Rhine, as you know, runs to the westward of this island. The boatman who ferried me knew about this chain, but thought it had been abandoned since traffic stopped. He says it runs right up into the Castle, and the moment a barge strikes against it, a big bell is automatically rung inside the stronghold, causing the Baron to laugh so loudly that they sometimes hear him over in Lorch."

"This is very interesting, Ebearhard, and an excellent feat of scouting must be set down to your credit. Say nothing to the men, because, although we give Furstenberg the go-by on this occasion, I shall pay my respects to Herman von Katznellenbogenstahleck on my return, and the knowledge you bring me will prove useful."

"Ha!" cried Greusel, "here are our infants returning, all in a body, Kurzbold at their head as usual. I imagine this morning they are going to depend on rhetoric, and allow their swords to remain in scabbard. They have evidently come to some momentous decision."

The three retired to the prow of the boat as the guild clambored on at the stern. The captain and two of his men had taken the skiff belonging to the barge, and were absent at Lorch, purchasing provisions. Roland stood at the prow of the barge, slightly in advance of his two lieutenants, and awaited the approach of Kurzbold, with seventeen men behind him.

"Commander," said the spokesman, with nothing of the late truculence in his tone, "we have just held a meeting of the guild, and unanimously agreed to ask you one question, and offer you one suggestion."

"I shall be pleased," replied Roland, "to answer the first if I think it desirable, and take the second into consideration."

He inclined his head to the delegation, and received a low bow in return. This was a most auspicious beginning, showing a certain improvement of method on the part of the majority.

"The question is, Commander, what have you done with the gold we captured yesterday?"

"A very proper inquiry," replied Roland, "that it gives me much pleasure to answer. I have placed the money in a custody which I believe to be absolute, arranging that if nothing happens to me, this money shall be properly divided in my presence."

"Do you deny, sir, that the money belongs to us?"

"Part of it undoubtedly does, but I, as leader of the expedition, am morally, if not legally, responsible to you all for its safe keeping. Our barge has stopped three times so far, and Captain Blumenfels tells me that he has had no real violence to complain of, but as we progress farther down the river, we are bound to encounter some Baron who is not so punctilious; for instance, the Margrave von Katznellenbogenstahleck, whose stronghold you doubtless saw from the latest meeting-place of the guild. Such a man as the Margrave is certain to do what you yourselves did without hesitation last night, that is, break open the lockers, and if gold were there you may depend it would not long remain in our possession after the discovery."

"You miss, or rather, evade the point, Commander. Is the gold ours, or is it yours?"

"I have admitted that part of it is yours."

"Then by what right do you assert the power to deal with it, lacking our consent? If you will pardon me for saying so, you, the youngest of our company, treat the rest of us as though we were children."

"If I possessed a child that acted at once so obstreperously and in so cowardly a manner as you did last night, I should cut a stick from the forest here, and thrash him with such severity that he would never forget it. As I have not done this to you, I deny that I treat you like children. The truth is that, although the youngest, I am your commander. We are engaged in acts of war, therefore military law prevails, and not the code of Justinian. It is my duty to protect your treasure and my own, and ensure that each man shall receive his share. After the division you may do what you please with the money, for you will then be under the common law, and I should not presume even to advise concerning its disposal."

"You refuse to tell us, then, what you have done with the gold?"

"I do. Now proceed with your suggestion."

211

"I fear I put the case too mildly when I called it a suggestion, considering the unsatisfactory nature of your reply to my question, therefore I withdraw the word 'suggestion,' and substitute the word 'command.'"

Kurzbold paused, to give his ultimatum the greater force. Behind him rose a murmur of approval.

"Words do not matter in the least. I deal with deeds. Out, then, with your command!" cried Roland, for the first time exhibiting impatience.

"The command unanimously adopted is this: the Castle of Furstenberg must be left alone. We know more of that Castle than you do, especially about its owner and his garrison. We have been gathering information as we journeyed, and have not remained sulking in the barge."

"Well, that is encouraging news to hear," said Roland. "I thought you were engaged in sampling wine."

"You hear the command. Will you obey?"

"I will not," said Roland decisively.

Ebearhard took a step forward to the side of his chief, and glanced at him reproachfully. Greusel remained where he was, but neither man spoke.

"You intend to attack Furstenberg?"

"Yes."

"When?"

"This afternoon."

Kurzbold turned to his following:

"Brethren," he said, "you have heard this conversation, and it needs no comment from me."

Apparently the discussion was to receive no comment from the others either. They stood there glum and disconcerted, as if the trend of affairs had taken an unexpected turn.

"I think," said one, "we had better retire and consult again."

This was unanimously agreed to, and once more they disembarked upon the island, and moved forward to their Witenagemot. Still Greusel and Ebearhard said nothing, but watched the men disappear through the trees. Roland looked at one after another with a smile.

"I see," he said, "that you disapprove of my conduct."

Greusel remained silent, but Ebearhard laughed and spoke.

"You came deliberately to the conclusion that it was unwise to attack Furstenberg. Now, because of Kurzbold's lack of courtesy, you deflect from your own mature judgment, and hastily jump into a course opposite to that which you marked out for yourself after sober, unbiased thought."

"My dear Ebearhard, the duty of a commander is to give, and not to receive, commands."

"Quite so. Command and suggestion are merely words, as you yourself pointed out, saying that they did not matter."

"In that, Ebearhard, I was wrong. Words do matter, although Kurzbold wasn't clever enough to correct me. For example, I hold no man in higher esteem than yourself, yet you might use words that would cause me instantly to draw my sword upon you, and fight until one or other of us succumbed."

Ebearhard laughed.

"You put it very flatteringly, Roland. Truth is, you'd fight till I succumbed, my swordsmanship being no match for yours. I shall say the words, however, that will cause you to draw your sword, and they are: Commander, I will stand by you whatever you do."

"And I," said Greusel curtly.

Roland shook hands in turn with the two men.

"Right," he cried. "If we are fated to go down, we will fall with banners flying."

After a time the captain returned with his supplies, but still the majority of the guild remained engaged in deliberation. Evidently discussion was not proceeding with that unanimity which Kurzbold always insisted was the case.

At noon Roland requested the captain to send some of his men with a meal for those in prolonged session, and also to carry them a cask which had been half-emptied either that morning or the night before.

"They will enjoy a picnic under the trees by the margin of the river," said Roland, as he and his two backers sat down in the empty cabin to their own repast.

"Do you think they are purposely delaying, so that you cannot cross over this afternoon?"

"'Tis very likely," said Roland. "I'll wait here until the sun sets, and then when they realize that I am about to leave them on an uninhabited island, without anything to eat, I think you will see them scramble aboard."

"But suppose they don't," suggested Greusel. "There are at least three of them able to swim across this narrow branch of the Rhine, and engage a boatman to take them off, should their signaling be unobserved."

"Again no matter. My plan for the undoing of the castles does not depend on force, but on craft. We three cannot carry away as much gold as can twenty-one, but our shares will be the same, and then we are not likely to find again so full a treasury as that at Rheinstein. My belief that these chaps would fight was dispelled by their conduct last night. Think of eighteen armed men flying before one sword!"

"Ah, you are scarce just in your estimate, Commander. They were under the influence of wine."

"True; but a brave man will fight, drunk or sober."

Although the sun sank out of sight, the men did not return. There had been more wine in the cask than Roland supposed, for the cheery songs of the guild echoed through the sylvan solitude. Roland told the captain to set his men at work and row round the top of the island into the main stream of the Rhine. The revelers had evidently appointed watchmen, for they speedily came running through the woods, and followed the movements of the boat from the shore, keeping pace with it. When the craft reached the opposite side of the island, the rowers drew in to the beach.

"Are you coming aboard?" asked Roland pleasantly.

"Will you agree to pass Furstenberg during the night?" demanded Kurzbold.

"No."

"Do you expect to succeed, as you did with the other castles?"

"Certainly; otherwise I shouldn't make the attempt."

"I was wrong," said Kurzbold mildly, "in substituting the word 'command' for 'suggestion,' which I first employed. There are many grave reasons for deferring an attempt on Furstenberg. In the heat of argument these reasons were not presented to you. Will you consent to listen to them if we go on board?"

"Yes; if you, on your part, will unanimously promise to abide by my decision."

"Do you think," said Kurzbold, "that your prejudice against me, which perhaps you agree does exist—"

"It exists," confessed Roland.

"Very well. Will you allow that prejudice to prevent you from rendering a decision in the men's favor?"

"No. If they present reasons that convince Greusel and Ebearhard against the attack on Furstenberg, I shall do what these two men advise, even although I myself believe in a contrary course. Thus you see, Herr Kurzbold, that my admitted dislike of you shall not come into play at all."

"That is quite satisfactory," said Kurzbold. "Will you tie up against the farther shore until your decision is rendered?"

"With pleasure," replied Roland; and accordingly the raiders tumbled impetuously on board the barge, whereupon the sailors bent to their long oars, and quickly reached the western bank, at a picturesque spot out of sight of any castle, where the trees came down the mountain-side to the water's edge. Here the sailors, springing ashore, tied their stout ropes to the tree-trunks, and the great barge lay broadside on to the land, with her nose pointing down the stream.

"You see," said Roland to his lieutenants, "without giving way in the least I allow you two the decision, and so I take it Furstenberg or ourselves will escape disaster on this occasion."

"Aside from all other considerations," replied the cautious Greusel, "I think it good diplomacy on this occasion to agree with the men, since they have stated their case so deferentially. They are improving, Commander."

"It really looks like it," he agreed. "You and Ebearhard had better go aft, and counsel them to begin the conference at once, for if we are to attack we must do so before darkness sets in. I'll remain here as usual at the prow."

Some of the men were strolling about the deck, but the majority remained in the cabin, down whose steps the lieutenants descended. Roland's impatience increased with the waning of the light.

Suddenly a cry that was instantly smothered rose from the cabin, then a shout:

"Treachery! Look out for yourself!"

Roland attempted to stride forward, but four men fell on him, pinioning his arms to his side, preventing the drawing of his weapon. Kurzbold, with half a dozen others, mounted on deck.

"Disarm him!" he commanded, and one of the men drew Roland's sword from its sheath, flinging it along the deck to Kurzbold's feet. The others now came up, bringing the two lieutenants, both gagged, with their arms tied behind them. Roland ceased his struggles, which he knew to be fruitless.

"We wish an amicable settlement of this matter," said Kurzbold, addressing the lieutenants, "and regret being compelled to use measures that may appear harsh. I do this only to prevent unnecessary bloodshed. Earlier in the day," he continued, turning to Roland, "when we found all appeals to you were vain, we unanimously deposed you from the leadership, which is our right, and also our duty."

"Not under martial law," said Roland.

"I beg to point out that there was no talk of martial law before we left Frankfort. It was not till later that we learned we had appointed an unreasoning tyrant over us. We have deposed him, and I am elected in his place, with John Gensbein as my lieutenant. We will keep you three here until complete darkness sets in, then put you ashore unarmed. Bacharach, on this side of the Rhine, is to be our next resting-place, and doubtless so clever a man as you, Roland, may say that we choose Bacharach because it is named for Bacchus, the god of drunkards. Nevertheless, to show our good intentions towards you, we will remain there all day to-morrow. You can easily reach Bacharach along the hilltops before daybreak. We have written a charter of comradeship which all have signed except yourselves. If at Bacharach you give us your word to act faithfully under my leadership, we will reinstate you in the guild, and return your swords. By way of recompense for this leniency, we ask you to direct the captain to obey my commands as he has done yours."

"Captain Blumenfels," said Roland to the honest sailor, who stood looking on in amaze at this turn of affairs, "you are to wait here until it is completely dark. See that no lights are burning to give warning to those in Furstenberg; and, by the way," added Roland, turning to his former company, "I advise you not to drink anything until you are well past the Castle. If you sing the songs of the guild within earshot of Furstenberg, you are like to sing on the other side of your mouths before morning. Don't forget that Margrave Hermann von Katznellenbogenstahleck is the chief hangman of Germany." Then once more to the captain:

"As the Castle of Furstenberg stands high above the river, and well back from it, you will be out of sight if you keep near this shore. However, you can easily judge your distance, because the towers are visible even in the darkness against the sky. No man on the ramparts of the Castle can discern you down here on the black surface of the water, so long as you do not carry a light."

"Roland, my deposed friend," said Kurzbold, "I fear you bear resentment, for you are giving the captain orders instead of telling him to obey mine."

"Kurzbold, you are mistaken. I resign command with great pleasure, and, indeed, Greusel and Ebearhard will testify that I had already determined to pass Furstenberg unseen. As my former lieutenants are disarmed, surely the company, with eighteen swords, is not so frightened as to keep them gagged and bound. 'Tis no wonder you wish to avoid the Laughing Baron, if that is all the courage you possess."

Stung by these taunts, Kurzbold gruffly ordered his men to release their prisoners, but when the gags were removed, and before the cords were cut, he addressed the lieutenants:

"Do you give me your words not to make any further resistance, if I permit you to remain unbound?"

"I give you my word on nothing, you mutinous dog!" cried Greusel; "and if I did, how could you expect me to keep it after such an example of treachery from you who pledged your faith, and then broke it? I shall obey my Commander, and none other."

"I am your Commander," asserted Kurzbold.

"You are not," proclaimed Greusel.

Ebearhard laughed.

"No need to question me," he said. "I stand by my colleagues."

"Gag them again," ordered Kurzbold.

"No, no!" cried Roland. "We are quite helpless. Give your words, gentlemen."

Gloomily Greusel obeyed, and merrily Ebearhard. Darkness was now gathering, and when it fell completely the three men were put off into the forest.

"You have not yet," said Kurzbold to Roland, "ordered the captain to obey me. I do not object to that, but it will be the worse for him and his men if they refuse to accept my instructions."

"Do you know this district, Captain Blumenfels?" asked Roland.

"Yes, mein Herr."

"Is there a path along the top that will lead us behind Furstenberg on to Bacharach?"

"Yes, mein Herr, but it is a very rough track."

"Is it too far for you to guide us there, and return before the moon rises?"

"Oh no, mein Herr, I can conduct you to the trail in half an hour if you consent to climb lustily."

"Very good. Herr Kurzbold, if you are not impatient to be off, and will permit the captain to direct us on our way, I will tell him to obey you."

"How long before you can return, captain?" asked Kurzbold.

"I can be back well within the hour, mein Herr."

"You will obey me if the late Commander orders you to do so?"

"Yes, mein Herr."

"Captain," said Roland, "I inform you in the hearing of these men that Herr Kurzbold occupies my place, and is to be obeyed by you until I resume command."

Kurzbold laughed.

"You mean until you are re-elected to membership in the guild, for we do not propose to make you commander again. Now, captain, to the hill, and see that your return is not delayed."

The four men disappeared into the dark forest.

"Captain," said Roland, when they reached the track, "I have taken you up here not that I needed your guidance, for I know this land as well as you do. You will obey Kurzbold, of course, but if he tells you to make for Lorch, allow your boat to drift, and do not get beyond the middle of the river until opposite Furstenberg. There is a buoyed chain—"

"I know it well," interrupted the captain. "I have many times avoided it, but twice became entangled with it, in spite of all my efforts, and was robbed by the Laughing Baron."

"Very well; I intend you to be entrapped by that chain to-night. Offer no resistance, and you will be safe enough. Do not attempt to help these lads should they be set upon, and it will be hard luck if I am not in command again before midnight. Keep close to this shore, but if they order you into the middle of the river, or across it, dally, my good Blumenfels, dally, until you are stopped by the chain for the third time."

When the captain returned to his barge, he found Kurzbold pacing the deck in a masterly manner, impatient to be off. For once the combatants, with an effort, were refraining from drink.

"We will open a cask," said Kurzbold, "as soon as we have passed the Schloss."

He ordered the captain to follow the shore as closely as was safe, and take care that they did not come within sight of Furstenberg's tall, round tower. All sat or reclined on the dark deck, saying no word as the barge slid silently down the swift Rhine. Suddenly the speed of the boat was checked so abruptly that one or two of the standing men were flung off their feet. From up on the hillside there tolled out the deep note of a bell. The barge swung round broadside on the current, and lay there with the water rushing like hissing serpents along its side, the bell pealing out a loud alarm that seemed to keep time with the shuddering of the helpless boat.

"What's wrong, captain?" cried Kurzbold, getting on his feet again and running aft.

"I fear, sir, 'tis an anchored chain."

"Can't you cut it?"

"That is impossible, mein Herr."

"Then get out your sweeps, and turn back. Where are we, do you think?"

"Under the battlements of Furstenberg Castle."

"Damnation! Put some speed into your men, and let us get away from here."

The captain ordered his crew to hurry, but all their efforts could not release the boat from the chain, against which it ground up and down with a tearing noise, and even the un-nautical swordsmen saw that the current was impelling it diagonally toward the shore, and all the while the deep bell tolled on.

"What in the fiend's name is the meaning of that bell?" demanded Kurzbold.

"It is the Castle bell, mein Herr," replied the captain.

Before Kurzbold could say anything more the air quivered with shout after shout of laughter. Torches began to glisten among the trees, and there was a clatter of horses' hoofs on the echoing rock. A more magnificent sight was never before presented to the startled eyes of so unappreciative a crowd. Along the zigzag road, and among the trees, spluttered the torches, each with a trail of sparks like the tail of a comet. The bearers were rushing headlong down the slope, for woe to the man who did not arrive at the water's edge sooner than his master.

The torchlight gleamed on flashing swords and glittering points of spears, but chief sight of all was the Margrave Hermann von Katznellenbogenstahleck, a giant in stature, mounted on a magnificent stallion, as black as the night, and of a size that corresponded with its prodigious rider. The Margrave's long beard and flowing hair were red; scarlet, one may say, but perhaps that was the fiery reflection from the torches. Servants, scullions, stablemen carried the lights; the men-at-arms had no encumbrance but their weapons, and the business-like way in which they lined up along the shore was a study in discipline, and a terror to any one unused to war. Above all the din and clash of arms rang the hearty, stentorian laughter of the Red Margrave actually echoing back in gusts of fiendish merriment from the hills on the other side of the Rhine.

Now the boat's nose came dully against the ledge of rock, to whose surface the swaying chain rose dripping from the water, sparkling like a jointed snake under the torchlight.

"God save us all!" cried the Margrave, "what rare show have we here? By my sainted patron, the Archbishop, merchants under arms! Whoever saw the like? Ha! stout Captain Blumenfels, do I recognize you? Once more my chain has caught you. This makes the third time, does it not, Blumenfels?"

"Yes, your Majesty."

"You may as well call me 'your Holiness' as 'your Majesty.' I'm contented with my title, the 'Laughing Baron,' Haw-haw-haw-haw! And so your merchants have taken to arms again? The lesson at the Lorely taught them nothing! Are there any ropes aboard, captain?"

"Plenty, my lord."

"Then fling a coil ashore. Now, my tigers," he roared to his men-at-arms, "hale me to land those damned shopkeepers."

With a clash of armor and weapons the brigands threw themselves on the boat, and in less time than is taken to tell it, every man of the guild was disarmed and flung ashore. Here another command of the Red Margrave gave them the outlaw's knot, as he termed it, a most painful tying-up of the body and the limbs until each victim was rigid as a red of iron. They were flung face downwards in a row, and beaten black and blue with cudgels, despite their screams of agony and appeals for mercy.

"Now turn them over on their backs," commanded the Margrave, and it was done. The glare of the pitiless torches fell upon contorted faces. The Baron turned his horse athwart the line of helpless men, and spurred that animal over it from end to end, but the intelligent horse, more merciful than its rider, stepped with great daintiness, despite its unusual size, and never trod on one of the prostrate bodies. During what followed, the Red Baron, shaking with laughter, marched his horse up and down over the stricken men.

"Now, unload the boat, but do not injure any of the sailors! I hope to see them often again. You cannot tell how we have missed you, captain. What are you loaded with this time? Sound Frankfort cloth?"

"Yes, your Majesty—I mean, my lord."

"No, you mean my Holiness, for I expect to be an Archbishop yet, if all goes well," and his laughter echoed across the Rhine. "Uplift your hatches, Blumenfels, and tell your men to help fling the goods ashore."

Delicately paced the fearful horse over the prone men, snorting, perhaps in sympathy, from his red nostrils, his jet-black coat a-quiver with the excitement of the scene. The captain obeyed the Margrave with promptness and celerity. The hatches were lifted, and his sailors, two and two, flung on the ledge of rock the merchant's bales. The men-at-arms, who proved to be men-of-all-work, had piled their weapons in a heap, and were carrying the bales a few yards inland. Through it all the Baron roared with laughter, and rode his horse along its living pavement, turning now at this end and now at the other.

"Do not be impatient," he cried down to them, "'twill not take long to strip the boat of every bale, then I shall hang you on these trees, and send back your bodies in the barge, as a lesson to Frankfort. You must return, captain," he cried, "for you cannot sell dead bodies to my liege of Cologne."

As he spoke a ruddy flush spread over the Rhine, as if some one had flashed a red lantern upon the waters. The glow died out upon the instant.

"What!" thundered the Margrave, "is that the reflection of my beard, or are Beelzebub and his fiends coming up from below for a portion of the Frankfort cloth? I will share with good brother Satan, but with no one else. Boil me if I ever saw a sight like that before! What was it, captain?"

"I saw nothing unusual, my lord."

"There, there!" exclaimed the Margrave, and as he spoke it seemed that a crimson film had fallen on the river, growing brighter and brighter.

"Oh, my lord," cried the captain, "the Castle is on fire!"

"Saints protect us!" shouted the Red Margrave, crossing himself, and turning to the west, where now both hearing and sight indicated that a furnace was roaring. The whole western sky was aglow, and although the flames could not be seen for the intervening cliff, every one knew there was no other dwelling that could cause such an illumination.

Spurring his horse, and calling his men to come on, the nobleman dashed up the steep acclivity, and when the last man had departed, Roland, followed by his two lieutenants, stepped from the forest to the right down upon the rocky plateau.

XIII. "A SENTENCE; COME, PREPARE!"

"Captain," said Roland quietly, "bring your crew ashore, and fling these bales on board again as quickly as you can."

An instant later the sailors were at work, undoing their former efforts.

"In mercy's name, Roland," wailed one of the stricken, "get a sword and cut our bonds."

"All in good time," replied Roland. "The bales are more valuable to me than you are, and we have two barrels of gold at the foot of the cliff to bring in, if they haven't sunk in the Rhine. Greusel, do you and Ebearhard take two of the crew, launch the small boat, and rescue the barrels if you can find them."

"Mercy on us, Roland! Mercy!" moaned his former comrades.

"I have already wasted too much mercy upon you," he said. "If I rescue you now, I shall be compelled to hang you in the morning as breakers of law, so I may as well leave you where you are, and allow the Red Margrave to save me the trouble. The loss of his castle will not make him more compassionate, especially if he learns you were the cause of it. You will then experience some refined tortures, I imagine; for, like myself, he may think hanging too good for you. I should never have fired his castle had it not been for your rebellion."

The men on the ground groaned but made no further appeal. Some of them were far-seeing enough to realize that an important change had come over the young man they thought so well known to them, who stood there with an air of indifference, throwing out a suggestion now and then for the more effective handling of the bales; suggestions carrying an impalpable force of authority that caused them to be very promptly obeyed. They did not know that this person whom they had regarded as one of themselves, the youngest at that, treating him accordingly, had but a day or two before received a tremendous assurance, which would have turned the head of almost any individual in the realm, old or young; the assurance that he was to be supreme ruler over millions of creatures like themselves; a ruler whose lightest word might carry their extinction with it.

Yet such is the strange littleness of human nature that, although this potent knowledge had been gradually exercising its effect on Roland's character, it was not the rebellion of the eighteen or their mutinous words that now made him hard as granite towards them. It was the trivial fact that four of them had dared to manhandle him; had made a personal assault upon him; had pinioned his helpless arms, and flung his sword, that insignia of honor, to the feet of Kurzbold, leader of the revolt.

The Lord's Anointed, he was coming to consider himself, although not yet had the sacred ointment been placed upon his head. A temporal Emperor and a vice-regent of Heaven upon earth, his hand was destined to hold the invisible hilt of the Almighty's sword of vengeance. The words "I will repay" were to reach their fulfillment through his action. Notwithstanding his youth, or perhaps because of it, he was animated by deep religious feeling, and this, rather than ambition, explained the celerity with which he agreed to the proposals of the Archbishops.

The personage the prisoners saw standing on the rock-ledge of Furstenberg was vastly different from the young man who, a comrade of comrades, had departed from Frankfort in their company. They beheld him plainly enough, for there was now no need of torches along the foreshore; the night was crimson in its brilliancy, and down the hill came a continuous roar, like that of the Rhine Fall seventy leagues away.

Into this red glare the small boat and its four occupants entered, and Roland saw with a smile that two well-filled casks formed its freight. The bales were now aboard the barge again, and the Commander ordered the crew to help the quartette in the small boat with the lifting of the heavy barrels. Greusel and Ebearhard clambered over the side, and came thus to the ledge where Roland stood, as the crew rolled the barrels down into the cabin.

"Lieutenants," said the Commander, "select two stout battle-axes from that heap. Follow the chain up the hill until you reach that point where it is attached to the thick rope. Cut the rope with your axes, and draw down the chain with you, thus clearing a passage for the barge."

The two men chose battle-axes, then turned to their leader.

"Should we not get our men aboard," they said, "before the barge is free?"

"These rebels are prisoners of the Red Margrave. They belong to him, and not to me. Where they are, there they remain."

The lieutenants, with one impulse, advanced to their Commander, who frowned as they did so. A cry of despair went up from the pinioned men, but Kurzbold shouted:

"Cut him down, Ebearhard, and then release us. In the name of the guild I call on you to act! He is unarmed; cut him down! 'Tis foul murder to desert us thus."

The cutting down could easily have been accomplished, for Roland stood at their mercy, weaponless since the émeute on the barge. Notwithstanding the seriousness of the occasion, the optimistic Ebearhard laughed, although every one else was grave enough.

"Thank you, Kurzbold, for your suggestion. We have come forward, not to use force, but to try persuasion. Roland, you cannot desert to death the men whom you conducted out of Frankfort."

"Why can I not?"

"I should have said a moment ago that you will not, but now I say you cannot. Kurzbold has just shown what an irreclaimable beast he is, and on that account, because birth, or training, or something has made you one of different caliber, you cannot thus desert him to the reprisal of that red fiend up the hill."

"If I save him now, 'twill be but to hang him an hour later. I am no hangman, while the Margrave is. I prefer that he should attend to my executions."

Again Ebearhard laughed.

"'Tis no use, Roland, pretending abandonment, for you will not abandon. I thoroughly favor choking the life out of Kurzbold, and one or two of the others, and will myself volunteer for the office of headsman, carrying, as I do, the ax, but let everything be done decently and in order, that a dignified execution may follow on a fair trial."

"Commander," shouted the captain from the deck of the barge, "make haste, I beg of you. The rope connecting with the Castle has been burnt, and the chain is dragging free. The current is swift, and this barge heavy. We shall be away within the minute."

"Get your crew ashore on the instant," cried Roland, "and fling me these despicable burdens aboard. A man at the head, another at the heels, and toss each into the barge. Is there time, captain, to take this heap of cutlery with us as trophies of the fray?"

"Yes," replied the captain, "if we are quick about it."

The howling human packages were hurled from ledge to barge; the strong, unerring sailors, accustomed to the task, heaved no man into the water. Others as speedily fell upon the heap of weapons, and threw them, clattering, on the deck. All then leaped aboard, and Roland, motioning his lieutenants to precede him, was the last to climb over the prow.

The chain came down over the stones with a clattering run, and fell with a great splash into the river. The barge, now clear, swung with the current stern foremost; the sailors got to their oars, and gradually drew their craft away from the shore. A little farther from the landing, those on deck, looking upstream, enjoyed an uninterrupted view of the magnificent conflagration. The huge stone Castle seemed to glow white hot. The roof had fallen in, and a seething furnace reddened the midnight sky. Like a flaming torch the great tower roared to the heavens. The whole hilltop resembled the crater of an active volcano. Timber floors and wooden partitions, long seasoned, proved excellent material for the incendiaries, and even the stones were crumbling away, falling into the gulf of fire, sending up a dazzling eruption of sparks, as section after section tumbled into this earthly Hades.

The long barge floated placidly down a river resembling molten gold.

The boat was in disarray, covered with bales of cloth not yet lowered into the hold, cluttered here and there with swords, battle-axes, and spears. In the various positions where they had been flung lay the helpless men, some on their faces, some on their backs. The deck was as light as if the red setting sun were casting his rays upon it. Roland seated himself on a bale, and said to the captain:

"Turn all these men face upward," and the captain did so.

"Ebearhard, you said execution should take place after a fair trial. There is no necessity to call witnesses, or to go through any court of law formalities. You two are perfectly cognizant of everything that has taken place, and no testimony will either strengthen or weaken that knowledge. As a preliminary, take Kurzbold, the new president, and Gensbein, his lieutenant, from among that group, and set them apart. Two members of the crew will carry out this order," which was carried out accordingly.

Roland rose, walked along the prostrate row, and selected, apparently at haphazard, four others, then said to the members of his crew:

"Place these four men beside their leader. Left to myself," he continued to his lieutenants, "I should hang the six. However, I shall take no hand in the matter. I appoint you, Joseph Greusel, and you, Gottlieb Ebearhard, as judges, with power of life and death. If your verdict on any or all of the accused is death, I shall use neither the ax nor the cord, but propose flinging them into the river, and if God wills them to reach the shore alive, their binding will be no hindrance to escape."

Kurzbold and his lieutenant broke out into alternate curses and appeals, protesting that Greusel and Ebearhard had not been expelled from the guild, and calling upon them by their solemn oath of brotherhood to release them now that they possessed the power. To these appeals the newly-appointed judges made no reply, and for once Ebearhard did not laugh.

The other four directed their supplications to Roland himself. They had been misled, they cried, and deeply regretted it. Already they suffered punishment of a severity almost beyond power of human endurance, and they feared their bones were broken with the cudgeling, since which assault their bonds grievously tortured them. All swore amendment, and their grim commander still remaining silent, they asked him in what respect they were more guilty than the dozen others whom seemingly he intended to spare. At last Roland replied.

"You four," he said sternly, "dared to lay hands upon me, and for that I demand from the judges a sentence of death."

Even his two lieutenants gazed at him in amazement, that he should make so much of an action which they themselves had endured and nothing said of it. Surely the laying-on of hands, even in rudeness, was not a capital crime, yet they saw to their astonishment that Roland was in deadly earnest.

The leader turned a calm face toward their scrutiny, but there was a frown upon his brow.

"Work while ye have the light," he said. "Judges, consider your decision, and deliver your verdict."

Greusel and Ebearhard turned their backs on every one, walked slowly aft, and down into the cabin. Roland resumed his seat on the bale of cloth, elbows on his knees, and face in his hands. All appeals had ceased, and deep silence reigned, every man aboard the boat in a state of painful tension. The fire in the distant castle lowered and lowered, and darkness was returning to the deck of the barge. At last the judges emerged from the cabin, and came slowly forward.

It was Greusel who spoke.

"We wish to know if only these six are on trial?"

"Only these six," replied Roland.

"Our verdict is death," said Greusel. "Kurzbold and Gensbein are to be thrown into the Rhine bound as they lie, but the other four receive one chance for life, in that the cords shall be cut, leaving their limbs free."

This seeming mercy brought no consolation to the quartette, for each plaintively proclaimed that he could not swim.

"I thank you for your judgment," said Roland, "which I am sure you must have formed with great reluctance. Having proven yourself such excellent judges, I doubt not you will now act with equal wisdom as advisers. A phrase of yours, Ebearhard, persists in my mind, despite all efforts to dislodge it. You uttered on the ledge of rock yonder something to the effect that we left Frankfort as comrades together. That is very true, and unless you override my resolution, I have come to the conclusion that if any of us are fated to die, the penalty shall be dealt by some other hand than mine. The twelve who lie here are scarcely less guilty than the six now under sentence, and I propose, therefore, to put ashore on the east bank Kurzbold and Gensbein, one a rogue, the other a fool. The sixteen who remain have so definitely proven themselves to be simpletons that I trust they will not resent my calling them such. If however, they abandon all claim to the comradeship that has been so much prated about, swearing by the Three Kings of Cologne faithfully to follow me, and obey my every word without cavil or argument, I will pardon them, but the first man who rebels will show that my clemency has been misplaced, and I can assure them that it shall not be exercised again. Captain, your sailors are familiar with knotted ropes. Bid them release all these men except the six condemned."

The boatmen, with great celerity, freed the prostrate captives from their bonds, but some of the mutineers had been so cruelly used in the cudgeling that it was necessary to assist them to their feet. The early summer daybreak was at hand, its approach heralded by the perceptible diluting of the darkness that surrounded them, and a ghastly, pallid grayness began to overspread the surface of the broad river. Down the stream to the west the towers of Bacharach could be faintly distinguished, looking like a dream city, the lower gloom of which was picked out here and there by points of light, each betokening an early riser.

It was a deeply dejected, silent group that stood in this weird half-light, awaiting the development of Roland's mind regarding them; he, the youngest of their company, quiet, unemotional, whose dominion no one now thought of disputing.

"Captain," he continued, "steer for the eastern shore. I know that Bacharach is the greatest wine mart on the Rhine, and well sustains the reputation of the drunken god for whom it is named, but we will nevertheless avoid it. There is a long island opposite the town, but a little farther down. I dare say you know it well. Place that island between us and Bacharach, and tie up to the mainland, out of view from the stronghold of Bacchus. He is a misleading god, with whom we shall hold no further commerce.

"Now, Joseph Greusel, and Gottlieb Ebearhard, do you two administer the oath of the Three Kings to these twelve men; but before doing so, give each one his choice, permitting him to say whether he will follow Kurzbold on the land or obey me on the water."

Here Kurzbold broke out again in trembling anger:

"Your pretended fairness is a sham, and your bogus option a piece of your own sneaking dishonesty. What chance have we townsmen, put ashore, penniless, in an unknown wilderness, far from any human habitation, knowing nothing of the way back to Frankfort? Your fraudulent clemency rescues us from drowning merely to doom us to starvation."

The daylight had so increased that all might see the gentle smile coming to Roland's lips, and the twinkle in his eye as he looked at the wrathful Kurzbold.

"A most intelligent leader of men are you, Herr Conrad. I suppose this dozen will stampede to join your leadership. They must indeed be proud of you when they learn the truth. I shall present to each of you, out of my own store of gold that came from the castle you so bravely attacked last night, one half the amount that is your due. This will be more money than any of you ever possessed before; each portion, indeed, excelling the total that you eighteen accumulated during your whole lives. I could easily bestow your share without perceptible diminution of the fund we three, unaided, extracted from the coffers of the Red Margrave. The reason I do not pay in full is this. When you reach Frankfort, I must be assured that you will keep your foolish tongues silent. If any man speaks of our labors, I shall hear of it on my return, and will fine that man his remaining half-share.

"It distresses me to expose your ignorance, Kurzbold, but I put you ashore amply provided with money, barely two-thirds of a league from Lorch, where you spent so jovial an evening, and where a man with gold in his pouch need fear neither hunger nor thirst. Lorch may be attained by a leisurely walker in less than half an hour; indeed, it is barely two leagues from this spot to Assmannshausen, and surely you know the road from that storehouse of red wine to the capital city of Frankfort, having once traversed it. A child of six, Kurzbold, might be safely put ashore where you shall set foot on land. Therefore, lieutenants, let each man know he will receive a bag of coin, and may land unmolested to accompany the brave and intelligent Kurzbold."

As he finished this declamation, that caused even some of the beaten warriors to laugh at their leader, the barge came gently alongside the strand, well out of sight of Bacharach. Each of the dozen swore the terrible, unbreakable oath of the Three Kings to be an obedient henchman to Roland.

"You may," said Roland, "depart to the cabin, where a flagon of wine will be served to every man, and also an early breakfast. After that you are permitted to lie down and relax your swollen limbs, meditating on the extract from Holy Writ which relates the fate of the blind when led by the blind."

When the dozen limped away, the chief turned to his prisoners.

"Against you four I bear resentment that I thought could not be appeased except by your expulsion, but reflection shows me that you acted under instruction from the foolish leader you selected, and therefore the principal, not the agent, is most to blame. I give you the same choice I have accorded to the rest. Unloose them, captain; and while this is being done, Greusel, get two empty bags from the locker, open one of the casks, and place in each bag an amount which you estimate to be one half the share which is Kurzbold's due."

The four men standing up took the oath, and thanked Roland for his mercy, hurrying away at a sign from him to their bread and wine.

"Send hither," cried Roland after them, "two of the men who have already refreshed themselves, each with a loaf of bread and a full flagon of wine. And now, captain, release Kurzbold and Gensbein."

When these two stood up and stretched themselves, the bearers of bread and wine presented them with this refreshment, and after they had partaken of it, Greusel gave them each a bag of gold, which they tied to their belts without a word, while Greusel and Ebearhard waited to escort them to land.

"We want our swords," said Kurzbold sullenly.

Ebearhard looked at his chief, but he shook his head.

"They have disgraced their swords," he said, "which now by right belong to the Margrave Hermann von Katznellenbogenstahleck. Put them ashore, lieutenant."

It was broad daylight, and the men had all come up from the cabin, standing in a silent group at the stern. Kurzbold, on the bank, foaming at the mouth with fury, shook his fist at them, roaring:

"Cowards! Pigs! Dolts! Asses! Poltroons!"

The men made no reply, but Ebearhard's hearty laugh rang through the forest.

"You have given us your titles, Kurzbold," he cried. "Send us your address whenever you get one!"

"Captain," said Roland, "cast off. Cross to this side of that island, and tie up there for the day. Set a man on watch, relieving the sentinel every two hours. We have spent an exciting night, and will sleep till evening."

"Your honor, may I first stow away these bales, and dispose of the battle-axes, spears, and broadswords, so to clear the deck?"

"You may do that, captain, at sunset. As for the bales, they make a very comfortable couch upon which I intend to rest."

XIV. THE PRISONER OF EHRENFELS

There is inspiration in the sight of armed men marching steadily together; men well disciplined, keeping step to the measured clank of their armor. Like a great serpent the soldiers of Cologne issued from the forest, coming down two and two, for the path was narrow. They would march four abreast when they reached the river road, and the evolutions which accomplished this doubling of the columns, without changing step or causing confusion, called forth praise from the two southern Archbishops.

A beautiful tableau of amity and brotherly love was presented to the troops as they looked up at the three Archbishops standing together on the balcony in relief against the gray walls of the Castle. The officers, who were on horseback, raised their swords sky-pointing from their helmets, for they recognized their overlord and his two notable confrères. With the motion of one man the three Archbishops acknowledged the salute. The troops cheered and cheered as the anaconda made its sinuous way down the mountainside, and company after company came abreast the Castle. The Archbishops stood there until the last man disappeared down the river road on his way to Coblentz.

"May I ask you," said Mayence, addressing Treves, "to conduct me to the flat roof of your Castle? Will you accompany us?" he inquired of Cologne.

Cologne and Treves being for once in agreement, the latter led the way, and presently the three stood on the broad stone plateau which afforded a truly striking panorama of the Rhine. The July sun sinking in the west transformed the river into a crimson flood, and at that height the cool evening breeze was delicious. Cologne stood with one hand on the parapet, and gazed entranced at the scene, but the practical Mayence paid no attention whatever to it.

"Your troublesome guest, Treves, has one more request to make, which is that you order his flag hoisted to the top of that pole."

Treves at once departed to give this command, while Cologne, with clouded brow, turned from his appreciation of the view.

"My Lord," he said, "you have requested the raising of a signal."

"Yes," was the reply.

"A signal which calls your men from the Lahn to the landing at Stolzenfels?"

"Yes," repeated Mayence.

"My Lord, I have kept my promise not only to the letter, but in the spirit as well. My troops are marching peaceably away, and will reach their barracks some time to-morrow. Although I exacted no promise from you, you implied there was a truce between us, and that your army, like my company, was not to be called into action of any kind."

"Your understanding of our pact is concisely stated, even though my share in that pact remained unspoken. A truce, did you say? Is it not more than that? I hoped that my seconding of the nomination you proposed proved me in complete accord with your views."

"I am not in effect your prisoner, then?"

"Surely not; so contrary to the fact is such an assumption that I implore you to accept my hospitality. The signal, which I see is now at the mast-head, calls for one barge only, and that contains no soldier, merely a captain and his ten stout rowers, whom you may at this moment, if you turn round, see emerging from the mouth of the Lahn. I present to you, and to the Countess von Sayn, my Schloss of Martinsburg for as long as you may require it. It is well furnished, well provisioned, and attended to by a group of capable servants, who are at your command. I suggest that you cross in my barge, in company with the Countess and her kinsman, the Reverend Father. You agree, I take it, to convoy the lady safely to her temporary restraint in Pfalz. It was her own request, you remember."

"I shall convoy her thither."

"I am trusting to you entirely. The distance is but thirteen leagues, and can be accomplished easily in a day. Once on the other side of the river she may despatch her kinsman, or some more trustworthy messenger, to her own Castle, and thus summon the two waiting-women who will share her seclusion."

"Is it your intention, my Lord, that her imprisonment shall—?"

The Archbishop of Mayence held up his thin hand with a gesture of deprecation.

"I use no word so harsh as 'imprisonment.' The penance, if you wish so to characterize it, is rather in the nature of a retreat, giving her needed opportunity for reflection, and, I hope, for regret."

"Nevertheless, my Lord, your action seems to me unnecessarily severe. How long do you propose to detain her?"

"I am pained to hear you term it severity, for her treatment will be of the mildest description. I thought you would understand that no other course was open to me. So far as I am personally concerned, she might have said what pleased her, with no adverse consequences, but she flouted the highest Court of the realm, and such contempt cannot be overlooked. As for the duration of her discipline, it will continue until the new Emperor is married, after which celebration the Countess is free to go whither she pleases. I shall myself call at Pfalz four days from now, that I may be satisfied the lady enjoys every comfort the Castle affords."

"And also, perhaps, to be certain she is there immured."

Mayence's thin lips indulged in a wry smile.

"I need no such assurance," he said, "since my Lord of Cologne has pledged his word to see that the order of the Court is carried out."

The conversation was here interrupted by the return of Treves. Already the great barge was half-way across the river. The surging, swift current swept it some distance below Stolzenfels, and the rowers, five a side, were working strenuously to force it into slower waters. Lord, lady, and monk crossed over to the mouth of the Lahn, and the barge returned immediately to convey across horses and escort.

As the valley of the Lahn opened out it presented a picture of quiet sylvan beauty, apparently uninhabited by any living thing. The Archbishop of Cologne rose, and, shading his eyes from the still radiant sun, gazed intently up the little river. No floating craft was anywhere in sight. He turned to the captain.

"Where is the flotilla from Mayence?" he asked.

"Flotilla, my Lord?"

"Yes; a hundred barges sailed down from Mayence in the darkness either last night or the night before, taking harbor here in the Lahn."

"My Lord, even one barge, manned as this is, could not have journeyed such a distance in so short a time, and, indeed, for a flotilla to attempt the voyage, except in daylight, would have been impossible. No barges have come down the Rhine for months, and had they ventured the little Lahn is too shallow to harbor them."

"Thank you, captain. I appear to be ignorant both of the history and the geography of this district. If I were to ask you and your stout rowers to take me down through the swiftest part of the river to Coblentz, how soon would we reach that town?"

"Very speedily, my Lord, but I could undertake no such voyage except at the command of my master. He is not one to be disobeyed."

"I quite credit that," said Cologne, sitting down again, the momentary desire to recall his marching troops, that had arisen when he saw the empty Lahn, dying down when he realized how effectually he had been outwitted.

When the horses were brought across, Father Ambrose, at the request of the Countess, rode back to Sayn, and sent forward the two waiting-women whom she required, and so well did he accomplish his task that they arrived at Schloss Martinsburg before ten of the clock that night. At an early hour next morning the little procession began its journey up the Rhine, his Lordship and the Countess in front; the six horsemen bringing up the rear.

The lady was in a mood of deep dejection; the regret which Mayence had anticipated as result of imprisonment already enveloped her. It was only too evident that the Archbishop of Cologne was bitterly disappointed, for he rode silently by her side making no attempt at conversation. They rested for several hours during midday, arriving at Caub before the red sun set, and now the Countess saw her pinnacled prison lying like an anchored ship in midstream.

At Caub they were met by a bearded, truculent-looking ruffian, who introduced himself to the Archbishop as the Pfalzgraf von Stahleck.

"You take us rather by surprise, Prince of Cologne," he said. "It is true that my overlord, the Archbishop of Mayence, called upon me several days ago while descending the Rhine in his ten-oared barge, and said there was a remote chance that a prisoner might shortly be given into my care. This had often happened before, for my Castle covers some gruesome cells that extend under the river,—cells with secret entrances not easily come by should any one search the Castle. It is sometimes convenient that a prisoner of State should be immured in one of them when the Archbishop has no room in his own Schloss Ehrenfels, so I paid little attention, and merely said the prisoner would receive a welcome on arrival. This morning there came one of the Archbishop's men from Stolzenfels, and both my wife and myself were astonished to learn that the prisoner would be here this evening under your escort, my Lord, and that it was a woman we were to harbor. Further, she was to be given the best suite of rooms we had in the Castle, and to be treated with all respect as a person of rank. Now, this apartment is in no state of readiness to receive such a lady, much less to house one of the dignity of your Lordship."

"It does not matter for me," replied the Archbishop. "Being, as I may say, part soldier, the bed and board of an inn is quite acceptable upon occasion."

"Oh no, your Highness, such a hardship is not to be thought of. The Castle of Gutenfels, standing above us, is comfortable as any on the Rhine. Its owner, the Count Palatine, is fellow-Elector of yours, and a very close friend of my overlord of Mayence, and I am told they vote together whenever my overlord needs his assistance."

"That is true," commented Cologne.

"My overlord sent word that anything I needed for the accommodation of her ladyship, he recognizing that my warning had been short, I should requisition from the Count Palatine, so at midday I went up to call upon him, not saying anything, of course, about State prisoners, male or female. The moment he heard that you, my Lord, were visiting this neighborhood, he begged me to tender to you, and to all your companions or following, the hospitality of his Castle for so long as you might honor him with your presence."

"The Count Palatine is very gracious, and I shall be glad to accept shelter and refreshment."

"He would have been here to greet your Highness, but I was unable to inform him at what hour you would arrive, so I waited for you myself, and will be pleased to guide you to the gates of Gutenfels."

The conversation was interrupted by a great clatter of galloping horses, descending the hill with reckless speed, and at its foot swinging round into the main street of the town.

"Ha!" cried the amateur jailer, "here is the Count Palatine himself;" and thus it is our fate to meet the fourth Elector of the Empire, who, added to the three Archbishops, formed a quorum so potent that it could elect or depose an Emperor at will.

The cavalry of the Count Palatine was composed of fifty fully-armed men, and their gallop through the town roused the echoes of that ancient bailiwick, which, together with the Castle, belonged to the Palatinate. The powerful noble extended a cordial welcome to his fellow-Elector, and together they mounted to the Castle of Gutenfels.

At dinner that night the Count Palatine proved an amiable host. Under his geniality the charming Countess von Sayn gradually recovered her lost good spirits, and forgot she was on her way to prison. After all, she was young, naturally joyous, and loved interesting company, especially that of the two Electors, who were well informed, and had seen much of the world. The Archbishop also shook off some of his somberness; indeed, all of it as the flagons flowed. Being asked his preference in wine, he replied that yesterday he had been regaled with a very excellent sample of Oberweseler.

"That is from this neighborhood," replied the Count. "Oberwesel lies but a very short distance below, on the opposite side of the river, but we contend that our beverage of Caub is at least equal, and sometimes superior. You shall try a good vintage of both. How did you come by Oberweseler so far north as Stolzenfels?"

"Simply because I was so forward, counting on the good nature of my friend of Treves, that I stipulated for Oberweseler."

"Ah! I am anxious to know why."

"For reasons of history, not of the palate. A fair English Princess was guest of Stolzenfels long ago, and this wine was served to her."

"In that case," returned the Count, "I also shall fall back on history, and first order brimming tankards of old Caub. Really, Madam," he said, turning to Hildegunde, "we should have had Royalty here to meet you, instead of two old wine-bibbers like his Highness and myself."

The girl looked startled at this mention of Royalty, bringing to her mind the turbulent events of yesterday. Nevertheless, with great composure, she smiled at her enthusiastic host.

"Still," went on the Count, "if we are not royal ourselves, 'tis a degree we are empowered to confer, and, indeed, may be very shortly called upon to bestow. That is true from what I hear, is it not, your Highness?"

"Yes," replied the Archbishop gravely.

"Well, as I was about to say, this Castle belonged to the Falkensteins, and was sold by them to the Palatinate. Rumor, legend, history, call it what you like, asserts that the most beautiful woman ever born on the Rhine was Countess Beatrice of Falkenstein. But when I drink to the toast I am about to offer I shall, Madam," he smiled at Hildegunde, "assert that the legend no longer holds, a contention I am prepared to maintain by mortal combat. Know then that the Earl of Cornwall, who was elected King of Germany in 1257, met Beatrice of Falkenstein in this Castle. The meeting was brought about by the Electors themselves, who, stupid matchmakers, attempted to coerce each into a marriage with the other. Beatrice refused to marry a foreigner.

"The Chronicles are a little vague about the most interesting part of the negotiations, but minutely plain about the outcome. In some manner the Earl and Beatrice met, and he became instantly enamored of her. This is the portion so deplorably slurred by these old monkish writers. I need hardly tell you that the Earl himself succeeded where the seven Electors failed. Beatrice became Cornwall's wife and Queen of Germany, and they lived happily ever afterwards.

"I give you the toast!" cried the chivalrous Count Palatine, rising. "To the cherished memory of the Royal lovers of Gutenfels!"

The Archbishop's eyes twinkled as he looked across the table at Hildegunde.

"This seems to be a time of Royal betrothals," he said, raising his flagon.

"'Seems' is the right word, Guardian," replied the Countess.

Then she sipped the ancient wine of Caub.

Next morning Hildegunde was early afoot. Notwithstanding her trouble of mind, she had slept well, and awakened with the birds, so great is the influence of youth and health. During her last conscious moments the night before, as she lay in the stately bed of the most noble room the Castle contained, she bitterly accused herself for the disastrous failure of the previous day. The Archbishop of Cologne had given her good counsel that was not followed, and his disappointment with the result, generously as he endeavored to conceal it, was doubtless the deeper because undiscussed. Thinking of coming captivity, a dream of grim Pfalz was expected, but instead the girl's spirit wandered through the sweet seclusion of Nonnenwerth, living again that happy, earlier time, free from politics and the tramp of armed men.

In the morning the porter, at her behest, withdrew bolt, bar, and chain, allowing exit into the fresh, cool air, and skirting the Castle, she arrived at a broad terrace which fronted it. A fleecy mist extending from shore to shore concealed the waters of the Rhine, and partially obliterated the little village of Caub at the foot of the hill. Where she stood the air was crystal clear, and she seemed to be looking out on a broad snow-field of purest white. Beyond Caub its surface was pierced by the dozen sharp pinnacles of her future prison, looking like a bed of spikes, upon which one might imagine a giant martyr impaled by the verdict of a cruel Archbishop.

Gazing upon this nightmare Castle, whose tusks alone were revealed, the girl formulated the resolution but faintly suggested the night before. On her release should ensue an abandonment of the world, and the adoption of a nun's veil in the convent opposite Drachenfels, an island exchanged for an island; turmoil for peace.

At breakfast she met again the jovial Count Palatine, and her more sober guardian, who both complimented her on the results of her beauty rest, the one with great gallantry, the other with more reserve, as befitted a Churchman. The Archbishop seemed old and haggard in the morning light, and it was not difficult to guess that no beauty sleep had soothed his pillow. It wrung the girl's heart to look at him, and again she accused herself for lack of all tact and discretion, wishing that her guardian took his disappointment more vengefully, setting her to some detested task that she might willingly perform.

The hospitable Count, eager that they should stop at least another night under his roof, pressed his invitation upon them, and the Archbishop gave a tacit consent.

"If the Countess is not too tired," said Cologne, "I propose that she accompany me on a little journey I have in view farther up the river. We will return here in the evening."

"I should be delighted," cried Hildegunde, "for all sense of fatigue has been swept away by a most restful night."

The good-natured Count left them to their own devices, and shortly afterwards guardian and ward rode together down the steep declivity to the river. The mist was already driven away, except a wisp here and there clinging to the gray surface of the water, trailing along as if drawn by the current, for the air was motionless, and there was promise of a sultry day. They proceeded in silence until a bend in the Rhine shut Caub and its sinister water-prison out of sight, and then it was the girl who spoke.

"Guardian," she said, "have I offended you beyond forgiveness?"

A gentle smile came to his lips as he gazed upon her with affection.

"You have not offended me at all, my dear," he said, "but I am grieved at thwarting circumstance."

"I have been thinking over circumstances too, and hold myself solely to blame for their baffling opposition. I will submit without demur to whatever length of imprisonment may please, and, if possible, soften the Archbishop of Mayence. After my release I shall ask your consent that I may forthwith join the Sisterhood at Nonnenwerth. I wish to divide my wealth equally between yourself and the convent."

The Archbishop shook his head.

"I could not accept such donation."

"Why not? The former Archbishop of Cologne accepted Linz from my ancestress Matilda."

"That was intended to be but a temporary loan."

"Well; call my benefaction temporary if you like, to be kept until I call for it, but meanwhile to be used at your discretion."

"It is quite impossible," said the Archbishop firmly.

"Does that mean you will not allow me to adopt the religious life?"

"It means, my child, that I should not feel justified in permitting this renunciation of the world until you knew more of what you were giving up."

"I know enough already."

"You think so, but your experience of it is too recent for us to expect unbiased judgment this morning. I should insist on a year, at least, and preferably two years, part of that time to be spent in Frankfort and in Cologne. I anticipate a great improvement in Frankfort when the new Emperor comes to the throne. If at the end of two years you are still of the same mind, I shall offer no further opposition."

"I shall never change my intention."

"Perhaps not. I am told that the determination of a woman is irrevocable, so a little delay does not much matter. Meanwhile, another problem passes my comprehension. I have thought and thought about it, and am convinced there is a misunderstanding somewhere, which possibly will be cleared away too late. I am quite certain that Father Ambrose did not meet Prince Roland in Frankfort."

"Do you, then, dispute the word of Father Ambrose?" asked the girl, quickly checking the accent of indignation that arose in her voice, for humility was to be her rôle ever after.

"Father Ambrose is at once both the gentlest and most truthful of men. He has undoubtedly seen somebody rob a merchant in Frankfort. He has undoubtedly been imprisoned among wine-casks; but that this thief and this jailer was Roland is incredible to me who know the young man, and physically impossible, for Prince Roland at that time was himself a prisoner, as, indeed, he is to-day. Prince Roland cannot be liberated from Ehrenfels without an order signed by Mayence, Treves, and myself. I alone have not the power to encompass his freedom, and Mayence is equally powerless although he is owner of the Castle. Some scoundrel is walking the streets of Frankfort pretending to be Roland."

"In that case, my Lord, he would not deny his identity when accosted on the bridge."

"A very clever point, my dear, but it does not overcome my difficulty.

There might be a dozen reasons why the rascal would not incriminate himself to any stranger who thus took him by surprise. However, it is useless to argue the question, for I persuade you as little as you persuade me. The practical thing is to fathom the misunderstanding, and remove it. Will you assist me in this?"

"Willingly, if I can, Guardian."

"Very well. I must first inform you that your imprisonment is likely to be very short. You are to know that the harmony supposed to exist in Stolzenfels is largely mythical: I left behind me the seeds of discord. I proposed that the glum niece of Treves, whom you met at our historic lunch, should be the future Empress. This nomination was seconded by Mayence himself, and received with unconcealed joy by my brother of Treves."

"Then for once the Court was unanimous? I think your choice an admirable one."

"The Archbishop of Mayence does not agree with you, my dear."

"Then why did he second your nomination?"

"Because he is so much more clever than Treves, who a few minutes later would have been the seconder."

"Why should his Lordship of Mayence think one thing and act another?"

"Why is he always doing it? No one can guess what Mayence really thinks, if he is judged by what he says. Were Treves' niece to become Empress, her uncle would speedily realize his power, and Mayence would lose his leadership. Could Mayence to-day secretly promote you to the position of Empress, he would gladly do so."

"But won't he at once look for some one else?"

"Certainly. That choice is now occupying his mind. His seconding of the nomination was merely a ruse to gain time, but if he proposes any one else he will find both Treves and myself against him. His only hope of circumventing the ambition of Treves is that something may happen, causing you to change your mind concerning Prince Roland."

"You forget, Guardian," protested the girl, "that his Lordship of Mayence said he would not permit me to marry Prince Roland after the way I had spoken and acted."

"He said that, my dear, under the influence of great resentment against you, but Mayence never allows resentment or any other feeling to stand in the way of his own interests. If you wrote him a contrite letter regretting your defiance of him, and expressing your willingness to bow to his wishes, I am very sure he would welcome the communication as a happy solution of the quandary in which he finds himself."

"You wish me to do this, Guardian?" she asked wistfully.

"Not until you are satisfied that Prince Roland is innocent of the charges you make against him."

"How can I receive such assurance?"

"Ah, now you come to the object of this apparently purposeless journey. I have had much experience in the world you are so anxious to renounce, and although I have seen the wicked prosper for a time, yet my faith has never been shaken in an overruling Providence, and what happened last night set me thinking so deeply that daylight stole in upon my meditations."

"Oh, my poor Guardian, I knew you had not slept, and all because of a worthless creature like myself, and a wicked creature, too, for I did not see the hand of Providence so visible to you."

"Surely, my dear, a moment's thought would reveal it to you. Remember how we came almost to the door of the prison, when a temporary reprieve was handed to us by that coarse reprobate, the Pfalzgraf. Your suite of rooms was not yet ready, and thus we found bestowed upon us another free day; a day of untrammeled liberty, quite unlooked for. Now, much may be done in a day. An Empire has been lost and won within a few hours. With this gift came a revelation. That wine-blotched Pfalzgraf would have shown no consideration for you: to him a prisoner is a prisoner, to be cast anywhere, lock the door, and have done, but a wholesome fear had been instilled into him by his overlord. The Archbishop of Mayence had taken thought for your comfort, ordering that the best rooms in the Castle should be placed at your disposal. Hence, after all that had passed, his Lordship felt no malignancy against you, and I dare say would have been glad to rescind the order for your imprisonment, were it not that he would never admit defeat."

"Oh, Guardian, what an imagination is yours! I am sure his Lordship of Mayence will never forgive me."

"His Lordship of Mayence, my dear, is in a dilemma from which no one except yourself can extricate him."

"His own cleverness will extricate him."

"Perhaps. Still, I'm not troubling about him. My thoughts are much too selfish for that. I wish you to lift me from my uncertainty."

"You mean about Prince Roland? I shall do whatever you ask of me."

"I place no command, but I proffer a suggestion."

"It shall be a command, nevertheless."

"We have left your own prison far behind, and are approaching that of Prince Roland. To the door of that detaining Castle I propose to lead you. I am forbidden by my compact with the other Electors to see Prince Roland or to hold any communication with him. The custodian of the Castle, who knows me well, will not refuse any request I make, even if I ask to see the young man himself. He will therefore not hesitate to admit you when I require him to do so. To take away any taint of surreptitiousness about my action, interfering, as one might say, with another man's house, I shall this evening write to the Archbishop of Mayence, tell him exactly what I have done, and why."

"Do you intend, then, that I should see Prince Roland and talk with him?"

"Yes."

"My dear Guardian!" cried the girl, her face flushing red, "what on earth can I say to him? How am I to excuse my intrusion?"

"A prisoner, I fancy, does not resent intrusion, especially if the intruder is—" The old man smiled as he looked at the girl, whose blush grew deeper and deeper; then, seeing her confusion, he added: "There are many things to say. Introduce yourself as the ward of his Lordship of Cologne; reveal that your guardian has confided to you that Prince Roland is to be the future Emperor; ask for some assurance from him that the property descending to you from your ancestors shall not be molested; or perhaps, better still, with the same introduction, tell him the story of Father Ambrose. Add that this has disquieted you: demand the truth, hearken to what the youth says for himself, thank him, and withdraw. It needs no long conversation, though I am prepared to hear that he wished to lengthen your stay. I am certain that five minutes face to face with him will completely overturn all Father Ambrose has said to his disparagement, and a few simple words from him will probably dispel the whole mystery. If someone is personating him in Frankfort it is more than likely he knows who it is."

They traveled a generous furlong together in silence, the girl's head bowed and her brow troubled. At last, as if with an effort, she cleared doubt away, and raised her head.

"I will do it," she said decisively.

The Archbishop heaved a deep sigh of relief. He knew now he was out of the wood.

"Is this Assmannshausen we are coming to?" she asked, as if to hint that the subject on which they had talked so earnestly was finally done with.

"No; this is Lorch, and that is the Castle of Nollich standing above it."

"I hope," said the girl, with a sigh of weariness, "that no English Princess about to marry an Emperor lodged there, or no Englishman who was to become an Emperor—"

The Archbishop interrupted the plaint with a hearty laugh, the first he had enjoyed for several days.

"The English seem an interfering race," she went on. "I wish they would attend to their own affairs."

"Nollich is uncontaminated," said the Archbishop, "though in olden days a reckless knight on horseback rode up to secure his lady-love, and I believe rode down again with her, and his route is still called the Devil's Ladder."

"Did the marriage turn out so badly?"

"No; I believe they lived happily ever after; but the ascent was so cliff-like that mountain sprites are supposed to have given their assistance."

"How much farther is Assmannshausen?"

"Less than two leagues. We will stop there and refresh ourselves. Are you tired?"

"Oh no; not in the least. I merely wish the ordeal was past."

"You are a brave girl, Hildegunde."

"I am anything but that, Guardian. Still, do not fear I shall flinch."

After partaking of the midday meal at Assmannshausen, the Countess proposed that they should leave their horses in the stable, and walk the short third of a league to Ehrenfels, and to this her guardian agreed.

He found more difficulty with the custodian than had been expected. The man objected, trembling. Without a written order from his master he dare not allow any one to visit the prisoner. He would be delighted to oblige his Lordship of Cologne, but he was merely a poor wretch who had no option in the matter.

"Very well," said Cologne. "I have just come from your master, who is stopping with my brother Treves at Stolzenfels. If you persist I must then request lodgings from you until such time as a speedy messenger can bring your master hither. This journey may cause him great inconvenience, and should such be the case, I fear you will fare ill with him."

"That may be, my Lord, but I must do my duty."

"Are you sure you have already done it on all occasions?" asked the Archbishop severely.

The man's face became ghastly in its pallor.

"I don't know what you mean, my Lord."

"Then I will quickly tell you what I mean. It is rumored that Prince Roland has been seen on the streets of Frankfort."

"How—how could that be, my Lord?"

"That is exactly what I wish to know. I believe the Prince is not in your custody."

"I assure you, my Lord," said the now thoroughly frightened man, "that his Highness is in his room."

"Very well; then conduct this lady thither. Although she does not know the Prince, a relative of hers who does asserts that he met his Highness in Frankfort. I said this was impossible if you had done that duty you prate so much about. The lady merely wishes to ask him for some explanation of this affair, so make your choice. Shall she go up with you now, or must I send for the other two Archbishops?"

There was but one comforting phrase in this remark, namely, that the lady did not know the Prince. Still, it was a dreadful risk, yet the custodian hesitated no longer. He took down a bunch of keys, and asked the Countess to follow him. Ascending the stair, he unlocked the door, and stood aside for the Countess to pass through.

Some one with wildly tousled hair sat sprawling in a chair; arms on the table, and head sunk forward down upon them. A full tankard of wine within his reach, and a flagon had been overset, sluicing the table with its contents, which still fell drip, drip, drip, to the floor.

The young man raised his head, aroused by the harsh unlocking of the door, and with the crash it made as his father flung it hard against the stone wall for the purpose of giving him warning, but the youth was in no condition to profit by this thoughtfulness, nor to understand the signals his father made from behind the frightened girl. He clutched wildly at the overturned flagon, and with an oath cried:

"Bring me more wine, you old—"

Staggering to his feet, he threw the flagon wide, then slipped on the spilled wine and fell heavily to the floor, roaring defiance at the world.

The panic-stricken girl shrank back, crying to the jailer:

"Let me out! Close the door quickly, and lock it!" an order obeyed with alacrity.

When Hildegunde emerged to the court her guardian asked no question. The horror in her face told all.

"I am sorry, my Lord," said the cringing custodian, "but his Highness is drunk."

"Does this—does this happen often?"

"Alas! yes, my Lord."

"Poor lad, poor lad! The sins of the fathers shall be visited on the children to the third and fourth generation. Hildegunde, forgive me. Let us away and forget it all."

The next morning the Countess began her imprisonment in Pfalz.

XV. JOURNEYS END IN LOVERS' MEETING

Roland slept until the sun was about an hour high over the western hills. He found the captain waiting patiently for him to awake, and then that useful martinet instantly set his crew at tying up the bales which had been torn open, placing them once more in the hold. He was about to do the same with the weapons captured from Furstenberg, but Greusel stepped forward, and asked him to put pikes, battle-axes, and the long swords into the cabin.

Roland nodded his approval, saying:

"They may prove useful instruments in case of an attack on the barge. Our own swords are just a trifle short for adding interest to an assault."

When once more the hatches were down, and the deck clear, supper was served. Shortly after sunset, Roland told the captain to cast off, directing him to keep to the eastern shore, passing between what might be called the marine Castle of Pfalz and the village of Caub, with the strictest silence he could enjoin upon his crew. Pfalz stands upon a rock in the Rhine, a short distance up the river from Caub, while above that village on the hill behind are situated the strong, square towers of Gutenfels.

"Don't you intend to pay a call upon Pfalzgrafenstein?" asked Ebearhard. "It is notoriously the most pestilent robber's nest between Mayence and Cologne."

"No," said Roland. "On this occasion Pfalz shall escape. You see, Ebearhard, on our first trip down the Rhine it is not my intention to fight if I can avoid conflict. The plan which proved successful with the four castles we have visited is impossible so far as Pfalz is concerned. If we attempted to enter this waterschloss by stealth, we would be discovered by those levying contributions on the barge. There is no cover to conceal us, so I shall give Pfalz the go-by, and also Gutenfels, because the latter is not a robber castle, but is owned by the Count Palatine, a true gentleman and no thief. The next object of our attentions will be Schonburg, on the western side of the river, near Oberwesel."

As the grotesque, hexagonal bulk of the Pfalz, with its numerous jutting corners and turrets, and over all the pentagonal tower, appeared dimly in the center of the Rhine, under the clear stars, the captain ordered his men to lie flat on the deck, himself following their example. Roland and his company were already seated in the cabin, and the great barge, lying so low in the water as to be almost invisible with its black paint, floated noiseless as a dream down the swift current.

Without the slightest warning came a shock, and every man on the lockers was flung to the floor of the cabin, with cries of dismay, for too well they recognized the preliminary to their disasters of the night before. Roland sprang up on deck, and found the boat swinging round broadside to the current, which had swept it so near to the Castle that at first it seemed to have struck against one of the outlying rocks. The fantastic form of the Pfalz hung over them, looking like some weird building seen in a nightmare, its sharp, pointed pinnacles outlined against the starlit sky.

The captain, muttering sonorous German oaths, ordered his men to the sweeps, but Roland saw at once that they were too close to the ledge of rock for any chance of escape. He hurried down into the cabin.

"Every man his sword, and follow me as silently as possible!"

Up on deck again, Roland said to the captain:

"Let your rowers help the chain to bring the barge alongside, but when the robbers appear, pretend to be getting away, although you must instantly obey them when ordered to cease your efforts."

The prow of the boat ground against the solid rock, jammed in between the stout chain and the low cliff. Roland was the first to spring ashore, and the rest nimbly followed him. With every motion of the barge the bell inside the Castle rang, and now they could hear the bestirring of the garrison, and clashing of metal, although the single door of the Pfalz had not yet been opened. This door stood six feet above the plateau of rock, and could be entered or quitted only by means of a ladder.

Roland led his men to a place of effective concealment along the western wall of the Pfalz, only just in time, for as he peered round the corner, his men standing back against the wall to the rear, he saw the flash of torches from the now-open door, and the placing of a stout ladder at a steep angle between the threshold and the floor of rock below. Most of the garrison, however, did not wait for this convenience, but leaped impetuously from doorway to rock. Others slid down the ladder, and all rushed headlong towards the barge, which made its presence known by the grinding of its side against the rock, and also by the despairing orders of the captain, and the hurrying footsteps of his men on deck.

More leisurely down the ladder came two officers, followed by one whom Roland recognized as lord of the Castle, Pfalzgraf Hermann von Stahleck, a namesake and relative of the Laughing Baron of Furstenberg, and quite as ruthless a robber as he.

"Cease your efforts at the prow," shouted the Pfalzgraf to the captain when he had descended the ladder, "and concentrate your force at the stern, swinging your boat round broadside on to the landing."

The captain obeyed, and presently the boat lay in such position as the nobleman desired. Now there was a great commotion as, at a word from the Pfalzgraf, the garrison fell on the barge, and began to wrench off the hatches, a task which they well knew how to perform.

"Follow as quietly as possible," whispered Roland to the two lieutenants behind him, who, under their breath, passed on word to the men. Roland ran nimbly up the ladder. No guard was set where none had ever been needed before. Greusel was the last to ascend, then the ladder was pulled up, and the massive door swung shut, bolted and chained.

The invaders found torches stuck here and there along the wall, and the picturesque courtyard, with its irregular balconies and stairways, seemed, in the flickering light, more spacious than was actually the case.

Although for the moment in safety, Roland experienced a sense of imprisonment as he gazed round the narrow limits of this enclosure. He had endeavored to count the number of men who followed the Pfalzgraf, but their impetuosity in seeking the barge prevented an accurate estimate, although he knew there were more than double the force that obeyed him, and therefore it would be suicidal to lead his untrained coterie against the seasoned warriors of Stahleck.

He ordered Greusel to take with him six men, and search the Castle, bringing into the courtyard whomsoever they might find; also to discover whether any window existed that looked out upon the eastern landing-place. The remainder of his men he grouped at the door, under command of Ebearhard.

"I fear, Ebearhard," he said, "that I boasted prematurely in thinking good luck would attend me now that I lead what appears to be an obedient following. Here we are in a trap, and unless we can escape through rat-holes, I admit that I fail to see for the moment how we are to get safely afloat again."

"We are in better fettle than the Pfalzgraf and his men outside," returned Ebearhard, "because this fortress is doubtless well supplied with provisions, and is considered impregnable, while the Pfalzgraf's impetuous chaps, who did not know enough to stay in comfortable quarters when they had them, are without shelter and without food. You have certainly done the best you could in the circumstances, and for those circumstances you are free of blame, since, not being a wizard, you could scarcely know of the chain."

"Indeed, Ebearhard, it is just in that respect I blame myself, neglecting your own good example, who discovered the chain at Furstenberg. This trap is a new invention, and, so far as I know, has never before been attempted on the Rhine. I might have remembered that Stahleck here is cousin to the Red Margrave, who likely has told him of the device. Indeed, the chances are that Stahleck himself was the contriver of the chain, for he seems a man of much more craft and intelligence than that huge, laughing animal farther up the river. I should have ordered the captain to tie up against the eastern bank, and then sent some men in a small boat to learn if the way was clear. No, Ebearhard, I blame myself for this muddle, and, through anxiety to pass the Pfalz, I have landed myself and my men within its walls. I must pace this courtyard for a time, and ponder what next to do. Go you, Ebearhard, with the men to the door. Allow no talking or noise. Listen intently, and report to me if you hear anything. You see, Ebearhard, the devil of it is that Stahleck, like his cousin with Cologne, swears allegiance to the Archbishop of Mayence, and here am I, after destroying the fief of one Archbishop, securely snared in the fief of another. I fear their Lordships' next meeting with me will not pass off so amicably as did the last."

"Next meeting?" cried Ebearhard in astonishment; "have you ever met the Archbishops?"

Roland gasped, realizing that his absorption in one subject had nearly caused him to betray his momentous secret.

"Ah, I remember," continued Ebearhard. "It was on account of the Archbishop's presence in Bonn that you returned from that town when first you journeyed up the Rhine."

"Yes," said Roland, with relief.

"It seems to me," went on Ebearhard consolingly, "that even if we may not leave the Castle, at least the Pfalzgraf cannot penetrate into the stronghold, therefore we are safe enough."

"Not so, Ebearhard," replied his chief. "The Pfalzgraf has the barge, remember, and it can carry his whole force to Caub or elsewhere, returning with ample provisions and siege instruments that will batter in the door despite all we can do. Nevertheless, let us keep up our hearts. Get you to the gate, Ebearhard. I must have time to think before Greusel returns."

Alone, with bent head, he paced back and forwards across the courtyard under the wavering light of the torches. Very speedily he concluded that no plan could be formed until Greusel made his report regarding the intricacies of the Castle.

"My luck is against me! My luck is against me!" he said aloud to himself, as if the sound of his own voice might suggest some way out of the difficulty.

"Luck always turns against a thief and a marauder," said a sweet and

257

clear voice behind him; "and how can it be otherwise, when the gallows-tree stands at the end of his journey."

Roland stopped in his walk, and turned abruptly towards the sound. He saw standing there, just descended from the stairway at her back, one quite evidently a lady; not more than eighteen, perhaps, but nevertheless with a flash of defiance in her somber eyes, which were bent fearlessly upon him. The two tirewomen accompanying her shrank timorously to the background, palpably panic-stricken, and ready to faint with fright.

"Ah, Madam, how came you here?" cried Roland, ignoring her insulting words, too much surprised by her beauty of face and form to think of aught else.

"I came here, because your bully upstairs hammered at my door and bade me open, which I would not do, defying him to break it down if he had the power. It so happened that he possessed the power, and used it."

"I deeply regret that you should have been disturbed, Madam. My lieutenant erred through over-zeal, and I ask your pardon for the offense."

The girl laughed.

"Why, sir, you are the politest of pirates, but, indeed, your lieutenant seems a harsh man. Without even removing his bonnet, he commanded me to betake myself to the courtyard and report to his chief, which obediently I have done."

"I did not guess that women inhabited this robber's nest. My lieutenant is searching for men in hiding, so please accept my assurance that you will suffer no further annoyance. You are surely not alone in this house?"

"Oh no. Her ladyship the Pfalzgraf's wife, and her entourage, have sought shelter in another part of the Castle, and presently they will all troop down here, prisoners to your most ungallant subordinate; that is, should their doors prove no stouter than mine, or if your furious men have not dislocated their shoulders."

"How came you to be absent from her ladyship's party?"

"Because, urbane pirate captain, I am an unwilling prisoner in this stronghold, being an obstreperous person, who refused to obey my superiors; those set in authority over me. Consequently am I immured in this dismal dungeon of the water-rats, and thus, youthful pirate, I welcome even so red-handed an outlaw as yourself."

"Then are we in like case, my lady of midnight beauty, for I, too, am a prisoner in Pfalzgrafenstein, and, when you came, was cogitating some plan of escape. Therefore, rebellious maiden, the sword of this red-handed freebooter is most completely at your service," and the speaker once more doffed his bonnet with a gallant sweep that caused the plume to kiss the flagstones at his feet, and he bowed low to the brave girl who had shown no fear of him.

XVI. MY LADY SCATTERS THE FREEBOOTERS AND CAPTURES THEIR CHIEF

Greusel appeared on one of the balconies, and called down to his leader.

"There are," he said, "a number of women in the western rooms of the Castle. They have bolted their doors, but tell me that the rooms contain the Pfalzgravine von Stahleck and other noble ladies, with their tirewomen. What am I to do?"

"Place a guard in the corridor, Greusel, to make sure that these ladies communicate with no one outside the fortress."

"I thought it well," explained Greusel, "not to break in the doors without definite instructions from you to that effect."

"Quite right. Tell the ladies we will not molest them."

"You molested me!" cried the handsome girl in the courtyard, her dark eyes flashing in the glow of the torches.

"This person," said the unemotional Greusel, betraying no eye for beauty, "called us every uncomplimentary name she could think of. We were the scum of the earth, according to her account."

The girl laughed scornfully.

"But I would not have dislodged her," continued Greusel, unperturbed, "had she not said there was a window in her room, which is on the eastern side of the Castle, overlooking the operations of the Pfalzgraf on the barge, and she proclaimed her determination to warn Stahleck that his Castle was filled with freebooters, as soon as she could make her voice heard above the din at the landing. Therefore I broke in the door, ordering her and the tirewomen to descend to the courtyard. On examining her room I find there is no such window as she described, and she could not communicate with the Count, so I advise that you send her back again."

Once more the young lady laughed, and exclaimed:

"I could not break down the door for myself, so compelled you and your clods to do it. I am immured here; a reluctant captive. You will not have me sent back to my cell, I hope, Commander?"

"No; if you are really my fellow-prisoner, and not one of the enemy."

"She may be deluding you also," warned Greusel.

"I will take the risk of that," replied Roland, smiling at the girl, who smiled back at him. She had a will of her own, but seemed sensitively responsive to fair treatment.

"Are there any men-servants?" asked Roland.

"Only three, and they are tottering with age," replied Greusel, "more frightened than the women themselves. Nevertheless, one of the retainers is important, being, as he told me, keeper of the treasure-house. I relieved him of his keys, and find that the strong-room is well supplied with bags of gold. 'Twill be the richest haul yet, excepting our two barrels of coin from—"

"Hush, hush!" cried Roland. "Mention no names. Did you discover any other exit excepting the door by which we entered?"

"No; but at the northern end there is a window through which a man of ordinary size might pass. It is, however, high above the rocks, and I discern floating in the tide a fleet of small boats."

"Ah," said Roland, "that is important."

"Taken in conjunction with the gold, most amiable robber," suggested the girl.

"Taken in conjunction with the gold," repeated Roland, smiling again; and adding, "Taken also in conjunction with a lady who, if I understand her, wishes to escape from the Pfalz."

"You are right," agreed the young girl archly. "Do I receive a share of the money?"

"Yes; if you join our band."

"Oh!" she cried, with a pout of feigned disappointment, "I thought you had already accepted me as a member. And what am I to call my new overlord, who acquires wealth so successfully that he does not wish the amount mentioned, or the place from which it was taken specified?"

"My name is Roland. Will you consent to a fair exchange?"

"I am called Hilda by my friends."

"Then, Hilda," said the young man, looking at her with admiration, "I welcome you as one of my lieutenants."

"One, indeed!" she exclaimed, with affected indignation. "I shall be first lieutenant or nothing."

"Up to this moment Herr Joseph Greusel, who so unceremoniously made your acquaintance, has been my chief lieutenant, but I willingly depose him, and give you his place."

"Do you hear that, Joseph?" Hilda called up to the man leaning over the balcony.

The deposed one made a grimace, but no reply.

"Set your guard, and come down, Greusel."

Presently Greusel appeared in the courtyard, followed by four men.

"I have left two on guard," he said.

"Right. What have you done with the servants?"

"Tied them up in a hard knot. I found a loft full of ropes."

"Right again. Take your four men, and stand guard at the door. Send Ebearhard to me."

Before Ebearhard arrived, Roland turned to the girl.

"Retire to your room," he said, "and bid your women gather together whatever you wish to carry with you."

"I'd rather stay where I am," protested Hilda, "being anxious to hear what your plans are. I confess I don't know how you can emerge from this Castle in safety."

"Fräulein Hilda, the first duty of a chief lieutenant is obedience."

"Refusing that, what will you do?"

"I shall call two of my men, cause you to be transported to your room, and order them to see that you do not leave it again."

"Remaining here when you have departed?"

"That, of course."

"You will take the gold, however."

"Certainly; the gold obeys me; doing what I ask of it."

For a few moments the girl stood there, gazing defiance at him, but although a slight smile hovered about his lips, she realized in some subtle way—woman's intuition, perhaps—that he meant what he said. Her eyes lowered, and an expression of pique came into her pretty face; then she breathed a long sigh.

"I shall go to my room," she said very quietly.

"I will call upon you the moment I have given some instructions to my third lieutenant."

"You need not trouble," she replied haughtily, speaking, however, as mildly as himself. "I remain a prisoner of the Pfalzgraf von Stahleck, who, though a distinguished pillager like yourself, nevertheless possesses some instincts of a gentleman."

With that, the young woman retired slowly up the stairway, and disappeared, followed by her two servants.

"Ebearhard," said Roland, when that official appeared, "Greusel has discovered a window to the north through which yourself and a number of your men can get down to the rocks with the aid of a cord, and he tells me there is a loft full of ropes. A flotilla of boats is tied up at the lower end of the Castle. He has visited the treasury, and finds it well supplied with bags of coin. I intend to effect a junction between those bags and that flotilla. Our position here is quite untenable, for there is probably some secret entrance to this Castle that we know nothing of. There are also a number of women within whom we cannot coerce, and must not starve. Truth to tell, I fear them more than I do the ruffians outside. Have any of the men-at-arms discovered that we pulled up the ladder and closed the door?"

"I think not, for in such case they would return from their pillages as quickly as did the Red Margrave when he found his house was ablaze. My opinion is that they are making a clean job of looting the barge."

"If that is so, our barrels of gold are gone, rendering it the more necessary that we should carry away every kreuzer our friend Stahleck possesses. Call, therefore, every man except one from the door. Greusel has the keys, and will lead you to the treasury. Hoist the bags to the north window. While your men are doing this, rive a stout rope so that you may all speedily descend to the rocks, except as many as are necessary to lower the bags. When this is accomplished, Greusel is to report to me from the balcony, and then descend, taking with him the man on guard at the door. Apportion men and bags in all the boats but one. That one I shall take charge of. Put Greusel in command of the flotilla, and tell him to convey his fleet as quietly as possible to the eastern shore; then paddle up in slack water until he is, say, a third of a league above Pfalz. There he must await my skiff. You will stand by that skiff until I join you. I shall likely be accompanied by three women, so retain the largest and most comfortable of the small boats."

Ebearhard raised his eyebrows at the mention of the women, but said nothing.

Roland went in person to the room occupied by the young woman, and knocked at her door, whereupon it was opened very promptly.

"Madam," he said, "there is opportunity for escape if you care to avail yourself of it."

The girl had been seated when he entered, but now she rose, speaking in a voice that was rather tremulous.

"Sir, I was wrong to disobey you when you had treated me so kindly. I shall therefore punish myself by remaining where I am."

"In that case, Madam, you will punish me as well; and, indeed, I deserve it, forgetting as I did for the moment that I addressed a lady. If you will give me the pleasure of escorting you, I shall conduct you in safety to whatever place of refuge you wish to reach."

"Sir, you are most courteous, but I fear my intended destination might take you farther afield than would be convenient for you."

"My time is my own, and nothing could afford me greater gratification than the assurance of your security. Tell me your destination."

"It is the Convent of Nonnenwerth, situated on an island larger than this, near Rolandseck."

"I shall be happy to convoy you thither."

"Again I thank you. It is my desire to join the Sisterhood there."

"Not to become a nun?" cried Roland, an intonation of disappointment in his voice.

"Yes; although to this determination my guardian is opposed."

"Alas," said Roland, with a sigh, "I confess myself in agreement with him so far as your taking the veil is concerned. Still, imprisonment seems an unduly harsh alternative."

The girl's seriousness fled, and she smiled at him.

"As you have had some experience of my obstinacy, and proposed an even harsher remedy than that—"

"Ah, you forget," interrupted Roland, "that I apologized for my lack of manners. I hope during our journey to Nonnenwerth I may earn complete forgiveness."

"Oh, you are forgiven already, which is magnanimous of me, when you recollect that the fault was wholly my own. I will join you in the courtyard at once if I may."

"Very well. I shall be down there after I have given final instructions to my men."

Roland arrived at the north window, and saw that the flotilla had already departed. He could discern Ebearhard standing with his hand on the prow of the remaining boat, so pulled up the rope, untied it from the ring to which it was fastened, and threw it down to his lieutenant.

"A rope is always useful," he whispered, "and we will puzzle the good Pfalzgraf regarding our exit."

In the courtyard he found the three women awaiting him. Quietly he drew back the heavy bolts, and undid the stout chains. Holding the door slightly ajar, he peered out at the scene on the landing, brightly illuminated by numerous torches which the servants held aloft.

The men-at-arms were enjoying themselves hugely, and the great heap of bales already on the rocks showed that they resolved not to leave even one package on the barge. The fact that they stood in the light prevented their seeing the exit of the quartette from the Castle, even had any been on the outlook.

Roland swung the door wide, placed the ladder in exactly the same position it had formerly occupied, assisted the three women to the ground, and then led them round the western side of the Castle through the darkness to Ebearhard and his skiff. Dipping their paddles with great caution, they kept well out of the torchlight radius.

As they left the shadow of the Castle, and came within sight of the party on the landing, they were somewhat startled by a lusty cheer.

"Ah," said Ebearhard, "they have discovered our barrels of gold."

"'Tis very likely," replied Roland.

"Still," added Ebearhard consolingly, "I think we have made a good exchange. There appears to be more money in Stahleck's bags than in our two barrels."

"By the Three Kings!" cried Roland, staring upstream, "the barge is getting away. They have looted her completely, and are giving her a parting salute. The robbers evidently bear no malice against our popular captain. Hear them inviting him to call again!"

They listened to the rattle of the big chain. It was more amenable than that at Furstenberg, confirming Roland in his belief that Stahleck was the inventor of the device. They saw half a dozen men paying out a rope, while the first section of the chain sank, leaving a passage-way for the barge. Silhouetted against the torchlight, the boatmen were getting ready with their sweeps, prepared to dip them into the water as soon as the vessel got clear of the rocky island.

"We will paddle alongside before they begin to row," said Roland; and Captain Blumenfels was gently hailed from the river, much to his astonishment.

"Make for the eastern bank, captain," whispered Roland, "and keep a lookout ahead for a number of small boats like this."

Presently, rowing up the river strenuously, close to the shore, the barge came upon the flotilla. Here Roland bade Hilda remain where she was, and leaving Ebearhard in charge of the skiff, he clambered up on the barge, ordering Greusel to range his boats alongside and fling aboard the treasure.

"Well, captain, did his Excellency of Pfalz leave you anything at all?"

"Not a rag," replied the captain. "The barge is empty as a drum."

"In that case there is nothing for it but a speedy return to Frankfort. I do not regret the cloth, which has been paid for over and over again, but I am mercenary enough to grudge Stahleck our two barrels of gold."

"Oh, as to the gold," replied the captain gravely, "I took the liberty of reversing your plan at Lorch."

"What plan?"

"Your honor poured gold into wine barrels, but I poured the red wine of Lorch into the gold barrels, and threw the empty cask overboard. Perhaps you know that the Pfalzgraf grows excellent white wine round his Castle of Stahleck, and despises the red wine of Lorch and Assmannshausen. He tasted the wine, which had not been improved by being poured into the dirty gold barrels, spat it out with an oath, and said we were welcome to keep it. He has also promised to send me a cask of good white wine to Frankfort."

"Captain, despite your quiet, unassuming manner, you are the most ingenious of men."

"Indeed, I but copied your honor's ingenuity."

"However it happened, you saved the gold, and that action alone will make a rich man of you, for you must accept my third share of the money."

By this time the bags had been heaved aboard. Greusel followed them, and stood ready to receive further orders.

"You will all make for Frankfort," said Roland, "keeping close as possible to this side of the river. No man is to be allowed ashore until you reach the capital. Captain, are there provisions enough aboard for the voyage?"

"Yes, your honor."

"Very well. Put every available person at the oars, and get past Furstenberg before daybreak. My men, who have not had an opportunity to distinguish themselves as warriors, will take their turn at the sweeps. You and Ebearhard," he continued, turning to Greusel, "will employ the time in counting the money and making a fair division. With regard to the two barrels, the captain will receive my third share, and also be one of us in the apportionment of the gold we secured to-night. It was through his thoughtfulness that the barrels were saved. Whatever portion you find me entitled to, place in the keeping of the merchant, Herr Goebel. And now I shall tie four bags to my belt for emergencies."

"Are you not coming with us, Roland?" asked Greusel anxiously.

"No. Urgent business requires my presence in the neighborhood of Bonn, but I shall meet you in the Kaiser cellar before a month is out."

Saying this, he shook hands with the captain and Greusel, and descended into the small boat, bidding farewell to Ebearhard.

"Urge them," were his last words, "to get well out of sight of Pfalz and Furstenberg before the day breaks, and as for the small boats, turn them loose; present them as a peace-offering to the Rhine."

In the darkness Prince Roland allowed his frail barque to float down the stream, using his paddle merely to keep it toward the east, so to avoid the chain. He found himself accompanied by a silent, spectral fleet; the empty boats that his men had sent adrift. To all appearance the little squadron lay motionless, while the dim Castle of Pfalz, with its score of pointed turrets piercing a less dark sky, seemed like a great ship moving slowly up the Rhine. When it had disappeared to the south, Roland ventured to speak, in a low voice.

"Madam," he said, "tell your women so to arrange what extra apparel you have brought to form a couch, where you may recline, and sleep for the rest of the night."

"Captain Roland," she replied, her gentle little laugh floating with so musical a cadence athwart the waters that he found himself regretting such a sweet voice should be kept from the world by the unappreciative walls of a convent,—"Captain Roland, I was never more awake than I am at this moment. Life has somehow become unexpectedly interesting. I experience the deliciously guilty feeling of belonging to a stealthy society of banditti. Do not, I beg of you, deprive me of that pleasure by asking me to sleep."

"In the morning, Madam, there will be little opportunity for rest. We must put all the distance we can between ourselves and the Pfalzgraf von Stahleck. I expect you to ride far and fast to-morrow."

"Do you intend, then, to abandon this boat?"

"I must, Madam. The river has been long so empty that this flotilla, which I cannot shake off, being unaccustomed to oars or paddle, will attract attention from both sides of the Rhine, and when the darkness lifts we are almost certain to be stopped. The boats will be recognized as belonging to the Pfalzgraf, and I wish to sever all connection between this night's work and my own future."

"What, then, do you propose?"

"As soon as day breaks we will come to land, and allow our boat to float away with the rest. Can you walk?"

"I love walking," cried the girl with enthusiasm. "I ask your pity for myself, immured in that windowless dungeon, situated on a tiny point of rock; I, who have roamed the hills and explored the valleys of my own land on foot, breathing the air of freedom with delight. Let me, therefore, I beg of you, remain awake that I may taste the pleasure of anticipation in my thoughts; or is such a wish disobedience on the part of your first lieutenant? I do not mean it so, and will quietly cry myself to sleep if you insist."

"Indeed, Hilda," said Roland, laughing, and abandoning the more formal title of "madam," "I am no such tyrant as you suppose. Besides, your office of first lieutenant has lapsed, because our men have all gone south, while we travel north."

"Then may I talk with you?"

"Nothing would please me better. I was thinking of your own welfare, and not of my desire, when I counseled slumber."

"Oh, I assure you I slept very well during the first part of the night, for, there being nothing else to do, I went to bed early, and was quite unconscious until the dreadful ringing of that alarm bell, which set the whole Castle astir."

"Why were you imprisoned?"

"Because—because," she replied haltingly, "I had chosen the religious life, the which my guardian opposed. He appeared to think that some experience of the rigors of the convent might make me less eager to immure myself in a nunnery, which, like Pfalz Castle, is also on a restricted island."

"Then his remedy has proved unavailing?"

"Quite. The Sisters will be very good to me, for I shall enrich their convent with my wealth. 'Twill be vastly different from incarceration in Pfalz."

"Hilda, I doubt that. Captivity is captivity, under whatever name you term it. I cannot understand why one who spoke so enthusiastically just now of hills and valleys and liberty should take the irrevocable step which you propose; a step that will rob you forever of those joys."

The girl remained silent, and he went on, speaking earnestly:

"I think in one respect you are like myself. You love the murmur of the trees, and the song of the running stream."

"I do, I do," she whispered, as if to herself.

"The air that blows around the mountain-top inspires you, and you cannot view the hills on the horizon without wishing to explore them, and learn what is on the other side."

There was light enough for him to see that the girl's head sank into her open hand.

"You, I take it, have never been restricted by discipline."

Her head came up quickly.

"You think that because of what I said in the courtyard?"

"No; my mind was running towards the future rather than to the past. The rigor of strict rules would prove as irksome to you as would a cage to a free bird of the forest."

"I fear you are in the right," she said with a sigh; and then, impatiently, "Oh, you do not understand the situation, and I cannot explain! The convent is merely a retreat for me; the lesser of two evils presented."

"You spoke of your land. Where is that land?"

"Do you know Schloss Sayn?" she asked.

"Sayn? Sayn?" he repeated. "Where have I heard that name before, and recently too? I thought I knew every castle on the Rhine, but I do not remember Sayn."

The girl laughed.

"You will find no fellow-craftsman there, Pirate Roland, if ever you visit it. The Schloss is not on the Rhine, and, perhaps on that account, rather than because of its owner's honesty, is free from the taint you suggest. It stands high in the valley of the Saynbach, more than half a league from this river."

"Ah, that accounts for my ignorance. I never saw Sayn Castle, although I seem to have heard of it. Are you its owner?"

"Yes; I told you I was wealthy."

"Where is the Schloss situated?"

"Below Coblentz, on the eastern side of the river."

"Then why not let me take you there instead of to the convent?"

"Willingly, if you had brought your barge-load of armed men, but in Sayn Castle I am helpless, commanding a peaceful retinue of servants who, although devoted to me, are useless when it comes to defense."

"I cannot account for it," said Roland in meditative tone, "but the thought of that convent becomes more and more distasteful. You will be free of your guardian, no doubt, but you merely exchange one whom you know for another whom you don't, and that other a member of your own sex."

"Do you disparage my sex, then?"

"No; but I cannot imagine any man being discourteous to you. Surely every gentleman with a sword by his side should spring at once to your defense."

The girl laughed.

"Ah, Captain Roland, you are very young, and, I fear, inexperienced, despite your filibustering. However, this lovely, still, summer night, with its warm, velvety darkness, was made for pleasant thoughts. Enough about myself. Let me hear something of you. Did you come up the river or down, with your barge?"

"We came down."

"How long since you adopted a career of crime? You do not seem to be a hardened villain."

"Believe me," protested Roland earnestly, "I am not, and I do not admit that my career is one of crime."

"Indeed," said the girl, laughing again, "I am not so gullible as you think. I could almost fancy that you were the incendiary of Furstenberg Castle."

"What!" exclaimed Roland in consternation. "How came you to learn of its destruction?"

"There!" cried the girl gleefully, "you have all but confessed. You are as startled as if I had said: 'I arrest you in the name of the Emperor!'"

"Who told you that Furstenberg Castle was burned?" demanded the young man sternly.

"Yesterday morning there came swiftly down the river, with no less than twelve oarsmen, a long, thin boat, traveling like the wind. It did not pause at Pfalz, but the man standing in the stern hailed the Castle, and shouted to the Pfalzgraf that Furstenberg had been burned by the outlaws of the Hunsruck. He was on his way to Bonn to inform the Archbishop of Cologne, and he carried also Imperial news for his Lordship: tidings that the Emperor is dead."

"Dead!" breathed Roland in horror, scarcely above his breath. "The Emperor dead! I wonder if that can be true."

"Little matter whether it is true or no," said the girl indifferently. "He doubtless passed away in a drunken sleep, and I am told his drunken son will be elected in his place."

"Madam!" said Roland harshly, awakened from his stupor by her words,

"I must inform your ignorance that the Emperor's son is not a drunkard, and, indeed, scarcely touches wine at all, being a most strenuous opposer to its misuse. How can one so fair, and, as I believed, so honest, repeat such unfounded slander?"

"Are you a partisan of his?"

"I come from Frankfort; have seen the Prince, and know I speak the truth."

"Ah, well," replied the girl lightly, "you and I will not quarrel over his Highness. I accept your amendment, and will never more bear false witness against him. After all, it makes slight difference one way or the other. An Emperor goes, and an Emperor is elected in his place as powerless as his predecessor. 'Tis the Archbishops who rule."

"You seem well versed in politics, Madam."

The girl leaned forward to him.

"Do not 'madam' me, I beg of you, Roland. I dare say rumor has prejudiced me against the young man, but I have promised not to speak slightingly of him again. I wish this veil of darkness was lifted, that I might see your face, to note the effect of anger. Do you know, I am disappointed in you, Roland? You spoke in such level tones in the courtyard that I thought anger was foreign to your nature."

"I am not angry," said Roland gruffly, "but I detest malicious gossip."

"Oh, so do I, so do I! I spoke thoughtlessly. I will kneel to the new Emperor and beg his pardon, if you insist."

Roland remained silent, and for a time they floated thus down the river, she trailing her fingers in the water, which made a pleasant ripple against them, looking up at him now and then. Perceptibly the darkness was thinning. One seemed to smell morning in the air. A bird piped dreamily in the forest at intervals, as if only half-awakened. The two women reclining in the prow were sound asleep.

Roland picked up the paddle, and with a strong, sweeping stroke turned the head of the boat towards the land. Now she could see his lowering brow, and if the sight pleased her, 'twas not manifested in her next remark.

She took her hand from the water, drew herself up proudly, and said:

"I shall not apologize to you again, and I hate your blameless Prince!"

"Madam, I ask for no apology, and whether you hate or like the Prince matters nothing to me, or, I dare say, to him, either."

"Cannot you even allow a woman her privilege of the last word?" she cried indignantly.

Roland's brow cleared, and a smile came to his lips, as he remained silent, thus bestowing upon her the prerogative she seemed to crave. Hilda lay back in the prow of the boat between her sleeping women, with hands clasped behind her head, and her eyes closed. More and more the light increased, and sturdily with his paddle Roland propelled the boat towards the shore, bringing it alongside the low bank at last. He sprang out on the turf, and with the paddle in one hand held the boat to land with the other.

"We are now," he said, "a short distance above St. Goarhausen, where I hope to purchase horses. Will you kindly disembark?"

The girl, without moving, or opening her eyes, said quietly:

"Please throw the paddle into the boat again. I shall make for Nonnenwerth in this craft, which is more comfortable than a saddle."

The paddle came rattling down upon the bottom of the skiff. Roland stooped, and before she knew what he was about, took Hilda in his arms, lifted her ashore, and laid her carefully on the grass.

"Come," he cried to the newly-awakened serving-women, "tumble out of that without further delay," and they obeyed him in haste.

He stepped into the skiff, flung their belongings on the sward, turned the prow to the west, and, leaping ashore, bestowed a kick upon the boat that impelled it like an arrow far out into the stream.

Hilda was standing on her feet now, speechless with indignation.

"Come along," urged Roland cheerfully, "breakfast awaits us when we earn it;" but seeing that she made no move, the frown furrowed his brow again.

"Madam," he said, "I tell you frankly that to be thwarted by petulance annoys me. It happens that time is of the utmost importance until we are much farther from Pfalz. If you think that the ownership of wealth and a castle gives you the right to flout a plain, ordinary man, you take a mistaken view of things. I care nothing for your castle, or for your wealth. You may be a lady of title for aught I know, but even that does not impress me. We must not stand here like two quarrelsome children. I will conduct you to the Adler Inn at St. Goarhausen, where I know from experience you will be taken care of. I shall then purchase four horses, and return to the inn after you have breakfasted. Three of these horses are at your disposal, also the fourth and myself, if you will condescend to make use of us. If not, I shall ask you to accept what money you need for your journey, so that you may travel north unmolested, while I take my way in the other direction."

"How can I repay the money," she demanded, "if I do not know who and what you are?"

"I shall send for it, either to your Castle of Sayn, or the Convent of Nonnenwerth. You need be under no obligation to me."

"But," cried the girl with a sob, "I am already under obligation to you; an obligation which I cannot repay."

"Oh yes, you can."

"How?"

"By coming with me, who will persuade you, as readily as you did with your guardian, who coerced you."

"I am an ungrateful simpleton," she murmured. "Of course your way is the right one, and I am quite helpless if you desert me."

"There," cried Roland, with enthusiasm, "you have more than repaid whatever you may owe."

After breakfasting at St. Goarhausen and purchasing the horses, they journeyed down the rough road that extended along the right bank of the Rhine. Roland and Hilda rode side by side, the other two following some distance to the rear. The young man maintained a gloomy silence, and the girl, misapprehending his thoughts, remained silent also, with downcast eyes, seeing nothing of the beautiful scenery they were passing. Every now and then Roland cast a sidelong glance at her, and his melancholy deepened as he remembered how heedlessly he had pledged his word to the three Archbishops regarding his marriage.

"I see," she said at last, "that I have offended you more seriously than I feared."

"No, no," he assured her. "There is a burden that I cannot cast from my mind."

"May I know what it is?"

"I dare not tell you, Hilda. I have been a fool. I am in the position of a man who must break his oath and live dishonored, or keep it, and remain for ever unhappy. Which would you do were you in my place?"

"Once given, I should keep my oath," she replied promptly, "unless those who accepted it would release me."

Roland shook his head.

"They will not release me," he said dolefully.

Again they rode together in silence, content to be near each other, despite the young man's alternations of elation and despair. 'Twas, all in all, a long summer's day of sweet unhappiness for each.

One of Roland's reasons for choosing the right bank of the Rhine was to avoid the important city of Coblentz, with its inevitable questioning, and it was late afternoon when they saw this town on the farther shore, passing it without hindrance.

"You will rest this night," she said, "in my Castle of Sayn, and then, as time is pressing, to-morrow you must return. We have met no interference even by this dangerous route, and I shall make my way alone without fear to Nonnenwerth, for I know you are anxious to be in Frankfort once more."

"I swear to you, Hilda, that if, without breaking my oath, I should never see Frankfort again, I would be the most joyous of men."

"Does your oath relate to Frankfort?"

"My oath relates to a woman," he said shortly.

"Ah," she breathed, "then you must keep it," and so they fell into silence and unhappiness again.

She had talked of security on the road they traversed, but turning a corner north of Vallandar they speedily found that a Rhine road is never safe.

Both reined in their horses as if moved by the same impulse, but to retreat now would simply draw pursuit upon them. Mounted on a splendid white charger, gorgeous with trappings, glittering with silver and gold, rode a dignified man in the outdoor habit of a general in times of peace.

Following him came an escort of twoscore horsemen; they in the full panoply of war; and behind them, on foot, in procession extending like a gigantic snake down the Rhine road, an army of at least three thousand men, the setting sun flashing fire from the points of their spears. Here and there, down the line, floated above them silken flags, and Roland recognized the device on the foremost one.

"God!" he shouted in dismay. "The Archbishop of Cologne!"

The girl uttered a little frightened cry, and edged her horse nearer to that of her escort.

"My guardian! My guardian!" she breathed. "I shall be rearrested!"

Seeing them standing as if stricken to stone, two horsemen detached themselves from the cavalry and galloped forward.

"Make way there, you fools!" cried the leader. "Get ye to the side; into the river; where you like; out of the path of my Lord the Archbishop."

Nevertheless Roland stood his ground, and dared even to frown at the officers of his Lordship.

"Stand aside you," he commanded in a tone of mastery, "and do not venture to intrude between the Archbishop and me."

The rider knew that no man who valued his head would dare use such language in the very presence of the Archbishop, unless he were the highest in the land. His dignified Lordship looked up to see the cause of this interruption, and of these angry words.

First came into his face an expression of amazement, then a smile melted the stern lips as he looked on Roland and recognized him. The impetuous horsemen faded away to the background. There was no answering smile on Roland's face. He reached out and clasped the hand of the girl.

"Now, by the Three Kings!" he whispered, "I shall break my oath."

Hilda glanced up at him, frightened by his vehemence, wincing under his iron grasp.

An unexpected sound interrupted the tension. The Archbishop had come to a stand, and "Halt! Halt! Halt!" rang out the word along the line of men, whose feet ceased to stir the dust of the road. The unexpected sound was that of hearty laughter from the dignified and mighty Prince of the Church.

"Forgive me, your Highness!" he cried, "but I laugh to think of the countenances of my somber brothers, Treves and Mayence, when they learn how sturdily you have kept your word with them. By the true Cross, Prince Roland, although we wished you to marry her, we had no thought that you would break into the Castle of Pfalz to win her hand. Ah, dear, what a pity 'tis we grow old! The impetuousness of youth outweighs the calculated wisdom of the three greatest prelates outside Rome. Judging by your fair face (and I have always held it to be beautiful, remember), you, Hildegunde Lauretta Priscilla Agnes, Countess of Sayn, are not moving northward to Nonnenwerth. I always insisted that the Saalhof at Frankfort was a more cheerful edifice than any nunnery on the Rhine, yet you never turned upon me such a glance of confidence as I see you bestow on your future Emperor."

"I hope, my Lord and Guardian," cried the girl, "that I have met you in time to deflect your course to my Castle of Sayn."

"Sweet Countess, I thank you for the invitation. My men can go on to their camp in the stronghold of my brother of Mayence, Schloss Martinsburg, and I shall gladly return with you to the hospitable hearth of Sayn. Indeed," said the Archbishop, lowering his voice, "I shall feel safer there than in enjoying the hospitality I had intended to accept."

"Are you not surprised to meet me?" asked the lady, with a laugh, adjusting words and manner to the new situation, which she more quickly comprehended than did her companion, who glanced with bewilderment from Countess to prelate, and back again.

The Archbishop waved his hand.

"Nothing you could do would surprise me, since your interview with the Court of Archbishops. I am on my way to Frankfort." Then, more seriously, to Prince Roland: "You heard of your father's death?"

"I learned it only this morning, my Lord. I shall return to Frankfort when I am assured that this gentlewoman is in a place of safety."

"Ah, Countess, there will be no lack of safety now! But will you not ease an old man's conscience by admitting he was in the right?"

The Countess looked up at Roland with a smile.

"Yes, dear Guardian," she said. "You were in the right."

XVII. "FOR THE EMPRESS, AND NOT FOR THE EMPIRE"

While the long line of troops stood at salute in single file, the Archbishop turned his horse to the north and rode past his regiments, followed by the Countess and Roland. His Lordship was accompanied to the end of the ranks by his general, who received final instructions regarding the march.

"You will encamp for the night not at Schloss Martinsburg, as I had intended, but a league or two up the Lahn. To-morrow morning continue your march along the Lahn as far as Limburg, and there await my arrival. We will enter Frankfort by the north gate instead of from the west."

The Archbishop sat on his horse for some minutes, watching the departing force, then called Roland to his right hand, and Hildegunde to his left, and thus the three set out on the short journey to Sayn.

"Your Highness," began the Archbishop, "I find myself in a position of some embarrassment. I think explanations are due to me from you both. Here I ride between two escaped prisoners, and I travel away from, instead of towards, their respective dungeons. My plain duty, on encountering you, was to place you in custody of a sufficient guard, marching you separately the one to Pfalz and the other to Ehrenfels. Having accomplished this I should report the case to my two colleagues, yet here am I actually compounding a misdemeanor, and assisting prisoners to escape."

"My Lord," spoke up Roland, "I am quite satisfied that my own imprisonment has been illegal, therefore I make no apology for circumventing it. Before entering upon any explanation, I ask enlightenment regarding the detention of my lady of Sayn. Am I right in surmising that she, like myself, was placed under arrest by the three Archbishops?"

"Yes, your Highness."

"On what charge?"

"High treason."

"Against whom?"

There was a pause, during which the Archbishop did not reply.

"I need not have asked such a question," resumed the Prince, "for high treason can relate only to the monarch. In what measure has her ladyship encroached upon the prerogative of the Emperor?"

"Your Highness forgets that there is such a thing as treason against the State."

"Are not members of the nobility privileged in this matter?"

"They cannot be, for the State is greater than any individual."

"I shall make a note of that, my Lord of Cologne. I believe you are in the right, and I hope so. During my lonely incarceration," the Prince laughed a little, "I have studied the condition of the State, arriving at the conclusion that the greatest traitors in our land are the three Archbishops, who, arrogating to themselves power that should belong to the Crown, did not use that power for suppressing those other treason-mongers, the Barons of the Rhine."

"What would you have us do with them?"

"You should disarm them. You should exact restitution of their illegally-won wealth. You should open the Rhine to honest commerce."

"That is easy to enunciate, and difficult to perform. If the Castles were disarmed, especially those on the left bank, a great injustice would be done that might lead to the extinction of many noble families. Why, the forests of Germany are filled with desperate outlaws, who respect neither life nor property. I myself have suffered but recently from their depredations. In broad daylight an irresistible band of these ruffians descended upon and captured the supposed impregnable Castle of Rheinstein, shamefully maltreating Baron Hugo von Hohenfels, tying him motionless, and nearly strangling him with stout ropes, after which the scoundrels robbed him of every stiver he possessed. The following midnight but one they descended on Furstenberg, a fief of my own, and not contenting themselves with robbery, brought red ruin on the Margrave by burning his Castle to the ground."

"My Lord, red ruin and the Red Margrave were made for each other. It was the justice of God that they should meet." The young man raised aloft his swordarm, shaking his clenched fist at the sky. "That hand held the torch that fired Furstenberg. The Castle was taken and burned by three sword makers from Frankfort, who never saw the Hunsruck or the outlaws thereof."

The Archbishop reined in his horse, and looked at the excited young man with amazement.

"You fired Furstenberg?"

"Yes; and effectively, my Lord. I shall rebuild it for you, but the Red Margrave I shall hang, as my predecessor Rudolph did his ancestor."

An expression of sternness hardened the Archbishop's face.

"Sir," he said, "I regret to hear you speak like this, and your safety lies in the fact that I do not believe a word of it. Even so, such wild words fill me with displeasure. I beg to remind you that the Election of an Emperor has not yet taken place, and I, for one, am likely to reconsider my decision. Still, as I said, I do not believe a word of your absurd tale."

"I believe every syllable of it!" cried the Countess with enthusiasm, "and glory that there is a mind brave enough, and a hand obedient to it, to smoke out a robber and a murderer."

The tension this astonishing revelation caused was relieved by a laugh from the Archbishop.

"My dear Hildegunde, you are forgetting your own ancestors. I venture that no woman of the House of Sayn talked thus when the Emperor Rudolph marched Count von Sayn to the scaffold. You would probably sing another song if asked to restore the millions amassed by Henry III. of Sayn and his successors; all accumulated by robbery as cruel as any that the Red Margrave has perpetrated."

"My Lord," said the Countess proudly, "you had no need to ask that question, for you knew the answer to it before you spoke. Every thaler I control shall be handed over to Prince Roland, to be used for the regeneration of his country."

Again the Archbishop laughed.

"Surely I knew that, my dear, and I should not have said what I did. I suppose you will not allow me to vote against his Highness at the coming Election."

"Indeed, you shall vote enthusiastically for him, because you know in your own heart he is the man Germany needs."

"Was there ever such a change of front?" cried the Archbishop. "Why, my dear, the charges you so hotly made against his Highness are as nothing to what he has himself confessed; yet now he is the savior of Germany, when previously—Ah, well, I must not play the tale-bearer."

"Prince Roland," cried the girl, "my kinsman, Father Ambrose, said he met you in Frankfort, although now I believe him to have been mistaken."

"Oh no; I encountered the good Father on the bridge."

"There now!" exclaimed the Archbishop, "what do you say to that, my lady?"

She seemed perplexed by the admission, but quickly replied to his Lordship:

"'Twas you said that could not be, as he was a close prisoner in Ehrenfels." She continued, addressing the Prince: "Father Ambrose asserted that you were a companion of drinkers and brawlers in a low wine cellar of Frankfort."

"Quite true; a score of them."

The girl became more and more perplexed.

"Did you imprison Father Ambrose?"

"Yes; in the lowest wine cellar, but only for a day or two. I am very sorry, Madam, but it was a stern necessity of war. He was meddling with affairs he knew nothing of, and there was no time for explanations. He, a man of peace, would not have sanctioned what there was to do even if I had explained."

"He says," continued the girl, "that he saw you rob a merchant of a bag of gold."

"That is untrue!" cried the Prince.

"My dear Hildegunde, what is the robbing of a bag of gold from a merchant when he admits having stolen gold by the castle full?"

"I robbed no merchant," protested the Prince. "How could Father Ambrose make such a statement?"

"He mounted an outside stairway on the Fahrgasse, and through lighted windows on the opposite side saw you place the point of your sword at the throat of an unarmed merchant, and take from him a bag of gold."

Roland, whose brow had been knitted into an angry frown, now threw back his head and laughed joyously.

"Oh, that was a mere frolic," he alleged.

It was the girl's turn to frown.

"When you took stolen treasure from thievish Barons and Margraves protected by scores of armed men, with the object of breaking their power, for the relief of commerce, I admired you, but to say that the despoiling of a helpless merchant is a frolic—"

"No, no, my dear, you do not understand," eagerly corrected the Prince, unconscious of the affectionate phrase that caused a flush to rise in the cheeks of his listener. "The merchant was, and is, my partner; a blameless man, Herr Goebel, who came near to being hanged on my behalf when these Archbishops took me captive. I sought from him a thousand thalers; he insisted on learning my plans for opening the Rhine, and still would not give the money until, reluctantly, I was obliged to confess myself son of the Emperor. This he could not credit, stipulating that before giving the money I must produce for him a safe-conduct, signed by the Emperor, and verified by the Great Seal of the Empire. This document I obtained at dire personal risk, through the aid of my mother. Here it is."

He thrust his hand into his doublet, and produced the parchment in question, delivering it to the lady, who, however, did not unfold it, but kept her eyes fixed upon him.

"This distrust annoyed me; it should not have done so, for he was merely acting in the cautious manner natural to a merchant. With a boyishness I now regret, I put my sword to his throat, demanding the money, which I received. I took only half of it, for my mother had given me five hundred thalers. Oh, no; I did not rob my friend Goebel, but merely tried to teach him that lack of faith is a dangerous thing."

If the old man who listened could have exchanged confidences with the young woman who listened, he would have learned they shared the same thought, which was that the young Prince spoke so straight-forwardly neither doubted him for a moment. The old man, it is true, felt that his talk was rather reckless of consequences, but, on the other hand, this in itself was complimentary, for, as he remembered, the Prince had been cautious enough when catechized by the three Archbishops together.

"I have often read," said Cologne, with a smile, "pathetic accounts of prisoners, who in extreme loneliness carved their names over and over again on stone as hard as the jailer's heart, but your Highness seems rather to have enjoyed yourself while so cruelly interned. May I further beg of you to enlighten us concerning a somewhat bibulous youth who at the present moment is enjoying, in every sense of the word, the hospitality of Ehrenfels Castle?"

It was now the Archbishop's turn to astonish the Prince.

"You knew of my device, then?"

"'Knew' is a little too strong. 'Suspect' more nearly fits the case. You won over your jailer, and some one else took your place as prisoner."

"Yes; a young man to whom I owe small thanks, and with whom I have an account to settle. He is son of the custodian, and thinks he has us both under his thumb, Heinrich drinks as if he were a fish or a Baron, but I shall cure him of that habit before it becomes firmly established."

"Am I correct in assuming that you found your liberty only after your interview with the three Electors?"

"Oh, bless you, no! I was free months before that time. Indeed, it is only since then that my substitute is practically useless. Heinrich might have passed for me at a pinch, but only because neither you nor your colleagues had seen me. I have kept him under lock and key ever since, because I dare not allow him abroad until the Election has taken place."

"I see. A very wise precaution. Well, your Highness, I shall say nothing of what you tell me; furthermore, I still promise you my vote; that is, if you will obey my orders until you are elected Emperor. I foresee we are not going to have the easy time with you that was anticipated, but this concerns Mayence and Treves, rather than myself, for I have no ambition to rule by proxy. And now, my lady of Sayn, when we journeyed southward that day from Gutenfels Castle I gave you some information regarding the mind of Mayence. You remember, perhaps, what I said about his quandary. I rather suspect that he admires you, notwithstanding your defiance of him; but there is nothing remarkable in that, for we all appreciate you, old and young. I, too, carry a document of safe-conduct, like Prince Roland here, although I see that his Highness has placed his safety in your hands."

The old man smiled, and Hildegunde found herself still carrying the parchment Roland had given her. For a moment she was confused, then smiled also, and offered it back; but the Prince shook his head. The Archbishop went on:

"Mayence sent down to me your written release, signed by himself and Treves. He asked me to attach a signature, and liberate you on my way to Frankfort, which I intended to do had this impetuous young man not forestalled me. By the way, Highness, how did you happen to meet Countess von Sayn in Pfalz?"

"We will tell you about that later, Guardian," said Hildegunde, before Roland could speak. "What instructions did his Lordship of Mayence give concerning me?"

"He asked me to bring you to my palace in Frankfort, and subtly expressed the hope you had changed your mind."

"You may assure him I have," said the Countess, again speaking rapidly; "but let us leave all details of that for the moment. I am then to go with you to the capital?"

"Yes; to-morrow morning."

"To remain until the coronation?"

"Certainly; if such is your wish. But do you not see something very significant in my brother Mayence's change of plan, for you know he did not intend to release you until after that event?"

"Yes, yes," replied the Countess breathlessly. "I see it quite clearly, but do not wish to discuss the matter at the present moment."

"Very well. I intended to enter Frankfort from the west, but meeting you so unexpectedly, I have deflected my troops up the Lahn to Limburg, at which town we will join them to-morrow night, thus following Father Ambrose's route to the capital."

"Ah, that will be very interesting. Prince Roland, you accompany us, I hope?"

"Of a surety," replied the young man confidently.

"No," quietly said the Archbishop.

"Why not?"

"Because I say no."

The young man almost an Emperor drew himself up proudly, and his lips pressed together into a firm line of determination.

"Does your Highness so quickly forget your promise?"

"What promise?" asked the Prince, scowling.

"In consideration of my keeping silence touching your recent outrageous career of fire and slaughter, and the enslavement of Heinrich, you promised to obey me until you became Emperor."

"I intend to obey all reasonable requests, but I very much desire to accompany the Countess from her Castle to the capital, I have never seen Limburg, or taken that route to Frankfort."

"It is a charming old city," replied the Archbishop dryly, "which you can visit any time at the expense of a day's ride. Meanwhile, I shall escort the Countess thither, and endeavor to entertain her with pleasing and instructive conversation during the journey."

The Prince continued to frown, yet bit his lip and repressed an angry retort.

"But," protested the girl, "would it not be much safer for his Highness to enter the city of Frankfort protected by your army?"

The Archbishop laughed a little.

"My dear Hildegunde, the presence of Prince Roland causes you to overlook a vast difference in the status of you both, but surely the exercise of a little imagination should present to you the true aspect of affairs. You are a free woman, and I hold the document by which you regained your liberty. Do not be deluded, therefore, by the apparent fact that his Highness can raise a clenched fist aloft and defy the heavens. It is not so. He wears fetters on his ankles, and manacles round his wrists. Roland is a prisoner, and must straightway immure himself. Your Highness, before us stands the stately Castle of Sayn, where presently you shall refresh yourself, and be furnished with an untired charger, on which to ride all night, that you may reach the gates of Ehrenfels early to-morrow morning. Once there, place the wine-loving Heinrich out of harm in the deepest dungeon, and take his place as prisoner. It is arranged that the three Archbishops personally escort you to Frankfort in the barge of Mayence, which will land you at the water-steps of the Royal Palace. If it were known that I had been even an hour in your company your chances of reaching the throne would be seriously jeopardized."

"Surely such haste is unnecessary," cried the girl. "He can set out tomorrow in one direction while we go in another. He traveled all last night, and for most part of it was paddling a boat containing four people; has ridden almost since daylight, and now to journey on horseback throughout the night is too much for human endurance."

The grave smile of the Archbishop shone upon her anxiety.

"For lack of a nail the shoe was lost," he said, "and you know the remainder of the warning. If Prince Roland cares to risk an Empire for a night's rest, I withdraw my objection."

The Prince suddenly wheeled his horse, and coming briskly round to the side of the girl, placed a hand on hers.

"A decision, Countess!" he cried. "Give me your decision. I shall always obey you!"

"Oh, the rashness of youth!" murmured the Archbishop.

The girl looked up at the young man, and he caught his breath and clasped her hand more tightly as he gazed into the depths of her glorious eyes.

"You must go," she sighed.

"Yes, alas!"

He raised her unresisting hand to his lips, and again turned his horse.

"You will obey?" asked the Archbishop.

"I will obey, my Lord."

He flashed from its scabbard, into the rays of the setting sun, the sword he had made, and elevating the hilt to his forehead, saluted the Archbishop.

"I shall see you at Ehrenfels, my Lord."

"Ah, do not go thus. Come to the Castle for an hour's rest at least."

The young man whirled his sword around, and caught it by the blade, touching the hilt with his lips as if it were a cross.

"I thank God," said he, "that I can willingly keep my oath."

Then, looking at the girl—"For the Empress, and not for the Empire!" he cried.

The sword seemed to drop into the scabbard of its own accord, as Roland set spurs to his steed and away.

XVIII. THE SWORD MAKER AT BAY

The heir-presumptive to the throne reached Frankfort very quietly in the Archbishop's barge, and was landed after nightfall at the water-steps of the Imperial Palace. The funeral of the Emperor took place almost as if it were a private ceremonial. Grave trouble had been anticipated, and the route of the procession for the short distance between Palace and Cathedral was thickly lined on either side by the troops of the three Archbishops. This precaution proved unnecessary. The dispirited citizens cared nothing for their late nominal ruler, and they manifested their undisguised hatred of the real rulers, the Archbishops, by keeping indoors while their soldiers marched the streets.

The condition of the capital was unique. It suffered from a famine of money rather than a famine of food. Frankfort starved in the midst of plenty. Never had the earth been more fruitful than during this year, and the coming autumn promised a harvest that would fill the granaries to overflowing, yet no one brought in food to Frankfort, for the common people had not the money to buy. The working population depended entirely upon the merchants and manufacturers, and with the collapse of mercantile business thousands were thrown out of employment, and this penniless mob was augmented by the speedy cessation of all manufacturing.

After the futile bread riots earlier in the year, put down so drastically by the Archbishops, the population of the city greatly diminished, and the country round about swarmed with homeless wanderers, who at least were sure of something to eat, but being city-bred, and consequently useless for agricultural employment, they gradually joined into groups and marauding bands, greatly to the menace of the provinces they traversed. Indeed, rumor had it that the robberies from certain castles on the Rhine, and the burning of Furstenberg, were the work of these free companies, consequently a sense of uneasiness permeated the Empire, whose rulers, great and small, began to foresee that a continuance of this state of things meant disaster to the rich as well as misery to the poor. Charity, spasmodic and unorganized, proved wholly unable to cope with the disaster that had befallen the capital city.

When darkness set in on the third night after Roland's return to Frankfort, he made his way out into the unlighted streets, acting with caution until certain he was not followed, then betook himself to the Palace belonging to the Archbishop of Cologne.

The porter at first refused him entrance, and Roland, not wishing to make himself known, declared he had an appointment with his Lordship. Trusting that the underling could not read, he presented his parchment safe-conduct, asking him to give that to his Lordship, with a message that the bearer awaited his pleasure. The suspicious servant, seeing the Grand Seal of the Empire upon the document, at once conducted Roland to a room on the ground floor, then departed with the manuscript to find his master.

The Archbishop returned with him, the Imperial scroll in his hand, and a distinctly perceptible frown on his brow. When the servant withdrew, closing the door, the prelate said:

"Highness, this is a very dangerous procedure on your part."

"Why, my Lord?"

"Because you are certain to have been followed."

"What matter for that?" asked the young man. "I am quite unknown in Frankfort."

"Prince Roland," said the Archbishop gravely, "until your Election is actually accomplished, you would be wise to do nothing that might arouse the suspicion of Mayence. This house is watched night and day, and all who come and go are noted. I dare say that within fifteen minutes Mayence will know you have visited me."

"My dear Archbishop, they cannot note an unknown man. The uneasiness of Frankfort has already taken hold of me, and therefore I saw to it that I was not followed."

"If you were not followed when you came, you will certainly be followed as you return."

"In that case, my Lord, the spies will track me to the innocent home of Herr Goebel, the merchant, in the Fahrgasse."

"They will shadow you when you leave his house."

"Then their industry will be rewarded by an enjoyable terminus; in other words, the drinking cellar of the Rheingold."

"Be assured, your Highness, that ultimately you will be traced to the Royal Palace."

"Again not so, my Lord. They will be led across the bridge into the mechanics' quarter of Sachsenhausen, and if the watch continues, they must make a night of it, for I shall enter my humble room there and go to bed."

"I see you have it all planned out," commented the discomfited Archbishop.

The young man laughed.

"I anticipate an interesting life, my Lord, because it is my habit to think before I act, and I notice that this apparently baffles the Electors. The truth is that you three are so subtle, and so much afraid of one another, so on the alert lest you be taken by surprise, that a straightforward action on my part throws all intrigue out of gear. Now, I'll warrant you cannot guess why I came here to-night."

"Oh, I know the reason very well."

"Do you? That astonishes me. What is the reason?"

"You came to see the Countess von Sayn."

"Ah, is the lady within? Why, of course, she must be. I remember now, she was to accompany you to Frankfort, and it naturally follows she is your guest."

"She is my guest, your Highness, and one reason why you cannot see her is because at this moment the lady converses with the Count Palatine, who has just arrived from Gutenfels. As the Countess and myself enjoyed his hospitality not long ago in that stronghold, I have invited him to be my guest until the coronation ceremonies are completed."

"My Lord, I regret that your hospitality halts when it reaches your future Emperor. Why may I not be introduced to the Count Palatine?"

"Such introduction must not take place except in the presence of the other Electors. I am very anxious, as you may perceive, that nothing shall be done to jeopardize your own prospects. We have arrived, your Highness, at a critical moment. History relates that more than one candidate has come to the very steps of the throne, only to be rejected at the last moment. I am too sincere a friend to risk such an outcome in your own case."

"Then you think it injudicious of me to see the Countess until after the Election?"

"I not only think it injudicious, your Highness, but I intend to prevent a meeting."

Again the young man laughed.

"'Tis blessed then that I came for no such purpose; otherwise I might be deeply disappointed."

"For what purpose did you come, Highness?"

"The Imperial Palace, my Lord, belongs no more to my mother. If she or I continue there to reside, we seem to be taking for granted that I shall be elected Emperor; an assumption unfair to the seven Electors, whose choice should be untrammeled by even a hint of influence. I beg of you, therefore, my Lord, to extend your hospitality to my mother. I have spoken to her on this subject, and she will gladly be your guest, happy, I am sure, to forsake that gloomy abode."

"I am honored, your Highness, by the opportunity you give me. I shall wait upon the Empress to-morrow at whatever hour it is convenient for her Majesty to receive me."

"You are most kind. I suggested that she should name an hour, and

295

midday was chosen."

The Archbishop bowed profoundly. The young man rose, and held out his hand, which the Archbishop took with cordiality. The Prince looked very straight-forwardly at his host, and the latter thought he detected a twinkle in his eye, as he said with decision:

"To-morrow I shall formally notify my Lord of Mayence that the Empress has chosen your Palace as her place of residence until after the coronation, and I shall request his Lordship to crave your permission that I may call here every day to see my mother."

Again Cologne bowed, and made no further protest, although Roland seemingly expected one, but as it did not come, the Prince continued:

"Here is my address in Sachsenhausen, should you wish a communication to reach me in haste; and kindly command your porter not to parley when I again demand speech with your Lordship. Good-night. I thank you, my Lord, for your courtesy," and the energetic youth disappeared before the slow-thinking Archbishop could call up words with which to reply.

Cologne did not immediately rejoin his guests, but stood a very figure of perplexity, muttering to himself:

"If our friend Mayence thinks that youngster is to be molded like soft clay, he is very much mistaken. I hope Roland will not cause him to feel the iron hand too soon. I wonder why Mayence is delaying the Election? Can it be that already he distrusts his choice, or is it the question of a wife?"

Meanwhile the front door of the Archbishop's Palace had clanged shut, and Roland strode across the square careless or unconscious of spies, looking neither to the right nor to the left. He made his way speedily to the Fahrgasse, walking down that thoroughfare until he came to Herr Goebel's door, where he knocked, and was admitted. Ushered into the room where he had parted from the merchant, he found Herr Goebel seated at his table as if he had never left it. The merchant, with a cry of delight, greeted the young man.

"Well, Herr Goebel, you see I have been a successful trafficker. Your bales of goods are all in Castle Pfalz, and I trust the barge returned safely to you with the money."

"It did indeed, your Highness."

"Has the coin been counted?"

"Yes; and it totals an enormous, almost unbelievable, sum, which I have set down here to the last stiver."

"That is brave news. Have any demands been made on you for its partition?"

"No, your Highness."

"Now, Herr Goebel, I have determined that all that money, which is in effect stolen property, shall go to the feeding of Frankfort's poor. Buying provender shrewdly, how long would this treasure keep hunger away from the gates of Frankfort?"

"That requires some calculation, your Highness."

"A month?"

"Surely so."

"Two months, perhaps?"

"'Tis likely; but I deal in cloth, not in food, and therefore cannot speak definitely without computation and the advice of those expert in the matter."

"Very well, Herr Goebel; get your computations made as soon as possible. Call together your merchants' guild, and ask its members—By the way," said Roland, suddenly checking himself, "give to me in writing the amount of gold I have sent you."

The unsuspecting merchant did so, and Roland's eyes opened with astonishment when he glanced at the total. He then placed the paper in the wallet he carried.

"You were perhaps about to suggest that a committee be appointed," ventured the merchant.

"Yes; a small but capable committee, of which you shall be chairman and treasurer. But first you will ask the merchants to subscribe, out of their known wealth, a sum equaling the gold I filched from the Barons."

The merchant's face fell, and took on a doleful expression.

"The times, your Highness, have long been very bad, none of us making money—"

The Prince held up his hand, and the merchant ceased his plaint.

"If I can strip a Baron of his wealth," he said, "I will not waste words over the fleecing of merchants. This contribution is to be given in the name of the three Archbishops, whose heavy hands came down on you after the late insurrection. The Archbishops have now nine thousand troops in Frankfort. If given leave, they will collect the sum three times over within a very few hours; so you, as chairman of the committee, may decide whether the fund shall be a voluntary contribution or an impost gathered by soldiery: it matters nothing to me. Have it proclaimed throughout the city that owing to the graciousness of the three Archbishops starvation is now at an end in Frankfort."

"Highness, with your permission, and all due deference, it seems rather unjust that we should contribute the cash and lose the credit."

"Yes, Herr Goebel; this is a very unjust world, as doubtless many of the starving people thought when they recollected that a few hundred of you possessed vast wealth while they were penniless. Nevertheless, there are good times ahead for all of us. Let me suggest that this money which I sent to you may prove sufficient and so the subscriptions of the merchants can be returned to them; that is, if the relief fund is honestly administered. So set to work early to-morrow with energy. You merchants have had a long vacation. I think the Rhine will be open before many weeks are past, and then you can turn to your money-making, but our first duty is to feed the hungry. Good-night, Herr Goebel."

He left the merchant as dazed as was the Archbishop. Once again outside he made directly for the wine cellar of the Rheingold. On reaching the steps he heard a roar of talk, lightened now and then by the sound of laughter. He paused a moment before descending. It was evident that the company was enjoying itself, and Roland soliloquized somewhat sadly:

"I am the disturbing element in that group. They seem to agree famously when by themselves. Ah, well, no matter. They will soon be rid of me!"

When Roland descended the stair, the proprietor greeted him with joy.

"I have missed you, Herr Roland," he said, "so you may imagine how much the guild has regretted your absence."

"Yes; I hear them bemoaning their fate."

The inn-keeper laughed.

"How many are here to-night?"

"There is a full house, Sir Roland."

"Really? Are Kurzbold and Gensbein within?"

"Oh, yes; and there is no scarcity of money, thanks to you, I understand."

"Rather, our thanks are for ever due to you, Herr Host, for sustaining us so long when we were penniless. We shall never forget that," and so with a semi-military salute to the gratified cellar-man, Roland pushed open the door and entered the banqueting room of the iron-workers' guild. An instant silence fell on the group.

"Good evening to you, gentlemen," said the Prince, taking off his hat, and with a twist of his shoulders flinging the cloak from them.

Instantly arose a great cheer, and Greusel, who occupied the chair at the head of the table, strode forward, took Roland's hat and cloak, and hung them up. After that he attempted to lead their Captain to the seat of honor.

"No, no, my dear lieutenant," said Roland, placing his hand affectionately on the other's shoulder, "a better man than I occupies the chair, and shall never be displaced by me."

The others, now on their feet, with the exception of Kurzbold and Gensbein, vociferously demanded that Roland take the chair. Smilingly he shook his head, and holding up his hand for silence, addressed them.

"Take your seats, comrades; and, Greusel, if you force me to give a command, I order you into that chair without further protest."

Greusel, with evident reluctance, obeyed.

"Truth to tell, brothers, I have but a few moments to stop. I merely dropped in to enjoy a sip of wine with you, and to offer a proposal that, within five minutes, will make me the most unpopular man in this room, therefore you see my wisdom in refusing a chair from which I should be very promptly ejected."

One of the members poured a tankard full of wine from a flagon, and handed it to Roland, who, saluting the company, drank.

"You did not divide the money, Greusel?"

"No, Roland. We gave each man five hundred thalers, to keep as best he might. We then concealed the rest of the gold between the bottom of the boat and its inner planking. Ebearhard and I construed your orders somewhat liberally, conceiving it was your desire to get our treasure and ourselves safely into Frankfort."

"Quite right," corroborated Roland.

"When morning came upon us, we soon discovered that the whole country was aroused, because of the destruction of Furstenberg and the looting of Sonneck. No one knew where the next raid would strike, and therefore the whole country-side was in a turmoil. Now, the only fact known to the despoiled was that a long black barge had appeared in front of the Castle while the attack was made from behind. We realized that it would be impossible for us to go up the river except in darkness, so in case of a search we concealed the treasure where it was not likely to be come at, and each day lay quiet at an unfrequented part of the river, rowing all night. Not until we reached the Main did we venture on a daylight voyage. It was agreed among us unanimously that the money should be placed in Herr Goebel's keeping until you returned."

"That was all excellently done," commented Roland. "I have just been to see Herr Goebel, and was surprised to learn how much we had actually taken. And now I ask you to make a great sacrifice. This city is starving. If we give that gold to its relief, the merchants of Frankfort will contribute an equal amount. I do not know how long such a total will keep the wolves from the doors of Frankfort; probably for six months. I shall learn definitely to-morrow." Here Roland outlined his plan of relief, which was received in silence.

Kurzbold spoke up.

"I should like to know how much the total is?"

"That is a matter with which you have nothing to do," growled Greusel; then, turning to Roland, who had not yet taken a seat, he said: "So far as my share is concerned, I agree."

"I agree," added Ebearhard; and so it went down along each side of the table until eighteen had spoken.

Kurzbold rose with a smile on his face.

"I don't know how it is, ex-Captain, that the moment you come among us there seems to arise a spirit of disputation."

"Curiously enough, Herr Kurzbold, that same thought arose in my mind as I listened to your hilarity before I entered. I beg to add, for your satisfaction, that this is my last visit to the guild, and never again shall I disturb its harmony."

"There is no lack of harmony," cried Ebearhard, laughing, as he rose. "The agreement has been practically unanimous—quite unanimous in fact, among those entitled to share in the great treasure. I believe Herr Kurzbold has a claim, if it has not been forfeited, to the loot of Rheinstein."

"Now, even the genial Ebearhard," continued Kurzbold, "although his words are blameless, speaks with a certain tone of acerbity, while my friend Greusel has become gruff as a bear."

"You need not labor that point, Herr Kurzbold," said Roland. "I have resigned."

"I just wished to remark," Kurzbold went on, "that I rose for the purpose of stating I had some slight share in something; stolen property; honor among thieves, you know. Are my rights to this share disputed?"

"No," said the chairman shortly.

"Very well," concluded Kurzbold, "as I am graciously permitted to speak in the august presence of our ex-Captain, I desire to say that whatever my share happens to be, I bestow it gladly, nay, exultantly, upon the poor of Frankfort."

With that Kurzbold sat down, and there was first a roar of laughter, followed by a clapping of hands. Gensbein rose, and said briefly:

"I do as Kurzbold does."

"Now," said Roland, "I want a number of volunteers to start out into the country early to-morrow morning, Greusel, you, as chairman, will designate the routes. Each man is to penetrate as far as he can along the main roads, asking the farmers to bring everything in the shape of food they have to sell. Tell them a vast sum has been collected, and that their cartloads will be bought entire the moment they enter the city. There will be no waiting for their money. Prompt payment, and everything eatable purchased immediately. Greusel, I put on you the hardest task. Penetrate into the forest south of the Main, and tell the charcoal-burners and woodmen to bring in material for kitchen fires. How many will volunteer?"

Every man rose. Roland thanked them. "I shall now divulge a secret, and you will see that when it was told to me I remembered your interests. It has been my privilege to meet, since I saw you, more than one man who is a ruler in this Empire."

"Did they tell you who is to be the new Emperor?" cried one.

"That is known only to the Electors. But what I was about to say is this. There are to be established by the Government ironworks on a scale hitherto unknown in any land. I believe, and did my best to inculcate that belief in others, that we are on the verge of an age of iron, and, knowing your skill, I am privileged to offer each of you the superintendency of a department, with compensation never before given so lavishly in Germany. I am also induced to believe that the new Emperor will bestow a title on each of you who desire such honor, so that there can be no question of your right to wear a sword. Greusel, you must receive reports from each of our food scouts, and I shall be glad to know the outcome, if you take the trouble to call upon me any hour after nine o'clock at night, at my old room in Sachsenhausen. And now, good-night, and good-luck to you all."

Roland went over the bridge, and so reached his room on the other side. He glanced around several times to satisfy himself he was not spied upon, and laughed at the apprehension of the Archbishop. Entering his room, he lit a lamp, took off his cloak and flung it on the bed, then unbuckled his sword-belt and hung it and the weapon on a peg, placing his cloak above them. He was startled by a loud knock at the door, and stood for a moment astonished, until it was repeated with the stern warning:

"Open in the name of the Archbishop!"

The young man strode forward, drew back the bolt, and flung open the door. An officer, with two soldiers behind him, came across the threshold, and at the side-motion of the officer's head a soldier closed and bolted the door. Roland experienced a momentary thrill of indignation at this rude intrusion, then he remembered he was a mechanic, and that his line must be the humble and deferential.

"You came to-night from the Imperial Palace. What were you doing there?"

"I was trying to gain admission, sir."

"For what purpose?"

"I wished," said Roland, rapidly outlining his defense in his own mind,

"I wished to see some high officer; some one of your own position, sir, but was not so fortunate as to succeed. I could not pass the sentries without a permit, which I did not then possess, but hope to acquire to-morrow."

"Again I ask, for what purpose?"

"For a purpose which causes me delight in meeting your excellency."

"I am no excellency. Come to the point! For what purpose?"

"To show the officer a sword of such superior quality that a man armed with it, and given a certain amount of skill, stands impregnable."

"Do you mean to tell me you went to the Royal Palace for the purpose of selling a second-hand sword?"

"Oh, no, my lord."

"Do not be so free with your titles. Call me Lieutenant."

"Well, Lieutenant, sir; I hope to get orders for a hundred, or perhaps a thousand of these weapons."

"Where did you go after leaving the Palace?"

"I went to the residence of that great Prince of the Church, the Archbishop of Cologne."

"Ah! You did not succeed in seeing his Lordship, I suppose?"

"Pardon me, Lieutenant, but I did. His Lordship is keenly interested in both weapons and armor."

"Did he give you an order for swords?"

"No, Lieutenant; he seems to be a very cautious man. He asked me to visit him in Cologne, or if I could not do that, to see his general, now in Frankfort. You understand, Lieutenant, the presence of the three Archbishops with their armies offers me a great opportunity, by which I hope to profit."

The officer looked at him with a puzzled expression on his face.

"Where next did you go?"

"I went to the house of a merchant in the Fahrgasse."

"Ah, that tale doesn't hold! Merchants are not allowed to wear swords."

"No, Lieutenant, but a merchant on occasion can supply capital that will enable a skilled workman to accept a large contract. If I should see the general of his Lordship to-morrow, and he gave me an order for, say, two thousand swords, I have not enough money to buy the metal, and I could not ask for payment until I delivered the weapons."

"Did the merchant agree to capitalize you?"

"He, too, was a cautious man, Lieutenant. He wished first to see the contract, and know who stood responsible for payment."

"Wise man," commented the officer; "and so, disheartened, I suppose, you returned here?"

"No, Lieutenant; the day has been warm, and I have traveled a good deal. I went from the merchant's house to the Rheingold tavern, there to drink a tankard of wine with my comrades, a score of men who have formed what they call the ironworkers' guild. I drank a tankard with them, and then came direct here, where I arrived but a few moments ago."

The officer was more and more puzzled. Despite this young man's deferential manner, his language was scarcely that of a mechanic, yet this certainly was his own room, and he had told the absolute truth about his wanderings, as one who has nothing to fear.

The Lieutenant stood for a space of time with eyes to the floor, as silent as the soldiers behind him. Suddenly he looked up.

"Show me the sword. I'll tell you where it's made!"

If he expected hesitation he was mistaken. Roland gave a joyful cry, swept aside the cloak, whisked forth the sword, flung it up, and caught it by the blade, then with a low bow handed it to the officer, who flashed it through the air, bent the blade between finger and thumb, then took it near the lamp and scrutinized it with the eye of an expert.

"A good weapon, my friend. Where was it made? I have never seen one like it."

"It was made by my own hands here in Frankfort. Of course I go first to those who know least about the matter, but if I can get an introduction to his Lordship of Mayence, his officers will know a sword when they see it; and I hope to-night fortune, in leading you to my door, has brought me an officer of Mayence."

The Lieutenant looked at him, and for the first time smiled. He handed back the weapon, signed to his men to unbolt the door, which they did, stepping out; then he said:

"I bid you good-night. Your answers have been satisfactory, but I set you down not as a mechanic, but a very excellent merchant of swords."

"Lieutenant," said Roland, "you do not flatter me." He raised his weapon in military salute. "I am no merchant, but a sword maker."

XIX. THE BETROTHAL IN THE GARDEN

Next morning Prince Roland sent a letter to the Archbishop of Mayence informing him that the Empress had taken up her abode in the Palace of her old friend, the Lord of Cologne, giving the reasons for this move and his own desertion of the Imperial Palace, and asking permission to call upon his mother each day. The messenger brought back a prompt reply, which commended the delicacy of his motives in leaving the Royal Palace, but added that, so far as the three Archbishops were concerned, the Saalhof was still at their disposal: of course Prince Roland's movements were quite untrammeled, and again, so far as concerned the three Archbishops, he was at liberty to visit whom he pleased, as often as he liked.

While waiting for the return of his messenger, Roland called upon Herr Goebel, and told him that twenty emissaries had gone forth in every direction from Frankfort to inform the farming community that a market had been opened in the city, and in exchange learned what the merchant had already done towards furthering the necessary organization.

"Oh, by the way, Herr Goebel," he cried, suddenly recollecting, "just write out and sign a document to this effect: 'I promise Herr Roland, sword maker of Sachsenhausen, to supply him with the capital necessary for carrying out his contract with his Lordship the Archbishop of Cologne.'"

Without demur the merchant indited the document, signed it, and gave it to the Prince.

"If any emissary of Mayence pays you a domiciliary visit, Herr Goebel, asking questions about me, carefully conceal my real status, and reply that I am an honest, skillful sword maker, anxious to revive the iron-working industry, and for this reason, being yourself solicitous for the welfare of Frankfort, you are risking some money."

In the afternoon Roland walked to the Palace of Cologne and boldly entered, with no attempt at secrecy, the doorkeeper on this occasion offering no impediment to his progress. He learned that the Empress, much fatigued, had retired to her room and must not be disturbed; that the Archbishop was consulting with the Count Palatine, while the Countess von Sayn was walking in the garden. Roland passed with some haste through the Palace, and emerged into the grounds behind it: grounds delightfully umbrageous, and of an extent surprisingly large, surrounded by a very high wall of stone, so solidly built that it might successfully stand a siege.

Roland found the girl sauntering very slowly along one of the most secluded alleys, whose gravel-path lay deeply in the shade caused by the thick foliage of over-hanging trees, which made a cool, green tunnel of the walk. Her head was slightly bowed in thought, her beautiful face pathetic in its weariness, and the young man realized, with a pang of sympathy, that she was still to all intents and purposes a prisoner, with no companions but venerable people. She could not, and indeed did not attempt to suppress an exclamation of delight at seeing him, stretching out both hands in greeting, and her countenance cleared as if by magic.

"I was thinking of you!" she cried, without a trace of coquetry.

"I judged your thoughts to be rather gloomy," he said, with a laugh, in which she joined.

"Gloomy only because I could see or hear nothing of you."

"Did you know I came yesterday?"

"No. Why did you not ask to see me?"

"I was informed you were entertaining the Count Palatine."

"Ah, yes. He is a delightful old man. I like him better and better as time goes on. My guardian and I were guests of his at Gutenfels just before I occupied the marine prison of Pfalz."

"So your guardian told me."

They were now walking side by side in this secluded, thickly-wooded avenue, just wide enough for two, running in a straight line from wall to wall the whole length of the property, in the part most remote from the house.

"Nothing disastrous has happened to you?" she asked. "I have had miserable forebodings."

"No; I am living a most commonplace life, quite uneventful."

"But why, why does the Archbishop of Mayence delay the Election?"

"I did not know he was doing so."

"Oh, my guardian is very anxious about it. Such postponement, I understand, never happened before. The State is without a head."

"Has your guardian spoken to Mayence about it?"

"Yes; and has been met by the most icy politeness. Mayence wishes this Election to take place with a full conclave of the seven Electors, three of whom have not yet arrived. But my guardian says they never arrive, and take no interest in Imperial matters. He pointed out to Mayence that a quorum of the Court is already in Frankfort, but his Lordship of the Upper Rhine merely protests that they must not force an Election, all of which my guardian thinks is a mere hiding of some design on the part of Mayence."

Prince Roland meditated on this for a few moments, then, as if shaking off his doubts, he said:

"It never occurs to one Archbishop that either of the others may be speaking the truth. There is so much mistrust among them that they nullify all united action, which accounts for the prostrate state of this city, the capital of one of the most prosperous countries under the sun. So far as I can see, taken individually, they are upright, trustworthy men. Now, to give you an instance. Your guardian last night was simply panic-stricken at my audacity in visiting him. He said I must not come again, refusing me permission to see you; he told you nothing of my conference with him: he felt certain I was being tracked by spies, and could not be made to understand that my presence here was of no consequence one way or another."

"Then why are you here now?"

"I am just coming to that. I asked your guardian to invite my mother as his guest. Have you met her yet?"

"No; they told me the Empress was too tired to receive any one. I am to be introduced at dinner to-night."

"Well, this morning I wrote to the Archbishop of Mayence, telling him of my interview with your guardian, the reason for it, and the results. His reply came promptly by return." Roland produced the document. "Just read that, and see whether you detect anything sinister in it."

She read the letter thoughtfully.

"That is honest enough on the surface."

"On the surface, yes; but why not below the surface as well? That is a frank assent to a frank request. I think that if the Archbishops would treat each other with open candor they would save themselves a good deal of anxiety."

"Perhaps," said the girl, very quietly.

"You are not convinced?"

"I don't know what to think." Then she looked up at him quickly. "Were you followed last night?"

"Ah!" ejaculated Roland, laughing a little "apparently not, so far as I could see, but the night was very dark." Then he related to her the incidents succeeding the return to his room, while she listened with breathless eagerness. "The Lieutenant," he concluded, "did not deny that he was in the service of Mayence when I hinted as much, but, on the other hand, he did not admit it. Of course, I knew by his uniform to whom he belonged. He conducted my examination with military abruptness, but skillfully and with increasing courtesy, although I proclaimed myself a mechanic."

"You a mechanic!" she said incredulously. "Do you think he believed it?"

"I see you doubt my histrionic ability, but when next he waits upon me I shall produce documentary evidence of my status, and, what is more, I'll take to my workshop."

310

"Do you possess a workshop?" cried the girl in amazement.

"Do I? Why, I am partner with a man named Greusel, and we own a workshop together. A gruff, clumsy individual, as you would think, but who, nevertheless, with his delicate hammer, would beat you out in metal a brooch finer than that you are wearing."

"Do you mean Joseph?"

"Yes," replied Roland, astonished. "What do you know of him?"

"Have you forgotten so soon? It was his stalwart shoulders that burst in my door at Pfalz, and you yourself told me his name was Joseph Greusel. Were all those marauders you commanded honest mechanics?"

"Every man of them."

"Then you must be the villain of the piece who led those worthy ironworkers astray?"

Roland laughed heartily.

"That is quite true," he said. "Have I fallen in your estimation?"

"No; to me you appeared as a rescuer. Besides, I come of a race of ruffians, and doubtless on that account take a more lenient view of your villainy than may be the case with others."

The young man stopped in his walk, and seized her hands again, which she allowed him to possess unresisting.

"Hilda," he said solemnly, "your guardian thought the Archbishop of Mayence had relented, and would withdraw his opposition to our marriage. Has Mayence said anything to corroborate that estimate?"

"Nothing."

"Has your guardian broached the subject to him?"

"Yes; but the attitude of my Lord of Mayence was quite inscrutable. Personally I think my guardian wrong in his surmise. The Archbishop of

311

Treves murmured that Mayence never forgives. I am certain I offended him too deeply for pardon. He wishes the future Empress to be a pliable creature who will influence her husband according to his Lordship's desires, but, as I have boasted several times, I belong to the House of Sayn."

"Hilda, will you marry me in spite of the Archbishops?"

"Roland, will you forego kingship for my sake?"

"Yes; a thousand times yes!"

"You said 'For the Empress; not for the Empire,' but if I am no Empress, you will as cheerfully wed me?"

"Yes."

"Then I say yes!"

He caught her in his arms, and they floated into the heaven of their first kiss, an ecstatic melting together. Suddenly she drew away from him.

"There is some one coming," she whispered.

"Nothing matters now," said Roland breathlessly. "There is no one in the world to-day but you and me."

Hildegunde drew her hands down her cheeks, as if to brush away their tell-tale color and their warmth.

"'Tis like," said Roland, "that you marry a poor man."

"Nothing matters now," she repeated, laughing tremulously. "I am said to be the richest woman in Germany. I shall build you a forge and enlist myself your apprentice. We will paint over the door 'Herr Roland and wife; sword makers.'"

Two men appeared at the end of the alley, and stood still; the one with a frown on his brow, the other with a smile on his lips.

"Oh!" whispered the Countess, panic striking from her face the color that her palms had failed to remove, "the Archbishop and the Count Palatine!"

His Lordship strode forward, followed more leisurely by the smiling Count.

"Prince Roland," said Cologne, "I had not expected this after our conference of last night."

"I fail to understand why, my Lord, when my parting words were 'Tell your porter to let me in without parley.' That surely indicated an intention on my part to visit the Palace."

"Your Highness knows that so far as I am concerned you are very welcome, and always shall be so, but at this juncture there are others to consider."

Roland interrupted.

"Read this letter, my Lord, and you will learn that I am here with the full concurrence of that generous Prince of the Church, Mayence."

Cologne, with knitted brow, scrutinized the communication.

"Your Highness is most courageous, but, if I may be permitted, just a trifle too clever."

"My Highness is not clever at all, but merely meets a situation as it arises."

"Prince Roland," said the Countess, her head raised proudly, "may I introduce to you my friend, and almost my neighbor, the Count Palatine of the Rhine?"

"Ah, pardon me," murmured the Archbishop, covered with confusion, but the jovial Count swept away all embarrassment by his hearty greeting.

"Prince Roland, I am delighted with the honor her ladyship accords me."

"And I, my Lord, am exceedingly gratified to meet the Count Palatine again."

"Again?" cried the Count in astonishment, "If ever we had encountered one another, your Highness, I certainly should not have been the one to forget the privilege."

The Prince laughed.

"It is true, nevertheless. My Lord Count, there is a namesake of mine in the precincts of your strong Castle of Gutenfels; a namesake who does more honor to the title than I do myself."

The Count Palatine threw back his head, and the forest garden echoed with boisterous laughter.

"You mean my black charger, Prince Roland!" he shouted. "A noble horse indeed. How knew you of him? If your Highness cares for horses allow me to present him to you."

"Never, my Lord Count. You are too fond of him yourself, and I have always had an affectionate feeling towards you for your love of that animal, which, indeed, hardly exceeds my own. I grasped his bridle-rein, and held the stirrup while you mounted."

"How is that possible?" asked the astonished Count.

"I cared for Prince Roland nearly a month, receiving generous wages, and, what I valued more, your own commendation, for you saw I was as fond of horses as you were."

"Good heavens! Were you that youth who came so mysteriously, and disappeared without warning?"

"Yes," laughed the Prince. "I know Gutenfels nearly as well as you do. I was a spy, studying the art of war and methods of fortification. I stopped in various capacities at nearly all the famous Castles of the Rhine, and this knowledge recently came in—"

"Your Highness, your Highness!" pleaded the Archbishop. "I implore you to remember that the Count Palatine is an Elector of the Empire, and, as I told last night, we are facing a crisis. Until that crisis is passed you will add to my already great anxiety by any lack of reticence on your part."

"By the Three Kings!" cried the Count, "this youth, if I may venture to call him so, has bound me to him with bands stronger than chain armor. I shall vote for him whoever falters."

"His Highness," said the Archbishop, with a propitiatory smile, "has been listening to the Eastern tales which our ancestors brought from the Crusades, and I fear has filled his head with fancies."

"Really, Archbishop, you misjudge me," said the young man; "I am the most practical person in the Empire. You interrupted my boasting to her ladyship of my handiwork. I would have you know I am a capable mechanic and a sword maker. What think you of that, my Lord?" he asked, drawing forth his weapon, and handing it to Cologne.

"An excellent blade indeed," said the latter, balancing it in his hand.

"Very well, my Lord, I made it and tempered it unassisted. I beg you to re-enter your palace, and write me out an order for a thousand of these weapons."

"If your Highness really wishes me to do this, and there is no concealed humorism in your request which I am too dull to fathom, you must accompany me to my study and dictate the document I am to indite. I shall wait till you bid farewell to the Countess."

A glance of mutual understanding flashed between the girl and himself, then Roland raised her hand to his lips, and although the onlookers saw the gallant salutation, they knew nothing of the gentle pressure with which the fingers exchanged their confidences.

"Madam," said the Prince, "it will be my pleasure and duty to wait upon my mother to-morrow. May I look forward to the happiness of presenting you to her?"

"I thank you," said the Countess simply, with a glance of appeal at her guardian. That good man sighed, then led the way into the house.

XX. THE MYSTERY OF THE FOREST

Roland left the palace with a sense of elation he had never before experienced, but this received a check as he saw standing in the middle of the square the Lieutenant of the night before. His first impulse was to avoid the officer, yet almost instinctively he turned and walked directly to him, which apparently nonplussed the brave emissary of Mayence.

"Good afternoon to you, sir," began Roland, as if overjoyed to see him. "Will you permit me to speak to you, sir?"

"Well?" said the Lieutenant curtly.

"My forge, which has been black and cold for many a long day, will soon be alight and warm again. What think you of this?" He handed to the Lieutenant his order for a thousand swords, and the officer made a mental note of the commission as an interesting point in armament that would be appreciated by his chief.

"You did not inform me last night who was the merchant you hoped would finance your enterprise."

"Hoped?" echoed Roland, his eyes sparkling. "'Tis more than hope, Herr Lieutenant. His name is Goebel, and he is one of the richest and chiefest traffickers of Frankfort. Why, my fortune is made! Read this, written in his own hand. I got it from him before midday, on my mere word that I was certain of an order from his Lordship."

"You are indeed much to be envied," said the Lieutenant coldly, returning the two documents.

"Ah, but I am just at the beginning. If you would favor me by smoothing the way to his Lordship, the Archbishop of Mayence, I in return—"

"Out upon you for a base-born, profit-mongering churl! Do you think that I, an officer, would demean myself by partnering a bagman!"

The Lieutenant turned on his heel, strode away and left him. Roland pursued his way with bowed head, as though stricken by the rebuff. Nearing the bridge, he saw a crowd around an empty cart, standing by which a man in rough clothing was cursing most vociferously.

At first he thought there had been an accident, but most of the people were laughing loudly; so, halting in the outskirts, he asked the cause of the commotion.

"'Tis but a fool farmer," said a man, "who came from the country with his load of vegetables. 'Tis safer to enter a lion's den unarmed than to come into Frankfort with food while people are starving. He has been plundered to the last leaf."

Roland shouldered his way through the crowd, and touched the frantic man on the shoulder.

"What was the value of your load?" he said.

"A misbegotten liar told me this morning that a market had opened in Frankfort, and that there was money to be had. No sooner am I in the town than everything I brought in is stolen."

"Yes, yes; I know all about that. My question is, How much is your merchandise worth?"

"Worth? Thirty thalers I expected to get, and now—"

"Thirty thalers," interrupted the Prince. "Here is your money. Get you gone, and tell your neighbors there is prompt payment for all the provender they can bring in."

The man calmed down as if a bucket of water had been thrown on him. He counted the payment with miserly care, testing each coin between his teeth, then mounted his cart without a word of thanks, and, to the disappointment of the gathering mob, drove away. Roland, seething with anger, walked directly to the house of Herr Goebel, and found that placid old burgher seated at his table.

"Ten thousand curses on your indolence!" he cried. "Where are your committee, and the emissaries empowered to carry out this scheme of relief I have ordered?"

"Committee? Emissaries?" cried the astonished man. "There has been no time!"

"Time, you thick-headed fool! I'll time you by hanging you to your own front door. There has been time for me to send my men out into the country; time for a farmer to come in with a cartload of produce, and be robbed here under your very nose! Maledictions on you, you sit here, well fed, and cry there is no time! If I had not paid the yeoman he would have gone back into the country crying we were all thieves here in Frankfort. Now listen to me. I drew my sword once upon you in jest. Should I draw it a second time it will be to penetrate your lazy carcass by running you through. If within two hours there is not a paymaster at every gate in Frankfort to buy and pay for each cartload of produce as it comes, and also a number of guides to tell that farmer where to deliver his goods, I'll give your town over to the military, and order the sacking of every merchant's house within its walls."

"It shall be done; it shall be done; it shall be done!" breathed the merchant, trembling as he rose, and he kept repeating the phrase with the iteration of a parrot.

"You owe me thirty thalers," said the Prince calming down; "the first payment out of the relief fund. Give me the money."

With quivering hands Herr Goebel, seeing no humor in the application, handed over the money, which the Prince slipped into his wallet.

Dusk had fallen when at last he reached his room in Sachsenhausen, and there he found awaiting him Joseph Greusel, in semi-darkness and in total gloom.

"Your housekeeper let me in," said the visitor.

"Good! I did not expect you back so soon. Have the others returned?"

"I do not know. I came direct here. I carry very ominous news, Roland, of impending disaster in Frankfort."

"Greater than at present oppresses it?"

"Civil war, fire, and bloodshed. Close the door, Roland; I am tired out, and I do not wish to be overheard."

The Prince obeyed the request, locking the door. Going to a cupboard, he produced a generous flagon of wine and a tankard, setting the same on a small table before Greusel, then he threw himself down in the one armchair the room possessed. Greusel filled the tankard, and emptied it without drawing breath. He plunged directly into his narrative.

"I had penetrated less than half a league into the forest when I was stopped by an armed man who stepped out from behind a tree. He wore the uniform of Mayence, and proclaimed me a prisoner. I explained my mission, but this had no effect upon him. He asked if I would go with him quietly, or compel him to call assistance. Being helpless, I said I would go quietly. Notwithstanding this, he bound my wrists behind me, then with a strip of cloth blindfolded me. Taking me by the arm, he led me through the forest for a distance impossible to calculate. I think, however, we walked not more than ten minutes. There was a stop and a whispered parley; a pause of a few minutes, and a further conference, which I partially heard. The commander before whom I must be taken was not ready to receive me. I should be placed in a tent, and a guard set over me.

"This was done. I asked that the cord, which hurt my wrists, might be removed, but instead, my ankles were tied together, and I sat there on the ground, leaning against a pole at the back of the tent. Here my conductor left me, and I heard him give orders to those without to maintain a strict watch, but to hold no communication with me.

"I imagine that the tent I occupied stood back to back with the tent of the commander, for after some time I heard the sound of voices, and it seemed to me voices of two men in authority. They had come to the back part of their tent, as if to speak confidentially, and their voices were low, yet I could hear them quite distinctly, being separated from them merely by two thicknesses of cloth. What I learned was this. There is concealed in the forest, within half an hour's quick march of the southern gate, a force of seven thousand soldiers. These soldiers belong to the Archbishop of Mayence, who commands an additional three thousand within the walls of Frankfort. Mayence holds the southern gate, as Treves holds the western and Cologne the northern. You see at once what that implies. Mayence can pour his troops into Frankfort, say, at midnight, and in the morning he has ten thousand soldiers as compared with the three thousand each commanded by the Archbishops of Treves and Cologne. That means civil war, and the complete crushing of the two northern Archbishops."

"I think you take too serious a view of the matter," commented Roland. "Mayence is undoubtedly a subtle man, who takes every precaution that he shall have his own way. The reason that there will be no civil war is this. I happen to know on very excellent authority that so far as the Electoral Court goes, Mayence is paramount. He does not need to conquer Cologne and Treves by force, because he is already supreme by his genius for intrigue. He is a born ruler, and his methods are all those of diplomacy as against those of arms. I dare say if occasion demanded it he would strike quick and strike effectually, but occasion does not demand. I am rather sure of my facts, and I know that the three Archbishops, together with the Count Palatine of the Rhine, are in agreement to elect my namesake, Prince Roland, Emperor of Germany."

"Yes," said Greusel, "I heard that rumor, and it is generally believed in Frankfort. Rumor, however, as usual, speaks falsely."

The Prince smiled at his pessimistic colleague, for that colleague was talking to the man who knew; nevertheless, he listened patiently, for of course he could not yet reveal himself to his somber lieutenant, who continued his narrative:

"The two men spoke of the unfortunate Prince, who is, I understand, still a prisoner in Ehrenfels."

Here Roland laughed outright.

"My dear Greusel, you are entirely mistaken. The Prince was never really a prisoner, and is at this moment in Frankfort, as free to do what he likes as

I am."

"I am sorry," said Greusel, "that you do not grasp the seriousness of the situation, but I have not yet come to the vital part of it, although I thought the very fact that seven thousand men threatened Frankfort would impress you."

"It does, Greusel," said Roland, remembering the distrust in which both the Countess and her guardian held Mayence, and also the close watch his Lordship was keeping over Frankfort, as evidenced by the domiciliary visit paid to himself by an officer of that potentate. "Go on, Greusel," he said more soberly, "I shall not interrupt you again."

"I gathered that Prince Roland actually had been chosen, but complications arose which I do not altogether understand. These complications relate to a woman, or two women; both of them equally objectionable to the Archbishop of Mayence. One of these two women was to marry the new Emperor, but rather than have this happen, Mayence determined that another than Prince Roland should be elected, the reason being that Mayence feared one Empress would be entirely under the influence of Cologne, if chosen, and the other under the influence of Treves. So his subtle Lordship is deluding both of these Electors. Cologne has been asked to bring to Frankfort the woman he controls, therefore he harbors the illusion that Mayence is reconciled to her. Treves also has been requested to bring the lady who is his relative; thus she, too, is in Frankfort, and Treves blindly believes Mayence is favorable to her cause.

"As a matter of fact Mayence will have neither, but has resolved to spring upon the Electoral Court at the last moment the name of the Grand Duke Karl of Hesse, a middle-aged man already married, and entirely under the dominance of his Lordship of Mayence."

"Pardon me, Greusel, I must interrupt, in spite of my disclaimer. What you say sounds very ingenious, but it cannot be carried out. Treves, Cologne, and the Count Palatine are already pledged to vote for Prince Roland, so is Mayence himself, and to change front at the last moment would be to forswear himself, and act as traitor to his colleagues. Now, he cannot afford to lose even one vote, and I believe that the Archbishop of Cologne will vote for Prince Roland through thick and thin. I think the same of the Count Palatine. Treves, of course, is always doubtful and wavering, but you see that the negative vote of the Archbishop of Cologne would render Mayence powerless and an Election impossible."

"Doubtless what you say is true, and now you have put your finger on the danger spot. Why has the Election been delayed beyond all precedent?"

"That I do not know," replied Roland.

"Then I will tell you. The Archbishop of Mayence has sent peremptory orders to the other three Electors, who are reported to be careless so far as Imperial affairs are concerned, and quite indifferent regarding the personality of the future Emperor. No one of these three Electors, however, dares offend so powerful a man as Mayence. If the Archbishop can overawe his colleagues nominally equal to him in position, each commanding an army, how think you can three small nobles, with no soldiers at their beck, withstand his requests, suavely given, no doubt, but with an iron menace behind them?"

"True, true," muttered Roland.

"Two of these nobles have already arrived, and are housed with the Archbishop of Mayence. The third is expected here within three days; four days at the farthest. Mayence will immediately convene the Electoral Court, when the Count Palatine, with the two Archbishops, may be astonished to find that for the first time in history, the whole seven are present in the Wahlzimmer. Mayence will ask Cologne to make the nomination, and he will put forward the name of Prince Roland. On a vote being taken the Prince will be in a minority of one. Mayence then shows his hand, nominating the Grand Duke Karl, who will be elected by a majority of one. Then may ensue a commotion in the Wahlzimmer, and accusations of bad faith, but remember that Cologne and Treves are taken completely by surprise. They cannot communicate with their commanders, for the three thousand troops which Mayence already has within Frankfort will have quietly surrounded the Town Hall that contains the Election Chamber, and Mayence's seven thousand men from the forest are pouring through the southern gate into the city, making straight for the Romer. Meanwhile the Grand Duke Karl, a man well known to the populace of Frankfort, appears on the balcony of the Kaisersaal, and is loudly acclaimed the new Emperor."

"Ah, Greusel, forgive my attitude of doubt. It is all as plain now as the Cathedral tower. Still, there will be no civil war. Treves and Cologne will gather up their troops and go home, once more defeated by a man cleverer and more unscrupulous than both of them put together. They are but infants in his hands."

"Have you any suggestion to make?" asked Greusel.

"No; there is nothing to be done. You see, the young Prince has no following. He is quite unknown in Frankfort. His name can arouse no enthusiasm, and, all in all, that strikes me as a very good thing. The Grand Duke Karl is popular, and I believe he will make a very good Emperor."

"You mean, Roland, that the Archbishop of Mayence will make a very good ruler, for he will be the real king."

"Well, after all, Joseph, there is much to be said in favor of Mayence. He is a man who knows what he wants, and, what is more, gets it, and that, after all is the main thing in life. If any one could sway the Archbishop so that he put his great talents to the benefit of his country, instead of thinking only of himself, what a triumph of influence that would be! By the Three Kings, I'd like to do it! I admire him. If I found opportunity and could persuade him to join us in the relief of Frankfort, and in opening the Rhine to commerce, we would give these inane merchants a lesson in organization."

Greusel rose from his chair, poured out another tankard full from the flagon, and drank it off.

"I must go down now and meet the guild," he said. "I have eaten nothing all day, and am as hungry as a wolf from the Taunus."

"Oh, how did you escape, by the way?"

"I didn't escape. I was led blindfolded into a tent, where my bandage was removed, and here a man in ordinary dress questioned me concerning my object in entering the forest. I told him exactly the truth, and explained what we were trying to do in Frankfort. I dare say I looked honest and rather stupid. He asked when I set out; in what direction I came; questioning me with a great affectation of indifference; wanted to know if I had met many persons, and I told him quite truthfully I met no one but the man I understood was a forester; a keeper, I supposed.'

"'There are a number of us,' he said, 'hunting the wild boar, and we do not wish the animal life of these woods to be disturbed. We shall not be here longer than a week, but I advise you to seek another spot for what timber you require.'

"He asked me, finally, if any one in Frankfort knew I had come to the forest, and I answered that the guild of twenty knew, and that we were all to meet to-night at the Rheingold tavern to report. He pondered for a while on this statement, and I suppose reached the conclusion that if I did not return to Frankfort, this score of men might set out in the morning to search for me, it being well known that the forest is dangerous on account of wild boars. So, as if it were of no consequence, he blindfolded me again, apologizing privately for doing so, saying it was quite unnecessary in the first instance, but as the guard had done so, he did not wish to censure him by implication.

"I answered that it did not matter at all, but desired him to order my wrists released, which was done."

"I must say," commented Roland, "that the Archbishop of Mayence is well served by his officers. Your examiner was a wise man."

"Yes," replied Greusel, "but nevertheless, I am telling my story here in Frankfort."

"No difference for that, because, as I have said, we can do nothing. Still, it is a blessing your examiner could not guess what you overheard in the other tent. He let you go thinking you had seen and learned nothing, and in doing so warded off a search party to-morrow."

XXI. A SECRET MARRIAGE

Blessed is he that expects nothing, for he shall not be disappointed. Roland walked with Greusel across the bridge and through the streets to the entrance of the Rheingold, and there stopped.

"I shall not go down with you," he said. "You have given me much to think of, and I am in no mood for a hilarious meeting. Indeed, I fear I should but damp the enthusiasm of the lads. Continue your good work to-morrow, and report to me at my room."

With this Roland bade Greusel good-night and turned away. He walked very slowly as far as the bridge, and there, resting his arms on the parapet, looked down at the dark water. He was astonished to realize how little he cared about giving up the Emperorship, and he recalled, with a glow of delight, his recent talk in the garden with Hildegunde, and her assurance that she lacked all ambition to become the first lady in the land so long as they two spent their lives together.

The bells of Frankfort tolling the hour of ten aroused him from his reverie, and brought down his thoughts from delicious dreams of romance to realms of reality. The precious minutes were passing over his head swiftly as the drops of water beneath his feet. There was little use of feeding Frankfort if it must be given over to fire and slaughter.

With a chill of apprehension he reviewed the cold treachery of Mayence, willing to levy the horrors of civil war upon an already stricken city so long as his own selfish purposes were attained.

"And yet," he said to himself, "there must be good in the man. I wish I knew his history. Perhaps he had to fight for every step he has risen in the world. Perhaps he has been baffled and defeated by deception; overcome by chicanery until his faith died within him. My faith would die within me were it not that when I meet a Mayence I encounter also the virtue of a Cologne, and the bluff honesty of a Count Palatine. How marvelous is this world, where the trickery of a Kurzbold and a Gensbein is canceled by the faithfulness unto death of a Greusel and an Ebearhard! Thus doth good balance evil, and then—and then, how Heaven beams upon earth in the angel glance of a good woman. God guide me aright! God guide me aright!" he repeated fervently, "and suppress in me all anger and uncharitableness."

He walked rapidly across the bridge into Sachsenhausen, past his room at the street corner, and on to the monastery of the Benedictines, whose little chapel stood open night and day for the prayers of those in trouble or in sadness, habited only by one of the elder brothers, who gave, if it were needed, advice, encouragement, or spiritual comfort. Removing his hat, the Prince entered into the silence on tiptoe, and kneeling before the altar, prayed devoutly for direction, asking the Almighty to turn the thoughts of His servant, Mayence, into channels that flowed towards peace and the relief of this unhappy city.

As he rose to his feet a weight lifted from his shoulders, and the buoyancy of youth drove away the depression that temporarily overcame him on hearing of the army threatening Frankfort. His plans were honest, his methods conciliatory, and the path now seemed clear before him. The monk in charge, who had been kneeling in a dark corner near the door, now came forward to intercept him.

"Will your Highness deny me in the chapel as you did upon the bridge?"

Roland stopped. In the gloom he had not recognized the ghostly Father.

"No, Father Ambrose, and I do now what I should have done then. I pray your blessing on the enterprise before me."

"My son, it is willingly given, the more willingly that I may atone in part my forgetting of the Holy Words: 'Judge not, that ye be not judged.' I grievously misjudged you, as I learn from both the Archbishop and my kinswoman. I ask your forgiveness."

"I shall forgive you, Father Ambrose, if you make full, not partial atonement. The consequences of your mistake have proved drastic and far-reaching. The least of these consequences is that it has cost me the

Emperorship."

"Oh," moaned the good man, "mea culpa, mea culpa! No penance put upon me can compensate for that disaster."

"You blame yourself overmuch, good Father. The penance I have to impose will leave me deeply in your debt. Now, to come from the least to the greatest of these results, so far as I am concerned, my marriage with your kinswoman, whom I love devotedly, is in jeopardy. Through her conviction that I was a thief, she braved the Archbishop of Mayence, who imprisoned her, and now his Lordship has determined that the Grand Duke Karl of Hesse shall be Emperor. Thus we arrive at the most important outcome of your error. Between the overwhelming forces of Mayence and the insufficient troops of Cologne and Treves there may ensue a conflict causing the streets of Frankfort to flow with blood."

The pious man groaned dismally.

"I have a plan which will prevent this. The day after to-morrow I shall renounce all claim to the throne; but being selfish, like the rest, I refuse to renounce all claim to the woman the Archbishops themselves chose as my wife, neither shall I allow the case to be made further the plaything of circumstance. Your kinswoman, no later ago than this afternoon, confessed her love for me and her complete disregard of any position I may hold in this realm. Now, Father Ambrose, I ask you several questions. Is it in consonance with the rules of the Church that a marriage be solemnized in this chapel?"

"Yes."

"Are you entitled to perform the ceremony?"

"Yes."

"Is it possible this ceremony can be performed to-morrow?"

"Yes."

"Will you therefore attend to the necessary preliminaries, of which I am vastly ignorant, and say at what hour the Countess and I may present ourselves in this chapel?"

"The Archbishop of Cologne is guardian to her ladyship. Will you bring me his sanction?"

"Ah, Father Ambrose, there is just the point. So far as concerns himself I doubt not that the Archbishop is the most unambitious of men, but to the marriage of his ward with a sword maker I fear he would refuse consent which he would gladly give to a marriage with an Emperor."

The monk hung his head, and pondered on the proposition. At last he said:

"Why not ask my Lord the Archbishop?"

"I dare not venture. Too much is at stake. She might be carried away to any castle in Germany. Remember that Cologne has already acquiesced in her imprisonment, and but that the iron chain of the Pfalzgraf brought me to her prison door—The iron chain, do I say? 'Twas the hand of God that directed me to her, and now, with the help of Him who guided me, not all the Archbishops in Christendom shall prevent our marriage. No, Father Ambrose, pile on yourself all the futile penances you can adopt. They are useless, for they do not remedy the wrong you have committed. And now, good-night to your Reverence!"

The young man strode towards the door.

"My son," said the quiet voice of the priest, "when you were on your knees just now did you pray for remission from anger?"

Roland whirled round.

"Mea culpa, as you said just now. Father Ambrose, I ask your pardon. I made an unfair use of your mistake to coerce you. You were quite right in relating what your own eyes saw here in Frankfort, and although the inference drawn was wrong, you were not to blame for that. I recognize your scruples, but nevertheless protest that already I possess the sanction of the Archbishop, which has never been withdrawn."

"Prince Roland, if you bring hither the Countess von Sayn to-morrow afternoon, when the bells strike three, I will marry you, and gladly accept whatever penances ensue. I fear the monk's robe has not crushed out all the impulses of the Sayn blood. In my case, perhaps, it has only covered them. And now, good-night, and God's blessing fall upon you and her you are to marry."

Roland went directly from the chapel to his own room, where he slept the sleep of one who has made up his mind. Nevertheless, it was not a dreamless sleep, for throughout the night he seemed to hear the tramp of armed men marching upon unconscious Frankfort, and this sound was so persistent, that at last he woke, yet still it continued. Springing up in alarm, and flinging wide the wooden shutters of his window, he was amazed to see that the sun was already high, while the sound that disturbed him was caused by a procession of heavy-footed horses, dragging over the cobble-stones carts well-laden with farm produce.

Having dressed and finished breakfast, he wrote a letter to the Archbishop of Mayence:

"My LORD ARCHBISHOP,—There are some important proposals which I wish to make to the Electors, and as it is an unwritten rule that I should not communicate with them separately, I beg of you to convene a meeting to-morrow, in the Wahlzimmer, at the hour of midday. Perhaps it is permissible to add, for your own information, that while my major proposition has to do with the relief of Frankfort, the minor suggestions I shall make will have the effect of clearing away obstacles that at present obstruct your path, and I venture to think that what I say will meet with your warmest approval."

It was so necessary that this communication should reach the Archbishop as soon as possible that Roland became his own messenger, and himself delivered the document at the Archbishop's Palace. As he turned away he was startled by a hand being placed on his shoulder with a weight suggesting an action of arrest rather than a greeting of friendship. He turned quickly, and saw the Lieutenant who had so discourteously used him in the square. There was, however, no menace in the officer's countenance.

"Still thrusting your sword at people?"

"Yes, Lieutenant, and very harmlessly. 'Tis a bloodless combat I wage with the sword. I praise its construction, and leave to superiors like yourself, sir, the proving of its quality."

"You are an energetic young man, and we of Mayence admire competence whether shown by mechanic or noble. Was the letter you handed in just now addressed to his Lordship?"

"Yes, Lieutenant."

"'Twill be quite without effect."

"It grieves me to hear you say so, sir."

"Take my advice, and make no effort to see the Archbishop until after the Election. I judge you to be a sane young fellow, for whom I confess a liking. You are the only man in Frankfort who has unhesitatingly told me the exact truth, and I have not yet recovered from my amazement. Now, when you return to your frugal room in Sachsenhausen you do not attempt to reach it by mounting the stairs with one step?"

"Naturally not, Lieutenant."

"Very well. When the Emperor is proclaimed, come you to me. I'll introduce you to my superior, and he, if impressed with your weapon, will take you a step higher, and thus you will mount until you come to an officer who may give you an astonishing order."

"I thank you, Lieutenant, and hope later to avail myself of your kindness."

The Lieutenant slapped him on the shoulder, and wished him good-luck. As Roland pushed his way through the crowd, he said to himself, with a sigh:

"I regret not being Emperor, if only for the sake of young fellows like that."

Frankfort was transformed as if a magician had waved his wand over it. The streets swarmed with people. Farmers' vehicles of every description added to the confusion, and Roland frowned as he noticed how badly organized had been the preparations for coping with this sudden influx of food, but he also saw that the men of Mayence had taken a hand in the matter, and were rapidly bringing method out of chaos. The uniforms of Cologne or Treves were seldom seen, while the quiet but firm soldiers of Mayence were everywhere ordering to their homes those already served, and clearing the way for the empty-handed.

At last Roland reached the Palace of Cologne, through a square thronged with people. Within he found his mother and the Countess, seated in a room whose windows overlooked the square, watching the stirring scene presented to them. Having saluted his mother, he greeted the girl with a quiet pressure of the hand.

"What is the cause of all this commotion?" asked the Empress.

Roland tapped his breast.

"I am the cause, mother," and he related the history of the relief committee, and if appreciation carries with it gratification, his was the advantage of knowing that the two women agreed he was the most wonderful of men.

"But indeed, mother," continued Roland, "I selfishly rob you of the credit. The beginning of all this was really your gift to me of five hundred thalers, that time I came to crave your assistance in procuring me this document I still carry, and without your thalers and the parchment, this never could have happened. So you see they have increased like the loaves and fishes of Holy Writ, and thus feed the multitude."

Her Majesty arose, smiling.

"Ah, Roland," she said, kissing him, "you always gave your mother more credit than she deserved. It wrung my heart at the time that I was so scant of money." Then, pleading fatigue, the Empress left the room.

"Hilda!" cried the young man, "when you and I discuss things, those things become true. Yesterday we agreed that the Imperial throne was not so enviable a seat as a chair by the domestic hearth. To-day I propose to secure the chair at the hearth, and to-morrow I shall freely give up the Imperial throne."

The girl uttered an exclamation that seemed partly concurrence and partly dismay, but she spoke no word, gazing at him intently as he strode up and down the room, and listening with eagerness. Walking backwards and forwards, looking like an enthusiastic boy, he very graphically detailed the situation as he had learned it from Greusel.

"Now you see, my dear, any opposition to the Archbishop of Mayence means a conflict, and supposing in that conflict our friends were to win, the victory would be scarcely less disastrous than defeat. I at once made up my mind, fortified by my knowledge of your opinion on the subject, that for all the kingships in the world I could not be the cause of civil dissension."

"That is a just and noble decision," she said, speaking for the first time.

Then, standing before her, the young man in more moderate tone related what had happened and what had been said in the chapel of the Benedictine Fathers. She looked up at him, earnest face aglow, during the first part of his recital, and now and then the sunshine of a smile flickered at the corners of her mouth as she recognized her kinsman in her lover's repetition of his words, but when it came to the question of a marriage, her eyes sank to the floor, and remained there.

"Well, Hilda," he said at last, "have you the courage to go with me, all unadvised, all unchaperoned, to the chapel this afternoon at three o'clock?"

She rose slowly, still without looking at him, placed her hands on his shoulders, then slipped them round his neck, laying her cheek beside his.

"It requires no courage, Roland," she whispered, "to go anywhere if you are with me. I need to call up my courage only when I think with a shudder of our being separated."

Some minutes elapsed before conversation was resumed.

"Where is the Archbishop?" asked Roland, in belated manner remembering his host.

"He and the Count Palatine went out together about an hour since. I think they were somewhat disturbed at the unusual commotion, and desired to know what it meant. Do you want to consult my guardian after all?"

"Not unless you desire me to do so?"

"I wish only what you wish, Roland."

"I am glad his Lordship is absent. Let us to the garden, Hilda, and discover a quiet exit if we can."

A stout door was found in the wall to the rear, almost concealed with shrubbery. The bolts were strong, and rusted in, but the prowess of Roland overcame them, and he drew the door partially open. It looked out upon a narrow alley with another high wall opposite. Roland looked up and down the lane, and saw it was completely deserted.

"This will do excellently," he said, shoving the door shut again, but without thrusting the bolts into position. He took her two hands in his.

"Dearest, noblest, sweetest of girls! I must now leave you. Await me here at half-past one. I go out by this door, for it is necessary I should know exactly where the alley joins a main street. It would be rather embarrassing if you were standing here, and Father Ambrose looking for us in the chapel, while I was frantically searching for and not finding the lane."

Some time in advance of the hour set, the impatient young man kept the appointment he had made, and when the Countess appeared exactly on the minute, he held open the door for her, then, drawing it shut behind him, they were both out in the city of Frankfort together. Roland's high spirits were such that he could scarcely refrain from dancing along at her side.

"I'd like to take your hand," he said, "and swing it, and show you the sights of the city, as if we were two young people in from the country."

"I am a country girl, please to remember," said the Countess. "I know nothing of Frankfort, or, indeed, of any other large town."

"I am glad of that, for there is much to see in Frankfort. We will make for the Cathedral, that beautiful red building, splendid and grand, where we should have been married with great and useless ceremony if I had been crowned Emperor. But I am sure the simple chapel in the working town of Sachsenhausen better suits a sword maker and his bride."

Now they came out into the busy street, which seemed more thronged than ever. In making their way to the Cathedral, the mob became so dense that progression was difficult. The current seemed setting in one direction, and it carried them along with it. Hildegunde took the young man's arm, and clung close to him.

"They are driving us, whether we will or no, towards our old enemy, the Archbishop of Mayence. That is his Palace facing the square. There is some sort of demonstration going on," cried Roland, as cheer after cheer ascended to the heavens. "How grim and silent the Palace appears, all shuttered as if it were a house of the dead! Somehow it reminds me of Mayence himself. I had pictured him occupying a house of gloom like that."

"Do you think we are in any danger?" asked the girl. "The people seem very boisterous."

"Oh, no danger at all. This mob is in the greatest good-humor. Listen to their heart-stirring cheers! The people have been fed; that is the reason of it."

"Is that why they cheer? It sounds to me like an ovation to the Archbishop! Listen to them: 'Long live Mayence! God bless the Archbishop!' There is no terror in those shouts."

Nevertheless his Lordship of Mayence had taken every precaution. The shutters of his Palace were tightly closed, and along the whole front of the edifice a double line of soldiers was ranged under the silent command of their officers. They stood still and stiffly as stone-graven statues in front of a Cathedral. The cheers rang unceasingly. Then, suddenly, as if the sinister Palace opened one eye, shutters were turned away from a great window giving upon the portico above the door. The window itself was then thrown wide. Cheering ceased, and in the new silence, from out the darkness there stepped with great dignity an old man, gorgeous in his long robes of office, and surmounting that splendid intellectual head rested the mitered hat of an Archbishop. After the momentary silence the cheers seemed to storm the very door of the sky itself, but the old man moved no muscle, and no color tinged his wan face.

"By the Kings," whispered Roland, during a temporary lull, "what a man! There stands power embodied, and yet I venture 'tis his first taste of popularity. I am glad we have seen this sight, both mob and master. How quick are the people to understand who is the real ruler of Germany! I wish he were my friend!"

Slowly the Archbishop raised his open hands, holding them for a moment in benediction over the vast assemblage. Once more the cheers died away, and every head was bowed, then the Archbishop was in his place no longer. Unseen hands closed the windows, and a moment later the shutters blinded it. The multitude began to dissolve, and the two wanderers found their way become clearer and clearer.

Together they entered the empty, red Cathedral, and together knelt down in a secluded corner. After some minutes passed thus Roland remembered that the hour of two had struck while they were gazing at the Archbishop. Gently he touched the hand of his companion. They rose, and walked slowly through the great church.

"There," he whispered, "is where the Emperor is crowned. The Archbishop of Mayence always performs that ceremony, so, after all, there is some justification for his self-assumed leadership."

Again out into the sunshine they walked to the Fahrgasse, and then to the bridge, where the Countess paused with an expression of delight at the beauty of the waterside city, glorified by the westering sun. Crossing the river, and going down the Bruckenstrasse of Sachsenhausen, Roland said:

"Referring to people who are not Emperors, that is my room at the corner, where I lived when supposed to be in prison."

"Is that where you made your swords?" she asked.

"No; Greusel's workshop and mine is farther along that side street. It is a grimy shop of no importance, but here, on the other side, we have an edifice that counts. That low building is the Benedictine monastery, and this is its little chapel."

The Countess made no comment, but stood looking at it for a few moments until her thoughts were interrupted by the solemn tones of a bell striking three. Roland went up the steps, and held open the door while she passed in, then, removing his hat, he followed her.

XXII. LONG LIVE THEIR MAJESTIES

The most anxious man in all Frankfort was not to be found among the mighty who ruled the Empire, or among the merchants who trafficked therein, or among the people who starved when there was no traffic. The most anxious man was a small, fussy individual of great importance in his own estimation, cringing to those above him, denouncing those beneath; Herr Durnberg, Master of the Romer, in other words, the Keeper of the Town Hall. The great masters whom this little master served were imperious and unreasonable. They gave him too little information regarding their intentions, yet if he failed in his strict duty towards them, they would crush him as ruthlessly as if he were a wasp.

Unhappy Durnberg! Every morning he expected the Electoral Court to be convened that day, and every evening he was disappointed. It was his first duty to lay out upon the table in that great room, the Kaisersaal, a banquet, to be partaken of by the newly-made Emperor, and by the seven potentates who elected him. It was also his duty to provide two huge tanks of wine, one containing the ruby liquor pressed out at Assmannshausen; the other the straw-colored beverage that had made Hochheim famous. These tanks were connected by pipes with the plain, unassuming fountain standing opposite the Town Hall in that square called the Romerberg. The moment an election took place Herr Durnberg turned off the flow of water from the fountain, and turned on the flow of wine, thus for an hour and a half there poured from the northward pointing spout of the fountain the rich red wine of Assmannshausen, and from the southern spout the delicate white wine of Hochheim. Now, wine will keep for a long time, but a dinner will not, so the distracted Durnberg prepared banquet after banquet for which there were no consumers.

At last, thought Herr Durnberg, his vigilance was about to be rewarded. There came up the broad, winding stair, to the landing on which opened the great doors of the Kaisersaal, two joyous-looking young people, evidently lovers, and with the hilt of his sword the youth knocked against the stout panels of the door. It was Herr Durnberg himself who opened, and he said haughtily—

"The Romer is closed, and will not be free to strangers until after the Election."

"We enter, nevertheless. I am Prince Roland, here to meet the Court of Electors, who convene at midday in the adjoining Wahlzimmer. You, Romermeister, will announce to their august Lordships that I am here, and, when their will is expressed, summon me to audience with them."

Herr Durnberg bowed almost to the polished floor, and flinging open both doors, retreated backwards, still bent double as he implored them to enter. Locking the doors, for the Electors would reach the Wahlzimmer through a private way, to be used by none but themselves, the bustling Durnberg produced two chairs, which he set by the windows in the front, and again running the risk of falling on his nose, bowed his distinguished visitors to seats where they might entertain themselves by watching the enormous crowd that filled the Romerberg from end to end, for every man in Frankfort knew an Election was impending, and it was after the banquet, when the wine began to flow in the fountain, that the new Emperor exhibited himself to his people by stepping from the Kaisersaal out upon the balcony in front of it.

"Do you feel any shyness about meeting this formidable conclave? Remember you have at least two good friends among them."

The girl placed her hand in his, and looked affectionately upon him.

"When you are with me, Roland, I am afraid of nothing."

"I should not ask you to pass through this ordeal were it not for your guardian. His astonishment at the announcement of our marriage will be so honest and unacted that even the suspicious Mayence cannot accuse him of connivance in what we have done. Of course, the strength of my position is that I have but carried out the formal request of their three Lordships; a request which has never been rescinded."

Before she could reply the hour of twelve rang forth. The deferential Herr Durnberg entered from the Wahlzimmer, and softly approached them.

"Your Highness," he said, "my Lords, the Electors, request your presence in the Wahlzimmer."

"How many are there, Romer-meister?"

"There are four, your Highness; the three Archbishops and the Count Palatine."

"Ah," breathed Roland, relieved that Mayence had not called up his reserve, and assured now that the seventh Elector had not arrived. With a glance of encouragement at his wife, Roland passed into the presence.

Herr Durnberg, anxious about the outcome, showed an inclination to close the door and remain inside, but a very definite gesture from Mayence wafted the good man to outer regions.

Mayence opened the proceedings.

"Yesterday I received a communication from your Highness, requesting me to convene this Court. I am as ignorant as my colleagues regarding the subjects to be placed before us. I therefore announce to you that we are prepared to listen."

"I thank you, my Lord of Mayence," began the Prince very quietly. "When first I had the honor of meeting your three Lordships in the Castle of Ehrenfels, I signed certain documents, and came to an agreement with you upon other verbal requests. I am not yet a man of large experience, but at that time, although comparatively few days have elapsed, I was a mere boy, trusting in the good faith of the whole world, knowing nothing of its chicanery. Since then I have been through a bitter school, learning bitter lessons, but I am nevertheless encouraged, in that for every man of treachery and deceit I meet two who are trustworthy."

"Pardon me," said Mayence suavely, "I did not understand that the discourse you proposed was to be a sermon. If your theme is a lecture on morality, I beg to remind you that this Wahlzimmer is a place of business, and what you say is better suited to a chapel or even a church, than to the Election Chamber of the Empire."

"I am sorry, my Lord," said Roland humbly, "if my introduction does not meet your approval. I assure you that the very opposite was my intention. My purpose is to show you why a change has come over me, and in order—"

"Once more I regret interrupting, but the reason for whatever change has occurred can be of little interest to any one but yourself. You begin by making vague charges of dishonesty, treachery, and what-not, against some person or persons unknown. May I ask you to be definite?"

"Is it your Lordship's wish that I should mention names?"

Cologne showed signs of uneasiness; Treves looked in bewilderment from one to another of his colleagues; the Count Palatine sat deeply interested, his elbows on the table, massive chin supported by huge hands.

"Your Highness is the best judge whether names should be mentioned or not," said Mayence, quite calmly, as if his withers were unwrung. "But you must see that if you hint at conspiracy and bafflement, certain inferences are likely to be drawn. Since the time you speak of there has been no opportunity for you to meet your fellow-men, therefore these inferences are apt to take the color that reference is made to one or the other of the three personages you did meet. I therefore counsel you either to abstain from innuendo or explain explicitly what you mean."

"I the more willingly bow to your Lordship's decision because it is characterized by that wisdom which accompanies every word your Lordship utters. I shall therefore designate good men and bad."

Mayence gazed at the young man in amazement, but merely said:

"Proceed, sir, on your perilous road."

"I am the head of a gang of freebooters. When this company left Frankfort under my command we appeared to be all of one mind. My gang consisted entirely of ironworkers, well-set-up young fellows in splendid physical condition, yet before I was gone a day on our journey I found myself confronted by mutiny. A man named Kurzbold was the leader of this rebellion; a treacherous hound, whom I sentenced to death. The two who stood by me were Greusel and Ebearhard, therefore I told you that when I met one villain I encountered two trustworthy men."

"When did this happen?" asked Mayence. "And what was the object of your freebooting expedition?"

"High Heaven!" cried the Archbishop of Cologne, unable longer to restrain his impatience when he saw the fatal trend of the Prince's confession, "what madness has overcome you? Can you not see the effect of these disturbing disclosures?"

The Prince smiled, and answered first the last question.

"'Tis an honest confession, my Lord, of what may be considered a dishonest practice. It is information that should be within your knowledge before you sit down to elect an Emperor.

"When did this happen, my Lord of Mayence?" he continued, turning to the chairman. "It happened when you thought I was your prisoner in Ehrenfels. Never for a day did you hold me there. I roamed the country at my pleasure. I examined leisurely and effectively the defenses of nearly every castle on the Rhine from the town of Bonn to your own city of Mayence. The object of our expedition, you ask? It was to loot the stolen treasure of the robber castles, and incidentally it resulted in the destruction by fire of Furstenberg. The marauding excursion ended at Pfalz, where I lightened the Pfalzgraf of his wealth, and liberated the Countess von Sayn, unlawfully imprisoned within that fortress."

"By the Three Kings!" cried the Count Palatine, bringing his huge fist down on the table like the blow of a sledge hammer, "you are a man, and I glory that it is my privilege to vote for you."

"I agree with my brother of Cologne," said Treves, speaking for the first time, "that this young man does not properly weigh the inevitable result of his terrible words. I vote, of course, with my Lord of Mayence, but such a vote will be most reluctantly given for a self-confessed burglar and incendiary."

"Be not too hasty, gentlemen," counseled Mayence. "We are not met here to cast votes. Your Highness, I complained a moment ago of lack of interest in your recital; I beg to withdraw that plea. After having heard you I agree that the Countess was unjustly imprisoned. She was accurate in her estimate of your character."

"I think not, my Lord, I do not regard myself as burglar, incendiary, thief, or robber. I call myself rather a restorer of stolen property. I shed no blood, which in itself is a remarkable feature of action so drastic as mine. The incendiarism was merely incidental, forced upon me by the fact that the Red Margrave tied up eighteen of my men, whom he proposed presently to hang. I diverted his attention from this execution by the first method that occurred to me, namely, the firing of his Castle. In my letter to you yesterday, my Lord, I promised to clear away certain obstacles from your path. I therefore remove one, by saying that an object of this conference is my own renunciation of the Emperorship, thus while I thank my Lord Count for his proffered franchise, I quiet the mind of my Lord of Treves by assuring him his defection has no terror for me. And now, my Lord of Mayence, will you listen carefully to my suggestion?"

"Prince Roland," replied his Lordship, almost with geniality, "I have never heard so graphic a narrator in my life. Proceed, I beg of you."

"When our band of cut-purses set out from Frankfort, they supposed the gold was to be shared equally among us. Mutiny taught me to use the arts of diplomacy, which I despise. I hoped to attain such influence over them that they would agree to abjure wealth for the benefit of Frankfort. I am happy to say that I accomplished my object, so that yesterday and to-day you have witnessed the results of my efforts; the relief of a starving city. I merely removed the wealth of robbers to benefit those whom they robbed. Knowing the dangerous feeling actuating this town against your Lordships, I caused proclamation to be made crediting this relief to the Archbishops.

"My Lord of Mayence, when yesterday I saw you appear on your own balcony, the most stern, the most dignified figure I ever beheld; when I heard the ringing cheers that greeted you; when I realized, as never before, the majesty of your genius, I cursed the stupid decree of Fate that denied me your friendship. What could we not have accomplished together for the Fatherland? I, with my youth and energy, under the tutelage of your wisdom and experience. You tasted there, probably for the first time in your life, the intoxicating cup of popularity, yet it affected you no more than if you had drunk of the fountain in the Romerberg.

"Now, my Lords, here is what I ask of you, and it will show how much I would have depended upon you had I been chosen to the position at first proposed to me. I request you, my Lord of Treves, to remove your three thousand troops to the other side of the Rhine."

"I shall do nothing of the sort," blurted Treves, amazed at the absurd proposal.

Roland went on, unheeding:

"I ask you, my Lord of Cologne, to march your troops to Assmannshausen."

"You indeed babble like the boy you said you were!" cried the indignant Cologne. "You show no grasp of statesmanship."

A faint smile quivered on the thin lips of Mayence at his colleagues' ill-disguised fear at leaving him the man in possession so far as Frankfort was concerned. The naive proposal which angered his two brethren merely amused Mayence. This young man's absurdity was an intellectual treat. Roland smiled in sympathy as he turned towards him, but his next words banished all expression of pleasure from the face of Mayence.

"I hope to succeed better with you, my Lord. Of course I recognize I have no standing with this Court since my refusal of the gift you intended to bestow. I ask you to draft into this city seven thousand men;" then after a pause: *"the seven thousand will not have far to march, my Lord."*

He caught an expression almost of fear in the Archbishop's eyes, which were quickly veiled, but his Lordship's tone was as unwavering as ever when he asked:

"What do you mean by that?"

"I mean that the city of Mayence is nearer to Frankfort than either Cologne or Treves."

"Your geographical point is undeniable. What am I to do with my ten thousand once they are here?"

"My Lord, I admire the rigid discipline of your men, and estimate from that the genius of organization possessed by your officers; a genius imparted, I believe, by you. No one knows better than I the state of confusion which this effort at relief has brought upon the city. I suggest that your capable officers divide this city into cantons, proclaim martial law, and deliver to every inhabitant rations of food as if each man, woman, and child were a member of your army. Meanwhile the merchants should be relieved of a task for which they have proved their incapacity, and turn their attention to commerce. This relief at best must be temporary. The vital task is to open the Rhine. The merchants will load every barge on the river with goods, and this flotilla the armies of Treves and Cologne will escort in safety to the latter city. In passing they will deliver an ultimatum to every castle, demanding a contribution in gold towards the further relief of Frankfort, until commerce readjusts itself, and assuring each nobleman that if this commerce is molested, his castle shall be forfeited, and himself imprisoned or hanged."

"Quite an effective plan, I think, your Highness, to which I willingly agree, if you can assure me of the support of my two colleagues, which I regret to say has already been refused."

His Lordship looked from one to another, but neither withdrew his declaration.

"Prince Roland," continued Mayence, "we seem to have reached a deadlock, and I fear its cause is that distrust of one human being toward another that you deplored a while ago. I confess myself, however, so pleased with the trend of your mind as exhibited in your conversation with us, that I am desirous to know what further proposals you care to make, now that our mutual good intentions have led us into an impasse."

"Willingly, my Lord. I propose that you at once proceed to the Election of an Emperor, for the delay in his choosing has already caused an anxiety and a tension dangerous to the peace of this country."

"Ah, that is easier said than done, your Highness. Having yourself eliminated the one on whom we were agreed, it seems to me you should at least suggest a substitute."

"Again willingly, my Lord. You should choose some quiet, conservative man, and, if possible, one well known to the citizens of Frankfort, and held in good esteem by the people everywhere. He should be a man of middle age—" Mayence's eyes began to close again, and his lips to tighten—"and if he had some experience in government, that would be all to the good. One already married is preferable to a bachelor, for then no delicate considerations regarding a woman can arise, as, I need not remind your Lordship, have arisen in my own case. A man of common sense should be selected, who would not make rash experiments with the ideals of the German people, as a younger and less balanced person might be tempted to do. That he should be a good Churchman goes without saying—"

"A truce, a truce!" cried Mayence sternly. "Again we are running into a moral catalogue impossible of embodiment. Is there any such man in your mind, or are you merely treating us to a counsel of perfection?"

"Notwithstanding my pessimism," said Roland, "I still think so well of my countrymen as to believe there are many such. Not to make any recommendation to those so much better qualified to judge than I, but merely to give a sample, I mention the Grand Duke Karl of Hesse, who fulfills every requirement I have named."

For what seemed to the onlookers a tense period of suspense, the old man seated and the young man standing gazed intently at one another. Mayence knew at once that in some manner unknown to him the Prince had fathomed his intentions; that his Highness alone knew why the Election had been delayed, yet the Prince conveyed this knowledge directly to the person most concerned, in the very presence of those whom Mayence desired to keep ignorant, without giving them the slightest hint anent the actual state

345

of affairs.

The favorable opinion which the Archbishop had originally formed of Roland in Ehrenfels during this conference became greatly augmented. Even the most austere of men is more or less susceptible to flattery, and yet in flattering him Roland had managed to convey his own sincerity in this laudation.

"We will suppose the Grand Duke Karl elected," Mayence said at last. "What then?"

"Why then, my Lord, the three differing bodies of troops at present occupying Frankfort would be withdrawn, and the danger line crossed over to the right side."

Mayence now asked a question that in his own mind was crucial. Once more he would tempt the young man to state plainly what he actually knew.

"Can your Highness give us any reason why you fear danger from the presence of troops commanded by three friendly men like my colleagues and myself?"

"My fear is that the hands of one or the other of you may be forced, and I can perhaps explain my apprehension better by citing an incident to which I have already alluded. I had not the slightest intention of burning Castle Furstenberg, but suddenly my hand was forced. I was responsible for the safety of my men. I hesitated not for one instant to fire the Castle. Of the peaceful intentions of my Lords the Archbishops there can be no question, but at any moment a street brawl between the soldiers, say, of Cologne and Treves, may bring on a crisis that can only be quelled by bloodshed. Do you see my point?"

"Yes, your Highness, I do, and your point is well taken. I repose such confidence in our future Emperor that voluntarily I shall withdraw my troops from Frankfort at once. Furthermore, I shall open the Rhine, by sending along its banks the ultimatum you propose, not supported by my army, but supported by the name of the Archbishop of Mayence, and I shall be interested to know what Baron on the Rhine dare flout that title. Will you accept my aid, Prince Roland?"

"I accept it, my Lord, with deep gratitude, knowing that it will prove effective."

His Lordship rose in his place.

"I said this was not an Electoral Court. I rise to announce my mistake. We Electors here gathered together form a majority. I propose to you the name of Prince Roland, son of our late Emperor."

"My Lord, my Lord!" cried Roland, raising his hand, "you do not know all."

"Patient Heaven!" cried the irritated Archbishop, "you make too much of us as father confessors. Do not tell us now you have been guilty of assassination!"

"No, my Lord, but you should know that I have married the Lady Hildegunde, Countess von Sayn, whom you have already rejected as Empress."

"Well, if you have accepted the dame, the balance is redressed. I am not sure but you made an excellent choice."

It was now the turn of the amazed Archbishop of Cologne to rise to his feet.

"What his Highness says is impossible. The Lady von Sayn has been in my care ever since she entered Frankfort, and I pledge my word she has never left my Palace!"

"We were married yesterday at three o'clock, in the chapel of the Benedictine Fathers, and in the presence of four of them. We left your Palace, my Lord, by a door which you may discover in the wall of your garden, near the summer-house, and my wife is present in the adjoining room to implore your forgiveness."

Cologne collapsed into his chair, and drew a hand across his bewildered brow. The situation appeared to amuse Mayence.

"I wish your Highness had withheld this information until I was sure that my brother of Treves will vote with me, as he promised. My Lord of Treves, you heard my proposition. May I count on your concurrence?"

Treves' house of cards fell so suddenly to the ground that under the compelling eyes of Mayence he could do no more than stammer his acquiescence.

"I vote for the Prince," he said in tones barely audible.

"And you, my Lord of Cologne?"

"Aye," said Cologne gruffly.

"The Count Palatine?"

"Yes," thundered the latter. "A choice that meets my full approval, and I speak now for the Empress as well as the Emperor."

"Durnberg!" cried Mayence, raising his voice.

The doors were instantly opened, and the cringing Romer-meister appeared.

"Is the banquet prepared?"

"Ready to lay on the table, my Lord."

"The wine for the fountains?"

"Needs but the turning of the tap, my Lord."

"Order up the banquet, turn the tap; and as the new Emperor is unknown to the people, cause heralds with trumpets to set out and proclaim the Election of Prince Roland of Frankfort."

"Yes, my Lord."

The Archbishop of Mayence led the way out into the grand Kaisersaal, and the new Empress rose from her chair, standing there, her face white as the costume she wore. Mayence advanced to her, bending his gray head over the hand he took in his own.

"Your Majesty," he said gravely, and this was her first hint of the outcome,

"I congratulate you upon your marriage, as I have already congratulated your husband."

"My Lord Archbishop," she said in uncertain voice, "you cannot blame me for obeying you."

"I think my poor commands would have been futile were it not for the assistance lent me by his Majesty."

The salutations of the others were drowned by the cheers of the great assemblage in the Romerberg. The red wine and white had begun to flow, and the people knew what had happened. In the intervals between the clangor of the trumpets, they heard that a Prince of their own town had been elected, so all eyes turned to the Romer, and cries of "The Emperor! The Emperor!" issued from every throat. The multitude felt that a new day was dawning.

"I believe," said Mayence, "that hitherto only the Emperor has appeared on the balcony, but to-day I suggest a precedent. Let Emperor and Empress appear before the people."

He motioned to Herr Durnberg, and the latter flung open the tall windows; then Roland taking his wife's hand, stepped out upon the balcony.

THE END

THE TRIUMPHS OF
EUGÈNE VALMONT

1. The Mystery of the Five Hundred Diamonds

When I say I am called Valmont, the name will convey no impression to the reader, one way or another. My occupation is that of private detective in London, but if you ask any policeman in Paris who Valmont was he will likely be able to tell you, unless he is a recent recruit. If you ask him where Valmont is now, he may not know, yet I have a good deal to do with the Parisian police.

For a period of seven years I was chief detective to the Government of France, and if I am unable to prove myself a great crime hunter, it is because the record of my career is in the secret archives of Paris.

I may admit at the outset that I have no grievances to air. The French Government considered itself justified in dismissing me, and it did so. In this action it was quite within its right, and I should be the last to dispute that right; but, on the other hand, I consider myself justified in publishing the following account of what actually occurred, especially as so many false rumours have been put abroad concerning the case. However, as I said at the beginning, I hold no grievance, because my worldly affairs are now much more prosperous than they were in Paris, my intimate knowledge of that city and the country of which it is the capital bringing to me many cases with which I have dealt more or less successfully since I established myself in London.

Without further preliminary I shall at once plunge into an account of the case which riveted the attention of the whole world a little more than a decade ago.

The year 1893 was a prosperous twelve months for France. The weather was good, the harvest excellent, and the wine of that vintage is celebrated to this day. Everyone was well off and reasonably happy, a marked contrast to the state of things a few years later, when dissension over the Dreyfus case rent the country in twain.

Newspaper readers may remember that in 1893 the Government of

France fell heir to an unexpected treasure which set the civilised world agog, especially those inhabitants of it who are interested in historical relics. This was the finding of the diamond necklace in the Château de Chaumont, where it had rested undiscovered for a century in a rubbish heap of an attic. I believe it has not been questioned that this was the veritable necklace which the court jeweller, Boehmer, hoped to sell to Marie Antoinette, although how it came to be in the Château de Chaumont no one has been able to form even a conjecture. For a hundred years it was supposed that the necklace had been broken up in London, and its half a thousand stones, great and small, sold separately. It has always seemed strange to me that the Countess de Lamotte-Valois, who was thought to have profited by the sale of these jewels, should not have abandoned France if she possessed money to leave that country, for exposure was inevitable if she remained. Indeed, the unfortunate woman was branded and imprisoned, and afterwards was dashed to death from the third storey of a London house, when, in the direst poverty, she sought escape from the consequences of the debts she had incurred.

I am not superstitious in the least, yet this celebrated piece of treasure-trove seems actually to have exerted a malign influence over everyone who had the misfortune to be connected with it. Indeed, in a small way, I who write these words suffered dismissal and disgrace, though I caught but one glimpse of this dazzling scintillation of jewels. The jeweller who made the necklace met financial ruin; the Queen for whom it was constructed was beheaded; that high-born Prince Louis René Edouard, Cardinal de Rohan, who purchased it, was flung into prison; the unfortunate Countess, who said she acted as go-between until the transfer was concluded, clung for five awful minutes to a London window-sill before dropping to her death to the flags below; and now, a hundred and eight years later, up comes this devil's display of fireworks to the light again!

Droulliard, the working man who found the ancient box, seems to have prised it open, and ignorant though he was—he had probably never seen a diamond in his life before—realised that a fortune was in his grasp. The baleful glitter from the combination must have sent madness into his brain, working havoc therein as though the shafts of brightness were those mysterious rays which scientists have recently discovered. He might quite easily have walked through the main gate of the Château unsuspected and unquestioned with the diamonds concealed about his person, but instead of this he crept from the attic window on to the steep roof, slipped to the eaves, fell to the ground, and lay dead with a broken neck, while the necklace, intact, shimmered in the sunlight beside his body. No matter where these jewels had been found the Government would have insisted that they belonged to the Treasury of the Republic; but as the Château de Chaumont was a historical monument, and the property of France, there could be no question regarding the ownership of the necklace. The Government at once claimed it, and ordered it to be sent by a trustworthy military man to Paris. It was carried safely and delivered promptly to the authorities by Alfred Dreyfus, a young captain of artillery, to whom its custody had been entrusted.

In spite of its fall from the tall tower neither case nor jewels were perceptibly damaged. The lock of the box had apparently been forced by Droulliard's hatchet, or perhaps by the clasp knife found on his body. On reaching the ground the lid had flown open, and the necklace was thrown out.

I believe there was some discussion in the Cabinet regarding the fate of this ill-omened trophy, one section wishing it to be placed in a museum on account of its historical interest, another advocating the breaking up of the necklace and the selling of the diamonds for what they would fetch. But a third party maintained that the method to get the most money into the coffers of the country was to sell the necklace as it stood, for as the world now contains so many rich amateurs who collect undoubted rarities, regardless of expense, the historic associations of the jewelled collar would enhance the intrinsic value of the stones; and, this view prevailing, it was announced that the necklace would be sold by auction a month later in the rooms of Meyer, Renault and Co., in the Boulevard des Italians, near the Bank of the Crédit-Lyonnais.

This announcement elicited much comment from the newspapers of all countries, and it seemed that, from a financial point of view at least, the decision of the Government had been wise, for it speedily became evident that a notable coterie of wealthy buyers would be congregated in Paris on the thirteenth (unlucky day for me!) when the sale was to take place. But we of the inner circle were made aware of another result somewhat more disquieting, which was that the most expert criminals in the world were also gathering like vultures upon the fair city. The honour of France was at stake. Whoever bought that necklace must be assured of a safe conduct out of the country. We might view with equanimity whatever happened afterwards, but while he was a resident of France his life and property must not be endangered. Thus it came about that I was given full authority to ensure that neither murder nor theft nor both combined should be committed while the purchaser of the necklace remained within our boundaries, and for this purpose the police resources of France were placed unreservedly at my disposal. If I failed there should be no one to blame but myself; consequently, as I have remarked before, I do not complain of my dismissal by the Government.

The broken lock of the jewel-case had been very deftly repaired by an expert locksmith, who in executing his task was so unfortunate as to scratch a finger on the broken metal, whereupon blood poisoning set in, and although his life was saved, he was dismissed from the hospital with his right arm gone and his usefulness destroyed.

When the jeweller Boehmer made the necklace he asked a hundred and sixty thousand pounds for it, but after years of disappointment he was content to sell it to Cardinal de Rohan for sixty-four thousand pounds, to be liquidated in three instalments, not one of which was ever paid. This latter amount was probably somewhere near the value of the five hundred and sixteen separate stones, one of which was of tremendous size, a very monarch of diamonds, holding its court among seventeen brilliants each as large as a filbert. This iridescent concentration of wealth was, as one might say, placed in my care, and I had to see to it that no harm came to the necklace or to its prospective owner until they were safely across the boundaries of France.

The four weeks previous to the thirteenth proved a busy and anxious time for me. Thousands, most of whom were actuated by mere curiosity, wished to view the diamonds. We were compelled to discriminate, and sometimes discriminated against the wrong person, which caused unpleasantness. Three distinct attempts were made to rob the safe, but luckily these criminal efforts were frustrated, and so we came unscathed to the eventful thirteenth of the month.

The sale was to begin at two o'clock, and on the morning of that day I took the somewhat tyrannical precaution of having the more dangerous of our own malefactors, and as many of the foreign thieves as I could trump up charges against, laid by the heels, yet I knew very well it was not these rascals I had most to fear, but the suave, well-groomed gentlemen, amply supplied with unimpeachable credentials, stopping at our fine hotels and living like princes. Many of these were foreigners against whom we could prove nothing, and whose arrest might land us into temporary international difficulties. Nevertheless, I had each of them shadowed, and on the morning of the thirteenth if one of them had even disputed a cab fare I should have had him in prison half an hour later, and taken the consequences, but these gentlemen are very shrewd and do not commit mistakes.

I made up a list of all the men in the world who were able or likely to purchase the necklace. Many of them would not be present in person at the auction rooms; their bidding would be done by agents. This simplified matters a good deal, for the agents kept me duly informed of their purposes, and, besides, an agent who handles treasure every week is an adept at the business, and does not need the protection which must surround an amateur, who in nine cases out of ten has but scant idea of the dangers that threaten him, beyond knowing that if he goes down a dark street in a dangerous quarter he is likely to be maltreated and robbed.

There were no less than sixteen clients all told, whom we learned were to attend personally on the day of the sale, any one of whom might well have made the purchase. The Marquis of Warlingham and Lord Oxtead from England were well-known jewel fanciers, while at least half a dozen millionaires were expected from the United States, with a smattering from Germany, Austria, and Russia, and one each from Italy, Belgium, and Holland.

Admission to the auction rooms was allowed by ticket only, to be applied for at least a week in advance, applications to be accompanied by satisfactory testimonials. It would possibly have surprised many of the rich men collected there to know that they sat cheek by jowl with some of the most noted thieves of England and America, but I allowed this for two reasons: first, I wished to keep these sharpers under my own eye until I knew who had bought the necklace; and, secondly, I was desirous that they should not know they were suspected.

I stationed trusty men outside on the Boulevard des Italians, each of whom knew by sight most of the probable purchasers of the necklace. It was arranged that when the sale was over I should walk out to the boulevard alongside the man who was the new owner of the diamonds, and from that moment until he quitted France my men were not to lose sight of him if he took personal custody of the stones, instead of doing the sensible and proper thing of having them insured and forwarded to his residence by some responsible transit company, or depositing them in the bank. In fact, I took every precaution that occurred to me. All police Paris was on the qui vive, and felt itself pitted against the scoundrelism of the world.

For one reason or another it was nearly half-past two before the sale began. There had been considerable delay because of forged tickets, and, indeed, each order for admittance was so closely scrutinised that this in itself took a good deal more time than we anticipated. Every chair was occupied, and still a number of the visitors were compelled to stand. I stationed myself by the swinging doors at the entrance end of the hall, where I could command a view of the entire assemblage. Some of my men were placed with backs against the wall, whilst others were distributed amongst the chairs, all in plain clothes. During the sale the diamonds themselves were not displayed, but the box containing them rested in front of the auctioneer and three policemen in uniform stood guard on either side.

Very quietly the auctioneer began by saying that there was no need for him to expatiate on the notable character of the treasure he was privileged to offer for sale, and with this preliminary, he requested those present to bid. Someone offered twenty thousand francs, which was received with much laughter; then the bidding went steadily on until it reached nine hundred thousand francs, which I knew to be less than half the reserve the Government had placed upon the necklace. The contest advanced more slowly until the million and a half was touched, and there it hung fire for a time, while the auctioneer remarked that this sum did not equal that which the maker of the necklace had been finally forced to accept for it. After another pause he added that, as the reserve was not exceeded, the necklace would be withdrawn, and probably never again offered for sale. He therefore urged those who were holding back to make their bids now. At this the contest livened until the sum of two million three hundred thousand francs had been offered, and now I knew the necklace would be sold. Nearing the three million mark the competition thinned down to a few dealers from Hamburg and the Marquis of Warlingham, from England, when a voice that had not yet been heard in the auction room was lifted in a tone of some impatience:—

'One million dollars!'

There was an instant hush, followed by the scribbling of pencils, as each person present reduced the sum to its equivalent in his own currency— pounds for the English, francs for the French, marks for the German, and so on. The aggressive tone and the clear-cut face of the bidder proclaimed him an American, not less than the financial denomination he had used. In a moment it was realised that his bid was a clear leap of more than two million francs, and a sigh went up from the audience as if this settled it, and the great sale was done. Nevertheless the auctioneer's hammer hovered over the lid of his desk, and he looked up and down the long line of faces turned towards him. He seemed reluctant to tap the board, but no one ventured to compete against this tremendous sum, and with a sharp click the mallet fell.

'What name?' he asked, bending over towards the customer.

'Cash,' replied the American; 'here's a cheque for the amount. I'll take the diamonds with me.'

'Your request is somewhat unusual,' protested the auctioneer mildly.

'I know what you mean,' interrupted the American; 'you think the cheque may not be cashed. You will notice it is drawn on the Crédit-Lyonnais, which is practically next door. I must have the jewels with me. Send round your messenger with the cheque; it will take only a few minutes to find out whether or not the money is there to meet it. The necklace is mine, and I insist on having it.'

The auctioneer with some demur handed the cheque to the representative of the French Government who was present, and this official himself went to the bank. There were some other things to be sold and the auctioneer endeavoured to go on through the list, but no one paid the slightest attention to him.

Meanwhile I was studying the countenance of the man who had made the astounding bid, when I should instead have adjusted my preparations to meet the new conditions now confronting me. Here was a man about whom we knew nothing whatever. I had come to the instant conclusion that he was a prince of criminals, and that a sinister design, not at that moment fathomed by me, was on foot to get possession of the jewels. The handing up of the cheque was clearly a trick of some sort, and I fully expected the official to return and say the draft was good. I determined to prevent this man from getting the jewel box until I knew more of his game. Quickly I removed from my place near the door to the auctioneer's desk, having two objects in view; first, to warn the auctioneer not to part with the treasure too easily; and, second, to study the suspected man at closer range. Of all evil-doers the American is most to be feared; he uses more ingenuity in the planning of his projects, and will take greater risks in carrying them out than any other malefactor on earth.

From my new station I saw there were two men to deal with. The bidder's face was keen and intellectual; his hands refined, lady-like, clean and white, showing they were long divorced from manual labour, if indeed they had ever done any useful work. Coolness and imperturbability were his beyond a doubt. The companion who sat at his right was of an entirely different stamp. His hands were hairy and sun-tanned; his face bore the stamp of grim determination and unflinching bravery. I knew that these two types usually hunted in couples—the one to scheme, the other to execute, and they always formed a combination dangerous to encounter and difficult to circumvent.

There was a buzz of conversation up and down the hall as these two men talked together in low tones. I knew now that I was face to face with the most hazardous problem of my life.

I whispered to the auctioneer, who bent his head to listen. He knew very well who I was, of course.

'You must not give up the necklace,' I began.

He shrugged his shoulders.

'I am under the orders of the official from the Ministry of the Interior. You must speak to him.'

'I shall not fail to do so,' I replied. 'Nevertheless, do not give up the box too readily.'

'I am helpless,' he protested with another shrug. 'I obey the orders of the Government.'

Seeing it was useless to parley further with the auctioneer, I set my wits to work to meet the new emergency. I felt convinced that the cheque would prove to be genuine, and that the fraud, wherever it lay, might not be disclosed in time to aid the authorities. My duty, therefore, was to make sure we lost sight neither of the buyer nor the thing bought. Of course I could not arrest the purchaser merely on suspicion; besides, it would make the Government the laughing-stock of the world if they sold a case of jewels and immediately placed the buyer in custody when they themselves had handed over his goods to him. Ridicule kills in France. A breath of laughter may blow a Government out of existence in Paris much more effectually than will a whiff of cannon smoke. My duty then was to give the Government full warning, and never lose sight of my man until he was clear of France; then my responsibility ended.

I took aside one of my own men in plain clothes and said to him,—

'You have seen the American who has bought the necklace?'

'Yes, sir.'

'Very well. Go outside quietly, and station yourself there. He is likely to emerge presently with the jewels in his possession. You are not to lose sight of either the man or the casket. I shall follow him and be close behind him as he emerges, and you are to shadow us. If he parts with the case you must be ready at a sign from me to follow either the man or the jewels. Do you understand?' 'Yes, sir,' he answered, and left the room.

It is ever the unforeseen that baffles us; it is easy to be wise after the event. I should have sent two men, and I have often thought since how admirable is the regulation of the Italian Government which sends out its policemen in pairs. Or I should have given my man power to call for help, but even as it was he did only half as well as I had a right to expect of him, and the blunder he committed by a moment's dull-witted hesitation—ah, well! there is no use of scolding. After all the result might have been the same.

Just as my man disappeared between the two folding doors the official from the Ministry of the Interior entered. I intercepted him about half-way on his journey from the door to the auctioneer.

'Possibly the cheque appears to be genuine,' I whispered to him.

'But certainly,' he replied pompously. He was an individual greatly impressed with his own importance; a kind of character with which it is always difficult to deal. Afterwards the Government asserted that this official had warned me, and the utterances of an empty-headed ass dressed in a little brief authority, as the English poet says, were looked upon as the epitome of wisdom.

'I advise you strongly not to hand over the necklace as has been requested,' I went on.

'Why?' he asked.

'Because I am convinced the bidder is a criminal.'

'If you have proof of that, arrest him.'

'I have no proof at the present moment, but I request you to delay the delivery of the goods.'

'That is absurd,' he cried impatiently. 'The necklace is his, not ours. The money has already been transferred to the account of the Government; we cannot retain the five million francs, and refuse to hand over to him what he has bought with them,' and so the man left me standing there, nonplussed and anxious. The eyes of everyone in the room had been turned on us during our brief conversation, and now the official proceeded ostentatiously up the room with a grand air of importance; then, with a bow and a flourish of the hand, he said, dramatically,—

'The jewels belong to Monsieur.'

The two Americans rose simultaneously, the taller holding out his hand while the auctioneer passed to him the case he had apparently paid so highly for. The American nonchalantly opened the box and for the first time the electric radiance of the jewels burst upon that audience, each member of which craned his neck to behold it. It seemed to me a most reckless thing to do. He examined the jewels minutely for a few moments, then snapped the lid shut again, and calmly put the box in his outside pocket, and I could not help noticing that the light overcoat he wore possessed pockets made extraordinarily large, as if on purpose for this very case. And now this amazing man walked serenely down the room past miscreants who joyfully would have cut his throat for even the smallest diamond in that conglomeration; yet he did not take the trouble to put his hand on the pocket which contained the case, or in any way attempt to protect it. The assemblage seemed stricken dumb by his audacity. His friend followed closely at his heels, and the tall man disappeared through the folding doors. Not so the other. He turned quickly, and whipped two revolvers out of his pockets, which he presented at the astonished crowd. There had been a movement on the part of every one to leave the room, but the sight of these deadly weapons confronting them made each one shrink into his place again.

The man with his back to the door spoke in a loud and domineering voice, asking the auctioneer to translate what he had to say into French and German; he spoke in English.

'These here shiners are valuable; they belong to my friend who has just gone out. Casting no reflections on the generality of people in this room, there are, nevertheless, half a dozen "crooks" among us whom my friend wishes to avoid. Now, no honest man here will object to giving the buyer of that there trinket five clear minutes in which to get away. It's only the "crooks" that can kick. I ask these five minutes as a favour, but if they are not granted I am going to take them as a right. Any man who moves will get shot.'

'I am an honest man,' I cried, 'and I object. I am chief detective of the French Government. Stand aside; the police will protect your friend.'

'Hold on, my son,' warned the American, turning one weapon directly upon me, while the other held a sort of roving commission, pointing all over the room. 'My friend is from New York and he distrusts the police as much as he does the grafters. You may be twenty detectives, but if you move before that clock strikes three, I'll bring you down, and don't you forget it.'

It is one thing to face death in a fierce struggle, but quite another to advance coldly upon it toward the muzzle of a pistol held so steadily that there could be no chance of escape. The gleam of determination in the man's eyes convinced me he meant what he said. I did not consider then, nor have I considered since, that the next five minutes, precious as they were, would be worth paying my life for. Apparently everyone else was of my opinion, for none moved hand or foot until the clock slowly struck three.

'Thank you, gentlemen,' said the American, as he vanished between the spring-doors. When I say vanished, I mean that word and no other, because my men outside saw nothing of this individual then or later. He vanished as if he had never existed, and it was some hours before we found how this had been accomplished.

I rushed out almost on his heels, as one might say, and hurriedly questioned my waiting men. They had all seen the tall American come out with the greatest leisure and stroll towards the west. As he was not the man any of them were looking for they paid no further attention to him, as, indeed, is the custom with our Parisian force. They have eyes for nothing but what they are sent to look for, and this trait has its drawbacks for their superiors.

I ran up the boulevard, my whole thought intent on the diamonds and their owner. I knew my subordinate in command of the men inside the hall would look after the scoundrel with the pistols. A short distance up I found the stupid fellow I had sent out, standing in a dazed manner at the corner of the Rue Michodière, gazing alternately down that short street and towards the Place de l'Opéra. The very fact that he was there furnished proof that he had failed.

'Where is the American?' I demanded.

'He went down this street, sir.'

'Then why are you standing here like a fool?'

'I followed him this far, when a man came up the Rue Michodière, and without a word the American handed him the jewel-box, turning instantly down the street up which the other had come. The other jumped into a cab, and drove towards the Place de l'Opéra.'

'And what did you do? Stood here like a post, I suppose?'

'I didn't know what to do, sir. It all happened in a moment.'

'Why didn't you follow the cab?'

'I didn't know which to follow, sir, and the cab was gone instantly while I watched the American.'

'What was its number?'

'I don't know, sir.'

'You clod! Why didn't you call one of our men, whoever was nearest, and leave him to shadow the American while you followed the cab?'

'I did shout to the nearest man, sir, but he said you told him to stay there and watch the English lord, and even before he had spoken both American and cabman were out of sight.'

'Was the man to whom he gave the box an American also?'

'No, sir, he was French.'

'How do you know?'

'By his appearance and the words he spoke.'

'I thought you said he didn't speak.'

'He did not speak to the American, sir, but he said to the cabman, "Drive to the Madeleine as quickly as you can."'

'Describe the man.'

'He was a head shorter than the American, wore a black beard and moustache rather neatly trimmed, and seemed to be a superior sort of artisan.'

'You did not take the number of the cab. Should you know the cabman if you saw him again?'

'Yes, sir, I think so.'

Taking this fellow with me I returned to the now nearly empty auction room and there gathered all my men about me. Each in his notebook took down particulars of the cabman and his passenger from the lips of my incompetent spy; next I dictated a full description of the two Americans, then scattered my men to the various railway stations of the lines leading out of Paris, with orders to make inquiries of the police on duty there, and to arrest one or more of the four persons described should they be so fortunate as to find any of them.

I now learned how the rogue with the pistols vanished so completely as he did. My subordinate in the auction room had speedily solved the mystery. To the left of the main entrance of the auction room was a door that gave private access to the rear of the premises. As the attendant in charge confessed when questioned, he had been bribed by the American earlier in the day to leave this side door open and to allow the man to escape by the goods entrance. Thus the ruffian did not appear on the boulevard at all, and so had not been observed by any of my men.

Taking my futile spy with me I returned to my own office, and sent an order throughout the city that every cabman who had been in the Boulevard des Italiens between half-past two and half-past three that afternoon, should report immediately to me. The examination of these men proved a very tedious business indeed, but whatever other countries may say of us, we French are patient, and if the haystack is searched long enough, the needle will be found. I did not discover the needle I was looking for, but I came upon one quite as important, if not more so.

It was nearly ten o'clock at night when a cabman answered my oft-repeated questions in the affirmative.

'Did you take up a passenger a few minutes past three o'clock on the Boulevard des Italiens, near the Crédit-Lyonnais? Had he a short black beard? Did he carry a small box in his hand and order you to drive to the Madeleine?'

The cabman seemed puzzled.

'He wore a short black beard when he got out of the cab,' he replied.

'What do you mean by that?'

'I drive a closed cab, sir. When he got in he was a smooth-faced gentleman; when he got out he wore a short black beard.'

'Was he a Frenchman?'

'No, sir; he was a foreigner, either English or American.'

'Was he carrying a box?'

'No, sir; he held in his hand a small leather bag.'

'Where did he tell you to drive?'

'He told me to follow the cab in front, which had just driven off very rapidly towards the Madeleine. In fact, I heard the man, such as you describe, order the other cabman to drive to the Madeleine. I had come alongside the curb when this man held up his hand for a cab, but the open cab cut in ahead of me. Just then my passenger stepped up and said in French, but with a foreign accent: "Follow that cab wherever it goes."'

367

I turned with some indignation to my inefficient spy.

'You told me,' I said, 'that the American had gone down a side street. Yet he evidently met a second man, obtained from him the handbag, turned back, and got into the closed cab directly behind you.'

'Well, sir,' stammered the spy, 'I could not look in two directions at the same time. The American certainly went down the side street, but of course I watched the cab which contained the jewels.'

'And you saw nothing of the closed cab right at your elbow?'

'The boulevard was full of cabs, sir, and the pavement crowded with passers-by, as it always is at that hour of the day, and I have only two eyes in my head.'

'I am glad to know you had that many, for I was beginning to think you were blind.'

Although I said this, I knew in my heart it was useless to censure the poor wretch, for the fault was entirely my own in not sending two men, and in failing to guess the possibility of the jewels and their owner being separated. Besides, here was a clue to my hand at last, and no time must be lost in following it up. So I continued my interrogation of the cabman.

'The other cab was an open vehicle, you say?'

'Yes, sir.'

'You succeeded in following it?'

'Oh, yes, sir. At the Madeleine the man in front redirected the coachman, who turned to the left and drove to the Place de la Concorde, then up the Champs-Elysées to the Arch and so down the Avenue de la Grande Armée, and the Avenue de Neuilly, to the Pont de Neuilly, where it came to a standstill. My fare got out, and I saw he now wore a short black beard, which he had evidently put on inside the cab. He gave me a ten-franc piece, which was very satisfactory.'

'And the fare you were following? What did he do?'

'He also stepped out, paid the cabman, went down the bank of the river and got on board a steam launch that seemed to be waiting for him.'

'Did he look behind, or appear to know that he was being followed?'

'No, sir.'

'And your fare?'

'He ran after the first man, and also went aboard the steam launch, which instantly started down the river.'

'And that was the last you saw of them?'

'Yes, sir.'

'At what time did you reach the Pont de Neuilly?'

'I do not know, sir; I was compelled to drive rather fast, but the distance is seven to eight kilometres.'

'You would do it under the hour?'

'But certainly, under the hour.'

'Then you must have reached Neuilly bridge about four o'clock?'

'It is very likely, sir.'

The plan of the tall American was now perfectly clear to me, and it comprised nothing that was contrary to law. He had evidently placed his luggage on board the steam launch in the morning. The handbag had contained various materials which would enable him to disguise himself, and this bag he had probably left in some shop down the side street, or else someone was waiting with it for him. The giving of the treasure to another man was not so risky as it had at first appeared, because he instantly followed that man, who was probably his confidential servant. Despite the windings of the river there was ample time for the launch to reach Havre before the American steamer sailed on Saturday morning. I surmised it was his intention to come alongside the steamer before she left her berth in Havre harbour, and thus transfer himself and his belongings unperceived by anyone on watch at the land side of the liner.

All this, of course, was perfectly justifiable, and seemed, in truth, merely a well-laid scheme for escaping observation. His only danger of being tracked was when he got into the cab. Once away from the neighbourhood of the Boulevard des Italiens he was reasonably sure to evade pursuit, and the five minutes which his friend with the pistols had won for him afforded just the time he needed to get so far as the Place Madeleine, and after that everything was easy. Yet, if it had not been for those five minutes secured by coercion, I should not have found the slightest excuse for arresting him. But he was accessory after the act in that piece of illegality—in fact, it was absolutely certain that he had been accessory before the act, and guilty of conspiracy with the man who had presented firearms to the auctioneer's audience, and who had interfered with an officer in the discharge of his duty by threatening me and my men. So I was now legally in the right if I arrested every person on board that steam launch.

With a map of the river before me I proceeded to make some calculations. It was now nearly ten o'clock at night. The launch had had six hours in which to travel at its utmost speed. It was doubtful if so small a vessel could make ten miles an hour, even with the current in its favour, which is rather sluggish because of the locks and the level country. Sixty miles would place her beyond Meulan, which is fifty-eight miles from the Pont Royal, and, of course, a lesser distance from the Pont de Neuilly. But the navigation of the river is difficult at all times, and almost impossible after dark. There were chances of the boat running aground, and then there was the inevitable delay at the locks. So I estimated that the launch could not yet have reached Meulan, which was less than twenty-five miles from Paris by rail. Looking up the timetable I saw there were still two trains to Meulan, the next at 10.25, which reached Meulan at 11.40. I therefore had time to reach St. Lazare station, and accomplish some telegraphing before the train left.

With three of my assistants I got into a cab and drove to the station. On arrival I sent one of my men to hold the train while I went into the telegraph office, cleared the wires, and got into communication with the lock master at Meulan. He replied that no steam launch had passed down since an hour before sunset. I then instructed him to allow the yacht to enter the lock, close the upper gate, let half of the water out, and hold the vessel there until I came. I also ordered the local Meulan police to send enough men to the lock to enforce this command. Lastly, I sent messages all along the river asking the police to report to me on the train the passage of the steam launch.

The 10.25 is a slow train, stopping at every station. However, every drawback has its compensation, and these stoppages enabled me to receive and to send telegraphic messages. I was quite well aware that I might be on a fool's errand in going to Meulan. The yacht could have put about before it had steamed a mile, and so returned back to Paris. There had been no time to learn whether this was so or not if I was to catch the 10.25. Also, it might have landed its passengers anywhere along the river. I may say at once that neither of these two things happened, and my calculations regarding her movements were accurate to the letter. But a trap most carefully set may be prematurely sprung by inadvertence, or more often by the over-zeal of some stupid ass who fails to understand his instructions, or oversteps them if they are understood. I received a most annoying telegram from Denouval, a lock about thirteen miles above that of Meulan. The local policeman, arriving at the lock, found that the yacht had just cleared. The fool shouted to the captain to return, threatening him with all the pains and penalties of the law if he refused. The captain did refuse, rung on full speed ahead, and disappeared in the darkness. Through this well-meant blunder of an understrapper those on board the launch had received warning that we were on their track. I telegraphed to the lock-keeper at Denouval to allow no craft to pass toward Paris until further orders. We thus held the launch in a thirteen-mile stretch of water, but the night was pitch dark, and passengers might be landed on either bank with all France before them, over which to effect their escape in any direction.

It was midnight when I reached the lock at Meulan, and, as was to be expected, nothing had been seen or heard of the launch. It gave me some satisfaction to telegraph to that dunderhead at Denouval to walk along the river bank to Meulan, and report if he learnt the launch's whereabouts. We took up our quarters in the lodgekeeper's house and waited. There was little sense in sending men to scour the country at this time of night, for the

371

pursued were on the alert, and very unlikely to allow themselves to be caught if they had gone ashore. On the other hand, there was every chance that the captain would refuse to let them land, because he must know his vessel was in a trap from which it could not escape, and although the demand of the policeman at Denouval was quite unauthorised, nevertheless the captain could not know that, while he must be well aware of his danger in refusing to obey a command from the authorities. Even if he got away for the moment he must know that arrest was certain, and that his punishment would be severe. His only plea could be that he had not heard and understood the order to return. But this plea would be invalidated if he aided in the escape of two men, whom he must know were wanted by the police. I was therefore very confident that if his passengers asked to be set ashore, the captain would refuse when he had had time to think about his own danger. My estimate proved accurate, for towards one o'clock the lock-keeper came in and said the green and red lights of an approaching craft were visible, and as he spoke the yacht whistled for the opening of the lock. I stood by the lock-keeper while he opened the gates; my men and the local police were concealed on each side of the lock. The launch came slowly in, and as soon as it had done so I asked the captain to step ashore, which he did.

'I wish a word with you,' I said. 'Follow me.'

I took him into the lock-keeper's house and closed the door.

'Where are you going?'

'To Havre.'

'Where did you come from?'

'Paris.'

'From what quay?'

'From the Pont de Neuilly.'

'When did you leave there?'

'At five minutes to four o'clock this afternoon.'

'Yesterday afternoon, you mean?'

'Yesterday afternoon.'

'Who engaged you to make this voyage?'

'An American; I do not know his name.'

'He paid you well, I suppose?'

'He paid me what I asked.'

'Have you received the money?'

'Yes, sir.'

'I may inform you, captain, that I am Eugène Valmont, chief detective of the French Government, and that all the police of France at this moment are under my control. I ask you, therefore, to be careful of your answers. You were ordered by a policeman at Denouval to return. Why did you not do so?'

'The lock-keeper ordered me to return, but as he had no right to order me, I went on.'

'You knew very well it was the police who ordered you, and you ignored the command. Again I ask you why you did so.'

'I did not know it was the police.'

'I thought you would say that. You knew very well, but were paid to take the risk, and it is likely to cost you dear. You had two passengers aboard?'

'Yes, sir.'

'Did you put them ashore between here and Denouval?'

'No, sir; but one of them went overboard, and we couldn't find him again.'

'Which one?'

'The short man.'

'Then the American is still aboard?'

'What American, sir?'

'Captain, you must not trifle with me. The man who engaged you is still aboard?'

'Oh, no, sir; he has never been aboard.'

'Do you mean to tell me that the second man who came on your launch at the Pont de Neuilly is not the American who engaged you?'

'No, sir; the American was a smooth-faced man; this man wore a black beard.'

'Yes, a false beard.'

'I did not know that, sir. I understood from the American that I was to take but one passenger. One came aboard with a small box in his hand; the other with a small bag. Each declared himself to be the passenger in question. I did not know what to do, so I left Paris with both of them on board.'

'Then the tall man with the black beard is still with you?'

'Yes, sir.'

'Well, captain, is there anything else you have to tell me? I think you will find it better in the end to make a clean breast of it.'

The captain hesitated, turning his cap about in his hands for a few moments, then he said,—

'I am not sure that the first passenger went overboard of his own accord. When the police hailed us at Denouval—'

'Ah, you knew it was the police, then?'

'I was afraid after I left it might have been. You see, when the bargain was made with me the American said that if I reached Havre at a certain time a thousand francs extra would be paid to me, so I was anxious to get along as quickly as I could. I told him it was dangerous to navigate the Seine at night, but he paid me well for attempting it. After the policeman called to us at Denouval the man with the small box became very much excited, and asked me to put him ashore, which I refused to do. The tall man appeared to be watching him, never letting him get far away. When I heard the splash in the water I ran aft, and I saw the tall man putting the box which the other had held into his handbag, although I said nothing of it at the time. We cruised back and forward about the spot where the other man had gone overboard, but saw nothing more of him. Then I came on to Meulan, intending to give information about what I had seen. That is all I know of the matter, sir.'

'Was the man who had the jewels a Frenchman?'

'What jewels, sir?'

'The man with the small box.'

'Oh, yes, sir; he was French.'

'You have hinted that the foreigner threw him overboard. What grounds have you for such a belief if you did not see the struggle?'

'The night is very dark, sir, and I did not see what happened. I was at the wheel in the forward part of the launch, with my back turned to these two. I heard a scream, then a splash. If the man had jumped overboard as the other said he did, he would not have screamed. Besides, as I told you, when I ran aft I saw the foreigner put the little box in his handbag, which he shut up quickly as if he did not wish me to notice.'

'Very good, captain. If you have told the truth it will go easier with you in the investigation that is to follow.'

I now turned the captain over to one of my men, and ordered in the foreigner with his bag and bogus black whiskers. Before questioning him I ordered him to open the handbag, which he did with evident reluctance. It was filled with false whiskers, false moustaches, and various bottles, but on top of them all lay the jewel case. I raised the lid and displayed that accursed necklace. I looked up at the man, who stood there calmly enough, saying nothing in spite of the overwhelming evidence against him.

'Will you oblige me by removing your false beard?'

He did so at once, throwing it into the open bag. I knew the moment I saw him that he was not the American, and thus my theory had broken down, in one very important part at least. Informing him who I was, and cautioning him to speak the truth, I asked how he came in possession of the jewels.

'Am I under arrest?' he asked.

'But certainly,' I replied.

'Of what am I accused?'

'You are accused, in the first place, of being in possession of property which does not belong to you.'

'I plead guilty to that. What in the second place?'

'In the second place, you may find yourself accused of murder.'

'I am innocent of the second charge. The man jumped overboard.'

'If that is true, why did he scream as he went over?'

'Because, too late to recover his balance, I seized this box and held it.'

'He was in rightful possession of the box; the owner gave it to him.'

'I admit that; I saw the owner give it to him.'

'Then why should he jump overboard?'

'I do not know. He seemed to become panic-stricken when the police at the last lock ordered us to return. He implored the captain to put him ashore, and from that moment I watched him keenly, expecting that if we drew near to the land he would attempt to escape, as the captain had refused to beach the launch. He remained quiet for about half an hour, seated on a camp chair by the rail, with his eyes turned toward the shore, trying, as I imagined, to penetrate the darkness and estimate the distance. Then suddenly he sprung up and made his dash. I was prepared for this, and instantly caught the box from his hand. He gave a half turn, trying either to save himself or to retain the box; then with a scream went down shoulders first into the water. It all happened within a second after he leaped from his chair.'

'You admit yourself, then, indirectly responsible for his drowning, at least?'

'I see no reason to suppose that the man was drowned. If able to swim he could easily have reached the river bank. If unable to swim, why should he attempt it encumbered by the box?'

'You believe he escaped, then?'

'I think so.'

'It will be lucky for you should that prove to be the case.'

'Certainly.'

'How did you come to be in the yacht at all?' 'I shall give you a full account of the affair, concealing nothing. I am a private detective, with an office in London. I was certain that some attempt would be made, probably by the most expert criminals at large, to rob the possessor of this necklace. I came over to Paris, anticipating trouble, determined to keep an eye upon the jewel case if this proved possible. If the jewels were stolen the crime was bound to be one of the most celebrated in legal annals. I was present during the sale, and saw the buyer of the necklace. I followed the official who went to the bank, and thus learned that the money was behind the cheque. I then stopped outside and waited for the buyer to appear. He held the case in his hand.'

'In his pocket, you mean?' I interrupted.

'He had it in his hand when I saw him. Then the man who afterwards jumped overboard approached him, took the case without a word, held up his hand for a cab, and when an open vehicle approached the curb he stepped in, saying, "The Madeleine." I hailed a closed cab, instructed the cabman to follow the first, disguising myself with whiskers as near like those the man in front wore as I had in my collection.'

'Why did you do that?'

'As a detective you should know why I did it. I wished as nearly as possible to resemble the man in front, so that if necessity arose I could pretend that I was the person commissioned to carry the jewel case. As a matter of fact, the crisis arose when we came to the end of our cab journey. The captain did not know which was his true passenger, and so let us both remain aboard the launch. And now you have the whole story.'

'An extremely improbable one, sir. Even by your own account you had no right to interfere in this business at all.'

'I quite agree with you there,' he replied, with great nonchalance, taking a card from his pocket-book, which he handed to me.

'That is my London address; you may make inquiries, and you will find I am exactly what I represent myself to be.'

The first train for Paris left Meulan at eleven minutes past four in the morning. It was now a quarter after two. I left the captain, crew, and launch in charge of two of my men, with orders to proceed to Paris as soon as it was daylight. I, supported by the third man, waited at the station with our English prisoner, and reached Paris at half-past five in the morning.

The English prisoner, though severely interrogated by the judge, stood by his story. Inquiry by the police in London proved that what he said of himself was true. His case, however, began to look very serious when two of the men from the launch asserted that they had seen him push the Frenchman overboard, and their statement could not be shaken. All our energies were bent for the next two weeks on trying to find something of the identity of the missing man, or to get any trace of the two Americans. If the tall American were alive, it seemed incredible that he should not have made application for the valuable property he had lost. All attempts to trace him by means of the cheque on the Crédit-Lyonnais proved futile. The bank pretended to give me every assistance, but I sometimes doubt if it actually did so. It had evidently been well paid for its services, and evinced no impetuous desire to betray so good a customer.

Robert Barr

We made inquiries about every missing man in Paris, but also without result.

The case had excited much attention throughout the world, and doubtless was published in full in the American papers. The Englishman had been in custody three weeks when the chief of police in Paris received the following letter:—

'Dear Sir,—On my arrival in New York by the English steamer Lucania, I was much amused to read in the papers accounts of the exploits of detectives, French and English. I am sorry that only one of them seems to be in prison; I think his French confrère ought to be there also. I regret exceedingly, however, that there is the rumour of the death by drowning of my friend Martin Dubois, of 375 Rue aux Juifs, Rouen. If this is indeed the case he has met his death through the blunders of the police. Nevertheless, I wish you would communicate with his family at the address I have given, and assure them that I will make arrangements for their future support.

'I beg to inform you that I am a manufacturer of imitation diamonds, and through extensive advertising succeeded in accumulating a fortune of many millions. I was in Europe when the necklace was found, and had in my possession over a thousand imitation diamonds of my own manufacture. It occurred to me that here was the opportunity of the most magnificent advertisement in the world. I saw the necklace, received its measurements, and also obtained photographs of it taken by the French Government. Then I set my expert friend Martin Dubois at work, and, with the artificial stones I gave him, he made an imitation necklace so closely resembling the original that you apparently do not know it is the unreal you have in your possession. I did not fear the villainy of the crooks as much as the blundering of the police, who would have protected me with brass-band vehemence if I could not elude them. I knew that the detectives would overlook the obvious, but would at once follow a clue if I provided one for them. Consequently, I laid my plans, just as you have discovered, and got Martin Dubois up from Rouen to carry the case I gave him down to Havre. I had had another box prepared and wrapped in brown paper, with my address in New York written thereon. The moment I emerged from the auction room, while my friend the cowboy

379

was holding up the audience, I turned my face to the door, took out the genuine diamonds from the case and slipped it into the box I had prepared for mailing. Into the genuine case I put the bogus diamonds. After handing the box to Dubois, I turned down a side street, and then into another whose name I do not know, and there in a shop with sealing wax and string did up the real diamonds for posting. I labelled the package "Books", went to the nearest post office, paid letter postage, and handed it over unregistered as if it were of no particular value. After this I went to my rooms in the Grand Hotel where I had been staying under my own name for more than a month. Next morning I took train for London, and the day after sailed from Liverpool on the Lucania. I arrived before the Gascoigne, which sailed from Havre on Saturday, met my box at the Customs house, paid duty, and it now reposes in my safe. I intend to construct an imitation necklace which will be so like the genuine one that nobody can tell the two apart; then I shall come to Europe and exhibit the pair, for the publication of the truth of this matter will give me the greatest advertisement that ever was.

'Yours truly,

'JOHN P HAZARD.'

I at once communicated with Rouen and found Martin Dubois alive and well. His first words were:—'I swear I did not steal the jewels.'

He had swum ashore, tramped to Rouen, and kept quiet in great fear while I was fruitlessly searching Paris for him. It took Mr. Hazard longer to make his imitation necklace than he supposed, and several years later he booked his passage with the two necklaces on the ill-fated steamer Burgoyne, and now rests beside them at the bottom of the Atlantic.

Full many a gem of purest ray serene,

The dark unfathomed caves of ocean bear.

2. The Siamese Twin of a Bomb-Thrower

The events previously related in 'The Mystery of the Five Hundred Diamonds' led to my dismissal by the French Government. It was not because I had arrested an innocent man; I had done that dozens of times before, with nothing said about it. It was not because I had followed a wrong clue, or because I had failed to solve the mystery of the five hundred diamonds. Every detective follows a wrong clue now and then, and every detective fails more often than he cares to admit. No. All these things would not have shaken my position, but the newspapers were so fortunate as to find something humorous in the case, and for weeks Paris rang with laughter over my exploits and my defeat. The fact that the chief French detective had placed the most celebrated English detective into prison, and that each of them were busily sleuth-hounding a bogus clue, deliberately flung across their path by an amateur, roused all France to great hilarity. The Government was furious. The Englishman was released and I was dismissed. Since the year 1893 I have been a resident of London.

When a man is, as one might say, the guest of a country, it does not become him to criticise that country. I have studied this strange people with interest, and often with astonishment, and if I now set down some of the differences between the English and the French, I trust that no note of criticism of the former will appear, even when my sympathies are entirely with the latter. These differences have sunk deeply into my mind, because, during the first years of my stay in London my lack of understanding them was often a cause of my own failure when I thought I had success in hand. Many a time did I come to the verge of starvation in Soho, through not appreciating the peculiar trend of mind which causes an Englishman to do inexplicable things—that is, of course, from my Gallic standpoint.

For instance, an arrested man is presumed to be innocent until he is proved guilty. In England, if a murderer is caught red-handed over his victim, he is held guiltless until the judge sentences him. In France we make no such foolish assumption, and although I admit that innocent men have sometimes been punished, my experience enables me to state very emphatically that this happens not nearly so often as the public imagines. In ninety-nine cases out of a hundred an innocent man can at once prove his innocence without the least difficulty. I hold it is his duty towards the State to run the very slight risk of unjust imprisonment in order that obstacles may not be thrown in the way of the conviction of real criminals. But it is impossible to persuade an Englishman of this. Mon Dieu! I have tried it often enough.

Never shall I forget the bitterness of my disappointment when I captured Felini, the Italian anarchist, in connection with the Greenwich Park murder. At this time—it gives me no shame to confess it—I was myself living in Soho, in a state of extreme poverty. Having been employed so long by the French Government, I had formed the absurd idea that the future depended on my getting, not exactly a similar connection with Scotland Yard, but at least a subordinate position on the police force which would enable me to prove my capabilities, and lead to promotion. I had no knowledge, at that time, of the immense income which awaited me entirely outside the Government circle. Whether it is contempt for the foreigner, as has often been stated, or that native stolidity which spells complacency, the British official of any class rarely thinks it worth his while to discover the real cause of things in France, or Germany, or Russia, but plods heavily on from one mistake to another. Take, for example, those periodical outbursts of hatred against England which appear in the Continental Press. They create a dangerous international situation, and more than once have brought Britain to the verge of a serious war. Britain sternly spends millions in defence and preparation, whereas, if she would place in my hand half a million pounds I would guarantee to cause Britannia to be proclaimed an angel with white wings in every European country.

When I attempted to arrive at some connection with Scotland Yard, I was invariably asked for my credentials. When I proclaimed that I had been chief detective to the Republic of France, I could see that this announcement made a serious impression, but when I added that the Government of France had dismissed me without credentials, recommendation, or pension, official sympathy with officialism at once turned the tables against me. And here I may be pardoned for pointing out another portentous dissimilarity between the two lands which I think is not at all to the credit of my countrymen.

I was summarily dismissed. You may say it was because I failed, and it is true that in the case of the Queen's necklace I had undoubtedly failed, but, on the other hand, I had followed unerringly the clue which lay in my path, and although the conclusion was not in accordance with the facts, it was in accordance with logic. No, I was not dismissed because I failed. I had failed on various occasions before, as might happen to any man in any profession. I was dismissed because I made France for the moment the laughing-stock of Europe and America. France dismissed me because France had been laughed at. No Frenchman can endure the turning of a joke against him, but the Englishman does not appear to care in the least. So far as failure is concerned, never had any man failed so egregiously as I did with Felini, a slippery criminal who possessed all the bravery of a Frenchman and all the subtlety of an Italian. Three times he was in my hands—twice in Paris, once in Marseilles—and each time he escaped me; yet I was not dismissed.

When I say that Signor Felini was as brave as a Frenchman, perhaps I do him a little more than justice. He was desperately afraid of one man, and that man was myself. Our last interview in France he is not likely to forget, and although he eluded me, he took good care to get into England as fast as train and boat could carry him, and never again, while I was at the head of the French detective force, did he set foot on French soil. He was an educated villain, a graduate of the University of Turin, who spoke Spanish, French, and English as well as his own language, and this education made him all the more dangerous when he turned his talents to crime.

Now, I knew Felini's handiwork, either in murder or in housebreaking, as well as I know my own signature on a piece of white paper, and as soon as I saw the body of the murdered man in Greenwich Park I was certain Felini was the murderer. The English authorities at that time looked upon me with a tolerant, good-natured contempt.

Inspector Standish assumed the manner of a man placing at my disposal plenty of rope with which I might entangle myself. He appeared to think me excitable, and used soothing expressions as if I were a fractious child to be calmed, rather than a sane equal to be reasoned with. On many occasions I had the facts at my finger ends, while he remained in a state of most complacent ignorance, and though this attitude of lowering himself to deal gently with one whom he evidently looked upon as an irresponsible lunatic was most exasperating, I nevertheless claim great credit for having kept my temper with him. However, it turned out to be impossible for me to overcome his insular prejudice. He always supposed me to be a frivolous, volatile person, and so I was unable to prove myself of any value to him in his arduous duties.

The Felini instance was my last endeavour to win his favour. Inspector Standish appeared in his most amiable mood when I was admitted to his presence, and this in spite of the fact that all London was ringing with the Greenwich Park tragedy, while the police possessed not the faintest idea regarding the crime or its perpetrator. I judged from Inspector Standish's benevolent smile that I was somewhat excited when I spoke to him, and perhaps used many gestures which seemed superfluous to a large man whom I should describe as immovable, and who spoke slowly, with no motion of the hand, as if his utterances were the condensed wisdom of the ages.

'Inspector Standish,' I cried, 'is it within your power to arrest a man on suspicion?'

'Of course it is,' he replied; 'but we must harbour the suspicion before we make the arrest.'

'Have confidence in me,' I exclaimed. 'The man who committed the Greenwich Park murder is an Italian named Felini.'

I gave the address of the exact room in which he was to be found, with cautions regarding the elusive nature of this individual. I said that he had been three times in my custody, and those three times he had slipped through my fingers. I have since thought that Inspector Standish did not credit a word I had spoken.

'What is your proof against this Italian?' asked the Inspector slowly.

'The proof is on the body of the murdered man, but, nevertheless, if you suddenly confront Felini with me without giving him any hint of whom he is going to meet, you shall have the evidence from his own lips before he recovers from his surprise and fright.'

Something of my confidence must have impressed the official, for the order of arrest was made. Now, during the absence of the constable sent to bring in Felini, I explained to the inspector fully the details of my plan. Practically he did not listen to me, for his head was bent over a writing-pad on which I thought he was taking down my remarks, but when I had finished he went on writing as before, so I saw I had flattered myself unnecessarily. More than two hours passed before the constable returned, bringing with him the trembling Italian. I swung round in front of him, and cried, in a menacing voice:—

'Felini! Regard me! You know Valmont too well to trifle with him! What have you to say of the murder in Greenwich Park?'

I give you my word that the Italian collapsed, and would have fallen to the floor in a heap had not the constables upheld him with hands under each arm. His face became of a pasty whiteness, and he began to stammer his confession, when this incredible thing happened, which could not be believed in France. Inspector Standish held up his finger.

'One moment,' he cautioned solemnly, 'remember that whatever you say will be used against you!'

The quick, beady black eyes of the Italian shot from Standish to me, and from me to Standish. In an instant his alert mind grasped the situation. Metaphorically I had been waved aside. I was not there in any official capacity, and he saw in a moment with what an opaque intellect he had to deal. The Italian closed his mouth like a steel trap, and refused to utter a word. Shortly after he was liberated, as there was no evidence against him. When at last complete proof was in the tardy hands of the British authorities, the agile Felini was safe in the Apennine mountains, and today is serving a life sentence in Italy for the assassination of a senator whose name I have forgotten.

Is it any wonder that I threw up my hands in despair at finding myself amongst such a people. But this was in the early days, and now that I have greater experience of the English, many of my first opinions have been modified.

I mention all this to explain why, in a private capacity, I often did what no English official would dare to do. A people who will send a policeman, without even a pistol to protect him, to arrest a desperate criminal in the most dangerous quarter of London, cannot be comprehended by any native of France, Italy, Spain, or Germany. When I began to succeed as a private detective in London, and had accumulated money enough for my project, I determined not to be hampered by this unexplainable softness of the English toward an accused person. I therefore reconstructed my flat, and placed in the centre of it a dark room strong as any Bastille cell. It was twelve feet square, and contained no furniture except a number of shelves, a lavatory in one corner, and a pallet on the floor. It was ventilated by two flues from the centre of the ceiling, in one of which operated an electric fan, which, when the room was occupied, sent the foul air up that flue, and drew down fresh air through the other. The entrance to this cell opened out from my bedroom, and the most minute inspection would have failed to reveal the door, which was of massive steel, and was opened and shut by electric buttons that were partially concealed by the head of my bed. Even if they had been discovered, they would have revealed nothing, because the first turn of the button lit the electric light at the head of my bed; the second turn put it out; and this would happen as often as the button was turned to the right. But turn it three times slowly to the left, and the steel door opened. Its juncture was completely concealed by panelling. I have brought many a scoundrel to reason within the impregnable walls of that small room.

Those who know the building regulations of London will wonder how it was possible for me to delude the Government inspector during the erection of this section of the Bastille in the midst of the modern metropolis. It was the simplest thing in the world. Liberty of the subject is the first great rule with the English people, and thus many a criminal is allowed to escape. Here was I laying plans for the contravening of this first great rule, and to do so I took advantage of the second great rule of the English people, which is, that property is sacred. I told the building authorities I was a rich man with a great distrust of banks, and I wished to build in my flat a safe or strong-room in which to deposit my valuables. I built then such a room as may be found in every bank, and many private premises of the City, and a tenant might have lived in my flat for a year and never suspected the existence of this prison. A railway engine might have screeched its whistle within it, and not a sound would have penetrated the apartments that surrounded it unless the door were open.

But besides M. Eugène Valmont, dressed in elegant attire as if he were still a boulevardier of Paris, occupier of the top floor in the Imperial Flats, there was another Frenchman in London to whom I must introduce you, namely, Professor Paul Ducharme, who occupied a squalid back room in the cheapest and most undesirable quarter of Soho. Valmont flatters himself he is not yet middle-aged, but poor Ducharme does not need his sparse gray beard to proclaim his advancing years. Valmont vaunts an air of prosperity; Ducharme wears the shabby habiliments and the shoulder-stoop of hopeless poverty. He shuffles cringingly along the street, a compatriot not to be proud of. There are so many Frenchmen anxious to give lessons in their language, that merely a small living is to be picked up by any one of them. You will never see the spruce Valmont walking alongside the dejected Ducharme.

'Ah!' you exclaim, 'Valmont in his prosperity has forgotten those less fortunate of his nationality.'

Pardon, my friends, it is not so. Behold, I proclaim to you, the exquisite Valmont and the threadbare Ducharme are one and the same person. That is why they do not promenade together. And, indeed, it requires no great histrionic art on my part to act the rôle of the miserable Ducharme, for when I first came to London, I warded off starvation in this wretched room, and my hand it was that nailed to the door the painted sign 'Professor Paul Ducharme, Teacher of the French Language'. I never gave up the room, even when I became prosperous and moved to Imperial Flats, with its concealed chamber of horrors unknown to British authority. I did not give up the Soho chamber principally for this reason: Paul Ducharme, if the truth were known about him, would have been regarded as a dangerous character; yet this was a character sometimes necessary for me to assume. He was a member of the very inner circle of the International, an anarchist of the anarchists. This malign organisation has its real headquarters in London, and we who were officials connected with the Secret Service of the Continent have more than once cursed the complacency of the British Government which allows such a nest of vipers to exist practically unmolested. I confess that before I came to know the English people as well as I do now, I thought that this complacency was due to utter selfishness, because the anarchists never commit an outrage in England. England is the one spot on the map of Europe where an anarchist cannot be laid by the heels unless there is evidence against him that will stand the test of open court. Anarchists take advantage of this fact, and plots are hatched in London which are executed in Paris, Berlin, Petersburg, or Madrid. I know now that this leniency on the part of the British Government does not arise from craft, but from their unexplainable devotion to their shibboleth—'The liberty of the subject.' Time and again France has demanded the extradition of an anarchist, always to be met with the question,—

'Where is your proof?'

I know many instances where our certainty was absolute, and also cases where we possessed legal proof as well, but legal proof which, for one reason or another, we dared not use in public; yet all this had no effect on the British authorities. They would never give up even the vilest criminal except on publicly attested legal evidence, and not even then, if the crime were political.

During my term of office under the French Government, no part of my duties caused me more anxiety than that which pertained to the political secret societies. Of course, with a large portion of the Secret Service fund at my disposal, I was able to buy expert assistance, and even to get information from anarchists themselves. This latter device, however, was always more or less unreliable. I have never yet met an anarchist I could believe on oath, and when one of them offered to sell exclusive information to the police, we rarely knew whether he was merely trying to get a few francs to keep himself from starving, or whether he was giving us false particulars which would lead us into a trap. I have always regarded our dealings with nihilists, anarchists, or other secret associations for the perpetrating of murder as the most dangerous service a detective is called upon to perform. Yet it is absolutely necessary that the authorities should know what is going on in these secret conclaves. There are three methods of getting this intelligence. First, periodical raids upon the suspected, accompanied by confiscation and search of all papers found. This method is much in favour with the Russian police. I have always regarded it as largely futile; first, because the anarchists are not such fools, speaking generally, as to commit their purposes to writing; and, second, because it leads to reprisal. Each raid is usually followed by a fresh outbreak of activity on the part of those left free. The second method is to bribe an anarchist to betray his comrades. I have never found any difficulty in getting these gentry to accept money. They are eternally in need, but I usually find the information they give in return to be either unimportant or inaccurate. There remains, then, the third method, which is to place a spy among them. The spy battalion is the forlorn hope of the detective service. In one year I lost three men on anarchist duty, among the victims being my most valuable helper, Henri Brisson. Poor Brisson's fate was an example of how a man may follow a perilous occupation for months with safety, and then by a slight mistake bring disaster on himself. At the last gathering Brisson attended he received news of such immediate and fateful import that on emerging from the cellar where the gathering was held, he made directly for my residence instead of going to his own squalid room in the Rue Falgarie. My concierge said that he arrived shortly after one o'clock in the morning, and it would seem that at this hour he could easily have made himself acquainted with the fact that he was followed. Still, as there was on his track that human panther, Felini, it is not strange poor Brisson failed to elude him.

Arriving at the tall building in which my flat was then situated, Brisson rang the bell, and the concierge, as usual, in that strange state of semi-somnolence which envelops concierges during the night, pulled the looped wire at the head of his bed, and unbolted the door. Brisson assuredly closed the huge door behind him, and yet the moment before he did so, Felini must have slipped in unnoticed to the stone-paved courtyard. If Brisson had not spoken and announced himself, the concierge would have been wide awake in an instant. If he had given a name unknown to the concierge, the same result would have ensued. As it was he cried aloud 'Brisson,' whereupon the concierge of the famous chief of the French detective staff, Valmont, muttered 'Bon! and was instantly asleep again.

Now Felini had known Brisson well, but it was under the name of Revensky, and as an exiled Russian. Brisson had spent all his early years in Russia, and spoke the language like a native. The moment Brisson had uttered his true name he had pronounced his own death warrant. Felini followed him up to the first landing—my rooms were on the second floor—and there placed his sign manual on the unfortunate man, which was the swift downward stroke of a long, narrow, sharp poniard, entering the body below the shoulders, and piercing the heart. The advantage presented by this terrible blow is that the victim sinks instantly in a heap at the feet of his slayer, without uttering a moan. The wound left is a scarcely perceptible blue mark which rarely even bleeds. It was this mark I saw on the body of the Maire of Marseilles, and afterwards on one other in Paris besides poor Brisson. It was the mark found on the man in Greenwich Park; always just below the left shoulder-blade, struck from behind. Felini's comrades claim that there was this nobility in his action, namely, he allowed the traitor to prove himself before he struck the blow. I should be sorry to take away this poor shred of credit from Felini's character, but the reason he followed Brisson into the courtyard was to give himself time to escape. He knew perfectly the ways of the concierge. He knew that the body would lie there until the morning, as it actually did, and that this would give him hours in which to effect his retreat. And this was the man whom British law warned not to incriminate himself! What a people! What a people!

After Brisson's tragic death, I resolved to set no more valuable men on the track of the anarchists, but to place upon myself the task in my moments of relaxation. I became very much interested in the underground workings of the International. I joined the organisation under the name of Paul Ducharme, a professor of advanced opinions, who because of them had been dismissed his situation in Nantes. As a matter of fact there had been such a Paul Ducharme, who had been so dismissed, but he had drowned himself in the Loire, at Orleans, as the records show. I adopted the precaution of getting a photograph of this foolish old man from the police at Nantes, and made myself up to resemble him. It says much for my disguise that I was recognised as the professor by a delegate from Nantes, at the annual Convention held in Paris, which I attended, and although we conversed for some time together he never suspected that I was not the professor, whose fate was known to no one but the police of Orleans. I gained much credit among my comrades because of this encounter, which, during its first few moments, filled me with dismay, for the delegate from Nantes held me up as an example of a man well off, who had deliberately sacrificed his worldly position for the sake of principle. Shortly after this I was chosen delegate to carry a message to our comrades in London, and this delicate undertaking passed off without mishap.

It was perhaps natural then, that when I came to London after my dismissal by the French Government, I should assume the name and appearance of Paul Ducharme, and adopt the profession of French teacher. This profession gave me great advantages. I could be absent from my rooms for hours at a time without attracting the least attention, because a teacher goes wherever there are pupils. If any of my anarchist comrades saw me emerging shabbily from the grand Imperial Flats where Valmont lived, he greeted me affably, thinking I was coming from a pupil.

The sumptuous flat was therefore the office in which I received my rich clients, while the squalid room in Soho was often the workshop in which the tasks entrusted to me were brought to completion.

I now come to very modern days indeed, when I spent much time with the emissaries of the International.

It will be remembered that the King of England made a round of visits to European capitals, the far-reaching results of which in the interest of peace we perhaps do not yet fully understand and appreciate. His visit to Paris was the beginning of the present entente cordiale, and I betray no confidence when I say that this brief official call at the French capital was the occasion of great anxiety to the Government of my own country and also of that in which I was domiciled. Anarchists are against all government, and would like to see each one destroyed, not even excepting that of Great Britain.

My task in connection with the visit of King Edward to Paris was entirely unofficial. A nobleman, for whom on a previous occasion I had been so happy as to solve a little mystery which troubled him, complimented me by calling at my flat about two weeks before the King's entry into the French capital. I know I shall be pardoned if I fail to mention this nobleman's name. I gathered that the intended visit of the King met with his disapproval. He asked if I knew anything, or could discover anything, of the purposes animating the anarchist clubs of Paris, and their attitude towards the royal function, which was now the chief topic in the newspapers. I replied that within four days I would be able to submit to him a complete report on the subject. He bowed coldly and withdrew. On the evening of the fourth day I permitted myself the happiness of waiting upon his lordship at his West End London mansion.

'I have the honour to report to your lordship,' I began, 'that the anarchists of Paris are somewhat divided in their opinions regarding His Majesty's forthcoming progress through that city. A minority, contemptible in point of number, but important so far as the extremity of their opinions are concerned, has been trying—'

'Excuse me,' interrupted the nobleman, with some severity of tone, 'are they going to attempt to injure the King or not?'

'They are not, your lordship,' I replied, with what, I trust, is my usual urbanity of manner, despite his curt interpolation. 'His most gracious Majesty will suffer no molestation, and their reason for quiescence—'

'Their reasons do not interest me,' put in his lordship gruffly. 'You are sure of what you say?'

'Perfectly sure, your lordship.'

'No precautions need be taken?'

'None in the least, your lordship.'

'Very well,' concluded the nobleman shortly, 'if you tell my secretary in the next room as you go out how much I owe you, he will hand you a cheque,' and with that I was dismissed.

I may say that, mixing as I do with the highest in two lands, and meeting invariably such courtesy as I myself am always eager to bestow, a feeling almost of resentment arose at this cavalier treatment. However, I merely bowed somewhat ceremoniously in silence, and availed myself of the opportunity in the next room to double my bill, which was paid without demur.

Now, if this nobleman had but listened, he would have heard much that might interest an ordinary man, although I must say that during my three conversations with him his mind seemed closed to all outward impressions save and except the grandeur of his line, which he traced back unblemished into the northern part of my own country.

The King's visit had come as a surprise to the anarchists, and they did not quite know what to do about it. The Paris Reds were rather in favour of a demonstration, while London bade them, in God's name, to hold their hands, for, as they pointed out, England is the only refuge in which an anarchist is safe until some particular crime can be imputed to him, and what is more, proven up to the hilt.

It will be remembered that the visit of the King to Paris passed off without incident, as did the return visit of the President to London. On the surface all was peace and goodwill, but under the surface seethed plot and counterplot, and behind the scenes two great governments were extremely anxious, and high officials in the Secret Service spent sleepless nights. As no 'untoward incident' had happened, the vigilance of the authorities on both sides of the Channel relaxed at the very moment when, if they had known their adversaries, it should have been redoubled. Always beware of the anarchist when he has been good: look out for the reaction. It annoys him to be compelled to remain quiet when there is a grand opportunity for strutting across the world's stage, and when he misses the psychological moment, he is apt to turn 'nasty', as the English say.

When it first became known that there was to be a Royal procession through the streets of Paris, a few fanatical hot-heads, both in that city and in London, wished to take action, but they were overruled by the saner members of the organisation. It must not be supposed that anarchists are a band of lunatics. There are able brains among them, and these born leaders as naturally assume control in the underground world of anarchy as would have been the case if they had devoted their talents to affairs in ordinary life. They were men whose minds, at one period, had taken the wrong turning. These people, although they calmed the frenzy of the extremists, nevertheless regarded the possible rapprochement between England and France with grave apprehension. If France and England became as friendly as France and Russia, might not the refuge which England had given to anarchy become a thing of the past? I may say here that my own weight as an anarchist while attending these meetings in disguise under the name of Paul Ducharme was invariably thrown in to help the cause of moderation. My rôle, of course, was not to talk too much; not to make myself prominent, yet in such a gathering a man cannot remain wholly a spectator. Care for my own safety led me to be as inconspicuous as possible, for members of communities banded together against the laws of the land in which they live, are extremely suspicious of one another, and an inadvertent word may cause disaster to the person speaking it.

Perhaps it was this conservatism on my part that caused my advice to be sought after by the inner circle; what you might term the governing body of the anarchists; for, strange as it may appear, this organisation, sworn to put down all law and order, was itself most rigidly governed, with a Russian prince elected as its chairman, a man of striking ability, who, nevertheless, I believe, owed his election more to the fact that he was a nobleman than to the recognition of his intrinsic worth. And another point which interested me much was that this prince ruled his obstreperous subjects after the fashion of Russian despotism, rather than according to the liberal ideas of the country in which he was domiciled. I have known him more than once ruthlessly overturn the action of the majority, stamp his foot, smite his huge fist on the table, and declare so and so should not be done, no matter what the vote was. And the thing was not done, either.

At the more recent period of which I speak, the chairmanship of the London anarchists was held by a weak, vacillating man, and the mob had got somewhat out of hand. In the crisis that confronted us, I yearned for the firm fist and dominant boot of the uncompromising Russian. I spoke only once during this time, and assured my listeners that they had nothing to fear from the coming friendship of the two nations. I said the Englishman was so wedded to his grotesque ideas regarding the liberty of the subject he so worshipped absolute legal evidence, that we would never find our comrades disappear mysteriously from England as had been the case in continental countries.

Although restless during the exchange of visits between King and President, I believe I could have carried the English phalanx with me, if the international courtesies had ended there. But after it was announced that members of the British Parliament were to meet the members of the French Legislature, the Paris circle became alarmed, and when that conference did not end the entente, but merely paved the way for a meeting of business men belonging to the two countries in Paris, the French anarchists sent a delegate over to us, who made a wild speech one night, waving continually the red flag. This aroused all our own malcontents to a frenzy. The French speaker practically charged the English contingent with cowardice; said that as they were safe from molestation, they felt no sympathy for their comrades in Paris, at any time liable to summary arrest and the torture of the secret cross-examination. This Anglo-French love-feast must be wafted to the heavens in a halo of dynamite. The Paris anarchists were determined, and although they wished the co-operation of their London brethren, yet if the speaker did not bring back with him assurance of such co-operation, Paris would act on its own initiative.

The Russian despot would have made short work of this blood-blinded rhetoric, but alas, he was absent, and an overwhelming vote in favour of force was carried and accepted by the trembling chairman. My French confrère took back with him to Paris the unanimous consent of the English comrades to whom he had appealed. All that was asked of the English contingent was that it should arrange for the escape and safe keeping of the assassin who flung the bomb into the midst of the English visitors, and after the oratorical madman had departed, I, to my horror, was chosen to arrange for the safe transport and future custody of the bomb-thrower. It is not etiquette in anarchist circles for any member to decline whatever task is given him by the vote of his comrades. He knows the alternative, which is suicide. If he declines the task and still remains upon earth, the dilemma is solved for him, as the Italian Felini solved it through the back of my unfortunate helper Brisson. I therefore accepted the unwelcome office in silence, and received from the treasurer the money necessary for carrying out the same.

I realised for the first time since joining the anarchist association years before that I was in genuine danger. A single false step, a single inadvertent word, might close the career of Eugène Valmont, and at the same moment terminate the existence of the quiet, inoffensive Paul Ducharme, teacher of the French language. I knew perfectly well I should be followed. The moment I received the money the French delegate asked when they were to expect me in Paris. He wished to know so that all the resources of their organisation might be placed at my disposal. I replied calmly enough that I could not state definitely on what day I should leave England. There was plenty of time, as the business men's representatives from London would not reach Paris for another two weeks. I was well known to the majority of the Paris organisation, and would present myself before them on the first night of my arrival. The Paris delegate exhibited all the energy of a new recruit, and he seemed dissatisfied with my vagueness, but I went on without heeding his displeasure. He was not personally known to me, nor I to him, but if I may say so, Paul Ducharme was well thought of by all the rest of those present.

I had learned a great lesson during the episode of the Queen's Necklace, which resulted in my dismissal by the French Government. I had learned that if you expect pursuit it is always well to leave a clue for the pursuer to follow. Therefore I continued in a low conversational tone:—

'I shall want the whole of tomorrow for myself: I must notify my pupils of my absence. Even if my pupils leave me it will not so much matter. I can probably get others. But what does matter is my secretarial work with Monsieur Valmont of the Imperial Flats. I am just finishing for him the translation of a volume from French into English, and tomorrow I can complete the work, and get his permission to leave for a fortnight. This man, who is a compatriot of my own, has given me employment ever since I came to London. From him I have received the bulk of my income, and if it had not been for his patronage, I do not know what I should have done. I not only have no desire to offend him, but I wish the secretarial work to continue when I return to London.'

There was a murmur of approval at this. It was generally recognised that a man's living should not be interfered with, if possible. Anarchists are not poverty-stricken individuals, as most people think, for many of them hold excellent situations, some occupying positions of great trust, which is rarely betrayed.

It is recognised that a man's duty, not only to himself, but to the organisation, is to make all the money he can, and thus not be liable to fall back on the relief fund. This frank admission of my dependence on Valmont made it all the more impossible that anyone there listening should suspect that it was Valmont himself who was addressing the conclave.

'You will then take the night train tomorrow for Paris?' persisted the inquisitive French delegate.

'Yes, and no. I shall take the night train, and it shall be for Paris, but not from Charing Cross, Victoria, or Waterloo. I shall travel on the 8.30 Continental express from Liverpool Street to Harwich, cross to the Hook of Holland, and from there make my way to Paris through Holland and Belgium. I wish to investigate that route as a possible path for our comrade to escape. After the blow is struck, Calais, Boulogne, Dieppe, and Havre will be closely watched. I shall perhaps bring him to London by way of Antwerp and the Hook.'

These amiable disclosures were so fully in keeping with Paul Ducharme's reputation for candour and caution that I saw they made an excellent impression on my audience, and here the chairman intervened, putting an end to further cross-examination by saying they all had the utmost confidence in the judgment of Monsieur Paul Ducharme, and the Paris delegate might advise his friends to be on the lookout for the London representative within the next three or four days.

I left the meeting and went directly to my room in Soho, without even taking the trouble to observe whether I was watched or not. There I stayed all night, and in the morning quitted Soho as Ducharme, with a gray beard and bowed shoulders, walked west to the Imperial Flats, took the lift to the top, and, seeing the corridor was clear, let myself in to my own flat. I departed from my flat promptly at six o'clock, again as Paul Ducharme, carrying this time a bundle done up in brown paper under my arm, and proceeded directly to my room in Soho. Later I took a bus, still carrying my brown paper parcel, and reached Liverpool Street in ample time for the Continental train. By a little private arrangement with the guard, I secured a compartment for myself, although up to the moment the train left the station, I could not be sure but that I might be compelled to take the trip to the Hook of Holland after all. If any one had insisted on coming into my compartment, I should have crossed the North Sea that night. I knew I should be followed from Soho to the station, and that probably the spy would go as far as Harwich, and see me on the boat. It was doubtful if he would cross. I had chosen this route for the reason that we have no organisation in Holland: the nearest circle is in Brussels, and if there had been time, the Brussels circle would have been warned to keep an eye on me. There was, however, no time for a letter, and anarchists never use the telegraph, especially so far as the Continent is concerned, unless in cases of the greatest emergency. If they telegraphed my description to Brussels the chances were it would not be an anarchist who watched my landing, but a member of the Belgian police force.

The 8.30 Continental express does not stop between Liverpool Street and Parkeston Quay, which it is timed to reach three minutes before ten. This gave me an hour and a half in which to change my apparel. The garments of the poor old professor I rolled up into a ball one by one and flung out through the open window, far into the marsh past which we were flying in a pitch dark night. Coat, trousers, and waistcoat rested in separate swamps at least ten miles apart. Gray whiskers and gray wig I tore into little pieces, and dropped the bits out of the open window.

I had taken the precaution to secure a compartment in the front of the train, and when it came to rest at Parkeston Quay Station, the crowd, eager for the steamer, rushed past me, and I stepped out into the midst of it, a dapper, well-dressed young man, with black beard and moustaches, my own closely cropped black hair covered by a new bowler hat. Anyone looking for Paul Ducharme would have paid small attention to me, and to any friend of Valmont's I was equally unrecognisable.

I strolled in leisurely manner to the Great Eastern Hotel on the Quay, and asked the clerk if a portmanteau addressed to Mr. John Wilkins had arrived that day from London. He said 'Yes,' whereupon I secured a room for the night, as the last train had already left for the metropolis.

Next morning, Mr. John Wilkins, accompanied by a brand new and rather expensive portmanteau, took the 8.57 train for Liverpool Street, where he arrived at half-past ten, stepped into a cab, and drove to the Savoy Restaurant, lunching there with the portmanteau deposited in the cloak room. When John Wilkins had finished an excellent lunch in a leisurely manner at the Café Parisien of the Savoy, and had paid his bill, he did not go out into the Strand over the rubber-paved court by which he had entered, but went through the hotel and down the stairs, and so out into the thoroughfare facing the Embankment. Then turning to his right he reached the Embankment entrance of the Hotel Cecil. This leads into a long, dark corridor, at the end of which the lift may be rung for. It does not come lower than the floor above unless specially summoned. In this dark corridor, which was empty, John Wilkins took off the black beard and moustache, hid it in the inside pocket of his coat, and there went up into the lift a few moments later to the office floor, I, Eugène Valmont, myself for the first time in several days.

Even then I did not take a cab to my flat, but passed under the arched Strand front of the 'Cecil' in a cab, bound for the residence of that nobleman who had formerly engaged me to see after the safety of the King.

You will say that this was all very elaborate precaution to take when a man was not even sure he was followed. To tell you the truth, I do not know to this day whether anyone watched me or not, nor do I care. I live in the present: when once the past is done with, it ceases to exist for me. It is quite possible, nay, entirely probable, that no one tracked me farther than Liverpool Street Station the night before, yet it was for lack of such precaution that my assistant Brisson received the Italian's dagger under his shoulder blade fifteen years before. The present moment is ever the critical time; the future is merely for intelligent forethought. It was to prepare for the future that I was now in a cab on the way to my lord's residence. It was not the French anarchists I feared during the contest in which I was about to become engaged, but the Paris police. I knew French officialdom too well not to understand the futility of going to the authorities there and proclaiming my object. If I ventured to approach the chief of police with the information that I, in London, had discovered what it was his business in Paris to know, my reception would be far from cordial, even though, or rather because, I announced myself as Eugène Valmont. The exploits of Eugène had become part of the legends of Paris, and these legends were extremely distasteful to those men in power. My doings have frequently been made the subject of feuilletons in the columns of the Paris Press, and were, of course, exaggerated by the imagination of the writers, yet, nevertheless, I admit I did some good strokes of detection during my service with the French Government. It is but natural, then, that the present authorities should listen with some impatience when the name of Eugène Valmont is mentioned. I recognise this as quite in the order of things to be expected, and am honest enough to confess that in my own time I often hearkened to narratives regarding the performances of Lecocq with a doubting shrug of the shoulders.

Now, if the French police knew anything of this anarchist plot, which was quite within the bounds of possibility, and if I were in surreptitious communication with the anarchists, more especially with the man who was to fling the bomb, there was every chance I might find myself in the grip of French justice. I must, then, provide myself with credentials to show that I was acting, not against the peace and quiet of my country, but on the side of law and order. I therefore wished to get from the nobleman a commission in writing, similar to that command which he had placed upon me during the King's visit. This commission I should lodge at my bank in Paris, to be a voucher for me at the last extremity. I had no doubt his lordship would empower me to act in this instance as I had acted on two former occasions.

Perhaps if I had not lunched so well I might have approached his lordship with greater deference than was the case; but when ordering lunch I permitted a bottle of Château du Tertre, 1878, a most delicious claret, to be decanted carefully for my delectation at the table, and this caused a genial glow to permeate throughout my system, inducing a mental optimism which left me ready to salute the greatest of earth on a plane of absolute equality. Besides, after all, I am the citizen of a Republic.

The nobleman received me with frigid correctness, implying disapproval of my unauthorised visit, rather than expressing it. Our interview was extremely brief.

'I had the felicity of serving your lordship upon two occasions,' I began.

'They are well within my recollection,' he interrupted, 'but I do not remember sending for you a third time.'

'I have taken the liberty of coming unrequested, my lord, because of the importance of the news I carry. I surmise that you are interested in the promotion of friendship between France and England.'

'Your surmise, sir, is incorrect. I care not a button about it. My only anxiety was for the safety of the King.'

Even the superb claret was not enough to fortify me against words so harsh, and tones so discourteous, as those his lordship permitted himself to use.

'Sir,' said I, dropping the title in my rising anger, 'it may interest you to know that a number of your countrymen run the risk of being blown to eternity by an anarchist bomb in less than two weeks from today. A party of business men, true representatives of a class to which the pre-eminence of your Empire is due, are about to proceed—'

'Pray spare me,' interpolated his lordship wearily, 'I have read that sort of thing so often in the newspapers. If all these estimable City men are blown up, the Empire would doubtless miss them, as you hint, but I should not, and their fate does not interest me in the least, although you did me the credit of believing that it would. Thompson, you will show this person out? Sir, if I desire your presence here in future I will send for you.'

'You may send for the devil!' I cried, now thoroughly enraged, the wine getting the better of me.

'You express my meaning more tersely than I cared to do,' he replied coldly, and that was the last I ever saw of him.

Entering the cab I now drove to my flat, indignant at the reception I had met with. However, I knew the English people too well to malign them for the action of one of their number, and resentment never dwells long with me. Arriving at my rooms I looked through the newspapers to learn all I could of the proposed business men's excursion to Paris, and in reading the names of those most prominent in carrying out the necessary arrangements, I came across that of W. Raymond White, which caused me to sit back in my chair and wrinkle my brow in an endeavour to stir my memory. Unless I was much mistaken, I had been so happy as to oblige this gentleman some dozen or thirteen years before. As I remembered him, he was a business man who engaged in large transactions with France, dealing especially in Lyons and that district. His address was given in the newspaper as Old Change, so at once I resolved to see him. Although I could not recall the details of our previous meeting, if, indeed, he should turn out to be the same person, yet the mere sight of the name had produced a mental pleasure, as a chance chord struck may bring a grateful harmony to the mind. I determined to get my credentials from Mr. White if possible, for his recommendation would in truth be much more valuable than that of the gruff old nobleman to whom I had first applied, because, if I got into trouble with the police of Paris, I was well enough acquainted with the natural politeness of the authorities to know that a letter from one of the city's guests would secure my instant release.

I took a hansom to the head of that narrow thoroughfare known as Old Change, and there dismissed my cab. I was so fortunate as to recognise Mr. White coming out of his office. A moment later, and I should have missed him.

'Mr. White,' I accosted him, 'I desire to enjoy both the pleasure and the honour of introducing myself to you.'

'Monsieur,' replied Mr. White with a smile, 'the introduction is not necessary, and the pleasure and honour are mine. Unless I am very much mistaken, this is Monsieur Valmont of Paris?'

'Late of Paris,' I corrected.

'Are you no longer in Government service then?'

'For a little more than ten years I have been a resident of London.'

'What, and have never let me know? That is something the diplomatists call an unfriendly act, monsieur. Now, shall we return to my office, or go to a café?'

'To your office, if you please, Mr. White. I come on rather important business.'

Entering his private office the merchant closed the door, offered me a chair, and sat down himself by his desk. From the first he had addressed me in French, which he spoke with an accent so pure that it did my lonesome heart good to hear it.

'I called upon you half a dozen years ago,' he went on, 'when I was over in Paris on a festive occasion, where I hoped to secure your company, but I could not learn definitely whether you were still with the Government or not.'

'It is the way of the French officialism,' I replied. 'If they knew my whereabouts they would keep the knowledge to themselves.'

'Well, if you have been ten years in London, Monsieur Valmont, we may now perhaps have the pleasure of claiming you as an Englishman; so I beg you will accompany us on another festive occasion to Paris next week. Perhaps you have seen that a number of us are going over there to make the welkin ring.'

'Yes; I have read all about the business men's excursion to Paris, and it is with reference to this journey that I wish to consult you,' and here I gave

Mr. White in detail the plot of the anarchists against the growing cordiality of the two countries. The merchant listened quietly without interruption until I had finished; then he said,—'I suppose it will be rather useless to inform the police of Paris?'

'Indeed, Mr. White, it is the police of Paris I fear more than the anarchists. They would resent information coming to them from the outside, especially from an ex-official, the inference being that they were not up to their own duties. Friction and delay would ensue until the deed was inevitable. It is quite on the cards that the police of Paris may have some inkling of the plot, and in that case, just before the event, they are reasonably certain to arrest the wrong men. I shall be moving about Paris, not as Eugène Valmont, but as Paul Ducharme, the anarchist; therefore, there is some danger that as a stranger and a suspect I may be laid by the heels at the critical moment. If you would be so good as to furnish me with credentials which I can deposit somewhere in Paris in case of need, I may thus be able to convince the authorities that they have taken the wrong man.'

Mr. White, entirely unperturbed by the prospect of having a bomb thrown at him within two weeks, calmly wrote several documents, then turned his untroubled face to me, and said, in a very confidential, winning tone:—'Monsieur Valmont, you have stated the case with that clear comprehensiveness pertaining to a nation which understands the meaning of words, and the correct adjustment of them; that felicity of language which has given France the first place in the literature of nations. Consequently, I think I see very clearly the delicacies of the situation. We may expect hindrances, rather than help, from officials on either side of the Channel. Secrecy is essential to success. Have you spoken of this to anyone but me?'

'Only to Lord Blank,' I replied; 'and now I deeply regret having made a confidant of him.'

'That does not in the least matter,' said Mr. White, with a smile; 'Lord Blank's mind is entirely occupied by his own greatness. Chemists tell me that you cannot add a new ingredient to a saturated solution; therefore your revelation will have made no impression upon his lordship's intellect. He has already forgotten all about it. Am I right in supposing that everything hinges on the man who is to throw the bomb?'

'Quite right, sir. He may be venal, he may be traitorous, he may be a coward, he may be revengeful, he may be a drunkard. Before I am in conversation with him for ten minutes, I shall know what his weak spot is. It is upon that spot I must act, and my action must be delayed till the very last moment; for, if he disappears too long before the event, his first, second, or third substitute will instantly step into his place.'

'Precisely. So you cannot complete your plans until you have met this man?'

'Parfaitement.'

'Then I propose,' continued Mr. White, 'that we take no one into our confidence. In a case like this there is little use in going before a committee. I can see that you do not need any advice, and my own part shall be to remain in the background, content to support the most competent man that could have been chosen to grapple with a very difficult crisis.'

I bowed profoundly. There was a compliment in his glance as well as in his words. Never before had I met so charming a man.

'Here,' he continued, handing me one of the papers he had written, 'is a letter to whom it may concern, appointing you my agent for the next three weeks, and holding myself responsible for all you see fit to do. Here,' he went on, passing to me a second sheet, 'is a letter of introduction to Monsieur Largent, the manager of my bank in Paris, a man well known and highly respected in all circles, both official and commercial. I suggest that you introduce yourself to him, and he will hold himself in readiness to respond to any call you may make, night or day. I assure you that his mere presence before the authorities will at once remove any ordinary difficulty. And now,' he added, taking in hand the third slip of paper, speaking with some hesitation, and choosing his words with care, 'I come to a point which cannot be ignored. Money is a magician's wand, which, like faith, will remove mountains. It may also remove an anarchist hovering about the route of a business man's procession.'

He now handed to me what I saw was a draft on Paris for a thousand pounds.

'I assure you, monsieur,' I protested, covered with confusion, 'that no thought of money was in my mind when I took the liberty of presenting myself to you. I have already received more than I could have expected in the generous confidence you were good enough to repose in me, as exhibited by these credentials, and especially the letter to your banker. Thanks to the generosity of your countrymen, Mr White, of which you are a most notable example, I am in no need of money.'

'Monsieur Valmont, I am delighted to hear that you have got on well amongst us. This money is for two purposes. First, you will use what you need. I know Paris very well, monsieur, and have never found gold an embarrassment there. The second purpose is this: I suggest that when you present the letter of introduction to Monsieur Largent, you will casually place this amount to your account in his bank. He will thus see that besides writing you a letter of introduction, I transfer a certain amount of my own balance to your credit. That will do you no harm with him, I assure you. And now, Monsieur Valmont, it only remains for me to thank you for the opportunity you have given me, and to assure you that I shall march from the Gare du Nord without a tremor, knowing the outcome is in such capable custody.'

And then this estimable man shook hands with me in action the most cordial. I walked away from Old Change as if I trod upon air; a feeling vastly different from that with which I departed from the residence of the old nobleman in the West End but a few hours before.

Next morning I was in Paris, and next night I attended the underground meeting of the anarchists, held within a quarter of a mile of the Luxembourg. I was known to many there assembled, but my acquaintance of course was not so large as with the London circle. They had half expected me the night before, knowing that even going by the Hook of Holland I might have reached Paris in time for the conclave. I was introduced generally to the assemblage as the emissary from England, who was to assist the bomb-throwing brother to escape either to that country, or to such other point of safety as I might choose. No questions were asked me regarding my doings of the day before, nor was I required to divulge the plans for my fellow-member's escape. I was responsible; that was enough. If I failed through no fault of my own, it was but part of the ill-luck we were all prepared to face. If I failed through treachery, then a dagger in the back at the earliest possible moment. We all knew the conditions of our sinister contract, and we all recognised that the least said the better.

The cellar was dimly lighted by one oil lamp depending from the ceiling. From this hung a cord attached to an extinguisher, and one jerk of the cord would put out the light. Then, while the main entry doors were being battered down by police, the occupants of the room escaped through one of three or four human rat-holes provided for that purpose.

If any Parisian anarchist does me the honour to read these jottings, I beg to inform him that while I remained in office under the Government of France there was never a time when I did not know the exit of each of these underground passages, and could during any night there was conference have bagged the whole lot of those there assembled. It was never my purpose, however, to shake the anarchists' confidence in their system, for that merely meant the removal of the gathering to another spot, thus giving us the additional trouble of mapping out their new exits and entrances. When I did make a raid on anarchist headquarters in Paris, it was always to secure some particular man. I had my emissaries in plain clothes stationed at each exit. In any case, the rats were allowed to escape unmolested, sneaking forth with great caution into the night, but we always spotted the man we wanted, and almost invariably arrested him elsewhere, having followed him from his kennel. In each case my uniformed officers found a dark and empty cellar, and retired apparently baffled. But the coincidence that on the night of every raid some member there present was secretly arrested in another quarter of Paris, and perhaps given a free passage to Russia, never seemed to awaken suspicion in the minds of the conspirators.

I think the London anarchists' method is much better, and I have ever considered the English nihilist the most dangerous of this fraternity, for he is cool-headed and not carried away by his own enthusiasm, and consequently rarely carried away by his own police. The authorities of London meet no opposition in making a raid. They find a well-lighted room containing a more or less shabby coterie playing cards at cheap pine tables. There is no money visible, and, indeed, very little coin would be brought to light if the whole party were searched; so the police are unable to convict the players under the Gambling Act. Besides, it is difficult in any case to obtain a conviction under the Gambling Act, because the accused has the sympathy of the whole country with him. It has always been to me one of the anomalies of the English nature that a magistrate can keep a straight face while he fines some poor wretch for gambling, knowing that next race day (if the court is not sitting) the magistrate himself, in correct sporting costume, with binoculars hanging at his hip, will be on the lawn by the course backing his favourite horse.

After my reception at the anarchists' club of Paris, I remained seated unobtrusively on a bench waiting until routine business was finished, after which I expected an introduction to the man selected to throw the bomb. I am a very sensitive person, and sitting there quietly I became aware that I was being scrutinised with more than ordinary intensity by someone, which gave me a feeling of uneasiness. At last, in the semi-obscurity opposite me I saw a pair of eyes as luminous as those of a tiger peering fixedly at me. I returned the stare with such composure as I could bring to my aid, and the man, as if fascinated by a look as steady as his own, leaned forward, and came more and more into the circle of light.

Then I received a shock which it required my utmost self-control to conceal. The face, haggard and drawn, was none other than that of Adolph Simard, who had been my second assistant in the Secret Service of France during my last year in office. He was a most capable and rising young man at that time, and, of course, he knew me well. Had he, then, penetrated my disguise? Such an event seemed impossible; he could not have recognised my voice, for I had said nothing aloud since entering the room, my few words to the president being spoken in a whisper. Simard's presence there bewildered me; by this time he should be high up in the Secret Service. If he were now a spy, he would, of course, wish to familiarise himself with every particular of my appearance, as in my hands lay the escape of the criminal. Yet, if such were his mission, why did he attract the attention of all members by this open-eyed scrutiny? That he recognised me as Valmont I had not the least fear; my disguise was too perfect; and, even if I were there in my own proper person, I had not seen Simard, nor he me, for ten years, and great changes occur in a man's appearance during so long a period. Yet I remembered with disquietude that Mr. White recognised me, and here tonight I had recognised Simard. I could not move my bench farther back because it stood already against the wall.

Simard, on the contrary, was seated on one of the few chairs in the room, and this he periodically hitched forward, the better to continue his examination, which now attracted the notice of others besides myself. As he came forward, I could not help admiring the completeness of his disguise so far as apparel was concerned. He was a perfect picture of the Paris wastrel, and what was more, he wore on his head a cap of the Apaches, the most dangerous band of cut-throats that have ever cursed a civilised city. I could understand that even among lawless anarchists this badge of membership of the Apache band might well strike tenor. I felt that before the meeting adjourned I must speak with him, and I determined to begin our conversation by asking him why he stared so fixedly at me. Yet even then I should have made little progress. I did not dare to hint that he belonged to the Secret Service; nevertheless, if the authorities had this plot in charge, it was absolutely necessary we should work together, or, at least, that I should know they were in the secret, and steer my course accordingly. The fact that Simard appeared with undisguised face was not so important as might appear to an outsider.

It is always safer for a spy to preserve his natural appearance if that is possible, because a false beard or false moustache or wig run the risk of being deranged or torn away. As I have said, an anarchist assemblage is simply a room filled with the atmosphere of suspicion. I have known instances where an innocent stranger was suddenly set upon in the midst of solemn proceedings by two or three impetuous fellow-members, who nearly jerked his own whiskers from his face under the impression that they were false. If

Simard, therefore, appeared in his own scraggy beard and unkempt hair it meant that he communicated with headquarters by some circuitous route. I realised, therefore, that a very touchy bit of diplomacy awaited me if I was to learn from himself his actual status. While I pondered over this perplexity, it was suddenly dissolved by the action of the president, and another substituted for it.

'Will Brother Simard come forward?' asked the president.

My former subordinate removed his eyes from me, slowly rose from his chair, and shuffled up to the president's table.

'Brother Ducharme,' said that official to me in a quiet tone, 'I introduce you to Brother Simard, whom you are commissioned to see into a place of safety when he has dispersed the procession.'

Simard turned his fishy goggle eyes upon me, and a grin disclosed wolf-like teeth. He held out his hand, which, rising to my feet, I took. He gave me a flabby grasp, and all the time his inquiring eyes travelled over me.

'You don't look up to much,' he said. 'What are you?'

'I am a teacher of the French language in London.'

'Umph!' growled Simard, evidently in no wise prepossessed by my appearance. 'I thought you weren't much of a fighter. The gendarmes will make short work of this fellow,' he growled to the chairman.

'Brother Ducharme is vouched for by the whole English circle,' replied the president firmly.

'Oh, the English! I think very little of them. Still, it doesn't matter,' and with a shrug of the shoulders he shuffled to his seat again, leaving me standing there in a very embarrassed state of mind; my brain in a whirl. That the man was present with his own face was bewildering enough, but that he should be here under his own name was simply astounding. I scarcely heard what the president said. It seemed to the effect that Simard would take me to his own room, where we might talk over our plans. And now Simard rose again from his chair, and said to the president that if nothing more were wanted of him, we should go. Accordingly we left the place of meeting together. I watched my comrade narrowly. There was now a trembling eagerness in his action, and without a word he hurried me to the nearest café, where we sat down before a little iron table on the pavement.

'Garçon!' he shouted harshly, 'bring me four absinthes. What will you drink, Ducharme?',

'A café-cognac, if you please.'

'Bah!' cried Simard; 'better have absinthe.'

Then he cursed the waiter for his slowness. When the absinthe came he grasped the half-full glass and swallowed the liquid raw, a thing I had never seen done before. Into the next measure of the wormwood he poured the water impetuously from the carafe, another thing I had never seen done before, and dropped two lumps of sugar into it. Over the third glass he placed a flat perforated plated spoon, piled the sugar on this bridge, and now quite expertly allowed the water to drip through, the proper way of concocting this seductive mixture. Finishing his second glass he placed the perforated spoon over the fourth, and began now more calmly sipping the third while the water dripped slowly into the last glass.

Here before my eyes was enacted a more wonderful change than the gradual transformation of transparent absinthe into an opaque opalescent liquid. Simard, under the influence of the drink, was slowly becoming the Simard I had known ten years before. Remarkable! Absinthe having in earlier years made a beast of the man was now forming a man out of the beast. His staring eyes took on an expression of human comradeship. The whole mystery became perfectly clear to me without a question asked or an answer uttered. This man was no spy, but a genuine anarchist. However it happened, he had become a victim of absinthe, one of many with whom I was acquainted, although I never met any so far sunk as he. He was into his fourth glass, and had ordered two more when he began to speak.

'Here's to us,' he cried, with something like a civilised smile on his gaunt face. 'You're not offended at what I said in the meeting, I hope?'

'Oh, no,' I answered.

'That's right. You see, I once belonged to the Secret Service, and if my chief was there today, we would soon find ourselves in a cool dungeon. We couldn't trip up Eugène Valmont.'

At these words, spoken with sincerity, I sat up in my chair, and I am sure such an expression of enjoyment came into my face that if I had not instantly suppressed it, I might have betrayed myself.

'Who was Eugène Valmont?' I asked, in a tone of assumed indifference.

Mixing his fifth glass he nodded sagely.

'You wouldn't ask that question if you'd been in Paris a dozen years ago. He was the Government's chief detective, and he knew more of anarchists, yes, and of Apaches, too, than either you or I do. He had more brains in his little finger than that whole lot babbling there tonight. But the Government being a fool, as all governments are, dismissed him, and because I was his assistant, they dismissed me as well. They got rid of all his staff. Valmont disappeared. If I could have found him, I wouldn't be sitting here with you tonight; but he was right to disappear. The Government did all they could against us who had been his friends, and I for one came through starvation, and was near throwing myself in the Seine, which sometimes I wish I had done. Here, garçon, another absinthe. But by-and-by I came to like the gutter, and here I am. I'd rather have the gutter and absinthe than the Luxembourg without it. I've had my revenge on the Government many times since, for I knew their ways, and often have I circumvented the police. That's why they respect me among the anarchists. Do you know how I joined? I knew all their passwords, and walked right into one of their meetings, alone and in rags.

'"Here am I," I said; "Adolph Simard, late second assistant to Eugène Valmont, chief detective to the French Government."

'There were twenty weapons covering me at once, but I laughed.

'"I'm starving," I cried, "and I want something to eat, and more especially something to drink. In return for that I'll show you every rat-hole you've got.

Lift the president's chair, and there's a trap-door that leads to the Rue Blanc. I'm one of you, and I'll tell you the tricks of the police."

'Such was my initiation, and from that moment the police began to pick their spies out of the Seine, and now they leave us alone. Even Valmont himself could do nothing against the anarchists since I have joined them.'

Oh, the incredible self-conceit of human nature! Here was this ruffian proclaiming the limitations of Valmont, who half an hour before had shaken his hand within the innermost circle of his order! Yet my heart warmed towards the wretch who had remembered me and my exploits.

It now became my anxious and difficult task to lure Simard away from this café and its absinthe. Glass after glass of the poison had brought him up almost to his former intellectual level, but now it was shoving him rapidly down the hill again. I must know where his room was situated, yet if I waited much longer the man would be in a state of drunken imbecility which would not only render it impossible for him to guide me to his room, but likely cause both of us to be arrested by the police. I tried persuasion, and he laughed at me; I tried threats, whereat he scowled and cursed me as a renegade from England. At last the liquor overpowered him, and his head sunk on the metal table and the dark blue cap fell to the floor.

I was in despair, but now received a lesson which taught me that if a man leaves a city, even for a short time, he falls out of touch with its ways. I called the waiter, and said to him,—

'Do you know my friend here?'

'I do not know his name,' replied the garçon, 'but I have seen him many times at this café. He is usually in this state when he has money.'

'Do you know where he lives? He promised to take me with him, and I am a stranger in Paris.'

'Have no discontent, monsieur. Rest tranquil; I will intervene.'

With this he stepped across the pavement in front of the café, into the street, and gave utterance to a low, peculiar whistle. The café was now nearly deserted, for the hour was very late, or, rather, very early. When the waiter returned I whispered to him in some anxiety,—

'Not the police, surely?'

'But no!' he cried in scorn; 'certainly not the police.'

He went on unconcernedly taking in the empty chairs and tables. A few minutes later there swaggered up to the café two of the most disreputable, low-browed scoundrels I had ever seen, each wearing a dark-blue cap, with a glazed peak over the eyes; caps exactly similar to the one which lay in front of Simard. The band of Apaches which now permeates all Paris has risen since my time, and Simard had been mistaken an hour before in asserting that Valmont was familiar with their haunts. The present Chief of Police in Paris and some of his predecessors confess there is a difficulty in dealing with these picked assassins, but I should very much like to take a hand in the game on the side of law and order. However, that is not to be; therefore, the Apaches increase and prosper.

The two vagabonds roughly smote Simard's cap on his prone head, and as roughly raised him to his feet.

'He is a friend of mine,' I interposed, 'and promised to take me home with him.'

'Good! Follow us,' said one of them; and now I passed through the morning streets of Paris behind three cut-throats, yet knew that I was safer than if broad daylight was in the thoroughfare, with a meridian sun shining down upon us. I was doubly safe, being in no fear of harm from midnight prowlers, and equally free from danger of arrest by the police. Every officer we met avoided us, and casually stepped to the other side of the street. We turned down a narrow lane, then through a still narrower one, which terminated at a courtyard. Entering a tall building, we climbed up five flights of stairs to a landing, where one of the scouts kicked open a door, into a room so miserable that there was not even a lock to protect its poverty. Here they allowed the insensible Simard to drop with a crash on the floor, thus they left us alone without even an adieu. The Apaches take care of their own—after a fashion.

I struck a match, and found part of a bougie stuck in the mouth of an absinthe bottle, resting on a rough deal table. Lighting the bougie, I surveyed the horrible apartment. A heap of rags lay in a corner, and this was evidently Simard's bed. I hauled him to it, and there he lay unconscious, himself a bundle of rags. I found one chair, or, rather, stool, for it had no back. I drew the table against the lockless door, blew out the light, sat on the stool, resting my arms on the table, and my head on my arms, and slept peacefully till long after daybreak.

Simard awoke in the worst possible humour. He poured forth a great variety of abusive epithets at me. To make himself still more agreeable, he turned back the rags on which he had slept, and brought to the light a round, black object, like a small cannon-ball, which he informed me was the picric bomb that was to scatter destruction among my English friends, for whom he expressed the greatest possible loathing and contempt. Then sitting up, he began playing with this infernal machine, knowing, as well as I, that if he allowed it to drop that was the end of us two.

I shrugged my shoulders at this display, and affected a nonchalance I was far from feeling, but finally put an end to his dangerous amusement by telling him that if he came out with me I would pay for his breakfast, and give him a drink of absinthe.

The next few days were the most anxious of my life. Never before had I lived on terms of intimacy with a picric bomb, that most deadly and uncertain of all explosive agencies. I speedily found that Simard was so absinthe-soaked I could do nothing with him. He could not be bribed or cajoled or persuaded or threatened. Once, indeed, when he talked with drunken affection of Eugène Valmont, I conceived a wild notion of declaring myself to him; but a moment's reflection showed the absolute uselessness of this course. It was not one Simard with whom I had to deal, but half a dozen or more. There was Simard, sober, half sober, quarter sober, drunk, half drunk, quarter drunk, or wholly drunk. Any bargain I might make with the one Simard would not be kept by any of the other six. The only safe Simard was Simard insensible through over-indulgence. I had resolved to get Simard insensibly drunk on the morning of the procession, but my plans were upset at a meeting of the anarchists, which luckily took place on an evening shortly after my arrival, and this gave me time to mature the plan which was actually carried out. Each member of the anarchists' club knew of Simard's slavery to absinthe, and fears were expressed that he might prove incapable on the day of the procession, too late for a substitute to take his place. It was, therefore, proposed that one or two others should be stationed along the route of the procession with bombs ready if Simard failed. This I strenuously opposed, and guaranteed that Simard would be ready to launch his missile. I met with little difficulty in persuading the company to agree, because, after all, every man among them feared he might be one of those selected, which choice was practically a sentence of death. I guaranteed that the bomb would be thrown, and this apparently was taken to mean that if Simard did not do the deed, I would.

This danger over, I next took the measurements, and estimated the weight, of the picric bomb. I then sought out a most amiable and expert pyrotechnist, a capable workman of genius, who with his own hand makes those dramatic firework arrangements which you sometimes see in Paris. As Eugène Valmont, I had rendered a great service to this man, and he was not likely to have forgotten it. During one of the anarchist scares a stupid policeman had arrested him, and when I intervened the man was just on the verge of being committed for life. France trembled in one of her panics, or, rather, Paris did, and demanded victims. This blameless little workman had indeed contributed with both material and advice, but any fool might have seen that he had done this innocently. His assistance had been invoked and secured under the pretence that his clients were promoting an amateur firework display, which was true enough, but the display cost the lives of three men, and intentionally so. I cheered up the citizen in the moment of his utmost despair, and brought such proof of his innocence to the knowledge of those above me that he was most reluctantly acquitted. To this man I now went with my measurement of the bomb and the estimate of its weight.

'Sir,' said I, 'do you remember Eugène Valmont?'

'Am I ever likely to forget him?' he replied, with a fervour that pleased me.

'He has sent me to you, and implores you to aid me, and that aid will wipe out the debt you owe him.'

'Willingly, willingly,' cried the artisan, 'so long as it has nothing to do with the anarchists or the making of bombs.'

'It has to do exactly with those two things. I wish you to make an innocent bomb which will prevent an anarchist outrage.'

At this the little man drew back, and his face became pale.

'It is impossible,' he protested; 'I have had enough of innocent bombs. No, no, and in any case how can I be sure you come from Eugène Valmont? No, monsieur, I am not to be trapped the second time.'

At this I related rapidly all that Valmont had done for him, and even repeated Valmont's most intimate conversation with him. The man was nonplussed, but remained firm.

'I dare not do it,' he said.

We were alone in his back shop. I walked to the door and thrust in the bolt; then, after a moment's pause, turned round, stretched forth my right hand dramatically, and cried,—'Behold, Eugène Valmont!'

My friend staggered against the wall in his amazement, and I continued in solemn tones,—'Eugène Valmont, who by this removal of his disguise places his life in your hands as your life was in his. Now, monsieur, what will you do?'

He replied,—'Monsieur Valmont, I shall do whatever you ask. If I refused a moment ago, it was because I thought there was now in France no Eugène Valmont to rectify my mistake if I made one.'

I resumed my disguise, and told him I wished an innocent substitute for this picric bomb, and he at once suggested an earthenware globe, which would weigh the same as the bomb, and which could be coloured to resemble it exactly.

'And now, Monsieur Valmont, do you wish smoke to issue from this imitation bomb?'

'Yes,' I said, 'in such quantity as you can compress within it.'

'It is easily done,' he cried, with the enthusiasm of a true French artist. 'And may I place within some little design of my own which will astonish your friends the English, and delight my friends the French?'

'Monsieur,' said I, 'I am in your hands. I trust the project entirely to your skill,' and thus it came about that four days later I substituted the bogus globe for the real one, and, unseen, dropped the picric bomb from one of the bridges into the Seine.

On the morning of the procession I was compelled to allow Simard several drinks of absinthe to bring him up to a point where he could be depended on, otherwise his anxiety and determination to fling the bomb, his frenzy against all government, made it certain that he would betray both of us before the fateful moment came. My only fear was that I could not stop him drinking when once he began, but somehow our days of close companionship, loathsome as they were to me, seemed to have had the effect of building up again the influence I held over him in former days, and his yielding more or less to my wishes appeared to be quite unconscious on his part.

The procession was composed entirely of carriages, each containing four persons—two Englishmen sat on the back seats, with two Frenchmen in front of them. A thick crowd lined each side of the thoroughfare, cheering vociferously. Right into the middle of the procession Simard launched his bomb. There was no crash of explosion. The missile simply went to pieces as if it were an earthenware jar, and there arose a dense column of very white smoke. In the immediate vicinity the cheering stopped at once, and the sinister word 'bomb' passed from lip to lip in awed whispers. As the throwing had been unnoticed in the midst of the commotion, I held Simard firmly by the wrist, determined he should not draw attention to himself by his panic-stricken desire for immediate flight.

'Stand still, you fool!' I hissed into his ear and he obeyed trembling.

The pair of horses in front of which the bomb fell rose for a moment on their hind legs, and showed signs of bolting, but the coachman held them firmly, and uplifted his hand so that the procession behind him came to a momentary pause. No one in the carriages moved a muscle, then suddenly the tension was broken by a great and simultaneous cheer. Wondering at this I turned my eyes from the frightened horses to the column of pale smoke in front of us, and saw that in some manner it had resolved itself into a gigantic calla lily, pure white, while from the base of this sprung the lilies of France, delicately tinted. Of course, this could not have happened if there had been the least wind, but the air was so still that the vibration of the cheering caused the huge lily to tremble gently as it stood there marvellously poised; the lily of peace, surrounded by the lilies of France! That was the design, and if you ask me how it was done, I can only refer you to my pyrotechnist, and say that whatever a Frenchman attempts to do he will accomplish artistically.

And now these imperturbable English, who had been seated immobile when they thought a bomb was thrown, stood up in their carriages to get a better view of this aerial phenomenon, cheering and waving their hats. The lily gradually thinned and dissolved in little patches of cloud that floated away above our heads.

'I cannot stay here longer,' groaned Simard, quaking, his nerves, like himself, in rags. 'I see the ghosts of those I have killed floating around me.'

'Come on, then, but do not hurry.'

There was no difficulty in getting him to London, but it was absinthe, absinthe, all the way, and when we reached Charing Cross, I was compelled to help him, partly insensible, into a cab. I took him direct to Imperial Flats, and up into my own set of chambers, where I opened my strong room, and flung him inside to sleep off his intoxication, and subsist on bread and water when he became sober.

I attended that night a meeting of the anarchists, and detailed accurately the story of our escape from France. I knew we had been watched, and so skipped no detail. I reported that I had taken Simard directly to my compatriot's flat; to Eugène Valmont, the man who had given me employment, and who had promised to do what he could for Simard, beginning by trying to break him of the absinthe habit, as he was now a physical wreck through over-indulgence in that stimulant.

It was curious to note the discussion which took place a few nights afterwards regarding the failure of the picric bomb. Scientists among us said that the bomb had been made too long; that a chemical reaction had taken place which destroyed its power. A few superstitious ones saw a miracle in what had happened, and they forthwith left our organisation. Then again, things were made easier by the fact that the man who constructed the bomb, evidently terror-stricken at what he had done, disappeared the day before the procession, and has never since been heard of. The majority of the anarchists believed he had made a bogus bomb, and had fled to escape their vengeance rather than to evade the justice of the law.

Simard will need no purgatory in the next world. I kept him on bread and water for a month in my strong room, and at first he demanded absinthe with threats, then grovelled, begging and praying for it. After that a period of depression and despair ensued, but finally his naturally strong constitution conquered, and began to build itself up again. I took him from his prison one midnight, and gave him a bed in my Soho room, taking care in bringing him away that he would never recognise the place where he had been incarcerated. In my dealings with him I had always been that old man, Paul Ducharme. Next morning I said to him:—'You spoke of Eugène Valmont. I have learned that he lives in London, and I advise you to call upon him. Perhaps he can get you something to do.'

Simard was overjoyed, and two hours later, as Eugène Valmont, I received him in my flat, and made him my assistant on the spot. From that time forward, Paul Ducharme, language teacher, disappeared from the earth, and Simard abandoned his two A's—anarchy and absinthe.

3. The Clue of the Silver Spoons

When the card was brought in to me, I looked upon it with some misgiving, for I scented a commercial transaction, and, although such cases are lucrative enough, nevertheless I, Eugène Valmont, formerly high in the service of the French Government, do not care to be connected with them. They usually pertain to sordid business affairs, presenting little that is of interest to a man who, in his time, has dealt with subtle questions of diplomacy upon which the welfare of nations sometimes turned.

The name of Bentham Gibbes is familiar to everyone, connected as it is with the much-advertised pickles, whose glaring announcements in crude crimson and green strike the eye throughout Great Britain, and shock the artistic sense wherever seen. Me! I have never tasted them, and shall not so long as a French restaurant remains open in London. But I doubt not they are as pronounced to the palate as their advertisement is distressing to the eye. If then, this gross pickle manufacturer expected me to track down those who were infringing upon the recipes for making his so-called sauces, chutneys, and the like, he would find himself mistaken, for I was now in a position to pick and choose my cases, and a case of pickles did not allure me. 'Beware of imitations,' said the advertisement; 'none genuine without a facsimile of the signature of Bentham Gibbes.' Ah, well, not for me were either the pickles or the tracking of imitators. A forged cheque! yes, if you like, but the forged signature of Mr. Gibbes on a pickle bottle was out of my line. Nevertheless, I said to Armand:—

'Show the gentleman in,' and he did so.

To my astonishment there entered a young man, quite correctly dressed in the dark frock-coat, faultless waistcoat and trousers that proclaimed a Bond Street tailor. When he spoke his voice and language were those of a gentleman.

'Monsieur Valmont?' he inquired.

'At your service,' I replied, bowing and waving my hand as Armand placed a chair for him, and withdrew.

'I am a barrister with chambers in the Temple,' began Mr. Gibbes, 'and for some days a matter has been troubling me about which I have now come to seek your advice, your name having been suggested by a friend in whom I confided.'

'Am I acquainted with him?' I asked.

'I think not,' replied Mr. Gibbes; 'he also is a barrister with chambers in the same building as my own. Lionel Dacre is his name.'

'I never heard of him.'

'Very likely not. Nevertheless, he recommended you as a man who could keep his own counsel, and if you take up this case I desire the utmost secrecy preserved, whatever may be the outcome.'

I bowed, but made no protestation. Secrecy is a matter of course with me.

The Englishman paused for a few moments as if he expected fervent assurances; then went on with no trace of disappointment on his countenance at not receiving them.

'On the night of the twenty-third, I gave a little dinner to six friends of mine in my own rooms. I may say that so far as I am aware they are all gentlemen of unimpeachable character. On the night of the dinner I was detained later than I expected at a reception, and in driving to the Temple was still further delayed by a block of traffic in Piccadilly, so that when I arrived at my chambers there was barely time for me to dress and receive my guests. My man Johnson had everything laid out ready for me in my dressing-room, and as I passed through to it I hurriedly flung off the coat I was wearing and carelessly left it hanging over the back of a chair in the dining-room, where neither Johnson nor myself noticed it until my attention was called to it after the dinner was over, and everyone rather jolly with wine.

'This coat contains an inside pocket. Usually any frock-coat I wear at an afternoon reception has not an inside pocket, but I had been rather on the rush all day.

'My father is a manufacturer whose name may be familiar to you, and I am on the directors' board of his company. On this occasion I took a cab from the city to the reception I spoke of, and had not time to go and change at my rooms. The reception was a somewhat bohemian affair, extremely interesting, of course, but not too particular as to costume, so I went as I was. In this inside pocket rested a thin package, composed of two pieces of cardboard, and between them rested five twenty-pound Bank of England notes, folded lengthwise, held in place by an elastic rubber band. I had thrown the coat across the chair-back in such a way that the inside pocket was exposed, leaving the ends of the notes plainly recognisable.

Over the coffee and cigars one of my guests laughingly called attention to what he termed my vulgar display of wealth, and Johnson, in some confusion at having neglected to put away the coat, now picked it up, and took it to the reception-room where the wraps of my guests lay about promiscuously. He should, of course, have hung it up in my wardrobe, but he said afterwards he thought it belonged to the guest who had spoken. You see, Johnson was in my dressing-room when I threw my coat on the chair in the corner while making my way thither, and I suppose he had not noticed the coat in the hurry of arriving guests, otherwise he would have put it where it belonged. After everybody had gone Johnson came to me and said the coat was there, but the package was missing, nor has any trace of it been found since that night.'

'The dinner was fetched in from outside, I suppose?'

'Yes.'

'How many waiters served it?'

'Two. They are men who have often been in my employ on similar occasions, but, apart from that, they had left my chambers before the incident of the coat happened.'

'Neither of them went into the reception-room, I take it?'

'No. I am certain that not even suspicion can attach to either of the waiters.'

'Your man Johnson——?'

'Has been with me for years. He could easily have stolen much more than the hundred pounds if he had wished to do so, but I have never known him to take a penny that did not belong to him.'

'Will you favour me with the names of your guests, Mr. Gibbes?'

'Viscount Stern sat at my right hand, and at my left Lord Templemere; Sir John Sanclere next to him, and Angus McKeller next to Sanclere. After Viscount Stern was Lionel Dacre, and at his right, Vincent Innis.'

On a sheet of paper I had written the names of the guests, and noted their places at the table.

'Which guest drew your attention to the money?'

'Lionel Dacre.'

'Is there a window looking out from the reception-room?'

'Two of them.'

'Were they fastened on the night of the dinner party?'

'I could not be sure; very likely Johnson would know. You are hinting at the possibility of a thief coming in through a reception-room window while we were somewhat noisy over our wine. I think such a solution highly improbable. My rooms are on the third floor, and a thief would scarcely venture to make an entrance when he could not but know there was a company being entertained. Besides this, the coat was there less than an hour, and it appears to me that whoever stole those notes knew where they were.'

'That seems reasonable,' I had to admit. 'Have you spoken to any one of your loss?';

'To no one but Dacre, who recommended me to see you. Oh, yes, and to Johnson, of course.'

I could not help noting that this was the fourth or fifth time Dacre's name had come up during our conversation.

'What of Dacre?' I asked.

'Oh, well, you see, he occupies chambers in the same building on the ground floor. He is a very good fellow, and we are by way of being firm friends. Then it was he who had called attention to the money, so I thought he should know the sequel.'

'How did he take your news?'

'Now that you call attention to the fact, he seemed slightly troubled. I should like to say, however, that you must not be misled by that. Lionel Dacre could no more steal than he could lie.'

'Did he show any surprise when you mentioned the theft?'

Bentham Gibbes paused a moment before replying, knitting his brows in thought.

'No,' he said at last; 'and, come to think of it, it appeared as if he had been expecting my announcement.'

'Doesn't that strike you as rather strange, Mr. Gibbes?'

'Really my mind is in such a whirl, I don't know what to think. But it's perfectly absurd to suspect Dacre. If you knew the man you would understand what I mean. He comes of an excellent family, and he is—oh! he is Lionel Dacre, and when you have said that you have made any suspicion absurd.'

'I suppose you caused the rooms to be thoroughly searched. The packet didn't drop out and remain unnoticed in some corner?'

'No; Johnson and myself examined every inch of the premises.'

'Have you the numbers of the notes?'

'Yes; I got them from the Bank next morning. Payment was stopped, and so far not one of the five has been presented. Of course, one or more may have been cashed at some shop, but none have been offered to any of the banks.'

'A twenty-pound note is not accepted without scrutiny, so the chances are the thief may find some difficulty in disposing of them.'

'As I told you, I don't mind the loss of the money at all. It is the uncertainty, the uneasiness caused by the incident which troubles me. You will comprehend how little I care about the notes when I say that if you are good enough to interest yourself in this case, I shall be disappointed if your fee does not exceed the amount I have lost.'

Mr. Gibbes rose as he said this, and I accompanied him to the door assuring him that I should do my best to solve the mystery. Whether he sprang from pickles or not, I realised he was a polished and generous gentleman, who estimated the services of a professional expert like myself at their true value.

I shall not set down the details of my researches during the following few days, because the trend of them must be gone over in the account of that remarkable interview in which I took part somewhat later. Suffice it to say that an examination of the rooms and a close cross-questioning of Johnson satisfied me he and the two waiters were innocent. I became certain no thief had made his way through the window, and finally I arrived at the conclusion that the notes were stolen by one of the guests. Further investigation convinced me that the thief was no other than Lionel Dacre, the only one of the six in pressing need of money at this time. I caused Dacre to be shadowed, and during one of his absences made the acquaintance of his man Hopper, a surly, impolite brute, who accepted my golden sovereign quickly enough, but gave me little in exchange for it. While I conversed with him, there arrived in the passage where we were talking together a huge case of champagne, bearing one of the best-known names in the trade, and branded as being of the vintage of '78. Now I knew that the product of Camelot Frères is not bought as cheaply as British beer, and I also had learned that two short weeks before Mr. Lionel Dacre was at his wits' end for money. Yet he was still the same briefless barrister he had ever been.

On the morning after my unsatisfactory conversation with his man Hopper, I was astonished to receive the following note, written on a dainty correspondence card:—

> '3 and 4 Vellum Buildings,
>
> 'Inner Temple, E.C.
>
> 'Mr. Lionel Dacre presents his compliments to Monsieur Eugène Valmont, and would be obliged if Monsieur Valmont could make it convenient to call upon him in his chambers tomorrow morning at eleven.'

Had the young man become aware that he was being shadowed, or had the surly servant informed him of the inquiries made? I was soon to know. I called punctually at eleven next morning, and was received with charming urbanity by Mr. Dacre himself. The taciturn Hopper had evidently been sent away for the occasion.

'My dear Monsieur Valmont, I am delighted to meet you,' began the young man with more of effusiveness than I had ever noticed in an Englishman before, although his very next words supplied an explanation that did not occur to me until afterwards as somewhat far-fetched. 'I believe we are by way of being countrymen, and, therefore, although the hour is early, I hope you will allow me to offer you some of this bottled sunshine of the year '78 from la belle France, to whose prosperity and honour we shall drink together. For such a toast any hour is propitious,' and to my amazement he brought forth from the case I had seen arrive two days before, a bottle of that superb Camelot Frères '78.

'Now,' said I to myself, 'it is going to be difficult to keep a clear head if the aroma of this nectar rises to the brain. But tempting as is the cup, I shall drink sparingly, and hope he may not be so judicious.'

Sensitive, I already experienced the charm of his personality, and well understood the friendship Mr. Bentham Gibbes felt for him. But I saw the trap spread before me. He expected, under the influence of champagne and courtesy, to extract a promise from me which I must find myself unable to give.

'Sir, you interest me by claiming kinship with France. I had understood that you belonged to one of the oldest families of England.'

'Ah, England!' he cried, with an expressive gesture of outspreading hands truly Parisian in its significance. 'The trunk belongs to England, of course, but the root—ah! the root—Monsieur Valmont, penetrated the soil from which this wine of the gods has been drawn.'

Then filling my glass and his own he cried:—

'To France, which my family left in the year 1066!'

I could not help laughing at his fervent ejaculation.

'1066! With William the Conqueror! That is a long time ago, Mr. Dacre.'

'In years perhaps; in feelings but a day. My forefathers came over to steal, and, lord! how well they accomplished it. They stole the whole country—something like a theft, say I—under that prince of robbers whom you have well named the Conqueror. In our secret hearts we all admire a great thief, and if not a great one, then an expert one, who covers his tracks so perfectly that the hounds of justice are baffled in attempting to follow them. Now even you, Monsieur Valmont (I can see you are the most generous of men, with a lively sympathy found to perfection only in France), even you must suffer a pang of regret when you lay a thief by the heels who has done his task deftly.'

'I fear, Mr. Dacre, you credit me with a magnanimity to which I dare not lay claim. The criminal is a danger to society.'

'True, true, you are in the right, Monsieur Valmont Still, admit there are cases that would touch you tenderly. For example, a man, ordinarily honest; a great need; a sudden opportunity. He takes that of which another has abundance, and he, nothing. What then, Monsieur Valmont? Is the man to be sent to perdition for a momentary weakness?'

His words astonished me. Was I on the verge of hearing a confession? It almost amounted to that already.

'Mr. Dacre,' I said, 'I cannot enter into the subtleties you pursue. My duty is to find the criminal.'

'Again I say you are in the right, Monsieur Valmont, and I am enchanted to find so sensible a head on French shoulders. Although you are a more recent arrival, if I may say so, than myself, you nevertheless already give utterance to sentiments which do honour to England. It is your duty to hunt down the criminal. Very well. In that I think I can aid you, and thus have taken the liberty of requesting your attendance here this morning. Let me fill your glass again, Monsieur Valmont.'

'No more, I beg of you, Mr. Dacre.'

'What, do you think the receiver is as bad as the thief?'

I was so taken aback by this remark that I suppose my face showed the amazement within me. But the young man merely laughed with apparently free-hearted enjoyment, poured some wine into his own glass, and tossed it off. Not knowing what to say, I changed the current of conversation.

'Mr. Gibbes said you had been kind enough to recommend me to his attention. May I ask how you came to hear of me?'

'Ah! who has not heard of the renowned Monsieur Valmont,' and as he said this, for the first time, there began to grow a suspicion in my mind that he was chaffing me, as it is called in England—a procedure which I cannot endure. Indeed, if this gentleman practised such a barbarism in my own country he would find himself with a duel on his hands before he had gone far. However, the next instant his voice resumed its original fascination, and I listened to it as to some delicious melody.

'I need only mention my cousin, Lady Gladys Dacre, and you will at once understand why I recommended you to my friend. The case of Lady Gladys, you will remember, required a delicate touch which is not always to be had in this land of England, except when those who possess the gift do us the honour to sojourn with us.'

I noticed that my glass was again filled, and bowing an acknowledgment of his compliment, I indulged in another sip of the delicious wine. I sighed, for I began to realise it was going to be very difficult for me, in spite of my disclaimer, to tell this man's friend he had stolen the money. All this time he had been sitting on the edge of the table, while I occupied a chair at its end. He sat there in careless fashion, swinging a foot to and fro. Now he sprang to the floor, and drew up a chair, placing on the table a blank sheet of paper. Then he took from the mantelshelf a packet of letters, and I was astonished to see they were held together by two bits of cardboard and a rubber band similar to the combination that had contained the folded bank notes. With great nonchalance he slipped off the rubber band, threw it and the pieces of cardboard on the table before me, leaving the documents loose to his hand.

'Now, Monsieur Valmont,' he cried jauntily, 'you have been occupied for several days on this case, the case of my dear friend Bentham Gibbes, who is one of the best fellows in the world.'

'He said the same of you, Mr. Dacre.'

'I am gratified to hear it. Would you mind letting me know to what point your researches have led you?'

'They have led me in a direction rather than to a point.'

'Ah! In the direction of a man, of course?'

'Certainly.'

'Who is he?'

'Will you pardon me if I decline to answer this question at the present moment?'

'That means you are not sure.'

'It may mean, Mr. Dacre, that I am employed by Mr. Gibbes, and do not feel at liberty to disclose the results of my quest without his permission.'

'But Mr. Bentham Gibbes and I are entirely at one in this matter. Perhaps you are aware that I am the only person with whom he has discussed the case beside yourself.'

'That is undoubtedly true, Mr. Dacre; still, you see the difficulty of my position.'

'Yes, I do, and so shall press you no further. But I also have been studying the problem in a purely amateurish way, of course. You will perhaps express no disinclination to learn whether or not my deductions agree with yours.'

'None in the least. I should be very glad to know the conclusion at which you have arrived. May I ask if you suspect any one in particular?'

'Yes, I do.'

'Will you name him?'

'No; I shall copy the admirable reticence you yourself have shown. And now let us attack this mystery in a sane and businesslike manner. You have already examined the room. Well, here is a rough sketch of it. There is the table; in this corner stood the chair on which the coat was flung. Here sat Gibbes at the head of the table. Those on the left-hand side had their backs to the chair. I, being on the centre to the right, saw the chair, the coat, and the notes, and called attention to them. Now our first duty is to find a motive. If it were a murder, our motive might be hatred, revenge, robbery—what you like. As it is simply the stealing of money, the man must have been either a born thief or else some hitherto innocent person pressed to the crime by great necessity. Do you agree with me, Monsieur Valmont?'

'Perfectly. You follow exactly the line of my own reasoning.'

'Very well. It is unlikely that a born thief was one of Mr. Gibbes's guests. Therefore we are reduced to look for a man under the spur of necessity; a man who has no money of his own but who must raise a certain amount, let us say, by a certain date. If we can find such a man in that company, do you not agree with me that he is likely to be the thief?'

'Yes, I do.'

'Then let us start our process of elimination. Out goes Viscount Stern, a lucky individual with twenty thousand acres of land, and God only knows what income. I mark off the name of Lord Templemere, one of His Majesty's judges, entirely above suspicion. Next, Sir John Sanclere; he also is rich, but Vincent Innis is still richer, so the pencil obliterates both names. Now we arrive at Angus McKeller, an author of some note, as you are well aware, deriving a good income from his books and a better one from his plays; a canny Scot, so we may rub his name from our paper and our memory. How do my erasures correspond with yours, Monsieur Valmont?'

'They correspond exactly, Mr. Dacre.'

'I am flattered to hear it. There remains one name untouched, Mr Lionel Dacre, the descendant, as I have said, of robbers.'

'I have not said so, Mr. Dacre.'

'Ah! my dear Valmont, the politeness of your country asserts itself. Let us not be deluded, but follow our inquiry wherever it leads. I suspect Lionel Dacre. What do you know of his circumstances before the dinner of the twenty-third?'

As I made no reply he looked up at me with his frank, boyish face illumined by a winning smile.

'You know nothing of his circumstances?' he asked.

'It grieves me to state that I do. Mr. Lionel Dacre was penniless on the night of the dinner.'

'Oh, don't exaggerate, Monsieur Valmont,' cried Dacre with a gesture of pathetic protest; 'his pocket held one sixpence, two pennies, and a halfpenny. How came you to suspect he was penniless?'

'I knew he ordered a case of champagne from the London representative of Camelot Frères, and was refused unless he paid the money down.'

'Quite right, and then when you were talking to Hopper you saw that case of champagne delivered. Excellent! excellent! Monsieur Valmont. But will a man steal, think you, even to supply himself with so delicious a wine as this we have been tasting? And, by the way, forgive my neglect, allow me to fill your glass, Monsieur Valmont.'

'Not another drop, if you will excuse me, Mr. Dacre.'

'Ah, yes, champagne should not be mixed with evidence. When we have finished, perhaps. What further proof have you discovered, monsieur?'

'I hold proof that Mr. Dacre was threatened with bankruptcy, if, on the twenty-fourth, he did not pay a bill of seventy-eight pounds that had been long outstanding. I hold proof that this was paid, not on the twenty-fourth, but on the twenty-sixth. Mr. Dacre had gone to the solicitor and assured him he would pay the money on that date, whereupon he was given two days' grace.'

'Ah, well, he was entitled to three, you know, in law. Yes, there, Monsieur Valmont, you touch the fatal point. The threat of bankruptcy will drive a man in Dacre's position to almost any crime. Bankruptcy to a barrister means ruin. It means a career blighted; it means a life buried, with little chance of resurrection. I see, you grasp the supreme importance of that bit of evidence. The case of champagne is as nothing compared with it, and this reminds me that in the crisis now upon us I shall take another sip, with your permission. Sure you won't join me?'

'Not at this juncture, Mr. Dacre.'

'I envy your moderation. Here's to the success of our search, Monsieur Valmont.'

I felt sorry for the gay young fellow as with smiling face he drank the champagne.

'Now, Monsieur,' he went on, 'I am amazed to learn how much you have discovered. Really, I think tradespeople, solicitors, and all such should keep better guard on their tongues than they do. Nevertheless, these documents at my elbow, which I expected would surprise you, are merely the letters and receipts. Here is the communication from the solicitor threatening me with bankruptcy; here is his receipt dated the twenty-sixth; here is the refusal of the wine merchant, and here is his receipt for the money. Here are smaller bills liquidated. With my pencil we will add them up. Seventy-eight pounds—the principal debt—bulks large. We add the smaller items and it reaches a total of ninety-three pounds seven shillings and fourpence. Let us now examine my purse. Here is a five-pound note; there is a golden sovereign. I now count out and place on the table twelve and sixpence in silver and two pence in coppers. The purse thus becomes empty. Let us add the silver and copper to the amount on the paper. Do my eyes deceive me, or is the sum exactly a hundred pounds? There is your money fully accounted for.'

'Pardon me, Mr. Dacre,' I said, 'but I observe a sovereign resting on the mantelpiece.'

Dacre threw back his head and laughed with greater heartiness than I had yet known him to indulge in during our short acquaintance.

'By Jove,' he cried, 'you've got me there. I'd forgotten entirely about that pound on the mantelpiece, which belongs to you.'

'To me? Impossible!'

'It does, and cannot interfere in the least with our century calculation. That is the sovereign you gave to my man Hopper, who, knowing me to be hard-pressed, took it and shamefacedly presented it to me, that I might enjoy the spending of it. Hopper belongs to our family, or the family belongs to him. I am never sure which. You must have missed in him the deferential bearing of a man-servant in Paris, yet he is true gold, like the sovereign you bestowed upon him, and he bestowed upon me. Now here, Monsieur, is the evidence of the theft, together with the rubber band and two pieces of cardboard. Ask my friend Gibbes to examine them minutely. They are all at your disposition, Monsieur, and thus you learn how much easier it is to deal with the master than with the servant. All the gold you possess would not have wrung these incriminating documents from old Hopper. I was compelled to send him away to the West End an hour ago, fearing that in his brutal British way he might assault you if he got an inkling of your mission.'

'Mr. Dacre,' said I slowly, 'you have thoroughly convinced me—'

'I thought I would,' he interrupted with a laugh.

'—that you did not take the money.'

'Oho, this is a change of wind, surely. Many a man has been hanged on a chain of circumstantial evidence much weaker than this which I have exhibited to you. Don't you see the subtlety of my action? Ninety-nine persons in a hundred would say: "No man could be such a fool as to put Valmont on his own track, and then place in Valmont's hands such striking evidence." But there comes in my craftiness. Of course, the rock you run up against will be Gibbes's incredulity. The first question he will ask you may be this: "Why did not Dacre come and borrow the money from me?" Now there you find a certain weakness in your chain of evidence. I knew perfectly well that Gibbes would lend me the money, and he knew perfectly well that if I were pressed to the wall I should ask him.'

'Mr. Dacre,' said I, 'you have been playing with me. I should resent that with most men, but whether it is your own genial manner or the effect of this excellent champagne, or both together, I forgive you. But I am convinced of another thing. You know who took the money.'

'I don't know, but I suspect.'

'Will you tell me whom you suspect?'

'That would not be fair, but I shall now take the liberty of filling your glass with champagne.'

'I am your guest, Mr. Dacre.'

'Admirably answered, monsieur,' he replied, pouring out the wine, 'and now I offer you a clue. Find out all about the story of the silver spoons.'

'The story of the silver spoons! What silver spoons?'

'Ah! That is the point. Step out of the Temple into Fleet Street, seize the first man you meet by the shoulder, and ask him to tell you about the silver spoons. There are but two men and two spoons concerned. When you learn who those two men are, you will know that one of them did not take the money, and I give you my assurance that the other did.'

'You speak in mystery, Mr. Dacre.'

'But certainly, for I am speaking to Monsieur Eugène Valmont.'

'I echo your words, sir. Admirably answered. You put me on my mettle, and I flatter myself that I see your kindly drift. You wish me to solve the mystery of this stolen money. Sir, you-do me honour, and I drink to your health.'

'To yours, monsieur,' said Lionel Dacre, and thus we drank and parted.

On leaving Mr. Dacre I took a hansom to a café in Regent Street, which is a passable imitation of similar places of refreshment in Paris. There, calling for a cup of black coffee, I sat down to think. The clue of the silver spoons! He had laughingly suggested that I should take by the shoulders the first man I met, and ask him what the story of the silver spoons was. This course naturally struck me as absurd, and he doubtless intended it to seem absurd. Nevertheless, it contained a hint. I must ask somebody, and that the right person, to tell me the tale of the silver spoons.

Under the influence of the black coffee I reasoned it out in this way. On the night of the twenty-third one of the six guests there present stole a hundred pounds, but Dacre had said that an actor in the silver spoon episode was the actual thief. That person, then, must have been one of Mr. Gibbes's guests at the dinner of the twenty-third. Probably two of the guests were the participators in the silver spoon comedy, but, be that as it may, it followed that one at least of the men around Mr. Gibbes's table knew the episode of the silver spoons. Perhaps Bentham Gibbes himself was cognisant of it. It followed, therefore, that the easiest plan was to question each of the men who partook of that dinner. Yet if only one knew about the spoons, that one must also have some idea that these spoons formed the clue which attached him to the crime of the twenty-third, in which case he was little likely to divulge what he knew to an entire stranger.

Of course, I might go to Dacre himself and demand the story of the silver spoons, but this would be a confession of failure on my part, and I rather dreaded Lionel Dacre's hearty laughter when I admitted that the mystery was too much for me. Besides this I was very well aware of the young man's kindly intentions towards me. He wished me to unravel the coil myself, and so I determined not to go to him except as a last resource.

I resolved to begin with Mr. Gibbes, and, finishing my coffee, I got again into a hansom, and drove back to the Temple. I found Bentham Gibbes in his room, and after greeting me, his first inquiry was about the case.

'How are you getting on?' he asked.

'I think I'm getting on fairly well,' I replied, 'and expect to finish in a day or two, if you will kindly tell me the story of the silver spoons.'

'The silver spoons?' he echoed, quite evidently not understanding me.

'There happened an incident in which two men were engaged, and this incident related to a pair of silver spoons. I want to get the particulars of that.' 'I haven't the slightest idea what you are talking about,' replied Gibbes, thoroughly bewildered. 'You will need to be more definite, I fear, if you are to get any help from me.'

'I cannot be more definite, because I have already told you all I know.'

'What bearing has all this on our own case?'

'I was informed that if I got hold of the clue of the silver spoons I should be in a fair way of settling our case.'

'Who told you that?'

'Mr. Lionel Dacre.'

'Oh, does Dacre refer to his own conjuring?'

'I don't know, I'm sure. What was his conjuring?'

'A very clever trick he did one night at dinner here about two months ago.'

'Had it anything to do with silver spoons?'

'Well, it was silver spoons or silver forks, or something of that kind. I had entirely forgotten the incident. So far as I recollect at the moment there was a sleight-of-hand man of great expertness in one of the music halls, and the talk turned upon him. Then Dacre said the tricks he did were easy, and holding up a spoon or a fork, I don't remember which, he professed his ability to make it disappear before our eyes, to be found afterwards in the clothing of some one there present. Several offered to bet that he could do nothing of the kind, but he said he would bet with no one but Innis, who sat opposite him. Innis, with some reluctance, accepted the bet, and then Dacre, with a great show of the usual conjurer's gesticulations, spread forth his empty hands, and said we should find the spoon in Innis's pocket, and there, sure enough, it was. It seemed a proper sleight-of-hand trick, but we were never able to get him to repeat it.'

'Thank you very much, Mr. Gibbes; I think I see daylight now.'

'If you do you are cleverer than I by a long chalk,' cried Bentham Gibbes as I took my departure.

I went directly downstairs, and knocked at Mr. Dacre's door once more. He opened the door himself, his man not yet having returned.

'Ah, monsieur,' he cried, 'back already? You don't mean to tell me you have so soon got to the bottom of the silver spoon entanglement?'

'I think I have, Mr. Dacre. You were sitting at dinner opposite Mr Vincent Innis. You saw him conceal a silver spoon in his pocket. You probably waited for some time to understand what he meant by this, and as he did not return the spoon to its place, you proposed a conjuring trick, made the bet with him, and thus the spoon was returned to the table.'

'Excellent! excellent, monsieur! that is very nearly what occurred, except that I acted at once. I had had experiences with Mr. Vincent Innis before. Never did he enter these rooms of mine without my missing some little trinket after he was gone. Although Mr. Innis is a very rich person, I am not a man of many possessions, so if anything is taken, I meet little difficulty in coming to a knowledge of my loss. Of course, I never mentioned these abstractions to him. They were all trivial, as I have said, and so far as the silver spoon was concerned, it was of no great value either. But I thought the bet and the recovery of the spoon would teach him a lesson; it apparently has not done so. On the night of the twenty-third he sat at my right hand, as you will see by consulting your diagram of the table and the guests. I asked him a question twice, to which he did not reply, and looking at him I was startled by the expression in his eyes. They were fixed on a distant corner of the room, and following his gaze I saw what he was staring at with such hypnotising concentration. So absorbed was he in contemplation of the packet there so plainly exposed, now my attention was turned to it, that he seemed to be entirely oblivious of what was going on around him. I roused him from his trance by jocularly calling Gibbes's attention to the display of money. I expected in this way to save Innis from committing the act which he seemingly did commit. Imagine then the dilemma in which I was placed when Gibbes confided to me the morning after what had occurred the night before. I was positive Innis had taken the money, yet I possessed no proof of it. I could not tell Gibbes, and I dare not speak to Innis. Of course, monsieur, you do not need to be told that Innis is not a thief in the ordinary sense of the word. He has no need to steal, and yet apparently cannot help doing so. I am sure that no attempt has been made to pass those notes. They are doubtless resting securely in his house at Kensington. He is, in fact, a kleptomaniac, or a maniac of some sort. And now, monsieur, was my hint regarding the silver spoons of any value to you?'

'Of the most infinite value, Mr. Dacre.'

'Then let me make another suggestion. I leave it entirely to your bravery; a bravery which, I confess, I do not myself possess. Will you take a hansom, drive to Mr. Innis's house on the Cromwell Road, confront him quietly, and ask for the return of the packet? I am anxious to know what will happen. If he hands it to you, as I expect he will, then you must tell Mr. Gibbes the whole story.'

'Mr. Dacre, your suggestion shall be immediately acted upon, and I thank you for your compliment to my courage.'

I found that Mr. Innis inhabited a very grand house. After a time he entered the study on the ground floor, to which I had been conducted. He held my card in his hand, and was looking at it with some surprise.

'I think I have not the pleasure of knowing you, Monsieur Valmont,' he said, courteously enough.

'No. I ventured to call on a matter of business. I was once investigator for the French Government, and now am doing private detective work here in London.'

'Ah! And how is that supposed to interest me? There is nothing that I wish investigated. I did not send for you, did I?'

'No, Mr. Innis, I merely took the liberty of calling to ask you to let me have the package you took from Mr. Bentham Gibbes's frock-coat pocket on the night of the twenty-third.'

'He wishes it returned, does he?'

'Yes.'

Mr. Innis calmly walked to a desk, which he unlocked and opened, displaying a veritable museum of trinkets of one sort and another. Pulling out a small drawer he took from it the packet containing the five twenty-pound notes. Apparently it had never been opened. With a smile he handed it to me.

'You will make my apologies to Mr. Gibbes for not returning it before. Tell him I have been unusually busy of late.'

'I shall not fail to do so,' said I, with a bow.

'Thanks so much. Good-morning, Monsieur Valmont.'

'Good-morning, Mr. Innis,'

And so I returned the packet to Mr. Bentham Gibbes, who pulled the notes from between their pasteboard protection, and begged me to accept them.

4. Lord Chizelrigg's Missing Fortune

The name of the late Lord Chizelrigg never comes to my mind without instantly suggesting that of Mr. T.A. Edison. I never saw the late Lord Chizelrigg, and I have met Mr. Edison only twice in my life, yet the two men are linked in my memory, and it was a remark the latter once made that in great measure enabled me to solve the mystery which the former had wrapped round his actions.

There is no memorandum at hand to tell me the year in which those two meetings with Edison took place. I received a note from the Italian Ambassador in Paris requesting me to wait upon him at the Embassy. I learned that on the next day a deputation was to set out from the Embassy to one of the chief hotels, there to make a call in state upon the great American inventor, and formally present to him various insignia accompanying certain honours which the King of Italy had conferred upon him. As many Italian nobles of high rank had been invited, and as these dignitaries would not only be robed in the costumes pertaining to their orders, but in many cases would wear jewels of almost inestimable value, my presence was desired in the belief that I might perhaps be able to ward off any attempt on the part of the deft-handed gentry who might possibly make an effort to gain these treasures, and I may add, with perhaps some little self-gratification, no contretemps occurred.

Mr. Edison, of course, had long before received notification of the hour at which the deputation would wait upon him, but when we entered the large parlour assigned to the inventor, it was evident to me at a glance that the celebrated man had forgotten all about the function. He stood by a bare table, from which the cloth had been jerked and flung into a corner, and upon that table were placed several bits of black and greasy machinery—cog wheels, pulleys, bolts, etc. These seemingly belonged to a French workman who stood on the other side of the table, with one of the parts in his grimy hand. Edison's own hands were not too clean, for he had palpably been examining the material, and conversing with the workman, who wore the ordinary long blouse of an iron craftsman in a small way. I judged him to be a man with a little shop of his own in some back street, who did odd jobs of engineering, assisted perhaps by a skilled helper or two, and a few apprentices. Edison looked sternly towards the door as the solemn procession filed in, and there was a trace of annoyance on his face at the interruption, mixed with a shade of perplexity as to what this gorgeous display all meant. The Italian is as ceremonious as the Spaniard where a function is concerned, and the official who held the ornate box which contained the jewellery resting on a velvet cushion, stepped slowly forward, and came to a stand in front of the bewildered American. Then the Ambassador, in sonorous voice, spoke some gracious words regarding the friendship existing between the United States and Italy, expressed a wish that their rivalry should ever take the form of benefits conferred upon the human race, and instanced the honoured recipient as the most notable example the world had yet produced of a man bestowing blessings upon all nations in the arts of peace. The eloquent Ambassador concluded by saying that, at the command of his Royal master, it was both his duty and his pleasure to present, and so forth and so forth.

Mr. Edison, visibly ill at ease, nevertheless made a suitable reply in the fewest possible words, and the étalage being thus at an end, the noblemen, headed by their Ambassador, slowly retired, myself forming the tail of the procession. Inwardly I deeply sympathised with the French workman who thus unexpectedly found himself confronted by so much magnificence. He cast one wild look about him, but saw that his retreat was cut off unless he displaced some of these gorgeous grandees. He tried then to shrink into himself, and finally stood helpless like one paralysed. In spite of Republican institutions, there is deep down in every Frenchman's heart a respect and awe for official pageants, sumptuously staged and costumed as this one was. But he likes to view it from afar, and supported by his fellows, not thrust incongruously into the midst of things, as was the case with this panic-stricken engineer. As I passed out, I cast a glance over my shoulder at the humble artisan content with a profit of a few francs a day, and at the millionaire inventor opposite him, Edison's face, which during the address had been cold and impassive, reminding me vividly of a bust of Napoleon, was now all aglow with enthusiasm as he turned to his humble visitor. He cried joyfully to the workman:—

'A minute's demonstration is worth an hour's explanation. I'll call round tomorrow at your shop, about ten o'clock, and show you how to make the thing work.'

I lingered in the hall until the Frenchman came out, then, introducing myself to him, asked the privilege of visiting his shop next day at ten. This was accorded with that courtesy which you will always find among the industrial classes of France, and next day I had the pleasure of meeting Mr. Edison. During our conversation I complimented him on his invention of the incandescent electric light, and this was the reply that has ever remained in my memory:—

'It was not an invention, but a discovery. We knew what we wanted; a carbonised tissue, which would withstand the electric current in a vacuum for, say, a thousand hours. If no such tissue existed, then the incandescent light, as we know it, was not possible. My assistants started out to find this tissue, and we simply carbonised everything we could lay our hands on, and ran the current through it in a vacuum. At last we struck the right thing, as we were bound to do if we kept on long enough, and if the thing existed. Patience and hard work will overcome any obstacle.'

This belief has been of great assistance to me in my profession. I know the idea is prevalent that a detective arrives at his solutions in a dramatic way through following clues invisible to the ordinary man. This doubtless frequently happens, but, as a general thing, the patience and hard work which Mr. Edison commends is a much safer guide. Very often the following of excellent clues had led me to disaster, as was the case with my unfortunate attempt to solve the mystery of the five hundred diamonds.

As I was saying, I never think of the late Lord Chizelrigg without remembering Mr. Edison at the same time, and yet the two were very dissimilar. I suppose Lord Chizelrigg was the most useless man that ever lived, while Edison is the opposite.

One day my servant brought in to me a card on which was engraved 'Lord Chizelrigg.'

'Show his lordship in,' I said, and there appeared a young man of perhaps twenty-four or twenty-five, well dressed, and of most charming manners, who, nevertheless, began his interview by asking a question such as had never before been addressed to me, and which, if put to a solicitor, or other professional man, would have been answered with some indignation. Indeed, I believe it is a written or unwritten law of the legal profession that the acceptance of such a proposal as Lord Chizelrigg made to me, would, if proved, result in the disgrace and ruin of the lawyer.

'Monsieur Valmont,' began Lord Chizelrigg, 'do you ever take up cases on speculation?'

'On speculation, sir? I do not think I understand you.'

His lordship blushed like a girl, and stammered slightly as he attempted an explanation.

'What I mean is, do you accept a case on a contingent fee? That is to say, monsieur—er—well, not to put too fine a point upon it, no results, no pay.'

I replied somewhat severely:—

'Such an offer has never been made to me, and I may say at once that I should be compelled to decline it were I favoured with the opportunity. In the cases submitted to me, I devote my time and attention to their solution. I try to deserve success, but I cannot command it, and as in the interim I must live, I am reluctantly compelled to make a charge for my time, at least. I believe the doctor sends in his bill, though the patient dies.'

The young man laughed uneasily, and seemed almost too embarrassed to proceed, but finally he said:—

'Your illustration strikes home with greater accuracy than probably you imagined when you uttered it. I have just paid my last penny to the physician who attended my late uncle, Lord Chizelrigg, who died six months ago. I am fully aware that the suggestion I made may seem like a reflection upon your skill, or rather, as implying a doubt regarding it. But I should be grieved, monsieur, if you fell into such an error. I could have come here and commissioned you to undertake some elucidation of the strange situation in which I find myself, and I make no doubt you would have accepted the task if your numerous engagements had permitted. Then, if you failed, I should have been unable to pay you, for I am practically bankrupt. My whole desire, therefore, was to make an honest beginning, and to let you know exactly how I stand. If you succeed, I shall be a rich man; if you do not succeed, I shall be what I am now, penniless. Have I made it plain now why I began with a question which you had every right to resent?'

'Perfectly plain, my lord, and your candour does you credit.'

I was very much taken with the unassuming manners of the young man, and his evident desire to accept no service under false pretences. When I had finished my sentence the pauper nobleman rose to his feet, and bowed.

'I am very much your debtor, monsieur, for your courtesy in receiving me, and can only beg pardon for occupying your time on a futile quest. I wish you good-morning, monsieur.'

'One moment, my lord,' I rejoined, waving him to his chair again. 'Although I am unprepared to accept a commission on the terms you suggest, I may, nevertheless, be able to offer a hint or two that will prove of service to you. I think I remember the announcement of Lord Chizelrigg's death. He was somewhat eccentric, was he not?'

'Eccentric?' said the young man, with a slight laugh, seating himself again—'well, rather!'

'I vaguely remember that he was accredited with the possession of something like twenty thousand acres of land?'

'Twenty-seven thousand, as a matter of fact,' replied my visitor.

'Have you fallen heir to the lands as well as to the title?'

'Oh, yes; the estate was entailed. The old gentleman could not divert it from me if he would, and I rather suspect that fact must have been the cause of some worry to him.'

'But surely, my lord, a man who owns, as one might say, a principality in this wealthy realm of England, cannot be penniless?'

Again the young man laughed.

'Well, no,' he replied, thrusting his hand in his pocket and bringing to light a few brown coppers, and a white silver piece. 'I possess enough money to buy some food tonight, but not enough to dine at the Hotel Cecil. You see, it is like this. I belong to a somewhat ancient family, various members of whom went the pace, and mortgaged their acres up to the hilt. I could not raise a further penny on my estates were I to try my hardest, because at the time the money was lent, land was much more valuable than it is today. Agricultural depression, and all that sort of thing, have, if I may put it so, left me a good many thousands worse off than if I had no land at all. Besides this, during my late uncle's life, Parliament, on his behalf, intervened once or twice, allowing him in the first place to cut valuable timber, and in the second place to sell the pictures of Chizelrigg Chase at Christie's for figures which make one's mouth water.'

'And what became of the money?' I asked, whereupon once more this genial nobleman laughed. 'That is exactly what I came up in the lift to learn if Monsieur Valmont could discover.'

'My lord, you interest me,' I said, quite truly, with an uneasy apprehension that I should take up his case after all, for I liked the young man already. His lack of pretence appealed to me, and that sympathy which is so universal among my countrymen enveloped him, as I may say, quite independent of my own will.

'My uncle,' went on Lord Chizelrigg, 'was somewhat of an anomaly in our family. He must have been a reversal to a very, very ancient type; a type of which we have no record. He was as miserly as his forefathers were prodigal. When he came into the title and estate some twenty years ago, he dismissed the whole retinue of servants, and, indeed, was defendant in several cases at law where retainers of our family brought suit against him for wrongful dismissal, or dismissal without a penny compensation in lieu of notice. I am pleased to say he lost all his cases, and when he pleaded poverty, got permission to sell a certain number of heirlooms, enabling him to make compensation, and giving him something on which to live. These heirlooms at auction sold so unexpectedly well, that my uncle acquired a taste, as it were, of what might be done. He could always prove that the rents went to the mortgagees, and that he had nothing on which to exist, so on several occasions he obtained permission from the courts to cut timber and sell pictures, until he denuded the estate and made an empty barn of the old manor house. He lived like any labourer, occupying himself sometimes as a carpenter, sometimes as a blacksmith; indeed, he made a blacksmith's shop of the library, one of the most noble rooms in Britain, containing thousands of valuable books which again and again he applied for permission to sell, but this privilege was never granted to him. I find on coming into the property that my uncle quite persistently evaded the law, and depleted this superb collection, book by book, surreptitiously through dealers in London. This, of course, would have got him into deep trouble if it had been discovered before his death, but now the valuable volumes are gone, and there is no redress. Many of them are doubtless in America, or in museums and collections of Europe.'

'You wish me to trace them, perhaps?' I interpolated.

'Oh, no; they are past praying for. The old man made tens of thousands by the sale of the timber, and other thousands by disposing of the pictures. The house is denuded of its fine old furniture, which was immensely valuable, and then the books, as I have said, must have brought in the revenue of a prince, if he got anything like their value, and you may be sure he was shrewd enough to know their worth. Since the last refusal of the courts to allow him further relief, as he termed it, which was some seven years ago, he had quite evidently been disposing of books and furniture by a private sale, in defiance of the law. At that time I was under age, but my guardians opposed his application to the courts, and demanded an account of the moneys already in his hands. The judges upheld the opposition of my guardians, and refused to allow a further spoliation of the estate, but they did not grant the accounting my guardians asked, because the proceeds of the former sales were entirely at the disposal of my uncle, and were sanctioned by the law to permit him to live as befitted his station. If he lived meagrely instead of lavishly, as my guardians contended, that, the judges said, was his affair, and there the matter ended.

'My uncle took a violent dislike to me on account of this opposition to his last application, although, of course, I had nothing whatever to do with the matter. He lived like a hermit, mostly in the library, and was waited upon by an old man and his wife, and these three were the only inhabitants of a mansion that could comfortably house a hundred. He visited nobody, and would allow no one to approach Chizelrigg Chase. In order that all who had the misfortune to have dealing with him should continue to endure trouble after his death, he left what might be called a will, but which rather may be termed a letter to me. Here is a copy of it.

'"MY DEAR TOM,—You will find your fortune between a couple of sheets of paper in the library.

'"Your affectionate uncle,

'"REGINALD MORAN, EARL OF CHIZELRIGG."'

'I should doubt if that were a legal will,' said I.

'It doesn't need to be,' replied the young man with a smile. 'I am next-of-kin, and heir to everything he possessed, although, of course, he might have given his money elsewhere if he had chosen to do so. Why he did not bequeath it to some institution, I do not know. He knew no man personally except his own servants, whom he misused and starved, but, as he told them, he misused and starved himself, so they had no cause to grumble. He said he was treating them like one of the family. I suppose he thought it would cause me more worry and anxiety if he concealed the money, and put me on the wrong scent, which I am convinced he has done, than to leave it openly to any person or charity.'

'I need not ask if you have searched the library?'

'Searched it? Why, there never was such a search since the world began!'

'Possibly you put the task into incompetent hands?'

'You are hinting, Monsieur Valmont, that I engaged others until my money was gone, then came to you with a speculative proposal. Let me assure you such is not the case. Incompetent hands, I grant you, but the hands were my own. For the past six months I have lived practically as my uncle lived. I have rummaged that library from floor to ceiling. It was left in a frightful state, littered with old newspapers, accounts, and what-not. Then, of course, there were the books remaining in the library, still a formidable collection.'

'Was your uncle a religious man?'

'I could not say. I surmise not. You see, I was unacquainted with him, and never saw him until after his death. I fancy he was not religious, otherwise he could not have acted as he did. Still, he proved himself a man of such twisted mentality that anything is possible.'

'I knew a case once where an heir who expected a large sum of money was bequeathed a family Bible, which he threw into the fire, learning afterwards, to his dismay, that it contained many thousands of pounds in Bank of England notes, the object of the devisor being to induce the legatee to read the good Book or suffer through the neglect of it.'

'I have searched the Scriptures,' said the youthful Earl with a laugh, 'but the benefit has been moral rather than material.'

'Is there any chance that your uncle has deposited his wealth in a bank, and has written a cheque for the amount, leaving it between two leaves of a book?'

'Anything is possible, monsieur, but I think that highly improbable. I have gone through every tome, page by page, and I suspect very few of the volumes have been opened for the last twenty years.'

'How much money do you estimate he accumulated?'

'He must have cleared more than a hundred thousand pounds, but speaking of banking it, I would like to say that my uncle evinced a deep distrust of banks, and never drew a cheque in his life so far as I am aware.

All accounts were paid in gold by this old steward, who first brought the receipted bill in to my uncle, and then received the exact amount, after having left the room, and waited until he was rung for, so that he might not learn the repository from which my uncle drew his store. I believe if the money is ever found it will be in gold, and I am very sure that this will was written, if we may call it a will, to put us on the wrong scent.'

'Have you had the library cleared out?'

'Oh, no, it is practically as my uncle left it. I realised that if I were to call in help, it would be well that the newcomer found it undisturbed.'

'You were quite right, my lord. You say you examined all the papers?'

'Yes; so far as that is concerned, the room has been very fairly gone over, but nothing that was in it the day my uncle died has been removed, not even his anvil.'

'His anvil?'

'Yes; I told you he made a blacksmith's shop, as well as bedroom, of the library. It is a huge room, with a great fireplace at one end which formed an excellent forge. He and the steward built the forge in the eastern fireplace of brick and clay, with their own hands, and erected there a second-hand blacksmith's bellows.'

'What work did he do at his forge?'

'Oh, anything that was required about the place. He seems to have been a very expert ironworker. He would never buy a new implement for the garden or the house so long as he could get one second-hand, and he never bought anything second-hand while at his forge he might repair what was already in use. He kept an old cob, on which he used to ride through the park, and he always put the shoes on this cob himself, the steward informs me, so he must have understood the use of blacksmith's tools. He made a carpenter's shop of the chief drawing-room and erected a bench there. I think a very useful mechanic was spoiled when my uncle became an earl.'

'You have been living at the Chase since your uncle died?'

'If you call it living, yes. The old steward and his wife have been looking after me, as they looked after my uncle, and, seeing me day after day, coatless, and covered with dust, I imagine they think me a second edition of the old man.'

'Does the steward know the money is missing?'

'No; no one knows it but myself. This will was left on the anvil, in an envelope addressed to me.'

'Your statement is exceedingly clear, Lord Chizelrigg, but I confess I don't see much daylight through it. Is there a pleasant country around Chizelrigg Chase?'

'Very; especially at this season of the year. In autumn and winter the house is a little draughty. It needs several thousand pounds to put it in repair.'

'Draughts do not matter in the summer. I have been long enough in England not to share the fear of my countrymen for a courant d'air. Is there a spare bed in the manor house, or shall I take down a cot with me, or let us say a hammock?'

'Really,' stammered the earl, blushing again, 'you must not think I detailed all these circumstances in order to influence you to take up what may be a hopeless case. I, of course, am deeply interested, and, therefore, somewhat prone to be carried away when I begin a recital of my uncle's eccentricities. If I receive your permission, I will call on you again in a month or two. To tell you the truth, I borrowed a little money from the old steward, and visited London to see my legal advisers, hoping that in the circumstances I may get permission to sell something that will keep me from starvation. When I spoke of the house being denuded, I meant relatively, of course. There are still a good many antiquities which would doubtless bring me in a comfortable sum of money. I have been borne up by the belief that I should find my uncle's gold. Lately, I have been beset by a suspicion that the old gentleman thought the library the only valuable asset left, and for this reason wrote his note, thinking I would be afraid to sell anything from that room. The old rascal must have made a pot of money out of those shelves. The catalogue shows that there was a copy of the first book printed in England by Caxton, and several priceless Shakespeares, as well as many other volumes that a collector would give a small fortune for. All these are gone. I think when I show this to be the case, the authorities cannot refuse me the right to sell something, and, if I get this permission, I shall at once call upon you.'

'Nonsense, Lord Chizelrigg. Put your application in motion, if you like. Meanwhile I beg of you to look upon me as a more substantial banker than your old steward. Let us enjoy a good dinner together at the Cecil tonight, if you will do me the honour to be my guest. Tomorrow we can leave for Chizelrigg Chase. How far is it?'

'About three hours,' replied the young man, becoming as red as a new Queen Anne villa. 'Really, Monsieur Valmont, you overwhelm me with your kindness, but nevertheless I accept your generous offer.'

'Then that's settled. What's the name of the old steward?'

'Higgins.'

'You are certain he has no knowledge of the hiding-place of this treasure?'

'Oh, quite sure. My uncle was not a man to make a confidant of anyone, least of all an old babbler like Higgins.'

'Well, I should like to be introduced to Higgins as a benighted foreigner. That will make him despise me and treat me like a child.'

'Oh, I say,' protested the earl, 'I should have thought you'd lived long enough in England to have got out of the notion that we do not appreciate the foreigner. Indeed, we are the only nation in the world that extends a cordial welcome to him, rich or poor.'

'Certainement, my lord, I should be deeply disappointed did you not take me at my proper valuation, but I cherish no delusions regarding the contempt with which Higgins will regard me. He will look upon me as a sort of simpleton to whom the Lord had been unkind by not making England my native land. Now, Higgins must be led to believe that I am in his own class; that is, a servant of yours. Higgins and I will gossip over the fire together, should these spring evenings prove chilly, and before two or three weeks are past I shall have learned a great deal about your uncle that you never dreamed of. Higgins will talk more freely with a fellow-servant than with his master, however much he may respect that master, and then, as I am a foreigner, he will babble down to my comprehension, and I shall get details that he never would think of giving to a fellow-countryman.'

The young earl's modesty in such description of his home as he had given me, left me totally unprepared for the grandeur of the mansion, one corner of which he inhabited. It is such a place as you read of in romances of the Middle Ages; not a pinnacled or turreted French château of that period, but a beautiful and substantial stone manor house of a ruddy colour, whose warm hue seemed to add a softness to the severity of its architecture. It is built round an outer and an inner courtyard and could house a thousand, rather than the hundred with which its owner had accredited it. There are many stone-mullioned windows, and one at the end of the library might well have graced a cathedral. This superb residence occupies the centre of a heavily timbered park, and from the lodge at the gates we drove at least a mile and a half under the grandest avenue of old oaks I have ever seen. It seemed incredible that the owner of all this should actually lack the ready money to pay his fare to town!

Old Higgins met us at the station with a somewhat rickety cart, to which was attached the ancient cob that the late earl used to shoe. We entered a noble hall, which probably looked the larger because of the entire absence of any kind of furniture, unless two complete suits of venerable armour which stood on either hand might be considered as furnishing. I laughed aloud when the door was shut, and the sound echoed like the merriment of ghosts from the dim timbered roof above me.

'What are you laughing at?' asked the earl.

'I am laughing to see you put your modern tall hat on that mediaeval helmet.'

'Oh, that's it! Well, put yours on the other. I mean no disrespect to the ancestor who wore this suit, but we are short of the harmless, necessary hat-rack, so I put my topper on the antique helmet, and thrust the umbrella (if I have one) in behind here, and down one of his legs. Since I came in possession, a very crafty-looking dealer from London visited me, and attempted to sound me regarding the sale of these suits of armour. I gathered he would give enough money to keep me in new suits, London made, for the rest of my life, but when I endeavoured to find out if he had had commercial dealings with my prophetic uncle, he became frightened and bolted. I imagine that if I had possessed presence of mind enough to have lured him into one of our most uncomfortable dungeons, I might have learned where some of the family treasures went to. Come up these stairs, Monsieur Valmont, and I will show you your room.'

We had lunched on the train coming down, so after a wash in my own room I proceeded at once to inspect the library. It proved, indeed, a most noble apartment, and it had been scandalously used by the old reprobate, its late tenant. There were two huge fireplaces, one in the middle of the north wall and the other at the eastern end. In the latter had been erected a rude brick forge, and beside the forge hung a great black bellows, smoky with usage. On a wooden block lay the anvil, and around it rested and rusted several hammers, large and small. At the western end was a glorious window filled with ancient stained glass, which, as I have said, might have adorned a cathedral. Extensive as the collection of books was, the great size of this chamber made it necessary that only the outside wall should be covered with book cases, and even these were divided by tall windows. The opposite wall was blank, with the exception of a picture here and there, and these pictures offered a further insult to the room, for they were cheap prints, mostly coloured lithographs that had appeared in Christmas numbers of London weekly journals, encased in poverty-stricken frames, hanging from nails ruthlessly driven in above them. The floor was covered with a litter of papers, in some places knee-deep, and in the corner farthest from the forge still stood the bed on which the ancient miser had died.

'Looks like a stable, doesn't it?' commented the earl, when I had finished my inspection. 'I am sure the old boy simply filled it up with this rubbish to give me the trouble of examining it. Higgins tells me that up to within a month before he died the room was reasonably clear of all this muck. Of course it had to be, or the place would have caught fire from the sparks of the forge. The old man made Higgins gather all the papers he could find anywhere about the place, ancient accounts, newspapers, and what not, even to the brown wrapping paper you see, in which parcels came, and commanded him to strew the floor with this litter, because, as he complained, Higgins's boots on the boards made too much noise, and Higgins, who is not in the least of an inquiring mind, accepted this explanation as entirely meeting the case.'

Higgins proved to be a garrulous old fellow, who needed no urging to talk about the late earl; indeed, it was almost impossible to deflect his conversation into any other channel. Twenty years' intimacy with the eccentric nobleman had largely obliterated that sense of deference with which an English servant usually approaches his master. An English underling's idea of nobility is the man who never by any possibility works with his hands. The fact that Lord Chizelrigg had toiled at the carpenter's bench; had mixed cement in the drawing-room; had caused the anvil to ring out till midnight, aroused no admiration in Higgins's mind. In addition to this, the ancient nobleman had been penuriously strict in his examination of accounts, exacting the uttermost farthing, so the humble servitor regarded his memory with supreme contempt. I realised before the drive was finished from the station to Chizelrigg Chase that there was little use of introducing me to Higgins as a foreigner and a fellow-servant. I found myself completely unable to understand what the old fellow said. His dialect, was as unknown to me as the Choctaw language would have been, and the young earl was compelled to act as interpreter on the occasions when we set this garrulous talking-machine going.

The new Earl of Chizelrigg, with the enthusiasm of a boy, proclaimed himself my pupil and assistant, and said he would do whatever he was told. His thorough and fruitless search of the library had convinced him that the old man was merely chaffing him, as he put it, by leaving such a letter as he had written. His lordship was certain that the money had been hidden somewhere else; probably buried under one of the trees in the park. Of course this was possible, and represented the usual method by which a stupid person conceals treasure, yet I did not think it probable. All conversations with Higgins showed the earl to have been an extremely suspicious man; suspicious of banks, suspicious even of Bank of England notes, suspicious of every person on earth, not omitting Higgins himself. Therefore, as I told his nephew, the miser would never allow the fortune out of his sight and immediate reach.

From the first the oddity of the forge and anvil being placed in his bedroom struck me as peculiar, and I said to the young man,—

'I'll stake my reputation that forge or anvil, or both, contain the secret. You see, the old gentleman worked sometimes till midnight, for Higgins could hear his hammering. If he used hard coal on the forge the fire would last through the night, and being in continual terror of thieves, as Higgins says, barricading the castle every evening before dark as if it were a fortress, he was bound to place the treasure in the most unlikely spot for a thief to get at it. Now, the coal fire smouldered all night long, and if the gold was in the forge underneath the embers, it would be extremely difficult to get at. A robber rummaging in the dark would burn his fingers in more senses than one. Then, as his lordship kept no less than four loaded revolvers under his pillow, all he had to do, if a thief entered his room was to allow the search to go on until the thief started at the forge, then doubtless, as he had the range with reasonable accuracy night or day, he might sit up in bed and blaze away with revolver after revolver. There were twenty-eight shots that could be fired in about double as many seconds, so you see the robber stood little chance in the face of such a fusillade. I propose that we dismantle the forge.'

Lord Chizelrigg was much taken by my reasoning, and one morning early we cut down the big bellows, tore it open, found it empty, then took brick after brick from the forge with a crowbar, for the old man had builded better than he knew with Portland cement. In fact, when we cleared away the rubbish between the bricks and the core of the furnace we came upon one cube of cement which was as hard as granite. With the aid of Higgins, and a set of rollers and levers, we managed to get this block out into the park, and attempted to crush it with the sledge-hammers belonging to the forge, in which we were entirely unsuccessful. The more it resisted our efforts, the more certain we became that the coins would be found within it. As this would not be treasure-trove in the sense that the Government might make a claim upon it, there was no particular necessity for secrecy, so we had up a man from the mines near by with drills and dynamite, who speedily shattered the block into a million pieces, more or less. Alas! there was no trace in its debris of 'pay dirt,' as the western miner puts it. While the dynamite expert was on the spot, we induced him to shatter the anvil as well as the block of cement, and then the workman, doubtless thinking the new earl was as insane as the old one had been, shouldered his tools, and went back to his mine.

The earl reverted to his former opinion that the gold was concealed in the park, while I held even more firmly to my own belief that the fortune rested in the library.

'It is obvious,' I said to him, 'that if the treasure is buried outside, someone must have dug the hole. A man so timorous and so reticent as your uncle would allow no one to do this but himself. Higgins maintained the other evening that all picks and spades were safely locked up by himself each night in the tool-house. The mansion itself was barricaded with such exceeding care that it would have been difficult for your uncle to get outside even if he wished to do so. Then such a man as your uncle is described to have been would continually desire ocular demonstration that his savings were intact, which would be practically impossible if the gold had found a grave in the park. I propose now that we abandon violence and dynamite, and proceed to an intellectual search of the library.'

'Very well,' replied the young earl, 'but as I have already searched the library very thoroughly, your use of the word "intellectual", Monsieur Valmont, is not in accord with your customary politeness. However, I am with you. 'Tis for you to command, and me to obey.'

'Pardon me, my lord,' I said, 'I used the word "intellectual" in contradistinction to the word "dynamite". It had no reference to your former search. I merely propose that we now abandon the use of chemical reaction, and employ the much greater force of mental activity. Did you notice any writing on the margins of the newspapers you examined?'

'No, I did not.'

'Is it possible that there may have been some communication on the white border of a newspaper?'

'It is, of course, possible.'

'Then will you set yourself to the task of glancing over the margin of every newspaper, piling them away in another room when your scrutiny of each is complete? Do not destroy anything, but we must clear out the library completely. I am interested in the accounts, and will examine them.'

It was exasperatingly tedious work, but after several days my assistant reported every margin scanned without result, while I had collected each bill and memorandum, classifying them according to date. I could not get rid of a suspicion that the contrary old beast had written instructions for the finding of the treasure on the back of some account, or on the fly-leaf of a book, and as I looked at the thousands of volumes still left in the library, the prospect of such a patient and minute search appalled me. But I remembered Edison's words to the effect that if a thing exist, search, exhaustive enough, will find it. From the mass of accounts I selected several; the rest I placed in another room, alongside the heap of the earl's newspapers.

'Now,' said I to my helper, 'if it please you, we will have Higgins in, as I wish some explanation of these accounts.'

'Perhaps I can assist you,' suggested his lordship drawing up a chair opposite the table on which I had spread the statements. 'I have lived here for six months, and know as much about things as Higgins does. He is so difficult to stop when once he begins to talk. What is the first account you wish further light upon?'

'To go back thirteen years I find that your uncle bought a second-hand safe in Sheffield. Here is the bill. I consider it necessary to find that safe.'

'Pray forgive me, Monsieur Valmont,' cried the young man, springing to his feet and laughing; 'so heavy an article as a safe should not slip readily from a man's memory, but it did from mine. The safe is empty, and I gave no more thought to it.'

Saying this the earl went to one of the bookcases that stood against the wall, pulled it round as if it were a door, books and all, and displayed the front of an iron safe, the door of which he also drew open, exhibiting the usual empty interior of such a receptacle.

'I came on this,' he said, 'when I took down all these volumes. It appears that there was once a secret door leading from the library into an outside room, which has long since disappeared; the walls are very thick. My uncle doubtless caused this door to be taken off its hinges, and the safe placed in the aperture, the rest of which he then bricked up.'

'Quite so,' said I, endeavouring to conceal my disappointment. 'As this strong box was bought second-hand and not made to order, I suppose there can be no secret crannies in it?'

'It looks like a common or garden safe,' reported my assistant, 'but we'll have it out if you say so.'

'Not just now,' I replied; 'we've had enough of dynamiting to make us feel like housebreakers already.'

'I agree with you. What's the next item on the programme?'

'Your uncle's mania for buying things at second-hand was broken in three instances so far as I have been able to learn from a scrutiny of these accounts. About four years ago he purchased a new book from Denny and Co., the well-known booksellers of the Strand. Denny and Co. deal only in new books. Is there any comparatively new volume in the library?'

'Not one.'

'Are you sure of that?'

'Oh, quite; I searched all the literature in the house. What is the name of the volume he bought?'

'That I cannot decipher. The initial letter looks like "M", but the rest is a mere wavy line. I see, however, that it cost twelve-and-sixpence, while the cost of carriage by parcel post was sixpence, which shows it weighed something under four pounds. This, with the price of the book, induces me to think that it was a scientific work, printed on heavy paper and illustrated.'

'I know nothing of it,' said the earl.

'The third account is for wallpaper; twenty-seven rolls of an expensive wallpaper, and twenty-seven rolls of a cheap paper, the latter being just half the price of the former. This wallpaper seems to have been supplied by a tradesman in the station road in the village of Chizelrigg.'

'There's your wallpaper,' cried the youth, waving his hand; 'he was going to paper the whole house, Higgins told me, but got tired after he had finished the library, which took him nearly a year to accomplish, for he worked at it very intermittently, mixing the paste in the boudoir, a pailful at a time as he needed it. It was a scandalous thing to do, for underneath the paper is the most exquisite oak panelling, very plain, but very rich in colour.'

I rose and examined the paper on the wall. It was dark brown, and answered the description of the expensive paper on the bill.

'What became of the cheap paper?' I asked.

'I don't know.'

'I think,' said I, 'we are on the track of the mystery. I believe that paper covers a sliding panel or concealed door.'

'It is very likely,' replied the earl. 'I intended to have the paper off, but I had no money to pay a workman, and I am not so industrious as was my uncle. What is your remaining account?'

'The last also pertains to paper, but comes from a firm in Budge Row, London, E.C. He has had, it seems, a thousand sheets of it, and it appears to have been frightfully expensive. This bill is also illegible, but I take it a thousand sheets were supplied, although of course it may have been a thousand quires, which would be a little more reasonable for the price charged, or a thousand reams, which would be exceedingly cheap.'

'I don't know anything about that. Let's turn on Higgins.'

Higgins knew nothing of this last order of paper either. The wallpaper mystery he at once cleared up. Apparently the old earl had discovered by experiment that the heavy, expensive wallpaper would not stick to the glossy panelling, so he had purchased a cheaper paper, and had pasted that on first. Higgins said he had gone all over the panelling with a yellowish-white paper, and after that was dry, he pasted over it the more expensive rolls.

'But,' I objected, 'the two papers were bought and delivered at the same time; therefore, he could not have found by experiment that the heavy paper would not stick.'

'I don't think there is much in that,' commented the earl; 'the heavy paper may have been bought first, and found to be unsuitable, and then the coarse, cheap paper bought afterwards. The bill merely shows that the account was sent in on that date. Indeed, as the village of Chizelrigg is but a few miles away, it would have been quite possible for my uncle to have bought the heavy paper in the morning, tried it, and in the afternoon sent for the commoner lot; but in any case, the bill would not have been presented until months after the order, and the two purchases were thus lumped together.'

I was forced to confess that this seemed reasonable.

Now, about the book ordered from Denny's. Did Higgins remember anything regarding it? It came four years ago.

Ah, yes, Higgins did; he remembered it very well indeed. He had come in one morning with the earl's tea, and the old man was sitting up in bed reading his volume with such interest that he was unaware of Higgins's knock, and Higgins himself, being a little hard of hearing, took for granted the command to enter. The earl hastily thrust the book under the pillow, alongside the revolvers, and rated Higgins in a most cruel way for entering the room before getting permission to do so. He had never seen the earl so angry before, and he laid it all to this book. It was after the book had come that the forge had been erected and the anvil bought. Higgins never saw the book again, but one morning, six months before the earl died, Higgins, in raking out the cinders of the forge, found what he supposed was a portion of the book's cover. He believed his master had burnt the volume.

Having dismissed Higgins, I said to the earl,—

'The first thing to be done is to enclose this bill to Denny and Co., booksellers, Strand. Tell them you have lost the volume, and ask them to send another. There is likely someone in the shop who can decipher the illegible writing. I am certain the book will give us a clue. Now, I shall write to Braun and Sons, Budge Row. This is evidently a French company; in fact, the name as connected with paper-making runs in my mind, although I cannot at this moment place it. I shall ask them the use of this paper that they furnished to the late earl.'

This was done accordingly, and now, as we thought, until the answers came, we were two men out of work. Yet the next morning, I am pleased to say, and I have always rather plumed myself on the fact, I solved the mystery before replies were received from London. Of course, both the book and the answer of the paper agents, by putting two and two together, would have given us the key.

After breakfast, I strolled somewhat aimlessly into the library, whose floor was now strewn merely with brown wrapping paper, bits of string, and all that. As I shuffled among this with my feet, as if tossing aside dead autumn leaves in a forest path, my attention was suddenly drawn to several squares of paper, unwrinkled, and never used for wrapping. These sheets seemed to me strangely familiar. I picked one of them up, and at once the significance of the name Braun and Sons occurred to me. They are paper makers in France, who produce a smooth, very tough sheet, which, dear as it is, proves infinitely cheap compared with the fine vellum it deposed in a certain branch of industry. In Paris, years before, these sheets had given me the knowledge of how a gang of thieves disposed of their gold without melting it. The paper was used instead of vellum in the rougher processes of manufacturing gold-leaf. It stood the constant beating of the hammer nearly as well as the vellum, and here at once there flashed on me the secret of the old man's midnight anvil work. He was transforming his sovereigns into gold-leaf, which must have been of a rude, thick kind, because to produce the gold-leaf of commerce he still needed the vellum as well as a 'clutch' and other machinery, of which we had found no trace.

'My lord,' I called to my assistant; he was at the other end of the room; 'I wish to test a theory on the anvil of your own fresh common sense.'

'Hammer away,' replied the earl, approaching me with his usual good-natured, jocular expression.

'I eliminate the safe from our investigations because it was purchased thirteen years ago, but the buying of the book, of wall covering, of this tough paper from France, all group themselves into a set of incidents occurring within the same month as the purchase of the anvil and the building of the forge; therefore, I think they are related to one another. Here are some sheets of paper he got from Budge Row. Have you ever seen anything like it? Try to tear this sample.'

'It's reasonably tough,' admitted his lordship, fruitlessly endeavouring to rip it apart.

'Yes. It was made in France, and is used in gold beating. Your uncle beat his sovereigns into gold-leaf. You will find that the book from Denny's is a volume on gold beating, and now as I remember that scribbled word which I could not make out, I think the title of the volume is "Metallurgy". It contains, no doubt, a chapter on the manufacture of gold-leaf.'

'I believe you,' said the earl; 'but I don't see that the discovery sets us any further forward. We're now looking for gold-leaf instead of sovereigns.'

'Let's examine this wallpaper,' said I.

I placed my knife under a corner of it at the floor, and quite easily ripped off a large section. As Higgins had said, the brown paper was on top, and the coarse, light-coloured paper underneath. But even that came away from the oak panelling as easily as though it hung there from habit, and not because of paste.

'Feel the weight of that,' I cried, handing him the sheet I had torn from the wall.

'By Jove!' said the earl, in a voice almost of awe.

I took it from him, and laid it, face downwards, on the wooden table, threw a little water on the back, and with a knife scraped away the porous white paper. Instantly there gleamed up at us the baleful yellow of the gold. I shrugged my shoulders and spread out my hands. The Earl of Chizelrigg laughed aloud and very heartily.

'You see how it is,' I cried. 'The old man first covered the entire wall with this whitish paper. He heated his sovereigns at the forge and beat them out on the anvil, then completed the process rudely between the sheets of this paper from France. Probably he pasted the gold to the wall as soon as he shut himself in for the night, and covered it over with the more expensive paper before Higgins entered in the morning.'

We found afterwards, however, that he had actually fastened the thick sheets of gold to the wall with carpet tacks.

His lordship netted a trifle over a hundred and twenty-three thousand pounds through my discovery, and I am pleased to pay tribute to the young man's generosity by saying that his voluntary settlement made my bank account swell stout as a City alderman.

5. The Absent-Minded Coterie

Some years ago I enjoyed the unique experience of pursuing a man for one crime, and getting evidence against him of another. He was innocent of the misdemeanour, the proof of which I sought, but was guilty of another most serious offence, yet he and his confederates escaped scot-free in circumstances which I now purpose to relate.

You may remember that in Rudyard Kipling's story, Bedalia Herodsfoot, the unfortunate woman's husband ran the risk of being arrested as a simple drunkard, at a moment when the blood of murder was upon his boots. The case of Ralph Summertrees was rather the reverse of this. The English authorities were trying to fasten upon him a crime almost as important as murder, while I was collecting evidence which proved him guilty of an action much more momentous than that of drunkenness.

The English authorities have always been good enough, when they recognise my existence at all, to look down upon me with amused condescension. If today you ask Spenser Hale, of Scotland Yard, what he thinks of Eugène Valmont, that complacent man will put on the superior smile which so well becomes him, and if you are a very intimate friend of his, he may draw down the lid of his right eye, as he replies,—

'Oh, yes, a very decent fellow, Valmont, but he's a Frenchman,' as if that said, there was no need of further inquiry.

Myself, I like the English detective very much, and if I were to be in a mêlée tomorrow, there is no man I would rather find beside me than Spenser Hale. In any situation where a fist that can fell an ox is desirable, my friend Hale is a useful companion, but for intellectuality, mental acumen, finesse— ah, well! I am the most modest of men, and will say nothing.

It would amuse you to see this giant come into my room during an evening, on the bluff pretence that he wishes to smoke a pipe with me. There is the same difference between this good-natured giant and myself as exists between that strong black pipe of his and my delicate cigarette, which I smoke feverishly when he is present, to protect myself from the fumes of his terrible tobacco. I look with delight upon the huge man, who, with an air of the utmost good humour, and a twinkle in his eye as he thinks he is twisting me about his finger, vainly endeavours to obtain a hint regarding whatever case is perplexing him at that moment. I baffle him with the ease that an active greyhound eludes the pursuit of a heavy mastiff, then at last I say to him with a laugh,—

'Come mon ami Hale, tell me all about it, and I will help you if I can.'

Once or twice at the beginning he shook his massive head, and replied the secret was not his. The last time he did this I assured him that what he said was quite correct, and then I related full particulars of the situation in which he found himself, excepting the names, for these he had not mentioned. I had pieced together his perplexity from scraps of conversation in his half-hour's fishing for my advice, which, of course, he could have had for the plain asking. Since that time he has not come to me except with cases he feels at liberty to reveal, and one or two complications I have happily been enabled to unravel for him.

But, staunch as Spenser Hale holds the belief that no detective service on earth can excel that centring in Scotland Yard, there is one department of activity in which even he confesses that Frenchmen are his masters, although he somewhat grudgingly qualifies his admission by adding that we in France are constantly allowed to do what is prohibited in England. I refer to the minute search of a house during the owner's absence. If you read that excellent story, entitled The Purloined Letter, by Edgar Allan Poe, you will find a record of the kind of thing I mean, which is better than any description I, who have so often taken part in such a search, can set down.

Now, these people among whom I live are proud of their phrase, 'The Englishman's house is his castle,' and into that castle even a policeman cannot penetrate without a legal warrant. This may be all very well in theory, but if you are compelled to march up to a man's house, blowing a trumpet, and rattling a snare drum, you need not be disappointed if you fail to find what you are in search of when all the legal restrictions are complied with. Of course, the English are a very excellent people, a fact to which I am always proud to bear testimony, but it must be admitted that for cold common sense the French are very much their superiors. In Paris, if I wish to obtain an incriminating document, I do not send the possessor a carte postale to inform him of my desire, and in this procedure the French people sanely acquiesce. I have known men who, when they go out to spend an evening on the boulevards, toss their bunch of keys to the concierge, saying,—

'If you hear the police rummaging about while I'm away, pray assist them, with an expression of my distinguished consideration.'

I remember while I was chief detective in the service of the French Government being requested to call at a certain hour at the private hotel of the Minister for Foreign Affairs. It was during the time that Bismarck meditated a second attack upon my country, and I am happy to say that I was then instrumental in supplying the Secret Bureau with documents which mollified that iron man's purpose, a fact which I think entitled me to my country's gratitude, not that I ever even hinted such a claim when a succeeding ministry forgot my services. The memory of a republic, as has been said by a greater man than I, is short. However, all that has nothing to do with the incident I am about to relate. I merely mention the crisis to excuse a momentary forgetfulness on my part which in any other country might have been followed by serious results to myself. But in France—ah, we understand those things, and nothing happened.

I am the last person in the world to give myself away, as they say in the great West. I am usually the calm, collected Eugène Valmont whom nothing can perturb, but this was a time of great tension, and I had become absorbed. I was alone with the minister in his private house, and one of the papers he desired was in his bureau at the Ministry for Foreign Affairs; at least, he thought so, and said,—

'Ah, it is in my desk at the bureau. How annoying! I must send for it!'

'No, Excellency,' I cried, springing up in a self-oblivion the most complete, 'it is here.' Touching the spring of a secret drawer, I opened it, and

467

taking out the document he wished, handed it to him.

It was not until I met his searching look, and saw the faint smile on his lips that I realised what I had done.

'Valmont,' he said quietly, 'on whose behalf did you search my house?'

'Excellency,' I replied in tones no less agreeable than his own, 'tonight at your orders I pay a domiciliary visit to the mansion of Baron Dumoulaine, who stands high in the estimation of the President of the French Republic. If either of those distinguished gentlemen should learn of my informal call and should ask me in whose interests I made the domiciliary visit, what is it you wish that I should reply?'

'You should reply, Valmont, that you did it in the interests of the Secret Service.'

'I shall not fail to do so, Excellency, and in answer to your question just now, I had the honour of searching this mansion in the interests of the Secret Service of France.'

The Minister for Foreign Affairs laughed; a hearty laugh that expressed no resentment.

'I merely wished to compliment you, Valmont, on the efficiency of your search, and the excellence of your memory. This is indeed the document which I thought was left in my office.'

I wonder what Lord Lansdowne would say if Spenser Hale showed an equal familiarity with his private papers! But now that we have returned to our good friend Hale, we must not keep him waiting any longer.

I well remember the November day when I first heard of the Summertrees case, because there hung over London a fog so thick that two or three times I lost my way, and no cab was to be had at any price. The few cabmen then in the streets were leading their animals slowly along, making for their stables. It was one of those depressing London days which filled me with ennui and a yearning for my own clear city of Paris, where, if we are ever visited by a slight mist, it is at least clean, white vapour, and not this horrible London mixture saturated with suffocating carbon. The fog was too thick for any passer to read the contents bills of the newspapers plastered on the pavement, and as there were probably no races that day the newsboys were shouting what they considered the next most important event—the election of an American President. I bought a paper and thrust it into my pocket. It was late when I reached my flat, and, after dining there, which was an unusual thing for me to do, I put on my slippers, took an easy-chair before the fire, and began to read my evening journal. I was distressed to learn that the eloquent Mr. Bryan had been defeated. I knew little about the silver question, but the man's oratorical powers had appealed to me, and my sympathy was aroused because he owned many silver mines, and yet the price of the metal was so low that apparently he could not make a living through the operation of them. But, of course, the cry that he was a plutocrat, and a reputed millionaire over and over again, was bound to defeat him in a democracy where the average voter is exceedingly poor and not comfortably well-to-do as is the case with our peasants in France. I always took great interest in the affairs of the huge republic to the west, having been at some pains to inform myself accurately regarding its politics, and although, as my readers know, I seldom quote anything complimentary that is said of me, nevertheless, an American client of mine once admitted that he never knew the true inwardness—I think that was the phrase he used—of American politics until he heard me discourse upon them. But then, he added, he had been a very busy man all his life.

I had allowed my paper to slip to the floor, for in very truth the fog was penetrating even into my flat, and it was becoming difficult to read, notwithstanding the electric light. My man came in, and announced that Mr. Spenser Hale wished to see me, and, indeed, any night, but especially when there is rain or fog outside, I am more pleased to talk with a friend than to read a newspaper.

'Mon Dieu, my dear Monsieur Hale, it is a brave man you are to venture out in such a fog as is abroad tonight.'

'Ah, Monsieur Valmont,' said Hale with pride, 'you cannot raise a fog like this in Paris!'

'No. There you are supreme,' I admitted, rising and saluting my visitor, then offering him a chair.

'I see you are reading the latest news,' he said, indicating my newspaper, 'I am very glad that man Bryan is defeated. Now we shall have better times.'

I waved my hand as I took my chair again. I will discuss many things with Spenser Hale, but not American politics; he does not understand them. It is a common defect of the English to suffer complete ignorance regarding the internal affairs of other countries.

'It is surely an important thing that brought you out on such a night as this. The fog must be very thick in Scotland Yard.'

This delicate shaft of fancy completely missed him, and he answered stolidly,—

'It's thick all over London, and, indeed, throughout most of England.'

'Yes, it is,' I agreed, but he did not see that either.

Still a moment later he made a remark which, if it had come from some people I know, might have indicated a glimmer of comprehension.

'You are a very, very clever man, Monsieur Valmont, so all I need say is that the question which brought me here is the same as that on which the American election was fought. Now, to a countryman, I should be compelled to give further explanation, but to you, monsieur, that will not be necessary.'

There are times when I dislike the crafty smile and partial closing of the eyes which always distinguishes Spenser Hale when he places on the table a problem which he expects will baffle me. If I said he never did baffle me, I would be wrong, of course, for sometimes the utter simplicity of the puzzles which trouble him leads me into an intricate involution entirely unnecessary in the circumstances.

I pressed my fingertips together, and gazed for a few moments at the ceiling. Hale had lit his black pipe, and my silent servant placed at his elbow the whisky and soda, then tiptoed out of the room. As the door closed my eyes came from the ceiling to the level of Hale's expansive countenance.

'Have they eluded you?' I asked quietly.

'Who?'

'The coiners.'

Hale's pipe dropped from his jaw, but he managed to catch it before it reached the floor. Then he took a gulp from the tumbler.

'That was just a lucky shot,' he said.

'Parfaitement,' I replied carelessly.

'Now, own up, Valmont, wasn't it?'

I shrugged my shoulders. A man cannot contradict a guest in his own house.

'Oh, stow that!' cried Hale impolitely. He is a trifle prone to strong and even slangy expressions when puzzled. 'Tell me how you guessed it.'

'It is very simple, mon ami. The question on which the American election was fought is the price of silver, which is so low that it has ruined Mr. Bryan, and threatens to ruin all the farmers of the west who possess silver mines on their farms. Silver troubled America, ergo silver troubles Scotland Yard.

'Very well, the natural inference is that someone has stolen bars of silver. But such a theft happened three months ago, when the metal was being unloaded from a German steamer at Southampton, and my dear friend Spenser Hale ran down the thieves very cleverly as they were trying to dissolve the marks off the bars with acid. Now crimes do not run in series, like the numbers in roulette at Monte Carlo. The thieves are men of brains. They say to themselves, "What chance is there successfully to steal bars of silver while Mr. Hale is at Scotland Yard?" Eh, my good friend?'

'Really, Valmont,' said Hale, taking another sip, 'sometimes you almost persuade me that you have reasoning powers.'

'Thanks, comrade. Then it is not a theft of silver we have now to deal with. But the American election was fought on the price of silver. If silver had been high in cost, there would have been no silver question. So the crime that is bothering you arises through the low price of silver, and this suggests that it must be a case of illicit coinage, for there the low price of the metal comes in. You have, perhaps, found a more subtle illegitimate act going forward than heretofore. Someone is making your shillings and your half-crowns from real silver, instead of from baser metal, and yet there is a large profit which has not hitherto been possible through the high price of silver. With the old conditions you were familiar, but this new element sets at nought all your previous formulae. That is how I reasoned the matter out.'

'Well, Valmont, you have hit it. I'll say that for you; you have hit it. There is a gang of expert coiners who are putting out real silver money, and making a clear shilling on the half-crown. We can find no trace of the coiners, but we know the man who is shoving the stuff.'

'That ought to be sufficient,' I suggested.

'Yes, it should, but it hasn't proved so up to date. Now I came tonight to see if you would do one of your French tricks for us, right on the quiet.'

'What French trick, Monsieur Spenser Hale?' I inquired with some asperity, forgetting for the moment that the man invariably became impolite when he grew excited.

'No offence intended,' said this blundering officer, who really is a good-natured fellow, but always puts his foot in it, and then apologises. 'I want someone to go through a man's house without a search warrant, spot the evidence, let me know, and then we'll rush the place before he has time to hide his tracks.'

'Who is this man, and where does he live?'

'His name is Ralph Summertrees, and he lives in a very natty little bijou residence, as the advertisements call it, situated in no less a fashionable street than Park Lane.'

'I see. What has aroused your suspicions against him?'

'Well, you know, that's an expensive district to live in; it takes a bit of money to do the trick. This Summertrees has no ostensible business, yet every Friday he goes to the United Capital Bank in Piccadilly, and deposits a bag of swag, usually all silver coin.'

'Yes, and this money?'

'This money, so far as we can learn, contains a good many of these new pieces which never saw the British Mint.'

'It's not all the new coinage, then?'

'Oh, no, he's a bit too artful for that. You see, a man can go round London, his pockets filled with new coinage five-shilling pieces, buy this, that, and the other, and come home with his change in legitimate coins of the realm—half-crowns, florins, shillings, sixpences, and all that.'

'I see. Then why don't you nab him one day when his pockets are stuffed with illegitimate five-shilling pieces?'

'That could be done, of course, and I've thought of it, but you see, we want to land the whole gang. Once we arrested him, without knowing where the money came from, the real coiners would take flight.'

'How do you know he is not the real coiner himself?'

Now poor Hale is as easy to read as a book. He hesitated before answering this question, and looked confused as a culprit caught in some dishonest act.

'You need not be afraid to tell me,' I said soothingly after a pause. 'You have had one of your men in Mr. Summertrees' house, and so learned that he is not the coiner. But your man has not succeeded in getting you evidence to incriminate other people.'

'You've about hit it again, Monsieur Valmont. One of my men has been Summertrees' butler for two weeks, but, as you say, he has found no evidence.'

'Is he still butler?'

'Yes.'

'Now tell me how far you have got. You know that Summertrees deposits a bag of coin every Friday in the Piccadilly bank, and I suppose the bank has allowed you to examine one or two of the bags.'

'Yes, sir, they have, but, you see, banks are very difficult to treat with. They don't like detectives bothering round, and whilst they do not stand out against the law, still they never answer any more questions than they're asked, and Mr. Summertrees has been a good customer at the United Capital for many years.'

'Haven't you found out where the money comes from?'

'Yes, we have; it is brought there night after night by a man who looks like a respectable city clerk, and he puts it into a large safe, of which he holds the key, this safe being on the ground floor, in the dining-room.'

'Haven't you followed the clerk?'

'Yes. He sleeps in the Park Lane house every night, and goes up in the morning to an old curiosity shop in Tottenham Court Road, where he stays all day, returning with his bag of money in the evening.'

'Why don't you arrest and question him?'

'Well, Monsieur Valmont, there is just the same objection to his arrest as to that of Summertrees himself. We could easily arrest both, but we have not the slightest evidence against either of them, and then, although we put the go-betweens in clink, the worst criminals of the lot would escape.'

'Nothing suspicious about the old curiosity shop?'

'No. It appears to be perfectly regular.'

'This game has been going on under your noses for how long?'

'For about six weeks.'

'Is Summertrees a married man?'

'No.'

'Are there any women servants in the house?'

'No, except that three charwomen come in every morning to do up the rooms.'

'Of what is his household comprised?'

'There is the butler, then the valet, and last, the French cook.'

'Ah,' cried I, 'the French cook! This case interests me. So Summertrees has succeeded in completely disconcerting your man? Has he prevented him going from top to bottom of the house?'

'Oh no, he has rather assisted him than otherwise. On one occasion he went to the safe, took out the money, had Podgers—that's my chap's name—help him to count it, and then actually sent Podgers to the bank with the bag of coin.'

'And Podgers has been all over the place?'

'Yes.'

'Saw no signs of a coining establishment?'

'No. It is absolutely impossible that any coining can be done there. Besides, as I tell you, that respectable clerk brings him the money.'

'I suppose you want me to take Podgers' position?'

'Well, Monsieur Valmont, to tell you the truth, I would rather you didn't. Podgers has done everything a man can do, but I thought if you got into the house, Podgers assisting, you might go through it night after night at your leisure.'

'I see. That's just a little dangerous in England. I think I should prefer to assure myself the legitimate standing of being the amiable Podgers' successor. You say that Summertrees has no business?'

'Well, sir, not what you might call a business. He is by the way of being an author, but I don't count that any business.'

'Oh, an author, is he? When does he do his writing?'

'He locks himself up most of the day in his study.'

'Does he come out for lunch?'

'No; he lights a little spirit lamp inside, Podgers tells me, and makes himself a cup of coffee, which he takes with a sandwich or two.'

'That's rather frugal fare for Park Lane.'

'Yes, Monsieur Valmont, it is, but he makes it up in the evening, when he has a long dinner with all them foreign kickshaws you people like, done by his French cook.'

'Sensible man! Well, Hale, I see I shall look forward with pleasure to making the acquaintance of Mr. Summertrees. Is there any restriction on the going and coming of your man Podgers?'

'None in the least. He can get away either night or day.'

'Very good, friend Hale, bring him here tomorrow, as soon as our author locks himself up in his study, or rather, I should say, as soon as the respectable clerk leaves for Tottenham Court Road, which I should guess, as you put it, is about half an hour after his master turns the key of the room in which he writes.'

'You are quite right in that guess, Valmont. How did you hit it?'

'Merely a surmise, Hale. There is a good deal of oddity about that Park Lane house, so it doesn't surprise me in the least that the master gets to work earlier in the morning than the man. I have also a suspicion that Ralph Summertrees knows perfectly well what the estimable Podgers is there for.'

'What makes you think that?'

'I can give no reason except that my opinion of the acuteness of Summertrees has been gradually rising all the while you were speaking, and at the same time my estimate of Podgers' craft has been as steadily declining. However, bring the man here tomorrow, that I may ask him a few questions.'

Next day, about eleven o'clock, the ponderous Podgers, hat in hand, followed his chief into my room. His broad, impassive, immobile smooth face gave him rather more the air of a genuine butler than I had expected, and this appearance, of course, was enhanced by his livery. His replies to my questions were those of a well-trained servant who will not say too much unless it is made worth his while. All in all, Podgers exceeded my expectations, and really my friend Hale had some justification for regarding him, as he evidently did, a triumph in his line.

'Sit down, Mr. Hale, and you, Podgers.'

The man disregarded my invitation, standing like a statue until his chief made a motion; then he dropped into a chair. The English are great on discipline.

'Now, Mr. Hale, I must first congratulate you on the make-up of Podgers. It is excellent. You depend less on artificial assistance than we do in France, and in that I think you are right.'

'Oh, we know a bit over here, Monsieur Valmont,' said Hale, with pardonable pride.

'Now then, Podgers, I want to ask you about this clerk. What time does he arrive in the evening?'

'At prompt six, sir.'

'Does he ring, or let himself in with a latchkey?'

'With a latchkey, sir.'

'How does he carry the money?'

'In a little locked leather satchel, sir, flung over his shoulder.'

'Does he go direct to the dining-room?'

'Yes, sir.'

'Have you seen him unlock the safe and put in the money?'

'Yes, sir.'

'Does the safe unlock with a word or a key?'

'With a key, sir. It's one of the old-fashioned kind.'

'Then the clerk unlocks his leather money bag?'

'Yes, sir.'

'That's three keys used within as many minutes. Are they separate or in a bunch?'

'In a bunch, sir.'

'Did you ever see your master with this bunch of keys?'

'No, sir.'

'You saw him open the safe once, I am told?'

'Yes, sir.'

'Did he use a separate key, or one of a bunch?'

Podgers slowly scratched his head, then said,—

'I don't just remember, sir.'

'Ah, Podgers, you are neglecting the big things in that house. Sure you can't remember?'

'No, sir.'

'Once the money is in and the safe locked up, what does the clerk do?'

'Goes to his room, sir.'

'Where is this room?'

'On the third floor, sir.'

'Where do you sleep?'

'On the fourth floor with the rest of the servants, sir.'

'Where does the master sleep?'

'On the second floor, adjoining his study.'

'The house consists of four stories and a basement, does it?'

'Yes, sir.'

'I have somehow arrived at the suspicion that it is a very narrow house. Is that true?'

'Yes, sir.'

'Does the clerk ever dine with your master?'

'No, sir. The clerk don't eat in the house at all, sir.'

'Does he go away before breakfast?'

'No, sir.'

'No one takes breakfast to his room?'

'No, sir.'

'What time does he leave the house?'

'At ten o'clock, sir.'

'When is breakfast served?'

'At nine o'clock, sir.'

'At what hour does your master retire to his study?'

'At half-past nine, sir.'

'Locks the door on the inside?'

'Yes, sir.'

'Never rings for anything during the day?'

'Not that I know of, sir.'

'What sort of a man is he?'

Here Podgers was on familiar ground, and he rattled off a description minute in every particular.

'What I meant was, Podgers, is he silent, or talkative, or does he get angry? Does he seem furtive, suspicious, anxious, terrorised, calm, excitable, or what?'

'Well, sir, he is by way of being very quiet, never has much to say for himself; never saw him angry, or excited.'

'Now, Podgers, you've been at Park Lane for a fortnight or more. You are a sharp, alert, observant man. What happens there that strikes you as unusual?'

'Well, I can't exactly say, sir,' replied Podgers, looking rather helplessly from his chief to myself, and back again.

'Your professional duties have often compelled you to enact the part of butler before, otherwise you wouldn't do it so well. Isn't that the case.'

Podgers did not reply, but glanced at his chief. This was evidently a question pertaining to the service, which a subordinate was not allowed to answer. However, Hale said at once,—

'Certainly. Podgers has been in dozens of places.'

'Well, Podgers, just call to mind some of the other households where you have been employed, and tell me any particulars in which Mr Summertrees' establishment differs from them.'

Podgers pondered a long time.

'Well, sir, he do stick to writing pretty close.'

'Ah, that's his profession, you see, Podgers. Hard at it from half-past nine till towards seven, I imagine?'

'Yes, sir.'

'Anything else, Podgers? No matter how trivial.'

'Well, sir, he's fond of reading too; leastways, he's fond of newspapers.'

'When does he read?'

'I've never seen him read 'em, sir; indeed, so far as I can tell, I never knew the papers to be opened, but he takes them all in, sir.'

'What, all the morning papers?'

'Yes, sir, and all the evening papers too.'

'Where are the morning papers placed?'

'On the table in his study, sir.'

'And the evening papers?'

'Well, sir, when the evening papers come, the study is locked. They are put on a side table in the dining-room, and he takes them upstairs with him to his study.'

'This has happened every day since you've been there?'

'Yes, sir.'

'You reported that very striking fact to your chief, of course?'

'No, sir, I don't think I did,' said Podgers, confused.

'You should have done so. Mr. Hale would have known how to make the most of a point so vital.'

'Oh, come now, Valmont,' interrupted Hale, 'you're chaffing us. Plenty of people take in all the papers!'

'I think not. Even clubs and hotels subscribe to the leading journals only. You said all, I think, Podgers?'

'Well, nearly all, sir.'

'But which is it? There's a vast difference.'

'He takes a good many, sir.'

'How many?'

'I don't just know, sir.'

'That's easily found out, Valmont,' cried Hale, with some impatience, 'if you think it really important.'

'I think it so important that I'm going back with Podgers myself. You can take me into the house, I suppose, when you return?'

'Oh, yes, sir.'

'Coming back to these newspapers for a moment, Podgers. What is done with them?'

'They are sold to the ragman, sir, once a week.'

'Who takes them from the study?'

'I do, sir.'

'Do they appear to have been read very carefully?'

'Well, no, sir; leastways, some of them seem never to have been opened, or else folded up very carefully again.'

'Did you notice that extracts have been clipped from any of them?'

'No, sir.'

'Does Mr. Summertrees keep a scrapbook?'

'Not that I know of, sir.'

'Oh, the case is perfectly plain,' said I, leaning back in my chair, and regarding the puzzled Hale with that cherubic expression of self-satisfaction which I know is so annoying to him.

'What's perfectly plain?' he demanded, more gruffly perhaps than etiquette would have sanctioned.

'Summertrees is no coiner, nor is he linked with any band of coiners.'

'What is he, then?'

'Ah, that opens another avenue of enquiry. For all I know to the contrary, he may be the most honest of men. On the surface it would appear that he is a reasonably industrious tradesman in Tottenham Court Road, who is anxious that there should be no visible connection between a plebian employment and so aristocratic a residence as that in Park Lane.'

At this point Spenser Hale gave expression to one of those rare flashes of reason which are always an astonishment to his friends.

'That is nonsense, Monsieur Valmont,' he said, 'the man who is ashamed of the connection between his business and his house is one who is trying to get into Society, or else the women of his family are trying it, as is usually the case. Now Summertrees has no family. He himself goes nowhere, gives no entertainments, and accepts no invitations. He belongs to no club, therefore to say that he is ashamed of his connection with the Tottenham Court Road shop is absurd. He is concealing the connection for some other reason that will bear looking into.'

'My dear Hale, the goddess of Wisdom herself could not have made a more sensible series of remarks. Now, mon ami, do you want my assistance, or have you enough to go on with?'

'Enough to go on with? We have nothing more than we had when I called on you last night.'

'Last night, my dear Hale, you supposed this man was in league with coiners. Today you know he is not.'

'I know you say he is not.'

I shrugged my shoulders, and raised my eyebrows, smiling at him.

'It is the same thing, Monsieur Hale.'

'Well, of all the conceited—' and the good Hale could get no further.

'If you wish my assistance, it is yours.'

'Very good. Not to put too fine a point upon it, I do.'

'In that case, my dear Podgers, you will return to the residence of our friend Summertrees, and get together for me in a bundle all of yesterday's morning and evening papers, that were delivered to the house. Can you do that, or are they mixed up in a heap in the coal cellar?'

'I can do it, sir. I have instructions to place each day's papers in a pile by itself in case they should be wanted again. There is always one week's supply in the cellar, and we sell the papers of the week before to the rag men.'

'Excellent. Well, take the risk of abstracting one day's journals, and have them ready for me. I will call upon you at half-past three o'clock exactly, and then I want you to take me upstairs to the clerk's bedroom in the third story, which I suppose is not locked during the daytime?'

'No, sir, it is not.'

With this the patient Podgers took his departure. Spenser Hale rose when his assistant left.

'Anything further I can do?' he asked.

'Yes; give me the address of the shop in Tottenham Court Road. Do you happen to have about you one of those new five-shilling pieces which you believe to be illegally coined?'

He opened his pocket-book, took out the bit of white metal, and handed it to me.

'I'm going to pass this off before evening,' I said, putting it in my pocket, 'and I hope none of your men will arrest me.'

'That's all right,' laughed Hale as he took his leave.

At half-past three Podgers was waiting for me, and opened the front door as I came up the steps, thus saving me the necessity of ringing. The house seemed strangely quiet. The French cook was evidently down in the basement, and we had probably all the upper part to ourselves, unless Summertrees was in his study, which I doubted. Podgers led me directly upstairs to the clerk's room on the third floor, walking on tiptoe, with an elephantine air of silence and secrecy combined, which struck me as unnecessary.

'I will make an examination of this room,' I said. 'Kindly wait for me down by the door of the study.'

The bedroom proved to be of respectable size when one considers the smallness of the house. The bed was all nicely made up, and there were two chairs in the room, but the usual washstand and swing-mirror were not visible. However, seeing a curtain at the farther end of the room, I drew it aside, and found, as I expected, a fixed lavatory in an alcove of perhaps four feet deep by five in width. As the room was about fifteen feet wide, this left two-thirds of the space unaccounted for. A moment later, I opened a door which exhibited a closet filled with clothes hanging on hooks. This left a space of five feet between the clothes closet and the lavatory. I thought at first that the entrance to the secret stairway must have issued from the lavatory, but examining the boards closely, although they sounded hollow to the knuckles, they were quite evidently plain matchboarding, and not a concealed door. The entrance to the stairway, therefore, must issue from the clothes closet. The right hand wall proved similar to the matchboarding of the lavatory as far as the casual eye or touch was concerned, but I saw at once it was a door. The latch turned out to be somewhat ingeniously operated by one of the hooks which held a pair of old trousers. I found that the hook, if pressed upward, allowed the door to swing outward, over the stairhead. Descending to the second floor, a similar latch let me in to a similar clothes closet in the room beneath. The two rooms were identical in size, one directly above the other, the only difference being that the lower room door gave into the study, instead of into the hall, as was the case with the upper chamber.

The study was extremely neat, either not much used, or the abode of a very methodical man. There was nothing on the table except a pile of that morning's papers. I walked to the farther end, turned the key in the lock, and came out upon the astonished Podgers.

'Well, I'm blowed!' exclaimed he.

'Quite so,' I rejoined, 'you've been tiptoeing past an empty room for the last two weeks. Now, if you'll come with me, Podgers, I'll show you how the trick is done.'

When he entered the study, I locked the door once more, and led the assumed butler, still tiptoeing through force of habit, up the stair into the top bedroom, and so out again, leaving everything exactly as we found it. We went down the main stair to the front hall, and there Podgers had my parcel of papers all neatly wrapped up. This bundle I carried to my flat, gave one of my assistants some instructions, and left him at work on the papers.

I took a cab to the foot of Tottenham Court Road, and walked up that street till I came to J. Simpson's old curiosity shop. After gazing at the well-filled windows for some time, I stepped aside, having selected a little iron crucifix displayed behind the pane; the work of some ancient craftsman.

I knew at once from Podgers's description that I was waited upon by the veritable respectable clerk who brought the bag of money each night to Park Lane, and who I was certain was no other than Ralph Summertrees himself.

There was nothing in his manner differing from that of any other quiet salesman. The price of the crucifix proved to be seven-and-six, and I threw down a sovereign to pay for it.

'Do you mind the change being all in silver, sir?' he asked, and I answered without any eagerness, although the question aroused a suspicion that had begun to be allayed,—

'Not in the least.'

He gave me half-a-crown, three two-shilling pieces, and four separate shillings, all the coins being well-worn silver of the realm, the undoubted inartistic product of the reputable British Mint. This seemed to dispose of the theory that he was palming off illegitimate money. He asked me if I were interested in any particular branch of antiquity, and I replied that my curiosity was merely general, and exceedingly amateurish, whereupon he invited me to look around. This I proceeded to do, while he resumed the addressing and stamping of some wrapped-up pamphlets which I surmised to be copies of his catalogue.

He made no attempt either to watch me or to press his wares upon me. I selected at random a little ink-stand, and asked its price. It was two shillings, he said, whereupon I produced my fraudulent five-shilling piece. He took it, gave me the change without comment, and the last doubt about his connection with coiners flickered from my mind.

At this moment a young man came in, who, I saw at once, was not a customer. He walked briskly to the farther end of the shop, and disappeared behind a partition which had one pane of glass in it that gave an outlook towards the front door.

'Excuse me a moment,' said the shopkeeper, and he followed the young man into the private office.

As I examined the curious heterogeneous collection of things for sale, I heard the clink of coins being poured out on the lid of a desk or an uncovered table, and the murmur of voices floated out to me. I was now near the entrance of the shop, and by a sleight-of-hand trick, keeping the corner of my eye on the glass pane of the private office, I removed the key of the front door without a sound, and took an impression of it in wax, returning the key to its place unobserved. At this moment another young man came in, and walked straight past me into the private office. I heard him say,—

'Oh, I beg pardon, Mr. Simpson. How are you, Rogers?'

'Hallo, Macpherson,' saluted Rogers, who then came out, bidding good-night to Mr. Simpson, and departed whistling down the street, but not before he had repeated his phrase to another young man entering, to whom he gave the name of Tyrrel.

I noted these three names in my mind. Two others came in together, but I was compelled to content myself with memorising their features, for I did not learn their names. These men were evidently collectors, for I heard the rattle of money in every case; yet here was a small shop, doing apparently very little business, for I had been within it for more than half an hour, and yet remained the only customer. If credit were given, one collector would certainly have been sufficient, yet five had come in, and had poured their contributions into the pile Summertrees was to take home with him that night.

I determined to secure one of the pamphlets which the man had been addressing. They were piled on a shelf behind the counter, but I had no difficulty in reaching across and taking the one on top, which I slipped into my pocket. When the fifth young man went down the street Summertrees himself emerged, and this time he carried in his hand the well-filled locked leather satchel, with the straps dangling. It was now approaching half-past five, and I saw he was eager to close up and get away.

'Anything else you fancy, sir?' he asked me.

'No, or rather yes and no. You have a very interesting collection here, but it's getting so dark I can hardly see.'

'I close at half-past five, sir.'

'Ah, in that case,' I said, consulting my watch, 'I shall be pleased to call some other time.'

'Thank you, sir,' replied Summertrees quietly, and with that I took my leave.

From the corner of an alley on the other side of the street I saw him put up the shutters with his own hands, then he emerged with overcoat on, and the money satchel slung across his shoulder. He locked the door, tested it with his knuckles, and walked down the street, carrying under one arm the pamphlets he had been addressing. I followed him some distance, saw him drop the pamphlets into the box at the first post office he passed, and walk rapidly towards his house in Park Lane.

When I returned to my flat and called in my assistant, he said,—

'After putting to one side the regular advertisements of pills, soap, and what not, here is the only one common to all the newspapers, morning and evening alike. The advertisements are not identical, sir, but they have two points of similarity, or perhaps I should say three. They all profess to furnish a cure for absent-mindedness; they all ask that the applicant's chief hobby shall be stated, and they all bear the same address: Dr. Willoughby, in Tottenham Court Road.'

'Thank you,' said I, as he placed the scissored advertisements before me.

I read several of the announcements. They were all small, and perhaps that is why I had never noticed one of them in the newspapers, for certainly they were odd enough. Some asked for lists of absent-minded men, with the hobbies of each, and for these lists, prizes of from one shilling to six were offered. In other clippings Dr. Willoughby professed to be able to cure absent-mindedness. There were no fees, and no treatment, but a pamphlet would be sent, which, if it did not benefit the receiver, could do no harm. The doctor was unable to meet patients personally, nor could he enter into correspondence with them. The address was the same as that of the old curiosity shop in Tottenham Court Road. At this juncture I pulled the pamphlet from my pocket, and saw it was entitled Christian Science and Absent-Mindedness, by Dr. Stamford Willoughby, and at the end of the article was the statement contained in the advertisements, that Dr Willoughby would neither see patients nor hold any correspondence with them.

I drew a sheet of paper towards me, wrote to Dr. Willoughby alleging that I was a very absent-minded man, and would be glad of his pamphlet, adding that my special hobby was the collecting of first editions. I then signed myself, 'Alport Webster, Imperial Flats, London, W.'

I may here explain that it is often necessary for me to see people under some other name than the well-known appellation of Eugène Valmont. There are two doors to my flat, and on one of these is painted, 'Eugène Valmont'; on the other there is a receptacle, into which can be slipped a sliding panel bearing any nom de guerre I choose. The same device is arranged on the ground floor, where the names of all the occupants of the building appear on the right-hand wall.

I sealed, addressed, and stamped my letter, then told my man to put out the name of Alport Webster, and if I did not happen to be in when anyone called upon that mythical person, he was to make an appointment for me.

It was nearly six o'clock next afternoon when the card of Angus Macpherson was brought in to Mr. Alport Webster. I recognised the young man at once as the second who had entered the little shop carrying his tribute to Mr. Simpson the day before. He held three volumes under his arm, and spoke in such a pleasant, insinuating sort of way, that I knew at once he was an adept in his profession of canvasser.

'Will you be seated, Mr. Macpherson? In what can I serve you?'

He placed the three volumes, backs upward, on my table.

'Are you interested at all in first editions, Mr. Webster?'

'It is the one thing I am interested in,' I replied; 'but unfortunately they often run into a lot of money.'

'That is true,' said Macpherson sympathetically, 'and I have here three books, one of which is an exemplification of what you say. This one costs a hundred pounds. The last copy that was sold by auction in London brought a hundred and twenty-three pounds. This next one is forty pounds, and the third ten pounds. At these prices I am certain you could not duplicate three such treasures in any book shop in Britain.'

I examined them critically, and saw at once that what he said was true. He was still standing on the opposite side of the table.

'Please take a chair, Mr. Macpherson. Do you mean to say you go round London with a hundred and fifty pounds worth of goods under your arm in this careless way?'

The young man laughed.

'I run very little risk, Mr. Webster. I don't suppose anyone I meet imagines for a moment there is more under my arm than perhaps a trio of volumes I have picked up in the fourpenny box to take home with me.'

I lingered over the volume for which he asked a hundred pounds, then said, looking across at him:—

'How came you to be possessed of this book, for instance?'

He turned upon me a fine, open countenance, and answered without hesitation in the frankest possible manner,—

'I am not in actual possession of it, Mr. Webster. I am by way of being a connoisseur in rare and valuable books myself, although, of course, I have little money with which to indulge in the collection of them. I am acquainted, however, with the lovers of desirable books in different quarters of London. These three volumes, for instance, are from the library of a private gentleman in the West End. I have sold many books to him, and he knows I am trustworthy. He wishes to dispose of them at something under their real value, and has kindly allowed me to conduct the negotiation. I make it my business to find out those who are interested in rare books, and by such trading I add considerably to my income.'

'How, for instance, did you learn that I was a bibliophile?'

Mr. Macpherson laughed genially.

'Well, Mr. Webster, I must confess that I chanced it. I do that very often. I take a flat like this, and send in my card to the name on the door. If I am invited in, I ask the occupant the question I asked you just now: "Are you interested in rare editions?" If he says no, I simply beg pardon and retire. If he says yes, then I show my wares.'

'I see,' said I, nodding. What a glib young liar he was, with that innocent face of his, and yet my next question brought forth the truth.

'As this is the first time you have called upon me, Mr. Macpherson, you have no objection to my making some further inquiry, I suppose. Would you mind telling me the name of the owner of these books in the West End?'

'His name is Mr. Ralph Summertrees, of Park Lane.'

'Of Park Lane? Ah, indeed.'

'I shall be glad to leave the books with you, Mr. Webster, and if you care to make an appointment with Mr. Summertrees, I am sure he will not object to say a word in my favour.'

'Oh, I do not in the least doubt it, and should not think of troubling the gentleman.'

'I was going to tell you,' went on the young man, 'that I have a friend, a capitalist, who, in a way, is my supporter; for, as I said, I have little money of my own. I find it is often inconvenient for people to pay down any considerable sum. When, however, I strike a bargain, my capitalist buys the book, and I make an arrangement with my customer to pay a certain amount each week, and so even a large purchase is not felt, as I make the instalments small enough to suit my client.'

'You are employed during the day, I take it?'

'Yes, I am a clerk in the City.'

Again we were in the blissful realms of fiction!

'Suppose I take this book at ten pounds, what instalment should I have to pay each week?'

'Oh, what you like, sir. Would five shillings be too much?'

'I think not.'

'Very well, sir, if you pay me five shillings now, I will leave the book with you, and shall have pleasure in calling this day week for the next instalment.'

I put my hand into my pocket, and drew out two half-crowns, which I passed over to him.

'Do I need to sign any form or undertaking to pay the rest?'

The young man laughed cordially.

'Oh, no, sir, there is no formality necessary. You see, sir, this is largely a labour of love with me, although I don't deny I have my eye on the future. I am getting together what I hope will be a very valuable connection with gentlemen like yourself who are fond of books, and I trust some day that

I may be able to resign my place with the insurance company and set up a choice little business of my own, where my knowledge of values in literature will prove useful.'

And then, after making a note in a little book he took from his pocket, he bade me a most graceful good-bye and departed, leaving me cogitating over what it all meant.

Next morning two articles were handed to me. The first came by post and was a pamphlet on Christian Science and Absent-Mindedness, exactly similar to the one I had taken away from the old curiosity shop; the second was a small key made from my wax impression that would fit the front door of the same shop—a key fashioned by an excellent anarchist friend of mine in an obscure street near Holborn.

That night at ten o'clock I was inside the old curiosity shop, with a small storage battery in my pocket, and a little electric glow-lamp at my buttonhole, a most useful instrument for either burglar or detective.

I had expected to find the books of the establishment in a safe, which, if it was similar to the one in Park Lane, I was prepared to open with the false keys in my possession or to take an impression of the keyhole and trust to my anarchist friend for the rest. But to my amazement I discovered all the papers pertaining to the concern in a desk which was not even locked. The books, three in number, were the ordinary day book, journal, and ledger referring to the shop; book-keeping of the older fashion; but in a portfolio lay half a dozen foolscap sheets, headed 'Mr. Rogers's List', 'Mr. Macpherson's', 'Mr Tyrrel's', the names I had already learned, and three others. These lists contained in the first column, names; in the second column, addresses; in the third, sums of money; and then in the small, square places following were amounts ranging from two-and-sixpence to a pound. At the bottom of Mr. Macpherson's list was the name Alport Webster, Imperial Flats, £10; then in the small, square place, five shillings. These six sheets, each headed by a canvasser's name, were evidently the record of current collections, and the innocence of the whole thing was so apparent that if it were not for my fixed rule never to believe that I am at the bottom of any case until I have come on something suspicious, I would have gone out empty-handed as I came in.

The six sheets were loose in a thin portfolio, but standing on a shelf above the desk were a number of fat volumes, one of which I took down, and saw that it contained similar lists running back several years. I noticed on Mr. Macpherson's current list the name of Lord Semptam, an eccentric old nobleman whom I knew slightly. Then turning to the list immediately before the current one the name was still there; I traced it back through list after list until I found the first entry, which was no less than three years previous, and there Lord Semptam was down for a piece of furniture costing fifty pounds, and on that account he had paid a pound a week for more than three years, totalling a hundred and seventy pounds at the least, and instantly the glorious simplicity of the scheme dawned upon me, and I became so interested in the swindle that I lit the gas, fearing my little lamp would be exhausted before my investigation ended, for it promised to be a long one.

In several instances the intended victim proved shrewder than old Simpson had counted upon, and the word 'Settled' had been written on the line carrying the name when the exact number of instalments was paid. But as these shrewd persons dropped out, others took their places, and Simpson's dependence on their absent-mindedness seemed to be justified in nine cases out of ten. His collectors were collecting long after the debt had been paid. In Lord Semptam's case, the payment had evidently become chronic, and the old man was giving away his pound a week to the suave Macpherson two years after his debt had been liquidated.

From the big volume I detached the loose leaf, dated 1893, which recorded Lord Semptam's purchase of a carved table for fifty pounds, and on which he had been paying a pound a week from that time to the date of which I am writing, which was November, 1896. This single document taken from the file of three years previous, was not likely to be missed, as would have been the case if I had selected a current sheet. I nevertheless made a copy of the names and addresses of Macpherson's present clients; then, carefully placing everything exactly as I had found it, I extinguished the gas, and went out of the shop, locking the door behind me. With the 1893 sheet in my pocket I resolved to prepare a pleasant little surprise for my suave friend Macpherson when he called to get his next instalment of five shillings.

Late as was the hour when I reached Trafalgar Square, I could not deprive myself of the felicity of calling on Mr. Spenser Hale, who I knew was then on duty. He never appeared at his best during office hours, because officialism stiffened his stalwart frame. Mentally he was impressed with the importance of his position, and added to this he was not then allowed to smoke his big, black pipe and terrible tobacco. He received me with the curtness I had been taught to expect when I inflicted myself upon him at his office. He greeted me abruptly with,—

'I say, Valmont, how long do you expect to be on this job?'

'What job?' I asked mildly.

'Oh, you know what I mean: the Summertrees affair.'

'Oh, that!' I exclaimed, with surprise. 'The Summertrees case is already completed, of course. If I had known you were in a hurry, I should have finished up everything yesterday, but as you and Podgers, and I don't know how many more, have been at it sixteen or seventeen days, if not longer, I thought I might venture to take as many hours, as I am working entirely alone. You said nothing about haste, you know.'

'Oh, come now, Valmont, that's a bit thick. Do you mean to say you have already got evidence against the man?'

'Evidence absolute and complete.'

'Then who are the coiners?'

'My most estimable friend, how often have I told you not to jump at conclusions? I informed you when you first spoke to me about the matter that Summertrees was neither a coiner nor a confederate of coiners. I secured evidence sufficient to convict him of quite another offence, which is probably unique in the annals of crime. I have penetrated the mystery of the shop, and discovered the reason for all those suspicious actions which quite properly set you on his trail. Now I wish you to come to my flat next Wednesday night at a quarter to six, prepared to make an arrest.'

'I must know who I am to arrest, and on what counts.'

'Quite so, mon ami Hale; I did not say you were to make an arrest, but merely warned you to be prepared. If you have time now to listen to the disclosures, I am quite at your service. I promise you there are some original features in the case. If, however, the present moment is inopportune, drop in on me at your convenience, previously telephoning so that you may know whether I am there or not, and thus your valuable time will not be expended purposelessly.'

With this I presented to him my most courteous bow, and although his mystified expression hinted a suspicion that he thought I was chaffing him, as he would call it, official dignity dissolved somewhat, and he intimated his desire to hear all about it then and there. I had succeeded in arousing my friend Hale's curiosity. He listened to the evidence with perplexed brow, and at last ejaculated he would be blessed.

'This young man,' I said, in conclusion, 'will call upon me at six on Wednesday afternoon, to receive his second five shillings. I propose that you, in your uniform, shall be seated there with me to receive him, and I am anxious to study Mr. Macpherson's countenance when he realises he has walked in to confront a policeman. If you will then allow me to cross-examine him for a few moments, not after the manner of Scotland Yard, with a warning lest he incriminate himself, but in the free and easy fashion we adopt in Paris, I shall afterwards turn the case over to you to be dealt with at your discretion.'

'You have a wonderful flow of language, Monsieur Valmont,' was the officer's tribute to me. 'I shall be on hand at a quarter to six on Wednesday.'

'Meanwhile,' said I, 'kindly say nothing of this to anyone. We must arrange a complete surprise for Macpherson. That is essential. Please make no move in the matter at all until Wednesday night.'

Spenser Hale, much impressed, nodded acquiescence, and I took a polite leave of him.

The question of lighting is an important one in a room such as mine, and electricity offers a good deal of scope to the ingenious. Of this fact I have taken full advantage. I can manipulate the lighting of my room so that any particular spot is bathed in brilliancy, while the rest of the space remains in comparative gloom, and I arranged the lamps so that the full force of their rays impinged against the door that Wednesday evening, while I sat on one side of the table in semi-darkness and Hale sat on the other, with a light beating down on him from above which gave him the odd, sculptured look of a living statue of Justice, stern and triumphant. Anyone entering the room would first be dazzled by the light, and next would see the gigantic form of Hale in the full uniform of his order.

When Angus Macpherson was shown into this room he was quite visibly taken aback, and paused abruptly on the threshold, his gaze riveted on the huge policeman. I think his first purpose was to turn and run, but the door closed behind him, and he doubtless heard, as we all did, the sound of the bolt being thrust in its place, thus locking him in.

'I—I beg your pardon,' he stammered, 'I expected to meet Mr. Webster.'

As he said this, I pressed the button under my table, and was instantly enshrouded with light. A sickly smile overspread the countenance of Macpherson as he caught sight of me, and he made a very creditable attempt to carry off the situation with nonchalance.

'Oh, there you are, Mr. Webster; I did not notice you at first.'

It was a tense moment. I spoke slowly and impressively.

'Sir, perhaps you are not unacquainted with the name of Eugène Valmont.'

He replied brazenly,—

'I am sorry to say, sir, I never heard of the gentleman before.'

At this came a most inopportune 'Haw-haw' from that blockhead Spenser Hale, completely spoiling the dramatic situation I had elaborated with such thought and care. It is little wonder the English possess no drama, for they show scant appreciation of the sensational moments in life.

'Haw-haw,' brayed Spenser Hale, and at once reduced the emotional atmosphere to a fog of commonplace. However, what is a man to do? He must handle the tools with which it pleases Providence to provide him. I ignored Hale's untimely laughter.

'Sit down, sir,' I said to Macpherson, and he obeyed.

'You have called on Lord Semptam this week,' I continued sternly.

'Yes, sir.'

'And collected a pound from him?'

'Yes, sir.'

'In October, 1893, you sold Lord Semptam a carved antique table for fifty pounds?'

'Quite right, sir.'

'When you were here last week you gave me Ralph Summertrees as the name of a gentleman living in Park Lane. You knew at the time that this man was your employer?'

Macpherson was now looking fixedly at me, and on this occasion made no reply. I went on calmly:—

'You also knew that Summertrees, of Park Lane, was identical with Simpson, of Tottenham Court Road?'

'Well, sir,' said Macpherson, 'I don't exactly see what you're driving at, but it's quite usual for a man to carry on a business under an assumed name. There is nothing illegal about that.'

'We will come to the illegality in a moment, Mr. Macpherson. You, and Rogers, and Tyrrel, and three others, are confederates of this man Simpson.'

'We are in his employ; yes, sir, but no more confederates than clerks usually are.'

'I think, Mr. Macpherson, I have said enough to show you that the game is, what you call, up. You are now in the presence of Mr. Spenser Hale, from Scotland Yard, who is waiting to hear your confession.'

Here the stupid Hale broke in with his—

'And remember, sir, that anything you say will be—'

'Excuse me, Mr. Hale,' I interrupted hastily, 'I shall turn over the case to you in a very few moments, but I ask you to remember our compact, and to leave it for the present entirely in my hands. Now, Mr Macpherson, I want your confession, and I want it at once.'

'Confession? Confederates?' protested Macpherson with admirably simulated surprise. 'I must say you use extraordinary terms, Mr—Mr—What did you say the name was?'

'Haw-haw,' roared Hale. 'His name is Monsieur Valmont.'

'I implore you, Mr. Hale, to leave this man to me for a very few moments. Now, Macpherson, what have you to say in your defence?'

'Where nothing criminal has been alleged, Monsieur Valmont, I see no necessity for defence. If you wish me to admit that somehow you have acquired a number of details regarding our business, I am perfectly willing to do so, and to subscribe to their accuracy. If you will be good enough to let me know of what you complain, I shall endeavour to make the point clear to you if I can. There has evidently been some misapprehension, but for the life of me, without further explanation, I am as much in a fog as I was on my way coming here, for it is getting a little thick outside.'

Macpherson certainly was conducting himself with great discretion, and presented, quite unconsciously, a much more diplomatic figure than my friend, Spenser Hale, sitting stiffly opposite me. His tone was one of mild expostulation, mitigated by the intimation that all misunderstanding speedily would be cleared away. To outward view he offered a perfect picture of innocence, neither protesting too much nor too little. I had, however, another surprise in store for him, a trump card, as it were, and I played it down on the table.

'There!' I cried with vim, 'have you ever seen that sheet before?'

He glanced at it without offering to take it in his hand.

'Oh, yes,' he said, 'that has been abstracted from our file. It is what I call my visiting list.'

'Come, come, sir,' I cried sternly, 'you refuse to confess, but I warn you we know all about it. You never heard of Dr. Willoughby, I suppose?'

'Yes, he is the author of the silly pamphlet on Christian Science.'

'You are in the right, Mr. Macpherson; on Christian Science and Absent-Mindedness.'

'Possibly. I haven't read it for a long while.'

'Have you ever met this learned doctor, Mr. Macpherson?'

'Oh, yes. Dr. Willoughby is the pen-name of Mr. Summertrees. He believes in Christian Science and that sort of thing, and writes about it.'

'Ah, really. We are getting your confession bit by bit, Mr. Macpherson. I think it would be better to be quite frank with us.'

'I was just going to make the same suggestion to you, Monsieur Valmont. If you will tell me in a few words exactly what is your charge against either Mr. Summertrees or myself, I will know then what to say.'

'We charge you, sir, with obtaining money under false pretences, which is a crime that has landed more than one distinguished financier in prison.'

Spenser Hale shook his fat forefinger at me, and said,—

'Tut, tut, Valmont; we mustn't threaten, we mustn't threaten, you know;' but I went on without heeding him.

'Take for instance, Lord Semptam. You sold him a table for fifty pounds, on the instalment plan. He was to pay a pound a week, and in less than a year the debt was liquidated. But he is an absent-minded man, as all your clients are. That is why you came to me. I had answered the bogus Willoughby's advertisement. And so you kept on collecting and collecting for something more than three years. Now do you understand the charge?'

Mr. Macpherson's head during this accusation was held slightly inclined to one side. At first his face was clouded by the most clever imitation of anxious concentration of mind I had ever seen, and this was gradually cleared away by the dawn of awakening perception. When I had finished, an ingratiating smile hovered about his lips.

'Really, you know,' he said, 'that is rather a capital scheme. The absent-minded league, as one might call them. Most ingenious. Summertrees, if he had any sense of humour, which he hasn't, would be rather taken by the idea that his innocent fad for Christian Science had led him to be suspected of obtaining money under false pretences. But, really, there are no pretensions about the matter at all. As I understand it, I simply call and receive the money through the forgetfulness of the persons on my list, but where I think you would have both Summertrees and myself, if there was anything in your audacious theory, would be an indictment for conspiracy. Still, I quite see how the mistake arises. You have jumped to the conclusion that we sold nothing to Lord Semptam except that carved table three years ago. I have pleasure in pointing out to you that his lordship is a frequent customer of ours, and has had many things from us at one time or another. Sometimes he is in our debt; sometimes we are in his. We keep a sort of running contract with him by which he pays us a pound a week. He and several other customers deal on the same plan, and in return for an income that we can count upon, they get the first offer of anything in which they are supposed to be interested. As I have told you, we call these sheets in the office our visiting lists, but to make the visiting lists complete you need what we term our encyclopaedia. We call it that because it is in so many volumes; a volume for each year, running back I don't know how long. You will notice little figures here from time to time above the amount stated on this visiting list. These figures refer to the page of the encyclopaedia for the current year, and on that page is noted the new sale, and the amount of it, as it might be set down, say, in a ledger.'

'That is a very entertaining explanation, Mr. Macpherson. I suppose this encyclopaedia, as you call it, is in the shop at Tottenham Court Road?'

'Oh, no, sir. Each volume of the encyclopaedia is self-locking. These books contain the real secret of our business, and they are kept in the safe at Mr. Summertrees' house in Park Lane. Take Lord Semptam's account, for instance. You will find in faint figures under a certain date, 102. If you turn to page 102 of the encyclopaedia for that year, you will then see a list of what Lord Semptam has bought, and the prices he was charged for them. It is really a very simple matter. If you will allow me to use your telephone for a moment, I will ask Mr Summertrees, who has not yet begun dinner, to bring with him here the volume for 1893, and, within a quarter of an hour, you will be perfectly satisfied that everything is quite legitimate.'

I confess that the young man's naturalness and confidence staggered me, the more so as I saw by the sarcastic smile on Hale's lips that he did not believe a single word spoken. A portable telephone stood on the table, and as Macpherson finished his explanation, he reached over and drew it towards him. Then Spenser Hale interfered.

'Excuse me,' he said, 'I'll do the telephoning. What is the call number of Mr. Summertrees?'

'140 Hyde Park.'

Hale at once called up Central, and presently was answered from Park Lane. We heard him say,—

'Is this the residence of Mr. Summertrees? Oh, is that you, Podgers? Is Mr. Summertrees in? Very well. This is Hale. I am in Valmont's flat—Imperial Flats—you know. Yes, where you went with me the other day. Very well, go to Mr. Summertrees, and say to him that Mr Macpherson wants the encyclopaedia for 1893. Do you get that? Yes, encyclopaedia. Oh, he'll understand what it is. Mr. Macpherson. No, don't mention my name at all. Just say Mr. Macpherson wants the encyclopaedia for the year 1893, and that you are to bring it. Yes, you may tell him that Mr. Macpherson is at Imperial Flats, but don't mention my name at all. Exactly. As soon as he gives you the book, get into a cab, and come here as quickly as possible with it. If Summertrees doesn't want to let the book go, then tell him to come with you. If he won't do that, place him under arrest, and bring both him and the book here. All right. Be as quick as you can; we're waiting.'

Macpherson made no protest against Hale's use of the telephone; he merely sat back in his chair with a resigned expression on his face which, if painted on canvas, might have been entitled 'The Falsely Accused.' When Hale rang off, Macpherson said,—

'Of course you know your own business best, but if your man arrests Summertrees, he will make you the laughing-stock of London. There is such a thing as unjustifiable arrest, as well as getting money under false pretences, and Mr. Summertrees is not the man to forgive an insult. And then, if you will allow me to say so, the more I think over your absent-minded theory, the more absolutely grotesque it seems, and if the case ever gets into the newspapers, I am sure, Mr Hale, you'll experience an uncomfortable half-hour with your chiefs at Scotland Yard.'

'I'll take the risk of that, thank you,' said Hale stubbornly.

'Am I to consider myself under arrest?' inquired the young man.

'No, sir.'

'Then, if you will pardon me, I shall withdraw. Mr. Summertrees will show you everything you wish to see in his books, and can explain his business much more capably than I, because he knows more about it; therefore, gentlemen, I bid you good-night.'

'No you don't. Not just yet awhile,' exclaimed Hale, rising to his feet simultaneously with the young man.

'Then I am under arrest,' protested Macpherson.

'You're not going to leave this room until Podgers brings that book.'

'Oh, very well,' and he sat down again.

And now, as talking is dry work, I set out something to drink, a box of cigars, and a box of cigarettes. Hale mixed his favourite brew, but Macpherson, shunning the wine of his country, contented himself with a glass of plain mineral water, and lit a cigarette. Then he awoke my high regard by saying pleasantly as if nothing had happened,—

'While we are waiting, Monsieur Valmont, may I remind you that you owe me five shillings?'

I laughed, took the coin from my pocket, and paid him, whereupon he thanked me.

'Are you connected with Scotland Yard, Monsieur Valmont?' asked Macpherson, with the air of a man trying to make conversation to bridge over a tedious interval; but before I could reply, Hale blurted out,—

'Not likely!'

'You have no official standing as a detective, then, Monsieur Valmont?'

'None whatever,' I replied quickly, thus getting in my oar ahead of Hale.

'This is a loss to our country,' pursued this admirable young man, with evident sincerity.

I began to see I could make a good deal of so clever a fellow if he came under my tuition.

'The blunders of our police', he went on, 'are something deplorable. If they would but take lessons in strategy, say, from France, their unpleasant duties would be so much more acceptably performed, with much less discomfort to their victims.'

'France,' snorted Hale in derision, 'why, they call a man guilty there until he's proven innocent.'

'Yes, Mr. Hale, and the same seems to be the case in Imperial Flats. You have quite made up your mind that Mr. Summertrees is guilty, and will not be content until he proves his innocence. I venture to predict that you will hear from him before long in a manner that may astonish you.'

Hale grunted and looked at his watch. The minutes passed very slowly as we sat there smoking, and at last even I began to get uneasy. Macpherson, seeing our anxiety, said that when he came in the fog was almost as thick as it had been the week before, and that there might be some difficulty in getting a cab. Just as he was speaking the door was unlocked from the outside, and Podgers entered, bearing a thick volume in his hand. This he gave to his superior, who turned over its pages in amazement, and then looked at the back, crying,—

'Encyclopaedia of Sport, 1893! What sort of a joke is this, Mr. Macpherson?'

There was a pained look on Mr. Macpherson's face as he reached forward and took the book. He said with a sigh,—

'If you had allowed me to telephone, Mr. Hale, I should have made it perfectly plain to Summertrees what was wanted. I might have known this mistake was liable to occur. There is an increasing demand for out-of-date books of sport, and no doubt Mr. Summertrees thought this was what I meant. There is nothing for it but to send your man back to Park Lane and tell Mr. Summertrees that what we want is the locked volume of accounts for 1893, which we call the encyclopaedia. Allow me to write an order that will bring it. Oh, I'll show you what I have written before your man takes it,' he said, as Hale stood ready to look over his shoulder.

On my notepaper he dashed off a request such as he had outlined, and handed it to Hale, who read it and gave it to Podgers.

'Take that to Summertrees, and get back as quickly as possible. Have you a cab at the door?'

'Yes, sir.'

'Is it foggy outside?'

'Not so much, sir, as it was an hour ago. No difficulty about the traffic now, sir.'

'Very well, get back as soon as you can.'

Podgers saluted, and left with the book under his arm. Again the door was locked, and again we sat smoking in silence until the stillness was broken by the tinkle of the telephone. Hale put the receiver to his ear.

'Yes, this is the Imperial Flats. Yes. Valmont. Oh, yes; Macpherson is here. What? Out of what? Can't hear you. Out of print. What, the encyclopaedia's out of print? Who is that speaking? Dr. Willoughby; thanks.'

Macpherson rose as if he would go to the telephone, but instead (and he acted so quietly that I did not notice what he was doing until the thing was done), he picked up the sheet which he called his visiting list, and walking quite without haste, held it in the glowing coals of the fireplace until it disappeared in a flash of flame up the chimney. I sprang to my feet indignant, but too late to make even a motion outwards saving the sheet. Macpherson regarded us both with that self-deprecatory smile which had several times lighted up his face.

'How dared you burn that sheet?' I demanded.

'Because, Monsieur Valmont, it did not belong to you; because you do not belong to Scotland Yard; because you stole it; because you had no right to it; and because you have no official standing in this country. If it had been in Mr. Hale's possession I should not have dared, as you put it, to destroy the sheet, but as this sheet was abstracted from my master's premises by you, an entirely unauthorised person, whom he would have been justified in shooting dead if he had found you housebreaking and you had resisted him on his discovery, I took the liberty of destroying the document. I have always held that these sheets should not have been kept, for, as has been the case, if they fell under the scrutiny of so intelligent a person as Eugène Valmont, improper inferences might have been drawn. Mr. Summertrees, however, persisted in keeping them, but made this concession, that if I ever telegraphed him or telephoned him the word "Encyclopaedia", he would at once burn these records, and he, on his part, was to telegraph or telephone to me "The Encyclopaedia is out of print," whereupon I would know that he had succeeded.

'Now, gentlemen, open this door, which will save me the trouble of forcing it. Either put me formally under arrest, or cease to restrict my liberty. I am very much obliged to Mr. Hale for telephoning, and I have made no protest to so gallant a host as Monsieur Valmont is, because of the locked door. However, the farce is now terminated. The proceedings I have sat through were entirely illegal, and if you will pardon me, Mr. Hale, they have been a little too French to go down here in old England, or to make a report in the newspapers that would be quite satisfactory to your chiefs. I demand either my formal arrest, or the unlocking of that door.'

In silence I pressed a button, and my man threw open the door. Macpherson walked to the threshold, paused, and looked back at Spenser Hale, who sat there silent as a sphinx.

'Good-evening, Mr. Hale.'

There being no reply, he turned to me with the same ingratiating smile,—

'Good-evening, Monsieur Eugène Valmont,' he said, 'I shall give myself the pleasure of calling next Wednesday at six for my five shillings.'

6. The Ghost with the Club-Foot

Celebrated critics have written with scorn of what they call 'the long arm of coincidence' in fiction. Coincidence is supposed to be the device of a novelist who does not possess ingenuity enough to construct a book without it. In France our incomparable writers pay no attention to this, because they are gifted with a keener insight into real life than is the case with the British. The superb Charles Dickens, possibly as well known in France as he is wherever the English language is read, and who loved French soil and the French people, probably probed deeper into the intricacies of human character than any other novelist of modern times, and if you read his works, you will see that he continually makes use of coincidence. The experience that has come to me throughout my own strange and varied career convinces me that coincidence happens in real life with exceeding frequency, and this fact is especially borne in upon me when I set out to relate my conflict with the Rantremly ghost, which wrought startling changes upon the lives of two people, one an objectionable, domineering man, and the other a humble and crushed woman. Of course, there was a third person, and the consequences that came to him were the most striking of all, as you will learn if you do me the honour to read this account of the episode.

So far as coincidence is concerned, there was first the arrival of the newspaper clipping, then the coming of Sophia Brooks, and when that much-injured woman left my flat I wrote down this sentence on a sheet of paper:—

'Before the week is out, I predict that Lord Rantremly himself will call to see me.'

Next day my servant brought in the card of Lord Rantremly.

I must begin with the visit of Sophia Brooks, for though that comes second, yet I had paid no attention in particular to the newspaper clipping until the lady told her story. My man brought me a typewritten sheet of paper on which were inscribed the words:—

'Sophia Brooks, Typewriting and Translating Office, First Floor, No. 51 Beaumont Street, Strand, London, W.C.'

I said to my servant,—

'Tell the lady as kindly as possible that I have no typewriting work to give out, and that, in fact, I keep a stenographer and typewriting machine on the premises.'

A few moments later my man returned, and said the lady wished to see me, not about typewriting, but regarding a case in which she hoped to interest me. I was still in some hesitation about admitting her, for my transactions had now risen to a higher plane than when I was new to London. My expenses were naturally very heavy, and it was not possible for me, in justice to myself, to waste time in commissions from the poor, which even if they resulted successfully meant little money added to my banking account, and often nothing at all, because the client was unable to pay. As I remarked before, I possess a heart the most tender, and therefore must greatly to my grief, steel myself against the enlisting of my sympathy, which, alas! has frequently led to my financial loss. Still, sometimes the apparently poor are involved in matters of extreme importance, and England is so eccentric a country that one may find himself at fault if he closes his door too harshly. Indeed, ever since my servant, in the utmost good faith, threw downstairs the persistent and tattered beggar-man, who he learned later to his sorrow was actually his Grace the Duke of Ventnor, I have always cautioned my subordinates not to judge too hastily from appearances.

'Show the lady in,' I said, and there came to me, hesitating, backward, abashed, a middle-aged woman, dressed with distressing plainness, when one thinks of the charming costumes to be seen on a Parisian boulevard. Her subdued manner was that of one to whom the world had been cruel. I rose, bowed profoundly, and placed a chair at her disposal, with the air I should have used if my caller had been a Royal Princess. I claim no credit for this; it is of my nature. There you behold Eugène Valmont. My visitor was a woman. Voilà!

'Madam,' I said politely, 'in what may I have the pleasure of serving you?'

The poor woman seemed for the moment confused, and was, I feared, on the verge of tears, but at last she spoke, and said,—

'Perhaps you have read in the newspapers of the tragedy at Rantremly Castle?'

'The name, madam, remains in my memory, associated elusively with some hint of seriousness. Will you pardon me a moment?' and a vague thought that I had seen the castle mentioned either in a newspaper, or a clipping from one, caused me to pick up the latest bunch which had come from my agent. I am imbued with no vanity at all; still it is amusing to note what the newspapers say of one, and therefore I have subscribed to a clipping agency. In fact, I indulge in two subscriptions—one personal; the other calling for any pronouncement pertaining to the differences between England and France; for it is my determination yet to write a book on the comparative characteristics of the two people. I hold a theory that the English people are utterly incomprehensible to the rest of humanity, and this will be duly set out in my forthcoming volume.

I speedily found the clipping I was in search of. It proved to be a letter to the Times, and was headed: 'Proposed Destruction of Rantremly Castle'. The letter went on to say that this edifice was one of the most noted examples of Norman architecture in the north of England; that Charles II had hidden there for some days after his disastrous defeat at Worcester. Part of the castle had been battered down by Cromwell, and later it again proved the refuge of a Stuart when the Pretender made it a temporary place of concealment. The new Lord Rantremly, it seemed, had determined to demolish this ancient stronghold, so interesting architecturally and historically, and to build with its stones a modern residence. Against this act of vandalism the writer strongly protested, and suggested that England should acquire the power which France constantly exerts, in making an historical monument of an edifice so interwoven with the fortunes of the country.

'Well, madam,' I said, 'all this extract alludes to is the coming demolition of Rantremly Castle. Is that the tragedy of which you speak?'

'Oh no,' she exclaimed; 'I mean the death of the eleventh Lord Rantremly about six weeks ago. For ten years Lord Rantremly lived practically alone in the castle. Servants would not remain there because the place was haunted, and well it may be, for a terrible family the Rantremlys have been, and a cruel, as I shall be able to tell you. Up to a month and a half ago Lord Rantremly was waited on by a butler older than himself, and if possible, more wicked. One morning this old butler came up the stairs from the kitchen, with Lord Rantremly's breakfast on a silver tray, as was his custom. His lordship always partook of breakfast in his own room. It is not known how the accident happened, as the old servant was going up the stairs instead of coming down, but the steps are very smooth and slippery, and without a carpet; at any rate, he seems to have fallen from the top to the bottom, and lay there with a broken neck. Lord Rantremly, who was very deaf, seemingly did not hear the crash, and it is supposed that after ringing and ringing in vain, and doubtless working himself into a violent fit of temper—alas! too frequent an occurrence—the old nobleman got out of bed, and walked barefooted down the stair, coming at last upon the body of his ancient servant. There the man who arrived every morning to light the fires found them, the servant dead, and Lord Rantremly helpless from an attack of paralysis. The physicians say that only his eyes seemed alive, and they were filled with a great fear, and indeed that is not to be wondered at, after his wicked, wicked life. His right hand was but partially disabled, and with that he tried to scribble something which proved indecipherable. And so he died, and those who attended him at his last moments say that if ever a soul had a taste of future punishment before it left this earth, it was the soul of Lord Rantremly as it shone through those terror-stricken eyes.'

Here the woman stopped, with a catch in her breath, as if the fear of that grim death-bed had communicated itself to her. I interjected calmness into an emotional situation by remarking in a commonplace tone,—'And it is the present Lord Rantremly who proposes to destroy the Castle, I suppose?'

'Yes.'

'Is he the son of the late lord?'

'No; he is a distant relative. The branch of the family to which he belongs has been engaged in commerce, and, I believe, its members are very wealthy.'

'Well, madam, no doubt this is all extremely interesting, and rather gruesome. In what way are you concerned in these occurrences?'

'Ten years ago I replied to an advertisement, there being required one who knew shorthand, who possessed a typewriting machine and a knowledge of French, to act as secretary to a nobleman. I was at that time twenty-three years old, and for two years had been trying to earn my living in London through the typing of manuscript. But I was making a hard struggle of it, so I applied for this position and got it. There are in the library of Rantremly Castle many documents relating to the Stuart exile in France. His lordship wished these documents sorted and catalogued, as well as copies taken of each. Many of the letters were in the French language, and these I was required to translate and type. It was a sombre place of residence, but the salary was good, and I saw before me work enough to keep me busy for years. Besides this, the task was extremely congenial, and I became absorbed in it, being young and romantically inclined. Here I seemed to live in the midst of these wonderful intrigues of long ago. Documents passed through my hands whose very possession at one period meant capital danger, bringing up even now visions of block, axe, and masked headsman. It seemed strange to me that so sinister a man as Lord Rantremly, who, I had heard, cared for nothing but drink and gambling, should have desired to promote this historical research, and, indeed, I soon found he felt nothing but contempt for it. However, he had undertaken it at the instance of his only son, then a young man of my own age, at Oxford University.

'Lord Rantremly at that time was sixty-five years old. His countenance was dark, harsh, and imperious, and his language brutal. He indulged in frightful outbursts of temper, but he paid so well for service that there was no lack of it, as there has been since the ghost appeared some years ago. He was very tall, and of commanding appearance, but had a deformity in the shape of a club-foot, and walked with the halting step of those so afflicted. There were at that time servants in plenty at the castle, for although a tradition existed that the ghost of the founder of the house trod certain rooms, this ghost, it was said, never demonstrated its presence when the living representative of the family was a man with a club-foot. Tradition further affirmed that if this club-footed ghost allowed its halting footsteps to be heard while the reigning lord possessed a similar deformity, the conjunction foreshadowed the passing of title and estates to a stranger. The ghost haunted the castle only when it was occupied by a descendant whose two feet were normal. It seems that the founder of the house was a club-footed man, and this disagreeable peculiarity often missed one generation, and sometimes two, while at other times both father and son had club-feet, as was the case with the late Lord Rantremly and the young man at Oxford. I am not a believer in the supernatural, of course, but nevertheless it is strange that within the past few years everyone residing in the castle has heard the club-footed ghost, and now title and estates descend to a family that were utter strangers to the Rantremlys.'

'Well, madam, this also sounds most alluring, and were my time not taken up with affairs more material than those to which you allude, I should be content to listen all day, but as it is—' I spread my hands and shrugged my shoulders.

The woman with a deep sigh said,—

'I am sorry to have taken so long, but I wished you to understand the situation, and now I will come direct to the heart of the case. I worked alone in the library, as I told you, much interested in what I was doing. The chaplain, a great friend of Lord Rantremly's son, and, indeed, a former tutor of his, assisted me with the documents that were in Latin, and a friendship sprang up between us. He was an elderly man, and extremely unworldly. Lord Rantremly never concealed his scorn of this clergyman, but did not interfere with him because of the son.

'My work went on very pleasantly up to the time that Reginald, the heir of his lordship, came down from Oxford. Then began the happiest days of a life that has been otherwise full of hardships and distress. Reginald was as different as possible from his father. In one respect only did he bear any resemblance to that terrible old man, and this resemblance was the deformity of a club-foot, a blemish which one soon forgot when one came to know the gentle and high-minded nature of the young man. As I have said, it was at his instance that Lord Rantremly had engaged me to set in order those historical papers. Reginald became enthusiastic at the progress I had made, and thus the young nobleman, the chaplain, and myself continued our work together with ever-increasing enthusiasm.

'To cut short a recital which must be trying to your patience, but which is necessary if you are to understand the situation, I may say that our companionship resulted in a proposal of marriage to me, which I, foolishly, perhaps, and selfishly, it may be, accepted. Reginald knew that his father would never consent, but we enlisted the sympathy of the chaplain, and he, mild, unworldly man, married us one day in the consecrated chapel of the castle.

'As I have told you, the house at that time contained many servants, and I think, without being sure, that the butler, whom I feared even more than Lord Rantremly himself, got some inkling of what was going forward. But, be that as it may, he and his lordship entered the chapel just as the ceremony was finished, and there followed an agonising scene. His lordship flung the ancient chaplain from his place, and when Reginald attempted to interfere, the maddened nobleman struck his son full in the face with his clenched fist, and my husband lay as one dead on the stone floor of the chapel. By this time the butler had locked the doors, and had rudely torn the vestments from the aged, half-insensible clergyman, and with these tied him hand and foot. All this took place in a very few moments, and I stood there as one paralysed, unable either to speak or scream, not that screaming would have done me any good in that horrible place of thick walls. The butler produced a key, and unlocked a small, private door at the side of the chapel which led from the apartments of his lordship to the family pew. Then taking my husband by feet and shoulders, Lord Rantremly and the butler carried him out, locking the door, and leaving the clergyman and me prisoners in the chapel. The reverend old gentleman took no notice of me. He seemed to be dazed, and when at last I found my voice and addressed him, he merely murmured over and over texts of Scripture pertaining to the marriage service.

'In a short time I heard the key turn again in the lock of the private door, and the butler entered alone. He unloosened the bands around the clergyman's knees, escorted him out, and once more locked the door behind him. A third time that terrible servant came back, grasped me roughly by the wrist, and without a word dragged me with him, along a narrow passage, up a stair, and finally to the main hall, and so to my lord's private study, which adjoined his bedroom, and there on a table I found my typewriting machine brought up from the library.

'I have but the most confused recollection of what took place. I am not a courageous woman, and was in mortal terror both of Lord Rantremly and his attendant. His lordship was pacing up and down the room, and, when I came in, used the most unseemly language to me; then ordered me to write at his dictation, swearing that if I did not do exactly as he told me, he would finish his son, as he put it. I sat down at the machine, and he dictated a letter to himself, demanding two thousand pounds to be paid to me, otherwise I should claim that I was the wife of his son, secretly married. This, placing pen and ink before me, he compelled me to sign, and when I had done so, pleading to be allowed to see my husband, if only for a moment, I thought he was going to strike me, for he shook his fist in my face, and used words which were appalling to hear. That was the last I ever saw of Lord Rantremly, my husband, the clergyman, or the butler. I was at once sent off to London with my belongings, the butler himself buying my ticket, and flinging a handful of sovereigns into my lap as the train moved out.'

Here the woman stopped, buried her face in her hands, and began to weep.

'Have you done nothing about this for the past ten years?'

She shook her head.

'What could I do?' she gasped. 'I had little money, and no friends. Who would believe my story? Besides this, Lord Rantremly retained possession of a letter, signed by myself, that would convict me of attempted blackmail, while the butler would swear to anything against me.'

'You have no marriage certificate, of course?'

'No.'

'What has become of the clergyman?'

'I do not know.'

'And what of Lord Rantremly's son?'

'It was announced that he had gone on a voyage to Australia for his health in a sailing ship, which was wrecked on the African coast, and everyone on board lost.'

'What is your own theory?'

'Oh, my husband was killed by the blow given him in the chapel.'

'Madam, that does not seem credible. A blow from the fist seldom kills.'

'But he fell backwards, and his head struck the sharp stone steps at the foot of the altar. I know my husband was dead when the butler and his father carried him out.'

'You think the clergyman was also murdered?'

'I am sure of it. Both master and servant were capable of any crime or cruelty.'

'You received no letters from the young man?'

'No. You see, during our short friendship we were constantly together, and there was no need of correspondence.'

'Well, madam, what do you expect of me?'

'I hoped you would investigate, and find perhaps where Reginald and the clergyman are buried. I realise that I have no proof, but in that way my strange story will be corroborated.'

I leaned back in my chair and looked at her. Truth to tell, I only partially credited her story myself, and yet I was positive she believed every word of it. Ten years brooding on a fancied injustice by a woman living alone, and doubtless often in dire poverty, had mixed together the actual and the imaginary until now, what had possibly been an aimless flirtation on the part of the young man, unexpectedly discovered by the father, had formed itself into the tragedy which she had told me.

'Would it not be well,' I suggested, 'to lay the facts before the present Lord Rantremly?'

'I have done so,' she answered simply.

'With what result?'

'His lordship said my story was preposterous. In examining the late lord's private papers, he discovered the letter which I typed and signed. He said very coldly that the fact that I had waited until everyone who could corroborate or deny my story was dead, united with the improbability of the narrative itself, would very likely consign me to prison if I made public a statement so incredible.'

'Well, you know, madam, I think his lordship is right.'

'He offered me an annuity of fifty pounds, which I refused.'

'In that refusal, madam, I think you are wrong. If you take my advice, you will accept the annuity.'

The woman rose slowly to her feet.

'It is not money I am after,' she said, 'although, God knows, I have often been in sore need of it. But I am the Countess of Rantremly, and I wish my right to that name acknowledged. My character has been under an impalpable shadow for ten years. On several occasions mysterious hints have reached me that in some manner I left the castle under a cloud. If Lord Rantremly will destroy the letter which I was compelled to write under duress, and if he will give me written acknowledgment that there was nothing to be alleged against me during my stay in the castle, he may enjoy his money in peace for all of me. I want none of it.'

'Have you asked him to do this?'

'Yes. He refuses to give up or destroy the letter, although I told him in what circumstances it had been written. But, desiring to be fair, he said he would allow me a pound a week for life, entirely through his own generosity.'

'And this you refused?'

'Yes, I refused.'

'Madam, I regret to say that I cannot see my way to do anything with regard to what I admit is very unjust usage. We have absolutely nothing to go upon except your unsupported word. Lord Rantremly was perfectly right when he said no one would credit your story. I could not go down to Rantremly Castle and make investigations there. I should have no right upon the premises at all, and would get into instant trouble as an interfering trespasser. I beg you to heed my advice, and accept the annuity.'

Sophia Brooks, with that mild obstinacy of which I had received indications during her recital, slowly shook her head.

'You have been very kind to listen for so long,' she said, and then, with a curt 'Good-day!' turned and left the room. On the sheet of paper underneath her address, I wrote this prophecy: 'Before the week is out, I predict that Lord Rantremly himself will call to see me.'

Next morning, at almost the same hour that Miss Brooks had arrived the day before, the Earl of Rantremly's card was brought in to me.

His lordship proved to be an abrupt, ill-mannered, dapper business man; purse-proud, I should call him, as there was every reason he should be, for he had earned his own fortune. He was doubtless equally proud of his new title, which he was trying to live up to, assuming now and then a haughty, domineering attitude, and again relapsing into the keen, incisive manner of the man of affairs; shrewd financial sense waging a constant struggle with the glamour of an ancient name. I am sure he would have shone to better advantage either as a financier or as a nobleman, but the combination was too much for him. I formed an instinctive dislike to the man, which probably would not have happened had he been wearing the title for twenty years, or had I met him as a business man, with no thought of the aristocratic honour awaiting him. There seemed nothing in common between him and the former holder of the title. He had keen, ferrety eyes, a sharp financial nose, a thin-lipped line of mouth which indicated little of human kindness. He was short of stature, but he did not possess the club-foot, which was one advantage. He seated himself before I had time to offer him a chair, and kept on his hat in my presence, which he would not have done if he had either been a genuine nobleman or a courteous business man.

'I am Lord Rantremly,' he announced pompously, which announcement was quite unnecessary, because I held his card in my hand.

'Quite so, my lord. And you have come to learn whether or no I can lay the ghost in that old castle to the north which bears your name?'

'Well, I'm blessed!' cried his lordship, agape. 'How could you guess that?'

'Oh, it is not a guess, but rather a choice of two objects, either of which might bring you to my rooms. I chose the first motive because I thought you might prefer to arrange the second problem with your solicitor, and he doubtless told you that Miss Sophia Brooks's claim was absurd; that you were quite right in refusing to give up or destroy the typewritten letter she had signed ten years ago, and that it was weakness on your part, without consulting him, to offer her an annuity of fifty-two pounds a year.'

Long before this harangue was finished, which I uttered in an easy and nonchalant tone of voice, as if reciting something that everybody knew, his lordship stood on his feet again, staring at me like a man thunderstruck. This gave me the opportunity of exercising that politeness which his abrupt entrance and demeanour had forestalled. I rose, and bowing, said,—

'I pray you to be seated, my lord.'

He dropped into the chair, rather than sat down in it.

'And now,' I continued, with the utmost suavity, stretching forth my hand, 'may I place your hat on this shelf out of the way, where it will not incommode you during our discourse?'

Like a man in a dream, he took his hat from his head, and passively handed it to me, and after placing it in safety I resumed my chair with the comfortable feeling that his lordship and I were much nearer a plane of equality than when he entered the room.

'How about the ghost with a club-foot, my lord?' said I genially. 'May I take it that in the City, that sensible, commercial portion of London, no spirits are believed in except those sold over the bars?'

'If you mean,' began his lordship, struggling to reach his dignity once more, 'if you mean to ask if there is any man fool enough to place credit in the story of a ghost, I answer no. I am a practical man, sir. I now possess in the north property representing, in farming lands, in shooting rights, and what not, a locked-up capital of many a thousand pounds. As you seem to know everything, sir, perhaps you are aware that I propose to build a modern mansion on the estate.'

'Yes; I saw the letter in the Times.'

'Very well, sir. It has come to a fine pass if, in this country of law and the rights of property, a man may not do what he pleases with his own.'

'I think, my lord, cases may be cited where the decisions of your courts have shown a man may not do what he likes with his own. Nevertheless, I am quite certain that if you level Rantremly Castle with the ground, and build a modern mansion in its place, the law will not hinder you.'

'I should hope not, sir, I should hope not,' said his lordship gruffly. 'Nevertheless, I am not one who wishes to ride roughshod over public opinion.

'I am chairman of several companies which depend more or less on popular favour for success. I deplore unnecessary antagonism. Technically, I might assert my right to destroy this ancient stronghold tomorrow if I wished to do so, and if that right were seriously disputed, I should, of course, stand firm. But it is not seriously disputed. The British nation, sir, is too sensible a people to object to the removal of an antiquated structure that has long outlived its usefulness, and the erection of a mansion replete with all modern improvements would be a distinct addition to the country, sir. A few impertinent busybodies protest against the demolition of Rantremly Castle, but that is all.'

'Ah, then you do intend to destroy it?' I rejoined, and it is possible that a touch of regret was manifest in my tones.

'Not just at present; not until this vulgar clamour has had time to subside. Nevertheless, as a business man, I am forced to recognise that a large amount of unproductive capital is locked up in that property.'

'And why is it locked up?'

'Because of an absurd belief that the place is haunted. I could let it tomorrow at a good figure, if it were not for that rumour.'

'But surely sensible men do not pay any attention to such a rumour.'

'Sensible men may not, but sensible men are often married to silly women, and the women object. It is only the other day that I was in negotiation with Bates, of Bates, Sturgeon and Bates, a very wealthy man, quite able and willing to pay the price I demanded. He cared nothing about the alleged ghost, but his family absolutely refused to have anything to do with the place, and so the arrangement fell through.'

'What is your theory regarding this ghost, my lord?'

He answered me with some impatience.

'How can a sane man hold a theory about a ghost? I can, however, advance a theory regarding the noises heard in the castle. For years that place has been the resort of questionable characters.'

'I understand the Rantremly family is a very old one,' I commented innocently, but his lordship did not notice the innuendo.

'Yes, we are an old family,' he went on with great complacency. 'The castle, as perhaps you are aware, is a huge, ramshackle place, honeycombed underneath with cellars. I dare say in the old days some of these cellars and caves were the resort of smugglers, and the receptacle of their contraband wares, doubtless with the full knowledge of my ancestors, who, I regret to admit, as a business man, were not too particular in their respect for law. I make no doubt that the castle is now the refuge of a number of dangerous characters, who, knowing the legends of the place, frighten away fools by impersonating ghosts.'

'You wish me to uncover their retreat, then?'

'Precisely.'

'Could I get accommodation in the castle itself?'

'Lord bless you, no! Nor within two miles of it. You might secure bed and board at the porter's lodge, perhaps, or in the village, which is three miles distant.'

'I should prefer to live in the castle night and day, until the mystery is solved.'

'Ah, you are a practical man. That is a very sensible resolution. But you can persuade no one in that neighbourhood to bear you company. You would need to take some person down with you from London, and the chances are, that person will not stay long.'

'Perhaps, my lord, if you used your influence, the chief of police in the village might allow a constable to bear me company. I do not mind roughing it in the least, but I should like someone to prepare my meals, and to be on hand in case of a struggle, should your surmise concerning the ghost prove correct.'

'I regret to inform you,' said his lordship, 'that the police in that barbarous district are as superstitious as the peasantry. I, myself, told the chief constable my theory, and for six weeks he has been trying to run down the miscreants, who, I am sure, are making a rendezvous of the castle. Would you believe it, sir, that the constabulary, after a few nights' experience in the castle, threatened to resign in a body if they were placed on duty at Rantremly? They said they heard groans and shrieks, and the measured beat of a club-foot on the oaken floors. Perfectly absurd, of course, but there you are! Why, I cannot even get a charwoman or labourer to clear up the evidences of the tragedy which took place there six weeks ago. The beds are untouched, the broken china and the silver tray lie today at the foot of the stairway, and everything remains just as it was when the inquest took place.'

'Very well, my lord, the case presents many difficulties, and so, speaking as one business man to another, you will understand that my compensation must be correspondingly great.'

All the assumed dignity which straightened up this man whenever I addressed him as 'my lord', instantly fell from him when I enunciated the word 'compensation'. His eyes narrowed, and all the native shrewdness of an adept skinflint appeared in his face. I shall do him the justice to say that he drove the very best bargain he could with me, and I, on my part, very deftly concealed from him the fact that I was so much interested in the affair that I should have gone down to Rantremly for nothing rather than forgo the privilege of ransacking Rantremly Castle.

When the new earl had taken his departure, walking to the door with the haughty air of a nobleman, then bowing to me with the affability of a business man, I left my flat, took a cab, and speedily found myself climbing the stair to the first floor of 51 Beaumont Street, Strand. As I paused at the door on which were painted the words, 'S. Brooks, Stenography, Typewriting, Translation', I heard the rapid click-click of a machine inside. Knocking at the door the writing ceased, and I was bidden to enter. The room was but meagrely furnished, and showed scant signs of prosperity. On a small side-table, clean, but uncovered, the breakfast dishes, washed, but not yet put away, stood, and the kettle on the hob by the dying fire led me to infer that the typewriting woman was her own cook. I suspected that the awkward-looking sofa which partly occupied one side of the room, concealed a bed. By the lone front window stood the typewriting machine on a small stand, and in front of it sat the woman who had visited me the morning before. She was now gazing at me, probably hoping I was a customer, for there was no recognition in her eyes.

'Good-morning, Lady Rantremly,' was my greeting, which caused her to spring immediately to her feet, with a little exclamation of surprise.

'Oh,' she said at last, 'you are Monsieur Valmont. Excuse me that I am so stupid. Will you take a chair?'

'Thank you, madam. It is I who should ask to be excused for so unceremonious a morning call. I have come to ask you a question. Can you cook?'

The lady looked at me with some surprise, mingled perhaps with so much of indignation as such a mild person could assume. She did not reply, but, glancing at the kettle, and then turning towards the breakfast dishes on the table by the wall, a slow flush of colour suffused her wan cheeks.

'My lady,' I said at last, as the silence became embarrassing, 'you must pardon the impulse of a foreigner who finds himself constantly brought into conflict with prejudices which he fails to understand. You are perhaps offended at my question. The last person of whom I made that inquiry was the young and beautiful Madame la Comtesse de Valérie-Moberanne, who enthusiastically clapped her hands with delight at the compliment, and replied impulsively,—

'"Oh, Monsieur Valmont, let me compose for you an omelette which will prove a dream," and she did. One should not forget that Louis XVIII himself cooked the truffes à la purée d'ortolans that caused the Duc d'Escars, who partook of the royal dish, to die of an indigestion. Cooking is a noble, yes, a regal art. I am a Frenchman, my lady, and, like all my countrymen, regard the occupation of a cuisinière as infinitely superior to the manipulation of that machine, which is your profession, or the science of investigation, which is mine.'

'Sir,' she said, quite unmollified by my harangue, speaking with a lofty pride which somehow seemed much more natural than that so intermittently assumed by my recent visitor, 'Sir, have you come to offer me a situation as cook?'

'Yes, madam, at Rantremly Castle.'

'You are going there?' she demanded, almost breathlessly.

'Yes, madam, I leave on the ten o'clock train tomorrow morning. I am commissioned by Lord Rantremly to investigate the supposed presence of the ghost in that mouldering dwelling. I am allowed to bring with me whatever assistants I require, and am assured that no one in the neighbourhood can be retained who dare sleep in the castle. You know the place very well, having lived there, so I shall be glad of your assistance if you will come. If there is any person whom you can trust, and who is not afraid of ghosts, I shall be delighted to escort you both to Rantremly Castle tomorrow.'

'There is an old woman,' she said, 'who comes here to clear up my room, and do whatever I wish done. She is so deaf that she will hear no ghosts, and besides, monsieur, she can cook.'

I laughed in acknowledgment of this last sly hit at me, as the English say.

'That will do excellently,' I replied, rising, and placing a ten-pound note before her. 'I suggest, madam, that you purchase with this anything you may need. My man has instructions to send by passenger train a huge case of provisions, which should arrive there before us. If you could make it convenient to meet me at Euston Station about a quarter of an hour before the train leaves, we may be able to discover all you wish to know regarding the mystery of Rantremly Castle.'

Sophia Brooks accepted the money without demur, and thanked me. I could see that her thin hands were trembling with excitement as she put the crackling banknote into her purse.

Darkness was coming on next evening before we were installed in the grim building, which at first sight seemed more like a fortress than a residence. I had telegraphed from London to order a wagonette for us, and in this vehicle we drove to the police station, where I presented the written order from Lord Rantremly for the keys of the castle. The chief constable himself, a stolid, taciturn person, exhibited, nevertheless, some interest in my mission, and he was good enough to take the fourth seat in the wagonette, and accompany us through the park to the castle, returning in that conveyance to the village as nightfall approached, and I could not but notice that this grave official betrayed some uneasiness to get off before dusk had completely set in. Silent as he was, I soon learned that he entirely disbelieved Lord Rantremly's theory that the castle harboured dangerous characters, yet so great was his inherent respect for the nobility that I could not induce him to dispute with any decisiveness his lordship's conjecture. It was plain to be seen, however, that the chief constable believed implicitly in the club-footed ghost. I asked him to return the next morning, as I should spend the night in investigation, and might possibly have some questions to ask him, questions which none but the chief constable could answer. The good man promised, and left us rather hurriedly, the driver of the wagonette galloping his horse down the long, sombre avenue towards the village outside the gates.

I found Sophia Brooks but a doleful companion, and of very little assistance that evening. She seemed overcome by her remembrances. She had visited the library where her former work was done, doubtless the scene of her brief love episode, and she returned with red eyes and trembling chin, telling me haltingly that the great tome from which she was working ten years ago, and which had been left open on the solid library table, was still there exactly as she had placed it before being forced to abandon her work. For a decade apparently no one had entered that library. I could not but sympathise with the poor lady, thus revisiting, almost herself like a ghost, the haunted arena of her short happiness. But though she proved so dismal a companion, the old woman who came with her was a treasure. Having lived all her life in some semi-slum near the Strand, and having rarely experienced more than a summer's-day glimpse of the country, the long journey had delighted her, and now this rambling old castle in the midst of the forest seemed to realise all the dreams which a perusal of halfpenny fiction had engendered in her imagination. She lit a fire, and cooked for us a very creditable supper, bustling about the place, singing to herself in a high key.

Shortly after supper Sophia Brooks, exhausted as much by her emotions and memories as by her long journey of that day, retired to rest. After being left to myself I smoked some cigarettes, and finished a bottle of superb claret which stood at my elbow. A few hours before I had undoubtedly fallen in the estimation of the stolid constable when, instead of asking him questions regarding the tragedy, I had inquired the position of the wine cellar, and obtained possession of the key that opened its portal. The sight of bin after bin of dust-laden, cobwebbed bottles, did more than anything else to reconcile me to my lonely vigil. There were some notable vintages represented in that dismal cavern.

It was perhaps half-past ten or eleven o'clock when I began my investigations. I had taken the precaution to provide myself with half a dozen so-called electric torches before I left London. These give illumination for twenty or thirty hours steadily, and much longer if the flash is used only now and then. The torch is a thick tube, perhaps a foot and a half long, with a bull's-eye of glass at one end. By pressing a spring the electric rays project like the illumination of an engine's headlight. A release of the spring causes instant darkness. I have found this invention useful in that it concentrates the light on any particular spot desired, leaving all the surroundings in gloom, so that the mind is not distracted, even unconsciously, by the eye beholding more than is necessary at the moment. One pours a white light over any particular substance as water is poured from the nozzle of a hose.

The great house was almost painfully silent. I took one of these torches, and went to the foot of the grand staircase where the wicked butler had met his death. There, as his lordship had said, lay the silver tray, and nearby a silver jug, a pair of spoons, a knife and fork, and scattered all around the fragments of broken plates, cups, and saucers. With an exclamation of surprise at the stupidity of the researchers who had preceded me, I ran up the stair two steps at a time, turned to the right, and along the corridor until I came to the room occupied by the late earl. The coverings of the bed lay turned down just as they were when his lordship sprang to the floor, doubtless, in spite of his deafness, having heard faintly the fatal crash at the foot of the stairs. A great oaken chest stood at the head of the bed, perhaps six inches from the wall. Leaning against this chest at the edge of the bed inclined a small, round table, and the cover of the table had slipped from its sloping surface until it partly concealed the chest lid. I mounted on this carven box of old black oak and directed the rays of electric light into the chasm between it and the wall. Then I laughed aloud, and was somewhat startled to hear another laugh directly behind me. I jumped down on the floor again, and swung round my torch like a searchlight on a battleship at sea. There was no human presence in that chamber except myself. Of course, after my first moment of surprise, I realised that the laugh was but an echo of my own. The old walls of the old house were like sounding-boards. The place resembled an ancient fiddle, still tremulous with the music that had been played on it. It was easy to understand how a superstitious population came to believe in its being haunted; in fact, I found by experiment that if one trod quickly along the uncovered floor of the corridor, and stopped suddenly, one seemed to hear the sound of steps still going on.

I now returned to the stair head, and examined the bare polished boards with most gratifying results. Amazed at having learnt so much in such a short time, I took from my pocket the paper on which the dying nobleman had attempted to write with his half-paralysed hand. The chief constable had given the document to me, and I sat on the stair head, spread it out on the floor and scrutinised it. It was all but meaningless. Apparently two words and the initial letter of a third had been attempted. Now, however grotesque a piece of writing may be, you can sometimes decipher it by holding it at various angles, as those puzzles are solved which remain a mystery when gazed at direct. By partially closing the eyes you frequently catch the intent, as in those pictures where a human figure is concealed among the outlines of trees and leaves. I held the paper at arm's length, and with the electric light gleaming upon it, examined it at all angles, with eyes wide open, and eyes half closed. At last, inclining it away from me, I saw that the words were intended to mean, 'The Secret'. The secret, of course, was what he was trying to impart, but he had apparently got no further than the title of it. Deeply absorbed in my investigation, I was never more startled in my life than to hear in the stillness down the corridor the gasped words, 'Oh, God!'

I swept round my light, and saw leaning against the wall, in an almost fainting condition, Sophia Brooks, her eyes staring like those of a demented person, and her face white as any ghost's could have been. Wrapped round her was a dressing-gown. I sprang to my feet.

'What are you doing there?' I cried.

'Oh, is that you, Monsieur Valmont? Thank God, thank God! I thought I was going insane. I saw a hand, a bodiless hand, holding a white sheet of paper.'

'The hand was far from bodiless, madam, for it belonged to me. But why are you here? It must be near midnight.'

'It is midnight,' answered the woman; 'I came here because I heard my husband call me three times distinctly, "Sophia, Sophia, Sophia!" just like that.'

'Nonsense, madam,' I said, with an asperity I seldom use where the fair sex is concerned; but I began to see that this hysterical creature was going to be in the way during a research that called for coolness and calmness. I was sorry I had invited her to come. 'Nonsense, madam, you have been dreaming.'

'Indeed, Monsieur Valmont, I have not. I have not even been asleep, and I heard the words quite plainly. You must not think I am either mad or superstitious.'

I thought she was both, and next moment she gave further evidence of it, running suddenly forward, and clutching me by the arm.

'Listen! listen!' she whispered. 'You hear nothing?'

'Nonsense!' I cried again, almost roughly for my patience was at an end, and I wished to go on with my inquiry undisturbed.

'Hist, hist!' she whispered; 'listen!' holding up her finger. We both stood like statues, and suddenly I felt that curious creeping of the scalp which shows that even the most civilised among us have not yet eliminated superstitious fear. In the tense silence I heard someone slowly coming up the stair; I heard the halting step of a lame man. In the tension of the moment I had allowed the light to go out; now recovering myself, I pressed the spring, and waved its rays backward and forward down the stairway. The space was entirely empty, yet the hesitating footsteps approached us, up and up. I could almost have sworn on which step they last struck. At this interesting moment Sophia Brooks uttered a piercing shriek and collapsed into my arms, sending the electric torch rattling down the steps, and leaving us in impenetrable darkness. Really, I profess myself to be a gallant man, but there are situations which have a tendency to cause annoyance. I carried the limp creature cautiously down the stairs, fearing the fate of the butler, and at last got her into the dining-room, where I lit a candle, which gave a light less brilliant, perhaps, but more steady than my torch. I dashed some water in her face, and brought her to her senses, then uncorking another bottle of wine, I bade her drink a glassful, which she did.

'What was it?' she whispered.

'Madam, I do not know. Very possibly the club-footed ghost of Rantremly.'

'Do you believe in ghosts, Monsieur Valmont?'

'Last night I did not, but at this hour I believe in only one thing, which is that it is time everyone was asleep.'

She rose to her feet at this, and with a tremulous little laugh apologised for her terror, but I assured her that for the moment there were two panic-stricken persons at the stair head. Taking the candle, and recovering my electric torch, which luckily was uninjured by its roll down the incline the butler had taken, I escorted the lady to the door of her room, and bade her good-night, or rather, good-morning.

The rising sun dissipated a slight veil of mist which hung over the park, and also dissolved, so far as I was concerned, the phantoms which my imagination had conjured up at midnight. It was about half-past ten when the chief constable arrived. I flatter myself I put some life into that unimaginative man before I was done with him.

'What made you think that the butler was mounting the stair when he fell?'

'He was going up with my lord's breakfast,' replied the chief.

'Then did it not occur to you that if such were the case, the silver pitcher would not have been empty, and, besides the broken dishes, there would have been the rolls, butter, toast, or what not, strewn about the floor?'

The chief constable opened his eyes.

'There was no one else for him to bring breakfast to,' he objected.

'That is where you are very much mistaken. Bring me the boots the butler wore.'

'He did not wear boots, sir. He wore a pair of cloth slippers.'

'Do you know where they are?'

'Yes; they are in the boot closet.'

'Very well, bring them out, examine their soles, and sticking in one of them you will find a short sliver of pointed oak.'

The constable, looking slightly more stupefied than ever, brought the slippers, and I heard him ejaculate: 'Well, I'm blowed!' as he approached me. He handed me the slippers soles upward, and there, as I have stated, was the fragment of oak, which I pulled out.

'Now, if you take this piece of oak to the top of the stair, you will see that it fits exactly a slight interstice at the edge of one of the planks. It is as well to keep one's eyes open, constable, when investigating a case like this.'

'Well, I'm blowed!' he said again, as we walked up the stair together.

I showed him that the sliver taken from the slipper fitted exactly the interstice I had indicated.

'Now,' said I to him, 'the butler was not going up the stairs, but was coming down. When he fell headlong he must have made a fearful clatter. Shuffling along with his burden, his slipper was impaled by this sliver, and the butler's hands being full, he could not save himself, but went head foremost down the stair. The startling point, however, is the fact that he was not carrying my lord's breakfast to him, or taking it away from him, but that there is someone else in the castle for whom he was caterer. Who is that person?'

'I'm blessed if I know,' said the constable, 'but I think you are wrong there. He may not have been carrying up the breakfast, but he certainly was taking away the tray, as is shown by the empty dishes, which you have just a moment ago pointed out.'

'No, constable; when his lordship heard the crash, and sprang impulsively from his bed, he upset the little table on which had been placed his own tray;

it shot over the oaken chest at the head of the bed, and if you look between it and the wall you will find tray, dishes, and the remnants of a breakfast.'

'Well, I'm blessed!' exclaimed the chief constable once again.

'The main point of all this,' I went on calmly, 'is not the disaster to the butler, nor even the shock to his lordship, but the fact that the tray the serving man carried brought food to a prisoner, who probably for six weeks has been without anything to eat.'

'Then,' said the constable, 'he is a dead man.'

'I find it easier,' said I, 'to believe in a living man than in a dead man's ghost. I think I heard his footsteps at midnight, and they seemed to me the footsteps of a person very nearly exhausted. Therefore, constable, I have awaited your arrival with some impatience. The words his late lordship endeavoured to write on the paper were "The Secret". I am sure that the hieroglyphics with which he ended his effort stood for the letter "R", and if he finished his sentence, it would have stood: "The secret room". Now, constable, it is a matter of legend that a secret room exists in this castle. Do you know where it is?'

'No one knows where the secret room is, or the way to enter it, except the Lords of Rantremly.'

'Well, I can assure you that the Lord of Rantremly who lives in London knows nothing about it. I have been up and about since daylight, taking some rough measurements by stepping off distances. I surmise that the secret room is to the left of this stairway. Probably a whole suite of rooms exists, for there is certainly a stair coinciding with this one, and up that stair at midnight I heard a club-footed man ascend. Either that, or the ghost that has frightened you all, and, as I have said, I believe in the man.'

Here the official made the first sensible remark I had yet heard him utter:—

'If the walls are so thick that a prisoner's cry has not been heard, how could you hear his footsteps, which make much less noise?'

'That is very well put, constable, and when the same thing occurred to me earlier this morning, I began to study the architecture of this castle. In the first place, the entrance hall is double as wide at the big doors as it is near the stairway. If you stand with your back to the front door you will at once wonder why the builders made this curious and unnecessary right angle, narrowing the farther part of the hall to half its width. Then, as you gaze at the stair, and see that marvellous carved oak newel post standing like a monumental column, you guess, if you have any imagination, that the stairway, like the hall, was once double as wide as it is now. We are seeing only half of it, and doubtless we shall find a similar newel post within the hidden room. You must remember, constable, that these secret apartments are no small added chambers. Twice they have sheltered a king.'

The constable's head bent low at the mention of royalty. I saw that his insular prejudice against me and my methods was vanishing, and that he had come to look upon me with greater respect than was shown at first.

'The walls need not be thick to be impenetrable to sound. Two courses of brick, and a space between filled with deafening would do it. The secret apartment has been cut off from the rest of the house since the castle was built, and was not designed by the original architect. The partition was probably built in a hurry to fulfil a pressing need, and it was constructed straight up the middle of the stair, leaving the stout planks intact, each step passing thus, as it were, through the wall. Now, when a man walks up the secret stairway, his footsteps reverberate until one would swear that some unseen person was treading the visible boards on the outside.'

'By Jove!' said the constable, in an awed tone of voice.

'Now, officer, I have here a pickaxe and a crowbar. I propose that we settle the question at once.'

But to this proposal the constable demurred.

'You surely would not break the wall without permission from his lordship in London?'

'Constable, I suspect there is no Lord Rantremly in London, and that we will find a very emaciated but genuine Lord Rantremly within ten feet of us. I need not tell you that if you are instrumental in his immediate rescue without the exercise of too much red tape, your interests will not suffer because you the more speedily brought food and drink to the lord paramount of your district.'

'Right you are,' cried the constable, with an enthusiasm for which I was not prepared. 'Where shall we begin?'

'Oh, anywhere; this wall is all false from the entrance hall to some point up here. Still, as the butler was carrying the meal upstairs I think we shall save time if we begin on the landing.'

I found the constable's brawn much superior to his brain. He worked like a sansculotte on a barricade. When we had torn down part of the old oak panelling, which it seemed such a pity to mutilate with axe and crowbar, we came upon a brick wall, that quickly gave way before the strength of the constable. Then we pulled out some substance like matting, and found a second brick wall, beyond which was a further shell of panelling. The hole we made revealed nothing but darkness inside, and although we shouted, there was no answer. At last, when we had hewn it large enough for a man to enter, I took with me an electric torch, and stepped inside, the constable following, with crowbar still in hand. I learned, as I had surmised, that we were in the upper hall of a staircase nearly as wide as the one on the outside. A flash of the light showed a door corresponding with the fireplace of the upper landing, and this door not being locked, we entered a large room, rather dimly lighted by strongly barred windows that gave into a blind courtyard, of which there had been no indication heretofore, either outside or inside the castle. Broken glass crunched under our feet, and I saw that the floor was strewn with wine bottles whose necks had been snapped off to save the pulling of the cork. On a mattress at the farther end of the room lay a man with gray hair, and shaggy, unkempt iron-gray beard. He seemed either asleep or dead, but when I turned my electric light full on his face he proved to be still alive, for he rubbed his eyes languidly, and groaned, rather than spoke:—

'Is that you at last, you beast of a butler? Bring me something to eat, in

Heaven's name!'

I shook him wider awake. He seemed to be drowsed with drink, and was fearfully emaciated. When I got him on his feet, I noticed then the deformity that characterised one of them. We assisted him through the aperture, and down into the dining-room, where he cried out continually for something to eat, but when we placed food before him, he could scarcely touch it. He became more like a human being when he had drunk two glasses of wine, and I saw at once he was not as old as his gray hair seemed to indicate. There was a haunted look in his eyes, and he watched the door as if apprehensive.

'Where is that butler?' he asked at last.

'Dead,' I replied.

'Did I kill him?'

'No; he fell down the stairway and broke his neck.'

The man laughed harshly.

'Where is my father?'

'Who is your father?'

'Lord Rantremly.'

'He is dead also.'

'How came he to die?'

'He died from a stroke of paralysis on the morning the butler was killed.'

The rescued man made no comment on this, but turned and ate a little more of his food. Then he said to me:—

'Do you know a girl named Sophia Brooks?'

'Yes. For ten years she thought you dead.'

'Ten years! Good God, do you mean to say I've been in there only ten years? Why, I'm an old man. I must be sixty at least.'

'No; you're not much over thirty.'

'Is Sophia—' He stopped, and the haunted look came into his eyes again.

'No. She is all right, and she is here.'

'Here?'

'Somewhere in the grounds. I sent her and the servant out for a walk, and told them not to return till luncheon time, as the constable and I had something to do, and did not wish to be interrupted.'

The man ran his hand through his long tangled beard.

'I should like to be trimmed up a bit before I see Sophia,' he said.

'I can do that for you, my lord,' cried the constable.

'My lord?' echoed the man. 'Oh, yes, I understand. You are a policeman, are you not?'

'Yes, my lord, chief constable.'

'Then I shall give myself up to you. I killed the butler.'

'Oh, impossible, my lord!'

'No, it isn't. The beast, as I called him, was getting old, and one morning he forgot to close the door behind him. I followed him stealthily out, and at the head of the stair planted my foot in the small of his back, which sent him headlong. There was an infernal crash. I did not mean to kill the brute, but merely to escape, and just as I was about to run down the stairway, I was appalled to see my father looking like—looking like—well, I won't attempt to say what he looked like; but all my old fear of him returned. As he strode towards me, along the corridor, I was in such terror that I jumped through the secret door and slammed it shut.'

'Where is the secret door?' I asked.

'The secret door is that fireplace. The whole fireplace moves inward if you push aside the carved ornament at the left-hand corner.'

'Is it a dummy fireplace, then?'

'No, you may build a fire in it, and the smoke will escape up the chimney. But I killed the butler, constable, though not intending it, I swear.'

And now the constable shone forth like the real rough diamond he was.

'My lord, we'll say nothing about that. Legally you didn't do it. You see, there's been an inquest on the butler and the jury brought in the verdict, "Death by accident, through stumbling from the top of the stair." You can't go behind a coroner's inquest, my lord.'

'Indeed,' said his lordship, with the first laugh in which he had indulged for many a year. 'I don't want to go behind anything, constable, I've been behind that accursed chimney too long to wish any further imprisonment.'

7. The Liberation of Wyoming Ed

A man should present the whole truth to his doctor, his lawyer, or his detective. If a doctor is to cure, he must be given the full confidence of the patient; if a lawyer is to win a case he needs to know what tells against his client as well as the points in his favour; if a secret agent is to solve a mystery all the cards should be put on the table. Those who half trust a professional man need not be disappointed when results prove unsatisfactory.

A partial confidence reposed in me led to the liberation of a dangerous criminal, caused me to associate with a robber much against my own inclination, and brought me within danger of the law. Of course, I never pretend to possess that absolute confidence in the law which seems to be the birthright of every Englishman. I have lived too intimately among the machinery of the law, and have seen too many of its ghastly mistakes, to hold it in that blind esteem which appears to be prevalent in the British Isles.

There is a doggerel couplet which typifies this spirit better than anything I can write, and it runs:—

No rogue e'er felt the halter draw,

With a good opinion of the law.

Those lines exemplify the trend of British thought in this direction. If you question a verdict of their courts you are a rogue, and that ends the matter. And yet when an Englishman undertakes to circumvent the law, there is no other man on earth who will go to greater lengths. An amazing people! Never understandable by the sane of other countries.

It was entirely my own fault that I became involved in affairs which were almost indefensible and wholly illegal.

My client first tried to bribe me into compliance with his wishes, which bribe I sternly refused. Then he partially broke down and, quite unconsciously as I take it, made an appeal to the heart—a strange thing for an Englishman to do. My kind heart has ever been my most vulnerable point. We French are sentimentalists. France has before now staked its very existence for an ideal, while other countries fight for continents, cash, or commerce. You cannot pierce me with a lance of gold, but wave a wand of sympathy, and I am yours.

There waited upon me in my flat a man who gave his name as Douglas Sanderson, which may or may not have been his legitimate title. This was a question into which I never probed, and at the moment of writing am as ignorant of his true cognomen, if that was not it, as on the morning he first met me. He was an elderly man of natural dignity and sobriety, slow in speech, almost sombre in dress. His costume was not quite that of a professional man, and not quite that of a gentleman. I at once recognised the order to which he belonged, and a most difficult class it is to deal with. He was the confidential servant or steward of some ancient and probably noble family, embodying in himself all the faults and virtues, each a trifle accentuated, of the line he served, and to which, in order to produce him and his like, his father, grandfather, and great-grandfather had doubtless been attached. It is frequently the case that the honour of the house he serves is more dear to him than it is to the representative of that house. Such a man is almost always the repository of family secrets; a repository whose inviolability gold cannot affect, threats sway, or cajolery influence.

I knew, when I looked at him, that practically I was looking at his master, for I have known many cases where even the personal appearance of the two was almost identical, which may have given rise to the English phrase, 'Like master, like man.' The servant was a little more haughty, a little less kind, a little more exclusive, a little less confidential, a little more condescending, a little less human, a little more Tory, and altogether a little less pleasant and easy person to deal with.

'Sir,' he began, when I had waved him to a seat, 'I am a very rich man, and can afford to pay well for the commission I request you to undertake. To ask you to name your own terms may seem unbusinesslike, so I may say at the outset I am not a business man. The service I shall ask will involve the utmost secrecy, and for that I am willing to pay. It may expose you to risk of limb or liberty, and for that I am willing to pay. It will probably necessitate the expenditure of a large sum of money; that sum is at your disposal.'

Here he paused; he had spoken slowly and impressively, with a touch of arrogance in his tone which aroused to his prejudice, the combativeness latent in my nature. However, at this juncture I merely bowed my head, and replied in accents almost as supercilious as his own:—

'The task must either be unworthy or unwelcome. In mentioning first the compensation, you are inverting the natural order of things. You should state at the outset what you expect me to do, then, if I accept the commission, it is time to discuss the details of expenditure.'

Either he had not looked for such a reply, or was loath to open his budget, for he remained a few moments with eyes bent upon the floor, and lips compressed in silence. At last he went on, without change of inflection, without any diminution of that air of condescension, which had so exasperated me in the beginning, and which was preparing a downfall for himself that would rudely shake the cold dignity which encompassed him like a cloak:—

'It is difficult for a father to confide in a complete stranger the vagaries of a beloved son, and before doing so you must pledge your word that my communication will be regarded as strictly confidential.'

'Cela va sans dire.'

'I do not understand French,' said Mr. Sanderson severely, as if the use of the phrase were an insult to him.

I replied nonchalantly,—

'It means, as a matter of course; that goes without saying. Whatever you care to tell me about your son will be mentioned to no one. Pray proceed, without further circumlocution, for my time is valuable.'

'My son was always a little wild and impatient of control. Although everything he could wish was at his disposal here at home, he chose to visit America, where he fell into bad company. I assure you there is no real harm in the boy, but he became implicated with others, and has suffered severely for his recklessness. For five years he has been an inmate of a prison in the West.

He was known and convicted under the name of Wyoming Ed.'

'What was his crime?'

'His alleged crime was the stopping, and robbing, of a railway train.'

'For how long was he sentenced?'

'He was sentenced for life.'

'What do you wish me to do?'

'Every appeal has been made to the governor of the State in an endeavour to obtain a pardon. These appeals have failed. I am informed that if money enough is expended it may be possible to arrange my son's escape.'

'In other words, you wish me to bribe the officials of the jail?'

'I assure you the lad is innocent.'

For the first time a quiver of human emotion came into the old man's voice.

'Then, if you can prove that, why not apply for a new trial?'

'Unfortunately, the circumstances of the case, of his arrest on the train itself, the number of witnesses against him, give me no hope that a new trial would end in a different verdict, even if a new trial could be obtained, which I am informed is not possible. Every legal means tending to his liberation has already been tried.'

'I see. And now you are determined to adopt illegal means? I refuse to have anything to do with the malpractice you propose. You objected to a phrase in French, Mr. Sanderson, perhaps one in Latin will please you better. It is "Veritas praevalebit," which means, "Truth will prevail." I shall set your mind entirely at rest regarding your son. Your son at this moment occupies a humble, if honourable, position in the great house from which you came, and he hopes in time worthily to fill his father's shoes, as you have filled the shoes of your father. You are not a rich man, but a servant. Your son never was in America, and never will go there. It is your master's son, the heir to great

English estates, who became the Wyoming Ed of the Western prison. Even from what you say, I do not in the least doubt he was justly convicted, and you may go back to your master and tell him so. You came here to conceal the shameful secret of a wealthy and noble house; you may return knowing that secret has been revealed, and that the circumstances in which you so solemnly bound me to secrecy never existed. Sir, that is the penalty of lying.'

The old man's contempt for me had been something to be felt, so palpable was it. The armour of icy reserve had been so complete that actually I had expected to see him rise with undiminished hauteur, and leave the room, disdaining further parley with one who had insulted him. Doubtless that is the way in which his master would have acted, but even in the underling I was unprepared for the instantaneous crumbling of this monument of pomp and pride. A few moments after I began to speak in terms as severe as his own, his trembling hands grasped the arms of the chair in which he sat, and his ever-widening eyes, which came to regard me with something like superstitious dread as I went on, showed me I had launched my random arrow straight at the bull's-eye of fact. His face grew mottled and green rather than pale. When at last I accused him of lying, he arose slowly, shaking like a man with a palsy, but, unable to support himself erect, sank helplessly back into his chair again. His head fell forward to the table before him, and he sobbed aloud.

'God help me!' he cried, 'it is not my own secret I am trying to guard.'

I sprang to the door, and turned the key in the lock so that by no chance might we be interrupted; then, going to the sideboard, I poured him out a liqueur glass full of the finest Cognac ever imported from south of the Loire, and tapping him on the shoulder, said brusquely:—

'Here, drink this. The case is no worse than it was half an hour ago. I shall not betray the secret.'

He tossed off the brandy, and with some effort regained his self-control.

'I have done my errand badly,' he wailed. 'I don't know what I have said that has led you to so accurate a statement of the real situation, but I have been a blundering fool. God forgive me, when so much depended on my making no mistake.'

'Don't let that trouble you,' I replied; 'nothing you said gave me the slightest clue.'

'You called me a liar,' he continued, 'and that is a hard word from one man to another, but I would not lie for myself, and when I do it for one I revere and respect, my only regret is that I have done it without avail.'

'My dear sir,' I assured him, 'the fault is not with yourself at all. You were simply attempting the impossible. Stripped and bare, your proposal amounts to this. I am to betake myself to the United States, and there commit a crime, or a series of crimes, in bribing sworn officials to turn traitor to their duty and permit a convict to escape.'

'You put it very harshly, sir. You must admit that, especially in new countries, there is lawlessness within the law as well as outside of it. The real criminals in the robbery of the railway train escaped; my young master, poor fellow, was caught. His father, one of the proudest men in England, has grown prematurely old under the burden of this terrible dishonour. He is broken-hearted, and a dying man, yet he presents an impassive front to the world, with all the ancient courage of his race. My young master is an only son, and failing his appearance, should his father die, title and estate will pass to strangers. Our helplessness in this situation adds to its horror. We dare not make any public move. My old master is one with such influence among the governing class of this country, of which he has long been a member, that the average Englishman, if his name were mentioned, would think his power limitless. Yet that power he dare not exert to save his own son from a felon's life and death. However much he or another may suffer, publicity must be avoided, and this is a secret which cannot safely be shared with more than those who know it now.'

'How many know it?'

'In this country, three persons. In an American prison, one.'

'Have you kept up communication with the young man?'

'Oh, yes.'

'Direct?'

'No; through a third person. My young master has implored his father not to write to him direct.'

'This go-between, as we may call him, is the third person in the secret? Who is he?'

'That I dare not tell you!'

'Mr. Sanderson, it would be much better for your master and his son that you should be more open with me. These half-confidences are misleading. Has the son made any suggestion regarding his release?'

'Oh yes, but not the suggestion I have put before you. His latest letter was to the effect that within six months or so there is to be an election for governor. He proposes that a large sum of money shall be used to influence this election so that a man pledged to pardon him may sit in the governor's chair.'

'I see. And this sum of money is to be paid to the third person you referred to?'

'Yes.'

'May I take it that this third person is the one to whom various sums have been paid during the last five years in order to bribe the governor to pardon the young man?'

Sanderson hesitated a moment before answering; in fact, he appeared so torn between inclination and duty; anxious to give me whatever information I deemed necessary, yet hemmed in by the instructions with which his master had limited him, that at last I waved my hand and said:—

'You need not reply, Mr. Sanderson. That third party is the crux of the situation. I strongly suspect him of blackmail. If you would but name him, and allow me to lure him to these rooms, I possess a little private prison of my own into which I could thrust him, and I venture to say that before he had passed a week in darkness, on bread and water, we should have the truth about this business.'

Look you now the illogical nature of an Englishman! Poor old Sanderson, who had come to me with a proposal to break the law of America, seemed horror-stricken when I airily suggested the immuring of a man in a dungeon here in England. He gazed at me in amazement, then cast his eyes furtively about him, as if afraid a trap door would drop beneath him, and land him in my private oubliette.

'Do not be alarmed, Mr. Sanderson, you are perfectly safe. You are beginning at the wrong end of this business, and it seems to me five years of contributions to this third party without any result might have opened the eyes of even the most influential nobleman in England, not to mention those of his faithful servant.'

'Indeed, sir,' said Sanderson, 'I must confess to you that I have long had a suspicion of this third person, but my master has clung to him as his only hope, and if this third person were interfered with, I may tell you that he has deposited in London at some place unknown to us, a full history of the case, and if it should happen that he disappears for more than a week at a time, this record will be brought to light.'

'My dear Mr. Sanderson, that device is as old as Noah and his ark. I should chance that. Let me lay this fellow by the heels, and I will guarantee that no publicity follows.'

Sanderson sadly shook his head.

'Everything might happen as you say, sir, but all that would put us no further forward. The only point is the liberation of my young master. It is possible that the person unmentioned, whom we may call Number Three, has been cheating us throughout, but that is a matter of no consequence.'

'Pardon me, but I think it is. Suppose your young master here, and at liberty. This Number Three would continue to maintain the power over him which he seems to have held over his father for the last five years.'

'I think we can prevent that, sir, if my plan is carried out.'

'The scheme for bribing the American officials is yours, then?'

'Yes, sir, and I may say I am taking a great deal upon myself in coming to you. I am, in fact, disobeying the implied commands of my master, but I have seen him pay money, and very large sums of money, to this Number Three for the last five years and nothing has come of it. My master is an unsuspicious man, who has seen little of the real world, and thinks everyone as honest as himself.'

'Well, that may be, Mr. Sanderson, but permit me to suggest that the one who proposes a scheme of bribery, and, to put it mildly, an evasion of the law, shows some knowledge of the lower levels of this world, and is not quite in a position to plume himself on his own honesty.'

'I am coming to that, Mr. Valmont. My master knows nothing whatever of my plan. He has given me the huge sum of money demanded by Number Three, and he supposes that amount has been already paid over. As a matter of fact, it has not been paid over, and will not be until my suggestion has been carried out, and failed. In fact, I am about to use this money, all of it if necessary, if you will undertake the commission. I have paid Number Three his usual monthly allowance, and will continue to do so. I have told him my master has his proposal under consideration; that there are still six months to come and go upon, and that my master is not one who decides in a hurry.'

'Number Three says there is an election in six months for governor. What is the name of the state?'

Sanderson informed me. I walked to my book-case, and took down a current American Year Book, consulted it, and returned to the table.

'There is no election in that State, Mr. Sanderson, for eighteen months. Number Three is simply a blackmailer, as I have suspected.'

'Quite so, sir,' replied Sanderson, taking a newspaper from his pocket. 'I read in this paper an account of a man immured in a Spanish dungeon. His friends arranged it with the officials in this way: The prisoner was certified to have died, and his body was turned over to his relatives. Now, if that could be done in America, it would serve two purposes. It would be the easiest way to get my young master out of the jail. It would remain a matter of record that he had died, therefore there could be no search for him, as would be the case if he simply escaped. If you were so good as to undertake this task you might perhaps see my young master in his cell, and ask him to write to this Number Three with whom he is in constant communication, telling him he was very ill. Then you could arrange with the prison doctor that this person was informed of my young master's death.'

'Very well, we can try that, but a blackmailer is not so easily thrown off the scent. Once he has tasted blood he is a human man-eating tiger. But still, there is always my private dungeon in the background, and if your plan for silencing him fails, I guarantee that my more drastic and equally illegal method will be a success.'

It will be seen that my scruples concerning the acceptance of this commission, and my first dislike for the old man had both faded away during the conversation which I have set down in the preceding chapter. I saw him under the stress of deep emotion, and latterly began to realise the tremendous chances he was taking in contravening the will of his imperious master. If the large sum of money was long withheld from the blackmailer, Douglas Sanderson ran the risk of Number Three opening up communication direct with his master. Investigation would show that the old servant had come perilously near laying himself open to a charge of breach of trust, and even of defalcation with regard to the money, and all this danger he was heroically incurring for the unselfish purpose of serving the interests of his employer. During our long interview old Sanderson gradually became a hero in my eyes, and entirely in opposition to the resolution I had made at the beginning, I accepted his commission at the end of it.

Nevertheless, my American experiences are those of which I am least proud, and all I care to say upon the subject is that my expedition proved completely successful. The late convict was my companion on the Arontic, the first steamship sailing for England after we reached New York from the west. Of course I knew that two or three years roughing it in mining camps and on ranches, followed by five years in prison, must have produced a radical effect not only on the character, but also in the personal appearance of a man who had undergone these privations. Nevertheless, making due allowance for all this, I could not but fear that the ancient English family, of which this young man was the hope and pride, would be exceedingly disappointed with him. In spite of the change which grooming and the wearing of a civilised costume made, Wyoming Ed still looked much more the criminal than the gentleman. I considered myself in honour bound not to make any inquiries of the young man regarding his parentage. Of course, if I had wished to possess myself of the secret, I had but to touch a button under the table when Sanderson left my rooms in the Imperial Flats, which would have caused him to be shadowed and run to earth. I may also add that the ex-prisoner volunteered no particulars about himself or his family. Only once on board ship did he attempt to obtain some information from me as we walked up and down the deck together.

'You are acting for someone else, I suppose?' he said.

'Yes.'

'For someone in England?'

'Yes.'

'He put up the money, did he?'

'Yes.'

There was a pause, during which we took two or three turns in silence.

'Of course, there's no secret about it,' he said at last. 'I expected help from the other side, but Colonel Jim has been so mighty long about it, I was afraid he'd forgotten me.'

'Who is Colonel Jim?'

'Colonel Jim Baxter. Wasn't it him gave you the money?'

'I never heard of the man before.'

'Then who put up the coin?'

'Douglas Sanderson,' I replied, looking at him sidewise as I mentioned the name. It had apparently no effect upon him. He wrinkled his brow for a moment, then said:—

'Well, if you never heard of Baxter, I never heard of Sanderson.'

This led me to suspect that Douglas Sanderson did not give me his own name, and doubtless the address with which he had furnished me was merely temporary. I did not cable to him from America regarding the success of the expedition, because I could not be certain it was a success until I was safely on English ground, and not even then, to tell the truth. Anyhow, I wished to leave no trail behind me, but the moment the Arontic reached Liverpool, I telegraphed Sanderson to meet us that evening at my flat.

He was waiting for me when Wyoming Ed and I entered together. The old man was quite evidently in a state of nervous tension. He had been walking up and down the room with hands clenched behind his back, and now stood at the end farthest from the door as he heard us approach, with his hands still clasped behind his back, and an expression of deep anxiety upon his rugged face. All the electric lamps were turned on, and the room was bright as day.

'Have you not brought him with you?' he cried.

'Brought him with me?' I echoed. 'Here is Wyoming Ed!'

The old man glared at him for a moment or two stupefied, then moaned:—

'Oh, my God, my God, that is not the man!'

I turned to my short-haired fellow traveller.

'You told me you were Wyoming Ed!'

He laughed uneasily.

'Well, in a manner of speaking, so I have been for the last five years, but

I wasn't Wyoming Ed before that. Say, old man, are you acting for Colonel Jim Baxter?'

Sanderson, on whom a dozen years seemed to have fallen since we entered the room, appeared unable to speak, and merely shook his head in a hopeless sort of way.

'I say, boys,' ejaculated the ex-convict, with an uneasy laugh, half-comic, half-bewildered, 'this is a sort of mix-up, isn't it? I wish Colonel Jim was here to explain. I say, Boss,' he cried suddenly, turning sharp on me, 'this here misfit's not my fault. I didn't change the children in the cradle. You don't intend to send me back to that hell-hole, do you?'

'No,' I said, 'not if you tell the truth. Sit down.'

The late prisoner seated himself in a chair as close to the door as possible, hitching a little nearer as he sat down. His face had taken on a sharp, crafty aspect like that of a trapped rat.

'You are perfectly safe,' I assured him. 'Sit over here by the table. Even if you bolted through that door, you couldn't get out of this flat. Mr. Sanderson, take a chair.'

The old man sank despondently into the one nearest at hand. I pressed a button, and when my servant entered, I said to him:—

'Bring some Cognac and Scotch whisky, glasses, and two syphons of soda.'

'You haven't got any Kentucky or Canadian?' asked the prisoner, moistening his lips. The jail whiteness in his face was now accentuated by the pallor of fear, and the haunted look of the escaped convict glimmered from his eyes. In spite of the comfort I had attempted to bestow upon him, he knew that he had been rescued in mistake for another, and for the first time since he left prison realised he was among strangers, and not among friends. In his trouble he turned to the beverage of his native continent.

'Bring a bottle of Canadian whisky,' I said to the servant, who disappeared, and shortly returned with what I had ordered. I locked the door after him, and put the key in my pocket.

'What am I to call you?' I asked the ex-convict.

With a forced laugh he said; 'You can call me Jack for short.'

'Very well, Jack, help yourself,' and he poured out a very liberal glass of the Dominion liquor, refusing to dilute it with soda. Sanderson took Scotch, and I helped myself to a petit verre of brandy.

'Now, Jack,' I began, 'I may tell you plainly that if I wished to send you back to prison, I could not do so without incriminating myself. You are legally dead, and you have now a chance to begin life anew, an opportunity of which I hope you will take advantage. If you were to apply three weeks from today at the prison doors, they would not dare admit you. You are dead. Does that console you?'

'Well, squire, you can bet your bottom dollar I never thought I'd be pleased to hear I was dead, but I'm glad if it's all fixed as you say, and you can bet your last pair of boots I'm going to keep out of the jug in future if I can.'

'That's right. Now, I can promise that if you answer all my questions truthfully, you shall be given money enough to afford you a new beginning in life.'

'Good enough,' said Jack briefly.

'You were known in prison as Wyoming Ed?'

'Yes, sir.'

'If that was not your name, why did you use it?'

'Because Colonel Jim, on the train, asked me to do that. He said it would give him a pull in England to get me free.'

'Did you know Wyoming Ed?'

'Yes, sir, he was one of us three that held up the train.'

'What became of him?'

'He was shot dead.'

'By one of the passengers?'

There was silence, during which the old man groaned, and bowed his head. Jack was studying the floor. Then he looked up at me and said:—

'You don't expect me to give a pal away, do you?'

'As that pal has given you away for the last five years, it seems to me you need not show very much consideration for him.'

'I'm not so sure he did.'

'I am; but never mind that point. Colonel Jim Baxter shot Wyoming Ed and killed him. Why?'

'See here, my friend, you're going a little too fast. I didn't say that.'

He reached somewhat defiantly for the bottle from Canada.

'Pardon me,' I said, rising quietly, and taking possession of the bottle myself, 'it grieves me more than I can say to restrict my hospitality. I have never done such a thing in my life before, but this is not a drinking bout; it is a very serious conference. The whisky you have already taken has given you a bogus courage, and a false view of things. Are you going to tell me the truth, or are you not?'

Jack pondered on this for a while, then he said:—

'Well, sir, I'm perfectly willing to tell you the truth as far as it concerns myself, but I don't want to rat on a friend.'

'As I have said, he isn't your friend. He told you to take the name of Wyoming Ed, so that he might blackmail the father of Wyoming Ed. He has done so for the last five years, living in luxury here in London, and not moving a finger to help you. In fact, nothing would appal him more than to learn that you are now in this country. By this time he has probably received the news from the prison doctor that you are dead, and so thinks himself safe for ever.'

'If you can prove that to me—' said Jack.

'I can and will,' I interrupted; then, turning to Sanderson, I demanded:—

'When are you to meet this man next?'

'Tonight, at nine o'clock,' he answered. 'His monthly payment is due, and he is clamouring for the large sum I told you of.'

'Where do you meet him? In London?'

'Yes.'

'At your master's town house?'

'Yes.'

'Will you take us there, and place us where we can see him and he can't see us?'

'Yes. I trust to your honour, Mr. Valmont. A closed carriage will call for me at eight, and you can accompany me. Still, after all, Mr Valmont, we have no assurance that he is the same person this young man refers to.'

'I am certain he is. He does not go under the name of Colonel Jim Baxter, I suppose?'

'No.'

The convict had been looking from one to the other of us during this colloquy. Suddenly he drew his chair up closer to the table.

'Look here,' he said, 'you fellows are square, I can see that, and after all's said and done, you're the man that got me out of clink. Now, I half suspicion you're right about Colonel Jim, but, anyhow, I'll tell you exactly what happened. Colonel Jim was a Britisher, and I suppose that's why he and Wyoming Ed chummed together a good deal. We called Jim Baxter Colonel, but he never said he was a colonel or anything else. I was told he belonged to the British army, and that something happened in India so that he had to light out He never talked about himself, but he was a mighty taking fellow when he laid out to please anybody. We called him Colonel because he was so straight in the back, and walked as if he were on parade. When this young English tenderfoot came out, he and the Colonel got to be as thick as thieves, and the Colonel won a good deal of money from him at cards, but that didn't make any difference in their friendship. The Colonel most always won when he played cards, and perhaps that's what started the talk about why he left the British army. He was the luckiest beggar I ever knew in that line of business. We all met in the rush to the new goldfields, which didn't pan out worth a cent, and one after another of the fellows quit and went somewhere else. But Wyoming Ed, he held on, even after Colonel Jim wanted to quit. As long as there were plenty of fellows there, Colonel Jim never lacked money, although he didn't dig it out of the ground, but when the population thinned down to only a few of us, then we all struck hard times. Now, I knew Colonel Jim was going to hold up a train. He asked me if I would join him, and I said I would if there wasn't too many in the gang. I'd been into that business afore, and I knew there was no greater danger than to have a whole mob of fellows. Three men can hold up a train better than three dozen. Everybody's scared except the express messenger, and it's generally easy to settle him, for he stands where the light is, and we shoot from the dark. Well, I thought at first Wyoming Ed was on to the scheme, because when we were waiting in the cut to signal the train he talked about us going on with her to San Francisco, but I thought he was only joking. I guess that Colonel Jim imagined that when it came to the pinch, Ed wouldn't back out and leave us in the lurch: he knew Ed was as brave as a lion. In the cut, where the train would be on the up grade, the Colonel got his lantern ready, lit it, and wrapped a thin red silk handkerchief round it. The express was timed to pass up there about midnight, but it was near one o'clock when her headlight came in sight. We knew all the passengers would be in bed in the sleepers, and asleep in the smoking car and the day coach. We didn't intend to meddle with them. The Colonel had brought a stick or two of dynamite from the mines, and was going to blow open the safe in the express car, and climb out with whatever was inside.

'The train stopped to the signal all right, and the Colonel fired a couple of shots just to let the engineer know we meant business. The engineer and fireman at once threw up their hands, then the Colonel turns to Ed, who was standing there like a man pole-axed, and says to him mighty sharp, just like if he was speaking to a regiment of soldiers:—

'"You keep these two men covered. Come on, Jack!" he says to me, and then we steps up to the door of the express car, which the fellow inside had got locked and bolted. The Colonel fires his revolver in through the lock, then flung his shoulder agin the door, and it went in with a crash, which was followed instantly by another crash, for the little expressman was game right through. He had put out the lights and was blazing away at the open door. The Colonel sprang for cover inside the car, and wasn't touched, but one of the shots took me just above the knee, and broke my leg, so I went down in a heap. The minute the Colonel counted seven shots he was on to that express messenger like a tiger, and had him tied up in a hard knot before you could shake a stick. Then, quick as a wink he struck a match, and lit the lamp. Plucky as the express messenger was, he looked scared to death, and now, when Colonel Jim held a pistol to his head, he gave up the keys and told him how to open the safe. I had fallen back against the corner of the car, inside, and was groaning with Pain. Colonel Jim was scooping out the money from the shelves of the safe, and stuffing it into a sack.

'"Are you hurt, Jack?" he cried.

'"Yes, my leg's broke."

'"Don't let that trouble you; we'll get you clear all right. Do you think you can ride your horse?"

'"I don't believe it," said I. "I guess I'm done for," and I thought I was.

'Colonel Jim never looked round, but he went through that safe in a way that'd make your hair curl, throwing aside the bulky packages after tearing them open, taking only cash, which he thrust into a bag he had with him, till he was loaded like a millionaire. Then suddenly he swore, for the train began to move.

'"What is that fool Ed doing?" he shouted, rising to his feet.

'At that minute Ed came in, pistol in each hand, and his face ablaze.

'"Here, you cursed thief!" he cried, "I didn't come with you to rob a train!"

'"Get outside, you fool!" roared Colonel Jim, "get outside and stop this train. Jack has got his leg broke. Don't come another step towards me, or I'll kill you!"

'But Ed, he walked right on, Colonel Jim backing, then there was a shot that rang like cannon fire in the closed car, and Ed fell forward on his face. Colonel Jim turned him over, and I saw he had been hit square in the middle of the forehead. The train was now going at good speed, and we were already miles away from where our horses were tied. I never heard a man swear like Colonel Jim. He went through the pockets of Ed, and took a bundle of papers that was inside his coat, and this he stuffed away in his own clothes. Then he turned to me, and his voice was like a lamb.

'"Jack, old man," he said, "I can't help you. They're going to nab you, but not for murder. The expressman there will be your witness. It isn't murder anyhow on my part, but self-defence. You saw he was coming at me when I warned him to keep away."

'All this he said in a loud voice, for the expressman to hear, then he bent over to me and whispered:—

'"I'll get the best lawyer I can for you, but I'm afraid they're bound to convict you, and if they do, I will spend every penny of this money to get you free. You call yourself Wyoming Ed at the trial. I've taken all this man's papers so that he can't be identified. And don't you worry if you're sentenced, for remember I'll be working night and day for you, and if money can get you out, you'll be got out, because these papers will help me to get the cash required. Ed's folks are rich in England, so they'll fork over to get you out if you pretend to be him." With that he bade me good-bye and jumped off the train. There, gentlemen, that's the whole story just as it happened, and that's why I thought it was Colonel Jim had sent you to get me free.'

There was not the slightest doubt in my mind that the convict had told the exact truth, and that night, at nine o'clock, he identified Major Renn as the former Colonel Jim Baxter. Sanderson placed us in a gallery where we could see, but could not hear. The old man seemed determined that we should not know where we were, and took every precaution to keep us in the dark. I suppose he put us out of earshot, so that if the Major mentioned the name of the nobleman we should not be any the wiser. We remained in the gallery for some time after the major had left before Sanderson came to us again, carrying with him a packet.

'The carriage is waiting at the door,' he said, 'and with your permission, Monsieur Valmont, I will accompany you to your flat.'

I smiled at the old man's extreme caution, but he continued very gravely:—

'It is not that, Monsieur Valmont. I wish to consult with you, and if you will accept it, I have another commission to offer.'

'Well,' said I, 'I hope it is not so unsavoury as the last.' But to this the old man made no response.

There was silence in the carriage as we drove back to my flat. Sanderson had taken the precaution of pulling down the blinds of the carriage, which he need not have troubled to do, for, as I have said, it would have been the simplest matter in the world for me to have discovered who his employer was, if I had desired to know. As a matter of fact, I do not know to this day whom he represented.

Once more in my room with the electric light turned on, I was shocked and astonished to see the expression on Sanderson's face. It was the face of a man who would grimly commit murder and hang for it. If ever the thirst for vengeance was portrayed on a human countenance, it was on his that night. He spoke very quietly, laying down the packet before him on the table.

'I think you will agree with me,' he said, 'that no punishment on earth is too severe for that creature calling himself Major Renn.'

'I'm willing to shoot him dead in the streets of London tomorrow,' said the convict, 'if you give the word.'

Sanderson went on implacably: 'He not only murdered the son, but for five years has kept the father in an agony of sorrow and apprehension, bleeding him of money all the time, which was the least of his crimes. Tomorrow I shall tell my master that his son has been dead these five years, and heavy as that blow must prove, it will be mitigated by the fact that his son died an honest and honourable man. I thank you for offering to kill this vile criminal. I intend that he shall die, but not so quickly or so mercifully.'

Here he untied the packet, and took from it a photograph, which he handed to the convict.

'Do you recognise that?'

'Oh yes; that's Wyoming Ed as he appeared at the mine; as, indeed, he appeared when he was shot.'

The photograph Sanderson then handed to me.

'An article that I read about you in the paper, Monsieur Valmont, said you could impersonate anybody. Can you impersonate this young man?'

'There's no difficulty in that,' I replied.

'Then will you do this? I wish you two to dress in that fashion. I shall give you particulars of the haunts of Major Renn. I want you to meet him together and separately, as often as you can, until you drive him mad or to suicide. He believes you to be dead,' said Sanderson, addressing Jack. 'I am certain he has the news, by his manner tonight. He is extremely anxious to get the lump sum of money which I have been holding back from him. You may address him, for he will recognise your voice as well as your person, but Monsieur Valmont had better not speak, as then he might know it was not the voice of my poor young master. I suggest that you meet him first together, always at night. The rest I leave in your hands, Monsieur Valmont.'

With that the old man rose and left us.

Perhaps I should stop this narration here, for I have often wondered if practically I am guilty of manslaughter.

We did not meet Major Renn together, but arranged that he should encounter Jack under one lamp-post, and me under the next. It was just after midnight, and the streets were practically deserted. The theatre crowds had gone, and the traffic was represented by the last 'buses, and a belated cab now and then. Major Renn came down the steps of his club, and under the first lamp-post, with the light shining full upon him, Jack the convict stepped forth.

'Colonel Jim,' he said, 'Ed and I are waiting for you. There were three in that robbery, and one was a traitor. His dead comrades ask the traitor to join them.'

The Major staggered back against the lamp-post, drew his hand across his brow, and muttered, Jack told me afterwards:—

'I must stop drinking! I must stop drinking!'

Then he pulled himself together, and walked rapidly towards the next lamp-post. I stood out square in front of him, but made no sound. He looked at me with distended eyes, while Jack shouted out in his boisterous voice, that had no doubt often echoed over the plain:—

'Come on, Wyoming Ed, and never mind him. He must follow.'

Then he gave a war whoop. The Major did not turn round, but continued to stare at me, breathing stertorously like a person with apoplexy. I slowly pushed back my hat, and on my brow he saw the red mark of a bullet hole. He threw up his hands and fell with a crash to the pavement.

'Heart failure' was the verdict of the coroner's jury.

8. Lady Alicia's Emeralds

Many Englishmen, if you speak to them of me, indulge themselves in a detraction that I hope they will not mind my saying is rarely graced by the delicacy of innuendo with which some of my own countrymen attempt to diminish whatever merit I may possess. Mr. Spenser Hale, of Scotland Yard, whose lack of imagination I have so often endeavoured to amend, alas! without perceptible success, was good enough to say, after I had begun these reminiscences, which he read with affected scorn, that I was wise in setting down my successes, because the life of Methuselah himself would not be long enough to chronicle my failures, and the man to whom this was said replied that it was only my artfulness, a word of which these people are very fond; that I intended to use my successes as bait, issue a small pamphlet filled with them, and then record my failures in a thousand volumes, after the plan of a Chinese encyclopaedia, selling these to the public on the instalment plan.

Ah, well; it is not for me to pass comment on such observations. Every profession is marred by its little jealousies, and why should the coterie of detection be exempt? I hope I may never follow an example so deleterious, and thus be tempted to express my contempt for the stupidity with which, as all persons know, the official detective system of England is imbued. I have had my failures, of course. Did I ever pretend to be otherwise than human? But what has been the cause of these failures? They have arisen through the conservatism of the English. When there is a mystery to be solved, the average Englishman almost invariably places it in the hands of the regular police. When these good people are utterly baffled; when their big boots have crushed out all evidences that the grounds may have had to offer to a discerning mind; when their clumsy hands have obliterated the clues which are everywhere around them, I am at last called in, and if I fail, they say:—

'What could you expect; he is a Frenchman.'

This was exactly what happened in the case of Lady Alicia's emeralds. For two months the regular police were not only befogged, but they blatantly sounded the alarm to every thief in Europe. All the pawnbrokers' shops of Great Britain were ransacked, as if a robber of so valuable a collection would be foolish enough to take it to a pawnbroker. Of course, the police say that they thought the thief would dismantle the cluster, and sell the gems separately. As to this necklace of emeralds, possessing as it does an historical value which is probably in excess of its intrinsic worth, what more natural than that the holder of it should open negotiations with its rightful owner, and thus make more money by quietly restoring it than by its dismemberment and sale piecemeal? But such a fuss was kicked up, such a furore created, that it is no wonder the receiver of the goods lay low, and said nothing. In vain were all ports giving access to the Continent watched; in vain were the police of France, Belgium, and Holland warned to look out for this treasure. Two valuable months were lost, and then the Marquis of Blair sent for me! I maintain that the case was hopeless from the moment I took it up.

It may be asked why the Marquis of Blair allowed the regular police to blunder along for two precious months, but anyone who is acquainted with that nobleman will not wonder that he clung so long to a forlorn hope. Very few members of the House of Peers are richer than Lord Blair, and still fewer more penurious. He maintained that, as he paid his taxes, he was entitled to protection from theft; that it was the duty of the Government to restore the gems, and if this proved impossible, to make compensation for them. This theory is not acceptable in the English Courts, and while Scotland Yard did all it could during those two months, what but failure was to be expected from its limited mental equipment?

When I arrived at the Manor of Blair, as his lordship's very ugly and somewhat modern mansion house is termed, I was instantly admitted to his presence. I had been summoned from London by a letter in his lordship's own hand, on which the postage was not paid. It was late in the afternoon when I arrived, and our first conference was what might be termed futile. It was take up entirely with haggling about terms, the marquis endeavouring to beat down the price of my services to a sum so insignificant that it would barely have paid my expenses from London to Blair and back. Such bargaining is intensely distasteful to me. When the marquis found all his offers declined with a politeness which left no opening for anger on his part, he endeavoured to induce me to take up the case on a commission contingent upon my recovery of the gems, and as I had declined this for the twentieth time, darkness had come on, and the gong rang for dinner. I dined alone in the salle à manger, which appeared to be set apart for those calling at the mansion on business, and the meagreness of the fare, together with the indifferent nature of the claret, strengthened my determination to return to London as early as possible next morning.

When the repast was finished, the dignified servingman said gravely to me,—

'The Lady Alicia asks if you will be good enough to give her a few moments in the drawing-room, sir.'

I followed the man to the drawing-room, and found the young lady seated at the piano, on which she was strumming idly and absentmindedly, but with a touch, nevertheless, that indicated advanced excellence in the art of music. She was not dressed as one who had just risen from the dining table, but was somewhat grimly and commonly attired, looking more like a cottager's daughter than a member of the great country family. Her head was small, and crowned with a mass of jet black hair. My first impression on entering the large, rather dimly lighted room was unfavourable, but that vanished instantly under the charm of a manner so graceful and vivacious, that in a moment I seemed to be standing in a brilliant Parisian salon rather than in the sombre drawing-room of an English country house. Every poise of her dainty head; every gesture of those small, perfect hands; every modulated tone of the voice, whether sparkling with laughter or caressing in confidential speech, reminded me of the grandes dames of my own land. It was strange to find this perfect human flower amidst the gloomy ugliness of a huge square house built in the time of the Georges; but I remembered now that the Blairs are the English equivalent of the de Bellairs of France, from which family sprang the fascinating Marquise de Bellairs, who adorned the Court of Louis XIV. Here, advancing towards me, was the very reincarnation of the lovely marquise, who gave lustre to this dull world nearly three hundred years ago. Ah, after all, what are the English but a conquered race! I often forget this, and I trust I never remind them of it, but it enables one to forgive them much. A vivid twentieth-century marquise was Lady Alicia, in all except attire. What a dream some of our Parisian dress artists could have made of her, and here she was immured in this dull English house in the high-necked costume of a labourer's wife. 'Welcome, Monsieur Valmont,' she cried, in French of almost faultless intonation. 'I am so glad you have arrived,' and she greeted me as if I were an old friend of the family. There was nothing of condescension in her manner; no display of her own affability, while at the same time teaching me my place, and the difference in our stations of life. I can stand the rudeness of the nobility, but I detest their condescension. No; Lady Alicia was a true de Bellairs, and in my confusion, bending over her slender hand, I said:—

'Madame la Marquise, it is a privilege to extend to you my most respectful salutations.'

She laughed at this quietly, with the melting laugh of the nightingale.

'Monsieur, you mistake my title. Although my uncle is a marquis, I am but Lady Alicia.'

'Your pardon, my lady. For the moment I was back in that scintillating Court which surrounded Louis le Grand.'

'How flatteringly you introduce yourself, monsieur. In the gallery upstairs there is a painting of the Marquise de Bellairs, and when I show it to your tomorrow, you will then understand how charmingly you have pleased a vain woman by your reference to that beautiful lady. But I must not talk in this frivolous strain, monsieur. There is serious business to be considered, and I assure you I looked forward to your coming, monsieur, with the eagerness of Sister Anne in the tower of Bluebeard.'

I fear my expression as I bowed to her must have betrayed my gratification at hearing these words, so confidentially uttered by lips so sweet, while the glance of her lovely eyes was even more eloquent than her words. Instantly I felt ashamed of my chaffering over terms with her uncle; instantly I forgot my resolution to depart on the morrow; instantly I resolved to be of what assistance I could to this dainty lady. Alas! the heart of Valmont is today as unprotected against the artillery of inspiring eyes as ever it was in his extreme youth.

'This house,' she continued vivaciously, 'has been practically in a state of siege for two months. I could take none of my usual walks in the gardens, on the lawns, or through the park, without some clumsy policeman in uniform crashing his way through the bushes, or some detective in plain clothes accosting me and questioning me under the pretence that he was a stranger who had lost his way. The lack of all subtlety in our police is something deplorable. I am sure the real criminal might have passed through their hands a dozen times unmolested, while our poor innocent servants, and the strangers within our gates, were made to feel that the stern eye of the law was upon them night and day.'

The face of the young lady was an entrancing picture of animated indignation as she gave utterance to this truism which her countrymen are so slow to appreciate. I experienced a glow of satisfaction.

'Yes,' she went on, 'they sent down from London an army of stupid men, who have kept our household in a state of abject terror for eight long weeks, and where are the emeralds?'

As she suddenly asked this question, in the most Parisian of accents, with a little outward spreading of the hand, a flash of the eye, and a toss of the head, the united effect was something indescribable through the limitations of the language I am compelled to use.

'Well, monsieur, your arrival has put to flight this tiresome brigade, if, indeed, the word flight is not too airy a term to use towards a company so elephantine, and I assure you a sigh of relief has gone up from the whole household with the exception of my uncle. I said to him at dinner tonight: "If Monsieur Valmont had been induced to take an interest in the case at first, the jewels would have been in my possession long before tonight."'

'Ah, my lady,' I protested, 'I fear you overrate my poor ability. It is quite true that if I had been called in on the night of the robbery, my chances of success would have been infinitely greater than they are now.'

'Monsieur,' she cried, clasping her hands over her knees, and leaning towards me, hypnotising me with those starry eyes, 'Monsieur, I am perfectly confident that before a week is past you will restore the necklace, if such restoration be possible. I have said so from the first. Now, am I right in my conjecture, monsieur, that you come here alone; that you bring with you no train of followers and assistants?'

'That is as you have stated it, my lady.'

'I was sure of it. It is to be a contest of trained mentality in opposition to our two months' experience of brute force.'

Never before had I felt such ambition to succeed, and a determination not to disappoint took full possession of me. Appreciation is a needed stimulant, and here it was offered to me in its most intoxicating form. Ah, Valmont, Valmont, will you never grow old! I am sure that at this moment, if I had been eighty, the same thrill of enthusiasm would have tingled to my fingers' ends. Leave the Manor of Blair in the morning? Not for the Bank of France!

'Has my uncle acquainted you with particulars of the robbery?'

'No, madame, we were talking of other things.'

The lady leaned back in her low chair, partially closed her eyes, and breathed a deep sigh.

'I can well imagine the subject of your conversation,' she said at last. 'The Marquis of Blair was endeavouring to impose usurer's terms upon you, while you, nobly scorning such mercenary considerations, had perhaps resolved to leave us at the earliest opportunity.'

'I assure you, my lady, that if any such conclusion had been arrived at on my part, it vanished the moment I was privileged to set foot in this drawing-room.'

'It is kind of you to say that, monsieur, but you must not allow your conversation with my uncle to prejudice you against him. He is an old man now, and, of course, has his fancies. You would think him mercenary, perhaps, and so he is; but then so, too, am I. Oh, yes, I am, monsieur, frightfully mercenary. To be mercenary, I believe, means to be fond of money. No one is fonder of money than I, except, perhaps, my uncle; but you see, monsieur, we occupy the two extremes. He is fond of money to hoard it; I am fond of money to spend it. I am fond of money for the things it will buy. I should like to scatter largesse as did my fair ancestress in France. I should love a manor house in the country, and a mansion in Mayfair. I could wish to make everyone around me happy if the expenditure of money would do it.'

'That is a form of money-love, Lady Alicia, which will find a multitude of admirers.'

The girl shook her head and laughed merrily.

'I should so dislike to forfeit your esteem, Monsieur Valmont, and therefore I shall not reveal the depth of my cupidity. You will learn that probably from my uncle, and then you will understand my extreme anxiety for the recovery of these jewels.'

'Are they very valuable?'

'Oh, yes; the necklace consists of twenty stones, no one of which weighs less than an ounce. Altogether, I believe, they amount to two thousand four hundred or two thousand five hundred carats, and their intrinsic value is twenty pounds a carat at least. So you see that means nearly fifty thousand pounds, yet even this sum is trivial compared with what it involves. There is something like a million at stake, together with my coveted manor house in the country, and my equally coveted mansion in Mayfair. All this is within my grasp if I can but recover the emeralds.'

The girl blushed prettily as she noticed how intently I regarded her while she evolved this tantalising mystery. I thought there was a trace of embarrassment in her laugh when she cried:—

'Oh, what will you think of me when you understand the situation? Pray, pray do not judge me harshly. I assure you the position I aim at will be used for the good of others as well as for my own pleasure. If my uncle does not make a confidant of you, I must take my courage in both hands, and give you all the particulars, but not tonight. Of course, if one is to unravel such a snarl as that in which we find ourselves, he must be made aware of every particular, must he not?'

'Certainly, my lady.'

'Very well, Monsieur Valmont, I shall supply any deficiencies that occur in my uncle's conversation with you. There is one point on which I should like to warn you. Both my uncle and the police have made up their minds that a certain young man is the culprit. The police found several clues which apparently led in his direction, but they were unable to find enough to justify his arrest. At first I could have sworn he had nothing whatever to do with the matter, but lately I am not so sure. All I ask of you until we secure another opportunity of consulting together is to preserve an open mind. Please do not allow my uncle to prejudice you against him.'

'What is the name of this young man?'

'He is the Honourable John Haddon.'

'The Honourable! Is he a person who could do so dishonourable an action?'

The young lady shook her head.

'I am almost sure he would not, and yet one never can tell. I think at the present moment there are one or two noble lords in prison, but their crimes have not been mere vulgar housebreaking.'

'Am I to infer, Lady Alicia, that you are in possession of certain facts unknown either to your uncle or the police?'

'Yes.'

'Pardon me, but do these facts tend to incriminate the young man?' Again the young lady leaned back in her chair, and gazed past me, a wrinkle of perplexity on her fair brow. Then she said very slowly:—

'You will understand, Monsieur Valmont, how loath I am to speak against one who was formerly a friend. If he had been content to remain a friend, I am sure this incident, which has caused us all such worry and trouble, would never have happened. I do not wish to dwell on what my uncle will tell you was a very unpleasant episode, but the Honourable John Haddon is a poor man, and it is quite out of the question for one brought up as I have been to marry into poverty. He was very headstrong and reckless about the matter, and involved my uncle in a bitter quarrel while discussing it, much to my chagrin and disappointment. It is as necessary for him to marry wealth as it is for me to make a good match, but he could not be brought to see that. Oh, he is not at all a sensible young man, and my former friendship for him has ceased. Yet I should dislike very much to take any action that might harm him, therefore I have spoken to no one but you about the evidence that is in my hands, and this you must treat as entirely confidential, giving no hint to my uncle, who is already bitter enough against Mr. Haddon.'

'Does this evidence convince you that he stole the necklace?'

'No; I do not believe that he actually stole it, but I am persuaded he was an accessory after the fact—is that the legal term? Now, Monsieur Valmont, we will say no more tonight. If I talk any longer about this crisis, I shall not sleep, and I wish, assured of your help, to attack the situation with a very clear mind tomorrow.'

When I retired to my room, I found that I, too, could not sleep, although I needed a clear mind to face the problem of tomorrow. It is difficult for me to describe accurately the effect this interview had upon my mind, but to use a bodily simile, I may say that it seemed as if I had indulged too freely in a subtle champagne which appeared exceedingly excellent at first, but from which the exhilaration had now departed. No man could have been more completely under a spell than I was when Lady Alicia's eyes first told me more than her lips revealed; but although I had challenged her right to the title 'mercenary' when she applied it to herself, I could not but confess that her nonchalant recital regarding the friend who desired to be a lover jarred upon me. I found my sympathy extending itself to that unknown young man, on whom it appeared the shadow of suspicion already rested. I was confident that if he had actually taken the emeralds it was not at all from motives of cupidity. Indeed that was practically shown by the fact that Scotland Yard found itself unable to trace the jewels, which at least they might have done if the necklace had been sold either as a whole or dismembered. Of course, an emerald weighing an ounce is by no means unusual. The Hope emerald, for example, weighs six ounces, and the gem owned by the Duke of Devonshire measures two and a quarter inches through its greatest diameter. Nevertheless, such a constellation as the Blair emeralds was not to be disposed of very easily, and I surmised no attempt had been made either to sell them or to raise money upon them. Now that I had removed myself from the glamour of her presence, I began to suspect that the young lady, after all, although undoubtedly possessing the brilliancy of her jewels, retained also something of their hardness. There had been no expression of sympathy for the discarded friend; it was too evident, recalling what had latterly passed between us, that the young woman's sole desire, and a perfectly natural desire, was to recover her missing treasure. There was something behind all this which I could not comprehend, and I resolved in the morning to question the Marquis of Blair as shrewdly as he cared to allow. Failing him, I should cross-question the niece in a somewhat dryer light than that which had enshrouded me during this interesting evening. I care not who knows it, but I have been befooled more than once by a woman, but I determined that in clear daylight I should resist the hypnotising influence of those glorious eyes. Mon Dieu! Mon Dieu! how easy it is for me to make good resolutions when I am far from temptation!

It was ten o'clock next morning when I was admitted to the study of the aged bachelor Marquis of Blair. His keen eyes looked through and through me as I seated myself before him.

'Well!' he said shortly.

'My lord,' I began deliberately, 'I know nothing more of the case than was furnished by the accounts I have read in the newspapers. Two months have elapsed since the robbery. Every day that passed made the detection of the criminal more difficult. I do not wish to waste either my time or your money on a forlorn hope. If, therefore, you will be good enough to place me in possession of all the facts known to you, I shall tell you at once whether or not I can take up the case.'

'Do you wish me to give you the name of the criminal?' asked his lordship.

'Is his name known to you?' I asked in return.

'Yes. John Haddon stole the necklace.'

'Did you give that name to the police?'

'Yes.'

'Why didn't they arrest him?'

'Because the evidence against him is so small, and the improbability of his having committed the crime is so great.'

'What is the evidence against him?'

His lordship spoke with the dry deliberation of an aged solicitor.

'The robbery was committed on the night of October the fifth. All day there had been a heavy rain, and the grounds were wet. For reasons into which I do not care to enter, John Haddon was familiar with this house, and with our grounds. He was well known to my servants, and, unfortunately, popular with them, for he is an openhanded spendthrift. The estate of his elder brother, Lord Steffenham, adjoins my own to the west, and Lord Steffenham's house is three miles from where we sit. On the night of the fifth a ball was given in the mansion of Lord Steffenham, to which, of course, my niece and myself were invited, and which invitation we accepted. I had no quarrel with the elder brother. It was known to John Haddon that my niece intended to wear her necklace of emeralds. The robbery occurred at a time when most crimes of that nature are committed in country houses, namely, while we were at dinner, an hour during which the servants are almost invariably in the lower part of the house. In October the days are getting short. The night was exceptionally dark, for, although the rain had ceased, not a star was visible. The thief placed a ladder against the sill of one of the upper windows, opened it, and came in. He must have been perfectly familiar with the house, for there are evidences that he went direct to the boudoir where the jewel case had been carelessly left on my niece's dressing table when she came down to dinner. It had been taken from the strong room about an hour before. The box was locked, but, of course, that made no difference. The thief wrenched the lid off, breaking the lock, stole the necklace, and escaped by the way he came.'

'Did he leave the window open, and the ladder in place?'

'Yes.'

'Doesn't that strike you as very extraordinary?'

'No. I do not assert that he is a professional burglar, who would take all the precautions against the discovery that might have been expected from one of the craft. Indeed, the man's carelessness in going straight across the country to his brother's house, and leaving footsteps in the soft earth, easily traceable almost to the very boundary fence, shows he is incapable of any serious thought.'

'Is John Haddon rich?'

'He hasn't a penny.'

'Did you go to the ball that night?'

'Yes, I had promised to go.'

'Was John Haddon there?'

'Yes; but he appeared late. He should have been present at the opening, and his brother was seriously annoyed by his absence. When he did come he acted in a wild and reckless manner, which gave the guests the impression that he had been drinking. Both my niece and myself were disgusted with his actions.'

'Do you think your niece suspects him?'

'She certainly did not at first, and was indignant when I told her, coming home from the ball, that her jewels were undoubtedly in Steffenham House, even though they were not round her neck, but latterly I think her opinion has changed.'

'To go back a moment. Did any of your servants see him prowling about the place?'

'They all say they didn't, but I myself saw him, just before dusk, coming across the fields towards this house, and next morning we found the same footprints both going and coming. It seems to me the circumstantial evidence is rather strong.'

'It's a pity that no one but yourself saw him. What more evidence are the authorities waiting for?'

'They are waiting until he attempts to dispose of the jewels.'

'You think, then, he has not done so up to date?'

'I think he will never do so.'

'Then why did he steal them?'

'To prevent the marriage of my niece with Jonas Carter, of Sheffield, to whom she is betrothed. They were to be married early in the New Year.'

'My lord, you amaze me. If Mr. Carter and Lady Alicia are engaged, why should the theft of the jewels interfere with the ceremony?'

'Mr. Jonas Carter is a most estimable man, who, however, does not move in our sphere of life. He is connected with the steel or cutlery industry, and is a person of great wealth, rising upwards of a million, with a large estate in Derbyshire, and a house fronting Hyde Park, in London. He is a very strict business man, and both my niece and myself agree that he is also an eligible man. I myself am rather strict in matters of business, and I must admit that Mr. Carter showed a very generous spirit in arranging the preliminaries of the engagement with me. When Alicia's father died he had run through all the money he himself possessed or could borrow from his friends. Although a man of noble birth, I never liked him. He was married to my only sister. The Blair emeralds, as perhaps you know, descend down the female line. They, therefore, came to my niece from her mother. My poor sister had long been disillusioned before death released her from the titled scamp she had married, and she very wisely placed the emeralds in my custody to be held in trust for her daughter. They constitute my niece's only fortune, and would produce, if offered in London today, probably seventy-five or a hundred thousand pounds, although actually they are not worth so much. Mr. Jonas Carter very amiably consented to receive my niece with a dowry of only fifty thousand pounds, and that money I offered to advance, if I was allowed to retain the jewels as security. This was arranged between Mr. Carter and myself.'

'But surely Mr. Carter does not refuse to carry out his engagement because the jewels have been stolen?'

'He does. Why should he not?'

'Then surely you will advance the fifty thousand necessary?'

'I will not. Why should I?'

'Well, it seems to me,' said I, with a slight laugh, 'the young man has very definitely checkmated both of you.'

'He has, until I have laid him by the heels, which I am determined to do if he were the brother of twenty Lord Steffenhams.'

'Please answer one more question. Are you determined to put the young man in prison, or would you be content with the return of the emeralds intact?'

'Of course I should prefer to put him in prison and get the emeralds too, but if there's no choice in the matter, I must content myself with the necklace.'

'Very well, my lord, I will undertake the case.'

This conference had detained us in the study till after eleven, and then, as it was a clear, crisp December morning, I went out through the gardens into the park, that I might walk along the well-kept private road and meditate upon my course of action, or, rather, think over what had been said, because I could not map my route until I had heard the secret which the Lady Alicia promised to impart. As at present instructed, it seemed to me the best way to go direct to the young man, show him as effectively as I could the danger in which he stood, and, if possible, persuade him to deliver up the necklace to me. As I strolled along under the grand old leafless trees, I suddenly heard my name called impulsively two or three times, and turning round saw the Lady Alicia running toward me. Her cheeks were bright with Nature's rouge, and her eyes sparkled more dazzlingly than any emerald that ever tempted man to wickedness.

'Oh, Monsieur Valmont, I have been waiting for you, and you escaped me. Have you seen my uncle?'

'Yes, I have been with him since ten o'clock.'

'Well?'

'Your ladyship, that is exactly the word with which he accosted me.'

'Ah, you see an additional likeness between my uncle and myself this morning, then? Has he told you about Mr. Carter?'

'Yes.'

'So now you understand how important it is that I should regain possession of my property?'

'Yes,' I said with a sigh; 'the house near Hyde Park and the great estate in Derbyshire.'

She clapped her hands with glee, eyes and feet dancing in unison, as she capered along gaily beside me; a sort of skippety-hop, skippety-hop, sideways, keeping pace with my more stately step, as if she were a little girl of six instead of a young woman of twenty.

'Not only that!' she cried, 'but one million pounds to spend! Oh, Monsieur Valmont, you know Paris, and yet you do not seem to comprehend what that plethora of money means!'

'Well, madame, I have seen Paris, and I have seen a good deal of the world, but I am not so certain you will secure the million to spend.'

'What!' she cried, stopping short, that little wrinkle which betokened temper appearing on her brow. 'Do you think we won't get the emeralds then?'

'Oh, I am sure we will get the emeralds. I, Valmont, pledge you my word. But if Mr. Jonas Carter before marriage calls a halt upon the ceremony until your uncle places fifty thousand pounds upon the table, I confess I am very pessimistic about your obtaining control of the million afterwards.'

All her vivacity instantaneously returned.

'Pooh!' she cried, dancing round in front of me, and standing there directly in my path, so that I came to a stand. 'Pooh!' she repeated, snapping her fingers, with an inimitable gesture of that lovely hand. 'Monsieur Valmont, I am disappointed in you. You are not nearly so nice as you were last evening. It is very uncomplimentary in you to intimate that when once I am married to Mr. Jonas I shall not wheedle from him all the money I want. Do not rest your eyes on the ground; look at me and answer!'

I glanced up at her, and could not forbear laughing. The witchery of the wood was in that girl; yes, and a perceptible trace of the Gallic devil flickered in those enchanting eyes of hers. I could not help myself.

'Ah, Madame la Marquise de Bellairs, how jauntily you would scatter despair in that susceptible Court of Louis!'

'Ah, Monsieur Eugène de Valmont,' she cried, mimicking my tones, and imitating my manner with an exactitude that amazed me, 'you are once more my dear de Valmont of last night. I dreamed of you, I assure you I did, and now to find you in the morning, oh, so changed!' She clasped her little hands and inclined her head, while the sweet voice sank into a cadence of melancholy which seemed so genuine that the mocking ripple of a laugh immediately following was almost a shock to me. Where had this creature of the dull English countryside learnt all such frou-frou of gesture and tone?

'Have you ever seen Sarah Bernhardt?' I asked.

Now the average English woman would have inquired the genesis of so inconsequent a question, but Lady Alicia followed the trend of my thought, and answered at once as if my query had been quite expected:—

'Mais non, monsieur. Sarah the Divine! Ah, she comes with my million a year and the house of Hyde Park. No, the only inhabitant of my real world whom I have yet seen is Monsieur Valmont, and he, alas! I find so changeable. But now, adieu frivolity, we must be serious,' and she walked sedately by my side.

'Do you know where you are going, monsieur? You are going to church. Oh, do not look frightened, not to a service. I am decorating the church with holly, and you shall help me and get thorns in your poor fingers.'

The private road, which up to this time had passed through a forest, now reached a secluded glade in which stood a very small, but exquisite, church, evidently centuries older than the mansion we had left. Beyond it were gray stone ruins, which Lady Alicia pointed out to me as remnants of the original mansion that had been built in the reign of the second Henry. The church, it was thought, formed the private chapel to the hall, and it had been kept in repair by the various lords of the manor.

'Now hearken to the power of the poor, and learn how they may flout the proud marquis,' cried Lady Alicia gleefully; 'the poorest man in England may walk along this private road on Sunday to the church, and the proud marquis is powerless to prevent him. Of course, if the poor man prolongs his walk then is he in danger from the law of trespass. On weekdays, however, this is the most secluded spot on the estate, and I regret to say that my lordly uncle does not trouble it even on Sundays. I fear we are a degenerate race, Monsieur Valmont, for doubtless a fighting and deeply religious ancestor of mine built this church, and to think that when the useful masons cemented those stones together, Madame la Marquise de Bellairs or Lady Alicia were alike unthought of, and though three hundred years divide them this ancient chapel makes them seem, as one might say, contemporaries. Oh, Monsieur Valmont, what is the use of worrying about emeralds or anything else? As I look at this beautiful old church, even the house of Hyde Park appears as naught,' and to my amazement, the eyes that Lady Alicia turned upon me were wet.

The front door was unlocked, and we walked into the church in silence. Around the pillars holly and ivy were twined. Great armfuls of the shrubs had been flung here and there along the walls in heaps, and a step-ladder stood in one of the aisles, showing that the decoration of the edifice was not yet complete. A subdued melancholy had settled down on my erstwhile vivacious companion, the inevitable reaction so characteristic of the artistic temperament, augmented doubtless by the solemnity of the place, around whose walls in brass and marble were sculptured memorials of her ancient race.

'You promised,' I said at last, 'to tell me how you came to suspect—'

'Not here, not here,' she whispered; then rising from the pew in which she had seated herself, she said:—

'Let us go, I am in no mood for working this morning. I shall finish the decoration in the afternoon.'

We came out into the cool and brilliant sunlight again, and as we turned homeward, her spirits immediately began to rise.

'I am anxious to know,' I persisted, 'why you came to suspect a man whom at first you believed innocent.'

'I am not sure but I believe him innocent now, although I am forced to the conclusion that he knows where the treasure is.'

'What forces you to that conclusion, my lady?'

'A letter I received from himself, in which he makes a proposal so extraordinary that I am almost disinclined to accede to it, even though it leads to the discovery of my necklace. However, I am determined to leave no means untried if I receive the support of my friend, Monsieur Valmont.'

'My lady,' said I, with a bow, 'it is but yours to command, mine to obey. What were the contents of that letter?'

'Read it,' she replied, taking the folded sheet from her pocket, and handing it to me.

She had been quite right in characterising the note as an extraordinary epistle. The Honourable John Haddon had the temerity to propose that she should go through a form of marriage with him in the old church we had just left. If she did that, he said, it would console him for the mad love he felt for her. The ceremony would have no binding force upon her whatever, and she might bring whom she pleased to perform it. If she knew no one that she could trust, he would invite an old college chum, and bring him to the church next morning at half-past seven o'clock. Even if an ordained clergyman performed the ceremony, it would not be legal unless it took place between the hours of eight in the morning, and three in the afternoon. If she consented to this, the emeralds were hers once more.

'This is the proposal of a madman,' said I, as I handed back the letter.

'Well,' she replied, with a nonchalant shrug of her shoulders, 'he has always said he was madly in love with me, and I quite believe it. Poor young man, if this mummery were to console him for the rest of his life, why should I not indulge him in it?'

'Lady Alicia, surely you would not countenance the profaning of that lovely old edifice with a mock ceremonial? No man in his senses could suggest such a thing!'

Once more her eyes were twinkling with merriment.

'But the Honourable John Haddon, as I have told you, is not in his senses.'

'Then why should you indulge him?'

'Why? How can you ask such a question? Because of the emeralds. It is only a mad lark, after all, and no one need know of it. Oh, Monsieur Valmont,' she cried pleadingly, clasping her hands, and yet it seemed to me with an undercurrent of laughter in her beseeching tones, 'will you not enact for us the part of clergyman? I am sure if your face were as serious as it is at this moment, the robes of a priest would become you.'

'Lady Alicia, you are incorrigible. I am somewhat of a man of the world, yet I should not dare to counterfeit the sacred office, and I hope you but jest. In fact, I am sure you do, my lady.'

She turned away from me with a very pretty pout.

'Monsieur Valmont, your knighthood is, after all, but surface deep. 'Tis not mine to command, and yours to obey. Certainly I did but jest. John shall bring his own imitation clergyman with him.'

'Are you going to meet him tomorrow?'

'Certainly I am. I have promised. I must secure my necklace.'

'You seem to place great confidence in the belief that he will produce it.'

'If he fails to do so, then I play Monsieur Valmont as my trump card. But, monsieur, although you quite rightly refuse to comply with my first request, you will surely not reject my second. Please meet me tomorrow at the head of the avenue, promptly at a quarter-past seven, and escort me to the church.'

For a moment the negative trembled on my tongue's end, but she turned those enchanting eyes upon me, and I was undone.

'Very well,' I answered.

She seized both my hands, like a little girl overjoyed at a promised excursion.

'Oh, Monsieur Valmont, you are a darling! I feel as if I'd known you all my life. I am sure you will never regret having humoured me,' then added a moment later, 'if we get the emeralds.'

'Ah,' said I, 'if we get the emeralds.'

We were now within sight of the house, and she pointed out our rendezvous for the following day, and with that I bade her good-bye.

It was shortly after seven o'clock next morning when I reached the meeting-place. The Lady Alicia was somewhat long in coming, but when she arrived her face was aglow with girlish delight at the solemn prank she was about to play.

'You have not changed your mind?' I asked, after the morning's greetings.

'Oh, no, Monsieur Valmont,' she replied, with a bright laugh. 'I am determined to recover those emeralds.'

'We must hurry, Lady Alicia, or we will be too late.'

'There is plenty of time,' she remarked calmly; and she proved to be right, because when we came in sight of the church, the clock pointed to the hour of half-past seven.

'Now,' she said 'I shall wait here until you steal up to the church and look in through one of the windows that do not contain stained glass. I should not for the world arrive before Mr. Haddon and his friend are there.'

I did as requested, and saw two young men standing together in the centre aisle, one in the full robes of a clergyman, the other in his ordinary dress, whom I took to be the Honourable John Haddon. His profile was toward me, and I must admit there was very little of the madman in his calm countenance. His was a well-cut face, clean shaven, and strikingly manly. In one of the pews was seated a woman—I learned afterwards she was Lady Alicia's maid, who had been instructed to come and go from the house by a footpath, while we had taken the longer road. I returned and escorted Lady Alicia to the church, and there was introduced to Mr. Haddon and his friend, the made-up divine. The ceremony was at once performed, and, man of the world as I professed myself to be, this enacting of private theatricals in a church grated upon me. When the maid and I were asked to sign the book as witnesses, I said:—

'Surely this is carrying realism a little too far?'

Mr. Haddon smiled, and replied:—

'I am amazed to hear a Frenchman objecting to realism going to its full length, and speaking for myself, I should be delighted to see the autograph of the renowned Eugène Valmont,' and with that he proffered me the pen, whereupon I scrawled my signature. The maid had already signed, and disappeared. The reputed clergyman bowed us out of the church, standing in the porch to see us walk up the avenue.

'Ed,' cried John Haddon, I'll be back within half an hour, and we'll attend to the clock. You won't mind waiting?'

'Not in the least, dear boy. God bless you both,' and the tremor in his voice seemed to me carrying realism one step further still.

The Lady Alicia, with downcast head, hurried us on until we were within the gloom of the forest, and then, ignoring me, she turned suddenly to the young man, and placed her two hands on his shoulders.

'Oh, Jack, Jack!' she cried.

He kissed her twice on the lips.

'Jack, Monsieur Valmont insists on the emeralds.'

The young man laughed. Her ladyship stood fronting him with her back towards me. Tenderly the young man unfastened something at the throat of that high-necked dress of hers, then there was a snap, and he drew out an amazing, dazzling, shimmering sheen of green, that seemed to turn the whole bleak December landscape verdant as with a touch of spring. The girl hid her rosy face against him, and over her shoulder, with a smile, he handed me the celebrated Blair emeralds.

'There is the treasure, Valmont,' he cried, 'on condition that you do not molest the culprit.'

'Or the accessory after the fact,' gurgled Lady Alicia in smothered tones, with a hand clasping together her high-necked dress at the throat.

'We trust to your invention, Valmont, to deliver that necklace to uncle with a detective story that will thrill him to his very heart.'

We heard the clock strike eight; then a second later smaller bells chimed a quarter-past, and another second after they tinkled the half-hour. 'Hallo!' cried Haddon, 'Ed has attended to the clock himself. What a good fellow he is.'

'I looked at my watch; it was twenty-five minutes to nine.

'Was the ceremony genuine then?' I asked.

'Ah, Valmont,' said the young man, patting his wife affectionately on the shoulder, 'nothing on earth can be more genuine than that ceremony was.'

And the volatile Lady Alicia snuggled closer to him.

APPENDIX: TWO SHERLOCK HOLMES PARODIES

1. The Adventures of Sherlaw Kombs

(With apologies to Dr. Conan Doyle, and his excellent book,

'A Study in Scarlet'.)

I dropped in on my friend, Sherlaw Kombs, to hear what he had to say about the Pegram mystery, as it had come to be called in the newspapers. I found him playing the violin with a look of sweet peace and serenity on his face, which I never noticed on the countenances of those within hearing distance. I knew this expression of seraphic calm indicated that Kombs had been deeply annoyed about something. Such, indeed, proved to be the case, for one of the morning papers had contained an article eulogising the alertness and general competence of Scotland Yard. So great was Sherlaw Kombs's contempt for Scotland Yard that he never would visit Scotland during his vacations, nor would he ever admit that a Scotchman was fit for anything but export.

He generously put away his violin, for he had a sincere liking for me, and greeted me with his usual kindness.

'I have come,' I began, plunging at once into the matter on my mind, 'to hear what you think of the great Pegram mystery.'

'I haven't heard of it,' he said quietly, just as if all London were not talking of that very thing. Kombs was curiously ignorant on some subjects, and abnormally learned on others. I found, for instance, that political discussion with him was impossible, because he did not know who Salisbury and Gladstone were. This made his friendship a great boon.

'The Pegram mystery has baffled even Gregory, of Scotland Yard.'

'I can well believe it,' said my friend, calmly. 'Perpetual motion, or squaring the circle, would baffle Gregory. He's an infant, is Gregory.'

This was one of the things I always liked about Kombs. There was no professional jealousy in him, such as characterises so many other men.

He filled his pipe, threw himself into his deep-seated armchair, placed his feet on the mantel, and clasped his hands behind his head.

'Tell me about it,' he said simply.

'Old Barrie Kipson,' I began, 'was a stockbroker in the City. He lived in Pegram, and it was his custom to—'

'COME IN!' shouted Kombs, without changing his position, but with a suddenness that startled me. I had heard no knock.

'Excuse me,' said my friend, laughing, 'my invitation to enter was a trifle premature. I was really so interested in your recital that I spoke before I thought, which a detective should never do. The fact is, a man will be here in a moment who will tell me all about this crime, and so you will be spared further effort in that line.'

'Ah, you have an appointment. In that case I will not intrude,' I said, rising.

'Sit down; I have no appointment. I did not know until I spoke that he was coming.'

I gazed at him in amazement. Accustomed as I was to his extraordinary talents, the man was a perpetual surprise to me. He continued to smoke quietly, but evidently enjoyed my consternation.

'I see you are surprised. It is really too simple to talk about, but, from my position opposite the mirror, I can see the reflection of objects in the street. A man stopped, looked at one of my cards, and then glanced across the street. I recognised my card, because, as you know, they are all in scarlet. If, as you say, London is talking of this mystery, it naturally follows that he will talk of it, and the chances are he wished to consult with me upon it. Anyone can see that, besides there is always—Come in!

There was a rap at the door this time.

A stranger entered. Sherlaw Kombs did not change his lounging attitude.

'I wish to see Mr. Sherlaw Kombs, the detective,' said the stranger, coming within the range of the smoker's vision.

'This is Mr. Kombs,' I remarked at last, as my friend smoked quietly, and seemed half-asleep.

'Allow me to introduce myself,' continued the stranger, fumbling for a card.

'There is no need. You are a journalist,' said Kombs.

'Ah,' said the stranger, somewhat taken aback, 'you know me, then.'

'Never saw or heard of you in my life before.'

'Then how in the world—'

'Nothing simpler. You write for an evening paper. You have written an article slating the book of a friend. He will feel badly about it, and you will condole with him. He will never know who stabbed him unless I tell him.'

'The devil!' cried the journalist, sinking into a chair and mopping his brow, while his face became livid.

'Yes,' drawled Kombs, 'it is a devil of a shame that such things are done. But what would you? as we say in France.'

When the journalist had recovered his second wind he pulled himself together somewhat. 'Would you object to telling me how you know these particulars about a man you say you have never seen?'

'I rarely talk about these things,' said Kombs with great composure. 'But as the cultivation of the habit of observation may help you in your profession, and thus in a remote degree benefit me by making your paper less deadly dull, I will tell you. Your first and second fingers are smeared with ink, which shows that you write a great deal. This smeared class embraces two sub-classes, clerks or accountants, and journalists. Clerks have to be neat in their work.

The ink smear is slight in their case. Your fingers are badly and carelessly smeared; therefore, you are a journalist. You have an evening paper in your pocket. Anyone might have any evening paper, but yours is a Special Edition, which will not be on the streets for half-an-hour yet. You must have obtained it before you left the office, and to do this you must be on the staff. A book notice is marked with a blue pencil. A journalist always despises every article in his own paper not written by himself; therefore, you wrote the article you have marked, and doubtless are about to send it to the author of the book referred to. Your paper makes a speciality of abusing all books not written by some member of its own staff. That the author is a friend of yours, I merely surmised. It is all a trivial example of ordinary observation.'

'Really, Mr. Kombs, you are the most wonderful man on earth. You are the equal of Gregory, by Jove, you are.'

A frown marred the brow of my friend as he placed his pipe on the sideboard and drew his self-cocking six-shooter.

'Do you mean to insult me, sir?'

'I do not—I—I assure you. You are fit to take charge of Scotland Yard tomorrow ——. I am in earnest, indeed I am, sir.'

'Then heaven help you,' cried Kombs, slowly raising his right arm.

I sprang between them.

'Don't shoot!' I cried. 'You will spoil the carpet. Besides, Sherlaw, don't you see the man means well. He actually thinks it is a compliment!'

'Perhaps you are right,' remarked the detective, flinging his revolver carelessly beside his pipe, much to the relief of the third party. Then, turning to the journalist, he said, with his customary bland courtesy—

'You wanted to see me, I think you said. What can I do for you, Mr Wilber Scribbings?'

The journalist started.

'How do you know my name?' he gasped.

Kombs waved his hand impatiently.

'Look inside your hat if you doubt your own name.'

I then noticed for the first time that the name was plainly to be seen inside the top-hat Scribbings held upside down in his hands.

'You have heard, of course, of the Pegram mystery—'

'Tush,' cried the detective; 'do not, I beg of you, call it a mystery. There is no such thing. Life would become more tolerable if there ever was a mystery. Nothing is original. Everything has been done before. What about the Pegram affair?'

'The Pegram—ah—case has baffled everyone. The Evening Blade wishes you to investigate, so that it may publish the result. It will pay you well. Will you accept the commission?'

'Possibly. Tell me about the case.'

'I thought everybody knew the particulars. Mr. Barrie Kipson lived at Pegram. He carried a first-class season ticket between the terminus and that station. It was his custom to leave for Pegram on the 5.30 train each evening. Some weeks ago, Mr. Kipson was brought down by the influenza. On his first visit to the City after his recovery, he drew something like £300 in notes, and left the office at his usual hour to catch the 5.30. He was never seen again alive, as far as the public have been able to learn. He was found at Brewster in a first-class compartment on the Scotch Express, which does not stop between London and Brewster. There was a bullet in his head, and his money was gone, pointing plainly to murder and robbery.'

'And where is the mystery, might I ask?'

'There are several unexplainable things about the case. First, how came he on the Scotch Express, which leaves at six, and does not stop at Pegram? Second, the ticket examiners at the terminus would have turned him out if he showed his season ticket; and all the tickets sold for the Scotch Express on the 21st are accounted for. Third, how could the murderer have escaped? Fourth, the passengers in the two compartments on each side of the one where the body was found heard no scuffle and no shot fired.'

'Are you sure the Scotch Express on the 21st did not stop between London and Brewster?'

'Now that you mention the fact, it did. It was stopped by signal just outside of Pegram. There was a few moments' pause, when the line was reported clear, and it went on again. This frequently happens, as there is a branch line beyond Pegram.'

Mr. Sherlaw Kombs pondered for a few moments, smoking his pipe silently.

'I presume you wish the solution in time for tomorrow's paper?'

'Bless my soul, no. The editor thought if you evolved a theory in a month you would do well.'

'My dear sir, I do not deal with theories, but with facts. If you can make it convenient to call here tomorrow at 8 a.m. I will give you the full particulars early enough for the first edition. There is no sense in taking up much time over so simple an affair as the Pegram case. Good afternoon, sir.'

Mr. Scribbings was too much astonished to return the greeting. He left in a speechless condition, and I saw him go up the street with his hat still in his hand.

Sherlaw Kombs relapsed into his old lounging attitude, with his hands clasped behind his head. The smoke came from his lips in quick puffs at first, then at longer intervals. I saw he was coming to a conclusion, so I said nothing.

Finally he spoke in his most dreamy manner. 'I do not wish to seem to be rushing things at all, Whatson, but I am going out tonight on the Scotch Express. Would you care to accompany me?'

'Bless me!' I cried, glancing at the clock, 'you haven't time, it is after five now.'

'Ample time, Whatson—ample,' he murmured, without changing his position. 'I give myself a minute and a half to change slippers and dressing-gown for boots and coat, three seconds for hat, twenty-five seconds to the street, forty-two seconds waiting for a hansom, and then seven minutes at the terminus before the express starts. I shall be glad of your company.'

I was only too happy to have the privilege of going with him. It was most interesting to watch the workings of so inscrutable a mind. As we drove under the lofty iron roof of the terminus I noticed a look of annoyance pass over his face.

'We are fifteen seconds ahead of our time,' he remarked, looking at the big clock. 'I dislike having a miscalculation of that sort occur.'

The great Scotch Express stood ready for its long journey. The detective tapped one of the guards on the shoulder.

'You have heard of the so-called Pegram mystery, I presume?'

'Certainly, sir. It happened on this very train, sir.'

'Really? Is the same carriage still on the train?'

'Well, yes, sir, it is,' replied the guard, lowering his voice, 'but of course, sir, we have to keep very quiet about it. People wouldn't travel in it, else, sir.'

'Doubtless. Do you happen to know if anybody occupies the compartment in which the body was found?'

'A lady and gentleman, sir; I put 'em in myself, sir.'

'Would you further oblige me,' said the detective, deftly slipping half-a-sovereign into the hand of the guard, 'by going to the window and informing them in an offhand casual sort of way that the tragedy took place in that compartment?'

'Certainly, sir.'

We followed the guard, and the moment he had imparted his news there was a suppressed scream in the carriage. Instantly a lady came out, followed by a florid-faced gentleman, who scowled at the guard. We entered the now empty compartment, and Kombs said:

'We would like to be alone here until we reach Brewster.'

'I'll see to that, sir,' answered the guard, locking the door.

When the official moved away, I asked my friend what he expected to find in the carriage that would cast any light on the case.

'Nothing,' was his brief reply.

'Then why do you come?'

'Merely to corroborate the conclusions I have already arrived at.'

'And might I ask what those conclusions are?'

'Certainly,' replied the detective, with a touch of lassitude in his voice. 'I beg to call your attention, first, to the fact that this train stands between two platforms, and can be entered from either side. Any man familiar with the station for years would be aware of that fact. This shows how Mr. Kipson entered the train just before it started.'

'But the door on this side is locked,' I objected, trying it.

'Of course. But every season ticket-holder carries a key. This accounts for the guard not seeing him, and for the absence of a ticket. Now let me give you some information about the influenza. The patient's temperature rises several degrees above normal, and he has a fever. When the malady has run its course, the temperature falls to three-quarters of a degree below normal. These facts are unknown to you, I imagine, because you are a doctor.'

I admitted such was the case.

'Well, the consequence of this fall in temperature is that the convalescent's mind turns towards thoughts of suicide. Then is the time he should be watched by his friends. Then was the time Mr. Barrie Kipson's friends did not watch him. You remember the 21st, of course. No? It was a most depressing day. Fog all around and mud under foot. Very good. He resolves on suicide. He wishes to be unidentified, if possible, but forgets his season ticket. My experience is that a man about to commit a crime always forgets something.'

'But how do you account for the disappearance of the money?'

'The money has nothing to do with the matter. If he was a deep man, and knew the stupidness of Scotland Yard, he probably sent the notes to an enemy. If not, they may have been given to a friend. Nothing is more calculated to prepare the mind for self-destruction than the prospect of a night ride on the Scotch express, and the view from the windows of the train as it passes through the northern part of London is particularly conducive to thoughts of annihilation.'

'What became of the weapon?'

'That is just the point on which I wish to satisfy myself. Excuse me for a moment.'

Mr. Sherlaw Kombs drew down the window on the right hand side, and examined the top of the casing minutely with a magnifying glass. Presently he heaved a sigh of relief, and drew up the sash.

'Just as I expected,' he remarked, speaking more to himself than to me. 'There is a slight dent on the top of the window-frame. It is of such a nature as to be made only by the trigger of a pistol falling from the nerveless hand of a suicide. He intended to throw the weapon far out of the window, but had not the strength. It might have fallen into the carriage. As a matter of fact, it bounced away from the line and lies among the grass about ten feet six inches from the outside rail. The only question that now remains is where the deed was committed, and the exact present position of the pistol reckoned in miles from London, but that, fortunately, is too simple to even need explanation.'

'Great heavens, Sherlaw!' I cried. 'How can you call that simple? It seems to me impossible to compute.'

We were now flying over Northern London, and the great detective leaned back with every sign of ennui, closing his eyes. At last he spoke wearily:

'It is really too elementary, Whatson, but I am always willing to oblige a friend. I shall be relieved, however, when you are able to work out the ABC of detection for yourself, although I shall never object to helping you with the words of more than three syllables. Having made up his mind to commit suicide, Kipson naturally intended to do it before he reached Brewster, because tickets are again examined at that point. When the train began to stop at the signal near Pegram, he came to the false conclusion that it was stopping at Brewster. The fact that the shot was not heard is accounted for by the screech of the air-brake, added to the noise of the train. Probably the whistle was also sounding at the same moment. The train being a fast express would stop as near the signal as possible. The air-brake will stop a train in twice its own length. Call it three times in this case. Very well. At three times the length of this train from the signal-post towards London, deducting half the length of the train, as this carriage is in the middle, you will find the pistol.'

'Wonderful!' I exclaimed.

'Commonplace,' he murmured.

At this moment the whistle sounded shrilly, and we felt the grind of the air-brakes.

'The Pegram signal again,' cried Kombs, with something almost like enthusiasm. 'This is indeed luck. We will get out here, Whatson, and test the matter.'

As the train stopped, we got out on the right-hand side of the line. The engine stood panting impatiently under the red light, which changed to green as I looked at it. As the train moved on with increasing speed, the detective counted the carriages, and noted down the number. It was now dark, with the thin crescent of the moon hanging in the western sky throwing a weird half-light on the shining metals. The rear lamps of the train disappeared around a curve, and the signal stood at baleful red again. The black magic of the lonesome night in that strange place impressed me, but the detective was a most practical man. He placed his back against the signal-post, and paced up the line with even strides, counting his steps. I walked along the permanent way beside him silently. At last he stopped, and took a tape-line from his pocket. He ran it out until the ten feet six inches were unrolled, scanning the figures in the wan light of the new moon. Giving me the end, he placed his knuckles on the metals, motioning me to proceed down the embankment. I stretched out the line, and then sank my hand in the damp grass to mark the spot.

'Good God!' I cried, aghast, 'what is this?'

'It is the pistol,' said Kombs quietly.

It was!!

Journalistic London will not soon forget the sensation that was caused by the record of the investigations of Sherlaw Kombs, as printed at length in the next day's Evening Blade. Would that my story ended here. Alas! Kombs contemptuously turned over the pistol to Scotland Yard. The meddlesome officials, actuated, as I always hold, by jealousy, found the name of the seller upon it. They investigated. The seller testified that it had never been in the possession of Mr Kipson, as far as he knew. It was sold to a man whose description tallied with that of a criminal long watched by the police. He was arrested, and turned Queen's evidence in the hope of hanging his pal. It seemed that Mr. Kipson, who was a gloomy, taciturn man, and usually came home in a compartment by himself, thus escaping observation, had been murdered in the lane leading to his house. After robbing him, the miscreants turned their thoughts towards the disposal of the body—a subject that always occupies a first-class criminal mind before the deed is done. They agreed to place it on the line, and have it mangled by the Scotch Express, then nearly due. Before they got the body half-way up the embankment the express came along and stopped. The guard got out and walked along the other side to speak with the engineer. The thought of putting the body into an empty first-class carriage instantly occurred to the murderers. They opened the door with the deceased's key. It is supposed that the pistol dropped when they were hoisting the body in the carriage.

The Queen's evidence dodge didn't work, and Scotland Yard ignobly insulted my friend Sherlaw Kombs by sending him a pass to see the villains hanged.

2. The Adventure of the Second Swag

The time was Christmas Eve, 1904. The place was an ancient, secluded manor house, built so far back in the last century as 1896. It stood at the head of a profound valley; a valley clothed in ferns waist deep, and sombrely guarded by ancient trees, the remnants of a primeval forest. From this mansion no other human habitation could be seen. The descending road which connected the king's highway with the stronghold was so sinuous and precipitate that more than once the grim baronet who owned it had upset his automobile in trying to negotiate the dangerous curves. The isolated situation and gloomy architecture of this venerable mansion must have impressed the most casual observer with the thought that here was the spot for the perpetration of dark deeds, were it not for the fact that the place was brilliantly illuminated with electricity, while the silence was emphasised rather than disturbed by the monotonous, regular thud of an accumulator pumping the subtle fluid into a receptive dynamo situated in an outhouse to the east.

The night was gloomy and lowering after a day of rain, but the very sombreness of the scene made the brilliant stained glass windows stand out like the radiant covers of a Christmas number. Such was the appearance presented by 'Undershaw', the home of Sir Arthur Conan Doyle, situated among the wilds of Hindhead, some forty or fifty miles from London. Is it any wonder that at a spot so remote from civilisation law should be set at defiance, and that the one lone policeman who perambulates the district should tremble as he passed the sinister gates of 'Undershaw'?

In a large room of this manor house, furnished with a luxuriant elegance one would not have expected in a region so far from humanising influences, sat two men. One was a giant in stature, whose broad brow and smoothly shaven strong chin gave a look of determination to his countenance, which was further enhanced by the heavy black moustache which covered his upper lip. There was something of the dragoon in his upright and independent bearing. He had, in fact, taken part in more than one fiercely fought battle, and was a member of several military clubs; but it was plain to be seen that his ancestors had used war clubs, and had transmitted to him the physique of a Hercules. One did not need to glance at the Christmas number of the Strand, which he held in his hand, nor read the name printed there in large letters, to know that he was face to face with Sir Arthur Conan Doyle.

His guest, an older man, yet still in the prime of life, whose beard was tinged with grey, was of less warlike bearing than the celebrated novelist, belonging, as he evidently did, to the civil and not the military section of life. He had about him the air of a prosperous man of affairs, shrewd, good-natured, conciliatory, and these two strongly contrasting personages are types of the men to whom England owes her greatness. The reader of the Christmas number will very probably feel disappointed when he finds, as he supposes, merely two old friends sitting amicably in a country house after dinner. There seems, to his jaded taste, no element of tragedy in such a situation. These two men appear comfortable enough, and respectable enough. It is true that there is whisky and soda at hand, and the box of cigars is open, yet there are latent possibilities of passion under the most placid natures, revealed only to writers of fiction in our halfpenny Press. Let the reader wait, therefore, till he sees these two men tried as by fire under a great temptation, and then let him say whether even the probity of Sir George Newnes comes scathless from the ordeal.

'Have you brought the swag, Sir George?' asked the novelist, with some trace of anxiety in his voice.

'Yes,' replied the great publisher; 'but before proceeding to the count would it not be wise to give orders that will insure our being left undisturbed?'

'You are right,' replied Doyle, pressing an electric button.

When the servant appeared he said: 'I am not at home to anyone. No matter who calls, or what excuse is given, you must permit none to approach this room.'

When the servant had withdrawn, Doyle took the further precaution of thrusting in place one of the huge bolts which ornamented the massive oaken door studded with iron knobs. Sir George withdrew from the tail pocket of his dress coat two canvas bags, and, untying the strings, poured the rich red gold on the smooth table.

'I think you will find that right,' he said; 'six thousand pounds in all.'

The writer dragged his heavy chair nearer the table, and began to count the coins two by two, withdrawing each pair from the pile with his extended forefingers in the manner of one accustomed to deal with great treasure. For a time the silence was unbroken, save by the chink of gold, when suddenly a high-keyed voice outside penetrated even the stout oak of the huge door. The shrill exclamation seemed to touch a chord of remembrance in the mind of Sir George Newnes. Nervously he grasped the arms of his chair, sitting very bolt upright, muttering:—

'Can it be he, of all persons, at this time, of all times?'

Doyle glanced up with an expression of annoyance on his face, murmuring, to keep his memory green:—

'A hundred and ten, a hundred and ten, a hundred and ten.'

'Not at home?' cried the vibrant voice. 'Nonsense! Everybody is at home on Christmas Eve!'

'You don't seem to be,' he heard the servant reply.

'Me? Oh, I have no home, merely rooms in Baker Street. I must see your master, and at once.'

'Master left in his motor car half an hour ago to attend the county ball, given tonight, at the Royal Huts Hotel, seven miles away,' answered the servant, with that glib mastery of fiction which unconsciously comes to those who are members, even in a humble capacity, of a household devoted to the production of imaginative art.

'Nonsense, I say again,' came the strident voice. 'It is true that the tracks of an automobile are on the ground in front of your door, but if you will notice the markings of the puncture-proof belt, you will see that the automobile is returning and not departing. It went to the station before the last shower to bring back a visitor, and since its arrival there has been no rain. That suit of armour in the hall spattered with mud shows it to be the casing the visitor wore. The blazonry upon it of a pair of scissors above an open book resting upon a printing press, indicates that the wearer is first of all an editor; second, a publisher; and third, a printer. The only baronet in England whose occupation corresponds with this heraldic device is Sir George Newnes.'

'You forget Sir Alfred Harmsworth,' said the servant, whose hand held a copy of Answers.

If the insistent visitor was taken aback by this unlooked-for rejoinder, his manner showed no trace of embarrassment, and he went on unabashed.

'As the last shower began at ten minutes to six, Sir George must have arrived at Haslemere station on the 6.19 from Waterloo. He has had dinner, and at this moment is sitting comfortably with Sir Arthur Conan Doyle, doubtless in the front room, which I see is so brilliantly lighted. Now if you will kindly take in my card—'

'But I tell you,' persisted the perplexed servant, 'that the master left in his motor car for the county ball at the Royal—'

'Oh, I know, I know. There stands his suit of armour, too, newly blackleaded, whose coat of arms is a couchant typewriter on an automobile rampant.'

'Great heavens!' cried Sir George, his eyes brightening with the light of unholy desire, 'you have material enough there, Doyle, for a story in our January number. What do you say?'

A deep frown marred the smoothness of the novelist's brow.

'I say,' he replied sternly, 'that this man has been sending threatening letters to me. I have had enough of his menaces.'

'Then triply bolt the door,' advised Newnes, with a sigh of disappointment, leaning back in his chair.

'Do you take me for a man who bolts when his enemy appears?' asked Doyle fiercely, rising to his feet. 'No, I will unbolt. He shall meet the Douglas in his hall!'

'Better have him in the drawing-room, where it's warm,' suggested Sir George, with a smile, diplomatically desiring to pour oil on the troubled waters.

The novelist, without reply, spread a copy of that evening's Westminster Gazette over the pile of gold, strode to the door, threw it open, and said coldly:—

'Show the gentleman in, please.'

There entered to them a tall, self-possessed, calm man, with clean-shaven face, eagle eye, and inquisitive nose.

Although the visit was most embarrassing at that particular juncture, the natural courtesy of the novelist restrained him from giving utterance to his resentment of the intrusion, and he proceeded to introduce the bidden to the unbidden guest as if each were equally welcome.

'Mr. Sherlock Holmes, permit me to present to you Sir George—'

'It is quite superfluous,' said the newcomer, in an even voice of exasperating tenor, 'for I perceive at once that one who wears a green waistcoat must be a Liberal of strong Home Rule opinions, or the editor of several publications wearing covers of emerald hue. The shamrock necktie, in addition to the waistcoat, indicates that the gentleman before me is both, and so I take it for granted that this is Sir George Newnes. How is your circulation, Sir George?'

'Rapidly rising,' replied the editor.

'I am glad of that,' asserted the intruder, suavely, 'and can assure you that the temperature outside is as rapidly falling.'

The great detective spread his hands before the glowing electric fire, and rubbed them vigorously together.

'I perceive through that evening paper the sum of six thousand pounds in gold.'

Doyle interrupted him with some impatience.

'You didn't see it through the paper; you saw it in the paper. Goodness knows, it's been mentioned in enough of the sheets.'

'As I was about to remark,' went on Sherlock Holmes imperturbably, 'I am amazed that a man whose time is so valuable should waste it in counting the money. You are surely aware that a golden sovereign weighs 123.44 grains, therefore, if I were you, I should have up the kitchen scales, dump in the metal, and figure out the amount with a lead pencil. You brought the gold in two canvas bags, did you not, Sir George?'

'In the name of all that's wonderful, how do you know that?' asked the astonished publisher.

Sherlock Holmes, with a superior smile, casually waved his hand toward the two bags which still lay on the polished table.

'Oh, I'm tired of this sort of thing,' said Doyle wearily, sitting down in the first chair that presented itself. 'Can't you be honest, even on Christmas Eve? You know the oracles of old did not try it on with each other.'

'That is true,' said Sherlock Holmes. 'The fact is, I followed Sir George Newnes into the Capital and Counties Bank this afternoon, where he demanded six thousand pounds in gold; but when he learned this would weigh ninety-six pounds seven ounces avoirdupois weight, and that even troy weight would make the sum no lighter, he took two small bags of gold and the rest in Bank of England notes. I came from London on the same train with him, but he was off in the automobile before I could make myself known, and so I had to walk up. I was further delayed by taking the wrong turning on the top and finding myself at that charming spot in the neighbourhood where a sailor was murdered by two ruffians a century or so ago.'

There was a note of warning in Doyle's voice when he said:—'Did that incident teach you no lesson? Did you not realise that you are in a dangerous locality?'

'And likely to fall in with two ruffians?' asked Holmes, slightly elevating his eyebrows, while the same sweet smile hovered round his thin lips. 'No; the remembrance of the incident encouraged me. It was the man who had the money that was murdered. I brought no coin with me, although I expect to bear many away.'

'Would you mind telling us, without further circumlocution, what brings you here so late at night?'

Sherlock Holmes heaved a sigh, and mournfully shook his head very slowly.

'After all the teaching I have bestowed upon you, Doyle, is it possible that you cannot deduct even so simple a thing as that? Why am I here? Because Sir George made a mistake about those bags. He was quite right in taking one of them to 'Undershaw', but he should have left the other at 221B, Baker Street. I call this little trip 'The Adventure of the Second Swag'. Here is the second swag on the table. The first swag you received long ago, and all I had for my share was some honeyed words of compliment in the stories you wrote. Now, it is truly said that soft words butter no parsnips, and, in this instance, they do not even turn away wrath. So far as the second swag is concerned, I have come to demand half of it.'

'I am not so poor at deduction as you seem to imagine,' said Doyle, apparently nettled at the other's slighting reference to his powers. 'I was well aware, when you came in, what your errand was. I deduced further that if you saw Sir George withdraw gold from the bank, you also followed him to Waterloo station.'

'Quite right.'

'When he purchased his ticket for Haslemere, you did the same.'

'I did.'

'When you arrived at Haslemere, you sent a telegram to your friend, Dr Watson, telling him of your whereabouts.'

'You are wrong there; I ran after the motor car.'

'You certainly sent a telegram from somewhere, to someone, or at least dropped a note in the post-box. There are signs, which I need not mention, that point irrevocably to such a conclusion.'

The doomed man, ruined by his own self-complacency, merely smiled in his superior manner, not noticing the eager look with which Doyle awaited his answer.

'Wrong entirely. I neither wrote any telegram, nor spoke any message, since I left London.'

'Ah, no,' cried Doyle. 'I see where I went astray. You merely inquired the way to my house.'

'I needed to make no inquiries. I followed the rear light of the automobile part way up the hill, and, when that disappeared, I turned to the right instead of the left, as there was no one out on such a night from whom I could make inquiry.'

'My deductions, then, are beside the mark,' said Doyle hoarsely, in an accent which sent cold chills up and down the spine of his invited guest, but conveyed no intimation of his fate to the self-satisfied later arrival.

'Of course they were,' said Holmes, with exasperating self-assurance.

'Am I also wrong in deducting that you have had nothing to eat since you left London?'

'No, you are quite right there.'

'Well, oblige me by pressing that electric button.'

Holmes did so with much eagerness, but, although the trio waited some minutes in silence, there was no response.

'I deduct from that,' said Doyle, 'that the servants have gone to bed. After I have quite satisfied all your claims in the way of hunger for food and gold, I shall take you back in my motor car, unless you prefer to stay here the night.'

'You are very kind,' said Sherlock Holmes.

'Not at all,' replied Doyle. 'Just take that chair, draw it up to the table and we will divide the second swag.'

The chair indicated differed from all others in the room. It was straight-backed, and its oaken arms were covered by two plates, apparently of German silver. When Holmes clutched it by the arms to drag it forward, he gave one half-articulate gasp, and plunged headlong to the floor, quivering. Sir George Newnes sprang up standing with a cry of alarm. Sir Arthur Conan Doyle remained seated, a seraphic smile of infinite satisfaction playing about his lips.

'Has he fainted?' cried Sir George.

'No, merely electrocuted. A simple device the Sheriff of New York taught me when I was over there last.'

'Merciful heavens! Cannot he be resuscitated?'

'My dear Newnes,' said Doyle, with the air of one from whose shoulders a great weight is lifted, 'a man may fall into the chasm at the foot of the Reichenbach Fall and escape to record his adventures later, but when two thousand volts pass through the human frame, the person who owns that frame is dead.'

'You don't mean to say you've murdered him?' asked Sir George, in an awed whisper.

'Well, the term you use is harsh, still it rather accurately sums up the situation. To speak candidly, Sir George, I don't think they can indite us for anything more than manslaughter. You see, this is a little invention for the reception of burglars. Every night before the servants go to bed, they switch on the current to this chair. That's why I asked Holmes to press the button. I place a small table beside the chair, and put on it a bottle of wine, whisky and soda, and cigars. Then, if any burglar comes in, he invariably sits down in the chair to enjoy himself, and so you see, that piece of furniture is an effective method of reducing crime. The number of burglars I have turned over to the parish to be buried will prove that this taking off of Holmes was not premeditated by me. This incident, strictly speaking, is not murder, but manslaughter. We shouldn't get more than fourteen years apiece, and probably that would be cut down to seven on the ground that we had performed an act for the public benefit.'

'Apiece!' cried Sir George. 'But what have I had to do with it?'

'Everything, my dear sir, everything. As that babbling fool talked, I saw in your eye the gleam which betokens avarice for copy. Indeed, I think you mentioned the January number. You were therefore accessory before the fact. I simply had to slaughter the poor wretch.'

Sir George sank back in his chair wellnigh breathless with horror. Publishers are humane men who rarely commit crimes; authors, however, are a hardened set who usually perpetrate a felony every time they issue a book. Doyle laughed easily.

'I'm used to this sort of thing,' he said. 'Remember how I killed off the people in "The White Company". Now, if you will help me to get rid of the body, all may yet be well. You see, I learned from the misguided simpleton himself that nobody knows where he is today. He often disappears for weeks at a time, so there really is slight danger of detection. Will you lend a hand?'

'I suppose I must,' cried the conscience-stricken man.

Doyle at once threw off the lassitude which the coming of Sherlock Holmes had caused, and acted now with an energy which was characteristic of him. Going to an outhouse, he brought the motor car to the front door, then, picking up Holmes and followed by his trembling guest, he went outside and flung the body into the tonneau behind. He then threw a spade and a pick into the car, and covered everything up with a water-proof spread. Lighting the lamps, he bade his silent guest get up beside him, and so they started on their fateful journey, taking the road past the spot where the sailor had been murdered, and dashing down the long hill at fearful speed toward London.

'Why do you take this direction?' asked Sir George. 'Wouldn't it be more advisable to go further into the country?'

Doyle laughed harshly.

'Haven't you a place on Wimbledon Common? Why not bury him in your garden?'

'Merciful motors!' cried the horrified man. 'How can you propose such a thing? Talking of gardens, why not have buried him in your own, which was infinitely safer than going forward at this pace.'

'Have no fear,' said Doyle reassuringly, 'we shall find him a suitable sepulchre without disturbing either of our gardens. I'll be in the centre of London within two hours.'

Sir George stared in affright at the demon driver. The man had evidently gone mad. To London, of all places in the world. Surely that was the one spot on earth to avoid.

'Stop the motor and let me off,' he cried. 'I'm going to wake up the nearest magistrate and confess.'

'You'll do nothing of the sort,' said Doyle. 'Don't you see that no person on earth would suspect two criminals of making for London when they have the whole country before them? Haven't you read my stories? The moment a man commits a crime he tries to get as far away from London as possible. Every policeman knows that, therefore, two men coming into London are innocent strangers, according to Scotland Yard.'

'But then we may be taken up for fast driving, and think of the terrible burden we carry.'

'We're safe on the country roads, and I'll slow down when we reach the suburbs.'

It was approaching three o'clock in the morning when a huge motor car turned out of Trafalgar Square, and went eastward along the Strand. The northern side of the Strand was up, as it usually is, and the motor, skilfully driven, glided past the piles of wood-paving blocks, great sombre kettles holding tar and the general débris of a re-paving convulsion. Opposite Southampton Street, at the very spot so graphically illustrated by George C.

Haité on the cover of the Strand Magazine, Sir Arthur Conan Doyle stopped his motor. The Strand was deserted. He threw pick and shovel into the excavation, and curtly ordered his companion to take his choice of weapons. Sir George selected the pick, and Doyle vigorously plied the spade. In almost less time than it takes to tell it, a very respectable hole had been dug, and in it was placed the body of the popular private detective. Just as the last spadeful was shovelled in place the stern voice of a policeman awoke the silence, and caused Sir George to drop his pick from nerveless hands.

'What are you two doing down there?'

'That's all right, officer,' said Doyle glibly, as one who had foreseen every emergency. 'My friend here is controller of the Strand. When the Strand is up he is responsible, and it has the largest circulation in the—I mean it's up oftener than any other street in the world. We cannot inspect the work satisfactorily while traffic is on, and so we have been examining it in the night-time. I am his secretary; I do the writing, you know.'

'Oh, I see,' replied the constable. 'Well, gentlemen, good morning to you, and merry Christmas.'

'The same to you, constable. Just lend a hand, will you?'

The officer of the law helped each of the men up to the level of the road.

As Doyle drove away from the ill-omened spot he said:—

'Thus have we disposed of poor Holmes in the busiest spot on earth, where no one will ever think of looking for him, and we've put him away without even a Christmas box around him. We have buried him for ever in the *Strand.*'

A PRINCE OF GOOD FELLOWS

To

Thomas Spencer Jerome

in his Villa of the Castle on the Island of Capri,

this book is respectfully dedicated, with

the hope that some of the facts

herein set forth may aid him

during his historical

researches.

The King Intervenes

Late evening had fallen on the grey walls of Stirling Castle, and dark night on the town itself, where narrow streets and high gables gave early welcome to the mirk, while the westward-facing turrets of the castle still reflected the departing glory of the sky.

With some suggestion of stealth in his movements, a young man picked his way through the thickening gloom of the streets. There was still light enough to show that, judging by his costume, he was of the well-to-do farmer class. This was proclaimed by his broad, coarse, bonnet and the grey check plaid which he wore, not looped to the shoulder and pinned there by a brooch, Highland fashion, but wrapped round his middle, with the two ends brought over the shoulders and tucked under the wide belt which the plaid itself made, the fringes hanging down at each knee, as a Lowland shepherd might have worn the garment. As he threaded his way through the tortuous streets, ever descending, he heard the clatter of a troop of horse coming up, and paused, looking to the right and left, as if desirous of escaping an encounter which seemed inevitable. But if such were his object, the stoppage, although momentary, was already too long, for ere he could deflect his course, the foremost of the horsemen was upon him, a well known noble of the Scottish Court.

"Out of the way, fellow!" cried the rider, and, barely giving him time to obey, the horseman struck at the pedestrian fiercely with his whip. The young man's agility saved him. Nimbly he placed his back against the wall, thus avoiding the horse's hoof and the rider's lash. The victim's right hand made a swift motion to his left hip, but finding no weapon of defence there, the arm fell back to his side again, and he laughed quietly to himself. The next motion of his hand was more in accordance with his station, for it removed his bonnet, and he stood uncovered until the proud cavalcade passed him.

When the street was once more clear and the echoing sounds had died away in the direction of the castle, the youth descended and descended until he came to the lower part of the town where, turning aside up a narrow lane, he knocked at the door of a closed and shuttered building, evidently an abiding place of the poorer inhabitants of Stirling. With some degree of caution the door was slightly opened, but when the occupant saw, by the flash of light that came from within, who his visitor was, he threw the portal wide and warmly welcomed the newcomer.

"Hey, guidman!" he cried, "ye're late the night in Stirling."

"Yes," said the young man stepping inside, "but the farm will see nothing of me till the morning. I've a friend in town who gives me a bed for myself and a stall for my horse, and gets the same in return when he pays a visit to the country."

"A fair exchange," replied the host as he closed and barred the door.

The low room in which the stranger found himself was palpably a cobbler's shop. Boots and shoes of various sizes and different degrees of ill repair strewed the floor, and the bench in the corner under a lighted cruzie held implements of the trade, while the apron which enveloped the man of the door proclaimed his occupation. The incomer seated himself on a stool, and the cobbler returned to his last, resuming his interrupted work. He looked up however, from time to time, in kindly fashion at his visitor, who seemed to be a welcome guest.

"Well," said the shoemaker with a laugh, "what's wrong with you?"

"Wrong with me? Nothing. Why do you think there is anything amiss?"

"You are flushed in the face; your breath comes quick as if you had been running, and there's a set about your lips that spells anger."

"You are a very observing man, Flemming," replied he of the plaid. "I have been walking fast so that I should have little chance of meeting any one. But it is as well to tell the whole truth as only part of it. I had a fright up the street. One of those young court sprigs riding to the castle tried to trample me under the feet of his horse, and struck at me with his whip for getting into his road, so I had just to plaster my back against somebody's front door and keep out of the way."

"It's easy to see that you live in the country, Ballengeich," replied the cobbler, "or you would never get red in the face over a little thing like that."

"I had some thought of pulling him off his horse, nevertheless," said the Laird of Ballengeich, whose brow wrinkled into a frown at the thought of the indignity he had suffered.

"It was just as well you left him alone," commented the cobbler, "for an unarmed man must even take whatever those court gallants think fit to offer, and if wise, he keeps the gap in his face shut, for fear he gets a bigger gap opened in his head. Such doings on the part of the nobles do not make them exactly popular. Still, I am speaking rather freely, and doubtless you are a firm friend of the new king?" and the shoemaker cast a cautious sidelong glance at his visitor.

"A friend of the king? I wonder to hear you! I doubt if he has a greater enemy than myself in all Scotland."

"Do you mean that, Ballengeich?" inquired the shoemaker, with more of interest than the subject appeared to demand, laying down his hammer as he spoke, and looking intently at his guest.

"I'd never say it, if it wasn't true," replied the laird.

It was some moments before the workman spoke, and then he surprised the laird by a remark which had apparently nothing to do with what had been said before.

"You are not a married man, I think you told me?"

"No, I am not. There's time enough for that yet," returned the other with a smile. "You see, I am new to my situation of responsibility, and it's as well not to take in the wife till you are sure you can support her."

"What like a house have you got, and how far is it from Stirling?"

"The house is well enough in its way; there's more room in it than I care to occupy. It's strongly built of stone, and could stand a siege if necessary, as very likely it has done in days long past, for it's a stout old mansion. It's near enough to Stirling for me to come in and see my friend the cobbler in the evening, and sleep in my own bed that night, if I care to do so."

"Is it in a lonely place?"

"I can hardly say that. It is at the top of a bit hill, yet there's room enough to give you rest and retirement if you should think of keeping retreat from the busy world of the town. What's on your mind, Flemming? Are you swithering whether you'll turn farmer or no? Let me inform you that it's a poor occupation."

"I'll tell you what's on my mind, Ballengeich, if you'll swear piously to keep it a secret."

"Indeed, I'll do nothing of the sort," replied the young man decisively. "An honest man's bare word is as good as his bond, and the strongest oath ever sworn never yet kept a rascal from divulging a secret intrusted to him."

"You're right in that; you're right in that," the cobbler hastened to add, "but this involves others as well as myself, and all are bound to each other by oaths."

"Then I venture to say you are engaged in some nefarious business. What is it? I'll tell nobody, and mayhap, young as I am, I can give you some plain, useful advice from the green fields that will counteract the pernicious notions that rise in the stifling wynds of the crowded town."

"Well, I'm not at all sure that we don't need it, for to tell the truth I have met with a wild set of lads, and I find myself wondering how long my head will be in partnership with my body."

"Is the case so serious as that?"

"Aye, it is."

"Then why not withdraw?"

"Ah, that's easier said than done. When you once shut a spring door on yourself, it isn't by saying 'I will' that you get out. You'll not have forgotten the first night we met, when you jumped down on my back from the wall of the Grey Friars' Church?"

"I remember it very distinctly, but which was the more surprised, you or I, I have never yet been able to settle. I know I was very much taken aback."

"Not so much as I," interrupted the cobbler dryly, "when you came plump on my shoulders."

"I was going to say," went on Ballengeich, "that I'm afraid my explanation about taking a short cut was rather incoherent."

"Oh, no more than mine, that I was there to catch a thief. It was none of my business to learn why you were in the kirkyard."

"By the way, did you ever hear any more of the thief you were after?"

"That's just the point I am coming to. The man we were after was his youthful majesty, James the Fifth, of Scotland."

"What, the king!" exclaimed the amazed laird.

"Just him, and no other," replied the cobbler, "and very glad I am that the ploy miscarried, although I fear it's to come on again."

"I never heard the like of this!"

"You may well say that. You see it is known that the king in disguise visits a certain house, for what purpose his majesty will be able to tell you better than I. He goes unattended and secretly, and this gives us our chance."

"But what in the name of the god of fools whoever he happens to be, would you do with Jamie once you got him?"

"'Deed there's many things that might be mended in this country, as you very well know, and the king can mend them if he likes, with a word. Now rather than have his throat cut, our leader thinks he will agree to reasonable reform."

"And supposing he doesn't agree, are you going to cut his throat?"

"I don't know what would happen if he proved stubborn. The moderate section is just for locking him by somewhere until he listens to wisdom."

"And it is in your mind that my house should become a prison for the king?"

"It seems to me worth considering."

"There seems to me very little worth considering in the matter. It is a mad scheme. Supposing the king promised under compulsion, what would be his first action the moment he returned to Stirling Castle? He would scour the country for you, and your heads would come off one by one like buttons from an old coat."

"That's what I said. 'Trust the word of a Stuart,' says I, 'it's pure nonsense!'"

"Oh I'm not sure but the word of a Stuart is as good as the word of any other man," replied Ballengeich with a ring of anger in his voice, at which the cobbler looked up surprised.

"You're not such an enemy of the king as you let on at first," commented the mender of shoes. "I doubt if I should have told you all this."

"Have no fear. I can pledge you that my word is as good as a Stuart's at least."

"I hope it's a good deal better."

"Your plan is not only useless, but dangerous, my friend. I told you I would give you my advice, and now you have it. Do you think James is a lad that you can tie to your bench stool here, lock your door, and expect to find him when you came back? You must remember that James has been in captivity before, when the Earl of Angus thought he had him secure in the stronghold of Falkland, and yet, Jamie, who was then but a lad of sixteen, managed to escape. Man Flemming, I must tell you about that some day."

"Tell me about what?" inquired the shoemaker.

"Oh well, it may not be true after all," said young Ballengeich in confusion, "but a friend of mine was gardener at Falkland and knew the whole story about James's escape. Never mind that; my advice to you is to shake hands with all such schemes, and turn your back on them."

"Oh, that's soon said," cried the cobbler with some impatience. "'Keep out of the fire and ye'll not be burnt,' says the branch on the tree to the faggot on the woodman's back. You see, Ballengeich, in this matter I'm between the cart-wheel and the hard road. My head's off if this ploy miscarries, as you've just told me, and my throat's cut if I withdraw from the secret conclave. It's but a choice between two hashings. There's a dead cobbler in any event."

"I see your difficulty," said the laird; "do you want to be helped out of it?"

"Does the toad want to get from under the harrow?"

"When is your next meeting, and where?"

"The meetings are held in this room, and the next will be on Wednesday night at eleven o'clock."

"Bless my soul!" cried Ballengeich. "Would nothing content you but to drink the whole bucketful? The rendezvous in your shop! Then whoever escapes, your head's on a pike."

"Aye," murmured the shoemaker dismally.

"It isn't taking very many of you to overturn the House of Stuart," said the laird, looking about the room, which was small.

"There's just one less than a dozen," replied the cobbler.

"Then we'll make up the number to the even twelve, hoping good luck will attend us, for we will be as many as the Apostles. Between now and Wednesday you might confer with your leaders, Flemming. Tell them you know a young man you can trust, who owns exactly the kind of house that James can be kept fast in, if he is captured. Say that your new conspirator will take the oath, or anything else they like to give, and add, what is more to the purpose, that he has a plot of his own which differs from theirs, in giving at least as much chance of success, and possesses the additional advantage of being safe. Whether his plan miscarries or not, there will be no need to fear a reprisal, and that is much to say in its favour."

"It is everything in its favour," said the shoemaker with a sigh of relief.

"Very well, then, I will meet you here on Wednesday night at this time, and learn whether or no they agree to have me as one of their number. If they refuse, there's no harm done; I shall say nothing, and the king will know no more about the matter than he does now."

"I could not ask better assurance than that," said the host cordially as his guest rose.

They shook hands, and the guidman of Ballengeich, after peering out into the darkness to see that the way was clear, took his leave.

The laird was prompt in keeping his appointment on the following Wednesday, and learned that the conspirators were glad of his assistance. The cobbler's tool-box had been pushed out of the way, and a makeshift table, composed of three boards and two trestles, occupied the centre of the room. A bench made up in similar fashion ran along the back wall, and there were besides, half a dozen stools. A hospitable pitcher of strong drink stood on the rude table, with a few small measures, cups and horns.

As if the weight of conspiracy had lain heavy on his shoulders, the young Laird of Ballengeich seemed older than he had ever looked before. Lines of care marked his brow, and his distraught manner proclaimed the plot-monger new to a dangerous business. The lights, however, were dim, and Ballengeich doubted if any there present would recognise him should they meet him in broad day, and this, in a measure, was comforting. The cobbler sat very quiet on his accustomed bench, the others occupying the stools and the board along the wall.

"We have been told," began the leader, who filled the chair at the head of the table, where he had administered the oath with much solemnity to their new member, "we have been told that you own a house which you will place at our disposal should the purpose for which we are gathered here together, succeed."

"I have such a house," said the laird, "and it is of course, placed freely at your service. But the plan you propose is so full of danger that I wondered if you have given the project the deep consideration it deserves. It will be a hazardous undertaking to get the king safely into my house, but let us suppose that done. How are you going to keep him there?"

"We will set a guard over him."

"Very good. Which of you are to be the guardsmen, and how many?"

The conspirators looked one at another, but none replied. At last the leader said,—

"It will be time to settle that when we have him safely under bolt."

"Pardon me, not so. The time to arrange all things is now. Everything must be cut and dried, or failure is certain. The moment the king is missing the country will be scoured for him. There will be no possible place of refuge for miles round that will not be searched for the missing monarch. We will suppose that four of you are guarding the king, two and two, turn about. What are the four, and myself, to say to the king's soldiers when they demand entrance to my house?"

"The king is but a boy, and when he sees death or compliance before him he will accede to our demands."

"He is a boy, it is true," agreed the laird, "but he is a boy, as I pointed out to my friend Flemming, who escaped from the clutches of the Earl of Angus, out of the stronghold of Falkland Palace, and who afterwards drove the earl and many of the Douglas leaders into English exile. That is the kind of boy you have to deal with. Suppose then, he gives consent to all you place before him? Do you think he will keep his word?"

"I doubt it," said the cobbler, speaking for the first time. "The word of a Stuart is not worth the snap of my finger."

"On the other hand, if he does not accede," continued Ballengeich, "what are we to do with him?"

"Cut his throat," replied the leader decisively.

"No, no," cried several others, and for a moment there was a clamour of discussion, all speaking at once, while the laird stood silently regarding the vociferous disputants. Finally their leader said,—

"What better plan have you to propose?"

"The king is a boy," spoke up Ballengeich, "as you have said." At the sound of his voice instant silence reigned. "But he is a boy, as I have told you, extremely difficult to handle with violence. I propose then to approach him peaceably. The fact that he is a boy, or a very young man at least, implies that his mind will be more impressionable than that of an older person whose ideas are set. I propose then that a deputation wait upon his majesty and place before him the evils that require remedying, being prepared to answer any question he may ask regarding the method of their amendment. If peaceable means fail, then try violence, say I, but it is hardly fair to the young man to approach him at the beginning of his reign with a dirk in the hand. His answer would likely be a reference to his headsman; that is a favourite Stuart mode of argument. I have some friends about the castle," continued the laird. "I supply them with various necessaries from the farm; and if I do say it myself, I am well thought of by some in authority. I can guarantee you, I am sure, a safe conduct for your mission."

"But if safe conduct be refused?" said the leader.

"In that case, no harm's done. I shall divulge the names of none here present, for indeed I know the name of none, except of my friend the cobbler."

"Will you head the delegation, and be its spokesman?"

"No. My power to serve you lies in the fact that I am well thought of in the palace. This power would be instantly destroyed were I known as disaffected. I would put it on this basis. My friend, Flemming, is the spokesman of ten others who have grievances to place before his majesty. Therefore, as a matter of friendship between Flemming and myself, I ask safe conduct for the eleven."

"Indeed," cried the cobbler, "I wish you would leave my name out of the affair, since no one else seems eager to put his own forward."

"I put mine forward in making the request," said Ballengeich.

"Aye, but not as one of the deputation."

"Very well," agreed the laird in an offhand manner, "if you make a point of it, I have no objection to saying that I shall make one of the concert. I only proposed to keep out of it, because it is always wise to have an unbiased person to put in his word at a critical moment, and it seems to me important to have such a person on the outside. But it shall be exactly as you please; I care little one way or the other. I have made my proposal, and with you rests the acceptance or the rejection of it. If you think it safer to kidnap a king than to have a friendly chat with him, amicably arranged beforehand, then all I can say is, that I don't in the least agree with you. Please yourselves; please yourselves. We have but one neck apiece, and surely we can risk it in the manner that brings us most content."

"There is wisdom in what the laird says," cried one of the more moderate party. "I never liked the kidnapping idea."

"Nor I," said the cobbler. "It was but a wild Hielan' notion."

"My project has this advantage," continued Ballengeich with nonchalant impartiality, "that if it does not succeed, you can then fall back upon abduction. Nothing in this proposal interferes with the ultimate carrying out of your first plan."

"It is putting our heads in the lion's mouth," objected the leader, but in the discussion that followed he was outvoted. Then came the choosing of the delegates, on which rock the enterprise was nearly wrecked, for there seemed to be no anxiety on the part of any four present to form the committee of expostulation which was to meet the monarch. At last it was decided that all should go, if Ballengeich could produce a written safe-conduct signed by the king, which would include eleven persons.

Within three days this document was placed in the hands of the cobbler by Ballengeich, who told him that it had been signed that morning. And he added that the king had expressed himself as well pleased to receive a deputation of his loyal subjects.

The cobbler handled the passport gingerly, as if he were not altogether assured of its potency to protect him.

"The conference is for Wednesday at midday," said Ballengeich. "Assemble some minutes before that hour in the courtyard of the castle, and you will be conducted to the Presence."

"Wednesday!" echoed the cobbler, his face turning pale. "Why Wednesday, the day of our weekly meetings? Did you suggest it?"

"It was the king's suggestion, of course," replied Ballengeich. "It is merely a coincidence, and is, I think, a good omen."

"I wish I were sure of it," moaned the cobbler.

Before the bell rang twelve the conspirators were gathered together in the courtyard of Castle Stirling; huddled would perhaps be the more accurate word, for they were eleven very frightened men. More than one cast longing looks towards the gate by which they had come in, but some places are easier to enter than to leave, and the portal was well guarded by stalwart soldiers.

As the bell slowly tolled twelve, an official came from the palace into the courtyard, searched the delegation for concealed weapons, and curtly commanded them to follow him. Climbing the stone stairway they were ushered into a large room containing a long oaken table with five chairs on one side and six on the other. At the head of the table was a high-backed seat resembling a throne. The official left them standing there alone, and after he had closed the door they heard the ominous sound of bolts being thrust into their places. The silence which followed seemed oppressive; almost suffocating. No man spoke, but each stood like a statue holding his cap in his hand. At last the tension was broken, but it would scarcely be correct to say that it was relieved. The heavy curtains parted and the king entered the room, clad in the imposing robes of his high state. A frown was on his brow, and he advanced straight from the doorway to the throne at the head of the table, without speaking or casting a glance at any one of the eleven. When he had seated himself he said gruffly,—

"There is a chair for each of you; sit down."

It is doubtful if any of the company, except the cobbler, at first recognised their ruler as the alleged Laird of Ballengeich; but at the sound of the monarch's voice several started and looked anxiously one at another. Again the king addressed them,—

"A week ago to-night I met you in Flemming's room. I appointed this day for the conference that the routine of your meetings might not be disturbed, as I thought it well that the last of your rebellious gatherings should be held in the Castle of Stirling, for I am resolved that this conclave shall be your final effort in treason. One of your number has stated that the word of a Stuart is not to be trusted. This reputation appears to have descended to me, and it is a pity I should not take advantage of it."

When the king ceased speaking he lifted a small mallet and smote a resounding bell, which was on the table before him. A curtain parted and two men entered bearing between them a block covered with black cloth; this they placed silently in the centre of the floor and withdrew. Again the king smote the bell and there entered a masked executioner with a gleaming axe over his shoulder. He took his place beside the block, resting the head of his axe on the floor.

"This," continued the king, "is the entertainment I have provided for you. Each of you shall taste of that," and he pointed to the heading block.

The cobbler rose unsteadily to his feet, drawing from his bosom with trembling fingers the parchment bearing the king's signature. He moistened his dry lips with his tongue, then spoke in a low voice.

"Sir," he said, "we are here under safe conduct from the king."

"Safe conduct to where?" cried James angrily, "that is the point. I stand by the document; read it; read it!"

"Sir, it says safe conduct for eleven men here present, under protection of your royal word."

"You do not keep to the point, cobbler," shouted the king bringing his fist down on the table. "Safe conduct to where? I asked. The parchment does not say safe conduct back into Stirling again. Safe conduct to Heaven, or elsewhere, was what I guaranteed."

"That is but an advocate's quibble, your majesty. Safe conduct is a phrase well understood by high and low alike. But we have placed our heads in the lion's mouth, as our leader said last Wednesday night, and we cannot complain if now his jaws are shut. Nevertheless I would respectfully submit to your majesty that I alone of those present doubted a Stuart's word, and am like to have my doubts practically confirmed. I would also point out to your majesty that my comrades would not have been here had I not trusted the Master of Ballengeich, and through him the king, therefore, I ask you to let me alone pay the penalty of my error, and allow my friends to go scatheless from the grim walls of Stirling."

"There is reason in what you say," replied the king. "Are you all agreed to that?" he asked of the others.

"No, by God," cried the leader springing to his feet and smiting the table with his fist as lustily as the king had done. "We stand together, or fall together. The mistake was ours as much as his, and we entered these gates with our eyes open."

"Headsman," said the king, "do your duty."

The headsman whipped off the black cloth and displayed underneath it a box containing a large jug surrounded by eleven drinking-horns. Those present, all now on their feet, glanced with amazement from the masked man to the king. The sternness had vanished from his majesty's face, as if a dark cloud had passed from the sun and allowed it to shine again. There sparkled in the king's eye all the jubilant mischief of the incorrigible boy, and his laughter rang to the ceiling. Somewhat recovering his gravity he stretched out his hand and pointed a finger at the cobbler.

"I frightened you, Flemming," he cried. "I frightened you; don't deny it. I'll wager my gold crown against a weaver's woollen bonnet, I frightened the whole eleven of you."

"Indeed," said the cobbler with an uneasy laugh, "I shall be the first to admit it."

"Your face was as white as a harvest moon in mid-sky, and I heard somebody's teeth chatter. Now the drink we have had at our meetings heretofore was vile, and no more fitted for a Christian throat than is the headsman's axe; but if you ever tasted anything better than this, tell me where to get a hogshead of it."

The headsman having filled their horns, the leader raised the flagon above his head and said,—

"I give you the toast of The King!"

"No, no," proclaimed the boyish monarch, "I want to drink this myself. I'll give you a toast. May there never come a time when a Scotchman is afraid to risk his head for what he thinks is right."

And this toast they drank together.

The King Dines

"When kings frown, courtiers tremble," said Sir Donald Sinclair to the Archbishop of St. Andrews, "but in Stirling the case seems reversed. The courtiers frown, and the king looks anxiously towards them."

"Indeed," replied the prelate, "that may well be. When a man invites a company to dine with him, and then makes the discovery that his larder is empty, there is cause for anxiety, be he king or churl. In truth my wame's beginning to think my throat's cut." And the learned churchman sympathetically smoothed down that portion of his person first named, whose rounded contour gave evidence that its owner was accustomed to ample rations regularly served.

"Ah well," continued Sir Donald, "his youthful majesty's foot is hardly in the stirrup yet, and I'm much mistaken in the glint of his eye and the tint of his beard, if once he is firmly in the saddle the horse will not feel the prick of the spur, should it try any tricks with him."

"Scotland would be none the worse of a firm king," admitted the archbishop, glancing furtively at the person they were discussing, "but James has been so long under the control of others that it will need some force of character to establish a will of his own. I doubt he is but a nought posing as a nine," concluded his reverence in a lower tone of voice.

"I know little of mathematics," said Sir Donald, "but yet enough to tell me that a nought needs merely a flourish to become a nine, and those nines among us who think him a nought, may become noughts should he prove a nine. There's a problem in figures for you, archbishop, with a warning at the end of it, like the flourish at the tail of the nine."

The young man to whom they referred, James, the fifth of that name, had been pacing the floor a little distance from the large group of hungry men who were awaiting their dinner with some impatience. Now and then the king paused in his perambulation, and gazed out of a window overlooking the courtyard, again resuming his disturbed march when his brief scrutiny was completed. The members of the group talked in whispers, one with another, none too well pleased at being kept waiting for so important a function as a meal.

Suddenly there was a clatter of horse's hoofs in the courtyard. The king turned once more to the window, glanced a moment at the commotion below, then gave utterance to an exclamation of annoyance, his right hand clenching angrily. Wheeling quickly to the guards at the door he cried,—

"Bring the chief huntsman here at once, and a prod in the back with a pike may make up for his loitering in the courtyard."

The men, who stood like statues with long axes at the doorway, made no move; but two soldiers, sitting on a bench outside, sprang to their feet and ran clattering down the stair. They returned presently with the chief huntsman, whom they projected suddenly into the room with a violence little to the woodman's taste, for he neglected to remove his bonnet in the royal presence, and so far forgot himself as to turn his head when he recovered his equilibrium, roundly cursing those who had made a projectile of him.

"Well, woodlander!" cried the king, his stern voice ringing down again from the lofty rafters of the great hall. "Are there no deer in my forests of the north?"

"Deer in plenty, your majesty," answered the fellow with a mixture of deference and disrespect, which in truth seemed to tinge the manners of all present. "There are deer in the king's forest, and yet a lack of venison in the king's larder!"

"What mean you by that, you scoundrel?" exclaimed the king, a flush overspreading his face, ruddy as his beard. "Have your marksmen lost their skill with bow and arrow, that you return destitute to the castle?"

"The marksmen are expert as ever, your majesty, and their arrows fly as unerringly to their billet, but in these rude times, your majesty, the sting of an arrow may not be followed by the whetting of a butcher's knife."

The king took an impatient step forward, then checked himself. One or two among the group of noblemen near the door laughed, and there was a ripple of suppressed merriment over the whole company. At first the frown on the king's brow deepened, and then as suddenly it cleared away, as a puff of wind scatters the mist from the heights of Stirling. When the king spoke again it was in a calm, even voice. "As I understand you, there was no difficulty in capturing the deer, but you encountered some obstacle between the forest and Stirling which caused you to return empty-handed. I hope you have not added the occupation of itinerant flesher to the noble calling of forest huntsman?"

"Indeed, your majesty," replied the unabashed hunter, "the profession of flesher was forced upon me. The deer we had slaughtered found it impossible to win by the gates of Arnprior."

"Ah! John Buchanan then happened to need venison as you passed?"

"Your majesty has hit the gold there. Buchanan not only needed it but took it from us."

"Did you inform him that your cargo was intended for the larder of the king?"

"I told him that in so many words, your majesty; and he replied that if James was king in Stirling, John was king in Kippen, and having the shorter name, he took the shorter method of supplying his kitchen."

"Made you any effort to defend your gear?"

"Truth to say, your majesty, that were a useless trial. The huntsman who will face the deer thinks no shame to turn his back on the wild boar, and Buchanan, when he demanded your majesty's venison, was well supported by a number of mad caterans with drawn swords in their hands, who had made up for a lack of good meat with a plenitude of strong drink. Resistance was futile, and we were fain to take the bannock that was handed to us, even though the ashes were upon it. Ronald of the Hills, a daft Heilan'man who knew no better, drew an arrow to his ear and would have pinned Buchanan to his own gate, resulting in the destruction of us all, had I not, with my stave, smote the weapon from his hand. Then the mad youth made such to-do that we had just to tie him up and bring him to Stirling on the horse's back like a sack of fodder."

"Your caution does credit to your Lowland breeding, Master huntsman, and the conduct of Ronald cannot be too severely condemned. Bring him here, I beg of you, that he may receive the king's censure."

Ronald was brought in, a wild, unkempt figure, his scanty dress disordered, bearing witness to the struggle in which he had but lately been engaged. His elbows were pinioned behind him, and his shock of red hair stood out like a heather broom. He scowled fiercely at the huntsman, and that cautious individual edged away from him, bound as he was.

"By my beard! as the men of the heathen East swear," said the king, "his hair somewhat matches my own in hue. Ronald, what is the first duty of a huntsman?"

"He speaks only the Gaelic, your majesty," explained the royal ranger.

"You have the Gaelic, MacNeish," continued the king, addressing one of his train. "Expound to him, I beg of you, my question. What is the first duty of a huntsman?"

MacNeish, stepping forward, put the question in Gaelic and received Ronald's reply.

"He says, your majesty, that a huntsman's first duty is to kill the game he is sent for."

"Quite right," and the king nodded approval. "Ask him if he knows as well the second duty of a huntsman."

Ronald's eye flashed as he gave his answer with a vehemence that caused the chief huntsman to move still farther away from him.

"He says, your majesty," translated MacNeish, "that the second duty of a huntsman is to cut the throat of any cateran who presumes to interfere with the progress of the provender from the forest to his master's kitchen."

"Right again," cried the king, smiting his thigh, "and an answer worthy of all commendation. Tell him this, MacNeish, that hereafter he is the chief huntsman to the Castle of Stirling. We will place this cowardly hellion in the kitchen where he will be safe from the hungry frenzy of a Buchanan, drunk or sober."

"But, your majesty—" protested the deposed ranger.

"To the kitchen with him!" sternly commandedry. "Strip off the woodlander's jacket he has disgraced and tie round him the strings of a scullion's apron, which will suit his middle better than the belt of a sword." Then the king, flashing forth his own weapon and stepping aside, swung it over the head of the Highlander, who stood like a statue in spite of the menace, and the sword came down with a deft accuracy which severed the binding cords without touching the person of the prisoner, freeing him at a stroke. A murmur of admiration at the dexterity of the king went up from the assemblage, every member of which was himself an expert with the weapon. The freed Highlander raised his brawny arms above his head and gave startling vent to the war-cry of his clan, "Loch Sloy! Loch Sloy!" unmindful of the presence in which he stood. Then he knelt swiftly and brought his lips to the buckle of the king's shoe.

"Gratitude in a MacFarlane!" sneered MacNeish.

"Aye," said the king, "and bravery too, for he never winked an eyelash when the sword swung above him; an admirable combination of qualities whether in a MacFarlane or a MacNeish. And now, gentlemen," continued his majesty, "although the affair of the huntsman is settled, it brings us no nearer our venison. If the cook will not to the king, then must the king to the cook. Gentlemen, to your arms and your horses! They say a Scotsman fights well when he is hungry; let us put the proverb to the test. We ride and dine with his majesty of Kippen."

A spontaneous cheer burst from every man in the great hall to the accompaniment of a rattle of swords. Most of those present were more anxious to follow the king to a contest than into a council chamber. When silence ensued, the mild voice of the archbishop, perhaps because it was due to his profession, put in a seasonable word; and the nobles scowled for they knew he had great influence with the king.

"Your majesty, if the Buchanans are drunk——"

"If they are drunk, my lord archbishop," interrupted James, "we will sober them. 'Tis a duty even the Church owes to the inebriate." And with that he led the way out of the hall, his reply clearing the brows of his followers.

A few minutes later a clattering cavalcade rode forth from the Castle of Stirling, through the town and down the path of Ballengeich, a score of soldiers bringing up the tail of the procession; and in due time the company came to the entrance of Arnprior Castle. There seemed like to be opposition at the gate, but Sir Donald, spurring his horse forward among the guard, scattered the members of it right and left, and, raising both voice and sword, shouted,—

"The king! The king! Make way for the King of Scotland!"

The defenders seeing themselves outnumbered, as the huntsmen had been in that locality a short time before, gave up their axes to the invaders as meekly as the royal rangers had given up their venison.

The king placed his own guard at the gate. Springing from his horse he entered the castle door, and mounted the stone steps, sword in hand, his retinue close at his heels. The great hall to which they ascended was no monk's chapel of silence. There was wafted to them, or rather blown down upon them like a fierce hurricane, the martial strains of "Buchanan for ever," played by pipers anything but scant of wind; yet even this tornado was not sufficient to drown the roar of human voices, some singing, others apparently in the heat of altercation, and during the height of this deafening clamour the king and his followers entered the dining-hall practically unobserved.

On the long oaken table, servitors were busily placing smoking viands soon to be consumed; others were filling the drinking-horns, while some of the guests were engaged in emptying them, although the meal had not yet begun. Buchanan, his back towards the incomers, his brawny hands on the table, leaning forward, was shouting to the company, commanding his guests to seat themselves and fall to while the venison was hot. There seemed

631

to be several loud voiced disputes going on regarding precedence. The first intimation that the bellowing laird had of the intruder's presence was the cold touch of steel on his bare neck. He sprang round as if a wasp had stung him, his right hand swinging instinctively to the hilt of his sword, but the point of another was within an inch of his throat, and his hand fell away from his weapon.

"The fame of your hospitality has spread abroad, Buchanan," spoke the clear voice of the king, "so we have come to test its quality."

The pipers had stopped in their march, and with the ceasing of the music, the wind from the bags escaped to the outer air with a long wailing groan. The tumult of discussion subsided, and all eyes turned towards the speaker, some of the guests hastily drawing swords but returning them again to the scabbards when they saw themselves confronted by the king. Buchanan steadied himself with his back against the table, and in the sudden silence it seemed long ere he found his tongue. At last he said,—

"Does the king come as a guest with a drawn sword in his hand?"

"As you get north of Stirling, Buchanan,' replied James with a smile, "it is customary to bring the knife with you when you go out to dine. But I am quite in agreement with the Laird of Arnprior in thinking the sword an ill ornament in a banqueting-hall, therefore bestow your weapons on Sir Donald here, and command your clan now present to disarm."

With visible reluctance Buchanan divested himself of sword and dirk, and his comrades, now stricken dumb, followed his example. The weapons were thrown together in a corner of the hall where some of the king's soldiers stood guard over them. His majesty's prediction regarding the sobering effect of his advent was amply fulfilled. The disarmed men looked with dismay on one another, for they knew that such a prelude might well have its grand finale at the block or the gibbet. The king, although seemingly in high spirits, was an unknown quantity, and before now there had been those in power who, with a smile on their lips, had sent doomed men to a scaffold.

"In intercepting my venison, Buchanan," continued the king with the utmost politeness, "you were actuated by one of two motives. Your intervention was either an insult to the king, or it was an intimation that you desired to become his cook. In which light am I to view your action, Buchanan?"

There was in the king's voice a sinister ring as he uttered this sentence that belied the smile upon his lips, and apprehension deepened as all present awaited Buchanan's reply. At the word "cook," he had straightened himself, and a deeper flush than the wine had left there, overspread his countenance; now he bowed with deference and said,—

"It has ever been my ambition to see your majesty grace with his presence my humble board."

"I was sure of it," cried James with a hearty laugh which brought relief to the anxious hearts of many standing before him. The king thrust his sword into a scabbard, and, with a clangour of hilt on iron, those behind him followed his example.

"And now," cried James, "let the king's men eat while the laird's men wait upon them. And as for you, John Buchanan, it is to-day my pleasure that you have the honour of being my cup-bearer."

Whether the honour thus thrust upon the Laird of Arnprior was as much to his liking as an invitation to sit down with his guest would have been, is questionable, but he served his majesty with good grace, and the king was loud in his praise of the venison, although his compliments fell sadly on the ears of the hungry men who watched it disappear so rapidly. At the end of the feast James rose with his flagon in his hand.

"I give you the king," he cried, "the King of Kippen. When I left Stirling I had made up my mind that there could be but one king in a country, but glorious Scotland shall have no such restriction, and I bestow upon Buchanan, whose ample cheer we have done justice to, the title of King of Kippen, so long as he does not fall into the error of supposing that Kippen includes all of Scotland, instead of Scotland including Kippen. And so, Laird of Arnprior, King of Kippen, we drink your good health, and when next my venison passes your door, take only that portion of it which bears the same relation to the whole, as the district of Kippen does to broad Scotland."

The toast was drunk with cheers, and when silence came, the King of Kippen, casting a rueful glance along the empty board, said,—

"I thank your majesty for your good wishes, but in truth the advice you give will be hard to follow, for I see I should have stolen twice the quantity of venison I did, because as I have not done so, I and my men are like to go hungry."

And thus Buchanan came into his title of King of Kippen, although he had to wait some time for his dinner on the day he acquired the distinction.

The King's Tryst

The king ruled. There was none to question the supremacy of James the Fifth. At the age of twenty-two he now sat firmly on his throne. He was at peace with England, friendly with France, and was pledged to take a wife from that country. His great grandfather, James the Second, had crushed the Black Douglas, and he himself had scattered the Red Douglas to exile. No Scottish noble was now powerful enough to threaten the stability of the throne. The country was contented and prosperous, so James might well take his pleasure as best pleased him. If any danger lurked near him it was unseen and unthought of.

The king, ever first in the chase, whether the quarry ran on four legs or on two, found himself alone on the road leading north-west from Stirling, having outstripped his comrades in their hunt of the deer. Evening was falling and James being some miles from Stirling Castle, raised his bugle to his lips to call together his scattered followers, but before a blast broke the stillness, his majesty was accosted by a woman who emerged suddenly and unnoticed from the forest on his left hand.

"My lord, the king;" she said, and her voice, like the sound of silver bells, thrilled with a note of inquiry.

"Yes, my lassie," answered the young man, peering down at his questioner, lowering his bugle, and reining in his frightened horse, which was startled by the sudden apparition before him. The dusk had not yet so far thickened but the king could see that his interlocutor was young and strikingly beautiful. Although dressed in the garb of the lower orders, there was a quiet and imposing dignity in her demeanour as she stood there by the side of the road. Her head was uncovered, the shawl she wore over it having slipped down to her shoulders, and her abundant hair, unknotted and unribboned, was ruddy as spun gold. Her complexion was dazzlingly fair, her eyes of the deepest blue, and her features perfection, except that her small mouth showed a trifle too much firmness, a quality which her strong but finely moulded chin corroborated and emphasised. The king, ever a connoisseur of womanly loveliness, almost held his breath as he gazed down upon the comely face upturned to him.

"They told me at Stirling," she said, "that you were hunting through this district, and I have been searching for you in the forest."

"Good heavens, girl!" cried the king; "have you walked all the way from Stirling?"

"Aye, and much further. It is nothing, for I am accustomed to it. And now I crave a word with your majesty."

"Surely, surely!" replied the king with enthusiasm, no thought of danger in this unconventional encounter even occurring to him. The natural prudence of James invariably deserted him where a pretty woman was concerned. Now, instead of summoning his train, he looked anxiously up and down the road listening for any sound of his men, but the stillness seemed to increase with the darkness, and the silence was profound, not even the rustle of a leaf disturbing it.

"And who, my girl, are you?" continued the king, noticing that her eyes followed his glance up and down the road with some trace of apprehension in them, and that she hesitated to speak.

"May it please your gracious majesty, I am humble tirewoman to that noble lady, Margaret Stuart, your honoured mother."

The king gave a whistle of astonishment.

"My mother!" he exclaimed. "Then what in the name of Heaven are you doing here and alone, so far from Methven?"

"We came from Methven yesterday to her ladyship's castle of Doune."

"Then her ladyship must have come to a very sudden resolution to travel, for the constable of Doune is in my hunting-party, and I'll swear he expected no visitors."

"My gracious lady did not wish Stuart the constable to expect her, nor does she now desire his knowledge of her presence in the castle. She commanded me to ask your majesty to request the constable to remain in Stirling, where, she understands, he spends most of his time. She begs your majesty to come to her with all speed and secrecy."

"I wonder what is wrong now?" mused the king. "I have not heard from her for nearly a year. She has quarrelled with her third husband, I suppose, for the Tudors are all daft where matrimony is concerned."

"What does your majesty say?" asked the girl.

"I was speaking to myself rather than to you, but I may add that I am ready to go anywhere if you are to be my guide. Lend me your hand and spring up here behind me. We will gallop to Doune at once."

The young woman drew back a step or two.

"No, no," she said. "The Lady Margaret is most anxious that your visit should be unknown to any but herself, so she begs you to dismiss your followers and lay your commands upon Constable Stuart of Doune."

"But my followers are all of them old enough to look after themselves," objected the king, "and the constable is not likely to leave Stirling where he has remained these many months."

"The Lady Margaret thought," persisted the girl, "that if your retinue returned to Stirling and learned of your continued absence, anxiety would ensue, and a search might be undertaken that would extend to Doune."

"How did my lady mother know I was hunting when you could not have learned of my excursion until you reached Stirling?" asked the king, with a glimmer of that caution which appeared to have deserted him.

The girl seemed somewhat nonplussed by the question, but she answered presently with quiet deliberation,—

"Her ladyship was much perturbed and feared I should not find you at the castle. She gave me various instructions, which she trusted I could accommodate to varying contingencies."

"My girl," said the king leaning towards her, "you do not speak like a serving-maid. What is your name?"

"I have been a gentlewoman, sire," she answered simply, "but women, alas, cannot control their fortunes. My name is Catherine. I will now forward to Doune, and wait for you at the further side of the new bridge the tailor has built over the Teith. If you will secure your horse somewhere before coming to the river, and meet me there on foot, I will conduct you to the castle. Will you come?"

"Of a surety," cried the king, in a tone that left no doubt of his intentions. "I shall overtake you long before you are at the bridge!" As he said this the girl fled away in the darkness, and then he raised his bugle to his lips and blew a blast that speedily brought answering calls.

James's unexplained absences were so frequent that his announcement of an intention not to return home that night caused no surprise among his company; so, bidding him good-night, they cantered off towards Stirling, while he, unaccompanied, set his face to the north-west, and his spurs to the horse's flanks, but his steed was already tired out and could not now keep pace with his impatience. To his disappointment, he did not overtake the girl, but found her waiting for him at the new bridge, and together they walked the short half mile to the castle. The young man was inclined to be conversational, but the girl made brief replies and finally besought his silence.

The night had proved exceedingly dark, and they were almost at the castle before its huge bulk loomed blackly before them. There was something so sinister in its dim, grim contour that for the first time since he set out on this night adventure, a suspicion that he was acting unwisely crossed the king's mind.

Still, he meditated, it was his mother's own castle, the constable of which was a warm friend of his—almost, as one might say, a relative, for Stuart was the younger brother of his mother's husband, so what could be amiss with this visit?

"You are not taking me to the main entrance," he whispered.

"No, to the postern door."

"But the postern door is situated in the wall high above my reach; it is intended for the exit of a possible messenger during a siege and not for the entrance of a guest."

"I am acting in accordance with my instructions," replied the girl. "A rope ladder descends from the postern door."

"A rope ladder! that sounds promising; will you ascend it?"

"Yes, sire, but meanwhile, I implore your majesty to be silent."

The king said no more until the rope ladder was in his hand.

"I hope it is strong," he murmured.

Then he mounted lightly up in the darkness, until he stood on the sill of the narrow doorway, when he reached forward his hand to assist his slower comrade in mounting, but she sprang past him without availing herself of his aid. In a low voice she begged pardon for preceding him. Then walked up and up a winding stone staircase, on whose steps there was barely room for two to pass each other. She pushed open a door and allowed some light to stream through on the turret stair, which disappeared in the darkness still further aloft.

The king found himself in a large square apartment either on the first or second story. It appeared in some sort to be a lady's boudoir, for the benches were cushioned and comfortable, and there were evidences, about on small tables, of tapestry work and other needle employment recently abandoned.

"Will your majesty kindly be seated," said the girl. "I must draw up the ladder, close the postern door, and then inform my lady that you are here."

She went out by the way they had entered and shut the door with a force that seemed to the king unnecessary, but he caught his breath an instant later as his quick ear seemed to tell him that a bolt had fallen. He rose at once, tried to open the door, and discovered it was indeed barred on the outside. One other exit remained to be tested; a larger door evidently communicating with another room or passage; that also he found locked. He returned to the middle of the room and stood there for a few moments with knitted brow.

"Trapped, Jamie, my lad! Trapped!" he muttered to himself. "Now what object can my mother have in this? Does she expect by such childish means to resume her authority over me? Does she hope that her third husband shall rule Scotland in my name as did her second, with me a prisoner? By Saint Andrew, no!"

The king seized a bench, raised it over his head and crashed it in bits against the larger door with a noise that reverberated through the castle.

"Open!" he cried; "open instantly!"

Then he paused, awaiting the result of his fury. Presently he thought he heard light footsteps coming along the passage and an instant later the huge key turned slowly in the lock. The door opened, and to his amazement he saw standing before him with wide frightened eyes, his guide, but dressed now as a lady.

"Madam," said the king sternly, "I ask you the meaning of this pleasantry?"

"Pleasantry," echoed the girl, staring at him with her hand upon a huge iron key, alert to run if this handsome maniac, strewn round by the wreckage of the bench he had broken, attempted to lay hands on her.

"Pleasantry?" she repeated; "that is a question I may well ask you. Who are you, sir, and what are you doing here?"

"Who I am, and what I am doing here, you know very well, because you brought me here. A change of garb does not change a well-remembered face," and the king bowed to his visitor with a return of his customary courtliness, now that his suspicions were allayed, for he knew how to deal with pretty women. "Madam, there is no queen in Scotland, but you are queen by right of nature, and though you doff your gown, you cannot change your golden crown."

The girl's hand unconsciously went up to her ruddy hair, while she murmured more to herself than to him,—

"This is some of Catherine's work."

"Catherine was your name in the forest, my lady, what is your name in the castle?"

"Isabel is my name in castle and forest alike. You have met my twin sister, Catherine. Why has she brought you here?"

"Like an obedient son, I am here at the command of my honourable mother; and your sister—if indeed goddesses so strangely fair, and so strangely similar can be two persons—has gone to acquaint my mother of my arrival."

The girl's alarm seemed to increase as the king's diminished. Trouble, dismay, and fear marred her perfect face, and as the king scrutinised her more minutely, he saw that the firm mouth and the resolute chin of her sister had no place in the more softened and womanly features of the lady before him.

"Your mother? Who is she?"

"First, Margaret Tudor, daughter of the King of England, second, Margaret Stuart, wife of the King of Scotland, third, Margaret Douglas, ill mate of the Earl of Angus; fourth, and let us hope finally, Margaret Stuart again, spouse of Lord Methven, and owner of this castle."

The girl swayed as if she would fall, all colour struck suddenly from her face. She leaned, nearly fainting, against the stone wall, passing her hand once or twice across her terror-filled eyes.

"Great God," she moaned, "do not tell me that you are James, King of Scotland, here, and alone, in this den of Douglases!"

"Douglas!" cried the king roused at the hated name. "How can there be Douglases in the Castle of Doune; my mother's house, constabled by my friend, young Stuart."

"Your mother's house?" said the girl with an uncanny laugh. "When has the Lady Margaret set foot in Doune? Not since she was divorced from my uncle, Archibald Douglas, Earl of Angus! And the constable? Aye, the constable is in Stirling. Doune Castle stands gloomy and alone, but in Stirling with the young king, there are masques, and hunting and gaiety. Young Stuart draws the revenues of his charge, but pays slight attention to the fulfilment of his duty."

"You are then Isabel Douglas? And now, to echo your own question, how came you here? If this is a den of Douglases, as you say, how comes my mother's castle to be officered by the enemies of her son?"

"That you ask such a question shows little foresight or knowledge of men. When your first step-father, and my uncle, Archibald Douglas, had control of this castle through your mother's name, he filled it with his own adherents."

"Naturally; nepotism was a well-known trait of my domineering stepfather, which did not add to his popularity in Scotland. Who can get office, or justice against a Douglas? was their cry. But did not young Stuart, when he was made constable, put in his own men?"

"The constable cares nothing for this stronghold so long as it furnishes money which he may spend gaily in Stirling."

"I see. So you and your sister found refuge among your underlings? and where so safe from search as within the king's mother's own fortress, almost under the shadow of Stirling? An admirable device. Why then do you jeopardise your safety by letting me into the secret?"

The girl sighed deeply with downcast eyes, then she flashed a glance at him which had something in it of the old Douglas hauteur.

"I fear," she said, "that it is not our safety which is jeopardised."

"You mean that I am in danger?"

"The same stronghold which gives immunity to a family of the Red Douglases can hardly be expected to confer security upon James the Fifth, their persecutor."

"No. Certainly that would be too much to expect. Are you then in this plot against me, my lady?"

"I have not heard of any plot. If there is one I know nothing of it. I merely acquaint you with some hint of my fears."

"Then I charge you as a loyal subject of the lawful king, to guide me from this stronghold, into which I have been cozened by treachery and falsehood."

Catherine, who had entered silently and unnoticed through the smaller door, now stepped forward, drew her sister into the room, took out the huge key, closed the door and locked it, then turned fiercely to the king. Her beautiful white right arm was bare to the elbow, the loose sleeve rolled up, and in her hand she held a dagger. With her back against the newly locked door, she said,—

"I'll be your majesty's guide from this castle, and your perjured soul shall find exit through a postern gate made by my dagger!"

"Oh, Catherine, Catherine," sobbed Isabel, weeping in fear and horror of the situation, "you cannot contemplate so awful a deed, a murder so foul, for however unworthy he may be, he is still the king."

"What is there foul in ridding the world of a reptile such as he? How many innocent lives has he taken to encompass his revenge? How many now of our name are exiled and starving because of his action? I shall strike the blow with greater surety, for in killing him I extinguish his treacherous race."

"No good can come from assassination, Catherine."

"What greater evil can spring from his death than from his life?"

"His killing will not bring back those whom he has slain; it will not cause our banished kinsmen to return. It will be a murder for revenge."

"And not the first in Scotland," said Catherine grimly.

The king had once more seated himself, and now, resting his chin on his open palm, listened to the discussion with the interested bearing of one who had little concern with its result. A half amused smile wreathed his lips, and once or twice he made a motion as if he would intervene, but on second thoughts kept silent.

"Do not attempt this fell deed, dear sister," pleaded Isabel earnestly. "Let us away as we intended. The horses are ready and waiting for us. Our mother is looking for our coming in her room. The night wears on and we must pass Stirling while it is yet dark, so there is no time to be lost. Dear sister, let us quit Scotland, as we purposed, an accursed land to all of our name, but let us quit it with unstained hands."

"Isabel, darling," said Catherine in a low voice that quavered with the emotion caused by her sister's distress and appeal, "what unlucky chance brought you to this fatal door at such a moment? Can you not understand that I have gone too far to retreat? Who, having caged the tiger, dare open again the gate and set him free? If for no other reason, the king must die because he is here and because I brought him here. Open the door behind you, Isabel, go down the circular stair, and at the postern step you will find the rope ladder by which I ascended. Get you to the courtyard and there wait for me, saying nothing."

"Catherine, Catherine, the king will pardon you. He will surely forgive what you have done in exchange for his life."

"Forgiveness!" cried Catherine, her eyes blazing again. "I want no forgiveness from the king of Scotland. Pardon! The tiger would pardon, till once he is free again. The king must die."

"I shall go as you have bid me, Catherine, but not to do your bidding. I shall arouse this castle and prevent an abominable crime."

Catherine laughed harshly.

"Whom would you call to your assistance? Douglases, Douglases, Douglases! How many of your way of thinking will you find in the castle? You know well, one only, and that is our mother, old and helpless. Rouse the castle, Isabel, if you will, and find a dead man, and perhaps a dead sister, when you break in this locked door."

The helpless Isabel sank her head against the wall and burst into a fury of weeping.

"Ladies," said the king soothingly, rising to his feet, "will you graciously condone my intervention in this dispute? You are discussing an important act, from the commission of which all sentiment should be eliminated; an act which requires the hard strong mind of a man brought to bear upon the pros and cons of its consummation. You are dealing with it entirely from the standpoint of the heart and not of the head, an error common with women, and one that has ever precluded their effective dealing with matters of State. You will pardon me, Lady Isabel, when I say that your sister takes a much more practical view of the situation than you do. She is perfectly right in holding that, having me prisoner here, it is impossible to allow me to go scatheless. There is no greater folly than the folly of half doing a thing."

"Does your majesty argue in favour of your own murder?" asked Isabel amazed, gazing at the young man through her tears.

"Not so, but still that is a consideration which I must endeavour to eliminate from my mind, if my advice is to be impartial, and of service to you. May I beg of you to be seated? We have the night before us, and may consider the various interesting points at our leisure, and thus no irremediable mistake need be made."

Isabel, wellnigh exhausted with the intensity of her feelings, sank upon the bench, but Catherine still stood motionless, dagger in hand, her back against the door. The king, seeing she did not intend to obey, went on suavely. There was a light of intense admiration in his eye as he regarded the standing woman.

"Ladies," he said, "can you tell me when last a King of Scotland—a James also—and a Catherine Douglas bore relation to each other in somewhat similar circumstances?"

The king paused, but the girl, lowering at him, made no reply, and after a few moments the young man went on.

"It was a year more than a century ago, when the life of James the First was not only threatened, but extinguished, not by one brave woman, but by a mob of cowardly assassins. Then Catherine Douglas nearly saved the life of her king. She thrust her fair young arm into the iron loops of a door, and had it shattered by those craven miscreants."

Isabel wept quietly, her face in her two open hands. But Catherine answered in anger,—

"Why did the Catherine Douglas of that day risk her life to save the king? Because James the First was a just monarch. Why does the Catherine Douglas of to-day wish to thrust her dagger into the false heart of James the Fifth? Because he has turned on the hand that nurtured him——"

"The hand that imprisoned him, Lady Catherine. Pardon my correction."

"He turned on the man who governed Scotland wisely and well."

"Again pardon me; he had no right to govern. I was the king, not Archibald Douglas. But all that is beside the question, and recrimination is as bad as sentiment for clouding cold reason. What I wished to point out is, that assassination of kings or the capture of them very rarely accomplishes its object. James the First was assassinated and as result two Stuarts, two Grahams and two Chamberses were tortured and executed; so his murderers profited little. My grandfather James the Third was carried off by the Boyds, but Sir Alexander Boyd was beheaded and his brother and nephew suffered forfeiture. I think I have shown then that violence is usually futile."

"Not so," answered Catherine; "your grandfather was assassinated, and the man who killed him is not known to this day. Your great-grandfather basely murdered the Black Douglas in Stirling, thus breaking his word of honour for he had given Douglas safe conduct, yet he profited by his act and crushed my kinsmen."

"I see, Lady Catherine, that you are too well versed in history for me to contend with you successfully on that subject," said the king with a silent laugh. "We will therefore restrict the inquiry to the present case, as wise people should. Tell me then, so that I may be the better able to advise you, what is your true object—revenge and my death, or the wringing from me of concessions for your family?"

"I could not wring concessions from you, because you could not make good those concessions unless I released you. I dare not release you, because I dare not trust you."

"I foresaw your difficulty, and so I told your sister that, having gone so far, you could not retreat. The issue is therefore narrowed down to death, and how it may best be accomplished. You have made the tactical mistake of forewarning me. I cannot understand why you did not mount my horse beside me and stab me in the back as we rode through the forest. Did this not occur to you, Lady Catherine?"

"It did, but there were objections. Your horse would doubtless have escaped me, and would have galloped riderless to Stirling; your body would have been found by break of day, and we but a few hours' march from Stirling. Here I expect you to lie undiscovered in this locked room till we are safe in England."

"That is clear reasoning," commented the king with impartiality, "but have you looked beyond? Who will be the successor of the throne? I have neither brother nor sister; my two uncles died before I was born, and I perish childless. I think you mentioned that you wished to extinguish our line. Very well; what follows? Who is heir to the throne?"

"It matters nothing to me," said Catherine firmly. "Whoever rules Scotland could not be a greater enemy to my race than you are."

"I am not so sure of that. I think your dagger-blow will bring consequences you do not look for, and that your kin, now exiled in England will find the stroke a savage one for them. You forget that the stern King of England is my uncle, and on this relationship may lay claim to the Scottish throne. Be that as it may, it will be no secret that a Douglas committed the murder; and think you Henry VIII will offer safe refuge to his nephew's assassins? You much misjudge him if you do. It would have been far better to have slain me in the forest. This castle business is but an ill-judged, ill thought-out plan. I am sorry to appear adversely critical, but such is my opinion, and it confirms me in the belief that women should leave steel and State alone."

"I dare not let you go," reiterated Catherine.

"Of a surety you dare not; that is what I have said from the beginning. On the other hand, I can make no concession, under coercion, that would save my life. You see we are both cowardly, each in a different way. And now having come to the absolutely logical conclusion that the king must die, you should turn your mind to the difficulties that confront you. I, you see, am also armed."

The king as he spoke took from his doublet a dagger almost similar to the one held by the girl. A gentle smile graced his lips as he ran his thumb along the edge, and then glanced up at the two in time to notice their consternation at this new element in the situation.

"If you enter a tiger's cage you should expect a touch of his claws, so, Lady Catherine, your task is more serious than you anticipated. There is furthermore another source of danger against you, and it is my sincere wish that in the struggle to come you may not be too severely handicapped. While the issue of our contest is still in doubt, your sister will assuredly unlock the door and give the alarm, hoping to prevent your contemplated crime, or my killing of you. I think it right that you should not be called upon to suffer this intervention, for, if you will permit me to say so, I admire your determination as much as I admire, in another way, the Lady Isabel's leaning towards mercy. I shall then, take this key from the larger door and place it, with your sister, outside on the narrow stairway. You have withdrawn the rope ladder so she cannot alarm the garrison."

"But I have not withdrawn it," said Catherine quickly. "My sister must not leave this room or she will bring interference."

"Then," said the king calmly, as he rose and took the key from the large door, "we shall at least make it impossible for her to open the way into the hall." And so saying, he stepped to the smaller door, which he opened, and before either of the women could prevent his action, or even grasp an inkling of his design, he stepped outside, key in hand, and thrust to their places the bolts of the stairway door.

The two girls looked at each other for a moment in silence, Isabel plainly panic-stricken, while in Catherine's face anger struggled with chagrin.

Each was quick to see the sudden consequences of this turning of the tables; the two were helpless prisoners in a remote portion of the castle, no one within its walls being acquainted with their whereabouts. The king, insulted, hoodwinked, and all but murdered, was now at liberty, free to ride the few short leagues that lay between Doune and Stirling, and before daybreak the fortress would be in the hands of an overwhelming force with the present garrison prisoners. In the awed stillness an unexpected sound came to them from the outside; the sound of a man endeavouring to suppress the hearty laughter that overmastered him. To be doomed is bad enough, but to be made the subject of levity was too much for the dauntless Catherine. She flung her dagger ringing to the stone floor with a gesture of rage, then sank upon a bench and gave way to tears; tears of bitter humiliation and rage.

"Ladies," said the king from the outside, "I beg that you will allow me to open the door." But, receiving no answer, the bolts were drawn once more; James again entered the apartment and gazed down upon two fair proud heads, crowned with ruddy hair.

"Dear ladies," said the king, "forgive me my untimely mirth. Both of you take matters much too seriously; a little laughter is necessary in this world. My Lady Catherine, I told you that I could grant no concessions under coercion, but now coercion has vanished and I enter this room a free man of my own will. Tell me, my girl, what is it you want? The rescinding of your father's exile? It is granted. The right to live unmolested in your own castle? It is granted. Safe conduct to England? It is granted. The privilege of remaining in Doune? It is granted. But do not ask me to rescind banishment against Archibald Douglas, Earl of Angus, for that I shall not concede. The Douglas ambition, and not the Scottish king, has wrecked the Douglas family, both Black and Red. But as far as concerns your own immediate kin, with one exception, I shall give anything you like to ask."

Catherine rose to her feet, threw back her auburn tresses, and said curtly,—

"We ask nothing but the privilege of leaving the country you rule."

The king bowed.

"And you, Lady Isabel?"

"I go with my sister and my mother."

"I grieve at your decision, ladies, and for the first time in my life envy England in getting an advantage over poor old Scotland, which I hope will not be irreparable, for I trust you will return. But if such be your determination, then go in peace, and in the daylight. Your journey shall not be molested by me. But, before you add finality to your intentions, I think it would be but fair to inform your lady mother that the king is anxious to be of service to her, and perhaps she may be content to accept what her daughters are apparently too proud to receive."

James placed the key once more in the lock, and turning to Catherine said,—

"My fair antagonist, I bid you good-night."

He stretched out his right hand, and she, with some hesitation and visible reluctance placed her palm in his. Then the king raised to his lips the hand which at one time seemed like to have stricken him.

"And you, sweet Isabel, whose gentle words I shall not soon forget, you will not refuse me your hand?"

"No, your majesty, if you will promise to think kindly of me."

The king, however, did not raise her hand to his lips, but placing an arm about her waist he drew her towards him and kissed her. Next moment he was hurrying down the stone steps, and the two were left alone together.

The King Investigates

The king, wishing to decide wisely, was troubled by a conflict of evidence, the bane of impartial judges all the world over. A courier from England had brought formal complaint that, while the two countries were ostensibly at peace, the condition along the border was practically a state of war. Raids were continually being made from the southern portion of Scotland across the boundary into England, and the robbers retreated unscathed to hide themselves among their hills, carrying their booty with them. These ruffians had long gone unpunished, and now England made friendly protest in the matter.

The king gathered his nobles about him and laid the case before them. Not a man among them but was older than himself, and therefore more experienced. James requested advice regarding the action it might be thought wise to take. Many of the nobles whose estates lay in the Lowlands of Scotland had themselves suffered from Highland cattle-lifters, and thus they were imbued with a fellow feeling for the raided English across the border. The English protest, they said, was courteously made. The evil was undoubted, and had existed unchecked for years, growing worse rather than better. Henry VIII, who now occupied the English throne, was a strong and determined man, and this continued source of irritation in the northern part of his realm might easily lead to a deplorable war between the two countries. In addition, James of Scotland was nephew to Henry of England, and the expostulation from uncle to nephew was of the mildest, without any threat even intimated.

The nobles thought that James might well put a stop to a state of things which no just man could approve, and thus do an act of justice which would at the same time please an august relative. James admitted that these were powerful arguments, but still if the Border robbers, who had many followers, resisted the Scottish force sent against them, there would be civil war, an outcome not to be looked forward to with light heart.

"In truth," said the king, "I would rather lead an army against England, with England in the right, than against my own countrymen, even if they were in the wrong."

This remark seemed to encourage certain gentlemen there present, who up to that moment had not spoken. The Earl of Bothwell, as the highest in rank among the silent phalanx, stepped forward and said,—

"Your majesty, there are always two sides to a question, and, with your permission, I should be glad to put in a word for those Border riders who have been so ruthlessly condemned by men who know nothing of them."

"It is for the purpose of hearing all there is to say that I called you together," rejoined the king. "Speak, my Lord of Bothwell."

"In the first place, your majesty, these Border men have had to stand the first brunt of all invasions into our country for centuries past. It is, therefore, little to be wondered at that they have small liking for the English. We are at peace with those to the south of us now, it is true; but how long that peace will remain unbroken, no man can say. There is, however, one thing certain, that if the King of Scotland exercises the power he undoubtedly possesses, and crushes the Border forces, he will have destroyed a staunch bulwark of his realm, and I quite agree with those gentlemen who have spoken so eloquently against the Borderers, that the King of England, and the people of England, will be well pleased."

This statement had a marked effect on King James, and it would have been well if those who agreed with the Earl of Bothwell had been as moderate in their denunciation. But some of them, apparently, could not forget the youth of the king, and, not having the sense to see that his majesty's desire was to render a just decision, thought he might be frightened by strong language.

"It is easy for those to speak well of the pike, who have not felt the prod of its point," cried Lord Maxwell angrily. "Few English invasions have reached Stirling, but every one of them have crossed the Border. What matters the lifting of some English cattle? The Southerners never scrupled to eat good Scottish beef whenever they set foot on Scottish soil. I would hang the English envoy for daring to come to a Scottish king with complaints of cattle lifting."

The king frowned slightly but said nothing, and then Adam Scott of Tushielaw had to thrust his bull neck into the noose.

"I give you fair warning," he cried, "that if the king's forces are turned against the Borderers, my sword helps my neighbours."

"And I say the same," shouted Cockburn of Henderland.

Some of the opposition were about to speak, but the king held up his hand for silence.

"That is treason," he said quietly. "Adam Scott, I have heard that you are called King of the Border. Scotland is blessed with a number of men who are king of this, or king of that, and I am sure I make no objection, as long as they do not forget the difference that exists between a king in name and a king in reality. I asked for advice, but not for threats."

Then to the whole assemblage he went on—

"Gentlemen, I thank you for your counsel. I shall give a soothing reply to my uncle's ambassador, keeping in mind the peace that exists between the two countries, and then I shall take what has been said on each side into consideration and let you know the result."

Accepting this as dismissal, those there congregated withdrew, save only Sir David Lyndsay, the king having made a sign for him to remain. "Well, Davie," he said, when they were alone, "what do you think of it all?"

"To tell truth, your majesty," answered the poet, "it's a knotty problem, not to be solved by rhyming brain. When the first spokesman finished I was entirely of his opinion, but, after that, the Earl of Bothwell's plea seemed equally weighty, and between the two I don't know what to think."

"That is the disadvantage of an unbiased mind, Davie. Now, with good, strong prejudices, one side or the other, the way would be clear, and yet I despise a man who doesn't know his own mind."

"Scott and Cockburn seemed to know their minds very well," ventured the poet, with a smile.

"Yes, and if one or two more of them had spoken as decidedly, I would have been off to the Border to-night at the head of my troops. It is a weakness of mine, but I can't put up with a threat very well."

"Kings are rarely called upon to thole a threat," said Sir David, with a laugh.

"I'm not so sure of that, Davie. Kings have to thole many things if they are to rule justly. Now, Davie, if you'll but tell me just what to do, it will be a great help, for then I can take the opposite direction with confidence."

But the poet shook his head.

"I cannot tell you," he said. "There seems much to be said for both sides."

"Then, Davie, send down to the town for the cobbler; send for Flemming, he is a common-sense, canny body; he shall be the Solomon of the occasion. That broad-faced hammer of his seems to rap out wisdom as well as drive pegs. Bring him up with you, and we'll place the case before him."

As the rhymster left the room, Sir Donald Sinclair came clanking in, seemingly in something of a hurry.

"Was it your majesty's pleasure," began Sir Donald, "to have detained Adam Scott and Cockburn?"

"No. Why do you ask?"

"Because they have mounted their horses and are off to the Border as fast as two good steeds can carry them."

"And where are Bothwell, Home, and Maxwell, and the Lairds of Fairniherst, Johnston and Buccleuch?"

"They are all closeted in the Earl of Bothwell's room, your majesty. Shall I take any action regarding them?"

"Oh no; do not meddle with them. You heard the opinions given a while since, Donald? What conclusion did you arrive at?"

"I am scarcely an impartial judge, your majesty. A soldier is ever for fighting, and I fear he pays little attention to the right or wrong of it."

"You would try a fall with the Border kings perhaps?"

"Yes, your majesty, I would."

"Then I need have no fear but the troops will respond if I call on them?"

"None in the least, your majesty."

"Well, I am glad to hear that, Sir Donald, and, meanwhile, I can think of the project without any doubt regarding my army."

When the cobbler came to the castle with Sir David, the king led the way to one of his small private rooms, and there sketched out the argument on both sides of the question with great impartiality.

"Now, Flemming," he said, at the conclusion, "what is there to do?"

For a long time the shoemaker made no reply; then he scratched his head in perplexed fashion. At last he said:

"It gets beyond me, your majesty. Thieving is not right unless it's done under cover of law, which these reiving lads to the South seem to take small account of. On the other hand, to destroy them root and branch may be leaving Scotland naked to her enemy. I admit I'm fairly in a corner."

Sir David Lyndsay laughed.

"You're as bad as I am, cobbler," he said.

"There is one point," commented the king, "that no one seems to have taken any notice of, and that is this: Those who speak against the Border marauders are those who know little of them except by hearsay; while the lords in their neighbourhood, who should know them well, stand up for them, and even threaten to draw sword on their behalf."

"That certainly speaks well for the villains," admitted the cobbler.

"Then what is your verdict," demanded the king.

"Well, I kind of think I should leave them alone," said Flemming cautiously.

"Do you agree with him, David?"

"I'm not sure but I do. It seems a choice of two evils."

The king laughed riotously and smote his thigh.

"Well, of all half-hearted counsellors, King James has the champion pair; and yet I had made up my mind before I asked the advice of either of you."

"And what was that?" inquired Sir David, "to attack them?"

"No."

"To leave them alone?" suggested the cobbler.

"No."

"What then?" cried both together.

"What then? Why, just to get a little surer information. Here are three men of open minds. I propose that for the next week, or thereabouts, we three shall be honest cattle merchants, who will mount our honest horses and take a quiet bit journey along the Border. The scenery, they tell me, is grand, and David here will make poems on it. It's a healthy country, and the cobbler has been bending too assiduously over broken shoes of late, so the fresh air and the exercise will do him good."

"Losh, your majesty!" cried the cobbler, in dismay, "I'm no horseman. I never rode any four-legged thing but a cobbler's bench, and that side-saddle fashion."

"Oh, you'll have learnt when we reach the Border," said the king, with a laugh. "Before two days are past you'll be riding as well as Sir David, who is at present the worst horseman in all Scotland."

"Pegasus is the steed I yearn to ride," returned the poet, with a wry face.

"Yes, and even it sometimes throws you, David. You'll never be the Psalmist your namesake was. Well, we'll look on it as agreed. Flemming shall be purse-bearer, and so our tour will be an economical one. Here is a purse well filled. You will look after the drover's costumes, make all disbursements, and take care that you do not betray us by undue lavishness."

Thus it came about that three supposed drovers took their way to the Border by a route which drovers were never known to travel before, and, besides this, they were travelling empty-handed towards England, whereas, real drovers faced the south with their herds before them, and the north with those herds sold or stolen. Not one of the three had in his vocabulary a single word pertaining to the cattle trade, and every man with whom they spoke knew at once that, whatever else they might be, they were not drovers, and so the ill-fated three went blundering through the free-booters' country, climbing hills and descending dales, and frightening honest folk with the questions they asked; questions about men whose names should be spoken in a whisper, and even then with a look of fear over the shoulder. Innkeepers who saw them approach with delight, watched them leave with relief, thanking God that no raider had happened inside to hear their innocent inquiries; yet the three themselves were enjoying an interesting and instructive journey, and the king had come to the conclusion that the devil was not so black as he was painted.

At last, they stumbled into a hostelry kept by a man whose name was Armstrong. Their horses were taken care of and the trio sat down to a hearty meal, as had been their luck all along the Border.

"Landlord, does this meat come from England?" asked the king.

The landlord caught his breath. He stood stock still for a moment and then replied,—

"I hope it is to your lordship's liking."

"Oh! I'm no lordship," said James, "but an honest drover body, trying to find new markets for my stock."

"I can see that," replied the landlord; "then you will know that this meat's raised by Scotchmen."

"Raised!" laughed the king. "Raised where? In Northumberland? Are you sure 'lift' is not the word you mean?"

"Sir," said the landlord, gravely, "there's no lifting of cattle hereabout. This is not the Highlands. All in the neighbourhood are honest farmers or foresters."

"Earning their bread by the sweat of their brow," put in Sir David Lyndsay.

"Doubtless, when the English are after them," suggested the cobbler.

The landlord did not join in their mirth, but merely said,—

"If your dinner is to your liking, my duty is done."

"Quite so," answered the king. "We were merely curious regarding the origin of your viands; but the question seems to be a ticklish one in this district."

"Oh, not at all," replied the innkeeper grimly. "If you question enough, you are sure to meet some one who will make you a suitable answer."

The landlord, seemingly not liking the turn of the conversation, disappeared, and during the rest of the meal they were waited upon by a lowering, silent woman, who scowled savagely at them, and made no reply to the raillery of the king, who was in the highest spirits. They had ridden far that morning since breakfasting, and it was well after midday when they drew away from a table that had been devoted to their satisfying. Sir David and Flemming showed little inclination to proceed with their journey.

"The poor beasts must have a rest," said the poet, although none of the three were horsemen enough to go out and see how the animals fared at the hands of the stableman. The king was accustomed to be waited upon, and the other two knew little and cared less about horses. As they sat there in great content they heard suddenly a commotion outside and the clatter of many hoofs on the stone causeway. The door burst in, and there came, trampling, half a dozen men, who entered with scant ceremony, led by a stalwart individual who cast a quick glance from one to the other of the three who were seated. His eye rested on the king, whom, with quick intuition, he took to be the leader of the expedition and, doffing his feathered bonnet in a salutation that had more of mockery than respect in it, he said: "I hear that, like myself, you're in the cattle trade, and that you're anxious to learn the prospect of doing business in this mountainous locality."

"You are quite right," replied the king.

"I have in my byres near by," continued the man, "some of the finest stirks that ever stood on four hoofs. Would you be willing to come and give me your opinion of them, and say how much you care to pay for as many as you need?"

Again the man swept his bonnet nearly to the floor, and his six men, who stood back against the wall, as if to give the speaker the stage in the centre of the floor, glanced one at another. The king, however, was unruffled, and he replied with a twinkle in his eye,—

"My good sir, you are mistaken, we are on the other side of the market. We are sellers and not buyers."

"So was Judas," said the incomer, his politeness giving way to an expression of fierceness and cruelty which went far to terrify two of the seated men. "Are you sure, sir, that the cattle you sell have not two legs instead of four?"

"I don't understand you," replied the king.

"Is it men or stirks, you would give to the butcher?"

"Still I do not understand you," repeated the king.

"Oh, very well. How much are you asking for your cattle?"

"We are here rather to see how much may be offered."

"I can well believe you. Still, you must know something of the price of beasts on hoofs. How much would you want for a good, fat stirk? Answer me that!"

The king glanced at his two companions, and his glance said as plainly as words, "Give me a hint, in heaven's name, regarding the cost of a beast;" but in all Scotland he could not have found two men who knew less about the subject.

"Oh, well," said the king, nonchalantly, not at all liking the turn affairs had taken, "I suppose we would be satisfied with twenty pounds," and this being received with a roar of laughter, he added hastily, "twenty pounds Scots."

"Oh," said the big man, "I was afraid you were going to demand that amount in English currency. It is evident you will do well at the trade, if you can find such buyers."

"Then make us an offer," suggested the king, with the air of a man willing to listen to reason.

"Where are your cattle?"

"They're in the north."

"What part of the north?"

"My good fellow," cried the king, his temper rising, "you have asked many questions and answered none. Who are you, and what right have you to make your demands in such a tone?"

"Ah, then there's some spirit among the three of you. I am glad to see that. Who am I? I am Johnny Armstrong. Did you ever hear tell of him? And I suspect that your cattle are grown in the high town of Stirling. Am I right in that? It is in Stirling that you can sell what you may lift on the Border, and your cattle will be paid for in king's gold. You are spies, my fine gentlemen, and know as little of cattle as I know of the king and the court."

The king rejoined calmly,—

"The country is at peace. There can be no spies except in a time of war."

"Is it even so? Then what are you three doing rampaging up and down my land on the Border?"

"That the lands may be yours we do not dispute, nor have we interfered with them. The highways are the king's, and we three are peaceful subjects of his, claiming, therefore, the right to travel on them as we will, so long as we infringe not his peace or the liberty of any man."

"Stoutly spoken and bravely, considering in what king's dominion you now find yourself. You have to learn that Johnny, and not Jamie, is king of the Border. And when you're in the hands of a man named Armstrong, you'll find how little a boy named Stuart can do for you. Tie them up!"

Before one of the three could move from the stool he occupied, they were set upon by the ruffians, and each Stirling man found his ankles fastened together and his elbows tied behind his back with a speed that amazed him.

"Bless my soul," moaned the poet, "all this in broad daylight, and in the king's dominion."

They were carried outside and flung thus helpless, face downward on horses, like so many sacks of corn, each before a mounted man. Armstrong sprung upon his horse and led his men from the high road into the forest, his followers numbering something like a score. The captives, from their agonising position on the horses, could see nothing of the way they were being taken, except that they journeyed on and on through dense woodland. They lost all knowledge of direction, and, by and by, came to the margin of a brawling stream, arriving at last, much to their relief, at a stronghold of vast extent, situated on a beetling rock that overhung the river. Here the three were placed on their feet again, and chattering women and children crowded round them, but, in no case, was there a word of pity or an expression of sympathy for their plight.

The striking feature of the castle was a tall square tower, which might be anything from seventy to a hundred feet in height; and connected with it were several stone buildings, some two stories and some three stories high. Round the castle, in a wide, irregular circle, had been built a stout stone wall, perhaps twenty feet high, wide enough on the top for half a dozen men to walk abreast. The space enclosed was tolerably flat, and large enough for a small army to exercise in. Leaning against the inside of this wall was an array of sheds, which provided stabling for the horses, and numerous stalls in which many cattle were lowing. The contour of the wall was broken by a gateway, through which the troop and their captives had entered. The inlet could be closed by a massive gate, which now stood open, and by a stout portcullis that hung ready to drop when a lever was pulled. But the most gruesome feature of this robber's lair was a stout beam of timber, which projected horizontally from the highest open window of the square tower. Attached to the further end of the beam was a thick rope, the looped end of which encircled the drawn neck of a man, whose lifeless body swayed like a leaden pendulum, helpless in the strong breeze. Seeing the eyes of the three directed to this pitiful object, Armstrong said to one of his men,—

"Just slip that fellow's head from the noose, Peter; we may need the rope again to-night." Then turning to his prisoners, Armstrong spoke like a courteous host anxious to exhibit to a welcome guest the striking features of his domain.

"That's but a grisly sight, gentlemen, to contemplate on a lowering evening."

The day was darkening to its close, and a storm, coming up out of the west, was bringing the night quicker than the hour sanctioned.

"But here is an ingenious contrivance," continued the freebooter, cheerfully, "which has commanded the admiration of many a man we were compelled to hang. You see there are so many meddlesome bodies in this world that a person like myself, who wishes to live in peace with all his fellows, must sometimes give the interferers a sharp bit lesson."

"I can well believe it," answered the king.

"An Englishman of great ingenuity had a plan for capturing us, but, as it stands, we captured him; and being a merciful man, always loth to hang, when anything else can be done, I set him at work here, and this is one of his constructions. As it's growing dark, come nearer that you may see how it works."

At the bottom of the tower, and close to it, there lay a wooden platform which afforded standing room for six or seven men. Peter got up on this platform and pulled a cord, which opened a concealed sluice-gate and resulted in a roar of pouring water. Gradually the platform lifted, and the king saw that it was placed on top of a tall pine-tree that had been cut in the form of a screw, the gigantic threads of which were well oiled. A whirling horizontal water-wheel, through the centre of which the big screw came slowly upwards, with Peter on the gradually elevating platform, formed the motive power of the contrivance.

"You understand the mechanism?" said Armstrong. "By pulling one cord, the water comes in on this side of the wheel and the platform ascends. Another cord closes the sluice and everything is stationary. A third cord opens the gate which lets the water drive the wheel in the opposite direction and then the platform descends. You see, I have taken away the old lower stairway that was originally built for the tower, and this is the only means of getting up and down from the top story. It does not, if you will notice, go entirely to the top, but stops at that door, fifty feet from the rock, into which Peter is now entering."

"It is a most ingenious invention," admitted the king. "I never saw anything like it before."

"It would be very useful in a place like Stirling," said Johnny, looking hard at his prisoner.

"I suppose it would," replied the king, in a tone indicating that it was no affair of his, "but you see I'm not a Stirling man myself. I belong rather to all Scotland; a man of the world, as you might say."

By this time Peter had climbed to the highest room of the tower, worked his way on hands and knees out to the end of the beam, and had drawn up to him the swaying body. With the deftness of expert practice, he loosened the noose and the body dropped like a plummet through the air, disappearing into the chasm below. Peter, taking the noose with him, crawled backward, like a crab, out of sight, and into the tower again. Armstrong, from below, had opened the other sluice, and the empty platform descended as leisurely and as tremblingly as it had risen. Armstrong himself cut the cords that bound the ankles of his captives.

"Now, gentlemen," he said, "if you will step on the platform I shall have the pleasure of showing you to your rooms."

Three armed men and the three prisoners moved upwards together.

"A fine sylvan view you have," said the king.

"Is it not!" exclaimed Armstrong, seemingly delighted that it pleased his visitor.

After the mechanical device had landed them some fifty feet above the rocks, they ascended several flights of stairs, a man with a torch leading the way. The prisoners were conducted to a small room, which had the roof of the tower for its ceiling. In a corner of the cell cowered a very abject specimen of the human race, who, when the others came, seemed anxious to attract as little attention as possible.

Armstrong, again, with his own hands removed the remaining cords from the prisoners, and the three stretched up their arms, glad to find them at liberty once more.

"Place the torch in its holder," said Johnny. "Now, gentlemen, that will last long enough to light you to your supper, which you will find on the floor behind you. I'm sure you will rest here comfortably for the night. The air is pure at this height, and I think you'll like this eagle's nest better than a dungeon under the ground. For my own part, I abhor a subterranean cell, and goodness knows I've been in many a one, but we're civilised folk here on the Border and try to treat our prisoners kindly."

"You must, indeed, earn their fervent gratitude," said the king.

"We should, we should," returned Johnny, "but I'm not certain that we do. Man is a thrawn beast as a rule. And now, you'll just think over your situation through the night, and be ready to answer me in the morning all the questions I'll ask of you. I'll be wanting to know who sent you here, and what news you have returned to him since you have been on the Border."

"We will give your request our deep consideration," replied the king.

"I'm glad to hear that. You see, we are such merciful people that we have but one rope to hang our enemies with, while we should have a dozen by rights. Still, I think we could manage three at a pinch, if your answers should happen to displease me. You will excuse the barring of the door, but the window is open to you if your lodgings are not to your liking. And so, good-night, the three of you."

"Good-night to you, Mr. Armstrong," said the king.

Peter had drawn in the rope, and its sinister loop lay on the floor, its further length resting on the window sill, and extending out to the end of the beam. The cobbler examined it with interest. "Come," cried the king, "there is little use letting a supper wait for the eating merely because we seem to have gone wrong in our inquiries about the cattle."

Neither the poet nor the cobbler had any appetite for supper, but the king was young and hungry, and did justice to the hospitality of the Armstrongs.

"Have you been here long?" he asked of the prisoner in the corner.

"A good while," answered the latter despondently. "I don't know for how long. They hanged my mate."

"I saw that. Do they hang many here about?"

"I think they do," replied the prisoner. "Some fling themselves down on the rocks, and others are starved to death. You see, the Armstrongs go off on a raid, and there's no one here to bring us food, for the women folk don't like to tamper with that machine that comes to the lower stair. I doubt if Johnny starves them intentionally, but he's kept away sometimes longer than he expects."

"Bless me," cried the king, "think of this happening in Scotland. And now, cobbler, what are we to do?"

"I'm wondering if this man would venture out to the end of the beam and untie the rope," suggested Flemming.

"Oh, I'll do that, willingly," cried the prisoner. "But what is the use of it;

it's about ten times too short, as the Armstrongs well know."

"Are we likely to be disturbed here through the night?" asked Flemming.

"Oh no, nor till late in the day to-morrow; they'll be down there eating and drinking till all hours, then they sleep long."

"Very well. Untie the other end of the rope, and see you crawl back here without falling."

As the prisoner obeyed instructions, Flemming rose to his feet and began feeling in his pockets, drawing forth, at last, a large brown ball.

"What is your plan, cobbler?" asked the king, with interest.

"Well, you see," replied Flemming, "the rope's short, but it's very thick."

"I don't see how that is to help us."

"There are nine or ten strands that have gone to the making of it, and I'm thinking that each of those strands will bear a man. Luckily, I have got a ball of my cobbler's wax here, and that will strengthen the strands, keep the knots from slipping, and make it easier to climb down."

"Cobbler!" cried the king, "if that lets us escape, I'll knight you."

"I care little for knighthood," returned the cobbler, "but I don't want to be benighted here."

"After such a remark as that, your majesty," exclaimed the poet, "I think you should have him beheaded, if he doesn't get us out of this safely."

"Indeed, Sir David," said the cobbler, as he unwound the rope, "if I don't get you out of here, the Armstrongs will save his majesty all trouble on the score of decapitation."

There was silence now as the three watched the deft hands of the cobbler, hurrying to make the most of the last rays of the flickering torch in the wall. He tested the strands and proved them strong, then ran each along the ball of wax, thus cementing their loose thread together. He knotted the ends with extreme care, tried their resistance thoroughly, and waxed them unsparingly.

It was a business of breathless interest, but at last the snake-like length of thin rope lay on the floor at his disposal. He tied an end securely to the beam just outside the window-sill so that there would be no sharp edge to cut the cord, then he paid out the line into the darkness, slowly and carefully that it might not became entangled.

"There," he said at last, with a sigh of satisfaction, "who's first for the rope. We three await your majesty's commands."

"Do you know the country hereabout?" asked the king of the man who had been prisoner longest.

"Every inch of it."

"Can you guide us safely to the north in the darkness?"

"Oh, yes, once I am down by the stream."

"Then," said the king, "go down by the stream. When you are on firm footing say no word, but shake the rope. If you prove a true guide to us this night we will pay you well."

"I shall be well paid with my liberty," replied the prisoner, crawling cautiously over the stone sill and disappearing in the darkness. The cobbler held the taut line in his hand. No man spoke, they hardly seemed to breathe until the cobbler said:

"He's safe. Your majesty should go next."

"The captain is the last to leave the ship," said the king; "over you go, Flemming." After the cobbler, Sir David descended, followed by the king; and they found at the bottom of the ravine some yards of line to spare.

Their adventures through that wild night and the next day, until they came to a village where they could purchase horses, form a story in themselves.

When the king reached Stirling, and was dressed once more in a costume more suited to his station than that which had been torn by the brambles of the Border, he called to him the chief minister of his realm.

"You will arrest immediately," he said, "Cockburn of Henderland, and

Adam Scott of Tushielaw, and have them beheaded."

"Without trial, your majesty?" asked the minister in amazement.

"Certainly not without trial, but see that the trial is as short as possible. Their crime is treason; the witnesses as many as you like to choose from our last council meeting. I love and adhere to the processes of law, but see that there is no mistake about the block being at the end of your trial." The minister made a note of this and awaited further instructions. "Place the Earl of Bothwell in the strongest room that Edinburgh Castle has vacant. Imprison Lord Maxwell and Lord Home and the Lairds of Fairniherst, Johnston and Buccleuch, in whatever stronghold is most convenient. Let these orders be carried out as speedily as possible."

The next man called into the royal presence was Sir Donald Sinclair.

"Have you five hundred mounted men ready for the road, Sir Donald?"

"Yes, your majesty, a thousand if you want them."

"Very well, a thousand I shall have, and I shall ride with you to the Border."

Nevertheless, when the king came to the inn where he had been captured, there were but twenty troopers with him. Sir Donald was the spokesman on that occasion. He said to the landlord, whose roving eye was taking count of the number of horses,—

"Go to Johnny Armstrong and tell him that the king, with twenty mounted men at his back, commands his presence here, and see that he comes quickly."

Johnny was not slow in replying to the invitation, and forty troopers rode behind him. The king sat on his horse, a little in advance of his squadron. As a mounted man, James looked well, and there was but little resemblance between him and the unfortunate drover, who had been taken prisoner at that spot two short weeks before.

"I have come promptly in answer to your majesty's call," said Armstrong, politely removing his bonnet, but making no motion to pay further deference to the King of Scotland.

"It gives me great pleasure to see you," replied the king, suavely. "You travel with a large escort, Mr. Armstrong?"

"Yes, your majesty, I am a sociable man and I like good company. The more stout fellows that are at my back, the better I am pleased."

"In this respect we are very much alike, Mr. Armstrong, as you will admit if you but cast your eyes to the rear of your little company."

At this, Johnny Armstrong violated a strict rule of royal etiquette and turned the back of his head to his king. He saw the forest alive with mounted men, their circle closing in upon him. He muttered the word: "Trapped!" and struck the spurs into his horse's flank. The stung steed pranced in a semi-circle answering his master's rein, but the fence of mounted steel was complete, every drawn sword a picket. Again Armstrong, laughing uneasily, faced the king, who still stood motionless.

"Your majesty has certainly the advantage of me as far as escort is concerned."

"It would seem so," replied James. "You travel with twoscore of men; I with a thousand."

"I have ever been a loyal subject of your majesty," said Armstrong, moistening his dry lips. "I hope I am to take no scathe for coming promptly and cordially to welcome your majesty to my poor district."

"You will be better able to answer your own question when you have replied to a few of mine. Have you ever met me before, Mr. Armstrong?"

The robber looked intently at the king.

"I think not," he said.

"Have you ever seen this man before?" and James motioned Sir David Lyndsay from the troop at his side.

Armstrong drew the back of his hand across his brow.

"I seem to remember him," he said, "but cannot tell where I have met him."

"Perhaps this third man will quicken your memory," and the cobbler came forward, dressed as he had been the night he was captured.

Armstrong gasped, and a greenish pallor overspread his face.

"What is your answer, Armstrong?" asked the king.

"I and my forty men will serve your majesty faithfully in your army if you grant us our lives."

"No thieves ride with any of Scotland's brigade, Armstrong."

"I will load your stoutest horse with gold until he cannot walk, if you spare our lives."

"The revenues of Scotland are sufficient as they are, Armstrong," replied the king.

"Harry of England will be glad to hear that the King of Scotland has destroyed twoscore of his stoutest warriors."

"The King of England is my relative, and I shall be happy to please him. The defence of Scotland is my care, and I have honest men enough in my army to see that it is secure. Have you anything further to say, Armstrong?"

"It is folly to seek grace at a graceless face. If we are for the tree, then to the tree with us. But if you make this fair forest bear such woeful fruit, you shall see the day when you shall die for lack of stout hearts like ours to follow you, as sure as this day is the fatal thirteenth."

The forty-one trees bore their burden, and thirteen years from that time the outlaw's prophecy was fulfilled.

The King's Gold

It is strange to record that the first serious difficulty which James encountered with the nobles who supported him, arose not over a question of State, but through the machinations of a foreign mountebank. The issue came to a point where, if the king had proceeded to punish the intriguer, his majesty might have stood alone while the lords of his court would have ranged themselves in support of the charlatan—a most serious state of things, the like of which has before now overturned a throne. In dealing with this unexpected crisis, the young king acted with a wisdom scarcely to be expected from his years. He directed the nobility as a skilful rider manages a mettlesome horse, sparing curb and spur when the use of the one might have unseated him, or the use of the other resulted in a frenzied bolt. Thus the judicious horseman keeps his saddle, yet arrives at the destination he has marked out from the beginning.

In the dusk of the evening, James went down the high street of Stirling, keeping close to the wall as was his custom when about to pay a visit to his friend the cobbler, for although several members of the court knew that he had a liking for low company, the king was well aware of the haughty disdain with which the nobles regarded those of the mechanical or trading classes. So he thought it best not to run counter to a prejudice so deeply rooted, and for this reason he restricted the knowledge of his visits to a few of his more intimate friends.

As the king was about to turn out of the main street he ran suddenly into the arms of a man coming from the shop of a clothier who made costumes for the court. As each started back from the unexpected encounter, the light from the mercer's shop window lit up the face of his majesty's opponent, and the latter saw that he had before him his old friend, Sir David Lyndsay.

"Ha, Davie!" cried the king, "it's surely late in the day to choose the colours for a new jacket."

"Indeed your majesty is in the right," replied Sir David, "but I was not selecting cloth; I was merely enacting the part of an honest man, and liquidating a reckoning of long standing."

"What, a poet with money!" exclaimed the king. "Who ever heard of such a thing? Man Davie, you might share the knowledge of your treasure-house with a friend. Kings are always in want of money. Is your gold mine rich enough for two?"

The king spoke jocularly, placing no particular meaning upon his words, and if Sir David had answered in kind, James would doubtless have thought no more about the matter, but the poet stammered and showed such evident confusion that his majesty's quick suspicions were at once aroused. He remembered that of late a change had come over the court. Scottish nobles were too poor to be lavish in dress, and frequently the somewhat meagre state of their wardrobe had furnished a subject for jest on the part of ambassadors from France or Spain. But when other foreigners less privileged than an ambassador had ventured to make the same theme one for mirth, they speedily found there was no joke in Scottish steel, which was ever at an opponent's service, even if gold were not. So those who were wise and fond of life, became careful not to make invidious comparisons between the gallants of Edinburgh and Stirling, and those of Paris and Madrid. But of late the court at Stirling had blossomed out in fine array, and although this grandeur had attracted the notice of the king and pleased him, he had given no thought to the origin of the new splendour.

The king instantly changed his mind regarding his visit to the cobbler, linked arm with the poet, and together they went up the street. This sudden reversion of direction gave the royal wanderer a new theme for thought and surmise. It seemed as if all the town was on the move, acting as surreptitiously as he himself had done a few moments previously. At first he imagined he had been followed, and the suspicion angered him. In the gloom he was unable to recognise any of the wayfarers, and each seemed anxious to avoid detection, passing hurriedly or slipping quietly down some less frequented alley or lane. Certain of the figures appeared familiar, but none stopped to question the king.

"Davie," cried James, pausing in the middle of the street, "you make a very poor conspirator."

"Indeed, your majesty," replied the poet earnestly, "no one is less of a conspirator than I."

"Davie, you are hiding something from me."

"That I am not, your majesty. I am quite ready to answer truly any question your majesty cares to ask."

"The trouble is, Davie, that my majesty has not yet got a clue which will lead to shrewd questioning, but as a beginning, I ask you, what is the meaning of all this court stir in the old town of Stirling?"

"How should I know, your majesty?" asked the poet in evident distress.

"There now, Davie, there now! The very first question I propound gets an evasive answer. The man who did not know would have replied that he did not. I dislike being juggled with, and for the first time in my life, Sir David Lyndsay, I am angered with you."

The knight was visibly perturbed, but at last he answered,—

"In this matter I am sworn to secrecy."

"All secrets reveal themselves at the king's command," replied James sternly. "Speak out; speak fully, and speak quickly."

"There is no guilt in the secret, your majesty. I doubt if any of your court would hesitate to tell you all, were it not that they fear ridicule, which is a thing a Scottish noble is loth to put up with whether from the king or commoner."

"Get on, and waste not so much time in the introduction," said his majesty shortly.

"Well, there came some time since to Stirling, an Italian chemist, who took up his abode and set up his shop in the abandoned refectory of the old Monastery. He is the author of many wonderful inventions, but none interests the court so much as the compounding of pure gold in a crucible from the ordinary earth of the fields."

"I can well believe that," cried the king. "I have some stout fighters in my court who fear neither man nor devil in battle, yet who would stand with mouth agape before a juggler's tent. But surely, Davie, you, who have been to the colleges, and have read much from learned books, are not such a fool as to be deluded by that ancient fallacy, the transmutation of any other metals into gold?"

Sir David laughed uneasily.

"I did not say I believed it, your majesty, still, a man must place some credence in what his eye sees done, as well as in what he reads from books; and after all, the proof of the cudgel is the rap on the head. I have beheld the contest, beginning with an empty pot and ending with a bar of gold."

"Doubtless. I have seen a juggler swallow hot iron, but I have never believed it went down his throttle, although it appeared to have done so. Did you get any share of the transmuted gold? That's the practical test, my Davie."

"That is exactly the test your barons applied. I doubt if their nobilities would take much interest in a scientific experiment were there no profit at the end of it. Each man entering the laboratory pays what he pleases to the money taker at the table, but it must not be less than one gold bonnet-piece. When all have entered, the doors are closed and locked. The amount of money collected is weighed against small bars of gold which the alchemist places in the opposite scale until the two are equally balanced. This bar of gold he then throws into the crucible."

"Oh, he puts gold into the crucible, does he? Where then is the profit? I thought these necromancers made gold from iron."

"Signor Farini's method is different, your majesty. He asserts that like attracts like, and that the gold in the crucible will take to itself the minute unseen particles which he believes exists in all soils; the intense heat burning away the dross and leaving the refined gold."

"I see; and how ends this experiment?"

"The residue is cooled and weighed. Sometimes it is double the amount of gold put in, sometimes treble; and I have known him upon occasion take from the crucible quadruple the gold of the bar, but never have I known a melting fall below double the amount collected by the man at the table. At the final act each noble has returned to him double or treble the gold he relinquished on entering."

"Where then arises the profit to your Italian? I never knew these foreigners to work for nothing."

"He says he does it for love of Scotland and hatred of England; an ancient enemy. Were but the Scottish nation rich, he thinks they could the better withstand incursions from the south."

"Well, Davie, that seems to me a most unsubstantial reason. Scotland's protection has been her poverty in all except hard knocks. Were she as wealthy as France it would be the greater temptation for Englishers to overrun the country. My grandfather, James the Third, had a black chest full of gold and jewels, yet he was murdered flying from defeat in battle. When does this golden wizard fire his cauldron, Davie?"

"To-night, your majesty. That is the reason the nobles of your court were making sly haste to his domicile."

"Ah, and Sir David Lyndsay was hurrying to the same spot so blindly that he nearly overran his monarch."

"It is even so, your majesty."

"Then am I hindering you from much profit, and you must even blame yourself for being so long in the telling. However, it is never too late to turn one bonnet-piece into two. So, Davie, lead the way, for I would see this alchemist turn out gold from a pot as a housewife boils potatoes."

"I fear, your majesty, that the doors will be shut."

"If they are, Davie, the king's name will open them. Lead the way; lead the way."

The doors were not shut but were just on the point of closing when Sir

David put his shoulder to them and forced his way in, followed closely by his companion. The king and his henchman found themselves in a small anteroom, furnished only with a bench and a table; on the latter was a yellow heap of bonnet-pieces of the king's own coinage. Beside this heap lay a scroll with the requisites for writing. The money-taker, a gaunt foreigner clad in long robes like a monk, closed the door and barred it securely, then returned to the table. He nodded to Sir David, and glanced with some distrust upon his plaid-covered companion.

"Whom have you brought to us, Sir Lyndsay?" asked the man suspiciously.

"A friend of mine, the Master of Ballengeich; one who can keep his own counsel and who wishes to turn an honest penny."

"We admit none except those connected with the court," demurred the money-taker.

"Well, in a manner, Ballengeich is connected with the court. He supplies the castle with the products of his farm."

The man shook his head.

"That will not do," he said, "my orders are strict. I dare not admit him."

"Is not my money as good as another's?" asked Ballengeich, speaking for the first time.

"No offence is meant to you, sir, as your friend Sir Lyndsay knows, but I have my orders and dare not exceed them."

"Do you refuse me admittance then?"

"I am compelled to do so, sir, greatly to my regret."

"Is not my surety sufficient?" asked Sir David.

"I am deeply grieved to refuse you, sir, but I cannot disobey my strict instructions."

"Oh, very well then," said the king impatiently, "we will stay no further question. Sir David here is a close friend of the king, and a friend of my own, therefore we will return to the castle and get the king's warrant, which, I trust, will open any door in Stirling."

The warder seemed nonplussed at this and looked quickly from one to the other; finally he said,—

"Will you allow me a moment to consult with my master?"

"Very well, so that you do not hold us long," replied the Master of Ballengeich.

"I shall do my errand quickly, for at this moment I am keeping the whole nobility of Scotland waiting."

The man disappeared, taking, however, the gold with him in a bag. In a short space of time he returned and bowing to the two waiting men he said,—

"My master is anxious to please you, Sir Lyndsay, and will accept the money of your friend." Whereupon the two placed upon the table five gold pieces each, and the amount was credited opposite their names upon the parchment.

Sir David, leading the way, drew aside one heavy curtain and then a second one, which allowed them to enter a long low-roofed room almost in total darkness, as far as the end to which they were introduced was concerned; but the upper portion of the hall was lit in lurid fashion. At the further end of the Refectory was a raised platform on which the heads of the Order had dined, during the prosperous days of the edifice, while the humbler brethren occupied, as was customary, the main body of the lower floor. Upon this platform stood a metal tripod, which held a basket of dazzling fire, and in this basket was set a crucible, now changing from red to white, under the constant exertions of two creatures who looked like imps from the lower regions rather than inhabitants of the upper world. These two strove industriously with a huge bellows which caused the fire to roar fiercely, and this unholy light cast its effulgence upon the faces of many notable men packed closely together in the body of the hall; it also shone on the figure of a tall man, the ghastly pallor of whose countenance was enhanced by a fringe of hair black as midnight. He had a nose like a vulture's beak, and eyes piercing in their intensity, as black as his midnight hair. His costume also resembled that of a monk in cut, but it was scarlet in hue; and the radiance of the furnace caused it to glow as if illumined by some fire from within.

At the moment the last two entered, Farini was explaining to his audience, in an accent palpably foreign, that he was a man of science, and that the devil gave him no aid in his researches, an assertion doubtless perfectly accurate. His audience listened to him with visible impatience, evidently anxious for talk to cease and practical work to begin.

The wizard held in his right hand the bag of gold that the king had seen taken from the outer room. Presently there entered through another curtained doorway, on what might be called the stage, the money-taker in the monk's dress, who handed to the necromancer the coins given him by Lyndsay and Ballengeich, which the wizard tossed carelessly into the bag. The attendant placed the scroll upon a table and then came forward with a weighing-machine held in his hand. The alchemist placed the gold from the bag upon one side of the scale, and threw into the other, bar after bar of yellow metal until the two were equal. Then the bag of gold was placed on the table beside the scroll, and the wizard carefully deposited the yellow bars within the crucible, the two imps now working the bellows more strenuously than ever.

The experiment was carried on precisely as Sir David had foretold, but there was one weird effect which the poet had not mentioned. When the necromancer added to the melting-pot huge lumps of what appeared to be common soil from the field, the mixture glared each time with a new colour. Once a vivid violet colour flamed up, which cast such a livid death-like hue on the faces of the knights there present, that each looked upon the other in obvious fear. Again the flame was pure white; again scarlet; again blue; again yellow. When at last the incantation was complete, the bellows-work was stopped. The coruscating caldron was lifted from the fire by an iron hook and chain, and set upon the stone floor to cool, bubbling and sparkling like a thing of evil; but the radiance became duller and duller as time went on, and finally its contents were poured out into a mould of sand, and there congealing, the result was lifted by tongs and laid upon the scale. The bag of gold was placed again in the opposite disc, but the heated metal far outweighed it. The wizard then unlocked a desk and threw coin after coin in the pan that held the bag, until at last the beam of the scale hung level. The secretary now pushed forward a table to the edge of the platform, and on the table placed a rush-light which served but to illuminate the parchment before him. With great rapidity he counted the gold pieces which were not in the bag, then whispered to his master.

The room was deathly still as the man in scarlet stepped forward to make his announcement.

"I regret," he said, "that our experiment has not been as successful as I had hoped. This doubtless has been caused by the poverty of the earth from which I took my material. I shall dig elsewhere against our next meeting, and then we may look for better results. To-night I can return to you but double the money you gave to my treasurer."

At this there went up what seemed to be a sigh of relief from the audience, which had been holding its breath with all the eagerness of a gambler, who had made a stake and awaited the outcome of the throw.

The necromancer, taking the parchment, called out name after name, and as each title was enunciated the bearer of it came to the edge of the platform and received from the secretary double the amount of gold pieces set down on the parchment. As each man secreted his treasure he passed along out of the hall; and so it came about that Sir David and Ballengeich, being the last on the list, received the remaining coins on the table, and silently took their departure.

The king spoke no word until they had entered the castle and were within his private room. Once there, the first thing he did was to pull from his pouch the coins he had received and examine them carefully one by one. There was no doubt about them, each was a good Scottish gold piece, with the king's profile and bonnet stamped thereon.

"You will find them genuine," said Sir David. "I had my own fears regarding them at first, thinking that this foreigner was trying the trick which Robert Cockran, the mason, accomplished so successfully during the reign of your grandfather, mixing the silver coins with copper and lead; but I had them tested by a goldsmith in Edinburgh and was assured the pieces are just what they claim to be."

"Prudent man!" exclaimed the king, throwing himself down on a seat and jingling the gold pieces. "Well, Davie, what do you think of it all? Give me an opinion as honest as the coin."

"Truth to tell, your majesty, I do not know what to think of it. It may be as he says, that the earth here contains particles of gold, that are drawn to the bars he throws in the melting-pot. If the man is a cheat, where can he hope for his profit?"

"Where indeed? I mind you told me he had other marvellous inventions; what are they?"

"He has a plan by which a man in full armour can enter the water and walk beneath it for any length of time without suffocating."

"Have you seen this tried?"

"No, your majesty; there has been no opportunity."

"What an admirable contrivance for invading Ireland! What are his plans as far as England is concerned? He seems, if I remember your tale aright, to have some animosity in that direction."

"He has constructed a pair of wings, and each soldier being provided with them can sail through the air across the Border."

"Admirable, admirable!" exclaimed the king nodding his head. "Now indeed is England ours, and France too for that matter, if his wings will carry so far. Have you seen these wings?"

"Yes, your majesty, but I have not seen them tried. They seem to be made of fine silk stretched on an extremely light framework, and are worked by the arms thrust up or down; thus, he says, a man may rise or fall at will."

"As to the falling, I believe him, and the rising I shall believe when I see it. Has our visit to-night then taught you nothing, David?"

"Nothing but what I knew before. What has it taught your majesty?"

"In the first place our charlatan does not want the king to know what he is doing, because when his subordinate refused me admittance and I said to him I would appeal to the king, he saw at once that this was serious, and wished to consult his master. His master was then willing to admit anyone so long as there was no appeal to the king. I therefore surmise he is most anxious to conceal his operations from me. What is your opinion, Davie?"

"It would seem that your majesty is in the right."

"Then again if he is a real scientist and has discovered an easy method of producing gold and is desirous to enrich Scotland, why should he object to a plain farmer like the Guidman of Ballengeich profiting by his production?"

"That is quite true, your majesty; but I suppose the line must be drawn somewhere, and I imagine he purposes to enrich only those of the highest rank, as being more powerful than the yeomen."

"Then we come back, Davie, to what I said before; why exclude the king who is of higher rank than any noble?"

"I have already confessed, your majesty, that I cannot fathom his motives."

"Well, you see at what we have arrived. This foreigner wishes to influence those who can influence the king. He wishes to have among his audience none but those belonging to the court. He has some project that he dare not place before the king. We will now return to the consideration of that project. In the first place, the man is not an Italian. Did a scholar like you, Davie, fail to notice that when he was in want of a word, it was a French word he used? He is therefore no Italian, but a Frenchman masquerading as an Italian. Therefore, the project, whatever it is, pertains to France, and it is his desire that this shall not be known. Now what does France most desire Scotland to do at this moment?"

"It thinks we should avenge Flodden; and many belonging to the court are in agreement with France on this point."

"Has your necromancer ever mentioned Flodden?"

"Once or twice he spoke of it with regret."

"I thought so," continued the king; "and now I hope you are beginning to see his design."

"What your majesty says is very ingenious; but if I may be permitted to raise an objection to the theory, I would ask your majesty why this was not done through the French ambassador? French gold has been used before now in the Scottish Court; and it seems to me that a great nation like France would not stoop to enlist the devices of a charlatan, if this man be a charlatan."

"Ah, now we enter the domain of State secrets, Davie, and there is where a king has an advantage over the commoner. Of course I know many things hidden from you which give colour to my surmise. Some while ago the French ambassador offered me a subsidy. Now I am not so avaricious as my grandfather, nor so lavish as my father, and I told the ambassador that I would depend on Scottish gold. I acquainted him with the success of my German miners in extracting gold from Leadhills in the Clydesdale, and I showed him my newly coined pieces. He was so condescendingly pleased and interested that he begged the privilege of having his own bars of metal coined in my mint, in order to disburse his expenses in the coin of the realm, and also to send some of our bonnet-pieces as specimens to France itself. This right of coinage I willingly bestowed upon him; firstly, because he asked it; secondly, I was glad to have some account of his expenditure. When I came in just now I examined these coins closely, and you imagined that I was suspicious of the purity of the metal. This was not so. I told my mint-master to coin all the bars the ambassador gave him, to keep a strict account of the issue, and to mark each piece with the letter 'F' on the margin. I find three of the coins which we received to-night bearing this private mark; therefore, they have passed through the hands of the French ambassador to the alchemist."

Sir David gave forth an exclamation of surprise. He left his seat, took the bonnet-pieces from his pocket and placed them under the lamp.

"Now," said the king, "you need sharp eyes to detect this mark, but there it is, and there, and there. Let us look a little closer into the object of France. The battle of Flodden was fought when I was little more than a year old; it destroyed the king, the flower of Scottish nobility, and ten thousand of her common soldiers. Who was responsible for this frightful calamity? My mother was strongly against the campaign, which was to bring the forces of her husband in contention with the forces of her brother, at that moment absent in France. The man who urged on the conflict was De la Motte, the French ambassador, standing ever at my father's side, whispering his treacherous, poisonous advice into an ear too willing to listen. England was not a bitter enemy, for England did not follow up her victory and march into Scotland, where none were left to command a Scottish army, and no Scottish army was left to obey. Scotland, on this occasion, was merely the catspaw of France. Now I am the son of an Englishwoman. The English king is my uncle, and France fears that I will keep the peace with my neighbour; so through his ambassador, he sounds me, and learns that such indeed is my intention. France resolves to leave me alone and accomplish its object by corrupting, with gold coined in my own mint, the nobles of my court, and, by God!" cried James in sudden anger, bringing his fist down on the table and making the coins jingle, "France is succeeding, through the blind stupidity of men who might have been expected to know their right hand from their left. The greatest heads of my realm are being cozened by a trickster; befooled in a way that any humble ploughman should be ashamed of. You see now why they wish to keep the silly proceedings from the king. I tell you, Davie, that Italian's head comes off, and thus in some small measure will I avenge Flodden."

Sir David Lyndsay sat meditatively silent for some moments while the king in angry impatience strode up and down the small limits of the room. When the heat of his majesty's temper had partially cooled, Sir David spoke with something of diplomatic shrewdness.

"I never before realised the depth and penetration of your majesty's mind. You have gone straight to the heart of this mystery, and have thrown light into its obscurest corner, as a dozen flaming torches would have illumined that dark laboratory in the Monastery. I have shared the stupidity of your nobles, which the clarity of your judgment now exposes so plainly; therefore, I feel that it would be presumption on my part to offer advice to your majesty in the further prosecution of this affair."

"No, Davie, no," said the king, stopping in his march and speaking with pleased cordiality, "no, I value your advice; you are an honest man, and it is not to be expected that the subtilty and craftiness of these foreigners should be as clear to you as the sunshine on a Highland hill. Speak out, Davie, and if you give me your counsel, I know it will be as wholesome as oatmeal porridge."

"Well, your majesty, you must meet subtilty with subtilty."

"I am not sure that the adage holds good, Davie," demurred the king. "You cannot outrace a Highlandman in his own glen, although you may fight him fairly in the open. Once this Frenchman's head is off, you stop his boiling-pot."

"That is quite true, your majesty, but if the French ambassador should put in a claim for his worthless carcass, you will find yourself on the eve of a break with France, if you proceed to his execution."

"But I shall have made France throw off its mask."

"It is not France I am thinking about, your majesty. Your own nobles have gone clean daft over this Italian. He is their goose that lays the golden eggs, and you saw yourself to-night with what breathless expectation they watched his experimenting. I am sure, your majesty, that they will stand by him, and that you will find not only France but Scotland arrayed against you. A moment's reflection will show you the danger. These meetings have been going on for months past, yet no whisper of their progress has reached your majesty's ears."

"That is true; even you yourself, Davie, kept silent."

"I swore an oath of silence, and honestly, I did not think that this gold-making was an affair of State."

"Very well. I will act with caution. The breath of the money-getter tarnishes the polish of the sword; and in my dealings I shall try to recollect that I have to do with men growing rapidly rich, as well as with nobles who should be too proud to accept unearned gold from any man. Now, Davie, I'll need your help in this, and in aiding me you will assist yourself, thus will virtue be its own reward, as is preached to us. I will give you as many gold pieces as you need, and instead of paying three pieces at the entrance, give the man three hundred. Urge all the nobles to increase their wagers; for thus we shall soon learn the depths of this yellow treasury. If I attempt to wring the neck of the goose before the eggs are laid, my followers would be justified in saying that the English part of my nature had got the better of the Scotch. Meanwhile, I will know nothing of this man's doings, and I hope for your sake, Davie, that the gold mine will prove as prolific as my own in the Clydesdale."

The nobles followed the example set to them by the lavish Sir David. They needed no urging from him to increase their stakes. The fever of the gambler was on each of them, and soon the alleged Italian began to be embarrassed in keeping up the pace he had set for himself. It required now an enormous sum to pay even double the amount taken at the door. The necromancer announced that the meetings would be held less often, but the nobles would not have it so. Then his experiments became less and less successful. One night the bonus amounted only to half the coins given to the treasurer, and then there were ominous grumblings. At the next meeting the bare amount paid in was given back, and the deep roar of resentment which greeted this proclamation made the foreigner tremble in his red robe. The ambassador was sending messenger after messenger to France, and looked anxiously for their return, while the necromancer did everything to gain time. At last there came an experiment which failed entirely; no gold was produced in the crucible. The alchemist begged for a postponement, but swords flashed forth and he was compelled on the spot to renew his incantation. If gold could be made on one occasion why not on another? cried the barons with some show of reason. The conjurer had conjured up a demon he could not control; the demon of greed.

The only man about the court who seemed to know nothing of what was going forward was the king himself. The French ambassador narrowly watched his actions, but James was the same free-hearted, jovial, pleasure-seeking monarch he had always been. He hunted and caroused, and was the life of any party of pleasure which sallied forth from the castle. He disappeared now and then, as was his custom, and could not be found, although his nobles winked at one another, while the perturbed French ambassador looked anxiously for the treasure ship that never came.

At last the nobles, who, in spite of their threatenings, had too much shrewdness to kill the gold-maker, hoping his lapse of power was only temporary, forced the question to a head and made appeal to the astonished king himself. Here was a man, they said, who could make gold and wouldn't. They desired a mandate to go forth, compelling him to resume the lucrative occupation he had abandoned.

The king expressed his amazement at what he heard, and summoned the mountebank before him. The gold-maker abandoned his robe of scarlet and appeared before James dressed soberly. He confessed that he knew the secret of extracting gold from ordinary soil, but submitted that he was not a Scottish citizen and therefore could not properly be coerced by the Scottish laws so long as he infringed none of the statutes. The king held that this appeal was well founded, and disclaimed any desire to coerce a citizen of a friendly state. At this the charlatan brightened perceptibly, and proportionately the gloom on the brows of the nobles deepened.

"But if you can produce gold, as you say, why do you refuse to do so?" demanded the king.

"I respectfully submit to your majesty," replied the mountebank, "that I have now perfected an invention of infinitely greater value than the gold-making process; an invention that will give Scotland a power possessed by no other nation, and which will enable it to conquer any kingdom, no matter how remote it may be from this land I so much honour. I wish, then, to devote the remaining energies of my life to the enlarging of this invention, rather than waste my time in what is, after all, the lowest pursuit to which a man may demean himself, namely, the mere gathering of money," and the speaker cast a glance of triumph at the disgruntled barons.

"I quite agree with you regarding your estimation of acquisitiveness," said the king cordially, giving no heed to the murmurs of his followers. "In what does this new invention consist?"

"It is simply a pair of wings, your majesty, made from the finest silk which I import from France. They may be fitted to any human being, and they give that human being the power which birds have long possessed."

"Well," said the king with a laugh, "I should be the last to teach a Scottish warrior to fly; still the ability to do so would have been, on several occasions, advantageous to us. Have you your wings at hand?"

"Yes, your majesty."

"Then you yourself shall test them in our presence."

"But I should like to spend, your majesty, some further time on preparation," demurred the man uneasily.

"I thought you said a moment ago that the invention was perfect."

"Nothing human is perfect, your majesty, and if I said so I spoke with the over-confidence of the inventor. I have, however, succeeded in sailing through the air, but cannot yet make way against a wind."

"Oh, you have succeeded so far as to interest us in a most attractive experiment. Bid your assistant bring them at once, and let us understand their principle. I rejoice to know that Scotland is to have the benefit of your great genius."

Farini showed little enthusiasm anent the king's confidence in him. He had, during the colloquy, cast many an anxious glance towards the French ambassador, apparently much to the annoyance of that high dignitary, for now the Frenchman, seeing his continued hesitation, said sharply,—

"You have heard his majesty's commands; get on your paraphernalia."

When the Italian was at last equipped, looking like a demon in a painting that hung in the chapel, the king led the way to the edge of Stirling cliff.

"There," he said, indicating a spot on the brow of the precipice, "you could not find in all Scotland a better vantage-point for a flight."

The terrified man stood for a moment on the verge of the appalling precipice; then he gave utterance to a remarkable pronouncement, the import of which was perhaps misunderstood because of the chattering of his teeth.

"Oh, not here, your majesty! Forgive me, and I will confess everything. The gold which I pretended to——"

"Fly, you fool!" cried the French ambassador, pushing the Italian suddenly between the shoulders and launching him into space. With a wild scream Farini endeavoured to support himself with his gauze-like wings, and for a moment seemed to hover in mid-air; but the framework cracked and the victim, whirling head over heels, fell like a plummet to the bottom of the cliff.

"I fear you have been too impetuous with him," said the king severely, although as his majesty glanced at Sir David Lyndsay the faint suspicion of a wink momentarily obscured his eye,—a temporary veiling of the royal refulgence, which passed unnoticed as every one else was gazing over the cliff at the motionless form of the fallen man.

"I am to blame, sire," replied the ambassador contritely, "but I think the villain is an impostor, and I could not bear to see your royal indulgence trifled with. However, I am willing to make amends for my imprudence, and if the scoundrel lives, I shall, at my own expense, transport him instantly to France, where he shall have the attendance of the best surgeons the country affords."

"That is very generous of you," replied the king.

And the ambassador, craving permission to retire, hastened to translate his benevolence into action.

Farini was still unconscious when the ambassador and his attendants reached him; but the French nobleman proved as good as his word, for he had the injured man, whose thigh-bone was broken, conveyed in a litter to Leith, and from there shipped to France. But it was many a day before the Scottish nobles ceased to deplore the untimely departure of their gold-maker.

The King A-Begging

Literary ambition has before now led men into difficulties. The king had completed a poem in thirteen stanzas entitled "The Beggar Man," and the prime requisite of a completed poem is an audience to listen to it. In spite of the fact that he wrote poetry, the king was a sensible person, and he knew that if he read his verses to the court, the members thereof were not the persons to criticise adequately the merits of such a composition; for you cannot expect a high noble, who, if he ever notices a beggar, merely does so to throw a curse at him, or lay the flat of his sword over his shoulders, to appreciate an epic which celebrates the free life led by a mendicant.

The king was well aware that he would receive ample praise for his production; king's goods are ever the best in the market, and though, like every other literary man, it was praise and not criticism that James wanted, still he preferred to have such praise from the lips of one who knew something of the life he tried to sing; therefore, as evening came on, the monarch dressed himself in his farmer costume, and, taking his thirteen stanzas with him, ventured upon a cautious visit to his friend the cobbler in the lower town of Stirling.

The cobbler listened with an attention which was in itself flattering, and paid his royal visitor the additional compliment of asking him to repeat certain of the verses, which the king in his own heart thought were the best. Then when the thirteenth stanza was arrived at, with the "No-that-bad" commendation, which is dear to the heart of the chary Scotchman, be he of high or low degree, Flemming continued,—

"They might be worse, and we've had many a poet of great reputation in Scotland who would not be ashamed to father them. But I'm thinking you paint the existence of a beggar in brighter colours than the life itself warrants."

"No, no, Flemming," protested the king earnestly. "I'm convinced that only the beggar knows what true contentment is. You see he begins at the very bottom of the ladder and every step he takes must be a step upward. Now imagine a man at the top, like myself; any move I make in the way of changing my condition must be downward. A beggar is the real king, and a king is but a beggar, for he holds his position by the favour of others. You see, Flemming, anything a beggar gets is so much to the good; and, as he has nothing to lose, not even his head—for who would send a beggar to the block—he must needs be therefore the most contented man on the face of the footstool."

"Oh, that's maybe true enough," replied Flemming, set in his own notion notwithstanding it was the king who opposed him; "but look you, what a scope a beggar has for envy, for there's nobody he meets that's not better off than himself."

"You go to extremes, Flemming. An envious man is unhappy wherever you place him; but I'm speaking of ordinary persons like ourselves, with charity and good-will toward all their fellow-kind. That man, I say, is happier as a beggar than as a king."

"Well, in so far as concerns myself, your majesty, I'd like to be sure of a roof over my head when the rain's coming down, and of that a beggar never can be. A king or a cobbler has a place to lay his head, at any rate."

"Aye," admitted the king, "but sometimes that place is the block. To tell you the truth, Flemming, I'm thinking of taking a week at the begging myself. A poet should have practical knowledge of the subject about which he writes. Give me a week on the road, Flemming, and I'll pen you a poem on beggary that will get warmer praise from you than this has had."

"I give your rhyming the very highest praise, and say that Gavin Douglas himself might have been proud had he put those lines together."

To this the king made no reply, and the cobbler, looking up at him, saw that a frown marred his brow. Then he remembered, as usual a trifle late, James's hatred of the Douglas name; a hatred that had been honestly earned by the Earl of Angus, head of that clan. Flemming was learning that it was as dangerous to praise, as to criticise a king. With native caution however, the cobbler took no notice of his majesty's displeasure, but added an amendment to his first statement.

"It would perhaps be more truthful to say that the verses are worthy of Sir David Lyndsay. In fact, although Sir David is a greater poet than Gavin Douglas, I doubt very much if in his happiest moments he could have equalled 'The Beggar Man.'"

In mentioning Sir David Lyndsay, Flemming had named the king's greatest friend, and the cobbler's desire to please could not have escaped the notice of a man much less shrewd than was James the Fifth. The king rose to his feet, checking a laugh.

"Man Flemming," he said, "I wonder at you! Have you forgotten that Sir David Lyndsay married Janet Douglas?"

The palpable dismay on the cobbler's countenance caused the young man to laugh outright.

"The cobbler should stick to his honesty, and not endeavour to tread the slippery path of courtiership. Flemming, if I wanted flattery I could get that up at the castle. I come down here for something better. If anything I could write were half so good as Sir David's worst, I should be a pleased man. But I'm learning, Flemming, I'm learning. This very day some of my most powerful nobles have presented me with a respectful petition. A year ago I should have said 'No' before I had got to the signature of it. But now I have thanked them for their attention to affairs of State, although between me and you and that bench, Flemming, it's a pure matter of their own greed and selfishness. So I've told them I will give the subject my deepest consideration, and that they shall have their answer this day fortnight. Is not that the wisdom of the serpent combined with the harmlessness of the dove?"

"It is indeed," agreed the cobbler.

"Very well; to-morrow it shall be given out that this petition will occupy my mind for at least a week, and during that time the king is invisible to all comers, high or low. To-morrow, Flemming, you'll get me as clean a suit of beggar's rags as you can lay your hands on. I'll come down here as the Master of Ballengeich, and leave these farmer's clothes in your care. I shall pass from this door as a beggar, and come back to it in the same condition a week or ten days hence, so see that you're at hand to receive me."

"Does your majesty intend to go alone?"

"Entirely alone, Flemming. Bless me, do you imagine I would tramp the country as a beggar with a troop of horse at my back?"

"Your majesty would be wise to think twice of such a project," warned the cobbler.

"Oh, well, I've doubled the number; I've thought four times about it; once when I was writing the poem, and three times while you were raising objections to my assertion that the beggar is the happiest man on earth."

"If your majesty's mind is fixed, then there's no more to be said. But take my advice and put a belt round your body with a number of gold pieces in it, for the time may come when you'll want a horse in a hurry, and perhaps you may be refused lodgings even when you greatly need them; in either case a few gold rascals will stand your friend."

"That's canny counsel, Flemming, and I'll act on it."

"And perhaps it might be as well to leave with some one in whom you have confidence, instructions so that you could be communicated with if your presence was needed hurriedly at Stirling."

"No, no, Flemming. Nothing can go wrong in a week. A beggar with a string tied to his legs that some one in Stirling can pull at his pleasure, is not a real beggar, but a slave. If they should want me sorely in Stirling before I return, they'll think the more of me once I am back."

And thus it came about that the King of Scotland, with a belt of gold around his waist in case of need, and garments concealing the belt which gave little indication that anything worth a robber's care was underneath, tramped the high roads and byways of a part of Scotland, finding in general a welcome wherever he went, for he could tell a story that would bring a laugh, and sing a song that would bring a tear, and all such rarely starve or lack shelter in this sympathetic world.

Only once did he feel himself in danger, and that was on what he thought to be the last day of his tramp, for in the evening he expected to reach the lower town of Stirling, even though he came to it late in the night. But the weather of Scotland has always something to say to the pedestrian, and it delights in upsetting his plans.

He was still more than two leagues from his castle, and the dark Forest of Torwood lay between him and royal Stirling, when towards the end of a lowering day, there came up over the hills to the west one of the fiercest storms he had ever beheld, which drove him for shelter to a wayside inn on the outskirts of the forest. The place of shelter was low and forbidding enough, but needs must when a Scottish storm drives, and the king burst in on a drinking company, bringing a swirl of rain and a blast of wind with him; so fierce in truth was the wind that one of the drinkers had to spring to his feet and put his shoulder to the door before the king could get it closed again. He found but scant welcome in the company. Those seated on the benches by the fire scowled at him; and the landlord seeing he was but a beggar, did not limit his displeasure to so silent a censure.

"What in the fiend's name," he cried angrily, "does the like of you want in here?"

The king nonchalantly shook the water from his rags and took a step nearer the fire.

"That is a very unnecessary question, landlord," said the young man with a smile, "nevertheless, I will answer it. I want shelter in the first place, and food and drink as soon as you can bring them."

"Shelter you can get behind a stone dyke or in the forest," retorted his host; "food and drink are for those who can pay for it. Get you gone! You mar good company."

"In truth, landlord, your company is none to my liking, but I happen to prefer it to the storm. Food and drink, you say, are for those who can pay; you see one of them before you, therefore, sir, hasten to your duty, or it may be mine to hurry you unpleasantly."

This truculence on the part of a supposed beggar had not the effect one might have expected of increasing the boisterousness of the landlord. That individual well knew that many beggars were better able to pay their way than was he himself when he took to journeying, so he replied more civilly,—

"I'll take your order for a meal when I have seen the colour of your money."

"Quite right," said the king, "and only fair Scottish caution." Then with a lack of that quality he had just commended, he drew his belt out from under his coat, and taking a gold piece from it, threw the coin on the table.

The entrance of the king and the manner of his reception exposed him to the danger almost sure to attend the display of so much wealth in such forbidding company. A moment later he realised the jeopardy in which his rashness had placed him, by the significant glances which the half-dozen rough men there seated gave to each other. He was alone and unarmed in a disreputable bothy on the edge of a forest, well known as the refuge of desperate characters. He wished that he had even one of the sharp knives belonging to his friend the cobbler, so that he might defend himself. However, the evil was done, if evil it was, and there was no help for it. James was never a man to cross a bridge before he came to it; so he set himself down to the steaming venison brought for his refreshment, and made no inquiry whether it were poached or not, being well aware that any question in that direction was as unnecessary as had been the landlord's first query to himself. He was young. His appetite, at all times of the best, was sharpened by his journey, and the ale, poor as it was, seemed to him the finest brew he had ever tasted. The landlord was now all obsequiousness, and told the beggar he could command the best in the house.

When the time came to retire, his host brought the king by a ladder to a loft which occupied the whole length of the building, and muttered something about the others sleeping here as well, but thanked Heaven there was room enough for an army.

"This will not do for me," said the beggar, coming down again. "I'll take to the storm first. What is this chamber leading out from the tap-room?"

"That is my own," replied the landlord, with some return of his old incivility, "and I'll give it up to no beggar."

The king without answering opened the door of the chamber and found himself in a room that could be barricaded. Taking a light with him he examined it more minutely.

"Is this matchlock loaded?" he asked, pointing to a clumsy gun, which had doubtless caused the death of more than one deer in the forest.

The landlord answered in surly fashion that it was, but the king tested the point for himself.

"Now," he said, "I rest here, and you will see that I am not disturbed. Any man who attempts to enter this room gets the contents of this gun in him, and I'll trust to my two daggers to take care of the rest."

He had no dagger with him, but he spoke for the benefit of the company in the tap-room. Something in his resolute manner seemed to impress the landlord, who grumbled, muttering half to himself and half to his companions, but he nevertheless retired, leaving the king alone, whereupon James fortified the door, and afterward slept unmolested the sleep of a tired man, until broad day woke him.

Wonderful is the change wrought in a man's feelings by a fair morning. A new day; a new lease of life. The recurrent morning must have been contrived to give discouraged humanity a fresh chance. The king, amazed to find that he had slept so soundly in spite of the weight of apprehension on his mind the night before, discovered this apprehension to be groundless in the clear light of the new day. The sulky villains of the tap-room were now honest fellows who would harm no one, and James laughed aloud at his needless fears; the loaded matchlock in the corner giving no hint of its influence towards a peaceful night. The landlord seemed, indeed, a most civil person, who would be the last to turn a penniless man from his door. James, over his breakfast, asked what had become of the company, and his host replied that they were woodlanders; good lads in their way, but abashed before strangers. Some of them had gone to their affairs in the forest and others had proceeded to St. Ninians, to enjoy the hanging set for that day.

"And which way may your honour be journeying?" asked the innkeeper, "for I see that you are no beggar."

"I am no beggar at such an inhospitable house as this," replied the wayfarer, "but elsewhere I am a beggar, that is to say, the gold I come by is asked for, and not earned."

"Ah, that's it, is it?" said the other with a nod, "but for such a trade you need your weapons by your side."

"The deadliest weapons," rejoined the king mysteriously, "are not always those most plainly on view. The sting of the wasp is generally felt before it is seen."

The landlord was plainly disturbed by the intelligence he had received, and now made some ado to get the change for the gold piece, but his guest replied airily that it did not matter.

"With whatever's coming to me," he said, "feed the next beggar that applies to you on a rainy night with less at his belt to commend him than I have."

"Well, good-day to you, and thank you," said the innkeeper. "If you're going Stirling way, your road's straight through the forest, and when you come to St. Ninians you'll be in time to see a fine hanging, for they're throttling Baldy Hutchinson to-day, the biggest man between here and the Border, yes, and beyond it, I warrant."

"That will be interesting," replied the king. "Good-day to you."

At the side of the wall, which ran from the end of the hostel and enclosed a bit of ground appertaining to it, James stooped ostensibly to tie his shoe, but in reality to learn if his late host made any move, for he suspected that the sinister company of the night before might not be so far away as the landlord had intimated. His stratagem was not without its reward. The back door opened, and he heard the landlord say in a husky whisper to some one unseen,—

"Run, Jock, as fast's you can to the second turning in the road, and tell Steenie and his men they'd best leave this chap alone; he's a robber himself."

The king smiled as he walked slowly north towards the forest and saw a bare-legged boy race at great speed across the fields and disappear at their margin. He resolved to give time for this message to arrive, so that he might not be molested, and therefore sauntered at a more leisurely rate than that at which a man usually begins a journey on an inspiring morning.

Entering the forest at last, he relaxed no precaution, but kept to the middle of the road with his stout stick ready in his hand. Whether Jock found his men or not he never learned, but at the second turning five stalwart ruffians fell upon him; two armed with knives, and three with cudgels. The king's early athletic training was to be put to a practical test. His first action was to break the wrist of one of the scoundrels who held a knife, but before he could pay attention to any of the others he had received two or three resounding blows from the cudgels, and now was fully occupied warding off their strokes, backing down the road to keep his assailants in front of him. His great agility gave him an advantage over the comparative clumsiness of the four yokels who pressed him, but he was well aware that an unguarded blow might lay him at their mercy. He was more afraid of the single knife than of the three clubs, and springing through a fortunate opening was delighted to crack the crown of the man who held the blade, stretching him helpless in a cart rut. The three who remained seemed in no way disheartened by the discomfiture of their comrades, but came on with greater fury. The king retreated and retreated baffling their evident desire to get in his rear, and thus the fighting four came to the corner of the road that James had passed a short time previously. One of the trio got in a nasty crack on the top of the beggar's bonnet, which brought him to his knees, and before he could recover his footing, a blow on the shoulder felled him. At this critical juncture there rose a wild shout down the road, for the fighting party, in coming round the turn, had brought themselves within view of a sturdy pedestrian forging along at a great pace, which he nevertheless marvellously accelerated on seeing the mêlée. For a moment the dazed man on the ground thought that the landlord had come to his rescue, but it was not so. It seemed as if a remnant of the storm had swept like a whirlwind among the aggressors, for the newcomer in the fray, with savage exclamations, which showed his delight in a tumult, scattered the enemy as a tornado drives before it the leaves of a forest. The king raised himself on his elbow and watched the gigantic stranger lay about him with his stick, while the five, with cries of terror, disappeared into the forest, for the two that were prostrate had now recovered wind enough to run.

"Losh," panted the giant, returning to the man on the road, "I wish I'd been here at the beginning."

"Thank goodness you came at the end," said the king, staggering unsteadily to his feet.

"Are you hurt?" asked the stranger.

"I'm not just sure yet," replied the king, removing his bonnet and rubbing the top of his head with a circular movement of his hand.

"Just a bit cloor on the croon," said the other in broad Lowland Scotch. "It stunners a man, but it's nothin' ava when ye can stan' on your ain feet."

"Oh, it's not the first time I've had to fight for my crown," said James with a laugh, "but five to one are odds a little more heavy than I care to encounter."

"Are ye able to walk on, for I'm in a bit o' a hurry, as ye'd have seen if your attention hadna been turned to the north."

"Oh, quite able," replied the king as they strode along together.

"What's wrong wi' those scamps to lay on a poor beggar man?" asked the stranger.

"Nothing, except that the beggar man is not so poor as he looks, and has a belt of gold about him, which he was foolish enough to show last night at the inn where these lads were drinking."

"Then the lesson hasn't taught you much, or you wouldn't say that to a complete stranger in the middle of a black forest, and you alone with him, that is, unless they've succeeded in reiving the belt away from you?"

"No, they have not robbed me, and to show you that I am not such a fool as you take me for, I may add that the moment you came up I resolved to give to my rescuer every gold piece that is in my belt. So you see, if you thought of robbing me, there's little use in taking by force what a man is more than willing to give you of his own free will."

The giant threw back his head and the wood resounded with his laughter.

"What I have said seems to amuse you," said the king not too well pleased at the boisterous merriment of his companion.

"It does that," replied the stranger, still struggling with his mirth; then striking the king on the shoulder, he continued, "I suppose there is not another man in all broad Scotland to-day but me, that wouldn't give the snap of his fingers for all the gold you ever carried."

"Then you must be wealthy," commented the king. "Yet it can't be that, for the richest men I know are the greediest."

"No, it isn't that," rejoined the stranger, "but if you wander anywhere about this region you will understand what I mean when I tell you that I'm Baldy Hutchinson."

"Baldy Hutchinson!" echoed the king, wrinkling his brows, trying to remember where he had heard that name before, then with sudden enlightenment,—

"What, not the man who is to be hanged to-day at St. Ninians?"

"The very same, so you see that all the gold ever minted is of little use to a man with a tightening rope round his neck." And the comicality of the situation again overcoming Mr. Hutchinson, his robust sides shook once more with laughter.

The king stopped in the middle of the road and stared at his companion with amazement.

"Surely you are aware," he said at last, "that you are on the direct road to St. Ninians?"

"Surely, surely," replied Baldy, "and you remind me, that we must not stand yammering here, for there will be a great gathering there to see the hanging. All my friends are there now, and if I say it, who shouldn't, I've more friends than possibly any other man in this part of Scotland."

"But, do you mean that you are going voluntarily to your own hanging? Bless my soul, man, turn in your tracks and make for across the Border."

Hutchinson shook his head.

"If I had intended to do that," he said, "I could have saved myself many a long step yesterday and this morning, for I was a good deal nearer the Border than I am at this moment. No, no, you see I have passed my word. The sheriff gave me a week among my own friends to settle my worldly affairs, and bid the wife and the bairns good-bye. So I said to the sheriff, 'I'm your man whenever you are ready for the hanging.' Now, the word of Baldy Hutchinson has never been broken yet, and the sheriff knew it, although I must admit he swithered long ere he trusted it on an occasion like this. But at last he said to me, 'Baldy,' says he, 'I'll take your plighted word. You've got a week before you, and you must just go and come as quietly as you can, and be here before the clock strikes twelve on Friday, for folk'll want to see you hanged before they have their dinners.' And that's what way I'm in such a hurry now, for I'm feared the farmers will be gathered, and that it will be difficult for me to place myself in the hands of the sheriff without somebody getting to jalouse what has happened."

"I've heard many a strange tale," said the king, "but this beats anything in my experience."

"Oh there's a great deal to be picked up by tramping the roads," replied Hutchinson sagely.

"What is your crime?" inquired his majesty.

"Oh, the crime's neither here nor there. If they want to hang a man, they'll hang him crime or no crime."

"But why should they want to hang a man with so many friends?"

"Well, you see a man may have many friends and yet two or three powerful enemies. My crime, as you call it, is that I'm related to the Douglases; that's the real crime; but that's not what I'm to be hanged for. Oh no, it's all done according to the legal satisfaction of the lawyers. I'm hanged for treason to the king; a right royal crime, that dubs a man a gentleman as much as if the king's sword slaps his bended back; a crime that better men than me have often suffered for, and that many will suffer for yet ere kings are abolished, I'm thinking. You see, as I said, I married into the Douglas family, and when the Earl of Angus let this young sprig of a king slip through his fingers, it was as much as one's very life was worth to whisper the name of Douglas. Now I think the Earl of Angus a good man, and when he was driven to England, and the Douglases scattered far and wide by this rapscallion callant with a crown on his head, I being an outspoken man, gave my opinion of the king, damn him, and there were plenty to report it. I did not deny it, indeed I do not deny it to-day, therefore my neck's like to be longer before the sun goes down."

"But surely," exclaimed the beggar, "they will not hang a man in Scotland for merely saying a hasty word against the king?"

"There's more happens in this realm than the king kens of, and all done in his name too. But to speak truth, there was a bit extra against me as well. A wheen of the daft bodies in Stirling made up a slip of a plot to trap the king and put him in hiding for a while until he listened to what they called reason. There were two weavers among them and weavers are always plotting; a cobbler, and such like people, and they sent word, would I come and help them. I was fool enough to write them a note, and entrusted it to their messenger. I told them to leave the king alone until I came to Stirling, and then I would just nab him myself, put him under my oxter and walk down towards the Border with him, for I knew that if they went on they'd but lose their silly heads. And so, wishing no harm to the king, I made my way to Stirling, but did not get within a mile of it, for they tripped me up at St. Ninians, having captured my letter. So I was sentenced, and it seems the king found out all about their plot as I knew he would, and pardoned the men who were going to kidnap him, while the man who wanted to stop such foolishness is to be hanged in his name."

"That seems villainously unfair," said the beggar. "Didn't the eleven try to do anything for you?"

"How do you know there were eleven?" cried Hutchinson, turning round upon him.

"I thought you said eleven."

"Well, maybe I did, maybe I did; yes, there were eleven of them. They never got my letter. Their messenger was a traitor, as is usually the case, and merely told them I would have nothing to do with their foolish venture; and that brings me to the point I have been coming to. You see although I would keep my word in any case, yet I'm not so feared to approach St. Ninians as another man might be. Young Jamie, the king, seems to have more sense in his noodle than he gets credit for. Some of his forbears would have snapped off the heads of that eleven without thinking more of the matter, but he seems to have recognised they were but poor silly bodies, and so let them go. Now the moment they set me at liberty, a week since, I got a messenger I could trust, and sent him to the cobbler, Flemming by name. I told Flemming I was to be hanged, but he had still a week to get me a reprieve. I asked him to go to the king and tell him the whole truth of the matter, so I'm thinking that a pardon will be on the scaffold there before me; still, the disappointment of the hundreds waiting to see the hanging will be great."

"Good God!" cried the beggar aghast, stopping dead in the middle of the road and regarding his comrade with horror.

"What's wrong with you?" asked the big man stopping also.

"Has it never occurred to you that the king may be away from the palace, and no one in the place able to find him?"

"No one able to find the King of Scotland? That's an unheard-of thing."

"Listen to me, Hutchinson. Let us avoid St. Ninians, and go direct to Stirling; it's only a mile or two further on. Let us see the cobbler before running your neck into a noose."

"But, man, the cobbler will be at St. Ninians, either with a pardon or to see me hanged, like the good friend he is."

"There will be no pardon at St. Ninians. Let us to Stirling; let us to Stirling. I know that the king has not been at home for a week past."

"How can you know that?"

"Never mind how I know it. Will you do what I tell you?"

"Not I! I'm a lad o' my word."

"Then you are a doomed man. I tell you the king has not been in Stirling since you left St. Ninians." Then with a burst of impatience James cried, "You stubborn fool, I am the king!"

At first the big man seemed inclined to laugh, and he looked over the beggar from top to toe, but presently an expression of pity overspread his countenance, and he spoke soothingly to his comrade.

"Yes, yes, my man," he said, "I knew you were the king from the very first. Just sit down on this stone for a minute and let me examine that clip you got on the top of the head. I fear me it's worse than I thought it was."

"Nonsense," cried the king, "my head is perfectly right; it is yours that is gone aglee."

"True enough, true enough," continued Hutchinson mildly, in the tone that he would have used towards a fractious child, "and you are not the first that's said it. But let us get on to St. Ninians."

"No, let us make direct for Stirling."

"I'll tell you what we'll do," continued Hutchinson in the same tone of exasperating tolerance. "I'll to St. Ninians and let them know the king's pardon's coming. You'll trot along to Stirling, put on your king's clothes and then come and set me free. That's the way we'll arrange it, my mannie."

The king made a gesture of despair, but remained silent, and they walked rapidly down the road together. They had quitted the forest, and the village of St. Ninians was now in view. As they approached the place more nearly, Hutchinson was pleased to see that a great crowd had gathered to view the hanging. He seemed to take this as a personal compliment to himself; as an evidence of his popularity.

The two made their way to the back of the great assemblage where a few soldiers guarded an enclosure within which was the anxious sheriff and his minor officials.

"Bless me, Baldy!" cried the sheriff in a tone of great relief, "I thought you had given me the slip."

"Ye thought naething o' the kind, sheriff," rejoined Baldy complacently. "I said I would be here, and here I am."

"You are just late enough," grumbled the sheriff. "The people have been waiting this two hours."

"They'll think it all the better when they see it," commented Baldy. "I was held back a bit on the road. Has there no message come from the king?"

"Could you expect it, when the crime's treason?" asked the sheriff impatiently, "but there's been a cobbler here that's given me more bother than twenty kings, and cannot be pacified. He says the king's away from Stirling, and this execution must be put by for another ten days, which is impossible."

"Allow me a word in your ear privately," said the beggar to the sheriff.

"I'll see you after the job's done," replied the badgered man. "I have no more places to give away, you must just stand your chances with the mob."

Baldy put his open hand to the side of his mouth and whispered to the sheriff:

"This beggar man," he said, "has been misused by a gang of thieves in Torwood Forest."

"I cannot attend to that now," rejoined the sheriff with increasing irritation.

"No, no," continued Baldy suavely, "it's no that, but he's got a frightful dunner on the top o' the head, and he thinks he's the king."

"I am the king," cried the beggar, overhearing the last word of caution, "and I warn you, sir, that you proceed with this execution at your peril. I am James of Scotland, and I forbid the hanging."

At this moment there broke through the insufficient military guard a wild unkempt figure, whose appearance caused trepidation to the already much-tried sheriff.

"There's the crazy cobbler again," he moaned dejectedly. "Now the fat's all in the fire. I think I'll hang the three of them, trial or no trial."

"Oh, your majesty!" cried the cobbler,—and it was hard to say which of the two was the more disreputable in appearance,—"this man Hutchinson is innocent. You will surely not allow the hanging to take place, now you are here."

"I'll not allow it, if I can prevent it, and can get this fool of a sheriff to listen."

"Fool of a sheriff! say you," stuttered that official in rising anger. "Here, guard, take these two ragamuffins into custody, and see that they are kept quiet till this hanging's done with. Hutchinson, get up on the scaffold; this is all your fault. Hangman, do your duty."

Baldy Hutchinson, begging the cobbler to make no further trouble, mounted the steps leading to the platform, the hangman close behind him. Before the guard could lay hands on the king, he sprang also up the steps, and took a place on the outward edge of the scaffold. Raising his hand, he demanded silence.

"I am James, King of Scotland," he proclaimed in stentorian tones. "I command you as loyal subjects to depart to your homes. There will be no execution to-day. The king reprieves Baldy Hutchinson."

The cobbler stood at the king's back, and when he had ended, lifted his voice and shouted,—

"God save the King!"

The mob heard the announcement in silence, and then a roar of laughter followed, as they gazed at the two tattered figures on the edge of the platform. But the laughter was followed by an ominous howl of rage, as they understood that they were like to be cheated of a spectacle.

"Losh, I'll king him," shouted the indignant sheriff, as he mounted the steps, and before the beggar or his comrade could defend themselves, that official with his own hands precipitated them down among the assemblage at the foot of the scaffold. And now the spirit of a wild beast was let loose among the rabble. The king and his henchman staggered to their feet and beat off, as well as they could, the multitude that pressed vociferously upon them. A soldier, struggling through, tried to arrest the beggarman, but the king nimbly wrested his sword from him, and circled the blade in the air with a venomous hiss of steel that caused the nearer portion of the mob to press back eagerly, as, a moment before, they had pressed forward. The man who swung a blade like that was certainly worthy of respect, be he beggar or monarch. The cobbler's face was grimed and bleeding, but the king's newly won sword cleared a space around him. And now the bellowing voice of Baldy Hutchinson made itself heard above the din.

"Stand back from him," he shouted. "They're decent honest bodies, even if they've gone clean mad."

But now these at the back of the crowd were forcing the others forward, and Baldy saw that in spite of the sword, his old and his new friend would be presently engulfed. He turned to one of the upright posts of the scaffold and gave it a tremendous shuddering kick; then reaching up to the cross-bar and exerting his Samson-like strength, he wrenched it with a crash of tearing wood down from its position, and armed with this formidable weapon he sprung into the mob, scattering it right and left with his hangman's beam.

"A riot and a rescue!" roared the sheriff. "Mount, Trooper MacKenzie, and ride as if the devil were after you to Stirling; to Stirling, man, and bring back with you a troop of the king's horse."

"We must stop that man getting to Stirling," said Baldy, "or he'll have the king's men on you. I'll clear a way for you through the people, and then you two must take leg bail for it to the forest."

"Stand where you are," said the beggar. "The king's horse is what I want to see."

"Dods, you'll see them soon enough. Look at that gallop!"

MacKenzie indeed had lost no time in getting astride his steed, and was now disappearing towards Stirling like the wind. The more timorous of the assemblage, fearing the oncoming of the cavalry, which usually made short work of all opposition, caring little who was trampled beneath horses' hoofs, began to disperse, and seek stations of greater safety than the space before the scaffold afforded.

"Believe me," said Baldy earnestly to his two friends, "you'd better make your legs save your throttle. This is a hanging affair for you as well as for me, for you've interfered with the due course of the law."

"It's not the first time I've done so," said the beggar with great composure, and shortly after they heard the thunder of horses' hoofs coming from the north.

"Thank God!" said the sheriff when he heard the welcome sound. The mob dissolved and left a free passage for the galloping cavalcade. The stout Baldy Hutchinson and his two comrades stood alone to receive the onset.

The king took a few steps forward, raised his sword aloft and shouted,—

"Halt, Sir Donald!"

Sir Donald Sinclair obeyed the command so suddenly that his horse's front feet tore up the turf as he reined back, while his sharp order to the troop behind him brought the company to an almost instantaneous stand.

"Sir Donald," said the king, "I am for Stirling with my two friends here. See that we are not followed, and ask this hilarious company to disperse quietly to their homes. Do it kindly, Sir Donald. There is no particular hurry, and they have all the afternoon before them. Bring your troop back to Stirling in an hour or two."

"Will your majesty not take my horse?" asked Sir Donald Sinclair.

"No, Donald," replied the king with a smile, glancing down at his rags. "Scottish horsemen have always looked well in the saddle; yourself are an example of that, and I have no wish to make this costume fashionable as a riding suit."

The sheriff who stood by with dropped jaw, now flung himself on his knees and craved pardon for laying hands on the Lord's anointed.

"The least said of that the better," remarked the king drily. "But if you are sorry, sheriff, that the people should be disappointed at not seeing a man hanged, I think you would make a very good substitute for my big friend Baldy here."

The sheriff tremulously asserted that the populace were but too pleased at this exhibition of the royal clemency.

"If that is the case then," replied his majesty, "we shall not need to trouble you. And so, farewell to you!"

The king, Baldy, and the cobbler took the road towards Stirling, and Sir Donald spread out his troop to intercept traffic in that direction. Advancing toward the bewildered crowd, Sir Donald spoke to them.

"You will go quietly to your homes," he said. "You have not seen the hanging, but you have witnessed to-day what none in Scotland ever saw before, the king intervene personally to save a doomed man; therefore, be satisfied, and go home."

Some one in the mob cried,—

"Hurrah for the poor man's king! Cheer, lads, cheer!" A great uproar was lifted to the skies; afar off the three pedestrians heard it, and Baldy, the man of many friends, taking the clamour as a public compliment to himself, waved his bonnet at the distant vociferous multitude.

The King's Visit

"No, no," said the king decisively, "Bring them in, bring them in. I'll have none cast into prison without at least a hearing. Have any of your men been killed?"

"No, your majesty," replied Sir Donald, "but some of them have wounds they will not forget in a hurry; the Highlandmen fought like tiger-cats."

"How many are there of them?" asked the king.

"Something more than a score, with a piper that's noisier than the other twenty, led by a breechless ruffian, although I must say he knows what to do with a sword."

"All armed, you say?"

"Every one of them but the piper. About half an hour ago they came marching up the main street of Stirling, each man with his sword drawn, and the pipes skirling death and defiance. They had the whole town at their heels laughing and jeering at them and imitating the wild Highland music. At first, they paid little attention to the mob that followed them, but in the square their leader gave a word in Gaelic, and at once the whole company swerved about and charged the crowd. There was instant panic among the townspeople, who fled in all directions out-screaming the pibroch in their fright. No one was hurt, for the Highlandmen struck them with the flat of their swords, but several were trampled under foot and are none the better for it."

"It serves them right," commented the king. "I hope it will teach them manners, towards strangers, at least. What followed?"

"A whistle from their leader collected his helots again, and so they marched straight from the square to the gates of the castle. The two soldiers on guard crossed pikes before them, but the leader, without a word, struck down their weapons and attempted to march in, brave as you please; who but they! There was a bit of a scuffle at the gate, then the bugle sounded and we surrounded them, trying to disarm them peaceably at first, but they fought like demons, and so there's some sore heads among them."

"You disarmed them, of course?"

"Certainly, your majesty."

"Very well; bring them in and let us hear what they have to say for themselves."

The doors were flung open, a sharp command was given, and presently there entered the group of Highlanders, disarmed and with their elbows tied behind their backs. A strong guard of the soldiery accompanied them on either side. The Highlanders were men of magnificent physique, a quality that was enhanced by the picturesque costume they wore, in spite of the fact that in some instances, this costume was in tatters, and the wearers cut and bleeding. But, stalwart as his followers were, their leader far outmeasured them in height and girth; a truly magnificent specimen of the human race, who strode up the long room with an imperial swagger such as had never before been seen in Stirling, in spite of the fact that his arms were pinioned. He marched on until he came before the king, and there took his stand, without any indication of bowing his bonneted head, or bending his sturdy bare knees. The moment the leader set his foot across the threshold, the unabashed piper immediately protruded his chest, and struck up the wild strain of "Failte mhic an Abba," or the Salute to the Chief.

"Stop it, ye deevil!" cried the captain of the guard. "How dare you set up such a squawking in the presence of the king?" and as the piper paid not the slightest attention to him, he struck the mouth-piece from the lips of the performer. This, however, did not cause a cessation of the music, for the bag under the piper's elbow was filled with wind and the fingers of the musician bravely kept up the strain on the reed chanter with its nine holes, and thus he played until his chief came to a stand before the king. The king gazed with undisguised admiration upon the foremost Highlander, and said quietly to the captain of the guard,—

"Unbind him!"

711

On finding his arms released, the mountaineer stretched them out once or twice, then folded them across his breast, making no motion however to remove his plumed bonnet, although every one else in the room except himself and his men were uncovered.

"You have come in from the country," began the king, a suspicion of a smile hovering about his lips, "to enjoy the metropolitan delights of Stirling. How are you satisfied with your reception?"

The big Highlandman made no reply, but frowned heavily, and bestowed a savage glance on several of the courtiers, among whom a light ripple of laughter had run after the king put his question.

"These savages," suggested Sir Donald, "do not understand anything but the Gaelic. Is it your majesty's pleasure that the interpreter be called?"

"Yes, bring him in."

When the interpreter arrived, the king said,—

"Ask this man if his action is the forefront of a Highland invasion of the Lowlands, or merely a little private attempt on his own part to take the castle by assault?"

The interpreter put the question in Gaelic, and was answered with gruff brevity by the marauder. The interpreter, bowing low to the king, said smoothly,—

"This man humbly begs to inform your majesty—"

"Speak truth, MacPherson!" cautioned the king. "Translate faithfully exactly what he says. Our friend here, by the look of him, does not do anything humbly, or fawn or beg. Translate accurately. What does he say?"

The polite MacPherson was taken aback by this reproof, but answered,—

"He says, your majesty, he will hold no communication with me, because I am of an inferior clan, which is untrue. The MacPhersons were a civilised clan centuries ago, which the MacNabs are not to this day, so please your majesty."

The MacNab's hand darted to his left side, but finding no sword to his grasp, it fell away again.

"You are a liar!" cried the chief in very passable English which was not to be misunderstood. "The MacPhersons are no clan, but an insignificant branch of the Chattan. 'Touch not the Cat' is your motto, and a good one, for a MacPherson can scratch but he cannot handle the broadsword."

MacPherson drew himself up, his face reddening with anger. His hand also sought instinctively the hilt of his sword, but the presence in which he stood restricted him.

"It is quite safe," he said with something like the spit of a cat, "for a heathen to insult a Christian in the presence of his king, and the MacNabs have ever shown a taste for the cautious cause."

"Tut, tut," cried the king with impatience, "am I to find myself involved in a Highland feud in my own hall? MacPherson, it seems this man does not require your interpreting, so perhaps it will further the peace of our realm if you withdraw quietly."

MacPherson with a low obeisance, did so; then to MacNab the king spoke,—

"Sir, as it appears you are acquainted with our language, why did you not reply to the question I put to you?"

"Because I would have you know it was not the proper kind of question to ask the like of me. I am a descendant of kings."

"Well, as far as that goes, I am a descendant of kings myself, though sorry I should be to defend all their actions."

"Your family only began with Robert the Bruce; mine was old ere he came to the throne."

"That may well be, still you must admit that what Robert lacked in ancestry, he furnished forth in ability."

"But the Clan MacNab defeated him at the battle of Del Rhi."

"True, with some assistance, which you ignore, from Alexander of Argyll. However, if this discussion is to become a competition in history, for the benefit of our ignorant courtiers, I may be allowed to add that my good ancestor, Robert, did not forget the actions of the MacNabs at Del Rhi, and later overran their country, dismantled their fortresses, leaving the clan in a more sane and chastened condition than that in which he found it. But what has all this to do with your coming storming into a peaceable town like Stirling?"

"In truth, your majesty," whispered Sir David Lyndsay, "I think they must have come to replenish their wardrobe, and in that they are not a moment too soon."

"I came," said the chief, who had not heard this last remark, "because of the foray you have mentioned. I came because Robert the Bruce desolated our country."

"By my good sword!" cried James, "speaking as one king to another, your revenge is somewhat belated, a lapse of two centuries should have outlawed the debt. Did you expect then to take Stirling with twenty men?"

"I expected King James the Fifth to rectify the wrong done by King Robert the First."

"Your expectation does honour to my reputation as a just man, but I have already disclaimed responsibility for the deeds of ancestors less remote than good King Robert."

"You have made proclamation in the Highlands that the chieftains must bring you proof of their right to occupy their lands."

"I have, and some have preferred to me their deeds of tenure, others prepared to fight; the cases have been settled in both instances. To which of these two classes do you belong, Chief of the Clan MacNab?"

"To neither. I cannot submit to you our parchments because Robert, your ancestor, destroyed them. I cannot fight the army of the Lowlands because my clan is small, therefore I, Finlay MacNab, fifth of my name, as you are fifth of yours, come to you in peace, asking you to repair the wrong done by your ancestor."

"Indeed!" cried the king. "If the present advent typifies your idea of a peaceful visit, then God forfend that I should ever meet you in anger."

"I came in peace and have been shamefully used."

"You must not hold that against us," said James. "Look you now, if I had come storming at your castle door, sword in hand, how would you have treated me, Finlay the Fifth?"

"If you had come with only twenty men behind you, I should treat you with all the hospitality of Glendochart, which far exceeds that of Stirling or any other part of your money-making Lowlands, where gold coin is valued more than a steel blade."

"It has all been a mistake," said the king with great cordiality. "The parchment you seek shall be given you, and I trust that your generosity, Lord of Glendochart, will allow me to amend your opinion of Stirling hospitality. I shall take it kindly if you will be my guests in the castle until my officers of law repair the harshness of my ancestor, Robert." Then, turning to the guard the king continued,—

"Unbind these gentlemen, and return to them their arms."

While the loosening of the men was rapidly being accomplished, the captain of the guard brought the chief his sword, and would have presented it to him, but the king himself rose and took the weapon in his own hand, tendering it to its owner. The chieftain accepted the sword and rested its point on the floor, then in dignified native courtesy, he doffed his broad, feathered bonnet.

"Sire," he said, with slow deliberation, "Scotland has a king that this good blade shall ever be proud to serve."

For three days, the MacNabs were the guests of the king in the castle, while the legal documents were being prepared. King and chieftain walked the town together, and all that Stirling had to show, MacNab beheld. The king was desirous of costuming, at his own expense, the portion of the clan that was now in his castle, whose disarray was largely due to his own soldiers, but he feared the proposal might offend the pride of Finlay the Fifth.

James's tact, however, overcame the difficulty.

"When I visit you, MacNab, over by Loch Tay, there is one favour I must ask; I want your tailors to make for me and the men of my following, suits of kilts in the MacNab tartan."

"Surely, surely," replied the chief, "and a better weaving you will get nowhere in the Highlands."

"I like the colour of it," continued the king. "There is a royal red in it that pleases me. Now there is a good deal of red in the Stuart tartan, and I should be greatly gratified if you would permit your men to wear my colours, as my men shall wear yours. My tailors here will be proud to boast that they have made costumes for the Clan MacNab. You know what tradesmen bodies are, they're pleased when we take a little notice of them."

"Surely," again replied MacNab, more dubiously, "and I shall send them the money for it when I get home."

"Indeed," said the king, "if you think I am going to have a full purse when I'm in the MacNab country, you're mistaken."

"I never suggested such a thing," replied the chief indignantly. "You'll count nane o' yer ain bawbees when you are with me."

"Ah, well," rejoined the king, "that's right, and so you will just leave me to settle with my own tailors here."

Thus the re-costuming came about, and all in all it was just as well that MacNab did not insist on his own tartan, for there was none of it in Stirling, while of the Stuart plaid there was a sufficiency to clothe a regiment.

On the last night, there was a banquet given which was the best that Stirling could bestow, in honour of the Clan MacNab. The great hall was decorated with the colours of the clan, and at the further end had been painted the arms of the MacNab—the open boat, with its oars, on the sea proper, the head of the savage, the two supporting figures and the Latin motto underneath, "Timor omnis abseto". Five pipers of the king's court had learned the Salute to the Chief, and now, headed by MacNab's own, they paced up and down the long room, making it ring with their war-like music. The king and the chieftain came in together, and as the latter took his place at his host's right hand, his impassive face betrayed no surprise at the splendid preparations which had been made for his reception. Indeed, the Highlanders all acted as if they had been accustomed to sit down to such a banquet every night. Many dainties were placed on the ample board cunningly prepared by foreign cooks, the like of which the Highlanders had never before tasted; but the mountaineers ate stolidly whatever was set in front of them, and if unusual flavours saluted their palates, the strangers made no sign of approval or the reverse. The red wine of Burgundy, grown old in the king's cellars, was new to most of them, and they drank it like water, emptying their tankards as fast as the attendant could refill them. Soon the ruddy fluid, whose potency had been under-estimated, began to have its effect, and the dinner table became noisy as the meal progressed, songs bursting forth now and then, with strange shouts and cries more familiar to the hills of Loch Tay than to the rafters of Stirling. The chief himself, lost the solemn dignity which had at first characterised him, and as he emptied flagon after flagon he boasted loudly of the prowess of his clan; foretold what he would do in future fields now that he was allied with the King of Scotland. Often forgetting himself, he fell into the Gaelic, roaring forth a torrent of words that had no meaning for many there present, then remembering the king did not understand the language, he expressed his pity for a man in such condition, saying the Gaelic was the oldest tongue in existence, and the first spoken by human lips upon this earth. It was much more expressive, he said, than the dialect of the Lowlands, and the only language that could fittingly describe war and battle, just as the pibroch was the only music suitable to strife, to all of which the smiling king nodded approval. At last MacNab sprang to his feet, holding aloft his brimming flagon, which literally rained Burgundy down upon him, and called for cheers for the King of Scotland, a worthy prince who knew well how to entertain a brother prince. Repeating this in Gaelic, his men, who had also risen with their chief, now sprang upon the benches, where standing unsteadily, they raised a series of yells so wild that a shudder of fear passed through many of the courtiers there present. The chief, calling to his piper, commanded him instantly to compose a pibroch for the king, and that ready musician, swelling with pride, marched up and down and round and round the great hall pouring forth a triumphal quickstep, with many wonderful flourishes and variations. Then at a word from the chief, each man placed his flagon on the table, whipped out his sword, swung it overhead, to the amazement of the courtiers, for it is not in accord with etiquette to show cold steel to the eyes of the king. Down came the blades instantly and together, each man splitting in two the goblet he had drunk from.

"You must all come to Loch Tay," cried the chief, "and I will show you a banqueting hall in honour of James the Fifth, such as you have never before seen." Then to the horror of the courtiers, he suddenly smote the king on the back with his open palm and cried, "Jamie, my lad, you'll come and visit me at Loch Tay?"

The smitten king laughed heartily and replied,—

"Yes, Finlay, I will."

The next day the MacNabs marched from the castle and down through the town of Stirling with much pomp and circumstance. They were escorted by the king's own guard, and this time the populace made no sneering remarks but thronged the windows and the roofs, cheering heartily, while the Highlanders kept proud step to the shrill music of the pipes. And thus the clansmen set faces towards the north on their long tramp home.

"What proud 'deevils' they are," said Sir David Lyndsay to the king after the northern company had departed. "I have been through the MacNab country from one end of it to the other, and there is not a decent hut on the hillside, let alone a castle fit to entertain a king, yet the chief gives an invitation in the heat of wine, and when he is sobered, he is too proud to admit that he cannot make good the words he has uttered."

"That very thing is troubling me," replied the king, "but it's a long time till July, and between now and then we will make him some excuse for not returning his visit, and thus avoid putting the old man to shame."

"But that too will offend him beyond repair," objected the poet.

"Well, we must just lay our heads together, Davie," answered the king, "and think of some way that will neither be an insult nor a humiliation. It might not be a bad plan for me to put on disguise and visit Finlay alone."

"Would you trust yourself, unaccompanied, among those wild caterans? One doesn't know what they might do."

"I wish I were as safe in Stirling as I should be among the MacNabs," replied the king.

However, affairs of state did not permit the carrying out of the king's intention. Embassies came from various countries, and the king must entertain the foreigners in a manner becoming their importance. This, however, gave James the valid excuse he required, and so he sent a commission to the chief of the MacNabs. "His majesty," said the head commissioner, "is entertaining the ambassadors from Spain and from France, and likewise a legate from the Pope. If he came north, he must at least bring with him these great noblemen with their retinues; and while he would have been glad to visit you with some of his own men, he could not impose upon the hospitality thus generously tendered, by bringing also a large number of strangers and foreigners."

"Tell his majesty," replied MacNab with dignity, "that whether he bring with him the King of Spain, the Emperor of France, or even the Pope himself, none of these princes is, in the estimation of MacNab, superior to James the Fifth, of Scotland. The entertainment therefore, which the king graciously condescends to accept, is certainly good enough for any foreigners that may accompany him, be their nobility ever so high."

When this reply was reported to the king he first smiled and then sighed.

"I can do nothing further," he said. "Return to MacNab and tell him that the Pope's legate desires to visit the Priory on Loch Tay. Tell the chief that we will take the boat along the lake on the day arranged. Say that the foreigners are anxious to taste the venison of the hills, and that nothing could be better than to give us a dinner under the trees. Tell him that he need not be at any trouble to provide us lodging, for we shall return to the Island Priory and there sleep."

In the early morning the king and his followers, the ambassadors and their train embarked on boats that had been brought overland for their accommodation, and sailed from the Island Priory the length of the beautiful lake; the numerous craft being driven through the water by strong northern oarsmen, their wild chaunting choruses echoing back from the picturesque mountains as they bent to their work. The evening before, horses for the party had been led through forests, over the hills, and along the strand, to the meeting-place at the other end of the lake. Here they were greeted by the MacNabs, pipers and all, and mounting the horses the gay cavalcade was led up the valley. The king had warned their foreign Highnesses that they were not to expect in this wilderness the niceties of Rome, Paris or Madrid, and each of the ambassadors expressed his delight at the prospect of an outing certain to contain so much that was novel and unusual to them.

A summer haze hung in the valley, and when the king came in sight of the stronghold of the MacNabs he rubbed his eyes in wonder, thinking the misty uncertainty of the atmosphere was playing wizard tricks with his vision. There, before them, stood the most bulky edifice, the most extraordinary pile he had ever beheld. Tremendous in extent, it seemed to have embodied every marked feature of a mediæval castle. At one end a great square keep arose, its amazing height looming gigantically in the gauze-like magic of the mist. A high wall, machicolated at the top, connected this keep with a small octagonal tower, whose twin was placed some distance to the left, leaving an opening between for a wide entrance. The two octagonal towers formed a sort of frame for a roaring waterfall in the background. From the second octagonal tower another extended lofty wall connected it with a round peel as high as the keep. This castle of a size so enormous that it made all others its beholders had ever seen shrink into comparative insignificance, was surrounded by a bailey wall; outside of that was a moat which proved to be a foaming river, fed by the volume of water which came down the precipice behind the castle. The lashing current and the snow-white cascade formed a striking contrast to the deep moss-green hue of the castle itself.

"We have many great strongholds in Italy," said the Pope's legate, "but never have I seen anything to compare with this."

"Oh," said MacNab slightingly, "we are but a small clan; you should see the Highland castles further north; they are of stone; indeed our own fortresses, which are further inland, are also of stone. This is merely our pleasure-house built of pine-trees."

"A castle of logs!" exclaimed the Pope's legate. "I never before heard of such a thing."

They crossed the bridge, passed between the two octagonal towers and entered the extensive courtyard, surrounded by the castle itself; a courtyard broad enough to afford manœvring ground for an army. The interior walls were as attractive as the outside was grim and forbidding. Balconies ran around three sides of the enclosure, tall thin, straight pine poles, rising three stories high, supporting them, each pole fluttering a flag at the top. The balconies were all festooned with branches of living green.

The air was tremulous with the thunder of the cataract and the courtyard was cut in two by a rushing torrent, spanned by rustic bridges. The walls were peopled by cheering clansmen, and nearly a score of pipers did much to increase the din. Inside, the king and his men found ample accommodation; their rooms were carpeted with moss and with flowers, forming a variety of colour and yielding a softness to the foot which the artificial piles of Eastern looms would have attempted to rival in vain. Here for three days the royal party was entertained. Hunting in the forest gave them prodigious appetites, and there was no criticism of the cooking. The supply of food and drink was lavish in the extreme; fish from the river and the loch, game from the moors and venison from the hills.

It was evening of the third day when the cavalcade set out again for the Priory; the chief, Finlay MacNab, accompanied his guests down the valley, and when some distance from the castle of logs, James smote him on the shoulder, copying thus his own astonishing action. "Sir Finlay," he cried, "a king's hand should be no less potent than a king's sword, and thus I create thee a knight of my realm, for never before has monarch been so royally entertained, and now I pause here to look once more on your castle of pine."

So they all stayed progress and turned their eyes toward the wooden palace they had left.

"If it were built of stone," said the Pope's legate, "it would be the strongest house in the world as it is the largest."

"A bulwark of bones is better than a castle of stones," said Sir Finlay. "That is an old Highland saying with us, which means that a brave following is the best ward. I will show you my bulwark of bones."

And with that, bowing to the king as if to ask permission, he raised his bugle to his lips and blew a blast. Instantly from the corner of the further bastion a torch flamed forth, and that torch lighted the one next it, and this its neighbour, so that speedily a line of fire ran along the outlines of the castle, marking out the square towers and the round, lining the curtain, the smaller towers, turrets and parapets. Then at the top of the bailey wall a circle of Highlanders lit torch after torch, and thus was the whole castle illumined by a circle of fire. The huge edifice was etched in flame against the sombre background of the high mountain.

"Confess, legate," cried the king, "that you never saw anything more beautiful even in fair Italy."

"I am willing to admit as much," replied the Roman.

Another blast from the bugle and all the torches on the castle itself disappeared, although the fire on the bailey wall remained intact, and the reason for this soon became apparent. From machicolated tower, keep, peel and curtain, the nimble Highlanders, torchless, scrambled down, cheering as they came. It seemed incredible that they could have attained such speed, picking their precarious way by grasping protruding branch or stump or limb, or by thrusting hand between the interstices of the timber, without slipping, falling and breaking their necks.

For a moment the castle walls were alive with fluttering tartans, strongly illuminated by the torches from the outer bailey. Each man held his breath while this perilous acrobatic performance was being accomplished, and silence reigned over the royal party until suddenly broken by the Italian.

"Highlander!" he cried, "your castle is on fire."

"Aye," said the Highlander calmly, raising his bugle again to his lips.

At the next blast those on the bailey wall thrust their torches, still burning among the chinks of the logs, and swarmed to the ground as speedily and as safely as those on the main building had done. Now the lighted torches that had been thrown on the roof of the castle, disappearing a moment from sight, gave evidence of their existence. Here and there a long tongue of flame sprung up and died down again.

"Can nothing be done to save the palace?" shouted the excitable Frenchman. "The waterfall; the waterfall! Let us go back, or the castle will be destroyed."

"Stand where you are," said the chief, "and you will see a sight worth coming north for."

Now almost with the suddenness of an explosion, great sheets of flame rose towering into a mountain of fire, as if this roaring furnace would emulate in height the wooded hills behind it. The logs themselves seemed to redden as the light glowed through every crevice between them. The bastions, the bailey walls, were great wheels of flame, encircling a palace that had all the vivid radiance of molten gold. The valley for miles up and down was lighter than the sun ever made it.

"Chieftain," said the legate in an awed whisper, "is this conflagration accident or design?"

"It is our custom," replied MacNab. "A monarch's pathway must be lighted, and it is not fitting that a residence once honoured by our king should ever again be occupied by anyone less noble. The pine tree is the badge of my clan. At my behest the pine tree sheltered the king, and now, at the blast of my bugle, it sends forth to the glen its farewell of flame."

The King Explores

James was pleased with himself. He had finished a poem, admitted by all the court to excel anything that Sir David Lyndsay ever wrote, and he had out-distanced James MacDonald, son of the Laird of Sleat, in a contest for the preference of the fairest lady in Stirling, and young MacDonald was certainly the handsomest sprig about the palace. So the double victory in the art of rhythm and of love naturally induced the king to hold a great conceit of himself. Poor Davie, who was as modest a man regarding his own merits as could be found in the realm, quite readily and honestly hailed the king his superior in the construction of jingling rhyme, but the strapping young Highlander was proud as any scion of the royal house, and he took his defeat less diffidently.

"If the king," he said boldly, "was plain Jamie Stuart, as I am Jamie MacDonald, we would soon see who was winner of the bonniest lass, and if he objected to fair play I'd not scruple to meet him sword in hand on the heather of the hills, but not on the stones of Stirling. It is the crown that has won, and not the face underneath it."

Now this was rank treason, for you must never talk of swords in relation to a king, except that they be drawn in his defence. The inexperienced young man made a very poor courtier, for he spoke as his mind prompted him, a reckless habit that has brought many a head to the block. Although MacDonald had a number of friends who admired the frank, if somewhat hot-headed nature of the youth, his Highland swagger often earned for him not a few enemies who would have been glad of his downfall. Besides this, there are always about a court plenty of sycophants eager to curry favour with the ruling power; and so it was not long after these injudicious utterances had been given forth that they were brought, with many exaggerations, to the ears of the king.

"You think, then," said his majesty to one of the tale-bearers, "that if Jamie had the chance he would run his iron through my royal person?"

"There is little doubt of it, your majesty," replied the parasite.

"Ah, well," commented James, "kings must take their luck like other folk, and some day Jamie and I may meet on the heather with no other witnesses than the mountains around us and the blue sky above us, and in that case I shall have to do the best I can. I make no doubt that MacDonald's position in Stirling is less pleasant than my own. He is practically a prisoner, held hostage here for the good conduct of his father, the firebrand of Sleat, so we must not take too seriously the vapouring of a youth whose leg is tied. I was once a captive myself to the Douglas, and I used words that would scarcely have been pleasant for my gaoler to hear had some kind friend carried them, so I have ever a soft side for the man in thrall."

To the amazement of the courtiers, who had shown some inclination to avoid the company of MacDonald after he had unburdened his soul, the king continued to treat the Highlander as affably as ever, but many thought his majesty was merely biding his time, which was indeed the case. The wiser heads about the court strongly approved of this diplomacy, as before they had looked askance at the king's rivalry with the irascible youth. They knew that affairs were not going well in the north, and so loose were the bonds restraining MacDonald, that at any moment he might very readily have escaped, ridden to the hills, and there augmented the almost constant warfare in those mountainous regions. Every clan that could be kept quiet was so much to the good, for although they fought mostly among themselves, there was ever a danger of a combination which might threaten the throne of Scotland. Very often the king recklessly offended those whom he should conciliate, but even the wiseacres were compelled to admit that his jaunty kindness frequently smoothed out what looked like a dangerous quarrel. The sage counsellors, however, thought the king should keep a closer watch on those Highland chieftains who were practically hostages in his court. But to this advice James would never listen. Having been a captive himself not so very long before, as he frequently remarked, he thus felt an intense sympathy for those in like condition, even though he himself kept them so through the necessity of internal politics, yet he always endeavoured to make the restraint sit as lightly as possible on his victims.

Some weeks after the ill-considered anti-royal threats had been made, their promulgator was one of a group in the courtyard of the castle, when the captain of the guard came forward and said the king wished to see him in his private chamber. MacDonald may have been taken aback by the unexpected summons, but he carried the matter off nonchalantly enough, with the air of one who fears neither potentate nor peasant, and so accompanied the captain; but the gossips nodded their heads sagely at one another, whispering that it would be well to take a good view of MacDonald's back, as they were little likely to see him soon again, and this whisper proved true, for next day MacDonald had completely disappeared, no one knew whither.

When James the laird's son, entered the presence of James the king, the latter said as soon as the captain had left them alone together,—

"Jamie, my man, you understand the Gaelic, so it is possible you understand those who speak it."

"If your majesty means the Highlanders, they are easily enough understood. They are plain, simple, honest bodies who speak what's on their minds, and who are always willing, in an argument, to exchange the wag of the tongue for a swoop of the black knife."

"I admit," said the king with a smile, "that they are a guileless pastoral people, easy to get on with if you comprehend them, but that is where I'm at a loss, and I thought your head might supplement my own."

"I am delighted to hear you want my head for no other purpose but that of giving advice," returned the Highlander candidly.

"Truth to tell, Jamie, your head would be of little use to me were it not on your shoulders. If the head were that of a winsome lassie I might be tempted to take it on my own shoulder, but otherwise I am well content to let heads remain where Providence places them."

Whether intentional or not, the king had touched a sore spot when he referred to the laying of a winsome lassie's head on his shoulder, and MacDonald drew himself up rather stiffly.

"In any ploy with the ladies," he said, "your majesty has the weight of an ermine cloak in your favour, and we all know how the lassies like millinery."

"Then, Jamie, in a fair field, you think you would have the advantage of me, as for example if our carpet were the heather instead of the weaving of an Eastern loom?"

"I just think that," said MacDonald stoutly.

The king threw back his head and laughed the generous laugh of the all-conquering man.

"E-god, Jamie, my man, we may put that to the test before long, but it is in the high realms of statesmanship I want your advice, and not in the frivolous courts of love. You may give that advice the more freely when I tell you that I have made up my mind what to do in any case, and am not likely to be swayed one way or other by the counsel I shall receive."

"Then why does your majesty wish to have my opinion?" asked the Highlander.

"Lord, I'll want more than your opinion before this is done with, but I may tell you at once that there's troublesome news from Skye."

"Are the MacLeods up again?"

"Aye, they're up and down. They're up in their anger and down on their neighbours. I cannot fathom the intricacies of their disputes, but it may interest you to know that some of your clan are engaged in it. I suspect that Alexander MacLeod of Dunvegan is behind all this, although he may not be an active participant."

"Ah, that is Allaster Crottach," said the young man, knitting his brows.

"Allaster, yes, but what does Crottach mean?" asked the king.

"It means the humpback."

"Yes, that's the man, and a crafty plausible old gentleman he is. He got a charter under the Great Seal, of all his lands, from my father, dated the fifteenth of June, 1468. This did not satisfy him, and when I came to the throne he asked for a similar charter from me, which I signed on the thirteenth of February last. Its conditions seemed to be most advantageous to him, for all that was required of him was that he should keep for my use a galley of twenty-six oars, and likewise keep the peace. I am not aware whether the galley has been built or not, but there is certainly very little peace where a MacLeod has a claymore in his hand. Now, Jamie, the MacLeods are your neighbours in Sleat, so tell me what you would do were the king's crown on your head?"

"I should withdraw their charter," said MacDonald.

"That seems but just," concurred the king, "still, I doubt if our friend the humpback places very much value on the writing of his august sovereign. He knows he holds his lands as he holds his sword, his grip on the one relaxing when he loses his grip on the other. We will suppose, however, the charter withdrawn and the MacLeod laughing defiance at us. What next, MacDonald?"

"Next! I would raise an army and march against him and make him laugh on the other side of his crooked mouth."

"Hum," said the king, "that means traversing the country of the Grahams, who would probably let us by; then we next meet the Stewarts, and for my name's sake perhaps they might not molest us. We march out of their country into the land of the MacNabs, and the chief is an old friend of mine, so we need fear no disturbance there. After that we must trust ourselves to the tender mercies of the Campbells, and the outcome would depend on what they could make by attacking us or by leaving us alone. Next the Clan Cameron confronts us, and are more likely than not to dispute our passage. After them the MacDonalds, and there, of course, you stand my friend. When at last we reached the Sound of Sleat, how many of us would be left, and how are we to get across to Skye with the MacLeods on the mainland to the north of us? I am thinking, Jamie, there are lions in that path."

"The lions are imaginary, your majesty. The Grahams, the Stewarts, the MacNabs would rise not against you, but for you, delighted to be led by their king. The Campbells themselves must join you, if your force were large enough to do without them. Among the MacDonalds alone I could guarantee you an army. You forget that the Highlandman is always anxious for warfare. Leave Stirling with a thousand men and you will have ten thousand before you are at the shores of Sleat."

The king meditated for a few moments, then he looked up at his comrade with that engaging smile of his.

"It may all be as you say, Jamie. Perhaps the Highlands would rise with me instead of against me, but a prudent commander must not ignore the possibility of the reverse. However, apart from all this I am desirous of quelling the military ardour of the Highlands, not of augmenting it. It's easy enough setting the heather on fire in dry weather, but he is a wise prophet who tells where the conflagration ends. I would rather carry a bucket of water than a sword, even though it may be heavier."

"If your majesty will tell me what you have resolved upon, then I shall very blithely give you my opinion on it. It is always easier to criticise the plans of another than to put forward sensible plans of one's own."

"You are right in that, Jamie, and the remark shows I have chosen a wise counsellor. Very well, then. I have never seen the renowned island of Skye. They tell me it is even more picturesque than Stirling itself. I propose then to don a disguise, visit Skye, and find out if I can what the turbulent islanders want. If I am not able to grant their desire, I can at least deal the better with them for being acquainted."

"Your majesty does not purpose going alone?" cried MacDonald in amazement.

"Certainly not. I shall be well guarded."

"Ah, that is a different matter, and exactly what I advised."

"You advised an army, which I shall not take with me. I shall be well guarded by my good right arm, and by the still more potent right arm, if I may believe his own statement, of my friend, Jamie MacDonald of Sleat."

With bent brows MacDonald pondered for a few moments, then

looking up, said,—

"Will your majesty trust yourself in the wilderness with a prisoner?"

"There is no question of any prisoner. If you refer to yourself, you have always been at liberty to come and go as pleased you. As for trusting, I trust myself to a good comrade, and a Highland gentleman."

The king rose as he spoke and extended his hand, which the other grasped with great cordiality.

"You will get yourself out of Stirling to-night," continued the king, "as quietly as possible, and hie you to my Castle of Doune, and there wait until I come, which may be in a day, or may be in a week. I will tell the court that you have gone to your own home, which will be true enough. That will keep the gossips from saying we have each made away with the other if we both leave together. You see, Jamie, I must have some one with me who speaks the Gaelic."

"My advice has been slighted so far," said MacDonald, "yet I must give you another piece of it. We are going into a kittleish country. I advise you to order your fleet into some safe cove on the west coast. It will do the west Highlanders good to see what ships you have, for they think that no one but themselves and Noah could build a boat. When we come up into my own country we'll get a gillie or two that can be depended on to wait on us, then if we are nipped, one or other of these gillies can easily steal a boat and make for the fleet with your orders to the admiral."

"That is not a bad plan, Jamie," said the king, "and we will arrange it as you suggest."

The court wondered greatly at the sudden disappearance of James MacDonald, but none dared to make inquiry, some thinking he had escaped to the north, others, that a dungeon in Stirling Castle might reveal his whereabouts. The king was as genial as ever, and the wiseacres surmised from his manner that he meditated going off on tramp again. The fleet was ordered to Loch Torridon, where it could keep a watchful eye on turbulent Skye. The king spent three days in settling those affairs of the realm which demanded immediate attention, left Sir Donald Sinclair in temporary command, and rode off to Doune Castle.

From this stronghold there issued next morning before daylight, two well-mounted young men, who struck in a northwesterly direction for the wild Highland country. Their adventures were many and various, but MacDonald's Gaelic and knowledge of the locality carried them scatheless to the coast, although much of the journey was done on foot, for before half the way was accomplished the insurmountable difficulty of the passes compelled them to relinquish their horses. As it was unadvisable for them to enter Skye in anything like state, the two travellers contented themselves with an ordinary fishing-boat, which spread sail when the winds were fair, and depended on the oars of the crew when the sea was calm. They were accompanied by two gillies, who were intended to be useful on any ordinary occasion, and necessary in case of emergency, for the boat and its crew were to wait in any harbour of Skye that was determined upon and carry news to Loch Torridon if the presence of the fleet was deemed necessary.

It was a beautiful evening, with the sea as smooth as glass, when the fishing-boat, with sails folded, propelled by the stalwart arms of the rowers, entered a land-locked harbour, guarded by bold headlands. The name given to the place by MacDonald was so unpronounceable in Gaelic that it completely baffled the Saxon tongue of the king, but although his majesty was not aware of the fact, his own presence was to remedy that difficulty, because the place was ever afterwards known as the Haven of the King—Portree.

The scattered village climbed up the steep acclivity, and as the royal party rounded the headland and came in sight of the place, it seemed as if the inhabitants knew a distinguished visitor was about to honour them with his presence, for the whole population, cheering and gesticulating, was gathered along the shore. The gillie, however, informed his master that the demonstration was probably on the occasion of the launch of the handsome ship which they now saw, covered with flags, riding placidly on the surface of the bay. She was evidently new for her sides were fresh from the axe, without stain of either weather or wave.

"It seems the boat is yours," said MacDonald to the king in English.

"It is the twenty-six oared galley that Allaster Crottach was bound by his agreement to build for you. My man tells me that it is to be taken to-morrow to Dunvegan Castle, so it is likely to be used by Allaster Crottach himself before your majesty sets foot in it, for if it had been intended only for the king it would have been left here so that it might be convenient to the mainland. It has been built by Malcolm MacLeod, the leader of all the people in these parts. He thinks himself the most famous boat-builder in the world, so Allaster has at least fulfilled one part of his agreement, and doubtless believes this to be the finest craft afloat."

"It is indeed a beautiful barge," assented the king, admiring the graceful lines of the ship. "But what is that long-haired, bare-legged cateran screaming about with his arms going like a windmill? The crowd evidently appreciates his efforts, for they are rapturous in their applause."

MacDonald held up his hand and the oarsmen paused, while the boat gently glided towards the shore. In the still air, across the water, the impassioned Gaelic words came clearly to the voyagers.

"He is saying," translated MacDonald, after a few moments listening, "that the MacLeods are like the eternal rocks of Skye, and their enemies like the waves of the sea. Their enemies dash against them and they remain unmoved, while the wave is shattered into infinitesimal spray. So do the MacLeods defy and scorn all who come against them."

The king shrugged his shoulders.

"The man forgets that the sea also is eternal, and that it ultimately wears away the cliff. This appears to be an incitement towards war, then?"

"Oh, not so," replied MacDonald. "The man is one of their poets, and he is reciting an epic he has written, doubtless in praise of Malcolm's boat-building."

"God save us!" cried the king. "Have we then poets in Skye?"

"The whole of the Highlands is a land of poetry, your majesty," affirmed MacDonald drawing himself up proudly, "although the very poor judges of the art in Stirling may not be aware of the fact."

The king laughed heartily at this.

"I must tell that to Davie Lyndsay," he said. "But here we have another follower of the muse who has taken the place of the first. Surely nowhere else is the goddess served by votaries so unkempt. What is this one saying?"

"He says that beautiful is the western sky when the sun sinks beneath the wave, but more beautiful still is the cheek of the Rose of Skye, the daughter of their chieftain."

"Ah, that is better and more reassuring. I think either of us, Jamie, would rather be within sight of the smiles of the Rose of Skye than within reach of the claymores of her kinsmen."

By this time the assemblage on shore became aware that visitors were approaching, and the declamation ceased. Malcolm MacLeod himself came forward on the landing to greet the newcomers. He was a huge man of about fifty, tall and well proportioned, with an honest but masterful face, all in all a magnificent specimen of the race, destined by nature to be a leader of men. He received his visitors with dignified courtesy.

"I am James MacDonald," explained that young man by way of introduction, "son of the Laird of Sleat. We heard you had built a boat for the king, and so have come to see it. This is James Stuart, a friend of mine from the Lowlands, and I have brought him with me that he may learn what boat-building really is."

"You are very welcome," said MacLeod, "and just in time, for they are taking her round the headland to Dunvegan to-morrow morning. Aye, she's a bonnie boat, if I do say it myself, for no one knows her and what she'll do better than I."

"The king should be proud of her," said MacDonald.

MacLeod tossed his shaggy head and replied with a sneer,—

"It's little the king knows about boats. He should be playing with a shallop in a tub of water, instead of meddling with men's affairs. Allaster Crottach is our king, and if he graciously pleases to tickle the lad in Stirling by saying he owns the boat, Allaster himself will have the using of her. I would not spike a plank for the king, but I'd build a fleet for Allaster if he wanted it. Has your friend the Gaelic? If he has, he may tell the king what I say, when he goes back to the Lowlands."

"No, he has no Gaelic, Malcolm, but I'll put into the English whatever you like to say."

And so he gave to the king a free rendition of MacLeod's remarks, toning them down a little, but James was shrewd enough to suspect from the manner of the man of Skye, that he held his nominal monarch in slight esteem.

Malcolm MacLeod took the strangers to his own house, which was the best in the village. Almost the entire population of the port had been working on the king's boat, and now that it was finished and launched, the place had earned a holiday. Malcolm was delighted to have visitors who could bear witness to the skill of his designing, appreciate the genius of the poets and listen to the skreigh of the piping. The strangers were most hospitably entertained and entered thoroughly into the spirit of the festivities. The morning after their arrival they cheered as lustily as the others when the twenty-six oars of the king's barge struck the water and the craft moved majestically out of the harbour. They seemed to have come into a land of good-will toward all mankind; high and low vying with each other to make their stay as pleasant as possible.

"Losh, Jamie," said the king to his friend two or three days after their arrival, "I might well have ignored your advice about the ships, as I did your base counsel about the army. I need no fleet here to protect me in Skye where every man is my friend."

"That is very true," replied MacDonald, "but you must not forget that no one has any suspicion who you are. Everyone is a friend of James Stuart of the Lowlands, but I hear nobody say a good word for the king."

"What have they against him?" asked the Guidman of Ballengeich with a frown, for it was not complimentary to hear that in a part of his own dominion he was thought little of.

"It isn't exactly that they have anything against the king," said MacDonald, perhaps not slow to prick the self-esteem of his comrade, "but they consider him merely a boy, of small weight in their affairs one way or another. They neither fear him nor respect him. The real monarch of these regions is the humpback in Dunvegan Castle; and even if they knew you were the king, your sternest command would have no effect against his slightest wish, unless you had irresistible force at the back of you."

"Ah, Jamie, you are simply trying to justify the bringing of the fleet round Scotland."

"Indeed and I am not. The only use to which you can put your fleet will be to get you away from here in case of trouble. As far as its force is concerned, these islanders would simply take to the hills and defy it."

"Ah, well," said the king, "I'll make them think better of me before I am done with them."

The week's festivities were to end with a grand poetical contest. All the bards of the island were scribbling; at any rate, those who could write. The poets who had not that gift were committing their verses to memory that they might be prepared to recite them before the judges, three famous minstrels, who were chosen from three districts on the island, thus giving variety and a chance of fairness to their decisions.

The king resolved to enter this competition, and he employed MacDonald every evening translating into the language of Skye, the poem which had been considered so good in Stirling, and MacDonald was to recite it for him at the contest. But this Homeric competition was endangered by disquieting news brought to the island by the fishermen. They reported that a powerful fleet had been seen rounding the northern coast of Scotland, and was now making towards the south. This unexpected intelligence seemed to change instantaneously the attitude of the islanders towards their two guests. Suspicion electrified the air. The news of the sighting of the fleet, coming so quickly on the advent of two strangers, who apparently had no particular business on the island, caused them to be looked upon as spies, and for a day or two they were in danger of being treated as such. The king's alertness of mind saved the situation. He had brought with him from Stirling, in case of emergencies, several sheets of blank parchment, each bearing the Great Seal of Scotland. Once more the useful MacDonald was his amanuensis. A proclamation in Gaelic was written and the signature of James the Fifth inscribed thereon. This document was enclosed with a communication, containing directions to the admiral of the fleet, and MacDonald entrusted the packet to one of his gillies, with orders that sail should be set for Loch Torridon, and the message given to the officer in command.

Three days later the ferment on the island was immeasurably increased when the guard on the headland reported that a ship of war was making direct for the harbour. A horseman was despatched full gallop to Dunvegan Castle to inform the head of the clan of the mysterious visit of the two men, followed so soon by the approach of a belligerent vessel. But before the messenger was ten miles on his way, the ceremony was over and done with. The big ship sailed majestically through the narrows, cast anchor and fired a salute. A well-manned boat was lowered and rowed to the shore. There stepped from the boat an officer in a splendid uniform, followed by a lieutenant and half a dozen men, one of whom carried the flag of Scotland. This company marched to the cross, which stood in the centre of the village, and the crowd sullenly followed, with Malcolm MacLeod at their head, not knowing what the action of the naval officer might portend, and in absence of definite orders from their chief, hesitating to oppose this inland march. Many of those on the fleet were Highlanders, and the second in command was one of them. This man mounted the three steps at the foot of the cross and stood with his back against the upright stone. His chief handed him a roll of parchment, and the subordinate officer in a loud voice, and in excellent Gaelic, cried,—

"A Proclamation from His Most Excellent Majesty, James the Fifth of Scotland! God save the King!"

At this the chief officer raised his sword in salute, and his men sent up a cheer, but the aggregation was not seconded by any of the large concourse there gathered together. Undaunted by this frigid reception the officer unrolled the manuscript and read its contents in a voice that reached to the furthest outskirts of the crowd:

> "I, James of Scotland, lawful King of this realm, do proclaim to all loyal subjects, that the safety and liberty of my land depends on an unconquerable fleet, and that the merit of the fleet consists in stout well-built ships, therefore the man whom I, the King, delight to honour is he whose skill produces the best sea-going craft, so I hereon inscribe the name of Malcolm MacLeod, master shipbuilder, a man who has designed and constructed a boat of which all Scotland has reason to be proud. The King's barge of twenty-six oars, planned by Malcolm MacLeod and built for him by the people of Skye, will be used as a model for all ship-builders in the Scottish navy."

The reader now looked up from his parchment and gazed over the assemblage.

"Is Malcolm MacLeod here?" he asked. "Let him step forward."

The giant, somewhat dazed, walking like a man in a dream, approached the foot of the cross. The officer rolled the proclamation and presented it to the shipbuilder, saying:—

"From the hand of the king, to the hand of Malcolm MacLeod."

Malcolm accepted it, muttering half with a smile, half with a frown,—

"E-god, the king knows a good boat when he gets it."

Then the officer uplifted his sword and cried,—

"God save the king;" and now the hills around re-echoed with the cheering.

The little company without another word retraced their steps to the small boat, and made for the ship which was now facing outward, anchor hoisted and sails spread once more, so the watching Highlanders had a view of a large vessel superbly managed, as the west wind which brought her into the harbour took her safely out again.

The royal young man had a striking lesson on the fickleness of the populace. Heretofore as MacDonald had truly said, no one had a good word to say for the king; now it was evident that James V. of Scotland was the greatest and wisest monarch that ever sat on a throne.

Malcolm MacLeod had been always so proud of his skill that this proclamation could hardly augment his self-esteem, but it suddenly changed his views regarding his august overlord. In conversation ever after it became, "I and the king," and he was almost willing to admit that James was very nearly as great a man as Alexander MacLeod of Dunvegan.

The enthusiasm was so great that several bards composed special poems in honour of the king of Scotland, and next day the effusions were to be heard at the cross, and the prizes awarded. The first thing done, however, after the departure of the ship, was to send another mounted messenger to Dunvegan Castle, so that the lord of the island might learn that no invasion was to be feared from the fleet. The parchment proclamation was sent on to the chief, ostensibly in explanation of the ship's visit, but probably because Malcolm was not loth to let the head of the clan know what the head of the country thought of his workmanship.

It was early next morning that the reading and reciting of the poems began, and so lengthy were these effusions that it was well past noon before the last had been heard. To the chagrin of James he found himself fifteenth on the list when the honours were awarded. MacDonald, endeavouring to keep a straight face, told the king of the judges' decision, adding,—

"It will be as well not to let Davie Lyndsay know of this."

"Oh, you may tell whom you please," cried the king. "I was sure you would bungle it in the Gaelic."

The king was pacing up and down the room in no very good humour, so the young Highlander thought it best not to reply. He was saved however, from the embarrassment of silence by the entrance of Malcolm MacLeod.

"You are in great good fortune," said Malcolm. "The messengers have returned with a score of horsemen at their backs, and Dunvegan himself invites you to the castle."

MacDonald seemed in no way jubilant over what his host considered the utmost honour that could be bestowed upon two strangers.

"What does he say?" demanded the king.

"He says that MacLeod of Dunvegan has invited us to his castle."

"Well, we will go then. I suppose we can get horses here, or shall we journey round by boat?"

"I understand," replied MacDonald, "that the chief has sent horses for us, and furthermore an escort of a score of men, so I'm thinking we have very little choice about the matter."

"Very well," returned the king with a shrug of indifference, "let us be off and see our new host. I wonder if he will be as easily flattered as the one we are leaving."

"I doubt it," said MacDonald seriously.

The King Drinks

The two young men mounted the small shaggy horses that had been provided for them by the forethought of their future host, MacLeod of Dunvegan. Apparently the king had forgotten all about his crushing defeat in the poetical contest of the day before, for he was blithe and gay, the most cheerful of those assembled, adventuring now and then scraps of Gaelic that he had picked up, and his pronunciation contributed much to the hilarity of the occasion.

MacDonald, on the other hand, was gloomy and taciturn, as if already some premonition of the fate that awaited him at Dunvegan cast its shadow before. The news of the great condescension of the laird in inviting two strangers to his castle had spread through all the land, and, early as was the hour, the whole population of the district had gathered to wish the travellers a cordial farewell. The escort, as the king called the score of men, who were to act as convoy from one port to the other; or the guard, as MacDonald termed them, sat on their horses in silence, awaiting the word of command to set forth.

At last this word was given, and the procession began its march amidst the cheers of the people and a skirling of the pipes. The distance was little more than seven leagues over a wild uninviting country. MacDonald sat his horse dejected and silent, for the prospect confronting him was far from alluring. The king was incognito, he was not; and he had begun to doubt the wisdom of having given his actual designation to the people of Skye, for the relations between this island and the mainland were at that time far from being of the most cordial description.

Dunvegan Castle was a grim stronghold in which the MacLeods sat so secure that all the efforts of all the MacDonalds, even if they were for once united, could not dislodge them. It was one of the most remote inhabited places in all Scotland, its next neighbour to the west being that new land of America discovered not yet fifty years. For the son of one Highland chieftain to come so completely into the power of another, his own people knowing practically nothing of his whereabouts, was a situation that did not commend itself to the young man. Allaster Crottach was celebrated more for craft than for violence. He had extended and consolidated his possessions with the skill of a diplomatist rather than by the arms of his soldiers, and MacDonald thought it quite likely that a slice of Sleat might be the ransom for his release. If through any incautious remark of his comrade the Crottach became aware that he held not only MacDonald of Sleat but also the King of Scotland, the fates only knew what might happen. The king, however, appeared to have no forebodings, but trotted along with great complacency, commenting now and then on the barrenness of the landscape.

The party had accomplished little more than half the distance, when, as they fronted a slight elevation, there came to them over the hills wild pipe music, louder than anything of that kind the king had ever heard.

"The MacLeod is evidently about to welcome us in state," said his majesty to MacDonald, "he must have the very monarch of pipers in his train."

"The MacRimmon," admitted MacDonald, "are acknowledged to be the best pipers in all the Highlands, and they are hereditary musicians to the MacLeod. The sounds we hear indicate that a number of pipers are playing in unison."

On reaching the brow of the hill they found this was indeed the case. There were from thirty to fifty pipers, but they evidently bore no greeting to the travellers, for the musical party was marching in the same direction as themselves, playing vigorously as they swung along. At the instance of the king, MacDonald made inquiries regarding this extraordinary spectacle. The taciturn commander of the guard answered briefly that it was the College of Pipers. The students were marching back to Bocraig on the other side of Loch Follart, where instruction in piping was bestowed by the MacRimmon; this excursion over the hills giving them training in piping and in tramping at the same time. The musical regiment took its way straight across the moors and so very soon was lost sight of by the two travellers, who kept to a track which was more or less of a road.

In due time the cavalcade reached Dunvegan Castle, and even a man accustomed to so stout a fortress as that of Stirling could not but be struck by the size, the strength, and the situation of this frowning stronghold; yet, extensive as it was, its proprietor evidently found it inadequate for his ambitions, as he was now building a massive tower which added a further dignity to the structure.

The king and his companion were received at the front entrance by an old man, whom each at once knew could not be their host, for his back had originally been straight enough, though now slightly stooped through age. He led them within, and up a stair direct to the apartments reserved for them. Their aged conductor spoke no English, so the burden of conversation fell on MacDonald. As soon as the latter perceived that he and his friend were to be separated, the king lodged at one end of the castle, and himself at the other, he protested against this arrangement, demanding two adjoining rooms. The old man replied that he was following instructions given, and if the rooms assigned were not satisfactory, his master would doubtless change them on the morrow.

"But, my good man," expostulated MacDonald, "we expect to be leaving the castle to-morrow."

"In that case," replied their cicerone with a scarcely perceptible shrug of the shoulders, "it makes but little difference for one night." The king inquiring into the purport of the discussion, quite agreed with the elderly guide, that the matter was of small moment.

"If our genial innkeeper intends to murder us," he said, "we shall be quite as helpless together as separate, for he has irresistible force at his command. If we are in a trap there is little use in snarling at the bars. By all accounts Dunvegan is a shrewd man, and I can see no object which he can attain by doing harm to either of us. If he had a son who was next heir to the position I hold, I confess I might sleep uneasily to-night; but as he must know that the king's fleet is hovering about his coast, and that his castle would make a most excellent target for it, as he cannot transport his house to the hills should the ships sail up the loch, I don't see what he can gain by maltreating two men, whom he must suspect of having some connection with the advent of the fleet."

"Oh, I have no thought," replied MacDonald, "that the Eagle of Dunvegan would fly so high as you suggest, but there are lowlier perches on which he may like to fix his talons. He has long cast covetous eyes across the Sound of Sleat to the mainland, and, whatever he knows or suspects, he is sure of one thing, which is that he has the son of the Laird of Sleat safely landed in his own house."

"How distrustful you Highlanders are of each other!" cried the young monarch laughing. "Bless me, Jamie, no bargain made in durance will hold; then you must remember you have me behind you, and I have all the power in Scotland behind me."

"That is very true, but the power of nothing is behind either of us if we cannot get word to the outside world. Last night on learning we were invited to this place, I searched for my gillies, but without success. My boat and its crew have been taken elsewhere. So you see there is at least a design to cut our communications. I'm thinking we'll see more of Loch Follart from this window for a while than of the field of Bannockburn from Stirling Towers."

"I quite agree with you, Jamie, that we're fairly nabbed, but the old gentleman who has us in thrall can make nothing by ill-using us. Sooner or later he must divulge his plan, whatever it is, before he can benefit from it, and when he does that it will be time enough to consider what course we are to pursue." Then turning suddenly towards their guide, who had been standing motionless during this conversation, the king said sharply in English,—

"Is your master at home?"

The old man made no reply, but looked at MacDonald as if for translation. The latter repeated the question in Gaelic and received an affirmative answer.

"He says the laird is at home. He has no English."

"I wasn't just sure of that, so I tested it by an abrupt question, thus locking the door after the horse was stolen, for we have spoken rather plainly before him, and so have proved ourselves in the beginning very poor conspirators. However, I care little what the next move is so long as it brings us something to eat. Clear your gloomy brow, Jamie, and tell them in the most culinary Gaelic that this is not a fast-day with us, and the ride across the moors has increased our appetites."

MacDonald followed his custodian down the long corridor, and the king entered the apartment assigned to him.

After sufficient time had elapsed to allow the travellers to remove the traces of travel from their persons, they were summoned to a small room where they found a most welcome and substantial meal set out for them. A generous flagon of wine stood by each trencher; it was the first the king had had an opportunity of tasting since he left his capital, and he seized upon the measure with some eagerness.

"Here's to the MacLeod!" he cried.

"I drink to the king, and good luck to him!" said MacDonald.

"I drink to anything, so long as the wine is sound," rejoined his majesty, enjoying a deep draught. "E-god, Jamie," he cried setting the flagon down again, "that's better claret than we have in Stirling."

"There is no reason why it shouldn't be excellent," replied MacDonald, "for the laird's own ships bring it direct from the coast of France to the coast of Skye, and there's little chance of adulteration between the two."

When the repast was finished the aged man who had received them at the door entered and announced that MacLeod of MacLeod was ready to greet them in his study. They followed him and were ushered into an oblong room somewhat larger than the one they had left. The king was astonished to find the walls lined with numerous volumes, some of the tomes massive in heavy binding. As books were not over-plentiful even in the realms of civilisation, he had not expected to find them in a corner of the world so remote.

Allaster the Hunchback sat by the side of a huge oaken table, and he did not rise from his chair when his visitors were presented to him, either because he wished the better to conceal the deformity which gave him his nickname, or because he did not consider his guests of such importance as to deserve a more courteous reception. He addressed them in excellent English, and the king constituted himself spokesman for the occasion, MacDonald standing by taciturn, in spite of the excellence of the wine, which indeed he had consumed somewhat sparingly.

"I understand," began MacLeod, "that you have honoured my poor rugged island of Skye with your presence for some days."

"The honour, sir, has been ours," replied the king with an inclination of his head. "I was visiting my friend MacDonald in Sleat and heard of the king's barge, so we came over to see it."

"This is your friend MacDonald of Sleat then?"

"Yes. May I have the pleasure of presenting Mr. James MacDonald to the MacLeod?"

The two Highlanders, one sitting, one standing, bowed somewhat distantly to each other as the king, with a flourish of his hand, made the introduction.

"Perhaps," continued MacLeod suavely, "your friend from Sleat will do a like obligement for yourself."

"I shall not put him to that trouble," said the king airily. "I am of such small account that it would be a pity to put upon a Highland chieftain the task of pronouncing my name. I am called the Guidman of Ballengeich, very much at your service, sir."

"Guidman, meaning farmer of course?" asked Dunvegan.

"Meaning small farmer," said the king with a graceful inclination of the head.

The tones of the MacLeod had not been too cordial from the first, but they became less so at this confession of low quality on the part of his visitor.

"You will forgive my ignorance, but where is Ballengeich?"

"It is a little steading near Stirling, but of more value than its size would indicate, for I am fortunate in possessing the custom of the court."

"You cater for the castle then?" asked MacLeod frigidly.

"Yes, in various ways."

MacLeod turned from his loquacious guest as if he desired to hold no further converse with him, and thus, however crafty he might be, he convinced the king that the castle had no suspicion whom it held. MacLeod said abruptly to his other visitor, fastening his piercing eyes upon him,—

"I heard you were prisoner at Stirling?"

"Prisoner, sir!" cried MacDonald angrily, the red colour mounting to the roots of his hair. But before he could speak further his garrulous companion struck in.

"What an absurd rumour. MacDonald a prisoner! I assure you he was no more a prisoner at Stirling Castle than he is at this moment in Dunvegan Castle."

"Ah," said McLeod turning again to the farmer, his eyes partially closing, examining the other with more severe scrutiny than had previously been the case. "He was at liberty to come and go as he pleased, then?"

"As free as air, sir; otherwise how could he have visited my slight holding and thus become acquainted with me?"

"I thought perhaps he had met you in the courtyard of Stirling with a sack of corn on your shoulder."

The king laughed heartily at this.

"I said a small farmer certainly, but I am not quite so unimportant as you seem to imply. I have a better horse to carry my corn than the one that to-day carried me to Dunvegan."

The laird ignored this disparagement of his cattle.

"You came to Skye then to see the king's boat, of which you had heard favourable report? The news of her seems to have travelled very quickly."

"Indeed and that's true," said the king complacently. "Information spreads rapidly in the Highlands."

"It seems to spread to the Lowlands as well. You heard the king's proclamation perhaps?"

"Yes, we heard the pronouncement."

"It's possible you came from the fleet?"

"No. We came overland."

"Had you heard of the fame of Malcolm's boat before you left Stirling?"

"I did not say we left Stirling. As a matter of fact we left the small village of Doune some miles to the north of it, and at that time had heard nothing either of Malcolm or his boat."

"Hum," ejaculated the laird, rummaging among his papers on the table. The king glancing in the direction of MacLeod's hands saw spread out the charter which he himself had signed, giving MacLeod tenure of his land, and beside it, as if this island magnate had been comparing the signatures was the recent draft of the proclamation commending Malcolm MacLeod's boat. This document Dunvegan passed to the Guidman of Ballengeich.

"You know the king's writing perhaps? Will you tell me whether this is, as I suspect, a forgery?"

James wrinkled his brows and examined the signature with minute care. "I have seen the writing of his majesty," he said at last, "but MacDonald here knows it better than I. What do you think of it, Jamie?" he continued, passing on the parchment to his friend. "Is this the real Mackay, or is it not?"

"It is," said MacDonald shortly and definitely.

"You say that is the actual signature of the king?" inquired MacLeod.

"I could swear it is as genuine as the one on your charter," replied

MacDonald.

"Well, now," said MacLeod leaning back in his chair, "will you resolve a mystery for me? How is it likely that James Fifth ever heard of Malcolm MacLeod's boat? and if he did, do you consider it probable that an august monarch would compliment a Highland cateran's skill with the axe?"

"James is a douce body," said the king, "and knows more of what is going on in his realm than folk who think themselves wiser might imagine."

"You hint, then," said MacLeod, drawing down his black brows, "that his majesty may have spies in Skye?"

"Truth to tell, Laird of Dunvegan, it is more than likely," admitted the king, with an air of great candour.

The frown on MacLeod's countenance deepened, and he said harshly,—

"You two gentlemen probably know the fate of spies when they are captured. Their fate is a short shrift, and a long rope."

"And quite properly so," rejoined the king promptly.

"I am glad that you are so well informed, and need no instruction from me," commented the Crottach with menace in his tone.

Suddenly the king's manner changed, and the air of authority which was natural to him asserted itself.

"MacLeod of Skye," he cried, "this discussion and beating about the bush is interesting, but nothing at all to the purpose. You are hinting that we two are spies, and I tell you there are no spies, and can be no spies on this island."

"I have only your word to set against my own doubts," said the MacLeod.

"My word and your doubts are both aside from the purpose. Your mind has become confused. Unless you are at war with James of Scotland, there can be spies neither in the domain you hold under his hand, nor in the kingdom over which he rules. Are you a rebel against your king, MacLeod of Skye?"

"That I am not," answered Allaster hastily, and with evident discomposure.

"Very well then. You see the absurdity of an argument on espionage. MacDonald and I have as much right on the island of Skye as you have, because it is part of the Kingdom of Scotland, and we are loyal, if humble subjects of his majesty."

"You are not come here then to report on the condition of Skye?"

"We came here of our own free will; the messengers of no man, and we are to report to no man. If the king should ask me any question regarding my visit to Skye, I would answer him, that I had met with the utmost courtesy, except from its chief. I would say that MacLeod of MacLeod was so ignorant regarding the usages of good society that he received us sitting down, and never asked us to be seated, an error in politeness which I was myself forced to amend. MacDonald, plant yourself on that chair beside you. I will take this one."

MacDonald promptly obeyed the command, and the king seated himself, throwing one leg over the other and leaning back in comfort.

"Now, my Lord of Skye," he said, "have you any further questions to ask, or any additional hints to bestow upon your guests, at present in your sullen presence upon your own invitation?"

The chieftain regarded the king in silence for a few moments, then said without change of countenance,—

"By God! you may be a small farmer, but you are a brave man. You are the first who has questioned the authority of the MacLeod on his own ground. So the case being without precedent, one has to be made, and that will require some thought. We will postpone the question until later. I trust you will both honour me with your presence at dinner this evening, but if you prefer it, you may sup alone in your own apartments."

"We are sociable travellers," said the king rising, for the laird's words had in them an inflection of dismissal, "and we will have great pleasure in accepting seats at your table."

Then with a bow to the man who still remained in his chair, the king and his comrade withdrew. They consulted together for a time in the room of the former, but reached no definite decision. MacDonald urged that they should come to an understanding with their host at once, and learn whether they were prisoners or free men, but the king held that Allaster should have the time for thinking over the situation which had been practically agreed on.

"There is no hurry," he said. "Each of us is younger than Allaster and so there is time to bide."

On being summoned to the great dining-hall that night, they found a company awaiting dinner numbering perhaps a score, all men. A piper was marching up and down the room making the timbers ring with his martial music. The MacLeod stood at the head of his table, a stalwart man whose massive head seemed sunk rather deep between his broad shoulders, but otherwise, perhaps because his costume was cunningly arranged, there was slight indication of the deformity with which he was afflicted. He greeted his guests with no great show of affability, and indicated the bench at his right hand as the seat of MacDonald. The young Highlander hesitated to take the place of preference, and glanced uneasily at his comrade.

"I am slightly deaf in my right ear," said the king good naturedly, "and as I should be grieved to miss any observations you may make, I will, with your permission, occupy the place you would bestow upon my friend."

MacLeod looked sternly at the speaker for a moment, but seeing that MacDonald, without protest moved speedily round to the left, he said at last,—

"Settle it as pleases you, but I should have thought a Highland chieftain took precedence of a Lowland huckster."

"Not a huckster exactly," explained the king with a smile. "My patrimony of Ballengeich may be small, but such as it is, I am the undisputed laird of it, while at best MacDonald is but the son of a laird, so because of my deaf ear, and according to your own rules of precedence, I think I may claim the place of honour at your right." And as the MacLeod, with an angry growl sat down, the king and MacDonald followed his example. The others took their places in some haste, and with more or less of disorder. It was plain that MacLeod preferred the silent Highlander to the more loquacious farmer of Ballengeich, for during the meal he addressed most of his remarks to the man on his left, although his advances were not as cordially received as perhaps they might have been. The king showed no resentment at this neglect, but concentrated his attention on the business at hand.

When the eating was done with, the servants placed three large flagons before their master and the two who sat on either side of him. These they filled to the brim with wine.

"Gentlemen," said MacLeod, "it is a custom in this castle that our guests, to show they are good men and true, each empty one of these flagons at a draught, and without drawing breath. Will you then accompany me to any toast you may care to name?"

"The wine I have already consumed at your hospitable board," said the king, "is the best that ever ran down a thirsty man's throat; but if I supplement it with so generous and instant an addition, I fear my legs will refuse their service, even if my head retain sense enough to give the command."

"That need not trouble you," said MacLeod, "for in the last hundred years no man has insulted this vintage by leaving the hall on his own feet. There stand your legs against the wall, Guidman of Ballengeich."

The king, glancing over his shoulder, saw standing against the wall a row of brawny gillies, each two of whom supported a stretcher, whose use was at once apparent.

"Very well," cried the king to his host; "give you a suitable toast, MacLeod, and I will enter with you the rosy realms of the red wine."

MacLeod then stood up.

"I give you," he said, "the King of Scotland. May he be blest with more wisdom than were some of his ancestors!" This he repeated in Gaelic, and the sentiment was received uproariously, for the wine was already making itself felt in the great hall.

If MacLeod had any design in offering this toast it did not appear on the surface, and if he expected a hesitancy on the part of his guests to do honour to it, he was disappointed, for each young man rose with the rest.

"Here's to the king!" cried the one on his right, "and may he imbibe wisdom as I imbibe wine." Then raising the flagon to his lips he drained it dry and set it with a crash on the table again.

MacLeod and MacDonald drank more slowly, but they ultimately achieved the same end. Then all seated themselves once more, and the drinking continued without the useless intervention of further talk. One by one the revellers sank under the table unnoticed by their noisy comrades, to be quickly pounced upon by the watchful stretcher-bearers, who, with a deftness evidently the result of much practice, placed the helpless individual on the carrier and marched off with him. This continuous disappearance of the fallen rapidly thinned the ranks of the combatants struggling with the giant Bacchus.

The king had been reluctant to enter this contest, fearing the red wine would loosen his tongue, but as the evening wore on he found all his resolution concentrated in a determination to walk to his bed. MacDonald proved no protection. Early in the bout his unaccustomed head descended gently upon the table and he was promptly carried off to rest.

At last MacLeod and the king sat alone in the hall, that looked larger now it was so nearly empty; and James, as a test of what sense remained to him, set himself to count the torches burning more and more dimly in the haze of their own smoke. But he gave up the attempt when he saw that they had increased by hundreds and thousands, and were engaged in a wild pyrotechnic dance to the rhythm of the last march that had been played on the pipes. He swayed over towards his host and smote him uncertainly on the shoulder.

"MacLeod," he cried, "I challenge you to stand, and I'll wager you I can walk further down the corridor with fewer collisions against either wall than any man in Skye."

With difficulty the king rose to his feet, and as he did so the stool on which he sat, because of a lurch against it, fell clattering to the floor.

"The very benches are drunk, MacLeod, and the table sways like a ship at sea. That stool is as insecure as a throne. Rise up if you can and see if yours is any better."

But the MacLeod sat helpless, glaring at him from under his shaggy eyebrows. Seeing him stationary the king laughed so heartily that he nearly unbalanced himself, and was forced to cling for support to the edge of the table. Then straightening himself to excessive rigidity he muttered,—

"Good-night, MacLeod. Sit there and see the rule of your house broken by your———" If the next word were "monarch," or "king," it was never uttered, for as James made his uncertain way towards the door, the expert gillies, who knew their business, came up behind him, swooped the stretcher against his unreliant legs, and they failing instantly, he fell backward on the stoutly woven web between the two poles. There was a guttural laugh from MacLeod, and the prone man helplessly waving his hands, shouted,—

"Unfair, by Saint Andrew, unfair! Curse the foe who attacks a man from the rear."

The King Sails

The young men awoke somewhat late next day with heads reasonably clear, a very practical testimonial to the soundness of their previous night's vintage.

"What's to be done?" asked the king.

MacDonald proposed that they should repair instantly to MacLeod and demand of him conveyance and safe conduct to the mainland.

"We can scarcely do that," demurred the king, "until we are sure that detention is intended. Let us put the matter at once to a practical test, and see if we are prevented from leaving the castle. If we are, then is the time for protest."

Acting on this suggestion, the two went outside and took the road by which they had come. They found an agile young gillie at their heels before they were out of sight of Dunvegan.

"Why are you following us?" asked MacDonald, in Gaelic.

"I was told to wait on your lordships," returned the man.

"We need no waiting on; turn back."

But the gillie shook his shaggy uncovered head and patiently trod in their footsteps.

"Let us see how far he will follow," said the king as he strode on. The gillie accompanied them for half an hour or more without making any protest, but at last he said to MacDonald that he thought it was time to return.

"We are going through to the coast we came from," replied MacDonald, "and do not intend to return."

At this the gillie drew from his belt a short black tube that looked like a practising chanter, which indeed it was, and on this he blew a few shrill notes.

Up to that moment the way had been clear, but now there appeared over the hill in front of them a dozen armed men, who approached carelessly as if they had merely happened to be in the neighbourhood, or were journeying together toward the castle.

"I think it is time to go back," suggested the gillie in a dull, uninterested voice.

"I think it is myself," replied MacDonald.

And so the futile excursion came to an end.

Once more in the castle they were confronted again by the question, What next?

"I am certain," said the king, "that if MacLeod is attempting to hold us, there is little use in making appeal to him, and we have small chance of getting word to the fleet. I propose then to coerce him. He was alone in his study yesterday, and he may be alone there now. A sword's point at a man's throat is an irresistible argument."

"But will he keep his word if he gives it under distress?" objected MacDonald.

"I think he will, but it is better not to put too strong a temptation on him. If we come on him alone we will make him sign a pass for us. Then we will gag and tie him securely, convey him, when the way is clear, to this room, where he will be less likely to be looked for. We will then give him the consolation that if his pass proves useless we will return and finish the business by sending him into a less troublesome world."

This advice was no sooner promulgated than it was acted upon. The pair traversed the corridors unseen until they came to the door of the study, then, slipping out their swords, they entered quickly unannounced. The sight which confronted them was so unexpected that each stood there with drawn sword in hand as if stricken into stone.

MacLeod was not in the room, but in his stead, beside the wall of books, her hand upraised, taking down a small vellum-covered volume, was the most beautiful young girl, of perhaps nineteen or twenty, that either of them had ever looked upon. She seemed surprised at their abrupt entrance and remained statuesquely in her position, as motionless as they. The young woman was the first of the three to recover her composure. Relinquishing the book to the shelf, the hand came down to her side, and she said in most charming, liquid tones, but in broken English,—

"You are looking for my father perhaps?"

The king, ever gallant, swept his hat from his head and bowed low, his alertness of mind saving the situation, for he answered quickly,—

"Indeed no, my lady. We thought the room was empty, so I implore you to pardon our intrusion. We were here yesterday, and my friend and I have just had a dispute regarding the size of these gigantic tomes on the lower shelf; my friend insisting that they exceeded our sword blades in length. Pardon me madam?" and the king stepped briskly to the largest book, laying his sword down its back as if in measurement.

"There, Jamie," he cried, "I have won the wager. I knew it was not more than three quarters the length of my blade."

The glance of fear to which the young woman had treated them departed from her face, and she smiled slightly at the young man's eagerness.

"I gather from your remark," he said, "that you are Miss MacLeod of Dunvegan. May I introduce my friend, James MacDonald of Sleat. My own name is James Stuart, and for a time we are your father's guests at Dunvegan."

The young lady with inimitable grace bowed her queenly head to each of them in turn. The men slipped their swords quietly back into their scabbards.

"I give you good welcome to Dunvegan," said the girl. "I regret that I do not speak fair the English."

"Indeed, my lady," rejoined the susceptible king, "it is the most charming English I ever heard."

The fair stranger laughed in low and most melodious cadence, like a distant cathedral's chime falling on the evening air.

"I am thinking you will be flattering me," she said, "but I know my English is not good, for there are few in these parts that I can speak to in it."

"I shall be delighted to be your teacher," replied the king with his most courteous intonation. He knew from experience that any offer of tutorship from him had always proved exceedingly acceptable to the more dainty sex, and this knowledge gave him unbounded confidence while it augmented his natural self-esteem.

"It is perhaps that you already speak the Gaelic?" suggested the young woman.

"Alas! no madam. But I should be overjoyed to learn and there, it may be, you will accept me in the part of pupil. You will find me a devoted and most obedient scholar. I am in a way what you might call a poet, and I am told on every hand that Gaelic is the proper medium for that art."

A puzzled expression troubled the face of the girl as she endeavoured to follow the communication addressed to her, but MacDonald sprang somewhat eagerly to the rescue, and delivered a long harangue in her native language. Her delight was instant, the cloud on her brow disappearing as if by magic under the genial influence of the accustomed converse. The king's physiognomy also underwent a change but the transformation was not so pleasing as that which had illumined the countenance of the girl. His majesty distinctly scowled at the intrepid subject who had so impetuously intervened, but the pair paid slight attention to him, conversing amiably together, much to their mutual pleasure.

Now, it is nowhere considered polite to use a language not understood by some one person in the party. This fact MacDonald knew perfectly well, and he doubtless would have acted differently if he had taken the time to think, but he had become so engrossed by the beauty of the lady, that, for the moment, every other consideration seemed to have fled from his mind. Miss MacLeod is to be excused because she probably supposed a Stuart to be more or less acquainted with the language, in spite of his former disclaimer, which it is not likely she fully comprehended. So she talked fluently and laughed lightly, while one of her auditors was consumed by an anger he dared not show.

The tension of the situation was changed rather than relieved, by the silent opening of the door, and the pause of MacLeod himself on the threshold, gazing dubiously at the group before him. The animation of the girl fell from her the moment she beheld her father, and the young men, turning, were confronted by the gloomy features of the chieftain. The MacLeod closed the door softly, and, without a word, walked to his chair beside the table. The girl, bowing slightly, with visible restraint, quitted the room, and, as she did so, MacDonald's alertness again proved his friend, for he tip-toed quickly to the door, before the king, accustomed to be waited upon rather than waiting, recollected himself; and held it open for the lady, making a gallant sweep with his bonnet as she passed out.

When the supple young man returned to his place beside the king he said in a whisper,—

"No sword's point play with the father of such a beauty, eh?"

To this remark his majesty made no reply, but said rather gruffly and abruptly to his host,—

"Do you hold us prisoners in this castle, sir?"

"That will depend on the answers I get from you," replied the MacLeod slowly. "Are you two or either of you, emissaries of the king?"

"We are not."

"Does the king know you are here?"

"Regarding the king, his knowledge or his doings, you had better address your inquiries to him personally. We have no authority to speak for his majesty."

"You are merely two private gentlemen, then, come all this distance to satisfy a love of travel and a taste for scenery?"

"You have stated the case with great accuracy, sir."

"Yesterday you spoke of my lack of manners in failing to ask you to be seated; I shall now refer to a breach of politeness on your own part. It is customary when strangers visit a province under an acknowledged ruler, that they should make a formal call upon the ruler before betaking themselves to other portions of his territory. You remained for several days in Skye without taking the trouble to inform me of your arrival."

"Sir," replied James haughtily, "I dispute your contention entirely. You are not the ruler of Skye."

"Who is then?"

"The King of Scotland, of course."

The MacLeod laughed in a fashion that somewhat resembled the snarl of an angry dog.

"Of course, as you say. No one disputes that James is king of all Scotland, and I would be the last to question his right, because I hold my lands under charter bearing his signature, carrying the Great Seal of the kingdom; nevertheless, the MacLeods held Skye long before the present royal family of Scotland were heard of, and I would have been MacLeod of MacLeod although James had never put his hand to this parchment. Meanwhile, I take the risk of detaining you until I learn more about you, and if the king makes objection, I shall apologise."

"You will apologise," said James sternly.

"Oh, it is easily done, and fair words smooth many a difficulty. I shall write to him if he complain, that I asked especially if you were his men, that you denied it, and so, both for his safety and my own, I considered it well to discover whether or not you were enemies of the realm. If the father of MacDonald is offended I shall be pleased to meet him either on sea or land, in anger or in friendship, and as for you, who talk so glibly of the king, I would warn you that many things happen in Skye that the king knows nothing of, besides the making of strong drink."

The king made him a courtier-like bow for this long speech, and answered lightly,—

"The cock crows blithely on his own midden. Your midden is here, while mine is far away, therefore the contest in crowing is somewhat uneven. Nevertheless I indulge in a final flapping of my wings and an effort of the throat when I say that you will apologise, not by writing at your ease in Dunvegan Castle, but on your bended knees at Stirling."

"That's as may be," said the MacLeod indifferently, and it was quite obvious that he remained unmoved by the threat. "Gentlemen, I have the honour to wish you good morning."

"One moment. Are we then to consider ourselves prisoners?"

"You may consider yourselves whatever best pleases you. If you make another attempt like the one you indulged in this morning, I shall clap you both in the deepest dungeons I possess. Some would even go so far as to call that imprisonment, but if each gives me his word of honour that he will make no attempt at escape, and also that he will not communicate with Stirling, then you are as free of my house and my grounds as if you were the most welcome of guests. But I warn you that if, when you pass your words, you attempt to tamper with any of my men, I shall know of it very soon after, and then comes the dungeon."

The king hesitated and looked at his friend, but MacDonald, who had taken no part in this conversation, seemed in an absent dream, his eyes gazing on vacancy, or perhaps beholding a vision that entranced him.

"What do you say, MacDonald?" enquired the king sharply.

MacDonald recovered himself with a start.

"To what?" he asked.

"To the terms proposed by our gaoler."

"I did not hear them; what are they?"

"Will you give your word not to escape?"

"Oh, willingly."

"And not to communicate with Stirling?"

"I don't care if I never see Stirling again."

The king turned to the chief.

"There is little difficulty, you see," he said, "with your fellow Highlander. I however, am supposed to be a Lowlander, and therefore cautious. I give you my word not to communicate with Stirling. As for the other proviso, I amend it as follows. I shall not leave this island without your knowledge and your company. If that is satisfactory, I pledge my faith."

"Perfectly satisfactory," answered the MacLeod, and with that the two young men took their departure.

Once more in the king's room, from which, earlier in the day they had set out so confidently, MacDonald flung himself upon a bench, but the king paced up and down the apartment. The former thought the latter was ruminating on the conditions that had been wrung from him, but the first words of the king proved his mistake.

"Jamie, you hardly gave me fair play, you and your Gaelic, with that dainty offspring of so grim a sire."

"Master of Ballengeich," replied the Highlander, "a man plays for his own hand. You should have learned the Gaelic long ago."

The king stopped abruptly in his walk.

"Why do you call me by that name?"

"Merely to show that in this ploy the royal prerogative is not brought into play; it is already settled that when I meet the king, I am defeated. It remains to be seen what luck plain James MacDonald has in a contest with plain James Stuart."

"Oh, it's to be a contest then?"

"Not unless you wish it so. I am content to exchange all the fair damsels of Stirling for this one Highland lassie."

"You'll exchange!" cried the king. "I make bold to say she is not yours to exchange."

"I intend to make her mine."

"Ah, we'll see about that, Jamie."

"We will, Ballengeich," said MacDonald with confident precision. And so the contest began.

The girl, who saw few in her father's castle to be compared with those whom she supposed to be mere visitors at Dunvegan, was at first equally charming to each. A younger sister was her almost constant companion, which was very well at first but latterly became irksome to both the suitors. Occasionally, however, one James or the other saw her alone and made the most of the opportunity presented, but the king soon found himself tremendously handicapped in the matter of language. The young lady possessed a keen sense of humour, and this, with the ever present knowledge that her English was not that of the schools, made her loth to adventure in that tongue before one accustomed to its polished use. This same sense of humour was equally embarrassing when the king madly plunged into the intricacies and ambushes of the Gaelic. His majesty was brave enough for anything and did not hesitate, as a forlorn hope, to call his scant knowledge of the Gaelic to his aid, but even he could see that the result was invariably unhappy, for although the girl made every endeavour to retain her composure, there were times when some unfortunate phrase made her slight frame quiver with suppressed merriment, and no one knew better than the baffled king, that laughter banishes sentiment. The serious Highlander, not less manly and handsome than his competitor, was gifted with an immeasurable advantage in his familiarity with every phase and inflection of his native vernacular. In his despair the king struck up a close friendship with Donald, the second son of the MacLeod, the elder son being absent on some foray or expedition, and his majesty made a frantic effort to learn the only speech with which his new comrade was equipped. But this race against time gave MacDonald long and uninterrupted conferences with his inamorata, and the king saw, too late, the futility of his endeavour. It might have been wiser if he had taken his lessons from the girl herself instead of from her brother, but his majesty was more proficient in teaching than in learning from the fair sex. He had come to the conclusion that his uninteresting rambles with Donald were not likely to further his quest, and was sitting in his room cogitating upon some new method of attack when MacDonald burst into the apartment with radiant face. The king looked up at his visitor with no great good nature, and said sharply,—

"Well, what is it?"

"Your majesty," cried MacDonald jubilantly, "I think I have found a method of escape, and that without in any way impugning our pledges."

"Oh, is that all," said the king, with the air of snubbing too enthusiastic a courtier. "I thought the house was on fire."

"And I thought, your majesty," returned MacDonald, "that this subject was ever uppermost in your mind."

The king rested his closed fist on his hip, leaned his head a little to one side and examined his rival critically.

"Why have you returned so unexpectedly to the phrase, your majesty?"

"Because, your majesty," answered MacDonald laughing, "the phrase, Guidman of Ballengeich, no longer matters."

"I do not understand you."

"It is to make myself understood that I have come so hurriedly. I beg then to inform your majesty, that Miss MacLeod has consented to become my wife. I have spoken to her father, who has somewhat grudgingly and conditionally given his consent. It occurred to me that if I wedded the daughter of your gaoler, I may have enough influence with the family to secure your majesty's release."

"I have no doubt," said the king, "that this was your object from the beginning. And so you have exchanged a temporary gaoler for one that will last you all your life."

The Highlander knit his brow and compressed his lips, as if to hold back some retort which later he might regret. There was a moment's constrained silence, then the king flung off his ill-humour as if it were a cloak.

"Forgive me, Jamie," he cried, springing to his feet. "Forgive the wounded vanity of the vanquished."

He extended his hand impetuously, which the other grasped with eager cordiality.

"Jamie, my lad, you were right. The crown weighs heavy when it is thrown into the scale, but with this lassie I well believe it would have made not an ounce of difference. Let the best man win, say I, and you're the victor, so you have my warmest congratulation. Still, Jamie, you must admit that the Gaelic is the cursedest lingo ever a poor Lowland-bred man tried to get his tongue round. So now you see, Jamie, we are even again. You think the crown defeated you at Stirling, and I hold the language defeated me in Skye; thus we are both able to retain a good opinion of ourselves, which is the splendid privilege of every Scotchman to hold. Your bravery deserves success, for it requires some courage to face your future father-in-law. What did the old curmudgeon say?"

"He gave little indication of pleasure or the reverse. He offered me my liberty, now that I had pledged it in another direction, but he refused to release you, so I declined to accept his clemency."

"Then my proposed rescue must await the marriage ceremony?"

"Not so. I have a more immediate and practical remedy. You have not forgotten the twenty-six oared barge which the MacLeod was to keep for the king, and which Malcolm MacLeod built for him."

"It is not very likely, when I issued a proclamation commending Malcolm as the greatest shipbuilder in the world."

"Well, Malcolm has arrived at Dunvegan to receive into his own hands once more that same proclamation. I asked him, in MacLeod's presence, if the fleet still lingered in Torridon Bay, and he answered that it did. MacLeod pricked up his ears at this, and thinking he was to get some information, now that I proposed myself as a member of his family, inquired if I knew why it remained so long. I said I had a suspicion of the cause. If Malcolm had not replied to the king's proclamation it was natural that the fleet would wait until he did. Old Alexander and Malcolm seemed surprised that a response was expected, Malcolm being but a simple yeoman. However, we wrote out a courteous reply to the king, in Gaelic, and Malcolm is to send it to the fleet as soon as he returns to the northern coast."

"I don't see how that is to help us," demurred his majesty.

"Here is my proposal. If you will now write out an order to the admiral commanding the fleet to appear before Dunvegan Castle, I will ride part of the way home with Malcolm, and suggest to him at parting, that perhaps none of the officers of the fleet understand Gaelic, or at least that none can read it, so I will fasten your letter to the other document, and tell Malcolm it is a translation of his Gaelic effusion. Neither Malcolm nor any of his friends at the port can read English, and as he is a simple minded man it is not likely that he will return and allow the laird a perusal. So in that way we may get word to the fleet. Even if the letter is discovered, you will have kept your word, for you promised only not to communicate with Stirling."

The king pronounced the device a feasible one, and set himself at once to the writing of the letter.

MacDonald succeeded in getting the unsuspicious Malcolm to take charge of the supposed English version of his note, and the king was left to await the result with whatever patience was vouchsafed him. The island had suddenly lost all interest for him and he fervently wished himself safely in Stirling once more. He complimented the girl on the excellent choice she had made, and she returned his compliment laughingly in Gaelic, glancing timidly at MacDonald as she asked him to be her interpreter.

Two or three days later there was a commotion in the castle. The guards on the western headlands reported the approach of numerous ships, and by-and-by from the castle wall itself the fleet could be seen sailing slowly up Loch

Follart. For the first time since they had known him, lines of deep anxiety marked the frowning brow of MacLeod as he stood gazing at the approaching vessels. Here were visitors who, if they proved not to his liking, he could scarcely threaten with the dungeons of Dunvegan.

"What do you make of this, MacDonald?" said the chieftain, turning to his future son-in-law, as if already he looked to him for support and counsel.

But MacDonald shook his head, in spite of the fact that his wife who-was-to-be, stood very close to him.

"All negotiations have been carried on by my friend here, and so to him I must refer you. He is the leader of our expedition of two."

During his brief acquaintance MacLeod had but thinly veiled his dislike of the Lowlander, who had always ventured to speak with him in a free and easy manner to which he was unaccustomed. Instead then of addressing his question to the other, he returned to his occupation of watching the ships manœuvring in the loch before him. But his air of expectancy seemed to indicate that he thought the usual glibness exhibited by the man at his right would bring forth some sort of explanation, but the king stood as silent as himself, his eyes fixed on the fleet. One by one the ships came to anchor and even an amateur in the art of naval warfare could see by the protruding guns that they were prepared for action.

MacLeod could restrain his impatience no longer, so without glancing at his visitor, he said,—

"Perhaps you, sir, can tell me the purport of all this display."

"Assuredly," answered the king with a trace of sternness in his tone that had hitherto been absent in his converse with his gaoler. "The fleet comes at the command of the king to take away your prisoners, if they are unharmed, or to batter down your castle if they have been molested."

"I suppose then I should be thankful they are unharmed?"

"You have reason," said the king shortly.

"His majesty must set great value on your heads if he sends his whole fleet to succour you."

"He does."

"How did he know you were here if you did not break your parole and communicate with Stirling?"

"The king knows there is more going on in Skye than the making of strong drink. I did not break my parole, neither did MacDonald."

"In spite of what you said to me, you must have told the king before you left Stirling where you were going."

"I did not."

"Then word must have been brought to him from Skye?"

"It was not."

"In that case the only conclusion I can come to is that the king is unaware of your presence here."

"He is well aware of it."

"You speak in riddles, my friend. However, I had no real wish to detain you, and you might have gone where you pleased any time this fortnight or more."

"So you say now."

"It's true enough, and if you wish to visit the fleet one of my boats will be ready to carry you the moment you give the order. I told you the first day that if you were a friend of the king's, or an emissary of his, you could go on your way unchecked. Did I not, MacDonald?"

"You said something of that sort, sir."

"You denied being a friend of the king's," persisted MacLeod, "and said you were but a small farmer near Stirling."

"I deny yet that I am a friend of the king. On the contrary, I don't mind confessing to you that I am the greatest enemy he has in the world, and it's well he knows it."

"You amaze me. Then you do not wish to meet the fleet."

"On the contrary, I do, and I ask you to order a suitable boat for me."

"You shall have the best boat in my possession," said MacLeod leaving them for a moment to give his command.

In a short time a large boat with ten oarsmen was waiting at the landing.

"They are ready for you," said MacLeod with an effort at geniality, which gave a most sinister effect to his face. "I am sorry to bid you good-bye, but I hope you bear away with you no ill will against Dunvegan."

"Sir," said the king ignoring his compliments, "that boat will not do for me."

"It is the best I have," said MacLeod looking at his truculent guest with new anxiety.

"The boat you must bring to the landing is the twenty-six oared barge, which Malcolm MacLeod built so well."

The MacLeod stepped back two paces.

"That boat is for the king," he said in a voice scarcely above a whisper.

"Yes, it is for the king, therefore the king demands it. Give the order instantly that it be brought to the landing, well manned with twenty-six rowers."

All colour left MacLeod's face. His next words were to MacDonald.

"Is this true?" he said.

"Yes," answered MacDonald, "it is true."

The girl, her wide eyes distended with fear, clutched the arm of her lover. Even she knew this was a case for the headsman, but MacLeod, with not a quiver in his voice, called down to his followers,—

"Bring round the king's barge, and see it is well manned. I myself will take the rudder."

The stern face of the king relaxed as he saw this chieftain stand straighter than ever before since he had known him, ready to take on his head whatever might befall.

The girl impetuously flung herself at the king's feet, and in her excitement forgetting the limitations of his learning, she poured forth a plea for her father in Gaelic. The king smiled as he stooped and raised the suppliant.

"My dear," he said, "I shall never hear that language without thinking of you, and of my own discomfiture. If it were not that MacDonald stands there with that dour Highland look on his face, it is I would kneel at your feet. Your father is to come with me to Stirling, for I have said he should, and I must keep my word with myself as well as I have kept it with him. Do not draw away your hand, in spite of MacDonald's scowls, for I have this to promise you. If you and he will accompany us to Stirling, I pledge to you the king's word that I shall grant you whatever you ask. So you see you need have no fear for your father's safety." Saying this, the king, with that courtly manner which so well became him, gave the hand of the girl into that of MacDonald.

Thus it came about that the MacLeod took a voyage he had not intended, and came so unscathed from it that he long outlived the man who was the cause of his journey.

The King Weds

Even a stranger in Stirling must have been impressed by the fact that something unusual was afoot, not to be explained by the mere preparation for ushering in the New Year. Inquiry soon solved the problem of the decorations and the rejoicings. James the Fifth, the most popular king Scotland had possessed since the days of Bruce, was about to be married, and most of his subjects thought it high time, for he had reached the mature age of twenty-six, and monarchs are expected to take a mate somewhat earlier than other folk. As the king, with a splendid retinue, was to depart shortly after the new year on a journey to France to claim his bride, the capital city flung its bunting to the breeze, and the inhabitants thereof pledged each other and the king in bumpers of exhilarating beverages; indeed all Scotland was following the example set to it by Stirling, for the marriage was extremely well liked throughout the land.

The king's father had linked himself to an English princess, and the Scottish people thought little of her. The precipitate marriage of this queen, only a few months after her husband's death, still further lowered her in public estimation. Scotland professed slight regard for Margaret of England, and was glad when her son refused the offer of his uncle, Henry the Eighth, to provide him with a wife. Indeed, James was at that moment the most sought-after young man in the world, so far as matrimony was concerned. The Pope, who now addressed him as Defender of the Faith, had a favourite candidate for his hand. Henry the Eighth was anxious that he should have all England to pick and choose from. The Emperor Charles the Fifth wished him to marry Princess Mary of Portugal; Francis the First of France was eager to supply him with a well-dowered bride. Never before had any youth such an embarrassment of choice, but James himself decided that he would go a-wooing to France, and his subjects universally applauded his preference. James's elderly relative, John, Duke of Albany, had married the heiress of De la Tour d'Auvergne, and the young king resolved to follow his example. Apart from this, James, in a manner, was pledged from the time he was three years of age, for Albany, when Regent of Scotland, had promised France that the young ruler should seek his consort in that country; so there had now been chosen for him Mary, daughter of the Duc de Vendôme, who was reported beautiful, and, what was more to the purpose in a thrifty nation, was known to be wealthy.

This courting by all Europe might have turned the head of a less sensible young man than James, but he well knew the reason that so many distinguished persons desired his alliance. Henry the Eighth was at loggerheads with France; the Emperor Charles and Francis the First were engaged in one of their customary aimless wars, the advantage as usual inclining rather to the emperor's side. Scotland was at peace with itself and with all the world. The Scots were excellent fighters in whatever part of the world they encountered an enemy, and the strong fleet which James the Fourth had builded was augmented by his son and might prove a powerful factor in European politics. France and Scotland had long been traditional friends, and so this new mating aroused enthusiasm in both countries.

Thus Stirling put on gay attire and her citizens went about with smiles on their faces, all except one, and that one was James himself, who became more and more gloomy as the time for his departure approached. He had no desire to take upon himself the trammels of the matrimonial estate, and although his uncle, the strenuous Henry, was ultimately to set an example before the world of the ease with which the restrictions of marriage were to be shuffled off, yet at this time Henry himself was merely an amateur at the business, engaged in getting rid of Catherine of Arragon, a task which he had not yet succeeded in accomplishing. James had postponed and re-postponed the fateful journey; but at last he saw it must be taken, or a friendly country, one of the proudest on earth, would be deliberately insulted in the face of the world. Not only this, but his own subjects were getting restive, and he knew as well as they that a disputed succession in the event of his early death might lead to civil war. So, making the best of the hard bargain which is imposed on princes, where what should be the most endearing ties of human affection are concerned, James set his face resolutely towards the south, and attended by a brilliant escort, sailed for France. After a stormy voyage, for the month was January, the royal party landed in France, and was met by a company of nobles, only less splendid than itself in that a king was one of the visitors; for Francis had remained at Loches, to welcome his brother sovereign at that great and sinister stronghold, where the Court of France for the moment held its seat. Both time and weather seemed unpropitious for joyous occasion. News arrived at Loches that the French army had suffered defeat in its invasion of the Duke of Savoy's territory, and these tidings exercised a depressing influence on the welcoming delegation.

As the united escorts of France and Scotland set out on their journey to Loches a flurry of damp snow filled the air, raw from off the Channel, and the road proved wellnigh impassable through depth of mud. The discontented countenance of the king, who was wont to be the life of any party of which he was a member, lowered the spirits of his Scottish followers to the level of those saddened by military defeat and the horsemen made their way through the quagmires of Northern France more like a slow funeral procession than wedding guests.

At the castle where they halted at the end of the first day's journey, the King speedily retired to the apartment assigned to him without a word of cheer even to the most intimate of his comrades.

The travellers had accomplished only about twelve leagues from the sea-coast on their first day's journey, and darkness had set in before the horsemen clattered through the narrow streets of a little town and came to the frowning gates of a great castle, whose huge tower in the glare of numerous torches loomed out white against the wintry sky. The chief room of the suite reserved for the king was the only cheerful object his majesty had seen that day. A roaring bonfire of bulky logs shed a flickering radiance on the tapestry that hung along the wall, almost giving animation to the knights pictured thereon, sternly battling against foes in anger, or merrily joisting with friends for pleasure at some forgotten tournament.

The king, probably actuated by the military instincts of his race urging him to get his bearings, even though he was in the care of a friendly country, strode to one of the windows and looked out. Dark as was the night and cloudy the sky, the landscape was nevertheless etched into tolerable distinctness by the snow that had fallen, and he saw far beneath him the depths of a profound valley, and what appeared to be a town much lower than the one through which he had just ridden. The stronghold appeared to stand on a platform of rock which was at least impregnable from this side. James turned from the wintry scene outside to the more alluring prospect within the apartment. A stout oaken table in the centre of the room was weighted with a sumptuous repast; and the king, with the stalwart appetite of youth and health augmented by a tiresome journey in keen air, forthwith fell to, and did ample justice to the providing of his unknown host. The choicest vintages of France did something to dispel that depression which had settled down upon him, and the outside glow of the great fire supplemented the inward ardour of good wine.

The king drew up his cushioned chair to the blaze, and while his attendants speedily cleared the board, a delicious drowsiness stole over him. He was partially aroused from this by the entrance of his poetical friend and confidant, Sir David Lyndsay.

"Your majesty," said the rhymster, "the constable of these towers craves permission to pay his respects to you, extending a welcome on behalf of his master, the King of France."

"Bring him in, Davie," cried James; "for in truth he has already extended the most cordial of welcomes, and I desire to thank him for my reception."

Shortly after Sir David Lyndsay ushered into the room a young man of about the same age as the king, dressed in that superb and picturesque costume which denoted a high noble of France, and which added the lustre of fine raiment to the distinguished court of Francis the First. The king greeted his visitor with that affability, which invariably drew even the most surly toward him, without relaxing the dignity which is supposed to be the heritage of a monarch.

"I am delighted to think," said the newcomer, "that the King of Scotland has honoured my house by making it his first halting-place in that realm which has ever been the friend of his country."

"Sir," replied James, "the obligation rests entirely upon me. After a stormy voyage and an inclement land journey, the hospitality of your board is one of the most grateful encounters I have ever met with. I plead an ignorance of geography which is deplorable; and cannot in the least guess where I am, beyond the fact that the boundaries of France encompass me."

"I shall not pretend," said the young man, "that my house is unworthy even of the distinguished guest which it now holds. Your majesty stands within historic walls, for in an adjoining apartment was born William, the founder of a great race of English kings. Scotchmen have defended this castle, and Scotchmen have assaulted it, so its very stones are linked with the fortunes of your country. Brave Henry the Fifth of England captured it, and France took it from his successor. My own family, like the Scotch, have both stood its guard and have been the foremost through a breach to sack it. I am but now employed in repairing the ravages of recent turmoil."

Here the King interrupted him, as if to mend the reputation of ignorance he had bestowed upon himself.

"I take it, then, that I speak to one of the renowned name of Talbot, and that this fortress is no other than the Castle of Falaise?" and the king impetuously extended his hand to him. "We both come of a stormy line, Talbot. Indeed we are even more intimately associated than you have hinted, for one of your name had the temerity to invade Scotland itself in the interests of Edward Baliol—yes, by the Rood, and successfully too."

"Ah, your majesty, it does not become the pride of our house to refer to Richard Talbot, for three years later the Scots took him prisoner, and he retired defeated from your country."

"Indeed," replied the king gaily, "if my memory serves me truly, we valued your valiant ancestor so highly that we made the King of England pay two thousand marks for him. We Scots are a frugal people; we weigh many of the blessings of life against good hard coin, and by Saint Andrew of Scotland, Talbot, I hold myself to-day no better than the rest, for, speaking as young man to young man, I think it unworthy of either king or peasant to take a woman to his bosom for aught save love of her."

"In that I cordially agree with your majesty," said Talbot, with a fervour that made the king glance at him with even more of sympathy than he had already exhibited. A wave of emotion seemed to overwhelm the sensitive James, and submerge for the moment all discretion; he appeared to forget that he spoke to a stranger and one foreign to him, yet James rarely mistook his man, and in this case his intuition was not at fault. To lay bare the secrets of his heart to one unknown to him shortly before, was an experiment of risk; but, as he had said, he spoke as young man to young man, and healthy youth is rarely cynical, no matter to what country it belongs. The heart knows nothing of nationality, and a true man is a true man wherever he hails from.

James sprang to his feet and paced the long room in an excess of excitement, a cloud on his brow; hands clenching and unclenching as he walked. Equally with the lowest in his realm he felt the need of a compassionate confidant. At last the words poured forth from him in an ecstasy of confession.

"Talbot," he cried, "I am on a journey that shames my very manhood. I have lived my life as others of my age, and whatever of contrition I may feel, that rests between my Maker and myself. I am as He formed me, and if I was made imperfect I may be to blame that I strove so little to overcome my deficiency, but, by God, I say it here, I never bought another nor sold myself. Now, on the contrary, I go to the loud marketplace; now I approach a woman I have never seen, and who has never seen me, to pledge our lives together, the consideration for this union set down on parchment, and a stipulated sum paid over in lands and gold."

The king stopped suddenly in his perambulation, raised his hands and said impressively,—

"I tell you, friend and host, I am no better than my fellows and worse than many of them, but when the priest mutters the words that bind, I say the man should have no thought in his mind, but of the woman who stands beside him; and she no thought in hers but of the man in whose hand she places her own."

"Then why go on with this quest?" cried young Talbot with an impetuosity equal to that of his guest.

"Why go on; how can I stop? The fate of kingdoms depends on my action. My honour is at stake. My pledged word is given. How can I withdraw?"

"Your majesty need not withdraw. My master, Francis, is the very prince of lovers, and every word you have uttered will awake an echo in his own heart, although he is our senior by twenty years. If I may venture to offer humbly such advice as occurs to me, you should tell him that you have come to France not to be chosen for, but to choose. France is the flower garden of the human race; here bloom the fairest lilies of womanhood, fit to grace the proudest throne in Christendom. Choice is the prerogative of kings."

"Indeed, Talbot, it is not," said the king dolefully.

"It should be so, and can be so, where a monarch boldly demands the right exercised unquestioned by the meanest hind. Whom shall you offend by stoutly claiming your right? Not France, for you will wed one of her daughters; not the king, for he is anxious to bestow upon you the lady you may prefer. Whom then? Merely the Duke of Vendôme, whose vaulting ambition it is to place a crown upon the head of his daughter, though its weight may crush her."

The king looked fixedly at the perturbed young man, and a faint smile chased away the sternness of his countenance.

"I have never known an instance," he said slowly, "where the burden of a crown was urged as an objection even by the most romantic of women."

"It would be so urged by Mary of Vendôme, were she allowed to give utterance to her wishes."

"You know her then?"

"I am proud to claim her as a friend, and to assert she is the very pearl of France."

"Ha, you interest me. You hint, then, that I come a bootless wooer? That is turning the tables indeed, and now you rouse an emulation which heretofore was absent in me. You think I cannot win and wear this jewel of the realm?"

"That you may wear it there is no doubt; that you may win it is another matter. Mary will place her listless hand in yours, knowing thus she pleases the king and her father, but it is rumoured her affections are fixed upon another."

"Sir, you stir me up to competition. Now we enter the lists. You bring the keen incentive of rivalry into play."

"Such, your majesty, was far from my intention. I spoke as a friend of the lady. She has no more choice in this bargain than you deplored the lack of a moment since."

The former gloom again overspread the king's face.

"There is the devil of it," he cried impatiently. "If I could meet her on even terms, plain man and woman, then if I loved her I would win her, were all the nobles of France in the scales against me. But I come to her chained; a jingling captive, and she approaches me alike in thrall. It is a cursed fate, and I chafe at the clanking links, though they hold me nevertheless. And all my life I can never be sure of her; the chiming metal ever between us. I come in pomp and display, as public as the street I walk on, and the union is as brazen as a slave market, despite cathedral bells and archbishop's blessing. Ah, well, there is nothing gained by ranting. Do you ride to Loches with me?"

"I follow your majesty a day behind, but hope to overtake you before you are well past Tours."

"I am glad of it. Good-night. I see you stand my friend, and before this comes to a climax we may have need to consult together. Good-night; good-night!"

Next morning early the itinerants were on horseback again, facing southward. The day was wild and stormy, and so was the next that followed it; but after leaving Tours they seemed to have entered an enchanted land, for the clouds were dispersed and the warm sun came forth, endowing the travellers with a genial climate like late springtime in Scotland. As they approached Loches even the king was amazed by the striking sight of the castle, a place formidable in its strength, and in extent resembling a small city.

The gay and gallant Francis received his fellow monarch with a cordiality that left no doubt of its genuine character. The French king had the geniality to meet James in the courtyard itself; he embraced him at the very gates as soon as James had dismounted from his horse. Notwithstanding his twenty years of seniority Francis seemed as young as the Scottish king.

"By Saint Denis, James," he cried, "you are a visitor of good omen, for you have brought fine weather with you and the breath of spring. All this winter we have endured the climate of Hades itself, without its warmth."

The two rulers stood together in the courtyard, entirely alone, for no man dare frequent their immediate neighbourhood; but in a circle some distance removed from their centre, the Scotch and the French fraternised together, a preeminent assemblage numbering a thousand or more; and from the balconies beautiful ladies looked down on the inspiring scene.

The gates were still open and the drawbridge down, when a horseman came clattering over the causeway, and, heedless of the distinguished audience, which he scattered to right and left, amid curses on his clumsiness, drew up his foaming horse in the very presence of royalty itself.

Francis cried out angrily at this interruption.

"Unmannerly varlet, how dare you come dashing through this throng like a drunken ploughman!"

The rider flung himself off the panting horse and knelt before his enraged master.

"Sire," he said, "my news may perhaps plead for me. The army of the Emperor Charles, in Provence, is broken and in flight. Spain has met a crushing defeat, and no foe insults the soil of France except by lying dead upon it."

"Now, my good fellow," cried the king with dancing eyes, "you are forgiven if you had ridden down half of my nobility."

The joyous news spread like wildfire, and cheer upon cheer rose to heaven like vocal flame to mark its advance.

"Brother," cried the great king to his newly arrived guest, placing an arm lovingly over his shoulder, his voice with suspicion of tremulousness about it, "you stalwart Scots have always brought luck to our fair land of France. This glad news is the more welcome to me that you are here when I receive it."

And so the two, like affectionate kinsmen, walked together into the castle which, although James did not then know it, was to be his home for many months.

There was a dinner of state that evening, so gay and on a scale so grand that James had little time or opportunity for reflection on his mission. Here indeed, as Talbot had truly said, was the flower garden of the human race; and the Scottish king saw many a proud lady to whom probably he would have been delighted to bend the knee. But his bride was not among the number. The Duchesse de Vendôme explained to the king that her daughter was suffering from a slight illness, and apart from this was anxious to greet her future husband in a conference more private than the present occasion afforded. This was certainly reasonable enough, and the important meeting took place the following afternoon.

Mary of Vendôme might truly be called the Pearl of France, if whiteness of visage gave claim to that title. The king found himself confronted by a drooping young woman whose stern mother gave her a support which was certainly needed. Her face was of the pallor of wax; and never once during that fateful interview did she raise the heavy lids from her eyes. That she had once been beautiful was undoubted, but now her face was almost gaunt in its excessive thinness. The death-like hue of her delicate skin, the fact that she seemed scarce to breathe, and that she never ventured to speak, gave her suitor the impression that she more resembled one preparing for the tomb than a young girl anticipating her bridal. She courtesied like one in a trance; but the keen eyes of the king saw the tightening of her mother's firm hand on her wrist while she made the obeisance which etiquette demanded. Short as was their formal greeting, it was too long for this anæmic creature, who would have sunk to the floor were it not for the clutch in which the determined mother held her. Even the king, self-contained as he usually was, found little to say beyond empty expressions of concern regarding her recent illness, ending with a brief remark to the effect that he hoped she would soon recover from her indisposition. But once the ordeal was over, James was filled with a frenzy to be alone, tortured as he was by an agony of mind which made any encounter with his fellows intolerable. He strode through the seemingly interminable corridors of the great castle, paying slight heed to his direction. All doors opened before him, and sentinels saluted as he passed. At last, not knowing where he was, or how to get outside, he said to one of the human statues who held a pike,—

"Tell me, good fellow, the quickest way to the outer air; some spot where I can be entirely alone?"

The guard, saluting, called a page, whispered a word to him, and the boy led the king to a door which gave access to a secluded garden, enclosed on every side by high battlements, yet nevertheless filled with great trees, under which ran paths both straight and winding. Beside one wall lay the longest walk of this little park, and up and down this gravelled way, his hands clasped behind him, the young king strode in more disturbance of mind than had ever before afflicted him.

"Oh, God save me; God save me!" he cried; "am I to be wedded to a ghost? That woman is not even alive, to say whether she is willing or no. Have I come to France to act the ghoul and rob the grave of its due? Saints in heaven, help me! What am I to do? I cannot insult France, yet I cannot chain my living body to that dead woman. Why is not Talbot here? He said he would overtake me at Tours, and yet is he not come. The Pearl of France, said he, the jewel of a toad's head, say I. My honour staked, and to that unbreathing image of tallow! Is this my punishment? Do the sins of our youth thus overtake us, and in such ghastly form? Bones of my ancestors, I will not wed the grave, though war and slaughter come of it. And yet—and yet, my faith is plighted; blindly, unknowingly plighted. Why does not Talbot come? He knew what my emotions would be on seeing that denizen of another world, and so warned me."

These muttered meditations were suddenly interrupted by a clear sweet voice from above.

"Écossais! Scottish knight! Please rescue for me my handkerchief, which I have, alas, let fall. Wrap a stone in it and throw it hither, I beg of you."

The startled king looked up and beheld, peering over at him from the battlements above, one of the most piquant and pretty, laughing faces he had ever seen. Innocent mischief sparkled in the luscious dark eyes, which regarded him from a seemingly inaccessible perch. A wealth of dark tousled hair made a midnight frame for a lovely countenance in the first flush of maidenly youth. Nothing could be more marked than the difference between the reality which thus came unexpectedly into view, and his sombre vision of another. There also sifted down to him from aloft, whisperings that were evidently protests, from persons unseen; but the minx who was the cause of them merrily bade her counsellors be quiet. She must get her handkerchief, she said, and the Scot was the only one to recover it. Fluttering white from one of the lower branches was a dainty bit of filmy lace, much too fragile a covering for the stone she had suggested. The despair which enveloped the king was dispelled as the mist vanishes before the beaming sun. He whipped out his thin rapier and deftly disentangled the light burden from the detaining branch. It fluttered to his hand and was raised gallantly to his lips, at which the girl laughed most joyfully, as if this action were intensely humorous. Other faces peeped momentarily over the balustrade to be as quickly withdrawn when they saw the stranger looking up at them; but the hussy herself, whoever she was, seemed troubled by no such timorousness, resting her arms upon the stone balustrade, with her chin above them, her inviting eyes gazing mockingly on the man below. The king placed the handkerchief in the bosom of his doublet, thrust home the rapier in its scabbard, grasped the lower branch of the tree and swung himself up on it with the agility of an acrobat. Now the insolence of those eyes was chased away by a look of alarm.

"No, no," she cried, "stay where you are. You are too bold, Scottish knight."

But she had to reckon with one who was a nimble wall climber, either up or down, whose expertness in descent had often saved him from the consequences of too ambitious climbing. The young man answered not a word, but made his way speedily up along the branches until he stood at a level with the parapet. Across the chasm which divided him from the wall he saw a broad platform, railed round with a stone balustrade, this elevated floor forming an ample promenade that was nevertheless secluded because of the higher castle walls on every side, walls that were unpierced by any window. A door at the farther end of the platform gave access to the interior of the palace. A short distance back from the balustrade stood a group of some half-dozen very frightened women. But the first cause of all this commotion remained in the forefront of the assemblage, angry and defiant.

"How dare you, sir?" she cried. "Go back, I command you." Then seeing he made no motion to obey her, but was measuring with his keen eye the distance between the bending limb on which he held his precarious position, and the parapet, something more of supplication came into her voice, and she continued,—

"My good fellow, place the handkerchief on the point of your sword and one of my women will reach for it. Be careful, I beg of you; that bough will break under your weight if you venture further. The outreached arm and the sword will span the space."

"Madam," said the king, "the sword's point is for my enemy. On bended knee must I present a lady that which belongs to her."

And with this, before further expostulation was possible, the young man made his perilous leap, clutched the parapet with his left arm, hung suspended for one breathless moment, then flung his right leg, a most shapely member, over the balustrade, and next instant was kneeling at her feet, offering the gosamer token. In the instant of crisis the young lady had given utterance to a little shriek which she instantly suppressed, glancing nervously over her shoulder. One of her women ran towards the door, but the girl peremptorily ordered her to return.

"The Scot will not eat you," she cried impatiently, "even if he is a savage."

"Madam, your handkerchief," explained the savage, still offering it.

"I shall not accept it," she exclaimed, her eyes blazing with resentment at his presumption.

The king sprang to his feet and swept off his plumed hat with the air of an Italian.

"Ten thousand thanks, madam, for your cherished gift." Saying which he thrust the slight web back into his doublet again.

"'Tis not a gift; render it to me at once, sir," she demanded with feminine inconsistency. She extended her hand, but the king, instead of returning the article in dispute, grasped her fingers unawares and raised them to his lips. She drew away her hand with an expression of the utmost contempt, but nevertheless stood her ground, in spite of the evident anxiety to be elsewhere of the bevy behind her.

"Sir, you are unmannerly. No one has ever ventured to treat me thus."

"Then I am delighted to be the first to introduce to you so amiable a custom. Unmannerly? Not so. We savages learn our manners from the charming land of France; and I have been told that in one or two instances, this country has known not only the fingers, but the lips to be kissed."

"I implore you, sir, to desist and take your departure the way you came; further, I warn you that danger threatens."

"I need no such warning, my lady. The danger has already encompassed me, and my heart shall never free itself from its presence, while remembrance of the lightning of those eyes abides with me."

The girl laughed with a trace of nervousness, and the rich colour mounted to her cheek.

"Sir, you are learning your lesson well in France."

"My lady, the lowest hind in my country could not do otherwise under such tutelage."

"You should turn your gifts to the service of your master. Go, woo for him poor Mary of Vendôme, and see if you can cure her who is dying of love for young Talbot of Falaise."

For a moment the king stood as if struck by the lightning he had just referred to, then staggering back a step, rested his hand on the parapet and steadied himself.

"Good God!" he muttered in low tones, "is that true?"

All coquetry disappeared from the girl as she saw the dramatic effect her words had produced. She moved lightly forward, then held back again, anxiety on her brow.

"Sir, what is wrong with you? Are you ill? Are you a friend of Talbot's?"

"Yes, I am a friend of his."

"And did you not know this? I thought every one knew it. Does not the King of Scotland know? What will he do when he learns, think you, or will it make a difference?"

"The King of Scotland is a blind fool; a conceited coxcomb, who thinks every woman that sees him must fall in love with him."

"Sir, you amaze me. Are you not a subject of his? You would not speak so in his hearing."

"Indeed and that I would, without hesitation, and he knows it."

"Is he so handsome as they say? Alas, I am thought too young to engage in court festivities, and in spite of my pleadings I was not allowed even to see his arrival."

The king had now recovered his composure, and there was a return of his gallant bearing.

"Madam, tell me your name, and I shall intercede that so rigid a rule for one so fair may be relaxed."

"Ah, now your impudence reasserts itself. My name is not for you. How can a humble Scottish knight hope to soften a rule promulgated by the King of France himself?"

"Madam, you forget that we are guests of France, and in this courteous country nothing is denied us. We meet with no refusals except from proud ladies like yourself. I shall ask my captain, he shall pass my request to the general, who will speak to the King of Scotland, and the king, when he knows how beautiful you are, will beg the favour from Francis himself."

The girl clasped her hands with exuberant delight.

"I wonder if it is possible," she said, leaning towards the gay cavalier, as if he were now her dearest friend—for indeed it was quite evident that she thought much of him in spite of his irregular approach. She was too young to feel the rules of etiquette otherwise than annoying bonds, and like an imprisoned wild bird, was willing to take any course that promised liberty.

"Your name, then, madam?"

"My name is Madeleine."

"I need not ask if you are noble."

"I am at least as noble as Mary of Vendôme, whom your king is to marry, if he is cruel enough."

At this point one of the women, who had stationed herself near the door, came running towards the group and warned them that somebody was approaching. The attendants, who had hitherto remained passive, probably with some womanly curiosity regarding the strange interview, now became wild with excitement, and joined their mistress in begging the stranger to depart.

"Not until I have whispered in your ear," he said stoutly.

"I cannot permit it; I cannot permit it. Go, go at once, I implore you."

"Then I escort you within the hall to meet whoever comes."

"Sir, you are importunate. Well, it doesn't matter; whisper."

He bent toward her and said:—

"Madeleine, you must meet me here alone at this time to-morrow."

"Never, never," she cried resolutely.

"Very well then; here I stay until you consent."

"You are cruel," she said, tears springing in her eyes. Then appealingly, as a knock sounded against the door, she added, "I promise. Go at once."

The young man precipitated himself over the parapet into the tree. The fortune which attends lovers and drunkards favoured him, and the last bending branch lowered him as gently to the gravel of the walk as if he were a son of the forest. He glanced upward, and saw that the luminous face, in its diaphanous environment of dark hair was again bent over the parapet, the lips apart and still, saying nothing, but the eloquent eyes questioning; indeed he fancied he saw in them some slight solicitude for his safety. He doffed his hat, kissed the tips of his fingers and wafted the salutation toward her, while a glow of satisfaction filled his breast as he actually saw a similar movement on the part of her own fair fingers, which was quickly translated into a gesture pointing to the garden door, and then she placed a finger-tip to her lips, a silent injunction for silence. He knew when to obey, as well as when to disobey, and vanished quickly through the door. He retreated in no such despairing phase of mind as he had advanced, but now paid some attention to the geography of the place that he might return unquestioning to his tryst. Arriving at the more public corridors of the palace, his first encounter was with the Constable of Falaise. Talbot's dress was travel-stained, and his youthful face wore almost the haggardness of age. He looked like a man who had ridden hard and slept little, finding now small comfort at the end of a toilsome journey. The king, with a cry of pleasure at the meeting, smote his two hands down on the shoulders of the other, who seemed unconsciously to shrink from the boisterous touch.

"Talbot," he cried, "you promised to overtake me at Tours, but you did not."

"It is not given to every man to overtake your majesty," said Talbot hoarsely.

"Constable of Falaise, you were not honest with me that night in your castle. I spoke to you freely from the bottom of my heart; you answered me from your lips outward."

"I do not understand your majesty," replied the young man grimly.

"Yes, you do. You love Mary of Vendôme. Why did you not tell me so?"

"To what purpose should I have made such a confession, even if it were the fact?"

"To the purpose of truth, if for nothing else. God's sake, man, is it thus you love in France! Cold Scotland can be in that your tutor. In your place, there had been a quick divorce between my sword and scabbard. Were my rival twenty times a king, I'd face him out and say, by Cupid's bow, return or fight."

"What! This in your castle to your guest?" exclaimed Talbot.

"No, perhaps not. You are in the right, constable, you are in the right. I had forgotten your situation for the moment. I should have been polite to him within my own walls, but I should have followed him across my marches and slit his gullet on the king's highway."

Notwithstanding his distraction of mind the newcomer smiled somewhat wanly at the impetuosity of the other.

"You must remember that while your foot presses French soil, you are still the guest of all true Frenchmen, nevertheless your majesty's words have put new life into my veins. Did you see Mary of Vendôme?"

"Yes, and there is not three months' life left to her unless she draws vitality from your presence. Man, man, why stand you here idling? Climb walls, force bolts, kidnap the girl and marry her in spite of all the world."

"Alas, there is not a priest in all France would dare to marry us, knowing her pledged to your majesty."

"Priests of France! I have priests in my own train who will, at a word from me, link you tighter than these stones are cemented together. God's will, Talbot, these obstacles but lend interest to the chase."

"Is it possible that you, having opportunity, care not to marry Mary of Vendôme?" cried the amazed young man, who could not comprehend that where his preference fell another might be indifferent; for she was, as he had said, the Pearl of France to him, and it seemed absurd to imagine that she might not be so to all the world.

"United Europe, with Francis and the Emperor Charles for once combined could not force me to marry where I did not love. I failed to understand this when I left Scotland, but I have grown in wisdom since then."

"Who is she?" asked the constable, with eager interest.

"Hark ye, Talbot," said the king, lowering his voice and placing an arm affectionately over the shoulder of the other. "You shall be my guide. Who is the Lady Madeleine of this court?"

"The Lady Madeleine? There are several."

"No, there is but one, the youngest, the most beautiful, the most witty, the most charming. Who is she?"

The constable wrinkled his brows in thought.

"That must be Madeleine de Montmorency. She is the youngest of her name, and is by many accounted beautiful. I never heard that she was esteemed witty until your majesty said so. Rather reserved and proud. Is that the lady?"

"Proud, yes. Reserved—um, yes, that is, perhaps not when she meets a man who knows enough to appreciate her. However, I shall speedily solve the riddle, and must remember that you do not see the lady through a lover's eyes. But I will not further keep you. A change of costume may prove to your advantage, and I doubt not an untroubled night's sleep will further it."

"Your majesty overwhelms me with kindness," murmured the young lover, warmly grasping the hand extended to him. "Have I your permission to tell Mary of Vendôme?"

"You have my permission to tell her anything, but you will bring her no news, for I am now on my way to see her."

The king gaily marched on, his head held high, a man not to be denied, and as he passed along all bowed at his coming, for everyone in the court admired him. There was something unexpectedly French in the dash of this young Scotchman. He strode across the court and up the steps which led into the Palais Vendôme. The duchess herself met him with a hard smile on her thin lips.

"Madam," he said bruskly, "I would see your daughter alone."

The grim duchesse hesitated.

"Mary is so shy," she said at last.

But the king interrupted her.

"I have a cure for that. Shyness flees in my presence. I would see your daughter alone, madam; send her to me."

There being no remedy when a king commands, the lady made the best of a dubious proceeding.

James was pacing up and down the splendid drawing-room when, from the further door the drooping girl appeared, still with downcast eyes, nun-like in her meek obedience. She came forward perhaps a third the length of the room, faltered, and stood.

"Mary," said the king, "they told me you were beautiful, but I come to announce to you that such is not my opinion. You are ambitious, it would seem, so I tell you frankly, you will never be Queen of Scotland."

For the first time in his presence the girl uncovered her eyes and looked up at him.

"Yes," said the king, "your eyes are fine. I am constrained to concede that much, and if I do not wed you myself it is but right I should nominate a candidate for your hand. There is a friend of mine for whom I shall use my influence with Francis and your father that they may persuade you to marry him. He is young Talbot, Constable of Falaise, a demented stripling who calls you the Pearl of France. Ah, now the colour comes to your cheeks. I would not have believed it. All this demureness then———" But the girl had sunk at his feet, grasped his hand and pressed it to her lips.

"Tut, tut," he cried hastily, "that is a reversal of the order of nature. Rise, and when I send young Talbot to you, see that you welcome him; and now, good-day to you."

As he passed through the outer room the duchesse lay in wait for him and began murmuring apologies for her daughter's diffidence.

"We have arranged all about the wedding, madam," said the king reassuringly as he left the palace.

The next day at the hour when the king had met Madeleine for the first time, he threaded his way eagerly through the mazes of the old castle until he came to the door that led him out into the Elysian garden. The weather still befriended him, being of an almost summer mildness.

For several minutes he paced impatiently up and down the gravel walk, but no laughing face greeted him from the battlements above. At last, swearing a good round Scottish oath he said, "I'll solve the mystery of the balcony," and seizing the lower branch of the tree, he was about to climb as he had done before, when a tantalizing silvery laugh brought his arms down to his sides again. It seemed to come from an arbour at the further end of the grounds, but when he reached there the place proved empty. He pretended to search among the bushes, but nevertheless kept an eye on the arbour, when his sharp ear caught a rustling of silk from behind the summer-house. He made a dash towards it, then reversed his direction, speeding like the wind, and next instant this illusive specimen of Gallic womanhood ran plump into his arms, not seeing where she was going, her head averted to watch the danger that threatened from another quarter.

Before she could give utterance to more than one exclamatory "Oh," he had kissed her thrice full on the lips. She struggled in his arms like a frightened bird, nobly indignant with shame-crimsoned cheeks, smiting him with her powerless little snowflake of a hand. Her royal lover laughed.

"Ha, my Madeleine, this is the second stage of the game. The hand was paradise on earth; the lips are the seventh heaven itself."

"Release me, you Scottish clown!" cried Madeleine, her black eyes snapping fire. "I will have you whipped from the court for your insolence."

"My dear, you could not be so cruel. Remember that poor Cupid's back is naked, and he would quiver under every stroke."

"I'd never have condescended to meet you, did I dream of your acting so. 'Tis intolerable, the forwardness of you beggarly Scots!"

"Nay, never beggarly, my dear, except where a woman is concerned, and then we beg for favours."

"You little suspect who I am or you would not venture to misuse me thus, and be so free with your 'my dears.'"

"Indeed, lass, in that you are mistaken. I not only found you in the garden, but I found your name as well. You are Madeleine de Montmorency."

She ceased to struggle, and actually laughed a little.

"How clever you are to have discovered so much in such a short time. Now let me go, and I will thank you; nay more, I promise that if you ask the Duke of Montmorency for his permission, and he grants it, I will see you as often as you please."

"Now Madeleine, I hold you to that, and I will seek an introduction to the duke at once."

She stepped back from him panting, and sank into a deep courtesy that seemed to be characterised more by ridicule than politeness.

"Oh, thank you, sir," she said. "I should dearly love to be an eavesdropper at your conference."

Before he could reply, the door opened by which he had entered the park.

"In the fiend's name, the king!" muttered James, in no manner pleased by the unwelcome interruption.

All colour left the girl's face, and she hastily endeavoured to arrange in brief measure the disordered masses of her hair, somewhat tangled in the struggle. As Francis advanced up the walk, the genial smile froze on his lips, and an expression of deep displeasure overshadowed his countenance, a look of stern resentment coming into his eyes that would have made any man in his realm quail before him. The girl was the first to break the embarrassing silence, saying breathlessly,—

"Your majesty must not blame this Scottish knight. It is all my fault, for I lured him hither."

"Peace, child," exclaimed Francis in a voice of cold anger. "You know not what you say. What do you here alone with the King of Scotland?"

"The King of Scotland!" echoed Madeleine, in surprise, her eyes opening wide with renewed interest as she gazed upon him. Then she laughed. "They told me the King of Scotland was a handsome man!"

James smiled at this imputation on his appearance, and even the rigour of the lord of France relaxed a trifle, and a gleam of affection for the wayward girl that was not to be concealed, rose in his eyes.

"Sire," said James slowly, "we are neither of us to blame. 'Tis the accident that brought us together must bear the brunt of consequence. I cannot marry Mary of Vendôme, and indeed I was about to beg your majesty to issue your command that she may wed your Constable of Falaise. If there is to be a union between France and Scotland other than now exists, this lady, and this lady alone, must say yes or no to it. Premising her free consent, I ask her hand in marriage."

"She is but a child," objected Francis, breathing a sigh, which had, however, something of relief in it.

"I am fully seventeen," expostulated Madeleine, with a promptness that made both men laugh.

"Sire, Youth is a fault, which alas, travels continually with Time, its antidote," said James. "If I have your good wishes in this project, on which, I confess, my heart is set, I shall at once approach the Duke of Montmorency and solicit his consent."

The face of Francis had cleared as if a ray of sunshine had fallen upon it.

"The Duke of Montmorency!" he cried in astonishment; "what has he to do with the marriage of my daughter?"

James murmured something that may have been a prayer, but sounded otherwise, as he turned to the girl, whose delight at thus mystifying the great of earth was only too evident.

"I told him he little suspected who I was," said Madeleine, with what might have been termed a giggle in one less highly placed; "but these confident Scots think they know everything. Indeed, it is all your own fault, father, in keeping me practically a prisoner, when the whole castle is throbbing with joy and festivity." Then the irrepressible princess buried her flushed face in her hands, and laughed and laughed, as if this were the most irresistible comedy in the world, instead of a grave affair of state, until at last the two monarchs were forced to laugh in sympathy.

"I could not wish her a braver husband," said Francis at last. "I see she has bewitched you as is her habit with all of us."

And thus it came about that James the Fifth of Scotland married the fair Madeleine of France.

THE END

About Author

Robert Barr (16 September 1849 – 21 October 1912) was a Scottish-Canadian short story writer and novelist.

Early years in Canada

Robert Barr was born in Barony, Lanark, Scotland to Robert Barr and Jane Watson. In 1854, he emigrated with his parents to Upper Canada at the age of four years old. His family settled on a farm near the village of Muirkirk. Barr assisted his father with his job as a carpenter, and developed a sound work ethic. Robert Barr then worked as a steel smelter for a number of years before he was educated at Toronto Normal School in 1873 to train as a teacher.

After graduating Toronto Normal School, Barr became a teacher, and eventually headmaster/principal of the Central School of Windsor, Ontario in 1874. While Barr worked as head master of the Central School of Windsor, Ontario, he began to contribute short stories—often based on personal experiences, and recorded his work. On August 1876, when he was 27, Robert Barr married Ontario-born Eva Bennett, who was 21. According to the 1891 England Census, the couple appears to have had three children, Laura, William, and Andrew.

In 1876, Barr quit his teaching position to become a staff member of publication, and later on became the news editor for the Detroit Free Press. Barr wrote for this newspaper under the pseudonym, "Luke Sharp." The idea for this pseudonym was inspired during his morning commute to work when Barr saw a sign that read "Luke Sharp, Undertaker." In 1881, Barr left Canada to return to England in order to start a new weekly version of "The Detroit Free Press Magazine."

London years

In 1881 Barr decided to "vamoose the ranch", as he called the process of immigration in search of literary fame outside of Canada, and relocated to London to continue to write/establish the weekly English edition of the Detroit Free Press. During the 1890s, he broadened his literary works, and started writing novels from the popular crime genre. In 1892 he founded the magazine The Idler, choosing Jerome K. Jerome as his collaborator (wanting, as Jerome said, "a popular name"). He retired from its co-editorship in 1895.

In London of the 1890s Barr became a more prolific author—publishing a book a year—and was familiar with many of the best-selling authors of his day, including :Arnold Bennett, Horatio Gilbert Parker, Joseph Conrad, Bret Harte, Rudyard Kipling, H. Rider Haggard, H. G. Wells, and George Robert Gissing. Barr was well-spoken, well-cultured due to travel, and considered a "socializer."

Because most of Barr's literary output was of the crime genre, his works were highly in vogue. As Sherlock Holmes stories were becoming well-known, Barr wrote and published in the Idler the first Holmes parody, "The Adventures of "Sherlaw Kombs" (1892), a spoof that was continued a decade later in another Barr story, "The Adventure of the Second Swag" (1904). Despite those jibes at the growing Holmes phenomenon, Barr remained on very good terms with its creator Arthur Conan Doyle. In Memories and Adventures, a serial memoir published 1923–24, Doyle described him as "a volcanic Anglo—or rather Scot-American, with a violent manner, a wealth of strong adjectives, and one of the kindest natures underneath it all".

In 1904, Robert Barr completed an unfinished novel for Methuen & Co. by the recently deceased American author Stephen Crane entitled The O'Ruddy, a romance.Despite his reservations at taking on the project, Barr reluctantly finished the last eight chapters due to his longstanding friendship with Crane and his common-law wife, Cora, the war correspondent and bordello owner.

Death

The 1911 census places Robert Barr, "a writer of fiction," at Hillhead, Woldingham, Surrey, a small village southeast of London, living with his wife, Eva, their son William, and two female servants. At this home, the author died from heart disease on 21 October 1912.

Writing Style

Barr's volumes of short stories were often written with an ironic twist in the story with a witty, appealing narrator telling the story. Barr's other works also include numerous fiction and non-fiction contributions to periodicals. A few of his mystery stories and stories of the supernatural were put in anthologies, and a few novels have been republished. His writings have also attracted scholarly attention. His narrative personae also featured moral and editorial interpolations within their tales. Barr's achievements were recognized by an honorary degree from the University of Michigan in 1900.

His protagonists were journalists, princes, detectives, deserving commercial and social climbers, financiers, the new woman of bright wit and aggressive accomplishment, and lords. Often, his characters were stereotypical and romanticized.

Barr wrote fiction in an episode-like format. He developed this style when working as an editor for the newspaper Detroit Press. Barr developed his skill with the anecdote and vignette; often only the central character serves to link the nearly self-contained chapters of the novels. (Source: Wikipedia)

NOTABLE WORKS

In a Steamer Chair and Other Stories (Thirteen short stories by one of the most famous writers in his day -1892)

"The Face And The Mask" (1894) consists of twenty-four delightful short stories.

In the Midst of Alarms (1894, 1900, 1912), a story of the attempted Fenian invasion of Canada in 1866.

From Whose Bourne (1896) Novel in which the main character, William Brenton, searches for truth to set his wife free.

One Day's Courtship (1896)

Revenge! (Collection of 20 short stories, Alfred Hitchcock-like style, thriller with a surprise ending)

The Strong Arm

A Woman Intervenes (1896), a story of love, finance, and American journalism.

Tekla: A Romance of Love and War (1898)

Jennie Baxter, Journalist (1899)

The Unchanging East (1900)

The Victors (1901)

A Prince of Good Fellows (1902)

Over The Border: A Romance (1903)

The O'Ruddy, A Romance, with Stephen Crane (1903)

A Chicago Princess (1904)

The Speculations of John Steele (1905)

The Tempestuous Petticoat (1905–12)

A Rock in the Baltic (1906)

The Triumphs of Eugène Valmont (1906)

The Measure of the Rule (1907)

Stranleigh's Millions (1909)

The Sword Maker (Medieval action/adventure novel, genre: Historical Fiction-1910)

The Palace of Logs (1912)

"The Ambassadors Pigeons" (1899)

"And the Rigor of the Game" (1892)

"Converted" (1896)

"Count Conrad's Courtship" (1896)

"The Count's Apology" (1896)

"A Deal on Change " (1896)

"The Exposure of Lord Stanford" (1896)

"Gentlemen: The King!"

"The Hour-Glass" (1899)

"An invitation" (1892)

" A Ladies Man"

"The Long Ladder" (1899)

"Mrs. Tremain" (1892)

" Transformation" (1896)

"The Understudy" (1896)

" The Vengeance of the Dead" (1896)

"The Bromley Gibbert's Story" (1896)

" Out of Thun" (1896)

"The Shadow of Greenback" (1896)

"Flight of the Red Dog" (fiction)

"Lord Stranleigh Abroad" (1913)

"One Day's Courtship and the Herald's of Fame" (1896)

"Cardillac"

"Dr. Barr's Tales"

"The Triumphs of Eugene Valmont"

CPSIA information can be obtained
at www.ICGtesting.com
Printed in the USA
LVHW090346140720
660560LV00013B/612

9 789390 194896

Feel the...

A Hot Pursuit

Hold on tight with these thrillingly seductive brand-new novels that are sure to take your breath away!

Cold Feet by Brenda Novak

'Novak's *Cold Feet* is a definite nail-biter... The plot is riveting, the ending delightfully unpredictable and the characters compelling.'
—*Romantic Times*

Internal Affair by Marie Ferrarella

'(*Internal Affair*)...sizzles with sexual tension, and the plot is edgy, dark and suspenseful. Ferrarella has penned a guaranteed page-turner!'
—*Romantic Times*

BRENDA NOVAK

Most writers say they've had stories running around in their head since they can remember, but that wasn't the case for Brenda. She grew up thinking she didn't have a creative bone in her body. It wasn't until she was 29 and married with three kids that she discovered writing. Now she has five children, three girls and two boys, and juggles her writing career with field trips and homework sessions, and trying to keep up with her active husband. Fortunately, her family is as involved in what she does as she is in their activities. Brenda loves to hear from her readers. You can contact her via her website at www.brendanovak.com.

MARIE FERRARELLA

Marie Ferrarella has earned a master's degree in Shakespearean comedy and, perhaps as a result, her writing is distinguished by humour and natural dialogue. Marie has one goal: to entertain, to make people laugh and feel good. 'That's what makes me happy,' she confesses. 'That, and a really good romantic evening with my husband.' She's keeping her fingers crossed that you enjoy reading her books as much as she's enjoyed writing them. Her novels are beloved by fans worldwide and have been translated into Spanish, Italian, German, Russian, Polish, Japanese and Korean.

A Hot Pursuit

MARIE FERRARELLA
BRENDA NOVAK

SILHOUETTE®

DID YOU PURCHASE THIS BOOK WITHOUT A COVER?
If you did, you should be aware it is **stolen property** as it was reported *unsold and destroyed* by a retailer. Neither the author nor the publisher has received any payment for this book.

All the characters in this book have no existence outside the imagination of the author, and have no relation whatsoever to anyone bearing the same name or names. They are not even distantly inspired by any individual known or unknown to the author, and all the incidents are pure invention.

All Rights Reserved including the right of reproduction in whole or in part in any form. This edition is published by arrangement with Harlequin Enterprises II B.V. The text of this publication or any part thereof may not be reproduced or transmitted in any form or by any means, electronic or mechanical, including photocopying, recording, storage in an information retrieval system, or otherwise, without the written permission of the publisher.

This book is sold subject to the condition that it shall not, by way of trade or otherwise, be lent, resold, hired out or otherwise circulated without the prior consent of the publisher in any form of binding or cover other than that in which it is published and without a similar condition including this condition being imposed on the subsequent purchaser.

Silhouette and Colophon are registered trademarks of Harlequin Books S.A., used under licence.

*First published in Great Britain 2005
Silhouette Books, Eton House, 18-24 Paradise Road,
Richmond, Surrey TW9 1SR*

A HOT PURSUIT © Harlequin Books S.A. 2005

The publisher acknowledges the copyright holders of the individual works as follows:

Cold Feet © Brenda Novak 2004
Internal Affair © Marie Rydzynski-Ferrarella 2003

ISBN 0 373 60289 8

009-0705

*Printed and bound in Spain
by Litografia Rosés S.A., Barcelona*

Cold Feet
BRENDA NOVAK

To my mother, Lavar Moffitt. I come from a long line of mentally tough women, and my mother is one of the toughest. As I grow older, I recognise more and more the foundation she has built for me and the debt of gratitude I owe her. I pray I will live up to the character she has tried to foster in me and, for my own children's sake, that I'll pass on her legacy…

ACKNOWLEDGEMENT

Many thanks to Detective Tom Bennett of Colorado for his help with the police and forensic details of this novel. Tom has spent more than thirty years in public service, working for the Arvada Police Department, and has investigated approximately 2000 felony cases. The recipient of numerous departmental honours, including the Medal of Valour, the highest honour the Arvada PD bestows on a police officer, Tom is a gifted detective and a honourable man.

CHAPTER ONE

"CALEB, SHE'S GONE. Disappeared. Vanished," Holly said.

Caleb Trovato could hear the distress in his ex-wife's voice, but he wasn't about to respond to it. Everything seemed to affect her far more acutely than it would anyone else, and by virtue of the fact that they were divorced—for the second time—he didn't have to ride her emotional roller coaster anymore.

He propped the phone up with his shoulder and swiveled back to his computer to check his e-mail, so the next few minutes wouldn't be a total waste. "Your sister's what—twenty-six? She'll turn up."

"How can you be so sure?"

"Susan's disappeared before. Remember that time she met some rich guy on an hour's layover in Vegas and let him talk her into a wild fling? We were positive something terrible had happened to her. Especially when the airline confirmed that she'd boarded the flight out of Phoenix."

"That was different," Holly retorted. "She called me the next day."

"Only because loverboy had started acting a little scary. She finally realized it might be a good thing to let someone know where she was. And she needed money to get home."

"That was almost five years ago, Caleb. She's changed.

She has a steady job at Nordstrom's cosmetics counter and she's kept her own apartment for almost a year."

The high pitch of Holly's voice brought back memories of the many outbursts he'd been forced to endure while they were married, and put his teeth on edge. "Listen, Holly, I'm sorry Susan's giving you a scare, but I'm really busy," he said, determined to escape this time. "I've got to go."

"Caleb, don't do this to me," she replied, openly crying. "I haven't bothered you for anything since our last divorce."

Caleb rolled his eyes. Wasn't that the general idea? It wasn't as if they had children together. And contrary to her claim of not bothering him, she called often. She called to borrow money. She called to ask how to file her income tax returns. She called to see if he could remember what happened to the X rays that had been taken of her leg when she'd had that waterskiing accident. She even called to see what his plans were for certain holidays.

"I don't understand what you want from me," he said in frustration.

"I haven't been able to reach Susan for almost a week. Mom and Dad haven't heard from her. Lance, the guy she's dating, hasn't heard from her. She hasn't called in at work—"

"Skipping work is nothing new for Susan, either," he pointed out.

"Caleb, she was living near the university."

At this Caleb sat forward, feeling his first flicker of alarm. Eleven women had been abducted and killed near the University of Washington over the past twelve years. Holly had lived right next door to one of them. That was how he'd met her. He'd been working for the Seattle Police Department, canvassing the apartment building of the strangler's ninth victim, looking for leads, and he'd knocked on Holly's door to check if she'd seen or heard anything.

But Caleb was certain the man who'd committed those murders was now dead. He should know. He'd spent three years on the task force investigating the case and another four continuing to help after he'd quit the Seattle PD. "Holly, the Sandpoint Strangler shot himself in his own backyard over a year ago."

She sniffed. "If you're so sure, why didn't you ever finish the book you were going to write about him?"

"There wasn't enough hard evidence to connect Ellis Purcell to the killings," Caleb admitted. "But you saw him drive away from your apartment building the night Anna was murdered. You're the one who gave us the partial plate number."

"But you could never place him inside the apartment."

"That doesn't mean he was innocent, Holly," Caleb said, making a halfhearted attempt to organize his desk while they talked. "Purcell couldn't account for his whereabouts during several of the murders. He failed two different lie-detector tests. The geographical profile done by the FBI indicated the killer lived within a five-block radius of him and his family. And he was secretive, kind of a recluse. I talked to him twice, Holly, and it always felt as though he was hiding something."

"I know all that, but when you worked for the department you searched his place three different times and never found anything."

"Some of the task force searched it. I was young enough, and new enough to the force, that I did what Gibbons told me, which was mainly behind-the-scenes grunt work. Gibbons was lead detective. He always dealt with the really important stuff. But the murders have stopped since Purcell's death," Caleb said. "That should tell you something."

"They stopped for several years after Anna's body was discovered, too," Holly argued.

"That's because the police were watching Purcell so closely he could scarcely breathe. The murders started up again as soon as that custodian, John Roach, killed a kindergarten teacher at Schwab Elementary downtown and almost everyone on the force, including Gibbons, suddenly believed we'd been barking up the wrong tree. But it was only wishful thinking."

"Then what about the woman who went missing from Spokane a couple of months ago?" Holly asked. "How do you explain that if the strangler's dead?"

"I haven't heard anything about it," he said.

"I just read an article the other day that said the police found some of that date rape drug on the floor of her car. Roach is in prison and Purcell is dead, but that sounds like the strangler to me."

Caleb still had several close friends on the force. If anything interesting had developed, Detective Gibbons or Detective Thomas would have called him. This case had meant a lot to all of them. "Have they found her body?"

"Not yet."

"Then they don't know anything. Roofies are only about two bucks per tablet, and they're easy to buy. We saw them in that pharmacy when we were in Mexico, remember?"

"So what about Susan?" she asked, with more than a hint of desperation.

She was baiting him, trying to tempt him back into her life. But it wasn't going to work this time. He no longer felt the same compulsion to rescue her that had drawn him to her in the first place. "I don't know what you want me to do."

"You used to be a cop, for God's sake! A good one. I want you to come out here and find her, Caleb."

Shoving his mouse away, Caleb turned in his new leather office chair to stare out the picture window that revealed a breathtaking view of San Francisco Bay. A panorama of blue-green, undulating ocean dotted with at least twenty colorful sailboats was spread out before him. "I live in California now, Holly." As if to prove how necessary it was that he remain in his current surroundings, he added, "I have someone coming to lay new carpet next week."

"This could mean Susan's life!" Holly cried.

Another over-the-top statement? Given Holly's penchant for theatrics, he figured it was.... "I'm not a cop anymore. I write true crime books. I don't know what you think I can do."

"I *know* what you can do," she said. "I married you twice, remember? It's almost uncanny how you turn up whatever you're looking for. It's a talent. You're...you're like one of those journalists who'll stop at nothing to uncover a story."

Caleb wasn't sure that was such a positive association, but he let it pass because she was still talking.

"You could come if you wanted to. Lord knows you've got the money."

"Money isn't the issue," he replied.

"Then what is?"

His hard-won freedom. He'd had to leave the Seattle area to get far enough away from Holly. He wasn't about to head back now, even though his parents still lived on Fidalgo Island, where he'd grown up, and he loved the place. "I can't leave. I'm in the middle of another book."

She seemed to sense that he wasn't going for the panicky stuff, and made an effort to rein in her emotions. "What's this one about?"

"A girl who murdered her stepfather."

She sniffled again. "Sounds fun."

At her sarcasm, he felt his lips twist into a wry grin. "It's a living. *Somebody* I know hated being a cop's wife and encouraged me to go for my dream of becoming a writer."

"And is that so bad? Now you're rich and famous."

But still divorced. No matter how much Holly professed to love him, he couldn't live with her. She was simply too obsessive. He'd married her the first time because he'd thought they could make a life together. He'd married her the second time because his sense of honor demanded it. But beyond their initial few months together, their relationship had been fractious at best, and they'd spent more days apart than they'd ever spent as a couple.

"You should come back here and do some more work on the Sandpoint Strangler," she said in a pouty voice.

"No, thanks. I've learned a bit since the early days." Caleb started doodling on an empty message pad. "Now I typically write about crimes that have already been solved—by someone else. It's a hell of a lot easier."

"You helped the police solve the murder of that one young runaway, then wrote a book about it, remember?"

He remembered. *Maria* had been the most satisfying project he'd worked on to date, because he felt he'd made a real difference in achieving justice for the victim and everyone involved. "That one happened to work out," he told Holly. "But it's always a gamble, and I don't think my publisher would appreciate the increased risk of having each book languish for years while I search high and low for a satisfying resolution."

"But you were fascinated by the Sandpoint Strangler."

He'd probably been more obsessed than fascinated. Even after leaving law enforcement, he'd continued to work the case, pro bono, with the hope of eventually putting it all in a book.

"You've said yourself, a hundred times, that working the investigation gave you an insider's view you simply couldn't achieve when you were writing about someone else's case," she went on. "I know a book about him would really sell. Nobody's done one yet."

"There're still too many unanswered questions to make for interesting reading, Holly. People like a definitive ending when they purchase a true crime book. They like logical sequences and answers. I can't give them that with the Sandpoint Strangler."

"Things change."

"I doubt there's enough new information to make much of a difference," he said.

"So you won't come?"

"Holly—"

"Where does that leave me with Susan, Caleb?" she asked, her veneer of control cracking and giving way to a sob.

Caleb pinched the bridge of his nose. He didn't want to let Holly's tears sway him, but her distress and what she'd said were beginning to make him wonder. Susan had been his sister, too, for a while. Although she'd been a real pain in the ass, always getting herself into one scrape or another, he still felt some residual affection for her.

"Have you called the police?" he asked.

"Of course. I'm frantic!"

He could tell. What he didn't know was whether or not her state of mind was justified. "What'd they say?"

"Nothing. They're as stumped as I am. There was no forced entry, no sign of a struggle at her apartment, no missing jewelry or credit cards—at least, that we could tell—and no activity on her bank account. I don't think they have any leads. They don't even know where to look."

"What about her car?"

"It's gone, but I know she didn't just drive off into the sunset. We would've heard from her by now. Unless..."

"Stop imagining the worst," he said. "There could be a lot of reasons for her disappearance. Maybe she met a rich college boy, and they're off cruising the Bahamas. It would be like her to show up tomorrow and say, 'Oh, you were worried? I didn't even think to call you.' He rubbed the whiskers on his chin, trying to come up with another plausible explanation. "Or maybe she's gotten mixed up in drugs. She was always—"

"She left her dogs behind, Caleb," Holly interrupted. "She wouldn't leave for days without asking someone to feed them. Not for a trip to the Caribbean. Not for the world's best party. Not for anything."

Holly had a point. Susan adored her schnauzers, to the tune of paying a veterinarian six thousand dollars—money she didn't really have—for extensive surgery when one darted across the street and was hit by a truck.

Caleb rocked back and draped an arm over his eyes. He didn't want to face it, but this wasn't sounding good. Even if the Sandpoint Strangler was no longer on the prowl, *something* had happened to Susan. And the longer she was missing, the tougher it would be to find her.

"When was the last time you saw her?" he asked in resignation.

"Six days ago."

Six days... Caleb propped his feet on the desk and considered the book he was writing. It wasn't going very well, anyway. After piecing the whole story together, he was actually feeling more sympathy for the girl who'd committed the crime than the abusive stepfather she'd poisoned.

"All right, I'll fly out first thing in the morning." He hung up and looked around his crisp, modern condo. *Shit. So much for putting some space between me and Holly.*

Somehow she always managed to reel him back in....

MADISON LIEBERMAN STARED at her father's photograph for a long time. He gazed back at her with fathomless dark eyes, his complexion as ruddy as a seaman's, his salt-and-pepper flattop as militarily precise as ever. He'd only been dead about a year, but already he seemed like a stranger to her. Maybe it was because she wondered so often if she'd ever really known him....

"Madison? Did you find it?"

Her mother's voice, coming from upstairs, pulled her away from the photograph, but she couldn't help glancing at it again as she hesitantly approached the small door that opened into the crawl space. She'd been raised in this home. The three-foot gap under the house provided additional storage for canned goods, emergency supplies, old baskets, arts and crafts and holiday decorations, among other things.

But it was damp, dark and crowded—perfect for spiders or, worse, rats. Which was one reason Madison generally avoided it. When she was a child, she'd been afraid her father would lock her in. Probably because he'd threatened to do so once, when she was only four years old and he'd caught her digging through the Christmas presents her mother had hidden there.

It wasn't the fear of spiders or rats, or even the fear of being locked in, that bothered her at age twenty-eight, however. Ever since the police and the media had started following her father around, suspecting him of being involved in the terrible murders near the university only a few blocks away, she'd been terrified of what she might find if she ever really looked....

"Madison?" Her mother's voice filtered down to her again.

"Give me a minute," she called in annoyance as she opened the small door. "It's a twenty-dollar punch bowl," she grumbled to herself. "Why can't she just let me buy her a new one?"

The smell of moist earth and rotting wood greeted her as she flipped on the dangling bulb overhead and peered inside. Years ago, her father had covered the bare, uneven ground with black plastic and made a path of wooden boards that snaked through the clutter. These makeshift improvements reminded her that this was *his* domain, one of the places he'd never liked her to go.

It didn't make the thought of snooping around any more appealing. Her half brothers, Johnny and Tye, her father's children by his first wife, stored things here occasionally, but she did her best to forget the dark yawning space even existed. She certainly didn't want to spend any portion of what had started out as a relaxing Sunday afternoon scrounging around this creepy place.

She considered telling her mother the punch bowl wasn't there. But ever since her father's suicide, her mother seemed to fixate on the smallest details. If Madison couldn't find it, she'd probably insist on looking herself, and Annette was getting too old to be crawling around on her hands and knees. Besides, Madison and her mother had stood by Ellis Purcell throughout the investigation that had ended with his death. Certainly Madison could have a little faith in him now. The police had searched the house about four years after the killings began and never found anything.

She wasn't going to find anything, either. Because her father was innocent. Of course.

Taking a deep, calming breath, she resisted the fresh wave of anxiety that seemed to press her back toward the entrance, and crawled inside. The punch bowl couldn't be far. It would only take a second to find it.

A row of boxes lined the wall closest to her. Some were labeled, others weren't. Madison quickly opened the ones that weren't labeled to discover some things her father had owned as a young man—old photo albums, school and college yearbooks, military stuff from his stint in Vietnam.

The photos and letters seemed so normal and far removed from the articles she'd read about Ellis in the newspapers that she finally began to relax. A lot of cobwebs hung overhead, almost iridescent in the ethereal glow of the dim lightbulb, but if there were spiders, they were off in the corners. Nothing jumped out to grab her. She saw no indication that anyone had been underneath the house since Johnny had come by to get his summer clothes out of storage two years ago.

Her father might have ended his life with one heck of a finale, but his death and the investigation, if not the suspicion, were behind them now. She could quit being afraid. She could move on and forget....

Shoving the memorabilia off to one side, she rummaged around some more and eventually came up with the punch bowl. She was about to drag it to the entrance when she remembered the box of Barbie dolls she'd packed up when she was twelve. They were probably down here, too, she realized. If she could find them, she could give them to her own daughter, Brianna, who'd just turned six.

Following the curve in the wooden path, Madison came across some leftover tiles from when they'd redone the bathroom, a dusty briefcase, an old ice-cream maker, and some of her baby things. Near the edge of the plastic, where bare dirt stretched into complete darkness, she found a few boxes that had belonged to her half brothers, along with the denim bedding her mother had bought when Johnny and Tye came to live with them.

As she pushed past Johnny's old stereo, she promised herself she'd write him again this week, even though he never answered her letters. He'd been in and out of prison for years, always on drug charges. But he had to be lonely. Tye stayed in touch with him, but her mother pretended he didn't exist. And he hated his own alcoholic mother who, last Madison had heard, was living somewhere in Pennsylvania in a halfway house.

She squinted in the dim light to make out the writing on several boxes: "Mother Rayma's tablecloths…" "Mother Rayma's dishes…" "Aunt Zelma's paintings."

No Barbies. Disappointed, Madison rocked back into a sitting position to save her knees from the hard planking, and hugged her legs to her chest, trying to figure out where that box might have gone. Brianna had had a difficult year, what with the divorce, their move to Whidbey Island thirty-five miles northwest of Seattle, her father's remarriage, and the expectation of a half sibling in the near future. Madison would love to have fifteen or more vintage Barbie dolls waiting in her back seat when she collected her daughter from her ex-husband's later today. Danny certainly lavished Brianna with enough toys.

Maybe she needed to dig deeper. Pushing several boxes out of the way, she slid the old mirror from the spare bedroom to the left, and the avocado bathroom accessories that had once decorated the upstairs bathroom to the right, to reach the stuff piled behind. She was pretty far from the light at the entrance, which made it difficult to see, but she was eventually rewarded for her efforts when she recognized her own childish writing on a large box tucked into the corner.

"There it is!" she murmured, wriggling the box out from behind an old Crock-Pot and some extra fabric that looked as if it was from the sixties and better off forgotten. "You're gonna love me for this, Brianna."

"Madison, what could possibly be taking so long?"

Madison jumped at the unexpected sound, knocking her head on a beam. "Ow."

"Are you okay?" her mother asked. Annette stood at the mouth of the crawl space, but Madison couldn't see her for all the junk between them.

"I'm fine." She batted away a few cobwebs to rub the sore spot on her forehead. "You can tell Mrs. Howell I found the punch bowl you said she could borrow."

"I use that punch bowl every Christmas. What's it doing all the way back there?"

"It wasn't back here. I've been looking for my old Barbies."

"Don't waste another minute on that," her mother said. "We gave them to Goodwill a long time ago."

"No, we didn't. They're right here."

"They are?"

"Sure." Madison pulled open the top flap of the box to prove it, and felt her heart suddenly slam against her chest. Her mother was right. There weren't any Barbies inside. Just a bunch of women's shoes and underwear, in various sizes. And a short coil of rope.

CHAPTER TWO

STUNNED, MADISON BLINKED at the jumble in the box as the pictures the police had shown her years earlier flashed through her mind—grotesque, heart-rending photos of women after the Sandpoint Strangler had finished with them. It made her dizzy and nauseous to even think about those poor women; it made her feel worse to believe her father might have—

No! Surely there was some mistake. The police had searched the crawl space. They would've found this stuff.

Steeling herself against overwhelming revulsion, Madison used a towel rod to poke through the box in hopes of finding some evidence that would refute the obvious.

In the bottom corner, she saw something that glittered, and forced herself to reach gingerly inside. It was a metal chain. When she pulled it out into the murky light, she could see it was a necklace with a gold locket on the end. But she was too terrified to open it. Her heart hammered against her ribs and her hands shook as she stared at it until, finally, she gathered the nerve to unhook the tiny clasp.

Inside, she saw an oval picture of Lisa and Joe McDonna. Lisa was victim number two. Madison knew because she'd memorized them all—by face and by name.

Closing her eyes, she put a hand to her stomach, attempting to override her body's reaction. But she retched anyway, several dry heaves that hurt her throat and her stomach. She'd hung on to her belief in Ellis's innocence for so long. She'd stood against the police, the media and popular opinion. She'd stayed in the same high school even after the kids had started taunting her and doing vengeful things, like throwing eggs and oranges at the house or writing "murderer" in the lawn with bleach. She'd held her head high and attended the University of Washington, just as she'd always planned. Through it all, she'd refused to consider the possibility of her father's culpability in the murders, even when the police produced an eyewitness who said she saw Ellis driving away from a neighbor's house the night that neighbor was murdered. The witness was old and could have been mistaken. There were a lot of blue Fords with white camper shells in Seattle. All the evidence was circumstantial.

But if he was innocent, how could such a personal item belonging to one of the victims have found its way inside the house?

"Ellis saved those Barbies, after all?" Annette said, her words suddenly sounding as though they had an echo. "I could've sworn we took them to Goodwill."

Madison couldn't breathe well enough to speak. After those hellish years in high school, she'd expected the scandal to die down, especially when the police couldn't find any DNA evidence. But the suspicion and hatred had gone on long after that, until it had destroyed her marriage. Her husband wanted to be seen as upwardly mobile and a man who had it all. Not the man who'd married the daughter of the Sandpoint Strangler.

"Madison?" her mother said, when she didn't respond.

She took a few bolstering breaths and managed an answer. "What?"

"Are you going to bring those Barbie dolls out or not? I'm sure Brianna will be thrilled to have them."

Madison wasn't about to let her mother see what the box really contained. Annette had been through enough already.

Wiping away the sweat beading on her upper lip, Madison struggled to distance herself from the whole tragic mess. She hadn't hurt those women. If her father had, she'd been as much a victim as anyone.

"It—it looks like there've been some rats in the box," she said. "I d-don't think we can give them to Brianna."

"That's too bad. Well, drag them out here anyway, and I'll get rid of them once and for all."

Madison breathed in through her nose and out through her mouth, struggling to remain calm and rational. "If it's okay with you, I'll just leave them here. They...there's a sticky web all over and I'm afraid there might be a black widow someplace."

"Oh boy, we wouldn't want to drag that out. You're right, just leave them. I'll hire someone to come down here and clean this out when I move."

When she moved... Ever since her father had shot himself in the backyard, Madison had been trying to talk her mother into relocating. Madison had a difficult time even coming to the house, what with all the bad memories; she couldn't imagine how Annette still lived here.

But now she wasn't so sure she wanted her mother to go anywhere. If Annette sold the house, Madison would either have to come forward with what she'd found, which was unimaginable, or she'd have to destroy it—something she wasn't sure her conscience would allow.

God, she'd thought the nightmare was over. Now she knew it would never be....

HOLLY MET CALEB at the airport on Monday morning. With her long, curly blond hair, he noticed her in the crowd almost as soon as he entered the arrivals lounge, and steeled himself for the moment she'd come rushing to meet him. Two years his senior, she was taller than most women, thin, and had a heart-shaped, angelic face. She looked good. She always *looked* good. But looks didn't matter with a woman whose emotions swung as widely as Holly's did.

He saw her pushing through the crowd as she made her way toward him. And then she was there, smiling in obvious relief. "Caleb, I'm so glad you came." She reached up to hug him, and he allowed it but quickly moved on, following the flow of the other passengers toward the baggage claim.

"You haven't heard from Susan?" he asked, glad to finally stretch his legs. First class had been full. He was too big for the narrow, cramped space allotted him in economy, but without advance booking he'd had to take what he could get.

"Not a word. I check my answering machine every hour, just in case. But..." She blinked rapidly, and he hoped she wasn't going to cry again. He hadn't come to be her emotional support. He just wanted to find Susan and get back to San Francisco.

"Have the Seattle police assigned any detectives to the case?"

"Two. Lynch and Jones. Do you know them?"

"I know Lynch better than Jones."

"They're driving me nuts," she said. "They keep talking about searching for fiber evidence and what not, but it doesn't seem like they're doing much of anything."

"This isn't television, Holly. Fiber evidence takes a long time. You have to track down all the people who visited Susan's apartment, and collect samples before you can send them to the lab for comparison. And you generally don't have a lab tech sitting there, twiddling his thumbs while waiting to help you. You have to take your place in line."

He dodged a woman who'd stopped right in front of him to dig through a bag. "Have you talked to your parents again?" he asked. Caleb knew relations between Holly and her adoptive parents were strained. They had been for most of her life. She hated her birth mother for giving her up, even though her birth mother had been barely sixteen. She hated her adoptive mother for not being her birth mother. And she was frequently jealous of Susan, who'd been born with the assistance of fertility drugs when Holly was seven.

"I called them last night to tell them you were coming," she said.

"What did they have to say about Susan's disappearance?"

"At first they said the same thing you did—she's done this before, she'll turn up. Now that it's been almost a week, they're worried. They're willing to hire a private investigator, if you think that's the best way to go. They wanted me to talk to you about it."

"I think we should do whatever we can as soon as possible."

"Okay." She scratched her arm through her sweater, looking uncertain. "You know how we were talking about the Sandpoint Strangler?"

"Yes?"

"There was something on the news earlier...."

They'd reached the luggage carousel. He slipped through the crowd to grab the small bag he'd packed in San Francisco. Besides a few clothes, he'd brought only his cell phone, his day planner and his laptop, so he could work if he got the chance. "What?" he asked, when he had his bag slung over his shoulder.

"Someone desecrated the grave of Ellis Purcell."

Caleb stiffened in surprise. "How? From what I remember, his widow and daughter went to great pains to keep its location a secret."

"I don't know. I just caught a clip while I was eating breakfast."

Caleb rubbed the stubble on his chin. He hadn't showered or shaved this morning. He'd had such an early flight, he'd simply rolled out of bed, pulled on a Fox Racing T-shirt, a pair of faded jeans and a Giants ball cap and headed south to the airport.

"It's probably just a coincidence," he said. But he had to admit it was strange that a woman would go missing from the Sandpoint Strangler's old hunting grounds a year after Ellis Purcell was dead. That she'd be related to Holly. And that Purcell's grave would be desecrated in the same week.

ALTHOUGH MONDAY AFTERNOON was warm, with a rare amount of sun for Seattle in September, the mortuary was cool. Too cool. It smelled of carnations, furniture polish and formaldehyde, which dredged up memories of every funeral Madison had ever attended—Aunt Zelma's, Grandma Rayma's, the skeletal-looking man who'd lived next door when she was five. She couldn't think of the old guy's name, but she remembered staring at his waxy face as he lay in his coffin.

Fortunately, she didn't have to deal with any memories of her father's funeral. They hadn't given him one. She, her mother, Tye and Johnny had simply sent out notices of his death to the few friends and family who'd remained supportive, and buried him without any type of viewing or wake. Because of the ongoing investigation, and the damage he'd done with his old rifle, it seemed prudent to handle things as quickly and quietly as possible.

Lawrence Howell, the manager of Sunset Lawn Funeral Home and Memorial Park, had helped make the arrangements. He sat across from Madison and her mother now, his short blond hair neatly combed, his face wearing the same somber expression he always wore.

Fortunately, Madison had been able to reach Joanna Stapley, a senior at South Whidbey High School who often baby-sat for her, in time to have her pick up Brianna from school, so she didn't have to cope with a wriggling six-year-old during such a difficult meeting.

"How could this have happened?" she asked when Mr. Howell had finished explaining what he'd told her on the phone when he'd reached her at her office earlier—that someone had dug up her father's coffin last night. "How could anyone have figured out where he was buried?"

Howell rested his elbows on his mahogany desk and clasped long white fingers in front of him. "As I told the gentleman who called me this morning—"

"What gentleman?" Annette demanded.

Madison put a comforting hand on her mother's arm. "Tye, Mom. I phoned him as soon as Mr. Howell contacted me. I thought he might want to be part of this."

"Is he coming?" she asked, obviously not pleased that Madison had included him.

"No, he said he has to work."

"What about his wife? Is she going to be here?"

"Sharon and the kids are visiting her mother in Spokane."

"Ellis never could count on his boys," Annette said, her lips compressed in disapproval. She didn't want Tye or his wife involved, yet she sounded affronted by their lack of support.

Mr. Howell, who'd waited politely through their exchange, cleared his throat. "As I was saying, I have no way of knowing how this happened. There was no headstone or anything else to mark your father's grave, Ms. Lieberman, just as you requested. Our files are kept private and are always locked up at night. There was no sign of forced entry into the mortuary here, where we keep the files. And it's been a year since the burial—a year in which we've had no hint of trouble."

"That's what I don't understand," Annette said, her eyes filling with tears. "Why now? What would anyone want with Ellis's body after all this time?"

"A year's not so long, Mom," Madison said before Howell could respond. "Whoever it was wants the same thing we've encountered before, to express their anger and contempt for…for what happened."

"I just want my husband to be able to rest in peace," her mother said. "Ellis was innocent. He never hurt those women."

Madison wished her mother's words didn't sound so hollow to her. She still wanted to believe them. But the locket she'd discovered under the house yesterday threatened the last of her faith, was leaching away the righteous anger that had sustained her so far. Without a strong conviction that her father was innocent, she had nothing to cling to, except the desire to protect her mother and Brianna from what was, most probably, the truth.

"Of course he was innocent," Howell said, his tone placating.

Madison was willing to bet Howell believed more in the extra money they'd paid him to keep her father's burial place a secret than he did in her father's innocence.

Just as she thought the call he'd made to them this morning, and what he might shortly suggest for her father's reburial, would come with a hefty price tag. They should've gone ahead with the cremation Madison had suggested from the first. But her mother wouldn't hear of it. Annette had never known anyone who'd been cremated. It seemed foreign to her—certainly nothing she was willing to do with her beloved husband's body.

"Fortunately, our security guard frightened the culprit away before he could open the casket," Howell added.

Madison rummaged through her purse to get her mother a tissue. Annette didn't used to cry so easily, but the past twelve years had taken quite a toll. "Why didn't the security guard catch him sooner?" she asked.

Howell politely turned his attention her way. "As you know, this is a big cemetery, Ms. Lieberman. Anthony, our security guard, circles the entire area several times a night, but he focuses mostly on the outer reaches. We buried your father close to the mortuary here, to throw off the media and anyone who might be looking for a fresh grave. Most folks buried near the mortuary have been dead sixty or seventy years, which means they're pretty well forgotten." He propped his fingertips together. "The lights on the building also serve as a deterrent."

"Did your security guard get a look at this guy?" Madison asked, handing the tissue to her mother.

"Anthony said he was wearing jeans and a blue jacket with a red Chinese dragon on the back, and he looked small, maybe a hundred and sixty pounds. But that's all he could see. As soon as Anthony started toward him in the security cart, he threw down his shovel and ran off." Howell bent to one side to cover a small cough. "We gave these details to the police this morning, of course."

"So this...guy, he—he just unearthed the coffin?"

Madison asked, her muscles aching with anxiety. How many other people had to deal with such a parade of unsettling incidents? "That's it?"

"He made a few pry marks on the coffin, but Anthony came along before he was able to get it open. We could have reburied your father easily enough, but I thought I'd better check with you and your mother to see if you'd like him moved now that...well, now that the media and everyone else seem to have taken a renewed interest."

"The media? How did the media find out?" Annette asked, her eyes wide with panic.

Howell unclasped his hands. "They must've heard the call go out when Anthony phoned the police."

Madison was still thinking about the guy in the Chinese dragon jacket. "So the police are looking for whoever did this?"

"We've made a report, as I said. Technically, there's a chance this...*disturbance* would be classified as a felony. Individual plots are personal property. But..." he hesitated, and this time his glance seemed to hold real compassion "...if you want the truth, Ms. Lieberman, I can't imagine the police will waste much time chasing down the crazy guy who did this when they're already so overworked and understaffed. I think you and your mother would be better off to simply move the coffin and put this unfortunate incident behind you."

Along with everything else, Madison thought bitterly. Only nothing from the past ever seemed to stay there.

CALEB STOOD AT THE ENTRANCE to Susan's bedroom Monday evening, surveying the clothes littering the floor, the perfume bottles and makeup strewn across the dresser, and her unmade bed. The place smelled like the expensive perfume so typical of Susan, which brought her back to him more clearly than he'd remembered her so far, and caused worry to claw at his gut. She hadn't been seen for a week, since last Monday. Where could she be?

Crossing to the dresser, he smoothed out a crinkled piece of paper to see that it was only a quick thank-you from a friend at work, then rifled through some change. He wasn't sure what he was looking for. Anything, really. Anything that might lead him to Susan.

Holly hovered behind him. "What are you doing?" she asked. "Why aren't you checking for pry marks on the window or something?"

He caught his ex-wife's eye in the mirror. It felt strange to be inside Susan's apartment with everything so quiet, so motionless. Even when Susan wasn't around, her dogs had always been here, barking and wagging a welcome. Now Holly had the schnauzers at her place, and other than a few visits from police, the apartment had been shut up. "I'm sure the detectives have done all that."

"So?"

"I'm focusing on my personal knowledge of Susan's behavior and habits."

"Which means…"

"I'm trying to figure out what she might have been wearing and doing the night she disappeared. When I talked to Detective Lynch a few minutes ago, he said you were the last person to see her on Monday afternoon. But she wasn't reported missing until Wednesday, when she didn't show up for work. That's a lot of time to change clothes."

Holly rearranged the slew of bottles and cosmetics on the dresser, putting them in some semblance of order. "There's no way to tell what she was wearing. For all we know, she was abducted in the middle of the night dressed in a pair of boxers and a T-shirt."

"I doubt she was taken from here."

Holly gave up on the mess and raised her eyebrows in surprise. "Just because there was no forced entry? Maybe someone came to the door," she said. "Maybe she knew who it was so she opened up. She might have even left with him. Detective Lynch seems to believe that's most likely what happened."

"Except that her car's gone," Caleb said.

Holly shrugged. "She and whoever she was with could have used her car."

"Susan wouldn't have wanted to drive if she had a man at the door with his own transportation. This was a woman who spent every dime she had on clothes and makeup and—" He indicated the perfumes, body lotions, mascara and eye shadow that covered almost every horizontal surface "—judging by the looks of this place, that hasn't changed over the past two years."

Holly pulled her hair into a ponytail. "I still don't think we can figure out what she was wearing. When I saw her on Monday, she was telling me about some hot new outfit she was going to buy. How are we supposed to place her in something we might never have seen?"

Caleb turned to study the room again, taking in the pajama bottoms draped over a chair, and noticing underwear on the floor near the bathroom. "Maybe we can't. But to me it looks like she took a shower, got dressed up and left for an evening out."

Holly frowned at his assessment and toyed with the hem of her turtleneck sweater. "What makes you say that?"

"I can still smell perfume in the air, as if she sprayed it last thing, and those panties look as though she just stepped out of them. If she was expecting someone, she would've at least tossed the underwear in the hamper, don't you think?"

"Susan was never much of a clean freak."

Caleb crossed to the closet, which was crammed full of blouses, slacks, suits, dresses, jackets, jeans and sweaters. There were even a few wigs and hairpieces on the shelf above. "Knowing Susan, she'd be anxious to wear the new clothes she told you about. Did she describe them to you?"

"Of course, but I wasn't really listening. She's always telling me about some new shade of eye shadow or clothes bargain."

He fingered a black sweater with faux fur at the wrists and collar. "Have you looked through her closet for anything with the tags still on it?"

"I haven't looked specifically for tags, but I know there are a few new things."

"Where are they?"

Holly started examining clothes at the back of the closet, but Caleb stopped her.

"Forget it," he said. "She wouldn't shove a hot new outfit all the way to the back. If she's got any new clothes that far back, she's never found an occasion to wear them, and they've probably been there for some time."

"So now what?"

"Maybe we could call Nordstrom to see what she's purchased lately. She'd probably put it on her charge card, wouldn't she?"

Holly didn't seem hopeful. "Except that her charge card's been maxed out since her first two weeks at work."

Of course. He hadn't taken Susan's spending habits into account. Still, there had to be some way to figure out what she'd bought and whether or not she was wearing it....

Caleb took another turn around the room, thinking. She

would've carried her purchase inside from the car, possibly tried it on, admired herself in the mirror and cut off the tags.

The tags...

Moving to the small garbage can on the other side of the nightstand, he found a crumpled Nordstrom bag with two tags inside. "Bingo," he said.

Holly took the tags from him. "What's so exciting about these?"

"We can use the SKU numbers to find out what Susan bought. Maybe she was wearing it when she went missing."

"What if she wasn't?"

He rubbed the back of his neck. "We have to start somewhere. Susan always liked the unique and ultra-trendy. Maybe she was wearing an outfit that really stood out."

Holly smiled up at him. "I knew I was right to have you come out here, Caleb."

"Slow down, Holly. We don't even know if this means anything."

"I'm sure you'll be able to help me," she said, and he hoped to God she was right.

CALEB GOT HIS WISH—at least in one regard. The short, worn-looking denim skirt and leopard-print halter top the Nordstrom saleswoman draped across the counter thirty minutes later was certainly conspicuous. He doubted that scrap of fabric the saleswoman called a skirt would cover much, but he had more to worry about than Susan's general lack of modesty.

"You're positive these items match the tags?" he asked.

"Check for yourself," the saleswoman—Deborah, according to her badge—held them up for comparison.

"Did you see anything like this in her apartment?" he asked Holly.

"No. I've never seen a halter top like this before in my life," she told him. "And I'd definitely remember it."

"I know Susan bought this because I sold it to her," Deborah insisted. "Just last week. She comes up here from cosmetics all the time or—" she looked slightly abashed "—she used to, anyway. And it was on clearance, so she got a great deal."

A great deal? Caleb touched the flimsy material. "Would someone really wear something like this in mid-September?" he asked. "Seattle doesn't exactly have beach weather."

"She was going clubbing," Deborah volunteered, trying to be helpful. "And it's so hot in those places. Especially when you're dancing, you know?"

Caleb knew all about clubs, but not because he'd visited one recently. He'd quickly grown tired of them after his divorce.

"It's too much of a long shot," Holly said. "Let's go."

She started for the door, but Caleb pulled her back. "Not so fast. It's better than nothing. I say we take a picture and add it to the flyers, just in case."

Holly studied the outfit with a critical eye, then sighed and shrugged. "If you say so."

"We'll take it," he told Deborah.

While he was paying for it, Holly looped her arm through his the way she used to while they were married. "This is just like old times," she murmured.

Caleb carefully extricated himself. "I'm not going to be in Seattle long," he said, and was determined to make sure she remembered that.

MADISON WAS EXHAUSTED by the time she returned home, but she felt a definite sense of relief the moment she drove off the Mukilteo-Clinton Ferry, which had brought her across Puget Sound from the mainland. After the unwelcome media attention she'd received during the past twelve years, and the crushing disappointment she'd experienced for her daughter's sake when Danny announced he was leaving her, she'd wanted to relocate as far from Seattle as possible. Start over. Forget. Or go into hiding until she was strong enough to face the world again.

But her divorce agreement stipulated that she couldn't move more than two hours away from Danny, who had joint custody of Brianna and lived on Mercer Island. And she felt too much responsibility toward her mother to leave without a backward glance. Annette was talking more favorably about moving than ever before, but she was still set in her ways and didn't want to go very far from the city where she'd been born and raised.

Whidbey became the compromise Madison had been searching for. With the island's sandy, saltwater beaches, damp, green woods, towering bluffs and spectacular views of Puget Sound and the Cascade Mountains, it felt remote. Yet it was still basically a suburb, with eateries and fast food, gas stations and convenience stores. And it was...familiar.

"Brianna!" Madison called as she let herself into the small cottage she'd used her divorce settlement to buy, along with her new business, the South Whidbey Realty Company. Located just off Maxwelton Beach, tucked into a stand of thick pine trees, the house itself reminded Madison of something from a Thomas Kinkade painting—romantic to the point of being whimsical. Built of redbrick and almost completely covered in ivy, the house was more than fifty years old. But it had always been well-loved and well-maintained, and the previous owners had done a fabulous job with the garden. The garage, which was detached, resembled an old carriage house and had been converted some years ago into a sort of minicottage.

"Hey? Where's my girl?" she called again, putting her briefcase next to the hall tree.

This time the television went off and Brianna came running, clutching Elizabeth, her stuffed rabbit, in one arm. "Mommy, you're home!"

"Yes, sweetie, I'm home." Madison gave her daughter a tight squeeze. "I'm sorry I had to be away. Grandma needed me. And then I had to swing by the office to pick up all the paperwork I didn't get around to today."

"Why couldn't I go with you to see Grandma? She loves it when I come to visit. And Elizabeth misses her."

"You and Elizabeth see her at least once a week, kiddo, and you weren't out of school yet," Madison said. But she wouldn't have taken Brianna to the Sunset Funeral Home and Memorial Park even if she'd been available. Madison tried to shield her daughter as much as possible from the taint of her grandfather's legacy.

Joanna Stapley appeared behind Brianna, toting a backpack. "Your timing's good," she said. "I just finished my homework."

"Perfect." Madison gave her a grateful smile and dug through her purse for the money to pay her. "Did anyone call while I was gone?"

"You had an ad call on the rental place."

"An ad call?" Brianna echoed. "What's an ad call?"

Madison shook her head. Her daughter was only six years old, but nothing slipped past her. "I'm trying to rent out the carriage house. Did the caller leave her name?" she asked Joanna.

"It was a he."

"Oh." For safety reasons, Madison had been hoping for a female tenant. But at this point, she knew she'd take anyone with good credit and solid references.

"What does it mean to rent out the carriage house?" Brianna asked.

"It means someone else will live there," Madison said.

"Why?"

To help her financially. When she'd purchased the house and her business, she'd planned for the eight months it would take her to learn what she needed to know and get her broker's license. But she hadn't expected business to be so slow once she actually took over. And she'd already lost her top agent, which meant she was down to three. It wasn't going to be easy to survive if the real estate market didn't pick up.

"Because it might be fun to have some company once in a while, don't you think?" she said to Brianna, even though company was really the last thing Madison wanted. She'd dealt with enough curious strangers to last her a lifetime.

Brianna scrunched up her face as though she wasn't quite sure about company, either, but Madison was more interested in what Joanna had to say. Danny had made some comments that led her to believe he and Leslie might sue for custody of Brianna *again*. Madison wanted to be ready for him. She needed to save what little money she had left from the divorce for a good attorney.

"Did he leave his name and number?" she asked.

Joanna frowned as she tried to remember. "Dwight... Sanderson, I think. His number's on the fridge."

"Good. I'm having trouble finding a tenant. Everyone wants to come for a visit, but the ferry can take as long as two hours, so we're not exactly in a prime location for people who work on the mainland."

"This guy definitely sounds interested."

"Thanks."

"No problem. If you need me again, just call my cell." The door slammed behind Joanna, then Madison heard the distinctive rattle of her Volkswagen bug as she pulled out of the drive.

"Dwight Sanderson," Madison mumbled to herself, heading straight to the kitchen.

"I don't want a man to live in the carriage house, Mommy," Brianna complained, trailing after her. "That's where you draw, and me and Elizabeth play."

"It's nice to have the extra room, but we can do without it," she replied.

"Daddy said we live in a closet."

Daddy doesn't know everything, Madison wanted to say, but she bit her tongue. "Our house isn't as big as his, but I like it here, don't you?"

Brianna nodded enthusiastically. "This is a cottage for princesses."

Hearing her own words come back at her from the day they'd moved in, Madison smiled. "Right. And we're princesses, so it's ideal."

"Will the man who moves in be a prince?" she asked.

Madison stared down at the Post-it note Joanna had stuck on the fridge, and thought about her father, her two half brothers and her ex-husband. She hadn't met very many princes in her life. She was beginning to believe they didn't exist.

"I doubt it," she said, and picked up the phone.

CHAPTER THREE

CALEB STOOD in the antique-filled living room of his parents' white Victorian, staring out the window at Guemes Channel and the wooded island beyond as he wondered what he was going to try next. He'd already spent three days doing everything he could think of to dig up some kind of lead on Susan. But he'd had no luck at all. Along with the police and the private investigator hired by Holly's parents, he and Holly had talked to Susan's friends, neighbors and work associates. They'd visited nightclub after nightclub with Susan's picture and checked her bank account again.

Still they'd come up empty.

"Holly called while you were in the shower," his mother said from the doorway.

Caleb glanced over his shoulder. Justine Trovato was in her early sixties, but she looked at least ten years younger. Today she'd pinned up her white hair and was wearing a tasteful pair of brown slacks and a silky blouse, with pearls at her neck and ears.

"If she calls back, tell her I need to do a few things on my own today," he said.

"If she calls back? Aren't you going to respond to her message? She thought you might need a ride somewhere."

Caleb didn't want to talk to Holly. They'd lost their tempers yesterday while canvassing the apartment building, and she'd stormed off for a couple of hours. She came back when she'd cooled off, but they were both pretty tense. He thought they could use some time apart. Which was the story of their whole relationship. "I'll rent a car."

"You know you can take my Cadillac." Justine moved into the room to straighten a doily, and Caleb immediately recognized the lavender fragrance she'd worn since he was small.

"I don't want to put you out. I don't really know my schedule."

"I'm sure I could live without a car for the day. Your father's out back tinkering in his shed. He could drive me in his little pickup if I need to go somewhere. Or there's always your sister."

Tamara, Caleb's older sister, lived next door with her husband and twin boys in a home his parents had helped them buy. "I appreciate the offer, Mom, but I'll feel more mobile if I have a car of my own."

"If it makes you more comfortable, dear."

More comfortable? Caleb wasn't feeling very comfortable about anything. He'd already spent far more time than he'd hoped it would take to find Susan—and he wasn't any closer than the day he'd arrived in Seattle.

She'll turn up.... He'd told Holly that when she first called him. But those words seemed terribly glib now. He was beginning to think that if Susan did turn up, she'd turn up dead. Otherwise they would've found some trace of her.

"Where are you planning to go?" his mother asked.

"I spoke to Detective Gibbons this morning and—"

"Oh, he called here yesterday saying he'd received a message from you."

"He got hold of me on my cell."

"Can he help?" His parents were as worried about Susan as he was. They'd met her at his wedding—the second time, they'd eloped—and had seen her at a few family functions since.

"He doesn't know much about Susan's case. It's not his to worry about."

"Then why did you contact him?"

"He worked on the Sandpoint Strangler task force with me."

"Those poor women." His mother shuddered. "But you're not interested in the Sandpoint Strangler anymore, are you? I thought you put that book aside."

Caleb had always been interested in the Sandpoint Strangler. Probably because he'd been brand-new to the police department when the killings first started, so he'd followed them from the very beginning. The Sandpoint Strangler was the biggest case he ever worked, too, and the most frustrating. He felt as though they'd come within inches of unraveling the whole mystery—only to have Ellis Purcell check out before they could hit pay dirt. When the killings stopped and the case went cold, the task force disbanded and the police naturally changed their focus to finding those rapists and murderers who were still living and breathing and capable of violence. Caleb had given up the search then, too. But he'd never stopped wondering how, exactly, the strange Mr. Purcell had managed to kill so many women and dump their bodies in such public places without leaving more of a trail. He'd since done several books about murderers: on Angel Maturino Resendiz, who was convicted of murdering a Houston woman but was linked by confessions and evidence to at least twelve other killings nationwide. On Robert L. Yates, Jr., who admitted to fifteen murders, and Aileen Wuornos, a female serial killer convicted of murdering six men while working as a prostitute along highways in central Florida. Or Jeffrey Dahmer, who'd been convicted of seventeen homicides, most in Milwaukee. Caleb had written several other books, as well, mostly isolated cases where a husband killed his wife for the insurance, or a wife killed the man who'd been cheating on her. Whoever did the killing always took a significant misstep somewhere.

But not Ellis Purcell.

"Holly told me something at the airport that's bothered me ever since," he said.

"What's that?" his mother asked.

"Ellis Purcell's grave was disturbed the night before I arrived."

"I read that in the paper."

"I'm wondering how whoever it was found out where he was buried."

His mother twisted the clasp of the necklace she was wearing around to the back. "Maybe someone in the family let it slip."

"Maybe," he said, jingling the change in the pocket of his chinos. But when he remembered Madison Lieberman and her mother, and how staunchly they'd supported Ellis throughout the whole affair, he doubted they'd revealed anything at all.

THAT AFTERNOON Caleb pulled his rental car, a silver-and-black convertible Mustang, in front of 433 Old Beachview Road, the small brick house that corresponded with the address Detective Gibbons had given him for Madison Lieberman. Then he bent his head to look at the place through the passenger-side window.

It was small but charming, not unlike Langley, the closest town, which boasted the highest density of bed-and-breakfasts, country inns and guest cottages in the state.

An arched entry covered with primroses partially concealed the front windows. But he didn't see activity anywhere, and there weren't any cars in the drive. Chances were Madison wasn't home.

The dull-gray mist that shrouded the island made it seem much later than midafternoon. Caleb glanced at the digital clock on his dash to see that it was just after three, close to the time school let out, and wondered if he should wait. When he'd still been researching her father's case a couple of years ago, Madison had been working as a Realtor and living in a house not far from Bill Gates's mansion on Mercer Island. But Detective Gibbons had told him this morning that she and her husband had split and Danny Lieberman had bought her out. Now she owned a small real estate company with office space only a few miles away, in Clinton.

Caleb parked next to a stand of pine trees and got out to have a look around. He'd never approached Madison Lieberman in person before. When he was an officer on the task force, he was new enough that he'd been relegated to the work least likely to bring him in contact with her. And since he'd quit the department and started writing full-time, he'd seen too many news clips of Madison turning her face resolutely away from the camera, read too many comments spoken in defense of her father, to harbor any illusions that she might be willing to cooperate with him. But, using his pseudonym, he *had* sent her, as well as Danny, several letters over the years. Danny had responded a time or two, but it quickly became apparent that he didn't have the answers Caleb needed. Madison had finally replied by threatening him with a restraining order if he so much as tried to speak with her.

He hoped she didn't feel quite so strongly about the issue now that her father was dead.

Shoving his keys in his pocket, he strode up the walk. The yard was generally well-kept but had once known a more diligent hand; he could tell that right away. A couple of hummingbird feeders and a birdbath sat in a meticulously tended herb garden off to the right, but the trees and shrubs everywhere else were overgrown and the grass was a little too long. What with being a single mom and trying to run a small business, Madison probably didn't have the time or money to maintain what had been in place before she came here. No doubt money was the reason for the For Rent sign Caleb saw attached to the small cottage at the side of the main house.

For rent... He hesitated briefly at the arch before changing direction and heading toward what had once been a garage. It was renovated now. Through a mullioned window exactly like those in the main house, he could see a studio apartment, complete with kitchen-living room, a single bedroom and a bath. A brown wicker couch with giant yellow-and-blue cushions faced a television in the large main room, which had a wooden floor and lots of rugs. A chair that matched the couch and the drapes sat off to the side, next to a rack of magazines. White cupboards lined the kitchen in the corner, which contained a round wooden table with plaid place mats in the same blue and yellow as the couch and drapes.

He could see only a slice of the bedroom and bath through two open doorways, but he could tell the bedroom was furnished with a four-poster bed, a fluffy down comforter and more pillows—these in red, white and blue. The bathroom had an old-style sink with brass fixtures.

He liked the place, he realized. It had the sort of country charm his mother had taught him to appreciate.

Taking a narrow path that led through the herb garden, he crossed over to the main house, where he saw a similar decorating theme. Madison's home wasn't quite as light and airy as the garage, certainly not as new, but it had a warm, cozy atmosphere.

The sound of a car pulling up made Caleb jerk away from the window and start toward the drive.

A petite woman he recognized as Madison Lieberman jumped out of a Toyota Camry as soon as she cut the engine. "Oh, my gosh! I never dreamed you'd beat me here," she exclaimed, obviously flushed from hurrying. A thin, strawberry-blond girl got out much more slowly, clinging to an old stuffed rabbit. "The ferry must be moving quickly today."

Caleb hadn't taken the ferry. He'd come south over Deception Pass from Fidalgo Island, which was due north. But he didn't correct her. He was enjoying the warmth of this reception—especially when he compared it to the "Get off my property" he'd most likely receive the moment he identified himself as the crime writer who'd contacted her before.

"Did you peek in the windows?" she asked.

He cleared his throat. "Actually, I did."

"I think you'd be very comfortable here."

Madison was much more attractive in person. Maybe it was because this was the first time Caleb had ever seen her smile. Only five foot four or so, she had a gymnast's body, which made him believe she stayed active, and almond-shaped brown eyes. Her hair was auburn—not his favorite color—but it looked soft and swayed gently around her chin in a stylish cut. And other than a few freckles sprinkled across her nose, her complexion was smooth and slightly golden.

"I know you're worried about privacy," she was saying, "but we'd never bother you. It's quiet here."

The little girl with Madison glared at him. He could

definitely see a family resemblance, mostly through the mouth. They both had full, pouty lips. "Is this your daughter?" he asked.

"It is. Say hello, Brianna," Madison prompted.

Brianna said nothing. She folded her arms around her stuffed toy and jutted out her sharp little chin.

"She's not happy about renting out the carriage house," Madison explained. "She called her father last night and he told her—" she waved her hand "—oh, never mind. I've got the key right here. Why don't we take a look inside?"

Caleb realized that now was probably a good time to explain that he wasn't who she thought he was. But he didn't see any need to hurry. It certainly wouldn't hurt to catch a glimpse of what Madison Lieberman was really like. That could only help him understand her family and, by extension, her father.

"Sounds good," he said, following her to what she'd labeled the carriage house.

Brianna glanced back at him several times, as if she thought she could scare him away with her dark looks. But he merely smiled and, when Madison swung the door wide, stepped past her.

The place smelled like an expensive candle store, Caleb decided as he began to notice several things he'd missed before—the vase of fresh wildflowers on the kitchen table, the small shower in the bathroom he'd been unable to see from the window, the mahogany entertainment center in the bedroom that housed another television.

"You know, from your voice, I thought you'd be older," Madison said as she watched him look around.

Opening what appeared to be a pantry, he pretended not to hear her. "How soon did you want to get someone in here?"

"As you can see, it's ready. I've had a phone installed and everything. You could move in tomorrow."

The hope in her voice and the modest car she was driving reinforced Caleb's impression that, considering Danny Lieberman's wealth, she hadn't managed to get a very good divorce settlement. "How long has it been on the market?"

"A little over a month. But I've lowered the price." She tucked a strand of hair behind one ear in a self-conscious movement. "I'm only asking eight hundred."

He nodded and walked back into the living room, wondering how to turn the conversation to her father—while feeling a peculiar reluctance to do so. "This place is small but…nice," he said.

Brianna was sitting on the couch with her stuffed rabbit and had spread several sheets of paper on the coffee table in front of her.

"These are very good," he said when he realized they were sketches, and that she meant for him to see them. "Who drew them?"

"My mom."

He studied the first, a pencil drawing of an old, gnarled hand gripping a cane, then the second, a set of clasped hands—one male, the other female—and the last, an intriguing pair of eyes. Were they Ellis Purcell's eyes? Caleb could have sworn they were. They seemed to hold all kinds of dark secrets.

He wondered if Madison knew those dark secrets, and if he'd ever be able to get them out of her.

"Brianna, what are you doing with my sketches?" Madison asked, coming up from behind.

"I think she's proud of you," Caleb said. "And it looks as though she has reason to be. You're very talented."

Madison quickly gathered up her drawings. "Thanks,

but it's just a hobby." After setting them aside, she clasped her hands in a businesslike manner. "So, do you like it? Do you want the place?"

He was about to explain that he hadn't really come to rent the carriage house when there was a knock on the door.

Brianna grabbed her stuffed rabbit and ran to open it. A tall, white-haired gentleman who looked to be in his late fifties stood on the stoop. "Is your mommy here?"

Brianna turned expectantly, and Madison approached the door. "Can I help you?"

"I'm Dwight Sanderson."

"Who?" she said.

Caleb watched the man's face cloud with confusion at Madison's startled reaction. "I spoke with you a few days ago and then again this morning, remember? I'm here to see the house."

"But—"

"I'm afraid you're too late," Caleb interrupted, joining them at the door. "It's already taken."

Madison blinked at him in surprise, and Caleb felt a good measure of surprise himself. What the hell did he think he was doing?

"I thought you were... Who *are* you?" Madison asked, turning to him.

"Caleb Trovato." He stuck out his hand, fairly confident she'd never recognize his name. He wrote under the pseudonym Thomas L. Wagner, his mother's grandfather's name, and had signed the letters he'd sent her and Danny the same way, since they'd been written in a professional capacity.

"Caleb Trovato," she repeated, hesitantly accepting his handshake. "If you called, my baby-sitter forgot to write it down."

Her fingers felt slim and dainty, and she was close enough that he could smell a hint of her perfume. "I didn't call. I just happened to see the sign as I was driving by. I actually live in San Francisco, but business has brought me here."

"For how long?"

"That remains to be seen."

"Oh." She glanced from him to Sanderson. "So is either of you willing to sign a lease?"

"I told you on the phone that I can't commit long-term," Sanderson said. "My situation is too tentative right now."

"I'll sign a lease," Caleb said, even though he knew he was crazy to offer. He'd recently furnished his new condo in San Francisco and planned to return there. But he couldn't miss this opportunity. Maybe now he'd finally be able to crack the Sandpoint Strangler case and achieve some closure—for himself, the public, the force and, most importantly, the families of the victims. Maybe he could even ease the foreboding that had settled over him since he'd learned of Susan's disappearance. If the deceased Purcell was really the Sandpoint Strangler, she certainly stood a better chance of being found alive. Random murders were rare. Most homicides of women were the result of a love relationship gone bad and, according to Holly, Susan hadn't been involved with anyone for over three years. She'd only been seeing Lance, the guy she was dating before she disappeared, for a couple of months.

In any case, Caleb could look for Susan from here just as easily as his parents' place on Fidalgo, and simply buy out the lease when he was ready to head home.

"Do you have any pets?" she asked.

"Would that be a problem?"

"Not necessarily. One dog or cat would be fine. I'm

not sure I'd be happy with a whole houseful of Doberman pinschers."

"No animals."

"Not even a hamster?"

"Not even a hamster."

"What about kids?" she asked.

He cocked an eyebrow. "You don't want a houseful of those, either?" He could understand it if they were all as sour as her daughter.

"I'd expect you to make sure they don't trample the flowerbeds."

"The flowerbeds are safe," he said. "I don't have any kids."

"Fine." She looked as though she wanted to smile but wouldn't allow it. "What kind of business brings you to Seattle, Mr. Trovato?"

He searched his mind, trying to come up with something that wouldn't give him away. "I'm a small-business consultant," he said, because it was the first thing he could think of.

"So you're regularly employed?"

"Definitely."

"And how long a lease are you willing to sign? A year?"

"Six months," he replied, letting her know by his tone that she wasn't getting any more out of him.

"And when would you like to move in?"

"Tomorrow morning, if that's okay with you."

"That's fine." Now she did smile, right before she turned back to Sanderson. "I've got your phone number, Mr. Sanderson," she said. "If Mr. Trovato's references don't check out, I'll give you a call."

Sanderson didn't appear too pleased with the situation, but there wasn't much he could do. Madison followed him out, probably to apologize for the wasted trip. Brianna stayed behind, still eyeing Caleb warily.

"You don't want me to live here?" he asked.

Her bottom lip came out. "No."

"Why not?"

"Because this is *our* house. My mommy draws here, and me and Elizabeth dance."

"I won't be staying long," he admitted. Then he remembered that Madison had started to tell him something out in the drive. "What did your dad have to say about the idea last night?"

Brianna tucked her stuffed bunny protectively under one slender arm. "He said you should never rent out part of your house."

"Why not?"

"Because you never know who might be moving in with you."

CHAPTER FOUR

POUNDING ON THE FRONT door dragged Madison from the depths of sleep.

She glanced, bleary-eyed, at the alarm clock on her nightstand. It was only eleven o'clock. Generally she wasn't in bed so early on a Friday night. She stayed up on weekends, handling paperwork, e-mail, or working on the computer. But this hadn't been a regular week. Ever since she'd found that box under her mother's house, she'd been so tired it felt as though someone had tied ten-pound weights to each limb. She'd climbed into bed a mere thirty minutes ago but was already sleeping like the dead.

Like the dead? Considering the recent disturbance of her father's grave, that seemed rather chilling. She rubbed her arms as she shivered and groped for her robe. The knocking continued.

"Mommy?" Brianna's confused voice came to her from the other room.

"Yes, honey?"

"Is it morning-time?"

"Not yet."

"Who's here?"

"I'm sure it's just our new renter. He probably can't find the remote for his television or doesn't know how to run the dishwasher or something." Madison tied the belt to her robe. "And he didn't bother to notice that our lights are out," she added under her breath.

"We shouldn't have let him move in," Brianna said, as if this incident proved the point she'd been trying to make from the start.

Brianna sounded like an echo of Danny. Sometimes Brianna also behaved a great deal like her father. Today she'd pouted and glowered at Mr. Trovato all afternoon while he was carrying in his belongings, which were rather sparse, along with a few groceries. "Try to go back to sleep, honey," she said.

Bang, bang, bang. The knocking was impatient. Demanding.

How could Brianna sleep with all that noise? "Give me a minute," Madison called out. As she stuffed her feet into the frumpy "housewife" slippers Danny had given her a year ago last Christmas, she pictured the diamond tennis bracelet he'd presented to his new wife the day she'd announced her pregnancy. After dropping out of college to finish putting him through school, Madison had come away from their seven-year marriage with probably a fifth of Danny's net worth, a real estate license and a pair of ugly house shoes, while Leslie was living in Madison's old mansion and dripping in diamonds. Somehow it didn't seem fair. But Madison didn't want Danny if he couldn't stand by her "for better or worse"—although she hated the fact that her daughter had lost the firm foundation of having both parents in the home.

"I'm coming," she said when she neared the door. "Who is it?"

There was no answer, but the banging didn't subside. It came in loud, staccato bursts that grated on Madison's nerves.

"Who is it?" she repeated more insistently, and

snapped on the porch light so she could peer through the peephole.

It definitely wasn't Caleb Trovato. She could see that right away. Mr. Trovato was probably six foot four, two hundred ten pounds of well-defined muscle. He was the kind of man who could turn a woman's head from forty feet away. This person was skinny to the point of looking emaciated. His hair was almost as dark as Mr. Trovato's, though not nearly as thick. And—

Her visitor moved and she caught a glimpse of his face.

Oh, God! It was Johnny.

Unlatching the safety chain, Madison opened the door for her half brother. "Johnny! What are you doing here?"

He sniffed as though he had allergies and shifted on the balls of his feet, regarding her with red-rimmed eyes. Behind him, headlights from some kind of car bore down on her, but the engine was off.

"I need a few bucks," he said, point-blank. "Can you help me out?"

Johnny and Tye had come to live with Madison and her parents for the first time when Johnny was fifteen and Tye was sixteen. From the beginning, they'd been in and out of trouble with her parents, the school, even the authorities, and didn't bother much with a little sister who was only eight. But for the eighteen months Johnny was living at the house, Madison had liked him a lot better than Tye, who was far more remote. She'd sort of idealized Johnny, because he did sometimes do her a kind deed. He'd let her play with the stray cats he brought home occasionally—before her mother made him turn them loose again. He'd share whatever candy filled his pockets. Tye ignored her completely.

"Are you alone?" she hedged, caught completely off

guard. Last she'd heard, Johnny was supposed to be in prison for another three years.

"Yeah."

"It doesn't look like you're alone." She shaded her eyes against the headlights and squinted, making out a shadowy figure sitting in the driver's seat of what was probably an old Buick Skylark.

"So I'm with a friend. Does it matter?" More nervous energy. More restless movements. From the way he was acting, he had to be on something.

Evidently there wasn't much about Johnny's lifestyle that had changed over the years. "When did you get out?"

He sniffled again. "Couple weeks ago, I guess."

He was so strung out, Madison wasn't sure he could tell one day from the next. Maybe he *hadn't* been released at all; maybe he'd escaped, and whoever was waiting in the car was his accomplice.

She tightened her robe, wondering what to do. If she gave Johnny money, he'd only use it to buy more drugs. But she had to help him. Except for Tye, she was his only family. And she felt guilty for having had the love and support of their father and for having a good mother when theirs was so neglectful and abusive.

"I've got twenty bucks," she said.

"Is that all?"

"That's all."

"Then how 'bout a drink? You got a beer for your brother?"

Madison hesitated. Johnny had his better moments, but he could also be unpredictable and moody. And, for all she knew, the person waiting in the car was another ex-convict. But Johnny *was* her half brother and he'd never done anything truly threatening to her in the past.

"Come in and I'll get you a Coke." She opened the door wider, to admit him, then locked it against whoever was waiting in the car.

"When was the last time you ate?" she asked as she led him to the kitchen.

He didn't answer. He was too busy staring at something in the hall.

Madison turned to see what that something was, and felt her stomach drop when she realized Brianna was standing there. "Go back to bed, sweetheart," she said. She didn't want her daughter around Johnny. The fact that he had a drug habit didn't necessarily make him dangerous. But they hadn't spent any time together in years, and Madison didn't feel she knew him all that well anymore.

"Who's *he?*" Brianna asked, peering at Johnny with the disdain she'd practiced on Caleb Trovato.

Johnny hooked his thumbs in the pockets of his filthy, tattered jeans and smiled. "Don't you remember me, pipsqueak? I saw you once, just before your grandpa blew his brains out."

"Johnny, don't," Madison said.

"Mommy, how do you blow your brains out?" Brianna asked.

Madison sent Johnny a look that was meant to silence him. "Never mind, honey. Grandpa went to heaven. You know that."

Johnny gave a disbelieving snort when she said "heaven," but Madison ignored him. Brianna was too little to understand everything that had happened, and she saw no reason to explain the gritty details, at least, not while Brianna was so young.

"You never could stand the truth," he said, shaking his head.

"There's no need to upset her. She's only six," Madison replied. But she didn't blame Johnny for being bitter. He'd been the one to find Ellis, and everyone knew Ellis had meant it to be that way. Just before Madison and her mother went on an all-day shopping trip, he'd called Johnny and said he needed to talk to him.

A few hours later, Johnny had found what was left of their father in Ellis's workshop.

"She doesn't look upset to me," he said.

Brianna was clinging to Elizabeth while giving him a challenging glare. "My name isn't pipsqueak," she told him. "And I don't think my father would like you very much."

Horrified, Madison gaped at her. "Brianna!"

"It's *true*."

"I don't care if it is," she said. "Johnny's your uncle. You're not to be rude to him or anyone else. Now please go back to bed."

Brianna didn't budge, so Madison gave her a frown designed to let her know there'd be serious consequences if she didn't obey. Finally, she turned and walked resolutely down the hall.

"I'll be there shortly to tuck you in," Madison called after her.

Johnny's twitching seemed to grow more extreme. "You're gonna have your hands full with that kid."

"Brianna's usually very sweet. It's just been lately, after I get her back from her father's, that I've run into these attitude problems." Anxious for Johnny to leave, she handed him a can of Coke. "Sorry I don't have any beer. I don't drink it."

He accepted what she offered him. "You wrote me about your divorce," he said.

"I wasn't sure you got that letter. You never answered it." He'd never answered any of her letters.

"I wanted to believe you were still living the good life." He said the words accusingly, as though she'd had some choice in the matter.

"No one lives a fairy tale." She leaned against the counter. "Does Tye know you're out?"

The can hissed as Johnny popped the top and took a long pull. "I went by his place a couple days ago. No one was home."

"His wife's been visiting her mother. Maybe he drove to Spokane to get her and the kids."

"Visiting her mom?" Johnny chuckled, scratching his shoulder, then his elbow, moving, always moving. "You mean she left him. Again."

Again? This was the first Madison had ever heard of any serious marital strife between Tye and Sharon. "Why would she leave?"

"They haven't been getting along."

"Are you sure?" she said, disappointed that Tye hadn't trusted her enough to share this information with her.

"You know Tye has a temper. They've been on and off for years." Johnny downed the rest of the soda, wiped his mouth on his sleeve and tossed the empty can toward the garbage. When he missed, it hit the floor with a rattle, and Madison quickly bent to pick it up.

"About that money..." he said.

She glanced down the hall to see Brianna poking her head out of her bedroom, and knew she needed to get her half brother on his way. "Here you go," she said, handing him a twenty.

He frowned at the bill. "You sure that's all you've got?"

She told herself to remain firm. But when she took in the state of his clothing and the old tennis shoes on his feet, she immediately began to second-guess her decision not to give him more. He looked so needy, so desperate. She hated watching him ruin his life. "Are you okay, Johnny?"

He blinked at her as though surprised by the question. "Does it matter?"

"Of course." She searched through the bottom of her purse. "Maybe I can scrounge together another few dollars."

"Thanks."

"No problem." She gave him an additional fistful of change, and he started for the door.

She should have breathed a sigh of relief and let him go, but something made her call him back. "Johnny?"

He peered over his shoulder at her. "Yeah?"

Except in general terms, Madison had never spoken to her brothers about the crimes their father had been accused of committing. Neither Johnny nor Tye had good feelings toward Ellis, so Madison had never expected them to be supportive. Her brothers were too busy trying to recover from their unhappy childhoods to worry about what was happening to their father—a father who'd let them down so badly. But she suddenly felt the need to talk to Johnny now, before he disappeared for another five years.

"Do you think he really did it?" she asked softly.

For a moment, Johnny looked more lucid than she'd seen him in years. "You mean Dad?"

She nodded. She longed to tell him what she'd found beneath the house. She had to tell *someone*. The burden of keeping the secret was too heavy. And there was no one else....

He stared at the floor for several seconds. "He did it."

"How do you know?"

"I don't want to talk about it," he said.

"You never heard or saw anything...out of the ordinary, did you?"

He was moving toward the door again. "I wasn't around."

"You showed up every once in a while, for short periods of time," she said, following him.

"I never saw anything."

Madison wished she could erase from her mind the image of opening that locket in the dank atmosphere of the crawl space. "Did you hear what happened to Dad's grave?" she asked as he opened the door and stepped outside.

He turned, scowling at her. "I don't want to know."

"But—"

"Look at me, Maddy," he said, calling her by the nickname the kids in the neighborhood had given her when she was young.

She met his gaze.

"You see what I am," he said. "I can't help you. I can't even help myself. You want a shoulder to cry on, call Tye. He's the one who never flinched, no matter how bad it got."

Then he hurried to the car, the motor revved and he was gone.

CALEB LEANED CLOSER to the house to avoid being seen by the men in the Buick Skylark. Who were they? And what did they want? Judging by the late hour, the rattletrap condition of their car and the "drifter" appearance of the guy who'd gone inside Madison's house, they weren't insurance salesmen.

He muttered the license plate number to himself a few more times, planning to have Detective Gibbons run a check on it in the morning, and started back to the cottage.

When he'd heard the car pull up, he'd been in bed watching television, and hadn't bothered to put on anything but a pair of jeans. It was chilly to be walking around without a shirt and shoes. But he hesitated when he passed Madison's window and glanced in to find her sitting at the kitchen table, her head in her hands. If he wasn't mistaken, she was crying. Even if she wasn't, there was something so weary, so hopeless about her posture....

Was she okay? His natural reluctance to intrude on her privacy warred with the desire to capitalize on a golden opportunity. After all, he'd moved in to get close to her.

Hurrying to the cottage house, he scribbled down the license plate number, put on a T-shirt and a pair of shoes and jogged back.

It took several seconds for her to answer his knock. When she finally came to the door, her cheeks were dry, but her eyes were red and damp.

Caleb studied her for a moment, wishing she were middle-aged and frumpy. That she was single and attractive only complicated matters. "Is something wrong?" he asked.

There was an insincere smile on her face and, when she spoke, her voice carried the high pitch of false cheer. "No, of course not. Why?"

He jerked his head toward the drive. "Those guys who were here. They didn't look very reputable. I thought maybe I should check on you."

"Oh." Her smile faltered. "That was just my brother Johnny."

Johnny Purcell. Caleb had come across that name years ago while he was researching Ellis. As a matter of fact, he'd interviewed Johnny once, in prison. But Johnny must have lost a lot of weight since then. Caleb hadn't recognized him.

"I know he doesn't look like much," she said. "But he's basically harmless. Fortunately, he doesn't come around very often. I'm sorry if he woke you."

"It's no problem. I wasn't sleeping. Is he in some sort of trouble?"

"No."

An awkward silence ensued, during which Caleb racked his brain for some other way to learn more about Johnny's visit.

Madison spoke first. "Did you get settled?"

"For the most part." He grinned, hoping to charm her. "I loaded up on the important things—peanut butter and bread."

"Well, if there's anything you need, a cup of sugar or an egg or whatever, feel free to ask."

"I appreciate that." He shoved his hands in the pockets of his jeans, wishing she'd invite him in for a cup of coffee. Other than moving onto the property, he hadn't considered *how* he was going to get close to Madison. Especially when she seemed so remote.

"Is Brianna asleep?" he asked.

"She's in bed. I don't know that she's asleep."

"I realize she feels I'm encroaching on her space, but with any luck she'll get used to having me around, don't you think?"

"I hope so," Madison said. "I know space shouldn't be an issue. She's got plenty of space. Especially at her father's. He lives in an eight-thousand-square-foot house, complete with a giant water fountain worthy of a casino."

"Sounds...ostentatious."

"It is." She finally gave him a genuine smile. "I hated living there. It felt like a mausoleum." She folded her arms, unwittingly revealing a fair amount of cleavage.

Caleb wished again that she was older, or significantly younger, or considerably overweight...

"Brianna's had a rough year," she was saying. "I'm guessing this is some sort of delayed reaction."

He pulled his attention away from the smooth skin of her breasts. "How long have you been divorced?"

"A little less than a year."

"It'll get easier."

"You sound as though you speak from experience."

"I went through a divorce two years ago." He didn't mention the first divorce. There'd been no one in between so it didn't count.

"I'm sorry."

"Don't be. Things are better now."

"They are for me, too," she said, but he didn't get the impression she really believed it.

Caleb considered being direct and simply asking if he could join her for a cup of coffee. With Susan missing, he felt the clock ticking. But he didn't dare come on too strong. If he frightened Madison or made her leery of him in any way, he'd only defeat his purpose.

"Well, thanks for checking on me," she said, and started backing up to close the door.

Caleb had no choice but to step off the porch. "Have a good night."

"You, too."

Reluctantly, he walked down the stone path that led to his new home, frustrated that he hadn't managed to wrangle any type of invitation out of her. Then he caught sight of her car. A nice car was important in the real estate business. He had no doubt that if she could afford it, she'd be driving a Mercedes instead of a Camry. "By the way," he said before she could close the door.

"Yes?"

"I'd like to hire someone to do my laundry and make me a few meals. I was wondering if you'd be interested."

"You're going to hire someone to cook and clean for you?"

He was if he could get her to take the job. "I'll be coming and going a lot."

"How much are you willing to pay?"

Caleb had always taken care of himself. He had no idea what such services should rightfully cost. But he wasn't afraid of being generous. He thought that helping her out financially might ease his conscience about having ulterior motives in befriending her. "Six hundred dollars a month sound fair?"

She coughed. "That's almost as much as you're paying in rent."

Evidently he'd been a little too generous. "That would include the price of groceries, of course."

Her teeth sank into the soft flesh of her bottom lip, distracting him again. "What constitutes 'a few meals'?"

"Dinner every night, unless you have other plans, and breakfast on the weekends." For a moment, he thought she'd refuse, and wished he'd asked her for less of a time commitment. She was trying to run a business and already seemed harried. But he needed to gain her confidence quickly. "I'm flexible, though. So if you think that's too much..."

"What kind of menu?" she asked.

"You can choose."

"Do you want me to bring it over to you?"

"If you'd prefer. But if you're open to company, I'd rather not eat alone."

She hesitated for another moment. "All right," she said at last. "I'm already cooking for Brianna and me. It won't take long to add an extra plate for dinner and do a few more loads of laundry each week. I think it might help Brianna adjust to having you here if she gets to know you a little."

"My laundry isn't difficult," he told her. "Mostly jeans and T-shirts."

"Sounds as though you live a pretty easy life, Mr. Trovato," she said.

"Call me Caleb."

"When would you like me to start, Caleb?"

He smiled as he moved away, feeling a sense of victory. It was only a matter of time before he knew everything Madison did. "How about tomorrow?"

CHAPTER FIVE

"CALEB, WHERE have you been? I've been calling your cell for the past hour."

Holly. Again. Between Caleb's run to his folks' house for his things that morning, and his trip to the grocery store in the afternoon, he'd met her at the university and helped pass out flyers with Susan's picture and description. Every time his ex-wife had called since then, he'd jumped for the phone, thinking she'd heard from someone who'd seen Susan. Shortly before Johnny had pulled up outside, Caleb had finally realized she was just stressed and worried and wanted to go over the same things she'd been saying all day. Only he'd already done everything he could until morning and didn't want to hold her hand anymore. He was comfortable in bed, once again flipping through satellite channels on television and enjoying the solitude.

"It's after midnight, Holly," he said. "Can't this wait until we get together in the morning?"

"No, it can't," she replied. "Someone called me about the flyer a little while ago."

At last! Caleb hit the off button and sat up, giving Holly his full attention. "Who was it?"

"I'll tell you all about it when I get there. I have something to show you."

"*Show* me?"

"I'm on my way."

"Wait, I'm not staying at my folks' place," he said before she could hang up.

"You're not?"

"No, I rented a small house."

Silence. Eventually she asked, "Why would you rent a place? You could've stayed here for free."

"Holly, we're divorced."

"I know that, Caleb. It isn't as though I'm asking you to sleep with me. I only offered to put you up for a few weeks. You're helping me, after all. I feel it's the least I can do."

"There's no need," he said. "I'm fine where I am."

"And where is that?"

"Whidbey Island."

"Whidbey! What made you move there?"

"It's closer to the mainland."

"If you wanted to be close to the mainland, why didn't you rent an apartment *on* the mainland?"

Caleb considered telling Holly that he was renting from Ellis Purcell's daughter, but decided not to. He didn't want her badgering him for information until he was ready to share it. Just because he *might* come across answers no one else had been able to glean didn't necessarily mean he would. It was possible that Madison was too secretive to let anything slip. It was also possible that she didn't know anything. But he was willing to bet against both of those possibilities. She'd been living with Ellis during his killing spree. At a minimum, she should be able to tell Caleb bits and pieces of conversation she'd overheard between her parents, whether her father was really at home when he'd claimed to be, whether she sometimes heard things go bump in the night, whether she ever saw him move something heavy that just might have resembled a dead body....

"This place is nice," he said instead.

"How much is it costing you?"

"It doesn't matter."

"Waste your money, then. I don't care," she said. "You're so stubborn. I don't know why I married you once, let alone twice."

He thought she might hang up in a huff, but she didn't. "Are you going to give me directions?" she asked after an extended silence.

A quick glance at the clock told him it was even later than he'd realized. But she'd said she had something to show him. "What do you have?" he asked.

"You'll see."

If she had a lead, he needed to know about it as soon as possible. He told her how to find him. Then he got up, dressed and put on some coffee.

Across the yard, he could see that the lights were still on in Madison's house, and he wondered what she was doing. Earlier, it had looked as though she carried the weight of the world on her shoulders....

Guilt about masquerading as a random renter flickered inside him. He could already tell Madison wasn't the ice princess he'd assumed from her television interviews and that one strongly worded letter. Her behavior wasn't strange, either, like her father's. Actually, she seemed pretty...normal. And there was no question she'd been through a lot.

Leaning against the wall, he stared out the window at her light. She might be nice. She might even be one of the most attractive women he'd ever met—but being nice and attractive didn't change the fact that the truth had to be told.

MADISON COULDN'T SLEEP. She was tired yet wound up, and didn't dare take a sleeping pill, for several reasons. Brianna could wake up in the night. Johnny, or whoever had been with him, could come back. And she wasn't yet comfortable with having a stranger living on her property. Especially one who knew she and Brianna were alone. Caleb Trovato's credit references had checked out; he seemed like a pretty solid citizen. But still...

Pulling out her sketchpad, she sat at the kitchen table and began to draw. She had tons of paperwork to take care of. She needed to review the purchase offers her agents had generated in the past week. As their broker, she was liable for any legal repercussions if they made a mistake. She also needed to revise the independent contractor agreement she was having her agents sign when they came to work for her, decide whether or not she was going to hire the young woman she'd interviewed this afternoon, and review the lease for the new copier she was buying for the office. But she was too tense to delve into work-related matters tonight.

Because she couldn't forget Johnny, she drew his eyes. Because she was worried about Brianna, she drew her daughter's full lips. She even sketched Danny's angry brow—something that had come to symbolize their relationship. The scratch of her pencil and her intense focus usually eased the stress knotting the muscles in her back and neck. But nothing seemed to help tonight. She still felt as though she were walking a tightrope with the ground frighteningly far below.

Her eyes slid to her briefcase. The urgency to make her business successful was part of the problem. Sales weren't going nearly as well as she'd hoped when she'd purchased South Whidbey Realty. She knew she was crazy to be wasting time while Brianna was sleeping, but Madison simply couldn't face the work she'd brought home with her.

Flipping to a new page, she considered drawing her mother's hands. But anything to do with her mother reminded Madison of her father, and she didn't want to confront her doubts about him. Not right now. Not in the middle of the night with the clock on the wall ticking and the rest of the house so silent.

She sorted through the faces she'd seen lately: an obese woman with beautiful blond hair she'd met at Brianna's school; a wiry, angular man who'd just started doing the janitorial work at the office building where she leased space; a baby she'd seen at the mall. None interested her enough to attempt them. But the gruff old man who worked on the ferry seemed to have potential—

A car pulled into the drive, and Madison's heart began to race. Was Johnny back? What could he possibly want now?

Dropping her pencil, she went to the window, but the car that parked behind Caleb's Mustang didn't look anything like the one Johnny had been riding in earlier. This car was a late-model Honda. And the person getting out of it was a woman—a tall woman who wasn't approaching her house.

A moment later, Caleb Trovato's door opened and he stepped out under the eaves. His broad shoulders blocked most of the light spilling from the cottage behind him, but Madison could see that his visitor was blond and most likely very pretty. Was she a friend? A lover? Coming this late she could even be a call girl.

No, Caleb would have no need to hire a prostitute, Madison decided. He probably had more female attention than he knew what to do with. He was ruggedly handsome. More than that, he carried himself with the sort of beguiling indifference most women found so appealing.

Most women, but not Madison. She'd trusted her father. She'd trusted Danny. She would have trusted Johnny and Tye, except they'd never let her get close enough. For some reason, when it came to men, she wasn't a very good judge of character. Which meant she was better off alone.

Even if she *wanted* a new love interest, how could she get close to anyone while guarding her father's terrible secret?

"THIS IS A CUTE PLACE," Holly said.

Caleb stretched out on the couch and flipped on the television. "Thanks."

"How did you find it?"

"I stumbled across the For Rent sign."

"So you leased it?" She snapped her fingers. "Like that?"

"Pretty much." He waved to the chair at the end of the couch. "Sit down and show me what you've got."

She didn't move toward the chair. "If you didn't want to stay with your mother or me, why not get a hotel? That's what most people do."

"Does it matter?" he asked, trying to head her off. She'd brought up the Sandpoint Strangler a number of times and was already frightened that Susan's disappearance might be connected. He didn't want to fuel her fears by admitting he suspected the same thing. At least until he had more to go on than gut instinct and a few wild coincidences.

She shook her head as she gazed around. "I just never expected it."

He buzzed past a commercial for dandruff shampoo.

"Don't make a big deal out of it, Holly. Now I have a place of my own while I'm here. That's it."

"And the downside is you're paying by the week?"

"*Forget* the cottage."

At the irritation in his voice, she propped her hands on her hips and faced him. "Why'd I have to fall in love with you?"

Caleb had asked himself the same question about her, many times. She'd just been so...lost when he met her. And he'd always been a sucker for a woman down on her luck. He liked feeling needed, liked taking care of others. Unfortunately, she'd exploited that tendency to its fullest.

"I wish I knew."

"I'll never understand you or what happened between us—"

"That's the beauty of being divorced," he interrupted. "We no longer have to analyze what's wrong with us. No more teary talks that carry on through the night. No more debilitating guilt. Surely you're as relieved as I am."

"But we loved each other."

Caleb scrubbed a hand over his jaw. "We just hated each other more."

"I never hated you," she said.

"God, Hol, would you let it go?" He blew out a sigh, hoping some of his frustration would go with it. "We couldn't be together for more than two days in a row. Now, do you have something on Susan or not?"

It took her a moment to regain control. But she managed to do so, for a change, and Caleb relaxed.

Leaving the remote control on the arm of the couch, he went to the refrigerator to get a beer. "Well?" he said when he'd popped the top and drunk almost half of it.

She finally sat down and stared at the television, probably so she wouldn't have to look at him. "I'm not sure if it'll tell us much in the end, but a woman named Jennifer Allred saw Susan the day after she and I had our nails done."

"Where?" He leaned one hip against the kitchen counter, enjoying the smooth taste of his Michelob Light and letting it siphon off some of the tension he'd been feeling only moments earlier.

"At a vegetarian pizza place not far from the university."

"She's sure it was Susan?"

Holly reached into her purse and withdrew a photograph. "She gave me this."

Surprised, Caleb left his beer on the counter and walked over to get a better look. "*How* did she give you this?" he asked. "I thought you said she *called* you."

"She did. Then she asked me to meet her on campus because she had some proof to give me."

"And you did it? Don't tell me you went there alone, Holly."

"What else was I supposed to do? Drag someone out of bed and coerce him or her into going with me? You weren't picking up."

He'd been outside creeping around, trying to figure out what was going on at Madison's—not the type of errand on which he wanted to carry a cell phone. "Twelve women, if you count Susan, have been snatched from that campus or the surrounding area! What were you thinking, meeting someone so late?"

"Oh, don't pretend you care about me," she said, coming right back at him. "If you cared, you never would've given up on me."

"Damn it, Holly, would you quit twisting the knife? I wanted to be there for you. I married you twice, remember? We aren't a good fit. I don't know how much more proof you need!" He hadn't planned on shouting, but she always managed to snap the control that was sufficient for every other situation and relationship.

She stared at him for several seconds, her glare challenging enough to make him believe they were going to end up in another of their famous rows. She was probably going to start in on the miscarriage. She always used that as some sort of trump card, as if he hadn't felt the loss of their baby just as deeply.

Instead, she covered her eyes and shook her head, obviously backing down. "Look at the picture, okay?"

Caleb felt the anger drain out of him. No one made him as crazy as Holly did. But this wasn't about their marriages or their divorces. This was about Susan, he reminded himself, gazing down at the picture. "I don't recognize any of these people," he said.

"That's because you've probably never seen them before. That's Jennifer and her two roommates. They're celebrating because the guy on the left just won an art grant."

"So what does this have to do with Susan?"

"Look behind them, in the background."

Caleb held the picture closer to the light, trying to make out the slightly blurred figure beyond the open door of the pizza place. It could have been any woman of Susan's general size, shape and coloring. But then he saw a slice of leopard print halter beneath a short black jacket and knew it was her.

"She's wearing just what I thought she was wearing," he said in amazement.

"Notice anything else?"

Caleb's blood ran cold. Next to Susan, parked at the curb, was a blue Ford pickup with a white camper shell. He cut his gaze to Holly. "Purcell's truck?"

"Or one just like it."

Another connection. At this stage, Caleb saw no benefit in keeping his reason for renting the cottage a secret. With the appearance of Purcell's truck in this picture with Susan, Holly's fears were already confirmed. "You wanted to know why I rented this place," he said.

"You're finally going to tell me?"

"Madison Lieberman lives next door. She's my landlady."

Holly's brows drew together as if she couldn't quite identify the name. "Madison Lieberman..."

"Ellis Purcell's daughter."

"Of course! I heard about her over and over when you were researching the Sandpoint Strangler. But she'd never talk to you. Has she changed her mind?"

"Not exactly. She doesn't even know that Caleb Trovato and Thomas L. Wagner are the same man. She was looking for a renter, and I happened to get here first. That's it." He tapped the picture against his palm. "Tell me how Jennifer came across one of our flyers."

"She's a graduate student at the university and saw it posted at the library."

Holly had insisted on putting her phone number on the flyer, which made sense because hers was local and not long distance. Also, Caleb knew a woman's name and number would seem less threatening. But Holly and this Jennifer woman had both been stupid to meet on campus so late at night—not that there was any point in arguing about it now. "What I don't understand is why she noticed something so obscure in one of her pictures," he said.

"Susan was involved in an argument that drew everyone's attention. When Jennifer saw the flyer, she looked through the pictures she'd taken that night and, voilà, there was Susan."

With a truck like Ellis Purcell's in the same vicinity. Was it another strange coincidence? Or did the police have a copycat killer on their hands?

"Did Jennifer say what the argument was about?" he asked.

"She wasn't sure. She thinks Susan bumped someone's fender while trying to park or something like that. Jennifer and her friends weren't really aware of anyone else until Susan screamed a curse. Then they all craned their heads to see what was going on. A male voice answered by calling her a stupid bitch. Then Susan got in her car and peeled off."

"What did the guy who called her a bitch look like?"

"He was beyond their view. After Susan left, Jennifer and her friends went back to their fun. She said if she hadn't seen the flyer, she probably wouldn't have thought about the incident again."

Caleb returned his attention to the picture, trying to figure out what it meant.

Holly watched him closely, fiddling with the cuff of her long-sleeved, black cotton blouse. "This might or might not have any relevance to my sister's disappearance, though, right?" she said. "I mean, for all we know that truck's a coincidence and Susan was arguing with Lance, the guy she was dating."

"At least this picture narrows down the time she could have disappeared," Caleb said. "Jennifer said this was taken on Tuesday?"

Holly nodded.

"She was reported missing when she didn't show up for work on Wednesday, which means she disappeared sometime Tuesday night or early Wednesday morning."

"Do you think it was Lance she was arguing with at the pizza place?" Holly persisted.

"We've talked to Lance. The last time he saw Susan was when they spent the night together on Saturday, remember?"

"That's what he *says*. Maybe he's afraid to tell us about the argument for fear it'll make him a suspect in the case."

"He's already a suspect," Caleb said. "In any homicide, the police look at the husband or boyfriend first, then extended family members and friends. But Gibbons doesn't believe Lance is our guy."

Her eyes narrowed. "When did you talk to Gibbons?"

"Last night."

"You didn't mention it to me."

"I haven't had a chance."

"We were passing out flyers together all day!"

"It's a moot point," he said. "Lance has a good alibi."

"For when?"

"For Monday *and* Tuesday nights." And for Wednesday and Thursday, as well, but Caleb didn't want to go into that.

"Where was he?" she asked.

Caleb raked his fingers through his hair, wondering how to frame his answer.

"What is it?" she pressed when he didn't respond right away. "You know something you're not telling me."

What the hell, he decided. The truth was the truth. "Lance is engaged to be married," he said. "He's been living with his fiancée and seeing Susan on the side."

"What?" Holly scrambled to her feet. "Susan told me he was living with his sister."

"If it makes you feel any better, his fiancée didn't know about Susan, either. She kicked him out as soon as she learned. But she maintains that he was home by six o'clock both Monday and Tuesday nights. She works evenings and needed him to sit with her mother, who just had surgery to replace a knee. The mother confirmed that she and Lance watched television together for several hours both nights."

"I can't believe it," Holly cried. "What scum! Men are all alike!"

"Hey, I never cheated on you," he said.

"You quit loving me. That's even worse." Burying her face in her hands, she dissolved into tears.

Her crying tugged at Caleb's heart, but he told himself not to feel any sympathy. He couldn't afford sympathy. Where Holly was concerned, the softer emotions always got him into trouble. But he couldn't stand to see her, or any woman, cry.

Leaving his beer on the counter, he went to see if he could get her to settle down. "Holly, you'll meet someone else," he told her.

She slipped her arms around his neck. His immediate impulse was to pull away, but she looked so crestfallen he couldn't bring himself to do it. "Someone who's more compatible with you than I am," he added, patting her awkwardly. "And we'll find Susan, okay? Don't give up hope. Not yet. She needs us to believe."

Holly clung to him, nestling her face into his neck. "What if we don't find her? I'll live my whole life never knowing what happened to my own sister. I've lost you already, Caleb. I can't bear to lose her, too. She's all I've got left."

Caleb thought of the other families suffering through the same kind of loss. He didn't relish the idea of lying to Madison Lieberman, but it seemed a small price to pay to resolve the mystery that had affected so many lives.

"I'm going to help you find Susan," he said. "Have some faith."

Holly shifted slightly in his arms, fitting her body more snugly to his. "If we don't find her, you'll eventually have to give up."

"We'll find her." He got the impression she was making her body accessible on purpose, and decided he'd given her all the comfort he could.

But when he tried to release her, she held on tight.

"Caleb?"

"What?"

"Is it *really* over between us? Because sometimes it doesn't feel like it is."

It had been more than two years since he'd made love to Holly. After his second divorce, he'd gone on a brief womanizing rampage, trying to repair what his failed marriage had done to his ego, he supposed. But he'd soon found the lifestyle too empty to bother with and had thrown himself back into his work. Now it had been ten months since he'd made love to *any* woman.

He had to admit he was beginning to feel his body's long neglect, but Caleb wasn't about to make another mistake with Holly. After their first divorce, a moment's weakness had left her pregnant and, for the baby's sake, he'd married her again. He certainly didn't want a repeat performance.

"It's really over," he said, putting her firmly away from him.

"Is there someone else?" she asked.

After tolerating Holly for so many years, Caleb suspected he wasn't naive enough to ever fall in love again. "No."

"You came back here to help me, even though we're through?"

He nodded. He had come to help her, and Susan. And because of Madison, he just might get lucky enough to solve the murders that had obsessed him for years.

CHAPTER SIX

MADISON WAS ON THE PHONE with Tye when Caleb knocked at her door for breakfast the following morning. Propping the receiver against her shoulder, she yelled for Brianna to let him in while she flipped the pancakes on the griddle.

"I can't believe Johnny's out," Tye said. "When did they release him?"

"He couldn't really tell me. I think he was on something."

Tye sighed. "That comes as no surprise."

Caleb knocked again. Evidently Brianna wasn't getting the door as she'd asked. Covering the phone a second time, Madison prompted her daughter to hurry.

Once she heard the patter of Brianna's feet finally heading down the hallway, she returned to their conversation. "I'm sorry. I thought you'd want to know," she said. "He tried stopping by your place before coming here. I guess you weren't home, but I'm sure he'll try again."

"Did he hit you up for money?"

Madison didn't want to admit that Johnny had asked for money, because she probably shouldn't have given him any. But letting him have what he wanted was the easiest way to deal with her conscience over everything that had happened—or not happened—in his life.

"He asked for a few bucks," she said.

"Did you give it to him?"

"What do you think?"

"Madison, we've talked about this before."

"I know." The emotions that made her give Johnny the money were so complex she couldn't have explained them if she'd tried. Especially because she felt some of the same guilt about Tye. He'd certainly turned out a lot better than Johnny, but he'd endured the same kind of childhood, and it had taken her years to get to know him well enough to feel comfortable calling him occasionally. "I won't give him any more," she said.

She could hear Brianna at the door, greeting Caleb with a chilly, "Oh, it's *you*." Momentarily distracted, Madison covered the phone to tell Brianna to mind her manners. But she was trying to get the pancakes off the griddle at the same time Tye was asking where she'd moved their father's coffin. She decided to have a talk with Brianna later. "He's at the Green Hill Cemetery in Renton," she told Tye.

Caleb's footsteps came down the hall and into the kitchen. She turned to wave a welcome, and ended up letting her gaze slide quickly over him instead. Not many men looked so good in a simple rugby shirt and a pair of faded jeans.

No wonder he had beautiful blond women visiting him in the middle of the night. The only mystery was that the woman hadn't stayed until morning and made him breakfast herself.

He gave her a devastating smile. "Smells great."

Madison told herself not to burn the food. "I hope you like pancakes."

"I like everything."

Suddenly remembering that she had Tye on the phone, she cleared her throat and told Caleb to have a seat. "I'll be with you in a second," she said. "I'm talking to my brother. I hope you don't mind."

"No problem." He removed the newspaper he'd been carrying under one arm and spread it out on the table.

Brianna sat directly across from him, twirling the fork at her place setting and glaring at him.

Madison threw her daughter a warning glance. Then she turned her attention back to Tye, because there was something she still wanted to ask him. Johnny had told her that Tye and Sharon were having problems, but Tye acted as though nothing had changed.

"Would you and Sharon like to drive over and have breakfast with us today?" she asked, trying to introduce the subject of Sharon as naturally as possible. Madison hoped, if he needed to talk, he might feel safe opening up to her. "It's nearly ready, but you don't live far. We could wait."

"Not today," he said. "The kids have soccer games."

"Oh." Madison poured more batter on the griddle, wondering what to say next. She wanted him to know he could trust her, but she didn't want him to think she was prying into his personal business. "Maybe Brianna and I could come and see them play."

"Next week would be better," he said.

"Next week" would probably never come. Madison wanted to see more of her nieces and nephews, but Tye was always so aloof. "Well, you know I'm here if you need anything, right? You'd call me if...if you ever felt like you wanted to talk, wouldn't you?"

"Of course," he said. But she knew he never would. Madison was fairly certain he still harbored some of the resentment he'd felt toward her when they were young. She had no idea what she could do to overcome it. She'd never mistreated Johnny or Tye. Some of the anger they felt toward Ellis for not being there when they needed him, and her mother for being such an unresponsive stepmother, had slopped over onto her.

"I'd better go," he said. "I don't want to make the kids late for their games. Thanks for telling me about Johnny."

"Sure." She hung up, feeling slightly hurt that Tye never wanted to include her in his life.

The rattle of the newspaper behind her reminded her that she had other things to think about.

She poured Caleb Trovato a cup of coffee and a glass of orange juice and motioned for Brianna to put down her fork and quit staring daggers at him.

"Thanks," he said, lowering the paper enough to look over it. He glanced at Brianna, grinned and went back to reading his paper.

Brianna's expression darkened the moment she realized her acute unhappiness at his presence caused Caleb no discomfort.

Madison decided she really had to talk to Danny about unifying their efforts to raise their daughter as a happy, well-adjusted child. "Did you sleep well?" she asked Caleb, cracking an egg into the skillet she'd just gotten out.

He folded the paper and set it to one side. "Very well. You?"

She was more than a little curious about Caleb's late-night visitor. But she wasn't about to mention it. She didn't want to seem like a nosy landlady—especially when she guarded her own privacy so carefully. "Fine, thanks."

"Was that the brother who came by last night?" he asked, nodding toward the telephone.

"No, that was Tye. He's a year older than Johnny."

"Do you have any other siblings?"

"Just the two brothers."

"They're both weird," Brianna volunteered, wrinkling her nose. "And Johnny stinks."

Embarrassed by Brianna's behavior, Madison grappled for patience. "Brianna, that's not polite. You're talking about your own uncles. And Johnny smells like smoke. That doesn't mean he stinks."

"He stinks to Elizabeth. And he stinks to Dad," she said smugly. "Dad says it's a wonder Johnny hasn't—"

"Let's not go into what your father has to say," Madison interrupted, knowing it wouldn't be nice. She added a pancake and a piece of bacon to Brianna's plate, and set the food in front of her in hopes she'd soon be too busy eating to speak.

But Brianna only stared at her food. "He doesn't like you, either," her daughter responded sullenly. "He said you couldn't see what was right in front of your eyes. He told Leslie that no-good son of a bitch father of yours nearly ruined his life."

Madison's jaw dropped. Brianna's words were obviously a direct quote, but that didn't make it any easier to hear them. "Brianna, you know better than to use that kind of language!"

"Dad says it," she said smugly.

"That doesn't make it right. Why don't you go to your room and see if you can remember what we talked about the last time you used a bad word."

Brianna spared her an angry glance before heading out of the kitchen, carrying Elizabeth smashed beneath one arm. She walked with her spine ramrod straight and her head held high, but it wasn't long before Madison heard sniffles coming from the direction of her bedroom.

Torn between going to her daughter and trying to remain firm, Madison closed her eyes and shook her head. "I'm sorry, Mr. Tro—"

"It's Caleb, remember?" he said gently.

"Caleb, I'm sorry. I'm afraid we're dealing with some...issues here. If you'd rather, I could bring your meals over to your place in the future."

"No, that's okay. Brianna doesn't bother me. I'm sure she's a great kid."

A lump swelled in Madison's throat. "She *is* a great kid. She's just a little out of her element right now. Her father remarried this past year, almost the day our divorce was final, which hasn't helped. The woman who's now her stepmother was already pregnant."

"That's a lot for a child to deal with."

Madison got another plate from the cupboard. "I'm afraid she's blaming me for all the changes, but I don't want to be too hard on her."

"A bright girl like Brianna will figure things out."

Madison scooped two eggs onto his plate. "I hope so."

"Here." Standing, he crossed the distance between them and guided her to Brianna's seat. "Why don't you sit down and relax a minute? I can get my own food."

Madison would have argued, but she'd been taking care of her mother and Brianna—and Danny before that—for so long, it felt good to let someone else take charge.

Using the fork Brianna had been so fixated on twirling, she began picking at the food she'd dished up for her daughter.

Caleb set a cup of coffee near her plate. "Sounds as though your ex-husband doesn't like your father much." Gathering his own plate, now heaped with food, he took his seat.

She put her fork aside and added some cream to her coffee. "My father's dead."

"I'm sorry to hear that." Caleb paused, his own coffee in hand. "When did he pass away?"

For her, Ellis had died just recently—the day she'd found that box. Somehow, letting go of the man she'd believed him to be felt worse than living without his physical presence. "It's been a year or so."

He took a sip. "That's too bad. How old was he?"

"Fifty-eight."

"Fifty-eight's pretty young. Did he have a heart attack?"

Normally Madison didn't like talking about her father. But Caleb was a complete stranger, which meant he had no stake in the situation. That seemed to make a difference. "He shot himself in our backyard."

His eyebrows drew together, and his gaze briefly touched her face. "That must have been terrible for you."

"It was." She remembered Johnny calling her the day it had happened. She'd felt shock and grief, of course, but also an incendiary anger. She'd believed the police and the media had finally badgered Ellis to the point where he could tolerate no more. She'd stood in the middle of the mall, her cell phone pressed tightly to her ear, her legs shaky as Johnny told her what he'd found. And once she'd hung up she had to break the news to her mother.

"Was he going through some type of depression?" Caleb asked. His attention was on his food, but the tone of his voice invited her confidence.

Madison wondered if telling him a little might bring her some solace. "My father was Ellis Purcell," she said.

Caleb set his coffee cup down with a clink. "Not the Ellis Purcell who was implicated in the killings over by the university."

"I'm afraid that's the one." Her father had been on the national news and in the papers so many times, it would've been much more surprising if Caleb *hadn't* recognized his name, but it was still a little disconcerting to have him clue in so fast.

Caleb didn't say anything for a moment, and Madison immediately regretted being so forthright. "I shouldn't have told you," she said.

There was a hesitancy in his expression that gave her the impression he agreed with her. But his words seemed to contradict that. "Why not?" he asked, stirring more sugar into his coffee before taking another sip.

She couldn't see his expression behind his cup. "Because I've spent years trying to escape the taint of it."

He put his coffee back on the table and finally looked at her. "I'm sorry," he said, the tone of his voice compassionate.

The ache that had begun deep inside her at the outset of the conversation seemed to intensify. She wanted to hang on to someone, to break away from her troubled past and be like other people. But it was impossible. Her father, or whoever had left those sickening souvenirs under the house, had seen to that. "That's what my ex-husband was referring to when he said what he did in front of Brianna," she explained.

"I see." Caleb cleared his throat. "How old were you when the first woman went missing?"

"Fifteen. I remember my mother talking about it one night. But it was just another story on the news to me then." She chuckled humorlessly. "Little did I know how much it would affect me later...."

He started eating his pancakes. "What was your father's reaction to the news?"

"He didn't really say anything. My mother was the one talking about it."

When Caleb had swallowed, he said, "Your father must not have been a suspect right away, then."

"No, he wasn't drawn into it until two years later, when some woman claimed she saw my father's truck leaving the house of her neighbor—who'd just been murdered. Then the police started coming over, asking questions. They contacted just about everyone who'd ever known us. They searched the house."

"What did they find?" he asked, pushing his plate away.

"Besides the fact that I was exchanging love letters with a boy my father had forbidden me to associate with, and I had just bought my first pair of sexy underwear?" She laughed. "Nothing."

Caleb's lips curved in a sympathetic smile. "They exposed all your girlish secrets, huh?"

"To this day I stay away from airports just in case security decides to rifle through my bags."

She'd meant her comments to sound flip but was afraid they didn't come across that way when Caleb remained serious. "So what do you think?" he asked.

"About what?"

"You probably knew your father as well as anyone." She could suddenly feel the depth of his focus, which seemed at odds with his casual pose. "Did he do it?"

She'd faced this question before, dozens of times. And she'd always had a ready, if passionate, answer. But that was before. Should she tell him what she'd believed throughout the investigation? Or should she admit that she might've been wrong all along?

She'd opened her mouth to tell him she didn't know *what* to think when the telephone interrupted.

"Excuse me," she said, and picked up the handset.

"Good news," Annette announced from the other end of the line, her voice cheerful.

"What's that?" Madison glanced down the hall toward Brianna's room, feeling as though she could use some good news at the moment.

"I've decided to sell the house."

"What?"

"I'm ready to move. I know it's taken me a while to come to this, but it's time."

A vision of her mother stumbling upon the shoes and underwear—and that locket and rope—flashed through Madison's mind. "There's no hurry, Mom," she said, turning away from Caleb. "Why don't you wait until spring?"

"Because I don't want to spend another Christmas here without Ellis. Do you think you can sell this house inside a couple of months?"

"I—I'm not sure."

"If not, maybe I'll rent it out. Now that I've made my decision, the memories are crowding so close."

"I understand. But..."

"But what?"

Madison looked at Caleb, wishing for the second time that she hadn't shared so many personal details with him. There was still a great deal to protect. She had to be more careful. "Don't start packing yet," she said.

"Why not?"

She groped for something that would sound logical. "Wait until I can help you."

"You're so busy. You just worry about getting this place sold. I'll have Toby next door help me."

"When?" Madison asked, her panic rising.

"He said he could do it the weekend following next."

The weekend following next...

She needed to move that box. And she needed to do it sometime in the next two weeks.

CALEB CURSED the untimely interruption of the telephone. He'd just had Madison talking to him about her father. She'd been open and warm, completely the opposite of what he'd expected her to be.

And then her mother had called.

He helped himself to another pancake and took his time eating, hoping they could return to their conversation as soon as Madison hung up. But when she got off the phone, she looked upset.

"How's your mother?" he asked, setting his napkin next to his plate as he finished.

"Fine."

"Does she live close?"

She gathered up the dishes. "Just beyond the university, for the time being."

"For the time being?"

She ran hot water in the sink. "She's talking about moving."

"Does that upset you?"

Madison glanced over at him and, if he wasn't mistaken, a wariness entered her eyes that hadn't been nearly as pronounced when they were talking earlier. "No, why?"

"You seem a little tense, that's all."

"I'm the one who's been telling her to move," she said. "It's tough to stay in the same house where everything went so wrong." Suddenly, she turned off the water. "Will you excuse me, please?"

"Of course."

She disappeared down the hall and, after a moment, he could hear her talking in a soft voice to her daughter. "Do you understand why I wasn't happy with what you said at the table, Bri?... Do you think you could try a little harder to remember your manners?... Okay, come give

Mommy a hug.... I know things haven't been easy lately, princess, but they'll get better.... Are you ready to eat?"

Caleb felt he should probably leave. There were several people he still needed to interview. And he wanted to talk to Jennifer Allred, the woman Holly had met last night, just to see if he could jog her memory for details. But the odd change that had come over Madison made him believe there was more to that phone call with her mother than she was saying, and he hoped to figure it out before he left.

"Breakfast was great," he said when she came back into the kitchen holding Brianna's hand.

"Thanks," she responded. "Have you always had someone cook and clean for you?"

He almost admitted that he hadn't, but he wanted to make it sound as though this type of arrangement wasn't anything new, so she'd relax around him even more. "Occasionally."

"Must be nice."

Brianna glowered at him, still sulky, as he carried the cream and sugar to the counter, searching for an excuse to linger. It was the weekend. He could probably spend more time with Madison if only he could think of something menial to do for her. He could fix something, wash her car, mow the grass—

The overgrown grass. Perfect.

"Any chance you'd like to work in the yard this afternoon?" he asked. "I've got a few hours. I thought I could mow the lawn and maybe trim some of the bushes while you and Brianna handled the weeds."

Madison set the frying pan in the soapy water and let her hands dangle in the sink. "Really?"

When he heard the gratitude in her voice, he felt less than an inch tall. But he had to stay focused, had to make this work. "If you don't mind my help."

She shook her head. "I don't mind at all. I'll even take some money off your rent, or trade you a couple of meals. I'm falling behind out there. My business takes every extra minute. I just lost my top agent and I've been trying to find someone to replace her. And my office manager doubles as typist for the agents, but she's a much better typist than she is a manager."

"We can do the grass ourselves," Brianna said, out of nowhere.

"Brianna..." Madison used her tone as another warning.

"Or you could help us," she added grudgingly.

Caleb grinned. "There's no need to compensate me." He knew it would only make him feel worse. "I think it'll be good to get out. I cut my folks' grass for years."

"Where do your folks live?"

"On Fidalgo Island."

"Really?" Madison's eyebrows rose. "That's not far."

"Farther than I'd want to drive to reach downtown," he said, so she wouldn't wonder why he'd rented her cottage, instead of staying with family.

"Do you often work downtown?"

"Not often. Once in a while."

"I see." Madison glanced at the clock over the table. "I'm afraid I have to run a few errands this morning. What time do you want to do the yard?"

"One o'clock okay?"

"Perfect."

He smiled. "See you then."

CHAPTER SEVEN

MADISON WAS NEARLY thirty minutes late returning from her errands. She'd had to deliver some tax returns to a loan agent for a buyer who was trying to purchase a vacation home outside Langley, and had gotten caught up talking to him about another deal they'd been working on, which had fallen apart. She'd also drawn up a purchase offer for one of her own listings, a small two-bedroom, two-bath located just down the street, even though she knew the buyer was coming in so low the seller would probably be offended and not even bother to counter. She was so busy managing the other agents and running the office that she didn't have the chance to get out and sell much, but she was doing everything she could to turn her business around, which meant she sometimes had to act as a regular agent, too.

Fortunately, once she and Brianna left the house, Brianna's mood had dramatically improved. Madison talked to her about being polite to guests and how important it was that Brianna, Madison and Danny treat each other with fairness and respect even though they were no longer living as a family. But it was difficult to tell whether Brianna actually grasped these concepts. It was the sort of stuff older children had problems sorting out. How could Madison expect a six-year-old to understand?

Pushing back the sleeve of her gray suit, she glanced

nervously at her watch as she pulled into the drive. She hoped Caleb hadn't given up on her.

As soon as she cut the engine, she could hear the steady roar of the lawnmower coming from the backyard, and felt a measure of relief. She loved where she lived and was anxious to get the grounds cleaned up. Because the previous owner had taken such meticulous care of the place, with Caleb's help it would soon look as good as it used to.

"You ready to do some weeding?" she asked Brianna as she got out.

Her daughter didn't move.

"You like working in the yard," Madison said, leaning back inside the car. "Come on. It'll be fun. We'll probably find some snails."

Reluctantly, Brianna climbed out.

The lawnmower fell silent and Caleb came around the house, carrying the grass bin. At her first sight of him, Brianna's expression darkened, but Madison had trouble fighting an appreciative smile. He'd obviously been working for some time—long enough to get too heated for his T-shirt, which he'd taken off and stuffed in his back pocket. Sweat gleamed on his golden torso, making the contours of his muscular chest and arms seem that much more defined.

Madison had seen a lot of sweaty, muscle-bound men at the gym when she was married to Danny. But from a sketch artist's standpoint, there was something truly beautiful about the way Caleb Trovato was put together. He looked far more natural than any of those men at the gym. When he moved, she could tell his tan ended at the waist, as though he'd gotten it from working or playing outdoors instead of baking naked in a tanning salon. And he seemed unconcerned with impressing others. He put down the bin and shrugged into his T-shirt the moment he saw them.

"There you are," he said.

"Sorry I'm late." Madison tried to hold the mental picture of his bare torso in her mind so she'd be able to recall it later. After being relatively uninspired over the past few weeks, she suddenly felt a jolt of creative energy. "I had to do a few things that just couldn't wait."

"No problem. I'm nearly finished in the back."

"I really appreciate your help," she said, and meant it. Having Caleb around, pitching in, made her life suddenly seem fuller, almost...normal.

He picked up the grass bin and emptied it in the green refuse container. "I found something I think you and your bunny might like," he said to Brianna.

Brianna had already dropped to her knees and situated Elizabeth beside her. She was digging in the dirt with a stick and pretending to ignore Caleb, but Madison could see her peeking at him, trying to figure out what he was talking about.

"Do you want to see what it is?" he asked when she didn't answer.

"No." She continued to dig.

Madison opened her mouth to remind her daughter of the talk they'd just had in the car. But Caleb gave her a quick shake of his head, indicating that he didn't need her to get involved.

"I'll bet Elizabeth would like to know," he said.

Brianna pretended to converse with Elizabeth, but ultimately shook her head.

"Okay." He started toward the mower with the empty bin.

Brianna rocked back on her haunches. "It's probably nothing we'd like, anyway," she called after him.

He didn't bother turning. "Whatever you say."

She frowned at his retreating form. "So, what is it?"

"Never mind."

"You're not going to tell?"

"You're not interested, remember? Even Elizabeth doesn't want to know."

Grabbing her stuffed animal, she stood up and ran after him. "What if Elizabeth's changed her mind?"

Madison retrieved her briefcase from the car, smiling at how easily Caleb had engaged Brianna's curiosity. Then she headed to the backyard to find them both kneeling over a shoebox covered with a piece of plastic Caleb had slit in several places.

"What is it?" she asked, unable to see because their heads blocked her view.

"It's a praying mantis," Brianna breathed, as though she'd never seen anything quite so wonderful. "See, Mom? It looks just like a green leaf."

"That's how it camouflages itself," Caleb explained. "Most of the time it blends in with the trees."

"Will it bite me?" Brianna asked.

"No."

"What does it eat?"

"Other insects."

"Yuck!"

"That's a good thing," Caleb said. "It helps keep the bad bugs in the garden from eating all the vegetables."

Brianna's nose was still wrinkled in distaste. "Ooo."

"Don't you find gnats and mosquitoes particularly appetizing?" he teased.

"What's *appetizing* mean?"

He chuckled. "Never mind. Do you want to hold it?"

Brianna shrank away from him. "I don't think so."

"Come on." He pulled back the plastic and gently

withdrew the mantis. "It won't hurt you. It has spiny legs that feel a little funny, but it's harmless."

Brianna remained skeptical at first, but the longer Caleb let the praying mantis perch on his hand, the more confident she became. "Okay."

He carefully transferred the insect to her just as Madison's cell phone rang. The LED readout identified the caller as Danny.

Taking a deep breath, she stepped away from Brianna and Caleb. "Hello?"

"You left a message on my voice mail this morning that you want to talk about Brianna," Danny said without the courtesy of a greeting. "What's going on?"

"I do want to talk, but I'm afraid now isn't a good time."

"What could possibly be wrong? God, she's six," he said.

Madison lowered her voice. "I have some very legitimate concerns, Danny. Our daughter is going through a difficult time, and I'm hoping you'll cooperate with me for her benefit."

"She'd be fine if only you'd let her come and live with us. She's perfectly happy when she's here. Ask Leslie."

"I don't need to ask Leslie anything," Madison said, irritated by the way he constantly discounted her feelings. "I know my own daughter. And I'm not going to give up my rights to her."

"Well, I don't want to conference with you about every little thing."

"Every *little* thing?" she replied. "Our *daughter* isn't a little thing."

"I think you just like to bother me, although I can't imagine why. When we were married you certainly didn't give a damn about anything other than protecting your beloved father."

Madison glanced up to see Caleb watching her. She didn't like him witnessing the discord between her and Danny, but she wasn't willing to end the conversation just yet. She was tired of Danny's unrelenting bitterness. He thought she'd ruined *his* life, but dealing with him wasn't easy.

"I'm going to pretend you never said that and say what I called to tell you in the first place," she said in carefully measured tones, thinking she might as well get it over with. "You're expressing opinions and attitudes in Brianna's presence that aren't good for her to hear. It's as simple as that."

"What opinions?"

"You're criticizing me in front of her, and I'm her mother."

"I haven't told her anything that isn't true," he said, and laughed.

Rolling her eyes, Madison consciously tried to sidestep an argument. "Just…just be careful of what you say in future, okay?"

"I'll do what I damn well please."

Another glance at Caleb and Brianna told Madison that her daughter was still absorbed with the mantis, but Caleb was watching her intently enough to suggest he recognized that something was wrong.

"Listen, we'll have to talk about this later," she said. "I've got someone here."

"Someone? Don't tell me you're finally starting to date."

She moved farther away from Caleb and Brianna and lowered her voice. "Whether I'm dating or not is none of your business. Anyway, I'm not seeing this guy. I'm renting to him."

The tension between them turned palpable. "You leased the cottage house?" Danny said, all sign of levity gone.

"I told you I was going to."

"And I told you I didn't want you to. Do you even know this guy?"

Madison curled the nails of her free hand into her palm. He thought he could walk out on her and still have a say in her choices; his presumption tested her patience, but she was determined not to lose her temper. "I'm getting to know him," she said calmly.

"So he's basically a stranger."

"A lot of people live in homes that are built closer together than my house is to the carriage house, Danny," she said. "If it helps, think of us as having a new neighbor."

"I'm taking you back to court," he snapped. "You'll be sorry you didn't listen to me when I cut my child support in half."

Disgusted that he'd threaten her with something that would hurt Brianna, Madison let her true opinion of him ooze into her voice. "You're pathetic, you know that?"

"Be careful. You really don't want to piss me off," he said, and hung up.

Madison was shaking by the time she hit the End button. Caleb was talking about the praying mantis again, but Brianna had finally clued in to the drama unfolding on the phone, despite his efforts to distract her.

"Was that Daddy?" she asked, watching her mother with wide, uncertain eyes.

Madison shoved her cell into her purse. "Yes, but don't worry, honey, everything's okay."

Brianna shaded her eyes against the sun. "Your face gets all red when you talk to Daddy."

Madison started moving toward the house. "It's a little hot in this suit. I'd better go change."

"I'll bet some ice cream would cool you down," Caleb said before she could get very far.

Brianna immediately jumped to her feet and clapped and danced. "I want some ice cream! Elizabeth wants ice cream, too!"

"I've got a yes from Brianna," he said. "What about you?"

Madison didn't want to go out for ice cream. After her conversation with Danny, she didn't want to go anywhere. Especially with her handsome renter. Letting another man into her life was like embracing a tornado. But she knew Caleb was trying to help her, so she made a conscious effort to let him. "Ice cream sounds good," she said.

THREE HOURS LATER, Caleb sat at a table at a McDonald's not far from Holly's house in Alderwood Manor, a suburb between Whidbey Island and Seattle. He tapped his pen on his leg, waiting impatiently for Detective Gibbons to answer his call as Holly inched forward in line. He'd spent most of the afternoon with Madison and Brianna, but he hadn't been able to get anything new out of Madison about her father or the murders. Even while they were having ice cream, she'd been too preoccupied by that phone call she'd received from her ex.

Caleb couldn't blame her. From what he'd overheard, Danny Lieberman was an ass.

When Gibbons finally came to the phone, Caleb had to yank the receiver away from his ear before the loud, foul-mouthed, twenty-year police veteran blasted out his eardrum.

"Trovato, what the hell are you doing calling me at home on a Saturday?"

Chuckling, Caleb leaned forward as Holly momentarily disappeared behind some hanging plants. When he'd ordered, she'd refused to eat, but he'd finally talked her into getting a hamburger and wanted to make sure she was still in line to order it. As soon as they finished a quick dinner, they were planning to canvass Susan's neighborhood again, just in case they'd missed someone or something. They didn't have a lot of other options. The private investigator was supposedly hard at work doing background checks on just about everyone who'd ever been associated with Susan, and the police were digging, too, searching for Susan's car, but no one seemed to be finding anything.

"What, you only accept calls when it's convenient, Gibbons?" he teased. "If I didn't know you better, I'd say you're in it strictly for the paycheck, man."

"You don't know what the hell you're talking about, as usual," he grumbled, but the old affection was still there. Caleb could feel it beneath the surface of everything that was said. "What do you want?"

Caleb wadded up his hamburger wrapper and shoved it inside his empty cup. "I have some evidence that might connect the Sandpoint Strangler case to—"

"The Sandpoint Strangler case!" he interrupted. "I have a woman who looks like Catherine Zeta Jones on her way over to fix me dinner, less than five minutes to clean up this dump, and you call me, acting like there's some kind of emergency on a case that's totally cold?"

Caleb had a hard time believing Gibbons could get a woman who even *remotely* resembled Catherine Zeta Jones to cook him dinner. Short, balding and a little on the heavy side, he had a blockish head with bulldog jowls.

To make things worse, he had a disconcerting way of shouting almost everything he said. "Just listen to me for a second, Gibbons. I think there might be a connection between the Strangler case and the Susan Michaelson disappearance."

"Don't give me that, Trovato."

"Susan Michaelson fits the profile. She's small, she's in the right age range and she was abducted from the same area."

"That could just as easily be coincidence as anything else. Quit looking for something exciting to put in one of those damn books you're writing these days."

Holly moved forward in line. Dressed in a denim jacket with fake fur at the collar, she studied the lighted menu overhead as though she hadn't seen it a million times. "I'm not working on a book right now. I'm trying to find Susan."

"Then why are you calling me? I'm not assigned to the Michaelson case."

"I think you should get yourself assigned to it, because I'm telling you there's a connection."

"Listen," Gibbons responded. "I'd give my right nut to know how that bastard Purcell did what he did. But you know as well as I do that the Sandpoint Strangler is dead. So, if that's all you've got, call me on Monday."

The phone clicked and Gibbons was gone.

"Damn," Caleb muttered, and dialed him again.

Gibbons answered on the first ring. "She just pulled up," he complained. "What the hell is it *this* time?"

Caleb came right to the point. "I've got a picture of Susan the night she disappeared."

His words were met with a few moments of silence, then, "How? Where?"

A doorbell rang in the background. While Gibbons let

his lady friend into the house, Caleb explained how he and Holly had come across the photo.

"So Tuesday night's the last time anyone saw her alive," Gibbons said.

"Anyone we've found so far."

"I want to see that picture."

"I thought you were too busy with Catherine Zeta Jones to get involved in someone else's case," Caleb said. "It's Saturday night, remember?"

"Kiss my ass, Trovato. I was heading back to the office in a couple of hours anyway."

"*There's* the hopeless workaholic I know and love."

"Criminals don't only work nine to five."

"Well, I've got something that'll get your attention. In the background of this picture, there's an '87 or '88 Ford, blue, with a white camper shell. It's identical to the one Purcell drove."

Gibbons gave an audible sigh, hesitated as though weighing this information, then said, "That could be a coincidence, too."

"Too many coincidences usually means there's no coincidence," Caleb said. "What's this I hear about a woman who's gone missing from Spokane?"

"That's probably completely unrelated."

"Holly says there was an article in the paper detailing the similarities. Some Rohypnol was found in her car, along with a piece of rope."

"We haven't even found her body yet. You're a cop, for hell's sake. Or you used to be," he added. "Don't start jumping to conclusions like everyone else. For all we know, that Spokane woman could be languishing on a beach somewhere."

"Or the Sandpoint Strangler is back in business."

"I think the Sandpoint Strangler is dead."

Caleb didn't mention that at one point Gibbons had thought the janitor at Schwab Elementary was the strangler.

"I guess it's possible that we're dealing with a copycat," Gibbons said. "Spokane's not in our jurisdiction, but I'll talk to Lieutenant Coughman and see if I can't help out a little with the Michaelson case. I know the lead detective was expecting the preliminary findings on some of the hair and fiber evidence recovered from her apartment, but I haven't heard anything yet."

"You find out, and I'll drop by in a few hours." Caleb saw Holly making her way toward him with a child-size hamburger and the change from his twenty. "One more thing," he said.

"What is it?"

"Would you do me a favor?"

"That depends on what it is."

Caleb pulled out the license plate number he'd written down last night. "I need you to run a plate."

"Why?"

"Just covering a few bases."

"I've gotta have a better reason than that, Trovato. You're not on the payroll anymore."

"I saw Johnny Purcell last night. He was in an old Buick Skylark with this plate."

Another long silence. Finally, Gibbons muttered, "What the hell. This is probably a waste, but...get me something to write with, will you, Kitten?"

"Kitten?" Caleb repeated.

"Go f—" Catching himself, probably for the lady's benefit, Gibbons lowered his voice. "Screw you," he said. Then he took down the plate number and hung up.

WHY, AFTER DRAGGING HER feet at every mention of moving, did her mother want to sell the house *now?*

Madison paced the floor of her living room, with the movie *Chocolat* on her DVD player, wondering what she should do. She felt a headache coming on, was exhausted from her busy day and her lack of sleep the night before, but she couldn't let herself rest. Neither could she concentrate on the movie. She had to make a decision about that box before her mother's neighbor started clearing out the crawl space.

House for sale... Nightmare in the making...

Madison rubbed her temples, hoping to ward off her headache. Her mother's neighborhood was a mixed bag of brick, wood and stucco homes, the timeless and well-maintained next to the old and dilapidated. But it was close to the university, had appealing narrow streets, rows of tall shady trees and, like the ivy-covered, redbrick buildings of the campus, gave the impression of traditional values and old money. Her mother's place should sell right away—except for the fact that it was the home of an alleged murderer and the location of a suicide. That would draw more curiosity seekers and ghouls than serious buyers.

The telephone rang, startling her. Snatching up the receiver so the sound wouldn't wake Brianna, she murmured a soft "Hello?" She'd expected it to be Danny again. Brianna had called him before bed to tell him about the praying mantis. Caleb was letting her keep it in her room until Monday, when she planned to take it to school to show the class.

"Sorry to bother you." It was Caleb Trovato. Madison knew instantly because of the flutter of excitement in her belly. "I saw your lights on and thought you might be hungry," he said. "I just ordered a pizza. Would you like to share it with me?"

Instinctively, Madison moved toward the window to peer through the wooden shutters she'd closed when she heard Caleb pull into the drive an hour or so earlier. She saw him standing at his living room window, one hand holding the phone to his ear, the other propped against the wall as he gazed out. She knew he'd seen her peeking at him when he smiled and gave her a small salute.

Closing the shutters, Madison stepped quickly away. Attractive didn't begin to describe Caleb Trovato, which was a big problem. She couldn't afford to get involved with anyone right now, least of all someone so smooth. Earlier this afternoon, he'd neutralized Brianna's resentment of him in just a few hours. And he'd charmed them both at the ice cream parlor. Given enough time and privacy, imagine what he could do with a lonely divorcée....

"I've already eaten," she said. "But I appreciate the offer."

"I was actually looking for company more than anything," he replied. "It's Saturday night, after all, and I don't know anyone in the immediate area."

Plotting to cover up her father's misdeeds was by nature a rather solitary endeavor, Madison thought sarcastically. "It's getting late...."

"It's only ten o'clock."

She could tell that "no" wasn't an answer Caleb heard very often. But she wasn't particularly concerned about his potential loneliness. She was more worried about insuring her life and Brianna's remained on a calm and even course. No extreme ups and downs. Just thoughtful decisions, solid parenting and a strong work ethic—no matter how good he looked standing in that window.

"Let me be honest, Caleb," she said. "You've been

very nice, and...and I really appreciate all the work you did in the yard today and the ice cream and all that. But I'd prefer to compensate you for your time and effort in rent or meals rather than feel obligated to you in...other ways."

"*Obligated* to me?"

He obviously didn't like the sound of that. Perhaps determination had prompted her to state her position a little too bluntly. "I feel bad turning you down after what you've done," she said. "But my life's a bit complicated. I'm a single mom, trying to run a business. I'm not interested in seeing anyone."

"I'm not asking for a relationship," he said, his tone slightly affronted. "I'm moving back to San Francisco at the end of my lease, so I won't be around long, anyway. I was just hoping we could be friends while I'm here."

She thought of how much she'd enjoyed their time together in the yard today and later at the ice cream parlor, and had to admit that being Caleb's friend was pretty tempting. Most of the friends she'd known growing up had either abandoned her or turned on her when the investigation destroyed her father's good name and reputation. Rhonda, her best friend since grade school, had hung in through the initial years—until the police became more and more convinced that Ellis was indeed their killer. Then she'd started pressuring Madison to assist in the investigation. She'd said she owed it to the women of Seattle. But when Madison had refused to do anything that could hurt her father, even Rhonda began to distance herself.

"You don't have any problems with being friends, do you?" Caleb asked.

"Of course not," Madison said. "I just don't want to

mislead you. As long as you understand my feelings, I'm perfectly okay with hanging out once in a while."

"Good. Sounds like we agree. So how 'bout a slice of pizza? It should be here any minute."

Madison smiled, thinking a distraction might actually be good for her. She couldn't do anything about that box at her mother's house until Brianna was staying with her father next weekend, anyway.

"Bring it over whenever you're ready," she said.

CHAPTER EIGHT

THAT COMMENT HE'D MADE on the phone about being friends really bothered Caleb. He took friendship seriously. Most of his friends had outlasted his two marriages. But at this point he had to use every avenue available to him to get close to Madison. Susan's life was possibly hanging in the balance, and Caleb was getting desperate. After spending a couple of hours down at the station with Detective Gibbons this evening, he'd learned that, so far, the hair and fiber analysis from the samples collected at Susan's apartment had yielded exactly nothing. All the hairs belonged to Susan or Holly or someone else who had a reason to be there. No unusual fibers, foot imprints or fingerprints offered any clues. And the forensics team had sprayed the apartment with luminol and determined that there wasn't any blood there, either.

Whatever happened to Susan had probably happened elsewhere. That fact had to be established, of course, but it was a very small step forward when they had no body, no crime scene, no suspect and no leads. They hadn't even found Susan's car....

A knock at the door told Caleb that the pizza had finally arrived. He handed the deliveryman thirty bucks, grabbed the pizza box and a bottle of wine he'd purchased on his way home, and headed directly to Madison's. With Brianna in bed asleep, he hoped this might be a good time to talk to her mom. Maybe he could persuade Madison to have a glass of wine, relax....

The smell of sausage and pepperoni rose to his nostrils while he waited on the front stoop, but did little to tempt his appetite. Like Madison, he'd eaten earlier. The pizza was only an excuse to get together with her—which, when he thought of it, bothered his conscience, too. He generally didn't pretend to be something he wasn't.

"Hi," she said when she opened the door. "Smells good."

Caleb's smile when he saw her was genuine; he didn't have to pretend he was glad to see her. "I brought some wine. I hope you'll have a glass with me."

She hesitated. "Maybe... Come in."

He could hear the television as he followed her into the kitchen, where she grabbed napkins, plates and glasses before waving him into the living room. "Are you comfortable over at the carriage house?" she asked.

"Actually I am. It's going to work out pretty well." He sat down and put a slice of pizza on a plate, which he passed to her, then nodded toward the film that was playing. "Looks like I interrupted you. What have you been watching?"

"*Chocolat.* Have you seen it?"

"No."

"It's fabulous."

He could've said the same for the way she looked, even though she certainly hadn't dressed up on his account. With her auburn hair in a short, messy ponytail, she was wearing a white long-john top and plaid pajama bottoms. No shoes. She'd already removed her makeup, which made the few freckles across her nose seem more pronounced.

He appreciated her fresh-scrubbed face. Not many

women possessed the inherent beauty to go so natural. But what really caught his attention was that she wasn't wearing a bra. She wasn't particularly big-busted, but the sight reminded him of just how long it had been since he'd seen, let alone touched, a woman in any intimate place. He had to drag his gaze away and remind himself that now was not the time. "Do you watch many movies?" he asked.

"Not really." She turned off the television. "I bought a real estate business when I moved here, and it keeps me busy. I don't go out much, and I only own a few DVDs. Mostly romantic comedies."

He could certainly understand why she might not have any thrillers in her collection. Uncorking the wine, he poured them each a glass. "So how's Brianna doing with her new pet?"

"She's crazy about it." Madison raised an eyebrow at him. "But I hope you're planning on helping her feed it. Looking for bugs isn't one of my favorite pastimes."

"Sure, I'll help," he said with a chuckle. "It only needs to be fed twice a day."

"*Twice* a day?"

"Come on," he teased. "Didn't those brothers of yours teach you anything?"

She accepted the glass he gave her but set it on the coffee table, next to her plate. "We weren't very close," she admitted.

He took a slice of pizza and grinned. "Maybe that's not entirely a bad thing. When I saw Johnny the other night, I got the impression he's caused some trouble in his lifetime."

She sat on the edge of the overstuffed chair not far from the sofa, and Caleb allowed himself another glance at her chest as she picked up her plate. "He has, but—in his defense—he didn't have a very good childhood."

"What happened?" he asked, wondering if she'd had a bad childhood, too.

She shrugged and swallowed her first bite. "Nothing too unusual. My father got his girlfriend pregnant in high school. They got married."

"Then the baby came." That statement seemed to stem the sexual awareness humming through him.

"Exactly. And they had Johnny right after Tye. But the marriage was too dysfunctional to survive. My father dropped out of school to become a truck driver, so he was gone a lot, and Peg—his wife—started drinking."

"That's too bad," he said, concentrating on his own pizza so he'd keep his eyes where they should be. "When did they split up?"

"Only a couple years later, I think. I'm not really sure of the details. My father was never much for conversation, and he probably didn't want to believe all the stuff he heard about Peg. But Tye and Johnny came to live with us when they were teenagers, and they told some pretty hair-raising stories."

Caleb traded the pizza for his glass of wine. He wasn't having any luck redirecting his attention, and it was easier to watch her over the rim of his glass. "Like what?"

She waited until she'd swallowed again, but she seemed to be enjoying the chance to talk. He could tell he'd chosen the right approach—targeting peripheral subjects, moving the conversation along, giving her a chance to drink some wine.

She tightened her ponytail, but her hair was pretty much falling out of it, anyway. "They said their mother once had a boyfriend who used to slug them if they made him angry," she said. "There might even have been sexual abuse, although the boys never talked about that."

She picked up her glass, studied it and finally took a sip. "They said there was usually nothing in the refrigerator except vodka and some moldy fast-food leftovers. One time Johnny called Peg to get him after school, and she was so drunk she told him he couldn't come home. Another time, when they were only ten and eleven, she dropped them off at a mall and never came back. When the place closed, the police finally brought them home."

"There's no excuse for that." Caleb's disgust helped check the attraction he was feeling. Unfortunately, the wine did not. "Why didn't the state take Tye and Johnny away from her?"

Madison finished the last of her pizza and set her plate aside. "Because she always knew how to pull it together when she really needed to, and her mother would occasionally step in and clean her place, make her look better than she really was."

"Did she ever dry out?"

"Not for long." Madison tossed a lap blanket over her legs and leaned back with her wine, folding one arm beneath the perfect breasts he found so fascinating. "Bottom line, I think she resented Johnny and Tye. I think she blamed them because she never found another man who was willing to take care of her."

"Why didn't your father step in and take over?"

She raised her glass to her lips again. "This is good," she said.

He smiled, beginning to feel a little warm.

"I don't think he realized how bad it was at the time, not that that's any excuse," she continued.

"Did he pay child support?"

"I'm sure he did."

"Maybe he thought that was enough."

"Maybe."

The wine rolled gently down Caleb's throat, easing the tension he'd felt earlier in the day. "What did your mother have to say about the boys?"

Madison pulled her blanket a little higher. "I'm ashamed to admit she was probably the reason my dad didn't get more involved with them. He didn't think it was fair to expect her to clean up a mess she hadn't done anything to create."

"Wow." He poured a little more wine into his glass and lifted the bottle to her in question, but she shook her head. "So you didn't get to know your brothers until they came to live with you?"

"I didn't have any contact with them until then. Once Peg's mother died, Peg called my dad to tell him she couldn't handle the boys anymore."

Caleb leaned forward, resting his elbows on his knees. "How did it go once they came to live at your place?"

"They didn't stay long. Johnny got busted for drugs and went to a juvenile detention center within the first eighteen months. Tye shut himself up in his room and listened to stoner music for hours on end. He didn't do his homework or interact with the family. He didn't have friends. It drove my mother nuts that he could simply cut everyone off like that."

"Was he on drugs, too?"

"Probably," she said with a shrug, and surprised Caleb by accepting when he once again offered her more wine. "Dad and Tye argued constantly."

"Did it ever come to blows?"

She sat back and faced him, her expression thoughtful. "Occasionally. Usually over schoolwork. My dad didn't want Tye to end up without an education, like him. And he didn't like the way Tye treated my mother." She sighed. "On the other hand, Tye didn't think my father had the right to tell him anything. Sometimes I could see hate flickering in his eyes when he spoke to my parents, and it was almost—" she hesitated, seeming to grope for the right words "—frightening."

Caleb couldn't help marveling at how different Madison was from the woman he'd expected her to be—and wishing she wasn't so nice. Then maybe he wouldn't have to feel like such a jerk for taking advantage of her. "Did *you* get along okay with Tye and Johnny?" he asked, feeling a bit protective in case the answer was no.

"I was only eight when they came to live with us, so I didn't really have much to do with them. I felt like a spectator most of the time. I heard the yelling and watched the fighting, but I couldn't do anything to stop what was going on around me. So I tried to tune it out."

"You and your brothers make my childhood seem like a party," he said. "Between the situation with Tye and Johnny and the investigation, how did you survive?"

He'd switched topics as smoothly as possible, but when she didn't answer right away, he feared she was going to say something about calling it a night.

Instead, she drank a little more wine. "I don't know. It all seems like a bad dream—a bad dream that lasted a very long time."

Her answer was too vague. He needed more. "How did your father deal with the investigation?"

She threw the blanket aside and started clearing up the mess. "At first he tried to protect my mother and me by cooperating with the police. But when he agreed to take a lie detector test and they claimed he failed it, he wouldn't cooperate anymore."

"They *claimed* he failed it?"

She looked up at him. "There's no law that says the police have to be truthful during an interrogation. Did you know that?"

Caleb tried not to think how darn pretty she was....

What was wrong with him? This was business. If only she'd put on her damn bra. "I didn't," he said, feeling more like Judas by the minute.

"I guess once my father learned that they didn't have to be honest, he assumed they weren't and never trusted them again," she said. "He thought they were out to get him."

He could tell she was no longer enjoying the conversation, but he had to keep pushing. Partially because he refused to let her beauty distract him from his real goal. "What did *you* think?"

"I believed him," she said. "I saw how the police were acting, knew they were definitely out to get *somebody*."

"But why your father?"

She shrugged and shifted positions, but he kept an expectant expression on his face, and she finally said, "He worked on the third victim's house, doing a renovation. Her name was Tatiana Harris. She lived pretty close to us, so that shouldn't have been particularly unusual. But the lady across the street claimed she saw my father's truck leaving Tatiana's house the night she was murdered."

"You mentioned something about that before. But you don't believe she saw what she claimed she saw?"

"I think she could've been confused about *when* she saw my father's truck. Or mistaken it for someone else's in the dark. I tried talking to her about it once, and she seemed a little dotty to me. But the police thought they'd found the connection they'd been searching for, and kept digging. From there, circumstantial evidence made my father look even guiltier. And then another woman, years later, claimed she saw my father's truck leaving another crime scene."

That was Holly, of course, who'd even managed to remember the first three digits of Purcell's license plate number. But Madison didn't add that license plate detail. Maybe she didn't want to face it.

"You don't believe her, either?"

"I don't know what to believe now." She toyed with her hair. "At the time I thought the second woman was just jumping on the bandwagon. The media had publicized the details of the case so much, everyone knew my father's blue Ford had supposedly been spotted at one of the crime scenes. Anyone who'd seen him in town or simply driving down the street could note his plate number."

So she did acknowledge the plate detail. Caleb set his glass on the table and leaned back. "But the police didn't look at it that way."

"No. Nine women had already been sexually assaulted and then murdered. Public pressure was such that they needed to solve the case as soon as possible." She gathered up the pizza box, on which she'd set their dirty plates, but before she could head to the kitchen, he stopped her with another question.

"Did your father ever think about hiring an independent specialist to administer a separate lie detector test?"

"Why would he bother?"

"To prove the police were wrong."

"I don't think it would've made any difference."

Caleb knew he should probably let the subject go—for tonight, anyway. She was growing agitated. But he needed answers, and he needed them fast. If only she'd tell him something he *didn't* already know... "Why wouldn't it?" he pressed.

"My father wasn't a very sophisticated man. He just wanted to be left in peace."

Just as she wanted to be left in peace. But she hadn't really answered his question. If Ellis *hadn't* been lying, why didn't he try to prove it?

Maybe winning her over would take too long. Maybe he needed to crack her cautious facade. "Do you ever think about the victims?" he asked.

She jerked as though he'd just poked her with something sharp, and he immediately realized he'd said what he'd said to remind himself of who she was. She appealed to him at such a gut level he regretted that he couldn't get to know her in any type of honest relationship.

"I try not to," she said.

"Did your father ever say anything about them?"

Ignoring his last question, she headed for the kitchen. "Thanks for the pizza, but I'd rather not talk about this anymore. It's hard enough to forget what happened to those poor women without dragging it all out in the open."

"I'm sorry," he said, following her.

She didn't answer.

"Madison?"

"It's late."

His calculated risk hadn't paid off. She hadn't given him any new information and was most definitely shutting him out. "Are we on for breakfast in the morning?"

"I don't think so. I promised Brianna I'd take her to the zoo, and we should probably get an early start. Maybe we'll just prorate your payment for meals by the number of days I actually cook."

"No problem," he said, because he didn't have a choice.

She led him down the hall and flicked on the porch light as soon as they reached the front door. "Watch that first step," she said politely as she held the door open for him.

Caleb started to go, then turned back to face her. "I don't want to go home like this," he said. It was probably the most honest thing he'd said so far.

"I don't know what you mean."

"What's wrong?"

"Nothing."

"You're upset."

"I'm not upset," she said.

"Then what?"

"I'm—" she lifted her hands helplessly "—disappointed."

Caleb leaned against the doorframe, wishing he could go back in time and take the evening a little more subtly. He'd grown impatient and pushed too hard. And he'd become frustrated by the fact that he *really* liked her when he didn't want to like her at all. "Are you going to tell me why?"

She sighed and folded her arms. "I guess I stupidly thought that when you offered to be my friend, you meant it."

His conscience wouldn't let him say he *did* want to be her friend, even though, on some level, it was true. If there'd never been a Sandpoint Strangler... If Susan weren't missing... "And now?"

"And now I know you're just like everyone else. You're only out to satisfy your morbid curiosity at my expense." She lifted her chin. "Well, I hope you were entertained."

Caleb didn't know how to respond. He let the silence stretch, torn between his duty and how he would have handled the situation if circumstances were different. "I owe you an apology," he said at last, but that sounded trite, even to his own ears. So he stepped close and ran a finger lightly over her soft cheek. "I'm really sorry, Madison."

She swatted his hand away and blinked several times in rapid succession, as though battling tears, and Caleb couldn't help pulling her into his arms.

She resisted at first, but he murmured, "It's okay, come here," and she finally relaxed against him. Only he didn't feel he'd improved matters. He couldn't promise to be a better friend. He couldn't declare his innocence. He was still living a lie.

He held her for several minutes—until he felt her tears fall on his forearm. Then he leaned away to wipe her cheeks and said what had been going through his mind all evening. "You're so beautiful, Madison. You know that?"

She stared up at him, her dark eyes luminous in the porch light. His gaze lowered to her lips. Then his heart began to pound and he did something he knew he was going to regret—he bent his head and kissed her.

CALEB'S KISS WAS SOFT and lingering, gentle. Letting her eyes close, Madison slipped her fingers into the hair at the nape of his neck and refused to think about anything. Not all the arguments against what she was doing. And certainly not her father. It was late, and they were completely alone. She felt as though she'd stolen this moment out of time and could do with it as she pleased. If she wanted only to *feel*—to feel and forget the shadow of violence in her life—she could do it right now.

Breathing in, she caught his slightly musky scent and liked it. When his arms tightened around her, she liked that, too. For the first time in a very long while, she seemed to be drowning in a sea of warm, pleasant sensations. She'd been cold for so long; she hadn't even realized how cold, until now.

His hand came up to brace her head as he parted her lips. She hesitated briefly as she remembered his pointed questions. But most people were curious about her father, and her disappointment in Caleb's earlier insensitivity was swept away by his touch. All of a sudden, she wasn't a rejected wife. She wasn't a single mother trying to run a struggling small business. She was young and wanton and desirable again....

You're so beautiful, Madison.

Sliding her other hand up over the muscles of his chest, she leaned into him as he kissed her more deeply. She wanted him to go on and on but, without warning, he pulled away.

"I shouldn't have done that," he said, closing his eyes as though he'd just made a huge mistake. "I had no idea."

She cupped his chin and made him open his eyes. "No idea of what?"

His breathing was a little erratic, giving her the impression that whatever had come over her had affected him just as much. "That you, of all people, could do this to me."

"Me, *of all people?* What's that supposed to mean?"

"Nothing," he said and left.

THE FOLLOWING MORNING, Caleb started packing. His big strategy had been a bust. He'd spent nearly the entire night thinking about Madison, and had decided he just wasn't cut out to use her. He was the guy who'd married a woman twice just to be sure he'd given her a fair shake. What made him believe he'd be able to divorce himself from the personal betrayal involved in what he had planned for Madison? She might be Ellis Purcell's daughter, but she was as deserving of loyalty and respect as anyone else.

He'd just have to find Susan without her. He wasn't *sure* there was any connection between the Sandpoint Strangler case and his ex-sister-in-law's disappearance, anyway. He'd only been working on a hunch. He'd buy out the lease and be on his way and never think of Madison Lieberman again.

Except that he knew he *would* think of her. After that kiss, he craved the taste of her—and wished like hell that they'd met under different circumstances.

His cell phone rang. He glanced over at it, reluctant to even check the caller ID, certain it was Holly or his mother. Yesterday he'd told Justine Trovato that he was renting a cottage from the daughter of Ellis Purcell. His mother knew what he wanted from Madison and hadn't liked his methods at all.

"*'What tangled webs we weave,'*" she'd quoted.

He should have listened to her.

Whoever had called simply hung up and tried again. Shoving the rest of his clothes into his bag with little regard for neatness, he finally grabbed his cell phone. The caller ID simply said "private."

"Hello?" he barked, curiously tense for someone who'd just gotten out of bed.

"There you are."

Gibbons. "Tell me you've found Susan," Caleb said.

For once the detective was noticeably reticent. "I'm afraid we have."

Dropping the tennis shoes he'd been trying to stuff into

his bag, which was nearly bursting its seams because he'd put his computer in there, too, he sank onto the bed. "But?"

"It isn't good news."

Those words seemed to echo through Caleb's head. He pictured his ex-sister-in-law coming toward him, grinning sheepishly, that time he and Holly had collected her from the airport after the stunt she'd pulled in Vegas, and closed his eyes, knowing instinctively what Gibbons was about to say.

"She's dead."

Jaw clenched, Caleb didn't bother to respond. His chest had constricted so tightly he could barely breathe, let alone speak.

"You there?" Gibbons asked after a few moments.

Caleb struggled to find his voice. "Have you or someone else notified the family?"

"Not yet. I thought maybe you should do it."

Thanks, he wanted to say. And yet he knew it was better for him to break the news than some stranger. "Right. I'll take care of it."

"Caleb?"

"What?"

"She was strangled."

Chills cascaded down Caleb's spine. "Then I was right."

"There's *something* going on. She was killed just like all the others, same fracture to the hyoid bone, same ligature marks, same..." He hesitated, obviously sensitive to the fact that because of the nature of his involvement, Caleb might not want to hear the gory details. "Same everything," he finished.

Which meant she'd been sexually assaulted with a foreign object and positioned for maximum shock value.

Caleb closed his eyes against the mental picture that was conjured up in his mind, and cursed. It felt as though he was living in some sort of alternate reality. How could the violence and horror he wrote about in the lives of others now reach out to touch him so personally? "Where did you find her?"

"Not far from where we found the others."

"Near the university?"

"Just off the Burke Gilman Trail, in some trees. A jogger saw a glimpse of white fabric—she was wrapped in a sheet—and went to investigate."

"How long has she been dead?"

"I don't have the coroner's report yet, of course, but looking at the body, I'd say at least ten days, maybe two weeks."

She'd been dead before Caleb ever reached Seattle. But what made the killer single Susan out?

"We'll know the time of death soon enough," Gibbons added, then covered the phone while he coughed. "Meanwhile, I need the next of kin to come down and ID the body."

Her parents were in Arizona, so Holly would have to do it. And Caleb knew, after two weeks, Susan wouldn't be a pretty sight. God, how was his ex-wife going to deal with seeing her sister like that?

"I'll bring Holly down to the morgue after...in a couple of hours," he said.

"That'll work."

Caleb sighed, wondering how to break the news.

"You get anywhere with Purcell's daughter?" Gibbons asked.

He'd nearly rounded first base, but that wasn't the kind of progress he'd been hoping for—and it certainly wasn't what Gibbons wanted to hear. "No, nothing that could help us."

"It's not too late."

"Too late for what?"

"We can catch this guy. There was a tire track at the scene."

"But do we have a vehicle to compare it against?" Caleb asked. Even DNA evidence wasn't any good unless the police could pinpoint a suspect and get a sample.

"Not yet, but according to a specialist on tire track impressions, it's probably from a truck."

"Oh, that narrows it down."

Any other time, Gibbons would have called him a smart ass. But he said only, "I want to check it against the tires on that blue Ford pick-up Purcell used to drive."

The blue Ford. There was a blue Ford in the picture Holly had acquired of Susan. And Susan had been strangled shortly after that photo was taken. "Do we know where the truck is?"

"I already checked with the DMV. It's still registered to the Purcells."

"So you're going to get another search warrant?"

"With Purcell dead, I don't think it's possible. Judges don't take the violation of people's constitutional rights lightly, and we both know Annette Purcell isn't capable of this murder. I was thinking it would be better to have you borrow the truck so I can take a quick peek."

"I can't borrow that truck," Caleb said.

"Why not?"

"Having me act as an agent for the police in order to obtain evidence could get you fired, for one thing. And I'm moving out of here."

"You're making this a bigger deal than it is," Gibbons replied. "I'm not going to touch the damn truck or its tires. The tread of this imprint is unusual enough that I should be able to get some idea from a visual inspection. If it checks out, I'll ask for a warrant. But I have to know I'm not out of my mind for wanting to see Purcell's vehicle when the man's already dead."

Caleb looked over at his packed bag. He'd been halfway out the door.... "Can't you see the truck's tires some other way?"

"I could if Purcell's widow ever drove it."

"Madison won't lend me her father's truck," Caleb said, remembering how difficult it had been for her to even talk about Ellis.

"She hasn't figured out who you really are, has she?"

"No."

"Then how do you know she won't do you a favor? You haven't asked her yet."

"She's trying to put her life back together. She's running a business, raising a kid. I can't—"

"Are you interested in solving this or not?" Gibbons interrupted.

"Of course." He wanted to solve it now more than ever. All the friends and family members of the various victims he'd met through the years suddenly seemed far closer to him. Instead of telling the story from a distance, he was now part of the actual picture—and the irony didn't escape him. To think that someone he knew, someone he cared about, had suffered as Susan must have suffered made him ill and showed him the difference between empathy and real understanding.

But he didn't want to use Madison. After last night, he knew that much.

"So what are you thinking?" Caleb asked.

"I don't know," Gibbons said. "Maybe we were wrong about Purcell. Maybe he wasn't the strangler, after all. Or maybe someone else has picked up where he left off. Someone close enough to know how he worked."

"Like who?" Caleb asked.

"Remember that license plate you had me run? The car you said Purcell's son was riding in a couple of nights ago?"

"Yeah?"

"It came back as stolen."

Caleb scrubbed a hand over his jaw. "You don't think Johnny's somehow involved, do you? He was in prison when some of those women were murdered."

"Well, he's not in prison anymore," Gibbons said. "They let him out three days before Susan disappeared."

CHAPTER NINE

THEY'D LEFT THE VIEWING room fifteen minutes earlier. Caleb and Holly had stared at Susan's body through a small window; they'd been separated from her by a wall and a glass panel, so Caleb knew he had to be imagining that he couldn't rid himself of the sweet, cloying scent of death. But he still would've headed directly home, stripped off his clothes and taken a long hot shower—with plenty of suds and vigorous scrubbing. Except he couldn't leave Holly. She was in no condition to be on her own, and her parents' flight from Phoenix wasn't arriving until later this evening.

"You okay?" he murmured as they sat on a bench in the hallway of the morgue. Holly had wept since he'd told her about Susan, but she seemed to be coming to the end of her tears. Her skin was splotchy, her eyes red and puffy, her hair somewhat tangled, but her face had taken on a stark expression that conveyed the depth of her grief far more effectively than simple crying.

She didn't answer him. She just wrapped her jacket more tightly around her.

"Hol?" He gave her shoulders a gentle squeeze.

"How can you even ask me that?" she said dully, her voice barely a whisper. "Of course I'm not okay."

"You have to get through this," he said. "Susan wouldn't want you to fall apart."

"Susan." Tears welled in her eyes again, but she didn't

curl into him as she had before. She sat on her hands and stared blankly at the floor.

Down the hall, Detective Gibbons stepped out of the autopsy room. "You're still here?" he said when he saw Caleb.

Caleb hadn't been able to get Holly to leave. She couldn't bear the sight of Susan as she was now. But the battered and badly decomposed corpse was all that remained of her sister. For Holly, walking away would sever that one last tie.

"You got a minute?" Gibbons asked. Though Gibbons's language and manner were pretty rough, he did wear a suit. It was a rather cheesy, three-piece affair—a throwback to professional fashion in the seventies—but it was a suit. And the way he straightened and buttoned his coat told Caleb that Gibbons wanted to talk to him alone.

Caleb was reluctant to abandon Holly. She seemed so fragile. But when he hesitated, she lifted her gaze to his and the tears that had pooled in her eyes brimmed and rolled down her cheeks. "Go. I want this bastard caught."

With a nod, Caleb got up and followed Gibbons into the coroner's office, where the smell of fresh-brewed coffee heartened him. He'd received Gibbons's call so early, he hadn't showered or shaved, and he felt rumpled and dirty, as though he'd been sleeping in his clothes.

Turning the bill of his ball cap to the back, he glanced around the empty room before propping himself against the coroner's desk. "Tell me you've found something," he said.

Gibbons sighed. "Autopsies take time—you know that. And they haven't even started yet. But judging by the injuries to her forearms, this young lady put up a good fight."

Susan would, Caleb thought; she had Holly's spirit. "Which means we have a chance of finding biological evidence under her nails, right?"

"Or on the sheet in which her body was wrapped. The forensics team has found a drop of blood that definitely doesn't belong to Susan."

"What can I do to help?" Caleb asked.

Reaching into his breast pocket, Gibbons pulled out a copy of the picture that had been taken at the pizza parlor, and handed it to him. "Take this and go back to the pizza place tonight," he said. "Show it around and see if you can find out who was driving that truck. And who was arguing with Susan."

"So you're officially on the case?" Caleb asked.

"Because Susan was killed in the same way as the victims of the Sandpoint Strangler, I'm not only on the case, I'm lead detective. The department doesn't want to waste resources by rebuilding everything I've already put together."

"No one knows more about the Sandpoint Strangler than you do."

Gibbons raised his brows. "Except maybe you. You're the one practically living with Madison Lieberman. Think you can get hold of Purcell's truck?"

Caleb let his breath seep slowly between his teeth as he considered the question. He hated the thought of embroiling Madison and Brianna in another painful investigation, this one centering on Johnny. She'd already been through more than enough. But he couldn't let whoever killed Susan get away with it. Especially when chances were likely that the sick bastard would strike again. "I'll figure something out," he said.

Gibbons clapped him on the back. "Good man."

MADISON LEANED CLOSE to the window to peer out at the dark drive as she finished drying the pans she'd used to make dinner. She knew Caleb was still gone. She'd been listening for his car for several hours and hadn't heard anything beyond the wash cycle of her dishwasher.

Where was he? It was getting late. He'd indicated that his work schedule wasn't especially grueling, yet he'd been gone from dawn until ten or eleven at night four days in a row. He hadn't even wanted dinner. He'd left a brief message on her answering machine Monday through Wednesday saying that he had to work late and not to expect him.

It wasn't until this morning, when she'd bumped into him as she was leaving to take Brianna to school, that she'd actually spoken to him. He'd been dressed in a dark suit, seemed far more somber than the man she'd thought she was getting to know, and had very little to say, except that he didn't want dinner again tonight.

Maybe he was avoiding her. Maybe that kiss had bothered him even more than she'd assumed. *That you, of all people, could do this to me.* What had he meant by that? Was he as afraid of intimacy as she was? Was he worried she might fall at his feet and try to extract some kind of commitment—over one silly kiss?

She shook her head. If so, he didn't understand that she wasn't open to the possibility of falling in love. She couldn't deal with the hope, the effort, the risk. Too much was riding on the next few years, for her business and her daughter.

"Mommy, look what I found!" Brianna said, charging into the kitchen.

Madison glanced through the window once more to find the drive still empty, then turned to see her daughter carrying a large photo album. There was anticipation on Brianna's little face. But Madison had to bite back a groan when she saw that it wasn't just any album. It was the album she'd hidden under her bed.

"See? It's my baby book!" she announced proudly. "Come on, Mommy, let's look at it."

The album contained pictures of Brianna's birth and infancy, and a few photos of when she was a toddler. Madison and Brianna used to spend a lot of time poring over this particular book. Like most children, Brianna was fascinated by pictures of herself and the concept that she hadn't always been as she was now. But there were also photos of Madison's father in there that Madison didn't want to see. Not now. She'd just taken down every picture of him.

"It's getting late, punkin," she said. "Why don't we look at that tomorrow?"

"No," Brianna said. "You promised you'd read me a bedtime story. I want to look at my pictures instead."

"But—"

"Please, Mommy?" Brianna wore such a beseeching expression that Madison couldn't refuse.

"For a little while," she said.

Brianna rewarded her with a beaming smile and started pulling her into the living room. "Come on, let's sit down."

Madison took a deep breath, steeling herself for the moments to follow, but it didn't help. Once they were seated on the couch and going through the album page by page, Brianna not only insisted on pointing at every person in every picture, she demanded Madison tell her all the old stories. How the doctor had missed the delivery when she was born and the nurse had to step in. How Daddy had fallen asleep in the chair by the bed and nearly slept through what had almost turned into an emergency. How Grandpa used to stand her up in the palm of his hand before she could even walk. How Grandma had once dressed her up in a snowsuit and taken her to Utah to visit Madison's Aunt Belinda, or Aunt Bee, as Brianna knew her.

By the time they'd gone through several pages, the memories crashed over Madison like waves, hard and fast, threatening to drag her out to sea. Through it all, she couldn't help wondering—what had gone wrong? If her father *had* killed those women, what had been so incredibly different about him that he could harm others, seemingly without remorse? Surely there must've been some clue that she'd missed. But she couldn't figure out what it would be. Her father had been quiet and difficult to know because of that, but not every strong, silent male becomes a mass murderer.

She knew he'd had a difficult childhood, that he was brought up in a strict household where corporal punishment was sometimes taken to the extreme. But other than maintaining a rigid belief in the father as patriarch of the home, he didn't seem too affected by the past. He went to bed early, got up before dawn, worked hard and took care of everything in the house with a fastidiousness seldom seen in the American world of "easy come, easy go." He'd been a simple man. Or so she'd thought.

"What's wrong, Mommy?" Brianna asked, frowning when Madison didn't turn the page.

Madison closed her eyes, remembering. Her father had never been demonstrative, but he'd always had a roll of Lifesavers in his pocket for Brianna. Whenever they visited Grandma and Grandpa's house, Grandpa had let Brianna help him husk corn or snap peas or tinker in the garage.

That she'd trusted her father enough to let him get so

close to Brianna terrified Madison now, just in case he'd been what everyone said he was.

"Mommy?" Brianna asked, sounding worried.

Madison pulled herself out of the sea of memories long enough to force a smile for her daughter. "What, honey?"

"What's wrong?"

"Nothing. I was just thinking."

Uncertainty flickered in Brianna's eyes, but Madison easily distracted her with the next picture. "This is when Grandma baked you a Barbie cake for your second birthday, and Grandpa made you that playhouse in the backyard. Do you remember?"

Brianna's forehead wrinkled. "Daddy said he built the playhouse."

"No, it was Grandpa." Her father had come over to build the playhouse because the guy Danny hired didn't show. Madison remembered being upset because it was Sunday, a day Danny didn't have to work, yet he'd been gone anyway. Madison knew her father found it strange that Danny wasn't more of a support to her. She'd thought Ellis was going to say something about it as he left that day. Instead, he'd squeezed her shoulder—for him, the equivalent of a long conversation.

With her father, so much went unsaid. And yet she'd always known he loved her....

"Mommy, why are you crying?" Brianna asked.

Madison hadn't realized she *was* crying. Dashing a hand across her cheeks, she searched for words that might make things clear for her daughter. But she knew Brianna wouldn't understand even if she tried to explain. Madison herself didn't understand, at least not fully. The fact that someone she loved and trusted so deeply could ruin the whole essence of who he was for reasons she couldn't begin to fathom was simply confusing and painful. And that was before she considered the victims and their families and friends....

"That's enough for tonight," she said, closing the book. "It's time for bed."

A knock at the door stole Brianna's attention. She hopped off the couch to answer, but Madison caught her by the arm. "You know it's not safe to go to the door alone, especially after dark. I'll see who it is. You get your pajamas on."

"Mo-om," Brianna complained.

"You have school in the morning."

Her daughter's scowl deepened.

"Even princesses need their sleep," Madison said.

"But it might be Caleb."

Madison arched an eyebrow at her. "I thought you didn't like Caleb. I thought you didn't want me to let him move in."

"*I* don't like him," she said quickly, "but Elizabeth does."

If not for the spell cast by that darn photo album, Madison might have laughed. "Elizabeth isn't even here," she pointed out.

"She's in the bedroom. I'll get her."

Brianna scampered off and Madison set the photo album aside, trying to convince herself that *she* wasn't excited by the prospect of seeing Caleb.

She should've known Caleb was much too handsome and charismatic to fit smoothly into her life.

She tried telling herself their kiss was nothing as she headed down the hall, but it didn't feel like nothing when she opened the door. Caleb stood there, still wearing the same suit he'd been wearing this morning, with his tie loosened and his hair slightly tousled as though it had been a long, hard day.

"Are you okay?" she asked.

His gaze briefly lowered to her lips before he met her eyes, and Madison had the strangest impulse to slip into his arms and let him kiss her again.

That's crazy. I'm *crazy.*

"Yes," he said. "Everything okay here?"

"Fine."

"Good." He hesitated for a moment, nodded and started walking away. But then Brianna came running. "Caleb! Caleb, where are you going? I'm right here!"

He turned and gave her a half smile. "I thought you'd be asleep, half-pint."

"We were just looking at pictures," she announced.

He reached into his pocket. "Well, I'm glad you're up because I brought you something."

"A surprise?"

"Sort of."

"Did you hear that, Elizabeth? He brought us a surprise!" Hugging her stuffed rabbit, she twirled around.

"Just a small one," he said and, her curiosity piqued, Madison leaned forward to see him drop a large nugget of pyrite in her child's hand.

Brianna's eyes went round. "Is it *gold?*"

"Oh, no. Gold is nothing compared to this," he said. "Haven't you ever heard the story 'Jack and the Beanstalk?'"

"I've heard it," she said. "Mommy reads it to me all the time."

"Then you know about his magic beans."

She nodded enthusiastically.

"This rock is like those beans. It's—" he looked around as though he was afraid he might be overheard and dropped his voice "—magic."

"It is?" she asked, completely taken in. "What can it do?"

"It can remind you of important things."

"Like what?" Her voice was filled with the awe and reverence he'd inspired.

"When you're scared or worried about something, anything at all, and there's nothing you can do to make it better, you hold this rock tightly in one hand, like this." He took the rock from her and made a fist around it. "And if you close your eyes and listen, it'll whisper to you."

"What will it say?"

"It will remind you of all the people who love you and it will tell you that everything is going to be okay."

"*Really?*" she breathed.

"You have to listen hard," he said.

"Oh, I will."

Madison put a hand to her mouth to cover a smile. "It's time for you to take your magic rock to bed," she said when she'd composed herself.

"But Caleb just got here," Brianna complained.

"Maybe you can see him tomorrow."

Brianna was too busy examining her rock to move, so Madison gave her a gentle nudge.

"Thanks," Brianna told Caleb. "I won't lose it."

He winked at her, and she skipped down the hall, talking to Elizabeth the whole way. "Look, Elizabeth. It's magic...."

Madison leaned against the doorjamb, thinking Caleb looked so handsome with his loosened tie and unbuttoned collar that he could start a new fashion trend—rumpled chic. "You got a rock for me?" she asked.

His lips curved into a sexy smile. "You want one, too?"

"Only if it's magic."

He reached into his pocket and pulled out a fifty-cent piece. "Looks like a magic coin is the best I can offer."

"Will it whisper to me when I'm worried or afraid?"

"You bet," he said.

"What will it say?"

He took her hand and put the coin in the center of her palm. "To call me."

She curled her fingers around the metal, which was warm from his touch, and let that warmth travel through her. "You might be a little tough to get hold of," she said. "You've been gone a lot lately."

With a sigh, he loosened his tie even more. "This has been a tough week."

"You want to talk about it?"

"Not really."

She waited, hoping he'd change his mind, but he changed the subject instead. "What's been happening around here?"

"Same old stuff." She grinned. "None of it magic."

"Has Johnny been around?"

"No. For all I know he's back in jail. It generally doesn't take him long." She tucked her hair behind one ear. "What you did for Brianna was really nice. What made you think of her?"

"Thinking of you and Brianna isn't the problem."

"I didn't know there was a problem, at least where we're concerned."

He glanced over his shoulder at his dark cottage. "There isn't. I'm just tired."

She could see that from the small lines of fatigue around his eyes and bracketing his mouth, but she was hesitant to let him leave while he seemed so…somber and unsettled. "Would you like a glass of wine before you go? It might help you relax."

"I don't know." His eyes grew thoughtful. "You'd probably be better off to send me straight home to bed. You know that, don't you?"

Madison imagined Caleb lying in bed, the sheet pulled only to his waist, his chest and arms bare, and felt a flutter of excitement that told her he was definitely right. Yet she opened the door wider. "But my magic coin is telling me you could use a drink."

CHAPTER TEN

WHILE MADISON WENT to tuck Brianna in for the night, Caleb sipped the wine she'd given him and circled her living room. He knew he should head directly to the cottage, get a good night's sleep, gain some perspective on everything that had happened—including Susan's funeral earlier today, which had been almost surreal—and call Madison in the morning to see if he could somehow borrow her father's truck. If he was going to help Gibbons and still maintain his integrity, he needed to be careful not to get too close.

Unfortunately, that was easier said than done. Caleb had blown his plan to keep a safe distance the minute he'd pulled into the drive—by going to Madison's house instead of his own. He'd just needed to assure himself that she, at least, was all right. But he hadn't been able to walk away. The moment he saw her, he'd remembered the taste of her kiss and wanted to bury his face in her neck, let her surround him with her scent, the softness of her skin, the warmth of her heart....

"Almost done," she called.

He could hear the water running in the bathroom, where she was helping Brianna brush her teeth. He finished his wine, considered leaving, ignored what was best—again—and turned on the television.

The news came blaring into the room. Irritated by the noise, he turned it off and sat down to look through the photo album he found on the table. The words *Our Little Princess* were affixed to the cover, along with a 5x7 photo of Brianna as a baby, and he couldn't help thinking that Susan's parents probably had a similar album about her somewhere.

Pulling the book into his lap, Caleb opened it to pictures of Madison in a hospital bed, smiling proudly as she cradled a red-faced newborn. Standing next to her was a man who had to be her ex-husband, Danny.

Caleb stripped off his jacket and rolled up his sleeves, then scrutinized the man she'd been speaking to on the phone a few days ago. Danny wasn't anything like he'd expected. Short and balding, he looked too old for Madison. And even though he was *in* the picture, his body language suggested he didn't necessarily want to be. While Caleb read joy on Madison's face at the birth of her first child, Danny seemed far less interested.

"What a guy," he muttered, and turned the page to find more hospital photos, these featuring Madison's parents. Danny's backside or leg appeared here and there, so Caleb knew he wasn't the person behind the lens. But neither was he posing with the others. From the relative positioning of everyone in the room, Caleb got the impression that there'd been no love lost between Madison's parents and her husband, even while she was married.

The next few pictures were of Grandpa and the baby. Caleb held the book closer as he examined Ellis Purcell. What could Ellis have been thinking as he looked at his wife, daughter and brand-new granddaughter? Was he feeling any remorse for the women he'd murdered so brutally? Or was his mind a million miles away, anticipating his next victim?

If so, Purcell had outsmarted them all.

Or maybe he hadn't outsmarted anybody. Maybe they'd

set their sights on the wrong guy from the beginning. Gibbons was becoming more and more suspicious of Johnny. He thought Johnny might've picked up where his father had left off. Who else would have access to Purcell's truck? Gibbons had argued. Who else would have known exactly how to position the body except someone with inside information?

Caleb couldn't answer those questions. But *he* wasn't convinced that Johnny was their man. In Caleb's mind, Johnny didn't have the nerve to do what this killer did. This killer was cool and cunning, far more controlled than Johnny. Stealing a car was one thing. Sexually assaulting and strangling a woman was another. That kind of brutality took a deep-seated rage....

"She's finally asleep," Madison said, emerging from the hall.

"I hope you don't mind," Caleb said, indicating the photo album. "It was on the table."

She frowned slightly but crossed the room and sat on the sofa a few feet away from him, wearing the same jeans and tight-fitting T-shirt she'd had on when he arrived. "Brianna dragged it out."

"I take it this is your ex," he said, turning back to the picture of Danny on the front page.

She made a face and scooted closer to look. "Handsome devil, isn't he?"

Caleb smiled at her sarcasm. "I'm guessing he must've had other attributes."

"Not really."

He raised his brows in question.

"I've decided he was an escape," she said. "An escape from everything that was going on in my life at the time. I didn't realize it when I married him, of course. But I had to face the truth shortly after. Especially because my marriage didn't really change anything, at least not for the better.''

"You mean you couldn't get along with a guy who frowns at the birth of his own daughter?" he asked with feigned surprise.

Madison laughed. "That passes as a smile for Danny."

"How did such a love match unravel?"

"We weren't ever what you could call a 'love match.' Danny's persistence and his confidence that we were meant to be together finally won me over. He was five years older and had his life all neatly planned out. He was also pretty understanding about the investigation—at first. And I'd just lost my best friend, so I was particularly vulnerable."

She brought her legs up and wrapped her arms around them. "Most of all, I was longing to settle down, have a family of my own and live what I hoped would be a 'normal' life. He claimed he wanted those things, too."

Caleb still couldn't believe Danny had managed to get a woman like Madison to even look at him. "What changed after you were married?"

"Danny was a lot more complex and difficult than I'd ever expected. Emotionally, he was like a child—everything revolved around him. He could never see how what was happening with my father affected *me,* only how it affected *him.* And after the first few years, two more bodies were discovered and the investigation intensified, so he stopped being as understanding."

"How long were you married?"

"Seven years." She drew an audible breath. "But we had detectives following us around toward the end. So that probably made a big difference to his behavior."

Caleb got up to pour himself some more wine. "You knew the police were following you?"

"Sometimes the detectives would sit at the curb out front and wave to us as we went in and out. I think they were trying to intimidate us."

That must have been after Caleb quit the force, because he'd never seen Danny in person. Gibbons had always kept him busy taking care of the hundreds of peripheral people who had to be interviewed. "Did it work?" he called from the kitchen.

"It was intimidating, sure," she said. "It would be intimidating for anyone. But I don't think they were very smart to bully us."

"Why?"

She accepted the glass of wine he brought back for her. "Their tactics only made me more determined to remain firm. Not that it did me any good. When the killings started up again, the police felt so much pressure to solve the case, they transferred that pressure to us, including Danny. Pretty soon the neighbors were accustomed to seeing detectives coming and going from my house, but they certainly weren't happy about it."

She paused to take a sip of wine. "They formed their own opinions," she continued, "and hinted that if I'd only cooperate and 'do the right thing' it would all be over and my 'poor husband' could hold up his head again. They quit inviting us to neighborhood barbecue parties. They wouldn't let their children play with Brianna or come to our house." She sighed and shifted position so she could stretch her legs out in front of her. "Danny couldn't tolerate all the negative attention."

"Why didn't the two of you take your baby and move somewhere else? Somewhere the murders and the investigation weren't so publicized?" Caleb asked, thinking that if he were Danny, he would've done anything to protect his family.

"By the time we realized things weren't going to die down, Danny had landed a fantastic job at Waskell, Bolchevik and Piedmont. You've probably heard of them."

"The big engineering firm downtown?"

She nodded. "He wasn't willing to walk away from that. His job came before everything."

"Does he have other family in town?"

"His parents and one brother live in Spokane, so they're not far."

Caleb held his glass up to the light, studying the pale gold of the chardonnay. "What about you?"

"What about me?"

"Didn't *you* want to leave Seattle?"

"No, leaving was never an option. I'm my mother's only child. I had to stay here and support her and my father."

He crossed his feet at the ankles, finally beginning to relax and distance himself from the reality of what had happened to Susan, and her funeral, and the whole past week. "What about your parents? Didn't they ever consider moving?" he asked.

"No."

"Why not?"

"Toward the end, they were convinced the police would plant some sort of evidence if one of the detectives ever gained access to the house."

Caleb pictured Madison with a young baby, a bad marriage, a needy mother, a murder suspect for a father, and Gibbons and Thomas always at her heels, invading her privacy.

"I admire you for standing by your parents," he said, and was surprised by the fact that he actually meant it. At one time he'd thought her callous and irresponsible for refusing to cooperate with the police. But now that he understood her situation better, he could see exactly why she'd done what she had. Few women were as loyal as Madison Lieberman. She'd even hung on to Danny for seven years.

"I did what I thought was best," she said. "But now…"

Caleb finished the last of his wine and slid down so he could rest his head on the back of the couch. "But now?"

"Now I think I might have made a huge mistake."

"How so?" He glanced over at her, noting her grave expression.

"Can I trust you, Caleb?"

"Trust me?" he repeated, feeling numb. *Sure, you can trust me* was a little too blatant a lie, even if he told it for the right reasons. "That depends on what you're going to trust me with," he said, hedging.

She placed her hand on his forearm and let it slip down. Unable to resist, he turned his hand palm up when she reached it, lacing his fingers securely through hers.

She looked down at their entwined hands, and he could tell that, like his, her breathing had gone a little shallow.

"Sometimes I wish I'd never been born to Ellis Purcell," she said.

Mesmerized by the contact, by the delicacy of her slim fingers, Caleb was feeling a very powerful physical response. It didn't help that it was late, they were alone…and the last thing he wanted was to return to an empty house to brood about Susan.

On impulse, he lifted her hand to his mouth and brushed a kiss across her knuckles. "I thought you said he didn't do it."

She shivered as though a tingle had traveled through her body—through places he wished he could touch.

"I said I didn't *think* he did it." She swallowed visibly,

her eyes on his mouth as he rubbed his lips lightly across the back of her hand. "But I didn't know then what I know now."

What was she saying? He'd been so preoccupied with touching her that he hadn't been paying as much attention to her words as he should. Letting go, he sat up. "You want to run that by me one more time?"

She seemed a little startled by his abrupt change. "Nothing. It's the wine, that's all," she said, grabbing her wineglass. "I don't know what I'm saying."

"Madison?"

"What?"

"You said you didn't know then what you know now. What did you mean by that?"

She put the photo album on the coffee table. "Never mind. My heart still tells me there's no way my father could have hurt those women."

"But can you always trust your heart?" he murmured, cupping her chin so she had to look up at him.

She lowered her lashes, and he sensed that she was feeling the same attraction he was.

"I don't know," she said, "but I think everyone comes face-to-face with that question at least once in a lifetime. Don't you?"

Caleb was pretty sure he was coming face to face with it now. His heart was telling him to protect Madison, to let himself care about her. But his head was telling him he'd been right all along. She knew something she wasn't saying.

And for Susan, and Holly, and all the women in Seattle who deserved to be safe, he had to find out what it was.

WHAT HAD SHE BEEN thinking, nearly telling Caleb about what she'd found in the crawl space? Obviously she was lonelier than she'd realized. He just seemed so caring, so safe, she was tempted to open up to him about her father. And Danny. Throughout her marriage and subsequent divorce, she hadn't had anyone to talk to—not about personal matters. She couldn't burden her mother with the sad little details of her failing marriage. Not when Annette was already overwhelmed by having her husband accused of sexual assault and murder. And because of the investigation and her focus on Brianna, Madison didn't have any close friends.

After a good night's sleep, she'd do better at keeping their conversations centered on inconsequential facts, she told herself. But she wasn't sure she'd be able to fall asleep right away. Her body was still humming with the aftereffects of Caleb's lips grazing her knuckles. Every time she closed her eyes, she imagined his mouth and hands on other parts of her body....

The telephone rang, startling her as she headed down the hall to her bedroom. She halfway hoped it was Caleb, despite wanting to keep some emotional distance between them.

When she answered, her mother's voice came on the line. "We're vindicated," she said. "At last."

Madison pulled the phone away to look down at it before bringing it back to her ear. "Did I miss something?" she asked.

"It's true. Haven't you heard?"

"Heard what?"

"It's been all over the news."

"I don't watch the news or read the papers," Madison said. "I've had enough of the press for the next ten years. So you might want to tell me what you're so excited about."

"The police have found another victim," her mother said. "Another woman's been strangled."

Madison's breath seemed to lodge in her throat. "You sound as though you think this is *good* news," she said when she could speak again.

"It *is* good news, for us. Don't you understand what it means?"

"It means another person has suffered untold depravity and violence. It means some other family has been deprived of a loved one."

"I'm sorry for all of that," her mother said tersely. "But I didn't do anything to cause it. And this proves that your father wasn't the Sandpoint Strangler, just as we've been saying all along."

"How?" Madison asked.

"This victim fit the same profile the earlier ones did. She was strangled and positioned just like the others. It's obviously the same killer."

Her knees suddenly weak, Madison felt behind her for the couch and sank down onto it. She didn't know what to think or how to feel. Relieved? Fearful? Doubtful? Hopeful? Somehow she seemed to be experiencing them all at once. "How do you know it's not a copycat?" she breathed.

"Because Ellis didn't kill those women, so there's nothing to copy. And now that it's happened again and he's gone, the police will have to turn their attention to finding the real killer, and the truth will finally come out."

"This doesn't make sense," Madison muttered to herself.

"What did you say?"

She swallowed hard. "Nothing. I— Where did they find her?"

"A few miles from the house."

"Who was she?"

"A twenty-six-year-old single woman who lived near the university and worked at Nordstrom. I think her name was Susan."

Susan. Madison closed her eyes. What if there was something in that box she'd found under the house that could've saved that woman? What if there was something that might help the police now? She had to take it to them, let them sort it out....

"Mom?"

"What, dear?"

"If...if I happened to stumble on something that would...that could possibly figure in the case, you'd want me to come forward with it, wouldn't you? Even if it made Dad look as though he might really have—"

"Madison!" her mother interrupted, her voice instantly sharp.

"What?"

"I don't think you understand what that investigation did to me, what it did to your father."

"I do, Mom. That's why I haven't said anything so far."

"Ellis was innocent! I'll go to my grave believing that."

"I loved him, too. I still love him. But—"

"Do you know why your father killed himself?" her mother asked, now openly weeping.

Madison thought she could come up with a few plausible reasons. She certainly knew what his critics would say. But she didn't bother answering. Her mother's question was rhetorical. "Why?"

"To put an end to what you and I were suffering. He hated that he couldn't save us from the harassment we were receiving from the police, the community, even our neighbors. So he ended it." She sniffed and gulped for the breath to continue. "He gave up his life so we could live normally again."

"He's gone now, Mom," Madison said softly. "We don't have to protect him anymore."

"I don't care. I won't betray him. And no daughter of mine would betray him, either."

Tension clawed at Madison's stomach. Her father was gone, couldn't have killed this latest victim. But because of that box there *had* to be a connection, didn't there? "You're not listening. I've found some articles that—"

"You could have a videotape and I wouldn't believe it," Annette cut in, her voice vehement.

Madison covered her eyes. "Faith is one thing, Mom. Sticking your head in the sand is another."

"All I know is what my heart tells me is true," her mother said.

Those words sounded like an echo of Madison's conversation earlier with Caleb. But it wasn't surprising, considering she and her mother had relied on that argument for years. "Can you always trust your heart?" she asked, repeating his question.

"If you can't trust your heart, what can you trust?" her mother said, and hung up.

CHAPTER ELEVEN

MADISON SHIVERED as she stood outside a few minutes later, waiting for Caleb to rouse himself from sleep and answer her knock. She tried to tell herself to go back home and go to bed. But she was too upset. Her mother would never forgive her if she turned that box over to the police.

But Madison wasn't sure she'd be able to forgive herself if she didn't.

It all came down to what *she* really believed, and she no longer knew what that was. Her father wasn't the type to hurt anyone. But if he hadn't murdered Lisa McDonna, why was her locket in the crawl space of his house?

Caleb opened the door wearing a pair of hastily donned jeans, judging by the top button, which was undone, and nothing else. His hair mussed from sleep, he flipped on the porch light and squinted against the sudden brightness. "Madison? Is something wrong?"

Suddenly, she felt awkward. When she was at home, it had seemed natural to come to him. She was so tired of being alone.

"I…" She fell silent because what she was feeling couldn't be distilled into a few simple words.

"Did something happen?" he asked.

She held out her hand to reveal the coin he'd given her. That was really all she'd come for, wasn't it? To collect on his promise that she could call him if she ever needed reassurance?

Taking her by the elbow, he guided her inside, closing the door behind them. They stood in the dim light of the living room, the shutters casting shadowed lines across Caleb's face. "Tell me what's wrong," he said.

"They found another p-poor woman." She shivered again, even though it was warm in the cottage.

Pulling her close, he put his arms around her. "You just heard?"

He seemed so solid and real, so in control at a time when she felt as if she was spinning out into space.

She closed her eyes and nodded, concentrating only on the heat flowing through her cheek, which she'd pressed to his bare chest. This was what she needed. This was all she needed. A few minutes of contact with another human being...

"Just tell me everything's going to be okay," she whispered.

He brushed back her hair and placed a featherlight kiss on her temple. "It might get worse before it gets better, Madison, but..." He hesitated, and she leaned back far enough to look up at him. "I'll be here if you need me," he finished, and she smiled because it sounded so much like a promise.

THE SLIGHTLY FLORAL SCENT of Madison's perfume and the softness of her body beneath the baggy sweats she was wearing kick-started Caleb's libido. He knew he'd be much better off sending her back to her own house—right away—but he couldn't seem to let go of her. She'd come to him for comfort, and he wanted to give her that much. Obviously she wasn't as insensitive about the suffering of others as he'd once believed.

Or maybe he couldn't let go of her because he needed a little comfort himself. The past four days hadn't been easy. He'd had a difficult time grasping the fact that such evil had touched his own life in a very personal way. Holly had been almost childlike in the way she'd clung to him, irritating yet sympathetic in her neediness. Her parents treated him as though he and Holly had never divorced, and had been leaning on him to deal with the police and also with the funeral home regarding Susan's burial. Beyond that, every extra minute had been spent helping Detective Gibbons. Caleb had been tracking down Johnny's friends, from previous schoolmates to cellmates, and some friends and neighbors of Tye's, too. He'd told them he was a private investigator working on a murder case and showed them pictures of Susan. And he'd haunted the pizza parlor and surrounding neighborhood, looking for the driver of that blue Ford in the picture—all to no avail.

He felt exhausted, frustrated, torn. Yet he still had some difficult decisions to make. Like how far he was willing to go to manipulate Madison into lending him Ellis's truck. He knew Gibbons would be calling him—if not tomorrow, then the next day.

"I just don't understand it," Madison murmured. The movement of her lips, tickling his bare skin, was enough to make his heart race. "I don't understand why anyone would want to hurt and humiliate another human being."

Caleb pressed her closer, enjoying the sensation of her against him while consciously working to keep his thoughts from turning sexual. Having Madison in his bed would give *him* a lot of comfort, but he was pretty sure sex wasn't the type of comfort *she* had in mind—and it certainly wasn't a memory she'd appreciate once she learned who he was. "Psychologists claim most violence is about power."

"I don't see how hurting someone or something weaker makes a man feel better about himself."

"Neither do I," he said, admiring the slight tilt at the end of her nose and the fullness of her lips. He remembered the softness of those lips all too well....

Before the temptation to abandon his morals could strike again, he stepped back, grabbed a sweatshirt he'd left on the couch earlier and held it out to her. "Put this on, and I'll walk you over to your place."

She pulled the sweatshirt over her head while he held the door.

"I'm sorry for waking you," she said as they crossed the drive.

Caleb jammed his hands in his pockets so that he wouldn't touch her. Now that he'd created some space between them, he needed to maintain it. If she cozied up to him again, he doubted he'd be able to stop himself from at least testing how she might respond to his desire for deeper intimacy. When the truth came out, she'd end up hating him for making love to her under such deception. But there *was* the argument that she was going to hate him anyway....

"No worries," he said. "My door's always open."

She smiled. "I like you, Caleb Trovato," she said. "I'm glad you moved in."

They'd reached her door. Caleb leaned a shoulder against the front of the house while she stood at the threshold.

He liked her, too. Which only made his next question that much more difficult to ask.

Fixing a picture of Susan's battered body in his mind, he called up the rage he felt at whoever had hurt her. "By the way," he said. "Any chance you know someone who owns a truck I could borrow?"

"What for?"

"I have a friend who's moving and could really use some help."

"When do you need it?"

"Tomorrow or Saturday, if possible."

She seemed somewhat hesitant, as though she was going to refuse him. But then her smile returned. "My dad's truck is just sitting in the garage. I'll see what I can do."

IT RAINED THE FOLLOWING day, tiny drops that quickly turned into a constant drizzle.

Madison grumbled at the damp, foggy weather, wishing she didn't have to drive over to the mainland to get her father's truck. But the memory of Caleb taking her into his arms when she was so upset last night made her want to go to the extra trouble. He'd been there for her. She wanted to be there for him.

"That's what friends are for," she muttered, and dashed out of the office building that housed her business, ducking beneath her briefcase until she could reach her car.

After starting the motor, she turned on her wiper blades, then backed out of her parking space. As soon as she was in line to catch the next ferry, she forced herself to do what she'd been dreading all morning—call her mother.

"Madison, is it you?" her mother asked. After their conversation the night before, Annette's voice was noticeably cool. "You're cutting in and out."

A moment later, Madison inched forward along with the other cars, and her cell reception improved. "Can you hear me now?"

"Yes. Are you in the car?"

"I'm about to cross over to the mainland. I'm on my way to your place."

"Are you showing the house?"

Madison felt a twinge of guilt, because she'd had several calls on her mother's house from both agents and buyers. Just as she'd feared, some of her callers seemed more interested in the house's dramatic history and getting a peek at it than in purchasing the property. Still, there'd been some legitimate calls, as well. Legitimate calls she hadn't returned. And she'd put off the people she'd already talked to, trying to avoid selling the house until she could decide what to do with the box hidden in the crawl space. "Not today," she said. "I'm getting some interest on it, though. Maybe I'll be able set up a tour for tomorrow or Sunday."

"So why are you coming here? Brianna's in school, isn't she?"

"I'm just dropping off the comps I said I'd put together for you."

"The comps?"

"The list of homes in your area that have sold in the past few months, along with the price of each."

"Oh, right. Okay."

"And—" Madison took a deep breath "—and I was hoping to borrow Dad's truck."

Dead silence. Madison knew it was her imagination, but it felt as though the temperature had dropped another ten degrees. "Mom?" she said, cranking up her heater.

"What's going on?" her mother demanded. "Why are you suddenly interested in the truck?"

"Nothing's going on. I want to lend it to a friend, that's all."

"You know how your father felt about that vehicle."

"Of course I know." Once that witness had placed Ellis's truck at Anna Tyler's apartment, he'd become increasingly afraid to drive it. He'd parked the truck in his garage to be sure no one had access to it. At the time, the police were so determined that Ellis was their strangler and so desperate to solve the case, Madison had believed her father's concerns to be legitimate. But now she had to wonder if his paranoia revolved around a fear that Seattle detectives would plant evidence—or find it.

"This has nothing to do with the police or anything else," she continued. "I'm just trying to help Caleb, my new renter."

Another long pause. "Do you have to help him like this?"

"Mom, I'm tired of being paranoid," Madison said. "Caleb needs the truck for only a few hours. For once I'd like to respond as a *normal* person would. For once I'd like to say, 'Sure, no problem,' as if we don't have anything to hide."

"We *don't* have anything to hide," her mother replied.

"Then why can't he borrow the truck?"

Madison could tell Annette didn't like being cornered, but she'd already decided to throw her support Caleb's way. She couldn't see how it would hurt anything to help him out.

"I'll leave the keys on the front porch," her mother said. Then, without a further word, she hung up.

MADISON STARED DOWN at the bulge beneath the mat on her mother's stoop. Evidently her mother wasn't going to soften and come to the door. Well, Madison wasn't about to let Annette's disapproval change her mind. She'd spent the past twelve years supporting and protecting her parents. Surely she could do a friend a favor.

She just wished that favor didn't entail entering the

garage where her father had ended his life. Situated at the very back of the property, the garage opened onto the alley. It was hidden by trees and overgrown with ivy. She hadn't been anywhere near it, or the workshop inside, since her father had shot himself. There hadn't been any reason to go there. Tye had cleaned up the mess, and her mother always parked in the front drive, closer to the house.

Bending, she left the folder of information she'd gathered for her mother on the step and removed the keys from beneath the mat. Then she rounded the house, opened the gate and stared out over the wide expanse of lawn dotted with ivy-covered trees.

This was where she'd grown up knowing a father who loved her....

A father who might have murdered eleven women.

She thought of the photo album Brianna had dragged out from under her bed, and felt her throat begin to burn. She simply couldn't reconcile those memories with what she'd found in the crawl space. She and Ellis might have had occasional differences while she was growing up, but those differences were nothing out of the ordinary. When she was a child, he'd let her follow him around all day and help him in the yard. He'd bought her a big piggy bank and always gave her his change. He'd even spent his "hard-earned money" on a swing set when she begged for the shiny metal kind that came from the store instead of the wooden one he'd planned to build. When she was a teenager, he'd provided her with a car and helped her maintain it. Sometimes he'd surprised her by filling it with gas.

A man like that couldn't be evil. He couldn't be a loving father *and* a twisted killer—could he? Wouldn't she have seen some evidence before now that her father was capable of such things? Wouldn't she have *known?*

Maybe the friends and relatives of killers like Ted Bundy felt the same way....

Whether Annette was really at the window or not, her mother's eyes seemed to bore holes in her back as Madison started across the yard. Her heels sank in the wet earth, slowing her progress, but she reached the safety of the overhang before the misty rain turned into pellet-size drops.

Unlocking the padlock, she turned the handle and used her shoulder to open the stiff, creaky door.

As she'd anticipated, it was mostly dark inside—dark and damp and close.

Leaving the padlock hanging, she stepped hesitantly across the threshold of her father's workshop and closed the door to keep out the rain. But what she found wasn't what she'd been expecting.

A wheel of jars containing various nails and screws hung from the ceiling. Her father's old black radio sat on the dusty window ledge, its antennae bent but still extended. A gray filing cabinet stood in the far corner, next to a scarred wooden desk. Which wasn't unusual. But there was also garbage tossed around, mostly sacks and cups from various fast-food restaurants. A dirty old pillow and blanket had been discarded on the floor. There were cigarette butts all over and a plastic lid teeming with ashes. And the whole place reeked of cigarette smoke and—marijuana.

What was going on? From the look of things, someone had recently been living inside the workshop. But how did he get in? Who was he? And what had happened to her father's guns? The rack that normally held his rifles and the shotgun that had ended his life was empty.

Her heart pounding in her ears, Madison opened the door she'd just come through and left it ajar, so she could make a quick exit if necessary. Then she peeked through the door that led to the two-stall garage.

There was no noise or movement. Whoever had been living in the workshop seemed to be gone now.

Slipping into the garage, she flipped the switch to the fluorescent light hanging from the ceiling. It buzzed and flickered, but even before it came on she could see that the window on the far side of the garage, facing away from the house, had been broken and was letting in the wind and rain.

So now she knew how whoever it was had gotten in....

Madison surveyed the place, taking in the empty stall to the right, the blue Ford parked on the left. Not far from the window she saw what appeared to be a filthy pair of jeans lying on the cement floor—and something else. Madison couldn't tell exactly what. She was just moving closer, trying to identify it, when the garage door suddenly rolled up.

Whirling, she found herself staring at Johnny.

"Johnny, you scared me to death," she said, putting her hand to her chest. "What are you doing here?"

He looked her up and down, then glanced beyond her. "Are you alone?"

Madison was breathing heavily, but she managed to nod. "Why?"

"I don't want your mother snooping around out here, hassling me."

Madison arched her brows. "She happens to own the place, remember?"

He shrugged. "My father was the one who paid the mortgage. I figure putting me up for a few weeks is the least he can do. It's tough for a guy like me to find a house these days."

Maybe that would change—if he was willing to work. "How have you been getting by?" she asked.

"One day at a time."

Madison thought of Ellis's guns and was willing to bet Johnny had pawned them. He'd probably taken other things that had belonged to their father, as well. "Did you ever get hold of Tye?"

"He doesn't want anything to do with me," he answered shortly. He crossed to the object she'd been trying to make out a few seconds earlier, and she immediately realized it was a small pipe, obviously for drugs. Of course.

"Why not?" she asked.

"I told you before, he and Sharon aren't getting along."

"You never told me why."

"Beats the hell out of me." He dug through the pockets of the discarded jeans and came up with a lighter. "Hey, you don't have twenty bucks, do ya?"

Madison felt a sinking sensation as she looked at her brother. He was never going to be in control of his life. He wouldn't even try. "No."

"Well, don't say anything about me being here to your mother."

Madison pinched the bridge of her nose, trying to quell her irritation. "Just tell me you're not on the run."

"What, you think I busted out of prison or something?" he said with a laugh. "I got out on good behavior. You can even call and check if you want."

She decided she believed him. "I'll give you a week. After that, you've got to find somewhere else. Mom's selling the house, and I'll be showing people through it."

"No shit." He shoved his straggly bangs out of his eyes, stuffed his pipe in the pocket of his jean jacket and searched for a cigarette. "And I was just growing fond of this place."

"Then you're the only one," she said, eager to leave. She didn't like being in Johnny's presence. She wanted to love him, did love him because he was her brother, but she couldn't relate to the type of person he'd become. He was throwing his life away, which was a terrible tragedy—but unless he *wanted* to change, she couldn't help him.

"So what brings you out here, all dressed up?" He spoke around the cigarette he was lighting.

Madison glanced down at her suit and the keys in her hand. "I need to use the truck."

"Oh, yeah?" He shoved his lighter back into his pocket and took a long drag. "Well, sorry it's a little low on gas. I didn't have the money to fill it up."

"You've been driving Dad's truck?"

"Why not?" he said. "Nobody else does."

"Where'd you get the keys?"

Smoked curled toward the ceiling from his cigarette as he clasped it between two dirty fingers and took another drag. "He always kept a spare out here. You didn't know?"

She shook her head.

"I guess there are a lot of things you never knew about dear old Dad, right?" He put his hands around his throat in a choking gesture and started making jerking motions and guttural noises, then laughed.

"I've got to go. I'm late for an important meeting," she said, and hurried to climb into the truck. She'd been planning to search it extensively, but she just wanted to get away. Besides, it looked completely clean. Leaving her own car parked out front, she backed out of the drive without bothering to wave.

CHAPTER TWELVE

CALEB SPENT THE MORNING trying to console Holly—who was still taking her sister's death very hard—and the afternoon with Gibbons, going over the evidence that had been found at the site of Susan's body. When he finally pulled into Madison's driveway, he found a shiny black Jaguar sitting in his parking spot. He might have wondered who drove such an expensive vehicle, but the license plate, "Lieber 1," gave him a pretty good indication.

The Jag's window slid smoothly down as he approached, and he immediately recognized the pasty-faced man he'd seen in Brianna's baby book.

"Can I help you?" Caleb asked.

Danny leaned away from the open window to save his expensive suit from the light rain as he studied Caleb. "Don't tell me *you're* the renter."

"Why not?" Caleb asked.

"Because a man your age ought to be able to afford his own place, that's why."

"I like it here," Caleb said carelessly.

"Where's Madison?"

"I'm assuming she's at work."

He made a show of checking his Rolex watch. "I pick up Brianna every other Friday at this time. She's supposed to be here."

"Did you try Madison's cell?"

"She's not answering."

"She must have caller ID," Caleb said.

Because he'd spoken with a smile, it took Danny a moment to realize he'd been insulted. When he caught on, a muscle jumped in his cheek. "If there's one thing I hate, it's a wise ass."

Caleb crouched down, so they'd be nearly at eye level, and rested his arms on the door. "That's interesting," he said, keeping his voice congenial, "because the one thing I hate is a man who bullies a woman."

"I don't know what you're talking about."

"I think you do."

Danny's eyes narrowed. "What happens between Madison and me is none of your business."

"You're right," Caleb said. "And if you want to keep it that way, I suggest you start treating her with some respect."

"You know nothing about our relationship."

"I know she's the mother of your child. That's enough to tell me you should be treating her better than you do."

"She won't have Brianna much longer," Danny said, but before Caleb could respond, Madison pulled into the drive—in her father's truck.

She did it, Caleb thought, standing. She got the truck. And now he had to take it to Gibbons....

His gaze automatically shifted toward the tires. He'd seen the plaster mold Gibbons had made of the track left near Susan's body, but he couldn't tell anything from this distance, especially in the rain. Comparing tire treads was usually a very difficult, laborious process. Only the fact that the mold revealed unique damage created by something sharp gave him any hope that Gibbons might be able to make a determination simply by looking.

"Sorry I'm late," she said, hurrying to help Brianna

out of the cab. "The ferry was backed up when I came across earlier, and that threw off my schedule for the whole afternoon."

"What are you doing with your father's truck?" Danny demanded, getting out of his car.

At the irritation in his voice, Brianna glanced uncertainly from her father to her mother. "Hi, Caleb," she said, sidling closer to him.

Caleb laid a reassuring hand on her shoulder.

"Caleb needs to borrow it," Madison said.

"For what?" Danny asked.

"He has a friend who's moving."

"I guess he's never heard of U-Haul."

"There's no need to rent a truck when I've got one available," she argued.

"Caleb gave me a magic rock," Brianna piped up.

Danny looked her way, and his face reddened when he saw her standing so close to Caleb. "Get your things, Brianna," he said curtly. "Leslie's waiting for us."

Madison's little girl hesitated briefly before running off.

"Please try to have her home earlier this Sunday," Madison said as her ex-husband slid into the Jag's soft-looking leather interior. "You've been bringing her back too late, which makes it hard for her to get up for school."

"I'll do as I damn well please," he snapped.

Madison leaned down to see through his open window. "The visitation papers say five o'clock, Danny."

He opened his mouth to make some sort of retort, but Brianna came charging out of the house at that moment. He glanced at his daughter, then at Caleb, and barely waited for Brianna to climb in before he threw the car into Reverse. Narrowly missing Caleb's Mustang and Madison's father's truck, he whipped out of the drive, leaving Caleb and Madison staring after him.

"THAT WENT WELL, don't you think?" Madison said sarcastically, wondering what was going to happen next.

"I don't think Brianna should spend any time with that guy," Caleb replied, his eyebrows lowered.

Madison chuckled as she watched Danny's car disappear. "He's normally not that bad. He's just bugged that I let you move in. When I do things he doesn't approve of, it reminds him that he no longer has control over me, which means he no longer has complete control of Brianna. That's why he's always coaxing Brianna to come and live with him. His new wife is pregnant, and Danny keeps trying to use the baby as a draw. 'Don't you want to live with your little sister? She's going to miss you when you're gone.'"

"In that photo album, he didn't even seem excited about her birth," Caleb said.

"He wasn't ready for children when we had her. He never got up with Brianna once during the night. Never baby-sat her on his own."

"So what's changed?"

"I guess he's grown up. He seems to be a much better father now."

"You can't tell he's grown up from the way he treats you."

"Like I said, he usually isn't quite *that* bad. I think he was showing off for your benefit."

"I'm not impressed."

"That's just how he is. Don't let him bother you. All I can do is save my dollars and cents for when he takes me back to court."

"Which might be sooner than you think," Caleb said. "He mentioned you might not have Brianna much longer."

"He always says that. But I'll fight him until my dying

day, if that's what it takes, and he knows it." She shifted her briefcase to her other hand, feeling eager to get out of her nylons. She couldn't let herself obsess over Brianna going with Danny. He'd brought Brianna home safely every time. She had to trust that he'd do so again.

Still, she said a silent prayer for her daughter's well-being and promised herself she'd call later and check up. "In any case, I'm free for the weekend," she said. "And the break couldn't have come at a better time. What do you want me to make us for dinner?"

"I was thinking steak and lobster."

"I don't have any lobster."

He slung an arm around her shoulders. "That's why I'm taking you out."

MADISON STARED AT HERSELF in the mirror, wondering if she was really daring enough to wear the tight little black dress. She'd bought it two years ago. She'd hoped it would help her and Danny's love life, their marriage in general, if she transformed herself from "tired mom" to "tempting siren." But Danny hadn't given her much of a chance to try before dropping his "I'm in love with someone else" bomb. Then the years of struggling to please him, to keep the family together, were over.

It really wasn't a "Danny" sort of dress, anyway. Formfitting and rather short, with spaghetti straps, it said "sleek and sophisticated," not "hard-core and raunchy," which was much more in line with Danny's sexual tastes.

Caleb, on the other hand, seemed like a man who'd appreciate a dress like this—and that made wearing it a little risky. But in some ways Madison didn't care. She was feeling better than she'd felt in ages, probably because she was opening herself up to new friendships. She'd won a small battle with the past when she'd taken her father's truck today. And she was actually able to laugh at Danny this evening instead of letting him upset her. Certainly that was progress, and it deserved some reward. What more appropriate reward was there than to feel five years younger and momentarily free from all the emotional baggage she'd been carrying?

She applied some glossy pink lipstick, stood back to assess the effect, and decided it was exactly the look she was going for. Then she began digging around in her makeup drawer for a matching shade of nail polish. Tonight she was going to paint her fingers and her toes, go barelegged and dab perfume right between her breasts.

"I'm getting hungry. Are you ready yet?" Caleb called from the living room. "You looked good before you went back there. What could be taking so long?"

What could be taking so long? Madison smiled at herself. It was just about time to show him.

CALEB KNEW HE WAS in trouble the second Madison emerged from the back of the house. She was all feminine curves, creamy skin and warm smiles, with a little shiny lipstick thrown in for good measure. And he'd been susceptible to her beauty *before* she'd gone and dressed like some kind of sex goddess.

He allowed himself to indulge in a brief fantasy—where he peeled down one of those skinny straps and let his lips skim her bare shoulder. But then he told himself to get a grip, and shoved his hands in his pockets to hide the fact that she'd had a very immediate effect on him.

"All set?" he said.

"I think so. I just need to find my house keys so I can lock up."

She crossed in front of him on her way to the kitchen,

and he breathed deeply as he caught a whiff of her perfume.

"You don't think I'm too dressed up, do you?" she asked, returning to the living room after she'd found her house keys.

He let his eyes climb her legs to the clingy black dress, her creamy shoulders, pouty lips and wide eyes, and began to say she might want to put on something that wouldn't interfere with his thinking. But that wasn't what came out. "You look perfect," he said.

"Good." Her smile seemed to have a direct link to his groin.

Just don't do anything your mother wouldn't approve of, he told himself. Fair-minded and conservative as Justine was, he knew that adhering to her standards would keep him well on this side of ethical. But he'd never been very good at listening to other people, even his mother.

Clearing his throat, he opened the door for Madison. "Let's go."

THE CANDLELIGHT at the restaurant cast everything in a golden glow that added to the surreal quality of the night. Madison reveled in the romantic lighting, the expensive wine Caleb had selected and the intimacy of their little table in the outer reaches of Rudy's Lobster Bay, an excellent seafood restaurant in downtown Seattle. Waiters and waitresses bustled past in tuxedos, yet she and Caleb seemed almost alone.

"Tell me about your childhood," Madison said, taking a bite of filet mignon smothered with mushrooms. "You told me you grew up on Fidalgo Island, but you haven't mentioned much about your family. Do you have siblings?"

"Just an older sister, Tamara. And believe me, with Tamara one sibling is more than enough."

"Why?"

"I never liked her much." He smiled ruefully.

Madison sipped her wine. "Seriously?"

"Maybe not completely, but she was a pain. She was one of those kids who had to tattle at every opportunity. No matter what I did, she ran to tell our parents."

"What did you do that made her want to tell on you?"

"Nothing big," he said, separating the meat of his lobster tail from the shell. "I once kicked a hole in the wall with my cowboy boots and tried to say I didn't know how it got there, but she didn't hesitate to set my parents straight."

"Why'd you kick the wall?"

"She was trying to make me dress up as a girl for Halloween and I wanted to be a cowboy," he said with a laugh. "I had the boots and everything, obviously."

"How old were you?"

"Five."

Madison enjoyed envisioning the rough-and-tumble little boy Caleb had probably been. A cowboy was definitely the better choice for his personality. "I see. Then you were perfectly justified."

He nodded as he began cutting his lobster. "My point exactly."

"Did you get in trouble for it?" she asked.

"Not as much trouble as I got in for other things."

"Like…"

"Like the time my sister was baby-sitting and told me I couldn't have any frogs in the house."

Madison held her glass while the waitress came around with more water. "I take it you didn't listen," she said to Caleb.

"I snuck several into my room because I couldn't see how a few frogs would hurt anything."

"And?"

He dipped some lobster meat in butter and offered it to her. She wasn't typically fond of seafood, which was why she'd ordered a steak. But he made lobster look downright tasty. Leaning over, she ate from his hand, enjoying the fact that he'd thought to share with her, more than the sweet tenderness of the meat.

His eyes lingered on her mouth, and it took him a moment to get back to his story. "And then the frogs got loose and when my mother came home, she stepped on one in the laundry room."

"Ick," Madison said with a shudder. "But I don't see how Tamara had anything to do with that."

"Oh, she was right there, saying, 'I told him not to do it, Mother, I told him you wouldn't like it.'"

Madison chuckled at his imitation of his tattletale sister and tried her steamed vegetables. They were as delicious as the rest of the food. "You must have been a little hellion."

"I don't think I was a hellion. Trouble just followed me around."

"What about your father?" she asked, taking a bite of her garlic mashed potatoes. "Didn't he ever stick up for you?"

"My mother's pretty formidable. He generally doesn't go against her, even for me."

"So she wears the pants in the family?"

"Not really. The power play between my parents isn't too out of whack. My mother's just so...organized and sure of herself, everyone naturally falls in line behind her. Sometimes I call her the Oracle."

"Because she's the font of all wisdom?"

"Exactly. She's always right, no matter what."

Madison couldn't help wishing her own mother was more "organized," more confident, so she wouldn't have to worry about her as much. But then, Caleb's mom hadn't been forced to deal with what Annette had.

"What do you think about that woman they found?" she asked, suddenly changing the subject.

"What woman?"

"The strangled woman."

He stopped eating for a moment. "What do you mean?"

"Have you been following the story?"

"A little."

"Do you think it's a copycat?"

He offered her another bite of lobster, but she waved it away. "I guess anything's possible," he said.

She nodded, thinking about the box waiting for her at her mother's house. She had to do something about it tonight. Tomorrow was Saturday morning—a likely time to have Toby start work.

But for now she was going to forget that her father had ever been involved in a murder investigation, and continue to enjoy herself.

"You're slowing down," Caleb said, nodding toward her plate. "Don't tell me you're full."

"I can't fit anything else inside this dress."

His eyes flicked over her. "It's worth it."

Madison felt a liquid warmth swirl through her. "I'm glad I finally had the chance to wear it. I bought it two years ago, but it's been buried at the back of my closet ever since."

"Sort of like carrying a concealed weapon, huh?"

"What?"

"Never mind," he said, chuckling. He paused for a

minute, then tipped his wineglass toward her. "You're sending me mixed signals. You know that, don't you?"

She leaned back, crossed her legs and took another sip of wine. "Mixed signals?" she repeated, as though she didn't already know perfectly well what he meant.

"You tell me you don't want a relationship, but you wear something that's—" he hesitated, then whistled softly "—guaranteed to stop me dead in my tracks."

"I didn't know this dress came with guarantees like that," she teased.

"It should have. Are you going to tell me what's up?"

She drank the last of her wine. "Okay, I admit to wanting to turn your head," she said. "I like the way you make me feel when you look at me, as though…"

"As though what?"

His voice was a little deeper, rougher than usual, and Madison had to work hard not to think about that kiss he'd given her at her door.

"Just 'as though,'" she said, slightly embarrassed. "But a little flirting is harmless, right? I mean, you're not interested in a relationship any more than I am. You're moving to San Francisco at the end of your lease. This is just a temporary…friendship."

He ate the last bite of his lobster. "I should probably tell you that this isn't feeling very much like friends to me."

"I'm not sure what it's feeling like to me," she said. "I was more or less robbed of the past twelve years. Maybe I'm trying to recapture some of the carefree fun I missed, some of the fun other people generally enjoy in their early twenties."

He held her gaze. "I guess I can understand that."

"Great." She smiled, eager to talk about something else. She didn't want to categorize their relationship or commit herself to any one mode of behavior. She liked looking at the night as an empty canvas, and refused to let the prudence that governed all her actions intercede at this juncture. "Then you won't mind taking me dancing."

He considered her for a few seconds. "Dancing."

"I want to have a night on the town, take a walk on the wild side for a change."

His eyebrows lifted. "How wild are you talking?"

Madison felt a sudden heady rush of excitement. "How wild are you willing to get?"

CHAPTER THIRTEEN

SHE WANTED TO GET *WILD*?

Caleb sat at the table he'd been lucky enough to snag as a small group left the crowded bar, which was pulsing with music and movement, and watched Madison walk away from him toward the ladies' room. He admired her legs for probably the millionth time, noticed a few other guys doing it, too, and knew there wasn't any way he'd be able to live up to his mother's standard of decency tonight. Ever since he'd seen Madison in that dress, he'd been interested in only one thing.

The waitress came by, but he waved her away because he was going to end the evening right now. If he allowed himself to show Madison Lieberman the meaning of wild as he saw it, he'd be taking misrepresentation to a whole new level. And when she eventually found out who he was, she wouldn't thank him. To say the least...

She emerged from the bathroom, and he stood up, planning to guide her out and drive her home. It was the right thing to do. If she wanted to go dancing, she could go with someone else. But when she reached him, she slipped her hand in his and said, "They're playing John Mayer's 'Wonderland.' I love that song. Can we dance?"

Caleb hesitated. He really didn't want to make the situation any more complicated than it already was. But she was looking up at him with those wide eyes, wearing an expression of such hopeful expectation that he couldn't bring himself to deny her.

Knowing he'd probably pay a high price for the next few minutes, he nodded and led her out onto the dance floor, where she put her arms around his neck and snuggled up to him. He could feel her breasts against his chest as John sang about the wonder of discovering a woman, and at that point he couldn't even *think* about leaving.

There was unethical...and then there was irresistible.

MADISON WAS EXHAUSTED when Caleb brought her home, but she'd had a wonderful time. She hadn't laughed so much since before she'd married Danny, and she didn't want the evening to end. Not yet. After Caleb went home she'd have to revert to her old life—become Ellis Purcell's daughter again and deal with the contents of the box beneath her mother's house. She still wasn't sure what to do with it. But she couldn't leave it where it was.

"Would you like to come in for a nightcap?" she asked as he walked her to the door, hoping to hold reality at bay a little longer.

He shook his head. "Not tonight."

"Why not?"

"It's late."

"You're going to be home by midnight, and you drank nothing but soda at the club," she said with a laugh. "I guess your idea of wild is about as tame as mine."

"I doubt it," he said dryly.

She raised her eyebrows. "What's that supposed to mean?"

"It means if I'd had anything stronger, or the situation was different, I wouldn't be going home right now. At least not by *my* choice."

She studied his handsome face, wondering at the

thoughts behind the dark eyes that had watched her so closely all night. "So you *do* want to stay?"

He didn't answer but extended his hand to her.

Butterflies filled Madison's stomach as she accepted it—a sensation that only grew more pronounced when he pulled her against him. "What do *you* think?" he breathed. Then he kissed her, much more powerfully than he had the first time.

Madison liked the barely leashed tension she felt in Caleb. She also liked the taste and smell of him. She immediately began to imagine his bare chest as she'd seen it that day in her yard, and couldn't resist slipping a hand beneath his shirt to feel the smooth skin at his waist.

As the wet warmth of his tongue moved against her own, her knees went weak and the butterflies in her stomach spread throughout her body. But before she could decide whether or not to let things go any further, he pushed her gently away from him.

"I want to stay, but not because I'm interested in a nightcap," he said, and walked toward his cottage.

Madison stared after him, too surprised to respond. She liked Caleb. She enjoyed his company and found him incredibly attractive. But she didn't know him very well, and her own life was...complicated.

"Caleb?" she called, torn between letting him go and asking him to stay.

He stopped a few feet away and turned.

"I—you're leaving at the end of your lease."

"I know," he said, and started moving again.

"If we were to make love, it would probably be a mistake."

He reached the cottage, opened his door and flipped on the light. "I know."

"That doesn't mean I'm not tempted."

It was difficult to tell from a distance, but she thought she saw him grin. "I know," he said and stepped inside.

"You could have acted a *little* more excited," Madison mumbled, chuckling as he closed the door. He hadn't pressed her or indicated in any way that being with her tonight was important to him. He'd only admitted that he wanted something significantly more intimate than meals and laundry, and it was probably a sad commentary on the state of her psyche that such nominal interest tempted her as much as it did.

"He's too disruptive to my peace of mind," she murmured to herself. She needed to be thinking about other things—like the women's shoes and underwear, and the locket, lurking beneath her mother's house. She'd decided she'd take care of that problem tonight, while Brianna was at Danny's. But the thought of driving there in the dark and sneaking into the damp crawl space while her mother slept and Johnny camped out in the garage chilled her blood.

The telephone rang. Madison glanced at it, surprised that anyone would call her so late, then hurried to pick up for fear it was something to do with Brianna.

"Hello?"

"Everything okay over there?"

Caleb. Madison smiled in spite of herself. "Everything's fine. Why wouldn't it be?"

"Just checking."

"I should've let old Mr. Sanderson move in. You know that, don't you?" She peeked outside to see him standing at his window again. The light in his living room provided a backdrop.

"You're probably right."

"Except that you've shown me a few things he never could have," she said.

"Like?"

"That I'm not dead from the neck down."

His chuckle was soft and stirring. "You seem perfectly vital and healthy to me."

"So tell me why you want to go back to San Francisco," she said. "What's there?"

"A whole other life."

"What does that entail? Friends? A job? A woman?"

"A view of the bay."

"That's it?"

"Pretty much."

"We have a good view of the water here, if you just walk across the street to the beach."

"I've noticed that," he said. "But to be honest, I'm partial to the view from this window."

Madison smiled. "What can you see?"

"Whatever you're willing to show me."

With his flirting, the feeling of weak knees and liquid warmth she'd experienced earlier, while he was kissing her, returned. Madison would never have thought herself bold enough to play along with him. But he was in his house and she was in hers and loosening up a bit seemed almost...safe. At least it was safer than having him any closer.

"So, if I were to unzip my dress and let it slip down a little, like this—" she lowered her zipper and let her dress fall to just above her breasts "—you could probably see that?"

"I could definitely see that." His voice had grown deeper, his expression—or what she could see of it—more intense. Somehow guessing at his reaction made what she was doing that much more titillating.

"And...if I were to lower it a little more, say to here—" she dropped her dress several inches more, to just *below* her breasts "—you could tell what kind of bra I'm wearing?"

"Black lace," he breathed. "My favorite."

The depth of his attention, which she could feel despite the distance, made her giddy. "And if I were to go a little farther..." she heard him suck air between his teeth as she followed suit "...you'd be able to tell if my panties match my bra?"

He groaned. "It's a thong. What are you doing wearing a thong?"

She laughed. "It sort of went with the dress."

"Oh, yeah? Turn around for me," he said. "Let me get a better look."

Taking a deep breath, she let the dress fall to the floor, stepped out of it and turned slowly in a circle.

"You're killing me," he said.

"Are you sure you don't want that nightcap?" she asked, scarcely able to get the words out for the pounding of her heart.

He didn't answer right away. Pressing his forehead to the glass, he closed his eyes. After a few seconds he finally said, "I can't."

"Why not?"

"Because..."

"Caleb?"

When he looked up, she took hold of the front clasp that fastened her lacy bra. She didn't know if she had the nerve to do what she wanted to. She'd never done a striptease in her life. But neither had she ever experienced such wanton desire. "Are you sure?" she asked. Before he could answer, she unsnapped the clasp and let her bra drop onto the floor with her dress.

Caleb's mouth fell open. He obviously hadn't expected

what she'd just done. But she didn't regret it. The appreciation on his face was worth it.

"Beautiful," he whispered. Then, after a brief silence, he added, "Throw on a robe and come over here."

The pounding of Madison's heart seemed to tap out, *Hurry over there...hurry over there...not every girl gets to be with a man like Caleb...don't miss out.* But she'd promised herself she'd make good decisions. She had a six-year-old to think about.

"I know this will probably punch a big hole in my sexy siren act," she said, "but I have no birth control. I haven't been with anybody since Danny."

"I bought some when we stopped for gas."

"You knew it might come to this *tonight?*" she asked, feeling slightly indignant.

He chuckled softly. "On some level."

She said nothing. She was thinking. *Make good decisions, avoid emotional upset, take no risks? Or go to Caleb?*

Somehow, making good decisions and avoiding unnecessary risk had never seemed so hopelessly unappealing. "You come over here," she said.

"I'm on my way." He hung up, and then it was too late to change her mind.

Suddenly far too nervous to remain as she was, Madison put on her bra and got her robe. She was just tying it when Caleb knocked.

That didn't take long. She wondered if she had the nerve to answer. She walked down the hall, backed away, bit her knuckle and, when he knocked again, finally opened the door.

He loomed above her, his face shadowed, the moon directly behind him. For the first time, she found his height a little intimidating. Or maybe it was the intensity of his expression. It seemed to suggest they'd gone too far to turn back now, even though they weren't even touching.

What am I doing? she asked herself. But she didn't wonder long. She stood back in silent invitation for him to enter, and the moment she closed the door, he slipped his hands inside her robe and around her waist, staring into her eyes as he drew her up against his hard length. He kissed her neck, curled one hand around her bottom, and she couldn't wait for his lips to find her mouth and his hands to seek all the places that begged to be touched.

"Caleb?"

"Hmm?" He sounded distracted as he pushed her robe off her shoulders and gazed down at what his hands revealed.

"If you're used to being with really experienced women, I'm not sure I—"

He caressed her lace-covered breasts, and she sucked in a quick breath. "You don't have anything to worry about," he said.

Lowering his head, he kissed the indentation beneath her collarbone, his breath hot, his lips barely grazing her skin. Then his hands sought the clasp of her bra, and Madison squeezed her eyes closed, waiting expectantly for that moment when he'd slip off her bra and actually touch her. But he didn't immediately do so.

She opened her eyes to look up at him. "What is it?" she asked, every nerve taut. She thought she might die if he backed out now.

"I want to go slow, but I don't think I have enough control right now." Surprise echoed through his voice. "I've never wanted anyone so much."

She was shaking; surely that told him how she felt.

"I'm already burning from the inside out, Caleb. And I want you to burn, too. Burn for me."

What had started out slow now moved very fast. "We'll do it again—slower—afterward, okay?" he promised. "Tell me I'll have another chance."

Madison would have told him almost anything. She murmured something and he said, "I know you might hate me for this later, Maddy, but I have to have you."

Madison smiled at the sound of her childhood name on his lips. "Why would I hate you?"

He didn't answer. He kicked her robe aside and removed her bra, leaving it where it landed. Her panties soon followed. Scooping her into his arms, he started toward the back of the house, but her bedroom seemed too far away. She made him stop so she could remove his clothes—his shirt, his pants, everything. And when she pressed against him, both of them fully naked, and felt him shaking like she was, she knew they weren't going to make it another foot. Arching into him, she breathed, "Take me now, Caleb. Right now."

She didn't need to ask twice. He waited only long enough to put on a condom before leaning her against the wall in the dark hallway and burying himself inside her. She cried out, clenching her hands in his hair. She felt herself stretch almost painfully to accept him, yet she wanted to draw him deeper, cling to him, lock her legs around him.

He lifted her and bore the bulk of her weight between him and the wall as he began to move, and the way he looked at her, the way he kissed her, made her feel as though more than their bodies touched.

Suddenly, Caleb was the *only* thing that mattered. Almost immediately Madison felt a spiraling sensation inside her, something she hadn't experienced for a long,

long time. She couldn't believe Caleb had the power to arouse her like this, so easily, so completely. But when she felt her body tense and that first wave roll through her, she cried out his name, determined that he wouldn't retain any more control than she had, and took him with her.

A moment later, they were breathing heavily, their hearts thudding in unison, their skin slick with sweat.

Caleb's eyes were closed, his forehead resting against hers. With his large body pressing her into the wall, Madison felt completely safe. And content... "That was incredible, Maddy," he whispered.

She could have said the same thing. But she was too busy reveling in the feel of him against her, inside her, everywhere.

He gathered her in his arms, as if to carry her to the bedroom, but before they'd moved an inch, he straightened. "Uh-oh."

Madison blinked up at him. "Uh-oh" wasn't what she'd expected.

"What is it?" she asked, suddenly a little self-conscious about her wild abandon.

He kissed her on the shoulder and gently lowered her to her feet. "Hurry and get dressed. Someone's here."

It took a few seconds for that piece of information to register, but when she listened, Madison could hear a car's engine. "Not now!"

She started to collect her clothes, but Caleb moved more quickly. He handed them to her on his way to the bathroom. She heard the toilet flush, then he reappeared and thrust his legs into his pants.

"I'll see who it is," he said.

"This late, it's got to be Johnny," she told him. "And—and you can't answer my door. It'll be too obvious that I'm...that we're... I don't want him to say anything to Danny or Brianna."

"I'll go out the back and walk around, as if I'm coming from the cottage," he said. "Keep your doors locked until I know it's safe."

"Okay." Hearing the back door close, she hurried to her room and pulled on some sweats so she could go to the kitchen and look out at the drive. What she saw when she got there was a new Ford Explorer. A short man with a neatly trimmed goatee and a stocky build had gotten out. It wasn't Johnny. It was Tye.

What was Tye doing here? He hadn't been over since she'd moved in and needed his help to set up her new television. Taking a moment to slow the pounding of her heart, she went to the door and threw it open. "Tye? What's going on?"

"Who the hell is this?" her brother said, jerking his head toward Caleb, who'd met him in the drive.

Madison didn't dare glance in Caleb's direction, afraid the look in her eyes would give away the fact that they'd just made love—or the fact that she wanted to make love with him again. "It's Caleb Trovato."

"Who's Caleb Trovato?"

"My, um, renter," she said, even though calling Caleb her renter suddenly seemed a remote term for a man she now knew more intimately than any other, except Danny.

"You didn't tell me you'd taken in a renter."

"I didn't think about it. The last time we talked, it was just after we'd moved Dad's grave, and I, um, had a lot on my mind." Her throat suddenly dry, she swallowed. "What are you doing here, anyway?" she asked, hoping to deflect his attention.

Tye shot Caleb a look that said he could leave, but Caleb propped his hands on his hips and stood his ground.

Madison's cheeks began to burn as she felt Caleb watching her. Falling into bed with a man she'd known only two weeks wasn't characteristic of her. She focused on her brother to avoid Caleb's possessive glance. "Is something wrong?"

"Isn't that Dad's truck?" he asked, motioning to the blue Ford parked in the drive.

She looked over to see the Ford sitting dark and empty as it had for the past few years, and felt an eerie chill down her spine. She didn't want her father's truck there, parked in the middle of the new life she was trying to build. But she liked the fact that she could overcome her fears enough to lend it to Caleb. That said something. "Yes. I'm borrowing it," she said, to keep things simple.

"Borrowing it," he repeated. "After all the time it's been locked up in that garage."

"Anything wrong with that?"

"I guess not," he said, but he didn't sound happy about it. "Have you heard from Sharon?" he asked.

"Sharon?" She could smell Caleb's cologne on her skin as she raised a hand to scratch her forehead, and quickly lowered her arm. "Don't you know where she is?"

"I can't find her."

"As in, something might have happened to her or—"

"Nothing happened," he interrupted irritably. "She left, that's all."

"But why?"

He waved a hand toward Caleb. "Can't you tell him to go home?"

"He is home," she said, but because she was afraid of what Tye might say or do, she asked Caleb for a few moments alone. "I'll call you later," she told him.

Despite the darkness where Caleb stood, she could see

that his mouth formed a grim line. He didn't answer. He just turned and walked away, and she was grateful for the space. She needed a chance to handle Tye on her own.

"Are you sleeping with that guy?" he asked as soon as she let him in.

Madison would bet the truth was written all over her face. Her body still tingled from Caleb's touch, but she said, "That's none of your business, Tye."

He followed her down the hall to the living room, prowling around once they got there as though he had too much pent-up energy.

"Do you want to tell me what's going on with Sharon?" she asked.

"We're having a little trouble at home," he admitted. "But it isn't anything we can't work out—if I could just find her."

Madison walked over and closed the shutters on the window that looked toward the cottage, as if she could separate Caleb from her regular life that easily. He was fantasy. Tye was part of reality. "Did she file for separation?" she asked.

He picked up the paper flower bouquet Brianna had made her for Mother's Day. "I don't know. I think she's trying to get a restraining order. I tell you, she's lost it. She's gone nuts or something."

"What about the kids?"

He put the arrangement back on the table. "She took them with her."

"When?"

"Yesterday morning. I thought she'd be home by now. But I haven't heard from her."

Madison sat in her overstuffed chair, still trying to recover from what had happened just before Tye arrived. How had she gone from "I'm not going to get involved with you" to hot, sweaty sex with Caleb in such a short time? "Have you called her parents?"

"I've tried. They won't talk to me. She told them I attacked her." He shook his head in disgust.

Madison couldn't picture her easygoing sister-in-law obsessing over something that wasn't true. "*Did* you attack her, Tye?"

He whirled to face her, his eyebrows knotted. "I can't believe you asked me that! Of course not."

She remembered how aloof and difficult he'd been as a teenager, and hated the fact that she didn't quite believe him. Somehow she doubted Sharon would take the kids and disappear without a good reason. Sharon had always talked as though she really loved Tye. "So where do you think she is?"

"I told you, I don't know. She's imagining things." He walked to the window and peered out through a crack in the shutters.

Madison could feel his pensive mood from across the room. Finally, he turned to face her. "I don't like that guy," he said.

He was talking about Caleb, but Madison didn't want to discuss Caleb with him, so changed the subject. "Have you seen Johnny lately?"

"No, have you?"

"This morning. He's living in my mother's garage."

He moved away from the window. "I never dreamed the old bitch would let him do that."

"She hasn't *let* him. She doesn't even know he's there. And don't call her an old bitch. She has her shortcomings, but she's not as bad as you think."

"She's worse," he muttered.

Madison chose to ignore that comment. "Anyway, Johnny can't stay there for long. She's selling the house and, judging by the number of interested parties, I think it's going to move very fast."

"Why would anyone want that place?"

"It's a prime piece of real estate."

Tye's forehead creased in consternation. "Isn't your mother terrified that once she moves the police will find some evidence that'll finally prove Ellis really did kill all those women? Then she won't be able to play the persecuted wife of a falsely accused man."

Madison threw a lap blanket over her legs, feeling a little chilled. "She believes Dad's innocent. You know that."

He rubbed his neck, disgusted or upset in some new way. "But surely she's found that box in the crawl space by now."

Madison thought for a moment that her heart had stopped beating.

"Madison?" he said when she didn't respond.

"How do you know about that box?" she breathed.

He paused, then said, "I'm the one who put it there."

CHAPTER FOURTEEN

SO MANY THOUGHTS converged in Madison's mind that at first she could only stare at her half brother. "What are you saying?" she asked when she'd recovered her voice.

"Nothing earth-shattering," Tye said with a shrug. "I found that stuff out in the workshop the day Dad died."

Had he really? But what other explanation could there be? Madison wasn't sure she wanted to ask herself that question, or confront the answer that came so readily to mind. She'd given the house keys to Tye when he agreed to clean up after Ellis shot himself. She'd gotten them back, of course, but he could easily have made copies. Which meant her father wasn't the only one who'd had access to the crawl space beneath the house. Ellis wasn't the only one familiar with the campus area. Ellis wasn't even the only one who drove the blue Ford. If Johnny knew about the spare key, certainly Tye did as well. And Tye hated their father. He probably wouldn't mind if Ellis took the blame for a crime he'd committed himself.

Even more chilling, what about her missing sister-in-law?

That Tye might have had something to do with the women who were murdered was a horrible possibility, one Madison couldn't quite bring herself to believe. Especially because he had no reason to tell her about the box if he thought it might implicate him in some way. Yet his calm acceptance of what was hidden beneath the house disturbed her.

"Why—" Madison began, but her voice broke, so she tried again. "Why didn't you say something before?"

"I knew it wouldn't be welcome news. Not when you and your mother had stood by Ellis through the whole thing."

"Didn't you feel you had a duty to go to the police?" she asked.

"What was the point? Dad wasn't going to hurt anyone else."

Faced with her own logic, Madison winced at how selfish it sounded. Even if Tye *hadn't* murdered those women, he'd shown no consideration for the victims, and she'd done her best to shove them out of her mind, too.

"How long have you known about the box?" he asked.

"Just a couple of weeks."

"So why didn't *you* report it?"

She'd thought it was to shelter Brianna and her mother from any further repercussions of the past. Now she knew there was more to it than that. Deep down, even though she'd seen the contents of that box, she couldn't believe her father had killed those women.

If you can't trust your heart, what can you trust? Maybe she wasn't so different from her mother, after all. "I still don't think he did it," she said.

"What?"

Madison's heart was not only beating again, it felt as though it might jump out of her chest. "I don't understand where that stuff came from, Tye," she said, trying to give him the benefit of the doubt. "But our father didn't kill those women."

He shook his head. "My God, what would it take to convince you?"

"Haven't you heard? Another woman was murdered."

"I know that. It's a copycat killing," he said.

"I don't think so." She hesitated, trying to search within the intuition that had kept her strong through the past—the same intuition she'd switched to "off" once she'd found that locket. "The original Sandpoint Strangler is still out there. I can *feel* it." She watched him closely, waiting for his response, and was greatly relieved when he merely scowled.

"But the evidence—"

"I don't care about the evidence." Throwing off the blanket, she got up.

"How can you say that?" he asked.

"Because I knew Dad."

"Where are you going?"

"To find my shoes so I can walk you out. Then I'm driving over to the house to get that box."

"What are you planning to do with it?"

"I'm going to destroy it," she said, in case he might object to anything else. But she wasn't going to destroy it. She was going to take it to the police.

THE HOUSE WAS AS DARK as Madison hoped it would be. She knew her mother sometimes had trouble sleeping and would lie on the couch and watch television until dawn. But there was no flicker in the window indicating a television might be in use—thank goodness.

After driving past the house twice, just to be sure, Madison parked in front of the neighbor's. She didn't want to risk waking her mother with the sound of her father's truck, which was the only vehicle available, since she'd left her own car here yesterday. And Madison certainly didn't want to go through the alley by the garage and risk waking Johnny. It was spooky back there.

Turning off her lights, she cut the engine and got out. It wasn't raining anymore, but the pavement shone like a mirror beneath the streetlights. Puddles filled every low spot and the entire area smelled of clean air and damp wood. She liked both scents. She just didn't like creeping up to her parents' house in the middle of the night.

It'll only take a few minutes, she told herself, fighting off the sick feeling in her stomach.

Shivering in spite of her warm-up suit, she rubbed her arms as she hurried to the house, moving as silently as possible. Her mother's car was where she always parked it, but there was steam coming off the hood, which told Madison it probably hadn't been sitting there long.

Where would Annette have gone so late at night? She pressed her palm to the hood. It was warm, all right. If her mother had been out, it was entirely possible that she'd just gone to bed and wasn't asleep yet. Madison would need to be extra cautious....

Good thing she'd decided to wait until Caleb's lights were off before she left. She might have arrived only to find her mother gone, with no clue as to when Annette might return.

Caleb... God, she'd made love to her sexy tenant, and was just beginning to realize that the ramifications could stretch far beyond one night, whether she wanted them to or not. That was why, when she called him after Tye had gone home, she'd told him she wanted to pretend it hadn't happened.

That he'd agreed so readily came as a surprise. She wasn't sure if she was relieved about that or upset. But she wouldn't think about him right now. She *couldn't* think about him. She needed to keep her mind on what she was doing.

Slipping through the gate and into the soggy backyard,

she glanced toward the garage to check for any hint of light—and saw nothing. She paused to listen as well, and heard only the steady drip, drip, drip coming from the downspouts.

With a bolstering breath, she searched her keys for the one to the back door—and dropped them in her hurry. The loud jangle as they hit the cement made panic clutch her insides.

She leaned against the house, waiting to see if perhaps a light would come on. When nothing happened, she squatted slowly and recovered her keys, going through them even more quickly this time. The sudden noise, exaggerated in the quiet night, had obviously rattled her because she was beginning to feel as though she was being watched.

She cast another furtive glance at the garage as she found the right key and inserted it into the lock. She was anxious to get inside. The thick clouds that had been covering the moon had rolled away and her shadow now fell across the lawn, looking strangely grotesque, like someone sneaking up on her from behind.

Bracing for the click, she turned the handle and slipped inside.

The heater was on. She could hear the steady hum of air blowing through vents as she closed the door behind her, but she heard nothing else. Her mother was asleep. There wasn't anyone around. She was fine. It would all be over in a few minutes.

Cutting through the kitchen, she headed for the stairs and took them as fast as she dared, quickly descending into the cool, pitch-black basement.

She blew on her hands to warm her cold fingers as she came around the foot of the stairs and stood in front of the door to the crawl space. She'd conquered the garage and her father's truck. She would conquer this, too. She just needed some light. She wished she had enough nerve to scramble under the house and drag that box out with only the bulb in the crawl space to guide her, but she couldn't make herself so much as open the door without first getting her bearings. Even if her mother woke up, she wouldn't see the light from here.

Madison felt a little less spooked once she'd dispelled the darkness. The room appeared as it always had, especially with that photograph of her father looking on. "Tell me I'm right to believe in you," she whispered, and crawled under the house.

It's almost over...it's almost over...

She made her way past the boxes and storage items she'd seen before. Her knees hurt as they knocked against the plank floor. She could hear her own breathing and movement, but then something else scurried off to her right, and she froze. What was it? A mouse? A rat? God, this place gave her the creeps.

But she *had* to get that box.

Finally she reached the end of the makeshift path, where the smell of mildew was strongest, and encountered the moist dirt that spread beneath the rest of the house. She heard another rustle, this one sounding as though it was caused by something much bigger than the average rodent. A squirrel? A possum? Surely it was her imagination that it sounded even bigger than that....

Madison caught her breath, listening. Drip, drip, drip, coming from somewhere beneath the house. She strained her eyes as she stared into the dark void before her. She couldn't see *anything*. But she had no doubt that anyone out there could see her.

Fear made her palms grow moist, but she refused to let

her imagination run away with her. The house had been locked. The sounds she heard were simply settling noises.

She quit trying to see where there was only blackness, and started shoving things out of the way. But the box wasn't where she'd left it. She had to search through the junk piled around her before she spotted it a few feet away, turned on its side.

The moment she touched it, she knew something was different. It felt light, far *too* light.

She didn't dare take the time to look. Not right then. Not when she was so close to the rustling and the dark.

She pulled it to the door, beneath the light, and opened the flaps to find—nothing. No women's underwear or shoes. No locket. And certainly no rope.

The box was empty.

"Tye?" she whispered, wondering if he'd beaten her to it, wondering if that scurrying was him.

No answer.

"Tye, if it's you, answer me."

Again, no response. The hair was standing up on the back of her neck. But she wasn't willing to ask a third time. Quickly shoving the empty box back under the house, she closed the door to the crawl space, flipped off the light and hurried away.

THE MOMENT CALEB HEARD a car pull into the drive, he yanked on his sweatshirt and headed for the door. He had no idea where Madison had been for the past two hours, but he was certainly going to find out. It was nearly three in the morning, for crying out loud. And there was a serial killer on the loose.

When he knew she'd caught sight of him standing at the edge of the drive, he slid his hands in his pockets and waited.

"Why are you awake?" she asked as soon as she'd killed the engine and climbed out of her father's truck.

Caleb hadn't realized until he saw Madison safe and whole just how worried he'd been. Maybe what had happened to Susan, along with all the atrocities he'd chronicled in the past, had skewered his perception of violent crime. But he hadn't been able to think of anything except the possibility that someone might hurt her while she was out so late at night. "I've been waiting for you," he said.

A perplexed expression crossed her face, replacing the tense, nervous look that had been there before. "What for?"

"You didn't tell me you were going out. Where have you been?"

There was more accusation in his words than Caleb had intended, and for a moment she looked as though she didn't know how to react. He thought she might come back with something like, "None of your business." They'd agreed to pretend their sexual encounter had never taken place. Considering his position, he was especially grateful for that. So why he was pushing things with her now, he didn't know. He just didn't want to lose anyone else he cared about.

"Am I *supposed* to let you know when I go out?" she asked. Her tone was measured, but she didn't fly off the handle the way Holly would have. Madison seemed to be giving him the benefit of the doubt.

He raked a hand through his hair and softened his voice. "I was worried," he said.

Her eyebrows drew together. "You're sending *me* mixed signals, you know that?" she said, stealing his line from the restaurant. "What's going on?"

Caleb tried to tell himself that making love to her had been a slip-up, the result of having been too long without a woman. But deep down he knew it wasn't that simple. If he'd had his way, she'd still be in his bed.

Briefly he considered telling her who he really was, but things had gone too far; he couldn't. Making her hate him wouldn't improve the situation. "Nothing," he said. "It's late, and we're both tired. That's all."

He started toward the cottage house, but she called him back. "Caleb?"

"Yeah?"

"Thanks for waiting up," she said. "It...it helped to have you here."

"I'd like to know where you went," he said.

She hesitated. "I'd...rather not say."

He wanted to press her, but now that he knew she was safe, the desire to touch her again felt much more immediate. "Are we still pretending what happened earlier didn't happen?" he asked.

She nodded.

Too bad. He figured that enjoying the rest of the night couldn't make matters any worse. Jerking his head toward the cottage house, he said, "Do you think we could start pretending in the morning?"

Her eyes met his. "Are you asking me to spend the night with you, Caleb?"

He was really climbing out on a limb. He might be able to attribute what had already happened to a thoughtless mistake, but that wouldn't explain the premeditation involved in asking her to stay with him now. "I am."

When she didn't answer right away, he was tempted to move closer to her, to convince her with his mouth and his hands. After her response to him earlier, he knew he'd stand a better chance that way. But, considering the circumstances, he needed her to come to him without coaxing.

"Just for tonight?" she asked.

"Just for tonight," he promised.

Finally, she said, "Okay," and Caleb closed his eyes in relief. He hadn't known until that moment just how much her answer meant to him.

MADISON BLINKED several times, trying to get her bearings. She felt satiated, content, but lonely without Caleb's warm body curled around her. Still, it was her own fault he wasn't there. She'd insisted on returning to her own bed at dawn. She knew better than to stay with Caleb any longer. The more time she spent with him, the more she wanted to spend with him. The more he touched her, the more she craved his touch.

But she couldn't help smiling as she remembered the many times he'd made love to her during the night. He'd been passionate and all-consuming one moment, gentle and loving the next. With him she'd experienced things she'd never experienced with anyone else—a mutual meeting of the mind, spirit and body. Somehow he already knew her better than Danny ever had.

The phone rang. She rolled over so she could reach the handset, hoping to hear his voice. She'd only been away from him for four hours, but it felt like four days. "Hello?" she answered sleepily.

"It's nearly ten o'clock," her mother said, sounding surprised. "What are you doing in bed? I want you to have an open house for me today, remember?"

Madison grimaced and tried not to yawn. "I thought you were mad at me."

"What gave you that idea?"

Um, the fact that you wouldn't come to the door yesterday? "Forget it," she said. If her mother wanted to pretend nothing had happened between them, Madison was more than game. She wasn't even surprised. It would've taken Annette more effort to do without her than to get past their little disagreement. "Can't we start next week?" she asked. She hadn't advertised it yet—and she couldn't show people around the property with her deadbeat brother sleeping in the garage.

"Next *week?*" her mother said.

Obviously not. "Never mind," Madison grumbled. She could always throw up a few signs. Unless she wanted to risk upsetting her mom again, she was stuck doing the open house. Which meant she'd have to visit the garage and tell Johnny to stay away for the day. "I'm getting up right now."

"But your car's here, remember? When will your friend be finished with the truck?"

Madison had almost forgotten that Caleb was going to be using the truck. "I'm not sure," she said. "I haven't even given him the keys yet."

Almost on cue, the doorbell rang. "I bet that's him right now," she said. She was sleeping in Caleb's T-shirt and a pair of his boxers. She liked the smell and feel of them because they reminded her of him. But she quickly stripped them off and put on her robe so he wouldn't know that.

When she reached the front door, a glance through the peek hole confirmed that it *was* Caleb. He was standing on the stoop, crisp and ready for the day.

Suddenly aware that she had nothing on beneath her robe, she tightened the belt and ran a self-conscious hand through her hair, trying to get it to lie down. "I'm talking to my mother," she explained as she let him in. "I'll be off the phone in a second, okay?"

"Who's that?" her mother asked.

"It's Caleb."

"The man who's living in the cottage?"

"Yes."

"How old is he?"

"He's…" Madison was about to hazard a guess—she knew Caleb wasn't far from her own twenty-eight—but he answered for her.

"Thirty-four."

It was then that Madison realized he could hear her mother, so she was a little embarrassed when Annette asked, "Is he single?" Especially because Caleb seemed different today than he had last night—more aloof, reserved, preoccupied. And he kept his distance. That was good, right? Her goals for today were to pull herself together, control her rampant emotions, get on track with her life. She was a responsible single mother, not a woman who had wild affairs with her tenant.

"He's divorced," she told her mother, because Annette would just ask again if she didn't answer. "These are for the truck," she said to Caleb, handing him the keys.

"Thanks." He moved to the counter. "I'll leave you my Mustang, in case you need to go anywhere while I'm gone."

"How long has he been divorced?" her mother asked.

Madison pressed the phone closer to her ear, wishing her mother would shut up. "I don't know."

"Two years," he said.

"Is he handsome?" Annette wanted to know.

God, was he, Madison thought. Handsome everywhere. After last night, she could definitely state that with authority. Not that she'd ever admit she possessed such intimate knowledge—not to her mother. "He's, um, never mind," she said. "I'll be over in a little bit. There's something I need to talk to you about."

"What's that?" her mother asked.

She'd assumed Caleb would leave, but he didn't. He was waiting for her to get off the phone. "We'll talk about it later."

"Tell me now."

Madison chose her words carefully. "I was wondering if...if you happened to find anything...strange under the house."

"I don't know what you're talking about."

She would if she'd found the contents of that box. "Has Toby started to help you pack?"

"Not yet."

"Has he been over at all?"

"No, why?"

"Never mind." It had to be Tye who'd taken that stuff, then. Madison felt her blood run cold as she remembered the scurrying under the house last night. What would Tye have done if she'd bumped into him in the dark?

Caleb was watching her closely, but Madison couldn't help murmuring a warning to her mother. "Mom, I think it might be time to get the locks changed on the house."

"Why?"

"Just get the locks changed. Right away, okay?"

"But—"

"Caleb's here," she interrupted. "I can't talk about this now." She covered the phone. "How long will you need the truck?"

"Just a couple of hours."

"I'll see you about one o'clock," she told her mother, and hung up before Annette could respond.

"Madison, are you okay?" Caleb asked, breaking into her thoughts. "You look...worried."

She let her eyes settle on him and, for once, decided to trust someone. "I'm afraid Tye might have had something to do with that woman who was murdered," she said.

CHAPTER FIFTEEN

CALEB GAPED IN SURPRISE at what Madison had just said. He knew he was getting close to her. In fact, after last night, they were considerably closer than his conscience could bear. He had to do something about that—apologize, move out, put some distance between them. But this took precedence. "What makes you think Tye might be involved?" he asked.

"I found something in the crawl space of my mother's house a couple of weeks ago."

Caleb's heart began to pound. This was exactly what he'd been hoping to learn from the beginning—inside information. He pictured Susan's pale face as he'd seen her lying in the morgue, and imagined he might be one step closer to avenging her murder. At the same time, he felt lousy about the means he was using to accomplish that goal. He seriously doubted Madison would have trusted him this much if they hadn't just slept together. "What was it?" he asked, angry that he'd put himself in such a situation.

"A box filled with women's shoes and underwear."

"Whose?"

"I think they belonged to those women who were murdered."

Caleb let his breath go in a rush. "What makes you think so?"

"There was a locket, too." Madison nibbled her lip

and, even as he waited with baited breath to hear what she was about to say, he couldn't help thinking about the way she'd kissed him last night, with such complete abandon. Neither could he forget her body moving beneath his, accepting him, exciting him, fulfilling him as she entwined her arms and legs with his and let him know she was enjoying their lovemaking as much as he was.

Willing his gaze away from her mouth, he looked into her eyes. He had to forget about last night, keep his distance before he made things any worse. "You say that as though it wasn't just any locket."

"It wasn't. It had Lisa and Joe McDonna's picture inside. Lisa was the Sandpoint Strangler's second victim."

She didn't have to tell him that. He knew exactly who Lisa McDonna was. He'd interviewed her husband and many of her friends. "Do you know where the locket and the other stuff came from? How it got under your mother's house?"

She suddenly looked alone and miserable, and he hated himself for betraying her. "Tye put it there the day my father...died. He said he found it in the workshop."

"What did you do with it?"

"Nothing. I was going to turn it over to the police, but when I went back to get it last night, everything inside the box was gone."

No! Caleb felt his muscles tense with frustration. "Where did it go?"

"Tye must've gotten to it before me. It had to be him. He's the only other person who knows about it."

"But how's he getting in and out of your mother's house? Does he have a key?"

"He could have one easily enough."

"Have you asked him?"

"I called him on his cell when I was driving home, but he didn't pick up."

Caleb wanted to move toward Madison, but he didn't dare. He was afraid he'd take her in his arms, and what had occurred in the hall last night would happen all over again. "Why would you doubt his word, Maddy? Why would you think him capable of murder?"

She frowned. "Because I know his dark side."

LESS THAN AN HOUR LATER, Caleb's cell phone rang while he was driving Ellis Purcell's truck to a bakery not far from the University of Washington, where he was to meet Detective Gibbons. He scowled as he looked down at the phone lying innocently on the seat beside him, and refused to answer. He couldn't believe he'd made the situation with Madison exponentially worse by sleeping with her.

Whoever was calling hung up, and silence fell. But a few minutes later, the ringing started again. Finally glancing at the LED readout, he realized it was his mother, and punched the talk button. He couldn't avoid her forever. She'd already left him several messages he hadn't returned because he didn't want to hear all the reasons he shouldn't be doing what he was doing. After last night, he was beginning to figure out a few of those reasons on his own.

Unfortunately, his hunch about Ellis's daughter possessing key information was also turning out to be right.

"Caleb?"

"Hi, Mom, what's up?"

"It's about time I got through to you," she said. "We talked more often when you were living in San Francisco."

"Sorry, I've been busy."

"With Ellis Purcell's daughter?"

He shook his head as guilt washed through him. "I'm meeting Detective Gibbons in a few minutes," he said, purposely sidestepping an answer.

"Holly called here last night," she said, switching subjects.

"She did? What for?"

"She'd just said goodbye to her parents at the airport and was feeling a little bereft. She's taking this all so hard." He heard the sympathy in his mother's voice. Caleb knew Justine was aware of Holly's shortcomings, but the ties they'd forged when they were a family didn't simply evaporate. "She said she dropped by your new place, but you weren't home."

Probably when he'd been out to dinner with Madison. "I'll give her a call," he said.

"That would be nice."

His call-waiting beeped. "I'd better go. Someone's trying to get through."

"Wait," she said. "I was hoping you could come to dinner this evening."

He thought about the contents of the box Madison had described last night. He wanted her to take him to her mother's house and let him search for it—or at least look for indications of who might have removed it. From what he'd overheard earlier, Madison's mother claimed she didn't know anything about that stuff. But Caleb wasn't completely convinced she was telling the truth. Annette was so loyal to Ellis he could easily imagine her destroying evidence that might prove her husband's guilt. And he wanted to question Tye and, of course, Johnny because he was living so close.

"Thanks for the invitation," he said. "I'd really like to see you and Dad, but I have other plans."

"With whom?"

"A friend."

"I'd like to meet Madison," his mother said, without skipping a beat. "Why don't you bring her over?"

Caleb pulled the phone away from his ear so he could catch the number of the person trying to reach him. It was Madison.

"I'm getting another call, Mom."

"So are you coming?"

"I can't bring Madison. Someone—Tamara or Dad—is bound to give me away."

"I'll talk to them before you get here, make sure that doesn't happen."

"I'll get back to you," he said and took Madison's call. "Hello?"

"Caleb?"

"Everything okay?"

"I think so. I wanted to tell you that Brianna called me from her father's house."

"What'd she have to say?"

"She asked me to tell you that the magic rock really works."

Caleb was glad he'd thought of Brianna when he'd found that piece of pyrite on the ground. But he was a little concerned that Brianna had felt the need to use its "magic." "What happened?"

"I guess she spilled her milk, and Leslie got upset," Madison said, worry creeping into her voice. "Brianna didn't get a chance to explain more than that because Danny walked in on the middle of the conversation and made her hang up."

"Did Brianna seem okay when she called?"

"For the most part."

"Is there any chance Danny would let us pick her up early?"

"No. I've tried that before."

"I wanted to bring her with us tonight."

"Are we going somewhere?"

Caleb knew they should avoid each other. He certainly had no business taking her to meet his family. But he couldn't resist. "My mother invited us over for dinner. I told her I'd ask you."

There was a slight hesitation. "Caleb..."

"Just as friends," he said.

"If Johnny's still living in the garage and won't leave, or my mother finds out he's ever been there, today might not go as smoothly as I'd like," she responded.

"Why don't I go there with you, make sure you don't run into any problems?"

"You really want to risk getting involved?"

He didn't want to risk having Johnny recognize him from that long-ago interview, but he couldn't let Madison go over to her mother's place alone, just in case her brother gave her trouble. On the hopeful side, Caleb had a hard time believing Johnny would be sitting inside the Purcells' garage in the middle of the day. "I'm not worried about it."

"If you're sure."

"I'm sure." He reached the Grateful Bread Company on 24th Street and could see Detective Gibbons, wearing his customary cheap suit, sitting inside with a cup of coffee. The detective got up and started toward him as soon as he spotted Caleb pulling into the small lot.

Caleb waved him away until he could hang up with Madison. "So will you come?"

"What time?" she asked.

"My parents usually eat around six, but I'll need to confirm. Do you think we can be finished at your mother's by then?"

"Unless we have Johnny problems."

"We'll hope for the best. I'll see you in a couple of hours." He ended the call and hopped out to find Detective Gibbons already circling the truck, checking each tire. "What do you think?" he asked. "Do they match the track you found near Susan's body?"

Gibbons had him get back in the truck and back up, then circled it again. Finally, he straightened and scratched his scalp. "I don't think so."

Caleb was surprised by the relief that flooded through him. He wanted to find Susan's killer, but he wanted that killer to have no connection with Madison. "You're sure?"

"I'm positive."

Crossing his arms and leaning against the truck, Caleb let some of the tension leave his body. "Then what do you make of the blue Ford that was spotted outside the pizza place?"

Gibbons waved his hand in a dismissive motion. "The make and model of Purcell's truck has been in all the papers. Our copycat's playing games, that's all."

"Our copycat doesn't have to read the paper for information, remember? From the way Susan's body was positioned, he already knows more than we ever revealed."

"I'm afraid our killer is close," Gibbons said. "Close to the investigation. Close to us."

Caleb thought of the trophies Madison had found under her mother's house. Johnny was close. So was Tye. "What about Madison's brothers?" he asked. "Have you learned any more about them than I was able to dig up?"

Gibbons shook his head. "Not really."

"They have alibis?"

"Tye's wife said he was home with her the night Susan was killed."

"When did you talk to her?"

"Two days ago. I talked to him, too. Showed him a picture of Susan. Said he's never seen her."

"Of course he'd say that."

"My thought exactly. So I visited some of the guys where he works, and some of the people who hang out at the same bar he does on weekends, just to get a general feel for what he's like."

Caleb knew Tye worked in construction the way his father had, and made a decent living as project manager for Stoddard Construction, one of the larger developers in the area. "Anybody have anything interesting to say?"

"Seems he has an explosive temper. Gets in fights all the time. But he's a hard worker and good at what he does, so they put up with him at Stoddard. Anyway, I don't see our perpetrator letting others see his temper."

"What about Johnny?"

"I still haven't tracked him down, but he's an unlikely suspect. I've confirmed that he was behind bars when at least two of the strangler's victims were killed."

Caleb considered this piece of information. "Are we sure they were the strangler's victims? The remains of some of those women weren't discovered until months after they died."

"Either way, I've decided he doesn't fit the profile." The detective straightened his tie, which was too short for a man his size. "His parole officer says he's not capable of executing such an organized, methodical murder."

Caleb had to agree. "What about Susan's autopsy? Have we learned anything there?"

"Asphyxiation was the cause of death, just as we expected. She was sexually assaulted with a broom handle or something similar. Only surprising thing was that the coroner couldn't find any Rohypnol in her blood."

"So she wasn't drugged like the others."

"The question is why."

"Maybe she wasn't an intended target."

"Or our copycat isn't as worried about his ability to overpower his victims as the original strangler was."

Pushing away from the truck, Caleb climbed behind the wheel. He hated that they weren't any closer to solving Susan's murder. He could barely think of her without feeling a terrible heaviness in his chest. But at least now he didn't have to worry about taking Madison to meet his mother. The investigation was heading in another direction entirely. She wasn't going to feel the heat of it. Which eased some of the guilt he felt about last night.

He rolled down his window. "So where do we go from here, Chief?"

"We keep searching," Gibbons said. "The news isn't all bleak. I found a message on my desk this morning from the lab. The DNA beneath Susan's nails is somewhat corrupted because of all the filth under there, too. Boy, did she put up a fight. But with time, they think they'll be able to create a profile."

"Really?" Maybe his promise to Susan wouldn't be an empty one, after all. Maybe, with a small amount of luck... "If they come through, we'll need the right suspect."

"Exactly." Gibbons thumped the door panel. "Thanks for getting the truck."

Caleb watched the detective heave himself into a nondescript beige sedan and drive out of the lot. They were making progress, but he was afraid it might be too little, too late. Their killer could strike again if he wasn't stopped soon. Where could they find the answers they needed?

Caleb's eyes lingered on the glove box before dropping

to the floor, which was bare except for a crushed paper cup. If the truck held any secrets, he wasn't sure he wanted to know them. But he felt obligated to search while he had the chance. Obligated to himself, the investigation and Susan.

Opening the glove box, he quickly rifled through its contents: an owner's manual, a service record, a stack of napkins and several receipts for gas, all from several years ago. Beneath the seat, he found a sack that still contained some french fries. The fries didn't appear to be very old, which suggested they were probably Johnny's trash—along with the cigarette butts in the ashtray.

Now Caleb just had to check beneath and behind the seat. He pulled out a coat with a Chinese dragon on the back, but it was a size small; that meant it probably belonged to Johnny, too.

Shoving it behind the seat again, he finally put the truck in reverse. He'd done what he needed to do and, thankfully, Madison was still in the clear.

TWO HOURS LATER, Caleb felt almost euphoric as he drove Madison over to her mother's place in Ellis's truck. The tires didn't seem to match the imprint left at the site of Susan's body. And Johnny and Tye were looking less like suspects than they had before. Which meant the shadow of violence that had so deeply affected Madison's life in the past probably wasn't going to overtake her again. It also meant that what Caleb had done in the name of justice should be forgivable, since there wouldn't be any negative consequences from his actions. He'd simply explain the truth to Madison and apologize. And make sure she understood that last night had nothing to do with any ulterior motives.

He'd tell her tonight, he decided, while there was still a chance she might forgive him.

"So who was the friend you helped move?" she asked, breaking the silence.

Caleb glanced over at her. She was dressed for business in a navy-blue suit, with her hair pulled back, and looked almost too cool and professional to be such a passionate lover. A grin tempted the corners of his lips as he remembered just how erotically she'd behaved. He'd never experienced sexual hunger like he had that first time at her place—unless it was later, at the cottage. But her question about the "move" he'd supposedly helped with this morning put him in an awkward position.

"Just someone I used to work with," he said, thinking of Gibbons. He didn't want to make up any more lies, but he couldn't tell her the truth right now. They were about to arrive at her mother's house, and the way Madison kept fidgeting with her purse strap told him she was nervous about what they might encounter. He'd wait until later, when he had her complete attention and plenty of time to convince her that last night was never part of his plan.

"When?" she asked.

"A couple of years ago."

"When you lived on Fidalgo?"

He cleared his throat. "No, I was just divorced and living in Seattle." He launched into another subject before she could press him for more details. "What do you think your mother will do if she finds out about Johnny staying in the garage?"

"She'll be furious with me for not kicking him out."

"But you didn't give Johnny permission to move in, did you?"

"No, his being there came as a complete surprise to

me. But I should've made him leave right away instead of giving him time."

"He might not have taken too kindly to that," Caleb said.

"I know. I was a little uncomfortable confronting him. But I can't show the house if he's living there, and my mother's getting really anxious to move."

Caleb wondered if Annette had taken those panties and shoes. And that locket. Lately he went back and forth about whether or not Ellis Purcell was really the Sandpoint Strangler. Susan's murder was too similar to the others to be a new killer, but what about the sightings of Purcell's truck at the scene of two of the previous murders? Either way, Caleb longed to know for sure—at last. He wanted to find out *how* the strangler had done what he'd done and managed to get away with it.

But whether or not Caleb ever learned the truth, Purcell's story was one he'd never write. He knew now that he would never capitalize on his relationship with Madison that way.

Reaching across the seat, he let his fingers close around hers. "Whatever's waiting for us at your mother's, we'll work it out," he said, and hoped his words would prove prophetic about the future in general.

CHAPTER SIXTEEN

THE GARAGE WAS EMPTY. Madison couldn't tell if Johnny was still living there or not. If he'd moved on, he certainly hadn't cleaned up after himself.

Caleb was in front of her. He'd insisted on going in first, and stood with his hands on his hips, surveying the mess. They'd entered from the alley so her mother wouldn't know they'd arrived. The autumn sun, streaming in behind them, warmed Madison's back, but she still didn't like the building's shadowy corners.

"What are you going to tell your mother about the broken window?" Caleb asked, using one foot to shove the glass into some semblance of a pile.

Madison frowned at the glittering shards on the cement. "Nothing. She won't come out here, so I don't have to worry about her seeing it before I have it replaced. I'm only trying to make sure a prospective buyer doesn't run into Johnny and mention him to her."

"How do you know she won't walk out here with someone who's taking a look at the yard?"

"Easy." She motioned toward the workshop and had to take a deep breath to be able to finish what she was about to say. "That's where my father shot himself."

The gravity in Caleb's gaze when it shifted to her face let her know that pumping her voice full of bravado hadn't concealed the fact that her father's suicide still hurt. If you'd loved someone who took his or her own life, did you ever really get over it? Did you ever get over the feeling of waste and betrayal?

"I'm sorry," he said. "You told me he'd shot himself in the backyard, or I'd read it somewhere, but I didn't realize it had happened in here."

She stared through the open door to the workshop, remembering the roar of the ball games her father had always listened to when he was there. "I never dreamed he'd be the type. My father made his share of mistakes, of course, especially when he was young. But he seemed so...stable. When I knew him, anyway."

"The investigation put him under a lot of pressure," Caleb pointed out.

She hiked her purse higher on her shoulder. "It upset him, sure. But not like it upset my mother and me."

"Maybe he just didn't let it show."

"That's what some people say. They assume he believed the police were about to arrest him and make him pay for his crimes. I..." She bit her lip and shook her head.

"You what?"

"I disagree. He didn't think the police were that close to an arrest. The D.A. was still refusing to prosecute because he didn't believe the state had a strong enough case."

"So why *would* your father do what he did?"

She shook her head again. "I guess he was just tired of the fight, or..." The ideas that had been percolating in her mind ever since Tye's visit bubbled to the forefront. "Or maybe he learned something he couldn't face."

"Like..."

"Maybe he stumbled on that box of underwear and shoes, found that locket and figured it had to be Tye who was killing those women."

Caleb walked back to her and placed his hands on her shoulders. "I realize it can't be easy to think your father could have committed such horrendous acts, Maddy. But I'm pretty sure Tye wasn't to blame."

"Why not?"

He seemed to search for the right words. "There's never been any evidence that it was him. At least that I've heard."

"What about the stuff in that box? He had access to my father's truck and...and the house, and he knows the area because he's lived here. He's also much angrier than my father ever was. As much as I'd rather not admit this, I could actually imagine him hurting someone. But the police have never even considered him."

"That you know of," he said.

"I don't think they ever really investigated anyone but my father."

"There must be a reason they kept coming back to him."

Madison sensed that Caleb was trying to be understanding, but she didn't feel he was listening to her with an open mind. "Finding that box is about the only scenario I can imagine that would make my father do something so...permanent," she said. "For one thing, he wouldn't willingly leave my mother. They were close, and she depended on him. He lived to take care of her. The last thing he did was sell the old car he'd been restoring so she'd have plenty of cash on hand. And...he loved me and Brianna. He wouldn't have wanted to do something that would hurt us, too."

"Madison, you're searching for reasons to explain a reality that's very painful for you. It's a natural reaction, and I understand how you feel, but—"

"No!" She grabbed his arms in a beseeching movement. "Think about it, Caleb. Could you go on, knowing that because of you, because of your early neglect, your son had turned into a brutal monster and raped and murdered eleven women?"

He opened his mouth to respond, but she pressed a finger over his lips. "Don't answer yet," she said. "My father was no killer. I need you to believe me."

Madison had never asked anyone to believe her. But it suddenly seemed terribly important that *someone* trust her instincts. And she wanted that someone to be Caleb. Maybe because Danny had never doubted that her father was as guilty as the police said. He'd patronized her occasionally, especially at first. He'd been upset about the inconveniences the investigation had brought him. But he'd never once validated her feelings on the matter, never once said, "You should know your own father."

"He wasn't a killer," she repeated.

The air between them seemed to crackle with the intensity of her emotions. *Please feel what I feel,* she wanted to add. But she refused to say more. She was probably asking too much as it was.

He tilted up her chin and gazed into her eyes, his expression skeptical, more of the same old "you're simply avoiding the truth" she got from everyone. But then something changed. "How can you be so sure," he asked, "when everything that's been found says you're wrong?"

The beat of Madison's heart reverberated in her fingertips. "The same way I'd know, if they ever accused you of such a heinous crime, that you didn't do it. I could *feel* it."

That made an impact, started a smoldering in his eyes. Lowering his head, he lightly brushed his lips against hers.

Madison let her eyelids close, reveling in the strength

of the arms that slid around her and the solidness of his chest as he gathered her to him. Caleb hadn't said he suddenly believed her father was innocent, but she could tell he *wanted* to side with her, which was a great deal more than she'd ever gotten from Danny. Caleb acted as though he believed in her, just like she believed in him.

"If I'm not careful, you're going to cost me my view of the bay," he murmured, kissing the side of her mouth, the indentation behind her ear, the column of her neck.

"Rent *is* pretty cheap at my place," she whispered.

"And the food is good."

"When I cook."

"There are other benefits." His hand came around to part her jacket and close over one breast.

Madison caught her breath. "We can't do this again, remember? I'm not ready for a relationship," she said, but the warmth of his hand was filtering through her thin blouse and lacy bra, and he was beginning to circle his thumb across the fabric directly covering her nipple, which made it pretty difficult to remember *why* she wasn't ready.

"What if we take it slow?" he said.

"Take *what* slow?" she asked, somehow confusing their conversation with the physical sensations that were drawing all of her body's energy into its very center.

"Anything you want," he answered with a lazy grin.

CALEB WAS RELUCTANT to let Madison go, but he certainly didn't want Johnny or someone else walking in on them. And he didn't want to take things any further in the garage where her father had killed himself. He hadn't meant to make any sexual advances. He'd only wanted to comfort her.

"We'd better clean up this place so we can let your mother know we're here," he said.

Madison didn't move. "Caleb, I have a six-year-old daughter and an ex-husband who will probably always do his best to make my life miserable."

He arched an eyebrow, wondering where she was going with this. "Okay."

"I also have an emotionally weak and rather clingy mother who has no one else and can be difficult sometimes."

He was beginning to catch on. What had passed between them had frightened her, and now she was running scared. "Are you making a point?" He handed her one of the black garbage bags he found on a shelf.

"Of course. My point is that you don't want to get involved with me. I failed miserably in my first marriage. Danny was unhappy with me from almost the first week."

Caleb located a broom in the corner next to a few garden utensils and started sweeping up the glass. He didn't have a very high opinion of Danny, so what Danny had thought or felt meant absolutely nothing to him. But that wasn't the issue. "Well, I failed at my first marriage *twice*, so if it makes you feel any better, I've got you beat," he said.

"How does someone fail twice at the same marriage?"

"It's easy. You remarry the person you just divorced and end up divorcing again."

"Were you still in love with her?"

"No, I made a stupid mistake. She wasn't willing to let our relationship go. She kept calling me, coming over, trying to seduce me. And it was too easy to fall back into the same routine."

Madison made a face that told him the mental picture

he'd just created wasn't a pleasant one. "You went on sleeping with her?"

He shook his head. "Not on a regular basis. I had a little too much to drink one night after our first divorce. She came over, it was late, and we ended up in bed together." He sighed and leaned on his broom. "She wound up pregnant, Maddy."

"So you married her again?"

"It was what she wanted," he said, searching the garage for a dustpan. "And with the baby coming...I thought it might make a difference. I wanted to at least try."

"But you told me when you moved in that you don't have any children."

"I don't." He took a deep breath because it wasn't easy for him to talk about the baby. When Holly miscarried, he'd been wanting kids for nearly five years, but she'd kept putting him off. "She lost the baby only a few weeks after the wedding. It happened while I was away on business."

"I'm sorry."

"Now I know it was for the best. We couldn't get along no matter how hard we tried. It's better that a child wasn't involved."

Madison twisted the empty garbage bag around her hands. "How long were you together after she lost the baby?"

"Almost a year, on and off." He gave up looking for a dustpan and swept the glass onto some paper. "So now you know why your failed marriage hardly frightens me."

"But I just pulled my life together again, Caleb, and I really can't get involved, with you or anyone else," she said. "It's simply not what's best for me or Brianna right now."

"How do you know what's best, Maddy? Have you got a crystal ball somewhere?" He rested the broom against the wall and moved toward her. "You can't exactly schedule the people who come into your life, you know. What, did you write in your day planner that three years from now you can meet someone?"

The fact that he didn't immediately back off, as he had earlier, seemed to take her by surprise. Her mouth opened and closed, twice, but nothing came out, and finally she began gathering up the wadded wrappers, napkins, empty paper cups and cigarette butts. "Maybe I did," she said at last. "In any case, you need to quit."

He tried to look puzzled. "Quit what?"

"Quit making me think about getting naked with you."

He laughed outright. "I wasn't the first one to take off my clothes last night."

"You took your clothes off quickly enough once you got the chance."

"True."

"And you goaded me into that little striptease in the first place."

"I won't deny that, either, but I'm certainly not going to help you run away from me just because you're a big chicken."

"I'm not a chicken. I'm being smart."

"If you can call letting fear get the best of you 'being smart.'"

Her brows knitted. "Stop twisting everything I say. I'm not going to sleep with you again."

He motioned for her to move away from the middle of the floor so he could pull the truck into one stall. "We'll see."

She caught him by the arm as he walked past her, her

hand cool against his skin. "*We'll see?* I can't believe you just said that."

He stared down at the freckles he liked so much. "Am I supposed to pretend I don't know what you want?"

She immediately released him. "You're supposed to respect my wishes."

"Okay," he said. "I'll respect your wishes. The next time anything happens between us, it'll be your move." He gave in to the smile tugging at his lips. "But that's not going to change a single thing."

CALEB WASN'T WEARING anything special. After they'd finished the open house and gone back home, he'd showered and changed from his faded jeans into a pair of chinos and a button-down shirt. But he looked so good and smelled so good that Madison couldn't keep her eyes from him as they left home in his Mustang and headed toward Highway 20, which would take them north to Fidalgo Island. After their conversation in her mother's garage, she didn't want to be so preoccupied with her tenant, but something significant had happened in those few moments, something even more monumental than last night. He'd offered her the emotional support she'd needed for so long, and that was a powerful aphrodisiac.

At least thinking about him kept her from dwelling on what had happened during the open house. Most of those who'd come through were more interested in the fact that Ellis Purcell had once lived in the house, and died in the backyard, than they were in actually making an offer. One woman had even said that he was eternally damned and his ghost would probably linger on the premises for generations.

That woman's rudeness hadn't been easy to tolerate. But it was Annette who'd nearly driven Madison crazy.

Her mother either fretted at her elbow, trying to defend Ellis at every opportunity, or fawned over Caleb, who'd been nice enough to mow the lawn and fix the fence while they were there. Annette had insisted on making him some lemonade, even though he'd told her water would be fine. She'd served him cake he'd initially refused. And after he came in from the yard, she had him relax in their most comfortable chair—and look through all of Madison's old photo albums.

"Wasn't she a cute baby?" her mother had gushed, over and over again.

Madison would roll her eyes and Caleb would grin because he knew perfectly well that she was squirming in her seat.

"You might have mowed my mother's lawn and suffered through my old photo album, but don't think that's going to change my mind," she said as they turned left onto the highway.

He cocked an eyebrow. "Did I miss the first half of this conversation? Because I don't have a clue what you're talking about."

"I'm saying I'm not going to sleep with you again."

His chuckle was a low rumble. "Sounds as though you can't think of anything else."

Maddy felt her face flush hot. He was right. She was completely infatuated with him. "It's the first time I've thought about it since the garage."

His smile said he knew she was lying, but he didn't call her on it, and she changed the subject before she could give any more away. "Did you see Johnny while you were out back?"

"No sign of him. But I did place a call to the police about the possibility that one of your brothers might have some tie to the murders."

Anxiety immediately tightened the muscles in Madison's shoulders and neck. "Did you tell them about the box?"

"No. I spoke to a Detective Gibbons, and said you had some suspicions from the way Tye and Johnny have been acting."

She grimaced, recognizing the name. "Gibbons was one of the detectives on my father's case. What did he say?"

Caleb reached out and squeezed her hand. "That they've already checked out Johnny *and* Tye and crossed them off the list of suspects."

"Only because they're sure it was my father!"

"Not anymore, they're not. Not after that other woman was strangled."

Madison missed the warmth of Caleb's hand when he returned it to the steering wheel. "So I don't have anything to worry about."

"That's what they told me."

"But who else could've taken the stuff out of that box?"

He seemed to consider the question. "Let's not worry about that stuff until we find it again, okay? Do you think you could get your mother out of the house tomorrow so I could look around?"

"I don't know. I'll try."

He switched radio stations, then leaned an elbow on the window ledge. "I was hoping for the chance to go under the house and take a look today. But your poor mother needed a distraction from all those strangers pouring through the door into what is normally her private space."

Madison blinked at him, surprised by his sensitivity. He hadn't seen Annette as overbearing, as she'd expected. He'd seen her as an insecure woman trying to cope with certain change, and he'd tried to help. "That's why you let her corner you?" she asked.

He shrugged. "I liked looking at your baby pictures."

Madison felt a flicker of guilt for not being more understanding of her mother. "I should've been more patient with her. It's not easy for her to open herself up to the kind of scrutiny she's received over the past decade or so."

"You should know," he said. "You were right there with her."

"That's probably why she wasn't willing to sell the house before now. Living with what's familiar, even if it's not good, is sometimes easier than taking a risk on the unknown."

Caleb cast Madison a meaningful look. "Seems I know someone else who's struggling with that."

"I'm just being cautious," she said. "It's not the same."

"Whatever you say." He turned his attention back to the road until they reached Deception Pass, the bridge that linked the two islands. Then they started winding around to the north side of Fidalgo Island, and he looked over at her again. "So why aren't you going to sleep with me tonight?"

"I thought you were thinking about other things," she said curtly.

He chuckled. "You've piqued my curiosity."

"Sleeping with you confuses me. I'm not planning to let myself get attached. And I don't do casual sex."

"Judging by last night, there wouldn't be anything casual about it."

And that would be the real reason. "Will I meet your sister today?" she asked, steering the conversation back to safe ground.

"I'm sure there won't be any way to avoid it. She lives next door."

Madison couldn't help laughing. "Tell me what she's like as an adult."

"Not much different than she was as a kid. She's still looking for a chance to run my life. My mother lovingly calls her a 'mother hen' but, believe me, Tamara takes the concept to new heights."

"Does she know how you feel about her?"

"No. And she wouldn't believe me even if I told her. That's one thing I *do* like about my sister. She's sort of indestructible."

Madison gazed out the window at Fidalgo Bay and a small cluster of fishing boats off in the distance. "It's pretty here."

"I've always liked it," he said as they stopped at a red light. They were approaching the small, quaint city of Anacortes.

"Then why did you leave?"

He turned from Commercial onto 12th Street. After a few blocks, Madison saw old, well-maintained homes on the left and Guemes Channel on the right. "I needed some space."

CHAPTER SEVENTEEN

CALEB'S PARENTS' HOUSE was a large white Victorian facing Guemes Channel. Madison loved it at first sight, especially the wraparound porch and the gingerbread that dripped from the eaves. As she got out of Caleb's car, she could see an arbor with climbing roses to the left. Stepping-stones led through it to what promised to be a very natural, beautiful yard.

"*This* is where you grew up?" she asked.

He waited for her to join him at the head of a redbrick walkway. "Yes. And if it looks like the kind of place where the children of the house would be forced to take piano lessons, it was."

Madison glanced at his hands, which were large and devoid of any jewelry. They didn't look like a musician's hands; they looked a lot more solid—like a quarterback's hands. "You can play the piano?"

"I didn't say I could play, only that I was forced to take lessons."

"For how long?"

"Five years. And they were the longest five years of my life. I'd have to sit and practice for forty-five minutes a day while all my buddies were out playing baseball. I hated it."

"How terrible to be so unloved," she said with a mocking smile.

He returned her grin. "I knew you'd understand."

"Just tell me one thing," she said. "How could you *not* learn to play in five years?"

His expression turned sheepish. "Unfortunately, I can be as stubborn as my mother. After all that time, my crowning achievement was a rather mediocre rendition of *Swan Lake*. I still have it memorized."

"What an accomplishment. You'll have to play it for me later."

"I don't think so. For me, that's sort of the equivalent of serenading you outside your window."

Madison feigned disappointment. "That isn't going to happen, either?"

"How'd you guess?"

She didn't have a chance to respond. A thin woman with beautiful white hair swept up with a gold clip had come to the door and was watching their advance. She smiled as soon as Madison looked at her, and Madison could immediately see the similarities between Caleb's facial features and those of his mother. She had the same sharp cheekbones, the same kind but shrewd eyes, the same generous mouth.

Madison particularly appreciated Caleb's mouth....

"Mom, this is Madison Lieberman," he said, embracing his mother as they stepped onto the porch. "Madison, this is Justine, the woman who scarred me with those piano lessons I was telling you about."

Justine rolled her eyes and took hold of Madison's hands. "Don't listen to that ungrateful boy. We're so glad you could come."

Her grip was warm and reassuring, her smile just short of radiant. She struck Madison as self-possessed and dignified. "I'm glad to be here." Caleb brushed past them and strolled inside.

"Then come in," Justine said. "My husband is just

getting cleaned up. He's been working in the back all day, trying to get the weeds pulled, but we'll have dinner soon. I hope you like salmon."

"That's my favorite fish." Madison followed her hostess into a house that smelled of broiled fish, mushrooms, onions and furniture polish—to find Caleb coming out of the kitchen with his mouth full.

"What are you eating?" his mother demanded. "You haven't been here ten seconds."

Caleb didn't look the least bit abashed. "Want a crescent roll?" he asked Madison, offering her the rest of what he'd momentarily tried to hide behind his back.

"No, thanks," she said, laughing. "I'll wait."

"Where are your manners?" Justine asked him, shaking her head. "We're waiting for Tamara and the kids."

"What'd I tell you?" Caleb said to Madison, finishing off his roll.

His mother's eyebrows lifted. "What's that supposed to mean?"

"Nothing," he said.

Madison could tell his mom knew better. "Tamara has always loved and pampered you," she insisted.

"When she wasn't getting me grounded for ditching school," he muttered.

Justine sighed and jerked her head toward Caleb. "It took all of us to manage this one."

"I can imagine," Madison said.

"But please don't assume that anything he does reflects on me," Justine replied drolly, leading her into a sitting room with wide front windows and an antique settee.

A knock at the door preceded two calls of "Grandma, we're here!" Then the screen door slammed shut. Little feet pounded down the hallway, and identical twin boys who seemed about eight years old came skidding around the corner, crying, "Uncle Caleb!"

Madison thought they were bent on tackling Caleb right there in front of the Russian tea set and lace draperies. But Caleb tossed the first boy over his shoulder and got the other in a headlock. "Well, if it isn't trouble," he said.

Turning so that Madison could see the boy dangling halfway down his back, he said, "This is my nephew Jacob."

Jacob didn't bother looking up at her. He was half-heartedly trying to free himself from his uncle's grasp. Like his brother, he was on the thin, gangly side and had the usual jumble of large and small teeth so characteristic of the age. But Madison suspected they'd grow up to be almost as handsome as their uncle.

Almost. Madison was beginning to believe no one was or ever would be as handsome as Caleb.

"And—" Caleb brought the red-faced boy in the headlock around "—this is Joey."

"I'm not Joey," the boy complained. The other was laughing too hard to care whether or not his uncle had gotten his name wrong.

"Don't believe 'em," Caleb warned in a conspiratorial whisper. "They love to screw with your mind."

Madison had the impression that it was Caleb who was trying to confuse her. "Hi, Joey," she said to the one he'd introduced as Jacob.

"She got you, Uncle Caleb," Joey squealed.

"So there's my long-lost brother," a tall, large-boned woman interrupted from the doorway. With her facial structure, dark hair and dark eyes, Madison knew it could only be Tamara. But the features that served Caleb so well looked too exaggerated for real beauty on his sister. "He's living in town now, but does he ever spend any time with us?" she asked facetiously. "Nooo. Does he ever come by? Nooo. Not unless he needs something."

Caleb gave her a grudging smile. "And here we have the woman responsible for having my new bicycle impounded just two days after my thirteenth birthday."

"You were riding in the street without using your handlebars," she said as primly as a schoolteacher.

"A crime if ever I heard one," Caleb responded.

"She won't let us ride without handlebars, either," one of the twins complained. "We lost our bikes for a whole month just for riding without helmets. And she still won't let us have skateboards. We're the only two kids in the whole school who don't have skateboards."

"Skateboards are dangerous," Tamara said.

"You're the *only* ones? I doubt it," Caleb said, surprising Madison by supporting his sister. He set Tamara's children down and hugged her, and Madison sensed that he didn't dislike her half as much as he pretended to. "Where's Mac?"

"He's running late," she said. "You know how he is, always on the phone. Most wives worry about losing their husbands to another woman. I've already lost mine to computers and cell phones." She glanced at Madison. "Is this your new lady friend?"

Madison stood and smiled. "I'm Madison Lieberman."

"I'm glad he's finally decided to bring home someone besides that crackpot he married," Tamara said. "After this past week I thought he was moving on to marriage and divorce number three." She flipped her long brown hair out of her eyes. "Holly's come by here twice over the last couple of days, Caleb."

"Tamara, let's not discuss Holly in front of Madison,

please," Justine said. "And unless you can say something nice, don't talk about her at all."

"I can't help it if the truth hurts," Tamara muttered as an older, raw-boned man entered the room.

"Ah, there you are, dear," Justine said, and introduced Madison to Caleb's father, Logan.

Logan shook her hand, but was far more reserved in his greeting than Justine had been. From beneath the ledge of a prominent brow, his eyes seemed to look right through her, and the lines on his forehead indicated that his intense expression was habitual. She decided it probably took a great deal to impress this man—or figure in his affections at all.

"You're Purcell's daughter, eh?" He rubbed his chin with a large callused hand, making a scratching sound.

She nodded, feeling a bit apprehensive about what he might ask her next. But when Justine took his hand, his face immediately mellowed. "That whole thing couldn't have been easy on you," he said. "We're happy to have you here."

Madison was pretty sure Justine was behind that sentiment. But Madison muttered the same polite remarks she'd been saying since she'd arrived, then had to repeat them one more time when Tamara's husband, Mac, finally showed up. Mac had just started to say, "Nice to meet you," when his cell phone rang, and he stepped out to take the call.

"See what I mean?" Tamara complained.

Caleb gave one of the twins a raspberry on the head. "What's this I hear about you having a girlfriend?"

"I don't have a girlfriend," the boy argued. "Joey's the one who has a girlfriend. He likes Sarah."

"I don't like Sarah!" Joey cried.

"Then why do you always give her your chocolate milk at lunch?" he challenged.

"Because I don't want it."

"Right," Jacob said. "I ask you for it every day, and you won't give it to me."

"That's because you're my stupid brother."

"Everyone knows you like her."

Joey's face went even redder than when Caleb had held him in that headlock. "Only because you told them."

"Did not."

"Did, too."

"Hey, what's wrong with liking a girl?" Caleb broke in, putting an arm around both children's waists and dragging them up against him. "Occasionally you meet one who's not half-bad," he added, winking at Madison.

"They just...they can't even play tetherball," Jacob said with disdain. "They spend their whole recess walking around the playground *talking*."

"So? Talking's bad?" Joey said.

"It's boring," Jacob retorted.

Justine gestured them to silence. "That's enough, boys. Your uncle Caleb tells me that Madison has a daughter who's just a bit younger than the two of you. I was sad that she couldn't make it tonight, but now I'm beginning to wonder if she isn't better off."

"You don't have to worry about Brianna," Caleb said, with what sounded suspiciously like pride. "She's tough. She could take these two, no problem. One look down her dainty little nose, and they'd be knocking themselves out trying to please her."

Madison thought of her daughter opening the door to Caleb that first morning and saying, "Oh, it's you," and nearly laughed. Her daughter *was* tough. She'd faced down an adult and let him know, in no uncertain terms, that she didn't approve. Of course, Caleb had won her over pretty easily since then. But Madison had difficulty believing any female could withstand his charm for long.

"If she's anything like her mother, she's probably darling," Justine said.

Madison felt a blush of pleasure at the compliment, but she liked Caleb's mother for more than her impeccable manners. She liked the air of authority Justine carried, and the high place she held in her family's esteem. Madison wished her own family hadn't been torn apart, especially in such an unusual way. The suspicion surrounding her father had separated her from almost everyone else, even friends of hers who'd suffered through calamities such as divorce, abuse or the death of a loved one.

"I'm ready for dinner. Can we eat?" Tamara said.

"Shouldn't we wait for Mac?" Justine asked.

"We can't do that or we'll all starve," her daughter replied.

THROUGH THE FIRST PART of dinner, Madison felt Caleb's eyes on her often and glanced up to see him smile. She loved that smile, even though it seemed to make a mockery of her puny attempts to hang on to her heart.

As the meal progressed, Caleb began looking out into the hallway, where Mac was talking to a client or someone else on his phone. Tamara had been carrying on as though her husband's extended absence from the table didn't bother her, but her smile had grown brittle and Madison was starting to realize how much it upset her. She could tell Caleb was coming to the same conclusion. Especially when, just before coffee and dessert, he excused himself from the dinner table and slipped out.

A few seconds later, he came back, and this time Mac was with him.

"Sorry that took so long," Tamara's husband said, completely nonchalant in his tardiness. "It was pretty important."

"On a Saturday?" Tamara said.

He shrugged. "Business is business."

Madison caught a subtle glance between Justine and Logan, but neither parent made any comment. Justine simply smiled and asked Mac if she could reheat his plate.

"No, thanks," he told her and turned to Caleb. "So how are things going on the case?"

Case? *What* case? Madison waited for Caleb's response, but everything became a little stilted at that point. Justine's fingers seemed to tighten on her wineglass. Tamara put down her fork, and Logan hesitated with his water halfway to his mouth.

Caleb was the only one who continued eating. "Work's going well, as usual. How about you, Mac? You getting that business you were telling me about off the ground?"

Everyone's eyes went to Mac, and the tension eased as he launched into a zealous explanation of why the next few months were going to make him a rich man in the import-export business. He rambled on and on, while everyone sat quietly, waiting for him to come to an end— or realize that he was going into far more detail than anyone cared to know.

Madison watched Tamara, mostly, and noticed the way her eyes flicked from her sons to her brother and finally to her husband. She was obviously struggling with some emotion, and Madison didn't have to be psychic to know that it was because of her husband's preoccupation with himself and his business.

"Are we all ready for coffee and ice cream?" Justine asked when Mac had finally finished eating.

"I don't think so," Tamara said. "Mac and I had better

get back. I have a lot of laundry to do and...and I was going to finish painting the downspouts before it got dark."

Mac's cell phone had vibrated twice while he ate. Each time he'd paused to check the caller ID, obviously tempted by what he might be missing. But each time, he'd looked at Caleb and pushed the End button. It was then that Madison knew Caleb had said more to him than a simple, "Your dinner's getting cold."

"*I* want dessert," Mac said. Then his phone vibrated again, and he changed his mind about dessert and left the room.

His "Hello, this is Mac Bly" floated back to them as he moved away.

Caleb reached over and took his sister's hand.

Madison saw that Tamara was fighting tears, and the sympathy of her family was only making it worse, so she quickly stood. "Maybe you wouldn't mind showing me your house, Tamara," she said, to offer the other woman an easy retreat.

Tamara glanced up at her in surprise. "Sure. Excuse us for a few minutes, will you?" she managed to say, and immediately ducked out of the room.

Madison hesitated, giving her a few seconds' lead.

"Is something wrong with Mom?" Jacob asked. At least Madison thought it was Jacob. The boys looked so much alike it was difficult to tell, but she was reasonably sure Jacob was the one in the blue shirt. Thank goodness Tamara hadn't dressed them alike.

"She's fine, dear," Justine said. "She's just eager to show Madison your pretty house. She's put a lot of work into that house, you know."

The way Justine said it indicated Tamara was the only

one working on the house, but she was certain the boys didn't pick up on that.

"Uh-oh," Joey groaned, nudging Jacob. "She's gonna be mad at us for not cleaning our rooms."

"I promise not to notice, okay?" Madison said at the door, and followed Tamara out.

She found Caleb's sister waiting for her on the back porch, wiping her eyes with her hand. "You going to be okay?" Madison asked, sitting down on the step next to her.

Tamara tried to shrug and ended up sniffing instead and wiping her eyes again. "Do you really want to see my house?"

"If you feel like showing it to me. Otherwise, we can just sit here until you're ready to go back inside, and you can give me a tour some other day." *If I'm ever invited back...* Strangely, Madison was disappointed by the thought that she might not have another opportunity to come to this place and be with these people.

Tamara nodded but didn't move, so Madison assumed the tour wasn't going to happen today.

"It shouldn't bother me, you know," Tamara muttered, sniffling again. "It's just...I can't get his attention for five minutes without an interruption, and the boys aren't having much better luck. If he says he'll come to one of their baseball games, he shows up when it's nearly over and then he spends the short time he's there standing in the background, where he can't even see, talking on the damn phone."

"My ex-husband was like that," Madison said.

Caleb's sister propped her chin in one hand, looking dejected. "Is that why you divorced him?"

"No, I was going through some other stuff at the time and didn't get around to considering our relationship, let alone acknowledging that I'd become very dissatisfied with it. He left me for another woman."

"I'm sorry."

Madison was surprised to find that it didn't bother her nearly as much as it used to. "Don't be. In many ways, he did me a favor. Now I'm not saddled with the guilt of calling it quits, which I would've had to do at some point."

"Maybe that's true for me, too, huh?" Tamara eyed her as though fearful she might agree.

"I don't get that impression," Madison said. "I think you and your husband still have a good chance of working out your relationship. He's just a little…preoccupied and needs to realize what he's taking for granted."

The door opened behind them and they both turned as Caleb stepped outside, looking as sexy as always, despite the dark scowl on his face.

"What did you say to Mac?" Tamara asked when she saw it was her brother.

Caleb leaned on the railing. "Obviously not enough."

"You kept him off the phone for nearly fifteen minutes. That's more of an accomplishment than you know."

"What's the problem between you two?" he asked. "I thought things were going well. That's what you always tell me."

"Isn't that what you want to hear?"

"When I ask, I'm looking for the truth."

"In a way, things are going well. He hasn't been unfaithful to me that I know of. He says he loves the boys and me. He just works twenty-four–seven, and in a good year he earns a living."

"In a good year?"

"Not every year is a good year."

"What about spending time with Jacob and Joey?"

"What about it?" She sniffed, looking resentful of her own tears. "I take care of them."

"That's what I thought." Caleb sighed as he gazed out over the backyard. "When did it get so bad?"

Tamara shrugged. "I can't name a particular time. It's something that's gotten progressively worse. He's just so intent on becoming rich."

"At the sacrifice of everything else?"

"I don't know," she said. "I haven't tested him on that yet."

A large tabby cat hopped up the steps and started purring as it rubbed against Caleb's legs. "Is that where the problems between you are going?" he asked.

Tamara didn't answer. "Look at that," she said, motioning to the cat. "Even my Tabby likes you better than me. Isn't that the story of my life?"

She'd said it jokingly, but Madison felt there might be a kernel of jealousy in those words.

"Are you serious?" Caleb said. "If you felt that way, why were you always working so hard to make sure nothing ever happened to me? 'Don't ride your bike in the street.' 'You're not tall enough to go on that roller coaster.' 'Don't go swimming in the creek without your life preserver.' 'Mom and Dad, Caleb snuck out again last night.'"

"You know why," she said gruffly.

He nudged her with his knee. "I don't think I do."

"What a bonehead," Tamara muttered to Madison. "Because I love you, silly. First you were my baby brother, the very center of our family. Then you became the standard for everything I wanted in a husband."

Caleb blinked, then pinched the back of his neck. "Ah, Tammy. How am I supposed to hold all that tattling against you when you say things like that?"

Madison was beginning to feel she was part of a conversation better suited to privacy. She got up to head back inside, but Caleb hooked an arm around her shoulders and pulled her to him as casually as though they'd been dating for months. "Will you tell my poor sister that I've been a jerk and I'm sorry?" he said.

Madison grinned down at Tamara. "Caleb says he's going to make up for all the grief he's put you through in the past. He'll stay with the boys next weekend and baby-sit while you and Mac get away and, hopefully, talk. He promises to keep in better touch in the future. And…" She paused to think, purposefully ignoring the are-you-nuts? expression on Caleb's face "…oh yes, if you ever need money, you know right where to come."

"Do you have any idea how hard it is to take care of those two boys?" he asked. In the face of baby-sitting, the promise of money was evidently minor, but she could tell he was only teasing, and it went far toward lightening the mood.

Tamara chuckled as she stood up, her tears now gone. "This girl's something special," she said. "I think you should hang on to her."

"Wait a second," he said as his sister started back inside the house. "You've hated every woman I've ever brought home."

"So has everyone else," she said.

"Not Mom and Dad."

"*Especially* Mom and Dad." She cast a know-it-all smile over her shoulder just before the screen door slammed shut.

CHAPTER EIGHTEEN

"THAT CAN'T BE TRUE," Caleb said in the wake of his sister's departure. "I have good taste in women."

Madison laughed at his hurt-little-boy expression. "What don't they like about your first wife?"

He pulled her down on the steps with him, keeping his arm around her, and Madison couldn't bring herself to move away, not when sitting so close allowed her to breathe in the aroma of his clean warm skin. "Let's see...I guess we could start with the fact that she's insecure and clingy."

"And?"

"Temperamental. Basically high-maintenance."

"So you married her because..."

"I was young and stupid."

Madison playfully elbowed him in the ribs. "Come on, there has to be *something* you liked about her."

He pretended to think hard. "I liked being needed for a change. As the baby of the family, I'd spent my life being raised by two more-than-capable women."

"Your mother and your sister."

"Exactly. I was ready to assert myself as the caregiver, and Holly wanted someone to take care of her. It seemed like the perfect fit—at first. But I guess you're right. I liked other things about her, too. I still do. I like the way she throws herself into everything wholeheartedly, usually without looking first. She's childlike in her exuberance for the things and people she loves."

Madison was beginning to regret she'd asked. She no longer felt she had the luxury of throwing herself into anything, least of all a relationship. She had to be cautious. Unlike Holly, she had to look before she leaped. Certainly she didn't compare well to the impetuous, trusting woman he'd married before....

"But I couldn't live with the moodiness," he continued. "And she became so obsessive. She'd get jealous when anyone, male or female, wanted a few minutes of my time. She'd even throw a fit if I spoke to my mother more than once a month on the phone. She was just too insecure. I kept thinking that if I changed or she changed or we both did, it might work. But we're just not compatible. I know that now."

"Why didn't you try for another kid? It sounds as though you were together long enough after the miscarriage. And from what I saw with your nephews, you like children."

He smiled wistfully. "I love kids. I always have. But—" he found a small pebble on the step beside him and tossed it into the yard "—things weren't right between us and I knew it."

"You'll have other opportunities," Madison said.

He turned to look at her. His eyes lingered on her face, then lowered to her breasts, and Madison felt her nipples tighten and tingle as though he'd touched her. "I hope so."

She cleared her throat. "How many children do you want?"

Lightly rubbing the side of her face with his thumb, he continued to gaze down at her. "Three. Maybe four. Unless my wife wants a dozen or so. That would be okay, too."

She laughed. "A *dozen?*"

"Think of all the Little League games," he said.

"I am! And the homework and dentist appointments and science projects and weddings—"

He waved airily. "Piece of cake."

She rolled her eyes. "You just complained about having to baby-sit your two nephews."

"You're not buying it, huh?"

"No, I'm not."

"Okay, I'd have to draw the line at six. What about you?"

"I'm happy with Brianna," she said. "I think I'm done."

His grin was slightly crooked, and the look in his eyes mocked her. "Liar. You want at least one or two more."

She shouldn't have continued smiling, because he'd caught her. But she couldn't help it. She smiled a lot when she was with Caleb. Most of the time he didn't even have to say anything funny. He just had to look at her. But he was right. She did want more babies. She wanted them with a man she loved and respected, a man who loved and respected her. She didn't want to risk another divorce, more heartache, a difficult childhood for those children.

She pursed her lips, bent on a little teasing of her own. "Okay, let me see. If I remember correctly, I've got a baby slotted for five years from now. But that's only if I happen to meet someone in three, as you mentioned earlier."

"I'm going to have to burn that damn day planner of yours," he said, getting up.

"Don't you do anything according to a schedule?" she asked.

Mac came hurrying out of the house, still on the phone. Caleb stepped aside to let him pass, but his gaze followed his brother-in-law across the lawn, and his expression wasn't a happy one. "And wind up like that?" he said, jerking his head toward Mac's retreating back. "Not if I can help it."

"CALEB, WHAT ARE YOU thinking?" Justine asked, her voice a harsh whisper as she trailed him into the kitchen.

He glanced longingly toward the door that led to the living room, where his sister, nephews, father and Madison were waiting so they could finish the game of dominoes they'd been playing together. "That I shouldn't have snuck in here for a second piece of cake and let you corner me," he grumbled.

She stood in front of the exit and folded her arms. "Don't try to be funny. I'm your mother, remember? I'm impervious to your charm."

"Oh, come on," he said with a grin.

"Obviously, you didn't learn anything from having lived in my house for eighteen years of your life," she said without so much as a responding smile. "Can't you see what's happening here?"

"Nothing's happening." He'd been having such a great time, he refused to think seriously about anything else right now. "We're playing bones. That's it. And I'm about to win."

"That's not it, Caleb. You can't look anywhere in the room except at Madison."

"So I like looking at her. She's an attractive woman."

"It's more than that," she argued. "Not only do you watch every move she makes, you touch her at every opportunity. And—"

"Mom, I don't want to talk about this," he said, and immediately started to walk around her.

She caught his arm. "I'm trying to tell you that you're falling in love with the very woman you set out to deceive, Caleb, and I can't imagine that it'll end well. What's Madison going to say when she finds out who you are? When she learns what your real motives have been?"

"Quit worrying, Mom. I don't plan to finish my book on her father, so there's no conflict of interest anymore. And this copycat we've been chasing isn't as close to Madison as we first thought. The way things are now, there's no reason not to tell her the truth."

"Then by all means get to it."

"I will."

"When?"

Soon. When it was safe. When he was sure it wouldn't turn her against him. "I'll know when the time is right."

Justine let him go, but sighed and shook her head. "Just tell me you haven't slept with her."

"Okay, I haven't slept with her," he said.

His mother dropped her head in one hand and began to rub her temples. "I don't deserve this."

"YOU'RE QUIET," Caleb said on the drive home. "You sleepy?"

Madison roused herself enough to smile, even though the steady *warp, warp, warp* of the tires was sending her into a contented trance. *Contented*... It had been a long time since she'd thought of herself that way. "I was just thinking," she said.

Lights from oncoming traffic illuminated Caleb's chiseled face, and she admired the hollow of his cheeks, the strong jaw.

"About what?"

"Everything. Your sister and her husband. Your parents. Your nephews."

He passed a slower moving car ahead of them while there was a break in the traffic. "What about them?"

"I like them. They're good people."

"Sorry about all that stuff with my sister," he said. "I had no idea Mac had become so neglectful of her and the kids."

"I was a little disappointed in him that he didn't come back and play dominoes with us," she said. "I know Tamara was hoping he would."

"Wasn't beating the rest of us enough?" he teased.

She proudly lifted her chin. "I told you I was good at dominoes."

"And you certainly proved it. I thought I had you right up until the last."

She adjusted her seat belt so she could lean against the door and watch him. "Do you think Tamara and Mac will work things out?"

"With time."

"Do you like Mac?"

"He's never been one of my favorites. But then I don't like Tamara, either, remember?"

Catching a flash of white teeth as he smiled, Madison laughed. "Which is why you rushed to her rescue when she was upset during dinner."

"I didn't rush to her rescue." He sounded offended at being so easily found out.

Maybe he didn't want to admit it, but he'd done exactly that. Perhaps he hadn't said *a lot* to Mac—he probably didn't feel it was his place to go too far—but he'd definitely taken steps to alleviate his sister's suffering.

"I think it's big of you to baby-sit the boys this next

weekend," she added, infusing her voice with a little arrogance.

"And I think it's big of you to help me," he retorted. "Because if I get stranded at my sister's house for the weekend, that's exactly where you'll be."

"Sorry, I'll have Brianna," she said breezily.

"I'm afraid that's not good enough. We can baby-sit together."

She considered him for several seconds, going through her options, then gave in. She didn't mind. As a matter of fact, she was looking forward to it. "Fine. Brianna will probably be so smitten with those boys she'll follow them around like a puppy."

"Her company will be good for them. The way they talk, you'd think girls were an alien species."

"You probably weren't like that," she joked.

"Maybe just a little," he admitted, but then his eyes took on a devilish light. "I don't think girls have cooties anymore, though."

Madison felt the heightened awareness that seemed to wash over at Caleb's slightest provocation. She wished he'd hold her hand. She was dying to touch him—anywhere. But he didn't, and it took her a full five minutes to gather enough nerve to make the first move. Clearing her throat to distract him, she slid closer and rested her hand on his thigh.

She was hoping he'd let her actions go unremarked, or simply respond by taking her hand. But she should have known he wasn't going to make anything easy on her. Arching a brow, he gazed down at his thigh, and her hand suddenly felt like a foreign object. "What's this?" he said.

"What's what?" she replied, groaning inside and feeling her face grow warm.

"Tell me what's going on."

She pulled her hand away. "Nothing's going on." Except an absolute fascination with him.

He chuckled softly. "You're not very good at hiding your emotions, you know that?"

"*You're* pretty good at it," she complained. "I think it must be a guy thing."

"Wait a second," he countered. "I'm not trying to hide anything." He made a point of reaching for her hand and tightly entwining their fingers, which satisfied her enough to make her feel significantly better. "I've made it perfectly clear what I want."

She batted her eyelashes at him. "A dozen babies? If that isn't enough to scare a woman, I don't know what is."

"How would you feel about one or two babies?" he asked.

"One or two doesn't scare me," she admitted. The prospect of having *his* baby excited her. Which was absolutely crazy. She'd known him only a few weeks, and already she was tempted to forget life's harder lessons.

"So what about it?" he asked, kissing her hand.

"What about what?" she responded, stalling, absolutely riveted to the sensation of his lips brushing across her knuckles.

"Will you come home with me tonight?"

No! Yes! Should she go with what she'd learned...or what she wanted?

"Well?"

The moment of truth. As she met his gaze, her entire body began to yearn. "Okay."

MADISON'S ANSWER STOLE Caleb's breath. He'd been half teasing, still expecting her to dodge him. But if he could trust the commitment in her eyes, she was serious.

Evidently he was getting a little ahead of himself. Rubbing the back of her hand against his cheek, he wondered how and when he was going to break the news of who he really was. Considering how quickly things were progressing, he needed to do it soon.

Just tell me you haven't slept with her.

Madison settled closer to him, despite the bucket seats, and laid her head on his shoulder. She was so near, so pliable and willing... And he wanted her.

If he didn't tell her, it might make everything worse later on.

If he did tell her, she might never speak to him again.

He drove for nearly twenty minutes, wrestling with himself. "Madison?" he finally said when they were nearly home.

"Hmm?"

She was half asleep, smelling like heaven and feeling like a dream come true. "Have you ever heard of Thomas L. Wagner?"

With a yawn, she sat up straight and combed her fingers through her hair. "That's the name of that crime-writer guy, isn't it?"

"He's written a few books. The one about Dahmer was probably his best." Caleb glanced at her to ascertain her reaction, and found her frowning.

"I've heard of him," she said, her voice completely flat.

"Have you ever read one of his books?"

"No, but I'll never forget him. He's slime."

Slime? "He's not that bad, is he?"

"Are you kidding? He's like a vulture, swooping in

after a catastrophe to pick the bones of any survivors. He gets rich off other people's pain."

He could see he'd definitely made a positive impression. "He just writes true-crime books. Some people like them. It gets the truth out in the open and sheds some light on the criminal mind."

"I guess," she said in a way that indicated she didn't agree but was playing neutral. "What about him?"

Caleb wasn't sure where to go next. *I'm that vulture?* "I heard he was doing a book about your father."

She shook her head. "He tried, but when the police were never able to solve the case, I think he dropped it. Thank goodness."

"Would a book about your father be so bad? Even if Wagner doesn't write one, someone else might someday."

"Maybe—or maybe not," she said. "In any case, I can wait. Fortunately, Wagner stopped contacting me. I think he moved out of the area."

"How do you know?"

"I happened to be standing in line at a little bookstore downtown when the guy in front of me was buying one of his books. I heard the cashier say Wagner is no longer local. He was lamenting the fact, of course. But I say good riddance."

"Right." Caleb cracked open his window because it was suddenly getting a little stuffy. Good riddance was the *last* thing he wanted her to say. Especially tonight. Which was why he decided that the truth could wait until morning.

"SOMETHING'S WRONG." Madison leaned forward as Caleb pulled into the drive. She was trying to figure out what it was about her house that seemed so...out of place. But a thick fog had descended just after they crossed Deception Pass, and it was so heavy she could barely make out the shape of the house, let alone any details.

"What do you mean?" Caleb asked.

"I didn't leave a light on, for one. I thought about it, but it was still daytime when we left, and I knew I wouldn't be coming home alone."

"Maybe it was already on and you just didn't realize it."

"Maybe," she said, but she didn't think so. Especially since there seemed to be several lights on, and... "Oh, my gosh. Is that my...is my window broken?"

"Where?"

She pointed to the kitchen window, the one that faced the cottage instead of the front lawn, and Caleb shifted to get a better look. "You're right," he said, and jammed the gearshift into park. The car lurched because he hadn't yet come to a complete stop, but that didn't keep him from jumping out and jogging over.

"Looks like someone tried to break in," he said as she hurried after him.

"*Tried* to break in or *did* break in?"

"I'm not sure. Give me your keys." He held out his hand, and she immediately relinquished her house key. "Get in the car and lock the doors," he said. "My cell phone's in there. Call the police if I don't come out in a minute or two."

"Maybe we should stay out here and call the police together," she said, thinking it might be smarter to play it safe. "I don't want you going in there if—"

"Whoever was here is probably long gone. Even if he was still inside when we arrived, I'm sure he heard the car and took off," Caleb said as he walked cautiously around to the front.

Madison didn't do as he told her. She ran to grab Caleb's cell and followed him, afraid to discover what might have been damaged or stolen. She hadn't been able to turn the real estate brokerage around as quickly as she'd expected when she bought it, and she wasn't sure she could withstand the financial setback of having to replace a lot of her belongings.

But everything looked as it always did—until Johnny came down the hall to confront them.

"Have a nice time?" he asked.

In what was obviously a knee-jerk reaction, Caleb nearly leveled him, but Madison managed to catch his arm before he let his fist fly. "It's okay. It's only my brother."

"What the *hell* is he doing breaking into your house?" Caleb demanded.

"Somebody cleaned up the garage," Johnny said. "I figured your mother was onto me, so I had a friend drop me off here."

"The same guy who brought you last time?"

"No, he got picked up for grand theft auto." He indicated Caleb with a nod of his head. "Who's this, anyway?"

Madison put a hand to her chest, trying to even out her pulse. "It's Caleb Trovato, my tenant."

"Caleb who?"

"Trovato."

"Like hell it is," Johnny said. "I've met this guy before."

"Johnny, you couldn't possibly know Caleb. He—"

"I'm telling you I know him. He came to the prison once, to interview me. But his name wasn't Caleb... whatever you said."

"What?" Madison thought she must have heard wrong. How could Johnny have met Caleb while he was in prison? "You must be confusing him with someone else. Caleb's from San Francisco."

"That's bullshit," Johnny muttered. "He's from right here in Seattle. He's—" he snapped his fingers impatiently "—I can't remember the name. But he's that big crime writer who made a mint off Dahmer's story. He was hoping to do the same with Dad, remember?"

"Thomas L. Wagner," Madison whispered, feeling numb. Sucker-punched. After her conversation with Caleb in the car, her words sounded like an echo and, when she turned to Caleb, she didn't have to ask if it was true. She knew from the look on his face.

"You lied to me," she said, and suddenly understood why a man like Caleb, who seemed to have it all, would be so interested in a struggling single mother who just happened to be the daughter of an accused murderer.

And she'd slept with him.... God, she was a fool, a dreamer, despite all previous reality checks!

"Madison, listen to me," Caleb said. "Give me a chance to explain."

"A chance to explain what?" she replied. "You knew who I was when you moved in, didn't you?"

"Of course. But then—"

"And you thought it was the perfect opportunity to find out everything you ever wanted to know about my father. You thought you'd slip in, see what you could learn while paying for a few weeks' rent, and the joke would be on me. Well, aren't you clever."

"It was never a joke," he said. "Sure, I thought it would be one way around your refusal to help me. I believed the people who've been hurt by the Sandpoint Strangler deserved some answers. I still believe that."

He reached out to grab her arm, but she knocked his hand away.

"What about *me?*" she asked. "Don't I deserve anything, Caleb? Not even the truth?"

"Because of you, I'm not going to write the book, Madison. I decided that almost the day I met you."

She closed her eyes, determined to fight the tears that seemed to be her heart's only recourse. "You offered to be my friend," she said hoarsely. "I trusted you."

"I *am* your friend."

She shook her head, scarcely able to swallow for the lump in her throat. "You're no friend of mine, Caleb or Thomas or—or whoever you are." She motioned toward the door. "Get your things from the cottage and get out of my life."

CHAPTER NINETEEN

CALEB HAD BEEN STANDING at his window, watching Madison's house ever since he'd left it. He'd seen her cover the broken window with plastic, but he hadn't seen Johnny come out yet. Madison was probably letting her brother stay the night. Caleb hated the thought of that. He didn't believe Johnny presented any real danger to her, but he knew Madison was already struggling to keep her business afloat and, with recent events, she didn't need anything else to worry about.

Who would've guessed Johnny still had enough brain cells to recognize him?

Damn. Caleb should have told her who he really was on the way home. But he'd mistakenly thought he'd have all night—and he'd let his libido get in the way. Now he wasn't sure she'd ever give him a chance to explain. He wasn't even sure explaining would do any good. He'd done exactly what she'd accused him of doing.

Only he'd come to care about her in the process. Didn't that count for something?

Turning to the television, which was on very low so he could hear anything that might happen outside, he stretched his neck. The stark expression in Madison's eyes when she'd heard his pseudonym and understood the truth still haunted him. He wanted to talk to her, didn't feel he could go to bed until he did. But he knew she was much less likely to listen to him while Johnny was there.

LONG AFTER JOHNNY went to sleep in Brianna's room, Madison sat in front of the television. But it wasn't on. Nothing was on except a lamp by the window. She knew she should've sent Johnny on his way. On one level, she was as frightened of him now as she'd been when she was just a kid and he and Tye were smoking pot out behind the garage and coaxing her to join them.

But how could she send her own brother away when he was broke and needed a place to spend the night? Besides, if she made Johnny leave or took him somewhere else, she'd be alone. And she didn't want to be alone right now. Her frustration and discomfort with Johnny seemed pretty minor in light of what she'd just learned about Caleb.

Drawing her knees up to her chest, she shivered against the cold. A ship's horn sounded outside, far off in the distance, and the dampness from the fog drifting in off the bay seemed to filter through the plastic covering the broken window and through every crevice in the house. But she didn't have the energy to get up and turn on the heat or even fetch herself a blanket. She was too busy replaying bits and pieces of conversation in her head, and remembering other things that should've given her some indication that Caleb wasn't what he'd said he was. His probing questions. His unusual work hours. The time he'd kissed her and said, "I never dreamed you, of all people, could do this to me."

Of all people... Damn him! He'd known who she was and what he wanted from her. And if he could get a little sex on the side, that made the joke even better, right?

She stiffened, feeling a renewed sense of betrayal when she thought of him borrowing her father's truck. He no doubt had ulterior motives for that, too. He'd probably gone through it with tweezers and a magnifying glass, looking for evidence. Exactly what her father had once feared might happen...

How could he?

Picking up the phone, she dialed his number.

He answered on the second ring.

"Caleb?"

"Madison! God, I'm glad it's you. Listen, I'm coming over there—"

"Just tell me something," she interrupted, keeping her voice as cold as her fingers and toes.

He hesitated, obviously leery. "What?"

"Did you really help a friend move when you borrowed my father's truck? Or did you make me walk into that garage—" her voice wobbled, so she paused until she could control it again "—and get that truck so you could search it?"

He didn't answer, but that was answer enough. Closing her eyes, she rubbed her forehead. "That's what I thought," she said and hung up.

The phone rang, but she just stared at it dully, as though the sound came from far away. She'd braved the place where her father had shot himself. She'd risked her mother's fragile peace of mind. All because she'd stupidly believed that Caleb was her friend. No, more than her friend...

The phone kept ringing. Madison refused to pick it up. She thought maybe the noise would wake Johnny, but she shouldn't have worried. As far as she could tell, he didn't stir.

Finally, silence fell. She thought Caleb had given up,

but the quiet didn't last long. A few minutes later, he knocked at the door.

"Madison, come on. I want to talk to you."

Madison felt wounded, exposed. She'd trusted Caleb. Yet their relationship had meant nothing to him. He'd merely been using her.

Bang, bang, bang. "I'm not going away, Madison. You might as well answer."

"Leave me alone," she called.

"Open up."

"Hey, I'm trying to sleep here," Johnny cried. "Who's making so much damn noise?"

"No one you need to worry about," Madison told him. Then, because she was tired of always being polite, she added, "So just stay out of it!"

To her surprise, he didn't respond.

"Madison?" Caleb hollered.

"Go away!"

"Not until you talk to me."

She could hear the determination in his voice, so she marched down the hall and threw open the door. "What do you want from me?"

He shoved a hand through his hair, which was sticking up as though he'd ruffled it a few times already. "I want you to calm down for a minute so we can work this out."

"There's nothing to work out, Caleb. I told you in the beginning that I wasn't ready for a relationship. I don't know how I let you change my mind. I guess it was too easy to have someone here who seemed to offer me some support. And then we were going out and dancing and...and I was meeting your mother...and—" closing her eyes, she shook her head "—I liked her. I liked your whole family."

"What went on between us wasn't something either

one of us decided to make happen, Madison." He tried to take her chin so she'd have to look at him, but as much as she craved physical contact, she jerked away.

"If you'll just think for a minute, you'll know what I'm saying is true," he said. "I didn't set out to seduce you."

"But you were certainly willing to take advantage of the unexpected windfall!"

His eyebrows drew together. "Last night was...it just got away from me."

"And tonight?"

"I would've made love to you tonight, too. I won't deny that. But I was planning on telling you the truth—soon. I tried to tell you in the car, remember? Only the minute I mentioned my pseudonym you reacted so negatively...." He sighed and dropped his hands. "It was stupid of me. I see that now. But I decided to wait for a better time."

"A better time would've been the day we met," she said.

"And you would have turned me away in a heartbeat."

"Exactly! I should have had that chance!"

He shifted on the balls of his feet, as though he was too edgy to stand still. "Madison, I know how you must feel, but the woman who went missing, the one who was just found dead, used to be my sister-in-law."

His what? Before Madison could respond, a car pulled into the drive. Caleb fell silent as he turned toward it, and Madison blinked against the sudden glare of headlights. When the engine died and the lights snapped off, she could make out a late-model Honda. The same tall blond woman who'd visited Caleb before was getting out of it.

"Shit," Caleb muttered.

The sick feeling in Madison's stomach intensified. "Don't tell me—it's your wife or girlfriend."

He gave her a look that said he wasn't *that* low. "I haven't been cheating on anyone. It's Holly, my *ex*-wife. Her sister's the woman who was just murdered."

That Caleb had personally known one of the victims somehow changed things, but Madison was still too upset to sort out why.

"Caleb, where have you been?" his ex-wife demanded, striding confidently up the drive in a black leather jacket and jeans. "I've been calling and calling you."

Caleb glanced at Madison, obviously eager to finish their conversation. But Holly demanded his attention. "Caleb?"

His eyebrows lowered into a dark line as she drew closer, but he turned to Madison. "Let me take care of whatever she wants, then I'll come over later and we'll talk some more, okay?"

Madison held up her hand, palm out. Some of her anger had dissipated. But something else was quickly replacing it—a sort of dull acceptance, a sense of inevitability. Had she really thought she'd found her prince at last? That she'd do any better the second time around? "Caleb, maybe—in your mind—you had good reason for using me," she said. "I think I can even understand it. But I just want to be left alone, okay?"

"Madison—"

"Good night," she said softly, and closed the door. Then she sagged against the wall and slid all the way to the floor. She had to take a hard line with Caleb. Softening would only get her hurt—again.

"WHAT WERE YOU DOING talking to Purcell's daughter this time of night?" Holly asked, scowling at Madison's closed door.

Caleb zipped up his windbreaker, wondering whether to knock again or give Madison time to cool off.

"Caleb?"

His muscles felt so taut he could barely move. "We had some business to take care of," he said.

"What kind of business? What was that about you using her?"

He didn't answer. Because of Holly's presence, he decided to give Madison the night to herself, and stepped off the porch. Maybe after she'd had a chance to rest and—

"It's nearly eleven." Holly's voice broke into his thoughts again. "What were you doing at her house at this time of night? Don't tell me you needed her to come over and fix a leaky faucet."

The bigger question, to Caleb, was what Holly thought *she* was doing appearing at his house so late. "I can handle my own leaky faucets," he grumbled. But he wasn't sure he could handle Madison cutting him out of her life.

He cast Holly a quick glance. "What do you want?"

She stiffened, obviously offended by his curt tone. "Is that any way to greet me?"

Caleb felt his jaw tighten and reminded himself that Holly's sister had just been murdered. He wanted to be sensitive to her loss. But she was using the investigation to call him day and night, usually for no good reason. *What are you doing? Where are you going? Can you stop by?* Surely there had to be someone else she could lean on. He was her *ex*-husband, for crying out loud. What about her parents? Her friends?

"It's the middle of the night, Holly," he said. "I wasn't expecting you." *And you interrupted at a really bad time.*

"But I've been trying and trying to reach you."

He'd turned off his cell phone because he hadn't wanted to hear from her.

She had to hurry to keep up with him as he trudged over to the cottage. "Are you going to tell me what you need?" he asked, and he'd insist on a good answer this time. He'd had it with, "I couldn't sleep," and "I miss you." He'd made it perfectly clear that their relationship was over.

She didn't answer right away, so he arched a brow to let her know he was waiting. "You're acting like you don't want me here," she said, pouting.

Her tone was accusatory enough to make him believe she was about to start an argument, and Caleb felt his control slipping. "Holly, I'm not capable of walking on eggshells tonight. If you have something to say, say it. But it had better be good. I'm not in the mood to—" he was about to say, "put up with you," but in deference to what had happened to Susan, he caught himself "—pry it out of you."

"What's bothering *you?*" She grabbed his arm and pulled him to a stop only a few steps from his front door.

He couldn't help looking back at Madison's house, to see that the shutters were tightly closed. Holly wanted to know what was bothering him? Losing Madison bothered him, even more than he'd thought it would.

Holly followed his gaze. "Wait a minute. Don't tell me there's something going on between you and...and Purcell's daughter. Are you sleeping with her?"

Caleb tensed at Holly's proprietary tone. "You act as though you have a right to ask me that, Hol."

"I do! You came here to help *me*. You're supposed to be searching for Susan's killer, not...not climbing into bed with Ellis Purcell's daughter!"

A muscle began to tick in Caleb's cheek. "Holly, don't push me, okay?" He jerked out of her grasp. "Now, I'm really tired. If you don't mind, I'm going inside to get some sleep. I'll call you tomorrow."

He started to move beyond her, but she reached for his jacket. "Wait...Caleb, don't be angry. I only came here tonight because Detective Gibbons called my place, looking for you."

He'd opened his door, but this succeeded in gaining his attention. "Why?" he asked, rounding on her.

"They've found Susan's car."

Caleb's jaw dropped. *"Where?"*

"Parked only a few blocks from Lance's place. Can you believe it? I think Lance has been lying the whole time. I think he killed Susan because she found out about his fiancée and threatened to tell her about their affair."

"Holly, Lance isn't even a plausible suspect. Our killer knows too much, which means he has to be someone closer to the case. Remember the Ford truck outside the pizzeria?"

"That could've been a coincidence."

"The way Susan's body was positioned was no coincidence. And if Lance did kill her, he'd have to be an idiot to park Susan's car so close to his house. But come in," he said, holding the door. "I'll give Gibbons a call. I want to see that car."

She didn't move right away. "You've changed, you know that?"

"Are you coming in?" he asked, refusing to spar with her.

Grudgingly, she stepped past him. "I think I was wrong about you. I don't think you're going to find this killer. He's much too smart."

MADISON COULDN'T SLEEP. She stared at the ceiling, tossed and turned, took a hot bath and went back to bed. But Caleb's face still lingered in her mind, and her heart threatened to break. They hadn't known each other long, but when they'd made love she'd felt like she was part of him. And tonight, when she'd met his family, it had seemed as though she belonged....

How could she have been so wrong?

Eventually, she gave up trying to drift off on her own and took two sleeping pills. She didn't have Brianna to worry about tonight. And, judging by the snoring in the next room, Johnny was so deeply asleep she doubted he'd wake before noon.

The medication was just starting to take effect when the doorbell rang. She heard it as a faint echo in the distance and eyed the digital clock near her bed. Two o'clock.

Caleb again, no doubt. With Johnny already here, it was too late to be anyone else. Except maybe Tye...

Madison wanted whoever it was to go away so she could sink into the oblivion that finally hovered so close. She needed to sleep, forget and wake with renewed perspective and resolve. But the bell rang again, accompanied by a loud knock, and she began to wonder if, by some chance, Danny had decided to bring Brianna home early.

"Johnny? Can you answer the door?" she called.

No reply. Just more snoring.

"Johnny?" Madison feared she was slurring her words. It required real effort to lift her eyelids, but picturing Brianna out in the cold got her up and moving.

She managed to find her robe. She had trouble shoving her arms into the sleeves and couldn't tie the belt, but she didn't care.

Another knock. Only now did Madison realize that

whoever stood at her door was actually giving it more of a light rap than a pounding. If not for being a mother, she probably wouldn't have heard it at all.

"Just a minute!" she called, and stumbled down the hall.

"Madison? It's me." It was a female voice, a voice Madison recognized.

Sharon? Quickly unfastening the latch, Madison opened the door and drew her sister-in-law inside. Then she poked her head out to see if Tye's wife was alone or if she'd brought the kids.

Madison couldn't see so much as a car in the drive—and she was fairly certain the sleeping pills had nothing to do with that.

"Are you okay?" she asked.

"I'm fine," Sharon replied, but it was misty and cold, and she wasn't wearing a coat. She hugged herself, rubbing her arms, as she trailed Madison into the kitchen.

Madison gave her a curious glance. "How did you get here?"

"I drove. My car's parked around the corner."

"Why'd you park it there?"

Sharon didn't answer, but the adrenaline boost of finding Tye's wife at the door helped counteract the sleeping pills. Madison smoothed down her hair, righted her robe and offered to make some tea.

Sharon accepted with a nod, and Madison put on the water.

"You're probably wondering what I'm doing here," she said when Madison didn't speak right away.

"I'm guessing you want to talk about Tye, but let's get you warm before we do that—or anything else." She went to the living room to retrieve the lap blanket, which she brought to the kitchen and draped over Sharon's shoulders. "Can I make you something to eat?"

Sharon gazed longingly at the refrigerator. "No, I'm not staying more than—"

"It'll only take a second."

"Okay," she said, and pulled the blanket more tightly around her. "I'd like that."

Madison collected the mayonnaise, mustard, lettuce, tomato, sliced meat and Swiss cheese from the refrigerator and set about making a sandwich. "What happened?" Sharon asked, eyeing the black plastic covering the window.

Madison followed her gaze. "Oh, that. We...had a little accident earlier." She turned her attention back to what she was doing. "Where are the kids?"

"They're—" Sharon dug at her cuticles, her expression furtive "—somewhere safe."

"Safe?" Madison glanced over her shoulder. "Why wouldn't they be safe here?"

Sharon's eyes met hers, but they looked haunted, worried. "I...I overheard something, Madison. Something that has me really scared."

Madison's pulse kicked up a notch. "Of what?" She finished making the sandwich, set it on a plate and put tea bags in two mugs of hot water. After carrying it all to the table, she pulled her chair close.

"Of Tye. And Johnny."

Madison peered down the hall to make sure it was empty. "Why?"

Sharon stared miserably at her food. "You know Tye's always had problems—a...a temper. When he gets angry, he sometimes says or does things he doesn't mean. It stems from what happened to him when he was a kid.

I've tried to be understanding about that. But last week, he...he just went too far."

Madison wished she'd never taken those sleeping pills. She was feeling more alert than she had a few minutes earlier, but her senses still seemed slightly dull. "In what way?"

Her sister-in-law took a bite of her sandwich. "The police came by several days ago," she said when she'd swallowed. "I heard them at the door, talking to Tye."

"What did they want?"

"To know if he'd seen Johnny."

Madison considered telling Sharon that Johnny was sleeping in Brianna's bedroom, but she was afraid the news might make her sister-in-law hurry away before she had a chance to say what she'd come to say. And Madison was hoping she'd be able to help her. This was the first time Tye's wife had ever reached out to her. "What did he tell them?"

"That he hadn't." She put the sandwich down. "But he *had*, Madison. Johnny came by the house several times. He even stopped in the day he got out of jail."

Madison remembered her conversation with Tye that Saturday morning when she'd cooked for Caleb. *I can't believe Johnny's out. When did they release him?* He'd lied to her, too.

"Why would Tye feel he needs to lie about whether or not he's seen Johnny?" she asked.

"I think it's because Johnny had something to do with that woman who was murdered. What else could it be?"

Madison twisted to glance down the hall again. "Johnny wouldn't hurt anyone," she said, lowering her voice. But she was remembering another conversation in which she'd told Caleb her father wouldn't have killed himself unless he'd found that box and thought Tye had murdered those women. What if it had actually been Johnny?

"You don't understand," Sharon said. "I heard them talking, just a few days after Johnny got out of prison. Tye was saying, 'Why'd you do it, man? That's stupid.' And Johnny said that something inside him just snapped. When I came in the room, they exchanged a look and shut up, and later Tye wouldn't tell me what they'd been talking about." She twisted her long, sandy-colored hair into a knot and pulled it over one shoulder. "But I knew whatever they were talking about wasn't good. Tye gave Johnny a pile of cash, told him to buy a car and get out of town."

Madison felt a shiver go down her spine. Johnny had been desperate for a mere twenty bucks when he first came to her place, which meant the money Tye had given him had already gone up his nose. Drugs made a person do crazy things. Could Sharon's story be true? "Is that why you left Tye?" she asked.

"No." Sharon stared at her food. "After the police talked to Tye, they wanted to talk to *me*."

"What'd you tell them?"

Sharon pressed her palms over her eyes before looking at Madison again. "Tye warned me to say I hadn't seen Johnny, either. I told him I didn't want to lie, that we could get into trouble doing that. And he grabbed my arm so hard, I thought he might break it. I've never seen such a fierce look on his face." She started to cry. "I told him he was hurting me, and he said it was nothing to what he'd do if I didn't tell the police exactly what he told me to say."

"So Tye's covering for Johnny?" Madison said. Was that why he'd visited the crawl space of her mother's house?

"Of course," Sharon continued after a sniffle. "I told the police what he forced me to say, but I wasn't sticking around. Not if my husband was going to risk himself and our whole family to cover for a murderer. Tye wasn't acting like himself. He was tense, angry. I was afraid he might hurt me or one of the kids."

"So you took them and disappeared." Madison stood up to get some tissues. "What made you come here?"

Sharon accepted the tissues and dabbed at her eyes. "I keep hearing television reports about that woman who was killed, wondering if I'm endangering someone else's life by not coming forward with what I know." She dug at her cuticles some more, even though they were already red and sore. "I don't want to turn on Tye. But I don't want to be responsible for—" Her voice caught and broke, and she buried her face in her hands.

Madison tried to comfort her. But she couldn't seem to do anything more than awkwardly pat her shoulder. She felt numb. "We have to go to the police," she said, sick at the thought. Johnny had had such a bad childhood. And despite all her negative memories, she had a few good ones of him, too. When Perry Little across the street made fun of her because she wasn't as developed as the other girls, Johnny had given him a fat lip. She remembered feeling quite vindicated when the other kids started teasing Perry because he couldn't talk right. And there'd been that time when Tye was so angry with her for leaving the rabbit cage open, and Johnny had stepped in to defend her. Johnny rarely stood up to Tye. That day Tye had been so surprised he'd stared blankly at them both, then simply turned and left.

It had to be the drugs, Madison decided. She knew Johnny had problems, but she also knew he wasn't innately violent.

"I can't go to the police," Sharon said. "What if...what if Tye does something to the children? I have to let him see the kids eventually. I'm afraid he might try to get back at me through them."

"The police will protect them," Madison said, and hoped beyond hope that it was true.

"You didn't see the look on his face."

Madison wished she hadn't taken those sleeping pills. They were making everything fuzzy again. "Don't worry. I'll turn him in myself." She had to, before anyone else was hurt. "Just do me one favor." She checked the hall a third time. Empty. "Write down the address where you're staying and a number where I can get in touch with you if I need to."

Sharon hesitated, but in the end gave Madison the information.

Madison let her sister-in-law out, and watched her disappear into the darkness, toward a car that was apparently parked around the corner. Then she walked as quietly as possible down the hall toward her bedroom. She had to get dressed so she could go to the police. She dared not call, not from here. Not with Johnny in the house. She wanted to get away from him while he was still sleeping soundly....

Only she didn't think he was sleeping anymore. When she reached his door, it was open, and she could no longer hear him snoring.

CHAPTER TWENTY

CALEB STOOD with Holly and Gibbons at Lance's front door. After Susan's car had been towed away around midnight, Gibbons had tried to get him and Holly to go home. It was late, past two o'clock. They probably should've listened. After what had happened with Madison earlier, Caleb wasn't in the mood to be out. But Detective Thomas's wife had just had a baby, so Gibbons would've been alone if they hadn't stayed with him. And Susan's car had been found so close to Lance's house that Caleb was as eager to catch him off guard as Gibbons was. He was beginning to wonder if he'd overrated the guy's intelligence.

According to Gibbons, Lance now lived with a buddy from work. Caleb wasn't particularly impressed by their small Renton neighborhood, but it seemed quiet enough. He'd seen a thousand streets exactly like this one, filled with inexpensive tract homes that alternated between four basic models. Most of the residences on Riley Way were well-maintained. But Lance and his roommate obviously didn't possess the same domestic ambitions as their neighbors. The front window had been broken and was covered with tape and newspaper. The yard was overgrown. And what sounded like a very large dog jumped against a wobbly fence, barking wildly in the backyard.

Caleb glanced at Gibbons when they received no response to their knock and banged again.

When the door finally opened a crack, the wafflelike imprint on Lance's face suggested they'd succeeded in surprising him. And the way he groaned as soon as he saw Gibbons left them in no doubt that he wasn't happy about it. "Oh, man! Not you again. What are you doing here? I've already answered all your questions."

"We need to speak with you again, if you have a minute," Gibbons said politely.

"Now?" He squinted in the porch light, which he'd flipped on only moments before. His short dark hair was bleached at the ends and that, taken together with his fake tan and slouchy posture, made him look like a misplaced beach boy. He was young—maybe twenty-five. "You can't go around waking people up in the middle of the night, you know," he said, his voice petulant.

"Who is it?" called another male voice from somewhere in the house.

"Don't worry, Ross, it's for me." The night was cold and he was wearing only a pair of jeans, but he stepped outside and closed the door behind him. "You know, I really don't like how you guys keep poking around in my life. I haven't done anything. I already told you that."

"You don't call *using* my sister something?" Holly said, immediately going on the offensive. "You don't call *killing* her something?"

Gibbons held up one hand. "I'll take care of this—"

"Look, I had a fling, okay?" Lance interrupted, scowling at Holly. "Screwing around on the side might not be right, but it doesn't make me a murderer!"

"What's the matter?" Holly retorted, leaning closer. "Did Susan find out about your fiancée and threaten to tell her about the two of you?"

"Holly," Caleb snapped, moving between them, "maybe you should wait in the car."

Holly lifted her chin and glared at him.

"Not another word or that's exactly where you'll be," he told her, using the weight of his gaze to get her to back off.

After a moment, she clamped her mouth shut and folded her arms, but continued to glare at all of them.

"I'm miserable, okay?" Lance said, changing his focus to Caleb and Gibbons. "I can't eat. I have trouble sleeping. I miss my fiancée, and I hate the fact that Susan's dead. But I'm telling you again, I never hurt her."

"Susan's car was found only two streets from here, on Lassiter," Gibbons said. "Any idea how it got there?"

Lance seemed honestly surprised. "That's not possible."

"Why not?" Gibbons asked.

"I would've seen it. I drive down that street every day. Where'd it come from?"

"That's what we're trying to find out," Caleb said.

"I wish I could help you," Lance replied. "But I don't know anything about it. I only know I didn't murder anyone."

"Then you probably wouldn't mind providing us with a DNA sample," Gibbons said.

Lance looked a little fearful at that suggestion. "What does it involve?"

The detective handed him his business card. "It's not difficult and it only takes a minute. Call me in the morning. We'll talk about it then."

Goose bumps rose on Lance's arms as he stood in the chill wind, staring down at Gibbons's card. "This is insane," he said. "I liked Susan. I never would've hurt her."

"Like hell! If it wasn't for you, she'd still be here,"

Holly said, but Caleb dragged her away before Lance could respond.

"Calm down," he told her.

"I'm telling you he's the one," she said. "He killed her because he didn't want her to tell his fiancée."

"He has an alibi," Gibbons pointed out.

"His fiancée's mother could be lying," she retorted.

"It's not him," Caleb said. Whoever murdered Susan had copied the strangler *too* well. And twelve years ago, Lance would've been only about thirteen.

MADISON HOVERED in the hall, wondering what to do. She needed to get dressed. She knew she'd feel much more secure and mobile if she had clothes on. But she was afraid to go to her room. She didn't want to pass Johnny's door on the way, didn't want to put herself in a place where she couldn't easily get out of the house if he came after her.

Except he wouldn't come after her. Madison wasn't even convinced that Sharon was right. If he'd killed Caleb's sister-in-law, he'd probably killed all the other women, too. Only he couldn't have. Johnny had been in jail when some of those women died—hadn't he? Without double-checking, there was no way to know for sure. He'd always drifted in and out of her life, and she didn't always know where he was. But he'd never tried to hurt her before, would have no reason to hurt her now.

Unless he knew she was going to the police. But he couldn't have heard her say anything about that. He'd been clear down the hall. She'd checked several times.

The floor creaked as she inched closer.

"Madison?"

She froze, heart pounding so loudly she was afraid he could hear it. What now? Should she answer him?

She didn't want him to get up, so she said, "Yes?"

"Who was that?"

"A friend of mine," she said, and cursed the false note in her own voice.

There was a moment of silence. "What did she want?"

Madison's legs were feeling peculiar, weak. She clung to the door frame to keep from sinking to the ground. "Just to talk."

"This late?"

"She couldn't sleep."

Madison licked dry lips, preparing for a "why?" or "what friend?" But he didn't say anything else.

Gathering her nerve, she said, "Good night."

Again he didn't respond. But he seemed to be going back to sleep, so she forced her legs to carry her to the bedroom as though nothing had changed. She'd get dressed and wait for a while, *then* she'd leave.

Unfortunately, finding the right clothes and getting them on proved more of a challenge than she had anticipated. The adrenaline running through her body was making her hands shake, and the pills she'd taken were starting to compound the problem. "Come on, come on," she whispered to herself.

She managed to don a pair of jeans and a sweater. But only with great concentration did she tie her tennis shoes. When she was finally dressed, she sat on the floor, trying to calm down while watching her digital alarm clock flip from one glowing numeral to the next: 2:43...2:44...2:45....

She made herself wait a full fifteen minutes. Then she shoved Sharon's number in her back pocket, grabbed a lightweight jacket and hurried into the hall—only to run full-tilt into Johnny.

MADISON TRIED TO DODGE Johnny and run. She couldn't see him in the pitch-black hallway, but she'd certainly felt their collision and could hear his ragged breathing. He was close. Probably too close. But if she could only get around him...

Bumping into the wall, she stumbled and nearly brushed past him. She had to get her keys, open the door, reach her car. But he clutched her by the shoulders before she could go anywhere, and yanked her back, surprising her with the strength of his grip.

"Johnny, let me go," she cried, twisting and pushing at him.

"I can't." His fingers curved painfully into her flesh. "Not until you tell me what Sharon wanted."

He knew. He'd known all along that it was Sharon. He'd been baiting her.

Madison tried not to panic. "Nothing. She didn't want anything except to...to talk about her problems with Tye." Again Madison attempted to wrench free, but the sleeping pills were making her light-headed. She felt dizzy, weak...terrified.

"You expect me to believe that's why you're creeping around?" His grip tightened. "Where are you going?"

"Nowhere. I—I couldn't sleep and—"

He gave her a little shake. "That's bullshit. What did Sharon say?"

"She's worried about you, Johnny."

"Don't lie to me! She's never liked me. Is she running to the police? Is that what's going on? Or is that what *you're* doing?"

"No, I—"

"Tye told me some detectives came around, asking questions about the night that woman was murdered. Now that Dad's gone, they're looking at me. Isn't that right? They think I had something to do with it."

Madison's mind raced, searching for options. But she knew he'd never trust a denial. "Sharon knows the truth, Johnny. It's over."

He went deathly still. "What truth? I didn't kill anyone. You have to believe me, Maddy."

Tears stung Madison's eyes. She *wanted* to believe him, but mere wanting didn't count. "All I know is that we have to make sure nobody else gets hurt. You...you need help."

"But it wasn't me! I swear I didn't do it." His voice sounded gravelly, torn.

"Johnny—"

"Maddy, listen to me."

She felt his grip weaken, knew she should take the opportunity to break away and dash for the door. But his denial and her memories of him from when she was a child were crowding close, confusing her.

Unless you want another fat lip, don't ever talk to my sister like that again....

Tye, she's just a kid. Leave her alone....

Haven't you ever seen a tadpole, Maddy? Want me to catch you one?

"Maddy?" he said.

Madison squeezed her eyes shut. She couldn't let herself remember those things. Johnny was a killer, *the* killer. At least that was what Sharon thought. And in some ways it made sense. His childhood had warped him, scarred him, and somehow their father had realized the truth. That was why Ellis shot himself....

"Dad thought it was you, too, didn't he?" she asked, making no effort to restrain her tears.

She felt his chest shudder against her and knew, despite the lack of light, that he was crying, too.

"He wouldn't believe me," he said. "I tried to tell him I'd never seen the stuff in that box, that I had nothing to do with it. But he...he just looked at me. And his face—" He shuddered again. "You have no idea what it was like seeing him that way. I'd always known he was disappointed in me, but right then I knew I was worse than dead to him."

Tears dripped off Madison's chin as she imagined the scene—the guilt her father must have experienced for not loving Johnny better. The pain Johnny must have known when confronted with their father's pure contempt.

"So you did what?" Madison could barely say the words for fear of Johnny's response because another, even more insidious thought had entered her mind. What if her father hadn't killed himself at all?

"I didn't do *anything*," Johnny insisted. "I told him he could go to hell if he didn't believe me, and I left."

"Then where did that box come from?"

"Dad said he found it buried in the woodpile. He figured I'd left it there, but I didn't. I wasn't lying—I'd never seen it before. Anyone could've hidden it there. Anyone!"

His grip was lax enough now that Madison could have gotten away. She knew that. But something made her hesitate. Maybe the sleeping pills were interfering with her thinking. Or maybe compassion wouldn't allow her to condemn her brother quite so soon. "Sharon overheard you and Tye—"

"I know, but we weren't talking about murder. We were talking about what I did the day I got out of prison. Tye was angry. He knew that since I'm on probation, they'd put me back in prison if anyone ever found out."

"Found out what?"

She couldn't see him, but she could imagine the tortured expression on his face. "That I...that I went to the cemetery."

His arms fell away from her, and he stepped back. But Madison didn't run. She didn't so much as flip on the light. Somehow she knew they both needed the darkness right now. "It was you who dug up Dad's coffin?" she said, her voice barely a whisper. "Why?"

"I was so angry, Madison. So...damn angry at him. Why wouldn't he believe me? I told him I didn't do it. For once, couldn't he have listened to me?"

She didn't answer. She couldn't speak, couldn't move. The passion in his voice was so real.

"I just wanted him to believe me," he said. "I *hate* going to sleep at night and seeing that...that damn look on his face." He drew a ragged breath that testified to the depth of his emotion. "I was high when I went to the cemetery. I wasn't thinking straight. Or I would've known it was far too late." His tone turned deadpan. "I couldn't convince him even when he was alive."

Poor Johnny. He lived with so many demons. Even now drugs stood between him and any kind of recovery. But he was no killer. He just didn't have it in him.

Putting her arms around him, Madison tried to draw him close, to offer him some of the support and comfort he'd never had.

At first he stiffened, tried to push her away. But then she said, "It's okay, Johnny. I believe you." And after a few moments, he was sobbing on her shoulder.

CALEB SAT AT HIS kitchen table with a cup of coffee and watched the sun rise. He'd arrived home nearly three hours ago, but he hadn't gone to bed. He had too much on his mind. Mostly Madison. And the investigation. Neither of which were going the way he'd hoped.

Did you really help a friend move when you borrowed my father's truck? Or did you make me walk into that garage and get that truck so you could search it?

He'd done worse than that. He'd made her walk into that garage so he could search Ellis's truck *and* have Gibbons check the tires. And it had all been for nothing.

With a yawn, he rubbed his tired eyes. After spending most of the night thinking about Madison, he'd finally decided that what had happened between them yesterday was probably for the best. Their relationship couldn't have gone anywhere. She wasn't emotionally available; she'd told him that several times. And he was going back to San Francisco. Better to get over his fascination with her now and focus on what he needed to do before he could return home.

Shoving his coffee away because the caffeine seemed to be making him sick, he called Gibbons.

"Shit, Trovato, don't you ever sleep?" Gibbons complained, picking up after the answering machine had come on.

Caleb felt a pang of guilt for waking him. Gibbons had already put in far more than his share of overtime. But Caleb was impatient. If he wasn't going to pursue a relationship with Madison, he wanted to get the hell out of Seattle. "I don't think—"

"Wait until the machine goes off."

They fell silent until Caleb heard a click, then it was Gibbons' turn to yawn, which he did loudly. "What is it?"

"I don't think we should waste any time with Lance Perkins."

Gibbons snorted. "Hell, I hope you didn't wake me up

just to tell me that. I know Lance isn't our man. He stood right in front of us, bare-chested. He didn't have a scratch on him. And I know Susan left marks."

"So where do we go from here?" Caleb asked.

"We get some sleep and recoup when we can think straight."

Caleb was too discouraged, too frustrated to sleep. But he didn't have any right to demand superhuman hours from Gibbons. This was just another case to him. There'd been plenty of such cases before, and there'd be plenty after.

"Call me when you get up," Caleb said, and disconnected. Then he slouched back in his chair, scowling at the gray clouds already scudding across the sky outside.

He'd wanted to search Madison's mother's house today, had hoped to find the contents of that box. He wasn't sure it would relate to Susan's disappearance in any way, but he knew it couldn't hurt to have a look. Maybe it would help the police finally solve the old case, finally prove Madison right—or wrong—about her father. But he'd lost her cooperation.

He'd lost a hell of a lot more than her cooperation....

The case. He needed to move on. What was he missing? What small detail had the killer left behind that would eventually be his undoing? Surely there had to be *something*.

According to the FBI profiler, the perpetrator was methodical, obsessive, manipulative. Like John Wayne Gacy, he probably managed to appear functional. Maybe he held a steady job, participated in community events. Which meant he could be one of a million different men living in Seattle.

Except this killer was probably impotent, judging by the way his victims had been sexually assaulted. And the profiler had given them one limiting physical factor—she'd said the killer wasn't very large. He was attacking small women to be sure he could physically overpower them, and he was using the date rape drug, Rohypnol, to improve his odds.

Caleb drummed his fingers on the table, asking himself the same questions he'd been asking all along. Who knew enough about the case to set up the crime scene? And who had the cunning, the complete self-absorption required to commit such crimes?

Johnny knew an awful lot about the case. He'd seen some of the crime-scene pictures. In an effort to get someone to talk, the police had shown the whole Purcell family those shocking photos. But Johnny's thinking was simply too disorganized. He lacked the control to get away with something like this.

Tye, on the other hand, appeared functional, even capable, and knew as much about the case as Johnny. But Caleb didn't believe he was their man, either. For one thing, he couldn't see Tye limiting his attacks to small women. Tye wasn't particularly tall, but he was muscular. And from what Gibbons had said, Madison's oldest brother had an explosive temper. An explosive temper would too easily tempt him beyond the veil of secrecy and premeditation required to commit the kind of murders they were dealing with.

Caleb took the picture of Susan standing outside the pizza place out of his wallet and stared down at her blurry profile. He knew Gibbons would be contacting Tye Purcell to ask him about the contents of the box missing from under the house. But Caleb didn't want to wait. Now that Madison knew who he really was, maybe the time had come to confront her brother face-to-face.

Tye lived in an older, rather depressed neighborhood of small, cookie-cutter houses, very few of which had a garage. Here and there, a carport had been finished off by homeowners seeking more living space. Tye's carport was still open, however, and housed a weight bench, which he happened to be using when Caleb arrived.

Pausing when he heard the car, Tye rested the barbells in the stand over his head and sat up, letting his hands dangle between his legs. "What are you doing here?" he asked as he watched Caleb approach.

It was nearly eight o'clock, which wasn't too early for a workday. But this was Sunday. Caleb had expected to find Tye in bed, but had wanted to catch him before he went out. "I have a few questions for you," he said.

"What kind of questions?" Suddenly indifferent, Tye started bench-pressing another set. It was chilly out, gray, overcast and a little windy, but Tye wore only a pair of karate pants and a T-shirt with the sleeves cut out. He had a Chinese dragon tattooed on his right biceps, very similar to the one embroidered on the jacket in his father's Ford, making Caleb wonder if he'd been wrong about the owner of that jacket. In any case, judging by the tattoo and the pants, Caleb guessed Tye was either taking or teaching karate. Which supported his gut feeling that if Tye wanted to hurt a woman, he wouldn't feel the need to use drugs....

Folding his arms, Caleb leaned against the corner of the house. He'd expected to see some sign of Tye's wife and kids. His wife had provided his alibi, after all. But except for Tye, the place seemed deserted. The only vehicle was Tye's Explorer parked out at the curb.

"Where's the wife and kids?" Caleb asked, noting the bikes, scooters and baseball gloves tossed against the shed that comprised the back wall of Tye's carport.

Tye paused with the barbell straight over his head. "Is

that one of your questions?" he asked, his muscles straining. "Because it's none of your damn business." The barbell clanged as he shoved it roughly into the stand and sat up, his eyes narrower than before. "Why don't you just tell me what the hell you're doing out here?"

"I know about the box of women's underwear and trinkets under the house," Caleb said.

Tye's eyebrows raised a notch. "So? What does that box mean to you?"

"My sister-in-law was just murdered, strangled like the women your father was accused of killing. I think there might be some connection."

Tye's face was devoid of emotion. "Was she killed before or after you moved in with Madison?"

"Before."

Tye swore softly under his breath. "Did Madison know that when she let you move in?"

"She knows it now."

"I hope she kicked your ass out," Tye said.

"Once I get the answers I need, I'm leaving anyway."

Tye stared at him for a moment. "Well, much as I'd like to help, that stuff belonged to my father. And if you know anything about the case, which I'm guessing you do, you know he's dead. You're wasting your time here."

"Humor me," Caleb said.

"How?"

"Where's the stuff in that box?"

Tye scowled darkly. "You said yourself that it was under the house."

"Until a couple weeks ago. Now it's gone." Caleb couldn't tell if Tye was surprised or not. He just kept stroking his goatee with his thumb and index finger.

"Well, I don't give a shit," he said at last. "That box has nothing to do with me."

"Then why didn't you take it to police?"

"Kiss my ass." Rolling back, he started yet another set, but Caleb didn't leave as he was obviously expected to. He dug into his pocket and retrieved the picture of Susan outside the pizzeria.

"Do you know this woman?" he asked, shoving the picture in front of Tye's face.

Tye grunted as he lifted the barbell for the twelfth time, arms shaking. When he put the weights away, he grabbed the photograph but only glanced at it briefly before handing it back. "What are you, a cop?"

"I used to be."

"Then you're a civilian just like me, which means you're trespassing and you've got no right to be here."

Caleb didn't respond because it was true.

"I'll tell you what I told the detectives who already came by," Tye said in a disgruntled voice. "I've never seen her before."

"Is that the truth?"

"What do you think?"

Caleb thought he was lying. He'd never considered Tye a real suspect in the killings, but there was something suspicious about his belligerent attitude and his reluctance to really look at Caleb.

"I have a woman who says she saw you there," Caleb said, folding the picture neatly. He meant Jennifer, but he was bluffing. When Caleb had met with Jennifer, he'd shown her a picture of Tye and been told she'd never seen him before. But that didn't prove Tye wasn't at the pizza place. She'd admitted she hadn't been able to tell *who* Susan was arguing with.

A muscle jumped in Tye's cheek. "What woman?"

"Someone who was there that night, too."

A door shut discreetly over at the neighbor's, but Caleb

didn't even look in that direction. He was too busy studying Tye's face.

"That's bullshit, man," Tye said.

"Is it?"

Silence. Tye stood, obviously agitated, but his mouth remained firmly closed.

"Have you had possession of your father's truck in the past few weeks, Tye?"

Now Madison's half brother looked positively furtive. He curled his fingers into fists, and Caleb straightened, preparing for anything...just in case. "No, I haven't," Tye muttered.

"I have a witness who says you drove your father's truck to the pizzeria that night," Caleb said, taking it one step further.

Tye's chest rose as if he'd inhaled deeply. Caleb got the impression he was about to reveal...something. But he didn't. "Get out of here," he said instead. "Get out of here right now or you'll be damn sorry you ever showed up."

Shit. Caleb's bluff hadn't paid off. He stared at Tye's angry face another long moment, then turned to leave.

He was only a few miles from Tye's neighborhood when an old Dodge came screaming up behind him. A chubby, middle-aged man honked and yelled for him to pull over.

Caleb rolled down his window. "What do you want?" he called above the wind as the man drove alongside him.

"Are you a detective?"

To keep things simple, Caleb nodded.

"That's what I thought." The guy braked to avoid a collision with the car ahead, and Caleb slowed to stay even with him. "I live right next to Tye Purcell," he hollered when it was safe to glance over again. "Pull off the road. I have some information for you."

"WHAT ARE YOU DOING?" Holly asked the moment Caleb answered his cell phone.

Caleb grimaced at the sound of her voice and changed lanes so he could speed up. "Heading home." *Racing home...*

"Where have you been?"

"Nowhere important," he said. After her behavior at Lance's last night, he was reluctant to share the grim information he'd just received. "Did you call for a reason?"

The phone went silent for a few seconds, then she said, "I left my purse in your car."

"I haven't seen it."

"It has to be there. I had it with me last night, and I haven't gone anywhere since."

Keeping one hand on the wheel, Caleb reached over to feel around the passenger seat. He found a few gum wrappers and a quarter wedged next to the console, but no purse. "It's not here, Holly."

"Then I must've left it at your house."

Wonderful. Another excuse to visit. "If it's there, I'll bring it over later, okay?" he said.

"Caleb, I need it right now."

"Holly, I'm tired." And he had to talk to Madison....
"Why—"

"I won't stay long," she promised.

He ground his teeth. He didn't want to see his ex-wife; he wanted to deal with what he'd found out. But he thought he'd be able to get rid of Holly more quickly and easily if he just gave her the damn purse. "Okay," he said. "But don't come for an hour or so. I'm in south Seattle and the ferry to Whidbey always takes awhile."

MADISON SCRUBBED HER FACE with her hand and blinked, trying to clear the blurriness from her eyes. Once she'd finally gone to sleep, she hadn't stirred for hours, thanks to the natural letdown of her emotions, combined with the effect of those sleeping pills. But then someone had knocked at the door, and she'd dragged herself out of bed to find the sun peeking through rain clouds and Caleb's ex-wife standing on her stoop.

"Can I help you?" Madison said, steadying herself with a hand on the lintel.

Holly didn't answer right away. Her gaze traveled slowly over Madison's robe to her well-worn slippers before returning to her face. "I left my purse at Caleb's house last night, but he isn't home."

Madison waited for her to make some sort of request, but Holly didn't add anything else. "I have an extra key," Madison said, "but I'm afraid I can't let you in without Caleb's permission. Have you tried calling him?"

Holly smiled. "Of course. He said he'd be here in a minute. I was just hoping you and I could have a little talk while I wait."

"A little talk about what?"

"Just a few things I think you should be aware of."

There was something about Holly's manner Madison didn't like or trust. And she wasn't eager to face any more unpleasant surprises. She felt sick every time she thought about her visit with Caleb at his parents' house and how wonderful it had been compared to the confrontation that had occurred afterward.

But basic good manners demanded she hear Holly out. She was certainly curious. "Come inside," she said, because it was beginning to sprinkle.

Feeling she needed a jolt of caffeine to help restore her

faculties, Madison led the way to the kitchen so she could make a pot of coffee.

"Nice place," Holly said, scratching one arm through her leather jacket as she came down the hall. "Did you decorate it yourself?"

"Yes." Madison motioned to the kitchen table. "Would you like to sit down?"

"No thanks." Caleb's ex-wife circled the room, gazing at the cupboards and appliances, examining the magnets and pictures on the fridge. "How long have you lived here?" she asked.

"Not quite a year."

"Since your divorce from Danny, the engineer?"

Madison was about to fill the coffeemaker with fresh grounds, but turned to stare at Holly instead. "How do you know anything about Danny? Or my divorce?"

"You're Ellis Purcell's daughter, aren't you?"

Madison curled her fingernails into her palms, feeling doubly betrayed that Caleb hadn't even bothered to keep quiet about the fact that he was playing her for a fool. "Did Caleb tell you that?"

"Of course. We're still *very* close." She took a picture off the refrigerator. "Is this your daughter?"

Holly held a photo of Brianna at the zoo. "Yes."

"What a cute little girl."

Her words were nice enough, but they were spoken almost tonelessly. And the way Holly stared at the picture made Madison want to yank it away. "She's a good girl. Most of the time, anyway," she said, watching Holly closely.

"I've always wanted a child."

Madison remembered Caleb telling her that he and Holly had lost a baby due to miscarriage. She would have felt sympathy except that Holly seemed so emotionally detached. Her comment had sounded like a casual observation.

"What is it you came to tell me, Holly?" Madison asked, anxious to bring their "little talk" to a close.

Holly tacked the picture back onto the fridge and turned. "Caleb's only interested in you because of who are you are," she said. "He thinks if he can solve this case, he'll finally reel in the one that got away. The big one. You know what I mean? That's all it is. It isn't you or—" she waved at the pictures of Brianna "—or your little girl that he likes."

Madison hated hearing what Holly was saying, but she couldn't argue with it because Holly was right. Caleb had only moved into the cottage because she was Ellis Purcell's daughter. But common sense told her that Holly wouldn't have shown up at her door unless she was feeling threatened in some way. "Holly, since you've been so candid with me, I think I'll do you the same favor," she said.

Holly's eyebrows shot up and she straightened, giving Madison the impression that she was surprised her revelation hadn't reduced Madison to tears. "What?"

"Caleb's over you. If you're smart, you'll forget him and move on with your life."

Which is exactly what I plan to do. But she knew forgetting Caleb was going to be much easier said than done. Especially when she heard a car turn in at the drive and her heart leaped into her throat at the thought that it was probably him.

CHAPTER TWENTY-ONE

THE IMPATIENCE CALEB FELT whenever Holly contacted him lately returned with a vengeance the moment he saw her car. Since it was Sunday, the ferry had been moving more quickly than usual. He'd made the drive from south Seattle in less than forty minutes, yet she'd beaten him here. Even after he'd told her to give him an hour. No wonder he'd moved to San Francisco.

Scowling, he put the Mustang in Park and cut the engine. He needed a few minutes alone with Madison, but he had to get rid of Holly first—wherever she was. He was fairly certain he'd locked the door to the cottage, so she couldn't be inside. And she wasn't sitting in her car.

He got out and started across the drive. When he'd cleared the arbor, he could see more of the cottage, where he expected to find Holly hunched against the rain, waiting for him under the eaves. But he saw no one until he was just a few feet away from Madison's house. Then the door opened and Holly dashed out, nearly running into him.

"Whoa, take it easy," he said, dodging her.

She glanced from him to Madison, who was standing in the doorway behind her. "You wouldn't even be here if it wasn't for me, Caleb," she said, her face full of fury.

"Holly—"

"I don't want to talk about it," she said, and marched to her car.

"What about your purse?" he called after her, but she'd already slammed her door and started the engine. Throwing the transmission in reverse, she gave it far more gas than necessary and tore out of the drive.

"THANKS FOR DETAILING my identity and your plans for me to your ex-wife," Madison said as the echo of Holly's squealing tires died away. "I guess I was the only one who didn't know, huh?"

"It wasn't like that," Caleb said.

"What was it like?"

"Would it make a difference if I told you?"

"Should it?"

He raked a hand through his hair. "I don't know," he said with a sigh. "But we need to talk." His somber expression and his tone told Madison that he wanted to discuss more than just their relationship.

Prickles of fear raced down her spine. Had he found something? Something she wouldn't like?

"Okay," she said, and held open the door, steeling herself for whatever would follow. But then Danny's Jaguar pulled into the drive, and Brianna got out.

"Hi, Caleb," she called and ran over the lawn to give him a big hug. "I'm home early!"

Madison waited her turn for a hug from Brianna, then crossed the wet lawn to collect Brianna's bag from Danny. "It's only ten o'clock," she said when he handed it to her. "What's going on?"

"I decided I'd better go in to the office today. I'm behind at work."

"You couldn't have called to let me know you were bringing Brianna home now?"

"You *asked* me to bring her home early," he said.

Madison sighed. "It would have been nice if you'd arranged it."

He shrugged and got back in his car. "I knew you'd be here," he said simply, and drove off.

Madison turned, trudging back to Caleb and Brianna. Caleb had lifted Brianna into his arms, and she was busy telling him all about the new fish her father had bought this weekend to add to her aquarium.

"Let's get out of the rain," Madison suggested, and felt the pressure of Caleb's hand on her back as they hurried inside. He pulled away to close the door, but not before she recognized that, no matter what he'd done, she still longed for his touch.

Evidently she was an even bigger fool than she'd thought.

"Well?" she said as he put Brianna down.

Caleb gave a subtle nod that let Madison know he was concerned about Brianna overhearing what he had to say. "Is there someplace we could be alone?"

"Johnny's here, too," she said.

"Then maybe I should go home. We can talk on the phone." But he didn't turn to leave right away. He stood there staring at her, making her feel self-conscious about her damp, tangled hair and hastily donned robe, even though he was mostly looking at her lips.

"Why's everyone up so early?" Johnny asked, stumbling into the living room with a yawn.

Grateful for the interruption, Madison broke eye contact with Caleb. "Brianna's home," she told him.

CALEB PEELED OFF his clothes on the way to his bedroom, planning to climb beneath the sheets and pass out for a few hours. But he still had to call Madison, prepare her for the fact that Tye would probably be arrested. He knew she'd have divided feelings. Horror that her own half brother could be capable of such violence. Sympathy for the way it was going to affect his wife and children. Vindication that she'd been right about her father all along.

Kicking off his jeans, he tossed them aside without caring where they landed, scooped the cordless phone off the nightstand and sank into bed in his boxers. Never had a mattress felt so good....

But he didn't have long to relax. Madison answered almost immediately. "Hello?"

He stared at the ceiling, picturing her almond-shaped eyes gazing up at him and her mouth curved into the same seductive smile as the night they'd gone dancing. "It's me."

She was silent for a moment, a silence fraught with tension. "What's happened?" she asked.

Closing his eyes, Caleb tried to separate what he felt for Madison from what he felt in general. "I'm afraid I have some news you might not want to hear."

"What is it?"

He could tell by the sound of her voice that she was bracing for the worst. "Tye might have a connection to my sister-in-law's murder."

His statement was met with silence. "I was afraid of that," she finally whispered. There was another long pause before she continued. "How did you find out?"

"I have a picture of Susan the night she disappeared. A blue Ford truck just like your father's is parked right next to her."

"There are a lot of trucks like my father's."

"Not with the same license plate. Tye's neighbor saw him driving your father's truck the night Susan disappeared. He said Tye brought it home and parked it out front for a while."

"Driving my dad's truck doesn't prove he hurt anyone," she said, but her voice held no conviction, and because of the locket and other things that had disappeared from under the house, Caleb knew she believed Tye was involved.

"We'll learn more later. I'll call you as soon as I hear anything."

"Does that mean he killed those other women, too?" she asked.

"Nothing's definite, yet. But it's possible."

He heard her sigh. "If so, he got away with it because of my father," she said. "Why would he kill again?"

"Sometimes there's no good explanation for homicidal behavior. To a psychopath, killing becomes a craving, an addiction. Serial killers feed on the power. Maybe the compulsion overcame him."

"Would he go to prison or..."

She let her words drift away, and Caleb knew she was thinking about the death penalty. "I won't lie to you. If the lab is able to come up with the DNA profile they've been working on, and it happens to match Tye's DNA, the district attorney will have a pretty strong case. And there'll probably be other evidence." He punched his pillow and rolled over. "I've called Gibbons. The police will be heading over to your brother's place as soon as they can procure a search warrant."

"I suspected Tye and yet...I can't believe it," she said. "When will we find out for sure?"

"Depends on the lab, but it shouldn't take more than another few days, maybe a week."

"Poor Sharon."

"Are *you* going to be okay?" he asked.

"I don't know. I'm relieved no one else will be hurt. And I'm numb enough right now that I just want it all to end. It's been part of my life, in one way or another, for far too long."

"I hope it'll be over soon."

"So you can write another book?" she said, her voice caustic.

"So I can go home," he said truthfully. He didn't need the headache of trying to sort out his feelings for her. He was torn between wanting to pursue a relationship and, now that things had turned sour, wanting to back away entirely. Holly had been a big mistake. He had no desire to make another.

"When will you leave?" Madison asked.

"Sometime soon."

Caleb sensed that she was softening toward him, and couldn't help taking advantage of it. "Madison, I want you to know that I didn't intend for what happened between us to—"

"Don't," she said. "I know. When we made love it was too honest for either of us to be pretending. But it's all too much right now. I—I don't know what to think about anything anymore."

He bit back the rest of what he wanted to say. He needed to give her time. She'd just learned that her brother might be going to prison—or worse. "What happened with Holly?" he asked when several seconds had passed in silence. "She was supposed to pick up her purse, but it's still here."

His call-waiting beeped, and he pulled the phone away to see who was trying to get through. He was eager to hear from Gibbons, to find out for sure that Tye was their man. But it was Holly.

"Speak of the devil," he said. "Holly's calling me on the other line."

"Then I'll let her explain."

"Okay."

He felt a nagging reluctance to let Madison go, even though there was nothing left to say. "I'll call you when I hear from Detective Gibbons," he said, forcing some finality into his voice.

"Caleb?"

"Yes?"

"Will you do me one favor?"

"What's that?"

"Don't leave without saying goodbye. After my father... Well, I hate that. I hate that I never got to say goodbye."

He closed his eyes. Despite his best efforts to push the memory away, he could still feel her body beneath his the night they'd made love. "I won't leave without saying goodbye," he said, although he knew it wouldn't be an easy moment.

She hung up and Caleb switched lines. "You never got your purse," he told Holly.

"I couldn't. I couldn't stand being around that woman another minute."

Caleb used one hand to rub both temples while he talked. "You mean Madison?"

"Who else?"

"There's nothing wrong with Madison, Holly."

"She thinks she has some sort of hold on you, Caleb. Can you believe she had the nerve to tell me you don't love me anymore, that I should move on?"

She laughed incredulously, but that only annoyed Caleb further. He'd told Holly the same thing in a million different ways. The fact that he'd divorced her for the second time and moved to another state wasn't enough? What he'd said in the cottage, when he'd told her they were over for good—that wasn't enough?

Maybe he'd been too gentle. Obviously, Holly didn't get it.

He gave up rubbing his temples. He was never going to relieve the tension humming through his body as long as he was talking to his ex-wife. "Holly, Madison's right," he said frankly.

"What?"

"We've talked about this before. We're finished. For good. Do you understand?"

"No, Caleb, I don't. You...you don't mean it. You came back to me last time."

"Last time there were—" he thought of the baby, dared not mention it "—other issues involved."

"I don't care. You came all the way back here, just because I needed you."

"Holly, I came back to help you out as a *friend*. I'll be going home in the next few days."

"You can't leave! What about finding Susan's killer?"

"I think we might have done that today."

He could tell by the sudden break in the conversation that this surprised her as much as he'd expected it to. "Who is it?" she asked.

"Tye Purcell."

"Madison's brother?"

"You remember him?"

"I remember everyone involved in the case, Caleb. I've been with you every step of the way since we first met. But then, *I* believe in 'till death do us part.'"

Hearing her voice rise, he hurried to cut her off before emotions could escalate any further. "I'm really tired. I've got to go, okay?"

"But you love me, Caleb. Admit it, *please*. You'll always love me."

"I don't love you, Holly. Not like you think."

He heard her sniff. "It's Madison, isn't it? You've fallen in love with her."

Caleb willed her words out of his head, willed Madison out of his heart. "What I feel for Madison is none of your business, Holly," he said, and disconnected.

MADISON TOUCHED Johnny's arm. He was sitting on the living room floor next to her, playing Candyland with Brianna, but he wasn't having an easy time relaxing. He kept glancing at the clock and jiggling his leg.

"You okay?" she asked.

"I'm fine."

Brianna squealed at getting a card with double red squares. "I'm going ahead of you," she taunted Johnny.

He shrugged, obviously indifferent to the game, agitation rolling off him in waves, but he took his turn. Madison supposed she had to admire her brother for even playing. She knew he'd only agreed because Brianna had begged him. But Madison had enough on her mind today without worrying about Johnny. Ever since Caleb had told her about Tye this morning, she'd been guessing and second-guessing about whether or not her brother could really have committed those horrible acts. And no matter how shocking, disturbing or overwhelming she found that possibility, her mind kept returning to Caleb.

Caleb's so handsome, Maddy. How did your date go last night? Her mother had asked her that on the phone earlier.

It wasn't really a date.

Did he kiss you?

I didn't call about Caleb. I called to tell you that I've got Brianna home, so I won't be showing the house today.

That's fine, dear. Do you think this Caleb is ready to find a wife?

Mom, that's enough!

But it was so nice of him to mow the lawn. They just don't make men like that anymore. You've got to snap him up while you can.

He's moving back to San Francisco.

When?

Soon. Too soon...

Don't let him get away, Maddy.

She'd known she could shut her mother up very quickly simply by telling Annette who Caleb really was. But something—misguided loyalty, no doubt—made her reluctant to ruin her mother's good opinion of him. She hadn't told Annette that Johnny had been the one to visit the cemetery, either, or that the police were now investigating Tye. What Johnny had done would hardly improve his relationship with her mother. And she didn't want to break the news about Tye, even to Johnny, until they knew for sure.

"What are you thinking?" Johnny asked.

She blinked and brought her attention back to the game. "Nothing. Is it my turn?"

He scrubbed his face, his palm rasping over several days' worth of whiskers. "It was your turn thirty seconds ago," he said as she drew a purple card and moved her plastic gingerbread man.

When they were talking privately earlier that day, she'd told Johnny she'd help him get on his feet. She'd promised to let him stay in the cottage after Caleb left, if he'd clean up and begin a rigorous rehabilitation program. But he hadn't made any commitments. To Madison's disappointment, the closeness and understanding they'd achieved the night before hadn't lasted. If anything, she felt Johnny resented her even more for having seen his weakness.

"Come on, Mom, go!" Brianna said.

"Sorry." Realizing it was her turn *again,* Madison offered her daughter a quick smile and picked up another card. "Oh, no!" She managed a groan for Brianna's benefit. "I have to go back."

Brianna laughed as she watched Madison move back to the purple "Plumpy" pictured on the card. "I'm going to win," her daughter cried gleefully, clapping her hands.

Madison knew she was *way* behind Brianna, and even Johnny, on their journey to the king's candy, but she wasn't worried about losing the game. She was afraid that, amidst the turmoil in her life, she was about to lose something much more important.

"It's your turn again, Mommy," Brianna said, her voice full of fresh impatience.

A honk sounded outside and Johnny scrambled to his feet. "That's my ride."

Madison frowned at him. He'd made a few calls earlier. She'd heard the drone of his voice in the other room while she was reading to Brianna, but he hadn't mentioned anything about leaving. "I didn't know you were going anywhere," she said. "Will you be coming back?"

"Not tonight. I'm gonna chill with a friend," he said, heading out.

Madison opened her mouth to tell him he might want to stay close, that they might have a family crisis on their hands. But she knew it wouldn't change his mind. He was his own walking crisis. And she didn't want to discuss what was happening with Tye until she heard more from Caleb.

"You're not quitting the game, too, are you, Mommy?" Brianna asked, clearly not pleased with Johnny's defection.

Madison sighed as the door slammed behind her half

brother, wondering when, if ever, she'd see him again. "No, I'm not going to quit," she said, and took her turn, only to land on the square labeled "Gooey Gumdrop—Stay Here until a Yellow Card is Drawn."

On her next three turns, she drew a green, a purple and then a red card. Brianna giggled each time she couldn't move, but Madison didn't think it was funny. The game felt a lot like her life. She couldn't continue happily on her way until she got over Caleb.

Unfortunately, she'd done exactly what she'd told herself not to do—and fallen in love.

HOLLY TURNED OFF her headlights and let the engine of her Honda idle as she sat behind the wheel, staring at the sleepy little house where Madison lived. Rain thrummed softly on her hood and beaded on her windshield, pearl-like in those fleeting moments when the moon's pale glow managed to slip through the clouds. Eventually, the drops began to quiver, then roll down the glass like tears. But there were no other sights or sounds to distract her. Only the beacon of light in Madison's kitchen where she sat alone at the table, bent over something Holly couldn't see because of the black plastic that covered half the window.

Madison Lieberman... Who would've thought Ellis Purcell's daughter would exact such perfect, if unwitting, revenge? Pretty, *petite* Madison.

Shaking her head, Holly laughed bitterly. Men liked their women small because it made them feel strong, powerful. Small women were *desirable*. Holly had large bones and height to rival most men's. The exact opposite of the petted girl she'd grown up with as her stepsister. Different from Susan in every way...

But that was nothing new. Holly had long since learned

that luck was never in her corner. If she wanted *anything,* she had to take matters into her own hands.

Getting out of the car, she pulled the black hood of her sweatshirt up over her hair. It wasn't easy to see through the trees that partially blocked her view of the house, but she dared not move the car any closer. Caleb wasn't a fool. After hearing his impatience with her on the phone, she was afraid of what he'd do if he caught her here.

But she needed to look things over. To think. To plan. Madison was something new, something she hadn't anticipated....

The smell of the sea hit her with the first blast of wind. She inhaled deeply as she made her way up the drive, crouching between the cars, moving steadily, deliberately, while gathering her calm and controlling her rage.

Caleb's car was to the right, Madison's to the left. They were parked side by side, as if they belonged to a married couple.

Holly grimaced and felt the hood of each car with the back of her hand. Cold. Just as she'd expected. It was nearly midnight.

With a frown, she hid in the arbor that concealed her from Madison's house, and craned her head to see Caleb's cottage. It was dark. He was there, in bed, without her.

She felt a sudden wave of debilitating sadness. Why did Caleb have to betray her like this? Why was he forcing her hand? It didn't make sense. She'd done everything for him, even going so far as to arrange her sister's death for his next book!

Absently rubbing the scratches on her arms where a few scabs remained, she closed her eyes, trying to shut out her last memories of Susan. If it hadn't been for Lance, the cheating bastard, her sister would never have shown up at her house so late at night. Susan would never have seen what she'd seen. But she *had* shown up and left Holly no choice. Susan was too perceptive, too persistent and inquisitive. She wouldn't let it go.

Still, Holly regretted that Susan was gone. Her stepsister was the only person in her life who'd stuck by her through thick and thin.

It's okay, she told herself when her throat started to tighten and burn. *I only did what I had to do.* And she'd been clever enough to make it all work to her advantage. She wasn't going to let Caleb slip away from her now. Madison would be a figure in his next book, nothing more, and Holly and Caleb would finally be together again.

Except Holly's rival wasn't only a woman. It was a child, too. She'd seen that picture on the fridge, known instantly how much Madison's daughter would appeal to Caleb. He'd wanted children for years....

Holly remembered the time she'd pretended to be pregnant. Sometimes it helped to pretend. Having a child would have made her life so much easier. Caleb wouldn't have left her if there'd been a baby.

Only she couldn't conceive. The abortion she'd given herself at sixteen had ruined any chance of that. But she wouldn't allow Madison to offer him what she couldn't.

Reality, as cold and harsh as the wind stinging her face, was too strong for pretending tonight. Holly knew she had to face the truth and deal with the gut-roiling jealousy that caused her real, physical pain—pain so acute she doubled over, barely biting back a groan.

"I'll fix it...I'll fix it...." She whispered those words like an incantation until she could believe her own promise. Until she could stand again. Until she could breathe.

She *would* fix it, she decided. She'd fix everything.

But how? Holly bit her lip as she tried to think. She could lure Caleb away from the house with a lie about some new piece of evidence. If she said Margie White, a friend of Susan's they'd already interviewed, had found something in her car, Caleb would rush right over to her house. Margie wouldn't know what he was talking about once he got there, of course, but Holly didn't need Margie to support the lie. She just needed time. When she saw Caleb again, she'd tell him that whoever had called her with the information had sounded just like Margie. She must have been mistaken, she'd say. Anyone could call based on that flyer they'd distributed, right? Maybe she'd even try to make it seem like a crank. And once Caleb was gone, she'd cut Madison's phone line, just in case things didn't go as smoothly as planned.

That was it, she decided. That was a good plan. With *that* plan, Madison and Brianna wouldn't figure in Caleb's affections for long.

CHAPTER TWENTY-TWO

THE RINGING OF the telephone interrupted a particularly good dream. Caleb was reluctant to wake fully, but he thought it might be Madison. *Why* he thought it might be her, he wasn't sure. Probably just wishful thinking.

"Hello?" Hearing the scratchy quality of his own voice, he cleared his throat and tried again. "Hello?"

"Wake up, Trovato."

Gibbons. Caleb tried not to feel disappointed. Shoving himself into a sitting position, he shot a glance at the clock to see that it was only one in the morning and not dawn, as he'd first assumed. "What is it? Did you arrest Tye Purcell?"

"No."

Caleb's disappointment grew exponentially. He'd been so sure they'd finally reached the end of the road, achieved resolution. "Why not?"

"Several reasons. Remember that drop of blood we found on the sheet beneath Susan's body?"

"Yeah."

"It's Type O, and Tye's Type B. It might take a few weeks to do a DNA comparison, but it only takes a minute to get a blood type."

"So that's it? We're back to square one?" Caleb propped the phone against his shoulder, got out of bed and yanked on his jeans. He needed a cup of coffee. He'd slept most of the day and half the night, but he still felt groggy as hell.

"Not yet. Holly just called me."

"Thank God she didn't call me," Caleb muttered, heading to the kitchen. He was so sick of hearing from his ex-wife he thought he could live the rest of his life without contact and be the better for it.

"You two having a lovers' quarrel?"

Caleb flipped on the kitchen light, wincing at the sudden brightness. "We don't have a lovers' anything. What'd she want?"

"She said a friend of Susan's named Margie called her and—"

"This late? Don't people do things in the middle of the day anymore?"

"That's what I'd like to know. According to Holly, Margie just found a note in her car signed by a man named Tye. She thinks it must've fallen out of Susan's purse a week or so before she died, when Margie and Susan went to lunch."

"Holly and I met Margie," Caleb said, scratching his bare chest with one hand while filling the coffeepot with the other. "She seemed pretty straight up, but—"

"Whether she's straight up or not, handwriting samples and maybe fingerprints should tell us whether the note is really from Tye," Gibbons interjected.

Caleb set the coffeepot on the counter. "But a note from Tye doesn't make sense. I thought you just said his blood type doesn't match the blood found on the sheet. Yet suddenly we have proof that he and Susan knew each other?"

"I'm as confused as you are."

Something didn't feel right. Caleb shook his head.

"You wanna meet me at Margie's house?" Gibbons asked.

Caleb changed the phone to his left hand so he could button his jeans with his right. "Are you *asking* me to come? When you found Susan's car, I had to twist your arm to let me join you."

"Yeah, well, you know I'm not supposed to bring civilians. An ex-cop is one thing. Holly's another. But Holly claims this woman won't talk to me tonight unless you're there. And I'd really like things to be easy for a change. If Tye *is* our killer, we've got to close in before he runs or hurts someone else."

"Why won't Margie talk to you without me?" Caleb asked. That didn't sound right, either. He'd only met her once, and they hadn't spoken since then.

"Who knows? Holly said Margie trusts you because she's met you before. I told her Margie shouldn't have any problem trusting me, but she repeated that she'd promised Margie you'd be there. You know how a woman thinks. If telling you once is good, repeating it fifty times is better, even if it doesn't make sense from the get-go."

"Where's Holly now?" Caleb asked.

"At home. She wanted to come, too, but I told her there was no way, not after the kind of behavior she exhibited at Lance Perkin's the other night."

"Did she give up?"

"Yeah. She said she'd stay out of it so long as you're going to be there. And believe me, I'd much rather have you present than her."

"Thanks, but I'm not dumb enough to believe that's much of a compliment," Caleb said dryly.

Gibbons chuckled. "We'll get this woman's statement and the note. That's it. If I need to arrest Tye, I'll take a couple of uniforms. When we questioned him today he nearly went ballistic."

"This note doesn't add up," Caleb muttered again.

"I've got to check it out whether it adds up or not," Gibbons said. "Are you coming?"

"I'm on my way." Lord knows he wasn't going to be able to sleep anymore tonight.

MADISON EXAMINED the sketch she'd just finished of Caleb's chest and shoulders, and scowled in frustration. His sculpted body easily lent itself to an artist's pencil. So did the raw-boned beauty of his face. But she'd been drawing for more than two hours and simply couldn't match the vision of him she held in her head.

She was still such an amateur, she thought in disgust, and dropped her pencil. But she'd drawn Caleb's mouth earlier, and felt she'd done a better job there. That sketch sat on the table at her elbow, tempting her eye again and again because his lips looked almost as sensual on paper as they did in real life. Almost. With Caleb, it was pretty tough to compete with reality.

Why she continued to torture herself by sketching him, Madison didn't know. She had so much work she needed to do. But drawing was the only thing that kept her from thinking too much about Tye and whether or not he'd be going to prison—or facing an even worse punishment.

Tomorrow would probably tell....

Pushing away from the table, she stood and stretched. She'd stayed up far too late. Her life might be in upheaval, but responsibilities didn't disappear. Tomorrow was Monday. Brianna had school, and Madison had to work. She'd checked earlier and already knew her voice mail was loaded with messages. Which was good. If business didn't pick up soon, she'd have a lot more to worry about than Tye getting arrested, or moving on without Caleb in her life.

Gathering her pads and pencils, Madison piled them neatly on the counter. Then she lingered in the kitchen, wiping off the faucet, cleaning the microwave and watering her plants, dreading the moment she actually had to call it a night. Everything seemed so quiet, so still, like the calm before a storm.

When she ran out of things to do, she started down the hall. But the crunch of tires on gravel outside drew her back. She'd heard Caleb leave about twenty minutes ago. She couldn't help hoping he was back. She liked knowing he was around.

Or maybe it was someone dropping off Johnny....

Standing to the side of the window, Madison watched a tall blond woman climb out of a familiar white Honda.

It wasn't Caleb or Johnny. It was Holly.

HOLLY SMILED WHEN Madison passed the window on her way to the door. She hadn't even had a chance to knock. Obviously Madison wasn't afraid of her. Not that Holly had expected her to be. Women weren't typically afraid of other women. Even during the media blitz following the other murders, Holly had never had trouble getting young women, complete strangers, to meet her somewhere or even come to her apartment. She'd bumped into Tatiana Harris at the grocery store and, simply by striking up a conversation and laughing at the stupid little comments Tatiana made about her husband, had talked her into going to a movie with her instead of straight home. Rosey Martin had gone home with her from the Laundromat to watch a video. Lori Schiller had agreed to meet her at a park. And there were others, including Anna Tyler, who'd lived next door.

Want to come over? We can do makeovers...manicures...have a drink...grab a bite to eat....

Women were so gullible—and catty and deceitful. They pretended to be your friend only to stab you in the back the moment you confided in them. Just like Rosie Wheeler and Paige Todd had done to her in high school.

Holly winced at the memory of the morning she'd shown up at school to find Baby Killer and Whore written in nail polish across her locker. She could still hear the whispers and muffled laughter, still feel the scorn that had nearly smothered her for months afterward. The other girls wouldn't include her, or even speak to her. But she'd show them.

She'd show Madison, too. Madison wouldn't take away the one person who made her feel complete. She hadn't felt the same anger when she believed Caleb loved her, hadn't bothered anyone the whole time they were married. There wasn't any reason to. When she had Caleb she had what all the other girls wanted and could simply laugh in their faces.

But if she was going to hang on to Caleb, she had to move fast. He wouldn't stay gone forever.

She reached the front step and heard the scrape of the deadbolt as Madison unlocked the door. "Is something wrong, Holly?" she asked, opening it slightly.

"Sorry to stop by so late," Holly said. "I wasn't going to bother you. I was just hoping to catch Caleb. But I don't see his car. I guess he's not home, huh?"

"He left about twenty minutes ago."

"That's too bad." She laughed. "I'm so out of it. I forgot my purse at his place again. Do you have any idea when he'll be back?"

"I'm afraid not. It might be smarter to call him tomorrow." She started to close the door.

Holly quickly put out a hand to stop her. "I'll do that. But before you go, I have something to tell you."

Madison seemed to hesitate. Holly could see only a slice of her face and body through the door, but it was enough to know she was wearing a pair of sweatpants and a cropped T-shirt. The T-shirt was faded and worn, but the way it hugged Madison's small breasts made Holly even angrier. She was trying to steal Caleb, tempt him. Women—they were always up to something.

"Holly, I don't think—" Madison began, but Holly cut her off.

"It's nothing like before. I would like to come in for a minute, though, if you don't mind. It's a little cold and damp out here." She rubbed her arms and shivered for added effect.

Madison still seemed skeptical. "Tomorrow would be better."

Holly backed up as though she was about to leave, purposely acting as nonconfrontational as possible. "Okay. I understand. I just wanted to tell you I've been out all night thinking. And you should know you were right earlier. I have to let go of Caleb. It's time. Past time, really, but—" she let her voice break, and swiped at the false tears gathering in her eyes "—sometimes it just hurts so badly. I still love him. I'll always love him. And…" She gulped as though the words were difficult for her. "And I'm afraid if he can't love me, no one else will be able to, either."

Compassion softened Madison's features. "I understand how you feel. Anyone who's gone through a divorce experiences some of the same insecurities. But you'll get over it and find your feet again."

"I'm not so sure of that," Holly said, and buried her face in her hands, sobbing brokenly.

Madison opened the door wider. "It takes time, Holly."

"You're probably right," she muttered. "I'm just so alone."

"You're not alone.... Why don't you come in, and I'll make us both some tea?"

"I wouldn't want to wake your little girl." Holly sniffed, finally lowering her hands from her face. "Or anyone else who might be staying with you."

"There's no one else, just Brianna. And we won't wake her."

Wiping her eyes, Holly followed Madison inside. The house smelled like homemade cookies. Madison was *so* domestic, with her pretty little girl, her natural beauty and charming house.

"Maybe Caleb will be home by the time you finish your tea, so you can get your purse," Madison was saying, her back to Holly now.

Holly felt in her pocket to make sure she hadn't lost the pills. She'd only be able to use them if she could get Madison to drink something. But Susan had proved that she didn't really need drugs. The shock would be enough.

"Maybe," Holly said. But she knew she'd be long gone by the time Caleb returned. She'd leave a surprise for him, though. And no one would suspect her.

No one ever suspected a woman.

FRUSTRATED, CALEB PUNCHED Holly's number into his cell phone again. He'd already called twice since leaving Whidbey Island and had gotten her answering machine both times. Where was she? She'd obviously been awake when she'd called Detective Gibbons only a half hour or so earlier. Even if she'd gone to bed, she wasn't a heavy sleeper. He knew that from when they were married. There were plenty of nights he'd awakened to find her staring at the ceiling or gone, off to the corner convenience store or out driving.

He glanced at her purse in the seat next to him and considered delivering it to her tomorrow, then decided against it. Her place was on the way to this Margie White's house, where he was supposed to meet Detective Gibbons. Taking it to her now, while it was so late and he was in a hurry, would be perfect. They'd have no time to talk, and she'd have no reason to contact him tomorrow. Especially if the police ended up proving that Tye *was* the one who'd murdered Susan. Then Caleb's obligation to the relationships of his past would be fulfilled; his trip to Seattle would be over.

He could easily conjure up the smell of San Francisco's crusty sourdough bread and the crabs and other seafood sold along the wharf, could feel the wind coming in off the bay. If picturing himself in his new home also felt a little lonely, he refused to acknowledge it. He just had to get back to work. At that point everything would be good again.

Slowing for the next off ramp, he exited Interstate 99 at Mill Creek and turned toward Alderwood Manor, where he used to live with Holly. The house they'd shared, which he'd given her as part of the divorce settlement, was nothing like the big estates on Mercer Island. But it had been new when they moved in and comfortable for a young couple just starting out. They'd both had great hopes when they'd bought that house.

He gazed at the quiet streets he'd frequented on and off for so long, feeling like a stranger now. Funny how things changed.

His cell phone rang. He glanced at the caller ID to see it was Gibbons before punching the Talk button.

"Where the hell are you?" the detective asked, nearly blasting out his eardrum.

Caleb jerked the phone back a few inches. Couldn't Gibbons say anything without shouting? "I've got to drop something by Holly's. I'll be there in a minute."

"I'll wait ten. Then I'm going to the door with or without you. I want to sleep sometime tonight."

"Good enough," Caleb said, and ended the call. But when he finally reached the small stucco, two-story home he'd shared with Holly, he found it dark. Evidently she'd gone to bed.

Shoving his phone in his pocket, he grabbed her purse and went to the door, leaving his car idling in the drive.

Susan's dogs barked as he waited impatiently for Holly to answer the bell, but seconds turned into minutes and she didn't appear.

He pushed the doorbell again, then knocked. Finally he tried the door handle. It was locked, but the small lockbox he'd bought to secure their spare key back when they were together was still right where he'd left it, inside the front flower planter. He doubted Holly knew how to change the combination. He'd always done that sort of thing. So he wasn't surprised when he pushed 1-9-4-3, the year of his mother's birth, and it opened.

"Holly, you home?" he called, poking his head inside the foyer as soon as he'd unlocked the door.

Susan's schnauzers growled low in their throats, but when he bent down and offered his hand for them to sniff, they remembered him. One even licked him. But there was no response from his ex-wife.

"Holly?" He stepped inside, immediately noticing that the house smelled different than it had when they were living together. He supposed that was normal, since his cologne, hair products and clothes were no longer part of the equation—since *he* was no longer part of the equation. But it didn't smell of perfume, like Susan's place, or feel-good food and crayons, like Madison's. Or even like the dogs. This scent was more...musty.

Once he flipped on a light, Caleb could see why. Piles of everything from clothes to magazines to books to papers covered all horizontal surfaces—even most of the floor—along with a thick layer of dust. The clutter seemed to be growing from the walls like some kind of space-eating plant, until only a narrow pathway remained, leading from room to room.

With Susan's murder, he could certainly understand why Holly wouldn't be worried about cleaning. But what he saw wasn't the result of days or weeks of neglect. It would take months, maybe even years, to collect so much junk. Holly must not have thrown anything away since he'd left her.

"Jeez, Holly," he muttered. She'd always been a packrat. They'd had a million arguments over cleaning out the garage and the closets. But now that she was living alone, without anyone to check her tendency to hang on to absolutely everything, she seemed to be taking it to new extremes.

He pulled a newspaper from the bottom of a stack of papers and grimaced at the date. It was thirteen months old.

Setting her purse on top of a box of envelopes and copy paper on the dining room table, he turned to go, counting himself lucky that he'd managed to miss her. But it seemed odd that she wouldn't be home when she'd told Gibbons she would be. There was something strange about the house in general. The mess, the shut-up feeling... What was going on with her?

Grudgingly, he turned back. He should at least let her

know he'd returned her purse. He'd placed it in a prominent spot, but there was still a good chance she'd never see it in the mess.

"Hello?" He rapped on the walls as he made his way up the stairs and down the hall toward the master suite.

Again, no answer.

The bedroom door stood ajar. "Holly?" He turned on the light, just in case she'd managed to sleep through the dogs barking, the bell-ringing and calling.

The bed was empty. Clothes were piled everywhere, and boxes of God-only-knew-what were stacked on the dresser, the nightstand, the cedar chest and the floor, making her room as difficult to navigate as the rest of the house. Next to a heap of what looked like clean laundry, he even found toys—a giant box of dolls and jump ropes and roller skates.

What was Holly doing with children's toys? And why was there so much paper, wadded into tight balls, strewn across the floor?

Curious, he picked one up and smoothed it out. Holly had written "Madison" over and over in red ink, scribbled it out until the paper tore, and started again. He ironed out another one to find more of the same. And another. And another. He was just wondering what the hell this was all about when Susan's dogs caught his eye. Growling playfully, they were fighting over some kind of leopard-print fabric.

Caleb's blood suddenly ran cold. That fabric looked like...

Bending closer, he took the article away, and saw that it was exactly what he'd feared—a halter top. Exactly like the one Susan had been wearing the night she disappeared. Exactly like the one Holly had said she'd never seen before.

Caleb's phone broke the silence. It was Detective Gibbons. "I don't know what's going on here," he said, "but I just dragged Margie White out of bed for nothing. She claims she never called Holly and doesn't know anything about a note from anyone named Tye."

CALEB'S HEART jackhammered against his chest as he dashed out of Holly's bedroom and pounded down the stairs. He took the halter top with him, but didn't bother locking the front door. Slamming it behind him, he jumped into his Mustang, popped the transmission into reverse and squealed out of the driveway.

He was at least thirty minutes away from Madison's, and Gibbons was even farther. Gibbons had just contacted the station. A car was on its way. But fear that they were already too late made it difficult for Caleb to breathe.

Holly says this woman won't talk to me tonight unless you're there....

She'd purposely drawn him away.

It's Madison, isn't it? You've fallen in love with her....

Madison...Madison...Madison, written all over those sheets in red ink...

Holly was crazy, obsessed.

He rounded the corner, then looked both ways before running a stoplight. "I'm coming, Maddy. I'm coming," he muttered, but he couldn't avoid the images dancing in his mind—images of finding Madison like Susan had looked.

Holly had seen pictures of the crime scene. She'd poured over every bit of evidence, right along with him. She could definitely have copied the Sandpoint Strangler, but now that he saw her as capable of doing what she'd done to Susan, bits and pieces of memories assaulted him one after the other, making him sick. He had a terrible feeling that Holly had been lying and manipulating him and everyone else for a long, long time, using the fact that she was a woman to evoke sympathy instead of suspicion.

He was driving a blue Ford truck with a white camper shell....

Holly had said that the first day they'd met. Now Caleb wondered if she'd been lying from the start. All the papers had mentioned the Ford. Cunning as she was, she could even have tracked down Purcell in order to come up with the partial plate number. She'd been the main reason the investigation had focused on Purcell.

I'm afraid our killer is close, Gibbons had said. *Close to the investigation. Close to us.*

Holly was close, all right. She'd stuck to Caleb like glue since he'd first knocked on her door about Anna Tyler's murder. Anna, the ninth victim, had been living next door to her. Talk about opportunity.

I think I was wrong about you. I don't think you're going to find this killer. He's much too smart....

Such calm, cool confidence wasn't the result of one freak, accidental murder. Caleb thought of all the pretending Holly had done, all the setting up. A person didn't turn into a cold-blooded killer overnight. She never would've been able to pull it off if she'd felt even a morsel of regret. She'd fed him misinformation, manipulated his emotions, used him to stay one step ahead of the investigation the whole time. And he'd looked everywhere but right in front of him.

"God!" he said, and smacked the steering wheel.

Only she'd finally slipped up. If she hadn't kept that halter top...

Did you see anything like this in her apartment, Holly?

No, I've never seen a halter top like that before in my life. I'd definitely remember it....

Grabbing his cell phone, he tried Madison's house again. "Pick up," he pleaded. "Pick up."

But it just rang and rang and rang....

CHAPTER TWENTY-THREE

"SO HOW MANY TIMES have you slept with Caleb?" Holly asked.

Startled by the question, which had come out of nowhere after fifteen minutes of small talk, Madison set her cup in its saucer with a clumsy *clank*. She blinked several times because Holly was no longer in clear focus, and shook her head. "I'm...I'm not going to answer that," she said, but her speech seemed hopelessly slurred. She wanted to tell Holly to leave, but the words eluded her. Probably because the room was spinning, scrambling her brain.

"*Have* you slept with him?" Holly persisted. "Has he made you shudder in ecstasy like he does me?"

Madison grimaced. The image of Caleb with Holly, especially in the present tense, made her nauseous.

"What? Don't you like thinking about what I'm going to do with Caleb later, when I console him over your death?" Holly said.

Her *death?* Was that supposed to be some kind of joke? If Madison wasn't mistaken, Holly was smiling faintly. But her eyes seemed strangely blank. They didn't act like windows to her soul; they were more like mirrors, reflecting Madison's image back at her.

And Holly didn't make sense. Nothing did. Madison could see Holly's words shimmering in the air between them, floating in space as though she could reach out and capture them with her hands.

Summoning all her mental energy, she focused hard on the question, because it seemed important that she reply. "Why are you trying to upset me?" she asked, and tried to take another sip of tea, but the cup was too heavy to lift.

"I'm not trying to upset you. I don't care about you at all. I'm just saying that Caleb takes making love pretty seriously. Once he goes to bed with me again, things will be different."

"Diff... differ..." Giving up on the longer word, Madison went for the more important one. "How?"

"He doesn't sleep with just anyone, like some men I know. Sex has meaning to him. He makes you feel as though you're the only woman in the world. It's very erotic."

Madison knew how erotic it was. She felt flushed just remembering. Or maybe she was coming down with the flu. Certainly something was wrong....

"Madison? Are you still with me?" Holly snapped her fingers in Madison's face.

Madison closed her eyes to stop the room from shifting. "Yes. Yes, I think so."

"Aren't you going to finish your tea?"

"No, I—" She used her hand to prop up her head, which suddenly seemed too large for her body. "I think it's time...for you...to go." There. She'd said it. It had taken supreme effort to remember all the words and string them together in the appropriate sequence. But she'd managed to say what needed to be said. She had to get back into bed, had to sleep until she felt better.

"To *go?*" Holly echoed. "That isn't very polite of you, now is it?"

Holly's laughter grew loud, then soft, then loud again. When her chair scraped the floor, Madison knew she'd gotten up, but she couldn't figure out what Holly was doing.

"Are...are you leaving?" she asked, having to take several breaths to get the whole sentence out.

"Of course not. At least not yet," Holly said. "I need to get my rope before I visit your daughter's room. But don't worry, it's just out in the car."

"Holly?" Madison felt disoriented, confused. Silence fell for an interminable time. Holly was gone, evidently. But then she was back and moving down the hall. Holly wanted to visit Brianna's room. Why? Holly was no friend....

At first Madison told herself it was all right; Brianna was at her father's. But then she heard Brianna's frightened voice calling, "Mommy? Mommy, who is this? Where are you?"

She lurched to her feet. "Brianna? Brianna, run, hide!" Madison used the table, the refrigerator, the wall to help her reach the hallway. She would have called out to her daughter again, warned her, but blackness was closing in on her fast, rolling toward her like a sudden storm.

BRIANNA SLIPPED UNDER her covers, away from the unfamiliar image of a stranger in her doorway. Her mother had said to run, to hide, but Brianna didn't know where to go. Her room had always been safe. What was happening? Why should she run?

She wanted to cry out for her mother again, but the blankets were thick and it was hard to breathe. She lay perfectly still, listening, trying to decide if Mommy was playing some kind of new game. But Mommy usually didn't trick her. And it was very late to be playing a game.

"Brianna? That's your name, isn't it? Come here, sweetheart." It was the stranger, a woman. Or maybe it was a monster with a woman's voice. That would be a very mean monster. Her mother *had* said to run and hide....

Brianna held her breath and squeezed her eyes shut as the she-monster patted the bed, searching for her among the blankets. She was drawing closer. Her hand nearly touched Brianna's arm, but Brianna slithered away and slipped into the crack between the bed and the wall, where she sometimes liked to stuff Elizabeth. It was their little hideout.

"Damn it! Come here." The monster grabbed her arm through the covers, and Brianna screamed. Jerking hard, she twisted free because of the blankets, and scooted under the bed. She stayed there on the floor in the corner, crying now because she knew this was no game. The she-monster was pulling away the bed, and there wasn't anywhere else to go.

BRIANNA'S SCREAM HELPED Madison force back the blackness, gave her the strength to keep fighting. She had to make her legs work, had to remain conscious long enough to be sure Brianna was all right.

Never had a hall seemed so long. Madison didn't think she was going to make it. She could hear her daughter whimpering, "Mommy...Mommy...Mommy..." and clung to that small voice.

"Shut up!" The woman. Angry. In Brianna's room.

Madison had to get there. And she had to do it *now*.

Now...now...now... The words inside her head echoed with urgency, but Madison could no longer walk. The world was spinning, tilting out of control. She was going to throw up. She wanted to sink to the floor and rest her head in her hands, let whatever lapped at her ankles suck her completely away.

Only she wouldn't give up until she knew her daughter was safe.

Falling to her knees, she crawled closer. She heard the squeak of the bed as someone pushed it around, heard low muttering, Brianna's crying....

Brianna, hang on. I'm coming. Mommy's coming.

Madison was breathless by the time she dragged herself into the doorway of Brianna's room. She could see a shape that had to be Holly down on her knees, trying to reach Brianna, who'd apparently crawled under the bed.

Gathering all her strength, Madison managed to find her feet again. *Get away from her. Get...away from...my daughter!* she shouted, but only inside her head. Then she launched herself at Holly.

Madison's movements weren't coordinated enough to do much damage, but she pushed Holly to the ground and their arms tangled. Holly tried to shove her off, to get up, but Madison used the weight of her body to pin her down. She could sense Holly's interest in Brianna, her desire to return to her daughter's bed.

Not at any cost, Madison told herself. Grabbing a fistful of Holly's long hair, she kept hold, focusing on only one thing, even as the darkness overcame her.

Don't let go...don't let go...don't ever let go....

She was just drifting off when she heard footsteps tramping down the hall and a male voice calling to her. Then Holly was wrenched away from her, screaming as she lost two fistfuls of hair, and the blackness became both silent and complete.

CALEB SAT NEXT TO Madison's hospital bed, a rectangle of pale yellow falling through the open door the only light. He was tense with worry despite the doctors' promises that she was going to be fine. Madison had been through so much. So much she didn't deserve. They all had.

Because of Holly.

Shaking his head, he swore under his breath, angry with himself for not realizing his ex-wife was insane. Gibbons had called to tell him he'd found a bunch of other things in Holly's attic—his own attic at one time—many of them belonging to women they'd long believed to be victims of Ellis Purcell.

He should have realized *somehow,* figured it out sooner. He'd known she had emotional problems. He'd just never imagined they were so severe, never imagined she was capable of doing what she'd done. He'd been too busy blaming himself for her problems because he couldn't love her the way she said she needed to be loved. Even after writing that book about the female serial killer Aileen Wuornos, he'd never considered that the Sandpoint Strangler could be a woman. What had happened was a classic example of looking beyond the mark. If a woman was going to kill, she typically used poison.

Holly *had* sedated her victims with drugs, he mused, which made it easy to sexually assault them with whatever she chose, whatever was handy at the time, and strangle them afterward. She was cunning, far more cunning than anyone he'd written about so far. She knew exactly how to make it look like a man's crime, how to cover her tracks.

Damn! He'd known there was some sort of link between the killer and Madison's family. He'd just never dreamed it was him....

Light crept through the window as the sun began to

rise. In the hallway, Caleb could hear movement, creaking wheels, the smooth voice of a woman over the intercom. Holding Madison's hand, he gently rubbed her delicate fingers. The effects of Rohypnol typically lasted for several hours, but according to blood tests run by the doctor when Madison first arrived, she hadn't ingested very much.

She'd been stirring for the past few minutes, so he wasn't surprised when she finally opened her eyes.

"Welcome back," he whispered, feeling relief pour through him.

"Caleb."

He squeezed her hand.

"Where's—" her eyebrows drew together "—where's Brianna?"

"She's with your mother." He pressed the back of her hand against his lips, enjoying the warm, reassuring feel of her skin. "They just left. Thanks to you, she's fine."

Tears trickled from the corners of Madison's eyes. "What happened? I—I can only remember Holly sitting at my kitchen table, drinking tea. And then...Brianna needing me."

Before he could answer, Caleb felt a presence at the door and turned to see that Johnny had returned from his trip to the cafeteria.

"She awake?" Johnny asked.

Caleb nodded.

"Johnny, you came back," Madison said.

"And it's a good thing," Caleb told her. "He arrived at your place before I could get there. He came before the police arrived. If it wasn't for him—" Caleb didn't want to think about what might have happened if Johnny hadn't shown up when he did.

"I didn't do much," Johnny said, chafing beneath the praise. "The cops came almost right away."

It would've taken Holly only a few minutes to add two more victims to her tally. But Caleb wasn't pointing out that grisly truth. He wanted to focus on the fact that everything was going to be okay. It was over. Holly was in jail. Even if she didn't get the death penalty for reason of insanity, she'd never set foot outside prison. She'd murdered nine women before he ever met her, another two while they were divorced the first time, and a woman in Spokane, as well as Susan, since he'd moved.

He felt terrible for her parents. After all they'd done to raise her and love her... And he felt even worse for her victims and their families.

"How long will I be here?" Madison asked, her eyes circling the room.

"Not long," Caleb assured her. "Holly slipped some date rape drug in your tea. The doctor wants to make sure you come out of it okay. Then he'll release you."

Her eyelashes fluttered to her cheeks. "Are you sure Brianna's okay?"

"I'm positive. But I want you to know something else before you fall asleep."

He watched her fight the weariness. "What's that?"

"You were right, Maddy. Your father never killed anyone."

Madison managed a fleeting smile, but he could tell she was struggling to remain conscious. "I'm so tired."

"Go ahead and sleep."

"Will you be here when I wake up?" With obvious effort, she raised her eyelids once again and met his gaze.

"Yes." He glanced at Johnny. "Tye and your mother are on their way. Your family will be waiting right here."

"My family," she said, and that faint smile returned as she drifted away.

THE NEXT TIME Madison woke, a nurse helped her dress, and Caleb drove her home. There were so many questions she wanted to ask about what had happened, so many nuances she didn't understand. But she felt as though she was living inside a bubble, or swimming underwater, completely out of touch with her normal environment and those around her. She knew Brianna was safe, Johnny was back and Caleb was with her. The rest could wait.

When they reached her place, Caleb insisted on carrying her inside. Leaning against his chest, she turned her face into his neck, comforted by the scent of him and the ease with which he bore her weight. As he tucked her into bed, she knew everything was going to be fine. Everything was going to be *better.* A feeling of hope and excitement told her she had something special to be happy about. She couldn't remember why—until she started to dream.

She was five and her father was pushing her on a swing in the backyard.... She was ten and finding a candy bar her father had slipped into her drawer to surprise her.... She was sixteen and getting into her car to find her father had filled it with gas, even though her mother had sworn she'd have to buy her own....

Simple things, but Ellis Purcell had been a simple man. He'd never asked for thanks or a great deal of attention. Not in life, not in her dreams. He was just there. And he was the man she'd always known—not a perfect man, but an innocent man, and a father who'd loved her.

Then her dream changed. Her father was walking toward her across the grass and she was going to meet him. He looked just as he had before he died, with his barrel chest and thick shoulders, salt-and-pepper flattop, calm brown eyes. He didn't wave or speak. But a lump grew in her throat as she reached him and put her arms around his neck. "I love you, Daddy," she murmured, and woke to find that she was crying.

"TAMARA WANTS TO TALK to you, too," Justine said. "Tamara, pick up the other line."

Caleb tossed the towel he'd been using to dry dishes across the kitchen to land on Madison's counter, and rolled his eyes. He didn't want to repeat everything he'd just told his mother, but his family was understandably shocked at the truth about Holly. *He* was shocked. There were moments when he still couldn't believe that the woman he'd lived with on and off for seven years had tried to kill Madison and Brianna, had succeeded in killing Susan, and had taken the lives of at least twelve others.

"My God, Caleb. What's happened is so unreal," Tamara said. "Poor Susan."

Caleb thought of Susan lying in the morgue. He'd been completely convinced by Holly's grief that day they'd identified the body. Her sadness had been so palpable, so real. Obviously she hadn't been grieving for the reasons he'd assumed.

"I should've known somehow," he said, finally speaking his thoughts aloud.

"Caleb, quit beating yourself up," Tamara said. "How could you have known? You never saw any proof of it, did you?"

"That depends on what you mean by proof. She was off balance. We all knew that. She was manipulative, obsessive."

"So? You were trained since you were small to shield and protect women. Of course you wouldn't even think of suspecting her. Lots of people are off balance, manipulative, obsessive, even certifiably insane, yet *they* don't become serial killers."

"She loved you, Caleb," his mother added, on the extension. "Make no mistake about that. I've never seen a woman so head over heels."

"Maybe she ingratiated herself with you because you were working on the case," Tamara said, "but it quickly turned into more than that."

No kidding, Caleb thought. Almost as soon as he and Holly had started dating, he'd tried to break if off and hadn't been able to.

"You were particularly susceptible to a needy woman like her," his mother said. "You've always been drawn to people you think you can help, and you tried to help her. Only she was too broken. I feel almost as sorry for her as I do for the people whose lives she destroyed. What would make a woman do what she's done?"

"Who can say?" he said. "I know she blames other women for almost every problem she's had in her life—her adoption, her unhappy childhood, her sister always stealing the limelight. She's always hated other women, distrusted them. But I never guessed that what she felt would be enough to turn her into a homicidal maniac."

"Caleb, at what point does any man look at his wife and wonder if she could be a cold-blooded killer?" Tamara asked. "No one is all good or all bad. We don't walk around with signs posted on our foreheads that label us good or evil, because we're all a mix to one degree or another. And Holly was so adept at pretending to be something she wasn't. Which is why I never liked her."

Cognitively, Caleb knew women were capable of violence. He'd done that book on Aileen Wuornos. But he'd also written a few other books about women who'd killed for more immediate reasons—because they'd been severely abused or stood to benefit financially. A violent woman who killed for power and control had never been part of his personal reality. And when he researched the crimes he wrote about, he was always dealing with a perpetrator who was a stranger to him, someone *else's* father, brother, cousin.

"What's going to happen to her now?" his mother asked.

"She'll go to prison."

"You're sure?"

He thought of the halter top in Holly's bedroom, the DNA evidence that should be forthcoming, and the tire imprint. Gibbons had called to tell him it matched an old Chevy belonging to Holly's neighbor. Evidently, she'd borrowed his truck when she'd dumped Susan's body. "There's plenty of evidence, so much that she knows she doesn't have a chance of fighting. Gibbons told me she confessed."

Madison's telephone beeped. Caleb glanced at the caller ID to see that her own mother was calling.

"I've got to go," he said.

"Does this mean you won't be baby-sitting for me this weekend?" Tamara asked.

Caleb smiled because he could tell she was joking, trying to lighten the mood. "Do you think you can get Mac to stay off the phone long enough to make leaving with him worthwhile?"

"He's promised to give up his cell phone for the whole weekend. We had a big fight yesterday. I threatened to leave him, and he swears he's going to do better."

"I like the doing better part. If he'll leave his phone at home, I'll gladly baby-sit. See you later," he said, and switched to the other line.

"How's Madison doing?" Annette Purcell asked.

Caleb went to the window and gazed out at Johnny in the yard. Caleb had promised Madison's brother forty dollars if he'd mow the lawn and trim the bushes. Caleb thought it might help keep his mind off his crack addiction and, for the moment, it seemed to be working. "She's still sleeping, but the doctor checked her just before we left the hospital and said she'll be fine. How's Brianna?"

"She's happy here. We just bought a new coloring book and some washable markers. Later we're going to look at some pictures of Grandpa."

Caleb could hear the pride in Annette's voice when she spoke of Ellis. She'd loved him and stuck by him through the whole thing. Her loyalty was impressive. It was tragic that Ellis had killed himself before this day could come. In a way, he was another of Holly's victims.

"I'm sorry about all you've gone through, Annette," he said. "And for my role in it." When they'd spoken at the hospital earlier, he'd told her who he was. She'd been upset at first, but she was too relieved to have Ellis's name cleared to hold it against him.

She was silent for a few seconds. "Everything's going to be fine now."

"I really thought it was Ellis," he said. "I came back here determined to finally prove myself right, and I nearly got your daughter and granddaughter killed."

"But you *didn't* get them killed. Do you realize that if you hadn't come back, we still wouldn't know the truth? Holly would still be preying on innocent people."

Caleb smiled. There was definitely some solace in that. As much as he hated the fact that he hadn't been able to save her past victims, his returning to Seattle *had* saved any future ones. "Thanks."

"Have you heard from Danny?" she asked.

"No."

"I guess I should call him." She sighed. "No one likes him much, but he *is* Brianna's father and should probably know what's going on."

Caleb chuckled. "Do you think he really intends to take Madison back to court for custody?"

"He might. He threatens often enough. But after what Madison just did for that child, I don't think there's a court in the country that would take Brianna away."

"I hope not," he said.

"Well, I've made some chicken soup for the both of you. I just wanted to let you know I'm on my way over."

"I'm sure it'll be good for Madison to see you—and Brianna."

"She's been asking about her mother. But she's been asking about you, too," Annette said. "Seems she's growing quite attached to you."

"You might mention to her that—" Caleb was about to tell Annette he was going back to San Francisco right away, as originally planned. But Madison called to him just then and suddenly San Francisco seemed very far from home.

"Never mind." He wasn't sure he could gain Madison's confidence again. He'd betrayed her trust and unwittingly put her in danger. But he did have a lease on the cottage. And it didn't run out for another five months.

CHAPTER TWENTY-FOUR

MADISON STUDIED CALEB as he came to stand in the doorway of her room. He was wearing a gray polo, a pair of jeans and a Giants cap, and the dark shadow covering his jaw indicated he hadn't shaved this morning. But he looked as good as always—strong, masculine, confident.

"How do you feel?" he asked, the muscles of his arms flexing as he hooked his fingers on the doorjamb over his head.

"I'm still tired," she admitted.

"You want to sleep some more? Or are you ready to eat something?"

She wriggled into a sitting position. "I want to talk."

He cocked an eyebrow, as though he was a little worried about what she might say.

"I need to understand what happened," she explained.

Letting go of the jamb, he moved closer, and she slid over so he could sit on the edge of the bed. "It was Holly," he said simply.

"How could that be? How could she kill her own sister?"

"Obviously she's not right. I arrived here just after the police arrested her. She was hysterical by then, cursing at the top of her lungs and blaming me. I couldn't get any coherent answers out of her. But I called Detective Gibbons from the hospital later, and he filled me in on a few things."

Madison blinked in surprise. Caleb had gone to the hospital with her when he finally had the killer for whom he'd been searching so long? "What did the detective say?" she asked.

"The day before Susan died, Susan and Lance, the guy she was dating, got into an argument. Susan suspected Lance was seeing someone else, which was true. Anyway, she was upset and showed up at Holly's house unexpectedly, late at night. Holly was gone and the door was locked, but Susan managed to fit through a window Holly had forgotten to close. While she was there, she found some Roofies hidden in a Tylenol bottle in the kitchen cupboard."

"Roofies?"

"Date rape drug."

"How did she know what they were?"

"The tablets are marked, and they're not as scarce as you might think. Susan was a partier. I'm sure she'd run into them before. Only, finding them at Holly's worried her. She started poking around, wondering what else she'd find, and discovered a jacket that belonged to the woman who was just murdered in Spokane. The police had made a big deal about it because—"

"It had her initials embroidered on the front," Madison interrupted. "I heard someone talking about it at work."

"Exactly." He leaned across her, propping himself up on one hand. "Susan confronted Holly. Holly said she'd bought the jacket at a garage sale, but she knew Susan would eventually figure it out and possibly even tell someone. She felt she had to do something. So she called Susan and told her she wanted to meet her at the Pie in the Sky Pizzeria the following night."

"Why such a public place?"

"She needed a place where she could convince Tye to meet her."

"*Tye?*" Madison exclaimed in surprise.

"Don't worry. He was as manipulated as the rest of us. Holly just wanted your father's truck and Susan seen in the same vicinity. She wanted to throw the police off track. And she wanted me back. She knew how interested I was in the old case, and was afraid I might not take enough interest in Susan's disappearance if it didn't tie in somehow."

"But I don't understand why he'd agree to meet her," Madison said. "Weren't they total strangers?"

"She promised to provide Tye with information that would prove your father innocent of the killings."

"Why would he bring the truck?"

"Because that's what the note she sent him said to do, so she'd be able to recognize him. When he arrived, no one came forward to meet him, of course. But Susan nearly backed into him when she was trying to park, which caused an argument between them."

"Tye never said anything about a note or anything else," Madison said.

"Can you blame him? Susan wound up dead, and *he'd* met her the night she was murdered, even argued with her. I'm sure Tye smelled a setup, but he didn't have any idea who'd sent that note, and after what happened to your father, he had no confidence that the police would believe him if he came forward."

"So Holly didn't even go to the pizza place that night."

"No."

"Then how did she kill Susan?"

"She simply called Susan, told her she couldn't make it and asked her to come to the house instead."

A creeping sensation made Madison shiver and pull the

blankets higher. "And Susan went to her house, after finding that jacket?"

Caleb sighed. "Holly's an incredible liar. And Susan had all their years as sisters working against her. She probably couldn't fathom that Holly could really be what the evidence seemed to suggest."

"Like I could never believe it of my father," Madison murmured. "Despite all that evidence."

"Even if Susan thought Holly capable of violence, she probably never dreamed her sister would harm *her*. There wasn't any Rohypnol in her blood, though, which leads us to believe she was leery enough to refuse a drink from Holly. She also put up a damn good fight."

"Poor Susan."

Caleb fell silent for a moment, and Madison knew he was feeling the same sympathy. But then she remembered something else. "Wait, what about the contents of that box under the house?" she asked. "The rope and the locket and—"

"Holly put that stuff in the woodpile behind your father's house after we got married the second time."

"Why?"

"She told Gibbons she'd decided to stop killing. Somehow being with me satisfied that urge, though I certainly wouldn't presume to understand her crazy logic."

"So she dumped those…trophies at my *parents'* place?" Madison asked.

"It was the safest place to put it," he replied. "Everyone already suspected your father. She'd made sure she set him up as her scapegoat years earlier. She'd seen the news reports of Tatiana Harris's neighbor claiming to have seen your father's truck leaving Tatiana's house. At that point, she merely dug up an old phone book that had your father listed, and made a point of driving by the house to get part of his license plate number. She must've done it right before she murdered Anna Tyler, the woman living next door to her, knowing the police would come knocking to see if she'd heard or seen anything."

"But my dad found that box and thought Johnny had killed those women! He—" Madison couldn't finish without breaking into tears. After her dream, she felt so close to her father.

Caleb nodded sadly and took her hand. "I'm sorry about that."

Rage at Holly and what she'd done burned inside Madison. She wondered if she'd ever be able to get over that anger. She knew others would tell her she had to forgive, for her own sake, but she also knew it was going to take time. How did a woman forgive a person who'd caused her father to commit suicide? Who'd tried to murder her daughter? Who'd nearly ruined her life in so many ways?

"Then Tye found it and hid it in the basement," he added, "which is where you found it."

She wiped away her angry tears. "But where did it go from there?"

"Your mother took it," he said. "When you were talking to her on the phone that day, telling her you'd found something, she knew where you must have found it. And she wasn't about to let anything that further implicated your father come to light."

"How do you know?"

"She told me this morning that she's turning it all over to police."

"So she did take it," Madison mumbled. "She was that certain my father was innocent."

"And now everyone else is, too," Caleb said.

Madison let her breath go in a long sigh. "I can't believe the nightmare that started twelve years ago is finally over."

"It's about time."

She glanced at the phone. "We need to tell Sharon."

"Sharon?"

"Tye's wife. She thinks Johnny was involved with the murders. She left Tye because she believed he was protecting Johnny."

"That's the only reason?"

Madison considered his question. "Probably not the only reason. Tye has his problems. But I know she loves him. I think their marriage is worth saving."

Madison could tell by the way he was looking at her that Caleb's mind was now moving in a different direction. "What?"

"That makes me think of something else that's worth saving," he said.

Hearing the subtle change in his voice, Madison hesitated before responding. "What's that?"

"I know you're angry about what I did, Maddy." He trailed his fingers up her arm, and she shivered at the unexpected pleasure. "You have every right to be. But I'm thinking you and I had something good. If you can forgive me, I'd like to stick around for a while and see what happens."

Madison's heart skipped a beat as her eyes met his. She knew what would happen. She'd get completely caught up in him. He was everything she'd ever wanted in a man. But she'd just been through the worst experience imaginable. How could she muster enough faith in the future to take such a risk right now? Especially with a man whose permanent address was three states away? If things went bad between them, he could simply pack up and leave. "Caleb, I—"

He immediately concealed the hope in his face, letting Madison know he anticipated her rejection. "You what?"

Madison felt as though she had a bowling ball sitting on her chest as she opened her mouth to continue. But she *had* to continue. She'd promised herself that she'd protect Brianna, protect them both. "I have to think about my daughter," she said. "She's dealt with so many changes already. With Danny always waiting in the wings, hoping to take my daughter away from me, I can't take any chances right now. I'm sorry."

Caleb stood, putting some distance between them, and she saw him take a deep breath, as though her answer had stung him. "I understand," he said shortly, his eyes now hooded. Then her mother hollered from the front door and Brianna came running toward the bedroom. The next thing Madison knew, Caleb was gone.

IT DIDN'T TAKE MADISON long to recover. She slept for most of Monday and Tuesday, but by Wednesday, when the glass company arrived to repair the window Johnny had broken, she was ready to take care of herself and Brianna and let her mother go home. She and Annette got along quite well. They'd had to stick together to get through the past, after all. But Madison was ready to be alone, or as alone as she could be with Johnny living in her house. She hadn't seen Caleb for several days, and she was having a tough time pretending it didn't matter.

"Mommy, when did you draw these?" Brianna asked.

Madison turned from admiring the new window as the repairman drove away to see that her daughter had found the sketches she'd done of Caleb's chest and lips. "A few days ago," she said, feeling her cheeks grow warm because her mother had also turned to look. "I was just doodling," she added quickly.

"Can I hang them up?" Brianna asked.

Madison opened her mouth to say no. The last thing she needed was a daily reminder of the man she'd fallen so deeply in love with. But Annette took a closer look and spoke before Madison could.

"I think they should go in your mommy's room," she said. "They're excellent."

"Thanks." Madison started cutting onions for homemade chili and blinked back tears she couldn't blame entirely on her task.

"Where is Caleb, anyway?" Brianna asked, wearing a frown. "I want to see him."

Madison decided the truth was probably best. "I think he moved back to San Francisco." She didn't know for sure because she hadn't been able to make herself go over to the cottage to check. She was afraid she'd find it as empty as she suspected it was.

"Can we go there?" Brianna asked.

"No, it's too far away," Madison said.

Brianna wrinkled her nose. "Why would he want to live there?"

"That's where his home is."

"But we're *here*. When's he coming back?"

Never was too permanent for a child, so Madison mumbled something about "someday."

"Speaking of Caleb," her mother murmured. "He sent you a check to buy out his lease. And his mother called while you were in the shower."

Caleb had sent her a check? Madison didn't feel right about taking his money when she'd asked him to leave. But she was more immediately concerned with the fact that Caleb's mother had called. "What did she say?"

"She wanted to make sure you're all right."

Madison had a definite soft spot where Justine Trovato

was concerned, but she needed to avoid anyone who had anything to do with Caleb, or getting over him would only be more difficult. "Did you tell her I'm fine?"

"No. I told her you'd call her back." Her mother waved at a slip of paper tacked to the fridge. "Her number's right there. And I put Caleb's check in the side pocket of your purse."

"Mom, you know I'd rather not deal with—" Madison started, but Brianna was watching her closely, so she stopped.

"I know what you told me," her mother replied. "But if you're going to shut him out, you're going to do it on your own because I can't help thinking that some risks are worth taking. And Caleb is one of them."

THAT EVENING, Madison sat in her bedroom, staring at the slip of paper with Justine Trovato's number. Annette had finally left. Johnny had gone over to Tye's because Sharon and the kids were back and Tye was trying to make up to his wife by fixing a few things around the house; he'd asked his brother to help. Brianna was in bed. So Madison was alone at last. She had the time and the opportunity to return Caleb's mother's call. But she knew talking to Justine would make her miss Caleb that much more....

After another few minutes, she took a deep breath and picked up the phone. She couldn't be so rude as not to call.

"Hello?"

"Mrs. Trovato?"

"No, it's Tamara."

"Oh, Tamara, I'm sorry I didn't recognize your voice. This is Madison."

"Madison, we've been worried about you. How are you?"

"Better."

"I'm glad to hear it. You must be tremendously relieved that Holly is now behind bars."

"I am." There was an awkward pause. "I'm just returning your mother's call."

"Wonderful. Hang on a second, I'll get Caleb."

"Wait! I said…what…why—" Madison sputtered.

"And you'd better make this count," Tamara added in a low voice. "He flies out in the morning."

"Tamara—"

"Hello?"

Madison's whole body tingled at the sound of Caleb's voice. Gripping the phone much too tightly, she licked suddenly dry lips and closed her eyes, feeling an overwhelming desire to see him again. "Caleb?"

"Maddy?"

She could hear his surprise, wondered what she was going to do now. Tell him that she'd sacrifice her good judgment—anything—to be with him again? How could she, after she'd already thought it through so many times and made her decision? "I, um, just called to tell you that I can't accept your buy-out check. A lessor has to buy out a lease only when he breaks the agreement. And you didn't do that. I'm letting you out of your lease," she said, proud of herself for thinking of an excuse so fast.

"I want you to have the money," he said. "It'll help you get by until you find another tenant."

"But—"

Brianna opened her door and poked her head inside the room. "Mommy?"

Madison jumped as though she'd been caught doing

something wrong. "What are you doing out of bed, Brianna?"

"I'm thirsty. Can I have a drink?"

"Of course." Madison decided she should end the call so she could take care of her daughter. They really had nothing more to discuss. But she couldn't bring herself to say goodbye. "Caleb, can you hang on for—"

"That's *Caleb?*" Brianna squealed, jumping up and down. "When's he coming home? Can I talk to him? I *knew* he'd call!"

Madison hesitated for a moment, wondering what to do now. "Brianna wants to say hello," she finally said.

"Put her on."

Madison handed her daughter the phone and Brianna eagerly clutched it to her ear. "Caleb, where did you go?...Why didn't you say goodbye to me?...When are you coming back?..."

Madison was supposed to be getting Brianna a glass of juice, but she was too caught up in what she was seeing and hearing, especially when Brianna's shoulders began to slump and her questions slowed. "But who's going to mow the grass?... Johnny doesn't even know what a praying mantis is...I don't want you to go to San Francisco...What about *me?* Elizabeth will miss you...."

Madison's heart ached as she watched and listened. Without even telling Caleb goodbye, her daughter gave her back the phone and started dragging Elizabeth out of the room. Her head was down, her request for a drink completely forgotten.

Brianna's dejection hit Madison hard. She was so busy trying to protect Brianna that she was denying her connection with someone she already cared about. She was denying herself, as well. Was she wrong? What if Caleb turned out to be an important part of their lives? Didn't she owe it to herself, to Brianna, to give him that chance?

Her pulse racing, Madison put the phone to her ear again. "Caleb?"

"Yes?"

She took a deep breath. "If I asked you to, would you come back?"

CALEB NEARLY DROPPED the phone. Shooting a glance at Tamara, who was hovering nearby, pacing and rubbing her hands, he turned his back on his sister, wishing for a moment of privacy. "Maddy, if I hadn't lied to you so I could move in, Holly would never have come after you and Brianna. I can't tell you how responsible I feel for that, how sorry I am."

"Caleb, getting to know you was worth everything that happened," she said. "My mother is happier than I've seen her in years, and Johnny and Tye have something of a fresh start—all because of this. I feel it's brought us closer as a family. Besides, Brianna is fine." She paused. "Except that she's crying in her room right now because she believes you're leaving town."

Caleb tensed. "Is she the only one who cares that I'm leaving?"

"God, you never make things easy for me, do you?"

He chuckled softly. "Say it, Maddy. Say it or I won't stay."

There was a long silence, then she said, "I'm in love with you, Caleb."

The words were almost a whisper, but they carried a tidal wave of emotion. Caleb let it wash over him, filling him with relief. He'd been trying to come to grips with the fact that he might never see her again, but he hadn't been able to do it. He'd thought of nothing but Madison and what she and Brianna had come to mean to him. Even if he'd been capable of forgetting her, his family wouldn't have let him. They talked of her constantly, encouraging him to stay in contact with her, encouraging him to wait until she was ready and then try again.

He grinned at Tamara, who was watching him with a self-satisfied smile. "I suppose I could work on Whidbey Island just as easily as in San Francisco," he said. "But you'd have to make a few concessions."

"Oh, yeah?" Her voice was slightly skeptical, as though she knew he was going to milk her confession for all it was worth. "What concessions would those be?"

Tamara squeezed his arm in support, then rushed to the door of the kitchen to call his mother.

"The cottage is a little drafty," he complained, sitting at the small telephone desk in his mother's kitchen.

"It is?" Madison replied.

He put his feet up. "Terribly."

"Which means..."

Justine Trovato hurried into the room, smiling. She was trailed by his father, who looked slightly amused, which was saying a lot for his father. Together with Tamara, they stood waiting expectantly, silently cheering for him. "I think I'd be much more comfortable living at your place," he said.

"With me?"

"Not without marrying her first, you're not," his mother said, obviously appalled, but he shook his head.

"Of course with you," he replied to Madison.

There was another slight hesitation on Madison's part. "What about Brianna?"

"What about her?" he said into the phone. "I love Brianna."

"And she loves you. But—"

"But what?" Folding his arms, Caleb pictured Madison's pretty face, her brow creased in consternation, and felt his grin broaden. She was backing right into his trap.

"We can't live together," Madison said. "Not unless...unless we get married."

"So you're proposing to me?" he said.

"No!"

He laughed at the embarrassment in her voice. "What if I was proposing to you? Would you say yes?"

His mother released a big sigh and nodded her approval. But he could hear Madison's quick intake of breath and thought maybe he was pushing too hard, too fast.

"You want to get *married?*" she said. "Already?"

"Does that frighten you?"

"It terrifies me. We haven't known each other very long."

"I'd be good to you, Maddy. I promise you that. I'd do my best to make you happy, and I'd love you for the rest of my life," he said, marveling at the fact that he wasn't embarrassed about making such promises despite having his entire family as an audience.

"He's not *too* hard to live with," Tamara chimed in.

Caleb knew Madison had heard her when she laughed. "But this is...this is so sudden," she said. "A moment ago, I thought I was never going to see you again."

"I don't think I could have left it at that," Caleb admitted. "I was hoping you'd call me, but I probably would've broken down and called you as soon as I reached San Francisco."

"I don't know what to say."

"Just say yes," he told her.

"We'll make it a lovely wedding," his mother said.

Madison paused for a second, a heartbeat, but it was

the longest moment of Caleb's life. "Yes," she said at last. "And tell your family yes, too.

"We're getting married," he announced, and they all started hugging each other. His mother began to cry and his father clapped him on the back.

"Now will you come home?" Madison asked.

He gave Tamara a high five. "My bags are already packed."

EPILOGUE

Eight months later...

THE SUN FELT SO WARM on Madison's face that she could scarcely keep her eyes open. The fact that she'd just finished another of Justine's big meals didn't help. They were all moving a little more slowly, even Mac, who had his arm around his wife and was chewing on a blade of grass not far from her and Caleb. He got up every few minutes to answer his cell phone, but overall he seemed to be giving Tamara more attention, which made Madison even happier.

"What did you say?" she murmured to Caleb, feeling his fingers comb gently through her hair while she lay in his lap, completely content just to be near him.

"I said Brianna needs a dog, don't you think?"

"A dog?" She turned to look across the yard, where Brianna was kicking a ball with Jacob and Joey. "She's only seven."

"So?" he said.

"A dog's a big responsibility. That's why we gave Susan's dogs to Tye, remember?"

"We gave Susan's dogs to Tye because he relates better to animals than he does people. And I didn't want to face those dogs every day of my life and think of Susan," he said.

Madison continued to watch the kids play. "But Brianna doesn't need a dog right now. She has a half sister at her father's house, and I'm due in three months, so she'll have another sibling. Do we have to do everything all at once?"

Caleb put a protective hand on her extended abdomen, which he did often. "The siblings are good, but I think she needs a pet, too."

"She has pets at Danny's."

Caleb grimaced. "She has fish at Danny's because Danny and Leslie are so afraid anything else will shed hair on their expensive furniture or stain their Persian rugs. And she only gets to see her fish every other weekend."

"But she's never mentioned wanting a dog to me," Madison pointed out.

Caleb called Brianna over. "Honey, you want a dog, right? You're lonely without a dog."

"I'm what?" Brianna said.

"Lonely."

"Oh, we're doing this now?" She wiped the smile off her face and managed a pleading expression, and it was all Madison could do not to roll her eyes.

"Mommy, I really, really, *really* want a dog. *Please...*"

"See?" Caleb said smugly.

Madison decided to play along. "Will you help take care of a dog?"

"I will," she said. "I'll give him food and water and brush his fur and—" she glanced at Caleb and lowered her voice to a whisper "—what else was I supposed to say, Daddy?"

Madison dropped the charade and cocked an eyebrow at her husband, while Tamara hooted with laughter. "You're busted, buddy," his sister said.

"What?" He spread out his hands, trying to play innocent.

"*Brianna* wants a dog?" Madison said.

"Okay, so she's not the *only* one who wants a dog."

"Our yard isn't equipped for a dog."

A devilish glint entered Caleb's eyes. "Then maybe it's time to move. Our family's outgrowing your little house, anyway. And once we have another baby and another, we're going to need the space."

"Caleb, I've told you, I'm not having six kids," Madison said. "I don't want to give up my business. I still believe I can get it turned around."

He leaned back on his palms. "You don't have to give up anything. I'll help you with the kids. I work from home, remember?"

She rolled onto her side and gazed up at him, admiring his sensual mouth. "You're in the middle of writing Holly's story. Granted, you're closer to this project than any in the past, but—"

"That's what'll make it so riveting."

"—half the time you don't even answer when we speak to you."

"I don't answer? Really?" He seemed genuinely surprised.

"What's going on out here?" Justine said, coming out of the house with Logan.

"Caleb is trying to talk Madison into a new house *and* a dog," Tamara said.

"Oh, is that all?" Justine teased. She took husband's hand and sobered as she looked at Madison. "What would Johnny do if you moved?"

"I think he'd be okay," Madison said. "Every day's a struggle for him, of course. But he's been clean and sober for almost six months, which is really saying something.

And he works with Tye, so Tye can help us keep an eye on him. It's probably time he lived on his own, anyway."

"So what do you say?" Caleb said, obviously not willing to let his petition for a dog go unanswered.

Madison gazed up at him, pictured his beautiful body the way she'd seen him when they'd showered together this morning, and grinned. She loved him so much. How could she say no? "What kind of dog do you want?"

* * * * *

Internal Affair
MARIE FERRARELLA

To the brave men and women
who put their lives on the line for us every day.
Thank you.

Chapter 1

"No!"

Every fiber of his muscular body tense and alert, Patrick Cavanaugh bolted upright in his bed, ready to fight, to protect. As adrenaline coursed through his veins, it took several moments before he realized he'd been dreaming. And it was *the* dream that plagued him. The one that he'd been having night after night for the past month. Ever since Ramirez had been shot right before his eyes. And killed.

Ramirez had been one step away from him.

One step away from being saved by him.

Awake now, Patrick shivered. His bedroom was cold. December in Aurora, California, tended to be bitterly cold at times. Because the dream had been so vivid, because he'd relived every second of it, his upper torso was covered with sweat, cooling him even more.

Getting back to sleep was impossible. Not now. Habit had him reaching for the pack of cigarettes on his nightstand. The pack of cigarettes that was no longer there. Not wanting anything to have a hold over him, he'd quit smoking the week after they had put Eduardo Ramirez into the ground. Twenty-two days and counting.

He sat for a moment, dragging his hand through his hair, trying to focus on the day before him. Dark thoughts hovered around him like the ghosts of years past, searching for a chink, a break in the armor he kept tightly wrapped around himself. Waiting to get to him.

Every man had his demons, he told himself. His were no bigger, no smaller than most.

It didn't help.

Patrick swallowed a halfhearted curse. He wondered what it felt like to wake up with a smile on his face, the way he knew his sister Patience did.

No use in going there, he thought. It wasn't anything he was about to find out. He'd always been the somber one in the family. Not without cause. Patience was the mystery, he'd decided long ago. Happy despite everything. Despite the home life they'd had growing up.

Any happiness that existed in their lives had come by way of his uncles Andrew and Brian and their families. It certainly hadn't come via his own, at least, not from his parents, Mike and Diane.

Patience was another story. She was the reason he'd plumbed the depths of his soul and discovered that he was a protector and capable of feeling an emotion other than anger. He had to, for Patience's sake.

Patrick narrowed his eyes, looking at the blue digital numbers. Six-thirty.

Time to get up, anyway, he thought. Time to get ready to serve and protect.

As he rose from his rumpled double bed, the sheet

tangled around his leg and then fell to the floor. He didn't bother picking it up. His whole bed looked like the scene of a battle.

And had been. Because last night, as he had almost every night since his partner's death, he'd fought the good fight. He'd led Ramirez and the other detectives and patrolmen into the crack house. Except that somehow, Ramirez had gotten in front of him just as shots were fired and all hell broke loose.

And he'd been too late to save Ramirez.

Again.

Don't go there, Patrick ordered himself coldly. He muttered another curse as he walked into the tiny adjacent bathroom, naked as the day he was born. He couldn't afford to think about Ramirez, couldn't afford to allow himself to dwell in the land of "what ifs." The guilt was still too raw, weighed too much. Dwelling on the pain left him winded and bleeding inside.

It was the beginning of a new week and he needed to be sharp. To survive the way others before him hadn't survived. He owed it to the department, but mostly to Patience. They had uncles and cousins, but he was the only immediate family she had. If he let this consume him, likely as not, he'd get himself killed. Leaving her alone.

Wasn't gonna happen. Yet.

Blowing out a deep breath, Patrick wrapped his anger around himself and stepped into the shower.

The shower handle was poised on cold. He pulled it and let the water hit him full blast. Jolting him into Monday.

"New assignment, Mag?"

Depositing the frying pan into the dishwasher, she

picked up the breakfast she'd prepared and placed it in front of her father. She'd been too preoccupied to hear his question. "What?"

Matthew McKenna pushed forward his coffee cup. An independent man, he lived alone now and liked his space. He liked it even more when his only daughter, his only child, dropped by before beginning her mornings. It wasn't something he took for granted. "Today, don't you start your new assignment?"

"Yes. Right."

The words came out like staccato gunfire. Mary Margaret McKenna—Maggi to those she considered part of her inner circle, or 3M to those who enjoyed honing in on her no-nonsense nature—poured coffee into her father's cup. She was bracing herself for the morning and the change of venue she was about to face.

She supposed that was why she'd stopped by this morning to make breakfast for her father. To touch base with what she considered to be her true self. Before she left that behind. Belatedly, she offered her father a smile along with cream for his coffee.

She was what she was because of her father. And because of him, in an indirect way, she had chosen the less-traveled path within her career. Patrolman Matthew McKenna had been one of Aurora's finest until a bullet had ended his career less than six months ago. The bullet had come from one of his own men. One of those awful things that happened in the heat of battle when shots went wild. The other policeman was found dead, a victim of one of the so-called suspects' deadly aim, or dumb luck, take your pick. But it was the service revolver in his hand that had fired the bullet which had found its way into Matthew's hip and left him with a slight limp. And a new appreciation for life.

She had been living in San Francisco when she'd gotten the call about her father. Without any hesitation, Maggi had handed in her resignation and come home to Aurora, to stand vigil over her father in the hospital and then nurse him back to health. When she was satisfied that he was on the mend, she put in for a job on the Aurora police force. It took little to work her way up. And when a position in Internal Affairs opened up, she applied for it.

The thought of spying on her fellow police officers bothered her. The thought of rogue police officers, giving the force a bad name, bothered her more. She took the position, signing on to work undercover. She still grappled with her own decision. It was a dirty job, she'd tell herself. But someone had to do it. For now, that someone was her.

Matthew sighed, looking at her over the rim of his cup. "You know, Mag, this isn't the kind of life your mother and I envisioned for you, dodging bullets and bad guys."

She finished her breakfast in three bites—toast, consumed mostly on her feet. Impatience danced through her, as it always did at the start of a new assignment. She thought of it as stage fright. A little always made you perform better.

"We all make our own way in the world, remember?" Maggie dusted off her fingers over the sink. "That was what you taught me."

Matthew shook his head. "I also taught you that there was no shame in taking the easy way, as long as it wasn't against the law."

Maggie laughed, partially to set him at ease. He worried too much. Just as much as she had when he had been the one to walk out the door wearing a badge. "Where's the fun in that?"

His expression was serious. "You think it's fun, my sitting here, wondering if you're going to walk in through that door again?"

Maggie refused to be drawn into a serious discussion. Not this morning. The seriousness of her work was bad enough. She needed an outlet, a haven where she could laugh, where she could put down her sword and shield and just be herself.

So instead, she winked at him. "I could move back up to San Francisco, take that burden away from you." Her grin widened as unspoken love entered her eyes. "You're old enough to live on your own now."

She'd moved back home to take care of him. And once he was on his feet, with the aid of a quad cane he hated, Maggi knew it was time for her to leave. But one thing after another seemed to get in the way and she remained, telling herself that she'd look for an apartment over the weekend. She'd finally moved out less than three weeks ago. But this still felt like home. She had a feeling it always would.

The somber expression refused to be teased away. "You know what I mean, Mary Margaret."

"Oh-uh, two names. Serious stuff." Inwardly she gritted her teeth together. She'd always hated her full name. Hearing it reminded her of eight years of dour-faced nuns looking down at her disapprovingly because she hadn't lived up to their expectations. All except for Sister Michael. Sister Michael had tried to encourage her to let her "better side out." She suspected that Sister Michael had probably been as much of a hellion in her day as she was accused of being in hers.

She'd turned to Sister Michael when her mother had

died and she felt she couldn't cry in front of her father. Couldn't cry because she was all that was keeping him together.

She crossed to him now and placed her arm around his shoulders. "Dad, you know damn well that you're my hero and I was honor-bound to grow up just like you."

The sigh was liberally laced with guilt. "I should have married Edna," he lamented. "She would have found a way to shave those rough edges off you."

"No, Edna would have turned out to be the reason I ran away from home."

Edna Grady was the woman his father had dated when she was fifteen. The widow had her cap set on marriage and would have stopped at nothing to arrive at that destination. She had a host of ideas about what their life was going to be like after the ceremony. It hadn't included having a stepdaughter under her roof. That was when her father had balked, terminating their relationship. Maggi had been eternally grateful when he had.

Maggi paused to kiss the top of her father's snow-white head, her heart swelling with love. He really was her rock, her pillar. "You did just fine raising me, Dad. You gave me all the right values. I'm just making sure they're in play, that's all. And that everyone else shares them."

While he applauded the principle, he didn't like the thought of his daughter risking her life every day. He vividly realized what his wife must have gone through all those years they were married and he was on the force.

He looked at her, disgruntled. "If I hadn't been shot, you would have been married by now."

"Divorced," she corrected, "I would have been divorced by now."

She firmly believed that. Maggi thought of Taylor Ramsford, the up-and-coming lawyer she'd met while working on the vice squad. He'd dazzled her with his wit, his charm, and they'd gotten engaged. But Taylor, it turned out, was not nearly the man she'd thought he was. Beneath the appealing exterior, there was nothing but a man who wanted to get ahead. A man centered on his own goals and nothing more. Marrying her had just been another goal. When she'd told him she was going home for an indefinite period of time to care for her father, he wouldn't stand for it.

"Your place is with me," he'd told her.

She'd known then that her place was anywhere *but* with him.

She gave her father a quick hug. "You know you're the only man for me."

He patted her hand affectionately. The day she was born, his partner had expressed his regret that his wife hadn't given birth to a son. Maggi was worth a hundred sons to him, and he told her so.

"Not that I'm not flattered, Mag, but I'm not going to live forever."

"Sure you are." She walked over to pick up her service revolver and holster from the bookcase in the family room where she'd left it. "And I don't need a man to survive. No woman this day and age does." She spared him a tolerant glance. "Catch up to the times, Dad."

He thought of his late wife. Maggi looked just like Annie had at her age. She'd had a way of making him feel that the sun rose and set around him without sacrificing a shred of her own independence. She'd been a rare woman. As was his daughter. He hoped to God that she'd find a man worthy of her someday.

"'Fraid it's too late. No new tricks for me. I'm the old-fashioned type, no changing that."

"Don't change a hair for me," she teased. Glancing at her watch, she knew she had to hit the road or risk getting stuck in ungodly traffic. She strapped on her holster, taking care to position the revolver to minimize the bulge it created. It was wreaking havoc on the linings of her jackets. "I've gotta go, Dad. Have a good day."

He nodded. It was time he got to work as well. To pass the time while he'd been convalescing, he'd taken to writing down some of his more interesting cases. Now he was at it in earnest, looking to crack the publishing world with a fictionalized novel.

Matthew rose from the table, walking Maggi to the front door. "Would I be threatening some chain of command if I told you to have the same?"

Have a good day. That wasn't possible, she thought. Her new assignment was taking her back undercover. Not to any seedy streets where the enemy was clearly defined the way her old job had been, but into the bowels of the homicide and burglary division of the Aurora force. She felt this was more dangerous. Because there were reputations at stake, and desperate people with a great deal to lose did desperate things when their backs were up against the wall.

Was Detective Patrick Cavanaugh a desperate man? Was that what had led him to betray the oath he'd taken the day he'd been sworn into the department? Had it been desperation or greed that had made him turn his back on his promise to serve and protect and made him serve only himself, protect only his own back?

Not your concern, Mag, she told herself. She wasn't judge and jury, she was only the investigator. Her job was to gather all the information she could and let someone else make the proper determination.

If that meant putting herself in front of a charging bull, well, she'd known this wasn't going to be a picnic when she'd signed on to help rid the force of dirty cops.

She frowned, thinking of what her superior had told her about Cavanaugh. The detective had a list of honors a mile long and he was braver than the day was long, but he was as hard as titanium to crack. And as friendly as a shark coming off a month-long hunger strike. The dark-haired, scowling detective went through partners the way most people went through paper towels. The only one who had managed to survive had been Eduardo Ramirez. Until the day he was shot. Ramirez had managed to last two years with Cavanaugh. According to what she'd read in his file, that was quite a record.

Detective First Class Patrick Cavanaugh was the product of a long blue line. His late father had been a cop, one of his uncles had been the chief of police and he was the nephew of the current chief of detectives. Not to mention that he had over half a dozen cousins on the force at the present time. Possibly covering his back. In any case, she knew extreme caution was going to have to be exercised. There could be a lot of toes involved.

She was Daniel, entering the lion's den, and all the lions were related.

But then, she'd always loved a challenge.

Maggi flashed a smile at her father, meant to put him at ease. "I'll see you tonight."

He watched as she slipped on her jacket, watched the

weapon disappear beneath the navy blue fabric. "I'll hold you to that."

She winked and kissed his cheek before leaving. "Count on it."

He did.

The call had reached him before he ever made it to the precinct. An overly curious jogger had seen something glistening in the river, catching the first rays of the dull morning sun. It turned out to be the sunroof of a sports car. An all but submerged sports car. He'd called in his find immediately.

A BMW sports car had gone over the railing and found its final resting place in the dark waters below. Patrick told dispatch he was on it and changed his direction, driving toward the river.

Even before he'd closed his cell phone, he'd been struck by the similarity of the case. Fifteen years ago, his aunt Rose's car was discovered nose down in the very same river. All the Cavanaughs had gathered at Uncle Andrew's house, trying to comfort his uncle and the others—Shaw, Callie, the twins—Clay and Teri—and Rayne. It was the only time he had seen his uncle come close to breaking down. Aunt Rose's body wasn't inside the car when it was fished out. Or in the river when they dragged it. Uncle Andrew refused to believe that she was dead, even when his father told him to move on with his life.

Patrick had been in the room when his father had said that to Andrew. They didn't realize he was there at first, but he was, just shy of the doorway. There was something there between the two men, something he hadn't seen before or since, something they never allowed to come out, except for that one time. His uncle came close to striking his father, then held himself in check at the last minute.

But then, his father had a way of getting under people's skins and rubbing them raw. It was what held him back. And turned him into a bitter drunk in his off hours. He never showed up for work under the influence, but the minute he was off duty, he went straight for a bottle. It was as if he was trying to drown something inside him that refused to die.

The tension between his father and his uncle that day had been so thick they might have come to blows if Uncle Andrew hadn't seen him standing there just then. The next minute, Uncle Andrew left, saying he wanted to go to the river to see what he could do to help find her. Uncle Brian went with him.

Eventually, everyone stopped believing that she was still alive, but he knew that Uncle Andrew never gave up hope. His uncle still believed his wife was alive, even to this day.

Hope was a strange thing, Patrick mused as he turned down the winding highway that fed on to the road by the river. It kept some people going, against all odds. He thought of his mother. Hope tortured others needlessly. His mother had stayed with his father until the day he died, hoping he would change. His father never had.

Patrick blocked the thoughts from his mind. This wasn't getting him anywhere. It was time for him to be a detective.

When he arrived at the site, there were ten or so curious passersby milling around the area, craning their necks for a view. They were held back by three patrolman who had been summoned to the scene. A bright yellow tape stretched across the area close to the retrieved vehicle, proclaiming it a crime scene.

He was really getting to hate the color yellow.

Exiting his car, Patrick nodded absently at the patrolmen and strode toward the recently fished out sports car. Except for a smashed left front light, the car seemed none the worse for wear. The driver's side door was hanging open, allowing him a view of the young woman inside. She was stretched out across her seat, her body tilted toward the passenger side. She was twenty, maybe twenty-one and had been very pretty before the water had stolen her last breath and filled her lungs, sealing the look of panic on her face.

He judged the woman in the trim navy suit bending over her to be a little older, though he wasn't sure by just how much. He didn't recognize her. Someone new in the coroner's office, he imagined. She looked a little young to be a doctor.

Or maybe he was just feeling old.

Patrick took a step back, partially turning toward the nearest patrolman. "Who's that?"

The officer glanced over his shoulder. "Detective McKenna. Says she's with you."

Irritation was close to the surface this morning. Okay, who the hell was playing games and why? "Nobody's with me," Patrick retorted tersely.

He thought he heard the patrolman mutter, "You said it, I didn't," but his attention was focused on the blonde kneeling beside the vehicle.

Crossing to her quickly, he wasted no time with preambles and niceties. He didn't like having his crime scene interfered with. "I thought I was assigned to this case."

Maggi raised her eyes from what she was doing. The

male voice was stern, definitely territorial. From what she'd been told, she'd expected nothing less. From her vantage point, six-three looked even taller than it ordinarily might have.

Patrick Cavanaugh.

Show time.

He was more formidable looking than his photograph, she thought. Also better looking. But that was neither here nor there. She was interested in beauty of the soul, not face or body. If she was, Maggi noted absently, someone might have said she'd hit the jackpot.

They'd said that Lucifer had been the most beautiful of the archangels.

"You are," Maggi replied mildly.

Because she didn't like the psychological advantage her position gave him, she rose to her feet, patently ignoring the extended hand he offered her. Ground rules had to be established immediately. She was her own person.

"Then what are you doing here?" Patrick demanded.

With the ease of someone slipping on a glove, she slid into the role she'd been assigned. Once upon a time, before the lure of the badge had gotten her, she'd entertained the idea of becoming an actress. Working undercover allowed her to combine both her loves.

"I guess they didn't tell you."

He had a crime scene to take charge of, he didn't have time for guessing games initiated by fluffy blondes compromising his crime scene. "Tell me what?"

"That I'm your new partner."

Chapter 2

"The hell you are."

Patrick glared at this woman who looked as if she would be more at home on some runway in Paris, modeling the latest in impractical lingerie than standing beside a waterlogged corpse, pretending to look for clues.

"Yes," Maggi replied with a smile. "The hell I am."

No one had notified him. He hated having things sprung on him without warning. In his experience, most surprises turned out bad.

"Since when?"

"Since this morning. Last night, actually," she corrected, "but it was too late to get started then."

He couldn't believe that someone actually believed that he and this woman could work together. He found working with another man difficult enough; working with a woman with all her accompanying quirks and baggage was out of the question.

"By whose authority?" he demanded.

"Captain Reynolds." She gave him the name of his direct superior, although the pairing had not originated with Reynolds. The order had come from John Halliday, the man in charge of Internal Affairs. A fair, honest man, if not the easiest to work with, Halliday had found a subtle way of getting her in so that not even Reynolds knew the true purpose behind her becoming Cavanaugh's new partner. "He said you wouldn't be thrilled."

Patrick's frown deepened. He knew why Reynolds hadn't said anything. It was because the captain didn't care for confrontations from within. Well, he couldn't just slide this blonde under his door and expect things to go well from there.

"Captain Reynolds has a gift for understatement." His voice was brittle. "I haven't seen you around."

His icy blue eyes seemed to go right through her. She could see why others might find him intimidating. "I've been there. Around," she clarified when he continued to stare at her. She shrugged casually. "I can't help it if you haven't noticed me."

Oh, he would have noticed her, Patrick thought. A woman who looked the way she did was hard to miss. She was the kind that made heads turn and married men stop to rethink their choice in a life partner. He wasn't given to socializing, but he would have noticed her.

Something didn't feel right, though. "How long have you been a detective?" Patrick asked.

"Three months."

Three months. A novice. What the hell was the captain thinking? Even a man as photo-op oriented as Reynolds had to know this was a bad idea. This woman needed training, aging, and that just wasn't his line.

Patrick waved her away. "Tell Captain Reynolds I don't do baby-sitting."

"I don't think that'll matter to him," she told him crisply. "He doesn't have any school-aged children." She indicated the vehicle next to her. "Now, why don't we just make the best of this and get back to work?"

Patrick looked at her sharply, about to make his rejection plainer since she seemed to have trouble assimilating it, when her words echoed in his brain. "We?"

"We," she repeated. There was more than ten inches difference between them in height. Maggi drew herself up as far as she could, refusing to appear cowed. "You've got to know that working with you isn't exactly my idea of being on a picnic."

His eyes were flat as he regarded her. "Then why do it?"

Halliday had told her to blend in, to stay quiet and gather as much information as possible about Cavanaugh and his dealings. The less attention drawn to herself, the better. But from what she'd managed to piece together about him, a man like Cavanaugh didn't respect sheep. He sheared them and went on. What he respected was someone who'd stand up to him, who'd go toe-to-toe without flinching. That kind of a person stood a chance of finding out something useful. Someone who blended in didn't.

Maggi had her battle plan laid out. "Because I go where they send me and I always follow orders."

His eyes pinned her to the spot. "Always?"

She met his stare head-on, his blue eyes against her own green. "Always."

Well, knowing Reynolds, that didn't exactly surprise him. He wondered if she was someone's daughter, someone's niece. Someone Reynolds owed a favor to.

You never knew when you had to call a favor in, especially when you had your eye on the political arena, the way Reynolds did.

"Terrific." He looked at her without attempting to hide his disgust. "A by-the-book, wet-behind-the-ears rookie."

She was far from a rookie, but this wasn't the time to get into that. For now, she left him with his assumptions. "Guess that's just your cross to bear," she quipped, turning her attention back to the victim.

He was accustomed to people withdrawing from him, to avoiding him whenever possible. This was something a little different. He wondered if stupidity guided her, or if she had some kind of different agenda. "You've got a smart mouth."

"Goes with my smart brain." Deciding that the corpse wasn't going anywhere, Maggi looked at the man whose soul she was going to have to crawl into. "I graduated top of my class from the academy."

If that was meant to impress him, she'd fallen short of her mark, he thought. He couldn't stomach newly minted detectives, spouting rhetoric and theories they'd picked up out of the safe pages of some textbook. "There's a whole world of difference between a classroom and what you find outside of it."

"I know." It was going to be slow going, finding his good side. From what she'd gleaned, he might not even have one. But she felt he'd be less antagonistic if he felt she had some sort of experience. "I was in Vice in San Francisco."

His eyes slid over her, taking full measure, seeing beneath the jacket and matching trousers. It took more than fabric to disguise her shape. She'd probably made one hell of a decoy. "Stopping it or starting it?"

Her grin was quick, lethal. "Now who's got the smart mouth?"

He looked away. "Difference being, I don't shoot mine off."

The wind kept insisting on playing with her hair. She pushed it away from her face, only to have it revisit less than a beat later. "I'll remember that. See? Learning already."

Annoyed, Patrick knew there was nothing he could do about the situation right now. If he ordered her away, he had a feeling she wouldn't retreat. He didn't want to go into a power struggle in front of the patrolmen. No one had to tell him that behind the sexy, engaging smile was a woman who'd gotten her way most of her life. You only had to look at her to know that.

He could wait. All that mattered was the end result. He didn't want a partner. He wanted to work alone. It required less effort, less coordination. And less would go wrong that way.

Patrick sighed. "Well, I need to learn something about you."

His eyes were intense, a light shade of blue that seemed almost liquid. She wondered if they could be warm on occasion, or if they always looked as if they were dissecting you. "Fire away."

"Your name. What is it?"

She realized that she'd skipped that small detail. She put her hand out now. "Margaret McKenna. My friends call me Maggi."

He made no effort to take her hand and she dropped it at her side. "What do people who aren't your friends call you?"

"The repeatable ones are McKenna, or 3M."

Despite himself, he was drawn in. "3M? Like the tape?"

Her gaze was unwavering. "No, because my full name is Mary Margaret McKenna."

He could see that the revelation pained her. She didn't like her name. That was fair enough—it didn't suit her. She didn't look like a Mary Margaret. Mary Margarets were subdued, given to shy smiles. Unless he missed his guess, the last time this woman had been subdued had probably been shortly before birth.

He laughed, his expression remaining unaffected. "Sounds like you should be starring in an off-Broadway revival of *Finian's Rainbow*."

Surprise nudged at her. She wouldn't have thought he'd know something like that. "You like musicals?"

"My sister does." Patrick stopped abruptly, realizing he'd broken his own rule about getting personal with strangers. And he meant for this woman to be a stranger. He didn't intend for her to remain in his company any longer than it took to get back to the station and confront Reynolds about his misguided, worse-than-usual choice of partners for him. "I work alone."

"So I was told." She'd also been told other things. Like the fact that he was a highly decorated cop who'd never been a team player. Now they were beginning to think that was because he was guarding secrets, secrets that had to do with lining his pockets. Rumors had been raised. Where there was smoke, there was usually fire and it was her job to put it out. "I won't get in your way."

"For that to be true, you'd have to leave."

From any other man, that might have been the beginning of a come-on, or at the very least, a slight flirtation. From Cavanaugh, she knew it meant that he regarded her as a pest. "All right, I won't get in your way much," she underscored.

He sincerely doubted that. But for the moment, he was stuck with this fledgling detective, and he didn't have any more time to waste on her.

Patrick took out a pair of rubber gloves from his jacket pocket and pulled them on. He nodded toward the vehicle that had been fished out. "What have you learned so far?"

"The victim seems to be in her early twenties, on her way to or from a party."

"How do you know?" The question came at her like a gunshot.

"Look at what she's wearing. A slinky, short black dress."

His glance was quick, concise, all-inclusive before reverting to Maggi. "Professional?"

Maggi paused. The panic on the victim's face made it difficult to see anything else. "A hooker? Maybe, but not cheap. A call girl maybe. The dress is subtle, subdued yet stylish."

He looked further into the vehicle. "Any ID?"

Maggi shook her head. "No purse. Might have been washed away, although I doubt it."

He looked at her sharply. Even a broken clock was right twice a day. "Why?"

She'd already been over the interior of the car and found nothing. "Because there's no registration inside the glove compartment. The glove compartment was completely empty. Not even a manual. Nobody keeps a glove compartment that clean."

If it was an attempt to hide identity, he thought, it was a futile one. "Ownership's easy enough to find out."

Maggi nodded. She gave him her thoughts on the subject. "It's a stalling tactic. Maybe whoever did this to her needed the extra time to try to fabricate an alibi."

His eyes made her feel like squirming when they penetrated that way. The man had to be hell on wheels in the interrogation room. "So you think this is a homicide, not an accident."

"That's the way the department's treating it or we wouldn't be here." She gave him an expression of sheer innocence.

He crossed his arms before him, looking down at her again. "Okay, Mary Margaret, what do you think the approximate time of death was?"

"Eleven twenty-three. Approximately," she said. He was trying to get her to lose her cool. Even if this wasn't about something bigger, she wasn't about to let him have the satisfaction.

"Woman's intuition?"

"Woman's vision," she corrected. "Twenty-twenty." Before he could ask her what she was talking about, Maggi reached over the body and held up the victim's right hand. The young woman was wearing an old-fashioned analog watch. The crystal wasn't broken, but it was obviously not water-resistant. It had stopped at precisely 11:23.

The CSI team arrived, equipped with their steel cases and apparatus intended to take the mystery out of death. Patrick stepped out of their way as they took possession of the vehicle and the victim within.

Maggi looked at him. "Want me to brief them?"

Something that could have passed for amusement flickered over him. "Asking for permission?"

She served his words back to him. "Trying not to get in your way."

Too late for that, he thought. Now they had to concentrate on getting her out of his way. Patrick gestured toward the head crime scene investigator. "Go ahead. That's Jack Urban."

Stepping around to the back of the vehicle, Patrick took out his notepad and carefully wrote down the license plate number before crossing to the nearest policeman. He handed the notepad to the man.

"See if these plates were run yet," he instructed. "Find out who the car belongs to. See if it was reported missing or stolen in the past twenty-four hours."

The policeman took the notepad without comment, retreating to his squad car.

The soft, light laugh that floated to him had Patrick looking back toward the crime scene. His so-called partner was talking to the head of the CSI team. Whatever she said had the man smiling like some living brain donor. Patrick shook his head. Obviously not everyone found his new partner as irritating as he did.

"I need to make a stop at the bank."

Patrick spared the woman sitting beside him in the front seat a look. It was cold outside and he had the windows of his car rolled up. He hadn't counted on the fact that along with the added warmth he'd be trapping the scent of her perfume within the vehicle.

Citing that they were partners until the captain tore them asunder, something Patrick was counting on happening in the very immediate future, the woman had hitched a ride back into town with him. When he'd asked her how she'd come to the crime scene in the first place, she'd told him that she'd caught a ride with one of the patrol cars.

The officers were still back at the scene, protecting

it from contamination as best they could. With them out of the picture, Patrick'd had no choice but to agree to let her come with him.

He didn't particularly like being agreeable.

He liked the idea of being a chauffeur even less.

"Why don't you do that after hours?" he bit off tersely.

She shifted in her seat. Again. The woman was nothing if not unharnessed energy, exuding enough for two people. She could have been her own partner, and should have been. Anything but his.

Maggi pointed to the building in the middle of the tree-lined block. "C'mon, Pat, we're passing it right now. It'll only take a minute."

She slid a glance in his direction. If looks could kill, she knew she would have been dead on the spot.

"All right, as long as you promise never to call me 'Pat' again."

"Deal." Like it or not, she was going to have to spend some time with him. She wanted it to be as stress free as she could make it. "So, what do you like being called?"

"I don't like being called at all."

No one said the assignments were going to be easy. "In the event that I have to get your attention," Maggi began gamely, "do you prefer 'hey you,' or shall I just throw sunflower seeds at you until I get you to turn around?"

He could see her doing it, too. She had that kind of bulldog quality about her. "Cavanaugh'll do."

"Not even Patrick?"

He slowed down. There was a parking spot almost directly across the street from the bank. Patrick guided the car into it, then pulled up the hand brake. Only then did he turn to look at her.

"Let's get something straight, McKenna. We're not friends, we're partners. We're not even going to be that for very long, so quit coming on like some Girl Scout and stop trying to sound like you're going to be my lifelong buddy."

She sat there quietly for a long moment, trying to get a handle on this man. "Losing Ramirez hit you pretty hard, didn't it?"

The look he shot her was darker than black. "The last thing I need or want is to ride around with Dr. Phil in the car. You want to analyze somebody—"

She held up her hand, not in surrender but to get him to curtail what he was about to say. "Sorry, just making conversation."

"Well, don't."

Unbuckling her seat belt, she turned to look at him. The intensity on her face took him by surprise. "You know, Cavanaugh, someday you just might need someone to watch your back for you."

"If and when I ever do, it sure as hell isn't going to be you."

She paused for a moment, and then she gave him a bright smile. "Roughage."

Had she lost her mind? What kind of a birdbrain were they cranking out of the academy these days? "What?"

"Morning roughage. Does wonders in clearing out all those poisons that seem to be running around all through you," she declared, getting out of the car. She paused to look in for a last second before closing the door. "I'll only be a minute."

Patrick frowned to himself. Even a minute seemed

too long to remain in the car, surrounded the way he was with her perfume. What he needed right now more than solitude was air. He got out.

When she looked at him curiously, he muttered, "I need to stretch my legs."

She pretended to glance down at them. "And long legs they are, too."

Not waiting for him, Maggi hurried across the street, wanting to put a little distance between herself and Mr. Personality before she said something she meant and blew everything. She held her hand up, stopping traffic as she darted toward the other side.

She supposed having him this ill-tempered made her job easier. It took away any qualms she might have about spying on him.

"Hey, didn't they teach you not to jaywalk at the academy while you were busy graduating at the top of your class?"

For less than two cents, she'd tell him what she thought of him. Exercising extreme control, Maggi turned around when she reached the curb. "You want to give me a ticket?"

"I don't want you risking your fool neck needlessly." What he wanted to do was give her her walking papers, but there was nothing he could do about that here.

Resigned, and far from happy about it, Patrick pushed the glass door open and crossed the threshold ahead of her. She looked surprised when he held the door for her.

"I see someone must have taught you manners somewhere along the line," she said.

"It's expedient. If I let the door go, you would probably walk into it and make the ER our next stop. We have to get back to the station."

She refused to let him get to her. She knew that was what he was after, to get to her so badly that she'd march into Reynolds's office and declare that she wouldn't work with him, the way all his other partners had. Except for Ramirez.

Ain't gonna happen, Cavanaugh, she thought as she walked by him.

"You can huff and puff all you want, Cavanaugh," she informed him brightly. "I'm not going anywhere."

With that, she picked out the shortest line. Patrick stopped by the small table with all the deposit and withdrawal slips, looking annoyed. Mercifully, this wasn't going to take long. Mondays were usually slow.

Except where homicides seemed to be concerned, she thought, thinking back to the crime scene they'd just left. Something like that made grabbing lunch a challenge to intestinal fortitude.

The teller in the window directly to her left screamed.

The next moment, the man standing before the window whirled around.

There was a gun in his hand.

"Everyone freeze," he announced loudly. "This is a holdup."

Chapter 3

The man's eyes bounced around like pinballs that had just been put into play. He seemed to aim his weapon at everyone in the bank at the same time. Patrick could almost hear the bank robber's nerves jangling.

"Get down!" the man shouted. "Everyone get down on the floor!" His gun moved erratically from person to person, turning each into a potential target, a potential victim. "Now!"

Patrick did a quick calculation. There were fourteen other people in the bank, not counting the bank robber. Five of them tellers. The gunman looked so rattled he could start firing away at any second. It had all the signs of becoming a bloodbath at the slightest provocation.

Going through the motions of dropping down to the floor, Patrick reached for his pistol.

The rest happened so fast he only had the opportunity to absorb it after the fact. Before he knew what she was doing, the partner the department had saddled him with cried out in what sounded like utter panic. His head jerked in her direction. The bank robber stared at her.

Maggi's eyes were wide as they were riveted on the bank robber and she was trembling. Her hands were raised above her head in total submission.

"Omigod, it's a gun." Panic escalated in her voice. "He's got a gun. Oh, please don't shoot me," she implored. "I just found out I'm pregnant. You'd be killing two people, not just one. Me and my baby. I don't want to die, mister. I've got everything to live for. Please don't kill me."

With each word she uttered, Maggi edged closer and closer to the bank robber. She was breathing heavily and still trembling.

"Shut up, you stupid bitch. Nobody's going to die, just do what I tell you." The bank robber looked panicked himself as he trained the gun on her.

"All right, all right—" Maggi's voice hitched "—if you promise you won't hurt me. Pretty please?"

The last two words she uttered were distinctively different from the rest. As she seemed to sag down right in front of him, Maggi grabbed hold of his gun hand. Catching him by surprise, she violently jerked his arm behind his back. In less than half a heartbeat, her own gun was in her other hand. She held it close enough to the robber's temple to get her point across.

"Drop the gun." He did as he was told, cursing her roundly. "Now apologize to the nice people and say you're sorry."

"What the—" At a loss for coherence, the bank robber let loose a string of profanities that only made Maggi shake her head.

"You kiss your mother with that mouth?" she marveled. Relieved that the situation was over, Maggi took a deep breath, trying to get a hold of her own nerves. They felt as if they'd been stretched to the limit. Adrenaline still raced through her veins. "Keep that up and we're going to have to wash your mouth out with soap, aren't we, Detective Cavanaugh?"

As if waiting for some kind of word of concurrence, Maggi raised her eyebrow toward Patrick. He merely grunted as he pulled the man's hands behind him and snapped handcuffs around his wrists. The look he gave her left Maggi short on description. Had she just stepped on his male pride?

The robber winced as the cuffs went on. "You're cops?"

"No, just into a little S&M," Maggi quipped. "We like to carry handcuffs with us." She winked broadly at Patrick, beginning to enjoy getting under his skin. "You never know when they might come in handy."

Using a handkerchief, she stooped down and picked up the man's weapon by the butt. Nothing fancy. She wondered if this was the man's first time. He'd certainly behaved that way.

"Next time you want money from a bank, do it right. Use a withdrawal slip." She tucked the gun in at her belt for the time being, then looked at Patrick. "Want me to call for backup?"

Patrick gave the cuffs a good tug, making sure they were secure. "You mean you're not going to fly off with him to the precinct?"

Maggi lifted a shoulder in a casual shrug. "My cape's at the dry cleaners."

Separating herself from the others, she took out her cell phone and put in a call for a squad car. The second she closed the phone, the bank manager was on her, telling her how grateful he was to her and her partner and asking if there was anything he could do to show his deep appreciation.

"Other than giving away a five-pound box of tens to charity, I'd say hire a security guard. The next time you might not be so lucky."

The man was still thanking her profusely as she crossed back to Patrick and the prisoner. It was hard to say which of the two men glared at her harder.

She didn't do recrimination well. "What's your problem?"

Patrick made the prisoner face the wall as they waited for the squad car to arrive. His voice was cold. "I don't like showboating."

"So I won't invite you to a boat show the next time there's one at the marina. Anything else?"

"Yes, did it ever occur to you that you could have gotten your head blown off?"

"Frankly, I didn't have time to think things through to their grisly end." Maggi moved her head from side to side. "See? It's still attached and in good working order."

"Just barely." The last thing he wanted was to lose another partner in the line of duty. He'd had enough department funerals to last a lifetime.

"That's all that counts." She kept her voice cheerful as approaching sirens grew louder. The cavalry had arrived. "Ah, that's always such a comforting sound." She looked at the prisoner. "Bet you don't think so, do you?"

"Bitch," the bank robber spit out. The next moment, he found himself spun around and held up an inch off the ground. The man's feet came in contact with air as Patrick yanked him up.

"What's your name?" Patrick growled at the man.

The bank robber fought for oxygen and against numbing panic. "Joe. Joe Wellington."

"Well, Joe, Joe Wellington, talk nice to the lady or the next time it won't be soap you'll be tasting in your mouth." Patrick's look was dark, malevolent. "Do I make myself clear?"

"Clear," the bank robber gasped out. His eyes were glassy as they regarded Patrick.

Filled with disgust, Patrick all but threw him down. He then became aware that Maggi was grinning at him like some damn Cheshire cat.

"And just when I thought you didn't like me," she said.

"I don't like you," he replied tersely. She didn't stop grinning. To say it got on his nerves gave new meaning to the word *understatement*. "What the hell are you talking about?"

"You defended my honor. I'm flattered."

He didn't want her making anything out of it. It had been purely reflexive reaction. "I did it to defend the honor of the badge. It wasn't done to flatter you."

"Call it a side effect."

He had no time to retort. The backup she'd summoned arrived that moment.

It was just as well, he decided. The sooner they got back to the precinct, the sooner things would get back to normal. Whatever that was.

"Buy you lunch?"

It was a little more than an hour later and the would-be bank robber had been sent to be processed through the system. Cavanaugh was writing up the report, annoyed at the time this took away from the homicide they were supposed to investigate.

He waved his hand at Maggi as if she were an annoying fruit fly buzzing around his head.

Maggi held up a twenty almost in front of his nose. "Now that I've had a chance to cash my check, I can afford to splurge a little. I feel like celebrating. Join me," she coaxed. She knew how dangerous the situation could have gotten, despite her earlier disclaimer to him. The fact that it hadn't gone badly, that she and everyone else were able to walk away, was a fantastic high she wasn't close to coming down from.

He ignored her and the bill she held up. "Not interested."

"Don't you eat?" She bent down until her face was level with his. The ends of her hair brushed against some of his files. "Can I buy you a can of oil?"

Patrick finally looked up. "Is that supposed to be cute?"

"Relatively speaking." She wasn't going to let him rob her of her moment. So little of what she did these days felt this good. The positive reactions she dealt with all squared themselves away on paper. That never produced a high. "C'mon, Cavanaugh, lighten up. We've still got the rest of the day to face together. It goes better on a full stomach." When he made no attempt to get up, she added, "My dad always says you can't trust a man who won't eat with you."

He laughed shortly. "I take it your father never saw *The Godfather.*"

Perched on the edge of his desk now, she hooted. "You *are* a movie buff."

He didn't like giving her points, didn't like her feeling

as if she knew something about him. The less you knew about each other, the less likely you were to get close.

"I told you, that's my sister's department. You can't help picking up a few things if it's always playing in the background."

That was the second time he'd mentioned his sister. She paused to study him for a moment. "Are you close, you and your sister?" And then she answered her own questions. "Silly question, I guess."

The computer network was down, temporarily halting the exchange of information that would allow him to get the name of the owner of the dead woman's sports car. Sometimes progress created nothing but stumbling blocks, he thought with annoyance. He didn't bother sparing Maggi a glance. "Only if you think that I'm going to give you an answer."

"So what are you, like, the Lone Ranger?"

It became obvious to him that subtlety was lost on her. She was probably the kind who had to be dislodged with a two-by-four or a crowbar. "The position of Tonto is not open."

Since he didn't look up, Maggi found herself staring at the top of his head. He had deep, straight black hair, the kind that tempted a woman to touch, to feather her fingers through it. She purposely slipped her hands under her as she sat.

"That's okay, I don't do sidekicks—I do partners."

He finally looked up. "Aside from catching bullets with your bare teeth?" The expression on his face grew darker. "What the hell were you thinking at the bank?"

Another wisecrack was on the tip of her tongue, but then, she decided to tell him the truth. She'd acted because she was afraid.

"That he was going to fire on you if you drew your

weapon the way you were planning to." And then, because it was getting too serious, she added, "I didn't want to lose a partner before I won you over with my sparkling personality."

"How did you know what I was going to do?"

"I saw it in your eyes," she said simply. "Sometimes, you can't go in like the Lone Ranger. Sometimes you have to go in like Fay Wray."

He stared at her. "Come again?"

"Fay Wray. The woman in *King Kong*." There was still no recognition in his face. "The screamer."

"You didn't scream."

"No, but I got properly hysterical. Enough to throw him off and get the drop on him." Because it was obviously causing friction, she didn't want to continue talking about the foiled bank robbery. "Anyway, it's over. C'mon, Cavanaugh." Playfully she tugged on his arm. "My stomach's rumbling."

He shrugged her off. "No one's stopping you from going to lunch."

"I hate to eat alone." She would have pouted prettily if she'd thought it would work, but she knew it wouldn't. Cavanaugh wasn't the type to go out of his way to please a woman.

He glanced at her before going back to his report. "Go to a crowded restaurant."

"I'd rather go to lunch with my partner." She didn't like being ignored and he was doing a royal job of it. This time, when she tugged on his arm, it was a hard jerk to get him to look at her again. "Hey, you owe me."

Her words more than her action earned his attention. He raised his head, his eyes penetrating her inner layers. "I *owe* you?"

She could see how he could make someone squirm. She felt like squirming and she wasn't the one who was supposed to be sitting on the hot seat.

"Sure, I told you I'd have your back and I did. Only it turned out to be your front, but—" she shrugged "—same difference. Now, are you going to come with me or do I push that chair of yours all the way to the elevator and *make* you come with me?"

He didn't have time for stupidity. He didn't know why he was bothering to answer her or even acknowledge her. "You wouldn't dare."

She grinned, her eyes gaining a mischievous glint he found oddly arousing. The blow to his gut came out of nowhere. He sent it back to the same address.

"Cavanaugh," she informed him, "I was the kid who never walked away from a dare."

He snorted. "You must have made your parents very proud."

"No, just gray." Maggi's eyes shifted down to the chair he was sitting in, then back to his face. "Your chair's got wheels and I know how to use them."

Patrick had every intention of continuing to say no, but the woman had the tendencies of an annoying gnat. He knew damn well that she'd keep after him until he either really snapped at her or gave in. And he had to admit the truth: he *was* hungry.

"Okay." Hitting the save button on the keyboard, he rose to his feet. "But you've got to stop sounding as if someone put your mouth in the fast forward mode." If it ever stopped moving, it might prove to be a tempting target.

Her mouth was quick to curve. "Deal."

Yeah, he thought, with the devil.

As he followed her out the door, he remembered

reading a passage that said something about the devil having the ability to assume a very pleasing shape. He watched the rhythmic sway of her hips.

Looked like the devil had definitely outdone himself this time.

Maggi offered him his choice of places. He picked a pizzeria that had more seats outside than in. She ate three slices with the December wind chilling her food. He seemed more interested in observing the people on the street than in listening to anything she said.

It was a power play, she knew that. She had invaded his territory and he was suspicious of her. He had no idea how suspicious he should have been, she thought. Or maybe he knew. The worst thing in the world was to underestimate your opponent. And he was that. Her opponent, her assignment. Not her partner. This kept life interesting. And damn complicated.

"You've got a healthy appetite," he commented when she reached for her fourth piece.

"He speaks. Wow."

"Forget I said anything."

"No, please, now that the floodgates have opened up, continue." When he made no comment, she shook her head. "You keep this up and I'm going to be forced to practice my ventriloquist act on you."

"Your what?"

"That's when the sane person makes the wooden creation beside her talk. In other words, putting words into your mouth. Like 'Thanks for the lunch, Maggi. Remind me to return the favor.'"

Patrick stared at her. She'd done a fair imitation of his voice, all without moving her lips.

"Want me to continue?" she offered.

"No, you made your point." He rose, passing a ten in her direction. "You're crazy."

"I said lunch was on me." She was on her feet, striding after him to the car. Catching up, she pushed the money back into his pocket. "Do we have to argue about this, too?"

He felt her hand as she withdrew it from his pants pocket. The tightening in his loins was purely instinctive. And annoying. As was she.

"Why not? You seem to like it."

She pulled open the door on her side and got in. "I'd like a little agreement better." Buckling her seat belt, she sighed. "Tell you what, I'll let you yell at me some more if you want to."

About to start the car, he paused to look at her. "I don't yell."

"Okay, growl. Lip-synch, something. Just talk. Say something, anything."

"Why?" Starting the car, he pulled out of the parking area.

"Because I want to get to know you. Partners should know something about each other and I really don't know anything about you, other than what I've heard and the fact that if these were Roman times, your scowl would put Zeus to shame."

He came to a stop at a red light. "Jupiter."

"What?"

The light turned green again and he stepped on the accelerator. "Zeus was a Greek god, Jupiter was the Roman equivalent."

So he knew something beyond police procedure. He didn't strike her as the kind of man who knew mythology. "Impressive. I'll still go with Zeus. You look more like a Greek god than a Roman god anyway."

She was flirting with him, he thought, but when he shot her a look, McKenna's expression was totally guileless. Was she putting him on? Didn't matter. She wasn't going to last long enough for that to become a problem.

"You were damn lucky today that things turned out the way they did and no one was hurt. Next time, you might not be so lucky."

"I've always been pretty lucky." His profile hardened even more. "Hey, don't underestimate the part luck plays when it comes to our line of work." She thought of the wound that had put her out of commission for a month a couple of years back. She'd kept that bit of information from her father. The man had enough on his mind. Thinking of it, she patted the region several inches below her shoulder. "Two inches to the left and this scar might have been the last one I ever got instead of just one of many."

"Scars? You're talking about scars?" What kind of a woman was she? As far as he knew, women didn't exactly go out of their way to draw attention to something that was considered to be a blemish.

"Sure. Don't you have any?"

"I have enough."

"Where?" she asked innocently.

"Out of the light of day."

For just the slightest second, she caught herself wondering just where on his very hard anatomy those scars were located. The next moment, she roused herself, hauling her mind back into focus. "Then you know what I'm talking about. About luck, I mean."

Turning right, he shook his head. "Mary Margaret, I'm beginning to think I don't have a damn clue what you're talking about most of the time."

She wished he wouldn't use her name, but she knew if she said anything, he would only do it more often. "The subject is luck. The visual aids are scars." Grabbing her jacket and blouse, she undid some buttons and pulled both articles back. "Like this one."

Patrick glanced in her direction and almost forgot to look back at the road. He'd only caught a glimpse, but that provided more than enough fodder. He swerved to avoid rear-ending the car in front of him.

"Damn it, Mary Margaret, you always go exposing your breasts to people you hardly know?"

All she'd shown him was a little more skin than had already been evident. "It's called cleavage and I'm not exposing myself, I'm showing you a scar that's well above the bad-taste line. If I was into exposing, there are other scars I could show you."

Patrick didn't have to look at her to know she was grinning. He heard it in her voice. He was about to ask her just where on her anatomy they were situated, but he didn't need to go there. The interior of the car was warm enough as it was.

Maggi moved the fabric back into place. "Anyway, my point is that luck has *everything* to do with it. And I've been luckier than most."

She not only had hair like a Barbie doll, but the intelligence of one as well, Patrick thought darkly.

"Luck has a nasty habit of running out when you least expect it."

"God, but you are Mr. Sunshine, aren't you?"

"Sunshine was never my department." This time, he took on the yellow light, making it through the intersection before it had a chance to turn red. The faster he got this annoying woman back to the precinct, the better. "That's the realm of cockeyed optimists."

"Would it help you to know that I can back up my cockeyed optimism?"

"How? A Ouija board?"

She glanced at her watch. They'd eaten lunch in less than twenty-five minutes. "We've got a little time left. Take me to the firing range."

"We've still got a homicide to solve," he reminded her.

"This'll only take a few minutes and it might make you feel a whole lot better."

What would make him feel a whole lot better, he thought, was finding out that she was just part of another one of his bad dreams.

Growling an oath under his breath, Patrick turned the car around.

Chapter 4

The fiftyish, barrel-chested man behind the desk at the firing range smiled warmly the moment he saw her walking in, transforming his round face from intimidating to surprisingly boyish in appearance. "Hey, back for more, Annie Oakley?"

Reaching behind his desk, the officer, Miles Baker, produced a box of ammunition before Maggi could make a formal request and slid it across the counter toward her.

Inclining her head, Maggi took the box from him. "Just here to see if my edge hasn't dulled."

Baker laughed. "Even dulled, you'd still be better than the rest of us." His deep-set brown eyes shifted toward Patrick. Since the other detective made no request for shells, he left a second box where it was. "Hey, you ever seen this lady in action?"

Against his will, Patrick thought about the incident at the bank. At the time, he'd been sure she'd lost her nerve. To be honest, McKenna had pulled her weapon out pretty quickly.

He looked at Maggi. "Depends on what you mean by action." He noted that she had the good grace to look just a shade uncomfortable.

Baker raised hamlike hands, warding off any stray thoughts. "Hey, I don't go there."

His denial was a bit too vehement. Patrick was willing to bet the man had had a sensual thought or two about the woman he was grinning at. Baker wouldn't have been human if he hadn't. Besides, Patrick had seen the way the man had brightened the second he'd recognized her.

"I'm talking about with a gun in her hand." Baker kissed the tips of his fingers before spreading them wide again as if to release the phantom kiss into the air. "Thing of beauty to watch."

Patrick still wasn't sure if the officer was referring to the way she shot or just McKenna in general. He supposed, if pinned down, he'd have to agree to the latter. But beauty had little to do with their line of work. If anything, it got in the way.

"Apparently that's why I'm here." Resigned, Patrick looked at what he hoped was his temporary partner expectantly. "Okay, you want to show me something, show me."

Though his expression remained impassive, she knew Cavanaugh was challenging her. Ordinarily she didn't go out of her way to prove anything about herself to anyone. She figured people who did were braggarts.

But this wasn't a case of bragging or showing off. This was a case of proving herself to the man she'd supposedly been partnered with. This was showing him that she could be trusted to at least cover his back when the time called for it. And, in her experience, one trust usually led to another.

At least, that was what she was counting on.

"All right." She turned on her heel to lead the way to the firing range. "Let's go."

"Hey, don't forget these." Leaning over the counter, Baker held up two sets of earphones. "Don't want to go around the rest of the day deaf, do you?"

Patrick doubled back and took both pairs from the officer. He handed one set to Maggi.

"All right, Mary Margaret," he said gamely, "impress me."

No pressure there. Going to the rear, Maggi chose a slot, then donned the earphones before pressing a button that sent her paper target flying down the field away from her.

Patrick watched as the blackened target became smaller and smaller. The woman with the gun made no effort to halt its progress. Just how far was she sending it?

"You planning on stopping that thing anytime soon? Nobody expects you to shoot at a perp fleeing the scene in Nevada."

The target still hadn't gone as far as she could shoot, but Maggi pressed the button to oblige Patrick. The paper target looked little bigger than a suspended stray piece of confetti.

Closing one eye, she took careful aim and fired.

Curious, Patrick didn't wait for her to discharge the weapon again. Holding his hand up to stop her from firing, he pressed the button to retrieve the target. When it came back, he saw that she'd hit it dead center. He felt he had to assume that it was just a freakish coincidence, but for argument's sake, he gave her the benefit of the doubt.

"Not bad," he conceded, releasing the target, "if you've got the time to line up your shot."

Maggi said nothing. Instead, reaching over him, she pressed the button again, sending the target back even farther away than before. This time, Patrick made no comment about the target's proximity but waited until she stopped it herself. And then, just when the target had reached the end of its run, she pressed for its return.

Once the line was activated again, Maggi began firing, sending off five rounds before the paper target came back to its place of origin.

Without a word, Patrick examined the target. She'd sent all five rounds into the same vicinity as the first. Two of the shots were almost on top of each other, the rest close enough to make the hole bigger.

Staring at it, Patrick had to admit to himself that she was impressive. But he'd never admit this to her.

"Not bad," he said again, "if the perp is running in a straight line and not firing back."

He was doing it to annoy her, Maggi thought. He wasn't the first man she'd had to prove herself to, and losing her temper wasn't part of the deal. She loaded a fresh clip into her weapon.

"I guess we'll just have to wait for the right occasion," she told him calmly.

"I guess. We done here?"

She squared her shoulders, feeling a slow boil begin. She could have gone on firing, but obviously it didn't prove anything to this lug. "We're done."

"Good." Patrick took off his earphones and walked back to the front desk.

He was a hard man, Maggi thought, but then she

already knew that. And she also knew that she'd made her point. Taking a deep breath, she hurried back to the front desk and handed in the remainder of the box of ammunition to Baker, as well as the earphones.

Baker looked surprised that she had cut her time so short.

"Fun time's over, Baker," she explained. "We've got to get back to the station."

The officer put the earphones away. "See you around, Annie Oakley," he chuckled.

Patrick stood at the door, waiting for her. "He knows you."

She walked out first. "We've talked."

He had a feeling she talked to everyone and everything, living or not. "So, how long have you had this supervision?"

It was a backhanded compliment. Nevertheless, she accepted it gladly. She barely suppressed the smile that rose to her lips, but Maggi knew he'd think she was preening. She walked briskly beside him to the car.

"I don't. What I had was a father who was on the job for twenty-two years. He put a gun in my hand when I was old enough to hold one and took me out to the firing range." She still remembered the first time. The weapon had weighed a ton, but she'd been far too proud to say anything.

"Some people would frown on that." He passed no judgments himself. People were free to live their lives any way they saw fit, as long as it didn't impinge on others. Or him.

"Yeah, well, my father wasn't exactly your average guy. He wanted me to have a healthy respect for guns and to know what one could or couldn't do."

Patrick heard the pride in her voice, and the affection. It was the same tone he heard in his cousins' voices when they talked about their fathers. He wondered what that was like, having a father you were close to, you were proud of. It seemed like such a foreign concept to him.

"A little bit of knowledge is a dangerous thing," he pointed out.

Her father had taught her how to take a gun apart first, piece by piece, and then clean it before reassembling it. She'd had to wait a long time before he allowed her to handle cartridges.

"Maybe, but enough of it sets you free," she countered.

"Whatever." Getting into the car, he waited until she buckled up. "So, how does your father feel about you being on the police force?"

"He worries." Maggi slid the metal tongue into the groove, snapping the belt into place. "He's a father first, a police officer second. But he's proud of me." She knew that without asking. It made her determined never to let him down. "He's the reason I joined up." She thought of the upbringing she'd had. Blue uniforms populated her everyday world. "I never knew anything else."

Starting the car, he backed out of his space. "What's your mother got to say about it?"

Maggi kept her face forward. "Nothing. She died when I was nine. He and his buddies raised me."

Her profile had gotten a little rigid. He'd hit a nerve, he thought. Miss Sunshine had a cloud on her horizon. Interesting. "His buddies?"

Maggi nodded. Her profile was relaxed again and she

was as animated as before. Just his luck. "The other police officers. I was their mascot."

He laughed to himself, taking a hard right. "That would explain it."

Maggi found she had to brace herself to keep from leaning toward the window. "Explain what?"

"The cocky attitude."

"I don't have a cocky attitude," she informed him. "I just know what I'm capable of and, since you're my partner, I wanted you to know, too," she added quickly before he could accuse her of showing off.

"You shouldn't have put yourself out."

Turning her head, she caught him sparing her a glance. She couldn't fathom what was in his eyes. "Why?"

"Because you're not going to be my partner for that long."

Guess again, Cavanaugh. "You know something I don't?"

Arriving at the station, he pulled into his spot and stopped the car. Sure shot or not, someone who looked like her didn't belong out in the field. It was like waving a red flag in front of every nut case in the area who wanted to get his rocks off. The sooner she wasn't his responsibility, the better.

Patrick got out, slamming the door. "Yeah, I know how long people in your position last, on the average." He took the front stairs to the entrance quickly, then paused at the door. She was right behind him.

Maggi grinned up at him as she walked through the door he held open for her. "Haven't you noticed, Cavanaugh? I'm not average."

Yeah, he thought as he followed her inside the building, *that's just the trouble, I've noticed.*

* * *

"Definitely died before she went into the water," the medical examiner, Dr. Stanley Ochoa, informed them with the slightly monotonous voice of a man who had been at his job too long.

Maggi couldn't help looking at the young woman on the table, stripped of her dignity and her clothes, every secret exposed except her identity and why she'd died.

Poor baby, you look like a kid. Maggi raised her eyes to the M.E. "And we know this how?"

Instead of answering immediately, Ochoa turned to Patrick. A hint of amusement flickered beneath his drooping mustache. "Eager little thing, isn't she?"

"And, oddly enough, not deaf or invisible," Maggi cheerfully informed the M.E. as she placed herself between the two men, both of whom towered over her. She missed the glimmer of a smile on Patrick's face. "Now, how do you know she didn't drown?"

"Simple. No water in the lungs. She wasn't breathing when she went over the side."

"Because she was already dead. Makes sense." Maggi looked at the gash on the woman's forehead. It looked as if there'd been a line of blood at one point. If she'd bled, that meant she'd still been alive when she'd sustained the blow. "That bump on her head— did she get it hitting her forehead against the steering wheel when she went over the railing?"

Ochoa dismissed the guess. "Might have, but at first glance it looks deeper than something she could have sustained from that kind of impact."

Patrick's face was expressionless. "The air bag was deployed."

Maggi bit the inside of her lip. She'd forgotten that detail and knew it made her look bad in his eyes. She regarded the victim again. "Could the air bag have suffocated her? She's a small woman."

Again the M.E. shook his head. "No, suffocation has different signs. This was a blunt force trauma to the head. Something heavy."

Because Cavanaugh wasn't saying anything, Maggi summarized what they'd just ascertained. "So someone killed her, then put her into the sports car and drove her into the river to make it look like an accident."

Ochoa nodded. The overhead light shone brightly on his forehead, accentuating his receding hairline. "Looks like."

Patrick had been regarding the victim in silence, as if he was conducting his own séance with her. He raised his eyes to look at the overweight medical examiner. "Anything else?"

"Not yet. I'm waiting on the blood work results and I haven't conducted the autopsy. Check back with me tomorrow."

Patrick was aware that Maggi wasn't beside him as he reached the door. Turning around, he saw her still standing by the table. He thought she was studying the victim for enlightenment until he saw the expression on her face.

With an annoyed sigh, he retraced his steps. "We don't mourn them, Mary Margaret, we just make sure whoever did this to them pays the price."

He probably thought she was weak, Maggi thought. The woman's death just seemed like such a sad waste. "Yeah, right." Squaring her shoulders, she walked out of the room.

The moment they were in the corridor, Patrick's cell phone rang. He had it out before it could ring a second time.

"Cavanaugh."

Curiosity ricocheted through her as she walked beside him, waiting for Cavanaugh to say something to the voice talking in his ear. She wanted to figure out the nature of his call. Her real assignment was still foremost in her mind, but she wanted to find the person who'd wantonly ended the life of the young woman on the table in the morgue.

If she was hoping for clues, she was disappointed. All Cavanaugh said before disconnecting was "Thanks."

Impatient, she tried not to sound it as she asked, "Well?"

He wasn't accustomed to answering to anyone. The only partner he'd ever gotten along with had always given him his space, waiting for him to say something but never really pressing him. But then, this woman wasn't Ramirez. What she was was a royal pain in the butt. "That was Goldsmith."

Maggi knew Goldsmith was the officer he'd asked to track down the sports car license. She was surprised that Cavanaugh recalled the man's name. He didn't strike her as the type to put names to people; he seemed more likely to just label everyone "them" and "me."

"And?"

The more she pushed, the more he felt like resisting. It wasn't a logical reaction, but this woman was pressing all the wrong buttons. Buttons that weren't supposed to be being pressed.

"C'mon, Cavanaugh, stop making me play twenty questions. Who does the car belong to?"

"Congressman Jacob Wiley."

She vaguely remembered the last election. Mind-numbing slogans had littered the airwaves, as well as most available and not-so-available spaces. But one of the few people she'd genuinely liked was Congressman Jake Wiley, "the people's candidate," according to the literature his people distributed.

"The family values man?" She glanced over her shoulder toward the morgue, reluctant to make the connection. Her father had taught her long ago not to jump to conclusions. There could be a great many explanations as to what a young, pretty girl was doing dead in a car that belonged to the congressman.

"One and the same," Patrick confirmed. He was already heading out the door again.

Maggi had to lengthen her stride to catch up.

Congressman Jacob Wiley had a build reminiscent of the quarterback he'd once been. Blessed with an engaging smile that instantly put its recipient at ease, he flashed it now at the two people his secretary ushered in. He'd been informed that they were from the local police and there was a hint of confusion in the way he raised his eyebrows as he rose from his cluttered desk to greet them.

Wiley extended his hand first to Maggi, then to Patrick. "Always glad to meet my constituents so I can thank them in person for their vote." His tone was affable.

Patrick's eyes were flat as he took full measure of the man before him. He found the smile a little too quick, the manner a little too innocent. "To set the record straight, I didn't vote for you."

"But I did," Maggi said to cut the potentially awkward moment. "You'll have to forgive my partner, Congressman. He left his manners in his other squad car. I'm afraid this is official business. We need to ask you a question."

"Ask away." Lacing his hands together, Wiley sat on the edge of his desk as if he was about to enter into a conversation with lifelong friends. "I believe in fully cooperating with the police."

She held up the digital photograph that had been printed less than half an hour ago. "Do you know this woman?"

Patrick watched the congressman's eyes as he took the photograph in his hands. There was horror on his face as he looked at the dead woman. "Oh, God, no." He turned his head away.

"Are you sure?" Patrick pressed, his voice low, steely. "She was found in your car."

Light eyebrows drew together in mounting confusion. "My car? My car's right outside." He pointed toward the window and the parking lot beyond.

Patrick's expression didn't change. "Navy blue sports car. Registered to you."

A light seemed to dawn in the older man's face. "Oh, right." As if to dissuade any rising suspicion, the man explained, "I have more than one car, detectives. I've got five kids, three of them drive. Of course, there's my wife," he tagged on. "But she prefers the Lincoln." He paused, sorting out his thoughts. "And then, sometimes I let one of my people borrow a car when they're running an errand for me."

Patrick made a notation in his notepad, deliberately making the congressman wait. "So at any given time of the day or night, you don't know where your cars are."

Wide, muscular shoulders rose and fell beneath a handmade suit. "I'm afraid not." Maggi began to take the photograph back, but Wiley stopped her at the last moment. "Wait, let me look at that again." The air was still as he studied the face in the photograph more closely. After a beat, the impact of death seemed to fade into the background. And then recognition filtered into his eyes. "This is Joan, no, Joanne, that's it. Joanne Styles." Wiley looked first at Maggi, then Patrick. "She works for me."

"Worked," Patrick corrected, taking the photograph back.

Disbelief was beginning to etch itself into the congressman's handsome face. "What happened to her?"

Patrick gave him just the minimal details. "She was found in the river this morning, in your sports car. It appears she went over the side of the road sometime last night."

Veering to the more sympathetic audience, Wiley looked at Maggi. "She drowned?"

"Someone would like to have us believe that," Patrick interjected, his eyes never leaving the man's face.

Confusion returned. "Then she didn't drown? She's alive?"

"Oh, she's dead all right," Patrick confirmed emotionlessly. "But she didn't die in the river. She died sometime before that."

"I don't understand."

"Neither do we. For the moment." Patrick pinned him with a look. "Where were you last night, Congressman, if you don't mind my asking?"

The congressman's friendly expression faded. "If you're suggesting what I think you're suggesting, I do mind your asking."

"Just doing our job, Congressman," Maggi interjected smoothly, her manner respectful. "Pulling together pieces of a puzzle. It might help us find Ms. Styles's killer if we could reconstruct the evening."

"Yes, of course. Sorry," he apologized to Patrick. "This has me a little rattled. I never knew anyone who was a murder victim before. I was at a political fund-raiser at the Hyatt Hotel." He looked at Patrick and added, "With several hundred other people."

"Was Ms. Styles there?" Maggi prodded gently.

"I imagine so, although I really couldn't say for certain. All of my staff was invited," he explained.

"Looks like those several hundred people certainly didn't help keep her alive, did they?" Patrick asked.

"If we could get a guest list, that would be very helpful. Could you tell us who was in charge of putting the fund-raiser together?" Maggi felt as if she was tap-dancing madly to exercise damage control.

"Of course. That would be Leticia Babcock." Picking up a pen, Wiley wrote down the name of the organization the woman worked for. Finished, he handed the paper to Maggi. He glanced at Patrick, but his words were directed to the woman before him. "Anything I can do, you only have to ask."

Patrick took the slip of paper from Maggi and tucked it into his pocket. His eyes never left the congressman's face. "Count on it."

Chapter 5

Hurrying to catch up to her partner, Maggi pulled the collar of her jacket up. It began to mist. The weather lately had been anything but ideal.

"You get more flies with honey than with vinegar, Cavanaugh."

Patrick reached his car and unlocked the driver's side. He looked at her over the roof. "I'm not interested in getting flies, Mary Margaret, I'm interested in getting a killer."

She blew out a breath as she got in on her side. "I wish you'd stop calling me that."

Patrick closed the door and flipped on the headlights. The sun had decided to hide behind dark clouds. They were in for a storm. "It's your name, isn't it?"

Her father had named her after his two sisters. She wished he'd been born an only child. "Yes it is. That doesn't mean I like hearing it—" Maggi turned in her seat to glare at him as she delivered the last word "—Pat."

The nickname she tossed at him was fraught with bad memories. Only his father had ever called him that, when the old man was especially drunk and reveling in the whole myth of "Pat and Mike," something Patrick gathered had come by way of a collection of Irish stories about two best friends. According to Uncle Andrew, a number of Irish-flavored jokes began that way, as well. In any case, he and his father didn't remotely fit the description of two friends, and it was only when he was in a drunken haze that his father could pretend that he'd created a home life for his family. In reality, home life was just barely short of a minefield, ready to go off at the slightest misstep.

Maggi sighed, trying to regain some ground. "All I'm saying is that the congressman was a great deal more cooperative when you weren't glaring at him."

He started up the car and got back on the road. "That's what you're here for, right? To win him over with your sunny disposition."

"Attila the Hun's disposition could be called sunny compared to yours."

To her surprise, she heard Patrick laugh softly to himself. "Looks like our first day isn't going very well, is it?"

She trod warily, afraid of being set up. "Could be better," she allowed. Maggi caught his grin out of the side of her eye.

"It'll get worse."

"If you're trying to get me to bail out, you're wasting your time."

"And why is that? Why are you so determined to work with me?" he wanted to know.

"You mean other than your sparkling personality, charm and wit?" She saw his expression darken another shade. The man could have posed for some kind of gothic novel, the kind given to sensuality. He'd be damn good-looking if he wasn't into scaring people off. Upbraiding herself, she curtailed her own impulse toward sarcasm. "I was assigned to you, Cavanaugh, and I don't back away from my assignments, no matter how much of a pain in the butt they might be."

Maggi watched his eyes in the rearview mirror. Instead of becoming incensed, he looked as if he was considering her words. "Fair enough."

She knew she should let it go, but she couldn't. A door had opened, and she didn't know when it could be opened again. She needed to move as much as she could through it.

"No, what's fair is if you give me a chance here," she told him tersely. "I've shown you that I don't fall apart in tense situations and that I'm a dead shot and all in under eight hours. If you were anyone else, that would definitely tip the scales way in my favor."

The woman could get impassioned when she wanted to. That was a minus. He'd always found that emotion got in the way of things. "I'm not anyone else."

She sank into her seat. "So I've been told."

Something in her tone worked its way under his skin, made half thoughts begin to form. It took a little effort on his part to ignore them. He had no idea why. "Make the best of it, Mary Margaret. What you see is what you get."

Not hardly. If that were the case, then there would be no need for her to go undercover to investigate the allegations Halliday had received from an anonymous source. The allegations that made Cavanaugh out to be a dirty cop on the take.

Even if she wasn't on the job, just one look would have told her that what you saw was definitely *not* what you got when it came to Patrick Cavanaugh.

Their next stop was the offices of Babcock and Anderson, which organized and handled the arrangements for fund-raisers of all types. The professional firm was run by Leticia Babcock, president and sole owner. There was no Anderson.

"I thought it sounded more aesthetically pleasing to have two names on the card," Leticia Babcock, a tall, slim woman in her mid-thirties informed them when they asked after the whereabouts of her partner. "Makes it sound as if the company has been around for ages." Because they'd requested to see the guest list, she scrolled through her records as she spoke to them. "Ah, here it is." She beamed. Stopping, she tapped the screen with a curved, flame-red nail. "We raised more than was originally hoped for. The gala was an amazingly rousing success. The congressman was very pleased."

Maggi could all but see the dollar signs in the other woman's eyes. "Congressman Wiley?"

"Yes." The dark-haired woman sat back in her chair, sizing up her visitors. "He was the one who came to me to organize it. Very generous man. Not bad-looking, either." Momentarily ignoring the tall, somber man standing beside her, she winked broadly at Maggi. "Too bad he's married." With a careful movement orchestrated to avoid chipping a nail, Leticia hit the Print key. The printer to the left of the highly polished teak desk came to life and began printing the list.

"That doesn't stop some men," Patrick indicated.

Leticia laughed. The sound carried no mirth. "Didn't stop my third husband, that was for sure. But I hear the congressman's a straight arrow." She sighed again and shook her head, as if lamenting the missed opportunity. She held out the pages to them. "Believe me, I left him enough of an opening."

Patrick glanced at down at the list the woman had provided for them. The names went on for several pages. And everyone was going to have to be checked out. He debated giving that assignment to McKenna, let her run solo with it.

"Five hundred guests," Maggi told him. "Don't bother counting them."

She was quick with numbers, he thought. Handy trait to have around. He looked at Leticia as he tapped the list. "He said his staff was there."

A small, slightly superior smile twisted her lips. "Yes, they were."

He watched the woman's eyes, looking for some telltale flicker. "Is that normal, to invite your reelection staff?"

"Not really, but like I said, the congressman's a very generous man." She ran down the benefits of attending. "There was a great deal of good food to eat. Some of those staff members probably ate better than they ever have in their lives. Not to mention networking."

"Networking?" Maggi asked before Patrick had a chance to.

"Yes, there are a lot of important, influential people attending these things. Everyone likes to be seen 'caring' about a popular cause. Doesn't hurt to be around them. You never know where your next big break is coming from.'' She looked from Maggi to Patrick, her manner terminating the session. "If there's anything else I can do for you, let me know."

He wasn't ready to leave just yet. Patrick took out the photograph of the dead woman and held it up to the organizer's face. "Did you see this woman at the party last night?"

Leticia shivered, making no move to take the photograph in her own hand.

"Not that I remember."

The very air had climbed up inside their lungs as they waited for her to go on.

"Is she...dead?"

"Very," he replied grimly, tucking the photograph away again.

"Thanks for your help," Maggi told the woman as they walked out. Patrick made an inaudible sound that could have passed for "Goodbye."

Outside the window, Maggi could see that the mist was getting heavier. She hoped it would hold off until she got home for the night.

She glanced at the papers he was holding. "Looks a little daunting."

"Looks can be deceiving."

Part of her wanted to ask if Patrick was on to something, but she knew he was just pulling her chain or maybe giving her some kind of encoded message. She wanted no part of either. As he pressed for the elevator, she looked at the list over his shoulder. "So, where do you want to start?"

He folded the list in half twice before lodging it beside the photograph. He never even looked at her. "At her apartment."

* * *

When she wasn't busy working or partying, Joanne Styles had spent her time in a tiny, cluttered studio apartment about two-thirds the size of the one Maggi had lived in when she was in San Francisco.

Standing in it now made Maggi entertain a very odd sense of déjà vu coupled with the thought "there but for the grace of God..."

Except that she would have never let her guard down enough to have someone do to her what had been done to Joanne.

Maggi supposed that was her inbred leeriness. It came from being raised in an atmosphere of law enforcement agents. Looking back, she knew that it was her leeriness that had gotten in her way with Tyler, urging her on to keep a part of herself in reserve, not allowing him to see all of her.

Lucky thing, too, considering the way that had turned out, she mused.

Patrick noticed the expression on his partner's face as she stood looking around. She seemed a million miles away. He ignored her for a moment, then heard himself asking, "What's wrong?"

"Nothing." Maggi took a moment to rouse herself before turning to squarely face him. "Just trying to put myself in her shoes, that's all."

He supposed there was nothing wrong in getting a female's perspective on all this. "Can't hurt."

She raised her eyes to his, humor playing along her lips. "Mellowing?"

She wore some kind of gloss, he realized, something that caught the overhead light and made her lips shimmer.

He was noticing the wrong things, Patrick told himself.

Not bothering to answer her, he nodded toward the laptop that stood open on the small, pressboard desk. There was every indication within the room that Joanne would have been returning to her apartment.

"She had a computer. Maybe there's some interesting e-mail that might tell us something. We can take it up to the lab," he said.

Maggi closed the lid and unplugged the computer. She spotted a carrying case haphazardly thrown under the desk and tucked the laptop into it. "Why the lab?"

"To read it." When she looked at him quizzically, he added, "There's probably a password they'll need to get by."

"I can get you through that," she said.

Patrick stopped rifling through the victim's closet. "You're a hacker?"

She shrugged carelessly. "I've been known to get into some systems."

He hadn't thought to catch McKenna in a contradiction so soon. "I thought you believed in the straight and narrow."

"I do." With the laptop safely put away, she began to go through the shallow center drawer. "I was also younger once."

Squatting, he looked from the victim's collection of shoes. Twelve pair. Shoes were obviously a weakness. Nothing unusual about that. "Guess not everyone starts out as a plaster saint."

"Guess not."

Maggi closed the center drawer. The desk wobbled dangerously and continued to do so with every move she made as she went through the other two drawers. It was the kind of desk that started out as pieces packed into a cardboard box along with simplistic photographs that were meant to be directions. It couldn't have been any cheaper if it had been constructed out of orange crates. "Looks like being a congressman's staff assistant doesn't pay all that much," she commented.

"Maybe she was in it for the fringe benefits."

Having found an album tucked into the rear corner of the closet, Patrick flipped through the plastic-covered pages until he found something worth looking at. He held up a page with a photograph mounted in the center. It displayed several young people, all smiling broadly and obviously celebrating. In the midst was the congressman. He had his arm draped around two staff members, one a male, the other was Joanne. A banner in the background proclaimed Wiley Is *Your* Congressman.

Maggi moved forward to look at it. Joanne seemed so happy. If this was the last election, that meant it was taken only a few weeks ago. "And maybe he's just a nice boss."

"Maybe."

From his tone, she knew he didn't believe it.

By the time they returned to the station, they had one more piece of information beyond the address book that Maggi had found in Joanne's desk and her laptop. Ochoa had called from the coroner's office to tell them that their victim had also been seven weeks pregnant.

Maggi watched as the rain teased the dormant windshield wipers of his car. They had just pulled into the precinct parking lot when he had gotten the call.

A baby. The killer had gotten two for the price of one. Her own charade in the bank came back to her. *You'll be killing two if you kill me.*

She sighed. "Puts a whole new spin on this, doesn't it?" she commented as Patrick put away his cell phone.

He opened the door. A whoosh of cold air and the smell of rain came in with them. "That it does, Mary Margaret, that it does."

She started to tell him again how much she hated to be called that, but then let it go. Some things in life remained the same. The more she voiced her dislike, the more he'd use the names. She was better off just putting up with it. With any luck, she'd find what she needed and terminate this charade Internal Affairs had assigned her before she gave in to the urge to strangle Cavanaugh.

A sense of urgency hovered over her as she hurried up the stairs into the building.

Patrick walked into his apartment, pushing the door shut. It slammed behind him, shuddering in the jamb. He stood in the dark for a moment, absorbing the solitude. And the quiet.

Especially the quiet.

Any way he looked at it, the week had been very long. He and McKenna had canvassed most of the people on the fund-raiser list as well as all those in the victim's address book.

Fortunately, that list had turned out to be a great deal shorter.

Unfortunately, although some of her girlfriends knew she was involved with someone, no one had a name for the mystery man. For all her perky, former cheerleader appearance, Joanne Styles chose to be rather closemouthed when it came to her love affair.

All he and McKenna could gather was that the mystery man had been relatively new in the young woman's life. So new she was afraid to talk about him because of the fear she might jinx it.

At least, that was what she'd told her friends. His money was still on the congressman. In that case, Styles might have been afraid to name him because Wiley had threatened to end the affair if anyone found out about the two of them. After all, he was the family values poster boy.

There was something about the man's wide smile that just rubbed him the wrong way.

He was letting his personal prejudice color his thinking, Patrick upbraided himself. But maybe it wasn't prejudice. Maybe it was a gut feeling. Like the gut feeling that he'd be a whole lot better off without McKenna as his partner.

As his thoughts shifted to her, he turned the light on. It just seemed wrong to have thoughts about her in the dark. McKenna was still working with Styles's computer, but so far, all the e-mail she'd managed to pull up was unenlightening. If Styles had communicated with her lover/possible killer, it wasn't from her own laptop. The mail there represented communications from and to former college friends and her family, all of whom lived back East somewhere.

He and McKenna had met with the member of the family who had flown out to claim the body. He had to admit that McKenna was better at talking to the distraught older sister than he was. It wasn't the dead that made him uncomfortable; it was the living.

The body had been released earlier today. There was no more information coming from the coroner's office. They'd learned as much as they could there. Besides the victim's own DNA, there was no one with whom to match the fetus's DNA. They had possible motive, but so far, no suspect they could remotely pin down.

Everyone, according to her friends and co-workers, liked Joanne.

Except for one person, he thought grimly, making his way out of his tie and into the kitchen. The father of Styles's baby. The man who had terminated them both.

Tossing the tie onto the back of a chair, Patrick opened his refrigerator. There was nothing except beer in it, but that was all right. Beer was all he wanted. Beer and some peace and quiet.

Going back into the living room, he sat down in front of the television set and left it off. He was vaguely aware of the sounds of cars beyond his window, tires passing through puddles as they made their way somewhere. Concentrating, he could block out the sound.

He couldn't block out the phone.

When he heard it ring, he stiffened. Taking another long gulp from the bottle, he debated letting the phone ring. Most of his work-related calls came through his cell phone. The telephone might mean telemarketers. Lately they had no shame, calling from early until late and invading the weekends. He told himself he needed to get caller ID.

But the telephone was also reserved for family or if there was some kind of an emergency. He stared at it, willing it to stop.

When the ringing went to the count of four, he yanked up the receiver. If it was a telemarketer, he promised himself one hell of a venting session. He could use someone to chew out after holding in his temper this entire week. His new partner had certainly tested him.

"Hello!"

"Patrick, you're barking." His sister's soft voice

filled his ear, the very sound of it soothing him. "Anything wrong?"

He sighed and then relaxed as he sank back into the cushions of the sofa. "Just a homicide case that refuses to cooperate."

"I haven't heard from you all week." Patience didn't add that she worried when she didn't hear from him. Patrick wasn't the type to weather guilt trips and she wasn't the type to bestow them. "How are you?"

"Busy. Tired."

They worked him too hard, she thought, and he never let anyone help him. She loved her brother dearly, but he made her crazy. She wished he was a little more like her cousins.

"Right, the homicide case. You work much too hard, Patrick. When are they going to give you a partner?"

At the mention of the word *partner,* he frowned. This was his haven and he didn't want to think about her when he was at home. "They did."

"Oh?"

He heard curiosity filling her voice. Good old Patience, as nosy as ever.

"Yeah, maybe that's why I need help," he muttered more into his beer than into the receiver.

They both knew what he was like. A hard man to please. That, unfortunately, he got from their father. Patience knew better than to say that to him. But she could say something.

"Give this one a chance, Patrick. Eduardo worked out after you stopped riding him."

"No way in hell this one's going to work out. She's a damn pain in the butt."

Patience's interest immediately increased one hundredfold. He could hear it in her voice.

"She?"

Too late Patrick realized his mistake.

Chapter 6

"Your new partner's a woman?"

Patrick could almost hear the wheels turning in his sister's head. "Temporarily."

"Temporarily?" He couldn't tell if it was confusion or amusement in her voice. "You mean it's a guy dressed as a woman? He's undercover?"

Served him right for opening his big mouth. Trouble was, around his family, he wasn't as vigilant as he was with everyone else. "No, I mean that she's my partner temporarily."

"Until you send her running for the hills and screaming," Patience said.

Patrick took another sip from the amber glass bottle before answering. "She doesn't have to scream."

If he thought he'd closed the subject, he should have known better. Patience had only begun exploring. "What's she like? Is she pretty?"

He frowned as an image of Maggi came unbidden into his head. "That has nothing to do with it," he fairly growled.

"Then she *is* pretty." Now she was grinning. He knew she was grinning. Damn, give Patience an inch and she constructed a regular road out of it. "On a scale of one to ten, what is she?"

An eleven.

The thought came out of nowhere and he shrugged it off as if it were some kind of killer bee buzzing around his head, looking for a tender spot to leave its stinger and die. So what if he noticed that McKenna was a step away from drop-dead gorgeous? He was a detective. He was supposed to notice things. Like the way McKenna's eyebrows drew together every time he called her by her first two names.

Or the way her mouth curved when she thought she was one jump ahead of him on something.

He took a longer drink from his bottle, as if that could wash away the image.

"A huge pain in the butt," he answered Patience. "Not unlike a certain sister can be some of the time. Like now."

"I like her already. What's her name?"

That she professed to like McKenna sight unseen didn't surprise him. Patience liked everyone. In his estimation, she was way too friendly. He worried about her. A lot.

"Don't get too attached," he warned. "She's not going to be around long enough for you to need to learn her name."

"Something you said?"

If only. McKenna appeared to have the hide of a

rhino. A definite contrast to her soft skin. He frowned. The beer was making him lax, leading his thoughts around in circles.

"Patience, you know I work better alone."

"No," she contradicted firmly, "you don't. You only think you do." A note of concern entered her voice. "You've got to stop thinking of yourself as a loner, Patrick."

"I *am* a loner."

They'd gone around about this before. It seemed to him that Patience refused to accept the fact that outside the family, he had no desire to meet anyone halfway.

"You're only a loner until the right woman comes along."

The conversation had taken a sharp turn. "Hey, hold it a second, how did this jump from being about work to my private life?"

Patience sighed softly. "Patrick, you don't have a life."

"That's what makes it private." He finished off his beer and thought about making dinner into a two-course meal by getting a second bottle. "Look, Patience, I'm dog tired and I feel like I've been chasing my own tail for a week—"

"Wouldn't have to do that if there was someone else to chase."

She was like an iron butterfly, soft but strong and determined. He wasn't in the mood for this tonight. "Enough."

"Okay then. Uncle Andrew says to say hi."

"Hi," he mumbled back, knowing there was more to come. With Andrew, there always was, but then, that was his way, and though words hadn't been said to the effect, he loved his uncle, both his uncles, far more than he ever had his own father.

"He also wants to know if you plan on showing up at his table ever again."

Well, that didn't take long, Patrick thought. He eyed the distance between the sofa and the kitchen, wondering if the trip was really worth it. For two cents, he could just sack out here on the sofa and forget about the second beer—he was that tired.

"I'll be there when I'll be there."

"That's what I told him."

He smiled to himself. "Good girl." He paused. Maybe he was just tired, but he thought there'd been something in her voice, something he couldn't place, ever since she'd called. "Everything okay with you?"

"Same as always," she told him cheerfully. "Up to my hips in dogs and cats and the occasional reptile."

His eyes battled to stay open, but he wasn't completely convinced. She sounded a tad too cheerful. "But you're okay."

"Couldn't be better."

Like a small stiletto, guilt slid through him, making tiny slits. "I could drop by tonight."

"What, and have your death on my conscience? No thank you. You sound like you're half-asleep already. Everything's fine, Patrick. Get your rest. I'll talk to you soon."

He let out a long sigh. He was damn tired, but that didn't negate his responsibility. His sister had been the recipient of some very unwanted attention by a man whose African Gray Parrot she'd successfully treated. When this admirer sent a dozen long-stemmed roses to her, she thought he was just grateful that she'd cured the bird, but other gifts followed even after she'd politely but firmly refused them. Was the man bothering her again?

"As long as you're sure everything's okay."

"Patrick, it was a harmless incident. I made too much of it. Fifteen years ago, Steven Jessen would have been called a persistent admirer, nothing more. These days people immediately assume someone with more than a mild interest in another person is a stalker. Forget it," she insisted. "I have."

He wasn't sure if she was just saying that to put him at ease. "Then he hasn't—"

"Nope, he hasn't," she countered quickly, "and I'm sure he won't. Any interest he had in me evaporated when he realized that I came with my own personal section of the Aurora police department." The last time he'd paid a visit to her pet clinic, she'd prominently displayed the group family photograph she had of her brother, cousins and uncles, all in police dress uniforms. That was more than a month ago and Steve hadn't been back since. "But, if you're feeling chatty, we can get back to the subject of your new partner. What did you say her name was again?"

"I didn't. Good night, Patience."

Patience laughed. "Good night, Patrick."

Just before he hung up, he heard dogs barking in the background and absently wondered if his sister was still in the clinic or had gone upstairs to her suite of rooms. Her own two German shepherds made enough noise to sound like a huge pack of dogs.

As far back as he could remember, Patience had always gravitated toward animals, turning them into pets and lavishing her affection on them. Different strokes for different folks, he supposed. As far as he was concerned, a pet rock represented too much work.

Patrick woke up with a start, so much sweat dampening his upper torso it was as if he'd spent the past three hours of troubled sleep on the top rack of a broiler instead of his own bed.

His nightmare was back. With a difference. Now it wasn't Ramirez who he saw being shot down in front of him. It was the woman.

McKenna.

Maggi.

Halfway through the dream, the crack house he and his partner were entering dissolved into the front of a bank. The same bank where she had risked her life to disarm the robber. Except that this time she didn't wrench the gun out of the man's hand. This time it discharged with the bullet hitting her in the forehead the way it had Ramirez.

His heart pounding, Patrick shot the robber dead as he raced to her side. But it was already too late. Maggi died in his arms, her green eyes staring up at him lifelessly. Staring into his soul.

Ripping things out.

He realized he was still breathing hard.

Patrick scrubbed his hands over his face, forcing himself to get a grip.

This just wasn't going to work. He'd tried, given it more time than he'd thought he would, but it just wasn't going to work.

Having a new partner was bad enough. Having a woman as his new partner was far worse. He'd grown up feeling too protective of his mother and sister to switch gears at this point in his life. And feeling protective about McKenna was just going to interfere with the way he responded to situations. He'd be too intent on watching her back to pay the right amount of attention to everything else. All it took was a moment's hesitation and all hell would break loose. He already knew that because of Ramirez. Because he'd been one step behind his partner instead of right there beside him.

It just wasn't going to work.

Four hours later, he was still saying the same thing, except out loud now and to the only man with the authority to make things right.

Patrick cornered his captain as soon as the man walked into the squad room. "It's not going to work."

Captain Reynolds waved him into his office and closed the door behind him before sitting down at his desk and leisurely opening up his container of imported coffee. He studied Patrick over the rim of the paper cup.

Reynolds forced a smile to his lips. "I'm assuming you're talking about your new partner."

"It's not to going to work," Patrick insisted again, his jaw clenched. He didn't want to live with another death on his conscience and she struck him as someone who could easily wind up dead.

The coffee was obviously too hot. Reynolds placed it back on his desk. "It's not that I don't respect your judgment, Cavanaugh, but given your track record as far as taking on new partners goes, I'd say your opinion is a little less than reliable in this matter."

His back against the wall, Patrick tried to strike up

a deal. "Look, I've always told you I work better alone, but if that can't be the case, at least give me another guy."

"McKenna comes highly recommended. She's got commendations up the wazoo from San Francisco—"

Commendations didn't impress him. It was all a matter of politics. Patrick cut his superior short. "I don't care if she's got a letter from the mayor, I don't want to work with her."

"Why?"

Patrick hated explaining himself, but he knew it was the only chance he had to get McKenna reassigned somewhere else. "Having a female around takes the edge off."

Reynolds grinned, as if amused. He blew on his coffee before taking a tentative sip. "This is a side of you I didn't know about. I didn't think you noticed women, Cavanaugh. I would have been a little worried if it wasn't for the fact that I don't think you really notice anything except the job you're working on." Taking another sip, longer this time, Reynolds replaced the container on his stained blotter. "Not that I'm complaining, mind you. You're damn good at what you do—lucky for you," he tagged on.

Patrick could read between the lines. "You're not going to reassign her, are you?"

"Nope."

Ordinarily he didn't push. But then, ordinarily he didn't ask for favors, either. He might as well go all the way. "Can I ask why?"

"Because I like having the best work for me and everyone else is happy in their little niches."

"I'm not happy," Patrick growled.

Reynolds shrugged. "You are never happy, that goes without saying." Obviously needing to keep the peace and give Cavanaugh a false sense of hope, he added, "Okay, tell you what. Give it a few more weeks. If you're still butting heads, I'll see what I can do. I have to say I'm surprised, though."

"Why?"

Draining half the container, Reynolds wiped his mouth with the napkin he'd brought in.

"Usually it's your partner in here, begging to be reassigned. I guess she doesn't find you as hard to work with as you find her. Either that, or she's got a hell of a lot more stick-to-itiveness than most of her predecessors."

She had a hell of a lot more something all right, Patrick thought, but he didn't know exactly what the label for it was.

"Whatever."

Annoyed, disgusted and more than vaguely unsettled, Patrick strode out of the office. He hated wasting time and he'd just wasted a precious amount of it trying to reason with a man who was far more interested in the kind of PR he could generate with the public than he was about the actual internal workings of his department.

His mood black, Patrick decided to go back to the morgue to review the original autopsy report on Joanne Styles to see if anything out of the ordinary struck him this time.

The morgue was deadly quiet. There were no autopsies in progress at the moment. The M.E. had handed Patrick his own copy of Joanne's autopsy before leaving the room. Patrick made himself as comfortable as possible, sitting down to read at a desk that was equally likely to hold the coroner's lunch as it was a victim's final effects.

The silence enveloped him as he read words that he'd gone over time and again already. Concentrating to the exclusion of everything else, the noise almost made him jump.

Maggi marched in at the far end of the room, hitting the door with the flat of her hand and sending it flying open. The door banged against the wall, summoning his attention.

She looked as if she were breathing fire. Her eyes had narrowed, boring small, burning holes into him before she ever reached him.

All in all, he had to admit she looked rather magnificent, like one of those paintings he'd seen by that artist who reveled in strong, beautiful, scantily clad women warriors. All she needed was a spear and a mythical steed.

It had taken Maggi several minutes to find out where Patrick was in the building. Her temper had increased with every second that passed and was now a hairbreadth away from reaching critical mass.

Facing him squarely, she demanded, "Who the hell do you think you are?"

He was as calm as she was angry. "Pay stub says Patrick Cavanaugh."

For two cents, she would have doubled her fists and beat on him even though the blows probably would have hurt her more than him.

"Don't get smart with me, Cavanaugh. I just heard you asked the captain for another partner."

Since the door was closed, she'd had to have heard that from Brooks, the only one in the squad who could read lips. Probably trying to cull favor with her, Patrick thought darkly.

"Asked, didn't receive."

Despite the fact that he'd been trained not to look away from a dangerous animal and he definitely placed his new partner in that category, Patrick lowered his eyes back to the folder on the table.

Incensed, resenting the way he insisted on treating her, Maggi swept the folder aside with the back of her hand. Pages rained down onto the floor. Her eyes blazed, daring him to pick them up. The pages remained where they were.

"Do you realize what kind of implications your asking for a new partner has? It makes me look incompetent. That you don't trust me to watch your back."

He felt something inside him stirring in response to the look on her face, to the fire in her eyes. He banked it down. Just pure animal reaction.

"All it says is that we're incompatible," he told her mildly, "and you wouldn't be the first partner to find yourself in that position." He bent down to pick up the pages, then placed them into the folder.

"If you have a problem with me, you *come* to me, you *talk* to me," she insisted. "You don't go behind my back and talk to the captain." She would have thought that someone like him would have respected that kind of a code. He wasn't a team player, he was a loner. Loners didn't run to their superiors with something.

He shrugged, his disinterest rankling her. "Like I

said, we're incompatible. If we weren't, I would have talked to you."

"Why?" Maggi spread her hands on the desk before him as she leaned into his face and demanded an answer. "Why are we incompatible? How do you even know? We've only been working together for a little more than a week and I haven't gone against you once, even when I felt you were wrong."

His interest was aroused despite himself. "When was that?"

Maggi waved away his question. "Doesn't matter. I'm your partner—you're supposed to talk to me."

He looked at her, his gaze steady. "I can't talk to you."

Her voice softened slightly. "Well, you're going to have to try, Cavanaugh. Because I am your partner and I am not going anywhere." She paused, needing an answer, something to hang his reactions on. If she understood, she could fix it. She needed him to trust her. "Is it because I'm a woman?"

Her face was too close, invading his space. Patrick leaned back in his chair, balancing it on two legs. "Partly."

Furious, Maggi struggled to swallow the scathing curse that rose to her lips. That wasn't going to do anything but lower her to his level, the bastard. Old-fashioned prejudice. She should have known. Cavanaugh was a throwback, a Neanderthal. Well, she wasn't about to let that get in the way of her assignment.

She held out her arms for inspection. "Look, two arms, two legs, all the same working parts as any other partner."

He looked at her pointedly. He'd never had a partner

with a twenty-five-inch waist before and he was willing to bet that her legs were a hell of a lot better looking than Ramirez's had ever been. Not to mention the obvious differences.

"Not really."

She met his look head-on. Sex, he was talking about sex. That was never going to be a problem between them. "That doesn't enter into this."

His eyes never left hers. "Doesn't it?"

Suddenly she heard a strange rushing noise in her ears. Maggi blocked it out, refusing to flinch, to give.

"No. I'm not letting it, and you shouldn't, either. We're not dating, Cavanaugh, we're working together. I know partners tend to get closer than some married people, but you certainly don't strike me as someone who'd leave himself open to that. You probably never even learned Ramirez's first name or knew anything about him."

His expression never changed. "Eduardo. He had a wife and three kids. Anything else you want to get wrong about me?"

She blew out a breath. Maybe the man did have feelings and she'd just stepped on them.

"Okay, look, I'm sorry. We'll start over." Before he could respond, she extended her hand to Patrick. "Hi, I'm Detective McKenna. According to the captain, we're supposed to be working together. You watch my back, I'll watch yours. You have any questions, any problems, call me. Anytime. We'll work something out. Deal?"

He regarded her hand for a moment before silently gripping it with his own.

Ochoa popped his head in. "Hey, you two just about

through in here? You're making enough racket to raise the dead." He pretended to look over to the steel drawers that were the temporary resting places for the bodies he had yet to examine.

"Just leaving, Dr. Ochoa." Maggi looked at Patrick pointedly. "See you later, *partner*."

The doctor paused to watch as the young detective made her exit. Sighing, he shook his head wistfully. "That woman's got one mighty fine rear view." He glanced at Patrick. "Wonder if she makes that much noise when she's making love."

Patrick rose. "I wouldn't know."

And it was something he damn well wasn't planning on finding out.

Chapter 7

It was the last booth in an out-of-the-way coffee shop that still believed that the only ingredient necessary for a decent cup of coffee was caffeine. John Halliday, the head of Internal Affairs, had elected to meet with her here for a progress report.

Maggi kept her eyes on the door rather than on the heavyset, aging man sitting opposite her. She was afraid someone she knew might walk in. To the untrained observer, she and John probably looked like a father sharing an early cup of black energy with his daughter before they hurried off to their separate worlds.

She warmed her hands around the cup, knowing that Halliday was waiting for an answer. She didn't have one to give him. It was lack of evidence she was finding herself up against, not proof of innocence. Exoneration by default was not what they were looking for.

"So far, nothing," she told him. "The man puts in

a long, full day, then goes home." The surface of her coffee shimmered, catching the weak overhead light just before she brought the cup to her lips. It was hotter than it was good.

The thin lips beneath the shaggy mustache drew together in a tight frown. "Are you getting close to him?"

"Not yet." And it wasn't for lack of trying. The half shrug beneath her gray jacket was curtailed frustration. "He's like a fortress."

Halliday's brown eyes were steady as they regarded her. "Are you familiar with the story about the Trojan horse?"

Maggi laughed softly to herself. "I guarantee that if Cavanaugh had been inside that fort with the Greeks, he would have burned the Trojan horse down before he'd ever allow them to bring it inside." She hoped Halliday knew better than to think she was throwing in the towel at this point.

"That's why I figured you were the best one for the job."

"Because I'm a woman?"

"Because you're good," he countered. His eyes swept over her in a manner she found almost unnervingly impartial. He was dissecting and reassembling her in the space of time it took to draw a long breath. "Of course, being an attractive woman doesn't hurt, either."

The coffee was growing on her. She took another long sip. "Thanks, but I don't think Cavanaugh's noticed."

Halliday's amusement surprised her. "Trust me, Maggi, dead men notice that you're attractive."

She tried to read between the lines. If he was looking for someone to go above and beyond the regulations, he'd selected the wrong woman. She wasn't about to give new meaning to the term "undercover" just to get the assignment done.

"You're not suggesting—"

"No," Halliday interrupted quickly. "I'm not. Just use a little of what they used to call feminine wiles in my day."

Right, as if that would work on a man like Cavanaugh. She grinned. "I think they still call them that, but I'm not sure I have them."

The look he gave her told her that he knew better. "And if I believe that, there's a bridge out there with my name on it."

Maggi finished her coffee and placed the cup down on the cracked saucer.

"You never know, there might be." Her smile faded as she glanced at her watch. It was getting late. The less explaining she had to do to Cavanaugh, the better. "I should get going." Sliding to the end of the booth, she sighed before she got up. "I'm beginning to feel like a spy."

Halliday signaled the waitress for a refill. "That's good, because you are."

Spies were only glamorous in the movies, Maggi thought. In real life, they felt ambivalent and gritty because of the secrets they were forced to carry around with them. Lines began to blur the moment people entered into the picture. Her assignment and her loyalties had been crystal clear when she'd started out, but now part of her couldn't help feeling like a voyeur.

That was because she was ascribing her own set of values to Cavanaugh, she reminded herself. And that was probably a fallacy that would lead her down the wrong road. Cavanaugh wasn't her. If he'd had her values, he wouldn't be under suspicion for being on the take to begin with.

"See you around." Rising, Maggi made her way past the waitress.

Patrick didn't bother glancing up when she walked into the cubicle. He could tell it was McKenna by the sound of her heels making contact with the vinyl flooring. She had a certain gait, just distinct enough to stick in his mind. He found that annoying, too.

"You're late."

"Stopped to get you breakfast." Maggi set down a white paper bag with a doughnut-shop logo imprinted on the side on his desk.

Breakfast. It reminded him of his phone call with his sister the other day and the fact that he hadn't been by his uncle's house for breakfast in several weeks. Retired, Uncle Andrew liked to gather his family together around the table whenever possible. Cooking was his passion now that his days on the force were over.

Patrick assuaged his conscience by reminding himself that he'd put in an appearance at Thanksgiving, although that had been partially a matter of self-preservation. Not to have shown up might have brought about a family schism. In all likelihood, his uncle would have sent one or more of his cousins to his apartment to drag him back to the table. Uncle Andrew took his holidays seriously.

He caught himself wanting to smile but resisted the urge. Instead, he moved the bag she'd brought to the side as if it were an annoyance that had fallen in his path.

"I don't do breakfast."

She'd picked up the jelly doughnuts on her way out

of the coffee shop to give herself an alibi. Even so, it bothered her to have him reject her offering.

"Save it for lunch, snack, wear it—I don't care." Reining in her temper, she sat down in the cubicle and swung her chair around to face him instead of her desk. What the hell was his problem, anyway? "I'm just trying to be nice here."

"No need."

The words were curt, meant to shut her out. Again. She felt like pounding on him.

Whoa, get a grip, Mag. You're not going to get anywhere if you lose your cool.

"You know," she began, measuring out her words, "you are a damn hard man to get close to."

This time, he raised his eyes to her. "We're not supposed to be close, Mary Margaret. We're just supposed to be working together."

"That doesn't seem to be going all that well, either, Paddy."

If she meant to get a rise out of him, she failed. He merely nodded toward the exit. "You know the way to the door."

This wasn't getting her anywhere. Determined to gain his confidence, she did a complete one-eighty and focused her attention on the homicide they were handling. "Okay, so where are we on the Styles case?"

Patrick never missed a beat. He indicated the time line on the back wall of the cubicle. They'd pieced it together from information they'd garnered since the body had been found.

"My money's on the congressman." He looked at her pointedly, waiting for her to contradict him. Waiting to cut her argument down.

She surprised him.

"I tend to agree, especially since we found out that Mrs. Wiley didn't attend the party and several other people thought they saw Wiley with Joanne at least once during the course of the evening. That makes his performance in the office about not recognizing her immediately a little suspect." She stopped, his scrutiny getting to her. "What are you staring at?"

Patrick shrugged, the movement careless. "Nothing. Just a little surprised that you're willing to come around, that's all."

"I'm not 'willing to come around,' Cavanaugh. I'm willing to let the evidence speak to me." Of all the prejudice, bigoted, thickheaded chauvinists, why did this one have to be her assignment? "What do you think—I've got a crush on the man and refuse to see any other viewpoint than the official party line?"

There was just the slightest hint of a smile on his lips. Or was that a badly concealed smirk? "Something like that."

"One, I don't get crushes." Even as she set him straight, she had a feeling her words were falling on deaf ears. "Two, I'm a police detective and a damn good one. That means I deal in facts and do my job to the best of my abilities."

"Nice to know." Leaning back in his chair, Patrick studied her for a long moment, trying to see beyond the long, blond silky hair and the mouth that always seemed to be moving. The mouth that was so quick to smile and generate a warm, seductive atmosphere around her. "Okay, if this was your case, what's your next move?"

"This *is* my case," she reminded him tersely. "But if you mean what would I do if I were the primary on it, I'd go back to see the congressman again, ask him a few more questions. Try to see if maybe I could jog his memory a little in light of the fact that at least three people saw him talking to Joanne Styles at some time during the party." She waited for him to shoot down her suggestion and braced herself to rebut him.

Instead, he rose from his chair. "Sounds like a plan to me." With that, he began to head for the door. He stopped only long enough to look over his shoulder. "You coming?"

"Yes."

The man was a trial, she thought as she grabbed her coat. A real trial.

"Of course I might have talked to her," Wiley allowed less than forty-five minutes later. He'd prefaced their audience by saying he only had five minutes before heading out for a meeting.

Wiley took a long drag of his cigarette before continuing. Beside him, a tall, slender air purifier was doing double duty in an attempt to help clear the air.

"But you have to understand, I talked to a great many people during the course of that party. During the course of any party. That's both the up- and downside of my position. I have to glad-hand a great deal. After a while, the names and faces begin to swim together." Though he made a point of looking at both of them, more than half his words were directed at Maggi. "Unfortunately for me, I don't have one of those photographic memories so I have to pretend that I know everyone to keep from offending someone. Sounds a little shallow, I know, but in my line of work I try to offend as few people as absolutely possible." He flashed a quick, disarming smile. "Every vote counts, you know."

Tapping his cigarette ash into the full ashtray on the corner of his desk, he seemed to note the way Maggi watched him. His grin was almost sheepish. "Yes, I know, it's a terrible habit."

There was no judgment intended on her part. "I was just thinking that this is supposed to be a smoke-free environment." According to state law, all public places of work in California were to be kept smoke free.

"Busted," Wiley admitted. He nodded at the tall, silent column. "Hence the air purifier. I'm really trying to cut down, but with the pace of the campaign and the stress of the job, I'm finding it difficult. But I guess it's better than drinking, and I never let myself be photographed with a cigarette." He looked as if he was debating snuffing out the cigarette, then decided not to. "Don't want to be a bad role model for the kids." The grin grew more sheepish. "I try to limit myself to five, but sometimes I cheat by emptying out the ashtray. That makes it look as if I haven't had any and, well..." His voice trailed off as he looked at Maggi.

Maggi's smile in response was soft, easy. "I understand."

To Patrick's disgust, his partner was really beginning to sound as if she was awestruck by the man. He would have thought after what she'd said in the office, just before they left for here, she could see through this tin demigod.

"Let me empty that for you," she offered.

Then, before the congressman could demur, Maggi took the ashtray and threw its contents into the wastepaper basket beside his desk. Wiley smiled at her.

It wasn't the smile of a predator, Patrick thought, trying to be fair. But with little effort, it could have been.

"If you don't remember speaking to her, then just how did she get into your car, Congressman?" Patrick wanted to know.

Rather than looking annoyed or cornered, Wiley simply spread his hands out in puzzled consternation.

"I really don't have an answer to that." All he could do was reiterate what he'd previously said. "As I already told you, I allow my staff access to my cars."

"There's no log, no record?" Patrick pressed.

The sheepish grin was back. That was for people like McKenna, Patrick thought. He just wasn't buying it.

"I'm afraid I'm lax that way."

From what he'd learned, Wiley was a very organized man. What he maintained didn't jibe with the established image.

"Can you remember who had it last?"

Wiley shook his head. "You'll have to ask my office manager, Travis Abbott. He handles the everyday details for me. But I just want you to know that everyone on my staff is trustworthy," he added as if he felt honor-bound to make the statement. "I've never had a pair of cuff links stolen, much less a car."

Maggi could feel herself being led further and further away from the heart of the original discussion. "This is a lot bigger than car theft, Congressman," she said.

The congressman sobered. "I know, murder." His hands folded before him, he shook his head. "I still can't believe it, one of my own people. It's so ugly."

"Uglier still when the victim was pregnant," Patrick told him.

Wiley's eyes widened in shock. "Pregnant? She was pregnant?"

"Coroner says seven weeks." Patrick's voice, like his expression, was grim.

Wiley covered his mouth, as if to keep back words wreathed in horror. "My God, that poor girl."

There was appeal in his eyes as he looked at Maggi, although it wasn't clear to her just what he was appealing to. She chalked it up to confusion.

"I had no idea." The congressman took another drag of his cigarette, a long one this time. Ashes hung suspended on the end of it, defying gravity. "I had no idea," he repeated quietly.

Just then, there was a knock on the door and a pert brunette they'd interviewed several days ago stuck her head in. She nodded toward them, then looked at Wiley.

"Sorry to bother you, Congressman, but you have a meeting with Mr. Donovan in less than half an hour and really should be going. Todd has the car waiting for you out front."

"Right." He rose, still appearing a little dazed. He extended his hand to Maggi out of purely ingrained habit.

As Patrick watched, Maggi brushed her hand against her jacket before shaking Wiley's hand. Had she done that because her hand was damp and she didn't want Wiley to know? Damn it, the last thing they needed now was a case of hero-worship getting in their way.

"I'm sorry I can't be more help," Wiley apologized.

"Don't underestimate yourself, Congressman," she said sweetly. "You've been a great deal of help."

Wiley smiled, nodded at Patrick and then hurried away to the waiting car.

Patrick lingered a moment before leaving the office. And then he walked out the door, struggling to hold on to a temper that seemed to come out of nowhere, flaring. As he punched the button for the elevator, he turned on her and demanded, "What the hell was that?"

"What?" She braced herself.

"Back there." He jerked a thumb at the office they'd walked out of. "Cleaning up after him, wiping your hand so that it wasn't offensive when you shook his. Are you opting to fill the dead girl's place?"

She stared at him, torn between taking umbrage and just laughing at him. "If I didn't know better, I'd say you sounded jealous."

Leave it to a woman to come up with the most ridiculous take on something. Her accusation almost didn't merit a response, but he decided to put her in her place. The elevator arrived and he walked in, jabbing for the first floor before she got in behind him. "To be jealous, I'd have to care."

"And you don't."

"All I care about is how the department comes off, having you do pirouettes around the man who likely killed what might very well have been his pregnant mistress." Arriving at the first floor, they got out.

Maggi hurried to keep up, silently damning his long legs. She was going to have to start working out again if she was going to finish this assignment in good condition.

"He didn't know she was pregnant," she told him as Patrick unlocked the car. "You can't fake that kind of look."

He got in but didn't buckle up. "You can fake any kind of a look, any kind of response."

Something drove her to egg him on. He was irritating the hell out of her. "And you'd know this why? Because of your vast acting experience?"

"Look, the guy's an operator. I'm not saying he's

not a good congressman, but he's a man married to a demanding wife, and this pretty young thing bats her eyes at him, making his blood rush and just like that—'' he snapped his fingers ''—he's off to the races.''

''I still say he was too stunned when you told him about the baby. That was real.'' About to buckle up, Maggi stopped. A strange look appeared on Cavanaugh's face, one she couldn't begin to read. ''What?''

Instead of saying anything, Patrick let actions do his talking for him. Very slowly, he extended his fingers and just barely touched her cheek, all the while looking into her eyes. Holding her prisoner.

Maggi felt her breath stop in her lungs.

Any demands she might have made as to what the hell he thought he was doing never made it to her lips.

Time stood still. Her pulse didn't as it went into rapid overdrive, hammering hard. When he finally leaned in to her, she felt herself going into a complete meltdown even before his lips touched hers.

At the last moment, he drew back. Disappointment created a huge void in her.

His eyes were knowing, as if he didn't need her to agree to the kiss. He was right and he knew it.

''Made you believe I was going to kiss you, didn't I?'' he asked.

Maggi felt as if she were stepping out of the *Twilight Zone* and still not sure if she would find solid ground or empty space beneath her feet. She stalled for time, trying to pull herself together.

''What?''

''Just now, you thought I was going to kiss you. Even though nothing's gone down between us, even though we mix together like oil and water. You still thought I was going to kiss you."

Maggi's breath returned in tiny dribbles and she husbanded it before saying in what she hoped was a normal voice, "The thought crossed my mind."

"Because I wanted it to."

And maybe, just maybe, he added silently, because the idea was not exactly abhorrent or foreign to him, either. It had buzzed around in the back of his mind now like an annoying itch. One he instinctively knew that, if he scratched, would just increase. He'd been testing himself more than the theory he was tendering to Maggi.

"And you weren't even predisposed to believe I'd do that. Wiley already knew you were buying his act, hook, line and sinker." When she cocked her head, silently asking for an explanation, he said, "You were practically playing his maid, for God's sake, dumping out his ashtray like that."

"I was playing detective," she countered with every fiber she could muster.

Damn, but he'd just about undone her. She should have pushed him away, should have laughed in his face, not just sat there holding her breath.

Waiting.

She should have had more than doughnuts for breakfast. Sugar always did make mush out of her brain.

Patrick's expression told her he wasn't buying what she was selling. "And how's that?"

It was her turn to play out the line and reel him in. "We need Wiley's DNA, don't we? To see if it matches the baby's."

"Yes, but—"

"Think the lab can get something useful from one

of these? I'm assuming there's got to be a little bit of saliva on at least one of them.''

And then, before he could ask her what she was talking about, Maggi opened her hand and produced three of the butts that had been in the congressman's ashtray.

Chapter 8

He stared at Maggi's opened hand. On her upturned palm, a smattering of ashes were mixed with the remnants of three cigarettes, smoked all the way down to the filters. "How did you get those?"

"I palmed them. From Wiley's ashtray." Taking out her handkerchief, she placed the evidence in the center, then carefully folded it and placed it back in her pocket. She made a mental note to have her jacket cleaned.

Patrick shook his head as he turned over the engine. "Damn but you're more resourceful than I gave you credit for."

Satisfied with herself, Maggi smiled. She supposed that was as close to a compliment as she was going to get from the man. "I'm a lot more things than you give me credit for. Apology accepted."

He studied her for a moment, then they left the parking area. "Hacker, thief, anything else I should know about you?"

Yes, that I'm really here to spy on you. The thought exploded in her chest with the force of a magnum bullet. She kept her face impassive and brazened it out. "Lots of things. You'll learn as we go along."

He had no idea why he found that promise sexy. Maybe it was because he found the woman sexy. Maybe because he'd rattled more than just her cage with that near kiss. He hadn't allowed it to come to proper fruition, not from any lack of interest on his part, but from a strong sense of survival. Sex had no business here, or in his life right now.

All he wanted was to be a good cop. Everything else, beyond his existing family ties, was just so much extra complication he wasn't willing to take on. And a relationship, any sort of a relationship, meant complications.

He set his mouth grimly and stared straight ahead as he wove his way through the traffic. "Let's get these to the lab."

His curt tone took her by surprise. Maggi tried to tell herself this made her job more challenging, more interesting, but right now she was getting more frustrated.

Nothing good ever came easy, her mother used to say to her. Too bad the woman hadn't lived long enough to make her own words come true, Maggi thought. One way or another, she was going to get some good out of this. She was either going to out a dirty cop or save the reputation of a clean, albeit ill-tempered, one.

She tried not to notice how the silence ate its way further into the interior of the car.

Processing the DNA evidence took longer than either one of them was happy about. While they waited, they went back to investigating the people who'd known Joanne, trying to catch a break, trying to find out if anyone knew the identity of her mysterious lover in case the DNA samples Maggi had brought turned out not to be a match.

When the call came from the lab, they lost no time in getting there.

For once the regular technician appeared too overwhelmed with work to give in to his normal flair for drama. Instead, he merely handed Patrick the sheet of paper that was the end result of testing and typing.

"Close," he pronounced.

Patrick looked at the summary. At first glance, it made no sense to him and might have just as well been written in Greek. "What do you mean, 'close'? It's either a match or it isn't."

Harry Everett paused to take a drink from the capped bottle of water that seemed to be in endless supply by his desk. "I mean the baby's DNA is not an exact match to what you gave me, but it's definitely in the same family."

"Same family, you mean like a brother or sister?" Maggi asked. She glanced at Patrick and wondered what he was thinking. He'd been so certain Wiley was the baby's father.

Harry leaned back in his chair. It creaked in response. "Son, daughter, mother, father. You know, the old definition of family."

"So it's not the congressman." Maggi deliberately kept an innocent expression on her face. She could tell by the rigid set of Cavanaugh's chin that this annoyed the hell out of him.

Harry's eyes shifted back and forth between two pages as he made one last comparison. "Doesn't look like it." He moved the printed page back, clearing the space for the next assignment he had to tackle. "Anything else I can do for you?"

"This'll do, thanks," Patrick muttered as he folded the sheet of paper and slid it into his breast pocket. He looked at Maggi as they left the lab and came to the only conclusion left to them. "If it's not the father, it's the son."

They'd interviewed Blake Wiley briefly, along with everyone else. Apparently he deserved a second look.

"Wiley's son is part of his staff," Maggi mentioned, thinking out loud. Before Patrick could say they already knew that, she told him something she didn't think he knew. She'd done her homework. "Only because he can't seem to find work anywhere else. It's one of those clichéd success stories. Dad makes good, son makes trouble. Doesn't have enough backbone to do anything on his own, can't handle living in the shadow of his famous father. Spends his whole life looking for himself when he hasn't gone anywhere." She smiled at him as they stopped by the elevator banks. "Have I impressed you yet?"

He frowned at her as he pressed for the down elevator. The doors opened instantly. The car hadn't gone to another floor while they were in the lab. "Takes a lot to impress me."

Maggi reached and pressed for the ground floor before he could. "I'll keep working on it."

Talk about getting under his skin. She'd managed to accomplish that in a record amount of time. "Why? Why would you want to impress me?"

Maggi gave him a half truth, just to see what he would say. "Because you're my Mount Everest. I don't climb to high places—they tend to make me dizzy—

but everyone's got to have a challenge and you're mine."

"Why?"

She laughed. When the elevator door opened again, there were several people waiting to get in. They threaded their way through.

"You know you're beginning to sound like an inquisitive five-year-old?" She saw that the observation didn't win any points with him. This time, she told him the truth, or a least a tiny piece of it. "Because I never met anyone who didn't like me—eventually."

Patrick noticed it had started to rain again. This kind of weather drove men to suicide. Or to relocate. He raised his collar. "So you're saying that you're out to get everyone you meet to like you?"

"More or less." She made the shrug look careless, but she had told him the truth. Because in an odd sort of way, it mattered to her. She *did* like to have people like her.

He looked around for the car. Seeing it, he started to lead the way. A steady light drizzle accompanied him through the crowded lot. "It's an impossible dream."

Hurrying after him, she raised her voice. "Hey, we've all got to have goals to keep us going. If it were easy, it wouldn't be a goal. It'd be a fact of life, and that's no fun."

Turning, he looked at her for a long moment, not knowing what to make of her, or the feelings that stirred up inside him. Since he was treading on unfamiliar ground, he retreated and found another path. "We've got a murderer to catch."

Maggi smiled at him. "That we do." She gestured toward the car. "Lead on, Macduff."

He said nothing, merely shook his head as he walked the rest of the way to the car.

She reached it first, waiting for him to open the doors. Once he did, she got in, quickly shutting the door and keeping the fine mist out. "By the way, when do I get to say I told you so?"

Buckled up, he refused to look in her direction. "Not anytime soon if you want to keep on living."

"I'll take that under advisement."

Unable to stop, he glanced at her. "That includes smirking."

"I wasn't smirking."

His frown deepened. Now she was lying outright. "Your mouth was curving."

"I smile a lot, or haven't you noticed?"

Turning, he looked behind them as he backed out. The rain made everything three times as hazardous. It seemed to him that no one knew how to handle a little precipitation in California. "Well, don't, it's distracting."

"What, smiling or smirking?"

"Both."

Maggi settled back in her seat. A bolt of lightning creased the brow of the sky. It looked like they were in for it. "Okay, then you try smiling."

Busy with watching the road, he thought he hadn't heard her correctly. "What?"

"If we both frown," Maggi explained, "there'll be no yin and yang."

He knew she was making another pitch for camaraderie. He needed a friend like he needed an extra toe. Both made navigating difficult. "There's not going to be a Starsky and Hutch, either."

Maggi's mouth dropped open. "You know about Starsky and Hutch?"

Another mistake. He sighed. "Do you *ever* stop talking?"

"Do you ever stop being grumpy?" she countered.

He wondered what the manual said about strangling your partner and if it ever fell in the realm of justifiable homicide.

Locating Blake Wiley proved to be relatively easy. They found him closeted with his secretary, examining the shape of her ear. She was on his lap at the time and he was using the taste approach. He was none too happy to see them and unhappier still when they sent his secretary back to her desk.

"Look, I already told you everything I know," he protested.

"Notice how he's telling the wall and not us?" Maggi said to Patrick.

For once, Patrick played along. "Why is that, do you suppose?"

Maggi got into Blake's face. "Could be he's afraid of making eye contact, afraid of what we might see if he did."

"My contacts," Blake retorted flippantly. "You'd see my contacts and nothing else. My father can have you up on harassment charges, you know."

"Hiding behind Daddy?" Patrick asked, deliberately baiting him. "Don't you get tired of that? Don't you ever wonder what it's like to stand up on your own two feet instead of letting him carry you?"

Blake became incensed. "You don't know what you're talking about."

"Don't I?" Patrick pressed.

The door to Blake's office flew open. "What's going on here?" Congressman Wiley asked as he entered.

"Does he always come in without knocking?" Patrick asked Blake. "No respect for your privacy, is there?" He was rewarded with an irritated, sullen look, directed not at him but at the congressman.

"Blake, what are they asking you?" Far from the smiling man they'd encountered the other two times, Wiley appeared worried as he looked from his son to the two detectives.

Patrick answered him before Blake could reply. "We're having an interesting conversation with your son." His eyes indicated the door behind Wiley. "You don't have to be here, Congressman. He's not a minor."

Blake snorted. There was nothing but contempt in his eyes as he looked at his father. "My father'll tell you I'm not very bright, either. At least, he doesn't think so."

Wiley clenched his hands at his sides impotently. It was clear that he wanted to say more but felt he couldn't. "Stop talking, Blake."

As Maggi watched, Patrick shook his head. "Now see, that might have been your first mistake, Congressman. You named him Blake. If you'd called him something ordinary, like Jim or Bill, he might have stood a chance in this world. But right there, you doomed him. You made him stand out for all the wrong reasons." Patrick glanced at Blake. "And he didn't like it."

Wiley appeared at a loss. "What the hell are you talking about?"

He noted that Maggi looked both surprised and impressed at his dabbling with psychology. "Just a little theory my partner and I were working on." He dropped the friendly tone. "The rest of it goes that your son here killed Joanne Styles."

Indignation reddened the congressman's cheeks. Or was that fear? Maggi wondered.

"That's ridiculous," Wiley cried.

"She was carrying his baby." Maggi had interjected so quietly, at first it was as if the congressman hadn't heard her. But when his eyes shifted toward her, she saw no surprise in them.

Figured it out, did you, Congressman?

Blake shifted in his seat as if it was suddenly becoming warmer than he liked. "Small detail I forgot to tell you, Dad." Though his mouth twisted in a mocking smirk, there was genuine fear in the younger man's eyes as they moved from person to person.

"Not another word," Wiley warned. "I'll get Christopher on the line." Picking up the telephone, he looked at Patrick. "He's not saying anything until I can get my lawyer in here."

"He doesn't have to say much." Maggi's tone was polite but firm. "We have the DNA, sir." Wiley looked sharply at his son. "He didn't give us his, we have yours."

Wiley looked stunned, then incredulous. "Mine?"

She could see the denial that was about to come. "You really should cut down on smoking, sir."

The light dawned, ushering in outrage and desperation. "You had no right to take those cigarette butts."

"I'm afraid that once you throw something out, it becomes public." Then, in case he'd forgotten, she added, "You had me throw out the cigarette butts. Our lab found that the baby's DNA was close enough to be tagged in the family." Both she and Patrick looked pointedly at Wiley's son.

Blake gripped the armrests hard enough that the leather groaned. "So I got her pregnant. That doesn't prove I killed her."

Patrick didn't bother talking to Blake. It wasn't the son who was pulling the strings here. "Now that we know what we're looking for, it'll speed things along. Just a matter of time, Congressman. Science has made wonderful strides. Even somebody as thickheaded as me knows that," Patrick said.

Maggi couldn't help wondering if Cavanaugh had thrown that in for her benefit.

"Can't hide from the evidence," Patrick continued. "Your son's best bet is to make a full statement now." He looked at Blake, getting his message across. "It might go easier on him if he cooperates."

Wiley closed his eyes for a moment and Maggi could see that he was genuinely suffering. Life had gotten out of hand for him.

When he opened his eyes, he looked ten years older. And determined. "All right, what's it going to take to make this go away?"

Patrick cocked his head as if he hadn't heard correctly. "What?"

"You heard me," Wiley said, exasperation echoing in his voice. He reached into his inside pocket for his personal checkbook. "What's it going to take? How much money do you want to just walk away from this?"

Maggi held her breath. This couldn't have gone any better if she'd orchestrated it. When Patrick looked at her, she spread her hands as if to say she was leaving the show up to him. She wasn't sure if his skeptical expression was intended for her or Wiley.

"Are you trying to buy us?" Patrick's emotionless tone gave nothing away.

"A little bluntly put, but yes." Wiley saw the look on Maggi's face. "Don't look so surprised. Everyone has a price. What's yours?"

Why wasn't McKenna saying anything? Patrick wondered. Why wasn't she protesting and tossing the offer back in Wiley's teeth? Patrick had no idea what kind of a game she was playing. He would have sworn that, despite the fact that she was a royal pain in the ass and irritatingly smug, his new partner was honest. But maybe that was something she'd wanted him to believe.

He kept her in view as he told Wiley, "I'm going to forget you said that, Congressman, because McKenna here seems to think you stand for something."

The desperation grew. Wiley struggled to keep it in check. He was a man on a tightrope, afraid of a misstep, afraid of falling onto the rocks below. "I *do* stand for something—family values—and I'm trying to keep my family together. This'll kill his mother and sister."

Despite the sincerity in Wiley's voice, Patrick wasn't buying it. "And this wouldn't have anything to do with keeping your campaign on track, or making sure that the opposition doesn't have any mud to fling when you're up for reelection?"

"No, damn it, it doesn't." Wiley's temper flared before he could get it under control. "Sorry." With effort, he tried again. "Don't you understand? He's my son. If he can't make it out in the work world, what chance is he going to have in prison?"

Almost trembling, Blake still spit out, "Your faith in me is touching, Dad."

The comment seemed to push the congressman over

the limit. He turned on his son. "If you'd ever given me something to work with, maybe I'd have some faith." Shutting his eyes, he seemed to center himself. The next moment, he was placing the checkbook on the desk, ready to write. "Now, what'll it be?"

Patrick placed his hand over the checkbook. "The truth, Congressman."

Wiley stared at him, frozen in disbelief.

"Since you're willing to buy our silence, you obviously know more about the situation than you've told us." He told Wiley something they both knew. "Knowing makes you an accessory after the fact."

"You're just trying for a bigger payoff." One look at the congressman told them that the man fervently hoped he was right. The alternative was something he couldn't deal with.

"Yeah," Patrick allowed, "I guess I am." He saw the look on Maggi's face. Did she think he was going to take Wiley up on his offer? How dumb did she think he was? Or did she have him pegged as a corrupt cop? Was that how they did things in San Francisco? "In a manner of speaking," he said slowly, his tone impassive, his eyes darkening. "I don't like liars, Congressman. And you lied."

"I'm not lying now. You've got a choice. You either take what I'm offering and walk away, or I'll ruin you," he promised. "I've got friends in all sorts of places, Detective, and I can make life hell for you."

Patrick looked unfazed. "We all make our own hell, Congressman." He took out his handcuffs. "And it looks like you've made yours."

"It was an accident," Blake suddenly burst out, jumping to his feet and getting in between Patrick and his father.

"Shut up, Blake." Wiley's voice rose an octave.

Maggi held up her hand to silence the congressman. To encourage his son. "Let him talk."

Blake began to sob, his voice bordering on hysteria as he said, "She wanted to get married, said if I didn't marry her she'd go to my father, tell him how I messed up. Again."

She knew it was absurd and that Cavanaugh would ridicule her, but she couldn't help it—she felt sorry for Blake.

"So you killed her?" Maggi prodded gently.

Wiley caught his son's arm, as if to physically pull him away from the confession. "Blake—"

Blake yanked his arm free. "What's the use?" His eyes shifted to Patrick. Imploring. "He said it'd go easier if I told the truth."

"Wait for Christopher," Wiley pleaded.

But it was too late for that. Years too late. Blake suddenly looked like a deflated doll. "I'm tired of taking orders, Dad."

They needed the confession before Wiley got to his son and sent for their lawyer. "How was it an accident?" Maggi coaxed.

Blake sank back down in the chair. "We argued. She came at me, beating me with her fists. I hit her." He looked at Maggi, his eyes begging her to believe him. "Just once, that's all, just to get her to stop. I didn't want to hurt her." He swallowed, remembering. "She lost her balance, fell, hitting her head on the coffee table. She wasn't breathing." Tears flowed down his cheeks, for himself, for the dead woman. "I tried to revive her, I did, but she just didn't come around. There was no pulse." He licked his lips nervously. "I panicked and called my father." He didn't look at the congressman but kept his eyes fixed on Maggi. "He told me what to do. I put her into the car, drove to the river and pushed it over the side." He looked at them, some of the terror he'd lived with evident in his eyes. "It was an accident," he ended helplessly.

Wiley was quick to pick up the slack. "You can see it wasn't premeditated. My son didn't want to kill her. He was just being inept, as always. What good would it do to arrest him?"

Patrick couldn't tell if the man was serious, if he really expected them to go along with what he was saying. "I'm afraid you've forgotten the way the system works, Congressman. Shame on you."

"God damn it, man, just let me give you this money." Quickly he wrote down a figure that would have assured them both of a life of leisure from this day forward. He held it up to Patrick. "You and your partner can split it any way you want to." When Patrick made no move to take the check, Wiley demanded, "What do you make?"

"Not nearly enough to put up with this kind of garbage," Patrick assured him. Taking Blake by the arm, he drew him up to his feet. "Blake Wiley, you're under arrest for the death of Joanne Styles." Putting the cuffs on him, Patrick glanced at Maggi, then nodded at Wiley. "You want to do the honors with the congressman?"

"Me?" Wiley demanded, stunned. "On what charge?"

"Take your pick. Obstructing justice, accessory after the fact." Patrick looked at him pointedly. "Bribing an officer of the law. And that's just for starters. Now, I hate reading the Miranda rights, so I'd appreciate it if you'd both listen closely."

As he began to recite, Patrick motioned Blake out of the office. Maggi followed close behind with the congressman. She spared him the indignity of being handcuffed.

All up and down the hallway, staff members emerged to stare incredulously at the strange parade as Patrick's voice droned on.

"You have the right to remain silent. If you give up that right, what you say can and will be held against you. You have the right to an attorney. If you cannot afford an attorney, the court will..."

Chapter 9

It took them hours to wade through the paperwork, the onslaught of lawyers and the sea of news reporters who'd swarmed in like sharks in a feeding frenzy. None of this fanfare tarnished Maggi's feeling that, in the end, this had been a job well-done. They had solved a homicide in a relatively short time. So many crimes went unsolved years after they had taken place.

The case also helped push other feelings into the background. Feelings that were now crowding her, elbowing out a place for themselves beside the satisfaction. Feelings of ambivalence over her true purpose for being here. Things had blurred since she'd come on the job.

Everything had been fine when she'd thought Cavanaugh was guilty, when she'd been pretty much assured by his aloof attitude that he was what the department feared he was.

But now she wasn't so sure.

She wasn't even half-sure. He'd turned down one hell of a substantial bribe right before her eyes.

Maggi sat at her desk, staring at the last page of the report she'd finished filing. Not seeing it at all.

Granted, the scene with the congressman could have played out as it had because she'd been there and she was, as far as Cavanaugh was concerned, still an untried commodity. Even allowing him to believe that she wasn't as straight as she'd initially let on might not have convinced him to take a chance. To accept the liberal bribe that had been waved under his nose. After all, how did he know she wouldn't turn him in?

The irony of the situation was not lost on her.

Something in her gut told Maggi he wouldn't have taken the bribe even if she hadn't been there to witness it. Something in her gut and in his eyes.

But the look in his eyes could have been faked, she argued. Cavanaugh might be more of an actor than was evident. As for her gut, well, she had her suspicions it was unduly influenced by other things. Things she wasn't even going to visit until after they'd died away.

Rising from her desk, she stretched, exhausted. She couldn't even remember the beginning of the day. It felt as if it had taken place a decade ago. Her stomach reminded her that lunch had been an unsatisfactory hamburger and dinner was only a thought. Still, the idea of falling straight into bed held a great of appeal.

"Want to go and grab a couple of beers to unwind?" When she jumped in response to the sound of his voice, he stepped back, afraid of colliding with her. "Hey, you okay, Mary Margaret?"

Turning, she looked at him. After all the evenings she'd tried to get him to come out with her, to perhaps maybe open up a little after hours, only to be flatly turned down, this invitation out of the blue caught her completely off guard.

"I didn't know you were there. Just tired," she explained when he looked at her dubiously.

He put his own interpretation on her words and started to leave. "Okay, rain check, then."

She made a grab for his arm. When he looked at her quizzically, she let the sleeve go. "No, a beer sounds great. I just didn't think you unwound."

"Even machines power down."

Her mouth curved. "So, is that what you are, a machine?"

"Some people think I am." He started to leave and looked at her expectantly. "You coming or not?"

"Coming," she responded. "Definitely coming." She found she had to hurry to keep up. It took effort. Cavanaugh had to be a laugh riot on a date, she thought. "Ever think of cutting down your stride? Not everyone has legs like a giraffe, you know."

He grinned. "Most people think of necks when they think of giraffes."

Her eyes met his. "Most people don't see the whole picture."

Patrick was already heading down the hall. "But you do."

She couldn't help wondering if he was baiting her. The evening ahead promised to be interesting at the very least. "I try."

"We'll see," he murmured, as if irritated once again.

Was he was putting her on some kind of notice, or just making conversation? In either case, tiny volts of electricity sparked the adrenaline in her veins to flow faster as she stepped into the elevator car beside Patrick.

* * *

They didn't go to the local police hangout the way she'd expected. Was he taking her to his place instead? Somehow, she didn't think so. He didn't strike her as the type who liked having his inner sanctum invaded.

Driving ahead of her, he led Maggi to a small bar, closer to where he lived. Fading neon lights proclaimed its name for all interested parties: Saints and Sinners, except that the second *S* was burned out, turning it into Saints and inners, which was a joke all its own. The bar was part of a strip mall that had seen better decades. Even in the dark, it evidently needed renovation.

After stopping her car beside his in the all but empty lot, she got out and took a longer look at the bar. The building had a sadness to it she found hard to shake. Did Cavanaugh have that same sadness?

She was getting too philosophical, she upbraided herself. What she needed was sleep, not a beer. But maybe he'd feel more inclined to share something with her tonight, closing the case and all. Sleep was just going to have to wait.

Maggi fell into step beside Patrick. "So this is where you hang out at the end of the day?"

He deliberately avoided giving her a direct answer. To hang out depicted a pattern, and he had no routine other than work and sleep. Everything else was just happenstance.

"This is where I go for beer if there's none in the refrigerator."

He was watching her as much as she was watching him, she thought. Was he sizing her up, wondering if he could let her in beyond the first layer of his armor? Or was he just trying to figure out if she was worth the effort of bedding?

She couldn't tell. Nothing in his eyes gave him away. She hoped there was nothing in hers that would betray her.

He led the way inside, holding the door open for her. Once he let it go, the room wrapped itself around her, shutting off the outer world. Making her a part of this one.

She saw three people sitting at the bar. But when she began to walk toward an empty stool, he motioned her toward one of the small tables. Taking a seat, he held up two fingers for the bartender to see. The tall, world-weary, broad-shouldered man behind the counter nodded, putting up two bottles of beer for the waitress to bus over to their table.

Maggi waited until the woman withdrew. She took one long sip to fortify herself. She needed a little push tonight to do what she had to do. Setting the bottle back down, she raised her eyes to his. "Did you mean it?"

"Mean what?" Patrick asked. He couldn't help wondering what made her tick, what made a woman like her opt to put her life on the line every day as she got out of bed.

The thought of her getting out of bed, of being in bed in the first place, sent hot pulses snaking through his body. He chalked it up to a pure physical reaction and reminded himself that he didn't act on those unless there was the promise of no repercussions. Being with McKenna would guarantee repercussions. He knew that without being told.

"Back at the congressman's office, when you called me your partner." She'd been surprised when he had. Surprised and oddly pleased. She shouldn't have been, she told herself, but the feeling had remained for more than a moment.

He shrugged, taking a drag from the bottle he preferred to the usual mug of beer. He liked wrapping his hand around the amber glass, feeling its weight. There was something basic about that. He liked basic things.

When he set the bottle back down again, he laughed. "I couldn't exactly call you my pain in the butt, now, could I? We were supposed to be a united front."

She studied his face and found herself getting sidetracked by its planes and rugged angles. "So I still haven't passed inspection as far as you're concerned."

He didn't answer right away. Instead, Patrick's ice-blue eyes swept over her. Maggi felt as if her clothes melted away. The thought sent shivers of anticipation up her spine. It'd been a long time since she'd been with a man. Maybe too long. But long or not, Cavanaugh couldn't be a candidate. There was a huge conflict of interest involved.

Lacing his hands behind his head, Patrick leaned back, his eyes still creating havoc inside the pit of her stomach. "Mary Margaret, I'm pretty willing to bet you could pass any inspection you wanted to."

She blinked, trying to sound urbane, feeling she was grasping at straws. "Are you coming on to me, Cavanaugh?"

He savored the seductive note in her voice, knowing it could go no further. He was still having trouble accepting her as his partner. Anything else couldn't begin to enter into it.

But a man was allowed fantasies.

His voice was as low as hers. "Just stating the obvious."

The job. She needed to get her mind back on the job, not on what it would feel like having his hands run along her body instead of just his eyes. She dug deep for a question.

"Weren't you tempted?" Too late she realized what he would think she meant and hurried to add, "When Wiley offered you that bribe."

His eyes remained on her face, raising her body temperature by slow increments. She shifted in her seat. "Were you?" he responded.

She wondered if drinking a single beer could make you feel unnaturally warm. She couldn't blame the rising heat or sensation of depleting air on an undue press of bodies. She'd rather think it was the beer than the company.

"I asked you first."

Distancing himself wasn't easy, but then he specialized in the not easy. "You give in once, they have you forever. They get control of your life."

The way he worded it reinforced her feelings that Patrick felt at odds with the immediate world. The man was a loner with a capital *L*. She sincerely doubted anyone would ever get complete control over this man. Not his work, not his family. He went through life solo even in a crowd. She found that rather sad.

Hoping to score a piece of information, another piece to the puzzle that was Patrick Cavanaugh, she said more than asked, "And control is important to you."

"Control," he told her, his eyes pinning her in place, his voice a whisper, "is everything."

Maggi wasn't sure exactly how it had happened. One moment, Cavanaugh was talking to her, the next moment, he was blowing the room apart.

He'd leaned in over the tiny, scarred table and was kissing her.

Or maybe she leaned into him. She wouldn't have

been able to testify as to the exact chain of events if she was on trial for her life. All she knew was that it had happened. And that she was ultimately grateful there was a table between them, that no other body parts were touching except for their lips, because she knew that restraint wouldn't have been a viable option for her if they were.

It barely was now.

A hunger had crawled up from her belly, clawing its way forward and seizing her in its viselike grip, disintegrating almost everything else in its path. Making confetti out of her resolve.

Her heart began to hammer audibly in her ears, drowning out the soft drone of voices until it was completely gone.

He tasted of beer. And sin. The path to which was tempting her beyond her wildest imagination.

She wanted to touch him, to place her hands about his face. Instead, Maggi gripped the sides of the wobbly table, anchoring herself to something real, something tangible, before she was completely swept away.

As she was afraid she would be.

He wasn't sure why he'd let his guard down and kissed her.

Maybe it was the word "tempted" that had triggered him. Because he had been.

Tempted ever since he'd proved his point to her in the car eons ago, halting a kiss at the very last possible moment. Wondering what it would have been like had he gone through with the aborted movement. It had been hovering about in the recesses of his mind all day.

Each time he thought of their almost kiss, the curiosity only became more pronounced.

And now he knew.

Kissing her was like stepping through some kind of time portal. A rip in the fabric of time that took him back to the days when he hadn't quite realized that the world was a hard, unforgiving place where bad things instead of good happened. Back to a time when he'd believed in the kind of world that his uncles tried to create, not the one that existed.

She made him want things.

Want her.

Abruptly he pulled back.

Dazed and struggling very hard not to be, Maggi looked at him with wide eyes that initially refused to focus.

"Afraid of what you found out?" she finally managed to ask, brazening the moment out. Surprised that she had a voice at all. And grateful that they were sitting, because the consistency of her body had turned to mostly sticky liquid.

He searched her face for a clue before asking, "What do you mean?"

"That you're human."

His laugh was short, dismissive. "Annual physical tells me that."

Maggi shook her head, hoping the man didn't have a clue as to how far he'd unraveled her. "No, your annual physical tells you that you're still breathing. The human part's trickier."

He surprised her by smiling at her comment. "You sound a lot like my uncle."

Good, he was talking family. The pleasure of that was dampened by the pragmatic feeling that she knew she needed to burrow in a little further, that this was the way to get him to trust her, bit by bit. "Andrew or Brian?"

He looked mildly surprised that she knew their names. "Doing a little digging into my life, Mary Margaret?"

She was almost getting used to the sound of that, of her names being waved at her like a red flag. Her annoyance had gone down several notches over the course of the past few days.

"Don't have to. You're a Cavanaugh, you come with a pedigree."

Which was also why she'd been told to tread lightly. Because, maverick or not, Patrick Cavanaugh had strong family ties, ties that went back several generations in the police department. Had he been anyone else, the investigation that was launched would have been public. But there were too many possible waves here to make swimming easy, hence the covert approach.

She nodded. "My father used to work with your uncle Andrew and he knew your uncle Brian, as well as your father."

He seemed not to hear her when she mentioned his father, but she had a feeling he did. Had there been bad blood between the two? Did that affect Patrick in some manner, turning him against the force to which his father had sworn allegiance?

Questions crowded her head, butting up against the sensations that were still rippling through her minutes after he'd withdrawn his mouth from hers.

Her body hummed, aching. Wanting.

"Want another?" he asked her.

She stared at him, her heart hammering hard again. Was he actually asking her if she wanted him to kiss her again? The word "yes" hovered on her lips, begging to be released.

"Beer," Patrick clarified. The lighting in the bar was several notches below dim, but he could have sworn he saw color creeping up her cheeks. Amusement nudged an elbow in his ribs.

For a moment, she'd thought...

Damn, what was wrong with her? She wasn't some nubile, untried virgin, being led off to the hayloft for her first tryst with the good-looking farmhand. Why was she acting like one?

Annoyed with herself, with him for rattling her this way, she cleared her throat. "No, this was nice, but I think one's a good place to stop." She looked at him pointedly.

Good advice, applied to the beer and to her, he told himself. For once they were in agreement.

Patrick inclined his head. "Well, then I guess we'd better call it a night."

"Right." Maggi was on her feet a little too fast. Wobbly or not, she needed to put some space between them. Fresh air might not be a bad idea, either. "Early day tomorrow." She was babbling, she thought, but she didn't want there to be silence between them right now. Silence was too sensual. "There's probably some *i*'s we forgot to dot and *t*'s we forgot to cross."

"I don't forget to dot *i*'s or cross *t*'s," he told her, throwing down several bills on the table.

Placing his hand at the small of her back, he ushered her out. Making it feel as if this was a date. But it wasn't, Maggi told herself. And it couldn't be.

"Sorry, don't know what came over me. I forgot you were perfect."

"Not perfect," he told her as he opened the door

then let her walk through first. "Just thorough. And careful."

Careful.

That was the key word here, she thought. The word she needed to hold on to. Because she'd slipped back there, slipped and very nearly lost her footing. Fraternizing with the enemy was strictly forbidden and, until she could find proof of it otherwise, Patrick Cavanaugh was still the enemy—a dirty cop who made them all look dirty by association. And cops like that had to be routed from the force and punished for the tarnish they caused and spread. She needed to remember that.

Flipping her collar up, Maggi turned around to look at him. The wind had picked up and the smell of more rain wafted through the air. The parking lot was all but empty. They might as well have been the last two people on the earth. It felt that way.

She took a deep breath, as if that could somehow fortify her against the man before her. "Thorough and careful," she echoed, letting amusement play along her lips as she thought of what had just happened inside the bar. "Always?"

He looked at her, at the way the light from the streetlamp was playing off her lips. He could taste just the barest hint of her lipstick. Something light, sweet, mingled with the bitter taste of beer.

He felt that tightening in his gut again and deliberately concentrated on shaking it off.

"No," he said quietly, "not always."

The wind picked up the words and feathered them across her face.

For one very long moment, she felt as if there was a war going on, a war she was destined to lose no matter which way it went.

If she gave in, allowed herself to be pulled in, she faced a huge ethical and moral dilemma. If she did the right thing, pulled back, everything would remain intact. Except what she was feeling.

The right thing felt all wrong.

Desperately searching for higher ground before she slid down a slippery slope, Maggi shoved her hands into her pockets and cleared her throat. She forced a smile to her lips as she looked at the man she had to remember was her assignment and nothing else. "So, this the way you usually celebrate closing a case with your partner?"

Patrick hunched his shoulders against the wind and mist. "Throwing back a couple of beers? No, not usually." He thought back. "Just a couple of times with Ramirez. He insisted on buying."

That wasn't what she meant and they both knew it. "And the other?"

Looking into her eyes, he smiled to himself. The woman was damn annoying, there was no question about that. So why did he find her, of all people, appealing? "No, never kissed Ramirez. Never even been tempted."

Did I tempt you?

Ripples of excitement undulated through her. She wanted to talk about what had just happened, to explore the sensation it had created and let it titillate her.

Damn it, Mag, you're behaving like a schoolgirl.

God knew she didn't feel like a schoolgirl. She felt like a woman. A woman who wanted what she knew she couldn't have. Moreover, what she *shouldn't* have. Hooking up with Patrick Cavanaugh promised nothing but complications. She had to remember that. She wasn't trying to get on his good side to form a lasting partnership, she was trying to draw information out of him. To get him to trust her enough to let something slip.

The bitter taste of bile rose to her mouth.

"It's late," she murmured. "We'd better get going. My father'll be standing at the window, watching for me." A fond smile played on her lips. "Trying to pretend he's not worried."

Patrick looked at her, mildly surprised. He would have thought she lived alone, with maybe a pet for company. A dog. She didn't look like a cat person. "You live with your father?"

"No, not anymore. I just promised I'd stop by on my way to my apartment, that's all."

"Not anymore?" he questioned.

"I did for a while. I came back to take care of him after he was shot." She still remembered how she'd felt getting the call. Like a mule had kicked her in her stomach. Which was why she let her father fuss over her. Everyone had their own way of dealing with tension. "Friendly fire," she said incredulously. "Technically, anyway."

About to walk away, Patrick jerked to attention. "What did you say?"

"Friendly fire," she repeated, wondering why he was looking at her so strangely. "The bullet came from a police-issued weapon, but they found one of the dead 'suspects' holding it. He must have gotten a hold of the gun somehow during the scuffle. It was a raid," she explained. "My dad was one of the backup cops on the scene." The look in Patrick's eyes told her she'd said something that had caught his attention, something she didn't realize she'd said. A lightning review of the conversation assured her that it had nothing to do with her cover. But still it was something. "What's the matter?"

Maybe something. Maybe nothing. "That's how my partner got killed," he told her. "Friendly fire."

"Except that in Ramirez's case, it really was so-called friendly fire," she pointed out. "Isn't the officer who did it undergoing counseling right now?"

Patrick raised his brow, obviously surprised.

"Hey, I like to know what I'm getting into. I asked around when I found out you were going to be my partner."

Patrick nodded absently. It was plausible. What still didn't feel plausible or right was Ramirez's death, over and above the obvious. More than a month later, there was still something about the way it had gone down that didn't sit right with him.

He told himself he had to let it go, to put that out of his mind. Just as he had to put the longing that was attempting to wrap long tentacles around him out of his mind. Because he knew he'd be out of his mind to give in. McKenna was his partner and that was bad enough. Making her anything more was crazy and asking for the kind of trouble he didn't need or want.

"See you," he tossed over his shoulder as he abruptly walked away.

"Count on it, Zorro," Maggi murmured, staring after him.

Who was *that masked man?* Had he just kissed her like that to throw her off? Because she certainly felt thrown off. No, kissing her to throw her off would have been the action of a man accustomed to winding women around his little finger. She'd be willing to bet her next year's pay that wasn't Cavanaugh's style.

So what the hell was going on here?

Damned if she knew.

Suddenly feeling very drained and weary, Maggi got into her car and drove to her father's home. She planned to pay a quick visit and then go straight to her apartment. What she needed right now, she counseled herself, was sleep. Things would be back to normal in the morning.

Or so she told herself.

Chapter 10

Morning came and went. Maggi put the evening before out of her mind and concentrated on her job. Both the one she was supposedly doing and her covert one. With no new homicide to work on, Reynolds made it a point to tell them that it was an ideal time to catch up on long-overdue paperwork.

As far as Maggi was concerned, there was never an ideal time to catch up on paperwork, especially when the cases initially had belonged to someone else.

The day dragged on longer than it should have. When she saw Patrick getting up from his desk, his computer shut down for the day, her antennae gratefully went up.

She swung her chair around to bar his way out of the cubicle. "Where're you going?"

Very deliberately, he took hold of her armrests and repositioned her, then walked out of the cubicle. "I'm taking off early."

Maggi was on her feet. "Hot date?"

Turning around, he looked at her. "No."

"Then what?"

Was it him, or did she sound eager? Maybe she just wanted to get out like he did. Sitting, shuffling papers all day could be mind numbing. It was for him. "Did it ever occur to you not to ask questions?"

"Not really," she told him cheerfully. "Knowledge is a wonderful thing."

"Curiosity killed the cat."

Looking down, she indicated her legs. She wore a skirt that showed them off to a far-from-modest advantage. It took Patrick a beat to draw his gaze away.

"Two legs, not four. I'm safe." Determined to learn what he was up to, leaving early like this, she gave it her best shot. "I thought that unless you're off on a trip to your proctologist to have that stick you've been harboring surgically removed, since there's no grisly homicide staring us in the face right now, maybe you'd like some company."

He wasn't looking forward to what he was about to do and it left him in a less-than-amenable mood. "I'm going to see Alicia Ramirez to see how she's getting along. And no, I wouldn't like some company."

Her eyes skimmed over his face, trying to read between the lines. She thought she detected something. A reluctance he was trying to hide from her. Maybe even from himself.

"But maybe you need some," she countered. "Alicia's your partner's widow, right?"

"Yeah. So?"

He sounded almost belligerent. She would have backed away if this wasn't about something bigger than just her own feelings.

"So it's still in the early days since he was killed. Your heart's obviously in the right place, but you really don't have the softest touch, Cavanaugh." She pretended to be cocky. "My touch is very soft. She might want a woman around."

Alicia Ramirez came from a large family. Her emotional support system was assured. He was going over for a different reason. He'd already put this off for too long. "I'm sure she's got plenty of women around."

"Then *you* might want a woman around." He looked at her sharply and she added, "To take over when the going gets awkward."

He supposed she might have a point. Though he liked Alicia, this wasn't something he looked forward to, just something that had to be done. His sense of honor demanded it. "You certainly have no problem taking over."

She laughed. "Funny, that's what my father always says."

He nodded. "Smart man."

"Yeah, he is," she said. There was no mistaking the affection in her voice. He couldn't remember ever feeling that way about his own father. Earliest memories involved hearing his father shouting and his cowering in his closet, trying to get away from the sound.

Maggi looked over to the secretarial assistant they had covering the front desk. "Terrance, if the captain asks, I'm taking a couple of hours personal time."

"Very good, Detective." The young man's bright hazel eyes shifted toward Patrick. "You, too, Detective?" His meaning was less than veiled.

"Apparently," Patrick muttered, even though he had already told Terrance earlier that he was going to be leaving early.

Patrick walked out of the room without another word.

Maggi grabbed her purse and hurried after him. If nothing else, this assignment was certainly keeping her on her toes physically. "Are we going together?"

Patrick was already on his way out of the building. "No."

He didn't need to be in an enclosed space with her. The effects of last night at the bar were still very present in his mind. He needed to dissipate, not reinforce, them.

She was almost trotting to keep up. "Then give me the address in case we get separated."

"We're not going to get separated," he snapped, then added as he slowed down, "no matter how much I try."

The backhanded admission nudged a smile from her. "Just trying to help, Cavanaugh."

They weren't going to go there, to some area of mutual dependency. He'd made the mistake of forming a relationship with his last partner and he wasn't about to leave himself open to that again.

"Get this straight, Mary Margaret, I don't need your help."

"Fair enough." But she stood her ground. "Then maybe Alicia Ramirez might."

There was no getting rid of the woman, he thought. And maybe, just this once, she was right. He wasn't at his best dealing with emotional situations or emotional women. He already knew that. With a sigh, Patrick rattled off the address to her.

Alicia Ramirez was a petite, dark-haired woman with huge, sad eyes that brightened when she saw her late husband's partner standing on her doorstep. She smiled warmly at him, opening the door all the way.

"Patrick, please, come in." Too polite to ask, Alicia looked at the woman beside him with a silent query in her eyes.

"This is Detective McKenna. She's—"

About to say that she was his new partner, Patrick couldn't quite get himself to do it. Perforce, life always went on, but for those left behind when the train pulled out of the station again, it was a difficult thing to accept. He didn't want to make it any worse for Alicia than it already was.

"I work with Detective Cavanaugh," Maggi explained, extending her hand to the woman. "I just wanted to tell you how sorry I am for your loss."

Bright tears shone in Alicia's eyes as she took Maggi's hand. "Thank you. Did you know my husband?"

"No," Maggi replied honestly. "But I heard very good things about him."

"That's because he was a very good man." Alicia led the way inside. The two-story house was in the kind of perpetual comfortable disarray that having three children under the age of ten sustained.

The kitchen was a little better, Patrick thought. The counters were cleared, the sink empty. It looked as if Alicia Ramirez was reclaiming her life a room at a time. Progress was slow.

"I—we," he amended, bringing Maggi into it because the situation begged for it, "didn't come to put you out," Patrick protested as Alicia insisted on serving them each tea. Obligingly, he accepted the cup she'd poured and kept it sitting in front of him on the table. "I just wanted to see how you were managing."

Alicia took a seat between them. Wrapping her hands around her cup, she took a sip of the dark liquid and let it warm her before answering.

"I'm managing." The smile on her lips was sad. "The kids keep me busy and my sisters come by every day to help out." She raised her eyes to Patrick. "I still can't—" Alicia pressed her lips together. Grief stole the last few words away from her.

He'd come to the conclusion long ago that he'd rather face bullets than tears. He hadn't known how to handle them when he'd seen his mother crying, when they had sprung up in Patience's eyes the time she'd turned to him for consolation. All he knew to do was fight what had caused them. Which was why at the age of ten, he'd pitted himself against his father and why he'd fought a bully teasing his sister in the schoolyard when he'd been one half the bully's size.

But there was no one he could take on here. Only a formless entity, a sadness that couldn't be vanquished with any amount of blows. He gave Alicia his handkerchief. A helplessness pervaded him that he neither tolerated nor knew what to do with.

Out of the corner of his eye he saw Maggi reaching across the table, putting her hand over Alicia's.

"It's okay to cry," Maggi told the woman softly. "It takes about a year for the tears to stop coming unexpectedly."

Alicia dried her eyes with the handkerchief. "You lost someone?"

"My mother." She was nine at the time. Sometimes it still felt like yesterday. "Only time I saw my father cry. Took me six months to stop blaming her for dying. Took longer to stop crying every time I thought of her." Maggi offered the other woman an encouraging smile. "It's rough, but it passes into something you can live with," she promised. "Something you can handle instead of having it handle you."

Alicia nodded. Folding it again, she offered the handkerchief back to Patrick along with an apologetic smile. "I'm sorry, you didn't come here to see this."

Patrick took the handkerchief, shifting slightly in his discomfort. He cleared his throat. "Actually, I came to see if you needed anything."

Alicia cocked her head slightly, not following him. "Needed anything?"

Though it was invading a private area, it was easier for him to talk about finances than trying to handle the woman's tears.

"I know that Ed must have left debts." His late partner had had trouble hanging on to a dollar. There was always some new venture, some surefire scheme that called to him. Patrick knew that he was treading on the woman's pride, but children were involved. And he felt responsible. If he'd just been a little faster, there would be no tears in this household. "If you need any money, Alicia, you just have to ask."

To his amazement, Alicia laughed softly. "Money is the one thing I don't need." He looked at her, puzzled. "Eddie was very smart when it came to money. He made a lot of good investments, put the money in the bank. First Republic," she murmured, her voice dying out. The sadness threatened to take her over again. "If only he was as smart about what he did for a living." And then she sighed. "That's not fair. He loved being a policeman."

She looked at Maggi. "Said it was what he'd wanted to be ever since he was a little boy. The only thing that meant more to him were me and the kids."

Alicia looked over toward the framed photograph on the mantel. It was of a handsome man wearing a dress uniform and a huge, bright smile. Her breath hitched. Another round of tears threatened to come and she struggled to hold them back.

The doorbell rang a second before they heard the sound of the front door being opened and someone calling out to Alicia.

"I'm in here," she called back. Overhead they heard the sound of small feet pounding down the stairs. "That's Teresa, one of my sisters," Alicia explained. Her mouth curved. "They take turns baby-sitting me. Teresa brings ice cream for the kids. They get excited every time she comes over."

Patrick was already rising. He'd overstayed his visit. "We'll get out of your hair."

Alicia was on her feet. She looked at Patrick's untouched cup of tea. "No, really, you can stay if you'd like."

If he saw her indicating the tea, he gave no sign. "Like I said, I just wanted to see how you were doing and to make sure that you knew if you needed anything, all you have to do is ask."

Alicia paused to kiss his cheek and then give him a grateful hug. After a beat, he closed his arms around her in response, though he was obviously a man uncomfortable with displays of emotion. "He was lucky to have you," Alicia said.

Maggi noted that Patrick's discomfort seemed to heighten. She slipped between them as Alicia released Patrick from the hug. "It was nice meeting you, Mrs. Ramirez."

"Alicia, please." She walked with them to the front

door. "And if you're ever in the neighborhood," she told Maggi, "you're welcome to stop by."

"Thank you." Maggi squeezed her hand. "I will."

They nodded at Alicia's sister as they passed her and let themselves out.

Maggi stepped off the front step, then turned to Patrick. "Don't much like tea, do you?"

He hoped it hadn't been overly obvious. "I'd rather drink poison."

She laughed. The sound was oddly comforting to him. But then it faded as she asked, "When are you going to stop blaming yourself?"

"What?"

She disregarded the sharp note in his voice. "I saw it in your eyes when she said Ramirez was lucky to have had you as a partner." He looked angry, like a bear whose wound was being probed. She didn't let that stop her. "I read the report, Cavanaugh. There was nothing you could do."

That wasn't the way he saw it. Ramirez had a family, a wife and kids who had depended on him. He didn't. "He took the bullet meant for me. I was supposed to be the one walking into that crack house first."

"You said it was friendly fire. What are you saying now—that you were supposed to be the one killed by our own side?"

"I was talking about fate, not intent." He waved his hand. Why was he trying to explain it to her anyway? There was something more important on his mind right now. "Never mind. Look, I'm going to go back to the station. You go home."

Maggi felt as if she as being dismissed. *Not that easy, fella.* She glanced at her watch. It was a little after five.

"You're off duty. Technically." She was beginning to get the impression that Cavanaugh felt he was never off duty. Which conflicted with her reasons for being assigned to the case in the first place. If he was so dedicated, could he really be dirty? "Why don't we go somewhere and I'll buy you a beer to wash the taste of that tea out of your mouth?"

It was tempting. So was doing something else to rid his mouth of the taste that was there. But right now, something bothered him more than the rebellion of his own hormones. What Alicia had told them wasn't sitting right with him.

"Some other time."

She deliberately moved in front of him, blocking the way to his car. "What's on your mind?"

Annoyed, he had to repress the desire to physically move her out of his way. "What?"

"I'm starting to know you, Cavanaugh." The funny part of it was, she was. What's more, she liked what she had learned. He exhibited all the warmth of a clay statue, but it was obvious that he cared about the welfare of his late partner's family. He got points for that. "I can see the little wheels in your head turning. Something's bothering you. What is it?"

"Other than a nagging partner?"

He'd called her his partner again. He was getting used to her. That was both good and bad, depending on what side of her guilt she was standing on. "Goes without saying."

Maybe two heads were better than one. At the very least, maybe he could use her as a sounding board. Just thinking of that surprised him. The whole concept of sharing his thoughts was foreign to him because he'd always gone it alone, always relied on his own instincts.

But maybe this time he was too close, too involved to be impartial. He cared about Ramirez, and about the welfare of the man's family. "Okay, I'll take you up on that beer."

Score one for the home team. "Great. Do I get to choose the place this time?"

"No."

"Didn't think so." She nodded toward his car. "You drive, I'll follow."

He was already getting in. "Wouldn't have it any other way."

Maggi bit her tongue to keep from commenting.

Chapter 11

This time Patrick took her to a place with more light, more noise, more anonymity. If she was interpreting body language correctly, no one here seemed to know him by name or by sight. The noise around them guaranteed their privacy.

She was secretly grateful he hadn't brought her back to the bar they'd been to last night. What had happened there was still very fresh in her mind and the velvety darkness would have only aided and abetted the desire that still hummed through her. A booth with a proper-sized table between them was a lot better.

She was also secretly disappointed.

Maggi waited until the waiter brought over their beers, bottles again, before she said anything. She had a feeling that if she didn't initiate the conversation, Cavanaugh would go on sitting there, not a syllable leaving his lips, until he decided it was time to get up and go.

"All right, I'm all ears."

She saw the way his eyes swept over her. For a second, she could almost feel them touching her as they passed. Her mouth grew a little drier. She felt less like a partner and a great deal more like a woman.

"Figuratively speaking," she felt bound to add. "Something's been bothering you since we were in Ramirez's house. What is it?" When he didn't begin to speak, frustration raised its head faster than she knew it should have. The man really knew how to press her buttons. A lot of them. "Talk to me, Cavanaugh. That's what I'm here for."

Even as she uttered the words, Maggi couldn't help wondering if the man she was sitting opposite had any idea how true those words were. That was what she was here for, to get him to talk to her. To wheedle into his confidence, not as a partner but as a spy.

She felt an unwanted shiver creeping through her system and banked it down.

Patrick sat for a long moment, regarding the neck on his bottle of beer. He hated what he was thinking. He wasn't outgoing, but his late partner had gotten to him, gotten his trust. Facing the possibility that he'd been fooled wasn't easy for him.

Finally he looked up. "He didn't have that kind of money."

"Ramirez?" she guessed.

He nodded slowly. "He always needed money. He was always into something that would get him rich, quick. Anytime he did anything right, anytime something panned out for him—and it wasn't often—" Patrick emphasized "—he told me about it. Told everyone about it. That man couldn't keep his mouth shut. That was just his way."

He needed to believe in his partner, she realized. It made Cavanaugh a little more real to her, a little less like some remote, two-dimensional being. It also made her want to help him hang on to his memory of the man.

"Maybe his wife's not asking for anything because of pride."

Patrick shook his head. "Alicia's not like that."

"You'd be surprised how much pride someone can have when it comes to preserving the reputation of someone they love." Patrick looked at her sharply. She'd only been throwing out words. *What are you thinking, Cavanaugh? Have I set off something in your head?* "A man's not a good provider for his wife and kids," she continued, pretending she hadn't noticed his reaction, "that brings his stock down."

He wasn't convinced. Something felt wrong. "It wouldn't have been something she would have kept from me." He thought of Ramirez. The first thing he remembered was the man's wide grin. The second was the sound of his voice, going on incessantly. Not unlike the woman in the booth with him now. "Partners get close. They spend a lot of time together—it's hard not to."

"And the two of you got close." It was hard picturing him getting close to anyone, Maggi thought. Maybe that was why he was resisting the idea they were silently waltzing around, because he'd gotten in close and put his faith in someone. And that someone had died.

He looked at her. "As close as I've ever gotten to someone who's not a member of my family."

His steady gaze held her prisoner. Needing to pull

back, Maggi tried to lighten the moment. "So I've got something to live for."

"Maybe."

There was no way to know what he was thinking now, she noted. His clear blue eyes gave nothing away.

Maggi struggled to keep her mind on the object of all this. "You do know how to put someone in what you think is their place, Cavanaugh." Maggi leaned forward, playing out her line, trying to reel him in a little closer. Ignoring the slight spasmodic twinges running up and down her conscience like a short circuit. "Okay, so if you were privy to everything Ramirez did that was aboveboard, maybe this wasn't."

"What are you saying?"

The man looked as if he could shoot lightning bolts from his eyes. She suddenly felt sorry for anyone on the wrong side of his temper. "That maybe Ramirez was getting something on the side. It's not the kind of thing he'd share with a partner."

Anger flared like unguarded flames. "You're saying he was dirty?"

She kept her voice light, low. "I'm spinning theories, not trying to get in a fight."

Patrick sucked in his breath. His voice had a dangerous ring to it as he said, "He wasn't the type."

Maggi didn't budge. "Everyone's the type if the situation is dire enough."

"Now you sound like Wiley." There was no missing his disgust.

"No," she insisted, "I sound like a realist."

Patrick started to leave the table. She grabbed his wrist. If looks could kill, she figured the one he shot her would have left her mortally wounded. But now that she'd gotten on to something, she was not about to back away.

"Follow me on this. The man had three kids, a wife, a mortgage, maybe a shoe box full of other debts. You said he was always getting into things that didn't pay off." Reluctantly Patrick sat down again. She continued holding his wrist. "Somebody offers to give him a little money to look the other way. He's a good guy but he's got creditors breathing down his neck, that kind of thing. So he does it." Seeing that she had his attention, Maggi slipped her hand from his wrist. "It's a one-time thing. Or so he tells himself. Except that once he's in, he's in. Like you said, he had no more control over the situation. It had control over him. So he goes along with it, putting aside money for the kids' college funds, a vacation, something pretty for his wife. And all it takes is not saying anything.

"But his conscience eats at him until he says 'that's it, I've had it.' Now whoever slipped Ramirez that money gets nervous. They know they've got a liability on their hands—"

"They?" He looked at her closely. Did she know something she wasn't telling him? After subjecting him to days of useless information and endless rhetoric, was there actually something useful she was holding back?

"Or he," Maggi allowed. "She, whatever. Bottom line is Ramirez has to be eliminated before he talks."

He hated to admit it, but the scenario fit. "And he gets killed."

"And he gets killed," she echoed.

He gazed at her intently. "So you think this is an inside thing?"

She raised her hands from the table, palms up. "I'm only spinning theories," she repeated. "But it does make sense." And it did, she thought, now that she'd put it out on the table. She only had to prove it. And then she had to see if perhaps Cavanaugh was a hell of a lot better actor than he let on and was actually part of all this. Damn, but this job was making her paranoid. "Puts a different light on 'friendly fire,' doesn't it?"

The theory put McKenna in a whole different light as well, he thought. "You're a lot darker than I thought you'd be."

"It's the lighting," she cracked, taking a drag from her bottle.

Why did she do that? he wondered. Why did she say something flippant to throw him off, keep him off balance? He didn't like it. "You know damn well what I mean."

Maggi sobered. "Yes, I do. I'm just not sure if it's a compliment or not."

"Neither am I." Leaning back, he contemplated the mouth of the empty bottle. He didn't like what she was saying, but he was too good a cop not to admit that, at least from the outside, it made sense. "We'd need proof. Evidence."

"Definitely."

He didn't know whether he wanted to dig deep and ruin a man's reputation because of principles. Ramirez had been one of the few people he'd allowed himself to call friend.

She saw the doubt on his face as he warred with his thoughts. Was he worried that an investigation would lead to his own dirty hands? Or was he just concerned for a man he'd privately considered a friend?

Instinct told her that if Patrick was dirty, he wouldn't contemplate shining a light on someone else so close to him.

But maybe that was what she wanted to think.

She hated admitting the possibility that her personal feelings were obstructing what she had to do. She needed distance here, at least for a few hours.

"Look, we're not going to settle anything tonight," she pointed out. "You can think about it and tomorrow, if you still agree there's some chance Ramirez was killed to keep him quiet, I'll help you dig."

He raised his eyes from the bottle. "You?"

"Well, you're going to need to get hold of bank records, information on file, things like that. We already know how proficient you are with a computer, so I figure you're going to need help."

There was no use protesting that he could manage alone, not when he was up against technology. Still, he didn't want her working with him, not on this. A man had to draw the line somewhere. How did he know he could trust her? "This isn't your concern."

Her eyes told him that she wasn't about to budge on this. "It's about a cop on the police force. How *isn't* it my concern?"

He thought of Ramirez, of seeing the life drain out of the man even as he held him in his arms, willing him back to life. "It could get ugly."

"I can do ugly."

"Not hardly," he said under his breath. For now, he wanted to table the discussion. "You hungry?"

She cocked her head. "You offering to buy or taking a survey?"

Something tightened in his gut. He figured it was in protest against hunger. "The former."

"Then I'm hungry." Maggi settled back in her seat, not bothering to suppress the smile on her face as he signaled for the waitress to come over.

Tiny, baby steps.

* * *

The telephone was ringing when he walked into his condo over an hour later. He and McKenna had gone their separate ways after dinner, although he'd had to struggle against the urge to ask her over to his place. The pretext of a nightcap wasn't even remotely in his thoughts. What he wanted was to find out if her skin was as smooth as it seemed. All over. If that look in her eyes hid a wildness instinct told him was there.

For a simple man, Patrick knew life had gotten incredibly complicated for him, and this bone about Ramirez was hard enough to chew on. He didn't need more.

Except Maggi was tormenting him. Need tormented him. A basic need as old as time. That's all it was, he told himself, taking off his holster. All he wanted was a little gut-wrenching, toe-curling, sweaty sex, nothing more.

The fact that he was contemplating having it with his partner made his mouth curve. Never thought he'd catch himself thinking that.

The phone kept ringing, an irritating noise scratching at the perimeter of his mind. Patrick thought of letting the machine get it, but his natural sense of urgency and order forced him to walk over to it and pick up the wireless receiver.

"Cavanaugh."

"Just wanted to put in my bid early for Christmas day."

The familiar voice drew out a smile as Patrick sank down on his sofa. The second he did, he felt as if he'd collapsed. He'd warred with a host of emotions that had made him more tired than a full day out in the field.

He put his feet up on the secondhand coffee table Patience had picked up for him at a garage sale. "You don't have to put in a bid, Uncle Andrew. It's a done deal, you know that."

"No, I don't," the other man informed him. "I didn't think I'd have to call and ask to see you, but apparently it looks like I have to. Your sister's looking well. She tells me she hasn't seen much of you, either."

Patrick grinned. There was something comforting about listening to his uncle's harping. He'd missed it. "Work. You know how it is."

He heard his uncle sigh and knew there was more than a little nostalgia echoing in the sound. "Yeah, I know how it is. Still doesn't give a man an excuse to cut out his family."

"No cutting," Patrick assured him, then teased, "trimming maybe."

"If I asked to see your clock-stopping mug at the table in the next say, three or four days, what do you think my chances would be?"

"Fair to good."

"But not perfect."

There were no birds on his uncle's antennae, Patrick thought fondly. Sometimes he wondered why the man opted to take early retirement. Andrew was still as sharp as ever. "No, not perfect."

Andrew hesitated for a moment. "You know, Patrick, if a case you're working on is giving you trouble, I'd be happy to have you bounce a few things off me. The brain still works pretty well."

Patrick glanced at a stack of mail on the corner of the table. It was beginning to pile up. He supposed he'd have to get around to going through it one of these days, before a utility company decided to shut off something he found useful. "So I've heard, but I just wrapped up a case."

Patrick could hear the trap snapping as soon as he made the admission. He'd been set up.

"Well, then, I guess you've got no excuse not to come over."

The private part of him liked leaving himself a little leeway, although he did enjoy going to his uncle's house for breakfast. His thoughts shifted to the conversation he'd had at dinner. "I'm working on something else right now."

"A new case?"

He heard the interest in his uncle's voice. Not being part of the force anymore, Uncle Andrew still had more connections than anyone Patrick knew. Maybe he'd heard something useful. But it was still too early to think of letting more people know about this. It chaffed him that McKenna was in on it.

"Not exactly." He paused. "I'll let you know if I need to ask you hypothetical questions."

"My best area," Andrew assured him. "Tomorrow's Saturday. Unless something comes up, you don't have to be in to work. Always a place for you at the table. Breakfast is eight-thirty. Try to make it."

"I'll try."

Patrick made himself a promise to do more than just try as he hung up. If his job kept him grounded, being around his uncle and cousins reminded him why he was still doing what he did, that there were times when the good guys actually did outnumber the bad.

With a sigh, he reached for the stack of mail.

"To what do I owe this unexpected pleasure?" Matthew McKenna moved back out of the way as he opened his front door farther. "Why didn't you use your key? You don't have to knock. This is still your house."

"I know and I appreciate that, Dad, but I didn't want to barge in." She winked. "You might have been entertaining a lady."

He shut the door, following her into the living room. "The only lady I want to entertain keeps making herself scarce." He looked at her pointedly.

She took off her jacket and tossed it on the side of the sofa. "Oh, Dad, don't act like I never come by."

His smile was fond. "Not nearly enough, Mag-pie, not nearly enough."

Maggi knew he wasn't trying to make her feel guilty, but she felt it just the same. Juggling family and work wasn't easy. "You and Mom should have had more kids."

He looked over toward the array of framed photographs on the wall along the stairway. They chronicled his life together with the two women who'd meant the most to him, his wife and his daughter. "Yes, we should have, but I'm afraid the good Lord didn't see it that way." He smiled at her. "He gave us all of heaven wrapped up in one little girl."

She gave him a warning look. "Dad, you keep that up and I'm leaving."

He laughed, raising his hands in mock surrender. "I'll behave. Is this one of your whirlwind visits, or can you stay for dinner?"

Her father's idea of dinner was taking something out of the freezer and introducing it to the microwave. "Already ate."

He was on his way to the kitchen to get her one of the diet soft drinks he kept on hand for her. "Alone?"

As she talked, she began to gather up the newspapers he'd left where he'd read them. The man needed a maid, she thought. "There were people in the restaurant."

"You went to a restaurant by yourself?" Returning, he handed her a can. "Why didn't you give me a call? I could have met you—"

He was fishing and she knew it. She tossed him a tidbit. "I wasn't by myself."

He beamed at her with satisfaction. "So, you did go with someone."

After placing the newspapers in the recycle bin, she turned around and looked at him. Amusement played along her lips.

"Were you this heavy-handed when you were investigating a crime?"

He shrugged carelessly, making himself comfortable on the sofa. "It's the father thing, brings out the clumsiness. I just want to see you happy."

"I *am* happy." Picking up the can again, she sat down opposite him. "I'm also curious."

"Oh, so this isn't just a casual visit. You've got questions. About?"

She looked at his left hip, remembering what had gone through her mind when she'd stood over him in the hospital, not sure if he was going to make it despite what the doctor had assured her. Her father had been shot in the shoulder and the hip and his chances were not the best. Twenty-nine or not, she wasn't ready to be an orphan yet.

"Are you sure that was an accident?"

His brows drew together. "You mean did I see the guy who shot me? No. There was a lot going down that day, Mag-pie. Shots were flying everywhere. One second, we were making a good bust, the next minute, all hell broke loose. The guy we were coming for had reinforcements. There were shooters everywhere. They matched the bullet I caught in my chest to the gun some dead punk was holding in his hand. Why?"

"Just trying to get a few things straight in my head. You said it was a policeman's service revolver," she reminded him.

"If you're asking me how the scum got a hold of it, I can't help you." He told her what she knew was in the report. "The guy it belonged to caught a bullet in the head."

This information had bothered her then and it bothered her now. "Why take his gun when there were obviously so many others on the scene?"

He lifted his right shoulder, letting it fall again. "A sick sense of humor, maybe. Or he lost his own weapon. Who knows? All I know is that every day I thank your mother for watching over me." He nodded upward. "Another inch over and we wouldn't be having this conversation." And then he looked at her more closely. "Why *are* we having this conversation?"

Talking to Cavanaugh had made her start to compare the two incidents. Both had been deemed as tragic mistakes. Both men had been shot with service revolvers, but that was where the similarities ended. Or did they? She couldn't get past the feeling that maybe there was a connection of some kind.

"I can't really put it into words, Dad. It's just a feeling I have."

"About?" he prodded gently.

"That maybe this is part of something else."

"Like what?"

She couldn't tell him about Ramirez, or her assignment, but she could talk to him about what had happened to him. "Like maybe someone tried to get you out of the way—you said the bullet almost cost you your life. Or if not out of the way, then at least off the force." She could feel an excitement building in her, but it had no outlet yet. "Is there anything you might know that could be a danger to someone?"

He laughed and shook his head. "You've been watching that TV show about the CIA again, haven't you?"

Maggi bit her tongue. Her father had no idea that she worked undercover for Internal Affairs and she meant to keep it that way. She wasn't sure exactly how he would take it, even if her motives were pure.

"Yeah, maybe I have. But if you think of anything, give me a call."

"You'll be the first to know." He dug himself out of the sofa and rose to his feet. "Now come in the kitchen and keep me company while I have my dinner. You can have some if you want."

She really hadn't eaten all that much at dinner. "What are you having?"

"Stroganoff. The brand you like," he added.

"Got an extra one in the freezer?"

He grinned. "Don't I always?"

She'd lost her taste for frozen dinners since she'd grown up, but here there was a bit of nostalgia attached to it. She felt like being nostalgic tonight, felt like remembering a time when dirty meant something that needed a little soap and water to come clean. "Okay, you twisted my arm."

He slipped his arm around her shoulder. "I thought I might."

Chapter 12

He'd had better ideas in his time.

Patrick frowned as he turned down a street. One side looked out onto a golf course, dormant now in deference to the inclement weather. The other, to his left, was lined with houses peering over a gray cinder-block wall. He was on his way to McKenna's apartment. She'd gotten to him at a weak point, when he'd been fresh from a visit to his uncle's.

Early this morning he'd swung by Patience's place. He'd picked her up and the two of them had breakfast with the others. Best medicine in the world. Going there helped ward off the darkness that threatened to seep into his soul. Not only did he get to see Shaw, Callie, the twins and Rayne, but two of his other cousins, as well, although Uncle Brian was a no-show.

Patrick hadn't done much talking, but he'd listened. And basked in the normalcy of the gathering. He'd lowered his guard just enough so that when McKenna called to ask him if he wanted to go ahead and start digging into Ramirez's records, he'd said the first thing that had come to his mind—yes.

The next thing he knew, he was listening to directions on how to get to her apartment. The radar that ordinarily saw him through dangerous, dicey moments kicked in immediately.

Dangerous and dicey. He figured she could be placed under that heading, although he was starting to think she belonged in a subcategory all her own.

"Why your apartment?"

"Do you have a computer?"

"No." He saw absolutely no use for one. Gadgets annoyed him. They required patience and reading, not to mention babying. If something was to work, it should do so at the flip of a switch, like a lightbulb or a television set, not because you were armed with an instructions manual big enough to choke a Clydesdale.

"I didn't think so," she said. He didn't particularly care for her smug tone. "The main thing you need if you're trying to get access to computer files is a computer."

He saw the woman five long days a week. Why was he even contemplating giving up his weekend to subject himself to more of the same? "Don't get smart with me, Mary Margaret."

He heard her laugh and instantly saw her in his mind's eye, her eyes bright, her mouth wide. Patrick wondered what the hell was happening to his control.

"Wouldn't dream of it."

He asked for a rain check. She talked him out of it. He placed several obstacles in the path; she knocked them down. The end result was that he found himself here, entering her apartment complex, searching for a parking place.

He told himself if he didn't find one in five minutes, he would just turn around and go back. But then a spot opened up. Grudgingly he took it.

Her ground-floor apartment faced the back of the complex. He had no trouble finding it. Apart from the identifying number on the door, his attention would have still been drawn to it. McKenna's door was completely gift wrapped in gold foil with a wreath topping it off.

The woman obviously had never found the word *restraint* in the dictionary.

Feeling surlier than usual, Patrick rang the doorbell. Christmas carols echoed in response. It figured.

Maggi unlocked the door even before his thumb was off the bell. "Hi, you showed up."

He tried not to notice that she was barefoot and her jeans fit her as if she'd just this moment painted them on. The powder-blue pullover she had on needed at least three inches to meet the top of her jeans. Her flat belly peeked out flirtatiously and made his palms itch.

"Told you I'd be here," he growled in response.

She opened the door wider. "I figured you'd come up with a last-minute excuse."

He gave her a look and remained where he was, on the opposite side of the threshold. "I could go."

Maggi stepped out of the way, her invitation clear. "Staying is easier."

"That's a matter of opinion," he muttered under his breath. He still thought coming here was a mistake, but he'd never been one to back away from something that made him uneasy.

Following her into the two-bedroom apartment, he

made it past the small kitchen before stopping dead. The whole apartment was saturated with toys of all shapes and sizes, wrapping paper and ribbons everywhere he looked.

And smack in the middle of the living room was a floor-to-ceiling Scotch pine jammed into a tree holder, its head slightly bent under the weight of the star affixed to it. There were decorations, multicolored lights and tinsel reflecting back at the viewer from every angle.

If there was a Santa Claus, he would have had less going on in his workshop than was happening here, Patrick thought.

"Someone die and leave you a toy shop?" He turned to look at her. "What are you doing with so many toys? You actually know this many kids?"

She led him to the rear of the room. There was a small desk against the wall. It hosted a computer and flat panel, leaving just enough room for a notepad. The printer sat on the floor to the right of the desk.

"No, not personally," she told him.

He looked around again. Action figures, dolls, stuffed animals. Did she have some kind of toy hangup? He didn't think he'd ever seen this many toys outside of FAO Schwartz toy store.

Patrick found himself wondering more and more about his new partner and liking it less and less. "Don't tell me Santa Claus is really a woman."

"These are for the kids at St. Agnes Shelter. That's the shelter for abused women and children," she explained. "I'm collecting for them." Innocence personified, Maggi turned her face up to his. "Care to make a donation?"

"I know what St. Agnes Shelter is."

She'd struck a chord, one he would have preferred not having struck. He was intimately familiar with the shelter she'd named. It had been around for twenty years. Long enough for him and his mother and sister to visit once. Flee to, actually. They'd been forced to go that time his father had completely lost control. Patrick remembered because it was shortly after his aunt Rose, uncle Andrew's wife, had disappeared.

His father's drinking binges had gone from bad to worse. When his mother tried to get him to stop, one thing had led to another until he was threatening to kill all of them. Despite that, Patrick knew his mother would have remained with his father, but Patrick had pleaded with her to think of herself and Patience. And told her that he would kill his father if anything happened to either one of them. In the end, more afraid of that than harm to herself, she'd gone, but only after he'd promised to come with her.

So he'd gone to the shelter with his mother and sister and had seen firsthand the sadness that existed in places like that. Everyone tried to cheer one another up, but the sadness had hung on like a steely specter, waiting for them, never letting go.

They'd gone home again, amid his father's promises to his mother that things would change. They had, but not of his choosing. His father was killed in the line of duty less than six months later.

Maggi looked at the dark, brooding man in her living room. Something was going on here, Maggi thought. More than just his cynicism. "Are you all right?"

"Yeah, fine." He waved a dismissive hand at her question. "I was just thinking that maybe I will make a donation."

He shrugged, drawing his eyes away from her face

before he did something stupid he'd regret. And then, because he'd been on the inside, because he'd seen the vacant eyes and the despair up close in children who were old before their time, he added, "That's a good thing you're doing."

An odd note stirred in his voice. She couldn't begin to interpret it. There was a lot of that going on when it came it Cavanaugh, she thought. Somehow, she was going to have to find a way to get closer to the man. So far, she hadn't a clue as to how.

"Thank you. That means a lot, coming from you."

His eyes narrowed as he maneuvered his way around the living room, his path impeded by piles of toys. "What's that supposed to mean?"

"Well, you don't exactly act as if you approve of me."

"You're all right. I mean, as far as cops go." Impatience began to break out of its bonds. "Can we get on with this?"

"Sure." She edged over to her computer, which was on, her cable connection already opened. "Where would you like to start?"

He looked around, at a loss. "How about finding a place to sit?"

"Sorry." Since the sofa was close to the desk, she cleared a place off for him, moving the brigade of stuffed animals closer together and over to one side. She grinned, gesturing toward the spot. "I'm sure that Big Bear and the others won't mind sharing their seat with you."

"Big Bear?" He stared at the large white polar bear with its silly grin and drooping head. "You named the stuffed animals?"

"Not me. The toy manufacturer beat me to it." The

bear looked as if it was going fall forward so she tucked it in beside the stuffed fox. "But I used to whenever my father gave me one." A fond look curved her mouth. "I was an only child—he liked to spoil me."

"Yeah, it shows."

If his words were any more weighed down with sarcasm, they would have made a hole in the floor. "Oh?"

"You like getting your own way."

Maggi tried not to take offense, but it wasn't easy. "That's called a forceful personality."

"That's called being a pain in the—" He sighed. If they were going to do anything productive, although he still wasn't sure what, then this was the wrong way to go. "Sorry, let's start over."

Maggi sat down at the computer, her back to him. "Fine by me."

He paused, unable to wrap his mind around his late partner and the possibility of wrongdoing, especially when his mind kept traveling the short path to the woman sitting at the computer.

The question came of its own accord, as if he had no say over the matter. "You've mentioned your father several times."

"Sorry, does that bother you?"

There was a touch of frost in her reply. He ignored it. "It's just that you never talk about your mother."

Maggi glanced toward the framed photo on the side table. It was of the three of them. The last one she had of her mother. "My mother died when I was nine. Car crash."

He'd heard her tell Alicia about her mother, he just hadn't realized she'd been that young when her mother died. "Sorry, didn't mean to..." Uncomfortable, Patrick let his voice trail off.

"Didn't mean to what, ask me a personal question? No problem. Just means we're getting closer together."

The look on his face was one of annoyed disgust. She would have been a little disappointed if he hadn't reacted at all.

"You're not going to be happy until we're joined at the hip, are you?" he asked.

"If I'm going to be your partner, I need to know how you think," she told him simply. *And if I'm going to get any answers for IA, that won't hurt, either.*

"Why?"

"So I can anticipate your next move. So I can be there to cover your back."

He'd wandered over to the side table and picked up the family photograph. They were all smiling. The smiles looked genuine. In the single shot he had of his immediate family, the only smile in the photograph belonged to Patience, who would have smiled standing next to the devil himself. His sister would probably like McKenna, he thought.

"You keep pushing me out in front and covering my back," he said.

"Sorry, does that bother you?" She turned around to glance at him and was surprised to discover that he was right behind her. "I'd take the lead but I get these Neanderthal vibes from you that tell me you wouldn't let a woman walk in front of you. It's a macho thing, am I right?"

Why the hell were her eyes getting to him when her wagging tongue was rubbing the very flesh off his body? Annoyed, he took a step back. "Which is why a man shouldn't be partnered with a woman."

Maggi sighed, her eyes fluttering shut for a second

as she sought strength. "That is so wrong I don't even know where to begin."

He laughed shortly. As if she was going to ever be quiet. "But you'll find a way, won't you?" He made a decision. "Look, this was a mistake." He began to back away. "I can—"

He was going to say that he could get the information he needed by himself. "Not easily," she interjected.

Ordinarily, what people thought had less than no effect on him, but for some reason, when it came to her, Patrick didn't like being cast in the role of an idiot. "Are you saying I can't get the information I need without you?"

"No," she contradicted. "What I'm saying is that it'll take you longer than if you let me help." She raised her eyes to his. "And I'm betting that you're smart enough to put whatever differences we still have aside to tackle this."

"Whatever differences we *still* have?" Patrick hooted incredulously. "Mary Margaret, there are nothing *but* differences between us."

Maggi tossed her head, sending her hair over her shoulder. She looked at him pointedly. "Oh, I think we found some common ground and it seems to be widening all the time." Before he could comment, she moved her swivel chair back to face the computer. "Okay, let's start out with the basics."

As he stood watching over her shoulder, Maggi called up Eduardo Ramirez's vital statistics via an internal program that had been installed by the Aurora police department some years earlier. The safeguards on it were brand-new. In an instant, they had Ramirez's social security number, his driver's license as well as a thumbnail sketch of his background and education.

In the area designated for any incidents reports, there was nothing. His record was surprisingly spotless, given their suspicions.

"You have access to that?"

She heard the doubt in his voice. Maggi indicated the screen. "You see it, don't you?"

Patrick was beginning to figure out how her mind worked. Sideways, like a sidewinder. "You're not answering my question," he persisted.

Maggi smiled to herself as she took in the information she'd pulled up. "Let's just say that if there's a paper trail of some sort, I can get access to almost anything we might need to clear this up."

She had already gotten into Patrick's banking records the night she'd received her assignment. But if Patrick was trafficking in something illegal and getting paid for it, he wasn't putting the money into anything that showed up on her radar. That fact didn't clear him, just made him harder to pin down. But then, if this mission had been easy, she wouldn't have been here.

"You really weren't kidding about being able to hack into data banks." The look he gave her wasn't quite accusing, just mystified. "Where did you learn how to do this?"

She didn't bother boring him with the fact that she had perfect recall. The kind that made people leery around you. "From a computer genius I knew in high school." She thought of Ronnie Rindle and smiled to herself. "He liked to challenge himself. His aspirations ended when he was caught starting a major upset on Wall Street by moving stock around and having false data show up in accounts." She still got cards from Ronnie at Christmas. "While he was behind bars, he found a new passion. Pottery. Keeps him out of trouble."

Patrick didn't quite follow her narrative. "And he passed on his mantel to you?"

Ronnie had tried to get her to join him, but she'd politely pointed out the very real danger of what he was doing. He'd been caught the very next day. "No, just gave me a few tips in gratitude."

"Gratitude?"

"He was kind of lonely. I was the only one who called him a genius, not a geek. He was a little odd, but nice."

Patrick had a feeling that she was the type of person who could find some good in almost anyone. They were as different as night and day. "For a felon."

"Reformed felon. Very good sculptor, really." Maggi looked back at the screen. "We've got Ramirez's social security number, shouldn't be too hard for us to get anything else. His wife said something about the money being in First Republic, didn't she?"

"You figure the money's just sitting in his bank account?"

"If your ex-partner got mixed up in this by accident, sure, why not? You make things too complicated, Cavanaugh. Only hardened criminals pay attention to safeguards and details. Besides, if Ramirez was accustomed to blowing money the way you said he was, he'd want it where he could get his hands on it easily enough."

But even now, she was frowning. A scan of the bank's records showed that the joint account held by Eduardo and Alicia Ramirez had less than a hundred and fifty dollars in it.

"This wouldn't take care of a week's groceries for

a family of four," Maggi commented. The money had to be somewhere else. But where?

"See if there's another account."

She'd already tried that. "Not with his name and social on it." Maggi bit her lip, tying again.

"Try his wife."

"That's what I'm doing." Glancing over her shoulder at him, she grinned. "You know what they say about great minds."

"Yeah, they're inside swelled heads." No one was going to accuse him of thinking like this woman.

Maggi shook her head. "Definitely need to work on your holiday spirit."

Patrick pointed at the flat panel. As far as he was concerned, Christmas was just another day, like all the rest. "Keep your mind on the screen," he told her tersely.

Maggi typed, her fingers flying, keying in codes. Watching her, Patrick marveled at how fast she was going. When he typed, it took him more than a minute to find every letter of a word.

Sitting back, Maggi looked at the information she'd manage to pull up. She was far from satisfied. "Okay, Alicia Ramirez has a checking account with almost a thousand dollars in it."

He thought of the way the woman had turned down his offer to help. "I guess it was just her pride, then," he surmised.

Still typing, Maggi wasn't ready to throw in the towel. "Maybe, maybe not."

There was something in her voice that put him on the alert. "You find something?"

Yes! "There's a third account." Satisfaction rippled through her as the information began to emerge. "Neither Ramirez nor his wife is the principle reportable social security number on it."

He didn't follow and hated feeling dumb. "Then how did you—?"

She turned the screen at an angle so he could see it, as well. "I tried to link either one of them up with another account. You know, like maybe in one of the kids' names."

"And?"

She tapped the top line of the screen. "You have any idea who Maria Cortez is?"

"No, why?"

"Well, she and Alicia have a joint account together and this Maria's social security number is the one that gets reported to the IRS. And whoever she is, she must be one rich lady."

Moving aside, Maggi indicated the bottom line of a series of entries, all made in a relatively short amount of time. And fairly recently.

The current balance in the account was close to two hundred thousand dollars.

Maggi shook her head as she looked at the figure. "If this does represent money that Ramirez was putting away in his wife's name, all I have to say is that the raises in your department must be phenomenal."

Chapter 13

She was having a hard time concentrating, what with Patrick behind her, moving back and forth like a brooding duck at a shooting gallery. Until now, she would have sworn that the man had been created without any nerves, but this clearly flew in the face of what she thought she knew about him.

It was obvious that what they were discovering about Ramirez bothered him. Why? Because she was getting close to something, or because this was about someone he'd allowed himself to think of as a friend? Did it disturb him because he thought his judgment was poor, or because it was Ramirez, a man he'd liked?

Whatever the answer, the relentless movement behind her began to grate on her nerves. When she hit a misstroke and had to backtrack, she bit off a curse. Trying to hold on to her temper, she glanced over her shoulder. "You know, I could do this a lot faster if you weren't pacing around like that."

Patrick stopped, not because she wanted him to but because he hadn't realized he was pacing. His own display of unrest annoyed him. "I thought nothing distracted you."

"So did I."

Her answer was barely audible and was meant more for herself than for him. She was becoming increasingly attuned to Patrick and not in a useful way. Maggi was afraid that it would make her want to tip the scales and the second she did, she became worse than useless to Internal Affairs.

Patrick pointed a finger at the screen. "Just work."

She caught the vein of distress beneath the royal command. "This is bothering you, isn't it?"

He raked his fingers through his hair, sending it into further disarray. Watching him, she found herself wanting to do the same, but she kept her fingers flying over the keyboard. It was safer that way.

"Wouldn't it bother you to find out you had a crooked partner?"

"Yes," Maggi deliberately turned around to look at him, "it would." She watched his face.

Nothing. Not a flinch, not a twitch, not an uncomfortable look. You're either very, very good, Cavanaugh, or you're innocent.

And she knew exactly which way she wanted to vote. Trouble was, you couldn't vote on facts. They either existed or they didn't. So far, there was nothing she could find to substantiate the rumors against him. But that didn't mean they weren't true, she reminded herself. Just that Cavanaugh was good at burying things.

It didn't take Maggi much more digging to discover the identity of Alicia Ramirez's partner on the joint account. Cortez turned out to be Alicia's maiden name. Maria Cortez was her mother.

Playing on the side of the angels, she asked, "Did Ramirez ever mention or hint that his mother-in-law was well-off?"

Patrick shook his head as he stared at a flickering light on her tree. She needed a new bulb, he thought absently. "He didn't say much about her except that she was a dragon lady and never forgave him for getting Alicia pregnant."

The more she heard about his late partner, the more she liked him. But then, she'd learned a long time ago that nothing was ever black or white. Dirty cops could be nice guys, too. "Pretty open, wasn't he?"

"That's my whole point." The frustration Patrick felt was barely contained beneath the surface. "If he'd gotten into something that wasn't aboveboard, he would have told me."

Still on the side of the angels, she pushed a little further. "Then maybe this is his mother-in-law's money."

He looked at the screen she'd pulled up, his expression darkening. "Not if she was making deposits up to six weeks ago."

She looked at the string of deposits that were listed. They'd stopped abruptly the third week in October. "Why?"

"Because I attended her funeral nine months ago."

Without saying a word, Maggi scrolled back to the beginning of the account. "This account was opened seven months ago."

Damn it, Ed, what the hell were you up to? What were you thinking? He looked at Maggi. It didn't make sense. "So tell me, how does a dead woman open a bank account?"

That she could answer. "It's very simple, really. Alicia goes in, saying she wants a joint account, but that her mother is too ill to come in and sign the papers. Wanting their business, the bank is more than happy to be accommodating. They give her a signature card to take home to mom, Alicia brings it back signed and voilà, a new account is opened, bearing mom's name." She stopped. He had that strange look in his eyes, the one that said he was examining her. "What?"

"How would you know that?" Patrick asked.

"I worked Fraud for a while in 'Frisco. You pick things up." She frowned as she viewed the screen again. There was no doubt about it—this did not look good. Wanting to see what he would do next, she placed the ball back in his court. "Now what?"

Patrick shoved his hands into his jeans. "Now I try to figure out what to do with this." He hated the kind of thoughts he was having. Ramirez had been one of the few people outside his family he'd trusted. Hell, he'd trusted the man more than he'd trusted his own father. What the hell did that say about his ability to read people? He slanted a glance at Maggi. "Those deposits wouldn't happen to be traceable, would they?"

Maggi shook her head. "Cash, every time." And then she paused, looking closer. "Interesting."

"What is?" Patrick leaned more closely over her, his hand on her shoulder as he looked at the screen.

She felt waves of warmth working their way through her, coming out of the blue. Trying to seduce her. *Not the time, Mag, not the time,* she warned herself. The waves kept coming.

Shifting, she got him to remove his hand. "The

handwriting on the deposit slips doesn't seem to match Alicia's." She pointed out the copies, then, hitting a button, she enlarged the portion that had caught her attention. "Hers is neat, precise." She shifted back to the deposit slips. "This is somebody dipping a chicken's foot in ink and making passes on a piece of paper. It actually makes my dad's handwriting look good."

Patrick's expression was grim as he looked at the samples she pointed out. "That's the way Ramirez used to write."

Ramirez made the deposits, probably to keep his wife innocent of what was going on. Maggi sincerely doubted the woman knew what her husband was really up to, other than trying to avoid reporting interest on an account.

Keeping his wife in the dark was one thing. Keeping his partner there was another matter. She was having a difficult time believing that Cavanaugh had no inkling of what Ramirez had been up to. After all, it wasn't as if Cavanaugh was mentally challenged or walked around, oblivious to things.

Maggi decided to go fishing. "You said he liked to talk. He ever approach you about this, make any vague references to feel you out?"

Patrick looked at her sharply. "No, he knew better than that."

She was pushing him, she thought, and he looked like he was on the edge. Maggi shoved with both hands. "You mean that he knew you were a straight shooter, right?"

He came close to telling her what she could do with her sarcastic tone, but stopped himself in time. He wasn't angry at her. He was angry at Ramirez for betraying him and for being stupid.

"I'm not pure as the driven snow," he informed her tersely. "I've got my share of black marks, but you don't get mixed up in something like that. One way or another, they'll get you."

Her eyes never left his face as she typed in more code. "You talking about the good guys or the bad?"

"Both." Bullets came from both directions. The way he saw it, if the good guys didn't catch you, the bad guys killed you. "Somebody gets greedy, somebody gets nervous." Cursing roundly, he moved away, needing space. Feeling frustrated. "Damn it, why didn't I see it?"

His anguish seemed genuine. So genuine she wanted to comfort him but knew that was both stupid and counterproductive. She needed him like this. If he was emotionally strung out, he was more likely to slip up. *If* there was anything to slip up about.

"Maybe because you're not clairvoyant."

He didn't need or want her sympathy. It changed nothing. Ramirez was dead not because he hadn't gone first into that building but because he hadn't been smart enough to pick up on things. He'd let the man down.

"I was his partner, the guy who was stuck with him for eight, ten, twelve hours a day. I should have felt it. He'd gotten quieter in the end." Patrick blew out a breath. Why hadn't Ramirez said anything? Why? "I just thought he and Alicia were having problems."

"I thought you said he always talked. Doesn't that mean he would have said something to you about it if he was having problems with his wife?"

A broad shoulder rose and fell. "Well, sometimes Ramirez kept a little something to himself. Chewed on it until he was ready to share." Now that he thought about it, things started to fall into place. Ramirez *had* looked as if he wanted to talk just before they'd gone on the raid, but then the man had waved it away. At the time, he hadn't thought anything of it. Maybe Ramirez had wanted to make a clean breast of his involvement. "He'd been preoccupied that last week."

"Maybe debating whether or not to get out."

And the wrong people had found out, Patrick thought, and decided to have him eliminated. He clenched his fists in his pockets. "Maybe."

She stopped pretending to type and turned to give him her full attention. "Any ideas on what he might have been mixed up in and who else might be involved?"

He frowned as he eyed her. "Right now, where I stand, everybody's a suspect." His meaning was clear.

The look in his eyes made her squirm inside, but she kept a mild expression on her face as she raised her hands in protest. "Hey, I'm the new kid on the block. I'm clean."

"This is a virus. It could have spread out in any direction." But he really didn't believe she was mixed up in something. She was the one doing the probing. If anything, he held that against her, but nothing else.

Patrick's words triggered a thought. Her father popped into her head. The accidental shooting had gotten her father off the force. Had that been on purpose? Had her father been about to stumble onto something and been blocked just in time?

"The trouble with conspiracy theories," she said aloud, "is that they start making you paranoid, get you looking over your shoulder all the time."

He thought of the way he'd been fooled. It wasn't

an image of himself he relished. "Maybe that's not such a bad thing."

She laughed shortly, thinking more of her line of work than anything he was facing. "Hell of a way to live."

"Key word here is 'live' and to keep on living." The image of his partner on the ground, already having taken his last breath, leaving behind a wife and three small children, ran through his head. "Maybe Ramirez should have been a little paranoid."

"Maybe he was. Maybe he tried to get out and that's when they had him shot."

She was on to something, he thought. And he needed to act on it. "I think I'll start by talking to Dugan."

"The guy who shot him?"

Mentally he was already out of the apartment and on his way. "Yeah, he's on disability."

Maggi was on her feet. The man definitely didn't know how to segue into anything. "Now? You're going to see him now?"

"Now's as good a time as any."

If he was going to question the man, she wanted to be there. This could all wind up being part of the same puzzle. She began to entertain the idea that maybe someone was throwing dirt on Cavanaugh to avoid any undue scrutiny.

"Give me a second to shut down my computer and unplug the tree."

Instinct told him to keep walking. He stopped anyway. "Why?"

"Because I'm going with you."

"He was my partner." He didn't want her tagging along. It was bad enough he had to put up with it during work hours.

She looked at him before answering, trying to figure out just what was going on in his head. "Yes, and you're mine."

Arguing with her would take up too much time. And he had a feeling that if he opted to walk out, she would be right there on his tail. He might as well keep her in his sights.

Sighing, Patrick gestured at the Christmas tree. "All right, go ahead, unplug it."

To his surprise, she began to crawl under the tree. He couldn't help watching as she snaked her way underneath, her small, tight posterior moving just enough to dry his mouth. He was only vaguely aware when the tree went dark after she hit the switch at the end of the abbreviated extension cord.

"You know, it must be five degrees hotter around this tree. Are you single-handedly trying to fund the energy company?"

Maggi wiggled back out from beneath the tree and rose to her feet. She'd managed to emerge a little closer to him than she'd anticipated. But to take a step back would have shown him that his proximity affected her. She remained where she was, at least for a beat.

"Hey, it's only one month out of the year. And it makes me happy."

The scent of something sweet and heady swirled around him. Cologne? Shampoo? Hadn't the woman ever heard of using scent-free products?

"I didn't think you needed anything to 'make' you happy," he said gruffly. "I thought you came that way."

"Never hurts to have a little reinforcement."

Her smile unfurled inside him like a cat stretching awake before a fireplace. "Whatever you say." If he didn't back off now, he knew he was done for. "Let's get going."

"Right."

Thank God he had backed away, or she would have had to, Maggi thought. She was going to have to remember to leave space between them. Lots and lots of space. Otherwise, the temptation to have no space at all would overwhelm her.

Another time and place, this would have been different, and she might have acted on what she was feeling, but here it wasn't going to work. Anything that might have been between them was doomed before she ever laid eyes on the brooding man. Allowing herself to go further down that road was only asking for trouble.

Why did trouble have to look so damn enticing?

Josh Dugan lived in a small wooden framed house that had once belonged to his parents and looked it. Like an aging former athlete, the two-story building sagged in a number of places and there were shingles missing from its roof.

"Well, if he's in on something illegal, he's not spending the money on home improvements, that's for sure," Maggi observed as Patrick rang the bell. "This place would have to have some major renovations just to be classified as a fixer-upper."

He made no comment, listening instead for the sound of someone coming on the other side. But there was nothing. After ringing again, Patrick knocked, hard.

A woman across the street was walking by with her dog. She stopped to look in their direction, curiosity painted on her weathered face. Pulling her terrier closer, she stopped and called out. "You two looking for Josh?"

Maggi walked down the rickety steps, crossing the wide residential street to reach her. "Yes, you know where he is?"

The other woman lifted her shoulders beneath a worn winter coat that had never been in style. "Gone."

Patrick frowned, joining Maggi. "What do you mean, gone?"

The woman seemed puzzled by the question. "Like, not there. I knocked on his door more than a couple of weeks ago to see if he wanted to come over for some Thanksgiving leftovers—never seem to be able to get rid of the stuff, you know?" she said, looking at Maggi.

Patrick suppressed an impatient sound. "What about Dugan?"

The expression on the woman's face told them she didn't like being rushed. "He wasn't home. Hasn't been home since, far as I can tell." As if to validate the information, she added, "I live across the street."

She pointed to a house that looked as if it had been a mirror image of Dugan's when the builder had finished his work. Now, the second house was in far better condition than the one belonging to the missing policeman. The woman's house squarely faced Dugan's. Her front windows would have allowed her a perfect view of Dugan's comings and goings. Patrick had a feeling she stationed herself at them with fair regularity.

"Do you remember when you last saw Officer Dugan?" Maggi asked.

The woman paused to think. "Just before then. Two and a half, three weeks ago, maybe."

"What was he doing?" Patrick pressed.

She shifted the leash from one hand to the other and

turned up her collar against the late afternoon wind. "Some men came over to see him. Friends from the squad I guess."

Patrick was on it immediately. "What makes you say that? Were they in uniform?"

The woman looked annoyed at the close questioning. "No, I said I guess."

Maggi intervened before Patrick's lack of people skills alienated the woman. "And you haven't seen him since?"

The woman frowned. A longing appeared in her eyes as she looked over to the other house. "No."

"Could you describe the men?" Maggi wanted to know.

Again the woman shrugged. "I dunno. They were men. Average height, dark hair, nothing special. Not like Josh," she added.

"How many were there?"

"Five. I remember because I wondered how they could all get into the car they were in. Like clowns in a circus, you know?"

Maggi nodded. "Did you notice what kind of a car?"

"Some foreign thing. Black, navy, I'm not sure."

It was obvious that the woman had exhausted her supply of useful information. Patrick took out a card and handed it to her. "If you think of anything else, give me a call."

Her hand curved around the card as she looked up at him. There was no mistaking the interest that had entered her brown eyes. "Can I give you a call if I don't think of anything else?"

"You might have to talk to his wife or one of his six kids first," Maggi told her cheerfully as she hooked her arm through Patrick's and drew him away. "Thanks for your help," she tossed over her shoulder.

"Thanks," he muttered to Maggi as the woman walked away.

"Don't mention it." She winked at him. "Told you I had your back." He was suddenly striding ahead of her with purpose, and she hurried to catch up. "Hey, where are you going?"

"To look around Dugan's. We've got probable cause now."

"We also have nothing," Patrick conceded thirty minutes later after they had searched the premises. He'd half expected to find Dugan's body in a pool of blood. It was getting to be that kind of a day. "He might have just gone on vacation."

Maggi stopped rummaging through the man's closet. "I thought he was in the middle of therapy with the department shrink."

"Can't think of better therapy than a vacation."

She caught something in his voice. "You don't believe he went on one, do you?"

"Nope."

Maggi stepped away from the closet and went to check the bureau drawers. "And you'd be right. Unless he went to a nudist colony." When Patrick lifted a brow, she nodded toward the open closet. "Suitcases are still in the closet."

"Maybe he had an extra one."

A half smile curved her mouth. "Men don't have extra suitcases. They also don't go anywhere without underwear. They shove it in at the last minute, but they take it." She closed the last of the drawers she'd opened. "His drawers are full."

He looked at her, curious despite himself. She kept doing that to him, he thought. "How do you know so much about how men pack?"

"Because I used to repack for one."

"Your father?"

"My fiancé."

The information stopped him in his tracks. He refused to speculate why. "You're engaged?"

"Was," Maggi corrected.

A wave of relief came out of nowhere. "What happened?"

She wondered if he'd even understand what she meant if she said, *Que sera, sera*. "My father caught a bullet, I caught a plane. My fiancé stayed where he was, nurturing his career."

"And you're not going back?"

"Nothing to go back to. Since when do you ask personal questions?"

"You must be rubbing off on me. And before you say anything, no, that's not a good thing."

Maggi forced herself to get her mind back on her work. She walked out of the bedroom. "I'm going to give this place another pass. Maybe there's something we're overlooking."

He was right behind her. "Like evidence of foul play?"

Maggi nodded. "Crossed my mind."

He doubted they had missed anything. The house was almost Spartan in its decor. "Easier to just take Dugan for a ride and do away with him somewhere else. Still, he might have decided to take off."

"Easy enough to verify, unless he decided to drive somewhere."

She was talking about her computer, he thought. "Back to your place?"

She was quick to grin. "Took the words right out of my mouth."

"That's a first."

There were other things he wanted to do with her mouth, things that had nothing to do with uttering words, but he kept that to himself. It was getting crowded there, amid all the things he was holding to himself, but he figured it was damn well safer that way. To release them into the light of day might just spell something else for him and he wasn't willing to go there yet.

Maybe never.

Chapter 14

She was getting too close.

Not to any dark, secret underbelly that Patrick Cavanaugh was suspected of having, just too close to the man himself. Too close to emotions that had absolutely no place in this kind of investigation. Not that she would allow them to cloud her judgment or stand in the way of her doing the right thing. She had too much integrity for that.

But Patrick did make it extremely difficult to concentrate, difficult to think of him as possibly being guilty of the allegations anonymously brought against him.

Just after she'd finished her shift, she'd been summoned to meet with her superior over another tepid cup of coffee at yet another out-of-the-way diner. She waited only long enough for the waitress to withdraw before expressing her doubts about the necessity of continuing the charade.

Maggi thought of the way Cavanaugh had looked when she'd suggested his late partner had been on the take. "The man can be colder than last week's toast, but he's a good cop," she insisted.

Halliday poured enough cream into his coffee to turn it a pale shade of tan. "Maybe that's what he wants you to think."

She didn't like the idea that Halliday thought she could be manipulated. "I don't think he 'wants' me to see anything. He doesn't care what I think of him, what anyone thinks of him. He's just out to do his job." It was stupid, but she felt protective of Cavanaugh. Felt the way, she realized, she would about a real partner she cared about.

If Halliday even noticed or was disturbed by her defense of the detective, he gave no indication. "It's early days and no one said he wasn't good at what he does. Maybe it's too soon for him to relax around you, to let his guard down."

She thought of the dark bar and the kiss across a wobbly table. And the way her heart had stood still. "I think he's as relaxed as he's going to get."

"Early days," Halliday repeated.

She felt a little as though she was telling tales out of school, but then, that was what she was supposed to be doing, right? Halliday had a right to know what she and Cavanaugh were investigating in their free time. And it might cast him in a good light. "There's more."

Halliday looked attentive. "Such as?"

Though the booths on either side of them were empty, she still leaned over the table and lowered her voice so that only Halliday could hear. "Cavanaugh suspects his late partner might have been on the take."

Halliday's eyes were flat as they regarded her. "Suspects, or wants you to suspect?"

She didn't want Halliday thinking that Cavanaugh was orchestrating anything. "He doesn't even want himself to suspect and he's been against my getting involved in this from the beginning."

The role of devil's advocate fit Halliday like a well-tailored, custom-made glove. "Because it'll point to his culpability."

"No," Maggi insisted, stopping just shy of being heated, "because Cavanaugh liked Ramirez, because he wants to help the man's wife and kids." She paused for a moment, knowing she was pulling things out of the air, setting them down out of order. "Let me start at the beginning."

Quickly she filled her superior in on what they'd learned about the situation, being careful to skip just how the information came into her hands. She had a feeling that unless there was a trial involved, Halliday didn't care about the means, only the end.

Halliday listened quietly, his hands wrapped around the almost cold cup of coffee. When she was finished, he nodded, as if sorting through the information and slipping the various pieces into different slots in his head. He fixed her with a meaningful look. "There are at least two sides to everything."

"And?" She realized she held her breath and willed herself to draw air back into her lungs.

"And with two sides, things can be turned around a full hundred and eighty degrees."

She knew where he was going with this and part of her actually resented it on Patrick's behalf. "Meaning he's dirty and he wants to draw attention away from himself and onto someone else."

Halliday's look went right through her, clear down to her bones. "Wouldn't that be the way you'd do it if it you were in his shoes?"

She sighed and stared at the table. The Formica surface had long since turned a yellow tinge, showing signs of wear as well as ingrained stains that she guessed were probably older than she was.

"Yes."

Her answer was quiet, swallowed up by the late afternoon din of people stopping by the diner for a quick bite before hurrying back to their lives. Right now, she envied them, envied what she imagined was the simplicity of their lives.

Halliday drained his cup, then set it down. He folded his hands before him, a theoretician stating his argument. "Don't you think it's rather odd that if Ramirez was dirty, Cavanaugh didn't know it? The two worked together for over two years. Cavanaugh isn't exactly fresh off the turnip truck."

No, she thought, he wasn't. He was one of the sharpest people she'd ever met. Which was why she was afraid that sooner rather than later, Cavanaugh was going to catch on to what she was doing.

"But if you're not looking for something, you might not see it," she insisted. And then her eyes widened as she thought she understood. "Is this why you're having me investigate him? Because of Ramirez?"

Halliday was quick to put her theory to rest. "No, we didn't know about Ramirez. But if it is true, it only solidifies our suspicions."

"I don't know. I'm still not buying it."

A hint of a smile played along his thin lips. "Doubt is good. Always doubt."

That was the problem. She was doubting. Doubting

Cavanaugh, doubting herself and doubting her ability to remain impartial no matter what.

If she couldn't properly defend Cavanaugh's reputation, even for herself, the least she could do was find out some information for the man she'd been sent to defame. "What about Dugan?"

There was a pause. The look in Halliday's eyes told her he was debating whether or not to answer.

"We're looking for him," he finally said. "The department's psychologist said he was a no-show for his appointment. That was over two weeks ago. Right now, from what you're telling me, it fits in with the puzzle, that Dugan shot Ramirez on purpose rather than by accident."

A thought came to her. "Maybe he didn't shoot Ramirez on purpose. Maybe he was aiming for Cavanaugh and got the other man by accident."

Halliday considered it. "It's a possibility." He wanted to get her reasoning, see if it fit in with his own. "Why would he be shooting at Cavanaugh?"

Maggi was getting up a full head of steam now. "Because they wanted Cavanaugh out of the way. Maybe they were afraid he was getting too close to the truth and if he found out, he'd turn them in."

Halliday's face was impassive. "Still want him to be innocent, don't you, McKenna?"

Maggi resented the veiled implication that she'd doctor details to suit her purpose. "No, I just want the truth and I don't want a good cop to be sacrificed."

Halliday suddenly seemed weary. "Nobody's sacrificing anyone, Detective. We're both after the truth."

She sincerely hoped so. As far as she knew, Halliday was an honorable man who had managed to keep above the taint that this kind of job dealt with.

But he had planted enough doubts in her mind to have her not only wondering about Cavanaugh, but about Halliday and what he wanted as well. Halliday was close to retiring. Was he after one last spectacular cleanup before he handed in his shield?

She wasn't sure of anything anymore.

It was time to leave. "Let me know if you ever find Dugan," she said, rising.

Halliday nodded. "And McKenna—"

"Yes?"

His eyes held hers and she couldn't shake the feeling that he was probing her. "This is a good thing you're doing."

She allowed the corners of her mouth to curve slightly. "If it's such a good thing, why do we have to keep meeting like a couple of clandestine lovers every time you want to debrief me?"

"It's just the way the system works."

Maggi pressed her lips together. "I'm beginning to think that maybe the system needs an overhaul," she commented just before she left.

She got into her car, feeling disgruntled and gritty. It had been that kind of a day. Just before she'd met with Halliday she and Cavanaugh had gone to see Alicia again, to confront her with what they had found. This time, Patrick hadn't hung back.

"We know about the bank account, Alicia. The joint one you have with your late mother." His eyes had narrowed. "The one that was opened after she died. Why is the account under her social security number?"

Alicia had looked upset, like a good little Catholic girl caught playing hooky instead of going to mass.

"Eddie said it was better that way, that we wouldn't have to pay taxes. I know it was wrong, but—" She stopped, the look on Patrick's face halting her flow of words. "What is it?"

"This goes deeper than just trying to avoid taxes, Alicia."

She'd looked from Maggi to her husband's partner, confusion on her pretty face. "I don't understand."

"We're afraid your husband might have been mixed up in something," Maggi had said tactfully, watching Alicia's expression.

"Something?" Alicia had echoed.

"Shady," Patrick put in.

The woman rose from sofa, her face clouding over. She seemed to understand the implication if not the actual details. "Get out of my house."

"Alicia—" Patrick began.

Alicia pointed to the door. "Get out of my house," she repeated. "You come here and trash my husband's name when he can't defend himself?" Outrage echoed in her voice. "Get out of my house!"

So they had left, convinced that Alicia knew nothing beyond what she'd said. That she'd opened the account because her husband had assured her it involved avoiding taxes and nothing more.

Even now, driving home, Maggi could remember the accusing look on the woman's face. She hated it. Hated anticipating the one she knew she would eventually see on Cavanaugh's face.

It had been one hell of a day.

Matthew McKenna opened the front door on the third ring. In the background, his favorite movie, *Unforgiven,* was playing. He knew the dialogue by heart. It only enhanced his enjoyment of the viewing experience.

The expression on his daughter's face had him forgetting all about Clint Eastwood. Concerned, he ushered her in. "You look like you lost your best friend."

Her smile seemed tired to him. "No, you're still here."

Matthew shut the door behind her. "Don't try to snow me, Mag-pie. What's up?"

She'd driven around for a bit after leaving the diner and Halliday. The adult thing would have been to drive home, but she didn't feel very adult right now. She felt like a child in need of comforting. In need of knowing that there were no monsters in the closet and that things were going to turn out for the best once morning came.

Shedding her coat, she dropped it on the back of the sofa. "I can't tell you that."

Picking up the remote, he shut off the video and then the set. He motioned her to the kitchen. He knew there were things about the job that people kept to themselves. He could respect that, but it was hard when his own daughter was the one involved.

For her sake, he tried to sound chipper. "What'll you have?"

Maggi dropped down into a chair. "A shoulder to lean on and a cup of hot chocolate."

"You've already got the shoulder, you knew that when you walked in. And as for the cup of hot chocolate, this sounds serious." Taking out a saucepan, he poured what he knew by practice was a ten-ounce glass of milk, then turned the burner on low. He sat down at the table, giving his daughter his full attention. "Okay, give me a hypothetical."

She cloaked her words as best she could. "Hypothetically, I think I've lost my way. The investigation

I'm on has me completely turned around and I don't know what to believe anymore."

Matthew covered her folded hands with one bearlike paw. He wasn't a large man, but his individual features were powerful looking.

He gave her the only advice he could. "Your instincts, Maggi, trust your instincts. You haven't gone wrong yet. How could you?" Getting up to tend to the milk, he paused long enough to wink at her. "You're my daughter."

She felt a little better even before the chocolate was poured.

Dashing around to get ready, Maggi belatedly registered the ringing in her brain. She dug into her pocket to retrieve her cell and put it against her ear. "Hello?"

"You up, Mary Margaret?"

Patrick's deep voice filled her ear, sending echoing waves through her, swirling around in her insides. She took a controlled breath before answering.

"Up and at 'em, why?"

"Because I need a ride in and I'm on your way." She heard the strain in his voice. He didn't like asking for favors.

"Car trouble?" she guessed, moving the conversation along. She paused before her reflection in the microwave door to run a hand through her too-flat hair.

"Yeah. Alternator died." His uncle had promised to come by this afternoon to take a look at it, just perpetuating the legend Uncle Andrew could do anything when he had to. Not like his own father who'd always put things off and accepted defeat before it ever arrived. To him, Andrew had always been the better man. "Can you pick me up or what?"

She was tempted to ask him just what comprised an "or what," but had a feeling that would just put him off. "Consider yourself picked up. It'll be a first for me," she heard herself saying, although for the life of her, she didn't know where this had come from. "I've never picked up a man before."

That he could readily believe. Women who looked like McKenna always had men hitting on them. They didn't need to think about picking up men. "Aren't you going to ask for the address?"

"I know where you live. Part of my self-orientation program," she added, picturing the scowl on his face as he thought of having his space invaded. "I told you, I like knowing what I'm getting into."

"And knowing my address helps?"

"Just part of the whole picture, Cavanaugh, just part of the whole picture."

Ramirez had been as invasive as she was. And yet, not quite the same way. He'd also never been remotely tempted to kiss Ramirez. The urge was still very much with him, getting in his way. "Anything else on that canvas I should know about?"

"Not that comes to mind," she told him cheerfully. "See you in twenty minutes."

She made it in fifteen.

Patrick lived in a modern, two-story condo in one of the newer residential areas in Aurora. That he owned property was in itself a surprise to her. From the bio she'd been given on him, she couldn't picture Patrick owning anything—not a pet, not a plant, certainly not a place to live. A home represented ties to something and the image he projected was of someone who wanted no ties to anything.

But she was learning that the image she'd gleaned from his department file didn't really do Patrick justice or cover nearly all the bases. Like the ties she'd discovered he had to his family. Or the fact that being with him in small, tight places did things to her respiratory system over and above the expected result that came of sharing oxygen.

After leaving her car in guest parking, she walked the short distance to his front door. The first thing she noticed was that, unlike a good many of his neighbors, Patrick's door had no wreath or any other sign of holiday decor on it.

No wreath, no lights, no token holly. This lack of festivity was definitely more in keeping with her image of Patrick Cavanaugh.

It struck her as sad.

She rang his bell. The door swung open a moment later. He was still buttoning his shirt. The obligatory tie was hanging out of his front pocket.

"You're early." Turning away, he picked up his gun and holster.

"Just three minutes." She peered into the house. "Can I come in?"

"No."

She raised an eyebrow in response.

"You're not going to be here long enough to come in."

Patrick was already reaching for his jacket and slipping it on. Maggi maneuvered around him to get a better view of the inside of the condo, stepping inside.

"Like you said, I'm early." The place looked neat. That surprised her. It was also relatively empty. That didn't.

Because he disliked it most, he put his tie on last. "You just want to snoop around."

She looked at him over her shoulder. A grin flashed. "Busted."

He tried to ignore the effect it had on him and tried to concentrate on the fact that she was yet again staging an invasion. "No, but that's what you're currently doing to a certain part of my anatomy."

Maggi barely paid attention to the protest. She swung around to face him. "You have no Christmas tree."

He knew he should be annoyed. Why he was amused made no sense to him. "Sharp. I can see why they made you a detective. With observation powers like yours, you could rise all the way to the top."

"But it's Christmas." Even her father put up a tree. He said it was to appease her, but she knew the tree made him think of her mother and the Christmases they had shared.

"Technically," he pointed out, "not for another few days." Patrick tried to remember the exact date on the calendar and couldn't. He glanced over to the wall next to the sink in the kitchen.

"So when are you going to put it up?"

Taking her by the arm, Patrick began to usher her out of the living room and toward the door again. "Does the twelfth of never ring a bell?" She had that look on her face, the one that could undo a knot the size of Baltimore. "Look, Mary Margaret, what do I want with a tree? There's one at my uncle's house. A big one," he emphasized. "That's where I go for Christmas."

"But you need a tree."

She was really getting worked up about this, wasn't

she? He found it oddly amusing. And kind of sweet. Not that he'd tell her. "Why?"

"Because it's a tradition."

He shrugged carelessly. "Maybe I'm not a lemming."

"This has nothing to do with going over a cliff—" Exasperation cut off her words. "What's wrong with you, don't you have a soul?"

For the first time since she'd met him, she heard Patrick laugh. The sound was warm and rich, embracing her like the feel of a sip of brandy going through her system on a particularly cold night. "You sound just like Patience."

"Patience. Your sister." She saw the affection in his eyes as he nodded. She knew it shouldn't mean anything to her to be compared to his sister, but it did. "I think I'd like to meet a female version of you."

He set her straight immediately. "Oh, no, Patience isn't anything like me. Fortunately for her," he said, surprising her. "She's the one who got all the 'soul' in the family. She's been after me for years to get a tree."

And he seemed to care a great deal about what his sister thought. Another surprise. "So why don't you?"

He shrugged again. "Too busy." On his way out the door, he stopped. "Wait, I forgot something."

"Your heart, Tin Man?" she suggested.

He gave her a reproving glance. "No, stay here."

The next moment, he disappeared into another room in the back. She was tempted to follow him but refrained. Instead, she stayed where she was, scanning his place.

She didn't like the thoughts finding their way into her head. The condo was new and she knew what decent houses went for in Aurora. This place was head and shoulders above decent. Not an easy thing to swing on even a detective's salary, given property taxes.

How did he afford a place like this?

There was no getting away from the conclusion, even though she wanted to. She was too good a cop to turn her back on it. Raising her voice, she decided to meet the challenge head-on.

"You've got a nice place here." She didn't bother trying to sound innocent. "Renting?"

"It's mine."

What little bit of hope she had evaporated like standing water in the hot sun. "How much did this set you back?"

Patrick walked out of the other room, a large red and blue wrapped box in his hands. His expression was dark. "Enough." He knew exactly what she was thinking and he resented it. "I also had enough after Patience and I sold our parents' home when my mother died." The house had too many bad memories for either one of them to want to live in it. Selling it was the only option they had.

She hadn't thought of that. "I didn't mean to imply—"

"Yes, you did." Angry, Patrick shoved a large box at her.

She stared at the glitter for a moment without saying anything. "What's this?"

"You asked me for a donation for the shelter's toy drive. Here's a donation." He snapped out his words like machine-gun fire. "It's one of those castles you build out of small building blocks. Good for girl or boy. The woman in the store wrapped it. Thought I'd save you the trouble."

Guilt tap-danced through her. She followed him outside. "I don't know what to say."

"Good." He slammed the door shut behind him. It locked automatically. "Keep it that way."

Chapter 15

Patrick wanted nothing more than to get on with the investigation into Ramirez's dealings, to find some kind of plausible explanation for the large deposits into the account bearing his wife's name.

Because the latter also bore the name of his old partner's late mother-in-law, he knew that kind of redemption of Ramirez's name was doomed. The excuse Ramirez had given his wife was flimsy, a lie for her to hold on to. Patrick knew Alicia loved her husband and didn't want to believe he was mixed up in something dirty.

He needed to get to the bottom of this, but because he wanted to carry out his investigation without attracting any undue attention, it had to be put on hold during work hours.

Like a racehorse pawing the ground at the starting gate, Patrick felt as if he was chafing at the bit, but there was nothing else he could do. Work had to come first.

He and McKenna were involved in a new homicide, one that mercifully wound up being open and shut. A young woman was found dead in her apartment, killed, it turned out, by the man who'd been stalking her. They had the suspect in handcuffs by the end of the day.

The incident made him think of Patience and the unwanted attention she'd garnered from the owner of one of her patients. Patience claimed that the whole thing had gone away after the man had seen a framed family photograph, the one in which they'd all worn their dress uniforms, but it didn't hurt to be too careful. She was the only sister he had.

He put in a call to her during the minimal lunch break he took, warning her to be careful. She gave him her word she would be. There were dogs barking in the background like a canine Greek chorus.

He knew that Patience took the situation a lot less seriously than he did. Patrick had a feeling she wasn't telling him everything, because she didn't want him to worry. However, he had no way of proving it. He hoped he was just being paranoid, but he strongly doubted it.

Some detective he made, he thought darkly now. Couldn't even catch his own sister in a lie.

With a sigh, he shut off the computer he rarely used. Outside the window, day was slipping gracefully into nightfall. Time to go home.

Maggi heard the click and looked Patrick's way. He'd been keeping her at arm's length since she'd stopped by to pick him up this morning. Nothing she said changed the scenario.

"Good work on the Miller case," Captain Reynolds

tossed the compliment their way as he walked past their desks.

"Thanks," Maggi murmured.

Cavanaugh, she noticed, said nothing, just barely nodding his head in acknowledgment. Of course, he didn't seem to need any kind of reinforcement, not like other mortals. He was in a class by himself.

Except that he took insults hard and she had insulted him this morning.

She had fences to mend.

"Want to go grab a beer?" she suggested, clearing off her desk. The squad room was almost empty now. All but one of the other detectives had gone home. She was vaguely aware that Reynolds had stopped to talk to the man.

"No."

"All right, I'll just drop you off home, then—"

He cut her off as he rose to his feet. "I've already got a ride."

Maggi sighed. He'd reverted to the way he was when she'd initially been coupled with him. Worse.

On her feet, she tried to block his way out. "Look, I'm sorry about this morning." She lowered her voice, afraid it might carry, knowing how much he hated having the smallest thing about his life made public. "I didn't mean I thought you were dirty. I guess I just got caught up in this whole conspiracy thing."

His eyes were flat, cold. "Apology accepted."

The hell it was. Maggi frowned as she watched him leave the squad room. "Doesn't sound it."

Barefoot, Patrick straddled the kitchen chair and set down the bottle he'd just gotten out of the refrigerator.

It took its place on the table next to the two empty bottles he'd finished off.

Thinking about the fact that Ed might have been on the take ate away at him.

How could he have misjudged someone so much?

He hadn't made that kind of a mistake since he'd thought of his father as being an honorable man. At least honorable in his own way. That image had been shattered when he'd accidentally overheard his father talking on the phone one day. As he stood in the shadows, listening, he heard his father try to convince Aunt Rose to run off with him. He'd been vaguely aware of some kind of trouble between Uncle Andrew and Aunt Rose. She had turned to his father just to vent. His father, always envious of what his two brothers had, had seen it as an opportunity for something more.

Whether that "something more" had ever happened, Patrick didn't know. All he knew was that he'd felt overwhelming disappointment that his father lacked the kind of family values, family loyalty he'd just taken for granted within the framework of the Cavanaughs. He remembered being disappointed in his aunt Rose, too, but then she'd gone missing shortly after that and things like blame and disappointment took a back seat to family grief.

Patrick took an extra long drag of his beer, savoring the ice-cold bitter brew as it flowed through his system. Looking to anesthetize himself.

He'd been wrong about his father and now it looked as if he was wrong about Ed, too. Showed what he knew. Nothing. Absolutely nothing.

He dragged a hand through his hair, finishing off the third bottle. Blinking, he looked down at the piece of paper on the table. He was working on a list of all the men he knew Ed had interacted with. Half-finished, the list was still long. Ramirez had had a lot of friends. And apparently some deadly enemies.

He heard the doorbell ring and groaned. He didn't feel like having company or talking to anyone. It was the middle of the week, not normally the time for visitors. But then, his cousins had a tendency to drop by without warning.

Maybe a little bit of company might be a good thing. He got up.

"Yeah, yeah, I'm coming," he called out as he heard the doorbell peal for the third time.

He wasn't prepared for what he saw when he opened the door.

It was a tree—a tall, skinny tree, its branches straining against the hemp that had been wound tightly around it. If the tree had taken on human form, he would have classified it as a runway model, all angles and malnutrition.

"What the hell?"

"Well, don't just stand there," a voice from behind the tree retorted. "Let me in."

Now it made sense. Sort of. "Mary Margaret, is that you?"

She peered around the tree she was holding. "Unless you believe in talking trees."

He had no idea why he felt like laughing. He was still incensed over what she'd intimated. At least, it had made a good excuse to be incensed. And a good excuse to keep her at arm's length, where she belonged.

"After being partnered with you, I'm starting to believe anything is possible."

"Good. Now help," she instructed, pushing the tree in his direction.

Patrick caught it in time and dragged the tree over the threshold. It was surprisingly light. Glancing back in her direction, he saw that Maggi had a six-pack of beer in one hand and some kind of aromatic large bag in the other. There was a red dragon embossed on the side. Was the woman moving in?

"What the hell is all this?" he demanded.

"Well, this—" she held up the six-pack "—and this—" she raised the bag "—are peace offerings."

He was willing to accept that, even though he wasn't entirely sure what she thought she was making peace over. But he was more interested in finding out why the woman was dragging around a scrawny tree in her wake. "And the tree?"

"Is something you need. Kitchen this way?" She walked toward the left before he could give her an answer. Patrick leaned the tree against the wall and hurried after her.

He managed to get in front of her. "Why would I need a tree?"

Scooting around him, she set the six-pack down on the table, noting the presence of the three empty bottles. Good thing she'd brought food, she thought. The man obviously had his sights set on a liquid dinner tonight.

"A Christmas tree," she corrected.

"A scrawny one," he pointed out.

"I tried to find a better one," she told him. "But it's almost Christmas. You wait too long, you have to settle."

He didn't want one in the first place. "Answer the question. Why the hell do I need a tree? A Christmas tree," he corrected himself before she could.

Maggi stopped unpacking the take-out dinner she'd brought and faced him. "Because Christmas is about love and forgiveness and being nice to people around you, I thought if you had a tree, you might remember the rest."

The absolute nerve of the woman amazed him. He frowned and gazed at the tree leaning against his living room wall. "I suppose you expect me to go out and buy decorations for it."

"Nope, got those in the car. Extras," she explained when he looked at her incredulously. "I have trouble resisting buying ornaments. They get cuter every year." And she had no willpower when it came to that. Over the years she had collected more than enough to decorate two trees and still have ornaments left over. "So I thought I'd bring over some of them for you."

The woman obviously took no prisoners. Except for maybe him. "Think of everything, don't you?"

She grinned. "I try." She folded the empty bag and left it on the counter. "So, are we friends again?"

"We weren't friends before," he said.

Maggi could only shake her head. "You are a hard man, Patrick Cavanaugh." She motioned him to the door. "C'mon, help me bring in the decorations."

He debated putting his foot down about that, but there didn't seem to be any solid ground beneath it. She'd come this far. He supposed letting her decorate the damn thing wouldn't hurt. With a shrug, he growled an "Okay," and walked out the front door.

The moment he did, a shot rang out, whizzing by his head. Missing him by less than an inch. He instantly grabbed Maggi's arm and pulled her down, blocking her with his body, the extra service revolver he kept strapped to his calf out in his hand.

There was no second shot.

Patrick looked around. He thought he saw someone

running in the distance. On his feet, he started to give chase.

"Stay here," he tossed over his shoulder.

But Maggi was beside him, matching him footfall for footfall, her own service revolver in her hand. "I'm not a civilian, Cavanaugh."

"No, just a damn pain who never listens," he snapped.

A quick surveillance of the area turned up nothing beyond a teen couple necking in a car in the girl's driveway. By the look on their faces, Patrick had managed to scare ten years out of each of them. He withdrew with a curt apology.

Just then, someone peeled out of the development, tires screeching. Patrick was too far away to get off a clear shot, or even see a license plate. The car was dark, blending into the night. Even its make was obscured.

Disgusted, he holstered his gun. "Now what the hell was all that about?"

The first thing that popped into her head was that he was being set up. Someone had tried to sabotage his reputation and since that wasn't happening quickly enough, they had resorted to plan B, trying to eliminate him. Or maybe that was the original plan, she thought, remembering the circumstances behind Ramirez's death.

She bit back the urge to tell him what she was thinking. She couldn't do that without risking the operation. And if he suspected that she'd been sent by IA to investigate him, he'd probably never speak to her again. She didn't want to risk that, either.

Damn, but this assignment was tying her up in knots, leaving her feeling conflicted.

She speculated the only way left open to her.

"Maybe someone thinks we're getting too close to finding out something about Ramirez."

It made sense. And troubled him, but there was nothing he could do about it tonight. He blew out a breath, centering himself. "You said something about decorations."

His defensiveness was gone. Maggi smiled to herself. At least the shooter had managed to get her closer to Cavanaugh again. And that was a good thing.

"You don't have to do this, you know."

He was addressing the words to her posterior as she stood up on the ladder she'd had him get out of his garage. What the tree lacked in breadth it made up for in height and she intended to decorate every scrawny inch of it. When he'd hooted at it, she'd informed him that the tree needed love and she figured he and the tree would be good for each other.

She gave him the answer he knew she would.

"Yes, I do." Holding on to the top of the ladder, she turned around so she was looking down at him with her back against the steps. She liked being taller. It gave her a certain advantage. "I'm an optimist, but I don't believe in magic."

He didn't trust the ladder and stood holding it, more than vaguely aware that he was bracketing her thighs. "Magic?"

Something warm and soft stirred through her as she gazed down at him. The words, meant to be light, had trouble leaving her mouth at more than a measured pace. Things were happening inside her, things that shouldn't. And she was enjoying them far too much.

"Yes, as in decorations magically going on the tree

by themselves because you sure as hell aren't going to put them on."

Thoughts crowded in his head that had nothing to do with police work, or shift partners, or even Christmas. "Think you know me?"

She took a step down, then another, careful not to lose her footing.

Too late for that, Mag, she mocked herself.

She ran her tongue along her lips, trying to fight the dryness. "I know that much about you."

The ladder swayed a little as she took another step down. Patrick immediately tightened his hold. "Careful, the damn thing's rickety."

"That's okay, so am I." The words all but floated from her mouth.

She was too close to him. Too close to do anything sensible. She could hear a rushing in her ears and wondered if that was her blood, making a break for it.

Unable to help himself, to push away the sudden shaft of desire that shot through him, Patrick cupped her face with his hands and brought his mouth down to hers.

She'd lied to him when she'd said that she didn't believe in magic. Because magic was exactly what was happening to her now. Everything about the moment was magic. And it swept her up so quickly she had no time to brace herself against it, no time to fend it off. And no desire to.

"You don't feel rickety," he told her, drawing back before he lost his resistance. What he really wanted to do was tear her clothes from her body and make love to her until he'd hopefully had his fill and was over these feelings.

"I thought you were a better judge of situations than

that," she breathed. "My heart's about to hammer out of my chest. Hasn't pounded like this since I tackled that perp running out of the First National Bank in 'Frisco."

As if to show him, she took his hand and placed it over her heart.

Maggie looked up into his eyes. Her pulse quickened, her loins ached.

Time stood perfectly still.

It was incredible. The woman was the last word in independence, in whatever the female version of macho was, and yet, right now, as he touched her, she felt delicate, frail.

His eyes held hers, knowing he should stop it here before it went any further.

Not that he didn't want to.

The fissures in the walls around his resolve doubled in size, widened until there was nothing to hold the dam back.

Patrick brought his mouth down to hers again. When she leaned her body into his, he knew there was no turning back.

Caution and clothing went flying, tossed to the winds on an impulse that had been waiting in the wings from the very first, waiting for the right unguarded moment. And it had arrived.

Restraint was a byword with him. Every movement he'd ever orchestrated had been carefully thought out, viewed from both sides, sometimes quickly, sometimes slowly, but always examined.

Until now.

Now he wasn't thinking. He was feeling, reacting. Wanting. There was something about this woman that got to him, that intoxicated him beyond logic and negated any good judgment he had. He'd unconsciously felt it from the first moment he'd laid eyes on her. His sense of survival had urged him to try to get her replaced, to push her away. But everything had failed.

And now there was no turning back.

He was glad.

Glad because she tasted like heaven and heaven had seemed like such a faraway place. It had never been anything he'd ever encountered. But she tasted of the promise of heaven and salvation and he wanted both more than he could say.

Maggi yanked the pullover he'd had on, dragging it off his torso and arms and pitching it carelessly aside. She had no idea where because all her attention was riveted to working the jeans off his hips. The black briefs he wore went down with them. He kicked them aside, his body cleaving to hers. He'd already made short work of her sweater and jeans before she'd ever started on his garments.

That left them both nude. Except for the hardware. A by-product of being on the force.

A mischievous smile played on her lips as she looked at him. *Now there was a sexy shot.* "Your weapon, Cavanaugh."

He glanced down. "Oh, you mean my gun."

Kneeling, he quickly removed it, then looked up at her with a grin that she found bone-scrapingly sexy. She wanted him more than she'd thought possible. She tried to chalk it up to abstinence, but knew she was lying to herself. It wasn't the lack of it that made her want to make love, it was the man.

The look in his eyes went right through her. "Since I'm already down here, let me do yours."

Maggi felt as if someone had struck a match and thrown it at her as she nodded.

Patrick unstrapped the holster from her thigh, slipping the leather from her. He carefully placed her secondary weapon beside his own, away from the field of play.

She expected him to rise. He remained where he was, his hands lightly resting on either side of her hips. Maggi felt herself begin to throb even as she moistened.

The next second she was digging her hands into his hair as he opened up gates leading to an ecstasy she'd never experienced before. Lines of flames shot through her like wildfire as she felt his tongue anointing the tender flesh between her legs. And then he was thrusting it in and out, causing shock waves to oscillate all through her.

She reached a climax before she fully realized what he was doing.

Clutching at his shoulder, Maggi dragged him back up to her level. "You don't play fair," she breathed.

"I don't 'play' at all."

He sealed his mouth to hers.

Damn it, he shouldn't want her this way, shouldn't surrender control over his actions to this formless thing that demanded fulfillment. But logic had no place here. Only desire.

The imprint of her body against his as he pressed her to him made him wild. He'd been hoping that once he knew he could have her, whatever he was grappling with would dissipate, go away. Not grow.

And yet it did.

With every kiss, every movement, the passion grew until it threatened to consume him completely. He should have taken her in his bedroom. He took her on the living room floor instead, beside a tree he'd never wanted, lit with lights he'd never asked for.

Kissing her until she was little more than pulsating flesh that twisted and writhed beneath him, he grasped her hands and held them above her head. He took her mouth, savaging it with kisses as he drove himself into her.

The soft sound that escaped her lips filled him with a sweetness. It drove the savagery away.

He stopped for a moment, looking down at her, not knowing what to think, not wanting to think at all.

Watching her eyes, he moved slower, then faster, until he wasn't conscious of making any effort at all. The effort made him. The moment made him. And he raced to embrace it. With her.

Chapter 16

Utterly exhausted, Patrick shifted his weight off Maggi. He felt as if he barely had the strength left for even that. The woman had completely drained him.

Who would have thought?

"If I'd known that was part of the tree-trimming ceremony, I might have gotten a Christmas tree a long time ago," he said.

In response to his carefully measured out words, he heard her laughing. Felt the sound bubbling up within her as her body moved against his.

He'd never known that listening to laughter could feel so good. So sexy.

Without thinking, he gathered her closer to him. "You find that funny?"

Maggi planted an elbow on his chest and raised herself up to look at him. A curtain of blond hair swept along his skin, tightening his gut. Laughter seemed to radiate from every part of her.

"I can't believe we just did this."

Neither could he.

Nor could he believe that he wanted her again. Just looking at her made his body hum, his cravings multiply. Why wasn't he sated? They'd just made love for longer than he could ever remember doing it. He should have been more than satisfied and on his way to being over whatever it was that kept drawing him to her.

What the hell was wrong with him? Why was she affecting him this way?

There was no answer to his question. Logic had left on winged feet.

"Then I guess we'll just have to review the evidence." Patrick cupped the back of her head with his hand and brought her mouth down to his.

This time, she was ready for it, braced, knowing that the wild ride ahead was going to sap her strength and send her mind reeling. This time, she wanted not to be alone in that first car on the roller coaster as it plunged and climbed its way ever faster over the slopes and peaks.

She kissed him back, long, hard. Sensuously.

The ride began slower, and by the time it was over, had brought the blood rushing through their veins to a new fever pitch.

Whatever he did, she did him one better, until by the end, Maggi knew his body better than he did. And in her heart, she had a feeling that he knew hers far better than she ever could. He had found pulse points she hadn't known existed, sent her flying almost out of control with a pass of his hand, with the lightest trace of his lips.

Nothing was sacred, nothing overlooked. Knees, elbows, fingertips, not to mention the soft, sensitive flesh in areas designed for lovemaking and ecstasy.

She sought out his secret places, determined to render him almost mindless with desire and pleasure, the way he had her. And when he moaned, she knew she had him. The thrill she felt increased a hundredfold.

He'd had his share of sexual encounters, but this, this was something new, something he hadn't realized was out there. This didn't just bring with it the burst of a crescendo at the end. This brought something much more with it.

It brought feelings, and with them a sense of protectiveness that he neither wanted nor knew what to do with.

But there was more.

Making love with her released something inside of him. It was formless, without a name, but moved over him like a low-lying fog, claiming him, obliterating his senses.

He felt he was entering a dark alley with only one path of retreat and that was behind him. What was in front was an unknown. He had no idea where to point his weapon, how to protect himself. The uneasy feeling that he was being taken prisoner without being able to defend himself was all too real.

Lacing his fingers through hers, he suddenly switched places with Maggi and, as he watched her, drove himself into her. He saw a host of emotions wash over her face. The same kind that he felt echoing within his own chest.

It scared the hell out of him.

And then there was no time for thought, no time for fear. There was only the race to the final place, the one that released volleys of lights and made everything else insignificant.

When it came to claim him, he felt her arch her back, driving her hips up to his and knew that she had reached a climax with him.

The quest for oxygen commanded his full attention.

Maggi slid off his slick body, her own body damp with the dew of lovemaking. She hardly had the strength to lift her head. He'd taken everything out of her and she had valiantly tried to do the same to him.

She could only hope she had succeeded in some small measure.

But as the euphoria receded into the shades, the reality that came in its wake dragged out questions that were quick to assault her. What the hell was she doing here, making love with a man she was supposed to be investigating?

Had she lost her mind?

The simple answer was yes, but that didn't negate what she had to do—leave as soon as possible.

She felt cold suddenly. "I think I should be going. Just as soon as I find my legs," she qualified.

He didn't want her to leave. Didn't want her to move a muscle. His arm tightened around her without any thought on his part.

"They have to be around here somewhere. I know I saw you come in with them."

It was on the tip of his tongue to tell her she could stay. To ask her if she *would* stay. But the very fact that he wanted her to chased the words away from his lips. This couldn't go any further than it had already gone and if she stayed, it would. He knew it would.

Pivoting herself on her palms, her arms still bracketing him, Maggi glanced over her shoulder. "Oh, there they are."

She was trying desperately to be flippant, but every word she uttered took effort. She couldn't remember ever feeling this drained. Or this happy, as if her whole body was humming a tune.

Dangerous, this is dangerous, not to mention unethical. Damn it, Mag, what were you thinking?

She wished her mind would shut up and let her enjoy the moment, but she knew it wouldn't. She was too disciplined for that.

Where the hell had her discipline been a few minutes ago?

Struggling for control of the situation, Maggi pushed herself off. She reached for her clothes, wishing she had something to wrap around herself other than her dignity, which had serious holes in it right now.

Still she did what she could. Rising, she held her clothes against her and looked down at him, forcing a smug smile she didn't feel to her lips.

"Well, my work here is done." Patrick was still lying on the floor, watching her. Maggi found it difficult not to let her gaze roam. He had one hell of a magnificent body. "Bathroom?"

"Through there." He pointed to the left.

"Thank you," she mustered with as much regal control as she could. With that, she withdrew.

He couldn't tear his eyes away. The M.E. was right, he thought. She made one hell of an exit.

Maggi was the first one to arrive in the squad room the next day. After she'd left Patrick's house, she knew there was no way she was going to fall asleep so she'd stayed up writing a formal report to Halliday, detailing her findings.

One thing she knew for certain: The man was one hell of a lover. The only time she smiled was when she tried to envision the expression on Halliday's face if he read that line.

Sleep had all but eluded her entirely. Every time she would almost drift off, her brain would intrude. There was no denying that she'd broken more rules than she could count and severely compromised herself and the operation. Moreover, she'd tainted any testimony she might offer on Patrick's behalf.

How the hell could she have slept with him?

How could she not? something within her whispered. That had to be the best time she'd ever had with or without her clothes on.

Her mind not on the report on the screen, Maggi stared away. Too bad last night didn't mean anything. At least, not to him.

Not to her, either, she insisted.

The silent argument continued to ricochet back and forth in her brain. Neither side won points.

The moment Patrick walked in, she was on her feet, crossing to him as if she was an arrow shot from a bow. "I need to talk to you."

He looked at her, not quite certain what to expect. Once dressed, she'd bolted out of his house so quickly last night, he was sure she must have broken some kind of speed record. He'd wanted to call her back. Drag her back. But common sense had finally prevailed and kept him where he was.

He'd slept poorly, dreaming of her. She'd be there one minute, gone the next and he'd spend the rest of the dream looking for her. Over and over again. He had no idea what it meant, only that he shouldn't have let last night happen.

There was an expression on her face now he couldn't fathom. He hated being in the dark.

"Okay." He followed Maggi to the coffee area. There were others in the squad room, but they were all in their cubicles, working. Still he lowered his voice before asking, "What's up?"

Maggi took a breath before answering. "I don't want you to get the wrong idea about last night."

His expression gave nothing away. "And what would be the wrong idea?"

"That it was about something." She thought she saw someone coming their way and paused, but the detective walked out. "It was just sex, pure and simple."

He thought of last night. He'd never known the human body could bend like that. She'd left him in awe. "There was nothing pure about it."

"What I mean is that there're no strings, no consequences."

Did she make love like that to every man? An unaccountable jealousy slashed through him before he regained control over himself.

"Aren't there?"

"No." Why did Cavanaugh look so annoyed? "I thought you'd be happy. Isn't that what all men want? No consequences?"

Until the second she'd uttered the words, he would have said yes. Would have thought that *was* what he wanted. But now that she was acting so cavalier about it, he felt his pride wounded.

"Don't presume to know what I want, or lump me in with everyone else."

"I didn't. I don't." She tried to find high ground as

everything sank around her. "It's just that I didn't want you to think there was anything going on."

"I don't think that."

A tiny salvo of regret lodged itself in her chest. *Isn't this what you want? What's wrong now?* "Good."

"Fine," he snapped. "Are we done with this conversation?"

"Completely." Her voice rose. Two could play this game. "Time's up. Nickel's been used."

He frowned. "If you ask me, your brain's been used and whoever used it forgot to put it back."

About to utter an equally mindless retort, she stopped herself and looked at him. "Are you angry with me for some reason?"

"Angry?" Yanking his mug to him, Patrick poured himself a cup of coffee. Even as he did so, he knew he was going to regret it. The coffee here could be used to retar worn-out roads. He glared at Maggi. "Why would I be angry with someone who insists on telling me she knows what I'm thinking?"

Without thinking, Maggi poured a cup for herself. Even as she did, she felt her stomach tightening in protest. "I wasn't insisting."

He laughed shortly. "Obviously you weren't on this side of the conversation."

She glared at him. He was such an ass. Why had she thought there were any feelings there? She wouldn't go to bed with him again if he were the last man on earth. In the galaxy.

"No, I was on the 'done' side." She closed her eyes, running her hand along her forehead. There were little men clog dancing inside her head. "You're giving me a headache."

He set his mug down, last night returning to him in

spades. He could feel his body responding and struggled to keep his thoughts in check. He only half succeeded. "You know the best thing for a headache?"

She raised her eyes to his and guessed at his answer, "A swift execution?"

She wasn't prepared to see the smile. Wasn't prepared for the way it went straight to her gut and unraveled her. "Hair of the dog that bit you."

"That's for a hangover."

His eyes shone as they washed over her. "Same principle." And then a stony expression took over his face as he saw the wary look come into her eyes. "Don't worry, Mary Margaret, I'm not about to jump your bones anytime the whim hits."

As if he could if she didn't want him to. But that was just the trouble. Even with all the obstacles she put in her way, even though she knew it was wrong, she still wanted him to. "I'm not worried about that."

He looked at her, puzzled. "Then what?"

She was worried about what he'd stirred up. About the way she'd compromised herself. And about the fact that she wanted to do it all again, every teeth-jarring second of it.

"Nothing," she bit off. Coffee in hand, she retreated to her desk on legs that were more than a little shaky.

What would Patrick say if he knew that he'd spent last night making love to someone whose primary function was not to be his partner, but to spy on him? Whose very existence in his life was a lie? At the very least, he would have felt betrayed and she couldn't blame him at all.

Maggi knew the right thing to do was to have herself removed from the case, but she refused to go that route. She wanted to clear Patrick's name. Every fiber of her being told her he was innocent of the charges lodged against him. At the very least, she owed him that much.

Patrick stood by the coffeemaker, staring at the back of her head as she returned to her cubicle. The best thing for him to do was go along with what she'd said. He didn't want ties and she was telling him that there weren't any.

So why did he feel so damn unsettled? So damn insulted?

Was it a matter of wanting what he couldn't have, or was it something else? But he'd never been like that before, never felt drawn to secure acquisitions. That just wasn't him.

But even as his mind counseled him to move along, to take the opportunity she'd offered him and forget this had ever happened, he felt himself resisting. Last night had been incredible. Since she didn't want anything permanent, what would it hurt to explore things a little further? To see if last night had been a fluke?

After a beat, he wandered over to her desk and perched on the edge of it. Her fingers flew madly across the keyboard. They moved even more wildly the second he sat down.

"Any faster and you're liable to melt them."

"They're heat resistant." He wasn't moving. She raised her eyes from the screen only because she dared herself to. "What's up?"

"I thought I'd do some nosing around, see if I can pick anything up." She knew he referred to looking further into Ramirez's dealings. "I want you to cover for me in case the captain comes looking around for me—"

"Why don't we just go to the local hangout after work? We're bound to hear more there. We're not in the middle of an investigation. It'd be kind of hard to explain where you are," she pointed out.

After a moment, Patrick nodded his agreement. Starting to rise, he stopped.

"Anything else on your mind?" Maggi asked.

About to say no, he changed his mind. Something was going on here, and he wasn't sure if he wanted it to or not. He figured if he could see how all this felt against a backdrop comprised of the people who meant something to him, then maybe he could make up his mind.

"What are you doing tomorrow night?"

"Christmas Eve? Wrapping a few last-minute presents, why?"

"My uncle Andrew has this Christmas party he's throwing. I thought maybe if you didn't have any other place to be..."

She wasn't sure just who was more stunned to hear the words, him or her. "Are you asking me out?"

"In," he corrected tersely. "I'm asking you in. Specifically, into my uncle's house. If you don't want to come—"

She cut him off. "I didn't say that." She'd heard about the parties Andrew Cavanaugh liked to throw. Boisterous, friendly. Warm. "Are you sure he wouldn't mind?"

"Not Uncle Andrew." He was willing to make book on that. His uncle was always after the next generation to settle down with someone. If he walked in with a woman, Andrew would be rendered speechless. At the moment, because of the improbability of the situation, the idea tickled Patrick. "He always says the more people, the better."

She gave up trying to concentrate on what she was

doing and pushed the keyboard away. "So you're trying to fill a quota?"

"Yes, no." She was getting him all tangled up again. He shouldn't have gone with impulse. Impulse wasn't his forte. "Damn it, woman, I'm inviting you to a Christmas party. You can come or not come—your choice."

Disgusted with himself and the way he was suddenly tripping over his own tongue, he began to walk away.

"Okay," she called after him.

Patrick stopped and slowly turned around. "Okay what?"

Because she didn't want anyone else listening, she got up and crossed to him. "Okay, I'll come. Do you want to give me the time and directions?"

She made it sound as if they were meeting a witness or going undercover. "Eight o'clock. And I'll pick you up."

"You don't have to...."

He blew out a breath. "I said I'll pick you up so I'll pick you up." He pinned her with a look. "Are you always this difficult?"

"No." Her mouth curved. "Not always." She searched his face for a clue. "Are you sure about this?"

"I wouldn't have invited you if I wasn't. I don't do or say things I don't want to."

Her grin grew wider as a warm feeling filtered through her. Telling herself that going to a party at Andrew Cavanaugh's was all in the line of duty, that maybe she would get more insight into Patrick that way, was a crock and she knew it. The upshot of the matter was that she was asking for trouble, but she couldn't help it. The temptation of seeing him surrounded by relatives was just too great.

"Okay, then."

"Cavanaugh, McKenna," the captain called out. Standing in the doorway of his office and holding a piece of paper aloft, he waved them over. "We've got another body."

Back to reality. Maggi sighed. There was something extra sad about having to deal with murder around the holidays.

"Whatever happened to "Tis the season to be jolly'?" Maggi asked.

"Some people have different ways of getting jolly," Patrick speculated.

She was already on her way to the captain's office. "That's got to be it."

Maggi's room looked as if a fashion tornado had been through it. Every dress she owned had been taken out and tried on in front of her mirror before joining the heap. Some had been unearthed three times before being permanently discarded.

In the end, she'd settled on her first choice. A curve-hugging electric blue velvet dress that came down to her ankle and was slit up the front well past her knees. It had a high collar, was cut to show off her arms and plunged beguilingly almost to her waist in the back. Her hair was down and her morale up as she surveyed the end result in the mirror.

She'd just slipped on her four-inch heels when she heard the doorbell. It took her longer than she was happy about to get to the door. But it was worth it once she opened it.

Patrick look one look at her and whatever he'd been about to say apparently vanished.

She grinned at the silent compliment. "Your mouth is hanging open, Cavanaugh."

He could feel the itch starting again. The one that had her name all over it. Walking in, he did a complete three-sixty around her. "You clean up good."

"There's that silver tongue again." She could feel herself beaming and told herself she was behaving like an idiot. "Thanks."

Walking in, he looked around. "Hey, it doesn't look like a toy factory exploded in here anymore."

Picking up her coat, she started to slip it on. "That's because I took all the toys in after work last night."

Patrick moved behind her, helping her with her coat when one of the sleeves got stuck. She looked up at him in surprise.

"How did you get started with that, collecting toys?" he clarified.

She'd been doing it for three years now. First up in San Francisco, then here. "I needed something to help balance out what I saw going on in the streets." She picked up her small clutch purse and headed for the front door. "There's a lot of reaffirmation to be found in the eyes of a child hugging a toy that they never expected to have even in their wildest dreams." She paused to lock the door. "It reminds me that there are more good guys than bad in this world."

He surprised her by taking her arm. "I wouldn't have thought you needed reminding."

"Even Pollyanna needs her batteries recharged once in a while."

"Pollyanna?"

He'd parked in the last spot available in guest parking. As they walked, the wind played with the ends of her hair, whipping them around. "Disney movie about a chirpy kid who only saw the good in everything."

Patrick opened the passenger side for her. "And you didn't star in it?"

"The part went to Hayley Mills." She didn't bother adding that it had been made before she was born.

"Who?"

She laughed and shook her head as she got in. "Never mind."

Patrick rounded the hood and got in on his side. "Just how much trivia is lodged in that brain of yours?"

Hiking her dress up in order to get comfortable, she noticed that Patrick made an effort not to look at the bit of thigh she'd accidentally flashed. It made her smile inside. "You really don't want to know."

The trouble was, Patrick thought as he started the car, he did.

Chapter 17

There were cars parked all up and down both sides of the cul-de-sac as well as two blocks in either direction. It was obvious to anyone who drove by that a party was in progress somewhere close by.

The site for the party wasn't difficult to pinpoint. Every light was on in the house in the middle of the block.

The sounds of muffled laughter emanated through the closed windows and door, beckoning them as they approached. A glance toward one of the windows on either side of the wreath-decorated door showed that the front room, and very probably the whole house, was filled to capacity and then some with celebrating people.

"Are you sure there's room for two more?" Maggi asked dubiously as Patrick knocked on the door.

The front door opened just then. The dark-haired

man in the doorway must have heard her. "Always room for more," he assured.

The man was tall and thin, and flecks of gray shot through his thick mane. So this was what Cavanaugh might look like in another two decades, Maggi thought. The man wore a light blue sweater that brought out his intense blue eyes. He was quick to take her hand, enveloping it in a strong, warm handshake.

"Andrew Cavanaugh," he introduced himself. "And you must be Maggi McKenna."

"Must be," she murmured as she eyed Patrick with no small surprise. "You mentioned me?"

Patrick shook his head. If anything, he was a shade more surprised than she at his uncle's greeting. "Not a word."

Andrew laughed, always tickled when he could still flex his detecting muscles. "Hey, just because I don't clock in every day at the station house anymore doesn't mean I don't still have my ways of finding things out."

As he spoke, he moved behind Maggi and began to help her with her coat. When the coat slipped off, he raised his eyes to his nephew's face and smiled his approval.

Andrew folded the coat over his arm and confided, "You have the honor of being the first woman Patrick's ever brought with him to a family function."

Tinged in long-suffering annoyance, Patrick's exhale was fairly audible.

"I think Uncle Brian's looking for you." He pointed to another man in the distance.

"We're going to have a nice long talk, you and me," Andrew promised Maggi before he slipped away with her coat.

The din around them was warm and comforting.

She'd always wished she was part of a large family and when she'd fantasized what holidays would be like, they'd been exactly like this.

"I like him."

Patrick lifted one shoulder in a half shrug. "Yeah, he's a great guy. Talks too much sometimes."

She gazed up at him, smiling. A collection of feelings danced through her. She let them dance. For now. "Not like some people."

He wasn't about to get drawn into any kind of discussion about his so-called shortcomings. He'd brought her here for one reason. To talk himself out of what he was starting to feel. He wanted to find lasting fault with her. So far, his uncle wasn't helping.

"Want something to drink?"

"Sounds good to me." As he turned to walk to the kitchen, she was quick to follow in his wake.

The kitchen proved to be currently the only room in the house that didn't look as if it was about to burst at the seams. She watched Patrick rummage through the refrigerator with no hesitation. He seemed more relaxed here than she'd ever seen him.

"You look at home here."

"I am." Taking out a fresh tray of ice cubes, he deposited them into the depleted bowl on the table, then refilled the tray with water before putting it back into the freezer. "I liked staying here better than in my own house. There was laughter here." Realizing he was exposing too much, he abruptly stopped talking. Instead, he nodded at the array of bottles on the table beside the bowl of ice cubes. "What'll you have?"

"White wine'll be fine."

He poured a glass for her, then selected red wine for himself.

Maggi smiled as she brought the wine to her lips. "What, no beer?"

"Beer's for everyday." He studied her as he spoke, wondering if this had ultimately been a mistake, bringing her here. "Wine's for special occasions."

"And whiskey's for drowning your sorrows." The statement came out of nowhere and she really had no idea why she said it. Or why he suddenly looked so annoyed, so distant.

"I don't drink whiskey."

She'd obviously stumbled into a sensitive area. "Sorry."

"No, I'm the one who's sorry," he said ruefully. There'd been no call for his harsh tone. She was just talking. No way could she have known what his life had been like, growing up with a functioning alcoholic for a father. "Didn't mean to snap at you. My father drank whiskey." A sense of self-preservation had him avoiding her eyes as he spoke. If he saw pity there, he didn't know if he could trust his reaction. "It was his oblivion of choice, which would have been fine if it had obliterated him. But a lot of times, getting drunk would just set him off. Some men get silly when they drink. Some get mean."

It wasn't hard to read between the lines. "And your father was the latter."

"Yeah." Even after all this time, it was a difficult thing for him to admit.

He didn't have to draw her a map. The subject was painful for him. Maggi abandoned it.

"So, was your uncle right?" He looked at her, puzzled. "Am I your first?"

He thought about the other night. She couldn't be talking about that. "What?"

"Am I the first one you ever brought to a family gathering?" she enunciated slowly.

He made an impatient face. "I don't keep track of those kind of things."

Yes you do, but you don't want to admit it. The warm feeling that slid over her was partially blocked by the specter of guilt that cast a shadow over everything in her life. None of this could go forward, she reminded herself. Because it was rooted in lies. Her lies.

Maggi jumped subjects again. She looked toward the threshold. Several people entered the kitchen. Someone had made a joke in the next room and a volley of laughter was heard. "Lot of people here. They're not all relatives, are they?"

He knew that to Uncle Andrew, sometimes it felt that way. "Hardly." Taking her arm to move her out of the way as more people came in search of libation, he ushered her into the living room. "There are eleven Cavanaugh cousins, counting my sister and me, and of course there's Uncle Andrew and Uncle Brian. The rest are assorted friends, mostly from the police force, but there're a few judges and people from the D.A.'s office. My cousin Janelle is an assistant D.A."

She tried to recall if she'd ever heard the name Janelle Cavanaugh. "Is she the only one who isn't on the police force?"

"Just her and Patience. Patience is a vet."

"Really? I love animals." Maggi looked around at the sea of people in the living room and the section of the family room she was privy to. She tried to find a woman who looked like a female version of Patrick. "Is she here?"

His brows drew together. "Yeah, she's here."

God, but he sounded guarded. What did he think she

was going to do, pump the woman for childhood stories about him?

"Do I get to meet her, or are you going to shove me into a box if she comes close?"

He made no effort to locate his sibling for her. Instead, he downed the rest of his drink, then set the glass on a nearby table. "What do you want to meet my sister for?"

"Because I'm your partner." Maybe fair exchange was the way to get him to relax. "I'll introduce you to my father if you drop by tomorrow."

"I don't know—"

The moment she'd said it, she knew she wanted him to come. No matter what the end result of all this was going to be, she wanted him to spend Christmas with her. "Tit for tat, Cavanaugh. I came to your family gathering, you can come to mine. Only difference is there'll be a lot more elbow room." Sold on the idea, Maggi was not about to take no for an answer. "Three o'clock. Bring your sister. I'm making a turkey and you can help us have fewer leftovers."

He didn't feel like standing in the middle of his uncle's house arguing with her. Things could be worked out later, when there was less than half the town within earshot.

"Okay, maybe. If she's not busy," he qualified.

"If she is, you can come by yourself. Unless you've made other plans." She looked up at him.

His uncle always made Christmas dinner, but he knew Uncle Andrew would understand if he went to Maggi's for Christmas. "No, no other plans."

"Patrick? Patrick, is that you?" Maggi turned around to see a petite young woman with Patrick's mouth approaching them. She had flame-red hair and her green eyes were wide with surprise. "I didn't recognize you with a woman standing next to you." Her eyes making a quick assessment, she smiled broadly as she put out her hand to Maggi. "Hi, I'm this big lug's younger, more attractive sister, Patience."

"I'm Maggi McKenna, his—"

"Partner," Patience completed in surprise. Her grin widened into one of glee. "Yes, I know." Her eyes shifted to her brother. "She doesn't look like a pain in the butt, Patrick," she observed innocently.

Patrick blew out a breath. The verdict was in. Coming here had *not* been a good idea. "Patience never learned to think before she spoke," he growled as he glared at his sister.

"That's okay, I like spontaneous," Maggi told the younger woman. She felt herself hitting it off with Patience instantly. "I get to find out a lot more that way."

"So, how do you like working with my brother?" Patience shifted so that her body blocked Patrick's. "You can be honest. I had to grow up with him."

Maggi crossed the minefield cautiously. "It's interesting."

Patience glanced over her shoulder at her brother. She nodded her approval. "Tactful, too. I think this one's a keeper, big brother." She turned back to Maggi. "Most of his partners start talking to their guns by the second week. Transfers usually come by the second month."

"Can't budge her with a crowbar," Patrick muttered as he picked up another wineglass. It was hours before he had to drive home. Right now he was thinking that he'd done smarter things in his life. Bringing Maggi here was a mistake.

Patience leaned into Maggi. "You hang in there,

girl," she cheered the other woman on. "He's got a rough surface, but once you scratch it, there's a pussycat underneath."

Maggi laughed. "I was thinking more along the lines of a mountain lion."

"Oh?" Patience raised an interested eyebrow in Maggi's direction. She looked from the woman to her brother and then smiled impishly. "Excuse me, I think I need some more wine."

"Less," Patrick informed her tersely as she started to walk away. "You need less wine."

Patience shook her head. "He never stops trying to boss me around. I'm twenty-six years old, Patrick," she told him fondly, then brushed a kiss across his cheek, "and can stand on my own two feet."

"Too much wine and you'll wind up not standing at all," he called after his sister's retreating form.

When he looked back at Maggi, she had that cat-got-into-the-cream look on her face.

"I'm glad you brought me. I'm finding out a lot about you." When he scowled at her, she just kept on talking. "For instance, I never would have thought you were the protective type."

Definitely a bad idea. Next time he had an impulse, he was going to sit on it until it passed. "I didn't bring you here so that you could spin theories about me."

She cocked her head. "Why did you bring me here?"

He struggled against a very strong desire that could not be acted upon here. Fortunately. "Does everything have to have a reason with you?"

Maggi's expression was the very personification of innocence. "I thought you liked logic."

He reached for the glass in her hand. "Let me go refill your glass."

Maggi looked down at her glass. "It's not empty yet."

But Patrick made his claim. He needed a couple of minutes to himself. Away from her. "No rule that it has to be." With that, he walked off.

Maggi sighed, staying where she was.

"Never saw him this skittish before. He must really like you."

The deep male voice was right behind her. Maggi turned around and found herself gazing up into Andrew's eyes. She shook her head. He read far too much into this. "I think I just rub him the wrong way."

"Then he wouldn't have brought you here, would he?"

"I'm afraid I really don't know quite what your nephew is capable of." She shrugged half-helplessly.

For now, Andrew decided to leave the subject alone. It was enough that Patrick had brought her. If it was meant to be, the rest would work itself out. Maybe with a little help from him, but not yet. All in all, she was a lovely young woman, just the kind he'd envisioned for his nephew. Her being in law enforcement didn't hurt, either.

Andrew regarded her thoughtfully. "McKenna, I used to know a McKenna. Matthew McKenna. Great cop."

Pleasure lit up within her. It always did when she heard something nice about her father. "Thank you, I'll tell him you said that. He's my father."

Andrew laughed, pleased. "Small world. Tell him hello for me. Better still, bring him around sometime." He gestured about the teeming area. "Always room."

She didn't want to get ahead of herself.

What ahead? Once reports are filed and he finds out what you've been up to, you're never going to see him again. He'll make sure of it.

She smiled politely. "Thank you, I really appreciate the invitation, but I think that depends on how Patrick feels."

He understood her reticence. Patrick was not always the easiest man to get along with. "He's a good kid. Turned out all right seeing as how he was always butting his head against a wall."

Her interest piqued, she looked at the older man. "Excuse me?"

Andrew couched it as well as he could. "My brother Mike had trouble with the ground rules when it came to raising kids. He never realized that you needed to praise 'em as well as correct them." He nodded at a late arrival who called out to him. "Nothing Patrick did was ever good enough. A lot of kids turn out bad with that kind of background."

"But he had you." Her observation caught him by surprise, but as he started to demur, Maggi said, "Anyone can see how he feels about you. Personally, I think you worked miracles with him." She kept an eye on the kitchen doorway, waiting for Patrick to return. She didn't want him to hear her talking to his uncle about him. "When I first met him, I wouldn't have guessed that he had any family ties at all."

"He runs deeper than most people know," Andrew told her.

Just then, she saw Patrick working his way toward them. He held a drink in each hand. He'd not only topped off her glass, but gotten a new one of his own as well. "I think I see my drink coming."

One of the things Andrew attributed his longevity to was his keen sense of survival. "I'd better slip away before he thinks we're conspiring against him." He smiled at her. "Nice talking to you."

By the time she said, "Same here," Andrew had already disappeared into the crowd.

But not soon enough for Patrick to miss his presence. He handed Maggi her glass. "What were you and Uncle Andrew talking about?"

She surprised herself with how easily she could slip into a lie.

"My dad." Maggi consoled herself with the fact that she hadn't told him a complete lie. Andrew *had* mentioned her father. "The two of them worked together a time or two."

Patrick groaned.

She didn't think what she'd said merited that kind of response. "What's wrong?"

"Cousins, six o'clock. A whole flock of them."

Before she knew it, Patrick took her hand and ushered her toward the patio door and the yard that lay beyond. But their path of escape was cut off. Too many bodies in the way to reach the exit in time.

His cousins descended on him before he ever had a chance.

Left with no choice, Patrick surrendered. He introduced her to his uncle Andrew's daughters, Callie, Teri and Rayne and braced himself.

The next five hours slipped by faster than she thought possible. And then she was saying good-night, promising to return some other day as Patrick all but hurried her into his car.

She didn't stop smiling all the way to her house, but

she had to admit, when they arrived there, she half expected Patrick to stop his car only long enough for her to get out. When he cut off the engine and walked her to her door, she knew she believed in the miracle of Christmas.

Maggi took out her key. "I had a wonderful time, Cavanaugh. Thanks for inviting me."

"You already said that," he reminded her. "In the car."

The man did not take thanks graciously, she thought. "Maybe it bears repeating."

There was a leaf in her hair. She'd brushed against a tree branch getting into his car. Patrick removed it, his fingers touching her hair. Needs rose a little higher. "And maybe you're just nervous."

Breathe, Mag, breathe. "What would I have to be nervous about?"

He nodded at the door behind her. He noticed she wasn't opening it. "Maybe you're afraid I'll ask myself in."

"And maybe I'm afraid you won't," she countered.

Somehow his hands found themselves around her waist. Even through the coat, she felt small. "Anybody ever tell you you're pushy?"

"I get that all the time." She took a breath. *Mistake number five hundred and twelve.* "So, would you like to come in?"

Yes, his brain responded. Which was exactly why he tried to refuse. "It's late. I'd better not."

He was wavering, she could see it. He was as uncertain about all this as she was. Two people in a boat made out of paper, approaching the rapids. She turned her face up to his. "Whatever you say."

He started to leave, he really did. His foot was poised

to pivot away from her and take the first step that would lead him from the apartment door to his car.

But somehow, he couldn't push off. Not when the moonlight was glistening along her lips. Not when every fiber of his being wanted him to kiss her.

"How come you don't have any mistletoe?"

She blinked. Had she heard him right? "What?"

"In your doorway. You have the door gift-wrapped with a wreath smack in the middle, but you don't have any mistletoe."

"I thought it might be overkill." She raised herself up ever so slightly, bringing her mouth even closer. Tantalizing him. "But if you'd like, you could pretend there's a mistletoe hanging right there." She pointed overhead.

He never took his eyes off her. "Works for me."

The next moment, he'd enveloped her in an embrace that shut out the world and opened the door to a far more intimate, dangerous place.

Chapter 18

As he assaulted her senses with openmouthed kisses, Patrick took the key from her. Though it felt as if his hands never left her body, somehow he managed to open her front door.

The instant he did, he moved them inside, away from prying eyes. She heard the door shut, felt the warm flare of intimacy taking hold.

The whole room was spinning as if she'd consumed more than her share of alcohol instead of the very little that she had. Maggi drew her head back, dragging in the air she so badly needed.

Something was happening here, she thought. Something very special. She didn't want to name it.

Maggi draped her arms around his neck. "Smooth," she commented, as her eyes indicated the door.

He turned on the light. He wanted to see her, all of her.

The soft nap of the velvet aroused him as it moved against his palms.

"Necessary." Where was the zipper on this thing? He couldn't find one. "You don't want to be arrested on Christmas Eve for indecent exposure."

Unable to hold back, Maggi rained kisses on his face, his throat. The eagerness built. Her heart started to hammer faster again. "Am I going to be indecently exposed?"

"Just as fast as I can figure out how to get this dress off you," he breathed.

Maggi took a step back. She smiled up into his eyes as she reached behind her neck and undid three tiny hooks that held her gown close to her. The two ends parted, sighing as they slid from her shoulders.

Patrick felt his body tighten like a string being drawn across the bridge of a violin. He tugged on the fabric still hugging her waist. The top of her dress sagged the rest of the way down to her hips. He placed his hands over them, bringing Maggi closer to him as his mouth covered hers.

The velvet moved from her hips and sank to the floor. When he finally looked at her an eon later, she stood before him wearing only her heels and a small gold locket around her neck.

Perfect.

Swallowing did nothing to alleviate the dryness in his mouth.

"Nothing indecent about this," he murmured.

The look in his eyes made her feel beautiful. And so eager she could barely stand it. Her hands flew as she unbuttoned, unzipped and pulled, bringing him to the same stage of undress as her within several hard heartbeats.

The rest became a blur of pleasuring, of reexploring and reclaiming. It was both familiar and new. And very, very special.

Trembling, she cleaved her body to his. Soft against hard. Desire spiked through her like an erratic pulse. She was certain he was going to take her right there, before the darkened Christmas tree. Heat traveling through her at lightning speed, she reached for him.

He chose that moment to sweep her from the floor and pick her up in his arms. His voice was low, raspy. "Your bedroom."

She wasn't even sure if she'd heard him. There was this rushing noise in her ears again and all she wanted was to make love with him right here, right now.

"What?"

"Your bedroom, woman," he growled. He didn't want to take her a second time on the floor, as if he was some kind of animal that couldn't contain himself. The least he could do was offer her the nicety of a bed. "Where is it?"

"Where I left it." For just a beat, her mind went blank. "Back there." She pointed vaguely to the rear, then framed his face with her hands as she kissed him hard, excitement racing through her at speeds so great Maggi didn't think she would ever catch her breath again.

As she felt him cross the threshold, she remembered the state in which she'd left the room. There were clothes all over the bed and draped on the chairs.

"It's messy," she warned.

"It's about to get messier."

Without looking, he used his elbow to clear away a space as he laid her down. The next second, he was there beside her, his body twining with hers.

She had no time to protest. Patrick's mouth was over hers, his hands sweeping along her body, making it hum songs she never thought it knew.

Clothes tumbled to the floor as she and Patrick twisted and turned, finding new places along each other's bodies, finding new highs.

She wanted this to go on forever. No tomorrows, no yesterdays; they were both framed in lies. All she wanted was now. Forever now.

Now was pure.

She tightened around him when he entered her, lifting her hips from the bed, losing herself entirely in the act. Praying that he would remember this moment when the rest happened.

"You keep looking at your watch, Mag-pie. You still have something in the oven?"

Preoccupied, Maggie had entered the kitchen to get a bottle of cider from the refrigerator. A few feet away was a long dining room table, formally set. Twelve close friends, both her father's and hers, milled around, catching up and waiting for dinner to be served.

But Patrick wasn't among them.

He's not coming. What did you expect? Flowers? Christmas presents? Snap out of it, Mag. You're a modern woman, not some Victorian wuss.

Her hormones were all over the board today. She felt like crying, like laughing. Like running to the window to watch for him. Like throwing up because she was so nervous.

All morning, she'd been completely out of synch. She chalked it up to rushing around so much. But she'd wanted everything to be perfect.

As if it mattered. The people out there didn't care. They were her friends.

And he was...

He was a definite unknown in all this.

Patrick had left her apartment shortly before two, despite the fact that she'd harbored the secret hope he would spend the night. But that would have meant waking up next to her on Christmas morning. Too much commitment on his part, she supposed.

Apparently so was showing up for Christmas dinner.

She turned around, sparkling cider bottle in hand. She wasn't about to lie to her father, even if she couldn't tell him the full story.

"No, Dad, I thought maybe my partner and his sister would show up." She closed the door. "I invited them over."

Matthew quietly studied his daughter as she spoke. "So you're getting along with him, this new partner of yours?"

She thought of last night. Of the way Cavanaugh had made her body sing. "Yes, Dad, I'm getting along with him."

Matthew's eyes never left his daughter's face. Something in her voice gave him pause. "But it's complicated, isn't it?"

She sighed, shaking her head, an amused smile on her lips. "Once in a while I wish you were a little less intuitive."

The microwave oven bell went off. Since he was closer, he opened the door and looked in. The rolls were ready. "I have to be. You never tell me anything. When you were a girl, you had all those girlie secrets of yours and I wasn't allowed in. Now that you're on the force, it's even worse."

She brushed a kiss across his cheek impulsively. She was more grateful for his existence in her life than she could ever put into words. "You know I can't talk about a case."

"I thought we were talking about your partner—" Matthew's eyebrows drew together. The light came on. "He's your case? You're working with Mike Cavanaugh's kid, aren't you?"

"You know I am."

She looked at her watch again. Cavanaugh was more than half an hour late. Something told her he wasn't going to show up no matter how long she held dinner. Maybe last night had scared him off. God knows the teeth-jarring intensity of making love with him scared the hell out of her. Even so, she had to resist the temptation to call him and demand to know why he was standing her up. If she did that, he'd have an inkling that having him over for dinner meant something more to her than another place setting at the table. The less she gave away, the better.

A little late for that, wouldn't you say, Mag?

She bet the bastard hadn't even told his sister she'd invited them.

Suddenly she squared her shoulders. She had guests who were waiting and a turkey to carve. "C'mon, Dad, it's time to eat. I'm not about to keep everyone else waiting for one rude man."

But as she began to walk out of the kitchen, Matthew drew her aside for one last father-daughter moment. "Men are funny, Mag-pie. Sometimes, when they stumble onto a good thing, instead of embracing it, they run."

Maggi raised her chin. "You don't need to make excuses for him."

"No—" he squeezed her hand "—but maybe you do."

"If you're bucking for Father of the Year, you've already got the award. Now get out there and start getting our guests seated—" she set the bottle of cider down on the sideboard "—while I go and bring in the turkey. Remember, Captain Reynolds sits as far away from me as possible. His teeth blind me when he smiles."

"Not a problem." He stopped only long enough to kiss the top of her head. "Attagirl, Maggi. You do me proud. But then, you always did."

She thought she'd gotten proper control over her emotions. That idea went out the window the second she saw him walking into the squad room. She had to struggle with the very strong urge to throw something heavy at him.

Bastard.

She took a deep breath. What the hell was the matter with her? She felt like some kind of Ping-Pong ball being lobbed back and forth over the net in a championship tournament.

It wasn't easy, but she managed to compose herself by the time he reached her desk. "Did you have a nice Christmas?"

He'd dreaded this ever since he'd gotten up this morning. Yesterday, he'd behaved like the kind of man he'd always despised. He'd acted like a coward. Instead of coming over to her house, or at least calling with some kind of half-assed excuse, he'd ignored the situation entirely in hopes it would go away.

Like it could.

"It was okay." Patrick felt as if he stared down at

a bomb he didn't know how to defuse. Because he didn't. Women were a complete unknown to him. Being close to Patience hadn't educated him in the slightest. But then, Patience had never stirred these kinds of emotions within him.

"I went to my uncle's," he began, then stopped abruptly, frustrated. He couldn't remember the last time he'd tried to render an excuse. "Look, I know I should have called—"

"There was so much noise, I probably wouldn't have heard anyway." She shrugged carelessly. "Hey, no big deal. I thought it might be nice, that's all. But you don't owe me an explanation." *Yes, you do, and you're doing a damn poor job of it.* "I told you once there're no strings and I meant it."

"Look, I'm sorry, okay?" He lowered his voice, not wanting anyone else to hear. "It's just that something's going on here, between us," he clarified when she looked at him in surprise, "something I can't begin to figure out."

Ditto. "Not everything can be reduced to a black-and-white equation you can plot out with graph paper, Cavanaugh. Some things just *are*," she emphasized. And then, because she wasn't up to dealing with her own feelings, she changed the subject to something they could both work with. "I've been doing a little more thinking about this thing concerning your ex-partner." There was still no word about the man who had supposedly shot him, and she had an uneasy feeling there wouldn't be. Dugan was still missing. "The bullet they dug out of his body, they logged that in as evidence, didn't they?"

"Sure. But they already know it belonged to Dugan's gun." Relieved to put the awkward situation on hold for the time being, he gratefully sank his teeth into the tidbit she offered up. "Why, what are you getting at?"

Maybe something, maybe nothing, she thought. "I'm just fishing. Follow me for a second," she urged. "Maybe the bullet didn't really come from Dugan's gun. Maybe someone else shot Ramirez and Dugan was 'persuaded' to take the fall for someone else. Someone higher up."

If that was true, Patrick thought, the very foundations of the department would come crumbling down. "Who?"

"That part I don't know yet." She smiled ruefully at him. "I guess being around you has gotten me slightly paranoid."

"Paranoid is better than oblivious." He sat down in the chair beside her desk, glad to be working. Glad not to let his thoughts drift too far into uncharted waters. Facing down an unknown enemy was a lot easier than dealing with unknown emotions. "I've tried talking to some of the other people who were there that day, as well as his old partner, Foster, and either no one else knows anything—"

She ended the sentence for him. "Or they're not saying anything."

"Exactly."

The day was slow. Maybe because of the season, Death had called a holiday and there were no new homicides on the board. It gave most of the detectives who hadn't taken the day off to be with their families time to play catch-up with their paperwork. No one would notice if they were missing for a while.

Maggi leaned forward. "What do you say we get on down to the evidence room and see what we can find?"

He'd been toying with the same idea, but he wanted to go alone. And after dark. "The sergeant there isn't just going to let us waltz in there."

Maggi rose from the desk. "You let me handle Sergeant Warren."

He followed her out of the squad room. "You know him?"

The man had been at her table yesterday. "According to my father, he was the man who held the camera when my parents gave me my first bath."

Patrick shook his head as they entered the stairwell that led down to the basement and the evidence room. "You're just one surprise after another, aren't you?"

"Keeps life interesting."

That was one way to put it, Patrick thought.

Sergeant Philip Warren was a corpulent man with a booming laugh, very little hair and six months to go before retirement. When he saw Maggi and her partner walking toward him, he set aside the copy of *Fish and Stream* and greeted them heartily. Visitors were scarce down in the bowels of the evidence room and Sergeant Warren liked to talk.

He winked broadly at Maggi. "Hey, long time no see. What's it been? Twenty, twenty-one hours?" he joked. "Great meal, Maggi, thanks again for having me over."

She smiled warmly. "Just a simple turkey dinner, Sergeant. This is my partner, Patrick Cavanaugh. He would have been there yesterday—" she couldn't help giving him one zinger "—but he was detained."

"You don't know what you missed out on," the sergeant confided. "It tasted like heaven." He patted his all-too-large belly fondly. "Gets me hungry just thinking about it."

Patrick had a feeling that the man grew hungry thinking about almost anything.

"So—" Getting himself as comfortable as possible, the sergeant looked from one to the other. "What can I do for you?"

"Has it been slow here, Phil?" she asked.

Patrick stared at her, surprised she was being so direct. When she'd said she knew the sergeant, he'd expected her to execute some kind of diversion to distract the man while he slipped into the evidence room and got the bullet in question.

"Having trouble keeping my eyes open, Maggi. It's always like this around the holidays. People even forget I'm down here."

"You know what you need?" she told him. "A quick run to the vending machine on the first floor. Get some energy food. Saw some of those chocolate marshmallow bars you're so partial to."

Warren seemed to understand immediately. His eyes shifted toward the man next to her and then back again. Maggi nodded, silently answering his question. Patrick was to be trusted. "Sounds like a good idea, but I don't have anyone to cover for me."

"That's okay, I can hang around for a bit, make sure anyone who might come along signs in first."

Warren was already coming around the desk. "You always were a good girl, Maggi." Standing close to her, he dropped his voice even though it was just the three of them here. "Ten minutes, Mag, can't give you more than that."

"More than enough," she assured him. "I'll be standing right here when you get back. And Phil?"

"Yeah?"

"Thanks."

The man nodded, making his way down the long hallway that led to the elevator bank at the end of the corridor. Maggi waited until she couldn't hear his footfalls any longer. She turned toward Patrick.

"Okay. Go."

He pushed open the door that led to the dark, ill-lit room. "One surprise after another," he murmured again.

Maggi stood guard, hoping no one would come. Hoping that Patrick would be able to find the proper area. She'd only been inside the evidence room once. It was comprised of rows and rows of gray metal shelves with carefully tagged evidence.

Human nature being what it was, it was easy to misfile things. Chances would have doubled of finding the evidence involved in Ramirez's shooting if she'd gone in with Cavanaugh, but she couldn't very well leave the desk unmanned. If a superior officer just happened to come by, the sergeant's job and subsequent pension would be on the line. That was no way to pay Warren back for going out on a limb.

She held her breath until Patrick came out of the room again. His expression was grim, but any questions she wanted to ask had to be put on hold. She heard the sergeant walking down the hall. He'd returned as promised, ten minutes to the second.

Warren laid his stash of six candy bars on the desk. "You were right. They had the marshmallow bars. Want one?"

"Thanks, I'll pass. I'm still working off my share of the chocolate cheesecake."

"You look just fine," the sergeant told her. "Doesn't she, Cavanaugh?"

"Just fine," Patrick echoed.

"I'll see you later," Maggi told the sergeant as he busily peeled back the wrapper on his snack. Warren nodded in response.

"Well?" she asked Patrick eagerly the second they put some distance between themselves and the evidence room.

"It's not there."

Her eyes widened. They weren't talking about an incident that had happened several years ago. This was recent. If the evidence was missing, it was on purpose. "The bullet? What do you mean it's not there? Are you sure you were in the right area?"

"Of course I'm sure." She could hear the frustration in his voice. He held open the stairwell door for her. "It's not there. Neither is Dugan's service revolver. They're both missing."

Her heels hit the metal stairs, echoing as she made her way to the first floor. "Or were taken."

He set his mouth firmly. "It's beginning to look like a conspiracy, isn't it?"

She sighed. "Hate that word, but yes, it does. Considering the kinds of deposits Ramirez made, this could be very, very big." She stopped at the top of the stairs and turned to look at him. "Are you sure he never said anything to you?"

He felt a flare of temper and banked it down. "I don't lie, Mary Margaret. I've got my faults, but that's not one of them."

No, she thought, *it's one of mine.*

"I know," she said quietly. She began to yank the

door open only to have him put his hand over the knob and do it for her.

"You're looking a little green around the gills. You okay?"

"Fine, terrific," she lied as her stomach suddenly lurched. This had to be what feeling seasick was like, she thought. Miserable. "Nothing a little antacid won't cure." She didn't want to think about her stomach. If she kept busy, this strange, queasy feeling would go away again the way it had yesterday. "Let's get started on making up a list of people in the department Ramirez had contact with."

That took them far beyond the realm of friends and the list that he had written up himself. "That could take forever."

She looked at him. "Got any better ideas?"

"Not at the moment." He blew out a breath. "Okay, let's get to it."

Chapter 19

The silence within the small, pale blue tiled bathroom was almost deafening.

Maggi stood staring at the slender stick in her hand. She wasn't sure just how much time had gone by. The darkened color at one end told her the same thing that the three other indicators now rudely housed inside her bathroom wastebasket had.

She was pregnant.

As if life wasn't already complicated enough.

Biting off several choice words about fate's rotten sense of humor, she threw the stick into the basket with the rest of the pregnancy testing paraphernalia.

Damn it, anyway.

She'd been throwing up for a week now, every morning like clockwork. The minute her eyes were open, her stomach insisted on crawling up into her throat. Once purged, she'd start to feel better and her nervousness would begin to fade. She'd gotten the kits just to put her own mind at ease, to convince herself that she was only experiencing some new kind of flu and nothing more.

Maggi took a deep breath as she struggled to pull herself together.

A baby. Cavanaugh's baby.

Ain't that a kick in the head?

Now she had two secrets to keep from him. She didn't want him to know she was carrying his baby, not when the situation was so dicey. There was no real indication that Patrick had any stronger feelings for her than those that lasted the duration of their lovemaking. If she told him about the baby and then he asked her to marry him, she'd never know if he had any feelings at all because, in her mind, the proposal would strictly be motivated because of the baby. And if she told him and he backed away from her, well, that would hurt too much to bear.

Silence was the best option. The only option.

Maggi looked at herself in the mirror. *Great little dilemma you've gotten yourself into, Mag.*

She had absolutely no idea what she was going to do beyond the next moment. She needed to get dressed and go on with her life for as long as she could.

Like a cadet reporting for duty, Maggi squared her shoulders. She had a report to file and a partner to back, although the latter, she suspected, would not be for very much longer.

Maggi ignored the pang she felt in her heart.

Hearing the almost furtive knock on his doorjamb, the tall, distinguished man sitting behind the desk looked up. The moment he did, every nerve ending in his body went on the alert.

His voice was deceptively calm, gracious. His ability to seem warm and outgoing had gotten him to where he was. And would eventually see him to where he wanted to be.

"What's up?"

Officer Foster licked his almost nonexistent lower lip. "We've got a problem."

The man's eyebrows moved together a fraction of an inch. "Close the door."

Foster quickly shut it behind him. He glanced at the chair in front of the desk but made no move to take it. He knew better than to sit without being invited. Or to talk out of turn even though the words were hovering in his mouth, vying for release.

The man at the desk closed the file he was looking over. "All right, what's wrong?"

The words flew out in a rush. "He's still nosing around, asking questions, talking to some of the guys. Taylor saw him and his partner coming out of the stairwell." Foster swallowed nervously. "They might have been down in the evidence room."

The man laughed shortly. "And they might have been groping each other in a dark, private place."

Unsure if the remark was meant to be humorous, Foster attempted a grin. A smile spasmodically came and went. "Wouldn't mind doing that myself with her, but not him. Cavanaugh's not like that. He doesn't mix business with pleasure. Hell, we're not even sure he has any pleasures."

There was no humor evident in the other man's dark eyes. "Has he talked to you?"

"Yeah, right at the start. I told him Ramirez was a square deal when we were working together." Foster added quickly, eager to show that he could keep his wits about him, "but I'm not sure he believed me."

The gaze was flat, the scrutiny deep. Unable to endure it, Foster shifted uneasily from one foot to the other.

"You've got the face of a damn angel," his superior retorted. "Why wouldn't he believe you?"

"That's why I came to you." Foster looked nervously over his shoulder, afraid the door would open at any moment and someone would overhear. "Because he says he wants to talk to me again when I've got a little time."

"Make the time," the man instructed quietly. His eyes pinned his subordinate. "And you know what to do."

Foster ran his fingertips over his sweaty palms. He'd been afraid of this. "I don't know if I can."

The other man didn't bother masking his disgust. Men like Foster were necessary drones, expendable pawns, and nothing more.

"Think of it as laying the foundations for your retirement plan." He shifted, leaning over his desk, holding Foster prisoner in his gaze. "You can either spend your golden years on some warm, inviting beach, or in a maximum security prison, courtesy of the state. The choice is yours. That is, if you actually make it to trial," he added significantly.

Foster knew what that meant. That he would meet a fate similar to Ramirez's, whose only misfortune was in being in the wrong place at the wrong time and whose conscience had finally gotten the better of him. Or like Dugan, whose body hadn't been found yet and probably would never be.

"The choice is yours," the man repeated softly, curdling the blood in Foster's veins.

Foster nodded, knowing what he had to do. Not liking it at all. He hadn't signed on for this. Garnering protection money from wealthy store owners who could well afford it in exchange for favors and protection was one thing. The cold-blooded elimination of problems, which was what he was being told to do, was a completely different matter.

But it all boiled down to self-defense. If he didn't do this, didn't defend himself against what might happen if Cavanaugh stumbled across the truth, he would die. That was guaranteed. And he knew he wasn't ready for that.

"Okay," Foster said, his mouth so dry he felt like choking, "I'll do it."

"Good man. Let me know how it goes. And Foster," he said just as the smaller man was about to leave.

"Yes?"

"Don't screw up."

"No, sir," Foster promised. He hurried out of the room, knowing he had to leave before he threw up.

Patrick's hands were clenched into fists at his sides as he walked down the long corridor.

He'd done nothing wrong, absolutely nothing wrong.

That still didn't ameliorate the uneasy feeling that insisted on dancing through him. He'd been summoned to appear before John Halliday, the head of IA.

Now.

A summons usually meant that he was either under investigation or required to give testimony about someone who was. Anticipation introduced a foul taste into his mouth. Either scenario was not one he remotely welcomed.

Although Internal Affairs was a necessary evil, like everyone else, Patrick thought of the people who worked for IA as belonging to the rat squad. They were people whose sole function was to ferret out the bad in everyone. A few well-placed chosen words could turn almost anything into a suspicious act.

And now those words would concern him.

Maybe this was about Ramirez, he thought. Could be someone higher up had gotten wind of the same thing he had about his late partner and was now doing some digging into the man's dealings. Which probably meant that he was also a suspect. Just as he figured Foster might be mixed up in all this. Only difference being that he assumed someone was innocent until he found evidence to the contrary. IA worked in the reverse. You were guilty until proved innocent.

It was a little like the KGB, Patrick thought as he stopped before Halliday's door. He paused before knocking. Damn, but he hated this. Any way he sliced it, he was about to walk into an unpleasant experience.

He hadn't even told Maggi where he was going. The less involved she was in this, the better.

There he went again, he upbraided himself, wanting to protect her. He was going to have to do something about that.

And while he was at it, he was going to have to do something about the way all his days seemed to wind up at her apartment. In her bed. And he was going to have to do something about the way he could think of nothing else but taking her into his arms and making love with her.

Patrick shook his head. He felt as if his own will had

been stolen and someone else's had wantonly been substituted. He didn't know whether to laugh and enjoy it while it lasted or run for the hills. Because he wanted it to last forever.

He still hadn't spent an entire night with her and there was still a part of himself he was holding back. But his hold was slipping. Eventually, he knew he'd lose his grip on it altogether. And give all of himself to her.

Patrick knocked and waited.

A deep voice on the other side of the door instructed a genial "Come in."

Braced and ready for anything, Patrick turned the knob and walked in.

And discovered that he wasn't really braced at all. Or ready for anything. Especially not for what he saw. Not for Maggi sitting there in the room.

"Leave her out of this," he snapped, forgoing any attempt at a perfunctory greeting. "Whatever you think you have on me, she has nothing to do with any of it. She hasn't even been my partner for very long."

"No, just long enough," Halliday responded. "Take a seat, Detective."

Patrick drew himself up even straighter, giving redwoods a run for their money. "I prefer to stand."

Halliday's eyes narrowed. "That wasn't a request. Sit, Detective Cavanaugh," he ordered. "You're making me nervous."

Reining in the very strong desire to grab Maggi's hand and just walk out of the office, Patrick sat down on the other chair. He kept his gaze fixed on the man who'd called him in. He hated the fact that Maggi was being dragged into this because of him.

Steepling his fingers, Halliday leaned back in his chair as he kept his eyes on his subject.

"I've heard some very good things about you, Cavanaugh. And some bad. It's up to me to figure out which are true, which aren't. I can't do that kind of thing without help." He paused significantly, letting the words sink in.

Patrick's eyes shifted to Maggi, trying to read her expression. She looked uneasy. What had gone down here? What had Halliday made her do? He would swear on his life that she wouldn't lie, wouldn't implicate him in anything just to save her own career.

So what was she doing here?

"What am I being accused of?" Patrick demanded abruptly.

In contrast, Halliday's voice was calm, soothing. "All in due time, Detective."

He wasn't about to wait while Halliday played games to amuse himself. "I've got a right to know *now.*"

Halliday merely smiled. "Most people sitting in that chair would be asking for legal counsel and to have their representative called in by now."

"I don't need a representative. I haven't done anything wrong," he growled through clenched teeth.

"You're not pure as the driven snow, Cavanaugh." The smile on Halliday's lips was unreadable. "I know you've bent your share of rules." He glanced down at the neatly typed report on his desk, the one signed by Mary Margaret McKenna. "But there's no evidence to prove that you're guilty of what you were initially accused of."

Patrick was losing patience fast. With little to no provocation, he'd leap over the desk and shake the answers out of Halliday.

"What?" Patrick demanded. "Just what the hell am I accused of? And by who?"

"It was an anonymous call, stating that you were responsible for Ramirez's death. And that you were up to your neck in dirty tricks. Scamming, bribery, collecting protection money from the locals. The man called you a dirty cop on the take and said that when Ramirez found out and was going to blow the whistle on you, you forced Dugan to kill him and make it look like an accident."

Patrick clutched at the armrests, all but breaking them off. "That's a lie."

Halliday moved his chair slightly to face Maggi. "That's what Detective McKenna tells me."

So that was it, they were grilling Maggi, trying to make her turn against him. Talk about misjudging characters. "Leave her out of this."

"I'm afraid I can't do that," Halliday informed him, his voice mild. "I was the one who sent her into this. To investigate you," he added when Cavanaugh continued to stare at him darkly. He indicated the report on his desk. "She's cleared you."

But Patrick's brain had stopped processing information, halted by Halliday's first remark. "You did what?"

"Bottom line is that you're cleared, Cavanaugh. You could run for president and withstand media microscrutiny based on the report McKenna turned in to me."

Patrick's eyes pinned Maggi to the wall. "You're with him?"

The accusation pierced her like two arrows.

"She's part of IA," Halliday told him. "Undercover, actually. Having her here while I talk to you flies in the face of protocol, but it was at her own insistence."

He glanced at Maggi. Halliday deemed himself to be a fair judge of people. "I imagine she was hoping to smooth things out."

Patrick rose to his feet, his expression stony. Ignoring Maggi, he addressed Halliday. "Am I free to go now?"

Halliday flipped Patrick's file closed. "Yes." But as Patrick began to leave, he added, "And Cavanaugh, leave the internal investigation to us. We'll be looking into Ramirez's connections and ties," he told him pointedly, "not you."

"Whatever you say," Patrick replied curtly.

Turning on his heel, he walked out of the room.

In the space of ten minutes, Patrick's entire universe had been turned completely upside down. The woman who had somehow managed to slip into his world through the cracks and become closer to him than he'd ever allowed anyone else to get, had been part of the rat squad all along, sent in to spy on him.

Spy on him. The words echoed inside his brain, mocking him.

Damn, so much for trusting his own instincts. He was worse than some wet-behind-the-ears recruit, he thought in utter self-disgust.

The clicking sound of heels hurrying along the vinyl flooring registered on the perimeter of his mind.

"Patrick, wait."

Patrick just kept walking down the hall as if he hadn't heard her. Maggi stepped up her pace until she managed to overtake him just shy of the elevator. She moved in front of him, preventing him access to the buttons.

"I said wait."

With both hands on her shoulders, he moved her

roughly aside, then punched the Down button. He'd never felt so explosive, so angry.

"Your report's filed, Mary Margaret," he spit. "You don't have to hang around me anymore."

The best thing was to walk away, to let him cool off. But the look of contempt in his eyes sliced her open from end to end. She had to make him understand.

"Patrick, please—" she caught hold of his arm "—let me explain."

He shrugged her off, curbing the impulse to shake her, to demand why she'd made him feel so much when all she was doing was spying on him. He knew it was unreasonable, but so were his emotions.

"Explain what?" he asked coldly. "There's nothing to explain. You were sent in to spy on me. You spied, it's over."

The last two words slammed into her. Never mind that she'd known they were coming, that she'd been trying to prepare herself for them all along. She didn't want it to be over. Not like this.

"Patrick, I had a job to do—"

"And you did it." His tone cut her off at the knees. "Very commendable." He turned from the elevator. The anger in his eyes took her breath away. "Tell me, did you get time and a half for sleeping with me? Or was that just a new part of the job description?"

He couldn't have hurt her more if he'd spent months orchestrating his words. She felt the sting of tears and pushed them back. "Don't be like that—"

"Oh? And how would you like me to be?"

Incensed, he grabbed Maggi by the arm and pulled her into an alcove, aiming for some semblance of privacy in this goldfish bowl he'd found himself in.

"You lied to me," he accused. "You burrowed your

hooks into me and pumped me for information any way you could." And then he told her the real source of his pain. The real source of the betrayal he felt. "I opened myself up to you the way I never had to anyone else before." Disgusted, he thrust her away from him, shaking his head as he mocked himself. "Damn it, I bought the whole puppet show, didn't I? The decorations, the Christmas tree, the toy drive—nice touch, by the way," he said sarcastically. "Did you find out that my mother, sister and I had to stay at a St. Agnes Shelter one year, was that what motivated you?" When he thought about how he'd felt, standing there in her living room, listening to her...his stomach just turned.

"No, I *do* collect toys for kids. All of that was real, *is* real," she insisted. "I didn't pretend to be anything I wasn't." She didn't want him to think that had been to manipulate him. Most of all, whether or not they were ever together again, she didn't want him to hate her.

Sheer contempt for her and her kind blazed in his eyes. "Except that what you were was part of the rat squad."

He knew better. He knew how the system worked. It was in place so that they could police themselves and keep them all clean, keep the public from doing the job for them.

"I couldn't tell you that. It was my job to clear you."

Did she think he was some kind of mental incompetent? They all knew how IA operated. "It was your job to find dirt that would stick."

"But I didn't."

"Damn straight you didn't, because there isn't any."

She felt herself getting angry in self-defense. "Evidence can always be manipulated, Cavanaugh, you know that."

"So if I didn't perform satisfactorily, you would have turned me in?"

Maggi threw her hands up in frustration. "That's not what I'm saying. Patrick, be reasonable."

"I am being reasonable." He glanced at his watch and then strode back to the elevator. When she attempted to block him, he growled, "Now get the hell out of my way."

Something was up. She could tell by the look on his face. "Where are you going?"

The elevator doors opened again. The car hadn't gone anywhere in the interim. Much like them, Patrick thought, anger eating away at him. "That's no longer any business of yours, is it?"

A sense of panic began to set in. What was he going to do? "I'm still your partner."

He got into the elevator and pressed the Close button. The look in his eyes forbade her to follow him in.

"Wrong. Again."

The elevator doors shut, underscoring the sinking feeling in the pit of her stomach.

Chapter 20

"Foster, you in here?"

Patrick's voice echoed back to him from within the confines of the empty warehouse he'd just entered. Filled with rusting metal rows that extended upward of two stories, the building had once held a profusion of boxed toys. Now it stood abandoned, as barren as the bankrupt toy store chain that had once required its contents.

He strained his eyes to see. Ramirez's old partner had called to tell him that he had some information for him but that Foster would only meet him here. The man feared reprisals. It was here or nowhere. Patrick had had no choice but to agree.

A movement on the left caught his attention. Foster, slight for his uniform, stepped out of the shadows. His sandy-colored hair looked darker in the poor light coming through barred windows with years of dirt and grime on them.

"Yeah, I'm here." Foster beckoned him away from the entrance. "Come on in."

Patrick left the door behind him standing open. He scanned the area as he approached. There was no sound except for Foster's breathing. Was the other man nervous? Did he feel threatened?

Was this just another wild-goose chase? Questions crowded Patrick's mind.

"Don't you think this is a little dramatic?" he asked. "A coffeehouse or diner would have been better." Foster's body was a symphony of motion. He *was* nervous, Patrick thought.

"I told you, I didn't want anyone overhearing us."

Patrick drew the only conclusion he could. "So there is something you want to tell me. Why didn't you say something when I questioned you the last time?"

"Couldn't." Foster became steadily more agitated as he talked. "Things've changed. But you can't say this came from me."

They were both aware of how the system worked. Guarantees couldn't be made. "I'll protect you for as long as I can, Foster, but I can't make any promises, you know that."

Foster struggled with what he knew he had to do. With what he didn't want to do. "Then maybe there's nothing to say."

No way was he going to let Foster out of here without the other man telling him what he knew. "Yes, there is. You wouldn't have gone in for this cheap movie effect if there wasn't."

For a second, the cornered-rabbit expression was gone. Foster looked around the dust-laden building. Nostalgia came over his thin features.

"My dad used to be the foreman here. Brought me around to play when I was a kid."

Patrick curbed his impatience. The man was stalling. Why? "In a warehouse?"

"He was a single dad and this was cheaper than having someone look after me after school. This place used to be where Melbourne Toys kept their inventory." Foster pointed toward shelves in the rear of the building. "That's where they kept the boxes with the action figures. I'd wait until no one was looking then work open the side of a box. A toy here, a toy there, nobody noticed."

The nostalgia gave way to a shrug. "Maybe it started here, I dunno. Thinking that it was all right to take something as long as nobody noticed. As long as you took from someone rich instead of the average guy in the street." Foster looked at Patrick, a defensive tone entering his voice. He was no longer talking about toys and petty theft. "We never took anything from the mom-and-pop places, only the ones who could afford it."

Was it just the two men, or did this involve more people? He had a hunch, he knew. But he needed more than just a hunch. Patrick tried to siphon the information from the other man carefully. "By took, you mean what?"

Foster sneered. "Don't play dumb, Cavanaugh. Money. What else would I be talking about? The owners paid us, we took care of them. Any tickets, any violations, they didn't get written up."

Patrick didn't have to be a genius to know how the operation worked. "And if they didn't pay, the violations were written up and fined even if they didn't exist."

"Something like that."

Time to push. "How many of you were there?" Fear entered Foster's eyes. "Ramirez's account was pretty healthy," Patrick said.

"Enough." As he spoke, Foster began to move around, to pace. "Eddie wasn't part of it, not the way you think. He stumbled onto what was going on and got paid to keep his mouth shut. When he didn't want to keep it that way any longer, things happened." Foster shrugged helplessly. "I'm sorry. He was a good guy."

Patrick could almost believe Foster regretted what had happened. But it was too late for regrets. "Who had him killed? How far up does this go?"

Foster shook his head. "Sorry, privileged information. On both counts."

"You're going to have to come clean." He wasn't going to allow the man to get away, not after this. One bad cop gave them all a bad name.

Foster's eyes became steely. "No, the only thing I have to do is this."

Patrick mentally cursed himself. His anger at McKenna's deceit had clouded his judgment, dulled that sixth sense of his that always warned him when something was about to go wrong. Or maybe it had just gotten impaired after totally going haywire because of Maggi.

It was the only explanation for why he didn't see it coming. Why he didn't see that he was walking into a trap.

Patrick found himself looking down the business end of the gun in Foster's hand.

Foster thought he could read what was going on in Cavanaugh's mind. "No, it's not regulation issue. It belongs to a dead man. Nobody's going to be able to trace this." His eyes narrowed slightly, but his voice wavered as he said, "Or find you."

A shot rang out. Foster screamed and the weapon he'd been aiming at Patrick went flying from his hands. Patrick made a dive for it. Only when he had the gun in his hands did he turn around to see the small figure running in through the warehouse entrance.

Maggi. Goddamn it, it was Maggi. Was she out of her mind?

"What the hell are you doing here?" he demanded roughly.

Maggi's eyes were on the fallen patrolman, watching for the one false move that would trip them up. "Tying up loose ends, saving you, take your pick." It was damn hard to sound flippant, what with her heart in her mouth and all.

Instinct had made her follow Patrick when he'd left the police station even while she'd counseled herself to give him some space. She knew she didn't like being crowded when she had to work something out for herself. But patience wasn't her long suit in this case.

Maggi was eternally grateful that just this once she hadn't listened to her head, but gone with her instincts and her heart. If she hadn't, Patrick could well be dead by now.

"How about dying alongside of him?"

The question came from the row of dust-encrusted shelves just behind them.

Captain Amos Reynolds stepped out, a gun in his hand. Contempt flared in his eyes as he glanced in Foster's direction. The latter looked as surprised as Maggi felt to see the senior officer.

This was bad, Maggi thought, very bad.

"Get up, you idiot. I knew you'd botch this," Reynolds said to the other man.

Foster began to take a step forward, but the look in Reynolds's eyes froze him in place. "I'm sorry, I'm sorry, she got the drop on me."

Anger and disgust creased the captain's handsome face. "Do you have any idea how pathetic that sounds?" He moved the barrel of his weapon to point at Foster. The other man jumped uneasily. "Three bodies are just as easy to get rid of as two." Smoothly Reynolds swung his hand back to aim at Patrick. "Drop your weapons, you two."

Patrick's hand only tightened on his. "You can't kill both of us."

Reynolds's gaze was unrelenting. "I can and I will unless you do exactly as I say. I'm not about to let you mess up something that's been going on for ten years. Everyone was protected, no one got hurt."

As if that made it right, Patrick thought. "Tell that to Ramirez," he spit.

Reynolds appeared unfazed. "That was unfortunate. It was only meant to be a warning, just a wound. But he moved." Reynolds looked in Maggi's direction. "It worked with your father."

Maggi's mouth dropped open. "My father?" Anger colored her cheeks. Reynolds wasn't fit to mention her father's name.

"Don't look so indignant." The soothing tone of Reynolds's voice only served to agitate her further. "He doesn't know anything. But he was starting to ask uncomfortable questions. Getting him off the force was the best way to deal with it." His smile was cold. "You don't worry about inconsistencies you've stumbled across when you're busy trying to cope with regaining the use of your leg."

All pretense at civility terminated. His eyes darkened. "Now I'm not going to ask you again. Drop your weapons." He took aim at Maggi. "Or she goes first."

Patrick had no other choice.

If he dropped his weapon, they'd be gunned down where they stood. He knew it.

It was going to be a matter of split-second timing. Shoving Maggi out of the way, he took dead aim and fired. Reynolds went down, spasmodically getting off one shot before he fell face forward to the floor. Dead.

Patrick whirled around and trained his weapon on Foster.

"Don't even think it," he warned. He kept his gun aimed at Foster as he warily approached the fallen captain. "Get his weapon, McKenna." When she made no answer, adrenaline kicked up another notch. He glanced in her direction. "McKenna?"

"Give me a second," she breathed, trying to gather herself up from her knees. Her shoulder felt as if it was on fire. Touching it, she looked down at her hand, which was covered in blood. Blood also oozed from her right shoulder, soaking its way into everything.

"Oh, my God, Maggi, you're hit."

Her teeth clamped down on her lower lip as she struggled to her feet. "Can't put nothing over on you, can I?" She sucked in air. Every breath hurt.

Guilt snapped its jaws around him. He should have pulled her down. Instead of sparing her, he'd pushed her right into Reynolds's line of fire.

"Is it bad?"

Trust Cavanaugh to understate something. It was almost funny. "Other than feeling like someone just set me on fire, no," she answered between clenched teeth. And then she stopped. "Listen." The sound of sirens in the distance pushed their way through the silence. "Better late than never, huh?"

She'd almost forgotten about that. On a hunch, she'd called for backup the moment she saw Foster. A man who didn't have anything to hide didn't go around meeting people in abandoned warehouses, didn't take these kinds of precautions.

It was getting hard to stay focused. "Don't let him get the drop on you again," she warned Patrick.

It was the last thing she said before the darkness claimed her.

Maggi had opened her eyes, but he didn't think she saw him. She looked so pale as she lay there on the gurney, so white she almost faded into the sheet.

He was afraid to say her name, afraid to call out to her and not have her respond. So as he sat beside her in the ambulance, he held on to her hand as tightly as he could. He willed her to hang on, silently forbidding her to slip away.

He'd never felt terrified before, not even when he'd been a small boy and his father had gone on a rampage, smashing things around the house, threatening to kill them all. Then his thoughts had been centered around protecting his mother and sister. But now there was nothing he could do to protect Maggi.

Nothing he could do to make her whole.

It was out of his hands and he hated the feeling of helplessness. Hated the fact that he was sitting here, maybe impotently watching her life slip away.

He wanted to yell, to rail.

He could do nothing.

Patrick bent very close to her ear, so that only she could hear him.

"I'm not going to let you go, you hear me? I forbid you to die. God damn it, Maggi, you can't do this to me. I love you."

Her face remained still and pale, her color a contrast to the blood spread out on her shirt.

Patrick closed his eyes and tried to remember how to pray.

Patience came flying down the long corridor. The moment she saw him, she threw her arms around her brother, embracing him. Patrick had called her less than twenty minutes ago. She'd broken speed limits to get here, using her cell phone to call the people who needed to be called as she drove to the hospital.

"How is she?" she asked breathlessly.

He shook his head. "I don't know. They won't tell me anything." He sighed, feeling like a man who was just about ready to leap out of his own skin. "She's in surgery."

There'd been no time for details when he'd called her. Only that Maggi had been shot and that he was in the hospital with her. "What happened?"

He'd been asking himself that same question over and over again in the past half hour.

"I thought she was clear. I shoved her out of the way. Reynolds was going to kill her." Stopping, Patrick dragged in air. It didn't help to calm him. Nothing would help until he knew Maggi was all right again. "Instead, I pushed her right into the line of fire."

Patience tried to lead him over to the chairs lined along the hallway. He didn't budge, remaining against the wall as if he was holding it up. Or maybe it was holding him up.

"She's going to be all right, Patrick. This is the best hospital in the county."

"Yeah, right," he said numbly.

But people died in good hospitals, didn't they? Oh God, what if...?

He couldn't bring himself to finish the sentence, even in his own mind.

They heard the sound of footsteps approaching quickly. The next moment, Matthew McKenna came racing down the hallway, his face as ashen as Maggi's had been when they had wheeled her into surgery.

He'd never met Maggi's father, but Patrick only had to take one look at the man's face before he knew. Straightening, he met the other man halfway.

"Are you Maggi's father?" There were suppressed tears in the man's eyes as he nodded. "I'm Patrick Cavanaugh, Maggi's partner. I'm the one who called you." Belatedly, he remembered he wasn't alone. "This is my sister, Patience."

"They told me at the front desk that she was in surgery. Do we know anything yet?" Patrick shook his head. Matthew tried to get control over his fears. "What happened?"

"She saved my life," Patrick replied simply. There was no doubt in his mind that if she hadn't shot the gun out of Foster's hand, he would have been dead right now.

Taking a breath, he pulled himself together and filled in his sister and Maggi's father as best he could about what had happened in the warehouse, ending with Foster's arrest and Maggi being taken into surgery. Reynolds had gone to the morgue in a body bag.

Matthew listened to it all in solemn silence. When Patrick finished, he nodded.

"I had a feeling all along that something wasn't right, but I had no way of proving it and I didn't want to let Maggi in on my suspicions. I knew she'd try to do something like this. Stubborn as all get-out, that girl. Thinks she's Joan of Arc the way she carries on about doing the right thing. I was afraid she'd take this into her own hands," Matthew McKenna said.

He didn't know, Patrick realized as he looked at Maggi's father. Matthew McKenna had no idea that his daughter worked for IA. She'd kept it from him.

"She's headstrong that way," Patrick agreed, not adding that it was also part of her job. Her being part of IA wasn't his secret to tell.

They heard several voices coming from around the bend. The next moment, Patrick saw his uncles Andrew and Brian heading toward them. He looked at Patience.

"I called them after you called me." She looked at Maggi's father. "Patrick told me that you know my uncles. I thought maybe you might need some company right now."

Matthew felt as if he'd aged ten years since he'd received the call from Patrick. He was grateful for Patience's thoughtfulness. He couldn't be distracted, but being around old comrades helped keep some of the demons at bay.

"Thank you."

Patience nodded. She glanced at her brother. If only there was someone she could call for him.

Patrick stood apart from the others, although it wasn't easy. The corridor had become crammed with people who knew Maggi, family friends and veterans of the force who had watched her grow up from a golden haired toddler into the woman she was, as well as people she worked with now. Carving out a space for himself was difficult, especially when everyone was trying to bolster each other.

He didn't care about other people's stories of miraculous recoveries or statistics that tipped the scales in her favor. None of that mattered. The only thing that mattered was what was going on behind the closed doors of the ground-floor operating room.

He felt as though he were standing in a time warp, holding his breath, vacillating between anger and fear.

When the blue-gowned internal surgeon finally made his way among them and asked, "Who's here for Maggi McKenna?" everyone replied in the affirmative and crowded around the physician.

Matthew pushed his way into the center. "I'm Maggi's father."

"How is she?" Patrick demanded, cutting the man off. He'd been the one the surgeon had briefed as quickly as he could about Maggi's situation. The surgeon wouldn't have even done that except that Patrick had rushed alongside of him as Maggi was being hurried into the operating room.

The surgeon looked close to exhaustion.

"She's one hell of a lucky girl. Half an inch closer and the wound would have been fatal." He seemed as relieved as the people crowded around him. "But we got the bullet out and she's going to be just fine, although she needs a lot of rest."

Patrick knew how receptive Maggi would be to that. The instant she started getting better, she would want to be back in active duty. "Don't worry, I'll sit on her if I have to."

"I wouldn't advise that if I were you." The surgeon smiled weakly, removing the surgical mask from around his neck. "At least not on her stomach."

There was something in the other man's voice that made Patrick wary. "Her stomach?"

"I'm sorry, little joke to ease the tension on my part. That's just my way of saying that the baby's fine, too."

"Baby?" Patrick echoed incredulously. For the second time that day, he felt as if he'd been punched straight in the gut. Taking the man's arm, he drew him over to the side. "She's pregnant?"

"Yes. Just barely." The surgeon's eyes searched Patrick's face. He must have made the assumption that Patrick was his patient's husband. "I'm sorry, did I just spoil the surprise?"

Feeling shaken and hardly aware of what he was doing, Patrick clapped the surgeon on the shoulder. "No, you did just fine, Doc. Just fine."

He left his hand there a moment longer before withdrawing it. Balance became a matter of intense concentration. Patrick felt as if someone had just taken away the ground from beneath his feet.

Chapter 21

Maggi's surgeon finally allowed Matthew and Patrick in to see her once she was out of recovery and safely in her room.

"But only for a few minutes," he cautioned before opening the door for them. "She's conscious but she's still very weak."

Matthew nodded solemnly as he passed the physician. The moment he saw his daughter, clear colored tubes running through her arms, his heart constricted. Positioning himself on one side of her, he took Maggi's hand in his, lightly kissed her forehead and said, "You're getting off the force."

Maggi smiled at her father. Her eyes flickered over Patrick. He was here. She hadn't imagined it. And he was all right. He and her baby were all right. That was all that mattered.

"Hi, Dad." Her voice sounded raspy and distant to

her own ear. "Didn't the doctor tell you not to get me upset?"

His grip tightened slightly around her hand. "I'm older. I'm not supposed to be upset first." Tears sprang to his eyes as he thought of what could have been. "Oh Mag-pie..." Unable to finish without cracking, his voice trailed off.

All the emotions she'd felt when she'd first gone to see him in the hospital returned. She wished she could have spared him this. "I know, Dad. I was standing on the other side of the railing not that long ago, remember?"

He nodded. "I like better being the one to get shot. You don't worry as much." He bent over and kissed her cheek. This wasn't over, but right now, she needed her rest. He glanced toward Patrick. The young man was restless. It was easy to see he wanted some time alone with her. "We'll talk later," Matthew promised.

"Won't do any good," she warned. A smattering of the sparkle had returned to her eyes and Matthew took heart in that.

"I'll be right outside if you need me." Feeling a rock had been lifted from his heart, Matthew slipped out and left Patrick alone with his daughter.

The words erupted out of Patrick the second the door was closed. "What the hell were you thinking, flying in like some goddamned superhero?"

"Probably the same thing you were when you went in." She was weak and it was costing her to talk. But things had to get said. "Y'know, a person shouldn't be afraid or be too proud to accept help, especially when there are guns pointed at him."

"You could have been killed," Patrick said.

"So could you," she countered though with far less energy than she would have wanted to. "And if you had been, it would have been my fault. I couldn't have that on my conscience."

"Why would it be your fault?"

She took a deep breath, fighting against the desire to close her eyes and drift off. "Because you weren't thinking straight after you walked out of Halliday's office. Anyone could see that."

Patrick struggled against the urge to shake her. To grab her and hold her close to him, never letting her go. Instead, he forced himself to remain where he was and just look at her. "Can you blame me?"

"Yeah, I can. You know how the job works."

"And you were only doing your job, right?" He didn't want to be having this same argument again. It led nowhere. And besides, she was right. "Sorry. It's behind us now and yes, I do know how the job works." He hadn't realized until this moment just how shaky he felt, as if his insides were one huge mass of undulating Jell-O. "And better someone fair and impartial like you than someone on the take and under Reynolds's thumb."

She took in a deep breath, trying to tack her words onto it. "Does it stop with Reynolds?"

To take his mind off her surgery, Patrick reported the matter to Brian, who, as chief of detectives, promised to take it from there.

"Too soon to tell, but it's a lot dirtier than we thought."

Bits and pieces of thoughts floated through her head. She thought of Alicia and her children. "What about Ramirez's wife?"

"I think I can keep her clean." Unless something drastic came to light to change the picture, the woman was safe. He paused. He didn't want to talk about the case or other people. Not when there was something so much bigger before them. "Doctor said you were going to be fine."

She smiled weakly. She'd never had a doubt. Not about herself. She supposed that was vain in a way, but her own mortality had never occurred to her. "I'm tough, like my dad."

"Baby's going to be fine, too." Each word had been measured out. He looked at her intently. "Is it mine?"

Her heart felt as if it had been pricked. Did he doubt her? The other deceptions didn't matter. This he should have known. "Do you have to ask?"

"Why didn't you tell me?"

She didn't look away. "Again, do you have to ask?" Maggi tried to read his expression and couldn't. A sinking feeling took hold, trespassing on the physical pain. If Patrick was happy about the situation, she would have known it, felt it. He obviously wanted nothing to do with her baby or her.

"I'm not going to ask you for anything except maybe input on the baby's name when the time comes." The scowl didn't leave his face. Her spirits sank a little lower. "You don't even have to do that if you don't want to."

He felt like the last man standing after a day-long blitzkrieg. So many emotions bounced around inside of him he couldn't begin to sort them out or even make heads or tails out of the mess. He was unaccustomed to having any emotions at all, much less a conflicting squadron. It had been one hell of a day. The woman he loved wasn't who he'd thought she was. On top of that, she had almost died saving his life. And then to discover that she was carrying his baby, well, it was just too much for him to handle. At least, right away.

"Baby's name is up to you," he told her, his voice distant, detached. "Seeing as how you've been calling all the shots so far."

"Not all the shots." She pulled her courage together, knowing she would never get another chance to be so nakedly honest, and knowing she had everything to lose. But she had to say it, had to tell him, no matter what the consequences. "I didn't plan on falling in love with you. I didn't even plan on liking you."

Love. He tried to absorb the word but couldn't, not when he felt so numbed.

"Yeah, well, plans don't always work out, do they?" He needed distance, time and distance, to be fair to her. To be fair to himself. He nodded toward the door. "The hall's full of people who want to see you. I've probably gone over my time limit." His voice was flat. "I'll see you later."

With that, he walked out of the room.

Maggi forced her tears back.

Patrick didn't remember walking out of the hospital. Didn't remember driving around in his car or where he and the next two hours eventually went.

His thoughts were all tied up in knots, much the way his gut was whenever he began to think of what might have happened to Maggi in the warehouse and how the scenario in the operating room might have turned out.

He could have lost her.

And lost himself.

Like a homing pigeon relying completely on programming and instinct, Patrick found himself returning to the precinct. Parking, he yanked up the hand brake. All the frustration he'd endured these past few hours came to a head, threatening to explode within him. Explode out of him.

Getting out of his car, he walked into the building and made his way up the stairwell until he reached the floor that housed IA.

Without sparing her a glance, he strode past Halliday's secretary.

About to go home, the woman looked up, taken completely by surprise. Belatedly she realized where he was going. "Wait, you can't go in there."

"Shoot me," Patrick snapped, leaving the woman utterly speechless.

John Halliday was on the phone when the door to his office was abruptly thrown open. The man in the doorway looked as if he was loaded for bear.

"Speak of the devil," Halliday murmured into the receiver. "He just walked in. I'll talk to you later." Hanging up, he rose from his chair. "Cavanaugh, I didn't expect to see you here."

Patrick curbed the urge to shout at the man, to let loose with a string of expletives. That would hardly release the fury he was experiencing. Instead, he measured out his words as evenly as he could.

"Maybe if I'd been here to begin with, you could have saved everyone a hell of a lot of time and effort." He stood toe-to-toe with the man, their eyes level. "You should have asked me directly. I would have cooperated with any investigation."

Halliday surprised him by laughing. "You don't exactly have the best reputation for working and playing well with others, Detective. Instead of answering questions, we figured you'd storm off, forewarned. We weren't sure if you really were in on it, the way the informant claimed, or how deep all of this went. Having someone on the inside was the best way to go. You know, sometimes things have to be done according to someone else's rules, not yours.

"By the way, you might be interested to know that the informant turned out to be Foster. He confessed half an hour ago. He's ready to flip on everyone, as long as we can guarantee that he'll stay alive."

But Halliday could see that Cavanaugh's reputation was the last thing on the man's mind. Halliday indicated the telephone. "That was her on the phone—McKenna—filing her last report. Woman's amazing. Flat on her back and she's still thinking about the job. I'm going to hate to lose her."

Patrick became alert. "Lose her?"

Halliday nodded. "She asked for a transfer. Said she didn't like dealing in lies anymore, even for a good cause."

Patrick told himself he didn't care. He knew he was lying. "Where does she want a transfer to?"

"She said she'd get back to me about that. Had to think about what to do with the rest of her life." Halliday looked at him pointedly. "You might like to help her with that."

"Me?"

Halliday snorted. "Give me a little credit here, Cavanaugh. All that emotion exploding out of you like lava from Mount Saint Helens isn't just because you think your honor's been impugned. I'm not saying anything else here, except that I don't think, off the record, that McKenna's the kind of woman any man in his right mind should allow to get away—provided she was interested in him in the first place.''

Halliday took his coat from the rack and slipped it on.

"Now, if there's nothing else, I'd like to go home to my wife and tell her I love her. I can't remember the last time I said that to her and she deserves to hear it. G'night, Cavanaugh."

Patrick walked out in front of him.

He drove home. To try to be alone with his thoughts. To try to pick up pieces of the life he'd had until McKenna had walked into it, messing everything up.

The first thing he saw when he let himself into his condo and turned on the light was the Christmas tree in the center of the living room.

The one that she had brought him.

It sagged like a little old man, its branches weighed down by the decorations she'd insisted he'd take. He'd been so wrapped up in his work, he'd forgotten to get rid of it.

Pine needles were scattered on the carpet like pale green dandruff. He hadn't remembered to water it, either. Nothing but a pain in the neck, that's what it was.

He remembered opening the door and seeing Maggi peering around it.

He touched a branch and was surprised to find that it wasn't as brittle as he'd thought it would be.

Having Maggi in his life meant always being surprised. If she wasn't in it anymore…

Turning on his heel, Patrick shut off the light and went back out.

* * *

Daylight tried to push its way through the white curtains her father had drawn shut before he'd left for the night.

Maggi stirred.

The slight motion brought an army of pain marching through her with huge combat boots. She felt worse today than yesterday.

Except for her heart.

That was as bad as ever. She expected it would be for a very long time to come.

Resisting the temptation of falling back into blessed oblivion, Maggi forced herself to open her eyes.

She wasn't alone in the room.

Startled, Maggi automatically reached for the weapon that wasn't there and cried out in pain from the effort before she could bite it back.

Patrick immediately stumbled out of the chair where he'd spent the night, remnants of sleep fleeing from his eyes.

"You want me to call the nurse? The doctor? What?"

Her head felt as if it were filled with cotton. Was this just another dream? She'd had several already, tiny vignettes in which Patrick had the dominant role. Sometimes he told her he loved her, sometimes he cursed her out. She was too exhausted, too emotionally drained to endure another go-around.

"Are you a dream?"

Her voice was strong. He could feel relief slipping through him. "Most people refer to me as a nightmare."

He saw her reach toward him and he took her hand in his as he sank back down in the chair he'd dragged over to her bedside.

Maggi swallowed. Someone had filleted her throat while she was asleep. Every word seemed to be scraping along raw skin.

"What are you doing here?"

"Getting a really bad backache."

He'd been in her room since one in the morning, having slipped in past security. The one nurse who had come in to check on Maggi's condition had been persuaded to allow him to stay. He figured she felt sorry for him. He was hoping Maggi would, too.

"Why are you here? Did you forget to get something else off your chest?" Maggi was too leery to allow herself to be happy that he'd come back. Not after the way he'd reacted to hearing about the baby.

"Yeah, I did. The cobwebs."

Maybe this was a dream. She could have sworn he was talking about cobwebs. "Excuse me?"

"The cobwebs from around my heart," he explained. He was doing his best to be romantic, but in his mouth, the words came out all wrong. "I've never used it very much except clinically. You know, for pumping blood through my veins and all. I never knew I could use it to feel with." He gave up the effort, knowing he'd made a mess of it. "Until you started putting me through hell."

Her mouth curved slightly. "You're not very good at this, are you?"

Still holding her hand, afraid to let it go, he blew out a breath. "The worst."

Still unsure where this was going, Maggi felt sorry for him. He looked as uncomfortable as a nudist about to deliver a speech at a fashion show. "Then maybe you should cut to the chase, Cavanaugh. What is it you're trying to say?"

Talking wasn't his thing; it never had been. "That I've said some things I didn't mean to."

"You're going to have to be more specific than that."

Restless, he dragged a hand through his hair. She should understand, not make him say it. "I didn't mean to be a jerk."

Her smile widened. He felt as if the sun had come out. "Go on, you're getting better."

He told her what was in this new organ that he had discovered. "When I saw you on that stretcher...when I thought you weren't going to make it...I didn't want to make it, either, Mary Margaret."

"You weren't shot."

"Didn't matter." As far as he was concerned, taking a bullet would have been a hell of a lot easier.

Something came back to her. She stared at him as the fog around her brain dissipated, allowing her to pull the fragments together. "Did you say something to me during the ambulance ride? I thought I heard you say 'I love you' but I figured I was out of my head."

He looked at her, his expression grim. "You weren't out of your head. I said it."

"And?"

"I meant it."

"Just then?" she prodded, watching his expression. Feeling hope bubbling up inside. "It was a pretty dramatic moment. People say things they don't mean in situations like that."

"Yeah, they do." He paused, then added, "But I don't."

"Then you love me."

"Yeah." He almost sounded as if he meant it begrudgingly.

"Say it, damn it."

He sighed, resigned to his fate. "I love you, Mary Margaret."

Maggi rolled her eyes. Why had he used her name? "Oh, please don't spoil it."

Patrick allowed himself a smile. "Sorry, that's how I think of you. That's what the priest is going to say when he marries us, isn't it? Do you Mary Margaret McKenna take—"

"Hold it." Maggi grabbed his hand, pulling his attention back to her. "Did I miss something here? How did we get from the ambulance to the church?"

He looked at her, knowing he was never going to feel about anyone the way he felt about her. Surprised that he did feel like this about anyone. "In big, giant steps, Mary Margaret, in big giant steps."

She hated being tethered like this. She wanted to get up, to throw her arms around him. With no other option, she played out the moment. "You realize you didn't even ask me. A girl likes to be asked."

He looked at her solemnly. "I didn't want to take a chance on you saying no."

How could he even think that? "Do you honestly think I would?"

"You're a constant surprise to me, Mary Margaret, a constant surprise."

"This isn't a surprise," she told him. "This is a sure thing." And then she grinned. "You can bet the farm this time."

"How about I just bet the rest of my life?"

"Works for me," she told him.

Shifting from the chair to the corner of her bed, Patrick took her into his arms, carefully avoiding the IVs she was still attached to.

"Yeah, me, too," Patrick agreed just before he kissed her.

* * * * *

If you liked Internal Affair, *you'll love Marie Ferrarella's next*
CAVANAUGH JUSTICE *romance,*
Dangerous Games,
coming to you from Silhouette Sensation in August 2005.
Don't miss it!

DYNASTIES: SUMMER IN SAVANNAH

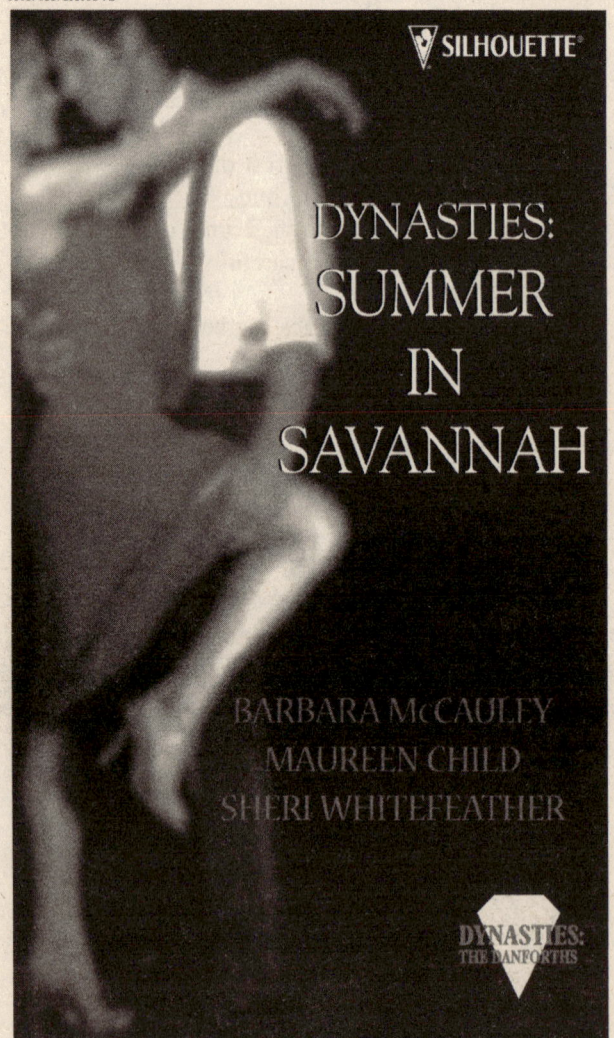

BARBARA McCAULEY
MAUREEN CHILD
SHERI WHITEFEATHER

DYNASTIES: THE DANFORTHS

On sale 20th May 2005

Available at most branches of WHSmith, Tesco, ASDA, Martins, Borders, Eason, Sainsbury's and all good paperback bookshops.

LOOK OUT FOR 3 FANTASTIC NOVELS IN 1 VOLUME

MILLS & BOON

Risqué Business

The fun starts after hours...

EMMA DARCY

Sharon Kendrick

Liz Fielding

On sale 1st July 2005

Available at most branches of WHSmith, Tesco, ASDA, Martins, Borders, Eason, Sainsbury's and all good paperback bookshops.

www.millsandboon.co.uk

Desert Heat

Susan Mallery
Alexandra Sellers

On sale 19th August 2005

Available at most branches of WHSmith, Tesco, ASDA, Martins, Borders, Eason, Sainsbury's and all good paperback bookshops.

SILHOUETTE

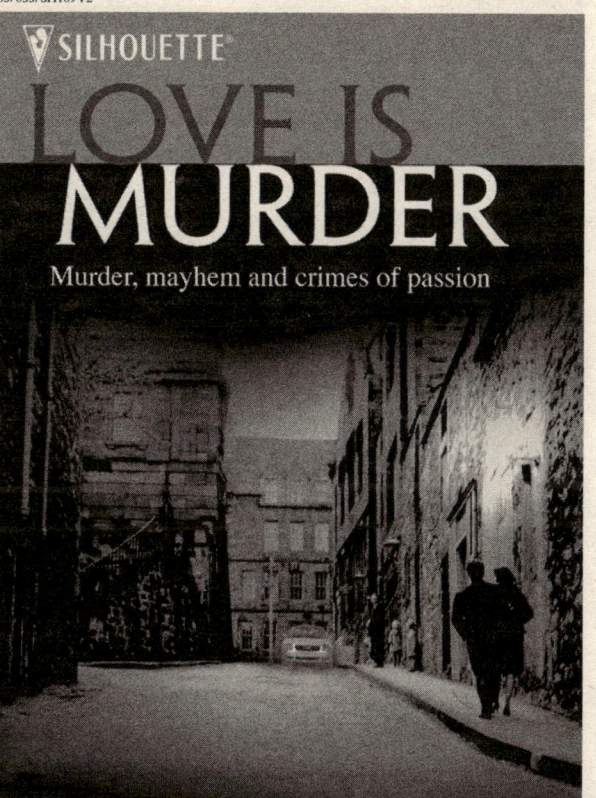

LOVE IS MURDER

Murder, mayhem and crimes of passion

REBECCA BRANDEWYNE
MAUREEN CHILD
LINDA WINSTEAD JONES

On sale 16th September 2005

Available at most branches of WHSmith, Tesco, ASDA, Martins, Borders, Eason, Sainsbury's and all good paperback bookshops.

2 FULL LENGTH BOOKS FOR £5.99

No.1 *New York Times* bestselling author

NORA ROBERTS

"Exciting, romantic, great fun."
—*Cosmopolitan*

SUSPICIOUS

PARTNERS and *NIGHT MOVES*

On sale 15th July 2005

Available at most branches of WHSmith, Tesco, ASDA, Martins, Borders, Eason, Sainsbury's and all good paperback bookshops.